The Works of Mark Twain

VOLUME 2

ROUGHING IT

This 1993 edition of *Roughing It* supersedes the
1972 edition as Volume 2 in The Works of Mark Twain.

THE MARK TWAIN PAPERS AND WORKS OF MARK TWAIN
is a comprehensive edition for scholars of the private papers
and published works of Mark Twain (Samuel L. Clemens).

THE MARK TWAIN LIBRARY
is a selected edition reprinted from the Papers and Works for
students and the general reader. Both series of books are published
by the University of California Press and edited by members of the

MARK TWAIN PROJECT
with headquarters in The Bancroft Library,
University of California, Berkeley.

Editorial work for all volumes is jointly supported by grants from the

NATIONAL ENDOWMENT FOR THE HUMANITIES,
an independent federal agency,
and by public and private donations to

THE FRIENDS OF THE BANCROFT LIBRARY.

THE MARK TWAIN PAPERS

Letters to His Publishers, 1867–1894
Edited with an Introduction by Hamlin Hill
1967

Satires & Burlesques
Edited with an Introduction by Franklin R. Rogers
1967

Which Was the Dream? and Other Symbolic
Writings of the Later Years
Edited with an Introduction by John S. Tuckey
1967

Hannibal, Huck & Tom
Edited with an Introduction by Walter Blair
1969

Mysterious Stranger Manuscripts
Edited with an Introduction by William M. Gibson
1969

Correspondence with Henry Huttleston Rogers, 1893–1909
Edited with an Introduction by Lewis Leary
1969

Fables of Man
Edited with an Introduction by John S. Tuckey
Text established by Kenneth M. Sanderson and Bernard L. Stein
Series Editor, Frederick Anderson
1972

Notebooks & Journals, Volume I (1855–1873)
Edited by Frederick Anderson, Michael B. Frank,
and Kenneth M. Sanderson
1975

Notebooks & Journals, Volume II (1877–1883)
Edited by Frederick Anderson, Lin Salamo, and Bernard L. Stein
1975

Notebooks & Journals, Volume III (1883–1891)
Edited by Robert Pack Browning, Michael B. Frank, and Lin Salamo
General Editor, Frederick Anderson
1979

Letters, Volume 1: 1853–1866
Editors: Edgar Marquess Branch, Michael B. Frank,
and Kenneth M. Sanderson
Associate Editors: Harriet Elinor Smith,
Lin Salamo, and Richard Bucci
1988

Letters, Volume 2: 1867–1868
Editors: Harriet Elinor Smith and Richard Bucci
Associate Editor: Lin Salamo
1990

Letters, Volume 3: 1869
Editors: Victor Fischer and Michael B. Frank
Associate Editor: Dahlia Armon
1992

THE MARK TWAIN LIBRARY

No. 44, The Mysterious Stranger
Edited by John S. Tuckey and William M. Gibson
1982

The Adventures of Tom Sawyer
Edited by John C. Gerber and Paul Baender
1982

Tom Sawyer Abroad · Tom Sawyer, Detective
Edited by John C. Gerber and Terry Firkins
1982

The Prince and the Pauper
Edited by Victor Fischer and Michael B. Frank
1983

A Connecticut Yankee in King Arthur's Court
Edited by Bernard L. Stein
1983

Adventures of Huckleberry Finn
Edited by Walter Blair and Victor Fischer
1985

*Huck Finn and Tom Sawyer among the Indians,
and Other Unfinished Stories*
Foreword and Notes by Dahlia Armon and Walter Blair
Texts established by Dahlia Armon, Paul Baender, Walter Blair,
William M. Gibson, and Franklin R. Rogers
1989

OTHER MARK TWAIN PROJECT
PUBLICATIONS

*The Devil's Race-Track: Mark Twain's Great Dark Writings
The Best from* Which Was the Dream? *and* Fables of Man
Edited by John S. Tuckey
1980

Union Catalog of Clemens Letters
Edited by Paul Machlis
1986

Union Catalog of Letters to Clemens
Edited by Paul Machlis,
with the assistance of Deborah Ann Turner
1992

Samuel L. Clemens in 1863 (above) and 1872.
Mark Twain Papers, The Bancroft Library (CU-MARK).

The Works of Mark Twain

General Editor, Robert H. Hirst

Contributing Editors for This Volume
Richard Bucci
Victor Fischer
Michael B. Frank
Kenneth M. Sanderson

A PUBLICATION OF THE
MARK TWAIN PROJECT OF THE BANCROFT LIBRARY

Mark Twain

ROUGHING IT

Illustrated by True Williams, Edward F. Mullen, and Others

Editors

HARRIET ELINOR SMITH

EDGAR MARQUESS BRANCH

Associate Editors

LIN SALAMO

ROBERT PACK BROWNING

UNIVERSITY OF CALIFORNIA PRESS

BERKELEY, LOS ANGELES, LONDON

1993

CENTER FOR
SCHOLARLY EDITIONS
AN APPROVED EDITION
MODERN LANGUAGE
ASSOCIATION OF AMERICA

UNIVERSITY OF CALIFORNIA PRESS
BERKELEY AND LOS ANGELES, CALIFORNIA

UNIVERSITY OF CALIFORNIA PRESS, LTD.
LONDON, ENGLAND

LIBRARY OF CONGRESS
CATALOGING-IN-PUBLICATION DATA

TWAIN, MARK, 1835–1910.
ROUGHING IT / EDITORS, HARRIET ELINOR SMITH, EDGAR MARQUESS
BRANCH ; ASSOCIATE EDITORS, LIN SALAMO, ROBERT PACK BROWNING ;
ILLUSTRATED BY TRUE WILLIAMS, EDWARD F. MULLEN, AND OTHERS.

P.   CM. — (THE WORKS OF MARK TWAIN ; 2)
INCLUDES BIBLIOGRAPHICAL REFERENCES.
ISBN 0-520-08498-5 (ALK. PAPER)
I. TWAIN, MARK, 1835–1910—JOURNEYS—WEST (U.S.) 2. AUTHORS,
AMERICAN—19TH CENTURY—JOURNEYS—WEST (U.S.) 3. WEST (U.S.)—
DESCRIPTION AND TRAVEL. I. SMITH, HARRIET ELINOR. II. BRANCH, EDGAR
MARQUESS, 1913–   . III. TITLE. IV. SERIES: TWAIN, MARK, 1835–1910.
WORKS. 1972 ; V. 2.
PS1300.F72   VOL. 2 1993 (RARE BK. COLL.)
[PS1318.A1 1993]
818'.409 S—DC20
[818'.303]
[B]
93-23042

SERIES DESIGN BY HARLEAN RICHARDSON
IN COLLABORATION WITH DAVE COMSTOCK

MANUFACTURED IN THE UNITED STATES OF AMERICA

Editorial work for this volume has been supported by a grant to
The Friends of The Bancroft Library from the

L. J. SKAGGS AND MARY C. SKAGGS FOUNDATION

and by matching funds from the
NATIONAL ENDOWMENT FOR THE HUMANITIES,
an independent federal agency.

Without such generous support, these editions could
not have been produced.

CONTENTS

ACKNOWLEDGMENTS

EDITORIAL WORK for this volume was made possible by the continuing generosity of the American taxpayer, and by the support of reviewers, panelists, Council, and staff members of the National Endowment for the Humanities, an independent federal agency, which has funded the Mark Twain Project by outright and matching grants since 1966. We are indeed grateful for this intellectual and material support, part of which the Endowment provided for the present volume by matching a major gift from the L. J. Skaggs and Mary C. Skaggs Foundation, without whose generous support this book could not have been produced.

The Endowment's recent grants were also made possible by an outpouring of private support for the Project. Without this self-imposed tax on Mark Twain's most loyal readers, neither this volume nor the Project itself would exist today. We therefore want to thank the following major donors: Betty G. Austin; The House of Bernstein, Inc.; J. Dennis Bonney; Edmund G. and Bernice Brown; Class of 1938, University of California, Berkeley; Chevron Corporation; Chronicle Books; Don L. Cook; the late Alice Gaddis; Launce E. Gamble; Dr. Orville J. Golub; Marion S. Goodin; Constance Crowley Hart; the late James D. Hart; William Randolph Hearst Foundation; Hedco Foundation; Janet S. and William D. Hermann; Kenneth E. Hill; Hal Holbrook; Koret Foundation; Mark Twain Foundation; Bobby for Frank and Georgiana Massa; Robert N. Miner; Jeanne G. O'Brien and the late James E. O'Brien; Connie J. and David H. Pyle; Catherine D. Rau; Verla K. Regnery Foundation; John W. and Barbara Rosston; Marion B. and Willis S. Slusser; Thomas More Storke Fund; Koji Tabei; Gretchen Trupiano; the late John Russell Wagner; Mrs. Paul L. Wattis; and two generous donors from California who prefer to remain anonymous.

Space prevents our listing every recent contributor here, but we do want to thank the following for their timely generosity: Jonathan Arac; Harold Aspiz; Howard G. Baetzhold; Lawrence I. Berkove; Paul Berkowitz; Kevin J. and Margaret A. Bochynski; Dr. and Mrs. Richard J. Borg; Harold I. and Beula Blair Boucher; Boone Brackett, M.D.; The Brick Row Book Shop; Richard Bridgman; Louis J. and Isabelle Budd; James E. Caron; William A. and Mildred Clayton; Jean R. and Sherman Chickering; Hennig Cohen; Marvin M. Cole; James L. Colwell; Frederick C. Crews; Sally J. Letchworth in memory of Susan Letchworth Dann; Dow Chemical Corporation Foundation; Victor A. Doyno; William J. Duhigg, Jr.; William W. Escherich; Dorothy D. Eweson; Shelley Fisher Fishkin; Friends of Caxton; Guy G. Gilchrist, Jr.; Jay E. Gillette; Dorothy Goldberg; Stephen L. and Barbara H. Golder; Shoji Goto; James C. Greene; John Mitchell Hardaway; Katherine Heller; Judith B. Herman; Mr. and Mrs. Stephen G. Herrick; Dr. and Mrs. David S. Hubbell; George J. Houlé Rare Books & Autographs; Hiroyoshi Ichikawa; Dr. Janice Beaty Janssen; Fred Kaplan; Lawrence Kearney; Dr. Charles C. Kelsey; Holger Kersten; Harlan Kessel; Paul R. and Elisa S. Kleven; Lucius Marion Lampton; J. William Larkin, Jr.; Jennifer S. Larson; Dr. Roger Keith Larson; Mary-Warren Leary; William S. Linn; Joseph H. Towson for Debbie L. Lopez; George J. Houlé in memory of Matthias (Matt) P. Lowman; The Honorable Thomas J. Mac Bride; William J. McClung; Hugh D. McNiven; James H. Maguire; Thomas A. Maik; Ronald R. Melen; Jay and Elise Miller; F. Van Dorn Moller; Ann Elizabeth and Robert Murtha; Makoto Nagawara; Suzanne Naiburg; Emily V. Nichols; Hiroshi Okubo; David Packard; Thelma Schoonmaker Powell; Reader's Digest Foundation; Taylor Roberts; Dr. Verne L. Roberts; Brandt Rowles; Kenneth M. Sanderson; John R. Shuman; Elinor Lucas Smith; Jeffrey Steinbrink; Forrest E. and Dorothy A. Tregea; Marlene Boyd Vallin; Robert W. Vivian; Willard D. Washburn; F. A. West; Merilynn Laskey Wilson; Edward O. Wolcott; Harold A. Wollenberg; Laurel A. and Jeffrey S. Wruble.

We thank the Mark Twain Committee of the Council of The Friends of The Bancroft Library, particularly its current members, for continuing efforts on our behalf: Janet S. Hermann and Barbara Boucke, co-chairs; Cindy A. Barber; A. D. Brugger; Edwin V. Glaser; Stephen G. Herrick; and Willis S. Slusser, as well as Kimberley L. Massingale, secretary to the Council. We thank Noel Polk for his careful scrutiny of the text and apparatus on behalf of the Committee on Scholarly Editions of the Modern Language Association. And we also thank the following individuals for documents and information that have enriched the annotation or helped establish the text: Fred Clagett; Kenneth D. Craven, Harry Ransome Humanities Research Center, University of Texas at Austin; James Gilreath and James H. Hutson, Library of Congress; Dorothy Goldberg; William Hare, New London County (Conn.) Historical Society; Jeffrey Kintop, Nevada State Library and Archives; Mitsuo Kodama, President, Iwaki Meisei University, Fukushima, Japan; Jo McIntyre, Mitchell Library, State Library of New South Wales, Sydney; Nancy S. MacKechnie, Vassar College Library; Michael H. Marleau; John Melton, John Carroll University, Cleveland; Spiro Peterson and Frank Jordan, Jr., Miami University English Department, Oxford, Ohio; Evelyn Walker, Rush Rhees Library, University of Rochester; Ronald G. Watt, Historical Department of the Church of Jesus Christ of Latter-day Saints; Geoffrey A. White, Hawaii State Archives; and Patricia C. Willis, Beinecke Rare Book and Manuscript Library, Yale University Library.

Professor Branch has received invaluable assistance over many years from the staff of the Miami University Library. We are especially indebted to Donald E. Oehlerts, former Director of the Miami University Libraries, and Judith A. Sessions, Dean and Miami University Librarian. We thank the entire staff of the Miami University Edgar Weld King Library, especially C. Martin Miller, Elizabeth Brice, Frances McClure, and James Bricker of Special Collections; Richard H. Quay and William Wortman of the Division of Humanities and Social Science; Documents Librarians Jean Sears, Margaret Lewis, and Judy Austin; and Sarah Barr, Karen Clift, and Scott Van Dam of the Interlibrary Loan Service. At the University of California, Berkeley, we have relied on the unsurpassed collections of western Americana in The Bancroft Library. For indispensable help with these collections we thank Anthony S. Bliss, Walter V. Brem, Jr., Franz Enciso, Vivian C. Fisher, Peter E. Hanff, Bonnie Hardwick, Irene M. Moran, David B. Rez, Terri A. Rinne, and William M. Roberts. We are likewise grateful to Philip Hoehn of the Map Room, and Leon D. Megrian, Jo Lynn Milardovich, and Rhio Barnhart of the Interlibrary Borrowing Service in the General Library.

Judith Abrams and Kathy Fallon each typed the text of *Roughing It* with exemplary accuracy. Fran Mitchell at the University of California Press coordinated production with her customary expertise. Christine Taylor and Janet Stephens of Wilsted and Taylor Publishing Services gave us valuable advice about book design, and expert typesetting that would have pleased Mark Twain. Allen McKinney, John Eastman, and Kevin McGehee of Graphic Impressions provided exceptionally fine photographs, particularly of the illustrations from the first edition and of the draft manuscript pages in the Introduction. Tina Espinosa, Kevin Kolb, John Parsons, and Susan Stanley of Eureka Cartography thoughtfully designed the maps.

We are, finally, grateful to our associates in the Mark Twain Project, both for their help with routine tasks and for their collaborative spirit. To edit Mark Twain in their company is to brave a continual stream of new-found information, exacting standards, and unsparing criticism, even-handedly applied to all. We thank Richard Bucci for his meticulous collation of newspaper and first-edition texts. We thank Kenneth M. Sanderson for applying his bibliographical expertise to the welter of *Roughing It* reprints. Michael B. Frank thoughtfully read and greatly improved the notes. Victor Fischer was an indispensable guide, often laying aside his own work to help solve problems with *Roughing It*. Several generations of editorial assistants cheerfully supported the work: Kandi B. Arndt, Scott Bean, Courtney L. Clark, Shawna L. Fleming, Laura Goodale, Simon J. Hernandez, Amy Horlings, Carol Kramer, Jane Murray, Kevin Skaggs, and Deborah Ann Turner. Administrative assistant Dorothy ("Sunny") Gottberg dispatched office business with unflagging energy and all-enduring patience. To each of these colleagues we renew our heartfelt thanks.

H. E. S.   E. M. B.   L. S.   R. P. B.

THE MINER'S DREAM.

ROUGHING IT

BY

MARK TWAIN
(SAMUEL L. CLEMENS)

FULLY ILLUSTRATED BY EMINENT ARTISTS

TO
CALVIN H. HIGBIE,
Of California,
An Honest Man, a Genial Comrade, and a Steadfast Friend,
THIS BOOK IS INSCRIBED
By the Author,
In Memory of the Curious Time
When We Two
WERE MILLIONAIRES FOR TEN DAYS.

PREFATORY

THIS book is merely a personal narrative, and not a pretentious history or a philosophical dissertation. It is a record of several years of variegated vagabondizing, and its object is rather to help the resting reader while away an idle hour than afflict him with metaphysics, or goad him with science. Still, there is information in the volume; information concerning an interesting episode in the history of the Far West, about which no books have been written by persons who were on the ground in person, and saw the happenings of the time with their own eyes. I allude to the rise, growth and culmination of the silver-mining fever in Nevada—a curious episode, in some respects; the only one, of its peculiar kind, that has occurred in the land; and the only one, indeed, that is likely to occur in it.

Yes, take it all around, there is quite a good deal of information in the book. I regret this very much; but really it could not be helped: information appears to stew out of me naturally, like the precious ottar of roses out of the otter. Sometimes it has seemed to me that I would give worlds if I could retain my facts; but it cannot be. The more I caulk up the sources, and the tighter I get, the more I leak wisdom. Therefore, I can only claim indulgence at the hands of the reader, not justification.

THE AUTHOR.

CONTENTS

CHAPTER 1

My brother had just been appointed Secretary of Nevada Territory—an office of such majesty that it concentrated in itself the duties and dignities of Treasurer, Comptroller, Secretary of State, and Acting Governor in the Governor's absence. A salary of eighteen hundred dollars a year and the title of "Mr. Secretary," gave to the great position an air of wild and imposing grandeur. I was young and ignorant, and I envied my brother. I coveted his distinction and his financial splendor, but particularly and especially the

ENVIOUS CONTEMPLATIONS.

long, strange journey he was going to make, and the curious new world he was going to explore. He was going to travel! I never had been away from home, and that word "travel" had a seductive charm for me. Pretty soon he would be hundreds and hundreds of miles away on the great plains and deserts, and among the mountains of the Far West, and would see buffaloes and Indians, and prairie dogs, and antelopes, and have all kinds of adventures, and maybe get hanged or scalped, and have ever such a fine time, and write home and tell us all about it, and be a hero. And he would see the gold mines and the silver mines, and maybe go about of an afternoon when his work was done, and pick up two or three pailfuls of shining slugs, and nuggets of gold and silver on the hillside. And by and by he would become very rich, and return home by sea, and be able to talk as calmly about San Francisco and the ocean, and "the Isthmus" as if it was nothing of any consequence to have seen those marvels face to face. What I suffered in contemplating his happiness, pen cannot describe. And so, when he offered me, in cold blood, the sublime position of private secretary under him, it appeared to me that the heavens and the earth passed away, and the firmament was rolled together as a scroll! I had nothing more to desire. My contentment was complete. At the end of an hour or two I was ready for the journey. Not much packing up was necessary, because we were going in the overland stage from the Missouri frontier to Nevada, and passengers were only allowed a small quantity of baggage apiece. There was no Pacific railroad in those fine times of ten or twelve years ago—not a single rail of it.

I only proposed to stay in Nevada three months—I had no thought of staying longer than that. I meant to see all I could that was new and strange, and then hurry home to business. I little thought that I would not see the end of that three-month pleasure excursion for six or seven uncommonly long years!

I dreamed all night about Indians, deserts, and silver bars, and in due time, next day, we took shipping at the St. Louis wharf on board a steamboat bound up the Missouri river.

We were six days going from St. Louis to "St. Joe"—a trip that was so dull, and sleepy, and eventless that it has left no more impression on my memory than if its duration had been six minutes instead of that many days. No record is left in my mind, now, concerning it, but a confused jumble of savage-looking snags, which we deliberately walked over with one wheel or the other; and of reefs which we butted and butted, and then retired from and

INNOCENT DREAMS.

climbed over in some softer place; and of sand-bars which we roosted on occasionally, and rested, and then got out our crutches and sparred over. In fact, the boat might almost as well have gone to St. Joe by land, for she was walking most of the time, anyhow—climbing over reefs and clambering over snags patiently and laboriously all day long. The captain said she was a "bully" boat, and all she wanted was more "shear" and a bigger wheel. I thought she wanted a pair of stilts, but I had the deep sagacity not to say so.

CHAPTER 2

THE first thing we did on that glad evening that landed us at St. Joseph was to hunt up the stage-office, and pay a hundred and fifty dollars apiece for tickets per overland coach to Carson City, Nevada.

The next morning, bright and early, we took a hasty breakfast, and hurried to the starting-place. Then an inconvenience presented itself which we had not properly appreciated before, namely, that one cannot make a heavy traveling trunk stand for twenty-five pounds of baggage—because it weighs a good deal more. But that was all we could take—twenty-five pounds each. So

LIGHT TRAVELING ORDER.

we had to snatch our trunks open, and make a selection in a good deal of a hurry. We put our lawful twenty-five pounds apiece all in one valise, and shipped the trunks back to St. Louis again. It was a sad parting, for now we had no swallow-tail coats and white kid gloves to wear at Pawnee receptions in the Rocky Mountains, and no stove-pipe hats nor patent-leather boots, nor anything else necessary to make life calm and peaceful. We were reduced to a war-footing. Each of us put on a rough, heavy suit of clothing, woolen army shirt and "stogy" boots included; and into the valise we crowded a few white shirts, some underclothing and such things. My brother, the Secretary, took along about four pounds of U. S. statutes and six pounds of Unabridged Dictionary; for we did not know—poor innocents—that such things could be bought in San Francisco on one day and received in Carson City the next. I was armed to the teeth with a pitiful little Smith & Wesson's seven-shooter, which carried a ball like a homœopathic pill, and it took the whole seven to make a dose for an adult. But I thought it was grand. It appeared to me to be a dangerous weapon. It only had one fault—you could not hit anything with it. One of our "conductors" practiced awhile on a cow with it, and as long as she stood still and behaved herself she was safe; but as soon as she

THE "ALLEN."

went to moving about, and he got to shooting at other things, she came to grief. The Secretary had a small-sized Colt's revolver strapped around him for protection against the Indians, and to guard against accidents he carried it uncapped. Mr. George Bemis was dismally formidable. George Bemis was our fellow-traveler. We had never seen him before. He wore in his belt an old original "Allen" revolver, such as irreverent people called a "pepper-box." Simply drawing the trigger back, cocked and fired the pistol. As the trigger came back, the hammer would begin to rise and the barrel to turn over, and presently down would drop the hammer, and away would speed the ball. To aim along the turning barrel and hit the thing aimed at was a feat which was probably never done with an "Allen" in the world. But George's was a reliable weapon, nevertheless, because, as one of the stage-drivers afterward said, "If she didn't get what she went after, she would fetch something else." And so she did. She went after a deuce of spades nailed against a tree, once, and fetched a mule standing about thirty yards to the left of it. Bemis did not want the mule; but the owner came out with a double-barreled shotgun and persuaded him to buy it, anyhow. It was a cheerful weapon—the "Allen." Sometimes all its six barrels would go off at once, and then there was no safe place in all the region round about, but behind it.

We took two or three blankets for protection against frosty weather in the mountains. In the matter of luxuries we were modest—we took none along but some pipes and five pounds of smok-

INDUCEMENTS TO PURCHASE.

ing tobacco. We had two large canteens to carry water in, between stations on the Plains, and we also took with us a little shot-bag of silver coin for daily expenses in the way of breakfasts and dinners.

By eight o'clock everything was ready, and we were on the other side of the river. We jumped into the stage, the driver cracked his whip, and we bowled away and left "the States" behind us. It was a superb summer morning, and all the landscape was brilliant with sunshine. There was a freshness and breeziness, too, and an exhilarating sense of emancipation from all sorts of cares and responsibilities, that almost made us feel that the years we had spent in the close, hot city, toiling and slaving, had been wasted and thrown away. We were spinning along through Kansas, and in the course of an hour and a half we were fairly abroad on the great Plains. Just here the land was rolling—a grand sweep of regular elevations and depressions as far as the eye could reach—like the stately heave and swell of the ocean's bosom after a storm. And everywhere were cornfields, accenting with squares of deeper green, this limitless expanse of grassy land. But presently this sea upon dry ground was to lose its "rolling" character and stretch away for seven hundred miles as level as a floor!

Our coach was a great swinging and swaying stage, of the most sumptuous description—an imposing cradle on wheels. It was drawn by six handsome horses, and by the side of the driver sat the "conductor," the legitimate captain of the craft; for it was his business to take charge and care of the mails, baggage, express matter, and passengers. We three were the only passengers, this trip. We sat on the back seat, inside. About all the rest of the coach was full of mail-bags—for we had three days' delayed mails with us. Almost touching our knees, a perpendicular wall of mail matter rose up to the roof. There was a great pile of it strapped on top of the stage, and both the fore and hind boots were full. We had twenty-seven hundred pounds of it aboard, the driver said—"a little for

THE FACETIOUS DRIVER.

Brigham, and Carson, and 'Frisco, but the heft of it for the Injuns, which is powerful troublesome 'thout they get plenty of truck to read." But as he just then got up a fearful convulsion of his countenance which was suggestive of a wink being swallowed by an earthquake, we guessed that his remark was intended to be facetious, and to mean that we would unload the most of our mail matter somewhere on the Plains and leave it to the Indians, or whosoever wanted it.

We changed horses every ten miles, all day long, and fairly flew over the hard, level road. We jumped out and stretched our legs every time the coach stopped, and so the night found us still vivacious and unfatigued.

After supper a woman got in, who lived about fifty miles further on, and we three had to take turns at sitting outside with the driver and conductor. Apparently she was not a talkative woman. She would sit there in the gathering twilight and fasten her steadfast

PLEASING NEWS.

eyes on a mosquito rooting into her arm, and slowly she would
raise her other hand till she had got his range, and then she would
launch a slap at him that would have jolted a cow; and after that
she would sit and contemplate the corpse with tranquil satisfaction—for she never missed her mosquito; she was a dead shot at
short range. She never removed a carcase, but left them there for

THE SPHYNX.

bait. I sat by this grim Sphynx
and watched her kill thirty
or forty mosquitoes—watched
her, and waited for her to say
something, but she never did.
So I finally opened the conversation myself. I said:

"The mosquitoes are pretty
bad, about here, madam."

"You bet!"

"What did I understand you
to say, madam?"

"You BET!"

Then she cheered up, and faced around and said:

"Danged if I didn't begin to think you fellers was deef and dumb. I did, b' gosh. Here I've sot, and sot, and sot, a bust'n muskeeters and wonderin' what was ailin' ye. Fust I thot you was deef and dumb, then I thot you was sick or crazy, or suthin', and then by and by I begin to reckon you was a passel of sickly fools that couldn't think of nothing to say. Wher'd ye come from?"

The Sphynx was a Sphynx no more! The fountains of her great deep were broken up, and she rained the nine parts of speech forty days and forty nights, metaphorically speaking, and buried us under a desolating deluge of trivial gossip that left not a crag or pinnacle of rejoinder projecting above the tossing waste of dislocated grammar and decomposed pronunciation!

How we suffered, suffered, suffered! She went on, hour after hour, till I was sorry I ever opened the mosquito question and gave her a start. She never did stop again until she got to her journey's end toward daylight; and then she stirred us up as she was leaving the stage (for we were nodding, by that time), and said:

"Now you git out at Cottonwood, you fellers, and lay over a couple o' days, and I'll be along some time to-night, and if I can do ye any good by edgin' in a word now and then, I'm right thar. Folks 'll tell you 't I've always ben kind o' offish and partic'lar for a gal that's raised in the woods, and I *am*, with the rag-tag and bob-tail, and a gal *has* to be, if she wants to *be* anything, but when people comes along which is my equals, I reckon I'm a pretty sociable heifer after all."

We resolved not to "lay by at Cottonwood."

CHAPTER 3

About an hour and a half before daylight we were bowling along smoothly over the road—so smoothly that our cradle only rocked in a gentle, lulling way, that was gradually soothing us to sleep, and dulling our consciousness—when something gave away under us! We were dimly aware of it, but indifferent to it. The coach stopped. We heard the driver and conductor talking together outside, and rummaging for a lantern, and swearing because they could not find it—but we had no interest in whatever had happened, and it only added to our comfort to think of those people out there at work in the murky night, and we snug in our nest with the curtains drawn. But presently, by the sounds, there seemed to be an examination going on, and then the driver's voice said:

"By George, the thoroughbrace is broke!"

This startled me broad awake—as an undefined sense of calamity is always apt to do. I said to myself: "Now, a thoroughbrace is probably part of a horse; and doubtless a vital part, too, from the dismay in the driver's voice. Leg, maybe—and yet how could he break his leg waltzing along such a road as this? No, it can't be his leg. That is impossible, unless he was reaching for the driver. Now, what can be the thoroughbrace of a horse, I wonder? Well, whatever comes, I shall not air my ignorance in this crowd, anyway."

Just then the conductor's face appeared at a lifted curtain, and his lantern glared in on us and our wall of mail matter. He said:

"Gents, you'll have to turn out a spell. Thoroughbrace is broke."

We climbed out into a chill drizzle, and felt ever so homeless and dreary. When I found that the thing they called a "thoroughbrace" was the massive combination of belts and springs which the coach rocks itself in, I said to the driver:

"I never saw a thoroughbrace used up like that, before, that I can remember. How did it happen?"

"Why, it happened by trying to make one coach carry three days' mail—that's how it happened," said he. "And right here is the very direction which is wrote on all the newspaper-bags which was to be put out for the Injuns for to keep 'em quiet. It's most uncommon lucky, becuz it's so nation dark I should 'a' gone by unbeknowns if that air thoroughbrace hadn't broke."

I knew that he was in labor with another of those winks of his, though I could not see his face, because he was bent down at work; and wishing him a safe delivery, I turned to and helped the rest get out the mail-sacks. It made a great pyramid by the roadside when it was all out. When they had mended the thoroughbrace we filled the two boots again, but put no mail on top, and only half as much inside as there was before. The conductor bent all the seat-backs down, and then filled the coach just half full of mail-bags from end to end. We objected loudly to this, for it left us no seats. But the conductor was wiser than we, and said a bed was better than seats, and moreover, this plan would protect his thoroughbraces. We never wanted any seats after that. The lazy bed was infinitely preferable. I had many an exciting day, subsequently, lying on it reading the statutes and the Dictionary, and wondering how the characters would turn out.

The conductor said he would send back a guard from the next station to take charge of the abandoned mail-bags, and we drove on.

It was now just dawn; and as we stretched our cramped legs full length on the mail-sacks, and gazed out through the windows across the wide wastes of greensward clad in cool, powdery mist, to where there was an expectant look in the eastern horizon, our perfect enjoyment took the form of a tranquil and contented ecstasy. The stage whirled along at a spanking gait, the breeze flapping curtains and suspended coats in a most exhilarating way; the cradle swayed and swung luxuriously, the pattering of the horses' hoofs, the cracking of the driver's whip, and his "Hi-yi! g'lang!" were music; the spinning ground and the waltzing trees appeared to give us a mute hurrah as we went by, and then slack up and look after us with interest, or envy, or something; and as we lay and smoked the pipe of peace and compared all this luxury with the years of tiresome city life that had gone before it, we felt that there

was only one complete and satisfying happiness in the world, and
we had found it.

After breakfast, at some station whose name I have forgotten,
we three climbed up on the seat behind the driver, and let the conductor have our bed for a nap. And by and by, when the sun made
me drowsy, I lay down on my face on top of the coach, grasping the
slender iron railing, and slept for an hour or more. That will give
one an appreciable idea of those matchless roads. Instinct will
make a sleeping man grip a fast hold of the railing when the stage
jolts, but when it only swings and sways, no grip is necessary.
Overland drivers and conductors used to sit in their places and
sleep thirty or forty minutes at a time, on good roads, while spinning along at the rate of eight or ten miles an hour. I saw them do
it, often. There was no danger about it; a sleeping man *will* seize
the irons in time when the coach jolts. These men were hard
worked, and it was not possible for them to stay awake all the time.

By and by we passed through Marysville, and over the Big Blue
and Little Sandy; thence about a mile, and entered Nebraska.
About a mile further on, we came to the Big Sandy—one hundred
and eighty miles from St. Joseph.

As the sun was going down, we saw the first specimen of an
animal known familiarly over two thousand miles of mountain

and desert—from Kansas clear
to the Pacific Ocean—as the
"jackass rabbit." He is well
named. He is just like any other
rabbit, except that he is from
one-third to twice as large, has
longer legs in proportion to his
size, and has the most preposterous ears that ever were
mounted on any creature *but*
a jackass. When he is sitting
quiet, thinking about his sins,
or is absent-minded or unappre-
hensive of danger, his majestic

MEDITATION.

ears project above him conspicuously; but the breaking of a twig
will scare him nearly to death, and then he tilts his ears back

gently and starts for home. All you can see, then, for the next minute, is his long gray form stretched out straight and "streaking it"
through the low sage-brush, head erect, eyes right, and ears just
canted a little to the rear, but showing you where the animal is, all
the time, the same as if he carried a jib. Now and then he makes a
marvelous spring with his long legs, high over the stunted sage-
brush, and scores a leap that would make a horse envious. Presently he comes down to a long, graceful "lope," and shortly he mysteriously disappears. He has crouched behind a sage-bush, and will
sit there and listen and tremble until you get within six feet of
him, when he will get under way again. But one must shoot at
this creature once, if he wishes to see him throw his heart into
his heels, and do the best he knows how. He is frightened clear

ON BUSINESS.

through, now, and he lays his long ears down on his back, straight-
ens himself out like a yard-stick every spring he makes, and
scatters miles behind him with an easy indifference that is
enchanting.

Our party made this specimen "hump himself," as the conductor said. The Secretary started him with a shot from the Colt; I
commenced spitting at him with my weapon; and all in the same
instant the old "Allen's" whole broadside let go with a rattling
crash, and it is not putting it too strong to say that the rabbit was
frantic! He dropped his ears, set up his tail, and left for San Francisco at a speed which can only be described as a flash and a vanish! Long after he was out of sight we could hear him whiz.

I do not remember where we first came across "sage-brush," but as I have been speaking of it I may as well describe it. This is easily done, for if the reader can imagine a gnarled and venerable live oak tree reduced to a little shrub two feet high, with its rough bark, its foliage, its twisted boughs, all complete, he can picture the "sage-brush" exactly. Often, on lazy afternoons in the mountains, I have lain on the ground with my face under a sage-bush, and entertained myself with fancying that the gnats among its foliage were lilliputian birds, and that the ants marching and countermarching

AUTHOR AS GULLIVER.

about its base were lilliputian flocks and herds, and myself some vast loafer from Brobdingnag waiting to catch a little citizen and eat him.

It is an imposing monarch of the forest in exquisite miniature, is the "sage-brush." Its foliage is a grayish green, and gives that tint to desert and mountain. It smells like our domestic sage, and "sage-tea" made from it tastes like the sage-tea which all boys are so well acquainted with. The sage-brush is a singularly hardy plant, and grows right in the midst of deep sand, and among barren rocks, where nothing else in the vegetable world would try to grow, except "bunch-grass."* The sage-bushes grow from three to six or seven feet apart, all over the mountains and deserts of the Far West, clear to the borders of California. There is not a tree of any kind in the deserts, for hundreds of miles—there is no vegetation at all in a regular desert, except the sage-brush and its cousin the "grease-wood," which is so much like the sage-brush that the difference amounts to little. Camp-fires and hot suppers in the deserts would be impossible but for the friendly sage-brush. Its trunk is as large as a boy's wrist (and from that up to a man's arm), and its crooked branches are half as large as its trunk—all good, sound, hard wood, very like oak.

When a party camps, the first thing to be done is to cut sage-brush; and in a few minutes there is an opulent pile of it ready for use. A hole a foot wide, two feet deep, and two feet long, is dug, and sage-brush chopped up and burned in it till it is full to the brim with glowing coals. Then the cooking begins, and there is no smoke, and consequently no swearing. Such a fire will keep all night, with very little replenishing; and it makes a very sociable camp-fire, and one around which the most impossible reminis-cences sound plausible, instructive, and profoundly entertaining.

Sage-brush is very fair fuel, but as a vegetable it is a distin-guished failure. Nothing can abide the taste of it but the jackass and his illegitimate child the mule. But their testimony to its nu-tritiousness is worth nothing, for they will eat pine knots, or an-thracite coal, or brass filings, or lead pipe, or old bottles, or any-thing that comes handy, and then go off looking as grateful as if they had had oysters for dinner. Mules and donkeys and camels have appetites that anything will relieve temporarily, but nothing satisfy. In Syria, once, at the head-waters of the Jordan, a camel took charge of my overcoat while the tents were being pitched, and examined it with a critical eye, all over, with as much interest as if

---

*"Bunch-grass" grows on the bleak mountain sides of Nevada and neighboring Territories, and offers excellent feed for stock, even in the dead of winter, wherever the snow is blown aside and exposes it; notwithstanding its unpromising home, bunch-grass is a better and more nutritious diet for cattle and horses than almost any other hay or grass that is known—so stock-men say.

A rough statement.

he had an idea of getting one made like it; and then, after he was done figuring on it as an article of apparel, he began to contemplate it as an article of diet. He put his foot on it, and lifted one of the sleeves out with his teeth, and chewed and chewed at it, gradually taking it in, and all the while opening and closing his eyes in a kind of religious ecstasy, as if he had never tasted anything as good as an overcoat before, in his life. Then he smacked his lips once or twice, and reached after the other sleeve. Next he tried the velvet collar, and smiled a smile of such contentment that it was plain to see that he regarded that as the daintiest thing about an overcoat. The tails went next, along with some percussion caps and cough candy, and some fig-paste from Constantinople. And then my newspaper correspondence dropped out, and he took a chance in that—manuscript letters written for the home papers. But he was treading on dangerous ground, now. He began to come across solid wisdom in those documents that was rather weighty on his stomach; and occasionally he would take a joke that would shake him up till it loosened his teeth; it was getting to be perilous times with him, but he held his grip with good courage and hopefully, till at last he began to stumble on statements that not even a camel could swallow with impunity. He began to gag and gasp, and his eyes to stand out, and his forelegs to spread, and in about a quarter of a minute he fell over as stiff as a carpenter's work-bench, and died a death of indescribable agony. I went and pulled the manuscript out of his mouth, and found that the sensitive creature had choked to death on one of the mildest and gentlest statements of fact that I ever laid before a trusting public.

I was about to say, when diverted from my subject, that occasionally one finds sage-bushes five or six feet high, and with a spread of branch and foliage in proportion, but two or two and a half feet is the usual height.

CHAPTER 4

As the sun went down and the evening chill came on, we made preparation for bed. We stirred up the hard leather letter-sacks, and the knotty canvas bags of printed matter (knotty and uneven because of projecting ends and corners of magazines, boxes and books). We stirred them up and redisposed them in such a way as to make our bed as level as possible. And we *did* improve it, too, though after all our work it had an upheaved and billowy look about it, like a little piece of a stormy sea. Next we hunted up our boots from odd nooks among the mail-bags where they had settled, and put them on. Then we got down our coats, vests, pantaloons and heavy woolen shirts, from the arm-loops where they had been swinging all day, and clothed ourselves in them—for, there being no ladies either at the stations or in the coach, and the weather being hot, we had looked to our comfort by stripping to our underclothing, at nine o'clock in the morning. All things being now ready, we stowed the uneasy Dictionary where it would lie as quiet as possible, and placed the water canteens and pistols where we could find them in the dark. Then we smoked a final pipe, and swapped a final yarn; after which, we put the pipes, tobacco and bag of coin in snug holes and caves among the mail-bags, and then fastened down the coach curtains all around, and made the place as "dark as the inside of a cow," as the conductor phrased it in his picturesque way. It was certainly as dark as any place could be—nothing was even dimly visible in it. And finally, we rolled ourselves up like silk-worms, each person in his own blanket, and sank peacefully to sleep.

Whenever the stage stopped to change horses, we would wake up, and try to recollect where we were—and succeed—and in a minute or two the stage would be off again, and we likewise. We began to get into country, now, threaded here and there with little streams. These had high, steep banks on each side, and every time we flew down one bank and scrambled up the other, our party inside got mixed somewhat. First we would all be down in a pile at the forward end of the stage, nearly in a sitting posture, and in a second we would shoot to the other end, and stand on our heads. And we would sprawl and kick, too, and ward off ends and corners of mail-bags that came lumbering over us and about us; and as the dust rose from the tumult, we would all sneeze in chorus, and the majority of us would grumble, and probably say some hasty thing, like: "Take your elbow out of my ribs!—can't you quit crowding?"

Every time we avalanched from one end of the stage to the other, the Unabridged Dictionary would come too; and every time it came it damaged somebody. One trip it "barked" the Secretary's elbow; the next trip it hurt me in the stomach, and the third it tilted Bemis's nose up till he could look down his nostrils—he said. The

THIRD TRIP OF THE UNABRIDGED.

pistols and coin soon settled to the bottom, but the pipes, pipe-stems, tobacco and canteens clattered and floundered after the Dictionary every time it made an assault on us, and aided and abetted the book by spilling tobacco in our eyes, and water down our backs.

Still, all things considered, it was a very comfortable night. It wore gradually away, and when at last a cold gray light was visible through the puckers and chinks in the curtains, we yawned and stretched with satisfaction, shed our cocoons, and felt that we had slept as much as was necessary. By and by, as the sun rose up and warmed the world, we pulled off our clothes and got ready for breakfast. We were just pleasantly in time, for five minutes afterward the driver sent the weird music of his bugle winding over the grassy solitudes, and presently we detected a low hut or two in the distance. Then the rattling of the coach, the clatter of our six horses' hoofs, and the driver's crisp commands, awoke to a louder and stronger emphasis, and we went sweeping down on the station at our smartest speed. It was fascinating—that old overland stage-coaching.

We jumped out in undress uniform. The driver tossed his gathered reins out on the ground, gaped and stretched complacently, drew off his heavy buckskin gloves with great deliberation and insufferable dignity—taking not the slightest notice of a dozen solicitous inquiries after his health, and humbly facetious and flattering accostings, and obsequious tenders of service, from five or six hairy and half-civilized station-keepers and hostlers who were nimbly unhitching our steeds and bringing the fresh team out of the stables—for in the eyes of the stage-driver of that day, station-keepers and hostlers were a sort of good enough low creatures, useful in their place, and helping to make up a world, but not the kind of beings which a person of distinction could afford to concern himself with; while, on the contrary, in the eyes of the station-keeper and the hostler, the stage-driver was a hero—a great and shining dignitary, the world's favorite son, the envy of the people, the observed of the nations. When they spoke to him they received his insolent silence meekly, and as being the natural and proper conduct of so great a man; when he opened his lips they all hung on his words with admiration (he never honored a particular individual with a remark, but addressed it with a broad generality to the horses, the stables, the surrounding country *and* the human underlings); when he discharged a facetious insulting personality at a hostler, that hostler was happy for the day; when he uttered his one jest—old as the hills, coarse, profane, witless, and inflicted on the same audience, in the same language, every time his coach drove up there—the varlets roared, and slapped their thighs, and swore it was the best thing they'd ever heard in all their lives. And how they would fly around when he wanted a basin of water, a gourd of the same, or a light for his pipe!—but they would instantly insult a passenger if he so far forgot himself as to crave a favor at their hands. They could do that sort of insolence as well as the driver they copied it from—for, let it be borne in mind, the overland driver had but little less contempt for his passengers than he had for his hostlers.

The hostlers and station-keepers treated the really powerful *conductor* of the coach merely with the best of what was their idea of civility, but the *driver* was the only being they bowed down to and worshipped. How admiringly they would gaze up at him in his high seat as he gloved himself with lingering deliberation, while some happy hostler held the bunch of reins aloft, and waited patiently for him to take it! And how they would bombard him with glorifying ejaculations as he cracked his long whip and went careering away.

The station buildings were long, low huts, made of sun-dried, mud-colored bricks, laid up without mortar (*adobes*, the Spaniards call these bricks, and Americans shorten it to " 'dobies"). The roofs, which had no slant to them worth speaking of, were thatched and then sodded or covered with a thick layer of earth, and from this sprung a pretty rank growth of weeds and grass. It was the first time we had ever seen a man's front yard on top of his house. The buildings consisted of barns, stable-room for twelve or fifteen horses, and a hut for an eating-room for passengers. This latter had bunks in it for the station-keeper and a hostler or two. You could rest your elbow on its eaves, and you had to bend in order to get in at the door. In place of a window there was a square hole about large enough for a man to crawl through, but this had no glass in it. There was no flooring, but the ground was packed hard. There was no stove, but the fire-place served all needful purposes. There were no shelves, no cupboards, no closets. In a corner stood an open sack of flour, and nestling against its base were a couple of black and venerable tin coffee-pots, a tin teapot, a little bag of salt, and a side of bacon.

By the door of the station-keeper's den, outside, was a tin washbasin, on the ground. Near it was a pail of water and a piece of yellow bar soap, and from the eaves hung a hoary blue woolen shirt, significantly—but this latter was the station-keeper's private towel, and only two persons in all the party might venture to use it—the stage-driver and the conductor. The latter would not, from a sense of decency; the former would not, because he did not choose to encourage the advances of a station-keeper. We had towels—in the valise; they might as well have been in Sodom and Gomorrah. We (and the conductor) used our handkerchiefs, and the driver his pantaloons and sleeves. By the door, inside, was fastened

A POWERFUL GLASS.

a small old-fashioned looking-glass frame, with two little fragments of the original mirror lodged down in one corner of it. This arrangement afforded a pleasant double-barreled portrait of you when you looked into it, with one-half of your head set up a couple of inches above the other half. From the glass frame hung the half of a comb by a string—but if I had to describe that patriarch or die, I believe I would order some sample coffins. It had come down from Esau and Samson, and had been accumulating hair ever since—along with certain impurities. In one corner of the room stood three or four rifles and muskets, together with horns and pouches of ammunition. The station-men wore pantaloons of coarse, country-woven stuff, and into the seat and the inside of the legs were sewed ample additions of buckskin, to do duty in place of leggings, when the man rode

AN HEIRLOOM.

horseback—so the pants were half dull blue and half yellow, and unspeakably picturesque. The pants were stuffed into the tops of high boots, the heels whereof were armed with great Spanish spurs, whose little iron clogs and chains jingled with every step. The man wore a huge beard and mustachios, an old slouch hat, a blue woolen shirt, no suspenders, no vest, no coat—in a leathern sheath in his belt, a great long "navy" revolver (slung on right side, hammer to the front), and projecting from his boot a horn-handled bowie knife. The furniture of the hut was neither gorgeous nor much in the way. The rocking-chairs and sofas were not present, and never had been, but they were represented by two three-legged stools, a pine-board bench four feet long, and two empty candle-boxes. The table was a greasy board on stilts, and the table-cloth and napkins had not come—and they were not look-

OUR LANDLORD.

ing for them, either. A battered tin platter, a knife and fork, and a tin pint cup, were at each man's place, and the driver had a queens-ware saucer that had seen better days. Of course this duke sat at

DIGNIFIED EXILE.

the head of the table. There was one isolated piece of table furniture that bore about it a touching air of grandeur in misfortune. This was the caster. It was German silver, and crippled and rusty, but it was so preposterously out of place there that it was suggestive of a tattered exiled king among barbarians, and the majesty of its native position compelled respect even in its degradation. There was only one cruet left, and that was a stopperless, fly-specked, broken-necked thing, with two inches of vinegar in it, and a dozen preserved flies with their heels up and looking sorry they had invested there.

The station-keeper up-ended a disk of last week's bread, of the shape and size of an old-time cheese, and carved some slabs from it which were as good as Nicolson pavement, and tenderer.

He sliced off a piece of bacon for each man, but only the experienced old hands made out to eat it, for it was condemned army bacon which the United States would not feed to its soldiers in the forts, and the stage company had bought it cheap for the sustenance of their passengers and employés. We may have found this condemned army bacon further out on the plains than the section I am locating it in, but we *found* it—there is no gainsaying that.

Then he poured for us a beverage which he called "*Slumgullion*," and it is hard to think he was not inspired when he named it.

DRINKING SLUMGULLION.

It really pretended to be tea, but there was too much dish-rag, and sand, and old bacon-rind in it to deceive the intelligent traveler. He had no sugar and no milk—not even a spoon to stir the ingredients with.

We could not eat the bread or the meat, nor drink the "slumgullion." And when I looked at that melancholy vinegar-cruet, I thought of the anecdote (a very, very old one, even at that day) of the traveler who sat down to a table which had nothing on it but a mackerel and a pot of mustard. He asked the landlord if this was all. The landlord said:

"*All!* Why, thunder and lightning, I should think there was mackerel enough there for six."

"But I don't like mackerel."

"Oh—then help yourself to the mustard."

In other days I had considered it a good, a very good, anecdote, but there was a dismal plausibility about it, here, that took all the humor out of it.

Our breakfast was before us, but our teeth were idle.

I tasted and smelt, and said I would take coffee, I believed. The station-boss stopped dead still, and glared at me speechless. At last, when he came to, he turned away and said, as one who communes with himself upon a matter too vast to grasp:

"*Coffee!* Well, if that don't go clean ahead of me, I'm d—d!"

We could not eat, and there was no conversation among the hostlers and herdsmen—we all sat at the same board. At least there was no conversation further than a single hurried request, now and then, from one employé to another. It was always in the same form, and always gruffly friendly. Its western freshness and novelty

A JOKE WITHOUT CREAM.

startled me, at first, and interested me; but it presently grew monotonous, and lost its charm. It was:

"Pass the bread, you son of a skunk!" No, I forget—skunk was not the word; it seems to me it was still stronger than that; I know it was, in fact, but it is gone from my memory, apparently. However, it is no matter—probably it was too strong for print, anyway. It is the landmark in my memory which tells me where I first encountered the vigorous new vernacular of the occidental plains and mountains.

We gave up the breakfast, and paid our dollar apiece and went back to our mail-bag bed in the coach, and found comfort in our pipes. Right here we suffered the first diminution of our princely state. We left our six fine horses and took six mules in their place. But they were wild Mexican fellows, and a man had to stand at the head of each of them and hold him fast while the driver gloved and got himself ready. And when at last he grasped the reins and gave the word, the men sprung suddenly away from the mules' heads and the coach shot from the station as if it had issued from a cannon. How the frantic animals did scamper! It was a fierce and furious gallop—and the gait never altered for a moment till we reeled off ten or twelve miles and swept up to the next collection of little station-huts and stables.

So we flew along all day. At 2 P.M. the belt of timber that fringes the North Platte and marks its windings through the vast level floor of the Plains came in sight. At 4 P.M. we crossed a branch of the river, and at 5 P.M. we crossed the Platte itself, and landed at Fort Kearny, *fifty-six hours out from St. Joe*—THREE HUNDRED MILES!

Now that was stage-coaching on the great overland, ten or twelve years ago, when perhaps not more than ten men in America, all told, expected to live to see a railroad follow that route to the Pacific. But the railroad is there, now, and it pictures a thousand odd comparisons and contrasts in my mind to read the following sketch, in the New York *Times*, of a recent trip over almost the very ground I have been describing. I can scarcely comprehend the new state of things:

ACROSS THE CONTINENT.

At 4:20 P. M., Sunday, we rolled out of the station at Omaha and started westward on our long jaunt. A couple of hours out, dinner was announced—an "event" to those of us who had yet to experience what it is to eat in one of PULLMAN'S hotels on wheels; so stepping into the car next forward of our sleeping palace, we found ourselves in the dining car. It was a revelation to us, that first dinner on Sunday; and though we con-

PULLMAN CAR DINING-SALOON.

tinued to dine for four days, and had as many breakfasts and suppers, our whole party never ceased to admire the perfection of the arrangements and the marvelous results achieved. Upon tables covered with snowy linen and garnished with services of solid silver, Ethiop waiters, flitting about in spotless white, placed as by magic a repast at which DELMONICO himself could have had no occasion to blush; and indeed in some respects it would be hard for that distinguished *chef* to match our *menu*; for, in addition to all that ordinarily makes up a first-chop dinner, had we not our antelope steak, (the gourmet who has not experienced *this*—bah! what does he know of the feast of fat things?) our delicious mountain brook-trout, our choice fruits and berries, and, sauce piquante and unpurchaseable, our sweet-scented appetite-compelling air of the prairies? You may depend upon it, we all did justice to the good things; and, as we washed them down with bumpers of sparkling Krug, while we sped along at the rate of thirty miles an hour, agreed it was the *fastest* living we had ever experienced. (We beat that, however, two days afterward, when we made *twenty-seven miles in twenty-seven minutes*, while our Champagne glasses filled to the brim spilled not a drop!) After dinner we repaired to our drawing-room car, and, as it was Sabbath eve, intoned some of the grand old hymns—"Praise God from whom," &c.; "Shining Shore," "Coronation," &c.—the voices of the men singers and of the women singers blending sweetly in the evening air, while our train, with its great, glaring

Polyphemus eye, lighting up long vistas of prairie, rushed into the night and the Wild. Then to bed in luxurious couches, where we slept the sleep of the just, and only awoke the next morning, (Monday,) at 8 o'clock, to find ourselves at the crossing of the North Platte, 300 miles from Omaha—*fifteen hours and forty minutes out.*

CHAPTER 5

ANOTHER night of alternate tranquillity and turmoil. But morning came, by and by. It was another glad awakening to fresh breezes, vast expanses of level greensward, bright sunlight, an impressive solitude utterly without visible human beings or human habitations, and an atmosphere of such amazing magnifying properties that trees that seemed close at hand were more than three miles away. We resumed undress uniform, climbed a-top of the

OUR MORNING RIDE.

flying coach, dangled our legs over the side, shouted occasionally at our frantic mules, merely to see them lay their ears back and scamper faster, tied our hats on to keep our hair from blowing away, and leveled an outlook over the world-wide carpet about us

for things new and strange to gaze at. Even at this day it thrills me
through and through to think of the life, the gladness and the wild

PRAIRIE DOGS.

sense of freedom that used to make the blood dance in my veins on
those fine overland mornings!

Along about an hour after breakfast we saw the first prairie-dog
villages, the first antelope, and the first wolf. If I remember rightly,
this latter was the regular *cayote* (pronounced ky-o-te) of the farther deserts. And if it *was*, he was not a pretty creature or respectable either, for I got well acquainted with his race afterward, and
can speak with confidence. The cayote is a long, slim, sick and
sorry-looking skeleton, with a gray wolf-skin stretched over it, a
tolerably bushy tail that forever sags down with a despairing

A CAYOTE.

expression of forsakenness and misery, a furtive and evil eye, and a long, sharp face, with slightly lifted lip and exposed teeth. He has a general slinking expression all over. The cayote is a living, breathing allegory of Want. He is *always* hungry. He is always poor, out of luck and friendless. The meanest creatures despise him, and even the fleas would desert him for a velocipede. He is so spiritless and cowardly that even while his exposed teeth are pretending a threat, the rest of his face is apologizing for it. And he is *so* homely!—so scrawny, and ribby, and coarse-haired, and pitiful. When he sees you he lifts his lip and lets a flash of his teeth out, and then turns a little out of the course he was pursuing, depresses his head a bit, and strikes a long, soft-footed trot through the sage-brush, glancing over his shoulder at you, from time to time, till he is about out of easy pistol range, and then he stops and takes a deliberate survey of you; he will trot fifty yards and stop again—another fifty and stop again; and finally the gray of his gliding body blends with the gray of the sage-brush, and he disappears. All this is when you make no demonstration against him; but if you do, he develops a livelier interest in his journey, and instantly electrifies his heels and puts such a deal of real estate between himself and your weapon, that by the time you have raised the hammer you see that you need a minie rifle, and by the time you have got him in line you need a rifled cannon, and by the time you have "drawn a bead" on him you see well enough that nothing but an unusually long-winded streak of lightning could reach him where he is now. But if you start a swift-footed dog after him, you will enjoy it ever so much—especially if it is a dog that has a good opinion of himself, and has been brought up to think he knows something about speed. The cayote will go swinging gently off on that deceitful trot of his, and every little while he will smile a fraudful smile over his shoulder that will fill that dog entirely full of encouragement and worldly ambition, and make him lay his head still lower to the ground, and stretch his neck further to the front, and pant more fiercely, and stick his tail out straighter behind, and move his furious legs with a yet wilder frenzy, and leave a broader and broader, and higher and denser cloud of desert sand smoking behind, and marking his long wake across the level plain! And all this time the dog is only a short twenty feet behind the cayote, and to save the soul of him he cannot understand why it is that he cannot get perceptibly closer; and he begins to get aggravated, and it makes him madder and madder to see how gently the cayote glides along and never pants or sweats or ceases to smile; and he grows still more and more incensed to see how shamefully he has been taken in by an entire stranger, and what an ignoble swindle that long, calm, soft-footed trot is; and next he notices that he is getting fagged, and that the cayote actually has to slacken speed a little to keep from running away from him—and *then* that town-dog is mad in earnest, and he begins to strain and weep and swear, and paw the sand higher than ever, and reach for the cayote with concentrated and desperate energy. This "spurt" finds him six feet behind the gliding enemy, and two miles from his friends. And then, in the instant that a wild new hope is lighting up his face, the cayote turns and smiles blandly upon him once more, and with a something about it which seems to say: "Well, I shall have to tear myself away from you, bub—business is business, and it will not do for me to be fooling along this way all day"—and forthwith there is a rushing sound, and the sudden splitting of a long crack through the atmosphere, and behold that dog is solitary and alone in the midst of a vast solitude!

It makes his head swim. He stops, and looks all around; climbs the nearest sand-mound, and gazes into the distance; shakes his head reflectively, and then, without a word, he turns and jogs along back to his train, and takes up a humble position under the hindmost wagon, and feels unspeakably mean, and looks ashamed, and hangs his tail at half-mast for a week. And for as much as a year after that, whenever there is a great hue and cry after a cayote, that dog will merely glance in that direction without emotion, and apparently observe to himself, "I believe I do not wish any of the pie."

The cayote lives chiefly in the most desolate and forbidding deserts, along with the lizard, the jackass rabbit and the raven, and gets an uncertain and precarious living, and earns it. He seems to subsist almost wholly on the carcases of oxen, mules and horses that have dropped out of emigrant trains and died, and upon windfalls of carrion, and occasional legacies of offal bequeathed to him by white men who have been opulent enough to have something better to butcher than condemned army bacon. He will eat anything in the world that his first cousins, the desert-frequenting tribes of Indians will, and they will eat anything they can bite. It is a curious fact that these latter are the only creatures known to history who will eat nitro-glycerine and ask for more if they survive.

The cayote of the deserts beyond the Rocky Mountains has a peculiarly hard time of it, owing to the fact that his relations, the Indians, are just as apt to be the first to detect a seductive scent on

SHOWING RESPECT TO RELATIVES.

the desert breeze, and follow the fragrance to the late ox it emanated from, as he is himself; and when this occurs he has to content himself with sitting off at a little distance watching those people strip off and dig out everything edible, and walk off with it. Then he and the waiting ravens explore the skeleton and polish the bones. It is considered that the cayote, and the obscene bird, and the Indian of the desert, testify their blood kinship with each other in that they live together in the waste places of the earth on terms of perfect confidence and friendship, while hating all other creatures and yearning to assist at their funerals. He does not mind going a hundred miles to breakfast, and a hundred and fifty to dinner, because he is sure to have three or four days between meals, and he can just as well be traveling and looking at the scenery as lying around doing nothing and adding to the burdens of his parents.

We soon learned to recognize the sharp, vicious bark of the cayote as it came across the murky plain at night to disturb our dreams among the mail-sacks; and remembering his forlorn aspect and his hard fortune, made shift to wish him the blessed novelty of a long day's good luck and a limitless larder the morrow.

CHAPTER 6

Our new conductor (just shipped) had been without sleep for twenty hours. Such a thing was very frequent. From St. Joseph, Missouri, to Sacramento, California, by stage-coach, was nearly nineteen hundred miles, and the trip was often made in fifteen days (the cars do it in four and a half, now), but the time specified in the mail contracts, and required by the schedule, was eighteen or nineteen days, if I remember rightly. This was to make fair allowance for winter storms and snows, and other unavoidable causes of detention. The stage company had everything under strict discipline and good system. Over each two hundred and fifty miles of road they placed an agent or superintendent, and invested him with great authority. His beat or jurisdiction of two hundred and fifty miles was called a "division." He purchased horses, mules, harness, and food for men and beasts, and distributed these things among his stage stations, from time to time, according to his judgment of what each station needed. He erected station buildings and dug wells. He attended to the paying of the station-keepers, hostlers, drivers and blacksmiths, and discharged them whenever he chose. He was a very, very great man in his "division"—a kind of Grand Mogul, a Sultan of the Indies, in whose presence common men were modest of speech and manner, and in the glare of whose greatness even the dazzling stage-driver dwindled to a penny dip. There were about eight of these kings, all told, on the overland route.

Next in rank and importance to the division-agent came the "conductor." His beat was the same length as the agent's—two hundred and fifty miles. He sat with the driver, and (when necessary) rode that fearful distance, night and day, without other rest or sleep than what he could get perched thus on top of the flying vehicle. Think of it! He had absolute charge of the mails, express

matter, passengers and stage-coach, until he delivered them to the
next conductor, and got his receipt for them. Consequently he had

to be a man of intelligence, decision and considerable executive ability. He was usually a
quiet, pleasant man, who attended closely to his duties, and
was a good deal of a gentleman.
It was not absolutely necessary
that the division-agent should
be a gentleman, and occasionally he wasn't. But he was always a general in administrative ability, and a bulldog in
courage and determination—
otherwise the chieftainship
over the lawless underlings of
the overland service would
never in any instance have been
to him anything but an equiva-

THE CONDUCTOR.

lent for a month of insolence and distress and a bullet and a coffin
at the end of it. There were about sixteen or eighteen conductors
on the overland, for there was a daily stage each way, and a conductor on every stage.

Next in *real* and official rank and importance, *after* the conductor, came my delight, the driver—next in real but not in *apparent*
importance—for we have seen that in the eyes of the common
herd the driver was to the conductor as an admiral is to the captain
of the flag-ship. The driver's beat was pretty long, and his sleeping-
time at the stations pretty short, sometimes; and so, but for the
grandeur of his position his would have been a sorry life, as well as
a hard and a wearing one. We took a new driver every day or every
night (for they drove backwards and forwards over the same piece
of road all the time), and therefore we never got as well acquainted
with them as we did with the conductors; and besides, they would
have been above being familiar with such rubbish as passengers,
anyhow, as a general thing. Still, we were always eager to get a
sight of each and every new driver as soon as the watch changed,

for each and every day we were either anxious to get rid of an unpleasant one, or loath to part with a driver we had learned to like
and had come to be sociable and friendly with. And so the first
question we asked the conductor whenever we got to where we
were to exchange drivers, was always, "Which is him?" The grammar was faulty, maybe, but we could not know, then, that it would
go into a book some day. As long as everything went smoothly, the
overland driver was well enough situated, but if a fellow driver got
sick suddenly it made trouble, for the coach *must* go on, and so the
potentate who was about to climb down and take a luxurious rest
after his long night's siege in the midst of wind and rain and darkness, had to stay where he was and do the sick man's work. Once,
in the Rocky Mountains, when I found a driver sound asleep on the
box, and the mules going at the usual break-neck pace, the conductor said never mind him, there was no danger, and he was doing
double duty—had driven seventy-five miles on one coach, and was
now going back over it on this without rest or sleep. A hundred and
fifty miles of holding back of six vindictive mules and keeping
them from climbing the trees! It sounds incredible, but I remember the statement well enough.

The station-keepers, hostlers, etc., were low, rough characters,
as already described; and from western Nebraska to Nevada a considerable sprinkling of them might be fairly set down as outlaws—
fugitives from justice, criminals whose best security was a section
of country which was without law and without even the pretense
of it. When the "division-agent" issued an order to one of these parties he did it with the full understanding that he might have to enforce it with a navy six-shooter, and so he always went "fixed" to
make things go along smoothly. Now and then a division-agent
was really obliged to shoot a hostler through the head to teach him
some simple matter that he could have taught him with a club if
his circumstances and surroundings had been different. But they
were snappy, able men, those division-agents, and when they tried
to teach a subordinate anything, that subordinate generally "got it
through his head."

A great portion of this vast machinery—these hundreds of men
and coaches, and thousands of mules and horses—was in the hands
of Mr. Ben Holladay. All the western half of the business was in his

THE SUPERINTENDENT AS A TEACHER.

hands. This reminds me of an incident of Palestine travel which is pertinent here, and so I will transfer it just in the language in which I find it set down in my Holy Land note-book:

No doubt everybody has heard of Ben Holladay—a man of prodigious energy, who used to send mails and passengers flying across the continent in his overland stage-coaches like a very whirlwind—two thousand long miles in fifteen days and a half, by the watch! But this fragment of history is not about Ben Holladay, but about a young New York boy by the name of Jack, who traveled with our small party of pilgrims in the Holy Land (and who had traveled to California in Mr. Holladay's overland coaches three years before, and had by no means forgotten it or lost his gushing admiration of Mr. H.) Aged nineteen. Jack was a good boy—a good-hearted and always well-meaning boy, who had been reared in the city of New York, and although he was bright and knew a great many useful things, his Scriptural education had been a good deal neglected—to such a degree, indeed, that all Holy Land history was fresh and new to him, and all Bible names mysteries that had never disturbed his virgin ear. Also in our party was an elderly pilgrim who was the reverse of Jack, in that he was learned in the Scriptures and an enthusiast concerning them. He was our encyclopedia, and we were never tired of listening to his speeches, nor he of making them. He never passed a celebrated locality, from Bashan to Bethlehem, without illuminating it with an oration. One day, when camped near the ruins of Jericho, he burst forth with something like this:

"Jack, do you see that range of mountains over yonder that bounds the Jordan valley? The mountains of Moab, Jack! Think of it, my boy—the actual mountains of Moab—renowned in Scripture history! We are actually standing face to face with those illustrious crags and peaks—and for all we know" [dropping his voice impressively], *"our eyes may be resting at this very moment upon the spot* WHERE LIES THE MYSTERIOUS GRAVE OF MOSES! Think of it, Jack!"

JACK AND THE ELDERLY PILGRIM.

"Moses *who?*" [falling inflection].

"Moses *who!* Jack, you ought to be ashamed of yourself—you ought to be ashamed of such criminal ignorance. Why, Moses, the great guide, soldier, poet, lawgiver of ancient Israel! Jack, from this spot where we stand, to Egypt, stretches a fearful desert three hundred miles in extent—and across that desert that wonderful man brought the children of Israel!—guiding them with unfailing sagacity for forty years over the sandy desolation and among the obstructing rocks and hills, and landed them at last, safe and sound, within sight of this very spot; and where we now stand they entered the Promised Land with anthems of rejoicing! It was a wonderful, wonderful thing to do, Jack! Think of it!"

"*Forty years! Only three hundred miles!* Humph! Ben Holladay would have fetched them through in thirty-six hours!"

The boy meant no harm. He did not know that he had said anything that was wrong or irreverent. And so no one scolded him or felt offended with him—and nobody *could* but some ungenerous spirit incapable of excusing the heedless blunders of a boy.

At noon on the fifth day out, we arrived at the "Crossing of the South Platte," *alias* "Julesburg," *alias* "Overland City," four hundred and seventy miles from St. Joseph—the strangest, quaintest, funniest frontier town that our untraveled eyes had ever stared at and been astonished with.

CHAPTER 7

It did seem strange enough to see a town again after what appeared to us such a long acquaintance with deep, still, almost lifeless and houseless solitude! We tumbled out into the busy street feeling like meteoric people crumbled off the corner of some other world, and wakened up suddenly in this. For an hour we took as much interest in Overland City as if we had never seen a town before. The reason we had an hour to spare was because we had to change our stage (for a less sumptuous affair, called a "mud-wagon") and transfer our freight of mails.

Presently we got under way again. We came to the shallow, yellow, muddy South Platte, with its low banks and its scattering flat sand-bars and pigmy islands—a melancholy stream straggling through the centre of the enormous flat plain, and only saved from being impossible to find with the naked eye by its sentinel rank of scattering trees standing on either bank. The Platte was "up," they said—which made me wish I could see it when it was down, if it could look any sicker and sorrier. They said it was a dangerous stream to cross, now, because its quicksands were liable to swallow up horses, coach and passengers if an attempt was made to ford it. But the mails had to go, and we made the attempt. Once or twice in midstream the wheels sunk into the yielding sands so threateningly that we half believed we had dreaded and avoided the sea all our lives to be shipwrecked in a "mud-wagon" in the middle of a desert at last. But we dragged through and sped away toward the setting sun.

Next morning, just before dawn, when about five hundred and fifty miles from St. Joseph, our mud-wagon broke down. We were to be delayed five or six hours, and therefore we took horses, by invitation, and joined a party who were just starting on a buffalo hunt. It was noble sport galloping over the plain in the dewy freshness of the morning, but our part of the hunt ended in disaster and disgrace, for a wounded buffalo bull chased the passenger Bemis

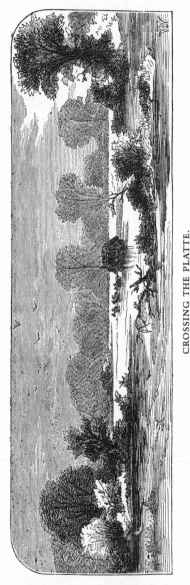

CROSSING THE PLATTE.

nearly two miles, and then he forsook his horse and took to a lone tree. He was very sullen about the matter for some twenty-four hours, but at last he began to soften little by little, and finally he said:

"Well, it was not funny, and there was no sense in those gawks making themselves so facetious over it. I tell you I was angry in earnest for a while. I should have shot that long gangly lubber they called Hank, if I could have done it without crippling six or seven other people—but of course I couldn't, the old 'Allen's' so confounded comprehensive. I wish those loafers had been up in the tree; they wouldn't have wanted to laugh so. If I had had a horse worth a cent—but no, the minute he saw that buffalo bull wheel on him and give a bellow, he raised straight up in the air and stood on his heels. The saddle began to slip, and I took him round the neck and laid close to him, and began to pray. Then he came down and stood up on the other end awhile, and the bull actually stopped pawing sand and bellowing to contemplate the inhuman spectacle. Then the bull made a pass at him and uttered a bellow that sounded perfectly frightful, it was so close to me, and that seemed to literally prostrate my horse's reason, and make a

AN INHUMAN SPECTACLE.

raving distracted maniac of him, and I wish I may die if he didn't
stand on his head for a quarter of a minute and shed tears. He was
absolutely out of his mind—he was, as sure as truth itself, and he
really didn't know what he was doing. Then the bull came charging at us, and my horse dropped down on all fours and took a fresh
start—and then for the next ten minutes he would actually throw
one hand-spring after another so fast that the bull began to get unsettled, too, and didn't know where to start in—and so he stood
there sneezing, and shoveling dust over his back, and bellowing
every now and then, and thinking he had got a fifteen-hundred-
dollar circus horse for breakfast, certain. Well, I was first out on his
neck—the horse's, not the bull's—and then underneath, and next
on his rump, and sometimes head up, and sometimes heels—but I
tell you it seemed solemn and awful to be ripping and tearing and
carrying on so in the presence of death, as you might say. Pretty
soon the bull made a snatch for us and brought away some of my
horse's tail (I suppose, but do not know, being pretty busy at the
time), but *something* made him hungry for solitude and suggested
to him to get up and hunt for it. And then you ought to have seen

A NEW DEPARTURE.

that spider-legged old skeleton go! and you ought to have seen the
bull cut out after him, too—head down, tongue out, tail up, bellowing like everything, and actually mowing down the weeds, and
tearing up the earth, and boosting up the sand like a whirlwind! By
George, it was a hot race! I and the saddle were back on the rump,
and I had the bridle in my teeth and holding on to the pommel with
both hands. First we left the dogs behind; then we passed a jackass
rabbit; then we overtook a cayote, and were gaining on an antelope
when the rotten girth let go and threw me about thirty yards off to
the left, and as the saddle went down over the horse's rump he gave
it a lift with his heels that sent it more than four hundred yards up
in the air, I wish I may die in a minute if he didn't. I fell at the foot
of the only solitary tree there was in nine counties adjacent (as any
creature could see with the naked eye), and the next second I had
hold of the bark with four sets of nails and my teeth, and the next
second after that I was astraddle of the main limb and blaspheming
my luck in a way that made my breath smell of brimstone. I *had*
the bull, now, if he did not think of *one* thing. But that one thing I
dreaded. I dreaded it very seriously. There was a possibility that the
bull might not think of it, but there were greater chances that he
would. I made up my mind what I would do in case he did. It was a
little over forty feet to the ground from where I sat. I cautiously unwound the lariat from the pommel of my saddle—"

"Your *saddle?* Did you take your saddle up in the tree with you?"

"Take it up in the tree with me? Why, how you talk. Of course I didn't. No man could do that. It *fell* in the tree when it came down."

"Oh—exactly."

"Certainly. I unwound the lariat, and fastened one end of it to the limb. It was the very best green raw-hide, and capable of sustaining tons. I made a slip-noose in the other end, and then hung it down to see the length. It reached down twenty-two feet—half way to the ground. I then loaded every barrel of the Allen with a double charge. I felt satisfied. I said to myself, if he never thinks of that one thing that I dread, all right—but if he does, all right anyhow—I am fixed for him. But don't you know that the very thing a man dreads is the thing that always happens? Indeed it is so. I watched the bull, now, with anxiety—anxiety which no one can conceive of who has not been in such a situation and felt that at any moment death might come. Presently a thought came into the bull's eye. I knew it! said I—if my nerve fails now, I am lost. Sure enough, it was just as I had dreaded, he started in to climb the tree—"

"What, the bull?"

"Of course—who else?"

"But a bull can't climb a tree."

"He can't, can't he? Since you know so much about it, did you ever see a bull try?"

"No! I never dreamt of such a thing."

"Well, then, what is the use of your talking that way, then? Because you never saw a thing done, is that any reason why it can't be done?"

"Well, all right—go on. What did you do?"

"The bull started up, and got along well for about ten feet, then slipped and slid back. I breathed easier. He tried it again—got up a little higher—slipped again. But he came at it once more, and this time he was careful. He got gradually higher and higher, and my spirits went down more and more. Up he came—an inch at a time—with his eyes hot, and his tongue hanging out. Higher and higher—hitched his foot over the stump of a limb, and looked up, as much as to say, 'You are my meat, friend.' Up again—higher and higher, and getting more excited the closer he got. He was within ten feet of me! I took a long breath,—and then said I, 'It is now or never.' I had the coil of the lariat all ready; I paid it out slowly, till it hung right over his head; all of a sudden I let go of the slack, and

SUSPENDED OPERATIONS.

the slip-noose fell fairly round his neck! Quicker than lightning I out with the Allen and let him have it in the face. It was an awful roar, and must have scared the bull out of his senses. When the smoke cleared away, there he was, dangling in the air, twenty foot from the ground, and going out of one convulsion into another faster than you could count! I didn't stop to count, anyhow—I shinned down the tree and shot for home."

"Bemis, is all that true, just as you have stated it?"

"I wish I may rot in my tracks and die the death of a dog if it isn't."

"Well, we can't refuse to believe it, and we don't. But if there were some proofs—"

"Proofs! Did I bring back my lariat?"

"No."

"Did I bring back my horse?"

"No."

"Did you ever see the bull again?"

"No."

"Well, then, what more do you want? I never saw anybody as particular as you are about a little thing like that."

I made up my mind that if this man was not a liar he only missed it by the skin of his teeth. This episode reminds me of an incident of my brief sojourn in Siam, years afterward. The European citizens of a town in the neighborhood of Bangkok had a prodigy among them by the name of Eckert, an Englishman—a person famous for the number, ingenuity and imposing magnitude of his lies. They were always repeating his most celebrated falsehoods, and always trying to "draw him out" before strangers; but they seldom succeeded. Twice he was invited to the house where I was visiting, but nothing could seduce him into a specimen lie. One day a planter named Bascom, an influential man, and a proud and sometimes irascible one, invited me to ride over with him and call on Eckert. As we jogged along, said he:

"Now, do you know where the fault lies? It lies in putting Eckert on his guard. The minute the boys go to pumping at Eckert he knows perfectly well what they are after, and of course he shuts up his shell. Anybody might know he would. But when we get there, we must play him finer than that. Let him shape the conversation to suit himself—let him drop it or change it whenever he wants to. Let him see that nobody is trying to draw him out. Just let him have his own way. He will soon forget himself and begin to grind out lies like a mill. Don't get impatient—just keep quiet, and let me play him. I will make him lie. It does seem to me that the boys must be blind to overlook such an obvious and simple trick as that."

Eckert received us heartily—a pleasant-spoken, gentle-mannered creature. We sat in the veranda an hour, sipping English ale, and talking about the king, and the sacred white elephant, the Sleeping Idol, and all manner of things; and I noticed that my comrade never led the conversation himself or shaped it, but simply followed Eckert's lead, and betrayed no solicitude and no anxiety about anything. The effect was shortly perceptible. Eckert began to grow communicative; he grew more and more at his ease, and more and more talkative and sociable. Another hour passed in the same way, and then all of a sudden Eckert said:

A WONDERFUL LIE.

"Oh, by the way! I came near forgetting. I have got a thing here to astonish you. Such a thing as neither you nor any other man ever heard of—I've got a cat that will eat cocoanut! Common green cocoanut—and not only eat the meat, but drink the milk. It is so— I'll swear to it."

A quick glance from Bascom—a glance that I understood—
then:

"Why, bless my soul, I never heard of such a thing. Man, it is
impossible."

"I knew you would say it. I'll fetch the cat."

He went in the house. Bascom said:

"There—what did I tell you? Now, that is the way to handle Eckert. You see, I have petted him along patiently, and put his suspi-
cions to sleep. I am glad we came. You tell the boys about it when
you go back. Cat eat a cocoanut—oh, my! Now, that is just his way,
exactly—he will tell the absurdest lie, and trust to luck to get out
of it again. Cat eat a cocoanut—the innocent fool!"

Eckert approached with his cat, sure enough.

Bascom smiled. Said he:

"I'll hold the cat—you bring a cocoanut."

Eckert split one open, and chopped up some pieces. Bascom
smuggled a wink to me, and proffered a slice of the fruit to puss.
She snatched it, swallowed it ravenously, and asked for more!

We rode our two miles in silence, and wide apart. At least I was
silent, though Bascom cuffed his horse and cursed him a good deal,
notwithstanding the horse was behaving well enough. When I
branched off homeward, Bascom said:

"Keep the horse till morning. And—you need not speak of this
—— foolishness to the boys."

CHAPTER 8

In a little while all interest was taken up in stretching our necks and watching for the "pony-rider"—the fleet messenger who sped across the continent from St. Joe to Sacramento, carrying letters nineteen hundred miles in eight days! Think of that for perishable horse and human flesh and blood to do! The pony-rider was usually a little bit of a man, brim full of spirit and endurance. No matter what time of the day or night his watch came on, and no matter whether it was winter or summer, raining, snowing, hailing, or sleeting, or whether his "beat" was a level straight road or a crazy trail over mountain crags and precipices, or whether it led through peaceful regions or regions that swarmed with hostile Indians, he must be always ready to leap into the saddle and be off like the wind! There was no idling-time for a pony-rider on duty. He rode fifty miles without stopping, by daylight, moonlight, starlight, or through the blackness of darkness—just as it happened. He rode a splendid horse that was born for a racer and fed and lodged like a gentleman; kept him at his utmost speed for ten miles, and then, as he came crashing up to the station where stood two men holding fast a fresh, impatient steed, the transfer of rider and mail-bag was made in the twinkling of an eye, and away flew the eager pair and were out of sight before the spectator could get hardly the ghost of a look. Both rider and horse went "flying light." The rider's dress was thin and fitted close; he wore a "roundabout" and a skull-cap, and tucked his pantaloons into his boot-tops like a race-rider. He carried no arms—he carried nothing that was not absolutely necessary, for even the postage on his literary freight was worth *two dollars an ounce.* He got but little frivolous correspondence to carry—his bag had business letters in it, mostly. His horse was stripped of all unnecessary weight, too. He wore a little wafer of a racing-saddle, and no visible blanket. He wore light shoes, or none at all. The little flat mail-pockets strapped under the rider's thighs would each hold about the bulk of a child's primer. They held many and many an important business chapter and newspaper letter, but these were written on paper as airy and thin as gold-leaf, nearly, and thus bulk and weight were economized. The stage-coach traveled about a hundred to a hundred and twenty-five miles a day (twenty-four hours), the pony-rider about two hundred and fifty. There were about eighty pony-riders in the saddle all the time, night and day, stretch-ing in a long, scattering procession from Missouri to California, forty flying eastward and forty toward the west, and among them making four

"HERE HE COMES!"

hundred gallant horses earn a stirring livelihood and see a deal of scenery every single day in the year.

We had had a consuming desire, from the beginning, to see a pony-rider, but somehow or other all that passed us and all that met us managed to streak by in the night, and so we heard only a whiz and a hail, and the swift phantom of the desert was gone before we could get our heads out of the windows. But now we were expecting one along every moment, and would see him in broad daylight. Presently the driver exclaims:

"HERE HE COMES!"

Every neck is stretched further, and every eye strained wider. Away across the endless dead level of the prairie a black speck appears against the sky, and it is plain that it moves. Well, I should think so! In a second or two it becomes a horse and rider, rising and falling, rising and falling—sweeping toward us nearer and nearer—growing more and more distinct, more and more sharply defined—nearer and still nearer, and the flutter of the hoofs comes faintly to the ear—another instant a whoop and a hurrah from our upper deck, a wave of the rider's hand, but no reply, and man and horse burst past our excited faces, and go winging away like a belated fragment of a storm!

So sudden is it all, and so like a flash of unreal fancy, that but for the flake of white foam left quivering and perishing on a mail-sack

CHANGING HORSES.

after the vision had flashed by and disappeared, we might have doubted whether we had seen any actual horse and man at all, maybe.

We rattled through Scott's Bluffs Pass, by and by. It was along here somewhere that we first came across genuine and unmistakable alkali water in the road, and we cordially hailed it as a first-class curiosity, and a thing to be mentioned with eclat in letters to the ignorant at home. This water gave the road a soapy appearance, and in many places the ground looked as if it had been white-washed. I think the strange alkali water excited us as much as any wonder we had come upon yet, and I know we felt very complacent and conceited, and better satisfied with life after we had added it to our list of things which *we* had seen and some other people had not. In a small way we were the same sort of simpletons as those who climb unnecessarily the perilous peaks of Mont Blanc and the Matterhorn, and derive no pleasure from it except the reflection that it isn't a common experience. But once in a while one of those parties trips and comes darting down the long mountain crags in a sitting posture, making the crusted snow smoke behind him, flit-ting from bench to bench, and from terrace to terrace, jarring the earth where he strikes, and still glancing and flitting on again, sticking an iceberg into himself every now and then, and tearing his clothes, snatching at things to save himself, taking hold of trees and fetching them along with him, roots and all, starting little rocks now and then, then big boulders, then acres of ice and snow and patches of forest, gathering and still gathering as he goes, adding and still adding to his massed and sweeping grandeur as he

RIDING THE AVALANCHE.

nears a three-thousand-foot precipice, till at last he waves his hat magnificently and rides into eternity on the back of a raging and tossing avalanche!

This is all very fine, but let us not be carried away by excitement, but ask calmly, how does this person feel about it in his cooler moments next day, with six or seven thousand feet of snow and stuff on top of him?

We crossed the sand hills near the scene of the Indian mail robbery and massacre of 1856, wherein the driver and conductor perished, and also all the passengers but one, it was supposed; but this must have been a mistake, for at different times afterward on the Pacific coast I was personally acquainted with a hundred and thirty-three or four people who were wounded during that massacre, and barely escaped with their lives. There was no doubt of the truth of it—I had it from their own lips. One of these parties told me that he kept coming across arrow-heads in his system for nearly seven years after the massacre; and another of them told me that he was stuck so literally full of arrows that after the Indians were gone and he could raise up and examine himself, he could not restrain his tears, for his clothes were completely ruined.

The most trustworthy tradition avers, however, that only one man, a person named Babbitt, survived the massacre, and he was desperately wounded. He dragged himself on his hands and knee (for one leg was broken) to a station several miles away. He did it during portions of two nights, lying concealed one day and part of another, and for more than forty hours suffering unimaginable anguish from hunger, thirst and bodily pain. The Indians robbed the coach of everything it contained, including quite an amount of treasure.

CHAPTER 9

WE passed Fort Laramie in the night, and on the seventh morning out we found ourselves in the Black Hills, with Laramie Peak at our elbow (apparently) looming vast and solitary—a deep, dark, rich indigo blue in hue, so portentously did the old colossus frown under his beetling brows of storm-cloud. He was thirty or forty miles away, in reality, but he only seemed removed a little beyond the low ridge at our right. We breakfasted at Horseshoe station, six hundred and seventy-six miles out from St. Joseph. We had now reached a hostile Indian country, and during the afternoon we passed La Prele station, and enjoyed great discomfort all the time we were in the neighborhood, being aware that many of the trees we dashed by at arm's length concealed a lurking Indian or two. During the preceding night an ambushed savage had sent a bullet through the pony-rider's jacket, but he had ridden on, just the same, because pony-riders were not allowed to stop and inquire into such things except when killed. As long as they had life enough left in them they had to stick to the horse and ride, even if the Indians had been waiting for them a week, and were entirely out of patience. About two hours and a half before we arrived at La Prele station, the keeper in charge of it had fired four times at an Indian, but he said with an injured air that the Indian had "skipped around so's to spile everything—and ammunition's blamed skurse, too." The most natural inference conveyed by his manner of speaking was, that in "skipping around," the Indian had taken an unfair advantage. The coach we were in had a neat hole through its front—a reminiscence of its last trip through this region. The bullet that made it wounded the driver slightly, but he did not mind it much. He said the place to keep a man "huffy" was down on the Southern Overland, among the Apaches, before the company moved the stage-line up on the northern route. He said the

Apaches used to annoy him all the time down there, and that he
came as near as anything to starving to death in the midst of abundance, because they kept him so leaky with bullet holes that he
"couldn't hold his vittles." This person's statements were not generally believed.

We shut the blinds down very tightly that first night in the hostile Indian country, and lay on our arms. We slept on them some,

INDIAN COUNTRY.

but most of the time we only lay on them. We did not talk much,
but kept quiet and listened. It was an inky-black night, and occasionally rainy. We were among woods and rocks, hills and gorges—
so shut in, in fact, that when we peeped through a chink in a curtain, we could discern nothing. The driver and conductor on top
were still, too, or only spoke at long intervals, in low tones, as is
the way of men in the midst of invisible dangers. We listened to
rain-drops pattering on the roof; and the grinding of the wheels
through the muddy gravel; and the low wailing of the wind; and all
the time we had that absurd sense upon us, inseparable from travel
at night in a close-curtained vehicle, the sense of remaining per-

fectly still in one place, notwithstanding the jolting and swaying of the vehicle, the trampling of the horses, and the grinding of the wheels. We listened a long time, with intent faculties and bated breath; every time one of us would relax, and draw a long sigh of relief and start to say something, a comrade would be sure to utter a sudden "Hark!" and instantly the experimenter was rigid and listening again. So the tiresome minutes and decades of minutes dragged away, until at last our tense forms filmed over with a dulled consciousness, and we slept, if one might call such a condition by so strong a name—for it was a sleep set with a hair-trigger. It was a sleep seething and teeming with a weird and distressful confusion of shreds and fag-ends of dreams—a sleep that was a chaos. Presently, dreams and sleep and the sullen hush of the night were startled by a ringing report, and cloven by *such* a long, wild, agonizing shriek! Then we heard—ten steps from the stage—

"Help! help! help!" [It was our driver's voice.]

"Kill him! Kill him like a dog!"

"I'm being murdered! Will no man lend me a pistol?"

"Look out! head him off! head him off!"

[Two pistol shots; a confusion of voices and the trampling of many feet, as if a crowd were closing and surging together around some object; several heavy, dull blows, as with a club; a voice that said appealingly, "Don't, gentlemen, please don't—I'm a dead man!" Then a fainter groan, and another blow, and away sped the stage into the darkness, and left the grisly mystery behind us.]

What a startle it was! Eight seconds would amply cover the time it occupied—maybe even five would do it. We only had time to plunge at a curtain and unbuckle and unbutton part of it in an awkward and hindering flurry, when our whip cracked sharply overhead, and we went rumbling and thundering away, down a mountain "grade."

We fed on that mystery the rest of the night—what was left of it, for it was waning fast. It had to remain a present mystery, for all we could get from the conductor in answer to our hails was something that sounded, through the clatter of the wheels, like "Tell you in the morning!"

So we lit our pipes and opened the corner of a curtain for a chimney, and lay there in the dark, listening to each other's story of how he first felt and how many thousand Indians he first thought had hurled themselves upon us, and what his remembrance of the subsequent sounds was, and the order of their occurrence. And we theorized, too, but there was never a theory that would account for our driver's voice being out there, nor yet account for his Indian murderers talking such good English, if they *were* Indians.

So we chatted and smoked the rest of the night comfortably away, our boding anxiety being somehow marvelously dissipated by the real presence of something to be anxious *about*.

We never did get much satisfaction about that dark occurrence. All that we could make out of the odds and ends of the information we gathered in the morning, was that the disturbance occurred at a station; that we changed drivers there, and that the driver that got off there had been talking roughly about some of the outlaws that infested the region ("for there wasn't a man around there but had a price on his head and didn't dare show himself in the settlements," the conductor said); he had talked roughly about these characters, and ought to have "drove up there with his pistol cocked and ready on the seat alongside of him, and begun business himself, because any softy would know they would be laying for him."

That was all we could gather, and we could see that neither the conductor nor the new driver were much concerned about the matter. They plainly had little respect for a man who would deliver offensive opinions of people and then be so simple as to come into their presence unprepared to "back his judgment," as they pleasantly phrased the killing of any fellow-being who did not like said opinions. And likewise they plainly had a contempt for the man's poor discretion in venturing to rouse the wrath of such utterly reckless wild beasts as those outlaws—and the conductor added:

"I tell you it's as much as Slade himself wants to do!"

This remark created an entire revolution in my curiosity. I cared nothing now about the Indians, and even lost interest in the murdered driver. There was such magic in that name, SLADE! Day or night, now, I stood always ready to drop any subject in hand, to listen to something new about Slade and his ghastly exploits. Even before we got to Overland City, we had begun to hear about Slade and his "division" (for he was a "division-agent") on the Overland;

and from the hour we had left Overland City we had heard drivers and conductors talk about only three things—"Californy," the Nevada silver mines, and this desperado Slade. And a deal the most of the talk was about Slade. We had gradually come to have a realizing sense of the fact that Slade was a man whose heart and hands and soul were steeped in the blood of offenders against his dignity; a man who awfully avenged all injuries, affronts, insults or slights, of whatever kind—on the spot if he could, years afterward if lack of earlier opportunity compelled it; a man whose hate tortured him day and night till vengeance appeased it—and not an ordinary vengeance either, but his enemy's absolute death—nothing less; a man whose face would light up with a terrible joy when he surprised a foe and had him at a disadvantage. A high and efficient servant of the Overland, an outlaw among outlaws and yet their relentless scourge, Slade was at once the most bloody, the most dangerous and the most valuable citizen that inhabited the savage fastnesses of the mountains.

CHAPTER 10

R EALLY and truly, two-thirds of the talk of drivers and conductors had been about this man Slade, ever since the day before we reached Julesburg. In order that the eastern reader may have a clear conception of what a Rocky Mountain desperado is, in his highest state of development, I will reduce all this mass of overland gossip to one straightforward narrative, and present it in the following shape:

Slade was born in Illinois, of good parentage. At about twenty-six years of age he killed a man in a quarrel and fled the country. At St. Joseph, Missouri, he joined one of the early California-bound emigrant trains, and was given the post of train-master. One day on the plains he had an angry dispute with one of his wagon-drivers, and both drew their revolvers. But the driver was the quicker artist, and had his weapon cocked first. So Slade said it was a pity to waste life on so small a matter, and proposed that the pistols be thrown on the ground and the quarrel settled by a fist-fight. The unsuspecting driver agreed, and threw down his pistol—whereupon Slade laughed at his simplicity, and shot him dead!

He made his escape, and lived a wild life for a while, dividing his time between fighting Indians and avoiding an Illinois sheriff, who had been sent to arrest him for his first murder. It is said that in one Indian battle he killed three savages with his own hand, and afterward cut their ears off and sent them, with his compliments, to the chief of the tribe.

Slade soon gained a name for fearless resolution, and this was sufficient merit to procure for him the important post of overland division-agent at Julesburg, in place of Mr. Jules, removed. For some time previously, the company's horses had been frequently stolen, and the coaches delayed, by gangs of outlaws, who were wont to laugh at the idea of any man's having the temerity to re-

sent such outrages. Slade resented them promptly. The outlaws
soon found that the new agent was a man who did not fear anything that breathed the breath of life. He made short work of all

A PROPOSED FIST-FIGHT.

offenders. The result was that delays ceased, the company's property was let alone, and no matter what happened or who suffered,
Slade's coaches went through, every time! True, in order to bring
about this wholesome change, Slade had to kill several men—
some say three, others say four, and others six—but the world was
the richer for their loss. The first prominent difficulty he had was
with the ex-agent Jules, who bore the reputation of being a reckless
and desperate man himself. Jules hated Slade for supplanting him,

FROM BEHIND THE DOOR.

and a good fair occasion for a fight was all he was waiting for. By
and by Slade dared to employ a man whom Jules had once discharged. Next, Slade seized a team of stage-horses which he accused Jules of having driven off and hidden somewhere for his own
use. War was declared, and for a day or two the two men walked
warily about the streets, seeking each other, Jules armed with a
double-barreled shotgun, and Slade with his history-creating revolver. Finally, as Slade stepped into a store, Jules poured the contents of his gun into him from behind the door. Slade was pluck,
and Jules got several bad pistol wounds in return. Then both men
fell, and were carried to their respective lodgings, both swearing
that better aim should do deadlier work next time. Both were bedridden a long time, but Jules got on his feet first, and gathering his
possessions together, packed them on a couple of mules, and fled
to the Rocky Mountains to gather strength in safety against the
day of reckoning. For many months he was not seen or heard of,
and was gradually dropped out of the remembrance of all save Slade

himself. But Slade was not the man to forget him. On the contrary, common report said that Slade kept a reward standing for his capture, dead or alive!

After a while, seeing that Slade's energetic administration had restored peace and order to one of the worst divisions of the road, the overland stage company transferred him to the Rocky Ridge division in the Rocky Mountains, to see if he could perform a like miracle there. It was the very paradise of outlaws and desperadoes. There was absolutely no semblance of law there. Violence was the rule. Force was the only recognized authority. The commonest misunderstandings were settled on the spot with the revolver or the knife. Murders were done in open day, and with sparkling frequency, and nobody thought of inquiring into them. It was considered that the parties who did the killing had their private reasons for it; for other people to meddle would have been looked upon as indelicate. After a murder, all that Rocky Mountain etiquette required of a spectator was, that he should help the gentleman bury his game—otherwise his churlishness would surely be remembered against him the first time he killed a man himself and needed a neighborly turn in interring him.

Slade took up his residence sweetly and peacefully in the midst of this hive of horse-thieves and assassins, and the very first time one of them aired his insolent swaggerings in his presence he shot him dead! He began a raid on the outlaws, and in a singularly short space of time he had completely stopped their depredations on the stage stock, recovered a large number of stolen horses, killed several of the worst desperadoes of the district, and gained such a dread ascendancy over the rest that they respected him, admired him, feared him, obeyed him! He wrought the same marvelous change in the ways of the community that had marked his administration at Overland City. He captured two men who had stolen overland stock, and with his own hands he hanged them. He was supreme judge in his district, and he was jury and executioner likewise—and not only in the case of offenses against his employers, but against passing emigrants as well. On one occasion some emigrants had their stock lost or stolen, and told Slade, who chanced to visit their camp. With a single companion he rode to a ranch, the owners of which he suspected, and opening the door, commenced firing, killing three, and wounding the fourth.

SLADE AS EXECUTIONER.

From a bloodthirstily interesting little Montana book* I take this paragraph:

> While on the road, Slade held absolute sway. He would ride down to a station, get into a quarrel, turn the house out of windows, and maltreat the occupants most cruelly. The unfortunates had no means of redress, and were compelled to recuperate as best they could. On one of these occasions, it is said, he killed the father of the fine little half-breed boy, Jemmy, whom he adopted, and who lived with his widow after his execution. Stories of Slade's hanging men, and of innumerable assaults, shootings, stabbings and beatings, in which he was a principal actor, form part of the legends of the stage line. As for minor quarrels and shootings, it is absolutely certain that a minute history of Slade's life would be one long record of such practices.

Slade was a matchless marksman with a navy revolver. The legends say that one morning at Rocky Ridge, when he was feeling comfortable, he saw a man approaching who had offended him some days before—observe the fine memory he had for matters like that—and, "Gentlemen," said Slade, drawing, "it is a good twenty-yard shot—I'll clip the third button on his coat!" Which he

---

*"The Vigilantes of Montana," by Prof. Thos. J. Dimsdale.

did. The bystanders all admired it. And they all attended the funeral, too.

On one occasion a man who kept a little whisky-shelf at the station did something which angered Slade—and went and made his will. A day or two afterward Slade came in and called for some brandy. The man reached under the counter (ostensibly to get a bottle—possibly to get something else), but Slade smiled upon him that peculiarly bland and satisfied smile of his which the neighbors had long ago learned to recognize as a death-warrant in

AN UNPLEASANT VIEW.

disguise, and told him "none of that!—pass out the high-priced article." So the poor barkeeper had to turn his back and get the high-priced brandy from the shelf; and when he faced around again he was looking into the muzzle of Slade's pistol. "And the next instant," added my informant, impressively, "he was one of the deadest men that ever lived."

The stage-drivers and conductors told us that sometimes Slade would leave a hated enemy wholly unmolested, unnoticed and unmentioned, for weeks together—had done it once or twice at any rate. And some said they believed he did it in order to lull the victims into unwatchfulness, so that he could get the advantage of them, and others said they believed he saved up an enemy that way, just as a school-boy saves up a cake, and made the pleasure go as far as it would by gloating over the anticipation. One of these cases was that of a Frenchman who had offended Slade. To the surprise of everybody Slade did not kill him on the spot, but let him alone for a considerable time. Finally, however, he went to the Frenchman's house very late one night, knocked, and when his enemy opened the door, shot him dead—pushed the corpse inside the door with his foot, set the house on fire and burned up the dead man, his widow and three children! I heard this story from several different people, and they evidently believed what they were saying. It may be true, and it may not. "Give a dog a bad name," etc.

Slade was captured, once, by a party of men who intended to lynch him. They disarmed him, and shut him up in a strong log house, and placed a guard over him. He prevailed on his captors to send for his wife, so that he might have a last interview with her. She was a brave, loving, spirited woman. She jumped on a horse and rode for life and death. When she arrived they let her in without searching her, and before the door could be closed she whipped out a couple of revolvers, and she and her lord marched forth defying the party. And then, under a brisk fire, they mounted double and galloped away unharmed!

In the fulness of time Slade's myrmidons captured his ancient enemy Jules, whom they found in a well-chosen hiding-place in the remote fastnesses of the mountains, gaining a precarious livelihood with his rifle. They brought him to Rocky Ridge, bound hand and foot, and deposited him in the middle of the cattle-yard with his back against a post. It is said that the pleasure that lit Slade's face when he heard of it was something fearful to contemplate. He examined his enemy to see that he was securely tied, and then went to bed, content to wait till morning before enjoying the luxury of killing him. Jules spent the night in the cattle-yard, and it is a region where warm nights are never known. In the morning Slade practiced on him with his revolver, nipping the flesh here and there, and occasionally clipping off a finger, while Jules begged him to kill him outright and put him out of his misery. Finally Slade reloaded, and walking up close to his victim, made some characteristic remarks and then dispatched him. The body lay there half a day, nobody venturing to touch it without orders, and then Slade detailed a party and assisted at the burial himself. But he first cut off the dead man's ears and put them in his vest pocket, where he carried them for some time with great satisfaction. That is the story as I have frequently heard it told and seen it in print in California newspapers. It is doubtless correct in all essential particulars.

In due time we rattled up to a stage station, and sat down to breakfast with a half-savage, half-civilized company of armed and bearded mountaineers, ranchmen and station employés. The most gentlemanly-appearing, quiet and affable officer we had yet found along the road in the Overland Company's service was the person who sat at the head of the table, at my elbow. Never youth stared and shivered as I did when I heard them call him SLADE!

Here was romance, and I sitting face to face with it!—looking upon it—touching it—hobnobbing with it, as it were! Here, right by my side, was the actual ogre who, in fights and brawls and various ways, *had taken the lives of twenty-six human beings,* or all men lied about him! I suppose I was the proudest stripling that ever traveled to see strange lands and wonderful people.

He was so friendly and so gentle-spoken that I warmed to him in spite of his awful history. It was hardly possible to realize that this pleasant person was the pitiless scourge of the outlaws, the rawhead-and-bloody-bones the nursing mothers of the mountains terrified their children with. And to this day I can remember nothing remarkable about Slade except that his face was rather broad across the cheek bones, and that the cheek bones were low and the lips peculiarly thin and straight. But that was enough to leave something of an effect upon me, for since then I seldom see a face possessing those characteristics without fancying that the owner of it is a dangerous man.

The coffee ran out. At least it was reduced to one tin-cupful, and Slade was about to take it when he saw that my cup was empty. He politely offered to fill it, but although I wanted it, I politely declined. I was afraid he had not killed anybody that morning, and might be needing diversion. But still with firm politeness he insisted on filling my cup, and said I had traveled all night and better deserved it than he—and while he talked he placidly poured the

UNAPPRECIATED POLITENESS.

fluid, to the last drop. I thanked him and drank it, but it gave me no comfort, for I could not feel sure that he would not be sorry, presently, that he had given it away, and proceed to kill me to distract his thoughts from the loss. But nothing of the kind occurred. We left him with only twenty-six dead people to account for, and I felt a tranquil satisfaction in the thought that in so judiciously taking care of No. 1 at that breakfast-table I had pleasantly escaped being No. 27. Slade came out to the coach and saw us off, first ordering certain reärrangements of the mail-bags for our comfort, and then we took leave of him, satisfied that we should hear of him again, some day, and wondering in what connection.

CHAPTER 11

AND sure enough, two or three years afterward, we did hear of him again. News came to the Pacific coast that the Vigilance Committee in Montana (whither Slade had removed from Rocky Ridge) had hanged him. I find an account of the affair in the thrilling little book I quoted a paragraph from in the last chapter—"The Vigilantes of Montana; being a Reliable Account of the Capture, Trial and Execution of Henry Plummer's Notorious Road Agent Band: By Prof. Thos. J. Dimsdale, Virginia City, M. T." Mr. Dimsdale's chapter is well worth reading, as a specimen of how the people of the frontier deal with criminals when the courts of law prove inefficient. Mr. Dimsdale makes two remarks about Slade, both of which are accurately descriptive, and one of which is exceedingly picturesque: "Those who saw him in his natural state only, would pronounce him to be a kind husband, a most hospitable host and a courteous gentleman; on the contrary, those who met him when maddened with liquor and surrounded by a gang of armed roughs, would pronounce him a fiend incarnate." And this: "From Fort Kearny, west, he was feared *a great deal more than the Almighty.*" For compactness, simplicity and vigor of expression, I will "back" that sentence against anything in literature. Mr. Dimsdale's narrative is as follows. In all places where italics occur, they are mine:

After the execution of the five men, on the 14th of January, the Vigilantes considered that their work was nearly ended. They had freed the country from highwaymen and murderers to a great extent, and they determined that, in the absence of the regular civil authority, they would establish a People's Court, where all offenders should be tried by Judge and Jury. This was the nearest approach to social order that the circumstances permitted, and, though strict legal authority was wanting, yet the people were firmly determined to maintain its efficiency, and to enforce its decrees. It may here be mentioned that the overt act which was the last round on the fatal ladder leading to the scaffold on which Slade perished,

*was the tearing in pieces and stamping upon a writ of this court, followed
by his arrest of the Judge, Alex. Davis, by authority of a presented Derringer, and with his own hands.*

J. A. Slade was himself, we have been informed, a Vigilanter; he openly
boasted of it, and said he knew all that they knew. He was never accused,
or even suspected of either murder or robbery, committed in this Territory, (the latter crime was never laid to his charge, in any place;) but that
he had killed several men in other localities, was notorious, and his bad
reputation in this respect was a most powerful argument in determining
his fate, when he was finally arrested for the offense above mentioned. On
returning from Milk River he became more and more addicted to drinking; until at last, it was a common feat for him and his friends to "take the
town." He and a couple of his dependants might often be seen on one
horse, galloping through the streets, shouting and yelling, firing revolvers,
etc. On many occasions he would ride his horse into stores; break up bars;
toss the scales out of doors, and use most insulting language to parties
present. Just previous to the day of his arrest, he had given a fearful beating
to one of his followers; but such was his influence over them that the man
wept bitterly at the gallows, and begged for his life with all his power. *It
had become quite common, when Slade was on a spree, for the shop-
keepers and citizens to close the stores and put out all the lights;* being
fearful of some outrage at his hands. For his wanton destruction of goods
and furniture, he was always ready to pay, when sober if he had money; but
there were not a few who regarded payment as small satisfaction for the
outrage, and these men were his personal enemies.

From time to time, Slade received warnings from men that he well
knew would not deceive him, of the certain end of his conduct. There was
not a moment, for weeks previous to his arrest, in which the public did not
expect to hear of some bloody outrage. The dread of his very name, and the
presence of the armed band of hangers-on, who followed him alone prevented a resistance, which must certainly have ended in the instant murder or mutilation of the opposing party.

Slade was frequently arrested by order of the court whose organization
we have described, and had treated it with respect by paying one or two
fines, and promising to pay the rest when he had money; but in the transaction that occurred at this crisis, he forgot even this caution, and goaded
by passion and the hatred of restraint, he sprang into the embrace of death.

Slade had been drunk and "cutting up" all night. He and his companions
had made the town a perfect hell. In the morning, J. M. Fox, the Sheriff, met
him, arrested him, took him into court, and commenced reading a warrant
that he had for his arrest, by way of arraignment. He became uncontrolla-
bly furious, and *seizing the writ, he tore it up, threw it on the ground and
stamped upon it.* The clicking of the locks of his companions' revolvers
was instantly heard and a crisis was expected. The Sheriff did not attempt

his retention; but being at least as prudent as he was valiant, he succumbed, leaving Slade the *master of the situation and the conqueror and ruler of the courts, law and law-makers.* This was a declaration of war, and

SLADE IN COURT.

was so accepted. The Vigilance Committee now felt that the question of social order and the preponderance of the law abiding citizens had then and there to be decided. They knew the character of Slade, and they were well aware that they must submit to his rule without murmur, or else that he must be dealt with in such fashion as would prevent his being able to wreak his vengeance on the Committee, who could never have hoped to live in the Territory secure from outrage or death, and who could never leave it without encountering his friends, whom his victory would have emboldened and stimulated to a pitch that would have rendered them reckless of consequences. The day previous, he had ridden into Dorris' store, and on being requested to leave, he drew his revolver and threatened to kill the gentleman who spoke to him. Another saloon he had led his horse into, and buying a bottle of wine, he tried to make the animal drink it. This was not considered an uncommon performance, as he had often entered saloons, and commenced firing at the lamps, causing a wild stampede.

A leading member of the committee met Slade, and informed him in the quiet earnest manner of one who feels the importance of what he is saying: "Slade, get your horse at once, and go home, or there will be —————— to pay." Slade started and took a long look with his dark and piercing eyes, at the gentleman— "what do you mean?" said he. "You have no right to ask me what I mean," was the quiet reply, "get your horse at once, and remember what I tell you." After a short pause he promised to do so, and actually got into the saddle; but, being still intoxicated, he began calling aloud to one after another of his friends, and, at last seemed to have forgotten the warning he had received and became again uproarious, shouting the name of a well known courtezan in company with those of two men whom he considered heads of the Committee, as a sort of challenge; perhaps, however, as a simple act of bravado. It seems probable that the intimation of personal danger he had received had not been forgotten entirely; though fatally for him, he took a foolish way of showing his remembrance of it. He sought out Alexander Davis, the Judge of the Court, and drawing a cocked Derringer, he presented it at his head, and told him that he should hold him as a hostage for his own safety. As the Judge stood perfectly quiet, and offered no resistance to his captor, no further outrage followed on this score. Previous to this, on account of the critical state of affairs, the Committee had met, and at last resolved to arrest him. His execution had not been agreed upon, and, at that time, would have been negatived, most assuredly. A messenger rode down to Nevada to inform the leading men of what was on hand, as it was desirable to show that there was a feeling of unanimity on the subject, all along the gulch.

The miners turned out almost en masse, leaving their work and forming in solid column, about six hundred strong, armed to the teeth, they marched up to Virginia. The leader of the body well knew the temper of his men, on the subject. He spurred on ahead of them, and hastily calling a meeting of the Executive, he told them plainly that the miners meant "business," and that, if they came up, they would not stand in the street to be shot down by Slade's friends; but that they would take him and hang him. The meeting was small, as the Virginia men were loath to act at all. This momentous announcement of the feeling of the Lower Town was made to a cluster of men, who were deliberating behind a wagon, at the rear of a store on Main street.

The Committee were most unwilling to proceed to extremities. All the duty they had ever performed seemed as nothing to the task before them; but they had to decide, and that quickly. It was finally agreed that if the whole body of the miners were of the opinion that he should be hanged, that the Committee left it in their hands to deal with him. Off, at hot speed, rode the leader of the Nevada men to join his command.

Slade had found out what was intended, and the news sobered him instantly. He went into P. S. Pfouts' store, where Davis was, and apologized for his conduct, saying that he would take it all back.

The head of the column now wheeled into Wallace street and marched up at quick time. Halting in front of the store, the executive officer of the Committee stepped forward and arrested Slade, who was at once informed of his doom, and inquiry was made as to whether he had any business to settle. Several parties spoke to him on the subject; but to all such inquiries he turned a deaf ear, being entirely absorbed in the terrifying reflections on his own awful position. He never ceased his entreaties for life, and to see his dear wife. The unfortunate lady referred to, between whom and Slade there existed a warm affection, was at this time living at their Ranch on the Madison. She was possessed of considerable personal attractions; tall, well-formed, of graceful carriage, pleasing manners, and was, withal, an accomplished horsewoman.

A messenger from Slade rode at full speed to inform her of her husband's arrest. In an instant she was in the saddle, and with all the energy that love and despair could lend to an ardent temperament and a strong physique, she urged her fleet charger over the twelve miles of rough and rocky ground that intervened between her and the object of her passionate devotion.

Meanwhile a party of volunteers had made the necessary preparations for the execution, in the valley traversed by the branch. Beneath the site of Pfouts and Russell's stone building there was a corral, the gate-posts of which were strong and high. Across the top was laid a beam, to which the rope was fastened, and a dry-goods box served for the platform. To this place Slade was marched, surrounded by a guard, composing the best armed and most numerous force that has ever appeared in Montana Territory.

The doomed man had so exhausted himself by tears, prayers and lamentations, that he had scarcely strength left to stand under the fatal beam. He repeatedly exclaimed, "my God! my God! must I die? Oh, my dear wife!"

On the return of the fatigue party, they encountered some friends of Slade, staunch and reliable citizens and members of the Committee, but who were personally attached to the condemned. On hearing of his sentence, one of them, a stout-hearted man, pulled out his handkerchief and walked away, weeping like a child. Slade still begged to see his wife, most piteously, and it seemed hard to deny his request; but the bloody consequences that were sure to follow the inevitable attempt at a rescue, that her presence and entreaties would have certainly incited, forbade the granting of his request. Several gentlemen were sent for to see him, in his last moments, one of whom, (Judge Davis) made a short address to the people; but in such low tones as to be inaudible, save to a few in his immediate vicinity. One of his friends, after exhausting his powers of entreaty, threw off his coat and declared that the prisoner could not be hanged until he himself was killed. A hundred guns were instantly leveled at him; whereupon he turned and fled; but, being brought back, he was compelled to resume his coat, and to give a promise of future peaceable demeanor.

Scarcely a leading man in Virginia could be found, though numbers of the citizens joined the ranks of the guard when the arrest was made. All lamented the stern necessity which dictated the execution.

Everything being ready, the command was given, "Men, do your duty," and the box being instantly slipped from beneath his feet, he died almost instantaneously.

The body was cut down and carried to the Virginia Hotel, where,

A WIFE'S LAMENTATION.

in a darkened room, it was scarcely laid out, when the unfortunate and bereaved companion of the deceased arrived, at headlong speed, to find that all was over, and that she was a widow. Her grief and heart-piercing cries were terrible evidences of the depth of her attachment for her lost husband, and a considerable period elapsed before she could regain the command of her excited feelings.

There is something about the desperado-nature that is wholly unaccountable—at least it looks unaccountable. It is this. The true desperado is gifted with splendid courage, and yet he will take the most infamous advantage of his enemy; armed and free, he will stand up before a host and fight until he is shot all to pieces, and yet when he is under the gallows and helpless he will cry and plead like a child. Words are cheap, and it is easy to call Slade a coward (all executed men who do not "die game" are promptly called cowards by unreflecting people), and when we read of Slade that he "had so exhausted himself by tears, prayers and lamentations, that he had scarcely strength left to stand under the fatal beam," the disgraceful word suggests itself in a moment—yet in frequently defying and inviting the vengeance of banded Rocky Mountain cut-throats by shooting down their comrades and leaders, and never offering to hide or fly, Slade showed that he was a man of peerless bravery. No coward would dare that. Many a notorious coward, many a chicken-livered poltroon, coarse, brutal, degraded, has made his dying speech without a quaver in his voice and been swung into eternity with what looked like the calmest fortitude, and so we are justified in believing, from the low intellect of such a creature, that it was not *moral* courage that enabled him to do it. Then, if moral courage is not the requisite quality, what could it have been that this stout-hearted Slade lacked?—this bloody, desperate, kindly-mannered, urbane gentleman, who never hesitated to warn his most ruffianly enemies that he would kill them whenever or wherever he came across them next! I think it is a conundrum worth investigating.

CHAPTER 12

JUST beyond the breakfast-station we overtook a Mormon emigrant train of thirty-three wagons; and tramping wearily along and driving their herd of loose cows, were dozens of coarse-clad and sad-looking men, women and children, who had walked as they were walking now, day after day for eight lingering weeks, and in that time had compassed the distance our stage had come in *eight days and three hours*—seven hundred and ninety-eight miles! They were dusty and uncombed, hatless, bonnetless and ragged, and they did look so tired!

After breakfast, we bathed in Horse Creek, a (previously) limpid, sparkling stream—an appreciated luxury, for it was very seldom that our furious coach halted long enough for an indulgence of that kind. We changed horses ten or twelve times in every twenty-four hours—changed mules, rather—six mules—and did it nearly every time in *four minutes*. It was lively work. As our coach rattled up to each station six harnessed mules stepped gayly from the stable; and in the twinkling of an eye, almost, the old team was out, and the new one in and we off and away again.

During the afternoon we passed Sweetwater Creek, Independence Rock, Devil's Gate and the Devil's Gap. The latter were wild specimens of rugged scenery, and full of interest—*we were in the heart of the Rocky Mountains, now.* And we also passed by "Alkali" or "Soda Lake," and we woke up to the fact that our journey had stretched a long way across the world when the driver said that the Mormons often came there from Great Salt Lake City to haul away saleratus. He said that a few days gone by they had shoveled up enough pure saleratus from the ground (it was a *dry* lake) to load two wagons, and that when they got these two wagon loads of a drug that cost them nothing, to Salt Lake, they could sell it for twenty-five cents a pound.

In the night we sailed by a most notable curiosity, and one we had been hearing a good deal about for a day or two, and were suffering to see. This was what might be called a natural ice-house. It was August, now, and sweltering weather in the daytime, yet at one of the stations the men could scrape the soil on the hillside under the lee of a range of boulders, and at a depth of six inches cut out pure blocks of ice—hard, compactly frozen, and clear as crystal!

Toward dawn we got under way again, and presently as we sat with raised curtains enjoying our early-morning smoke and contemplating the first splendor of the rising sun as it swept down the long array of mountain peaks, flushing and gilding crag after crag and summit after summit, as if the invisible Creator reviewed his gray veterans and they saluted with a smile, we hove in sight of South Pass City. The hotel-keeper, the postmaster, the blacksmith, the mayor, the constable, the city marshal and the principal citizen and property holder, all came out and greeted us cheerily, and we gave him good-day. He gave us a little Indian news, and a little Rocky Mountain news, and we gave him some Plains information in return. He then retired to his lonely grandeur and we climbed on up among the bristling peaks and the ragged clouds. South Pass City consisted of four log cabins, one of which was unfinished, and the gentleman with all those offices and titles was the chiefest of the ten citizens of the place. Think of hotel-keeper, postmaster, blacksmith, mayor, constable, city marshal and principal citizen all condensed into one person and crammed into one skin. Bemis said he was "a perfect Allen's revolver of dignities." And he said that if he were to die as postmaster, or as blacksmith, or as postmaster and blacksmith both, the people might stand it; but if he were to die all over, it would be a frightful loss to the community.

Two miles beyond South Pass City we saw for the first time that mysterious marvel which all western untraveled boys have heard of and fully believe in, but are sure to be astounded at when they see it with their own eyes, nevertheless—banks of snow in dead summer time. We were now far up toward the sky, and knew all the time that we must presently encounter lofty summits clad in the "eternal snow" which was so commonplace a matter of mention in books, and yet when I did see it glittering in the sun on stately

THE CONCENTRATED INHABITANT.

domes in the distance and knew the month was August and that
my coat was hanging up because it was too warm to wear it, I was
full as much amazed as if I never had heard of snow in August before. Truly, "seeing is believing"—and many a man lives a long life
through, *thinking* he believes certain universally received and well
established things, and yet never suspects that if he were confronted by those things once, he would discover that he did not
really believe them before, but only thought he believed them.

In a little while quite a number of peaks swung into view with
long claws of glittering snow clasping them; and with here and
there, in the shade, down the mountain side, a little solitary patch
of snow looking no larger than a lady's pocket-handkerchief, but
being in reality as large as a "public square."

And now, at last, we were fairly in the renowned SOUTH PASS,
and whirling gayly along high above the common world. We were
perched upon the extreme summit of the great range of the Rocky
Mountains, toward which we had been climbing, patiently climb-

THE SOUTH PASS.

ing, ceaselessly climbing, for days and nights together—and about us was gathered a convention of Nature's kings that stood ten, twelve, and even thirteen thousand feet high—grand old fellows who would have to stoop to see Mount Washington, in the twilight. We were in such an airy elevation above the creeping populations of the earth, that now and then when the obstructing crags stood out of the way it seemed that we could look around and abroad and contemplate the whole great globe, with its dissolving views of mountains, seas and continents stretching away through the mystery of the summer haze.

As a general thing the Pass was more suggestive of a valley than a suspension bridge in the clouds—but it strongly suggested the latter at one spot. At that place the upper third of one or two majestic purple domes projected above our level on either hand and gave us a sense of a hidden great deep of mountains and plains and valleys down about their bases which we fancied we might see if we could step to the edge and look over. These Sultans of the fastnesses were turbaned with tumbled volumes of cloud, which shredded away from time to time and drifted off fringed and torn, trailing their continents of shadow after them; and catching presently on an intercepting peak, wrapped it about and brooded there—then shredded away again and left the purple peak, as they had left the purple domes, downy and white with new-laid snow. In passing, these monstrous rags of cloud hung low and swept along right over the spectator's head, swinging their tatters so nearly in his face that his impulse was to shrink when they came closest. In the one place I speak of, one could look below him upon a world of diminishing crags and cañons leading down, down, and away to a vague plain with a thread in it which was a road, and bunches of feathers in it which were trees,—a pretty picture sleeping in the sunlight—but with a darkness stealing over it and glooming its features deeper and deeper under the frown of a coming storm; and then, while no film or shadow marred the noon brightness of his high perch, he could watch the tempest break forth down there and see the lightnings leap from crag to crag and the sheeted rain drive along the cañon-sides, and hear the thunders peal and crash and roar. We had this spectacle; a familiar one to many, but to us a novelty.

We bowled along cheerily, and presently, at the very summit (though it had been all summit to us, and all equally level, for half an hour or more), we came to a spring which spent its water through two outlets and sent it in opposite directions. The conductor said that one of those streams which we were looking at, was just starting on a journey westward to the Gulf of California and the Pacific Ocean, through hundreds and even thousands of miles of desert solitudes. He said that the other was just leaving its home among the snow-peaks on a similar journey eastward—and we knew that long after we should have forgotten the simple rivulet it would still be plodding its pa-

THE PARTED STREAM.

tient way down the mountain sides, and cañon-beds, and between the banks of the Yellowstone; and by and by would join the broad Missouri and flow through unknown plains and deserts and unvisited wildernesses; and add a long and troubled pilgrimage among snags and wrecks and sand-bars; and enter the Mississippi, touch the wharves of St. Louis and still drift on, traversing shoals and rocky channels, then endless chains of bottomless and ample bends, walled with unbroken forests, then mysterious byways and secret passages among woody islands, then the chained bends again, bordered with wide levels of shining sugar-cane in place of the sombre forests; then by New Orleans and still other chains of bends—and finally, after two long months of daily and nightly harassment, excitement, enjoyment, adventure, and awful peril of parched throats, pumps and evaporation, pass the Gulf and enter into its rest upon the bosom of the tropic sea, never to look upon its snow-peaks again or regret them.

I freighted a leaf with a mental message for the friends at home, and dropped it in the stream. But I put no stamp on it and it was held for postage somewhere.

On the summit we overtook an emigrant train of many wagons, many tired men and women, and many a disgusted sheep and cow. In the wofully dusty horseman in charge of the expedition I recognized John ——. Of all persons in the world to meet on top of the Rocky Mountains thousands of miles from home, he was the last one I should have looked for. We were school-boys together and warm friends for years. But a boyish prank of mine had disruptured this friendship and it had never been renewed. The act of which I speak was this. I had been accustomed to visit occasionally an editor whose room was in the third story of a building and overlooked the street. One day this editor gave me a watermelon which I made preparations to devour on the spot, but chancing to look out of the window, I saw John standing directly under it and an irresistible

desire came upon me to drop the melon on his head, which I immediately did. I was the loser, for it spoiled the melon, and John never forgave me and we dropped all intercourse and parted, but now met again under these circumstances.

We recognized each other simultaneously, and hands were grasped as warmly as if no coldness had ever existed between us, and no allusion was made to any. All animosities were buried and the simple fact of meeting a familiar face in that isolated spot so far from home, was

IT SPOILED THE MELON.   sufficient to make us forget all things but pleasant ones, and we parted again with sincere "good-byes" and "God bless you" from both.

We had been climbing up the long shoulders of the Rocky Mountains for many tedious hours—we started *down* them, now. And we went spinning away at a round rate too.

We left the snowy Wind River Mountains and Uinta Mountains behind, and sped away, always through splendid scenery but occasionally through long ranks of white skeletons of mules and oxen—monuments of the huge emigration of other days—and here and there were up-ended boards or small piles of stones which

GIVEN OVER TO THE CAYOTE AND THE RAVEN.

the driver said marked the resting-place of more precious remains. It was the loneliest land for a grave! A land given over to the cayote and the raven—which is but another name for desolation and utter solitude. On damp, murky nights, these scattered skeletons gave forth a soft, hideous glow, like very faint spots of moonlight starring the vague desert. It was because of the phosphorus in the bones. But no scientific explanation could keep a body from shivering when he drifted by one of those ghostly lights and knew that a skull held it.

At midnight it began to rain, and I never saw anything like it— indeed, I did not even see this, for it was too dark. We fastened down the curtains and even caulked them with clothing, but the rain streamed in in twenty places, notwithstanding. There was no escape. If one moved his feet out of a stream, he brought his body under one; and if he moved his body he caught one somewhere else. If he struggled out of the drenched blankets and sat up, he was bound to get one down the back of his neck. Meantime the stage was wandering about a plain with gaping gullies in it, for the driver could not see an inch before his face nor keep the road, and the storm pelted so pitilessly that there was no keeping the horses still. With the first abatement the conductor turned out with lanterns to look for the road, and the first dash he made was into a chasm about fourteen feet deep, his lantern following like a meteor. As soon as he touched bottom he sang out frantically:

"Don't come here!"

To which the driver, who was looking over the precipice where he had disappeared, replied, with an injured air: "Think I'm a dam fool?"

"DON'T COME HERE!"   "THINK I'M A DAM FOOL?"

The conductor was more than an hour finding the road—a matter which showed us how far we had wandered and what chances we had been taking. He traced our wheel-tracks to the imminent verge of danger, in two places. I have always been glad that we were not killed that night. I do not know any particular reason, but I have always been glad.

In the morning, the tenth day out, we crossed Green river, a fine, large, limpid stream—stuck in it, with the water just up to the top of our mail-bed, and waited till extra teams were put on to haul us up the steep bank. But it was nice cool water, and besides it could not find any fresh place on us to wet.

At the Green river station we had breakfast—hot biscuits, fresh antelope steaks, and coffee—the only decent meal we tasted between the United States and Great Salt Lake City, and the only one we were ever really thankful for. Think of the monotonous execrableness of the thirty that went before it, to leave this one simple breakfast looming up in my memory like a shot-tower after all these years have gone by!

At 5 P.M. we reached Fort Bridger, one hundred and seventeen miles from the South Pass, and one thousand and twenty-five miles from St. Joseph. Fifty-two miles further on, near the head of Echo Cañon, we met sixty U. S. soldiers from Camp Floyd. The day before, they had fired upon three hundred or four hundred Indians, whom they supposed gathered together for no good purpose. In the fight that had ensued, four Indians were captured, and the main body chased four miles, but nobody killed. This looked like business. We had a notion to get out and join the sixty soldiers, but upon reflecting that there were four hundred of the Indians, we concluded to go on and join the Indians.

Echo Cañon is twenty miles long. It was like a long, smooth, narrow street, with a gradual descending grade, and shut in by enormous perpendicular walls of coarse conglomerate, four hundred feet high in many places, and turreted like mediæval castles. This was the most faultless piece of road in the mountains, and the driver said he would "let his team out." He did, and if the Pacific express trains whiz through there now any faster than we did then in the stage-coach, I envy the passengers the exhilaration of it. We fairly seemed to pick up our wheels and fly—and the mail matter was lifted up free from everything and held in solution! I am not given to exaggeration, and when I say a thing I mean it.

However, time presses. At four in the afternoon we arrived on the summit of Big Mountain, fifteen miles from Salt Lake City, when all the world was glorified with the setting sun, and the most stupendous panorama of mountain peaks yet encountered burst on our sight. We looked out upon this sublime spectacle from under the arch of a brilliant rainbow! Even the overland stage-driver stopped his horses and gazed!

Half an hour or an hour later, we changed horses, and took supper with a Mormon "Destroying Angel." "Destroying Angels," as I understand it, are Latter-Day Saints who are set apart by the church to conduct permanent disappearances of obnoxious citizens. I had heard a deal about these Mormon Destroying Angels

and the dark and bloody deeds they had done, and when I entered
this one's house I had my shudder all ready. But alas for all our ro-
mances, he was nothing but a loud, profane, offensive, old black-
guard! He was murderous enough, possibly, to fill the bill of a De-
stroyer, but would you have *any* kind of an Angel devoid of

THE "DESTROYING ANGEL."

dignity? Could you abide an Angel in an unclean shirt and no suspenders? Could you respect an Angel with a horse-laugh and a
swagger like a buccaneer?

There were other blackguards present—comrades of this one.
And there was one person that looked like a gentleman—Heber C.
Kimball's son, tall and well made, and thirty years old, perhaps. A
lot of slatternly women flitted hither and thither in a hurry, with
coffee-pots, plates of bread, and other appurtenances to supper,
and these were said to be the wives of the Angel—or some of
them, at least. And of course they were; for if they had been hired
"help" they would not have let an angel from above storm and
swear at them as he did, let alone one from the place this one
hailed from.

This was our first experience of the western "peculiar institution," and it was not very prepossessing. We did not tarry long to observe it, but hurried on to the home of the Latter-Day Saints, the stronghold of the prophets, the capital of the only absolute monarch in America—Great Salt Lake City. As the night closed in we took sanctuary in the Salt Lake House and unpacked our baggage.

CHAPTER 13

We had a fine supper, of the freshest meats and fowls and vegetables—a great variety and as great abundance. We walked about the streets some, afterward, and glanced in at shops and stores; and there was fascination in surreptitiously staring at every creature we took to be a Mormon. This was fairy-land to us, to all intents and purposes—a land of enchantment, and goblins, and awful mystery. We felt a curiosity to ask every child how many mothers it had, and if it could tell them apart; and we experienced a thrill every time a dwelling-house door opened and shut as we passed, disclosing a glimpse of human heads and backs and shoulders—for we so longed to have a good satisfying look at a Mormon family in all its comprehensive ampleness, disposed in the customary concentric rings of its home circle.

By and by the Acting Governor of the Territory introduced us to other "Gentiles," and we spent a sociable hour with them. "Gentiles" are people who are not Mormons. Our fellow-passenger, Bemis, took care of himself, during this part of the evening, and did not make an overpowering success of it, either, for he came into our room in the hotel about eleven o'clock, full of cheerfulness, and talking loosely, disjointedly and indiscriminately, and every now and then tugging out a ragged word by the roots that had more hiccups than syllables in it. This, together with his hanging his coat on the floor on one side of a chair, and his vest on the floor on the other side, and piling his pants on the floor just in front of the same chair, and then contemplating the general result with superstitious awe, and finally pronouncing it "too many for *him*" and going to bed with his boots on, led us to fear that something he had eaten had not agreed with him.

But we knew afterward that it was something he had been drinking. It was the exclusively Mormon refresher, "valley tan." Valley tan (or, at least, one form of valley tan) is a kind of whisky, or first cousin to it; is of Mormon invention and manufactured only in Utah. Tradition says it is made of (imported) fire and brimstone. If

EFFECTS OF "VALLEY TAN."

I remember rightly no public drinking saloons were allowed in the kingdom by Brigham Young, and no private drinking permitted among the faithful, except they confined themselves to "valley tan."

Next day we strolled about everywhere through the broad, straight, level streets, and enjoyed the pleasant strangeness of a city of fifteen thousand inhabitants with no loafers perceptible in it; and no visible drunkards or noisy people; a limpid stream rippling and dancing through every street in place of a filthy gutter; block after block of trim dwellings, built of "frame" and sunburned

brick—a great thriving orchard and garden behind every one of
them, apparently—branches from the street stream winding and
sparkling among the garden beds and fruit trees—and a grand general air of neatness, repair, thrift and comfort, around and about
and over the whole. And everywhere were workshops, factories,
and all manner of industries; and intent faces and busy hands were
to be seen wherever one looked; and in one's ears was the ceaseless
clink of hammers, the buzz of trade and the contented hum of
drums and fly-wheels.

The armorial crest of my own State consisted of two dissolute
bears holding up the head of a dead and gone cask between them
and making the pertinent remark, "UNITED, WE STAND—(HIC!)—
DIVIDED, WE FALL." It was always too figurative for the author of

ONE CREST.

THE OTHER.

this book. But the Mormon crest was easy. And it was simple,
unostentatious, and fitted like a glove. It was a representation of a
GOLDEN BEEHIVE, with the bees all at work!

The city lies in the edge of a level plain as broad as the State of
Connecticut, and crouches close down to the ground under a curving wall of mighty mountains whose heads are hidden in the
clouds, and whose shoulders bear relics of the snows of winter all
the summer long. Seen from one of these dizzy heights, twelve or
fifteen miles off, Great Salt Lake City is toned down and diminished till it is suggestive of a child's toy-village reposing under the
majestic protection of the Chinese wall.

On some of those mountains, to the southwest, it had been raining every day for two weeks, but not a drop had fallen in the city. And on hot days in late spring and early autumn the citizens could quit fanning and growling and go out and cool off by looking at the luxury of a glorious snow-storm going on in the mountains. They could enjoy it at a distance, at those seasons, every day, though no snow would fall in their streets, or anywhere near them.

Salt Lake City was healthy—an extremely healthy city. They declared there was only one physician in the place and he was arrested every week regularly and held to answer under the vagrant act for having "no visible means of support." [They always give you

THE VAGRANT.

a good substantial article of truth in Salt Lake, and good measure and good weight, too. Very often, if you wished to weigh one of their airiest little commonplace statements you would want the hay scales.]

We desired to visit the famous inland sea, the American "Dead Sea," the great Salt Lake—seventeen miles, horseback, from the city—for we had dreamed about it, and thought about it, and talked about it, and yearned to see it, all the first part of our trip; but now when it was only arm's length away it had suddenly lost nearly every bit of its interest. And so we put it off, in a sort of general way, till next day—and that was the last we ever thought of it. We dined with some hospitable Gentiles; and visited the foundation of the prodigious temple; and talked long with that shrewd Connecticut Yankee, Heber C. Kimball (since deceased), a saint of

HEBER KIMBALL

high degree and a mighty man of commerce. We saw the "Tithing-House," and the "Lion House," and I do not know or remember how many more church and government buildings of various kinds and curious names. We flitted hither and thither and enjoyed every hour, and picked up a great deal of useful information and entertaining nonsense, and went to bed at night satisfied.

The second day, we made the acquaintance of Mr. Street (since deceased) and put on white shirts and went and paid a state visit to the king. He seemed a quiet, kindly, easy-mannered, dignified, self-possessed old gentleman of fifty-five or sixty, and had a gentle craft in his eye that probably belonged there. He was very simply dressed and was just taking off a straw hat as we entered. He talked about Utah, and the Indians, and Nevada, and general American matters and questions, with our Secretary and certain government officials who came with us. But he never paid any attention to me,

BRIGHAM YOUNG

notwithstanding I made several attempts to "draw him out" on Federal politics and his high-handed attitude toward Congress. I thought some of the things I said were rather fine. But he merely looked around at me, at distant intervals, something as I have seen a benignant old cat look around to see which kitten was meddling with her tail. By and by I subsided into an indignant silence, and so sat until the end, hot and flushed, and execrating him in my heart for an ignorant savage. But he was calm. His conversation with those gentlemen flowed on as sweetly and peacefully and musically as any summer brook. When the audience was ended and we were retiring from the presence, he put his hand on my head, beamed down on me in an admiring way and said to my brother:

"Ah—your child, I presume? Boy, or girl?"

CHAPTER 14

Mr. Street was very busy with his telegraphic matters—and considering that he had eight or nine hundred miles of rugged, snowy, uninhabited mountains, and waterless, treeless, melancholy deserts to traverse with his wire, it was natural and needful that he should be as busy as possible. He could not go comfortably along and cut his poles by the roadside, either, but they had to be hauled by ox teams across those exhausting deserts—and it was two days' journey from water to water, in one or two of them. Mr. Street's contract was a vast work, every way one looked at it; and yet to comprehend what the vague words "eight hundred miles of rugged mountains and dismal deserts" mean, one must go over the ground in person—pen and ink descriptions cannot convey the dreary reality to the reader. And after all, Mr. S.'s mightiest difficulty turned out to be one which he had never taken into the account at all. Unto Mormons he had sub-let the hardest and heaviest half of his great undertaking, and all of a sudden they concluded that they were going to make little or nothing, and so they tranquilly threw their poles overboard in mountain or desert, just as it happened when they took the notion, and drove home and went about their customary business! They were under written contract to Mr. Street, but they did not care anything for that. They said they would "admire" to see a "Gentile" force a Mormon to fulfil a losing contract in Utah! And they made themselves very merry over the matter. Street said—for it was he that told us these things:

"I was in dismay. I was under heavy bonds to complete my contract in a given time, and this disaster looked very much like ruin.

It was an astounding thing; it was such a wholly unlooked-for difficulty, that I was entirely nonplussed. I am a business man—have always been a business man—do not know anything *but* business—and so you can imagine how like being struck by lightning it was to find myself in a country where *written contracts were worthless!*—that main security, that sheet-anchor, that absolute necessity, of business. My confidence left me. There was no use in making new contracts—that was plain. I talked with first one prominent citizen and then another. They all sympathized with me, first rate, but they did not know how to help me. But at last a Gentile said, 'Go to Brigham Young!—these small fry cannot do you any good.' I did not think much of the idea, for if the *law* could not help me, what could an individual do who had not even anything to do with either making the laws or executing them? He might be a very good patriarch of a church and preacher in its tabernacle, but something sterner than religion and moral suasion was needed to handle a hundred refractory, half-civilized subcontractors. But what was a man to do? I thought if Mr. Young could not do anything else, he might probably be able to give me some advice and a valuable hint or two, and so I went straight to him and laid the whole case before him. He said very little, but he showed strong interest all the way through. He examined all the papers in detail, and whenever there seemed anything like a hitch, either in the papers or my statement, he would go back and take up the thread and follow it patiently out to an intelligent and satisfactory result. Then he made a list of the contractors' names. Finally he said:

"'Mr. Street, this is all perfectly plain. These contracts are strictly and legally drawn, and are duly signed and certified. These men manifestly entered into them with their eyes open. I see no fault or flaw anywhere.'

"Then Mr. Young turned to a man waiting at the other end of the room and said: 'Take this list of names to So-and-so, and tell him to have these men here at such-and-such an hour.'

"They were there, to the minute. So was I. Mr. Young asked

them a number of questions, and their answers made my statement good. Then he said to them:

"'You signed these contracts and assumed these obligations of
your own free will and accord?'

"'Yes.'

"'Then carry them out to the letter, if it makes paupers of you!
Go!'

"And they *did* go, too! They are strung across the deserts now,
working like bees. And I never hear a word out of them. There is a
batch of governors, and judges, and other officials here, shipped

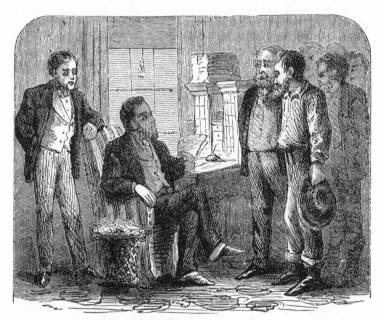

THE CONTRACTORS BEFORE THE KING.

from Washington, and they maintain the semblance of a republican form of government—but the petrified truth is that Utah is an
absolute monarchy and Brigham Young is king!"

Mr. Street was a fine man, and I believe his story. I knew him
well during several years afterward in San Francisco.

Our stay in Salt Lake City amounted to only two days, and therefore we had no time to make the customary inquisition into the
workings of polygamy and get up the usual statistics and deduc-
tions preparatory to calling the attention of the nation at large
once more to the matter. I had the will to do it. With the gushing
self-sufficiency of youth I was feverish to plunge in headlong and
achieve a great reform here—until I saw the Mormon women.

I WAS TOUCHED.

Then I was touched. My heart was wiser than my head. It warmed
toward these poor, ungainly and pathetically "homely" creatures,
and as I turned to hide the generous moisture in my eyes, I said,
"No—the man that marries one of them has done an act of Christian charity which entitles him to the kindly applause of mankind,
not their harsh censure—and the man that marries sixty of them

has done a deed of open-handed generosity so sublime that the nations should stand uncovered in his presence and worship in
silence."*

_____

*For a brief sketch of Mormon history, and the noted Mountain Meadows mas-
sacre, see Appendices A and B.

CHAPTER 15

It is a luscious country for thrilling evening stories about assassinations of intractable Gentiles. I cannot easily conceive of anything more cosy than the night in Salt Lake which we spent in a Gentile den, smoking pipes and listening to tales of how Burton galloped in among the pleading and defenceless "Morrisites" and shot them down, men and women, like so many dogs. And how Bill Hickman, a Destroying Angel, shot Drown and Arnold dead for bringing suit against him for a debt. And how Porter Rockwell did this and that dreadful thing. And how heedless people often come to Utah and make remarks about Brigham, or polygamy, or some other sacred matter, and the very next morning at daylight such parties are sure to be found lying up some back alley, contentedly waiting for the hearse.

And the next most interesting thing is to sit and listen to these Gentiles talk about polygamy; and how some portly old frog of an elder, or a bishop, marries a girl—likes her, marries her sister—likes her, marries another sister—likes her, takes another—likes her, marries her mother—likes her, marries her father, grandfather, great grandfather, and then comes back hungry and asks for more. And how the pert young thing of eleven will chance to be the favorite wife and her own venerable grandmother have to rank away down toward D 4 in their mutual husband's esteem, and have to sleep in the kitchen, as like as not. And how this dreadful sort of thing, this hiving together in one foul nest of mother and daughters, and the making a young daughter superior to her own mother in rank and authority, are things which Mormon women submit to because their religion teaches them that the more wives a man has on earth, and the more children he rears, the higher the place they will all have in the world to come—and the warmer, maybe, though they do not seem to say anything about that.

According to these Gentile friends of ours, Brigham Young's
harem contains twenty or thirty wives. They said that some of

FAVORITE WIFE AND D 4.

them had grown old and gone out of active service, but were comfortably housed and cared for in the hennery—or the Lion House,
as it is strangely named. Along with each wife were her children—
fifty altogether. The house was perfectly quiet and orderly, when
the children were still. They all took their meals in one room, and
a happy and homelike sight it was pronounced to be. None of our
party got an opportunity to take dinner with Mr. Young, but a Gentile by the name of Johnson professed to have enjoyed a sociable
breakfast in the Lion House. He gave a preposterous account of the
"calling of the roll," and other preliminaries, and the carnage that
ensued when the buckwheat cakes came in. But he embellished
rather too much. He said that Mr. Young told him several smart
sayings of certain of his "two-year-olds," observing with some
pride that for many years he had been the heaviest contributor in
that line to one of the eastern magazines; and then he wanted to

show Mr. Johnson one of the pets that had said the last good thing, but he could not find the child. He searched the faces of the children in detail, but could not decide which one it was. Finally he gave it up with a sigh and said:

"I thought I would know the little cub again but I don't." Mr. Johnson said further, that Mr. Young observed that life was a sad,

NEEDED MARKING.

sad thing—"because the joy of every new marriage a man contracted was so apt to be blighted by the inopportune funeral of a less recent bride." And Mr. Johnson said that while he and Mr. Young were pleasantly conversing in private, one of the Mrs. Youngs came in and demanded a breast-pin, remarking that she had found out that he had been giving a breast-pin to No. 6, and *she*, for one, did not propose to let this partiality go on without making a satisfactory amount of trouble about it. Mr. Young reminded her that there was a stranger present. Mrs. Young said that if the state of things inside the house was not agreeable to the stranger, he could find room outside. Mr. Young promised the breast-pin, and she went away. But in a minute or two another Mrs.

Young came in and demanded a breast-pin. Mr. Young began a re-
monstrance, but Mrs. Young cut him short. She said No. 6 had got
one, and No. 11 was promised one, and it was "no use for him to try
to impose on her—she hoped she knew her rights." He gave his
promise, and she went. And presently three Mrs. Youngs entered
in a body and opened on their husband a tempest of tears, abuse,
and entreaty. They had heard all about No. 6, No. 11, and No. 14.
Three more breast-pins were promised. They were hardly gone
when nine more Mrs. Youngs filed into the presence, and a new
tempest burst forth and raged round about the prophet and his
guest. Nine breast-pins were promised, and the weird sisters filed
out again. And in came eleven more, weeping and wailing and
gnashing their teeth. Eleven promised breast-pins purchased peace
once more.

"That is a specimen," said Mr. Young. "You see how it is. You see
what a life I lead. A man *can't* be wise all the time. In a heedless
moment I gave my darling No. 6—excuse my calling her thus, as
her other name has escaped me for the moment—a breast-pin. It
was only worth twenty-five dollars—that is, *apparently* that was
its whole cost—but its ultimate cost was inevitably bound to be a
good deal more. You yourself have seen it climb up to six hundred
and fifty dollars—and alas, even that is not the end! For I have
wives all over this Territory of Utah. I have dozens of wives whose
numbers, even, I do not know without looking in the family Bible.
They are scattered far and wide among the mountains and valleys
of my realm. And mark you, every solitary one of them will hear of
this wretched breast-pin, and every last one of them will have one
or die. No. 6's breast-pin will cost me twenty-five hundred dollars
before I see the end of it. And these creatures will compare these
pins together, and if one is a shade finer than the rest, they will all
be thrown on my hands, and I will have to order a new lot to keep
peace in the family. Sir, you probably did not know it, but all the
time you were present with my children your every movement
was watched by vigilant servitors of mine. If you had offered to give
a child a dime, or a stick of candy, or any trifle of the kind, you
would have been snatched out of the house instantly, provided it
could be done before your gift left your hand. Otherwise it would
be absolutely necessary for you to make an exactly similar gift to

all my children—and knowing by experience the importance of the thing, I would have stood by and seen to it myself that you did it, and did it thoroughly. Once a gentleman gave one of my children a tin whistle—a veritable invention of Satan, sir, and one which I have an unspeakable horror of, and so would you if you had eighty or ninety children in your house. But the deed was done—the man escaped. I knew what the result was going to be, and I thirsted for vengeance. I ordered out a flock of Destroying Angels, and they hunted the man far into the fastnesses of the Nevada mountains. But they never caught him. I am not cruel, sir—I am not vindictive except when sorely outraged—but if I had caught him, sir, so help me Joseph Smith, I would have locked him into the nursery till the brats whistled him to death! By the slaughtered body of St. Parley Pratt (whom God assoil!) there was never anything on this earth like it! *I* knew who gave the whistle to the child, but I could not make those jealous mothers believe me. They believed *I* did it, and the result was just what any man of reflection could have foreseen: I had to order a hundred and ten whistles—I think we had a hundred and ten children in the house then, but some of them are off at college now—I had to order a hundred and ten of those shrieking things, and I wish I may never speak another word if we didn't have to talk on our fingers entirely, from that time forth until the children got tired of the whistles. And if ever another man gives a whistle to a child of mine and I get my hands on him, I will hang him higher than Haman! That is the word with the bark on it! Shade of Nephi! *You* don't know anything about married life. I am rich, and everybody knows it. I am benevolent, and everybody takes advantage of it. I have a strong fatherly instinct and all the foundlings are foisted on me. Every time a woman wants to do well by her darling, she puzzles her brain to cipher out some scheme for getting it into my hands. Why, sir, a woman came here once with a child of a curious lifeless sort of complexion (and so had the woman), and swore that the child was mine and she my wife—that I had married her at such-and-such a time in such-and-such a place, but she had forgotten her number, and of course I could not remember her name. Well, sir, she called my attention to the fact that the child looked like me, and really it did seem to resemble me—a common thing in the Territory—and, to cut the story

short, I put it in my nursery, and she left. And by the ghost of Orson
Hyde, when they came to wash the paint off that child it was an
Injun! Bless my soul, you don't know anything about married life.

A REMARKABLE RESEMBLANCE.

It is a perfect dog's life, sir—a perfect dog's life. You can't econo-
mize. It isn't possible. I have tried keeping one set of bridal attire
for all occasions. But it is of no use. First you'll marry a combination of calico and consumption that's as thin as a rail, and next
you'll get a creature that's nothing more than the dropsy in disguise, and then you've got to eke out that bridal dress with an old
balloon. That is the way it goes. And think of the wash-bill—(excuse these tears)—nine hundred and eighty-four pieces a week!
No, sir, there is no such a thing as economy in a family like mine.
Why, just the one item of cradles—think of it! And vermifuge!
Soothing syrup! Teething rings! And 'papa's watches' for the babies to play with! And things to scratch the furniture with! And
lucifer matches for them to eat, and pieces of glass to cut themselves with! The item of glass alone would support *your* family, I
venture to say, sir. Let me scrimp and squeeze all I can, I still can't
get ahead as fast as I feel I ought to, with my opportunities. Bless

you, sir, at a time when I had seventy-two wives in this house, I groaned under the pressure of keeping thousands of dollars tied up in seventy-two bedsteads when the money ought to have been out at interest; and I just sold out the whole stock, sir, at a sacrifice, and built a bedstead seven feet long and ninety-six feet wide. But it was a failure, sir. I could *not* sleep. It appeared to me that the whole seventy-two women snored at once. The roar was deafening. And then the danger of it! That was what I was looking at. They would all draw in their breath at once, and you could actually see the walls of the house suck in—and then they would all exhale their breath at once, and you could see the walls swell out, and strain, and hear the rafters crack, and the shingles grind together. My friend, take an old man's advice, and *don't* encumber yourself with a large family—mind, I tell you, don't do it. In a small

THE FAMILY BEDSTEAD.

family, and in a small family only, you will find that comfort and that peace of mind which are the best at last of the blessings this world is able to afford us, and for the lack of which no accumulation of wealth, and no acquisition of fame, power, and greatness can ever compensate us. Take my word for it, ten or eleven wives is all you need—never go over it."

Some instinct or other made me set this Johnson down as being unreliable. And yet he was a very entertaining person, and I doubt if some of the information he gave us could have been acquired from any other source. He was a pleasant contrast to those reticent Mormons.

CHAPTER 16

ALL men have heard of the Mormon Bible, but few except the "elect" have seen it, or, at least, taken the trouble to read it. I brought away a copy from Salt Lake. The book is a curiosity to me, it is such a pretentious affair, and yet so "slow," so sleepy; such an insipid mess of inspiration. It is chloroform in print. If Joseph Smith composed this book, the act was a miracle—keeping awake while he did it was, at any rate. If he, according to tradition, merely translated it from certain ancient and mysteriously-engraved plates of copper, which he declares he found under a stone, in an out-of-the-way locality, the work of translating was equally a miracle, for the same reason.

The book seems to be merely a prosy detail of imaginary history, with the Old Testament for a model; followed by a tedious plagiarism of the New Testament. The author labored to give his words and phrases the quaint, old-fashioned sound and structure of our King James's translation of the Scriptures; and the result is a mongrel—half modern glibness, and half ancient simplicity and gravity. The latter is awkward and constrained; the former natural, but grotesque by the contrast. Whenever he found his speech growing too modern—which was about every sentence or two—he ladled in a few such Scriptural phrases as "exceeding sore," "and it came to pass," etc., and made things satisfactory again. "And it came to pass" was his pet. If he had left that out, his Bible would have been only a pamphlet.

The title-page reads as follows:

THE BOOK OF MORMON: AN ACCOUNT WRITTEN BY THE HAND OF
  MORMON, UPON PLATES TAKEN FROM THE PLATES OF NEPHI.
  Wherefore it is an abridgment of the record of the people of Nephi, and
also of the Lamanites; written to the Lamanites, who are a remnant of the
House of Israel; and also to Jew and Gentile: written by way of command-

ment, and also by the spirit of prophecy and of revelation. Written and sealed up, and hid up unto the Lord, that they might not be destroyed; to come forth by the gift and power of God unto the interpretation thereof: sealed by the hand of Moroni, and hid up unto the Lord, to come forth in due time by the way of Gentile; the interpretation thereof by the gift of God. An abridgment taken from the Book of Ether also; which is a record of the people of Jared; who were scattered at the time the Lord confounded the language of the people when they were building a tower to get to Heaven.

"Hid up" is good. And so is "wherefore"—though why "wherefore?" Any other word would have answered as well—though in truth it would not have sounded so Scriptural.

Next comes

THE TESTIMONY OF THREE WITNESSES.

Be it known unto all nations, kindreds, tongues, and people unto whom this work shall come, that we, through the grace of God the Father, and our Lord Jesus Christ, have seen the plates which contain this record, which is a record of the people of Nephi, and also of the Lamanites, their brethren, and also of the people of Jared, who came from the tower of which hath been spoken; and we also know that they have been translated by the gift and power of God, for his voice hath declared it unto us; wherefore we know of a surety that the work is true. And we also testify that we have seen the engravings which are upon the plates; and they have been shewn unto us by the power of God, and not of man. And we declare with words of soberness, that an angel of God came down from heaven, and he brought and laid before our eyes, that we beheld and saw the plates, and the engravings thereon; and we know that it is by the grace of God the Father, and our Lord Jesus Christ, that we beheld and bear record that these things are true; and it is marvellous in our eyes, nevertheless the voice of the Lord commanded us that we should bear record of it; wherefore, to be obedient unto the commandments of God, we bear testimony of these things. And we know that if we are faithful in Christ, we shall rid our garments of the blood of all men, and be found spotless before the judgment-seat of Christ, and shall dwell with him eternally in the heavens. And the honour be to the Father, and to the Son, and to the Holy Ghost, which is one God. Amen.

OLIVER COWDERY,
DAVID WHITMER,
MARTIN HARRIS.

Some people have to have a world of evidence before they can come anywhere in the neighborhood of believing anything; but for me, when a man tells me that he has "seen the engravings which are upon the plates," and not only that, but an angel was there at the time, and saw him see them, and probably took his receipt for it, I am very far on the road to conviction, no matter whether I ever heard of that man before or not, and even if I do not know the name of the angel, or his nationality either.

Next is this:

AND ALSO THE TESTIMONY OF EIGHT WITNESSES.

Be it known unto all nations, kindreds, tongues, and people unto whom this work shall come, that Joseph Smith, Jun., the translator of this work, has shewn unto us the plates of which hath been spoken, which have the appearance of gold; and as many of the leaves as the said Smith has translated, we did handle with our hands; and we also saw the engravings thereon, all of which has the appearance of ancient work, and of curious workmanship. And this we bear record with words of soberness, that the said Smith has shewn unto us, for we have seen and hefted, and know of a surety that the said Smith has got the plates of which we have spoken. And we give our names unto the world, to witness unto the world that which we have seen; and we lie not, God bearing witness of it.

CHRISTIAN WHITMER,	HIRAM PAGE,
JACOB WHITMER,	JOSEPH SMITH, Sen.
PETER WHITMER, Jun.	HYRUM SMITH,
JOHN WHITMER,	SAMUEL H. SMITH.

And when I am far on the road to conviction, and eight men, be they grammatical or otherwise, come forward and tell me that they have seen the plates too; and not only seen those plates but "hefted" them, I *am* convinced. I could not feel more satisfied and at rest if the entire Whitmer family had testified.

The Mormon Bible consists of fifteen "books"—being the books of Jacob, Enos, Jarom, Omni, Mosiah, Zeniff, Alma, Helaman, Ether, Moroni, two "books" of Mormon, and three of Nephi.

In the first book of Nephi is a plagiarism of the Old Testament, which gives an account of the exodus from Jerusalem of the "children of Lehi;" and it goes on to tell of their wanderings in the wilderness, during eight years, and their supernatural protection by one of their number, a party by the name of Nephi. They finally reached the land of "Bountiful," and camped by the sea. After they

had remained there "for the space of many days"—which is more
Scriptural than definite—Nephi was commanded from on high to
build a ship wherein to "carry the people across the waters." He
travestied Noah's ark—but he obeyed orders in the matter of the
plan. He finished the ship *in a single day*, while his brethren stood
by and made fun of it—and of him, too—"saying, our brother is a
fool, for he thinketh that he can build a ship." They did not wait for
the timbers to dry, but the whole tribe or nation sailed the next
day. Then a bit of genuine nature cropped out, and is revealed by
outspoken Nephi with Scriptural frankness—they all got on a
spree! They, "and also their wives, began to make themselves
merry, insomuch that they began to dance, and to sing, and to

THE MIRACULOUS COMPASS.

speak with much rudeness; yea, they were lifted up unto exceeding rudeness."

Nephi tried to stop these scandalous proceedings; but they tied
him neck and heels, and went on with their lark. But observe how

Nephi the prophet circumvented them by the aid of the invisible powers:

> And it came to pass that after they had bound me, insomuch that I could not move, the compass, which had been prepared of the Lord, did cease to work; wherefore, they knew not whither they should steer the ship, insomuch that there arose a great storm, yea, a great and terrible tempest, and we were driven back upon the waters for the space of three days; and they began to be frightened exceedingly, lest they should be drowned in the sea; nevertheless they did not loose me. And on the fourth day, which we had been driven back, the tempest began to be exceeding sore.
>
> And it came to pass that we were about to be swallowed up in the depths of the sea.

Then they untied him.

> And it came to pass after they had loosed me, behold, I took the compass, and it did work whither I desired it. And it came to pass that I prayed unto the Lord; and after I had prayed, the winds did cease, and the storm did cease, and there was a great calm.

Equipped with their compass, these ancients appear to have had the advantage of Noah.

Their voyage was toward a "promised land"—the only name they give it. They reached it in safety.

Polygamy is a recent feature in the Mormon religion, and was added by Brigham Young after Joseph Smith's death. Before that, it was regarded as an "abomination." This verse from the Mormon Bible occurs in Chapter II. of the book of Jacob:

> For behold, thus saith the Lord, this people begin to wax in iniquity; they understand not the scriptures; for they seek to excuse themselves in committing whoredoms, because of the things which were written concerning David, and Solomon his son. Behold, David and Solomon truly had many wives and concubines, which thing was abominable before me, saith the Lord; wherefore, thus saith the Lord, I have led this people forth out of the land of Jerusalem, by the power of mine arm, that I might raise up unto me a righteous branch from the fruit of the loins of Joseph. Wherefore, I the Lord God, will not suffer that this people shall do like unto them of old.

However, the project failed—or at least the modern Mormon end of it—for Brigham "suffers" it. This verse is from the same chapter:

Behold, the Lamanites your brethren, whom ye hate, because of their filthiness and the cursings which hath come upon their skins, are more righteous than you; for they have not forgotten the commandment of the Lord, which was given unto our fathers, that they should have, save it were one wife; and concubines they should have none.

The following verse (from Chapter IX. of the book of Nephi) appears to contain information not familiar to everybody:

And now it came to pass that when Jesus had ascended into heaven, the multitude did disperse, and every man did take his wife and his children, and did return to his own home.

And it came to pass that on the morrow, when the multitude was gathered together, behold, Nephi and his brother whom he had raised from the dead, whose name was Timothy, and also his son, whose name was Jonas, and also Mathoni, and Mathonihah, his brother, and Kumen, and Kumenonhi, and Jeremiah, and Shemnon, and Jonas, and Zedekiah, and Isaiah; now these were the names of the disciples whom Jesus had chosen.

In order that the reader may observe how much more grandeur and picturesqueness (as seen by these Mormon twelve) accompanied one of the tenderest episodes in the life of our Savior than other eyes seem to have been aware of, I quote the following from the same "book"—Nephi:

And it came to pass that Jesus spake unto them, and bade them arise. And they arose from the earth, and he said unto them, blessed are ye because of your faith. And now behold, my joy is full. And when he had said these words, he wept, and the multitude bear record of it, and he took their little children, one by one, and blessed them, and prayed unto the Father for them. And when he had done this he wept again, and he spake unto the multitude, and saith unto them, behold your little ones. And as they looked to behold, they cast their eyes towards heaven, and they saw the heavens open, and they saw angels descending out of heaven as it were, in the midst of fire; and they came down and encircled those little ones about, and they were encircled about with fire; and the angels did minister unto them, and the multitude did see and hear and bear record; and they know that their record is true, for they all of them did see and hear, every man for himself; and they were in number about two thousand and five hundred souls; and they did consist of men, women, and children.

And what else would they be likely to consist of?

The book of Ether is an incomprehensible medley of "history," much of it relating to battles and sieges among peoples whom the reader has possibly never heard of; and who inhabited a country which is not set down in the geography. There was a King with the remarkable name of Coriantumr, and he warred with Shared, and Lib, and Shiz, and others, in the "plains of Heshlon;" and the "valley of Gilgal;" and the "wilderness of Akish;" and the "land of Moron;" and the "plains of Agosh;" and "Ogath," and "Ramah," and the "land of Corihor," and the "hill Comnor," by "the waters of Ripliancum," etc., etc., etc. "And it came to pass," after a deal of fighting, that Coriantumr, upon making calculation of his losses, found that "there had been slain two millions of mighty men, and also their wives and their children"—say 5,000,000 or 6,000,000 in all—"and he began to sorrow in his heart." Unquestionably it was time. So he wrote to Shiz, asking a cessation of hostilities, and offering to give up his kingdom to save his people. Shiz declined, except upon condition that Coriantumr would come and let him cut his head off first—a thing which Coriantumr would not do. Then there was more fighting for a season; then *four years* were devoted to gathering the forces for a final struggle—after which ensued a battle, which, I take it, is the most remarkable set forth in history,—except, perhaps, that of the Kilkenny cats, which it resembles in some respects. This is the account of the gathering and the battle:

7. And it came to pass that they did gather together all the people, upon all the face of the land, who had not been slain, save it was Ether. And it came to pass that Ether did behold all the doings of the people; and he beheld that the people who were for Coriantumr, were gathered together to the army of Coriantumr; and the people who were for Shiz, were gathered together to the army of Shiz; wherefore they were for the space of four years, gathering together the people, that they might get all who were upon the face of the land, and that they might receive all the strength which it was possible that they could receive. And it came to pass that when they were all gathered together, every one to the army which he would, with their wives and their children; both men, women, and children being armed with weapons of war, having shields, and breast-plates, and head-plates, and being clothed after the manner of war, they did march forth one against another, to battle; and they fought all that day, and conquered not. And it came to pass that when it was night they were weary, and retired to their camps; and after they had

retired to their camps, they took up a howling and a lamentation for the loss of the slain of their people; and so great were their cries, their howlings and lamentations, that it did rend the air exceedingly. And it came to pass that on the morrow they did go again to battle, and great and terrible was that day; nevertheless they conquered not, and when the night came again, they did rend the air with their cries, and their howlings, and their mournings, for the loss of the slain of their people.

8. And it came to pass that Coriantumr wrote again an epistle unto Shiz, desiring that he would not come again to battle, but that he would take the kingdom, and spare the lives of the people. But behold, the spirit of the Lord had ceased striving with them, and satan had full power over the hearts of the people, for they were given up unto the hardness of their hearts, and the blindness of their minds that they might be destroyed; wherefore they went again to battle. And it came to pass that they fought all that day, and when the night came they slept upon their swords; and on the morrow they fought even until the night came; and when the night came they were drunken with anger, even as a man who is drunken with wine; and they slept again upon their swords; and on the morrow they fought again; and when the night came they had all fallen by the sword save it were fifty and two of the people of Coriantumr, and sixty and nine of the people of Shiz. And it came to pass that they slept upon their swords that night, and on the morrow they fought again, and they contended in their mights with their swords, and with their shields, all that day; and when the night came there were thirty and two of the people of Shiz, and twenty and seven of the people of Coriantumr.

9. And it came to pass that they ate and slept, and prepared for death on the morrow. And they were large and mighty men, as to the strength of men. And it came to pass that they fought for the space of three hours, and they fainted with the loss of blood. And it came to pass that when the men of Coriantumr had received sufficient strength, that they could walk, they were about to flee for their lives, but behold, Shiz arose, and also his men, and he swore in his wrath that he would slay Coriantumr, or he would perish by the sword; wherefore he did pursue them, and on the morrow he did overtake them; and they fought again with the sword. And it came to pass that when they had all fallen by the sword, save it were Coriantumr and Shiz, behold Shiz had fainted with loss of blood. And it came to pass that when Coriantumr had leaned upon his sword, that he rested a little, he smote off the head of Shiz. And it came to pass that after he had smote off the head of Shiz, that Shiz raised upon his hands and fell; and after that he had struggled for breath, he died. And it came to pass that Coriantumr fell to the earth, and became as if he had no life. And the Lord spake unto Ether, and said unto him, go forth. And he went forth, and beheld that the words of the Lord had all been fulfilled; and he finished his record; and the hundredth part I have not written.

It seems a pity he did not finish, for after all his dreary former chapters of commonplace, he stopped just as he was in danger of becoming interesting.

The Mormon Bible is rather stupid and tiresome to read, but there is nothing vicious in its teachings. Its code of morals is unobjectionable—it is "smouched"* from the New Testament and no credit given.

---

*Milton.

CHAPTER 17

Aᴛ the end of our two days' sojourn, we left Great Salt Lake City hearty and well fed and happy—physically superb but not so very much wiser, as regards the "Mormon question," than we were when we arrived, perhaps. We had a deal more "information" than we had before, of course, but we did not know what portion of it was reliable and what was not—for it all came from acquaintances of a day—strangers, strictly speaking. We were told, for instance, that the dreadful "Mountain Meadows massacre" was the work of the Indians entirely, and that the Gentiles had meanly tried to fasten it upon the Mormons; we were told, likewise, that the Indians were to blame, partly, and partly the Mormons; and we were told,

THREE SIDES TO A QUESTION.

likewise, and just as positively, that the Mormons were almost if not wholly and completely responsible for that most treacherous and pitiless butchery. We got the story in all these different shapes, but it was not till several years afterward that Mrs. Waite's book, "The Mormon Prophet," came out with Judge Cradlebaugh's trial of the accused parties in it and revealed the truth that the latter version was the correct one and that the Mormons *were* the assassins. All our "information" had three sides to it, and so I gave up the idea that I could settle the "Mormon question" in two days. Still I have seen newspaper correspondents do it in one.

I left Great Salt Lake a good deal confused as to what state of things existed there—and sometimes even questioning in my own mind whether a state of things existed there at all or not. But presently I remembered with a lightening sense of relief that we had learned two or three trivial things there which we could be certain of; and so the two days were not wholly lost. For instance, we had learned that we were at last in a pioneer land, in absolute and tangible reality. The high prices charged for trifles were eloquent of

New York.	St. Louis.	Overland City.	Salt Lake City.

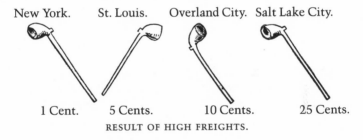

1 Cent.	5 Cents.	10 Cents.	25 Cents.

RESULT OF HIGH FREIGHTS.

high freights and bewildering distances of freightage. In the east, in those days, the smallest moneyed denomination was a penny and it represented the smallest purchasable quantity of any commodity. West of Cincinnati the smallest coin in use was the silver five-cent piece and no smaller quantity of an article could be bought than "five cents' worth." In Overland City the lowest coin appeared to be the ten-cent piece; but in Salt Lake there did not seem to be any money in circulation smaller than a quarter, or any smaller quantity purchasable of any commodity than twenty-five cents' worth. We had always been used to half dimes and "five cents' worth" as the minimum of financial negotiations; but in Salt Lake if one wanted a cigar, it was a quarter; if he wanted a chalk pipe, it was a quarter; if he wanted a peach, or a candle, or a

newspaper, or a shave, or a little Gentile whisky to rub on his
corns to arrest indigestion and keep him from having the tooth-
ache, twenty-five cents was the price, every time. When we looked
at the shot-bag of silver, now and then, we seemed to be wasting
our substance in riotous living, but if we referred to the expense
account we could see that we had not been doing anything of the
kind. But people easily get reconciled to big money and big prices,
and fond and vain of both—it is a descent to little coins and cheap
prices that is hardest to bear and slowest to take hold upon one's
toleration. After a month's acquaintance with the twenty-five-
cent minimum, the average human being is ready to blush every
time he thinks of his despicable five-cent days. How sunburnt
with blushes I used to get in gaudy Nevada, every time I thought of
my first financial experience in Salt Lake. It was on this wise
(which is a favorite expression of great authors, and a very neat
one, too, but I never hear anybody *say* on this wise when they are
talking). A young half-breed with a complexion like a yellow-
jacket asked me if I would have my boots blacked. It was at the Salt
Lake House the morning after we arrived. I said yes, and he blacked
them. Then I handed him a silver five-cent piece, with the benevolent air of a person who is conferring wealth and blessedness
upon poverty and suffering. The yellow-jacket took it with what I
judged to be suppressed emotion, and laid it reverently down in
the middle of his broad hand. Then he began to contemplate it,
much as a philosopher contemplates a gnat's ear in the ample field
of his microscope. Several mountaineers, teamsters, stage-drivers,
etc., drew near and dropped into the tableau and fell to surveying
the money with that attractive indifference to formality which is
noticeable in the hardy pioneer. Presently the yellow-jacket
handed the half dime back to me and told me I ought to keep my
money in my pocket-book instead of in my soul, and then I
wouldn't get it cramped and shriveled up so!

What a roar of vulgar laughter there was! I destroyed the mongrel reptile on the spot, but I smiled and smiled all the time I was
detaching his scalp, for the remark he made *was* good for an
"Injun."

Yes, we had learned in Salt Lake to be charged great prices without letting the inward shudder appear on the surface—for even al-

ready we had overheard and noted the tenor of conversations among drivers, conductors, and hostlers, and finally among citizens of Salt Lake, until we were well aware that these superior beings despised "emigrants." We permitted no tell-tale shudders and winces in our countenances, for we wanted to seem pioneers, or Mormons, half-breeds, teamsters, stage-drivers, Mountain

A SHRIVELED QUARTER.

Meadows assassins—anything in the world that the plains and Utah respected and admired—but we were wretchedly ashamed of being "emigrants," and sorry enough that we had white shirts and could not swear in the presence of ladies without looking the other way.

And many a time in Nevada, afterward, we had occasion to remember with humiliation that we were "emigrants," and consequently a low and inferior sort of creatures. Perhaps the reader has visited Utah, Nevada, or California, even in these latter days, and while communing with himself upon the sorrowful banishment of those countries from what he considers "the world," has had his wings clipped by finding that *he* is the one to be pitied, and that there are entire populations around him ready and willing to do it for him—yea, who are complacently doing it for him already, wherever he steps his foot. Poor thing, they are making fun of his hat; and the cut of his New York coat; and his conscientiousness about his grammar; and his feeble profanity; and his consumingly ludicrous ignorance of ores, shafts, tunnels, and other things

AN OBJECT OF PITY.

which he never saw before, and never felt enough interest in to read about. And all the time that he is thinking what a sad fate it is to be exiled to that far country, that lonely land, the citizens around him are looking down on him with a blighting compassion because he is an "emigrant" instead of that proudest and blessedest creature that exists on all the earth, a "Forty-Niner."

The accustomed coach life began again, now, and by midnight it almost seemed as if we never had been out of our snuggery among the mail-sacks at all. We had made one alteration, however. We had provided enough bread, boiled ham and hard boiled eggs to last double the six hundred miles of staging we had still to do.

And it was comfort in those succeeding days to sit up and contemplate the majestic panorama of mountains and valleys spread out below us and eat ham and hard boiled eggs while our spiritual natures reveled alternately in rainbows, thunderstorms, and peerless sunsets. Nothing helps scenery like ham and eggs. Ham and eggs, and after these a pipe—an old, rank, delicious pipe—ham and eggs and scenery, a "down grade," a flying coach, a fragrant pipe and a contented heart—these make happiness. It is what all the ages have struggled for.

CHAPTER 18

AT eight in the morning we reached the remnant and ruin of what had been the important military station of "Camp Floyd," some forty-five or fifty miles from Salt Lake City. At 4 P.M. we had doubled our distance and were ninety or a hundred miles from Salt Lake. And now we entered upon one of that species of deserts whose concentrated hideousness shames the diffused and diluted horrors of Sahara—an "*alkali*" desert. For sixty-eight miles there was but one break in it. I do not remember that this was really a break; indeed it seems to me that it was nothing but a watering depot *in the midst* of the stretch of sixty-eight miles. If my memory serves me, there was no well or spring at this place, but the water was hauled there by mule and ox teams from the further side of the desert. There was a stage station there. It was forty-five miles from the beginning of the desert, and twenty-three from the end of it.

We plowed and dragged and groped along, the whole livelong night, and at the end of this uncomfortable twelve hours we finished the forty-five-mile part of the desert and got to the stage station where the imported water was. The sun was just rising. It was easy enough to cross a desert in the night while we were asleep; and it was pleasant to reflect, in the morning, that we in actual person *had* encountered an absolute desert and could always speak knowingly of deserts in presence of the ignorant thenceforward. And it was pleasant also to reflect that this was not an obscure, back country desert, but a very celebrated one, the metropolis itself, as you may say. All this was very well and very comfortable and satisfactory—but now we were to cross a desert in *daylight*. This was fine—novel—romantic—dramatically adventurous—

this, indeed, was worth living for, worth traveling for! We would write home all about it.

This enthusiasm, this stern thirst for adventure, wilted under the sultry August sun and did not last above one hour. One poor little hour—and then we were ashamed that we had "gushed" so. The poetry was all in the anticipation—there is none in the reality. Imagine a vast, waveless ocean stricken dead and turned to ashes; imagine this solemn waste tufted with ash-dusted sage-bushes; imagine the lifeless silence and solitude that belong to such a place; imagine a coach, creeping like a bug through the midst of this shoreless level, and sending up tumbled volumes of dust as if it were a bug that went by steam; imagine this aching monotony of toiling and plowing kept up hour after hour, and the shore still as far away as ever, apparently; imagine team, driver, coach and passengers so deeply coated with ashes that they are all one colorless color; imagine ash-drifts roosting above moustaches and eyebrows like snow accumulations on boughs and bushes. This is the reality of it.

The sun beats down with dead, blistering, relentless malignity; the perspiration is welling from every pore in man and beast, but scarcely a sign of it finds its way to the surface—it is absorbed before it gets there; there is not the faintest breath of air stirring; there is not a merciful shred of cloud in all the brilliant firmament; there is not a living creature visible in any direction whither one searches the blank level that stretches its monotonous miles on every hand; there is not a sound—not a sigh—not a whisper—not a buzz, or a whir of wings, or distant pipe of bird—not even a sob from the lost souls that doubtless people that dead air. And so the occasional sneezing of the resting mules, and the champing of the bits, grate harshly on the grim stillness, not dissipating the spell but accenting it and making one feel more lonesome and forsaken than before.

The mules, under violent swearing, coaxing and whip-cracking, would make at stated intervals a "spurt," and drag the coach a hundred or maybe two hundred yards, stirring up a billowy cloud of dust that rolled back, enveloping the vehicle to the wheel-tops or higher, and making it seem afloat in a fog. Then a rest followed, with the usual sneezing and bit-champing. Then another "spurt" of a hundred yards and another rest at the end of it. All day long we kept this up, without water for the mules and without ever changing the team. At least we kept it up ten hours, which, I take it, is a day, and a pretty honest one, in an alkali desert. It was from four in the morning till two in the afternoon. And it was so hot! and so close! and our water canteens went dry in the middle of the day and we got so thirsty! It was so stupid and tiresome and dull! and the tedious hours did lag and drag and limp along with such a cruel deliberation! It was so trying to give one's watch a good long undisturbed spell and then take it out and find that it had been fooling away the time and not trying to get ahead any! The alkali dust cut through our lips, it persecuted our eyes, it ate through the delicate membranes and made our noses bleed and *kept* them bleeding— and truly and seriously the romance all faded far away and disappeared, and left the desert trip nothing but a harsh reality—a thirsty, sweltering, longing, hateful reality!

Two miles and a quarter an hour for ten hours—that was what we accomplished. It was hard to bring the comprehension away down to such a snail-pace as that, when we had been used to making eight and ten miles an hour. When we reached the station on the farther verge of the desert, we were glad, for the first time, that the Dictionary was along, because we never could have found language to tell how glad we were, in any sort of dictionary but an unabridged one with pictures in it. But there could not have been found in a whole library of dictionaries language sufficient to tell how tired those mules were after their twenty-three-mile pull. To try to give the reader an idea of how *thirsty* they were, would be to "gild refined gold or paint the lily."

Somehow, now that it is there, the quotation does not seem to fit—but no matter, let it stay, anyhow. I think it is a graceful and attractive thing, and therefore have tried time and time again to work it in where it *would* fit, but could not succeed. These efforts have kept my mind distracted and ill at ease, and made my narra-

tive seem broken and disjointed, in places. Under these circumstances it seems to me best to leave it in, as above, since this will
afford at least a temporary respite from the wear and tear of trying
to "lead up" to this really apt and beautiful quotation.

CHAPTER 19

ON the morning of the sixteenth day out from St. Joseph we arrived at the entrance of Rocky Cañon, two hundred and fifty miles from Salt Lake. It was along in this wild country somewhere, and far from any habitation of white men, except the stage stations, that we came across the wretchedest type of mankind I have ever seen, up to this writing. I refer to the Goshoot Indians. From what we could see and all we could learn, they are very considerably inferior to even the despised Digger Indians of California; inferior to all races of savages on our continent; inferior to even the Terra del Fuegans; inferior to the Hottentots, and actually inferior in some respects to the Kytches of Africa. Indeed, I have been obliged to

GOSHOOT INDIANS HANGING AROUND STATIONS.

look the bulky volumes of Wood's "Uncivilized Races of Men" clear through in order to find a savage tribe degraded enough to take rank with the Goshoots. I find but one people fairly open to that shameful verdict. It is the Bosjesmans (Bushmen) of South Africa. Such of the Goshoots as we saw, along the road and hanging about the stations, were small, lean, "scrawny" creatures; in complexion a dull black like the ordinary American negro; their faces and hands bearing dirt which they had been hoarding and accumulating for months, years, and even generations, according to the age of the proprietor; a silent, sneaking, treacherous looking race; taking note of everything, covertly, like all the other "Noble Red Men" that we (do not) read about, and betraying no sign in their countenances; indolent, everlastingly patient and tireless, like all other Indians; prideless beggars—for if the beggar instinct were left out of an Indian he would not "go," any more than a clock without a pendulum; hungry, always hungry, and yet never refusing anything that a hog would eat, though often eating what a hog would decline; hunters, but having no higher ambition than to kill and eat jackass rabbits, crickets and grasshoppers, and embezzle carrion from the buzzards and cayotes; savages who, when asked if they have the common Indian belief in a Great Spirit show a something which almost amounts to emotion, thinking whisky is referred to; a thin, scattering race of almost naked black children, these Goshoots are, who produce nothing at all, and have no villages, and no gatherings together into strictly defined tribal communities—a people whose only shelter is a rag cast on a bush to keep off a portion of the snow, and yet who inhabit one of the most rocky, wintry, repulsive wastes that our country or any other can exhibit.

The Bushmen and our Goshoots are manifestly descended from the self-same gorilla, or kangaroo, or Norway rat, whichever animal-Adam the Darwinians trace them to.

One would as soon expect the rabbits to fight as the Goshoots, and yet they used to live off the offal and refuse of the stations a few months and then come some dark night when no mischief was expected, and burn down the buildings and kill the men from ambush as they rushed out. And once, in the night, they attacked the stage-coach when a District Judge, of Nevada Territory, was the only passenger, and with their first volley of arrows (and a bullet or two) they riddled the stage curtains, wounded a horse or two and mortally wounded the driver. The latter was full of pluck, and so was his passenger. At the driver's call Judge Mott swung himself out, clambered to the box and seized the reins of the team, and away they plunged, through the racing mob of skeletons and under

THE DRIVE FOR LIFE.

a hurtling storm of missiles. The stricken driver had sunk down on the boot as soon as he was wounded, but had held on to the reins and said he would manage to keep hold of them until relieved. And after they were taken from his relaxing grasp, he lay with his head between Judge Mott's feet, and tranquilly gave directions about the road; he said he believed he could live till the miscreants were outrun and left behind, and that if he managed that, the main dif-ficulty would be at an end, and then if the Judge drove so and so (giving directions about bad places in the road, and general course) he would reach the next station without trouble. The Judge dis-tanced the enemy and at last rattled up to the station and knew that the night's perils were done; but there was no comrade-in-arms for him to rejoice with, for the soldierly driver was dead.

Let us forget that we have been saying harsh things about the Overland drivers, now. The disgust which the Goshoots gave me, a disciple of Cooper and a worshipper of the Red Man—even of the scholarly savages in the "Last of the Mohicans" who are fittingly associated with backwoodsmen who divide each sentence into two equal parts: one part critically grammatical, refined and choice of language, and the other part just such an attempt to talk like a hunter or a mountaineer, as a Broadway clerk might make after eating an edition of Emerson Bennett's works and studying frontier life at the Bowery Theatre a couple of weeks—I say that the nausea which the Goshoots gave me, an Indian worshipper, set me to examining authorities, to see if perchance I had been over-estimating the Red Man while viewing him through the mellow moonshine of romance. The revelations that came were disenchanting. It was curious to see how quickly the paint and tinsel fell away from him and left him treacherous, filthy and repulsive—and how quickly the evidences accumulated that wherever one finds an Indian tribe he has only found Goshoots more or less modified by circumstances and surroundings—but Goshoots, after all. They deserve pity, poor creatures; and they can have mine—at this distance. Nearer by, they never get anybody's.

There is an impression abroad that the Baltimore and Washington Railroad Company and many of its employés are Goshoots; but it is an error. There is only a plausible resemblance, which, while it is apt enough to mislead the ignorant, cannot deceive parties who have contemplated both tribes. But seriously, it was not only poor wit, but very wrong to start the report referred to above; for however innocent the motive may have been, the necessary effect was to injure the reputation of a class who have a hard enough time of it in the pitiless deserts of the Rocky Mountains, Heaven knows! If we cannot find it in our hearts to give those poor naked creatures our Christian sympathy and compassion, in God's name let us at least not throw mud at them.

CHAPTER 20

O<small>N</small> the seventeenth day we passed the highest mountain peaks we had yet seen, and although the day was very warm the night that followed upon its heels was wintry cold and blankets were next to useless.

On the eighteenth day we encountered the eastward-bound telegraph-constructors at Reese river station and sent a message to his Excellency Gov. Nye at Carson City (distant one hundred and fifty-six miles).

On the nineteenth day we crossed the Great American Desert— forty memorable miles of bottomless sand, into which the coach wheels sunk from six inches to a foot. We worked our passage most of the way across. That is to say, we got out and walked. It was a dreary pull and a long and thirsty one, for we had no water. From one extremity of this desert to the other, the road was white with the bones of oxen and horses. It would hardly be an exaggeration to say that we could have walked the forty miles and set our feet on a bone at every step! The desert was one prodigious graveyard. And the log-chains, wagon tyres, and rotting wrecks of vehicles were almost as thick as the bones. I think we saw log-chains enough rusting there in the desert, to reach across any State in the Union. Do not these relics suggest something of an idea of the fearful suffering and privation the early emigrants to California endured?

At the border of the desert lies Carson Lake, or the "Sink" of the Carson, a shallow, melancholy sheet of water some eighty or a hundred miles in circumference. Carson river empties into it and is lost—sinks mysteriously into the earth and never appears in the light of the sun again—for the lake has no outlet whatever.

There are several rivers in Nevada, and they all have this mysterious fate. They end in various lakes or "sinks," and that is the last of them. Carson Lake, Humboldt Lake, Walker Lake, Mono Lake, are all great sheets of water without any visible outlet. Water is always flowing into them; none is ever seen to flow out of them, and yet they remain always level full, neither receding nor overflowing. What they do with their surplus is only known to the Creator.

On the western verge of the desert we halted a moment at Ragtown. It consisted of one log house and is not set down on the map.

This reminds me of a circumstance. Just after we left Julesburg, on the Platte, I was sitting with the driver, and he said:

"I can tell you a most laughable thing indeed, if you would like to listen to it. Horace Greeley went over this road once. When he was leaving Carson City he told the driver, Hank Monk, that he

GREELEY'S RIDE.

had an engagement to lecture at Placerville and was very anxious to go through quick. Hank Monk cracked his whip and started off at an awful pace. The coach bounced up and down in such a terrific

way that it jolted the buttons all off of Horace's coat, and finally
shot his head clean through the roof of the stage, and then he yelled
at Hank Monk and begged him to go easier—said he warn't in as
much of a hurry as he was a while ago. But Hank Monk said, 'Keep
your seat, Horace, and I'll get you there on time!'—and you bet you
he did, too, what was left of him!"

A day or two after that we picked up a Denver man at the cross
roads, and he told us a good deal about the country and the Gregory
Diggings. He seemed a very entertaining person and a man well
posted in the affairs of Colorado. By and by he remarked:

"I can tell you a most laughable thing indeed, if you would like
to listen to it. Horace Greeley went over this road once. When he
was leaving Carson City he told the driver, Hank Monk, that he
had an engagement to lecture at Placerville and was very anxious
to go through quick. Hank Monk cracked his whip and started off
at an awful pace. The coach bounced up and down in such a terrific
way that it jolted the buttons all off of Horace's coat, and finally
shot his head clean through the roof of the stage, and then he yelled
at Hank Monk and begged him to go easier—said he warn't in as
much of a hurry as he was a while ago. But Hank Monk said, 'Keep
your seat, Horace, and I'll get you there on time!'—and you bet you
he did, too, what was left of him!"

At Fort Bridger, some days after this, we took on board a cavalry
sergeant, a very proper and soldierly person indeed. From no other
man during the whole journey, did we gather such a store of concise and well-arranged military information. It was surprising to
find in the desolate wilds of our country a man so thoroughly acquainted with everything useful to know in his line of life, and yet
of such inferior rank and unpretentious bearing. For as much as
three hours we listened to him with unabated interest. Finally he
got upon the subject of trans-continental travel, and presently
said:

"I can tell you a most laughable thing indeed, if you would like
to listen to it. Horace Greeley went over this road once. When he
was leaving Carson City he told the driver, Hank Monk, that he
had an engagement to lecture at Placerville and was very anxious
to go through quick. Hank Monk cracked his whip and started off

at an awful pace. The coach bounced up and down in such a terrific way that it jolted the buttons all off of Horace's coat, and finally shot his head clean through the roof of the stage, and then he yelled at Hank Monk and begged him to go easier—said he warn't in as much of a hurry as he was a while ago. But Hank Monk said, 'Keep your seat, Horace, and I'll get you there on time!'—and you bet you he did, too, what was left of him!"

When we were eight hours out from Salt Lake City a Mormon preacher got in with us at a way station—a gentle, soft-spoken, kindly man, and one whom any stranger would warm to at first sight. I can never forget the pathos that was in his voice as he told, in simple language, the story of his people's wanderings and unpitied sufferings. No pulpit eloquence was ever so moving and so beautiful as this outcast's picture of the first Mormon pilgrimage across the plains, struggling sorrowfully onward to the land of its banishment and marking its desolate way with graves and watering it with tears. His words so wrought upon us that it was a relief to us all when the conversation drifted into a more cheerful channel and the natural features of the curious country we were in came under treatment. One matter after another was pleasantly discussed, and at length the stranger said:

"I can tell you a most laughable thing indeed, if you would like to listen to it. Horace Greeley went over this road once. When he was leaving Carson City he told the driver, Hank Monk, that he had an engagement to lecture at Placerville and was very anxious to go through quick. Hank Monk cracked his whip and started off at an awful pace. The coach bounced up and down in such a terrific way that it jolted the buttons all off of Horace's coat, and finally shot his head clean through the roof of the stage, and then he yelled at Hank Monk and begged him to go easier—said he warn't in as much of a hurry as he was a while ago. But Hank Monk said, 'Keep your seat, Horace, and I'll get you there on time!'—and you bet you he did, too, what was left of him!"

Ten miles out of Ragtown we found a poor wanderer who had lain down to die. He had walked as long as he could, but his limbs had failed him at last. Hunger and fatigue had conquered him. It would have been inhuman to leave him there. We paid his fare to

Carson and lifted him into the coach. It was some little time before
he showed any very decided signs of life; but by dint of chafing him
and pouring brandy between his lips we finally brought him to a
languid consciousness. Then we fed him a little, and by and by he
seemed to comprehend the situation and a grateful light softened
his eye. We made his mail-sack bed as comfortable as possible, and
constructed a pillow for him with our coats. He seemed very
thankful. Then he looked up in our faces, and said in a feeble voice
that had a tremble of honest emotion in it:

"Gentlemen, I know not who you are, but you have saved my
life; and although I can never be able to repay you for it, I feel
that I can at least make one hour of your long journey lighter. I
take it you are strangers to this great thoroughfare, but I am entirely familiar with it. In this connection I can tell you a most
laughable thing indeed, if you would like to listen to it. Horace
Greeley—"

I said, impressively:

"Suffering stranger, proceed at your peril. You see in me the melancholy wreck of a once stalwart and magnificent manhood. What
has brought me to this? That thing which you are about to tell.

BOTTLING AN ANECDOTE.

Gradually but surely, that tiresome old anecdote has sapped my
strength, undermined my constitution, withered my life. Pity my

helplessness. Spare me only just this once, and tell me about young George Washington and his little hatchet for a change."

We were saved. But not so the invalid. In trying to retain the anecdote in his system he strained himself and died in our arms.

I am aware, now, that I ought not to have asked of the sturdiest citizen of all that region, what I asked of that mere shadow of a man; for, after seven years' residence on the Pacific coast, I know that no passenger or driver on the Overland ever corked that anecdote in, when a stranger was by, and survived. Within a period of six years I crossed and recrossed the Sierras between Nevada and California thirteen times by stage and listened to that deathless incident four hundred and eighty-one or eighty-two times. I have the list somewhere. Drivers always told it, conductors told it, landlords told it, chance passengers told it, the very Chinamen and vagrant Indians recounted it. I have had the same driver tell it to me two or three times in the same afternoon. It has come to me in all the multitude of tongues that Babel bequeathed to earth, and flavored with whisky, brandy, beer, cologne, sozodont, tobacco, garlic, onions, grasshoppers—everything that has a fragrance to it through all the long list of things that are gorged or guzzled by the sons of men. I never have smelt any anecdote as often as I have smelt that one; never have smelt any anecdote that smelt so variegated as that one. And you never could learn to know it by its smell, because every time you thought you had learned the smell of it, it would turn up with a different smell. Bayard Taylor has written about this hoary anecdote, Richardson has published it; so have Jones, Smith, Johnson, Ross Browne, and every other correspondence-inditing being that ever set his foot upon the great overland road anywhere between Julesburg and San Francisco; and I have heard that it is in the Talmud. I have seen it in print in nine different foreign languages; I have been told that it is employed in the inquisition in Rome; and I now learn with regret that it is going to be set to music. I do not think that such things are right.

Stage-coaching on the Overland is no more, and stage-drivers are a race defunct. I wonder if they bequeathed that bald-headed anecdote to their successors, the railroad brakemen and conductors, and if these latter still persecute the helpless passenger with it until he concludes, as did many a tourist of other days, that the real grandeurs of the Pacific coast are not Yo Semite and the Big Trees, but Hank Monk and his adventure with Horace Greeley.*

---

*And what makes that worn anecdote the more aggravating, is, that the adventure it celebrates *never occurred.* If it were a good anecdote, that seeming demerit would be its chiefest virtue, for creative power belongs to greatness; but what ought to be done to a man who would wantonly contrive so flat a one as this? If *I* were to suggest what ought to be done to him, I should be called extravagant—but what does the thirteenth chapter of Daniel say? Aha!

CHAPTER 21

We were approaching the end of our long journey. It was the morning of the twentieth day. At noon we would reach Carson City, the capital of Nevada Territory. We were not glad, but sorry. It had been a fine pleasure trip; we had fed fat on wonders every day; we were now well accustomed to stage life, and very fond of it; so the idea of coming to a stand-still and settling down to a humdrum existence in a village was not agreeable, but on the contrary depressing.

Visibly our new home was a desert, walled in by barren, snow-clad mountains. There was not a tree in sight. There was no vegetation but the endless sage-brush and greasewood. All nature was gray with it. We were plowing through great deeps of powdery alkali dust that rose in thick clouds and floated across the plain like smoke from a burning house. We were coated with it like millers; so were the coach, the mules, the mail-bags, the driver—we and the sage-brush and the other scenery were all one monotonous color. Long trains of freight wagons in the distance enveloped in ascending masses of dust suggested pictures of prairies on fire.

These teams and their masters were the only life we saw. Otherwise we moved in the midst of solitude, silence and desolation. Every twenty steps we passed the skeleton of some dead beast of burthen, with its dust-coated skin stretched tightly over its empty ribs. Frequently a solemn raven sat upon the skull or the hips and contemplated the passing coach with meditative serenity.

CONTEMPLATION.

By and by Carson City was pointed out to us. It nestled in the edge of a great plain and was a sufficient number of miles away to look like an assemblage of mere white spots in the shadow of a grim range of mountains overlooking it, whose summits seemed lifted clear out of companionship and consciousness of earthly things.

We arrived, disembarked, and the stage went on. It was a "wooden" town; its population two thousand souls. The main street consisted of four or five blocks of little white frame stores which were too high to sit down on, but not too high for various other purposes; in fact, hardly high enough. They were packed close together, side by side, as if room were scarce in that mighty plain. The sidewalk was of boards that were more or less loose and inclined to rattle when walked upon. In the middle of the town, opposite the stores, was the "plaza" which is native to all towns beyond the Rocky Mountains—a large, unfenced, level vacancy, with a liberty pole in it, and very useful as a place for public auctions, horse trades, and mass meetings, and likewise for teamsters to camp in. Two other sides of the plaza were faced by stores, offices and stables. The rest of Carson City was pretty scattering.

We were introduced to several citizens, at the stage-office and on the way up to the Governor's from the hotel—among others, to a Mr. Harris, who was on horseback; he began to say something, but interrupted himself with the remark:

"I'll have to get you to excuse me a minute; yonder is the witness that swore I helped to rob the California coach—a piece of impertinent intermeddling, sir, for I am not even acquainted with the man."

Then he rode over and began to rebuke the stranger with a six-shooter, and the stranger began to explain with another. When the pistols were emptied, the stranger resumed his work (mending a whip-lash), and Mr. Harris rode by with a polite nod, homeward bound, with a bullet through one of his lungs, and several in his hips; and from them issued little rivulets of blood that coursed down the horse's sides and made the animal look quite picturesque. I never saw Harris shoot a man after that but it recalled to mind that first day in Carson.

This was all we saw that day, for it was two o'clock, now, and according to custom the daily "Washoe Zephyr" set in; a soaring dust-drift about the size of the United States set up edgewise came with it, and the capital of Nevada Territory disappeared from view. Still, there were sights to be seen which were not wholly uninter-

esting to new comers; for the vast dust-cloud was thickly freckled
with things strange to the upper air—things living and dead, that

THE WASHOE ZEPHYR.

flitted hither and thither, going and coming, appearing and disappearing among the rolling billows of dust—hats, chickens and
parasols sailing in the remote heavens; blankets, tin signs, sage-
brush and shingles a shade lower; door-mats and buffalo robes
lower still; shovels and coal scuttles on the next grade; glass doors,
cats and little children on the next; disrupted lumber yards, light
buggies and wheelbarrows on the next; and down only thirty or
forty feet above ground was a skurrying storm of emigrating roofs
and vacant lots.

It was something to see that much. I could have seen more, if I
could have kept the dust out of my eyes.

But seriously a Washoe wind is by no means a trifling matter. It
blows flimsy houses down, lifts shingle roofs occasionally, rolls up
tin ones like sheet music, now and then blows a stage-coach over
and spills the passengers; and tradition says the reason there are so
many bald people there, is, that the wind blows the hair off their
heads while they are looking skyward after their hats. Carson

streets seldom look inactive on summer afternoons, because there
are so many citizens skipping around their escaping hats, like
chambermaids trying to head off a spider.

The "Washoe Zephyr" (Washoe is a pet nickname for Nevada) is
a peculiarly Scriptural wind, in that no man knoweth "whence it
cometh." That is to say, where it *originates*. It comes right over the
mountains from the west, but when one crosses the ridge he does
not find any of it on the other side! It probably is manufactured on
the mountain-top for the occasion, and starts from there. It is a
pretty regular wind, in the summer time. Its office hours are from
two in the afternoon till two the next morning; and anybody venturing abroad during those twelve hours needs to allow for the
wind or he will bring up a mile or two to leeward of the point he is
aiming at. And yet the first complaint a Washoe visitor to San
Francisco makes, is that the sea winds blow so, there! There is a
good deal of human nature in that.

THE GOVERNOR'S HOUSE.

We found the state palace of the Governor of Nevada Territory to
consist of a white frame one-story house with two small rooms in
it and a stanchion supported shed in front—for grandeur—it compelled the respect of the citizen and inspired the Indians with awe.
The newly arrived Chief and Associate Justices of the Territory,
and other machinery of the government, were domiciled with less

splendor. They were boarding around privately, and had their offices in their bedrooms.

The Secretary and I took quarters in the "ranch" of a worthy
French lady by the name of Bridget O'Flannigan, a camp follower
of his Excellency the Governor. She had known him in his prosperity as commander-in-chief of the Metropolitan Police of New
York, and she would not desert him in his adversity as Governor of
Nevada. Our room was on the lower floor, facing the plaza, and
when we had got our bed, a small table, two chairs, the government fire-proof safe, and the Unabridged Dictionary into it, there
was still room enough left for a visitor—maybe two, but not without straining the walls. But the walls could stand it—at least the
partitions could, for they consisted simply of one thickness of
white "cotton domestic" stretched from corner to corner of the
room. This was the rule in Carson—any other kind of partition

DARK DISCLOSURES.

was the rare exception. And if you stood in a dark room and your
neighbors in the next had lights, the shadows on your canvas told
queer secrets sometimes! Very often these partitions were made of
old flour sacks basted together; and then the difference between

the common herd and the aristocracy was, that the common herd
had unornamented sacks, while the walls of the aristocrat were
overpowering with rudimental fresco—*i. e.*, red and blue mill
brands on the flour sacks. Occasionally, also, the better classes embellished their canvas by pasting pictures from *Harper's Weekly* on
them. In many cases, too, the wealthy and the cultured rose to spit-
toons and other evidences of a sumptuous and luxurious taste.* We
had a carpet and a genuine queensware washbowl. Consequently
we were hated without reserve by the other tenants of the O'Flannigan "ranch." When we added a painted oil-cloth window curtain,
we simply took our lives into our own hands. To prevent bloodshed I removed up stairs and took up quarters with the untitled
plebeians in one of the fourteen white pine cot-bedsteads that
stood in two long ranks in the one sole room of which the second
story consisted.

THE IRISH BRIGADE.

*Washoe people take a joke so hard that I must explain that the above description
was only the rule; there were many honorable exceptions in Carson—plastered
ceilings and houses that had considerable furniture in them.—M. T.

It was a jolly company, the fourteen. They were principally voluntary camp followers of the Governor, who had joined his retinue
by their own election at New York and San Francisco and came
along, feeling that in the scuffle for little Territorial crumbs and
offices they could not make their condition more precarious than
it was, and might reasonably expect to make it better. They were
popularly known as the "Irish Brigade," though there were only
four or five Irishmen among all the Governor's retainers. His good-
natured Excellency was much annoyed at the gossip his henchmen
created—especially when there arose a rumor that they were paid
assassins of his, brought along to quietly reduce the Democratic
vote when desirable!

Mrs. O'Flannigan was boarding and lodging them at ten dollars
a week apiece, and they were cheerfully giving their notes for it.
They were perfectly satisfied, but Bridget presently found that
notes that could not be discounted were but a feeble constitution
for a Carson boarding house. So she began to harry the Governor to
find employment for the "Brigade." Her importunities and theirs
together drove him to a gentle desperation at last, and he finally
summoned the Brigade to the presence. Then, said he:

"Gentlemen, I have planned a lucrative and useful service for
you—a service which will provide you with recreation amid noble
landscapes, and afford you never ceasing opportunities for enriching your minds by observation and study. I want you to survey a
railroad from Carson City westward to a certain point! When the
legislature meets I will have the necessary bill passed and the re-
muneration arranged."

"What, a railroad over the Sierra Nevada Mountains?"

"Well, then, survey it eastward to a certain point!"

RECREATION.

He converted them into surveyors,
chain-bearers and so on, and turned them
loose in the desert. It was "recreation"
with a vengeance! Recreation on foot,
lugging chains through sand and sage-
brush, under a sultry sun and among cattle bones, cayotes and tarantulas. "Romantic adventure" could go no further.
They surveyed very slowly, very deliber-

ately, very carefully. They returned every night during the first
week, dusty, footsore, tired, and hungry, but very jolly. They
brought in great store of prodigious hairy spiders—tarantulas—
and imprisoned them in covered tumblers up stairs in the "ranch."
After the first week, they had to camp on the field, for they were
getting well eastward. They made a good many inquiries as to the
location of that indefinite "certain point," but got no information.
At last, to a peculiarly urgent inquiry of "How far eastward?" Gov.
Nye telegraphed back:

"To the Atlantic Ocean, blast you!—and then bridge it and go
on!"

This brought back the dusty toilers, who sent in a report and
ceased from their labors. The Governor was always comfortable
about it; he said Mrs. O'Flannigan would hold him for the Brigade's board anyhow, and he intended to get what entertainment
he could out of the boys; he said, with his old-time pleasant twin-
kle, that he meant to survey them into Utah and then telegraph
Brigham to hang them for trespass!

The surveyors brought back more tarantulas with them, and so
we had quite a menagerie arranged along the shelves of the room.
Some of these spiders could straddle over a common saucer with
their hairy, muscular legs, and when their feelings were hurt, or

THE TARANTULA.

their dignity offended, they were the wickedest-looking desperadoes the animal world can furnish. If their glass prison-houses
were touched ever so lightly they were up and spoiling for a fight
in a minute. Starchy?—proud? Indeed, they would take up a straw
and pick their teeth like a member of Congress. There was as usual
a furious "zephyr" blowing the first night of the Brigade's return,

and about midnight the roof of an adjoining stable blew off, and a corner of it came crashing through the side of our ranch. There was a simultaneous awakening, and a tumultuous muster of the Brigade in the dark, and a general tumbling and sprawling over each other in the narrow aisle between the bed-rows. In the midst of the turmoil, Bob H—— sprung up out of a sound sleep, and knocked down a shelf with his head. Instantly he shouted:

"Turn out, boys—the tarantulas is loose!"

No warning ever sounded so dreadful. Nobody tried, any longer, to leave the room, lest he might step on a tarantula. Every man groped for a trunk or a bed, and jumped on it. Then followed the strangest silence—a silence of grisly suspense it was, too—waiting, expectancy, fear. It was as dark as pitch, and one had to imagine the spectacle of those fourteen scant-clad men roosting gingerly on trunks and beds, for not a thing could be seen. Then came occasional little interruptions of the silence, and one could recognize a man and tell his locality by his voice, or locate any other sound a sufferer made by his gropings or changes of position. The occasional voices were not given to much speaking—you simply heard a gentle ejaculation of "Ow!" followed by a solid thump, and you knew the gentleman had felt a hairy blanket or something touch his bare skin and had skipped from a bed to the floor. Another silence. Presently you would hear a gasping voice say:

"Su-su-something's crawling up the back of my neck!"

Every now and then you could hear a little subdued scramble and a sorrowful "O Lord!" and then you knew that somebody was getting away from something he took for a tarantula, and not losing any time about it, either. Directly a voice in the corner rang out wild and clear:

"I've got him! I've got him!" [Pause, and probable change of circumstances.] "No, he's got me! Oh, ain't they *never* going to fetch a lantern!"

The lantern came at that moment, in the hands of Mrs. O'Flannigan, whose anxiety to know the amount of damage done by the assaulting roof had not prevented her waiting a judicious interval, after getting out of bed and lighting up, to see if the wind was done, now, up stairs, or had a larger contract.

The landscape presented when the lantern flashed into the room
was picturesque, and might have been funny to some people, but
was not to us. Although we were perched so strangely upon boxes,

LIGHT THROWN ON THE SUBJECT.

trunks and beds, and so strangely attired, too, we were too earnestly distressed and too genuinely miserable to see any fun about
it, and there was not the semblance of a smile anywhere visible. I
know I am not capable of suffering more than I did during those
few minutes of suspense in the dark, surrounded by those creeping, bloody-minded tarantulas. I had skipped from bed to bed and
from box to box in a cold agony, and every time I touched anything
that was furzy I fancied I felt the fangs. I had rather go to war than
live that episode over again. Nobody was hurt. The man who
thought a tarantula had "got him" was mistaken—only a crack in
a box had caught his finger. Not one of those escaped tarantulas
was ever seen again. There were ten or twelve of them. We took
candles and hunted the place high and low for them, but with no
success. Did we go back to bed then? We did nothing of the kind.
Money could not have persuaded us to do it. We sat up the rest of
the night playing cribbage and keeping a sharp lookout for the
enemy.

CHAPTER 22

IT was the end of August, and the skies were cloudless and the weather superb. In two or three weeks I had grown wonderfully fascinated with the curious new country, and concluded to put off my return to "the States" awhile. I had grown well accustomed to wearing a damaged slouch hat, blue woolen shirt, and pants crammed into boot-tops, and gloried in the absence of coat, vest and braces. I felt rowdyish and "bully," (as the historian Josephus phrases it, in his fine chapter upon the destruction of the Temple). It seemed to me that nothing could be so fine and so romantic. I had become an officer of the government, but that was for mere sublimity. The office was an unique sinecure. I had nothing to do and no salary. I was private secretary to his majesty the Secretary and there was not yet writing enough for two of us. So Johnny K—— and I devoted our time to amusement. He was the young son of an Ohio nabob and was out there for recreation. He got it. We had heard a world of talk about the marvelous beauty of Lake Tahoe, and finally curiosity drove us thither to see it. Three or four members of the Brigade had been there and located some timber lands on its shores and stored up a quantity of provisions in their camp. We strapped a couple of blankets on our shoulders and took an axe apiece and started—for we intended to take up a wood ranch or so ourselves and become wealthy. We were on foot. The reader will find it advantageous to go horseback. We were told that the distance was eleven miles. We tramped a long time on level ground, and then toiled laboriously up a mountain about a thousand miles high and looked over. No lake there. We descended on the other side, crossed the valley and toiled up another mountain three or four thousand miles high, apparently, and looked over again. No lake yet. We sat down tired and perspiring, and hired a couple of Chinamen to curse those people who had beguiled us.

Thus refreshed, we presently resumed the march with renewed
vigor and determination. We plodded on, two or three hours
longer, and at last the lake burst upon us—a noble sheet of blue
water lifted six thousand three hundred feet above the level of the
sea, and walled in by a rim of snow-clad mountain peaks that towered aloft full three thousand feet higher still! It was a vast oval,
and one would have to use up eighty or a hundred good miles in
traveling around it. As it lay there with the shadows of the mountains brilliantly photographed upon its still surface I thought it
must surely be the fairest picture the whole earth affords.

We found the small skiff belonging to the Brigade boys, and
without loss of time set out across a deep bend of the lake toward
the landmarks that signified the locality of the camp. I got Johnny
to row—not because I mind exertion myself, but because it makes
me sick to ride backwards when I am at work. But I steered. A

three-mile pull brought us to
the camp just as the night fell,
and we stepped ashore very
tired and wolfishly hungry. In a
"cache" among the rocks we
found the provisions and the
cooking utensils, and then, all
fatigued as I was, I sat down on
a boulder and superintended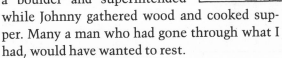
while Johnny gathered wood and cooked sup-
per. Many a man who had gone through what I
had, would have wanted to rest.

I STEERED.

It was a delicious supper—hot bread, fried ba-
con, and black coffee. It was a delicious solitude we were in, too.
Three miles away was a saw-mill and some workmen, but there
were not fifteen other human beings throughout the wide circumference of the lake. As the darkness closed down and the stars
came out and spangled the great mirror with jewels, we smoked
meditatively in the solemn hush and forgot our troubles and our
pains. In due time we spread our blankets in the warm sand between two large boulders and soon fell asleep, careless of the
procession of ants that passed in through rents in our clothing and

explored our persons. Nothing could disturb the sleep that fettered us, for it had been fairly earned, and if our consciences had any sins on them they had to adjourn court for that night, anyway. The wind rose just as we were losing consciousness, and we were lulled to sleep by the beating of the surf upon the shore.

It is always very cold on that lake shore in the night, but we had plenty of blankets and were warm enough. We never moved a muscle all night, but waked at early dawn in the original positions, and got up at once, thoroughly refreshed, free from soreness, and brim full of friskiness. There is no end of wholesome medicine in such an experience. That morning we could have whipped ten such people as we were the day before—sick ones at any rate. But the world is slow, and people will go to "water cures" and "movement cures" and to foreign lands for health. Three months of camp life on Lake Tahoe would restore an Egyptian mummy to his pristine vigor, and give him an appetite like an alligator. I do not mean the oldest and driest mummies, of course, but the fresher ones. The air up there in the clouds is very pure and fine, bracing and delicious. And why shouldn't it be?—it is the same the angels breathe. I think that hardly any amount of fatigue can be gathered together that a man cannot sleep off in one night on the sand by its side. Not under a roof, but under the sky; it seldom or never rains there in the summer time. I know a man who went there to die. But he made a failure of it. He was a skeleton when he came, and could barely stand. He had no appetite, and did nothing but read tracts and reflect on the future. Three months later he was sleeping out of doors regularly,

THE INVALID.

eating all he could hold, three times a day, and chasing game over mountains three thousand feet high for recreation. And he was a skeleton no longer, but weighed part of a ton. This is no fancy sketch, but the truth. His disease was consumption. I confidently commend his experience to other skeletons.

I superintended again, and as soon as we had eaten breakfast we got in the boat and skirted along the lake shore about three miles and disembarked. We liked the appearance of the place, and so we claimed some three hundred acres of it and stuck our "notices" on a tree. It was yellow pine timber land—a dense forest of trees a hundred feet high and from one to five feet through at the butt. It was necessary to fence our property

THE RESTORED.

or we could not hold it. That is to say, it was necessary to cut down trees here and there and make them fall in such a way as to form a

sort of enclosure (with pretty wide gaps in it). We cut down three trees apiece, and found it such heart-breaking work that we decided to "rest our case" on those; if they held the property, well and good; if they didn't, let the property spill out through the gaps and go; it was no use to work ourselves to death merely to save a few acres of land. Next day we came back to build a house—for a house was also necessary, in order to hold the property. We decided to build a substantial log house and excite the envy of the Brigade boys; but by the time we had cut and trimmed the first log it seemed unnecessary to be so elaborate, and so we concluded to build it of saplings. However, two saplings, duly cut and trimmed, compelled recognition of the fact that

OUR HOUSE.

a still modester architecture would satisfy the law, and so we concluded to build a "brush" house. We devoted the next day to this work, but we did so much "sitting around" and discussing, that by the middle of the afternoon we had achieved only a half-way sort of affair which one of us had to watch while the other cut brush, lest if both turned our backs we might not be able to find it again, it had such a strong family resemblance to the surrounding vegetation. But we were satisfied with it.

We were land owners now, duly seized and possessed, and within the protection of the law. Therefore we decided to take up our residence on our own domain and enjoy that large sense of independence which only such an experience can bring. Late the next afternoon, after a good long rest, we sailed away from the Brigade camp with all the provisions and cooking utensils we could carry off—borrow is the more accurate word—and just as the night was falling we beached the boat at our own landing.

CHAPTER 23

I F there is any life that is happier than the life we led on our timber ranch for the next two or three weeks, it must be a sort of life which I have not read of in books or experienced in person. We did not see a human being but ourselves during the time, or hear any sounds but those that were made by the wind and the waves, the sighing of the pines, and now and then the far-off thunder of an avalanche. The forest about us was dense and cool, the sky above us was cloudless and brilliant with sunshine, the broad lake before us was glassy and clear, or rippled and breezy, or black and storm-tossed, according to Nature's mood; and its circling border of mountain domes, clothed with forests, scarred with land-slides, cloven by cañons and valleys, and helmeted with glittering snow, fitly framed and finished the noble picture. The view was always fascinating, bewitching, entrancing. The eye was never tired of gazing, night or day, in calm or storm; it suffered but one grief, and that was that it could not look always, but must close sometimes in sleep.

We slept in the sand close to the water's edge, between two protecting boulders, which took care of the stormy night-winds for us. We never took any paregoric to make us sleep. At the first break of dawn we were always up and running foot-races to tone down excess of physical vigor and exuberance of spirits. That is, Johnny was—but I held his hat. While smoking the pipe of peace after breakfast we watched the sentinel peaks put on the glory of the sun, and followed the conquering light as it swept down among the shadows, and set the captive crags and forests free. We watched the tinted pictures grow and brighten upon the water till every little detail of forest, precipice and pinnacle was wrought in and finished, and the miracle of the enchanter complete. Then to "business."

That is, drifting around in the boat. We were on the north shore. There, the rocks on the bottom are sometimes gray, sometimes white. This gives the marvelous transparency of the water a fuller

AT BUSINESS.

advantage than it has elsewhere on the lake. We usually pushed out a hundred yards or so from shore, and then lay down on the thwarts, in the sun, and let the boat drift by the hour whither it would. We seldom talked. It interrupted the Sabbath stillness, and marred the dreams the luxurious rest and indolence brought. The shore all along was indented with deep, curved bays and coves, bordered by narrow sand-beaches; and where the sand ended, the steep mountain sides rose right up aloft into space—rose up like a vast wall a little out of the perpendicular, and thickly wooded with tall pines.

So singularly clear was the water, that where it was only twenty or thirty feet deep the bottom was so perfectly distinct that the boat seemed floating in the air! Yes, where it was even *eighty* feet deep. Every little pebble was distinct, every speckled trout, every hand's-breadth of sand. Often, as we lay on our faces, a granite boulder, as large as a village church, would start out of the bottom apparently, and seem climbing up rapidly to the surface, till presently it threatened to touch our faces, and we could not resist the impulse to seize an oar and avert the danger. But the boat would float on, and the boulder descend again, and then we could see that when we had been exactly above it, it must still have been twenty or thirty feet below the surface. Down through the transparency of these great depths, the water was not *merely* transparent, but dazzlingly, brilliantly so. All objects seen through it had a bright, strong vividness, not only of outline, but of every minute detail, which they would not have had when seen simply through the same depth of atmosphere. So empty and airy did all spaces seem below us, and so strong was the sense of floating high aloft in midnothingness, that we called these boat-excursions "balloon-voyages."

We fished a good deal, but we did not average one fish a week. We could see trout by the thousand winging about in the emptiness under us, or sleeping in shoals on the bottom, but they would not bite—they could see the line too plainly, perhaps. We frequently selected the trout we wanted, and rested the bait patiently and persistently on the end of his nose at a depth of eighty feet, but he would only shake it off with an annoyed manner, and shift his position.

We bathed occasionally, but the water was rather chilly, for all it looked so sunny. Sometimes we rowed out to the "blue water," a mile or two from shore. It was as dead blue as indigo there, because of the immense depth. By official measurement the lake in its centre is one thousand five hundred and twenty-five feet deep!

Sometimes, on lazy afternoons, we lolled on the sand in camp, and smoked pipes and read some old well-worn novels. At night, by the camp-fire, we played euchre and seven-up to strengthen the mind—and played them with cards so greasy and defaced that only a whole summer's acquaintance with them could enable the student to tell the ace of clubs from the jack of diamonds.

We never slept in our "house." It never recurred to us, for one thing; and besides, it was built to hold the ground, and that was enough. We did not wish to strain it.

By and by our provisions began to run short, and we went back to the old camp and laid in a new supply. We were gone all day, and reached home again about nightfall, pretty tired and hungry. While Johnny was carrying the main bulk of the provisions up to our "house" for future use, I took the loaf of bread, some slices of bacon, and the coffee-pot, ashore, set them down by a tree, lit a fire, and went back to the boat to get the frying pan. While I was at this, I heard a shout from Johnny, and looking up I saw that my fire was galloping all over the premises!

Johnny was on the other side of it. He had to run through the flames to get to the lake shore, and then we stood helpless and watched the devastation.

The ground was deeply carpeted with dry pine-needles, and the fire touched them off as if they were gunpowder. It was wonderful to see with what fierce speed the tall sheet of flame traveled! My coffee-pot was gone, and everything with it. In a minute and a half

FIRE AT LAKE TAHOE.

the fire seized upon a dense growth of dry manzanita chaparral six
or eight feet high, and then the roaring and popping and crackling
was something terrific. We were driven to the boat by the intense
heat, and there we remained, spell-bound.

Within half an hour all before us was a tossing, blinding tempest
of flame! It went surging up adjacent ridges—surmounted them
and disappeared in the cañons beyond—burst into view upon
higher and farther ridges, presently—shed a grander illumination
abroad, and dove again—flamed out again, directly, higher and still
higher up the mountain side—threw out skirmishing parties of
fire here and there, and sent them trailing their crimson spirals
away among remote ramparts and ribs and gorges, till as far as the
eye could reach the lofty mountain-fronts were webbed as it were
with a tangled net-work of red lava streams. Away across the water
the crags and domes were lit with a ruddy glare, and the firmament
above was a reflected hell!

Every feature of the spectacle was repeated in the glowing mirror
of the lake! Both pictures were sublime, both were beautiful; but
that in the lake had a bewildering richness about it that enchanted
the eye and held it with the stronger fascination.

We sat absorbed and motionless through four long hours. We
never thought of supper, and never felt fatigue. But at eleven
o'clock the conflagration had traveled beyond our range of vision,
and then darkness stole down upon the landscape again.

Hunger asserted itself now, but there was nothing to eat. The
provisions were all cooked, no doubt, but we did not go to see. We
were homeless wanderers again, without any property. Our fence
was gone, our house burned down; no insurance. Our pine forest
was well scorched, the dead trees all burned up, and our broad acres
of manzanita swept away. Our blankets were on our usual sand-
bed, however, and so we lay down and went to sleep. The next
morning we started back to the old camp, but while out a long way
from shore, so great a storm came up that we dared not try to land.
So I baled out the seas we shipped, and Johnny pulled heavily
through the billows till we had reached a point three or four miles
beyond the camp. The storm was increasing, and it became evident
that it was better to take the hazard of beaching the boat than go
down in a hundred fathoms of water; so we ran in, with tall white-

caps following, and I sat down in the stern-sheets and pointed her head on to the shore. The instant the bow struck, a wave came over the stern that washed crew and cargo ashore, and saved a deal of trouble. We shivered in the lee of a boulder all the rest of the day, and froze all the night through. In the morning the tempest had gone down, and we paddled down to the camp without any unnecessary delay. We were so starved that we ate up the rest of the Brigade's provisions, and then set out to Carson to tell them about it and ask their forgiveness. It was accorded, upon payment of damages.

We made many trips to the lake after that, and had many a hairbreadth escape and blood-curdling adventure which will never be recorded in any history.

CHAPTER 24

I RESOLVED to have a horse to ride. I had never seen such wild, free, magnificent horsemanship outside of a circus as these picturesquely-clad Mexicans, Californians and Mexicanized Americans displayed in Carson streets every day. How they rode! Leaning just gently forward out of the perpendicular, easy and nonchalant, with broad slouch-hat brim blown square up in front, and long *riata* swinging above the head, they swept through the town like the wind! The next minute they were only a sailing puff of dust on the far desert. If they trotted, they sat up gallantly and gracefully, and seemed part of the horse; did not go jiggering up and down after the silly Miss-Nancy fashion of the riding-schools. I had quickly learned to tell a horse from a cow, and was full of anxiety to learn more. I was resolved to buy a horse.

While the thought was rankling in my mind, the auctioneer came skurrying through the plaza on a black beast that had as many humps and corners on him as a dromedary, and was necessarily uncomely; but he was "going, going, at twenty-two!—horse, saddle and bridle at twenty-two dollars, gentlemen!" and I could hardly resist.

A man whom I did not know (he turned out to be the auctioneer's brother) noticed the wistful look in my eye, and observed that that was a very remarkable horse to be going at such a price; and added that the saddle alone was worth the money. It was a Spanish saddle, with ponderous *tapaderas*, and furnished with the ungainly sole-leather covering with the unspellable name. I said I had half a notion to bid. Then this keen-eyed person appeared to me to be "taking my measure;" but I dismissed the suspicion when he spoke, for his manner was full of guileless candor and truthfulness. Said he:

"I know that horse—know him well. You are a stranger, I take it, and so you might think he was an American horse, maybe, but I assure you he is not. He is nothing of the kind; but—excuse my speaking in a low voice, other people being near—he is, without the shadow of a doubt, a Genuine Mexican Plug!"

"YOU MIGHT THINK HE WAS AN AMERICAN HORSE."

I did not know what a Genuine Mexican Plug was, but there was something about this man's way of saying it, that made me swear inwardly that I would own a Genuine Mexican Plug, or die.

"Has he any other—er—advantages?" I inquired, suppressing what eagerness I could.

He hooked his forefinger in the pocket of my army-shirt, led me to one side, and breathed in my ear impressively these words:

"He can out-buck anything in America!"

"Going, going, going—at *twent–ty*-four dollars and a half, gen—"

"Twenty-seven!" I shouted, in a frenzy.

"And sold!" said the auctioneer, and passed over the Genuine Mexican Plug to me.

I could scarcely contain my exultation. I paid the money, and put the animal in a neighboring livery-stable to dine and rest himself.

In the afternoon I brought the creature into the plaza, and certain citizens held him by the head, and others by the tail, while I mounted him. As soon as they let go, he placed all his feet in a bunch together, lowered his back, and then suddenly arched it upward, and shot me straight into the air a matter of three or four feet! I came as straight down again, lit in the saddle, went instantly

UNEXPECTED ELEVATION.

up again, came down almost on the high pommel, shot up again, and came down on the horse's neck—all in the space of three or four seconds. Then he rose and stood almost straight up on his hind feet, and I, clasping his lean neck desperately, slid back into the saddle, and held on. He came down, and immediately hoisted his heels into the air, delivering a vicious kick at the sky, and stood

on his forefeet. And then down he came once more, and began the
original exercise of shooting me straight up again. The third time
I went up I heard a stranger say:

"Oh, *don't* he buck, though!"

While I was up, somebody struck the horse a sounding thwack
with a leathern strap, and when I arrived again the Genuine Mexican Plug was not there. A Californian youth chased him up and
caught him, and asked if he might have a ride. I granted him that
luxury. He mounted the Genuine, got lifted into the air once, but
sent his spurs home as he descended, and the horse darted away
like a telegram. He soared over three fences like a bird, and disappeared down the road toward the Washoe Valley.

I sat down on a stone, with a sigh, and by a natural impulse one
of my hands sought my forehead, and the other the base of my
stomach. I believe I never appreciated, till then, the poverty of the
human machinery—for I still needed a hand or two to place elsewhere. Pen cannot describe how I was jolted up. Imagination cannot conceive how disjointed I was—how internally, externally and

UNIVERSALLY UNSETTLED.

universally I was unsettled, mixed up and ruptured. There was a
sympathetic crowd around me, though.

One elderly-looking comforter said:

"Stranger, you've been taken in. Everybody in this camp knows that horse. Any child, any Injun, could have told you that he'd buck; he is the very worst devil to buck on the continent of America. You hear *me*. I'm Curry. *Old* Curry. Old *Abe* Curry. And moreover, he is a simon-pure, out-and-out, genuine d—d Mexican plug, and an uncommon mean one at that, too. Why, you turnip, if you had laid low and kept dark, there's chances to buy an *American* horse for mighty little more than you paid for that bloody old foreign relic."

I gave no sign; but I made up my mind that if the auctioneer's brother's funeral took place while I was in the Territory I would postpone all other recreations and attend it.

After a gallop of sixteen miles the Californian youth and the Genuine Mexican Plug came tearing into town again, shedding foam-flakes like the spume-spray that drives before a typhoon, and, with one final skip over a wheelbarrow and a Chinaman, cast anchor in front of the "ranch."

Such panting and blowing! Such spreading and contracting of the red equine nostrils, and glaring of the wild equine eye! But was the imperial beast subjugated? Indeed he was not. His lordship the Speaker of the House thought he was, and mounted him to go down to the Capitol; but the first dash the creature made was over

RIDING THE PLUG.

a pile of telegraph poles half as high as a church; and his time to the Capitol—one mile and three-quarters—remains unbeaten to this day. But then he took an advantage—he left out the mile, and only did the three-quarters. That is to say, he made a straight cut across lots, preferring fences and ditches to a crooked road; and when the Speaker got to the Capitol he said he had been in the air so much he felt as if he had made the trip on a comet.

In the evening the Speaker came home afoot for exercise, and got the Genuine towed back behind a quartz wagon. The next day I loaned the animal to the Clerk of the House to go down to the

WANTED EXERCISE.

Dana silver mine, six miles, and *he* walked back for exercise, and got the horse towed. Everybody I loaned him to always walked back; they never could get enough exercise any other way. Still, I continued to loan him to anybody who was willing to borrow him,

my idea being to get him crippled, and throw him on the borrower's hands, or killed, and make the borrower pay for him. But somehow nothing ever happened to him. He took chances that no other
horse ever took and survived, but he always came out safe. It was
his daily habit to try experiments that had always before been considered impossible, but he always got through. Sometimes he mis-
calculated a little, and did not get his rider through intact, but *he*
always got through himself. Of course I had tried to sell him; but
that was a stretch of simplicity which met with little sympathy.
The auctioneer stormed up and down the streets on him for four
days, dispersing the populace, interrupting business, and destroying children, and never got a bid—at least never any but the
eighteen-dollar one he hired a notoriously substanceless bummer
to make. The people only smiled pleasantly, and restrained their
desire to buy, if they had any. Then the auctioneer brought in his
bill, and I withdrew the horse from the market. We tried to trade
him off at private vendue next, offering him at a sacrifice for
second-hand tombstones, old iron, temperance tracts—any kind
of property. But holders were stiff, and we retired from the market
again. I never tried to ride the horse any more. Walking was good
enough exercise for a man like me, that had nothing the matter
with him except ruptures, internal injuries, and such things. Finally I tried to *give* him away. But it was a failure. Parties said
earthquakes were handy enough on the Pacific coast—they did not
wish to own one. As a last resort I offered him to the Governor for
the use of the "Brigade." His face lit up eagerly at first, but toned
down again, and he said the thing would be too palpable.

Just then the livery-stable man brought in his bill for six weeks'
keeping—stall-room for the horse, fifteen dollars; hay for the
horse, two hundred and fifty! The Genuine Mexican Plug had
eaten a ton of the article, and the man said he would have eaten a
hundred if he had let him.

I will remark here, in all seriousness, that the regular price of
hay during that year and a part of the next was really two hundred
and fifty dollars a ton. During a part of the previous year it had sold
at five hundred a ton, in gold, and during the winter before that
there was such scarcity of the article that in several instances
small quantities had brought eight hundred dollars a ton in coin!

The consequence might be guessed without my telling it: people turned their stock loose to starve, and before the spring arrived Carson and Eagle Valleys were almost literally carpeted with their carcases! Any old settler there will verify these statements.

I managed to pay the livery bill, and that same day I gave the Genuine Mexican Plug to a passing Arkansas emigrant whom fortune delivered into my hand. If this ever meets his eye, he will doubtless remember the donation.

Now whoever has had the luck to ride a real Mexican plug will recognize the animal depicted in this chapter, and hardly consider him exaggerated—but the uninitiated will feel justified in regarding his portrait as a fancy sketch, perhaps.

CHAPTER 25

ORIGINALLY, Nevada was a part of Utah and was called Carson County; and a pretty large county it was, too. Certain of its valleys produced no end of hay, and this attracted small colonies of Mormon stock-raisers and farmers to them. A few orthodox Americans straggled in from California, but no love was lost between the two classes of colonists. There was little or no friendly intercourse; each party staid to itself. The Mormons were largely in the majority, and had the additional advantage of being peculiarly under the protection of the Mormon government of the Territory. Therefore they could afford to be distant, and even peremptory toward their neighbors. One of the traditions of Carson Valley illustrates the condition of things that prevailed at the time I speak of. The hired girl of one of the American families was Irish, and a Catholic; yet it was noted with surprise that she was the only person outside of the Mormon ring who could get favors from the Mormons. She asked kindnesses of them often, and always got them. It was a mystery to everybody. But one day as she was passing out at the door, a large bowie knife dropped from under her apron, and when her mistress asked for an explanation she observed that she was going out to "borry a wash-tub from the Mormons!"

In 1858 silver lodes were discovered in "Carson County," and then the aspect of things changed. Californians began to flock in, and the American element was soon in the majority. Allegiance to Brigham Young and Utah was renounced, and a temporary Territorial government for "Washoe" was instituted by the citizens. Gov. Roop was the first and only chief magistrate of it. In due course of time Congress passed a bill to organize "Nevada Territory," and President Lincoln sent out Gov. Nye to supplant Roop.

At this time the population of the Territory was about twelve or fifteen thousand, and rapidly increasing. Silver mines were being vigorously developed and silver mills erected. Business of all kinds was active and prosperous and growing more so day by day.

BORROWING MADE EASY.

The people were glad to have a legitimately constituted government, but did not particularly enjoy having strangers from distant States put in authority over them—a sentiment that was natural enough. They thought the officials should have been chosen from among themselves—from among prominent citizens who had earned a right to such promotion, and who would be in sympathy with the populace and likewise thoroughly acquainted with the needs of the Territory. They were right in viewing

the matter thus, without doubt. The new officers were "emigrants," and that was no title to anybody's affection or admiration either.

The new government was received with considerable coolness.
It was not only a foreign intruder, but a poor one. It was not even
worth plucking—except by the smallest of small-fry office-seekers
and such. Everybody knew that Congress had appropriated only
twenty thousand dollars a year in greenbacks for its support—
about money enough to run a quartz mill a month. And everybody
knew, also, that the first year's money was still in Washington,
and that the getting hold of it would be a tedious and difficult
process. Carson City was too wary and too wise to open up a credit
account with the imported bantling with anything like indecent
haste.

There is something solemnly funny about the struggles of a
new-born Territorial government to get a start in this world. Ours
had a trying time of it. The Organic Act and the "instructions"
from the State Department commanded that a legislature should
be elected at such-and-such a time, and its sittings inaugurated at
such-and-such a date. It was easy to get legislators, even at three
dollars a day, although board was four dollars and fifty cents, for
distinction has its charm in Nevada as well as elsewhere, and there
were plenty of patriotic souls out of employment; but to get a legislative hall for them to meet in was another matter altogether.
Carson blandly declined to give a room rent-free, or let one to the
government on credit.

FREE RIDES.

But when Curry heard of the difficulty, he came forward, solitary
and alone, and shouldered the Ship of State over the bar and got her

afloat again. I refer to "Curry—*Old* Curry—Old *Abe* Curry." But for him the legislature would have been obliged to sit in the desert. He offered his large stone building just outside the capital limits, rent-free, and it was gladly accepted. Then he built a horse-railroad from town to the Capitol, and carried the legislators gratis. He also furnished pine benches and chairs for the legislature, and covered the floors with clean saw-dust by way of carpet and spittoon combined. But for Curry the government would have died in its tender infancy. A canvas partition to separate the Senate from the House of Representatives was put up by the Secretary, at a cost of three dollars and forty cents, but the United States declined to pay for it. Upon being reminded that the "instructions" permitted the payment of a liberal rent for a legislative hall, and that that money was saved to the country by Mr. Curry's generosity, the United States said that did not alter the matter, and the three dollars and forty cents would be subtracted from the Secretary's eighteen-hundred-dollar salary—and it *was!*

The matter of printing was from the beginning an interesting feature of the new government's difficulties. The Secretary was sworn to obey his volume of written "instructions," and these commanded him to do two certain things without fail, viz.:

1. Get the House and Senate journals printed; and,

2. For this work, pay one dollar and fifty cents per "thousand" for composition, and one dollar and fifty cents per "token" for press-work, in greenbacks.

It was easy to swear to do these two things, but it was entirely impossible to do more than one of them. When greenbacks had gone down to forty cents on the dollar, the prices regularly charged everybody by printing establishments were one dollar and fifty cents per "thousand" and one dollar and fifty cents per "token," in *gold*. The "instructions" commanded that the Secretary regard a paper dollar issued by the government as equal to any other dollar issued by the government. Hence the printing of the journals was discontinued. Then the United States sternly rebuked the Secretary for disregarding the "instructions," and warned him to correct his ways. Wherefore he got some printing done, forwarded the bill to Washington with full exhibits of the

high prices of things in the Territory, and called attention to a
printed market report wherein it would be observed that even
hay was two hundred and fifty dollars a ton. The United States
responded by subtracting the printing-bill from the Secretary's
suffering salary—and moreover remarked with dense gravity that
he would find nothing in his "instructions" requiring him to purchase hay!

Nothing in this world is palled in such impenetrable obscurity
as a U. S. Treasury Comptroller's understanding. The very fires of
the hereafter could get up nothing more than a fitful glimmer in it.
In the days I speak of he never could be made to comprehend why
it was that twenty thousand dollars would not go as far in Nevada,
where all commodities ranged at an enormous figure, as it would
in the other Territories, where exceeding cheapness was the rule.
He was an officer who looked out for the little expenses all the
time. The Secretary of the Territory kept his office in his bedroom,
as I before remarked; and he charged the United States no rent, although his "instructions" provided for that item and he could have
justly taken advantage of it (a thing which I would have done with
more than lightning promptness if I had been Secretary myself).
But the United States never applauded this devotion. Indeed, I
think my country was ashamed to have so improvident a person in
its employ.

Those "instructions" (we used to read a chapter from them
every morning, as intellectual gymnastics, and a couple of chapters in Sunday school every Sabbath, for they treated of all subjects under the sun and had much valuable religious matter in
them along with the other statistics) those "instructions" commanded that pen-knives, envelops, pens and writing-paper be
furnished the members of the legislature. So the Secretary made
the purchase and the distribution. The knives cost three dollars
apiece. There was one too many, and the Secretary gave it to
the Clerk of the House of Representatives. The United States
said the Clerk of the House was not a "member" of the legislature, and took that three dollars out of the Secretary's salary, as
usual.

White men charged three or four dollars a "load" for sawing up stove-wood. The Secretary was sagacious enough to know that the United States would never pay any such price as that; so he got an Indian to saw up a load of office wood at one dollar and a half. He made out the usual voucher, but signed no name to it—simply appended a note explaining that an Indian had done the work, and had done it in a very capable and satisfactory way, but could not sign the voucher owing to lack of ability in the necessary direction. The Secretary had to pay that dollar and a half. He thought the United States would admire both his economy and his honesty in getting the work done at half price and not putting a pretended Indian's signature to the voucher, but the United States did not see it in that light. The United States was too much accustomed to employing dollar-and-a-half thieves in all manner of official capacities to regard his explanation of the voucher as having any foundation in fact.

But the next time the Indian sawed wood for us I taught him to make a cross at the bottom of the voucher—it looked like a cross that had been drunk a year—and then I "witnessed" it and it went through all right. The United States never said a word. I was sorry

SATISFACTORY VOUCHER.

I had not made the voucher for a thousand loads of wood instead of one. The government of my country snubs honest simplicity but fondles artistic villainy, and I think I might have developed into a very capable pickpocket if I had remained in the public service a year or two.

That was a fine collection of sovereigns, that first Nevada legislature. They levied taxes to the amount of thirty or forty thousand dollars and ordered expenditures to the extent of about a million.

Yet they had their little periodical explosions of economy like all
other bodies of the kind. A member proposed to save three dollars
a day to the nation by dispensing with the Chaplain. And yet that
short-sighted man needed the Chaplain more than any other member, perhaps, for he generally sat with his feet on his desk, eating
raw turnips, during the morning prayer.

The legislature sat sixty days, and passed private toll-road fran-

NEEDS PRAYING FOR.

chises all the time. When they adjourned it was estimated that
every citizen owned about three franchises, and it was believed
that unless Congress gave the Territory another degree of longi-
tude there would not be room enough to accommodate the toll-
roads. The ends of them were hanging over the boundary line
everywhere like a fringe.

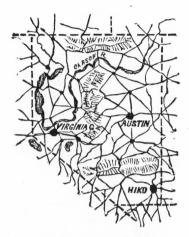

MAP OF TOLL-ROADS.

The fact is, the freighting business had grown to such important proportions that there was nearly as much excitement over suddenly acquired toll-road fortunes as over the wonderful silver mines.

CHAPTER 26

By and by I was smitten with the silver fever. "Prospecting parties" were leaving for the mountains every day, and discovering and taking possession of rich silver-bearing lodes and ledges of quartz. Plainly this was the road to fortune. The great "Gould & Curry" mine was held at three or four hundred dollars a foot when we arrived; but in two months it had sprung up to eight hundred. The "Ophir" had been worth only a mere trifle, a year gone by, and now it was selling at nearly *four thousand dollars a foot!* Not a mine could be named that had not experienced an astonishing advance in value within a short time. Everybody was talking about these marvels. Go where you would, you heard nothing else, from morning till far into the night. Tom So-and-so had sold out of the "Amanda Smith" for forty thousand dollars—hadn't a cent when he "took up" the ledge six months ago. John Jones had sold half his interest in the "Bald Eagle and Mary Ann" for sixty-five thousand dollars, gold coin, and gone to the States for his family. The widow Brewster had "struck it rich" in the "Golden Fleece" and sold ten feet for eighteen thousand dollars—hadn't money enough to buy a crape bonnet when Sing-Sing Tommy killed her husband at Baldy Johnson's wake last spring. The "Last Chance" had found a "clay casing" and knew they were "right on the ledge"—consequence, "feet" that went begging yesterday were worth a brick house apiece to-day, and seedy owners who could not get trusted for a drink at any bar in the country yesterday were roaring drunk on champagne to-day and had hosts of warm personal friends in a town where they had forgotten how to bow or shake hands from long-continued want of practice. Johnny Morgan, a common loafer, had gone to sleep in the gutter and waked up worth a hundred thousand dollars in consequence of the decision in the "Lady

Franklin and Rough and Ready" lawsuit. And so on—day in and day out the talk pelted our ears and the excitement waxed hotter and hotter around us.

I would have been more or less than human if I had not gone mad like the rest. Cart-loads of solid silver bricks, as large as pigs of lead, were arriving from the mills every day, and such sights as that

UNLOADING SILVER BRICKS.

gave substance to the wild talk about me. I succumbed and grew as frenzied as the craziest.

Every few days news would come of the discovery of a bran-new mining region; immediately the papers would teem with accounts of its richness, and away the surplus population would scamper to take possession. By the time I was fairly inoculated with the disease, "Esmeralda" had just had a run and "Humboldt" was beginning to shriek for attention. "Humboldt! Humboldt!" was the new cry, and straightway Humboldt, the newest of the new, the richest of the rich, the most marvelous of the marvelous discoveries in silver-land, was occupying two columns of the public prints to "Esmeralda's" one. I was just on the point of starting to Esmeralda, but turned with the tide and got ready for Humboldt. That the reader

may see what moved me, and what would as surely have moved
him had he been there, I insert here one of the newspaper letters of
the day. It and several other letters from the same calm hand were
the main means of converting me. I shall not garble the extract, but
put it in just as it appeared in the *Daily Territorial Enterprise:*

But what about our mines? I shall be candid with you. I shall express an
honest opinion, based upon a thorough examination. Humboldt county is
the richest mineral region upon God's footstool. Each mountain range is
gorged with the precious ores. Humboldt is the true Golconda.

The other day an assay of mere *croppings* yielded exceeding *four thousand dollars to the ton.* A week or two ago an assay of just such surface
developments made returns of *seven thousand* dollars to the ton. Our
mountains are full of rambling prospectors. Each day and almost every
hour reveals new and more startling evidences of the profuse and intensi-
fied wealth of our favored county. The metal is not silver alone. There are
distinct ledges of auriferous ore. A late discovery plainly evinces cinna-
bar. The coarser metals are in gross abundance. Lately evidences of bitu-
minous coal have been detected. My theory has ever been that coal is a
ligneous formation. I told Col. Whitman, in times past, that the neighborhood of Dayton (Nevada) betrayed no present or previous manifestations
of a ligneous foundation, and that hence I had no confidence in his lauded
coal mines. I repeated the same doctrine to the exultant coal discoverers
of Humboldt. I talked with my friend Captain Burch on the subject. My
pyrrhonism vanished upon his statement that in the very region referred
to he had seen petrified trees of the length of two hundred feet. Then is the
fact established that huge forests once cast their grim shadows over this
remote section. I am firm in the coal faith. Have no fears of the mineral
resources of Humboldt county. They are immense—incalculable.

Let me state one or two things which will help the reader to better comprehend certain items in the above. At this time, our near
neighbor, Gold Hill, was the most successful silver mining locality
in Nevada. It was from there that more than half the daily shipments of silver bricks came. "Very rich" (and scarce) Gold Hill ore
yielded from a hundred to four hundred dollars to the ton; but the
usual yield was only twenty to forty dollars per ton—that is to say,
each hundred pounds of ore yielded from one dollar to two dollars.
But the reader will perceive by the above extract, that in Humboldt
from one-fourth to nearly half the mass was silver! That is to say,
every one hundred pounds of the ore had from *two hundred* dollars

up to about *three hundred and fifty* in it. Some days later this same correspondent wrote:

I have spoken of the vast and almost fabulous wealth of this region—it is incredible. The intestines of our mountains are gorged with precious ore to plethora. I have said that nature has so shaped our mountains as to furnish most excellent facilities for the working of our mines. I have also told you that the country about here is pregnant with the finest mill sites in the world. But what is the mining history of Humboldt? The Sheba mine is in the hands of energetic San Francisco capitalists. It would seem that the ore is

combined with metals that render it difficult of reduction with our imperfect mountain machinery. The proprietors have combined the capital and labor hinted at in my exordium. They are toiling and probing. Their tunnel has reached the length of one hundred feet. From primal assays alone, coupled with the development of the mine and public confidence in the continuance of effort, the stock had reared itself to eight hundred dollars market value. I do not know that one ton of the ore has been converted into current metal. I do know that there are many lodes in this

VIEW IN HUMBOLDT MOUNTAINS.

section that surpass the Sheba in primal assay value. Listen a moment to the calculations of the Sheba operators. They purpose transporting the ore concentrated to Europe. The conveyance from Star City (its locality) to Virginia City will cost seventy dollars per ton; from Virginia to San Francisco, forty dollars per ton; from thence to Liverpool, its destination, ten dollars per ton. Their idea is that its conglomerate metals will reimburse them their cost of original extraction, the price of transportation, and the expense of reduction, and that then a ton of the raw ore will net them twelve hundred dollars. The estimate may be extravagant. Cut it in twain, and the product is enormous, far transcending any previous developments of our racy Territory.

A very common calculation is that many of our mines will yield five hundred dollars to the ton. Such fecundity throws the Gould & Curry, the Ophir and the Mexican, of your neighborhood, in the darkest shadow. I have given you the estimate of the value of a single developed mine. Its richness is indexed by its market valuation. The people of Humboldt county are *feet* crazy. As I write, our towns are near deserted. They look as languid as a consumptive girl. What has become of our sinewy and athletic fellow-citizens? They are coursing through ravines and over mountain tops. Their tracks are visible in every direction. Occasionally a horseman will dash among us. His steed betrays hard usage. He alights before his adobe dwelling, hastily exchanges courtesies with his townsmen, hurries to an assay office and from thence to the District Recorder's. In the morning, having renewed his provisional supplies, he is off again on his wild and unbeaten route. Why, the fellow numbers already his feet by the thousands. He is the horse-leech. He has the craving stomach of the shark or anaconda. He would conquer metallic worlds.

This was enough. The instant we had finished reading the above article, four of us decided to go to Humboldt. We commenced getting ready at once. And we also commenced upbraiding ourselves for not deciding sooner—for we were in terror lest all the rich mines would be found and secured before we got there, and we might have to put up with ledges that would not yield more than two or three hundred dollars a ton, maybe. An hour before, I would have felt opulent if I had owned ten feet in a Gold Hill mine whose ore produced twenty-five dollars to the ton; now I was already annoyed at the prospect of having to put up with mines the poorest of which would be a marvel in Gold Hill.

CHAPTER 27

Hurry, was the word! We wasted no time. Our party consisted of four persons—a blacksmith sixty years of age, two young lawyers, and myself. We bought a wagon and two miserable old horses. We put eighteen hundred pounds of provisions and mining tools in the wagon and drove out of Carson on a chilly December afternoon. The horses were so weak and old that we soon found that it would be better if one or two of us got out and walked. It was an improvement. Next, we found that it would be better if a third man got out. That was an improvement also. It was at this time that I volunteered to drive, although I had never driven a harnessed horse before and many a man in such a position would have felt fairly excused from such a responsibility. But in a little while it was found that it would be a fine thing if the driver got out and walked also. It was at this time that I resigned the position of driver, and never resumed it again. Within the hour, we found that it would not only be better, but was absolutely necessary, that we four, taking turns, two at a time, should put our hands against the end of

GOING TO HUMBOLDT.

the wagon and push it through the sand, leaving the feeble horses little to do but keep out of the way and hold up the tongue. Perhaps it is well for one to know his fate at first, and get reconciled to it. We had learned ours in one afternoon. It was plain that we had to walk through the sand and shove that wagon and those horses two hundred miles. So we accepted the situation, and from that time forth we never rode. More than that, we stood regular and nearly constant watches pushing up behind.

We made seven miles, and camped in the desert. Young Clagett (now member of Congress from Montana) unharnessed and fed and watered the horses; Oliphant and I cut sage-brush, built the fire and brought water to cook with; and old Mr. Ballou the black-smith did the cooking. This division of labor, and this appoint-ment, was adhered to throughout the journey. We had no tent, and so we slept under our blankets in the open plain. We were so tired that we slept soundly.

We were fifteen days making the trip—two hundred miles; thir-teen, rather, for we lay by a couple of days, in one place, to let the horses rest. We could really have accomplished the journey in ten days if we had towed the horses behind the wagon, but we did not think of that until it was too late, and so went on shoving the horses and the wagon too when we might have saved half the labor. Parties who met us, occasionally, advised us to put the horses *in* the wagon, but Mr. Ballou, through whose iron-clad earnestness no sarcasm could pierce, said that that would not do, because the pro-visions were exposed and would suffer, the horses being "bitumi-nous from long deprivation." The reader will excuse me from translating. What Mr. Ballou customarily meant, when he used a long word, was a secret between himself and his Maker. He was one of the best and kindest hearted men that ever graced a humble sphere of life. He was gentleness and simplicity itself—and unself-ishness, too. Although he was more than twice as old as the eldest of us, he never gave himself any airs, privileges, or exemptions on that account. He did a *young* man's share of the work; and did his share of conversing and entertaining from the general stand-point of *any* age—not from the arrogant, overawing summit-height of sixty years. His one striking peculiarity was his Partingtonian

fashion of loving and using big words *for their own sakes,* and independent of any bearing they might have upon the thought he was
purposing to convey. He always let his ponderous syllables fall
with an easy unconsciousness that left them wholly without of-
fensiveness. In truth his air was so natural and so simple that one
was always catching himself accepting his stately sentences as
meaning something, when they really meant nothing in the world.
If a word was long and grand and resonant, that was sufficient to
win the old man's love, and he would drop that word into the most
out-of-the-way place in a sentence or a subject, and be as pleased
with it as if it were perfectly luminous with meaning.

   We four always spread our common stock of blankets together
on the frozen ground, and slept side by side; and finding that our
foolish, long-legged hound pup had a deal of animal heat in him,
Oliphant got to admitting him to the bed, between himself and

BALLOU'S BEDFELLOW.

Mr. Ballou, hugging the dog's warm back to his breast and finding
great comfort in it. But in the night the pup would get stretchy and
brace his feet against the old man's back and shove, grunting complacently the while; and now and then, being warm and snug,
grateful and happy, he would paw the old man's back simply in excess of comfort; and at yet other times he would dream of the chase
and in his sleep tug at the old man's back hair and bark in his ear.
The old gentleman complained mildly about these familiarities, at
last, and when he got through with his statement he said that such

a dog as that was not a proper animal to admit to bed with tired
men, because he was "so meretricious in his movements and so organic in his emotions." We turned the dog out.

It was a hard, wearing, toilsome journey, but it had its bright
side; for after each day was done and our wolfish hunger appeased
with a hot supper of fried bacon, bread, molasses and black coffee,
the pipe-smoking, song-singing and yarn-spinning around the evening camp-fire in the still solitudes of the desert was a happy, care-
free sort of recreation that seemed the very summit and culmination of earthly luxury. It is a kind of life that has a potent charm

PLEASURES OF CAMPING OUT.

for all men, whether city
or country-bred. We are
descended from desert-
lounging Arabs, and countless ages of growth toward
perfect civilization have
failed to root out of us the no-
madic instinct. We all confess to a gratified thrill at the thought of
"camping out."

Once we made twenty-five miles in a day, and once we made forty miles (through the Great American Desert), and ten miles beyond—fifty in all—in twenty-three hours, without halting to eat, drink or rest. To stretch out and go to sleep, even on stony and frozen ground, after pushing a wagon and two horses fifty miles, is a delight so supreme that for the moment it almost seems cheap at the price.

We camped two days in the neighborhood of the "Sink of the Humboldt." We tried to use the strong alkaline water of the Sink, but it would not answer. It was like drinking lye, and not weak lye, either. It left a taste in the mouth, bitter and every way execrable, and a burning in the stomach that was very uncomfortable. We put molasses in it, but that helped it very little; we added a pickle, yet the alkali was the prominent taste, and so it was unfit for drinking. The coffee we made of this water was the meanest compound man has yet invented. It was really viler to the taste than the unameliorated water itself. Mr. Ballou, being the architect and builder of the beverage, felt constrained to endorse and uphold it, and so drank half a cup, by little sips, making shift to praise it faintly the while, but finally threw out the remainder, and said frankly it was "too technical for *him*."

But presently we found a spring of fresh water, convenient, and then, with nothing to mar our enjoyment, and no stragglers to interrupt it, we entered into our rest.

CHAPTER 28

AFTER leaving the Sink, we traveled along the Humboldt river a little way. People accustomed to the monster mile-wide Mississippi, grow accustomed to associating the term "river" with a high degree of watery grandeur. Consequently, such people feel rather disappointed when they stand on the shores of the Humboldt or the Carson and find that a "river" in Nevada is a sickly rivulet which is just the counterpart of the Erie Canal in all respects save that the canal is twice as long and four times as deep. One of the pleasantest and most invigorating exercises one can contrive is to run and jump across the Humboldt river till he is overheated, and then drink it dry.

On the fifteenth day we completed our march of two hundred miles and entered Unionville, Humboldt County, in the midst of a driving snow-storm. Unionville consisted of eleven cabins and a liberty pole. Six of the cabins were strung along one side of a deep cañon, and the other five faced them. The rest of the landscape was made up of bleak mountain walls that rose so high into the sky from both sides of the cañon that the village was left, as it were, far down in the bottom of a crevice. It was always daylight on the mountain-tops a long time before the darkness lifted and revealed Unionville.

We built a small, rude cabin in the side of the crevice and roofed it with canvas, leaving a corner open to serve as a chimney, through which the cattle used to tumble occasionally, at night, and mash our furniture and interrupt our sleep. It was very cold weather and fuel was scarce. Indians brought brush and bushes several miles on their backs; and when we could catch a laden Indian it was well—and when we could not (which was the rule, not the exception), we shivered and bore it.

I confess, without shame, that I expected to find masses of silver lying all about the ground. I expected to see it glittering in the sun on the mountain summits. I said nothing about this, for some instinct told me that I might possibly have an exaggerated idea about it, and so if I betrayed my thought I might bring derision upon myself. Yet I was as perfectly satisfied in my own mind as I could be of anything, that I was going to gather up, in a day or two, or at furthest a week or two, silver enough to make me satisfactorily wealthy—and so my fancy was already busy with plans for spending this money. The first opportunity that offered, I sauntered carelessly away from the cabin, keeping an eye on the other boys, and stopping and contemplating the sky when they seemed to be observing me; but as soon as the coast was manifestly clear, I fled away as guiltily as a thief might have done and never halted till I was far beyond sight and call. Then I began my search with a feverish excitement that was brim full of expectation—almost of certainty. I crawled about the ground, seizing and examining bits of stone, blowing the dust from them or rubbing them on my clothes, and then peering at them with anxious hope. Presently I found a bright fragment and my heart bounded! I hid behind a boulder and polished it and scrutinized it with a nervous eagerness and a delight that was more pronounced than absolute certainty itself could have afforded. The more I examined the fragment the more I was convinced that I had found the door to fortune. I marked the spot and carried away my specimen. Up and down the rugged mountain side I searched, with always increasing interest and always augmenting gratitude that I had come to Humboldt and come in time. Of all the experiences of my life, this secret search among the hidden treasures of silver-land was the nearest to unmarred ecstasy. It was a delirious revel. By and by, in the bed of a shallow rivulet, I found a deposit of shining yellow scales, and my breath almost forsook me! A gold mine, and in my simplicity I had been content with vulgar silver! I was so excited that I half believed my overwrought imagination was deceiving me. Then a fear came upon me that people might be observing me and would guess my secret. Moved by this thought, I made a circuit of the place, and ascended a knoll to reconnoitre. Solitude. No creature was near. Then I returned to my mine, fortifying myself against possible disappointment, but my fears were groundless—the shining scales

THE SECRET SEARCH.

were still there. I set about scooping them out, and for an hour I
toiled down the windings of the stream and robbed its bed. But at
last the descending sun warned me to give up the quest, and I
turned homeward laden with wealth. As I walked along I could not
help smiling at the thought of my being so excited over my fragment of silver when a nobler metal was almost under my nose. In
this little time the former had so fallen in my estimation that once
or twice I was on the point of throwing it away.

The boys were as hungry as usual, but I could eat nothing. Neither could I talk. I was full of dreams and far away. Their conversation interrupted the flow of my fancy somewhat, and annoyed me
a little, too. I despised the sordid and commonplace things they
talked about. But as they proceeded, it began to amuse me. It grew
to be rare fun to hear them planning their poor little economies
and sighing over possible privations and distresses when a gold
mine, all our own, lay within sight of the cabin and I could point it
out at any moment. Smothered hilarity began to oppress me, presently. It was hard to resist the impulse to burst out with exultation
and reveal everything; but I did resist. I said within myself that I
would filter the great news through my lips calmly and be serene

as a summer morning while I watched its effect in their faces. I said:

"Where have you all been?"

"Prospecting."

"What did you find?"

"Nothing."

"Nothing? What do you think of the country?"

"Can't tell, yet," said Mr. Ballou, who was an old gold miner, and had likewise had considerable experience among the silver mines.

"Well, haven't you formed any sort of opinion?"

"Yes, a sort of a one. It's fair enough here, maybe, but overrated. Seven-thousand-dollar ledges are scarce, though. That Sheba may be rich enough, but we don't own it; and besides, the rock is so full of base metals that all the science in the world can't work it. We'll not starve, here, but we'll not get rich, I'm afraid."

"So you think the prospect is pretty poor?"

"No name for it!"

"Well, we'd better go back, hadn't we?"

"Oh, not yet—of course not. We'll try it a riffle, first."

"Suppose, now—this is merely a supposition, you know—suppose you could find a ledge that would yield, say, a hundred and fifty dollars a ton—would that satisfy you?"

"Try us once!" from the whole party.

"Or suppose—merely a supposition, of course—suppose you were to find a ledge that would yield two thousand dollars a ton—would *that* satisfy you?"

"Here—what do you mean? What are you coming at? Is there some mystery behind all this?"

"Never mind. I am not saying anything. You know perfectly well there are no rich mines here—of course you do. Because you have been around and examined for yourselves. Anybody would know that, that had been around. But just for the sake of argument, suppose—in a kind of general way—suppose some person were to tell you that two-thousand-dollar ledges were simply contemptible—contemptible, understand—and that right yonder in sight of this very cabin there were piles of pure gold and pure silver—oceans of it—enough to make you all rich in twenty-four hours! Come!"

"I should say he was as crazy as a loon!" said old Ballou, but wild with excitement, nevertheless.

"Gentlemen," said I, "I don't say anything—*I* haven't been around, you know, and of course don't know anything—but all I ask of you is to cast your eye on *that,* for instance, and tell me what you think of it!" and I tossed my treasure before them.

"CAST YOUR EYE ON *THAT!*"

There was an eager scramble for it, and a closing of heads together over it under the candle-light. Then old Ballou said:

"Think of it? I think it is nothing but a lot of granite rubbish and nasty glittering mica that isn't worth ten cents an acre!"

So vanished my dream. So melted my wealth away. So toppled my airy castle to the earth and left me stricken and forlorn.

Moralizing, I observed, then, that "all that glitters is not gold."

Mr. Ballou said I could go further than that, and lay it up among my treasures of knowledge, that *nothing* that glitters is gold. So I learned then, once for all, that gold in its native state is but dull, unornamental stuff, and that only low-born metals excite the admiration of the ignorant with an ostentatious glitter. However, like the rest of the world, I still go on underrating men of gold and glorifying men of mica. Commonplace human nature cannot rise above that.

CHAPTER 29

Tᴙᴜᴇ knowledge of the nature of silver mining came fast enough. We went out "prospecting" with Mr. Ballou. We climbed the mountain sides, and clambered among sage-brush, rocks and snow till we were ready to drop with exhaustion, but found no silver— nor yet any gold. Day after day we did this. Now and then we came upon holes burrowed a few feet into the declivities and apparently abandoned; and now and then we found one or two listless men still burrowing. But there was no appearance of silver. These holes were the beginnings of tunnels, and the purpose was to drive them hundreds of feet into the mountain, and some day tap the hidden ledge where the silver was. Some day! It seemed far enough away, and very hopeless and dreary. Day after day we toiled, and climbed and searched, and we younger partners grew sicker and still sicker of the promiseless toil. At last we halted under a beetling rampart of rock which projected from the earth high upon the mountain. Mr. Ballou broke off some fragments with a hammer, and examined them long and attentively with a small eye-glass; threw them away and broke off more; said this rock was quartz, and quartz was the sort of rock that contained silver. *Contained* it! I had thought that at least it would be caked on the outside of it like a kind of veneering. He still broke off pieces and critically examined them, now and then wetting the piece with his tongue and applying the glass. At last he exclaimed:

"We've got it!"

We were full of anxiety in a moment. The rock was clean and white, where it was broken, and across it ran a ragged thread of blue. He said that that little thread had silver in it, mixed with base metals, such as lead and antimony, and other rubbish, and that there was a speck or two of gold visible. After a great deal of effort we managed to discern some little fine yellow specks, and judged that a couple of tons of them massed together might make a gold dollar, possibly. We were not jubilant, but Mr. Ballou said

"WE'VE GOT IT!"

there were worse ledges in the world than that. He saved what he called the "richest" piece of the rock, in order to determine its value by the process called the "fire-assay." Then we named the mine "Monarch of the Mountains" (modesty of nomenclature is not a prominent feature in the mines), and Mr. Ballou wrote out and stuck up the following "notice," preserving a copy to be entered upon the books in the mining recorder's office in the town.

NOTICE.

We the undersigned claim three claims, of three hundred feet each (and one for discovery), on this silver-bearing quartz lead or lode, extending north and south from this notice, with all its dips, spurs, and angles, variations and sinuosities, together with fifty feet of ground on either side for working the same.

We put our names to it and tried to feel that our fortunes were made. But when we talked the matter all over with Mr. Ballou, we felt depressed and dubious. He said that this surface quartz was not all there was of our mine; but that the wall or ledge of rock called the "Monarch of the Mountains," extended down hundreds and hundreds of feet into the earth—he illustrated by saying it was like a curb-stone, and maintained a nearly uniform thickness—say twenty feet—away down into the bowels of the earth, and was perfectly distinct from the casing rock on each side of it; and that it kept to itself, and maintained its distinctive character always, no matter how deep it extended into the earth or how far it stretched itself through and across the hills and valleys. He said it might be a mile deep and ten miles long, for all we knew; and that wherever we bored into it above ground or below, we would find gold and silver in it, but no gold or silver in the meaner rock it was cased between. And he said that down in the great depths of the ledge was its richness, and the deeper it went the richer it grew. Therefore, instead of working here on the surface, we must either bore down into the rock with a shaft till we came to where it was rich—say a hundred feet or so—or else we must go down into the valley and bore a long tunnel into the mountain side and tap the ledge far under the earth. To do either was plainly the labor of months; for we could blast and bore only a few feet a day—some five or six. But this was not all. He said that after we got the ore out it must be hauled in wagons to a distant silver mill, ground up, and the silver extracted by a tedious and costly process. Our fortune seemed a century away!

But we went to work. We decided to sink a shaft. So, for a week we climbed the mountain, laden with picks, drills, gads, crowbars, shovels, cans of blasting powder and coils of fuse and strove with might and main. At first the rock was broken and loose and we dug it up with picks and threw it out with shovels, and the hole progressed very well. But the rock became more compact, presently, and gads and crowbars came into play. But shortly nothing could make an impression but blasting powder. That was the weariest work! One of us held the iron drill in its place and another would strike with an eight-pound sledge—it was like driving nails on a

INCIPIENT MILLIONAIRES.

large scale. In the course of an hour or two the drill would reach a depth of two or three feet, making a hole a couple of inches in diameter. We would put in a charge of powder, insert half a yard of fuse, pour in sand and gravel and ram it down, then light the fuse and run. When the explosion came and the rocks and smoke shot into the air, we would go back and find about a bushel of that hard, rebellious quartz jolted out. Nothing more. One week of this satisfied me. I resigned. Clagett and Oliphant followed. Our shaft was only twelve feet deep. We decided that a tunnel was the thing we wanted.

So we went down the mountain side and worked a week; at the end of which time we had blasted a tunnel about deep enough to hide a hogshead in, and judged that about nine hundred feet more of it would reach the ledge. I resigned again, and the other boys only held out one day longer. We decided that a tunnel was not what we wanted. We wanted a ledge that was already "developed." There were none in the camp.

We dropped the "Monarch" for the time being.

Meantime the camp was filling up with people, and there was a constantly growing excitement about our Humboldt mines. We fell victims to the epidemic and strained every nerve to acquire more "feet." We prospected and took up new claims, put "notices" on them and gave them grandiloquent names. We traded some of our "feet" for "feet" in other people's claims. In a little while we owned largely in the "Gray Eagle," the "Columbiana," the "Branch Mint," the "Maria Jane," the "Universe," the "Root-Hog-or-Die," the "Samson and Delilah," the "Treasure Trove," the "Golconda," the "Sultana," the "Boomerang," the "Great Republic," the "Grand Mogul," and fifty other "mines" that had never been molested by a shovel or scratched with a pick. We had not less than thirty thousand "feet" apiece in the "richest mines on earth" as the frenzied cant phrased it—and were in debt to the butcher. We were stark mad with excitement—drunk with happiness—smothered under mountains of prospective wealth—arrogantly compassionate toward the plodding millions who knew not our marvelous cañon—but our credit was not good at the grocer's.

It was the strangest phase of life one can imagine. It was a beggars' revel. There was nothing doing in the district—no mining—no milling—no productive effort—no income—and not enough money in the entire camp to buy a corner lot in an eastern village, hardly; and yet a stranger would have supposed he was walking among bloated millionaires. Prospecting parties swarmed out of

town with the first flush of dawn, and swarmed in again at nightfall laden with spoil—rocks. Nothing but rocks. Every man's pockets were full of them; the floor of his cabin was littered with them;
they were disposed in labeled rows on his shelves.

CHAPTER 30

I MET men at every turn who owned from one thousand to thirty thousand "feet" in undeveloped silver mines, every single foot of which they believed would shortly be worth from fifty to a thousand dollars—and as often as any other way they were men who had not twenty-five dollars in the world. Every man you met had his new mine to boast of, and his "specimens" ready; and if the opportunity offered, he would infallibly back you into a corner and offer as a favor to *you*, not to *him*, to part with just a few feet in the "Golden Age," or the "Sarah Jane," or some other unknown stack of croppings, for money enough to get a "square meal" with, as the phrase went. And you were never to reveal that he had made you the offer at such a ruinous price, for it was only out of friendship for you that he was willing to make the sacrifice. Then he would fish a piece of rock out of his pocket, and after looking mysteriously around as if he feared he might be waylaid and robbed if caught with such wealth in his possession, he would dab the rock against his tongue, clap an eye-glass to it, and exclaim:

"Look at that! Right there in that red dirt! See it? See the specks of gold? And the streak of silver? That's from the 'Uncle Abe.' There's a hundred thousand tons like that in sight! Right in sight, mind you! And when we get down on it and the ledge comes in solid, it will be the richest thing in the world! Look at the assay! I don't want you to believe *me*—look at the assay!"

Then he would get out a greasy sheet of paper which showed that the portion of rock assayed had given evidence of containing silver and gold in the proportion of so many hundreds or thousands of dollars to the ton. I little knew, then, that the custom was to hunt out the *richest* piece of rock and get it assayed! Very often, that piece, the size of a filbert, was the only fragment in a ton that had a particle of metal in it—and yet the assay made it pretend to represent the average value of the ton of rubbish it came from!

"DO YOU SEE IT?"

On such a system of assaying as that, the Humboldt world had gone crazy. On the authority of such assays its newspaper correspondents were frothing about rock worth four and seven thousand dollars a ton!

And does the reader remember, a few pages back, the calculations, of a quoted correspondent, whereby the ore is to be mined and shipped all the way to England, the metals extracted, and the gold and silver contents received back by the miners as clear profit, the copper, antimony and other things in the ore being sufficient to pay all the expenses incurred? Everybody's head was full of such "calculations" as those—such raving insanity, rather. Few people took *work* into their calculations—or outlay of money either; except the work and expenditures of other people.

We never touched our tunnel or our shaft again. Why? Because we judged that we had learned the *real* secret of success in silver mining—which was, *not* to mine the silver ourselves by the sweat of our brows and the labor of our hands, but to *sell* the ledges to the dull slaves of toil and let them do the mining!

Before leaving Carson, the Secretary and I had purchased "feet" from various Esmeralda stragglers. We had expected immediate returns of bullion, but were only afflicted with regular and constant "assessments" instead—demands for money wherewith to develop the said mines. These assessments had grown so oppressive that it seemed necessary to look into the matter personally. Therefore I projected a pilgrimage to Carson and thence to Esmeralda. I bought a horse and started, in company with Mr. Ballou and a gentleman named Ollendorff, a Prussian—not the party who has inflicted so much suffering on the world with his wretched foreign grammars, with their interminable repetitions of questions which never have occurred and are never likely to occur in any conversation among human beings. We rode through a snow-storm for two or three days, and arrived at "Honey Lake Smith's," a sort of isolated inn on the Carson river. It was a two-story log house situated on a small knoll in the midst of the vast basin or desert through which the sickly Carson winds its melancholy way. Close to the house were the Overland stage stables, built of sun-dried bricks. There was not another building within several leagues of the place. Toward sunset about twenty hay wagons arrived and camped around the house and all the teamsters came in to supper—a very, very rough set. There were one or two Overland stage-drivers there, also, and half a dozen vagabonds and stragglers; consequently the house was well crowded.

We walked out, after supper, and visited a small Indian camp in the vicinity. The Indians were in a great hurry about something, and were packing up and getting away as fast as they could. In their broken English they said, "By'm-by, heap water!" and by the help of signs made us understand that in their opinion a flood was coming. The weather was perfectly clear, and this was not the rainy season. There was about a foot of water in the insignificant river—or maybe two feet; the stream was not wider than a back alley in a village, and its banks were scarcely higher than a man's head. So,

FAREWELL SWEET RIVER.

where was the flood to come from? We canvassed the subject awhile and then concluded it was a ruse, and that the Indians had some better reason for leaving in a hurry than fears of a flood in such an exceedingly dry time.

At seven in the evening we went to bed in the second story—with our clothes on, as usual, and all three in the same bed, for every available space on the floors, chairs, etc., was in request, and even then there was barely room for the housing of the inn's guests. An hour later we were awakened by a great turmoil, and springing out of bed we picked our way nimbly among the ranks of snoring teamsters on the floor and got to the front windows of the long room. A glance revealed a strange spectacle, under the moonlight. The crooked Carson was full to the brim, and its waters were raging and foaming in the wildest way—sweeping around the sharp bends at a furious speed, and bearing on their surface a chaos of logs, brush and all sorts of rubbish. A depression, where its bed had once been, in other times, was already filling, and in one or two places the water was beginning to wash over the main bank. Men were flying hither and thither, bringing cattle and wagons close up to the house, for the spot of high ground on which it stood extended only some thirty feet in front and about a hundred in the rear. Close to the old river bed just spoken of, stood a little log stable, and in this our horses were lodged. While we looked, the waters increased so fast in this place that in a few minutes a torrent was roaring by the little stable and its margin encroaching steadily on the logs. We suddenly realized that this flood was not a mere holiday spectacle, but meant damage—and not only to the small log stable but to the Overland buildings close to the main river, for the waves had now come ashore and were creeping about

THE RESCUE.

the foundations and invading the great hay-corral adjoining. We ran down and joined the crowd of excited men and frightened animals. We waded knee-deep into the log stable, unfastened the horses and waded out almost *waist-*deep, so fast the waters increased. Then the crowd rushed in a body to the hay-corral and began to tumble down the huge stacks of baled hay and roll the bales up on the high ground by the house. Meantime it was discovered that Owens, an overland driver, was missing, and a man ran to the large stable, and wading in, boot-top deep, discovered him asleep in his bed, awoke him, and waded out again. But Owens was drowsy and resumed his nap; but only for a minute or two, for presently he turned in his bed, his hand dropped over the side and came in contact with the cold water! It was up level with the mattrass! He waded out, breast-deep, almost, and the next moment the sunburned bricks melted down like sugar and the big building crumbled to a ruin and was washed away in a twinkling.

At eleven o'clock only the roof of the little log stable was out of water, and our inn was on an island in mid-ocean. As far as the eye could reach, in the moonlight, there was no desert visible, but only a level waste of shining water. The Indians were true prophets, but how did they get their information? I am not able to answer the question.

We remained cooped up eight days and nights with that curious crew. Swearing, drinking and card playing were the order of the day, and occasionally a fight was thrown in for variety. Dirt and vermin—but let us forget those features; their profusion is simply inconceivable—it is better that they remain so.

There were two men—however, this chapter is long enough.

CHAPTER 31

THERE were two men in the company who caused me particular discomfort. One was a little Swede, about twenty-five years old, who knew only one song, and he was forever singing it. By day we were all crowded into one small, stifling bar-room, and so there was no escaping this person's music. Through all the profanity, whisky-guzzling, "old sledge" and quarreling, his monotonous song meandered with never a variation in its tiresome sameness, and it seemed to me, at last, that I would be content to die, in order to be rid of the torture. The other man was a stalwart ruffian called "Arkansas," who carried two revolvers in his belt and a bowie knife projecting from his boot, and who was always drunk and always suffering for a fight. But he was so feared, that nobody would accommodate him. He would try all manner of little wary ruses to entrap somebody into an offensive remark, and his face would light up now and then when he fancied he was fairly on the scent of a fight, but invariably his victim would elude his toils and then he would show a disappointment that was almost

"MR. ARKANSAS."

pathetic. The landlord, Johnson, was a meek, well-meaning fellow, and Arkansas fastened on him early, as a promising subject, and gave him no rest day or night, for a while. On the fourth morning, Arkansas got drunk and sat himself down to wait for an opportunity. Presently Johnson came in, just comfortably sociable with whisky, and said:

"I reckon the Pennsylvania 'lection—"

Arkansas raised his finger impressively and Johnson stopped. Arkansas rose unsteadily and confronted him. Said he:

"Wha-what do you know a-about Pennsylvania? Answer me that. Wha-what do you know 'bout Pennsylvania?"

"I was only goin' to say—"

"You was only goin' to *say*. *You* was! You was only goin' to say— *what* was you goin' to say? That's it! That's what *I* want to know. *I* want to know wha-what you (*'ic*) what you know about Pennsylvania, since you're makin' yourself so d—d free. Answer me that!"

"Mr. Arkansas, if you'd only let me—"

"Who's a henderin' you? Don't you insinuate nothing agin me!—don't you do it. Don't you come in here bullyin' around, and cussin' and goin' on like a lunatic—don't you do it. 'Coz *I* won't *stand* it. If fight's what you want, out with it! I'm your man! Out with it!"

Said Johnson, backing into a corner, Arkansas following, menacingly:

"Why, *I* never said nothing, Mr. Arkansas. You don't give a man no chance. I was only goin' to say that Pennsylvania was goin' to have an election next week—that was all—that was everything I was goin' to say—I wish I may never stir if it wasn't."

"Well then why d'n't you say it? What did you come swellin' around that way for, and tryin' to raise trouble?"

"Why *I* didn't come swellin' around, Mr. Arkansas—I just—"

"I'm a liar am I! Ger-reat Cæsar's ghost—"

"Oh, please, Mr. Arkansas, I never meant such a thing as that, I wish I may die if I did. All the boys will tell you that I've always spoke well of you, and respected you more'n any man in the house. Ask Smith. Ain't it so, Smith? Didn't I say, no longer ago than last night, that for a man that was a gentleman *all* the time and every way you took him, give me Arkansas? I'll leave it to any gentleman here if them warn't the very words I used. Come, now, Mr. Arkansas, le's take a drink—le's shake hands and take a drink. Come up—everybody! It's my treat. Come up, Bill, Tom, Bob, Scotty—come up. I want you all to take a drink with me and Arkansas—*old* Arkansas, I call him—bully old Arkansas. Gimme your hand agin. Look at him, boys—just take a *look* at him. Thar stands the whitest man in America!—and the man that denies it has got to fight *me*, that's all. Gimme that old flipper agin!"

They embraced, with drunken affection on the landlord's part and unresponsive toleration on the part of Arkansas, who, bribed by a drink, was disappointed of his prey once more. But the foolish landlord was so happy to have escaped butchery, that he went on talking when he ought to have marched himself out of danger. The consequence was that Arkansas shortly began to glower upon him dangerously, and presently said:

"Lan'lord, will you p-please make that remark over agin if you please?"

"I was a sayin' to Scotty that my father was up'ards of eighty year old when he died."

"Was that *all* that you said?"

"Yes, that was all."

"Didn't say nothing but that?"

"No—nothing."

Then an uncomfortable silence.

Arkansas played with his glass a moment, lolling on his elbows on the counter. Then he meditatively scratched his left shin with his right boot, while the awkward silence continued. But presently he loafed away toward the stove, looking dissatisfied; roughly shouldered two or three men out of a comfortable position; occupied it himself, gave a sleeping dog a kick that sent him howling under a bench, then spread his long legs and his blanket-coat tails apart and proceeded to warm his back. In a little while he fell to grumbling to himself, and soon he slouched back to the bar and said:

"Lan'lord, what's your idea for rakin' up old personalities and blowin' about your father? Ain't this company agreeable to you? Ain't it? If this company ain't agreeable to you, p'r'aps we'd better leave. Is that your idea? Is that what you're coming at?"

"Why bless your soul, Arkansas, I warn't thinking of such a thing. My father and my mother—"

"Lan'lord, *don't* crowd a man! Don't do it. If nothing 'll do you but a disturbance, out with it like a man (*'ic*)—but *don't* rake up old bygones and fling 'em in the teeth of a passel of people that wants to be peaceable if they could git a chance. What's the matter with you this mornin', anyway? I never see a man carry on so."

"Arkansas, I reely didn't mean no harm, and I won't go on with it if it's onpleasant to you. I reckon my licker's got into my head, and what with the flood, and havin' so many to feed and look out for—"

"So *that's* what's a ranklin' in your heart, is it? You want us to leave do you? There's too many on us. You want us to pack up and swim. Is that it? Come!"

"Please be reasonable, Arkansas. Now *you* know that I ain't the man to—"

"Are you a threatenin' me? Are you? By George, the man don't live that can skeer me! Don't you try to come that game, my chicken—'cuz I can stand a good deal, but I won't stand that. Come out from behind that bar till I clean you! You want to drive us out, do you, you sneakin' underhanded hound! Come out from behind that bar! *I'll* learn you to bully and badger and browbeat a gentleman that's forever trying to befriend you and keep you out of trouble!"

"Please, Arkansas, please don't shoot! If there's got to be bloodshed—"

"Do you hear that, gentlemen? Do you hear him talk about bloodshed? So it's blood you want, is it, you ravin' desperado! You'd made up your mind to murder somebody this mornin'—I knowed it perfectly well. I'm the man, am I? It's me you're goin' to murder, is it? But you can't do it 'thout I get one chance first, you thievin' black-hearted, white-livered son of a nigger! Draw your weepon!"

With that, Arkansas began to shoot, and the landlord to clamber over benches, men and every sort of obstacle in a frantic desire to escape. In the midst of the wild hubbub the landlord crashed through a glass door, and as Arkansas charged after him the landlord's wife suddenly appeared in the doorway and confronted the desperado with a pair of scissors! Her fury was magnificent. With head erect and flashing eye she stood a moment and then advanced, with her weapon raised. The astonished ruffian hesitated, and then fell back a step. She followed. She backed him step by step into the middle of the bar-room, and then, while the wondering

AN ARMED ALLY.

crowd closed up and gazed, she gave him such another tongue-lashing as never a cowed and shamefaced braggart got before, per-haps! As she finished and retired victorious, a roar of applause shook the house, and every man ordered "drinks for the crowd" in one and the same breath.

The lesson was entirely sufficient. The reign of terror was over, and the Arkansas domination broken for good. During the rest of the season of island captivity, there was one man who sat apart in a state of permanent humiliation, never mixing in any quarrel or uttering a boast, and never resenting the insults the once cringing crew now constantly leveled at him, and that man was "Arkansas."

By the fifth or sixth morning the waters had subsided from the land, but the stream in the old river bed was still high and swift and

there was no possibility of crossing it. On the eighth it was still too
high for an entirely safe passage, but life in the inn had become
next to insupportable by reason of the dirt, drunkenness, fighting,
etc., and so we made an effort to get away. In the midst of a heavy
snow-storm we embarked in a canoe, taking our saddles aboard

CROSSING THE FLOOD.

and towing our horses after us by their halters. The Prussian, Ollendorff, was in the bow, with a paddle, Ballou paddled in the middle, and I sat in the stern holding the halters. When the horses lost
their footing and began to swim, Ollendorff got frightened, for
there was great danger that the horses would make our aim uncertain, and it was plain that if we failed to land at a certain spot the
current would throw us off and almost surely cast us into the main
Carson, which was a boiling torrent, now. Such a catastrophe
would be death, in all probability, for we would be swept to sea in
the "Sink" or overturned and drowned. We warned Ollendorff to
keep his wits about him and handle himself carefully, but it was

useless; the moment the bow touched the bank, he made a spring and the canoe whirled upside down in ten-foot water. Ollendorff seized some brush and dragged himself ashore, but Ballou and I had to swim for it, encumbered with our overcoats. But we held on to the canoe, and although we were washed down nearly to the Carson, we managed to push the boat ashore and make a safe landing. We were cold and water-soaked, but safe. The horses made a landing, too, but our saddles were gone, of course. We tied the animals in the sage-brush and there they had to stay for twenty-four hours. We baled out the canoe and ferried over some food and blankets for them, but we slept one more night in the inn before making another venture on our journey.

The next morning it was still snowing furiously when we got away with our new stock of saddles and accoutrements. We mounted and started. The snow lay so deep on the ground that there was no sign of a road perceptible, and the snow-fall was so thick that we could not see more than a hundred yards ahead, else we could have guided our course by the mountain ranges. The case looked dubious, but Ollendorff said his instinct was as sensitive as any compass, and that he could "strike a bee-line" for Carson City and never diverge from it. He said that if he were to straggle a single point out of the true line his instinct would assail him like an outraged conscience. Consequently we dropped into his wake happy and content. For half an hour we poked along warily enough, but at the end of that time we came upon a fresh trail, and Ollendorff shouted proudly:

"I knew I was as dead certain as a compass, boys! Here we are, right in somebody's tracks that will hunt the way for us without any trouble. Let's hurry up and join company with the party."

So we put the horses into as much of a trot as the deep snow would allow, and before long it was evident that we were gaining on our predecessors, for the tracks grew more distinct. We hurried along, and at the end of an hour the tracks looked still newer and fresher—but what surprised us was, that the *number* of travelers in advance of us seemed to steadily increase. We wondered how so large a party came to be traveling at such a time and in such a solitude. Somebody suggested that it must be a company of soldiers from the fort, and so we accepted that solution and jogged along a little faster still, for they could not be far off now. But the tracks still multiplied, and we began to think the platoon of soldiers was miraculously expanding into a regiment—Ballou said they had already increased to five hundred! Presently he stopped his horse and said:

"Boys, these are our own tracks, and we've actually been circussing round and round in a circle for more than two hours, out here in this blind desert! By George this is perfectly hydraulic!"

ADVANCE IN A CIRCLE.

Then the old man waxed wroth and abusive. He called Ollendorff all manner of hard names—said he never saw such a lurid fool as he was, and ended with the peculiarly venomous opinion that he "did not know as much as a logarithm!"

We certainly had been following our own tracks. Ollendorff and his "mental compass" were in disgrace from that moment. After all our hard travel, here we were on the bank of the stream again, with the inn beyond dimly outlined through the driving snow-fall. While we were considering what to do, the young Swede landed

from the canoe and took his pedestrian way Carson-wards, singing
his same tiresome song about his "sister and his brother" and "the
child in the grave with its mother," and
in a short minute faded and disappeared
in the white oblivion. He was never
heard of again. He no doubt got bewildered and lost, and Fatigue delivered
him over to Sleep and Sleep betrayed
him to Death. Possibly he followed our
treacherous tracks till he became exhausted and dropped.

THE SONGSTER.

Presently the Overland stage forded
the now fast receding stream and
started toward Carson on its first trip since the flood came. We hesitated no longer, now, but took up our march in its wake, and trotted merrily along, for we had good confidence in the driver's bump
of locality. But our horses were no match for the fresh stage team.
We were soon left out of sight; but it was no matter, for we had the
deep ruts the wheels made for a guide. By this time it was three in
the afternoon, and consequently it was not very long before night
came—and not with a lingering twilight, but with a sudden shut-
ting down like a cellar door, as is its habit in that country. The
snow-fall was still as thick as ever, and of course we could not see
fifteen steps before us; but all about us the white glare of the snow-
bed enabled us to discern the smooth sugar-loaf mounds made by
the covered sage-bushes, and just in front of us the two faint
grooves which we knew were the steadily filling and slowly disappearing wheel-tracks.

Now those sage-bushes were all about the same height—three
or four feet; they stood just about seven feet apart, all over the vast
desert; each of them was a mere snow-mound, now; in *any* direction that you proceeded (the same as in a well laid out orchard) you
would find yourself moving down a distinctly defined avenue,
with a row of these snow-mounds on either side of it—an avenue
the customary width of a road, nice and level in its breadth, and
rising at the sides in the most natural way, by reason of the
mounds. But we had not thought of this. Then imagine the chilly
thrill that shot through us when it finally occurred to us, far in the

night, that since the last faint trace of the wheel-tracks had long
ago been buried from sight, we might now be wandering down a
mere sage-brush avenue, miles away from the road and diverging
further and further away from it all the time. Having a cake of ice
slipped down one's back is placid comfort compared to it. There
was a sudden leap and stir of blood that had been asleep for an
hour, and as sudden a rousing of all the drowsing activities in our
minds and bodies. We were alive and awake at once—and shaking
and quaking with consternation, too. There was an instant halting
and dismounting, a bending low and an anxious scanning of the
road-bed. Useless, of course; for if a faint depression could not be
discerned from an altitude of four or five feet above it, it certainly
could not with one's nose nearly against it.

CHAPTER 32

We seemed to be in a road, but that was no proof. We tested this by walking off in various directions—the regular snow-mounds and the regular avenues between them convinced each man that *he* had found the true road, and that the others had found only false ones. Plainly the situation was desperate. We were cold and stiff and the horses were tired. We decided to build a sage-brush fire and camp out till morning. This was wise, because if we were wandering from the right road and the snow-storm continued another day our case would be the next thing to hopeless if we kept on.

All agreed that a camp-fire was what would come nearest to saving us, now, and so we set about building it. We could find no matches, and so we tried to make shift with the pistols. Not a man in the party had ever tried to do such a thing before, but not a man in the party doubted that it *could* be done, and without any trouble—because every man in the party had read about it in books many a time and had naturally come to believe it, with trusting simplicity, just as he had long ago accepted and believed *that other* common book-fraud about Indians and lost hunters making a fire by rubbing two dry sticks together.

We huddled together on our knees in the deep snow, and the horses put their noses together and bowed their patient heads over us; and while the feathery flakes eddied down and turned us into a group of white statuary, we proceeded with the momentous experiment. We broke twigs from a sage-bush and piled them on a little cleared place in the shelter of our bodies. In the course of ten or fifteen minutes all was ready, and then, while conversation ceased and our pulses beat low with anxious suspense, Ollendorff applied his revolver, pulled the trigger and blew the pile clear out of the county! It was the flattest failure that ever was.

This was distressing, but it paled before a greater horror—the horses were gone! I had been appointed to hold the bridles, but in my absorbing anxiety over the pistol experiment I had unconsciously dropped them and the released animals had walked off in

A FLAT FAILURE.

the storm. It was useless to try to follow them, for their footfalls could make no sound, and one could pass within two yards of the creatures and never see them. We gave them up without an effort at recovering them, and cursed the lying books that said horses would stay by their masters for protection and companionship in a distressful time like ours.

We were miserable enough, before; we felt still more forlorn, now. Patiently, but with blighted hope, we broke more sticks and piled them, and once more the Prussian shot them into annihilation. Plainly, to light a fire with a pistol was an art requiring practice and experience, and the middle of a desert at midnight in a snow-storm was not a good place or time for the acquiring of the accomplishment. We gave it up and tried the other. Each man took a couple of sticks and fell to chafing them together. At the end of half an hour we were thoroughly chilled, and so were the sticks. We bitterly execrated the Indians, the hunters and the books that had betrayed us with the silly device, and wondered dismally what was next to be done. At this critical moment Mr. Ballou fished out four matches from the rubbish of an overlooked pocket. To have found four gold bars would have seemed poor and cheap good luck

THE LAST MATCH.

compared to this. One cannot think how good a match looks under such circumstances—or how lovable and precious, and sacredly beautiful to the eye. This time we gathered sticks with high hopes; and when Mr. Ballou prepared to light the first match, there was an amount of interest centred upon him that pages of writing could not describe. The match burned hopefully a moment, and then went out. It could not have carried more regret with it if it had been a human life. The next match simply flashed and died. The wind puffed the third one out just as it was on the imminent verge of success. We gathered together closer than ever, and developed a solicitude that was rapt and painful, as Mr. Ballou scratched our last hope on his leg. It lit, burned blue and sickly, and then budded into a robust flame. Shading it with his hands, the old gentleman bent gradually down and every heart went with him—everybody, too, for that matter—and blood and breath stood still. The flame touched the sticks at last, took gradual hold upon them—hesitated—took a stronger hold—hesitated again—held its breath five heart-breaking seconds, then gave a sort of human gasp and went out.

Nobody said a word for several minutes. It was a solemn sort of silence; even the wind put on a stealthy, sinister quiet, and made no more noise than the falling flakes of snow. Finally a sad-voiced conversation began, and it was soon apparent that in each of our hearts lay the conviction that this was our last night with the living. I had so hoped that I was the only one who felt so. When the others calmly acknowledged their conviction, it sounded like the summons itself. Ollendorff said:

"Brothers, let us die together. And let us go without one hard feeling towards each other. Let us forget and forgive bygones. I know that you have felt hard towards me for turning over the canoe, and for knowing too much and leading you round and round in the snow—but I meant well; forgive me. I acknowledge freely that I have had hard feelings against Mr. Ballou for abusing me and calling me a logarithm, which is a thing I do not know what, but no doubt a thing considered disgraceful and unbecoming in America, and it has scarcely been out of my mind and has hurt me a great deal—but let it go; I forgive Mr. Ballou with all my heart, and—"

Poor Ollendorff broke down and the tears came. He was not alone, for I was crying too, and so was Mr. Ballou. Ollendorff got his voice again and forgave me for things I had done and said. Then he got out his bottle of whisky and said that whether he lived or died he would never touch another drop. He said he had given up all hope of life, and although ill-prepared, was ready to submit humbly to his fate; that he wished he could be spared a little longer, not for any selfish reason, but to make a thorough reform in his character, and by devoting himself to helping the poor, nursing the sick, and pleading with the people to guard themselves against the evils of intemperance, make his life a beneficent example to the young, and lay it down at last with the precious reflection that it had not been lived in vain. He ended by saying that his reform should begin at this moment, even here in the presence of death, since no longer time was to be vouchsafed wherein to prosecute it to men's help and benefit—and with that he threw away the bottle of whisky.

Mr. Ballou made remarks of similar purport, and began the reform he could not live to continue, by throwing away the ancient pack of cards that had solaced our captivity during the flood and made it bearable. He said he never gambled, but still was satisfied

DISCARDED VICES.

that the meddling with cards in any way was immoral and injurious, and no man could be wholly pure and blemishless without eschewing them. "And therefore," continued he, "in doing this act I already feel more in sympathy with that spiritual saturnalia necessary to entire and obsolete reform." These rolling syllables touched him as no intelligible eloquence could have done, and the old man sobbed with a mournfulness not unmingled with satisfaction.

My own remarks were of the same tenor as those of my comrades, and I know that the feelings that prompted them were heartfelt and sincere. We were all sincere, and all deeply moved and earnest, for we were in the presence of death and without hope. I threw away my pipe, and in doing it felt that at last I was free of a hated vice and one that had ridden me like a tyrant all my days. While I yet talked, the thought of the good I might have done in the world and the still greater good I might *now* do, with these new incentives and higher and better aims to guide me if I could only be spared a few years longer, overcame me and the tears came again. We put our arms about each other's necks and awaited the warning drowsiness that precedes death by freezing.

It came stealing over us presently, and then we bade each other a last farewell. A delicious dreaminess wrought its web about my yielding senses, while the snow-flakes wove a winding sheet about my conquered body. Oblivion came. The battle of life was done.

CHAPTER 33

I DO not know how long I was in a state of forgetfulness, but it seemed an age. A vague consciousness grew upon me by degrees, and then came a gathering anguish of pain in my limbs and through all my body. I shuddered. The thought flitted through my brain, "this is death—this is the hereafter."

Then came a white upheaval at my side, and a voice said, with bitterness:

"Will some gentleman be so good as to kick me behind?"

It was Ballou—at least it was a towzled snow image in a sitting posture, with Ballou's voice.

I rose up, and there in the gray dawn, not fifteen steps from us, were the frame buildings of a stage station, and under a shed stood our still saddled and bridled horses!

An arched snow-drift broke up, now, and Ollendorff emerged from it, and the three of us sat and stared at the houses without speaking a word. We really had nothing to say. We were like the profane man who could not "do the subject justice," the whole situation was so painfully ridiculous and humiliating that words were tame and we did not know where to commence anyhow.

The joy in our hearts at our deliverance was poisoned; well-nigh dissipated, indeed. We presently began to grow pettish by degrees, and sullen; and then, angry at each other, angry at ourselves, angry at everything in general, we moodily dusted the snow from our clothing and in unsociable single file plowed our way to the horses, unsaddled them, and sought shelter in the station.

I have scarcely exaggerated a detail of this curious and absurd adventure. It occurred almost exactly as I have stated it. We actually went into camp in a snow-drift in a desert, at midnight in a storm, forlorn and hopeless, within fifteen steps of a comfortable inn.

For two hours we sat apart in the station and ruminated in dis-

CAMPING IN THE SNOW.

gust. The mystery was gone, now, and it was plain enough why the horses had deserted us. Without a doubt they were under that shed a quarter of a minute after they had left us, and they must have overheard and enjoyed all our confessions and lamentations.

After breakfast we felt better, and the zest of life soon came back. The world looked bright again, and existence was as dear to us as ever. Presently an uneasiness came over me—grew upon me—assailed me without ceasing. Alas, my regeneration was not complete—I wanted to smoke! I resisted with all my strength, but the flesh was weak. I wandered away alone and wrestled with myself an hour. I recalled my promises of reform and preached to myself persuasively, upbraidingly, exhaustively. But it was all vain, I shortly found myself sneaking among the snow-drifts hunting for my pipe. I discovered it after a considerable search, and crept away to hide myself and enjoy it. I remained behind the barn a good while, asking myself how I would feel if my braver, stronger, truer comrades should catch me in my degradation. At last I lit the pipe, and no human being can feel meaner and baser than I did then. I was ashamed of being in my own pitiful company. Still dreading discovery, I felt that perhaps the further side of the barn would be somewhat safer, and so I turned the corner. As I turned the one corner, smoking, Ollendorff turned the other with his bottle to his lips, and between us sat unconscious Ballou deep in a game of "solitaire" with the old greasy cards!

Absurdity could go no farther. We shook hands and agreed to say no more about "reform" and "examples to the rising generation."

The station we were at was at the verge of the Twenty-six-Mile Desert. If we had approached it half an hour earlier the night before, we must have heard men shouting there and firing pistols; for they were expecting some sheep drovers and their flocks and knew that they would infallibly get lost and wander out of reach of help unless guided by sounds. While we remained at the station, three of the drovers arrived, nearly exhausted with their wanderings, but two others of their party were never heard of afterward.

We reached Carson in due time, and took a rest. This rest, together with preparations for the journey to Esmeralda, kept us

IT WAS THUS WE MET.

there a week, and the delay gave us the opportunity to be present
at the trial of the great land-slide case of Hyde *vs.* Morgan—an episode which is famous in Nevada to this day. After a word or two of
necessary explanation, I will set down the history of this singular
affair just as it transpired.

CHAPTER 34

THE mountains are very high and steep about Carson, Eagle and Washoe Valleys—very high and very steep, and so when the snow gets to melting off fast in the spring and the warm surface-earth begins to moisten and soften, the disastrous land-slides commence. The reader cannot know what a land-slide is, unless he has lived in that country and seen the whole side of a mountain taken off some fine morning and deposited down in the valley, leaving a vast, treeless, unsightly scar upon the mountain's front to keep the circumstance fresh in his memory all the years that he may go on living within seventy miles of that place.

Gen. Buncombe was shipped out to Nevada in the invoice of Territorial officers, to be U. S. Attorney. He considered himself a lawyer of parts, and he very much wanted an opportunity to manifest it—partly for the pure gratification of it and partly because his salary was Territorially meagre (which is a strong expression.) Now the older citizens of a new territory look down upon the rest of the world with a calm, benevolent compassion, as long as it keeps out of the way—when it gets in the way they snub it. Sometimes this latter takes the shape of a practical joke.

One morning Dick Hyde rode furiously up to Gen. Buncombe's door in Carson City and rushed into his presence without stopping to tie his horse. He seemed much excited. He told the General that he wanted him to conduct a suit for him and would pay him five hundred dollars if he achieved a victory. And then, with violent gestures and a world of profanity, he poured out his griefs. He said it was pretty well known that for some years he had been farming (or ranching as the more customary term is,) in Washoe District, and making a successful thing of it, and furthermore it was known that his ranch was situated just in the edge of the valley, and that

Tom Morgan owned a ranch immediately above it on the mountain side. And now the trouble was that one of those hated and dreaded land-slides had come and slid Morgan's ranch, fences, cabins, cattle, barns and everything down on top of *his* ranch and

exactly covered up every single vestige of his property, to a depth of about thirty-eight feet. Morgan was in possession and refused to vacate the premises—said he was occupying his own cabin and not interfering with anybody else's— and said the cabin was standing on the same dirt and same ranch it had always stood on, and he would like to see anybody make him vacate.

TAKING POSSESSION.

"And when I reminded him," said Hyde, weeping, "that it was on top of my ranch and that he was trespassing, he had the infernal meanness to ask me why didn't I *stay* on my ranch and hold possession when I see him a coming! Why didn't I *stay* on it, the blathering lunatic—by George, when I heard that racket and looked up that hill it was just like the whole world was a ripping and a tearing down that mountain side—splinters, and cord-wood, thunder and lightning, hail and snow, odds and ends of hay stacks, and awful clouds of dust!—trees going end over end in the air, rocks as big as a house jumping 'bout a thousand feet high and busting into ten million pieces, cattle turned inside out and a coming head on with their tails hanging out between their teeth!—and in the midst of all that wrack and destruction sot that cussed Morgan on his gate-post, a wondering why I didn't *stay and hold possession!* Laws bless me, I just took one glimpse, General, and lit out'n the county in three jumps exactly.

"But what grinds me is that that Morgan hangs on there and won't move off'n that ranch—says it's his'n and he's going to keep it—likes it better'n he did when it was higher up the hill. Mad! Well, I've been so mad for two days I couldn't find my way to town—been wandering around in the brush in a starving condition—got anything here to drink, General? But I'm here *now*, and I'm a going to law. You hear *me!*"

Never in all the world, perhaps, were a man's feelings so outraged as were the General's. He said he had never heard of such high-handed conduct in all his life as this Morgan's. And he said there was no use in going to law—Morgan had no shadow of right to remain where he was—nobody in the wide world would uphold him in it, and no lawyer would take his case and no judge listen to it. Hyde said that right there was where he was mistaken—everybody in town sustained Morgan; Hal Brayton, a very smart lawyer, had taken his case; the courts being in vacation, it was to be tried before a referee, and ex-Governor Roop had already been appointed to that office and would open his court in a large public hall near the hotel at two that afternoon.

The General was amazed. He said he had suspected before that the people of that Territory were fools, and now he knew it. But he said rest easy, rest easy and collect the witnesses, for the victory was just as certain as if the conflict were already over. Hyde wiped away his tears and left.

At two in the afternoon referee Roop's court opened, and Roop appeared throned among his sheriffs, the witnesses, and spectators, and wearing upon his face a solemnity so awe-inspiring that some of his fellow-conspirators had misgivings that maybe he had not comprehended, after all, that this was merely a joke. An unearthly stillness prevailed, for at the slightest noise the judge uttered sternly the command:

"Order in the court!"

And the sheriffs promptly echoed it. Presently the General elbowed his way through the crowd of spectators, with his arms full of law-books, and on his ears fell an order from the judge which

was the first respectful recognition of his high official dignity that
had ever saluted them, and it trickled pleasantly through his whole
system:

"Way for the United States Attorney!"

The witnesses were called—legislators, high government officers, ranchmen, miners, Indians, Chinamen, negroes. Three-
fourths of them were called by the defendant Morgan, but no matter, their testimony invariably went in favor of the plaintiff Hyde.
Each new witness only added new testimony to the absurdity of a
man's claiming to own another man's property because his farm
had slid down on top of it. Then the Morgan lawyers made their
speeches, and seemed to make singularly weak ones—they did
really nothing to help the Morgan cause. And now the General,
with exultation in his face, got up and made an impassioned effort;

A GREAT EFFORT.

he pounded the table, he banged the law-books, he shouted, and
roared, and howled, he quoted from everything and everybody, poetry, sarcasm, statistics, history, pathos, bathos, blasphemy, and

wound up with a grand war-whoop for free speech, freedom of the press, free schools, the Glorious Bird of America and the principles of eternal justice! [Applause.]

When the General sat down, he did it with the conviction that if there was anything in good strong testimony, a great speech and believing and admiring countenances all around, Mr. Morgan's case was killed. Ex-Governor Roop leant his head upon his hand for some minutes, thinking, and the still audience waited for his decision. Then he got up and stood erect, with bended head, and thought again. Then he walked the floor with long, deliberate strides, his chin in his hand, and still the audience waited. At last he returned to his throne, seated himself, and began, impressively:

"Gentlemen, I feel the great responsibility that rests upon me this day. This is no ordinary case. On the contrary it is plain that it is the most solemn and awful that ever man was called upon to decide. Gentlemen, I have listened attentively to the evidence, and have perceived that the weight of it, the overwhelming weight of it, is in favor of the plaintiff Hyde. I have listened also to the remarks of counsel, with high interest—and especially will I commend the masterly and irrefutable logic of the distinguished gentleman who represents the plaintiff. But gentlemen, let us beware how we allow mere human testimony, human ingenuity in argument and human ideas of equity to influence us at a moment so solemn as this. Gentlemen, it ill becomes us, worms as we are, to meddle with the decrees of Heaven. It is plain to me that Heaven, in its inscrutable wisdom, has seen fit to move this defendant's ranch for a purpose. We are but creatures, and we must submit. If Heaven has chosen to favor the defendant Morgan in this marked and wonderful manner; and if Heaven, dissatisfied with the position of the Morgan ranch upon the mountain side, has chosen to remove it to a position more eligible and more advantageous for its owner, it ill becomes us, insects as we are, to question the legality of the act or inquire into the reasons that prompted it. No—Heaven created the ranches and it is Heaven's prerogative to reärrange them, to experiment with them, to shift them around at its pleasure. It is for us to submit, without repining. I warn you that

REÄRRANGING AND SHIFTING.

this thing which has happened is a thing with which the sacrilegious hands and brains and tongues of men must not meddle.
Gentlemen, it is the verdict of this court that the plaintiff, Richard
Hyde, has been deprived of his ranch by the visitation of God! And
from this decision there is no appeal."

Buncombe seized his cargo of law-books and plunged out of the
court room frantic with indignation. He pronounced Roop to be a
miraculous fool, an inspired idiot. In all good faith he returned at
night and remonstrated with Roop upon his extravagant decision,
and implored him to walk the floor and think for half an hour, and
see if he could not figure out some sort of modification of the verdict. Roop yielded at last and got up to walk. He walked two hours
and a half, and at last his face lit up happily and he told Buncombe
it had occurred to him that the ranch underneath the new Morgan
ranch still belonged to Hyde, that his title to the ground was just
as good as it had ever been, and therefore he was of opinion that
Hyde had a right to dig it out from under there and—

The General never waited to hear the end of it. He was always an impatient and irascible man, that way. At the end of two months the fact that he had been played upon with a joke had managed to bore itself, like another Hoosac Tunnel, through the solid adamant of his understanding.

CHAPTER 35

WHEN we finally left for Esmeralda, horseback, we had an addition to the company in the person of Capt. John Nye, the Governor's brother. He had a good memory, and a tongue hung in the middle. This is a combination which gives immortality to conversation. Capt. John never suffered the talk to flag or falter once during the hundred and twenty miles of the journey. In addition to his conversational powers, he had one or two other endowments of a marked character. One was a singular "handiness" about doing anything and everything, from laying out a railroad or organizing a political party, down to sewing on buttons, shoeing a horse, or setting a broken leg, or a hen. Another was a spirit of accommodation that prompted him to take the needs, difficulties and perplexities of anybody and everybody upon his own shoulders at any and all times, and dispose of them with admirable facility and alacrity—hence he always managed to find vacant beds in crowded inns, and plenty to eat in the emptiest larders. And finally, wherever he met a man, woman or child, in camp, inn or desert, he either knew such parties personally or had been acquainted with a relative of the same. Such another traveling comrade was never seen before. I cannot forbear giving a specimen of the way in which he overcame difficulties. On the second day out, we arrived, very tired and hungry, at a poor little inn in the desert, and were told that the house was full, no provisions on hand, and neither hay nor barley to spare for the horses—we must move on. The rest of us wanted to hurry on while it was yet light, but Capt. John insisted on stopping awhile. We dismounted and entered. There was no welcome for us on any face. Capt. John began his blandishments, and within twenty minutes he had accomplished the following things, viz.: found old acquaintances in three teamsters; discovered that he used to go to school with the landlord's mother; recognized his wife as a lady whose life he had saved once in California, by stopping her runaway horse; mended a child's broken toy and won the favor of its mother, a guest of the inn; helped the hostler bleed a horse, and prescribed for another horse that had the "heaves;" treated the entire party three times at the landlord's bar; produced a later paper than anybody had seen for a week and sat himself down to read the news to a deeply interested audience. The result, summed up, was as follows: The hostler found plenty of feed for our horses; we had a trout supper, an exceedingly sociable time after it, good beds to sleep in, and a surprising breakfast in the morning—and when we left, we left lamented by all! Capt. John had some bad traits, but he had some uncommonly valuable ones to offset them with.

WE LEFT LAMENTED.

Esmeralda was in many respects another Humboldt, but in a little more forward state. The claims we had been paying assessments on were entirely worthless, and we threw them away. The principal one cropped out of the top of a knoll that was fourteen feet high, and the inspired Board of Directors were running a tunnel under that knoll to strike the ledge. The tunnel would have to be seventy feet long, and would then strike the ledge at the same depth that a *shaft* twelve feet deep would have reached! The Board were living on the "assessments." [N. B.—This hint comes too late for the enlightenment of New York silver miners; they have already learned all about this neat trick by experience.] The Board had no desire to strike the ledge, knowing that it was as barren of silver as a curb-stone. This reminiscence calls to mind Jim Townsend's tunnel. He had paid assessments on a mine called the "Daley" till he was well-nigh penniless. Finally an assessment was levied to run a tunnel two hundred and fifty feet on the Daley, and Townsend went up on the hill to look into matters. He found the Daley cropping out of the apex of an exceedingly sharp-pointed peak, and a couple of men up there "facing" the proposed tunnel. Townsend made a calculation. Then he said to the men:

"So you have taken a contract to run a tunnel into this hill two hundred and fifty feet to strike this ledge?"

"Yes, sir."

"Well, do you know that you have got one of the most expensive and arduous undertakings before you that was ever conceived by man?"

"Why no—how is that?"

"Because this hill is only twenty-five feet through from side to side; and so you have got to build two hundred and twenty-five feet of your tunnel on trestle-work!"

The ways of silver mining Boards are exceedingly dark and sinuous.

PICTURE OF TOWNSEND'S TUNNEL.

We took up various claims, and *commenced* shafts and tunnels on them, but never finished any of them. We had to do a certain amount of work on each to "hold" it, else other parties could seize our property after the expiration of ten days. We were always hunting up new claims and doing a little work on them and then waiting for a buyer—who never came. We never found any ore that would yield more than fifty dollars a ton; and as the mills charged fifty dollars a ton for *working* ore and extracting the silver, our pocket-money melted steadily away and none returned to take its place. We lived in a little cabin and cooked for ourselves; and altogether it was a hard life, though a hopeful one—for we never ceased to expect fortune and a customer to burst upon us some day.

At last, when flour reached a dollar a pound, and money could not be borrowed on the best security at less than *eight per cent a month* (I being without the security, too), I abandoned mining and went to milling. That is to say, I went to work as a common laborer in a quartz mill, at ten dollars a week and board.

CHAPTER 36

I HAD already learned how hard and long and dismal a task it is to burrow down into the bowels of the earth and get out the coveted ore; and now I learned that the burrowing was only half the work; and that to get the silver out of the ore was the dreary and laborious other half of it. We had to turn out at six in the morning and keep at it till dark. This mill was a six-stamp affair, driven by steam. Six tall, upright rods of iron, as large as a man's ankle, and heavily shod

QUARTZ MILL IN NEVADA.

with a mass of iron and steel at their lower ends, were framed together like a gate, and these rose and fell, one after the other, in a ponderous dance, in an iron box called a "battery." Each of these rods or stamps weighed six hundred pounds. One of us stood by the battery all day long, breaking up masses of silver-bearing rock with a sledge and shoveling it into the battery. The ceaseless dance of the stamps pulverized the rock to powder, and a stream of water that trickled into the battery turned it to a creamy paste. The minutest particles were driven through a fine wire screen which fitted close around the battery, and were washed into great tubs warmed by super-heated steam—amalgamating pans, they are called. The mass of pulp in the pans was kept constantly stirred up by revolving "mullers." A quantity of quicksilver was kept always in the battery, and this seized some of the liberated gold and silver particles and held on to them; quicksilver was shaken in a fine shower into the pans, also, about every half hour, through a buckskin sack. Quantities of coarse salt and sulphate of copper were added, from time to time, to assist the amalgamation by destroying base metals which coated the gold and silver and would not let it unite with the quicksilver. All these tiresome things we had to attend to constantly. Streams of dirty water flowed always from the pans and were carried off in broad wooden troughs to the ravine. One would not suppose that atoms of gold and silver would float on top of six inches of water, but they did; and in order to catch them, coarse blankets were laid in the troughs, and little obstructing "riffles" charged with quicksilver were placed here and there across the troughs also. These riffles had to be cleaned and the blankets washed out every evening, to get their precious accumulations—and after all this eternity of trouble one-third of the silver and gold in a ton of rock would find its way to the end of the troughs in the ravine at last and have to be worked over again some day. There is nothing so aggravating as silver milling. There never was any idle time in that mill. There was always something to do. It is a pity that Adam could not have gone straight out of Eden into a quartz mill, in order to understand the full force of his doom to "earn his bread by the sweat of his brow." Every now and then, during the day, we had to scoop some pulp out of the pans, and tediously "wash" it in a horn spoon—wash it little by little over the edge till at last nothing was left but some little dull globules of quicksilver in the bottom. If they were soft and yielding, the pan needed some salt or some sulphate of copper or some other chemical rubbish to assist digestion; if they were crisp to the touch and would retain a dint, they were freighted with all the silver and gold they could seize and hold, and consequently the pans needed a fresh charge of quicksilver. When there was nothing else to do, one could always "screen tailings." That is to say, he could shovel up the dried sand that had washed down to the ravine through the troughs and dash it against an upright wire screen to free it from

ANOTHER PROCESS OF AMALGAMATION.

pebbles and prepare it for working over. The process of amalgamation differed in the various mills, and this included changes in style of pans and other machinery, and a great diversity of opinion existed as to the best in use, but none of the methods employed, involved the principle of milling ore without "screening the tailings." Of all recreations in the world, screening tailings on a hot day, with a long-handled shovel, is the most undesirable.

At the end of the week the machinery was stopped and we "cleaned up." That is to say, we got the pulp out of the pans and batteries, and washed the mud patiently away till nothing was left but the long accumulating mass of quicksilver, with its imprisoned treasures. This we made into heavy, compact snow-balls, and piled them up in a bright, luxurious heap for inspection. Making these snow-balls cost me a fine gold ring—that and ignorance together; for the quicksilver invaded the ring with the same facility with which water saturates a sponge—separated its particles and the ring crumbled to pieces.

We put our pile of quicksilver balls into an iron retort that had a pipe leading from it to a pail of water, and then applied a roasting heat. The quicksilver turned to vapor, escaped through the pipe into the pail, and the water turned it into good wholesome quicksilver again. Quicksilver is very costly, and they never waste it. On opening the retort, there was our week's work—a lump of pure white, frosty looking silver, twice as large as a man's head. Perhaps a fifth of the mass was gold, but the color of it did not show— would not have shown if two-thirds of it had been gold. We melted it up and made a solid brick of it by pouring it into an iron brick-mould.

By such a tedious and laborious process were silver bricks obtained. This mill was but one of many others in operation at the time. The first one in Nevada was built at Egan Cañon and was a

FIRST QUARTZ MILL IN NEVADA.

small insignificant affair and compared most unfavorably with some of the immense establishments afterward located at Virginia City and elsewhere.

From our bricks a little corner was chipped off for the "fire-assay"—a method used to determine the proportions of gold, silver and base metals in the mass. This is an interesting process. The chip is hammered out as thin as paper and weighed on scales so fine and sensitive that if you weigh a two-inch scrap of paper on them and then write your name on the paper with a coarse, soft pencil and weigh it again, the scales will take marked notice of the addition. Then a little lead (also weighed) is rolled up with the flake of silver and the two are melted at a great heat in a small vessel called a cupel, made by compressing bone ashes into a cup-shape in a steel mould. The base metals oxydize and are absorbed with the lead into the pores of the cupel. A button or globule of perfectly pure gold and silver is left behind, and by weighing it and noting the loss, the assayer knows the proportion of base metal the brick contains. He has to separate the gold from the silver now. The button is hammered out flat and thin, put in the furnace and kept some time at a red heat; after cooling it off it is rolled up like a quill and heated in a glass vessel containing nitric acid; the acid dissolves the silver and leaves the gold pure and ready to be weighed on its own merits. Then salt water is poured into the vessel containing the dissolved silver and the silver returns to palpable form again and sinks to the bottom. Nothing now remains but to weigh it; then the proportions of the several metals contained in the brick are known, and the assayer stamps the value of the brick upon its surface.

The sagacious reader will know now, without being told, that the speculative miner, in getting a "fire-assay" made of a piece of rock from his mine (to help him sell the same), was not in the habit of picking out the least valuable fragment of rock on his dump-pile, but quite the contrary. I have seen men hunt over a pile of nearly worthless quartz for an hour, and at last find a little piece as large as a filbert, which was rich in gold and silver—and this was reserved for a fire-assay! Of course the fire-assay would demonstrate that a ton of such rock would yield hundreds of dollars—and on such assays many an utterly worthless mine was sold.

Assaying was a good business, and so some men engaged in it, occasionally, who were not strictly scientific and capable. One assayer got such rich results out of all specimens brought to him that in time he acquired almost a monopoly of the business. But like all men who achieve success, he became an object of envy and suspicion. The other assayers entered into a conspiracy against him, and let some prominent citizens into the secret in order to show that they meant fairly. Then they broke a little fragment off a carpenter's grindstone and got a stranger to take it to the popular scientist and get it assayed. In the course of an hour the result came—whereby it appeared that a ton of that rock would yield $1,284.40 in silver and $366.36 in gold!

Due publication of the whole matter was made in the paper, and the popular assayer left town "between two days."

I will remark, in passing, that I only remained in the milling business one week. I told my employer I could not stay longer without an advance in my wages; that I liked quartz milling, indeed was infatuated

A SLICE OF RICH ORE.

with it; that I had never before grown so tenderly attached to an occupation in so short a time; that nothing, it seemed to me, gave such scope to intellectual activity as feeding a battery and screening tailings, and nothing so stimulated the moral attributes as retorting bullion and washing blankets—still, I felt constrained to ask an increase of salary.

He said he was paying me ten dollars a week, and thought it a good round sum. How much did I want?

I said about four hundred thousand dollars a month, and board, was about all I could reasonably ask, considering the hard times.

I was ordered off the premises! And yet, when I look back to those days and call to mind the exceeding hardness of the labor I performed in that mill, I only regret that I did not ask him seven hundred thousand.

Shortly after this I began to grow crazy, along with the rest of the population, about the mysterious and wonderful "cement mine," and to make preparations to take advantage of any opportunity that might offer to go and help hunt for it.

CHAPTER 37

It was somewhere in the neighborhood of Mono Lake that the marvelous Whiteman cement mine was supposed to lie. Every now and then it would be reported that Mr. W. had passed stealthily through Esmeralda at dead of night, in disguise, and then we would have a wild excitement—because he must be steering for his secret mine, and now was the time to follow him. In less than three hours after daylight all the horses and mules and donkeys in the vicinity would be bought, hired or stolen, and half the community would be off for the mountains, following in the wake of Whiteman. But W. would drift about through the mountain gorges for days together, in a purposeless sort of way, until the provisions of the miners ran out, and they would have to go back home. I have known it reported at eleven at night, in a large mining camp, that Whiteman had just passed through, and in two hours, the streets, so quiet before, would be swarming with men and animals. Every individual would be trying to be very secret, but yet venturing to whisper to just one neighbor that W. had passed through. And long before daylight—this in the dead of winter—the stampede would be complete, the camp deserted, and the whole population gone chasing after W.

The tradition was that in the early immigration, more than twenty years ago, three young Germans, brothers, who had survived an Indian massacre on the Plains, wandered on foot through the deserts, avoiding all trails and roads, and simply holding a westerly direction and hoping to find California before they starved or died of fatigue. And in a gorge in the mountains they sat down to rest one day, when one of them noticed a curious vein of cement running along the ground, shot full of lumps of dull yellow metal. They saw that it was gold, and that here was a fortune to be acquired in a single day. The vein was about as wide as a curb-stone, and fully two-thirds of it was pure gold. Every pound of the wonderful cement was worth well-nigh two hundred dollars. Each of the brothers loaded himself with about twenty-five pounds of it, and then they covered up all traces of the vein, made a rude drawing of the locality and the principal landmarks in the vicinity, and started westward again. But troubles thickened about them. In their wanderings one brother fell and broke his leg, and the others were obliged to go on and leave him to die in the wilderness. Another, worn out and starving, gave up by and by, and lay down to die, but after two or three weeks of incredible hardships, the third reached the settlements of California exhausted, sick, and his mind deranged by his sufferings. He had thrown away all his cement but a few fragments, but these were sufficient to set everybody wild with excitement. However, he had had enough of the cement country, and nothing could induce him to lead a party thither. He was entirely content to work on a farm for wages. But he gave Whiteman his map, and described the cement region as well as he could, and thus transferred the curse to that gentleman—for when I had my one accidental glimpse of Mr. W. in Esmeralda, he had been hunting for the lost mine, in hunger and thirst,

THE SAVED BROTHER.

poverty and sickness, for twelve or thirteen years. Some people believed he had found it, but most people believed he had not. I saw a piece of cement as large as my fist which was said to have been given to Whiteman by the young German, and it was of a seductive nature. Lumps of virgin gold were as thick in it as raisins in a slice of fruit cake. The privilege of working such a mine one week would be sufficient for a man of reasonable desires.

A new partner of ours, a Mr. Higbie, knew Whiteman well by sight, and a friend of ours, a Mr. Van Dorn, was well acquainted with him, and not only that, but had Whiteman's promise that he should have a private hint in time to enable him to join the next cement expedition. Van Dorn had promised to extend the hint to us. One evening Higbie came in greatly excited, and said he felt certain he had recognized Whiteman, up town, disguised and in a pretended state of intoxication. In a little while Van Dorn arrived and confirmed the news; and so we gathered in our cabin and with heads close together arranged our plans in impressive whispers.

We were to leave town quietly, after midnight, in two or three small parties, so as not to attract attention, and meet at dawn on the "divide" overlooking Mono Lake, eight or nine miles distant. We were to make no noise after starting, and not speak above a whisper under any circumstances. It was believed that for once Whiteman's presence was unknown in the town and his expedition unsuspected. Our conclave broke up at nine o'clock, and we set about our preparations diligently and with profound secrecy. At eleven o'clock we saddled our horses, hitched them with their long *riatas* (or lassos), and then brought out a side of bacon, a sack of beans, a small sack of coffee, some sugar, a hundred pounds of flour in sacks, some tin cups and a coffee-pot, frying pan and some few other necessary articles. All these things were "packed" on the back of a led horse—and whoever has not been taught, by a Spanish adept, to pack an animal, let him never hope to do the thing by natural smartness. That is impossible. Higbie had had some experience, but was not perfect. He put on the pack saddle (a thing like a saw-buck), piled the property on it and then wound a rope all over and about it and under it, "every which way," taking a hitch in it every now and then, and occasionally surging back on it till the horse's sides sunk in and he gasped for breath—but every time the lashings grew tight in one place they loosened in another. We never did get the load tight all over, but we got it so that it would do, after a fashion, and then we started, in single file, close order, and without a word. It was a dark night. We kept the middle of the road, and proceeded in a slow walk past the rows of cabins, and whenever a miner came to his door I trembled for fear the light would shine on us and excite curiosity. But nothing happened. We began the long winding ascent of the cañon, toward the "divide," and presently the cabins began to grow infrequent, and the intervals between them wider and wider, and then I began to breathe tolerably freely and feel less like a thief and a murderer. I was in the rear, leading the pack horse. As the ascent grew steeper he grew proportionately less satisfied with his cargo, and began to pull back on his *riata* occasionally and delay progress. My comrades were passing out of sight in the gloom. I was getting anxious. I coaxed and bullied the pack horse till I presently got him into a trot, and then the tin cups and pans strung about his person frightened him and he ran. His *riata* was wound around the pommel of my saddle, and so, as he went by he dragged me from my horse and the two animals traveled briskly on without me. But I was not alone—the loosened cargo tumbled overboard from the pack horse and fell close to me. It was abreast of almost the last cabin. A miner came out and said:

"Hello!"

I was thirty steps from him, and knew he could not see me, it was so very dark in the shadow of the mountain. So I lay still. Another head appeared in the light of the cabin door, and presently the two men walked toward me. They stopped within ten steps of me, and one said:

" 'St! Listen."

I could not have been in a more distressed state if I had been escaping justice with a price on my head. Then the miners appeared to sit down on a boulder, though I could not see them distinctly enough to be very sure what they did. One said:

"I heard a noise, as plain as I ever heard anything. It seemed to be about there—"

A stone whizzed by my head. I flattened myself out in the dust like a postage stamp, and thought to myself if he mended his aim ever so little he would probably hear another noise. In my heart, now, I execrated secret expeditions. I promised myself that this

ON A SECRET EXPEDITION.

should be my last, though the Sierras were ribbed with cement veins. Then one of the men said:

"I'll tell you what! Welch knew what he was talking about when he said he saw Whiteman to-day. I heard horses—that was the noise. I am going down to Welch's, right away."

They left and I was glad. I did not care whither they went, so they went. I was willing they should visit Welch, and the sooner the better.

As soon as they closed their cabin door my comrades emerged from the gloom; they had caught the horses and were waiting for a clear coast again. We remounted the cargo on the pack horse and got under way, and as day broke we reached the "divide" and joined Van Dorn. Then we journeyed down into the valley of the lake, and feeling secure, we halted to cook breakfast, for we were tired and sleepy and hungry. Three hours later the rest of the population filed over the "divide" in a long procession, and drifted off out of sight around the borders of the lake!

Whether or not my accident had produced this result we never knew, but at least one thing was certain—the secret was out and Whiteman would not enter upon a search for the cement mine this time. We were filled with chagrin.

We held a council and decided to make the best of our misfortune and enjoy a week's holiday on the borders of the curious lake. Mono, it is sometimes called, and sometimes the "Dead Sea of California." It is one of the strangest freaks of Nature to be found in any land, but it is hardly ever mentioned in print and very seldom visited, because it lies away off the usual routes of travel and besides is so difficult to get at that only men content to endure the roughest life will consent to take upon themselves the discomforts of such a trip. On the morning of our second day, we traveled around to a remote and particularly wild spot on the borders of the lake, where a stream of fresh, ice-cold water entered it from the mountain side, and then we went regularly into camp. We hired a large boat and two shotguns from a lonely ranchman who lived some ten miles further on, and made ready for comfort and recreation. We soon got thoroughly acquainted with the lake and all its peculiarities.

MONO LAKE.

CHAPTER 38

Mono Lake lies in a lifeless, treeless, hideous desert, eight thousand feet above the level of the sea, and is guarded by mountains two thousand feet higher, whose summits are always clothed in clouds. This solemn, silent, sailless sea—this lonely tenant of the loneliest spot on earth—is little graced with the picturesque. It is an unpretending expanse of grayish water, about a hundred miles in circumference, with two islands in its centre, mere upheavals of rent and scorched and blistered lava, snowed over with gray banks and drifts of pumice stone and ashes, the winding sheet of the dead volcano, whose vast crater the lake has seized upon and occupied.

The lake is two hundred feet deep, and its sluggish waters are so strong with alkali that if you only dip the most hopelessly soiled garment into them once or twice, and wring it out, it will be found as clean as if it had been through the ablest of washerwomen's hands. While we camped there our laundry work was easy. We tied the week's washing astern of our boat, and sailed a quarter of a mile, and the job was complete, all to the wringing out. If we threw the water on our heads and gave them a rub or so, the white lather would pile up three inches high. This water is not good for bruised places and abrasions of the skin. We had a valuable dog. He had raw places on him. He had more raw places on him than sound ones. He was the rawest dog I almost ever saw. He jumped overboard one day to get away from the flies. But it was bad judgment. In his condition, it would have been just as comfortable to jump into the fire. The alkali water nipped him in all the raw places simultaneously, and he struck out for the shore with considerable interest. He yelped and barked and howled as he went—and by the time he got to the shore there was no bark to him—for he had barked the bark all out of his inside, and the alkali water had cleaned the bark all

RATHER SOAPY.

off his outside, and he probably wished he had never embarked in any such enterprise. He ran round and round in a circle, and pawed the earth and clawed the air, and threw double summersets, some-

A BARK UNDER FULL SAIL.

times backwards and sometimes forwards, in the most extraordinary manner. He was not a demonstrative dog, as a general thing, but rather of a grave and serious turn of mind, and I never saw him take so much interest in anything before. He finally struck out over the mountains, at a gait which we estimated at about two hundred and fifty miles an hour, and he is going yet. This was about nine years ago. We look for what is left of him along here every day.

A white man cannot drink the water of Mono Lake, for it is nearly pure lye. It is said that the Indians in the vicinity drink it sometimes, though. It is not improbable, for they are among the purest liars I ever saw. [There will be no additional charge for this joke, except to parties requiring an explanation of it. This joke has received high commendation from some of the ablest minds of the age.]

There are no fish in Mono Lake—no frogs, no snakes, no polly-wogs—nothing, in fact, that goes to make life desirable. Millions of wild ducks and sea-gulls swim about the surface, but no living thing exists *under* the surface, except a white feathery sort of worm, one-half an inch long, which looks like a bit of white thread frayed out at the sides. If you dip up a gallon of water, you will get about fifteen thousand of these. They give to the water a sort of grayish-white appearance. Then there is a fly, which looks some-thing like our house fly. These settle on the beach to eat the worms that wash ashore—and any time, you can see there a belt of flies an inch deep and six feet wide, and this belt extends clear around the lake—a belt of flies one hundred miles long. If you throw a stone among them, they swarm up so thick that they look dense, like a cloud. You can hold them under water as long as you please—they do not mind it—they are only proud of it. When you let them go, they pop up to the surface as dry as a patent office report, and walk off as unconcernedly as if they had been educated especially with a view to affording instructive entertainment to man in that par-ticular way. Providence leaves nothing to go by chance. All things have their uses and their part and proper place in Nature's econ-omy: the ducks eat the flies—the flies eat the worms—the Indians eat all three—the wild-cats eat the Indians—the white folks eat the wild-cats—and thus all things are lovely.

Mono Lake is a hundred and fifty miles in a straight line from the ocean—and between it and the ocean are one or two ranges of mountains—yet thousands of sea-gulls go there every season to lay their eggs and rear their young. One would as soon expect to find sea-gulls in Kansas. And in this connection let us observe another instance of Nature's wisdom. The islands in the lake being merely huge masses of lava, coated over with ashes and pumice stone, and utterly innocent of vegetation or anything that would burn; and sea-gulls' eggs being entirely useless to anybody unless they be cooked, Nature has provided an unfailing spring of boiling water on the largest island, and you can put your eggs in there, and in four minutes you can boil them as hard as any statement I have made during the past fifteen years. Within ten feet of the boiling spring is a spring of pure cold water, sweet and wholesome. So, in that island you get your board and washing free of charge—and if nature had gone further and furnished a nice American hotel clerk who was crusty and disobliging, and didn't know anything about the time tables, or the railroad routes—or—anything—and was proud of it—I would not wish for a more desirable boarding house.

A MODEL BOARDING HOUSE.

Half a dozen little mountain brooks flow into Mono Lake, but *not a stream of any kind flows out of it.* It neither rises nor falls, apparently, and what it does with its surplus water is a dark and bloody mystery.

There are only two seasons in the region round about Mono Lake—and these are, the breaking up of one winter and the beginning of the next. More than once (in Esmeralda) I have seen a perfectly blistering morning open up with the thermometer at ninety degrees at eight o'clock, and seen the snow fall fourteen inches deep and that same identical thermometer go down to forty-four degrees under shelter, before nine o'clock at night. Under favorable circumstances it snows at least once in every single month in the year, in the little town of Mono. So uncertain is the climate in summer that a lady who goes out visiting cannot hope to be prepared for all emergencies unless she takes her fan under one arm and her snow shoes under the other. When they have a Fourth of July procession it generally snows on them, and they do say that as a general thing when a man calls for a brandy toddy there, the barkeeper chops it off with a hatchet and wraps it up in a paper, like maple sugar. And it is further reported that the old soakers haven't any teeth—wore them out eating gin cocktails and brandy punches. I do not endorse that statement—I simply give it for what it is worth—and it is worth—well, I should say, millions, to any man who can believe it without straining himself. But I do endorse the snow on the Fourth of July—because I know that to be true.

CHAPTER 39

ABOUT seven o'clock one blistering hot morning—for it was now dead summer time—Higbie and I took the boat and started on a voyage of discovery to the two islands. We had often longed to do this, but had been deterred by the fear of storms; for they were frequent, and severe enough to capsize an ordinary row-boat like ours without great difficulty—and once capsized, death would ensue in spite of the bravest swimming, for that venomous water would eat a man's eyes out like fire, and burn him out inside, too, if he shipped a sea. It was called twelve miles, straight out to the islands—a long pull and a warm one—but the morning was so quiet and sunny, and the lake so smooth and glassy and dead, that we could not resist the temptation. So we filled two large tin canteens with water (since we were not acquainted with the locality of the spring said to exist on the large island), and started. Higbie's brawny muscles gave the boat good speed, but by the time we reached our destination we judged that we had pulled nearer fifteen miles than twelve.

We landed on the big island and went ashore. We tried the water in the canteens, now, and found that the sun had spoiled it; it was so brackish that we could not drink it; so we poured it out and began a search for the spring—for thirst augments fast as soon as it is apparent that one has no means at hand of quenching it. The island was a long, moderately high hill of ashes—nothing but gray ashes and pumice stone, in which we sunk to our knees at every step—and all around the top was a forbidding wall of scorched and blasted rocks. When we reached the top and got within the wall, we found simply a shallow, far-reaching basin, carpeted with ashes, and here and there a patch of fine sand. In places, picturesque jets of steam shot up out of crevices, giving evidence that although this ancient crater had gone out of active business, there was still some fire left in its furnaces. Close to one of these jets of steam stood the

LIFE AMID DEATH.

only tree on the island—a small pine of most graceful shape and most faultless symmetry; its color was a brilliant green, for the steam drifted unceasingly through its branches and kept them always moist. It contrasted strangely enough, did this vigorous and beautiful outcast, with its dead and dismal surroundings. It was like a cheerful spirit in a mourning household.

We hunted for the spring everywhere, traversing the full length of the island (two or three miles), and crossing it twice—climbing ash-hills patiently, and then sliding down the other side in a sitting posture, plowing up smothering volumes of gray dust. But we found nothing but solitude, ashes and a heart-breaking silence. Finally we noticed that the wind had risen, and we forgot our thirst in a solicitude of greater importance; for, the lake being quiet, we had not taken pains about securing the boat. We hurried back to a point overlooking our landing place, and then—but mere words cannot describe our dismay—the boat was gone! The chances were that there was not another boat on the entire lake. The situation

was not comfortable—in truth, to speak plainly, it was frightful.
We were prisoners on a desolate island, in aggravating proximity
to friends who were for the present helpless to aid us; and what was
still more uncomfortable was the reflection that we had neither
food nor water. But presently we sighted the boat. It was drifting
along, leisurely, about fifty yards from shore, tossing in a foamy
sea. It drifted, and continued to drift, but at the same safe distance
from land, and we walked along abreast it and waited for fortune to
favor us. At the end of an hour it approached a jutting cape, and
Higbie ran ahead and posted himself on the utmost verge and prepared for the assault. If we failed there, there was no hope for us. It
was driving gradually shoreward all the time, now; but whether it
was driving fast enough to make the connection or not was the momentous question. When it got within thirty steps of Higbie I was
so excited that I fancied I could hear my own heart beat. When, a
little later, it dragged slowly along and seemed about to go by, only
one little yard out of reach, it seemed as if my heart stood still; and
when it was exactly abreast him and began to widen away, and he
still standing like a watching statue, I knew my heart did stop. But

A JUMP FOR LIFE.

when he gave a great spring, the next instant, and lit fairly in the
stern, I discharged a war-whoop that woke the solitudes!

But it dulled my enthusiasm, presently, when he told me he had not been caring whether the boat came within jumping distance or not, so that it passed within eight or ten yards of him, for he had made up his mind to shut his eyes and mouth and swim that trifling distance. Imbecile that I was, I had not thought of that. It was only a long swim that could be fatal.

The sea was running high and the storm increasing. It was growing late, too—three or four in the afternoon. Whether to venture toward the mainland or not, was a question of some moment. But we were so distressed by thirst that we decided to try it, and so Higbie fell to work and I took the steering-oar. When we had pulled a mile, laboriously, we were evidently in serious peril, for the storm had greatly augmented; the billows ran very high and were capped with foaming crests, the heavens were hung with black, and the wind blew with great fury. We would have gone back, now, but we did not dare to turn the boat around, because as soon as she got in the trough of the sea she would upset, of course. Our only hope lay in keeping her head on to the seas. It was hard work to do this, she plunged so, and so beat and belabored the billows with her rising and falling bows. Now and then one of Higbie's oars would trip on the top of a wave, and the other one would snatch the boat half around in spite of my cumbersome steering apparatus. We were drenched by the sprays constantly, and the boat occasionally shipped water. By and by, powerful as my comrade was, his great exertions began to tell on him, and he was anxious that I should change places with him till he could rest a little. But I told him this was impossible; for if the steering-oar were dropped a moment while we changed, the boat would slue around into the trough of the sea, capsize, and in less than five minutes we would have a hundred gallons of soap-suds in us and be eaten up so quickly that we could not even be present at our own inquest.

But things cannot last always. Just as the darkness shut down we came booming into port, head on. Higbie dropped his oars to hurrah—I dropped mine to help—the sea gave the boat a twist, and over she went!

The agony that alkali water inflicts on bruises, chafes and blistered hands, is unspeakable, and nothing but greasing all over will modify it—but we ate, drank and slept well, that night, notwithstanding.

In speaking of the peculiarities of Mono Lake, I ought to have mentioned that at intervals all around its shores stand picturesque turret-looking masses and clusters of a whitish, coarse-grained rock that resembles inferior mortar dried hard; and if one breaks off fragments of this rock he will find perfectly shaped and thoroughly petrified gulls' eggs deeply imbedded in the mass. How did they get there? I simply state the fact—for it is a fact—and leave the geological reader to crack the nut at his leisure and solve the problem after his own fashion.

At the end of a week we adjourned to the Sierras on a fishing excursion, and spent several days in camp under snowy Castle Peak, and fished successfully for trout in a bright, miniature lake whose surface was between ten and eleven thousand feet above the level of the sea; cooling ourselves during the hot August noons by sitting on snow banks ten feet deep, under whose sheltering edges *fine grass and dainty flowers flourished luxuriously;* and at night entertaining ourselves by almost freezing to death. Then we returned to Mono Lake, and finding that the cement excitement was over for the present, packed up and went back to Esmeralda. Mr. Ballou reconnoitred awhile, and not liking the prospect, set out alone for Humboldt.

About this time occurred a little incident which has always had a sort of interest to me, from the fact that it came so near "instigating" my funeral. At a time when an Indian attack had been expected, the citizens hid their gunpowder where it would be safe and yet convenient to hand when wanted. A neighbor of ours hid six cans of rifle powder in the bake-oven of an old discarded cooking stove which stood on the open ground near a frame out-house or shed, and from and after that day never thought of it again. We hired a half-tamed Indian to do some washing for us, and he took up quarters under the shed with his tub. The ancient stove reposed within six feet of him, and before his face. Finally it occurred to him that hot water would be better than cold, and he went out and fired up under that forgotten powder magazine and set on a kettle of water. Then he returned to his tub. I entered the shed presently and threw down some more clothes, and was about to speak to him when the stove blew up with a prodigious crash, and disappeared, leaving not a splinter behind. Fragments of it fell in the streets full two hundred yards away. Nearly a third of the shed roof over our heads was destroyed, and one of the stove lids, after cutting a small stanchion half in two in front of the Indian, whizzed between us and drove partly through the weather-boarding beyond. I was as white as a sheet and as weak as a kitten and speechless. But the Indian betrayed no trepidation, no distress, not even discomfort. He simply stopped washing, leaned forward and surveyed the clean, blank ground a moment, and then remarked:

"STOVE HEAP GONE!"

"Mph! Dam stove heap gone!"—and resumed his scrubbing as placidly as if it were an entirely customary thing for a stove to do. I will explain, that "heap" is "Injun-English" for "very much." The reader will perceive the exhaustive expressiveness of it in the present instance.

CHAPTER 40

I NOW come to a curious episode—the most curious, I think, that had yet accented my slothful, valueless, heedless career. Out of a hillside toward the upper end of the town, projected a wall of reddish looking quartz-croppings, the exposed comb of a silver-bearing ledge that extended deep down into the earth, of course. It was owned by a company entitled the "Wide West." There was a shaft sixty or seventy feet deep on the under side of the croppings, and everybody was acquainted with the rock that came from it— and tolerably rich rock it was, too, but nothing extraordinary. I will remark here, that although to the inexperienced stranger all the quartz of a particular "district" looks about alike, an old resident of the camp can take a glance at a mixed pile of rock, separate the fragments and tell you which mine each came from, as easily as a confectioner can separate and classify the various kinds and qualities of candy in a mixed heap of the article.

All at once the town was thrown into a state of extraordinary excitement. In mining parlance the Wide West had "struck it rich!" Everybody went to see the new developments, and for some days there was such a crowd of people about the Wide West shaft that a stranger would have supposed there was a mass meeting in session there. No other topic was discussed but the rich strike, and nobody thought or dreamed about anything else. Every man brought away a specimen, ground it up in a hand mortar, washed it out in his horn spoon, and glared speechless upon the marvelous result. It was not hard rock, but black, decomposed stuff which could be crumbled in the hand like a baked potato, and when spread out on a paper exhibited a thick sprinkling of gold and particles of "native" silver. Higbie brought a handful to the cabin, and when he had washed it out his amazement was beyond description. Wide

West stock soared skywards. It was said that repeated offers had been made for it at a thousand dollars a foot, and promptly refused. We have all had the "blues"—the mere sky-blues—but mine were indigo, now—because I did not own in the Wide West. The world seemed hollow to me, and existence a grief. I lost my appetite, and ceased to take an interest in anything. Still I had to stay, and listen to other people's rejoicings, because I had no money to get out of the camp with.

The Wide West company put a stop to the carrying away of "specimens," and well they might, for every handful of the ore was worth a sum of some consequence. To show the exceeding value of the ore, I will remark that a sixteen-hundred-pound parcel of it was sold, just as it lay, at the mouth of the shaft, at *one dollar a pound;* and the man who bought it "packed" it on mules a hundred and fifty or two hundred miles, over the mountains, to San Francisco, satisfied that it would yield at a rate that would richly compensate him for his trouble. The Wide West people also commanded their foreman to refuse any but their own operatives permission to enter the mine at any time or for any purpose. I kept up my "blue" meditations and Higbie kept up a deal of thinking, too, but of a different sort. He puzzled over the "rock," examined it with a glass, inspected it in different lights and from different points of view, and after each experiment delivered himself, in soliloquy, of one and the same unvarying opinion in the same unvarying formula:

"It is *not* Wide West rock!"

He said once or twice that he meant to have a look into the Wide West shaft if he got shot for it. I was wretched, and did not care whether he got a look into it or not. He failed that day, and tried again at night; failed again; got up at dawn and tried, and failed again. Then he lay in ambush in the sage-brush hour after hour, waiting for the two or three hands to adjourn to the shade of a boulder for dinner; made a start once, but was premature—one of the men came back for something; tried it again, but when almost at the mouth of the shaft, another of the men rose up from behind the boulder as if to reconnoitre, and he dropped on the ground and lay quiet; presently he crawled on his hands and knees to the mouth of the shaft, gave a quick glance around, then seized the rope and slid down the shaft. He disappeared in the gloom of a "side drift" just as a head appeared in the mouth of the shaft and somebody shouted "Hello!"—which he did not answer. He was not disturbed any

more. An hour later he entered the cabin, hot, red, and ready to burst with smothered excitement, and exclaimed in a stage whisper:

"I knew it! We are rich! IT'S A BLIND LEAD!"

I thought the very earth reeled under me. Doubt— conviction—doubt again— exultation—hope, amazement, belief, unbelief— every emotion imaginable swept in wild procession through my heart and brain, and I could not speak a word. After a moment or two of this mental fury, I shook myself to rights, and said:

"Say it again!"

"It's a blind lead!"

"Cal., let's—let's burn the house—or kill somebody! Let's

INTERVIEWING THE "WIDE WEST."

get out where there's room to hurrah! But what is the use? It is a hundred times too good to be true."

"It's a blind lead, for a million!—hanging wall—foot wall—clay casings—everything complete!" He swung his hat and gave three cheers, and I cast doubt to the winds and chimed in with a will. For I was worth a million dollars, and did not care "whether school kept or not!"

But perhaps I ought to explain. A "blind lead" is a lead or ledge that does not "crop out" above the surface. A miner does not know where to look for such leads, but they are often stumbled upon by accident in the course of driving a tunnel or sinking a shaft. Higbie

knew the Wide West rock perfectly well, and the more he had examined the new developments the more he was satisfied that the

WORTH A MILLION.

ore could not have come from the Wide West vein. And so had it
occurred to him alone, of all the camp, that there was a blind lead
down in the shaft, and that even the Wide West people themselves
did not suspect it. He was right. When he went down the shaft, he
found that the blind lead held its independent way through the
Wide West vein, cutting it diagonally, and that it was enclosed in
its own well-defined casing-rocks and clay. Hence it was public
property. Both leads being perfectly well defined, it was easy for
any miner to see which one belonged to the Wide West and which
did not.

We thought it well to have a strong friend, and therefore we
brought the foreman of the Wide West to our cabin that night and
revealed the great surprise to him. Higbie said:

"We are going to take possession of this blind lead, record it and establish ownership, and then forbid the Wide West company to take out any more of the rock. You cannot help your company in this matter—nobody can help them. I will go into the shaft with you and prove to your entire satisfaction that it *is* a blind lead. Now we propose to take you in with us, and claim the blind lead in our three names. What do you say?"

What could a man say who had an opportunity to simply stretch forth his hand and take possession of a fortune without risk of any kind and without wronging any one or attaching the least taint of dishonor to his name? He could only say, "Agreed."

The notice was put up that night, and duly spread upon the recorder's books before ten o'clock. We claimed two hundred feet each—six hundred feet in all—the smallest and compactest organization in the district, and the easiest to manage.

No one can be so thoughtless as to suppose that we slept, that night. Higbie and I went to bed at midnight, but it was only to lie broad awake and think, dream, scheme. The floorless, tumbledown cabin was a palace, the ragged gray blankets silk, the furni-

MILLIONAIRES LAYING PLANS.

ture rosewood and mahogany. Each new splendor that burst out of my visions of the future whirled me bodily over in bed or jerked me to a sitting posture just as if an electric battery had been applied to me. We shot fragments of conversation back and forth at each other. Once Higbie said:

"When are you going home—to the States?"

"To-morrow!"—with an evolution or two, ending with a sitting position. "Well—no—but next month, at furthest."

"We'll go in the same steamer."

"Agreed."

A pause.

"Steamer of the 10th?"

"Yes. No, the 1st."

"All right."

Another pause.

"Where are you going to live?" said Higbie.

"San Francisco."

"That's me!"

Pause.

"Too high—too much climbing"—from Higbie.

"What is?"

"I was thinking of Russian Hill—building a house up there."

"Too much climbing? Shan't you keep a carriage?"

"Of course. I forgot that."

Pause.

"Cal., what kind of a house are you going to build?"

"I was thinking about that. Three-story and an attic."

"But what *kind*?"

"Well, I don't hardly know. Brick, I suppose."

"Brick—bosh."

"Why? What is your idea?"

"Brown stone front—French plate glass—billiard-room off the dining-room—statuary and paintings—shrubbery and two-acre grass plat—greenhouse—iron dog on the front stoop—gray horses—landau, and a coachman with a bug on his hat!"

"By George!"

A long pause.

"Cal., when are you going to Europe?"

"Well—I hadn't thought of that. When are you?"

"In the spring."

"Going to be gone all summer?"

"All summer! I shall remain there three years."

"No—but are you in earnest?"

"Indeed I am."

"I will go along too."

"Why of course you will."

"What part of Europe shall you go to?"

"All parts. France, England, Germany—Spain, Italy, Switzerland, Syria, Greece, Palestine, Arabia, Persia, Egypt—all over—everywhere."

"I'm agreed."

"All right."

"Won't it be a swell trip!"

"We'll spend forty or fifty thousand dollars trying to make it one, anyway."

Another long pause.

"Higbie, we owe the butcher six dollars, and he has been threatening to stop our—"

"Hang the butcher!"

"Amen."

And so it went on. By three o'clock we found it was no use, and so we got up and played cribbage and smoked pipes till sunrise. It was my week to cook. I always hated cooking—now, I abhorred it.

The news was all over town. The former excitement was great—this one was greater still. I walked the streets serene and happy. Higbie said the foreman had been offered two hundred thousand dollars for his third of the mine. I said I would like to see myself selling for any such price. My ideas were lofty. My figure was a million. Still, I honestly believe that if I had been offered it, it would have had no other effect than to make me hold off for more.

I found abundant enjoyment in being rich. A man offered me a three-hundred-dollar horse, and wanted to take my simple, unendorsed note for it. That brought the most realizing sense I had yet had that I was actually rich, beyond shadow of doubt. It was followed by numerous other evidences of a similar nature—among which I may mention the fact of the butcher leaving us a double supply of meat and saying nothing about money.

By the laws of the district, the "locators" or claimants of a ledge were obliged to do a fair and reasonable amount of work on their new property within ten days after the date of the location, or the property was forfeited, and anybody could go and seize it that chose. So we determined to go to work the next day. About the middle of the afternoon, as I was coming out of the post office, I met a Mr. Gardiner, who told me that Capt. John Nye was lying dangerously ill at his place (the "Nine-Mile Ranch"), and that he

DANGEROUSLY SICK.

and his wife were not able to give him nearly as much care and attention as his case demanded. I said if he would wait for me a moment, I would go down and help in the sick room. I ran to the cabin to tell Higbie. He was not there, but I left a note on the table for him, and a few minutes later I left town in Gardiner's wagon.

CHAPTER 41

CAPT. NYE was very ill indeed, with spasmodic rheumatism. But the old gentleman was himself—which is to say, he was kind-hearted and agreeable when comfortable, but a singularly violent wild-cat when things did not go well. He would be smiling along pleasantly enough, when a sudden spasm of his disease would take him and he would go out of his smile into a perfect fury. He would groan and wail and howl with the anguish, and fill up the odd chinks with the most elaborate profanity that strong convictions and a fine fancy could contrive. With fair opportunity he could swear very well and handle his adjectives with considerable judgment; but when the spasm was on him it was painful to listen to him, he was so awkward. However, I had seen him nurse a sick man himself and put up patiently with the inconveniences of the situation, and consequently I was willing that he should have full license now that his own turn had come. He could not disturb me, with all his raving and ranting, for my mind had work on hand, and it labored on diligently, night and day, whether my hands were idle or employed. I was altering and amending the plans for my house, and thinking over the propriety of having the billiard-room in the attic, instead of on the same floor with the dining-room; also, I was trying to decide between green and blue for the upholstery of the drawing-room, for, although my preference was blue I feared it was a color that would be too easily damaged by dust and sunlight; likewise while I was content to put the coachman in a modest livery, I was uncertain about a footman—I needed one, and was even resolved to have one, but wished he could properly appear and perform his functions out of livery, for I somewhat dreaded so much show; and yet, inasmuch as my late grandfather had had a coachman and such things, but no liveries, I felt rather drawn to beat him;—or beat his ghost, at any rate; I was also systematizing the

European trip, and managed to get it all laid out, as to route and length of time to be devoted to it—everything, with one exception—namely, whether to cross the desert from Cairo to Jerusalem per camel, or go by sea to Beirut, and thence down through the country per caravan. Meantime I was writing to the friends at home every day, instructing them concerning all my plans and intentions, and directing them to look up a handsome homestead for my mother and agree upon a price for it against my coming, and also directing them to sell my share of the Tennessee land and tender the proceeds to the widows' and orphans' fund of the typographical union of which I had long been a member in good standing. [This Tennessee land had been in the possession of the family many years, and promised to confer high fortune upon us some day; it still promises it, but in a less violent way.]

When I had been nursing the Captain nine days he was somewhat better, but very feeble. During the afternoon we lifted him into a chair and gave him an alcoholic vapor bath, and then set about putting him on the bed again. We had to be exceedingly careful, for the least jar produced pain. Gardiner had his shoulders and I his legs; in an unfortunate moment I stumbled and the patient fell heavily on the bed in an agony of torture. I never heard a man swear so in my life. He raved like a maniac, and tried to snatch a revolver from the table—but I got it. He ordered me out of the house, and swore a world of oaths that he would kill me wherever he caught me when he got on his feet again. It was simply a passing fury, and meant nothing. I knew he would forget it in an hour, and maybe be sorry for it, too; but it angered me a little, at the moment. So much so, indeed, that I determined to go back to Esmeralda. I thought he was able to get along alone, now, since he was on the war path. I took supper, and as soon as the moon rose, began my nine-mile journey, on foot. Even millionaires needed no horses, in those days, for a mere nine-mile jaunt without baggage.

As I "raised the hill" overlooking the town, it lacked fifteen minutes of twelve. I glanced at the hill over beyond the cañon, and in the bright moonlight saw what appeared to be about half the population of the village massed on and around the Wide West croppings. My heart gave an exulting bound, and I said to myself, "They have made a new strike to-night—and struck it richer than

ever, no doubt." I started over there, but gave it up. I said the
"strike" would keep, and I had climbed hills enough for one night.
I went on down through the town, and as I was passing a little German bakery, a woman ran out and begged me to come in and help
her. She said her husband had a fit. I went in, and judged she was
right—he appeared to have a hundred of them, compressed into
one. Two Germans were there, trying to hold him, and not making
much of a success of it. I ran up the street half a block or so and
routed out a sleeping doctor, brought him down half dressed, and
we four wrestled with the maniac, and doctored, drenched and bled
him, for more than an hour, and the poor German woman did the
crying. He grew quiet, now, and the doctor and I withdrew and left
him to his friends.

It was a little after one o'clock. As I entered the cabin door, tired
but jolly, the dingy light of a tallow candle revealed Higbie, sitting
by the pine table gazing stupidly at my note, which he held in his
fingers, and looking pale, old, and haggard. I halted, and looked at
him. He looked at me, stolidly. I said:

"Higbie, what—what is it?"

"We're ruined—we didn't do the work—THE BLIND LEAD'S
RELOCATED!"

It was enough. I sat down sick, grieved—broken-hearted, indeed. A minute before, I was rich and brim full of vanity; I was a
pauper now, and very meek. We sat still an hour, busy with
thought, busy with vain and useless self-upbraidings, busy with
"Why *didn't* I do this, and why *didn't* I do that," but neither spoke
a word. Then we dropped into mutual explanations, and the mystery was cleared away. It came out that Higbie had depended on
me, as I had on him, and as both of us had on the foreman. The folly
of it! It was the first time that ever staid and steadfast Higbie had
left an important matter to chance or failed to be true to his full
share of a responsibility.

But he had never seen my note till this moment, and this moment was the first time he had been in the cabin since the day he
had seen me last. He, also, had left a note for me, on that same fatal
afternoon—had ridden up on horseback, and looked through the
window, and being in a hurry and not seeing me, had tossed the

WORTH NOTHING.

note into the cabin through a broken pane. Here it was, on the floor, where it had remained undisturbed for nine days:

Don't fail to do the work before the ten days expire. W. has passed through and given me notice. I am to join him at Mono Lake, and we shall go on from there to-night. He says he will find it this time, sure.   CAL.

"W." meant Whiteman, of course. That thrice accursed "cement!"

That was the way of it. An old miner, like Higbie, could no more withstand the fascination of a mysterious mining excitement like this "cement" foolishness, than he could refrain from eating when he was famishing. Higbie had been dreaming about the marvelous cement for months; and now, against his better judgment, he had gone off and "taken the chances" on my keeping secure a mine worth a million undiscovered cement veins. They had not been followed this time. His riding out of town in broad daylight was such a commonplace thing to do that it had not attracted any attention. He said they prosecuted their search in the fastnesses of the mountains during nine days, without success; they could not find the cement. Then a ghastly fear came over him that something might have happened to prevent the doing of the necessary work to hold the blind lead (though indeed he thought such a thing hardly possible), and forthwith he started home with all speed. He would have reached Esmeralda in time, but his horse broke down and he had to walk a great part of the distance. And so it happened that as he came into Esmeralda by one road, I entered it by another. His was the superior energy, however, for he went straight to the Wide West, instead of turning aside as I had done—and he arrived there about five or ten minutes too late! The "notice" was already up, the "relocation" of our mine completed beyond recall, and the crowd rapidly dispersing. He learned some facts before he left the ground. The foreman had not been seen about the streets since the night we had located the mine—a telegram had called him to California on a matter of life and death, it was said. At any rate he had done no work and the watchful eyes of the community were taking note of the fact. At midnight of this woful tenth day, the ledge would be "relocatable," and by eleven o'clock the hill was black with men prepared to do the relocating. That was the crowd I had seen when I fancied a new "strike" had been made—idiot that I was. [We three had the same right to relocate the lead that other people had, provided we were quick enough.] As midnight was announced, fourteen men, duly armed and ready to back their proceedings, put up their "notice" and proclaimed their ownership of the blind lead, under the new name of the "Johnson." But A. D. Allen our partner (the foreman) put in a sudden appearance about that time, with a cocked revolver in his hand, and said his name must be added to the list, or he would "thin out the Johnson company some." He was a manly, splendid, determined fellow, and known to be as good as his word, and therefore a compromise was effected. They put in his name for a hundred feet, reserving to themselves the customary two hundred feet each. Such was the history of the night's events, as Higbie gathered from a friend on the way home.

ENFORCING A COMPROMISE.

Higbie and I cleared out on a new mining excitement the next morning, glad to get away from the scene of our sufferings, and after a month or two of hardship and disappointment, returned to Esmeralda once more. Then we learned that the Wide West and the Johnson companies had consolidated; that the stock, thus united, comprised five thousand feet, or shares; that the foreman, apprehending tiresome litigation, and considering such a huge concern unwieldy, had sold his hundred feet for ninety thousand dollars in gold and gone home to the States to enjoy it. If the stock was worth such a gallant figure, with five thousand shares in the corporation, it makes me dizzy to think what it would have been worth with only our original six hundred in it. It was the difference between six hundred men owning a house and five thousand owning it. We would have been millionaires if we had only worked with pick and spade one little day on our property and so secured our ownership!

It reads like a wild fancy sketch, but the evidence of many witnesses, and likewise that of the official records of Esmeralda District, is easily obtainable in proof that it is a true history. I can always have it to say that I was absolutely and unquestionably worth a million dollars, once, for ten days.

A year ago my esteemed and in every way estimable old millionaire partner, Higbie, wrote me from an obscure little mining camp in California that after nine or ten years of buffetings and hard striving, he was at last in a position where he could command twenty-five hundred dollars, and said he meant to go into the fruit business in a modest way. How such a thought would have insulted him the night we lay in our cabin planning European trips and brown stone houses on Russian Hill!

CHAPTER 42

Wᴴᴀᴛ to do next?

It was a momentous question. I had gone out into the world to shift for myself, at the age of thirteen (for my father had endorsed for friends; and although he left us a sumptuous legacy of pride in his fine Virginian stock and its national distinction, I presently found that I could not live on that alone without occasional bread to wash it down with). I had gained a livelihood in various vocations, but had not dazzled anybody with my successes; still the list was before me, and the amplest liberty in the matter of choosing, provided I wanted to work—which I did not, after being so wealthy. I had once been a grocery clerk, for one day, but had consumed so much sugar in that time that I was relieved from further duty by the proprietor; said he wanted me outside, so that he could have my custom. I had studied law an entire week, and then given it up because it was so prosy and tiresome. I had engaged briefly in the study of blacksmithing, but wasted so much time trying to fix the bellows so that it would blow itself, that the master turned me adrift in disgrace, and told me I would come to no good. I had been a bookseller's clerk for a while, but the customers bothered me so much I could not read with any comfort, and so the proprietor gave me a furlough and forgot to put a limit to it. I had clerked in a drug store part of a summer, but my prescriptions were unlucky, and we appeared to sell more stomach pumps than soda water. So I had to go. I had made of myself a tolerable printer, under the impression that I would be another Franklin some day, but somehow had missed the connection thus far. There was no berth open in the Esmeralda *Union*, and besides I had always been such a slow compositor that I looked with envy upon the achievements of apprentices of two years' standing; and when I took a "take," foremen were in the habit of suggesting that it would be wanted "some time during

the year." I was a good average St. Louis and New Orleans pilot and
by no means ashamed of my abilities in that line; wages were two

ONE OF MY FAILURES.

hundred and fifty dollars a month and no board to pay, and I did
long to stand behind a wheel again and never roam any more—but
I had been making such an ass of myself lately in grandiloquent
letters home about my blind lead and my European excursion that
I did what many and many a poor disappointed miner had done before; said "It is all over with me now, and I will never go back home
to be pitied—and snubbed." I had been a private secretary, a silver
miner and a silver mill operative, and amounted to less than nothing in each, and now—

What to do next?

I yielded to Higbie's appeals and consented to try the mining
once more. We climbed far up on the mountain side and went to
work on a little rubbishy claim of ours that had a shaft on it eight
feet deep. Higbie descended into it and worked bravely with his
pick till he had loosened up a deal of rock and dirt and then I went
down with a long-handled shovel (the most awkward invention yet
contrived by man) to throw it out. You must brace the shovel for-

ward with the side of your knee till it is full, and then, with a skil-
ful toss, throw it backwards over your left shoulder. I made the toss
and landed the mess just on the edge of the shaft and it all came
back on my head and down the back of my neck. I never said a
word, but climbed out and walked home. I inwardly resolved that I
would starve before I would make a target of myself and shoot rubbish at it with a long-handled shovel. I sat down, in the cabin, and

gave myself up to solid misery—
so to speak. Now in pleasanter
days I had amused myself with
writing letters to the chief paper
of the Territory, the Virginia *Daily
Territorial Enterprise*, and had always been surprised when they appeared in print. My good opinion
of the editors had steadily declined; for it seemed to me that
they might have found something
better to fill up with than my literature. I had found a letter in the
post office as I came home from
the hillside, and finally I opened it.
Eureka! [I never did know what
Eureka meant, but it seems to be
as proper a word to heave in as any
when no other that sounds pretty

TARGET SHOOTING.

offers.] It was a deliberate offer to me of Twenty-Five Dollars a
week to come up to Virginia and be city editor of the *Enterprise*.

I would have challenged the publisher in the "blind lead" days—
I wanted to fall down and worship him, now. Twenty-Five Dollars
a week—it looked like bloated luxury—a fortune—a sinful and
lavish waste of money. But my transports cooled when I thought of
my inexperience and consequent unfitness for the position—and
straightway, on top of this, my long array of failures rose up before
me. Yet if I refused this place I must presently become dependent
upon somebody for my bread, a thing necessarily distasteful to a
man who had never experienced such a humiliation since he was
thirteen years old. Not much to be proud of, since it is so com-

mon—but then it was all I had to *be* proud of. So I was scared into being a city editor. I would have declined, otherwise. Necessity is the mother of "taking chances." I do not doubt that if, at that time, I had been offered a salary to translate the Talmud from the original Hebrew, I would have accepted—albeit with diffidence and some misgivings—and thrown as much variety into it as I could for the money.

I went up to Virginia and entered upon my new vocation. I was a rusty looking city editor, I am free to confess—coatless, slouch

hat, blue woolen shirt, pantaloons stuffed into boot-tops, whiskered half down to the waist, and the universal navy revolver slung to my belt. But I secured a more Christian costume and discarded the revolver. I had never had occasion to kill anybody, nor ever felt a desire to do so, but had worn the thing in deference to popular sentiment, and in order that I might not, by its absence, be offensively conspicuous, and a subject of remark. But the other editors, and all the printers, carried revolvers. I asked the chief editor and proprietor (Mr. Goodman, I will call him, since it describes him as well as any name could do) for some instructions with regard to my duties, and he told me to go all over town and ask all sorts of people all sorts of questions, make notes of the information gained, and write them out for publication. And he added:

AS CITY EDITOR.

"Never say 'We learn' so-and-so, or 'It is reported,' or 'It is rumored,' or 'We understand' so-and-so, but go to headquarters and get the absolute facts, and then speak out and say 'It *is* so-and-so.' Otherwise, people will not put confidence in your news. Unassailable certainty is the thing that gives a newspaper the firmest and most valuable reputation."

It was the whole thing in a nut-shell; and to this day when I find a reporter commencing his article with "We understand," I gather

a suspicion that he has not taken as much pains to inform himself
as he ought to have done. I moralize well, but I did not always practice well when I was a city editor; I let fancy get the upper hand of
fact too often when there was a dearth of news. I can never forget
my first day's experience as a reporter. I wandered about town
questioning everybody, boring everybody, and finding out that nobody knew anything. At the end of five hours my note-book was
still barren. I spoke to Mr. Goodman. He said:

"Dan used to make a good thing out of the hay wagons in a dry
time when there were no fires or inquests. Are there no hay wagons in from the Truckee? If there are, you might speak of the renewed activity and all that sort of thing, in the hay business, you
know. It isn't sensational or exciting, but it fills up and looks
business-like."

I canvassed the city again and found one wretched old hay truck
dragging in from the country. But I made affluent use of it. I multi-

THE ENTIRE MARKET.

plied it by sixteen, brought it into town from sixteen different directions, made sixteen separate items out of it, and got up such another sweat about hay as Virginia City had never seen in the world
before.

This was encouraging. Two nonpareil columns had to be filled,
and I was getting along. Presently, when things began to look dismal again, a desperado killed a man in a saloon and joy returned
once more. I never was so glad over any mere trifle before in my
life. I said to the murderer:

"Sir, you are a stranger to me, but you have done me a kindness this day which I can never forget. If whole years of gratitude can be to you any slight compensation, they shall be yours. I was in trouble and you have relieved me nobly and at a time when all seemed dark and drear. Count me your friend from this time forth, for I am not a man to forget a favor."

A FRIEND INDEED.

If I did not really say that to him I at least felt a sort of itching desire to do it. I wrote up the murder with a hungry attention to details, and when it was finished experienced but one regret—namely, that they had not hanged my benefactor on the spot, so that I could work him up too.

Next I discovered some emigrant wagons going into camp on the plaza and found that they had lately come through the hostile Indian country and had fared rather roughly. I made the best of the item that the circumstances permitted, and felt that if I were not confined within rigid limits by the presence of the reporters of the other papers I could add particulars that would make the article much more interesting. However, I found one wagon that was going on to California, and made some judicious inquiries of the proprietor. When I learned, through his short and surly answers to my cross-questioning, that he was certainly going on and would not be in the city next day to make trouble, I got ahead of the other papers, for I took down his list of names and added his party to the killed and wounded. Having more scope here, I put this wagon through an Indian fight that to this day has no parallel in history.

My two columns were filled. When I read them over in the morning I felt that I had found my legitimate occupation at last. I reasoned within myself that news, and stirring news, too, was

what a paper needed, and I felt that I was peculiarly endowed with
the ability to furnish it. Mr. Goodman said that I was as good a reporter as Dan. I desired no higher commendation. With encouragement like that, I felt that I could take my pen and murder all the
immigrants on the plains if need be and the interests of the paper
demanded it.

CHAPTER 43

However, as I grew better acquainted with the business and learned the run of the sources of information I ceased to require the aid of fancy to any large extent, and became able to fill my columns without diverging noticeably from the domain of fact.

I struck up friendships with the reporters of the other journals, and we swapped "regulars" with each other and thus economized work. "Regulars" are permanent sources of news, like courts, bullion returns, "clean-ups" at the quartz mills, and inquests. Inasmuch as everybody went armed, we had an inquest about every day, and so this department was naturally set down among the "regulars." We had lively papers in those days. My great competitor among the reporters was Boggs of the *Union*. He was an excellent reporter. Once in three or four months he would get a little intoxicated, but as a general thing he was a wary and cautious drinker although always ready to tamper a little with the enemy. He had the advantage of me in one thing; he could get the monthly public school report and I could not, because the principal hated the *Enterprise*. One snowy night when the report was due, I started out sadly wondering how I was going to get it. Presently, a few steps up the almost deserted street I stumbled on Boggs and asked him where he was going.

"After the school report."

"I'll go along with you."

"No, *sir*. I'll excuse you."

"Just as you say."

A saloon-keeper's boy passed by with a steaming pitcher of hot punch, and Boggs snuffed the fragrance gratefully. He gazed fondly after the boy and saw him start up the *Enterprise* stairs. I said:

"I wish you could help me get that school business, but since you can't, I must run up to the *Union* office and see if I can get

them to let me have a proof of it after they have set it up, though I
don't begin to suppose they will. Good night."

"Hold on a minute. I don't mind getting the report and sitting
around with the boys a little, while you copy it, if you're willing to
drop down to the principal's with me."

"Now you talk like a rational being. Come along."

We plowed a couple of blocks through the snow, got the report and
returned to our office. It was a short document and soon copied.
Meantime Boggs helped himself to the punch. I gave the manuscript
back to him and we started out to get an inquest, for we heard pistol
shots near by. We got the particulars with little loss of time, for it
was only an inferior sort of bar-room murder, and of little interest to
the public, and then we separated. Away at three o'clock in the
morning, when we had gone to press and were having a relaxing concert as usual—for some of the printers were good singers and others
good performers on the guitar and on that atrocity the accordeon—
the proprietor of the *Union* strode in and desired to know if anybody
had heard anything of Boggs or the school report. We stated the case,
and all turned out to help hunt for the delinquent. We found him
standing on a table in a saloon, with an old tin lantern in one hand

AN EDUCATIONAL REPORT.

and the school report in the other, haranguing a gang of intoxicated Cornish miners on the iniquity of squandering the public moneys on education "when hundreds and hundreds of honest hard-working men are literally starving for whisky." [Riotous applause.] He had been assisting in a regal spree with those parties for hours. We dragged him away and put him to bed.

Of course there was no school report in the *Union,* and Boggs held me accountable, though I was innocent of any intention or de-sire to compass its absence from that paper and was as sorry as any one that the misfortune had occurred.

But we were perfectly friendly. The day that the school report was next due, the proprietor of the "Genesee" mine furnished us a buggy and asked us to go down and write something about the property—a very common request and one always gladly acceded to when people furnished buggies, for we were as fond of pleasure excursions as other people. In due time we arrived at the "mine"— nothing but a hole in the ground ninety feet deep, and no way of getting down into it but by holding on to a rope and being lowered with a windlass. The workmen had just gone off somewhere to dinner. I was not strong enough to lower Boggs's bulk; so I took an unlighted candle in my teeth, made a loop for my foot in the end of the rope, implored Boggs not to go to sleep or let the windlass get the start of him, and then swung out over the shaft. I reached the bottom muddy and bruised about the elbows, but safe. I lit the can-dle, made an examination of the rock, selected some specimens and shouted to Boggs to hoist away. No answer. Presently a head appeared in the circle of daylight away aloft, and a voice came down:

"Are you all set?"

"All set—hoist away."

"Are you comfortable?"

"Perfectly."

"Could you wait a little?"

"Oh certainly—no particular hurry."

"Well—good-bye."

"Why? Where are you going?"

"After the school report!"

And he did. I staid down there an hour, and surprised the workmen when they hauled up and found a man on the rope instead of a bucket of rock. I walked home, too—five miles—up hill. We had no school report next morning; but the *Union* had.

NO PARTICULAR HURRY.

Six months after my entry into journalism the grand "flush times" of Silverland began, and they continued with unabated splendor for three years. All difficulty about filling up the "local department" ceased, and the only trouble now was how to make the lengthened columns hold the world of incidents and happenings that came to our literary net every day. Virginia had grown to be the "livest" town, for its age and population, that America had ever produced. The sidewalks swarmed with people—to such an extent, indeed, that it was generally no easy matter to stem the human tide. The streets themselves were just as crowded with quartz wagons, freight teams and other vehicles. The procession was endless. So great was the pack, that buggies frequently had to wait half an hour for an opportunity to cross the principal street. Joy sat on every countenance, and there was a glad, almost fierce, intensity in every eye, that told of the money-getting schemes that were seething in every brain and the high hope that held sway in every heart. Money was as plenty as dust; every individual considered himself wealthy, and a melancholy countenance was nowhere to be seen. There were military companies, fire companies, brass bands, banks, hotels, theatres, "hurdy-gurdy houses," wide-open gambling palaces, political pow-wows, civic processions, street fights, murders, inquests, riots, a whisky mill every fifteen steps, a Board of Aldermen, a Mayor, a City Surveyor, a City Engineer, a Chief of the Fire Department, with First, Second and Third Assistants, a Chief of Police, City Marshal and a large police force, two Boards of Mining Brokers, a dozen breweries and half a dozen jails and station-houses in full operation, and some talk of building a church. The "flush times" were in magnificent flower! Large fireproof brick buildings were going up in the principal streets, and the wooden suburbs were spreading out in all directions. Town lots soared up to prices that were amazing.

The great "Comstock lode" stretched its opulent length straight through the town from north to south, and every mine on it was in diligent process of development. One of these mines alone employed six hundred and seventy-five men, and in the matter of elections the adage was, "as the 'Gould & Curry' goes, so goes the city." Laboring men's wages were four and six dollars a day, and they worked in three "shifts" or gangs, and the blasting and picking and shoveling went on without ceasing, night and day.

The "city" of Virginia roosted royally midway up the steep side of Mount Davidson, seven thousand two hundred feet above the level of the sea, and in the clear Nevada atmosphere was visible from a distance of fifty miles! It claimed a population of fifteen thousand to eighteen thousand, and all day long half of this little army swarmed the streets like bees and the other half swarmed among the drifts and tunnels of the "Comstock," hundreds of feet down in the earth directly under those same streets. Often we felt our chairs jar, and heard the faint boom of a blast down in the bowels of the earth under the office.

The mountain side was so steep that the entire town had a slant to it like a roof. Each street was a terrace, and from each to the next street below the descent was forty or fifty feet. The fronts of the houses were level with the street they faced, but their rear first floors were propped on lofty stilts; a man could stand at a rear first floor window of a C street house and look down the chimneys of the row of houses below him facing D street. It was a laborious climb, in that thin atmosphere, to ascend from D to A street, and you were panting and out of breath when you got there; but you could

BIRD'S EYE VIEW OF VIRGINIA AND MOUNT DAVIDSON.

turn around and go down again like a house a-fire—so to speak.
The atmosphere was so rarified, on account of the great altitude,
that one's blood lay near the surface always, and the scratch of a
pin was a disaster worth worrying about, for the chances were that
a grievous erysipelas would ensue. But to offset this, the thin atmosphere seemed to carry healing to gunshot wounds, and therefore, to simply shoot your adversary through both lungs was a
thing not likely to afford you any permanent satisfaction, for he
would be nearly certain to be around looking for you within the
month, and not with an opera glass, either.

From Virginia's airy situation one could look over a vast, far-
reaching panorama of mountain ranges and deserts; and whether
the day was bright or overcast, whether the sun was rising or setting, or flaming in the zenith, or whether night and the moon held
sway, the spectacle was always impressive and beautiful. Over your
head Mount Davidson lifted its gray dome, and before and below
you a rugged cañon clove the battlemented hills, making a sombre
gateway through which a soft-tinted desert was glimpsed, with the
silver thread of a river winding through it, bordered with trees
which many miles of distance diminished to a delicate fringe; and
still further away the snowy mountains rose up and stretched their
long barrier to the filmy horizon—far enough beyond a lake that
burned in the desert like a fallen sun, though that, itself, lay fifty
miles removed. Look from your window where you would, there
was fascination in the picture. At rare intervals—but very rare—
there were clouds in our skies, and then the setting sun would gild
and flush and glorify this mighty expanse of scenery with a bewildering pomp of color that held the eye like a spell and moved the
spirit like music.

CHAPTER 44

My salary was increased to forty dollars a week. But I seldom drew it. I had plenty of other resources, and what were two broad twenty-dollar gold pieces to a man who had his pockets full of such and a cumbersome abundance of bright half dollars besides? [Paper money has never come into use on the Pacific coast.] Reporting was lucrative, and every man in the town was lavish with his money and his "feet." The city and all the great mountain side were riddled with mining shafts. There were more mines than miners. True, not ten of these mines were yielding rock worth hauling to a mill, but everybody said, "Wait till the shaft gets down where the ledge comes in solid, and then you will see!" So nobody was discouraged. These were nearly all "wild cat" mines, and wholly worthless, but nobody believed it then. The "Ophir," the "Gould & Curry," the "Mexican," and other great mines on the Comstock lead in Virginia and Gold Hill were turning out huge piles of rich rock every day, and every man believed that his little wild cat claim was as good as any on the "main lead" and would infallibly be worth a thousand dollars a foot when he "got down where it came in solid." Poor fellow, he was blessedly blind to the fact that he never would see that day. So the thousand wild cat shafts burrowed deeper and deeper into the earth day by day, and all men were beside themselves with hope and happiness. How they labored, prophesied, exulted! Surely nothing like it was ever seen before since the world began. Every one of these wild cat mines—not mines, but holes in the ground over imaginary mines—was incorporated and had handsomely engraved "stock" and the stock was salable, too. It was bought and sold with a feverish avidity in the boards every day. You could go up on the mountain side, scratch around and find a ledge (there was no lack of

them), put up a "notice" with a grandiloquent name in it, start a
shaft, get your stock printed, and with nothing whatever to prove

A NEW MINE.

that your mine was worth a straw, you could put your stock on the
market and sell out for hundreds and even thousands of dollars. To
make money, and make it fast, was as easy as it was to eat your dinner. Every man owned "feet" in fifty different wild cat mines and
considered his fortune made. Think of a city with not one solitary
poor man in it! One would suppose that when month after month
went by and still not a wild cat mine (by wild cat I mean, in general
terms, *any* claim not located on the mother vein, *i. e.*, the "Comstock") yielded a ton of rock worth crushing, the people would begin to wonder if they were not putting too much faith in their prospective riches; but there was not a thought of such a thing. They
burrowed away, bought and sold, and were happy.

New claims were taken up daily, and it was the friendly custom
to run straight to the newspaper offices, give the reporters forty or
fifty "feet," and get them to go and examine the mine and publish

a notice of it. They did not care a fig what you said about the property so you said something. Consequently we generally said a word or two to the effect that the "indications" were good, or that the ledge was "six feet wide," or that the rock "resembled the Comstock" (and so it did—but as a general thing the resemblance was not startling enough to knock you down). If the rock was moderately promising, we followed the custom of the country, used strong adjectives and frothed at the mouth as if a very marvel in silver discoveries had transpired. If the mine was a "developed" one, and had no pay ore to show (and of course it hadn't), we praised the tunnel; said it was one of the most infatuating tunnels in the land; driveled and driveled about the tunnel till we ran entirely out of ecstasies—but never said a word about the rock. We would squander half a column of adulation on a shaft, or a new wire rope, or a dressed pine windlass, or a fascinating force pump, and close with a burst of admiration of the "gentlemanly and efficient Superintendent" of the mine—but never utter a whisper about the rock. And those people were always pleased, always satisfied. Occasionally we patched up and varnished our reputation for discrimination and stern, undeviating accuracy, by giving some old abandoned claim a blast that ought to have made its dry bones rattle—and then somebody would seize it and sell it on the fleeting notoriety thus conferred upon it.

There was *nothing* in the shape of a mining claim that was not salable. We received presents of "feet" every day. If we needed a hundred dollars or so, we sold some; if not, we hoarded it away, satisfied that it would ultimately be worth a thousand dollars a foot. I had a trunk about half full of "stock." When a claim made a stir in the market and went up to a high figure, I searched through my pile to see if I had any of its stock—and generally found it.

The prices rose and fell constantly; but still a fall disturbed us little, because a thousand dollars a foot was our figure, and so we were content to let it fluctuate as much as it pleased till it reached it. My pile of stock was not all given to me by people who wished their claims "noticed." At least half of it was given me by persons who had no thought of such a thing, and looked for nothing more than a simple verbal "thank you;" and you were not even obliged by law to furnish that. If you are coming up the street with a couple of baskets of apples in your hands, and you meet a friend, you naturally invite him to take a few. That describes the condition of

"TAKE A FEW?"

things in Virginia in the "flush times." Every man had his pockets full of stock, and it was the actual *custom* of the country to part with small quantities of it to friends without the asking. Very often it was a good idea to close the transaction instantly, when a man offered a stock present to a friend, for the offer was only good and binding at that moment, and if the price went to a high figure shortly afterward the procrastination was a thing to be regretted. Mr. Stewart (Senator, now, from Nevada) one day told me he would give me twenty feet of "Justis" stock if I would walk over to his office. It was worth five or ten dollars a foot. I asked him to make the offer good for next day, as I was just going to dinner.

He said he would not be in town; so I risked it and took my dinner instead of the stock. Within the week the price went up to seventy dollars and afterward to a hundred and fifty, but nothing could make that man yield. I suppose he sold that stock of mine and placed the guilty proceeds in his own pocket. [My revenge will be found in the accompanying portrait.] I met three friends one afternoon, who said they had been buying "Overman" stock at auction at eight dollars a foot. One said if I would come up to his office he would give me fifteen feet; another said he would add fifteen; the third said he would do the same. But I was going after an inquest and could not stop. A few weeks afterward they sold all their "Overman" at six hundred dollars a foot and generously came around to tell me about it—and also to urge me to accept of the next forty-five feet of it that people tried to force on me. These are actual facts, and I could make the list a long one and still confine myself strictly to the truth. Many a time friends gave us as much as twenty-five feet of stock that was selling at twenty-five dollars a foot, and they thought no more of it than they would of offering a guest a cigar. These were "flush times" indeed! I thought they were going to last always, but somehow I never was much of a prophet.

To show what a wild spirit possessed the mining brain of the community, I will remark that "claims" were actually "located" in excavations for cellars, where the pick had exposed what seemed to be quartz veins—and not cellars in the suburbs, either, but in the very heart of the city; and forthwith stock would be is-

PORTRAIT OF MR. STEWART.

sued and thrown on the market. It was small matter who the cellar belonged to—the "ledge" belonged to the finder, and unless the U. S. government interfered (inasmuch as the government holds the primary right to mines of the noble metals in Nevada—or at least did then), it was considered to be his privilege to work it. Imagine a stranger staking out a mining claim among the costly shrubbery in your front yard and calmly proceeding to lay waste the ground with pick and shovel and blasting powder! It has been often done in California. In the middle of one of the principal business streets of Virginia, a man "located" a mining claim and began a shaft on it. He gave me a hundred feet of the stock and I sold it for a fine suit of clothes because I was afraid somebody would fall down the shaft and sue for damages. I owned in another claim that was located in the middle of another street; and to show how absurd people can be, that "East India" stock (as it was called) sold briskly although there was an ancient tunnel running directly under the claim and any man could go into it and see that it did not cut a quartz ledge or anything that remotely resembled one.

One plan of acquiring sudden wealth was to "salt" a wild cat claim and sell out while the excitement was up. The process was

SELLING A MINE.

simple. The schemer located a worthless ledge, sunk a shaft on it, bought a wagon load of rich "Comstock" ore, dumped a portion of it into the shaft and piled the rest by its side, above ground. Then he showed the property to a simpleton and sold it to him at a high figure. Of course the wagon load of rich ore was all that the victim ever got out of his purchase. A most remarkable case of "salting" was that of the "North Ophir." It was claimed that this vein was a remote "extension" of the original "Ophir," a valuable mine on the "Comstock." For a few days everybody was talking about the rich developments in the North Ophir. It was said that it yielded perfectly pure silver in small, solid lumps. I went to the place with the owners, and found a shaft six or eight feet deep, in the bottom of which was a badly shattered vein of dull, yellowish, unpromising rock. One would as soon expect to find silver in a grindstone. We got out a pan of the rubbish and washed it in a puddle, and sure enough, among the sediment we found half a dozen black, bullet-looking pellets of unimpeachable "native" silver. Nobody had ever heard of such a thing before; science could not account for such a queer novelty. The stock rose to sixty-five dollars a foot, and at this figure the world-renowned tragedian, McKean Buchanan, bought a commanding interest and prepared to quit the stage once more— he was always doing that. And then it transpired that the mine had been "salted"—and not in any hackneyed way, either, but in a singularly bold, barefaced and peculiarly original and outrageous fashion. On one of the lumps of "native" silver was discovered the minted legend, "TED STATES OF," and then it was plainly apparent that the mine had been "salted" with melted half dollars! The lumps thus obtained had been blackened till they resembled native silver, and were then mixed with the shattered rock in the bottom of the shaft. It is literally true. Of course the price of the stock at once fell to nothing, and the tragedian was ruined. But for this calamity we might have lost McKean Buchanan from the stage.

CHAPTER 45

The "flush times" held bravely on. Something over two years before, Mr. Goodman and another journeyman printer, had borrowed forty dollars and set out from San Francisco to try their fortunes in the new city of Virginia. They found the *Territorial Enterprise*, a poverty-stricken weekly journal, gasping for breath and likely to die. They bought it, type, fixtures, good-will and all, for a thousand dollars, on long time. The editorial sanctum, news-room, press-room, publication office, bed-chamber, parlor, and kitchen were all compressed into one apartment and it was a small one, too. The editors and printers slept on the floor, a Chinaman did their cooking, and the "imposing-stone" was the general dinner table. But now things were changed. The paper was a great daily, printed by steam; there were five editors and twenty-three compositors; the subscription price was sixteen dollars a year; the advertising rates were exorbitant, and the columns crowded. The paper was clearing from six to ten thousand dollars a month, and the "Enterprise Building" was finished and ready for occupation—a stately fire-proof brick. Every day from five all the way up to eleven columns of "live" advertisements were left out or crowded into spasmodic and irregular "supplements."

The "Gould & Curry" company were erecting a monster hundred-stamp mill at a cost that ultimately fell little short of a million dollars. Gould & Curry stock paid heavy dividends—a rare thing, and an experience confined to the dozen or fifteen claims located on the "main lead," the "Comstock." The Superintendent of the Gould & Curry lived, rent-free, in a fine house built and furnished by the company. He drove a fine pair of horses which were a present from the company, and his salary was twelve thousand dollars a year. The Superintendent of another of the great mines traveled in grand state, had a salary of twenty-eight thousand dollars a year, and in a lawsuit in after days claimed that he was to have had one per cent on the gross yield of the bullion likewise.

Money was wonderfully plenty. The trouble was, not how to get it,—but how to spend it, how to lavish it, get rid of it, squander it. And so it was a happy thing that just at this juncture the news came over the wires that a great U. S. Sanitary Commission had been formed and money was wanted for the relief of the wounded sailors and soldiers of the Union languishing in the eastern hospitals. Right on the heels of it came word that San Francisco had responded superbly before the telegram was half a day old. Virginia rose as one man! A Sanitary Committee was hurriedly organized, and its chairman mounted a vacant cart in C street and tried to make the clamorous multitude understand that the rest of the committee were flying hither and thither and working with all their might and main, and that if the town would only wait an hour, an office would be ready, books opened, and the Commission prepared to receive contributions. His voice was drowned and his information lost in a ceaseless roar of cheers, and demands that the money be received *now*—they swore they would not wait. The chairman pleaded and argued, but, deaf to all entreaty, men plowed their way through the throng and rained checks and gold coin into the cart and skurried away for more. Hands clutching money, were thrust aloft out of the jam by men who hoped this eloquent appeal would cleave a road their strugglings could not open. The very Chinamen and Indians caught the excitement and dashed their half dollars into the cart without knowing or caring what it was all about. Women plunged into the crowd, trimly attired, fought their way to the cart with their coin, and emerged again, by and by, with their apparel in a state of hopeless dilapidation. It was the wildest mob Virginia had ever seen and the most determined and ungovernable; and when at last it abated its fury and dispersed, it had not a penny in its pocket. To use its own phraseology, it came there "flush" and went away "busted."

After that, the Commission got itself into systematic working order, and for weeks the contributions flowed into its treasury in a generous stream. Individuals and all sorts of organizations levied upon themselves a regular weekly tax for the Sanitary fund, graduated according to their means, and there was not another grand

COULDN'T WAIT.

universal outburst till the famous "Sanitary Flour Sack" came our
way. Its history is peculiar and interesting. A former schoolmate of
mine, by the name of Reuel Gridley, was living at the little city of
Austin, in the Reese river country, at this time, and was the Democratic candidate for mayor. He and the Republican candidate
made an agreement that the defeated man should be publicly presented with a fifty-pound sack of flour by the successful one, and
should carry it home on his shoulder. Gridley was defeated. The
new mayor gave him the sack of flour, and he shouldered it and carried it a mile or two, from Lower Austin to his home in Upper Austin, attended by a band of music and the whole population. Arrived
there, he said he did not need the flour, and asked what the people
thought he had better do with it. A voice said:

   "Sell it to the highest bidder, for the benefit of the Sanitary fund."

The suggestion was greeted with a round of applause, and Gridley mounted a dry-goods box and assumed the role of auctioneer. The bids went higher and higher, as the sympathies of the pioneers awoke and expanded, till at last the sack was knocked down to a mill man at two hundred and fifty dollars, and his check taken. He was asked where he would have the flour delivered, and he said:

"Nowhere—sell it again."

Now the cheers went up royally, and the multitude were fairly in the spirit of the thing. So Gridley stood there and shouted and perspired till the sun went down; and when the crowd dispersed he had sold the sack to three hundred different people, and had taken in eight thousand dollars in gold. And still the flour sack was in his possession.

The news came to Virginia, and a telegram went back:

"Fetch along your flour sack!"

Thirty-six hours afterward Gridley arrived, and an afternoon mass meeting was held in the Opera House, and the auction began. But the sack had come sooner than it was expected; the people were not thoroughly aroused, and the sale dragged. At nightfall only five thousand dollars had been secured, and there was a crestfallen feeling in the community. However, there was no disposition to let the matter rest here and acknowledge vanquishment at the hands of the village of Austin. Till late in the night the principal citizens were at work arranging the morrow's campaign, and when they went to bed they had no fears for the result. At eleven the next morning a procession of open carriages, attended by clamorous bands of music and adorned with a moving display of flags, filed along C street and was soon in danger of blockade by a huzzaing multitude of citizens. In the first carriage sat Gridley, with the flour sack in prominent view, the latter splendid with bright paint and gilt lettering; also in the same carriage sat the mayor and the recorder. The other carriages contained the Common Council, the editors and reporters, and other people of imposing consequence. The crowd pressed to the corner of C and Taylor streets, expecting the sale to begin there, but they were disappointed, and also unspeakably surprised; for the cavalcade moved on as if Virginia had ceased to be of importance, and took its way over the "divide," toward the small town of Gold Hill. Telegrams had gone ahead to Gold Hill, Silver City and Dayton, and those communities were at fever heat and rife for the

THE GREAT "FLOUR SACK" PROCESSION.

conflict. It was a very hot day, and wonderfully dusty. At the end of a short half hour we descended into Gold Hill with drums beating and colors flying, and enveloped in imposing clouds of dust. The whole population—men, women and children, Chinamen and Indians, were massed in the main street, all the flags in town were at the mast head, and the blare of the bands was drowned in cheers. Gridley stood up and asked who would make the first bid for the National Sanitary Flour Sack. Gen. W. said:

"The Yellow Jacket silver mining company offers a thousand dollars, coin!"

A tempest of applause followed. A telegram carried the news to Virginia, and fifteen minutes afterward that city's population was massed in the streets devouring the tidings—for it was part of the programme that the bulletin boards should do a good work that day. Every few minutes a new dispatch was bulletined from Gold Hill, and still the excitement grew. Telegrams began to return to us from Virginia beseeching Gridley to bring back the flour sack; but such was not the plan of the campaign. At the end of an hour Gold Hill's small population had paid a figure for the flour sack that awoke all the enthusiasm of Virginia when the grand total was displayed upon the bulletin boards. Then the Gridley cavalcade moved on, a giant refreshed with new lager beer and plenty of it—for the people brought it to the carriages without waiting to measure it—and within three hours more the expedition had carried Silver City and Dayton by storm and was on its way back covered with glory. Every move had been telegraphed and bulletined, and as the procession entered Virginia and filed down C street at half past eight in the evening the town was abroad in the thoroughfares, torches were glaring, flags flying, bands playing, cheer on cheer cleaving the air, and the city ready to surrender at discretion. The auction began, every bid was greeted with bursts of applause, and at the end of two hours and a half a population of fifteen thousand souls had paid in coin for a fifty-pound sack of flour a sum equal to forty thousand dollars in greenbacks! It was at a rate in the neighborhood of three dollars for each man, woman and child of the population. The grand total would have been twice as large, but the streets were very narrow, and hundreds who wanted to bid could not get within a block of the stand, and could not make themselves heard. These grew tired of waiting and many of them went home long before the auction was over. This was the greatest day Virginia ever saw, perhaps.

Gridley sold the sack in Carson City and several California towns; also in San Francisco. Then he took it east and sold it in one or two Atlantic cities, I think. I am not sure of that, but I know that he finally carried it to St. Louis, where a monster Sanitary Fair was being held, and after selling it there for a large sum and helping on the enthusiasm by displaying the portly silver bricks which Nevada's donation had produced, he had the flour baked up into small cakes and retailed them at high prices.

It was estimated that when the flour sack's mission was ended it had been sold for a grand total of a hundred and fifty thousand dollars in greenbacks! This is probably the only instance on record where common family flour brought three thousand dollars a pound in the public market.

It is due to Mr. Gridley's memory to mention that the expenses of his Sanitary flour sack expedition of fifteen thousand miles, going and returning, were paid in large part, if not entirely, out of his own pocket. The time he gave to it was not less than three months. Mr. Gridley was a soldier in the Mexican war and a pioneer Californian. He died at Stockton, California, in December, 1870, greatly regretted.

CHAPTER 46

THERE were nabobs in those days—in the "flush times," I mean. Every rich strike in the mines created one or two. I call to mind several of these. They were careless, easy-going fellows, as a general thing, and the community at large was as much benefited by their riches as they were themselves—possibly more, in some cases.

Two cousins, teamsters, did some hauling for a man, and had to take a small segregated portion of a silver mine in lieu of three hundred dollars cash. They gave an outsider a third to open the mine, and they went on teaming. But not long. Ten months afterward the mine was out of debt and paying each owner eight to ten thousand dollars a month—say a hundred thousand dollars a year.

One of the earliest nabobs that Nevada was delivered of wore six thousand dollars' worth of diamonds in his bosom, and swore he was unhappy because he could not spend his money as fast as he made it.

A NABOB.

Another Nevada nabob boasted an income that often reached sixteen thousand dollars a month; and he used to love to tell how he had worked in the very mine that yielded it, for five dollars a day, when he first came to the country.

The silver and sage-brush State has knowledge of another of these pets of fortune—lifted from actual poverty to affluence almost in a single night—who was able to offer a hundred thousand dollars for a position of high official distinction, shortly afterward, and did offer it—but failed to get it, his politics not being as sound as his bank account.

Then there was John Smith. He was a good, honest, kind-hearted soul, born and reared in the lower ranks of life, and miraculously ignorant. He drove a team, and owned a small ranch—a ranch that paid him a comfortable living, for although it yielded but little hay, what little it did yield was worth from two hundred and fifty to three hundred dollars in gold per ton in the market. Presently Smith traded a few acres of the ranch for a small undeveloped silver mine in Gold Hill. He opened the mine and built a little unpretending ten-stamp mill. Eighteen months afterward he retired from the hay business, for his mining income had reached a most comfortable figure. Some people said it was thirty thousand dollars a month, and others said it was sixty thousand dollars. Smith was very rich at any rate.

And then he went to Europe and traveled. And when he came back he was never tired of telling about the fine hogs he had seen in England, and the gorgeous sheep he had seen in Spain, and the fine cattle he had noticed in the vicinity of Rome. He was full of the wonders of the old world, and advised everybody to travel. He said a man never imagined what surprising things there were in the world till he had traveled.

One day, on board ship, the passengers made up a pool of five hundred dollars, which was to be the property of the man who should come nearest to guessing the run of the vessel for the next twenty-four hours. Next day, toward noon, the figures were all in the purser's hands in sealed envelops. Smith was serene and happy, for he had been bribing the engineer. But another party won the prize! Smith said:

"Here, that won't do! He guessed two miles wider of the mark than I did."

The purser said, "Mr. Smith, you missed it further than any man on board. We traveled two hundred and eight miles yesterday."

"Well, sir," said Smith, "that's just where I've got you, for I guessed two hundred and nine. If you'll look at my figgers again you'll find a 2 and two 0's, which stands for 200, don't it?—and after 'em you'll find a 9 (2009), which stands for two hundred and nine. I reckon I'll take that money, if you please."

The Gould & Curry claim comprised twelve hundred feet, and it all belonged originally to the two men whose names it bears. Mr. Curry owned two-thirds of it—and he said that he sold it out for twenty-five hundred dollars, in cash, and an old plug horse that ate up his market value in hay and barley in seventeen days by the watch. And he said that Gould sold out for a pair of second-hand government blankets and a bottle of whisky that killed nine men in three hours, and that an unoffending stranger that smelt the cork was disabled for life. Four years afterward the mine thus disposed of was worth in the San Francisco market seven million six hundred thousand dollars in gold coin.

In the early days a poverty-stricken Mexican who lived in a cañon directly back of Virginia City, had a stream of water as large as a man's wrist trickling from the hillside on his premises. The Ophir Company segregated a hundred feet of their mine and traded it to him for the stream of water. The hundred feet proved to be the richest part of the entire mine; four years after the swap, its market value (including its mill) was one million five hundred thousand dollars.

An individual who owned twenty feet in the Ophir mine before its great riches were revealed to men, traded it for a horse, and a very sorry-looking brute he was, too. A year or so afterward, when Ophir stock went up to three thousand dollars a foot, this man, who had not a cent, used to say he was the most startling example of magnificence and misery the world had ever seen—because he was able to ride a sixty-thousand-dollar horse—yet could not scrape up cash enough to buy a saddle, and was obliged to borrow one or ride bareback. He said if fortune were to give him another sixty-thousand-dollar horse it would ruin him.

A youth of nineteen, who was a telegraph operator in Virginia on a salary of a hundred dollars a month, and who, when he could not make out German names in the list of San Francisco steamer arrivals, used to ingeniously select and supply substitutes for them out of an old Berlin city directory, made himself rich by watching the mining telegrams that passed through his hands and buying and selling stocks accordingly, through a friend in San Francisco.

Once when a private dispatch was sent from Virginia announcing a rich strike in a prominent mine and advising that the matter be

MAGNIFICENCE AND MISERY.

kept secret till a large amount of the stock could be secured, he bought forty "feet" of the stock at twenty dollars a foot, and afterward sold half of it at eight hundred dollars a foot and the rest at double that figure. Within three months he was worth a hundred and fifty thousand dollars, and had resigned his telegraphic position.

Another telegraph operator who had been discharged by the company for divulging the secrets of the office, agreed with a moneyed man in San Francisco to furnish him the result of a great Virginia mining lawsuit within an hour after its private reception by the parties to it in San Francisco. For this he was to have a large percentage of the profits on purchases and sales made on it by his fellow-conspirator. So he went, disguised as a teamster, to a little wayside telegraph office in the mountains, got acquainted with the operator, and sat in the office day after day, smoking his pipe, complaining that his team was fagged out and unable to travel—and meantime listening to the dispatches as they passed clicking through the machine from Virginia. Finally the private dispatch announcing the result of the lawsuit sped over the wires, and as soon as he heard it he telegraphed his friend in San Francisco:

"Am tired waiting. Shall sell the team and go home."

It was the signal agreed upon. The word "waiting" left out, would have signified that the suit had gone the other way. The mock teamster's friend picked up a deal of the mining stock, at low figures, before the news became public, and a fortune was the result.

For a long time after one of the great Virginia mines had been incorporated, about fifty feet of the original location were still in the hands of a man who had never signed the incorporation papers. The stock became very valuable, and every effort was made to find this man, but he had disappeared. Once it was heard that he was in New York, and one or two speculators went east but failed to find him. Once the news came that he was in the Bermudas, and straightway a speculator or two hurried east and sailed for Bermuda—but he was not there. Finally he was heard of in Mexico, and a friend of his, a barkeeper on a salary, scraped together a little money and sought him out, bought his "feet" for a hundred dollars, returned and sold the property for seventy-five thousand dollars.

But why go on? The traditions of Silverland are filled with instances like these, and I would never get through enumerating them were I to attempt to do it. I only desired to give the reader an idea of a peculiarity of the "flush times" which I could not present so strikingly in any other way, and which some mention of was necessary to a realizing comprehension of the time and the country.

I was personally acquainted with the majority of the nabobs I have referred to, and so, for old acquaintance sake, I have shifted their occupations and experiences around in such a way as to keep the Pacific public from recognizing these once notorious men. No longer notorious, for the majority of them have drifted back into poverty and obscurity again.

In Nevada there used to be current the story of an adventure of two of her nabobs, which may or may not have occurred. I give it for what it is worth:

Col. Jim had seen somewhat of the world, and knew more or less of its ways; but Col. Jack was from the back settlements of the States, had led a life of arduous toil, and had never seen a city. These two, blessed with sudden wealth, projected a visit to New York,—Col. Jack to see the sights, and Col. Jim to guard his unsophistication from misfortune. They reached San Francisco in the night, and sailed in the morning. Arrived in New York, Col. Jack said:

"I've heard tell of carriages all my life, and now I mean to have a ride in one; I don't care what it costs. Come along."

They stepped out on the sidewalk, and Col. Jim called a stylish barouche. But Col. Jack said:

"*No*, sir! None of your cheap-John turn-outs for me. I'm here to have a good time, and money ain't any object. I mean to have the nobbiest rig that's going. Now here comes the very trick. Stop that yaller one with the pictures on it—don't you fret—I'll stand all the expenses myself."

So Col. Jim stopped an empty omnibus, and they got in. Said Col. Jack:

"Ain't it gay, though? Oh, no, I reckon not! Cushions, and windows, and pictures, till you can't rest. What would the boys say if they could see us cutting a swell like this in New York? By George, I wish they *could* see us."

Then he put his head out of the window, and shouted to the driver:

"Say, Johnny, this suits *me!*—suits yours truly, you bet you! I want this shebang all day. I'm *on* it, old man! Let 'em out! Make 'em go! We'll make it all right with *you*, sonny!"

The driver passed his hand through the strap-hole, and tapped for his fare—it was before the gongs came into common use. Col. Jack took the hand, and shook it cordially. He said:

"You twig me, old pard! All right between gents. Smell of *that*, and see how you like it!"

And he put a twenty-dollar gold piece in the driver's hand. After a moment the driver said he could not make change.

"Bother the change! Ride it out. Put it in your pocket."

Then to Col. Jim, with a sounding slap on his thigh:

"*Ain't* it style, though? Hanged if I don't hire this thing every day for a week."

The omnibus stopped, and a young lady got in. Col. Jack stared a moment, then nudged Col. Jim with his elbow:

"Don't say a word," he whispered. "Let her ride, if she wants to. Gracious, there's room enough."

The young lady got out her porte-monnaie, and handed her fare to Col. Jack.

"What's this for?" said he.

"Give it to the driver, please."

"Take back your money, madam. We can't allow it. You're welcome to ride here as

A FRIENDLY DRIVER.

long as you please, but this shebang's chartered, and we can't let you pay a cent."

The girl shrunk into a corner, bewildered. An old lady with a basket climbed in, and proffered her fare.

"Excuse me," said Col. Jack. "You're perfectly welcome here, madam, but we can't allow you to pay. Set right down there, mum, and don't you be the least uneasy. Make yourself just as free as if you was in your own turn-out."

Within two minutes, three gentlemen, two fat women, and a couple of children, entered.

"Come right along, friends," said Col. Jack; "don't mind *us*. This is a free blow-out." Then he whispered to Col. Jim, "New York ain't no sociable place, I don't reckon—it ain't no *name* for it!"

He resisted every effort to pass fares to the driver, and made everybody cordially welcome. The situation dawned on the people, and they pocketed their money, and delivered themselves up to covert enjoyment of the episode. Half a dozen more passengers entered.

ASTONISHES THE NATIVES.

"Oh, there's *plenty* of room," said Col. Jack. "Walk right in, and make yourselves at home. A blow-out ain't worth anything *as* a blow-out, unless a body has company." Then in a whisper to Col. Jim: "But *ain't* these New Yorkers friendly? And ain't they cool about it, too? Icebergs ain't anywhere. I reckon they'd tackle a hearse, if it was going their way."

More passengers got in; more yet, and still more. Both seats were filled, and a file of men were standing up, holding on to the cleats overhead. Parties with bas-

COL. JACK "WEAKENS."

kets and bundles were climbing up on the roof. Half-suppressed laughter rippled up from all sides.

"Well, for clean, cool, out-and-out cheek, if this don't bang anything that ever I saw, I'm an Injun!" whispered Col. Jack.

A Chinaman crowded his way in.

"I weaken!" said Col. Jack. "Hold on, driver! Keep your seats, ladies and gents. Just make yourselves free—everything's paid for.
Driver, rustle these folks around as long as they're a mind to go—
friends of ours, you know. Take them everywheres—and if you
want more money, come to the St. Nicholas, and we'll make it all
right. Pleasant journey to you, ladies and gents—go it just as long
as you please—it shan't cost you a cent!"

The two comrades got out, and Col. Jack said:

"Jimmy, it's the sociablest place *I* ever saw. The Chinaman
waltzed in as comfortable as anybody. If we'd staid awhile, I reckon
we'd had some niggers. B' George, we'll have to barricade our doors
to-night, or some of these ducks will be trying to sleep with us."

CHAPTER 47

SOMEBODY has said that in order to know a community, one must observe the style of its funerals and know what manner of men they bury with most ceremony. I cannot say which class we buried with most eclat in our "flush times," the distinguished public benefactor or the distinguished rough—possibly the two chief grades or grand divisions of society honored their illustrious dead about equally; and hence, no doubt the philosopher I have quoted from would have needed to see two representative funerals in Virginia before forming his estimate of the people.

There was a grand time over Buck Fanshaw when he died. He was a representative citizen. He had "killed his man"—not in his own quarrel, it is true, but in defence of a stranger unfairly beset by numbers. He had kept a sumptuous saloon. He had been the proprietor of a dashing helpmeet whom he could have discarded without the formality of a divorce. He had held a high position in the fire department and been a very Warwick in politics. When he died there was great lamentation throughout the town, but especially in the vast bottom-stratum of society.

On the inquest it was shown that Buck Fanshaw, in the delirium of a wasting typhoid fever, had taken arsenic, shot himself through the body, cut his throat, and jumped out of a four-story window and broken his neck—and after due deliberation, the jury, sad and tearful, but with intelligence unblinded by its sorrow, brought in a verdict of death "by the visitation of God." What could the world do without juries?

Prodigious preparations were made for the funeral. All the vehicles in town were hired, all the saloons put in mourning, all the municipal and fire-company flags hung at half-mast, and all the firemen ordered to muster in uniform and bring their machines duly draped in black. Now—let us remark in parenthesis—as all

the peoples of the earth had representative adventurers in the Silverland, and as each adventurer had brought the slang of his nation
or his locality with him, the combination made the slang of Nevada the richest and the most infinitely varied and copious that
had ever existed anywhere in the world, perhaps, except in the
mines of California in the "early days." Slang was the language of
Nevada. It was hard to preach a sermon without it, and be understood. Such phrases as "You bet!" "Oh, no, I reckon not!" "No Irish
need apply," and a hundred others, became so common as to fall
from the lips of a speaker unconsciously—and very often when
they did not touch the subject under discussion and consequently
failed to mean anything.

After Buck Fanshaw's inquest, a meeting of the short-haired
brotherhood was held, for nothing can be done on the Pacific coast
without a public meeting and an expression of sentiment. Regret-
ful resolutions were passed and various committees appointed;
among others, a committee of one was deputed to call on the minister, a fragile, gentle, spirituel new fledgling from an eastern theological seminary, and as yet unacquainted with the ways of the

COMMITTEEMAN AND MINISTER.

mines. The committeeman, "Scotty" Briggs, made his visit; and in
after days it was worth something to hear the minister tell about

it. Scotty was a stalwart rough, whose customary suit, when on weighty official business, like committee work, was a fire helmet, flaming red flannel shirt, patent-leather belt with spanner and revolver attached, coat hung over arm, and pants stuffed into boot-tops. He formed something of a contrast to the pale theological student. It is fair to say of Scotty, however, in passing, that he had a warm heart, and a strong love for his friends, and never entered into a quarrel when he could reasonably keep out of it. Indeed, it was commonly said that whenever one of Scotty's fights was investigated, it always turned out that it had originally been no affair of his, but that out of native goodheartedness he had dropped in of his own accord to help the man who was getting the worst of it. He and Buck Fanshaw were bosom friends, for years, and had often taken adventurous "pot luck" together. On one occasion, they had thrown off their coats and taken the weaker side in a fight among strangers, and after gaining a hard-earned victory, turned and found that the men they were helping had deserted early, and not only that, but had stolen their coats and made off with them! But to return to Scotty's visit to the minister. He was on a sorrowful mission, now, and his face was the picture of woe. Being admitted to the presence he sat down before the clergyman, placed his fire-hat on an unfinished manuscript sermon under the minister's nose, took from it a red silk handkerchief, wiped his brow and heaved a sigh of dismal impressiveness, explanatory of his business. He choked, and even shed tears; but with an effort he mastered his voice and said in lugubrious tones:

"Are you the duck that runs the gospel-mill next door?"

"Am I the—pardon me, I believe I do not understand?"

With another sigh and a half-sob, Scotty rejoined:

"Why you see we are in a bit of trouble, and the boys thought maybe you would give us a lift, if we'd tackle you—that is, if I've got the rights of it and you are the head clerk of the doxology-works next door."

"I am the shepherd in charge of the flock whose fold is next door."

"The which?"

"The spiritual adviser of the little company of believers whose sanctuary adjoins these premises."

Scotty scratched his head, reflected a moment, and then said:

"You ruther hold over me, pard. I reckon I can't call that hand. Ante and pass the buck."

"How? I beg pardon. What did I understand you to say?"

"Well, you've ruther got the bulge on me. Or maybe we've both got the bulge, somehow. You don't smoke me and I don't smoke you. You see, one of the boys has passed in his checks and we want to give him a good send-off, and so the thing I'm on now is to roust out somebody to jerk a little chin-music for us and waltz him through handsome."

"My friend, I seem to grow more and more bewildered. Your observations are wholly incomprehensible to me. Cannot you simplify them in some way? At first I thought perhaps I understood you, but I grope now. Would it not expedite matters if you restricted yourself to categorical statements of fact unencumbered with obstructing accumulations of metaphor and allegory?"

Another pause, and more reflection. Then, said Scotty:

"I'll have to pass, I judge."

"How?"

"You've raised me out, pard."

"I still fail to catch your meaning."

"Why, that last lead of yourn is too many for me—that's the idea. I can't neither trump nor follow suit."

The clergyman sank back in his chair perplexed. Scotty leaned his head on his hand and gave himself up to thought. Presently his face came up, sorrowful but confident.

"I've got it now, so's you can savvy," he said. "What we want is a gospel-sharp. See?"

"A what?"

"Gospel-sharp. Parson."

"Oh! Why did you not say so before? I am a clergyman—a parson."

"Now you talk! You see my blind and straddle it like a man. Put it there!"—extending a brawny paw, which closed over the minister's small hand and gave it a shake indicative of fraternal sympathy and fervent gratification.

"Now we're all right, pard. Let's start fresh. Don't you mind my snuffling a little—becuz we're in a power of trouble. You see, one of the boys has gone up the flume—"

"Gone where?"

"Up the flume—threw up the sponge, you understand."

"Thrown up the sponge?"

"Yes—kicked the bucket—"

"Ah—has departed to that mysterious country from whose bourne no traveler returns."

"Return! I reckon not. Why pard, he's *dead!*"

"Yes, I understand."

"Oh, you do? Well I thought maybe you might be getting tangled some more. Yes, you see he's dead again—"

"*Again!* Why, has he ever been dead before?"

"Dead before? No! Do you reckon a man has got as many lives as a cat? But you bet you he's awful dead now, poor old boy, and I wish I'd never seen this day. I don't want no better friend than Buck Fanshaw. I knowed him by the back; and when I know a man and like him, I freeze to him—you hear *me.* Take him all round, pard, there never was a bullier man in the mines. No man ever knowed Buck Fanshaw to go back on a friend. But it's all up, you know, it's all up. It ain't no use. They've scooped him."

"Scooped him?"

"Yes—death has. Well, well, well, we've got to give him up. Yes indeed. It's a kind of a hard world, after all, *ain't* it? But pard, he was a rustler! You ought to seen him get started once. He was a bully boy with a glass eye! Just spit in his face and give him room according to his strength, and it was just beautiful to see him peel and go in. He was the worst son of a thief that ever drawed breath. Pard, he was *on* it! He was on it bigger than an Injun!"

"On it? On what?"

"On the shoot. On the shoulder. On the fight, you understand. *He* didn't give a continental for *any*body. *Beg* your pardon, friend, for coming so near saying a cuss-word—but you see I'm on an awful strain, in this palaver, on account of having to cramp down and draw everything so mild. But we've got to give him up. There ain't any getting around that, I don't reckon. Now if we can get you to help plant him—"

"Preach the funeral discourse? Assist at the obsequies?"

"Obs'quies is good. Yes. That's it—that's our little game. We are going to get the thing up regardless, you know. He was always nifty himself, and so you bet you his funeral ain't going to be no slouch—solid silver door-plate on his coffin, six plumes on the hearse, and a nigger on the box in a biled shirt and a plug hat—how's that for high? And we'll take care of *you*, pard. We'll fix you all right. There'll be a kerridge for you; and whatever you want, you just 'scape out and we'll 'tend to it. We've got a shebang fixed up for you to stand behind, in No. 1's house, and don't you be afraid. Just go in and toot your horn, if you don't sell a clam. Put Buck through as bully as you can, pard, for anybody that knowed him will tell you that he was one of the whitest men that was ever in the mines. You can't draw it too strong. He never could stand it to see things going wrong. He's done more to make this town quiet and peaceable than any man in it. I've seen him lick four Greasers in eleven minutes, myself. If a thing wanted regulating, *he* warn't

SCOTTY REGULATING MATTERS.

a man to go browsing around after somebody to do it, but he would prance in and regulate it himself. He warn't a Catholic. Scasely. He was down on 'em. His word was, 'No Irish need apply!' But it didn't make no difference about that when it came down to what a man's rights was—and so, when some roughs jumped the Catholic bone-yard and started in to stake out town lots in it he *went* for 'em! And he *cleaned* 'em, too! I was there, pard, and I seen it myself."

"That was very well indeed—at least the impulse was— whether the act was strictly defensible or not. Had deceased any religious convictions? That is to say, did he feel a dependence upon, or acknowledge allegiance to a higher power?"

More reflection.

"I reckon you've stumped me again, pard. Could you say it over once more, and say it slow?"

"Well, to simplify it somewhat, was he, or rather had he ever been connected with any organization sequestered from secular concerns and devoted to self-sacrifice in the interests of morality?"

"All down but nine—set 'em up on the other alley, pard."

"What did I understand you to say?"

"Why, you're most too many for me, you know. When you get in with your left I hunt grass every time. Every time you draw, you fill; but I don't seem to have any luck. Let's have a new deal."

"How? Begin again?"

"That's it."

"Very well. Was he a good man, and—"

"There—I see that; don't put up another chip till I look at my hand. A good man, says you? Pard, it ain't no name for it. He was the best man that ever—pard, you would have doted on that man. He could lam any galoot of his inches in America. It was him that put down the riot last election before it got a start; and everybody said he was the only man that could have done it. He waltzed in with a spanner in one hand and a trumpet in the other, and sent fourteen men home on a shutter in less than three minutes. He had that riot all broke up and prevented nice before anybody ever got a chance to strike a blow. He was always for peace, and he would *have* peace—he could not stand disturbances. Pard, he was a great loss to this town. It would please the boys if you could chip in something like that and do him justice. Here once when the Micks got to throwing stones through the Methodis' Sunday school windows, Buck Fanshaw, all of his own notion, shut up his saloon and took a couple of six-shooters and mounted guard over the Sunday school. Says he, 'No Irish need apply!' And they didn't. He was the bulliest man in the mountains, pard! He could run faster, jump higher, hit harder, and hold more tangle-foot whisky without spilling it than any man in seventeen counties. Put that in, pard—it'll please the boys more than anything you could say. And you can say, pard, that he never shook his mother."

"Never shook his mother?"

NEVER SHOOK HIS MOTHER.

"That's it—any of the boys will tell you so."

"Well, but why *should* he shake her?"

"That's what *I* say—but some people does."

"Not people of any repute?"

"Well, some that averages pretty so-so."

"In my opinion the man that would offer personal violence to his own mother, ought to—"

"Cheese it, pard; you've banked your ball clean outside the string. What I was a drivin' at, was, that he never *throwed off* on his mother—don't you see? No indeedy. He give her a house to live in, and town lots, and plenty of money; and he looked after her and took care of her all the time; and when she was down with the small-pox I'm d—d if he didn't set up nights and nuss her himself! *Beg* your pardon for saying it, but it hopped out too quick for yours truly. You've treated me like a gentleman, pard, and I ain't the man to hurt your feelings intentional. I think you're white. I think you're a square man, pard. I like you, and I'll lick any man that don't. I'll lick him till he can't tell himself from a last year's corpse! Put it *there!*" [Another fraternal hand-shake—and exit.]

The obsequies were all that "the boys" could desire. Such a marvel of funeral pomp had never been seen in Virginia. The plumed hearse, the dirge-breathing brass bands, the closed marts of business, the flags drooping at half-mast, the long, plodding procession of uniformed secret societies, military battalions and fire companies, draped engines, carriages of officials, and citizens in vehicles and on foot, attracted multitudes of spectators to the sidewalks, roofs and windows; and for years afterward, the degree of grandeur attained by any civic display in Virginia was determined by comparison with Buck Fanshaw's funeral.

Scotty Briggs, as a pall-bearer and a mourner, occupied a prominent place at the funeral, and when the sermon was finished and the last sentence of the prayer for the dead man's soul ascended, he responded, in a low voice, but with feeling:

"Amen. No Irish need apply."

As the bulk of the response was without apparent relevancy, it was probably nothing more than a humble tribute to the memory of the friend that was gone; for, as Scotty had once said, it was "his word."

Scotty Briggs, in after days, achieved the distinction of becoming the only convert to religion that was ever gathered from the Virginia roughs; and it transpired that the man who had it in him

SCOTTY AS A SUNDAY SCHOOL TEACHER.

to espouse the quarrel of the weak out of inborn nobility of spirit was no mean timber whereof to construct a Christian. The making him one did not warp his generosity or diminish his courage; on the contrary it gave intelligent direction to the one and a broader field to the other. If his Sunday school class progressed faster than the other classes, was it matter for wonder? I think not. He talked to his pioneer small fry in a language they understood! It was my large privilege, a month before he died, to hear him tell the beautiful story of Joseph and his brethren to his class "without looking at the book." I leave it to the reader to fancy what it was like, as it fell, riddled with slang, from the lips of that grave, earnest teacher, and was listened to by his little learners with a consuming interest that showed that they were as unconscious as he was that any violence was being done to the sacred proprieties!

CHAPTER 48

The first twenty-six graves in the Virginia cemetery were occupied by *murdered* men. So everybody said, so everybody believed, and so they will always say and believe. The reason why there was so much slaughtering done, was, that in a new mining district the rough element predominates, and a person is not respected until he has "killed his man." That was the very expression used.

If an unknown individual arrived, they did not inquire if he was capable, honest, industrious, but—had he killed his man? If he had not, he gravitated to his natural and proper position, that of a man of small consequence; if he had, the cordiality of his reception was graduated according to the number of his dead. It was tedious work struggling up to a position of influence with bloodless hands; but when a man came with the blood of half a dozen men on his soul, his worth was recognized at once and his acquaintance sought.

In Nevada, for a time, the lawyer, the editor, the banker, the chief desperado, the chief gambler, and the saloon-keeper, occupied the same level in society, and it was the highest. The cheapest and easiest way to become an influential man and be looked up to by the community at large, was to stand behind a bar, wear a cluster-diamond pin, and sell whisky. I am not sure but that the saloon-keeper held a shade higher rank than any other member of society. His opinion had weight. It was his privilege to say how the elections should go. No great movement could succeed without the countenance and direction of the saloon-keepers. It was a high favor when the chief saloon-keeper consented to serve in the legislature or the board of aldermen. Youthful ambition hardly aspired so much to the honors of the law, or the army and navy as to the dignity of proprietorship in a saloon.

To be a saloon-keeper and kill a man was to be illustrious. Hence the reader will not be surprised to learn that more than one man was killed in Nevada under hardly the pretext of provocation, so impatient was the slayer to achieve reputation and throw off the

THE MAN WHO HAD KILLED A DOZEN.

galling sense of being held in indifferent repute by his associates. I knew two youths who tried to "kill their men" for no other reason—and got killed themselves for their pains. "There goes the man that killed Bill Adams" was higher praise and a sweeter sound in the ears of this sort of people than any other speech that admiring lips could utter.

The men who murdered Virginia's original twenty-six cemetery-occupants were never punished. Why? Because Alfred the Great, when he invented trial by jury, and knew that he had admirably framed it to secure justice in his age of the world, was not aware that in the nineteenth century the condition of things would be so entirely changed that unless he rose from the grave and altered the jury plan to meet the emergency, it would prove the most ingenious and infallible agency for *defeating* justice that human wisdom could contrive. For how could he imagine that we simpletons would go on using his jury plan after circumstances had stripped it of its usefulness, any more than he could imagine that we would go on using his candle-clock after we had invented chronometers? In his day news could not travel fast, and hence he could easily find a jury of honest, intelligent men who had not heard of the case they were called to try—but in our day of telegraphs and newspapers his plan compels us to swear in juries composed of fools and rascals, because the system rigidly excludes honest men and men of brains.

I remember one of those sorrowful farces, in Virginia, which we call a jury trial. A noted desperado killed Mr. B., a good citizen, in the most wanton and cold-blooded way. Of course the papers were full of it, and all men capable of reading, read about it. And of course all men not deaf and dumb and idiotic, talked about it. A jury-list was made out, and Mr. B. L., a prominent banker and a valued citizen, was questioned precisely as he would have been questioned in any court in America:

"Have you heard of this homicide?"

"Yes."

"Have you held conversations upon the subject?"

"Yes."

"Have you formed or expressed opinions about it?"

"Yes."

"Have you read the newspaper accounts of it?"

"Yes."

"We do not want you."

A minister, intelligent, esteemed, and greatly respected; a merchant of high character and known probity; a mining superintendent of intelligence and unblemished reputation; a quartz mill owner of excellent standing, were all questioned in the same way, and all set aside. Each said the public talk and the newspaper reports had not so biased his mind but that sworn testimony would overthrow his previously formed opinions and enable him to render a verdict without prejudice and in accordance with the facts. But of course such men could not be trusted with the case. Ignoramuses alone could mete out unsullied justice.

When the peremptory challenges were all exhausted, a jury of twelve men was empaneled—a jury who swore they had neither

THE UNPREJUDICED JURY.

heard, read, talked about nor expressed an opinion concerning a murder which the very cattle in the corrals, the Indians in the sage-brush and the stones in the streets were cognizant of! It was a jury composed of two desperadoes, two low beer-house politicians, three barkeepers, two ranchmen who could not read, and three dull, stupid, human donkeys! It actually came out afterward, that one of these latter thought that incest and arson were the same thing.

The verdict rendered by this jury was, Not Guilty. What else could one expect?

The jury system puts a ban upon intelligence and honesty, and a premium upon ignorance, stupidity and perjury. It is a shame that we must continue to use a worthless system because it *was* good a thousand years ago. In this age, when a gentleman of high social standing, intelligence and probity, swears that testimony given under solemn oath will outweigh, with him, street talk and newspaper reports based upon mere hearsay, he is worth a hundred jurymen who will swear to their own ignorance and stupidity, and justice would be far safer in his hands than in theirs. Why could not the jury law be so altered as to give men of brains and honesty an *equal ϴhance* with fools and miscreants? Is it right to show the present favoritism to one class of men and inflict a disability on

another, in a land whose boast is that all its citizens are free and
equal? I am a candidate for the legislature. I desire to tamper with
the jury law. I wish to so alter it as to put a premium on intelligence and character, and close the jury box against idiots, black-
legs, and people who do not read newspapers. But no doubt I shall
be defeated—every effort I make to save the country "misses fire."

My idea, when I began this chapter, was to say something about
desperadoism in the "flush times" of Nevada. To attempt a portrayal of that era and that land, and leave out the blood and carnage,
would be like portraying Mormondom and leaving out polygamy.
The desperado stalked the streets with a swagger graded according
to the number of his homicides, and a nod of recognition from him
was sufficient to make a humble admirer happy for the rest of the
day. The deference that was paid to a desperado of wide reputation,
and who "kept his private graveyard," as the phrase went, was
marked, and cheerfully accorded. When he moved along the side-

A DESPERADO GIVING REFERENCE.

walk in his excessively long-tailed frock-coat, shiny stump-toed
boots, and with dainty little slouch hat tipped over left eye, the

small-fry roughs made room for his majesty; when he entered the restaurant, the waiters deserted bankers and merchants to over-whelm him with obsequious service; when he shouldered his way to a bar, the shouldered parties wheeled indignantly, recognized him, and—apologized. They got a look in return that froze their marrow, and by that time a curled and breast-pinned barkeeper was beaming over the counter, proud of the established acquain-tanceship that permitted such a familiar form of speech as:

"How 're ye, Billy, old fel? Glad to see you. What'll you take—the old thing?"

The "old thing" meant his customary drink, of course.

The best known names in the Territory of Nevada were those be-longing to these long-tailed heroes of the revolver. Orators, gover-nors, capitalists and leaders of the legislature enjoyed a degree of fame, but it seemed local and meagre when contrasted with the fame of such men as Sam Brown, Jack Williams, Billy Mulligan, Farmer Pease, Sugarfoot Mike, Pock-Marked Jake, El Dorado Johnny, Jack McNabb, Joe McGee, Jack Harris, Six-fingered Pete, etc., etc. There was a long list of them. They were brave, reckless men, and traveled with their lives in their hands. To give them their due, they did their killing principally among themselves, and seldom molested peaceable citizens, for they considered it small credit to add to their trophies so cheap a bauble as the death of a man who was "not on the shoot," as they phrased it. They killed each other on slight provocation, and hoped and expected to be killed themselves—for they held it almost shame to die otherwise than "with their boots on," as they expressed it.

I remember an instance of a desperado's contempt for such small game as a private citizen's life. I was taking a late supper in a res-taurant one night, with two reporters and a little printer named—Brown, for instance—any name will do. Presently a stranger with a long-tailed coat on came in, and not noticing Brown's hat, which was lying in a chair, sat down on it. Little Brown sprang up and be-came abusive in a moment. The stranger smiled, smoothed out the hat, and offered it to Brown with profuse apologies couched in caustic sarcasm, and begged Brown not to destroy him. Brown threw off his coat and challenged the man to fight—abused him, threatened him, impeached his courage, and urged and even implored him to fight; and in the meantime the smiling stranger placed himself under our protection in mock distress. But presently he assumed a serious tone, and said:

"Very well, gentlemen, if we must fight, we must, I suppose. But don't rush into danger and then say I gave you no warning. I am more than a match for all of you when I get started. I will give you proofs, and then if my friend here still insists, I will try to accommodate him."

The table we were sitting at was about five feet long, and unusually cumbersome and heavy. He asked us to put our hands on the dishes and hold them in their places a moment—one of them was a large oval dish with a portly roast on it. Then he sat down, tilted up one end of the table, set two of the legs on his knees, took the end of the table between his teeth, took his hands away, and pulled down with his teeth till the table came up to a level position, dishes and all! He said he could lift a keg of nails with his teeth. He

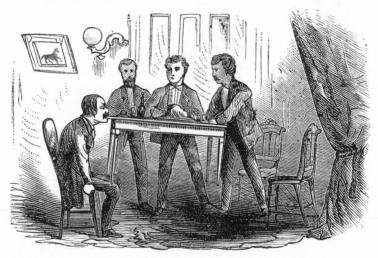

SATISFYING A FOE.

picked up a common glass tumbler and bit a semi-circle out of it. Then he opened his bosom and showed us a net-work of knife and bullet scars; showed us more on his arms and face, and said he believed he had bullets enough in his body to make a pig of lead. He was armed to the teeth. He closed with the remark that he was Mr.

—— of Cariboo—a celebrated name whereat we shook in our shoes. I would publish the name, but for the suspicion that he might come and carve me. He finally inquired if Brown still thirsted for blood. Brown turned the thing over in his mind a moment, and then—asked him to supper.

With the permission of the reader, I will group together, in the next chapter, some samples of life in our small mountain village in the old days of desperadoism. I was there at the time. The reader will observe peculiarities in our *official* society; and he will observe also, an instance of how, in new countries, murders breed murders.

CHAPTER 49

An extract or two from the newspapers of the day will furnish a photograph that can need no embellishment:

FATAL SHOOTING AFFRAY.—An affray occurred, last evening, in a billiard saloon on C street, between *Deputy Marshal Jack Williams* and Wm. Brown, which resulted in the immediate death of the latter. There had been some difficulty between the parties for several months.

An inquest was immediately held, and the following testimony adduced:

Officer GEO. BIRDSALL, sworn, says:—I was told Wm. Brown was drunk and was looking for Jack Williams; so soon as I heard that I started for the parties to prevent a collision; went into the billiard saloon; saw Billy Brown running around, saying if anybody had anything against him to show cause; he was talking in a boisterous manner, and officer Perry took him to the other end of the room to talk to him; Brown came back to me; remarked to me that he thought he was as good as anybody, and knew how to take care of himself; he passed by me and went to the bar; don't know whether he drank or not; Williams was at the end of the billiard-table, next to the stairway; Brown, after going to the bar, came back and said he was as good as any man in the world; he had then walked out to the end of the first billiard-table from the bar; I moved closer to them, supposing there would be a fight; as Brown drew his pistol I caught hold of it; he had fired one shot at Williams; don't know the effect of it; caught hold of him with one hand, and took hold of the pistol and turned it up; think he fired once after I caught hold of the pistol; I wrenched the pistol from him; walked to the end of the billiard-table and told a party that I had Brown's pistol, and to stop shooting; I think four shots were fired in all; after walking out, Mr. Foster remarked that Brown was shot dead.

Oh, there was no excitement about it—he merely "remarked" the small circumstance!

Four months later the following item appeared in the same paper (the *Enterprise*). In this item the name of one of the city officers above referred to (*Deputy Marshal Jack Williams*) occurs again:

ROBBERY AND DESPERATE AFFRAY.—On Tuesday night, a German named Charles Hurtzal, engineer in a mill at Silver City, came to this place, and visited the hurdy-gurdy house on B street. The music, dancing and Teutonic maidens awakened memories of Faderland until our German friend was carried away with rapture. He evidently had money, and was spending it freely. Late in the evening Jack Williams and Andy Blessington invited him down stairs to take a cup of coffee. Williams proposed a game of cards and went up stairs to procure a deck, but not finding any returned. On the stairway he met the German, and drawing his pistol knocked him down and rifled his pockets of some seventy dollars. Hurtzal dared give no alarm, as he was told, with a pistol at his head, if he made any noise or exposed them, they would blow his brains out. So effectually was he frightened that he made no complaint, until his friends forced him. Yesterday a warrant was issued, but the culprits had disappeared.

This efficient city officer, Jack Williams, had the common reputation of being a burglar, a highwayman and a desperado. It was said that he had several times drawn his revolver and levied money contributions on citizens at dead of night in the public streets of Virginia.

Five months after the above item appeared, Williams was assassinated while sitting at a card table one night; a gun was thrust through the crack of the door and Williams dropped from his chair riddled with balls. It was said, at the time, that Williams had been for some time aware that a party of his own sort (desperadoes) had sworn away his life; and it was generally believed among the people that Williams's friends and enemies would make the assassination memorable—and useful, too—by a wholesale destruction of each other.*

---

*However, one prophecy was verified, at any rate. It was asserted by the desperadoes that one of their brethren (Joe McGee, *a special policeman*) was known to be the conspirator chosen by lot to assassinate Williams; and they also asserted that doom had been pronounced against McGee, and that he would be assassinated in exactly the same manner that had been adopted for the destruction of Williams—a prophecy which came true a year later. After twelve months of distress (for McGee saw a fancied assassin in every man that approached him), he made the last of many efforts to get out of the country unwatched. He went to Carson and sat down in a saloon to wait for the stage—it would leave at four in the morning. But as the night waned and the crowd thinned, he grew uneasy, and told the barkeeper that assassins were on his track. The barkeeper told him to stay in the middle of the room, then, and not go near the door, or the window by the stove. But a fatal fascination seduced him to the neighborhood of the stove every now and then, and repeatedly the bar-

It did not so happen, but still, times were not dull during the next twenty-four hours, for within that time a woman was killed by a pistol shot, a man was brained with a slung shot, and a man named Reeder was also disposed of permanently. Some matters in the *Enterprise* account of the killing of Reeder are worth noting— especially the accommodating complaisance of a Virginia justice of the peace. The italics in the following narrative are mine:

MORE CUTTING AND SHOOTING.—The devil seems to have again broken loose in our town. Pistols and guns explode and knives gleam in our streets as in early times. When there has been a long season of quiet, people are slow to wet their hands in blood; but once blood is spilled, cutting and shooting come easy. Night before last Jack Williams was assassinated, and yesterday forenoon we had more bloody work, growing out of the killing of Williams, and on the same street in which he met his death. It appears that Tom Reeder, a friend of Williams, and George Gumbert were talking, at the meat market of the latter, about the killing of Williams the previous night, when Reeder said it was a most cowardly act to shoot a man in such a way, giving him "no show." Gumbert said that Williams had "as good a show as he gave Billy Brown," meaning the man killed by Williams last March. Reeder said it was a d—d lie, that Williams had no show at all. At this, Gumbert drew a knife and stabbed Reeder, cutting him in two places in the back. One stroke of the knife cut into the sleeve of Reeder's coat and passed downward in a slanting direction through his clothing, and entered his body at the small of the back; another blow struck more squarely, and made a much more dangerous wound. Gumbert gave himself up to the officers of justice, and was shortly after discharged by Justice Atwill, *on his own recognizance,* to appear for trial at six o'clock in the evening. In the meantime Reeder had been taken into the office of Dr. Owens, where his wounds were properly dressed. *One of his wounds was considered quite dangerous, and it was thought by many that it would prove fatal. But being considerably under the influence of liquor, Reeder did not feel his wounds as he otherwise would, and he got up and went into the street.* He went to the meat market and renewed his quarrel with Gumbert, threatening his life. Friends tried to

---

keeper brought him back to the middle of the room and warned him to remain there. But he could not. At three in the morning he again returned to the stove and sat down by a stranger. Before the barkeeper could get to him with another warning whisper, some one outside fired through the window and riddled McGee's breast with slugs, killing him almost instantly. By the same discharge the stranger at McGee's side also received attentions which proved fatal in the course of two or three days.

interfere to put a stop to the quarrel and get the parties away from each other. In the Fashion Saloon Reeder made threats against the life of Gumbert, saying he would kill him, and it is said that *he requested the officers not to arrest Gumbert, as he intended to kill him.* After these threats Gumbert went off and procured a double-barreled shot gun, loaded with buck-shot or revolver balls, and went after Reeder. Two or three persons were assisting him along the street, trying to get him home, and had him just in front of the store of Klopstock & Harris, when Gumbert came across toward him from the opposite side of the street with his gun. He came up within about ten or fifteen feet of Reeder, and called out to those with him to "look out! get out of the way!" and they had only time to heed the warning, when he fired. Reeder was at the time attempting to screen himself behind a large cask, which stood against the awning post of Klopstock & Harris's store, but some of the balls took effect in the lower part of his breast, and he reeled around forward and fell in front of the cask. Gumbert then raised his gun and fired the second barrel, which missed Reeder and entered the ground. At the time that this occurred, there were a great many persons on the street in the vicinity, and a number of them called out to Gumbert, when they saw him raise his gun, to "hold on," and "don't shoot!" The cutting took place about ten o'clock and the shooting about twelve. After the shooting the street was instantly crowded with the inhabitants of that part of the town, some appearing much excited and laughing—declaring that it looked like the "good old times of '60." Marshal Perry and officer Birdsall were near when the shooting occurred, and Gumbert was immediately arrested and his gun taken from him, when he was marched off to jail. Many persons who were attracted to the spot where this bloody work had just taken place, looked bewildered and seemed to be asking themselves what was to happen next, appearing in doubt as to whether the killing mania had reached its climax, or whether we were to turn in and have a grand killing spell, shooting whoever might have given us offence. It was whispered around that it was not all over yet—five or six more were to be killed before night. Reeder was taken to the Virginia City Hotel, and doctors called in to examine his wounds. They found that two or three balls had entered his right side; one of them appeared to have passed through the substance of the lungs, while another passed into the liver. Two balls were also found to have struck one of his legs. As some of the balls struck the cask, the wounds in Reeder's leg were probably from these, glancing downwards, though they might have been caused by the second shot fired. After being shot, Reeder said when he got on his feet—smiling as he spoke—"It will take better shooting than that to kill me." The doctors consider it almost impossible for him to recover, but as he has an excellent constitution he may survive, notwithstanding the number and dangerous character of the wounds he has received. The town appears to be perfectly quiet at present, as though the late stormy times had cleared our moral atmosphere; but who can tell in what quarter clouds are lowering or plots ripening?

Reeder—or at least what was left of him—survived his wounds two days! Nothing was ever done with Gumbert.

Trial by jury is the palladium of our liberties. I do not know what a palladium is, having never seen a palladium, but it is a good thing no doubt at any rate. Not less than a hundred men have been murdered in Nevada—perhaps I would be within bounds if I said three hundred—and as far as I can learn, only two persons have suffered the death penalty there. However, four or five who had no money and no political influence have been punished by imprisonment— one languished in prison as much as eight months, I think. However, I do not desire to be extravagant—it may have been less.

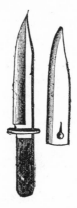

CHAPTER 50

THESE murder and jury statistics remind me of a certain very extraordinary trial and execution of twenty years ago; it is a scrap of history familiar to all old Californians, and worthy to be known by other peoples of the earth that love simple, straightforward justice unencumbered with nonsense. I would apologize for this digression but for the fact that the information I am about to offer is apology enough in itself. And since I digress constantly anyhow, perhaps it is as well to eschew apologies altogether and thus prevent their growing irksome.

Capt. Ned Blakely—that name will answer as well as any other fictitious one (for he was still with the living at last accounts, and may not desire to be famous)—sailed ships out of the harbor of San Francisco for many years. He was a stalwart, warm-hearted, eagle-eyed veteran, who had been a sailor nearly fifty years—a sailor from early boyhood. He was a rough, honest creature, full of pluck, and just as full of hard-headed simplicity, too. He hated trifling conventionalities—"business" was the word, with him. He had all a sailor's vindictiveness against the quips and quirks of the law, and steadfastly believed that the first and last aim and object of the law and lawyers was to defeat justice.

He sailed for the Chincha Islands in command of a guano ship. He had a fine crew, but his negro mate was his pet—on him he had for years lavished his admiration and esteem. It was Capt. Ned's first voyage to the Chinchas, but his fame had gone before him— the fame of being a man who would fight at the dropping of a handkerchief, when imposed upon, and would stand no nonsense. It was a fame well earned. Arrived in the islands, he found that the staple of conversation was the exploits of one Bill Noakes, a bully, the mate of a trading ship. This man had created a small reign of terror there. At nine o'clock at night, Capt. Ned, all alone, was pacing his deck in the starlight. A form ascended the side, and approached him. Capt. Ned said:

"Who goes there?"

"I'm Bill Noakes, the best man in the islands."

"What do you want aboard this ship?"

"I've heard of Capt. Ned Blakely, and one of us is a better man than t'other—I'll know which, before I go ashore."

"You've come to the right shop—I'm your man. I'll learn you to come aboard this ship without an *invite*."

He seized Noakes, backed him against the mainmast, pounded his face to a pulp, and then threw him overboard.

IMPARTING INFORMATION.

Noakes was not convinced. He returned the next night, got the pulp renewed, and went overboard head first, as before. He was satisfied.

A week after this, while Noakes was carousing with a sailor crowd on shore, at noonday, Capt. Ned's colored mate came along, and Noakes tried to pick a quarrel with him. The negro evaded the trap, and tried to get away. Noakes followed him up; the negro began to run; Noakes fired on him with a revolver and killed him.

Half a dozen sea-captains witnessed the whole affair. Noakes retreated to the small after-cabin of his ship, with two other bullies,
and gave out that death would be the portion of any man that in-
truded there. There was no attempt made to follow the villains;
there was no disposition to do it, and indeed very little thought of
such an enterprise. There were no courts and no officers; there was
no government; the islands belonged to Peru, and Peru was far
away; she had no official representative on the ground; and neither
had any other nation.

However, Capt. Ned was not perplexing his head about such
things. They concerned him not. He was boiling with rage and furious for justice. At nine o'clock at night he loaded a double-
barreled gun with slugs, fished out a pair of handcuffs, got a ship's
lantern, summoned his quartermaster, and went ashore. He said:

"Do you see that ship there at the dock?"

"Ay-ay, sir."

"It's the Venus."

"Ay-ay, sir."

"You—you know *me*."

"Ay-ay, sir."

"Very well, then. Take the lantern. Carry it just under your chin.
I'll walk behind you and rest this gun-barrel on your shoulder,
p'inting forward—so. Keep your lantern well up, so's I can see
things ahead of you good. I'm going to march in on Noakes—and
take him—and jug the other chaps. If you flinch—well, you know
me."

"Ay-ay, sir."

In this order they filed aboard softly, arrived at Noakes's den, the
quartermaster pushed the door open, and the lantern revealed the
three desperadoes sitting on the floor. Capt. Ned said:

"I'm Ned Blakely. I've got you under fire. Don't you move without orders—any of you. You two kneel down in the corner; faces to
the wall—now. Bill Noakes, put these handcuffs on; now come up
close. Quartermaster, fasten 'em. All right. Don't stir, sir. Quartermaster, put the key in the outside of the door. Now, men, I'm going
to lock you two in; and if you try to burst through this door—well,
you've heard of *me*. Bill Noakes, fall in ahead, and march. All set.
Quartermaster, lock the door."

Noakes spent the night on board Blakely's ship, a prisoner under strict guard. Early in the morning Capt. Ned called in all the sea-captains in the harbor and invited them, with nautical ceremony,

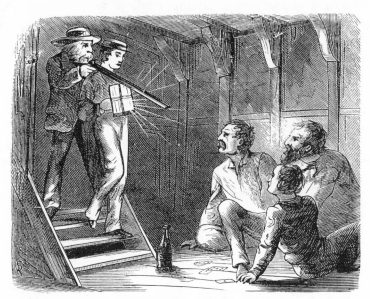

A WALKING BATTERY.

to be present on board his ship at nine o'clock to witness the hang-ing of Noakes at the yard-arm!

"What! The man has not been tried."

"Of course he hasn't. But didn't he kill the nigger?"

"Certainly he did; but you are not thinking of hanging him with-out a trial?"

"*Trial!* What do I want to try him for, if he killed the nigger?"

"Oh, Capt. Ned, this will *never* do. Think how it will sound."

"Sound be hanged! *Didn't he kill the nigger?*"

"Certainly, certainly, Capt. Ned,—nobody denies that,—but—"

"Then I'm going to *hang* him, that's all. Everybody I've talked to talks just the same way you do. Everybody says he killed the nig-ger, everybody knows he killed the nigger, and yet every lubber of you wants him *tried* for it. I don't understand such bloody foolish-ness as that. *Tried!* Mind you, I don't object to trying him, if it's got to be done to give satisfaction; and I'll be there, and chip in and help, too; but put it off till afternoon—put it off till afternoon, for I'll have my hands middling full till after the burying—"

"Why, what do you mean? Are you going to hang him *anyhow*—and try him afterward?"

"Didn't I *say* I was going to hang him? I never saw such people as you. What's the difference? You ask a favor, and then you ain't satisfied when you get it. Before or after's all one—*you* know how the trial will go. He killed the nigger. Say—I must be going. If your mate would like to come to the hanging, fetch him along. I like him."

There was a stir in the camp. The captains came in a body and pleaded with Capt. Ned not to do this rash thing. They promised that they would create a court composed of captains of the best character; they would empanel a jury; they would conduct everything in a way becoming the serious nature of the business in hand, and give the case an impartial hearing and the accused a fair trial. And they said it would be murder, and punishable by the American courts if he persisted and hung the accused on his ship. They pleaded hard. Capt. Ned said:

"Gentlemen, I'm not stubborn and I'm not unreasonable. I'm always willing to do just as near right as I can. How long will it take?"

"Probably only a little while."

"And can I take him up the shore and hang him as soon as you are done?"

"If he is proven guilty he shall be hanged without unnecessary delay."

"*If* he's proven guilty. Great Neptune, *ain't* he guilty? This beats my time. Why you all *know* he's guilty."

But at last they satisfied him that they were projecting nothing underhanded. Then he said:

"Well, all right. You go on and try him and I'll go down and overhaul his conscience and prepare him to go—like enough he needs it, and I don't want to send him off without a show for hereafter."

This was another obstacle. They finally convinced him that it was necessary to have the accused in court. Then they said they would send a guard to bring him.

"No, sir, I prefer to fetch him myself—he don't get out of *my* hands. Besides, I've got to go to the ship to get a rope, anyway."

The court assembled with due ceremony, empaneled a jury, and presently Capt. Ned entered, leading the prisoner with one hand and carrying a Bible and a rope in the other. He seated himself by the side of his captive and told the court to "up anchor and make sail." Then he turned a searching eye on the jury, and detected Noakes's friends, the two bullies. He strode over and said to them confidentially:

"You're here to interfere, you see. Now you vote right, do you hear?—or else there'll be a double-barreled inquest here when this trial's off, and your remainders will go home in a couple of baskets."

The caution was not without fruit. The jury was a unit—the verdict, "Guilty."

Capt. Ned sprung to his feet and said:

"Come along—you're my meat *now*, my lad, anyway. Gentlemen you've done yourselves proud. I invite you all to come and see that I do it all straight. Follow me to the cañon, a mile above here."

The court informed him that a sheriff had been appointed to do the hanging, and—

Capt. Ned's patience was at an end. His wrath was boundless. The subject of a sheriff was judiciously dropped.

When the crowd arrived at the cañon, Capt. Ned climbed a tree and arranged the halter, then came down and noosed his man. He opened his Bible, and laid aside his hat. Selecting a chapter at random, he read it through, in a deep bass voice and with sincere solemnity. Then he said:

"Lad, you are about to go aloft and give an account of yourself; and the lighter a man's manifest is, as far as sin's concerned, the better for him. Make a clean breast, man, and carry a log with you that'll bear inspection. You killed the nigger?"

No reply. A long pause.

The captain read another chapter, pausing, from time to time, to impress the effect. Then he talked an earnest, persuasive sermon to him, and ended by repeating the question:

"Did you kill the nigger?"

No reply—other than a malignant scowl. The captain now read the first and second chapters of Genesis, with deep feeling— paused a moment, closed the book reverently, and said with a perceptible savor of satisfaction:

"There. Four chapters. There's few that would have took the pains with you that I have."

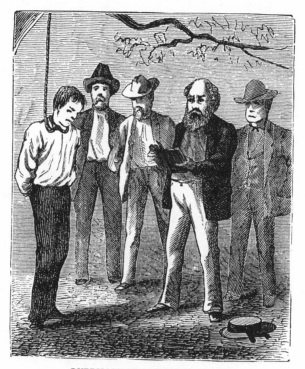

OVERHAULING HIS MANIFEST.

Then he swung up the condemned, and made the rope fast; stood by and timed him half an hour with his watch, and then delivered the body to the court. A little after, as he stood contemplating the motionless figure, a doubt came into his face; evidently he felt a twinge of conscience—a misgiving—and he said with a sigh:

"Well, p'raps I ought to burnt him, maybe. But I was trying to do for the best."

When the history of this affair reached California (it was in the "early days") it made a deal of talk, but did not diminish the captain's popularity in any degree. It increased it, indeed. California had a population then that "inflicted" justice after a fashion that was simplicity and primitiveness itself, and could therefore admire appreciatively when the same fashion was followed elsewhere.

CHAPTER 51

Vice flourished luxuriantly during the hey-day of our "flush times." The saloons were overburdened with custom; so were the police courts, the gambling dens, the brothels and the jails—unfailing signs of high prosperity in a mining region—in any region for that matter. Is it not so? A crowded police court docket is the surest of all signs that trade is brisk and money plenty. Still, there is one other sign; it comes last, but when it does come it establishes beyond cavil that the "flush times" are at the flood. This is the birth of the "literary" paper. The *Weekly Occidental*, "devoted to literature," made its appearance in Virginia. All the literary people were engaged to write for it. Mr. F. was to edit it. He was a felicitous skirmisher with a pen, and a man who could say happy things in a crisp, neat way. Once, while editor of the *Union*, he had disposed of a labored, incoherent, two-column attack made upon him by a cotemporary, with a single line, which, at first glance, seemed to contain a solemn and tremendous compliment—viz.: "THE LOGIC OF OUR ADVERSARY RESEMBLES THE PEACE OF GOD,"—and left it to the reader's memory and after-thought to invest the remark with another and "more different" meaning by supplying for himself and at his own leisure the rest of the Scripture—"*in that it passeth understanding.*" He once said of a little, half-starved, wayside community that had no subsistence except what they could get by preying upon chance passengers who stopped over with them a day when traveling by the overland stage, that in their church service they had altered the Lord's Prayer to read: "Give us this day our daily stranger!"

We expected great things of the *Occidental*. Of course it could not get along without an original novel, and so we made arrangements to hurl into the work the full strength of the company. Mrs. F. was an able romancist of the ineffable school—I know no other name to apply to a school whose heroes are all dainty and all per-

fect. She wrote the opening chapter, and introduced a lovely
blonde simpleton who talked nothing but pearls and poetry and
who was virtuous to the verge of eccentricity. She also introduced
a young French Duke of aggravated refinement, in love with the
blonde. Mr. F. followed next week, with a brilliant lawyer who set
about getting the Duke's estates into trouble, and a sparkling
young lady of high society who fell to fascinating the Duke and im-
pairing the appetite of the blonde. Mr. D., a dark and bloody editor
of one of the dailies, followed Mr. F., the third week, introducing a
mysterious Rosicrucian who transmuted metals, held consulta-
tions with the devil in a cave at dead of night, and cast the horo-
scope of the several heroes and heroines in such a way as to provide

THE HEROES AND HEROINES OF THE STORY.

plenty of trouble for their future careers and breed a solemn and
awful public interest in the novel. He also introduced a cloaked
and masked melodramatic miscreant, put him on a salary and set
him on the midnight track of the Duke with a poisoned dagger. He
also created an Irish coachman with a rich brogue and placed him
in the service of the society-young-lady with an ulterior mission to
carry billets-doux to the Duke.

About this time there arrived in Virginia a dissolute stranger
with a literary turn of mind—rather seedy he was, but very quiet
and unassuming; almost diffident, indeed. He was so gentle, and

his manners were so pleasing and kindly, whether he was sober or intoxicated, that he made friends of all who came in contact with him. He applied for literary work, offered conclusive evidence that he wielded an easy and practiced pen, and so Mr. F. engaged him at once to help write the novel. His chapter was to follow Mr. D.'s, and mine was to come next. Now what does this fellow do but go off and get drunk and then proceed to his quarters and set to work with his imagination in a state of chaos, and that chaos in a condition of extravagant activity. The result may be guessed. He scanned the chapters of his predecessors, found plenty of heroes and heroines already created, and was satisfied with them; he decided to introduce no more; with all the confidence that whisky in-

DISSOLUTE AUTHOR.

spires and all the easy complacency it gives to its servant, he then launched himself lovingly into his work: he married the coachman to the society-young-lady for the sake of the scandal; married the Duke to the blonde's stepmother, for the sake of the sensation; stopped the desperado's salary; created a misunderstanding between the devil and the Rosicrucian; threw the Duke's property into the wicked lawyer's hands; made the lawyer's upbraiding conscience drive him to drink, thence to *delirium tremens*, thence to suicide; broke the coachman's neck; let his widow succumb to contumely, neglect, poverty and consumption; caused the blonde to drown herself, leaving her clothes on the bank with the customary note pinned to them forgiving the Duke and hoping he would be happy; revealed to the Duke, by means of the usual strawberry mark on left arm, that he had married his own long-lost mother and destroyed his long-lost sister; instituted the proper and necessary suicide of the Duke and the Duchess in order to compass poetical justice; opened the earth and let the Rosicrucian through, accompanied with the accustomed smoke and thunder and smell of brimstone, and finished with the promise that in the next chapter, after holding a general inquest, he would take up the surviving character of the novel and tell what became of the devil!

It read with singular smoothness, and with a "dead" earnestness that was funny enough to suffocate a body. But there was war when it came in. The other novelists were furious. The mild stranger, not yet more than half sober, stood there, under a scathing fire of vituperation, meek and bewildered, looking from one to another of his assailants, and wondering what he could have done to invoke such a storm. When a lull came at last, he said his say gently and appealingly—said he did not rightly remember what he had written, but was sure he had tried to do the best he could, and knew his object had been to make the novel not only pleasant and plausible but instructive and—

The bombardment began again. The novelists assailed his ill-chosen adjectives and demolished them with a storm of denunciation and ridicule. And so the siege went on. Every time the stranger tried to appease the enemy he only made matters worse. Finally he offered to rewrite the chapter. This arrested hostilities. The indignation gradually quieted down, peace reigned again and the sufferer retired in safety and got him to his own citadel.

But on the way thither the evil angel tempted him and he got drunk again. And again his imagination went mad. He led the heroes and heroines a wilder dance than ever; and yet all through it ran that same convincing air of honesty and earnestness that had marked his first work. He got the characters into the most extraordinary situations, put them through the most surprising performances, and made them talk the strangest talk! But the chapter cannot be described. It was symmetrically crazy; it was artistically absurd; and it had explanatory foot-notes that were fully as curious as the text. I remember one of the "situations," and will offer it as an example of the whole. He altered the character of the brilliant lawyer, and made him a great-hearted, splendid fellow; gave him fame and riches, and set his age at thirty-three years. Then he made the blonde discover, through the help of the Rosicrucian and the melodramatic miscreant, that while the Duke loved her money ardently and wanted it, he secretly felt a sort of leaning toward the society-young-lady. Stung to the quick, she tore her affections from him and bestowed them with tenfold power upon the lawyer, who responded with consuming zeal. But the parents would none of it. What they wanted in the family was a Duke; and a Duke they were determined to have; though they confessed that next to the Duke the lawyer had their preference. Necessarily the blonde now went into a decline. The parents were alarmed. They pleaded with her to marry the Duke, but she steadfastly refused, and pined on. Then they laid a plan. They told her to wait a year and a day, and if at the end of that time she still felt that she could not marry the Duke, she might marry the lawyer with their full consent. The result was as they had foreseen: gladness came again, and the flush of returning health. Then the parents took the next step in their scheme. They had the family physician recommend a long sea voyage and much land travel for the thorough restoration of the blonde's strength; and they invited the Duke to be of the party. They judged that the Duke's constant presence and the lawyer's protracted absence would do the rest—for they did not invite the lawyer.

So they set sail in a steamer for America—and the third day out, when their sea-sickness called truce and permitted them to take their first meal at the public table, behold there sat the lawyer! The

UNLOOKED-FOR APPEARANCE OF THE LAWYER.

Duke and party made the best of an awkward situation; the voyage
progressed, and the vessel neared America. But, by and by, two
hundred miles off New Bedford, the ship took fire; she burned to
the water's edge; of all her crew and passengers, only thirty were
saved. They floated about the sea half an afternoon and all night
long. Among them were our friends. The lawyer, by superhuman
exertions, had saved the blonde and her parents, swimming back
and forth two hundred yards and bringing one each time—(the girl
first). The Duke had saved himself. In the morning two whaleships
arrived on the scene and sent their boats. The weather was stormy
and the embarkation was attended with much confusion and excitement. The lawyer did his duty like a man; helped his exhausted and insensible blonde, her parents and some others into a
boat (the Duke helped himself in); then a child fell overboard at the
other end of the raft and the lawyer rushed thither and helped half
a dozen people fish it out, under the stimulus of its mother's
screams. Then he ran back—a few seconds too late—the blonde's
boat was under way. So he had to take the other boat, and go to the
other ship. The storm increased and drove the vessels out of sight
of each other—drove them whither it would. When it calmed, at
the end of three days, the blonde's ship was seven hundred miles
north of Boston and the other about seven hundred south of that
port. The blonde's captain was bound on a whaling cruise in the
North Atlantic and could not go back such a distance or make a
port without orders; such being nautical law. The lawyer's captain
was to cruise in the North Pacific, and *he* could not go back or
make a port without orders. All the lawyer's money and baggage
were in the blonde's boat and went to the blonde's ship—so his
captain made him work his passage as a common sailor. When
both ships had been cruising nearly a year, the one was off the coast
of Greenland and the other in Behring's Strait. The blonde had long
ago been well-nigh persuaded that her lawyer had been washed
overboard and lost just before the whaleships reached the raft, and
now, under the pleadings of her parents and the Duke she was at
last beginning to nerve herself for the doom of the covenant, and
prepare for the hated marriage. But she would not yield a day before the date set. The weeks dragged on, the time narrowed, orders
were given to deck the ship for the wedding—a wedding at sea

among icebergs and walruses. Five days more and all would be over. So the blonde reflected, with a sigh and a tear. Oh where was

THE STORM INCREASED.

her true love—and why, why did he not come and save her? At that moment he was lifting his harpoon to strike a whale in Behring's Strait, five thousand miles away, by the way of the Arctic Ocean, or twenty thousand by the way of the Horn—that was the reason. He struck, but not with perfect aim—his foot slipped and he fell in the whale's mouth and went down his throat. He was insensible five days. Then he came to himself and heard voices; daylight was streaming through a hole cut in the whale's roof. He climbed out and astonished the sailors who were hoisting blubber up a ship's side. He recognized the vessel, flew aboard, surprised the wedding party at the altar and exclaimed:

"Stop the proceedings—I'm here! Come to my arms, my own!"

There were foot-notes to this extravagant piece of literature wherein the author endeavored to show that the whole thing was within the possibilities; he said he got the incident of the whale traveling from Behring's Strait to the coast of Greenland, five thousand miles in five days, through the Arctic Ocean, from Charles Reade's "Love Me Little, Love Me Long," and considered that that established the fact that the thing could be done; and he instanced Jonah's adventure as proof that a man could live in a whale's belly, and added that if a preacher could stand it three days a lawyer could surely stand it five!

JONAH OUTDONE.

There was a fiercer storm than ever in the editorial sanctum now, and the stranger was peremptorily discharged, and his manuscript flung at his head. But he had already delayed things so much that there was not time for some one else to rewrite the chapter, and so the paper came out without any novel in it. It was but a feeble, struggling, stupid journal, and the absence of the novel probably shook public confidence; at any rate, before the first side of the next issue went to press, the *Weekly Occidental* died as peacefully as an infant.

An effort was made to resurrect it, with the proposed advantage of a telling new title, and Mr. F. said that *The Phenix* would be just

the name for it, because it would give the idea of a resurrection
from its dead ashes in a new and undreamed of condition of splendor; but some low-priced smarty on one of the dailies suggested
that we call it the *Lazarus*; and inasmuch as the people were not
profound in Scriptural matters but thought the resurrected Lazarus
and the dilapidated mendicant that begged in the rich man's gateway were one and the same person, the name became the laughing
stock of the town, and killed the paper for good and all.

I was sorry enough, for I was very proud of being connected with
a literary paper—prouder than I have ever been of anything since,
perhaps. I had written some rhymes for it—poetry I considered
it—and it was a great grief to me that the production was on the
"first side" of the issue that was not completed, and hence did not
see the light. But time brings its revenges—I can put it in here; it
will answer in place of a tear dropped to the memory of the lost *Occidental.* The idea (not the chief idea, but the vehicle that bears it)
was probably suggested by the old song called "The Raging Canal,"
but I cannot remember now. I do remember, though, that at that
time I thought my doggerel was one of the ablest poems of the age:

THE AGED PILOT MAN.

On the Erie Canal, it was,
   All on a summer's day,
I sailed forth with my parents
   Far away to Albany.

From out the clouds at noon that day
   There came a dreadful storm,
That piled the billows high about,
   And filled us with alarm.

A man came rushing from a house,
   Saying, "Snub up* your boat I pray,
Snub up your boat, snub up, alas,
   Snub up while yet you may."

Our captain cast one glance astern,
   Then forward glancèd he,
And said, "My wife and little ones
   I never more shall see."

---

*The customary canal technicality for "tie up."

Said Dollinger the pilot man,
  In noble words, but few,—
"Fear not, but lean on Dollinger,
  And he will fetch you through."

The boat drove on, the frightened mules
  Tore through the rain and wind,
And bravely still, in danger's post,
  The whip-boy strode behind.

"Come 'board, come 'board," the captain cried,
  "Nor tempt so wild a storm;"
But still the raging mules advanced,
  And still the boy strode on.

Then said the captain to us all,
  "Alas, 'tis plain to me,
The greater danger is not there,
  But here upon the sea.

So let us strive, while life remains,
  To save all souls on board,
And then if die at last we must,
  Let . . . . I *cannot* speak the word!"

DOLLINGER.

Said Dollinger the pilot man,
　　Tow'ring above the crew,
"Fear not, but trust in Dollinger,
　　And he will fetch you through."

"Low bridge! low bridge!" all heads went down,
　　The laboring bark sped on;
A mill we passed, we passed a church,
　　Hamlets, and fields of corn;
And all the world came out to see,
　　And chased along the shore
Crying, "Alas, alas, the sheeted rain,
　　The wind, the tempest's roar!
Alas, the gallant ship and crew,
　　Can *nothing* help them more?"

"LOW BRIDGE!"

And from our deck sad eyes looked out
　　Across the stormy scene:
The tossing wake of billows aft,
　　The bending forests green,
The chickens sheltered under carts
　　In lee of barn the cows,

The skurrying swine with straw in mouth,
  The wild spray from our bows!

   "She balances!
    She wavers!
Now let her go about!
  If she misses stays and broaches to,
We're all"—[then with a shout,]
   "Hurray! hurray!
   Avast! belay!
   Take in more sail!
   Lord, what a gale!
Ho, boy, haul taut on the hind mule's tail!"

SHORTENING SAIL.

"Ho! lighten ship! ho! man the pump!
  Ho, hostler, heave the lead!
And count ye all, both great and small,
  As numbered with the dead!
For mariner for forty year,
  On Erie, boy and man,
I never yet saw such a storm,
  Or one 't with it began!"

So overboard a keg of nails
    And anvils three we threw,
Likewise four bales of gunny sacks,
    Two hundred pounds of glue,
Two sacks of corn, four ditto wheat,
    A box of books, a cow,
A violin, Lord Byron's works,
    A rip-saw and a sow.

LIGHTENING SHIP.

A curve! a curve! the dangers grow!
    "Labbord!—stabbord!—s-t-e-a-d-y!—so!—
Hard-a-port, Dol!—hellum-a-lee!
    Haw the head mule!—the aft one gee!
Luff!—bring her to the wind!"

"A quarter-three!—'tis shoaling fast!
    Three feet large!—t-h-r-e-e feet!—
Three feet scant!" I cried in fright
    "Oh, is there no retreat?"

Said Dollinger, the pilot man,
    As on the vessel flew,
"Fear not, but trust in Dollinger,
    And he will fetch you through."

A panic struck the bravest hearts,
   The boldest cheek turned pale;
For plain to all, this shoaling said
A leak had burst the ditch's bed!
And, straight as bolt from crossbow sped,
Our ship swept on, with shoaling lead,
   Before the fearful gale!

"Sever the tow-line! Cripple the mules!"
   Too late! . . . . . There comes a shock!
     *   *   *   *   *   *
Another length, and the fated craft
   Would have swum in the saving lock!

Then gathered together the shipwrecked crew
   And took one last embrace,
While sorrowful tears from despairing eyes
   Ran down each hopeless face;
And some did think of their little ones
   Whom they never more might see,
And others of waiting wives at home,
   And mothers that grieved would be.

THE MARVELOUS RESCUE.

But of all the children of misery there
   On that poor sinking frame,

But one spake words of hope and faith,
    And I worshipped as they came:
Said Dollinger the pilot man,—
    (O brave heart, strong and true!)—
"Fear not, but trust in Dollinger,
    For he will fetch you through."

Lo! scarce the words have passed his lips
    The dauntless prophet say'th,
When every soul about him seeth
    A wonder crown his faith!

For straight a farmer brought a plank,—
    (Mysteriously inspired)—
And laying it unto the ship,
    In silent awe retired.

Then every sufferer stood amazed
    That pilot man before;
A moment stood. Then wondering turned,
    And speechless walked ashore.

CHAPTER 52

SINCE I desire, in this chapter, to say an instructive word or two about the silver mines, the reader may take this fair warning and skip, if he chooses. The year 1863 was perhaps the very top blossom and culmination of the "flush times." Virginia swarmed with men and vehicles to that degree that the place looked like a very hive—that is when one's vision could pierce through the thick fog of alkali dust that was generally blowing in summer. I will say, concerning this dust, that if you drove ten miles through it, you and your horses would be coated with it a sixteenth of an inch thick and present an outside appearance that was a uniform pale yellow color, and your buggy would have three inches of dust in it, thrown there by the wheels. The delicate scales used by the assayers were enclosed in glass cases intended to be air-tight, and yet some of this dust was so impalpable and so invisibly fine that it would get in, somehow, and impair the accuracy of those scales.

Speculation ran riot, and yet there was a world of substantial business going on, too. All freights were brought over the mountains from California (a hundred and fifty miles) by pack-train partly, and partly in huge wagons drawn by such long mule teams that each team amounted to a procession, and it did seem, sometimes, that the grand combined procession of animals stretched unbroken from Virginia to California. Its long route was traceable clear across the deserts of the Territory by the writhing serpent of dust it lifted up. By these wagons, freights over that hundred and fifty miles were two hundred dollars a ton for small lots (same price for all express matter brought by stage), and a hundred dollars a ton for full loads. One Virginia firm received one hundred tons of freight a month, and paid ten thousand dollars a month freightage. In the winter the freights were much higher. All the bullion was

SILVER BRICKS.

shipped in bars by stage to San Francisco (a bar was usually about twice the size of a pig of lead and contained from fifteen hundred to three thousand dollars according to the amount of gold mixed with the silver), and the freight on it (when the shipment was large) was one and a quarter per cent of its intrinsic value. So, the freight on these bars probably averaged something more than twenty-five dollars each. Small shippers paid two per cent. There were three stages a day, each way, and I have seen the out-going stages carry away a third of a ton of bullion each, and more than once I saw them divide a two-ton lot and take it off. However, these were extraordinary events.* Two tons of silver bullion would be in the

---

*Mr. Valentine, Wells Fargo's agent, has handled all the bullion shipped through the Virginia office for many a month. To his memory—which is excellent—we are indebted for the following exhibit of the company's business in the Virginia office since the first of January, 1862: From January 1st to April 1st, about $270,000 worth of bullion passed through that office; during the next quarter, $570,000; next quarter, $800,000; next quarter, $956,000; next quarter, $1,275,000; and for the quarter ending on the 30th of last June, about $1,600,000. Thus in a year and a half, the Virginia office only shipped $5,330,000 in bullion. During the year 1862 they shipped $2,615,000, so we perceive the average shipments have more than doubled in the last six months. This gives us room to promise for the Virginia office $500,000 a month for the year 1863 (though perhaps, judging by the steady increase in the business, we are underestimating, somewhat). This gives us $6,000,000 for the year. Gold Hill and Silver City together can beat us—we will give them $10,000,000. To Dayton, Empire City, Ophir and Carson City, we will allow an aggregate of $8,000,000, which is not over the mark, perhaps, and may possibly be a little under it. To Esmeralda we give $4,000,000. To Reese River and Humboldt $2,000,000, which is liberal now, but may not be before the year is out. So we prognosticate that the yield of bullion this year will be about $30,000,000. Placing the number of mills in the Territory at 100, this gives to each the labor of producing $300,000 in bullion during the twelve months. Allowing them to run 300 days in the year, (which none of them more than do) this makes their work average $1,000 a day. Say the mills average 20 tons of rock a day and this rock worth $50 as a general thing, and you

neighborhood of forty bars, and the freight on it over a thousand dollars. Each coach always carried a deal of ordinary express matter besides, and also from fifteen to twenty passengers at from twenty-five to thirty dollars a head. With six stages going all the time, Wells, Fargo and Co.'s Virginia City business was important and lucrative.

All along under the centre of Virginia and Gold Hill, for a couple of miles, ran the great Comstock silver lode—a vein of ore from fifty to eighty feet thick between its solid walls of rock—a vein as

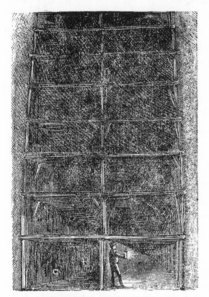

TIMBER SUPPORTS.

wide as some of New York's streets. I will remind the reader that in Pennsylvania a coal vein only eight feet wide is considered ample.

Virginia was a busy city of streets and houses above ground. Under it was another busy city, down in the bowels of the earth, where a great population of men thronged in and out among an intricate maze of tunnels and drifts, flitting hither and thither under a winking sparkle of lights, and over their heads towered a vast web of interlocking timbers that held the walls of the gutted Comstock apart. These timbers were as large as a man's body, and the framework stretched upward so far that no eye could pierce to its top through the closing gloom. It was like peering up through the clean-picked ribs and bones of some colossal skeleton. Imagine such a framework two miles long, sixty feet wide, and higher than any church spire in America.

---

have the actual work of our 100 mills figured down "to a spot"—$1,000 a day each, and $30,000,000 a year in the aggregate.—*Enterprise.*
[A considerable overestimate.—M. T.]

Imagine this stately lattice-work stretching down Broadway, from the St. Nicholas to Wall street, and a Fourth of July procession, reduced to pigmies, parading on top of it and flaunting their flags, high above the pinnacle of Trinity steeple. One can imagine that, but he cannot well imagine what that forest of timbers cost, from the time they were felled in the pineries beyond Washoe Lake, hauled up and around Mount Davidson at atrocious rates of freightage, then squared, let down into the deep maw of the mine and built up there. Twenty ample fortunes would not timber one of the greatest of those silver mines. The Spanish proverb says it requires a gold mine to "run" a silver one, and it is true. A beggar with a silver mine is a pitiable pauper indeed if he cannot sell.

I spoke of the underground Virginia as a city. The Gould & Curry is only one single mine under there, among a great many others; yet the Gould & Curry's streets of dismal drifts and tunnels were five miles in extent, altogether, and its population five hundred miners. Taken as a whole, the underground city had some thirty miles of streets and a population of five or six thousand. In this present day some of those populations are at work from twelve to sixteen hundred feet under Virginia and Gold Hill, and the signal-bells that tell them what the superintendent above ground desires them to do are struck by telegraph as we strike a fire alarm. Sometimes men fall down a shaft, there, a thousand feet deep. In such cases, the usual plan is to hold an inquest.

If you wish to visit one of those mines, you may walk through a tunnel about half a mile long if you prefer it, or you may take the quicker plan of shooting like a dart down a shaft, on a small platform. It is like tumbling down through an empty steeple, feet first. When you reach the bottom, you take a candle and tramp through drifts and tunnels where throngs of men are digging and blasting; you watch them send up tubs full of great lumps of stone—silver ore; you select choice specimens from the mass, as souvenirs; you admire the world of skeleton timbering; you reflect frequently that you are buried under a mountain, a thousand feet below daylight; being in the bottom of the mine you climb from "gallery" to "gallery," up endless ladders that stand straight up and down; when your legs fail you at last, you lie down in a small box-car in a

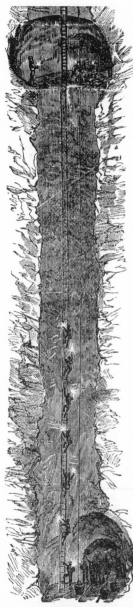

FROM GALLERY TO
GALLERY.

cramped "incline" like a half-up-ended
sewer and are dragged up to daylight feeling as if you are crawling through a coffin
that has no end to it. Arrived at the top,
you find a busy crowd of men receiving the
ascending cars and tubs and dumping the
ore from an elevation into long rows of
bins capable of holding half a dozen tons
each; under the bins are rows of wagons
loading from chutes and trap-doors in the
bins, and down the long street is a procession of these wagons wending toward the
silver mills with their rich freight. It is all
"done," now, and there you are. You need
never go down again, for you have seen it
all. If you have forgotten the process of reducing the ore in the mill and making the
silver bars, you can go back and find it
again in my Esmeralda chapters if so
disposed.

Of course these mines cave in, in places,
occasionally, and then it is worth one's
while to take the risk of descending into
them and observing the crushing power
exerted by the pressing weight of a settling
mountain. I published such an experience
in the *Enterprise*, once, and from it I will
take an extract:

AN HOUR IN THE CAVED MINES.—We journeyed down into the Ophir mine, yesterday, to
see the earthquake. We could not go down the
deep incline, because it still has a propensity to
cave in places. Therefore we traveled through
the long tunnel which enters the hill above the
Ophir office, and then by means of a series of
long ladders, climbed away down from the first
to the fourth gallery. Traversing a drift, we
came to the Spanish line, passed five sets of
timbers still uninjured, and found the earth-

quake. Here was as complete a chaos as ever was seen—vast masses of earth and splintered and broken timbers piled confusedly together, with scarcely an aperture left large enough for a cat to creep through. Rubbish was still falling at intervals from above, and one timber which had braced others earlier in the day, was *now* crushed down out of its former position, showing that the caving and settling of the tremendous mass was still going on. We were in that portion of the Ophir known as the "north mines." Returning to the surface, we entered a tunnel leading into the Central, for the purpose of getting into the main Ophir. Descending a long incline in this tunnel, we traversed a drift or so, and then went down a deep shaft from whence we proceeded into the fifth gallery of the Ophir. From a side-drift we crawled through a small hole and got into the midst of the earthquake again—earth and broken timbers mingled together without regard to grace or symmetry. A large portion of the second, third and fourth galleries had caved in and gone to destruction—the two latter at seven o'clock on the previous evening.

At the turn-table, near the northern extremity of the fifth gallery, two big piles of rubbish had forced their way through from the fifth gallery, and from the looks of the timbers, more was about to come. These beams are solid—eighteen inches square; first, a great beam is laid on the floor, then upright ones, five feet high, stand on it, supporting another horizontal beam, and so on, square above square, like the framework of a window. The superincumbent weight was sufficient to mash the ends of those great upright beams fairly into the solid wood of the horizontal ones three inches, compressing and bending the upright beam till it curved like a bow. Before the Spanish caved in, some of their twelve-inch horizontal timbers were compressed in this way until they were only five inches thick! Imagine the power it must take to squeeze a solid log together in that way. Here, also, was a range of timbers, for a distance of twenty feet, tilted six inches out of the perpendicular by the weight resting upon them from the caved galleries above. You could hear things cracking and giving way, and it was not pleasant to know that the world overhead was slowly and silently sinking down upon you. The men down in the mine do not mind it, however.

Returning along the fifth gallery, we struck the safe part of the Ophir incline, and went down it to the sixth; but we found ten inches of water there, and had to come back. In repairing the damage done to the incline, the pump had to be stopped for two hours, and in the meantime the water gained about a foot. However, the pump was at work again, and the flood-water was decreasing. We climbed up to the fifth gallery again and sought a deep shaft, whereby we might descend to another part of the sixth, out of reach of the water, but suffered disappointment, as the men had gone to dinner, and there was no one to man the windlass. So, having seen the earthquake, we climbed out at the Union incline and tunnel, and adjourned, all dripping with candle grease and perspiration, to lunch at the Ophir office.

During the great flush year of 1863, Nevada [claims to have] produced $25,000,000 in bullion—almost, if not quite, a round million to each thousand inhabitants, which is very well, considering that she was without agriculture and manufactures.* Silver mining was her sole productive industry.

---

*Since the above was in type, I learn from an official source that the above figure is too high, and that the yield for 1863 did not exceed $20,000,000. However, the day for large figures is approaching; the Sutro Tunnel is to plow through the Comstock lode from end to end, at a depth of two thousand feet, and then mining will be easy and comparatively inexpensive; and the momentous matters of drainage, and hoisting and hauling of ore will cease to be burdensome. This vast work will absorb many years, and millions of dollars, in its completion; but it will early yield money, for that desirable epoch will begin as soon as it strikes the first end of the vein. The tunnel will be some eight miles long, and will develop astonishing riches. Cars will carry the ore through the tunnel and dump it in the mills and thus do away with the present costly system of double handling and transportation by mule teams. The water from the tunnel will furnish the motive power for the mills. Mr. Sutro, the originator of this prodigious enterprise, is one of the few men in the world who is gifted with the pluck and perseverance necessary to follow up and hound such an undertaking to its completion. He has converted several obstinate Congresses to a deserved friendliness toward his important work, and has gone up and down and to and fro in Europe until he has enlisted a great moneyed interest in it there.

CHAPTER 53

Every now and then, in these days, the boys used to tell me I ought to get one Jim Blaine to tell me the stirring story of his grandfather's old ram—but they always added that I must not mention the matter unless Jim was drunk at the time—just comfortably and sociably drunk. They kept this up until my curiosity was on the rack to hear the story. I got to haunting Blaine; but it was of no use, the boys always found fault with his condition; he was often moderately but never satisfactorily drunk. I never watched a man's condition with such absorbing interest, such anxious solicitude; I never so pined to see a man uncompromisingly drunk before. At last, one evening I hurried to his cabin, for I learned that this time his situation was such that even the most fastidious could find no fault with it—he was tranquilly, serenely, symmetrically drunk—not a hiccup to mar his voice, not a cloud upon his brain thick enough to obscure his memory. As I entered, he was sitting upon an empty powder-keg, with a clay pipe in one hand and the other raised to command silence. His face was round, red, and very serious; his throat was bare and his hair tumbled; in general appearance and costume he was a stalwart miner of the period. On the pine table stood a candle, and its dim light revealed "the boys" sitting here and there on bunks, candle-boxes, powder-kegs, etc. They said:

"Sh—! Don't speak—he's going to commence."

THE STORY OF THE OLD RAM.

I found a seat at once, and Blaine said:

"I don't reckon them times will ever come again. There never was a more bullier old ram than what he was. Grandfather

fetched him from Illinois—got him of a man by the name of
Yates—Bill Yates—maybe you might have heard of him; his father was a deacon—Baptist—and he was a rustler, too; a man had
to get up ruther early to get the start of old Thankful Yates; it
was him that put the Greens up to jining teams with my grandfather when he moved West. Seth Green was prob'ly the pick of

JIM BLAINE.

the flock; he married a Wilkerson—Sarah Wilkerson—good cretur, she was—one of the likeliest heifers that was ever raised in
old Stoddard, everybody said that knowed her. She could heft a
bar'l of flour as easy as I can flirt a flap-jack. And spin? Don't
mention it! Independent? Humph! When Sile Hawkins come a
browsing around her, she let him know that for all his tin he
couldn't trot in harness alongside of *her*. You see, Sile Hawkins
was—no, it warn't Sile Hawkins, after all—it was a galoot by the
name of Filkins—I disremember his first name; but he *was* a
stump—come into pra'r meeting drunk, one night, hooraying for
Nixon, becuz he thought it was a primary; and old deacon Fer-

guson up and scooted him through the window and he lit on old
Miss Jefferson's head, poor old filly. She was a good soul—had a
glass eye and used to lend it to old Miss Wagner, that hadn't any,
to receive company in; it warn't big enough, and when Miss Wagner warn't noticing, it would get twisted around in the socket,
and look up, maybe, or out to one side, and every which way,
while t'other one was looking as straight ahead as a spy-glass.
Grown people didn't mind it, but it most always made the children cry, it was so sort of scary. She tried packing it in raw cotton, but it wouldn't work, somehow—the cotton would get loose

HURRAH FOR NIXON.

and stick out and look so kind of awful that the children couldn't
stand it no way. She was always dropping it out, and turning up
her old dead-light on the company empty, and making them on-
comfortable, becuz *she* never could tell when it hopped out,

being blind on that side, you see. So somebody would have to
hunch her and say, 'Your game eye has fetched loose, Miss Wagner
dear'—and then all of them would have to sit and wait till she
jammed it in again—wrong side before, as a general thing, and
green as a bird's egg, being a bashful cretur and easy sot back before
company. But being wrong side before warn't much differ-

MISS WAGNER.

ence, anyway, becuz her own eye
was sky-blue and the glass one was
yaller on the front side, so whichever way she turned it it didn't
match nohow. Old Miss Wagner
was considerable on the borrow,
she was. When she had a quilting,
or Dorcas S'iety at her house she
gen'ally borrowed Miss Higgins's
wooden leg to stump around on; it
was considerable shorter than her
other pin, but much *she* minded
that. She said she couldn't abide

crutches when she had company, becuz they were so slow; said
when she had company and things had to be done, she wanted to
get up and hump herself. She was as bald as a jug, and so she used
to borrow Miss Jacops's wig—Miss Jacops was the coffin-
peddler's wife—a ratty old buzzard, he was, that used to go roosting around where people was sick, waiting for 'em; and there that
old rip would sit all day, in the shade, on a coffin that he judged
would fit the can'idate; and if it was a slow customer and kind
of uncertain, he'd fetch his rations and a blanket along and sleep
in the coffin nights. He was anchored out that way, in frosty
weather, for about three weeks, once, before old Robbins's place,
waiting for him; and after that, for as much as two years, Jacops
was not on speaking terms with the old man, on account of his
disapp'inting him. He got one of his feet froze, and lost money,
too, becuz old Robbins took a favorable turn and got well. The
next time Robbins got sick, Jacops tried to make up with him,
and varnished up the same old coffin and fetched it along; but
old Robbins was too many for him; he had him in, and 'peared

to be powerful weak; he bought the coffin for ten dollars and Jacops was to pay it back and twenty-five more besides if Robbins
didn't like the coffin after he'd tried it. And then Robbins died,
and at the funeral he bursted off the lid and riz up in his shroud
and told the parson to let up on the performances, becuz he could
not stand such a coffin as that. You see he had been in a trance
once before, when he was young, and he took the chances on another, cal'lating that if he made the trip it was money in his
pocket, and if he missed fire he couldn't lose a cent. And by
George he sued Jacops for the rhino and got jedgment; and he set
up the coffin in his back parlor and said he 'lowed to take his
time, now. It was always an aggravation to Jacops, the way that
miserable old thing acted. He moved back to Indiany pretty
soon—went to Wellsville—Wellsville was the place the Hoga-
dorns was from. Mighty fine family. Old Maryland stock. Old
Squire Hogadorn could carry around more mixed licker, and cuss
better than most any man I ever see. His second wife was the
widder Billings—she that was Becky Martin; her dam was deacon Dunlap's first wife. Her oldest child, Maria, married a missionary and died in grace—et up by the savages. They et *him*,
too, poor feller—biled him. It warn't the custom, so they say, but

WAITING FOR A CUSTOMER.

they explained to friends of his'n that went down there to bring
away his things, that they'd tried missionaries every other way
and never could get any good out of 'em—and so it annoyed all
his relations to find out that that man's life was fooled away just
out of a dern'd experiment, so to speak. But mind you, there ain't

WAS TO BE THERE.

anything ever reely lost; everything that people can't understand and don't see the reason
of does good if you only hold
on and give it a fair shake;
Prov'dence don't fire no blank
ca'tridges, boys. That there
missionary's substance, unbeknowns to himself, actu'ly converted every last one of them
heathens that took a chance
at the barbacue. Nothing ever
fetched them but that. Don't
tell *me* it was an accident that
he was biled. There ain't no
such a thing as an accident.
When my uncle Lem was leaning up agin a scaffolding once,
sick, or drunk, or suthin, an
Irishman with a hod full of bricks fell on him out of the third
story and broke the old man's back in two places. People said it
was an accident. Much accident there was about that. He didn't
know what he was there for, but he was there for a good object.
If he hadn't been there the Irishman would have been killed.
Nobody can ever make me believe anything different from that.
Uncle Lem's dog was there. Why didn't the Irishman fall on the
dog? Becuz the dog would a seen him a coming and stood from
under. That's the reason the dog warn't appinted. A dog can't
be depended on to carry out a special providence. Mark my
words it was a put-up thing. Accidents don't happen, boys. Uncle Lem's dog—I wish you could a seen that dog. He was a reg-
lar shepherd—or ruther he was part bull and part shepherd—

splendid animal; belonged to parson Hagar before uncle Lem got him. Parson Hagar belonged to the Western Reserve Hagars; prime family; his mother was a Watson; one of his sisters married a Wheeler; they settled in Morgan County, and he got nipped by the machinery in a carpet factory and went through in less than a quarter of a minute; his widder bought the piece of carpet that had his remains wove in, and people come a hundred mile to 'tend the funeral. There was fourteen yards in the piece. She wouldn't let them roll him up, but planted him just so—full length. The church was middling small where they preached the funeral, and they had to let one end of the coffin stick out of the window. They didn't bury him—they planted one end, and let him stand up, same as a monument. And they nailed a sign on it and put—put on—put on it—sacred to—the m-e-m-o-r-y—of fourteen y-a-r-d-s—of three-ply—car - - - pet—containing all that was—m-o-r-t-a-l—of—of—W-i-l-l-i-a-m—W-h-e—"

THE MONUMENT.

Jim Blaine had been growing gradually drowsy and drowsier—his head nodded, once, twice, three times—dropped peacefully upon his breast, and he fell tranquilly asleep. The tears were running down the boys' cheeks—they were suffocating with suppressed laughter—and had been from the start, though I had never noticed it. I perceived that I was "sold." I learned then that Jim Blaine's peculiarity was that whenever he reached a certain stage of intoxication, no human power could keep him from setting out, with impressive unction, to tell about a wonderful adventure which he had once had with his grandfather's old ram—and the mention of the ram in the first sentence was as far as any man had ever heard him get, concerning it. He always maundered off, interminably, from one thing to another, till his whisky got the best of him and he fell asleep. What the thing was that happened to him and his grandfather's old ram is a dark mystery to this day, for nobody has ever yet found out.

CHAPTER 54

O_F course there was a large Chinese population in Virginia—it is the case with every town and city on the Pacific coast. They are a harmless race when white men either let them alone or treat them no worse than dogs; in fact they are almost entirely harmless anyhow, for they seldom think of resenting the vilest insults or the cruelest injuries. They are quiet, peaceable, tractable, free from drunkenness, and they are as industrious as the day is long. A disorderly Chinaman is rare, and a lazy one does not exist. So long as a Chinaman has strength to use his hands he needs no support from anybody; white men often complain of want of work, but a Chinaman offers no such complaint; he always manages to find something to do. He is a great convenience to everybody—even to the worst class of white men, for he bears the most of their sins, suffering fines for their petty thefts, imprisonment for their robberies, and death for their murders. Any white man can swear a Chinaman's life away in the courts, but no Chinaman can testify against a white man. Ours is the "land of the free"—nobody denies that—nobody challenges it. [Maybe it is because we won't let other people testify.] As I write, news comes that in broad daylight in San Francisco, some boys have stoned an inoffensive Chinaman to death, and that although a large crowd witnessed the shameful deed, no one interfered.

There are seventy thousand (and possibly one hundred thousand) Chinamen on the Pacific coast. There were about a thousand in Virginia. They were penned into a "Chinese quarter"—a thing which they do not particularly object to, as they are fond of herding together. Their buildings were of wood; usually only one story high, and set thickly together along streets scarcely wide enough for a wagon to pass through. Their quarter was a little removed from the rest of the town. The chief employment of Chinamen in towns is to wash clothing. They always send a bill, like this below, pinned to the clothes. It is mere ceremony, for it does not enlighten the customer much. Their price for washing was $2.50 per dozen—rather cheaper than white people could afford to wash for at that time. A very common sign on the Chinese houses was: "See Yup, Washer and Ironer;" "Hong Wo, Washer;" "Sam Sing & Ah Hop, Washing." The house servants, cooks, etc., in California and Nevada, were chiefly Chinamen. There were few white servants and no Chinawomen so employed. Chinamen make good house servants, being quick, obedient, patient, quick to learn and tirelessly industrious. They do not need to be taught a thing twice, as a general thing. They are imitative. If a Chinaman were to see his master break up a centre table, in a passion, and kindle a fire with it, that Chinaman would be likely to resort to the furniture for fuel forever afterward.

All Chinamen can read, write and cipher with easy facility—pity but all our petted *voters* could. In California they rent little patches of ground and do a deal of gardening. They will raise surprising crops of vegetables on a sand pile. They waste nothing. What is rubbish to a Christian, a Chinaman carefully preserves and makes useful in one way or another. He gathers up all the old oyster and sardine cans that white people throw away, and procures marketable tin and solder from them by melting. He gathers up old bones and turns them into manure. In California he gets a living out of old mining claims that white men have abandoned as exhausted and worthless—and then the officers come down on him once a month with an exorbitant swindle to which the legislature has given the broad, general name of "foreign" mining tax, but it is usually inflicted on no foreigners but Chinamen. This swindle has in some cases been repeated once or twice on the same victim in the course of the same month—but the public treasury was not additionally enriched by it, probably.

Chinamen hold their dead in great reverence—they worship their departed ancestors, in fact. Hence, in China, a man's front yard, back yard, or any other part of his premises, is made his family burying ground, in order that he may visit the graves at any and

IMITATION.

all times. Therefore that huge empire is one mighty cemetery; it is ridged and wrinkled from its centre to its circumference with graves—and inasmuch as every foot of ground must be made to do its utmost, in China, lest the swarming population suffer for food, the very graves are cultivated and yield a harvest, custom holding this to be no dishonor to the dead. Since the departed are held in such worshipful reverence, a Chinaman cannot bear that any indignity be offered the places where they sleep. Mr. Burlingame said that herein lay China's bitter opposition to railroads; a road could not be built anywhere in the empire without disturbing the graves of their ancestors or friends.

A Chinaman hardly believes he could enjoy the hereafter except his body lay in his beloved China; also, he desires to receive, himself, after death, that worship with which he has honored his dead that preceded him. Therefore, if he visits a foreign country, he makes arrangements to have his bones returned to China in case he dies; if he hires to go to a foreign country on a labor contract, there is always a stipulation that his body shall be taken back to China if he dies; if the government sells a gang of Coolies to a foreigner for the usual five-year term, it is specified in the contract that their bodies shall be restored to China in case of death. On the Pacific coast the Chinamen all belong to one or another of several great companies or organizations, and these companies keep track of their members, register their names, and ship their bodies home when they die. The See Yup Company is held to be the largest of these. The Ning Yeong Company is next, and numbers eighteen thousand members on the coast. Its headquarters are at San Francisco, where it has a costly temple, several great officers (one of whom keeps regal state in seclusion and cannot be approached by common humanity), and a numerous priesthood. In it I was shown a register of its members, with the dead and the date of their shipment to China duly marked. Every ship that sails from San Francisco carries away a heavy freight of Chinese corpses—or did, at least, until the legislature, with an ingenious refinement of Christian cruelty, forbade the shipments, as a neat underhanded way of deterring Chinese immigration. The bill was offered, whether it passed or not. It is my impression that it passed. There was another bill—it became a law—compelling every incoming Chinaman to be vaccinated on the wharf and pay a duly appointed quack (no decent doctor would defile himself with such legalized robbery) ten dollars for it. As few importers of Chinese would want to go to an expense like that, the law-makers thought this would be another heavy blow to Chinese immigration.

What the Chinese quarter of Virginia was like—or, indeed, what the Chinese quarter of any Pacific coast town was and is like— may be gathered from this item which I printed in the *Enterprise* while reporting for that paper:

CHINATOWN.—Accompanied by a fellow reporter, we made a trip through our Chinese quarter the other night. The Chinese have built their portion of the city to suit themselves; and as they keep neither carriages nor wagons, their streets are not wide enough, as a general thing, to admit of the passage of vehicles. At ten o'clock at night the Chinaman may be seen in all his glory. In every little cooped-up, dingy cavern of a hut, faint with the odor of burning Josh-lights and with nothing to see the gloom by save the sickly, guttering tallow candle, were two or three yellow, long-tailed vagabonds, coiled up on a sort of short truckle-bed, smoking opium, motionless and with their lustreless eyes turned inward from excess of satisfaction—or rather the recent smoker looks thus, immediately after having passed the pipe to his neighbor—for opium-smoking is a comfortless operation, and requires constant attention. A lamp sits on the bed, the length of the long pipe-stem from the smoker's mouth; he puts a pellet of opium on the end of a wire, sets it on fire, and plasters it into the pipe much as a Christian would fill a hole with putty; then he applies the bowl to the lamp and proceeds to smoke—and the stewing and frying of the drug and the gurgling of the juices in the stem would wellnigh turn the stomach of a statue. John likes it, though; it soothes him, he takes about two dozen whiffs, and then rolls over to dream, Heaven only knows what, for we could not imagine by looking at the soggy creature. Possibly in his visions he travels far away from the gross world and his regular washing, and feasts on succulent rats and birds'-nests in Paradise.

Mr. Ah Sing keeps a general grocery and provision store at No. 13 Wang street. He lavished his hospitality upon our party in the friendliest way. He had various kinds of colored and colorless wines and brandies, with unpronounceable names, imported from China in little crockery jugs, and which he offered to us in dainty little miniature wash-basins of porcelain. He offered us a mess of birds'-nests; also, small, neat sausages, of which we could have swallowed several yards if we had chosen to try, but we suspected that each link contained the corpse of a mouse, and therefore refrained. Mr. Sing had in his store a thousand articles of merchandise, curious to behold, impossible to imagine the uses of, and beyond our ability to describe.

His ducks, however, and his eggs, we could understand; the former were split open and flattened out like codfish, and came from China in that shape, and the latter were plastered over with some kind of paste which kept them fresh and palatable through the long voyage.

We found Mr. Hong Wo, No. 37 Chow-chow street, making up a lottery scheme—in fact we found a dozen others occupied in the same way in various parts of the quarter, for about every third Chinaman runs a lottery, and the balance of the tribe "buck" at it. "Tom," who speaks faultless English, and used to be chief and only cook to the *Territorial Enterprise,* when the establishment kept bachelor's hall two years ago, said that "Sometime Chinaman buy ticket one dollar hap, ketch um two tree hundred, sometime no ketch um anyting; lottery like one man fight um seventy—may-be he whip, may-be he get whip heself, welly good." However, the percentage being sixty-nine against him, the chances are, as a general thing, that "he get whip heself." We could not see that these lotteries differed in any respect from our own, save that the figures being Chinese, no ignorant white man might ever hope to succeed in telling "t'other from which;" the manner of drawing is similar to ours.

Mr. See Yup keeps a fancy store on Live Fox street. He sold us fans of white feathers, gorgeously ornamented; perfumery that smelled like Limburger cheese, Chinese pens, and watch-charms made of a stone unscratchable with steel instruments, yet polished and tinted like the inner

CHINESE LOTTERY.

coat of a sea-shell.* As tokens of his esteem, See Yup presented the party with gaudy plumes made of gold tinsel and trimmed with peacocks' feathers.

We ate chow-chow with chop-sticks in the celestial restaurants; our comrade chided the moon-eyed damsels in front of the houses for their want of feminine reserve; we received protecting Josh-lights from our hosts and "dickered" for a pagan God or two. Finally, we were impressed with the genius of a Chinese book-keeper; he figured up his accounts on a machine like a gridiron with buttons strung on its bars; the different rows represented units, tens, hundreds and thousands. He fingered them with incredible rapidity—in fact, he pushed them from place to place as fast as a musical professor's fingers travel over the keys of a piano.

They are a kindly disposed, well-meaning race, and are respected and well treated by the upper classes, all over the Pacific coast. No

---

*A peculiar species of the "jade-stone"—to a Chinaman peculiarly precious.

Californian *gentleman or lady* ever abuses or oppresses a Chinaman, under any circumstances, an explanation that seems to be
much needed in the east. Only the scum of the population do it—
they and their children; they, and, naturally and consistently, the
policemen and politicians, likewise, for these are the dust-licking
pimps and slaves of the scum, there as well as elsewhere in
America.

CHAPTER 55

I BEGAN to get tired of staying in one place so long. There was no longer satisfying variety in going down to Carson to report the proceedings of the legislature once a year, and horse-races and pumpkin-shows once in three months; (they had got to raising pumpkins and potatoes in Washoe Valley, and of course one of the first achievements of the legislature was to institute a ten-thousand-dollar Agricultural Fair to show off forty dollars' worth of those pumpkins in—however, the Territorial legislature was usually spoken of as the "asylum"). I wanted to see San Francisco. I wanted to go somewhere. I wanted—I did not know *what* I wanted. I had the "spring fever" and wanted a change, principally, no doubt. Besides, a convention had framed a State Constitution; nine men out of every ten wanted an office; I believed that these gentlemen would "treat" the moneyless and the irresponsible among the population into adopting the Constitution and thus well-nigh killing the country (it could not well carry such a load as a State government, since it had nothing to tax that could stand a tax, for undeveloped mines could not, and there were not fifty developed ones in the land, there was but little realty to tax, and it did seem as if nobody was ever going to think of the simple salvation of inflicting a money penalty on murder). I believed that a State government would destroy the "flush times," and I wanted to get away. I believed that the mining stocks I had on hand would soon be worth a hundred thousand dollars, and thought if they reached that before the Constitution was adopted, I would sell out and make myself secure from the crash the change of government was going to bring. I considered a hundred thousand dollars sufficient to go home with decently, though it was but a small amount compared to what I had been expecting to return with. I felt rather down-hearted about it, but I tried to comfort myself with the reflection that with such a sum I could not fall into want. About this time a schoolmate of mine whom I had not seen since boyhood, came tramping in on foot from Reese river, a very allegory of Poverty. The son of wealthy parents, here he was, in a strange land, hungry, bootless, mantled in an ancient horse-blanket, roofed with a brimless hat, and so generally and so extravagantly dilapidated that he could have "taken the shine out of the Prodigal Son himself," as he pleasantly remarked. He wanted to borrow forty-six dollars—twenty-six to take him to San Francisco, and twenty for something else; to buy some soap with, maybe, for he needed it. I found I had but little more than the amount wanted, in my pocket; so I stepped in and borrowed forty-six dollars of a banker (on twenty days' time, without the formality of a note), and gave it him, rather than walk half a block to the office,

AN OLD FRIEND.

where I had some specie laid up. If anybody had told me that it would take me two years to pay back that forty-six dollars to the banker (for I did not expect it of the Prodigal, and was not disappointed), I would have felt injured. And so would the banker.

I wanted a change. I wanted variety of some kind. It came. Mr. Goodman went away for a week and left me the post of chief editor. It destroyed me. The first day, I wrote my "leader" in the forenoon. The second day, I had no subject and put it off till the afternoon. The third day I put it off till evening, and then copied an elaborate editorial out of the "American Cyclopedia," that steadfast friend of the editor, all over this land. The fourth day I "fooled around" till

midnight, and then fell back on the Cyclopedia again. The fifth day
I cudgeled my brain till midnight, and then kept the press waiting
while I penned some bitter personalities on six different people.
The sixth day I labored in anguish till far into the night and
brought forth—nothing. The paper went to press without an editorial. The seventh day I resigned. On the eighth, Mr. Goodman returned and found six duels on his hands—my personalities had
borne fruit.

Nobody, except he has tried it, knows what it is to be an editor.
It is easy to scribble local rubbish, with the facts all before you; it
is easy to clip selections from other papers; it is easy to string out
a correspondence from any locality; but it is unspeakable hardship
to write editorials. *Subjects* are the trouble—the dreary lack of
them, I mean. Every day, it is drag, drag, drag—think, and worry
and suffer—all the world is a dull blank, and yet the editorial columns *must* be filled. Only give the editor a *subject*, and his work
is done—it is no trouble to write it up; but fancy how you would
feel if you had to pump your brains dry every day in the week, fifty-
two weeks in the year. It makes one low spirited simply to think of
it. The matter that each editor of a daily paper in America writes
in the course of a year would fill from four to eight bulky volumes
like this book! Fancy what a library an editor's work would make,
after twenty or thirty years' service. Yet people often marvel that
Dickens, Scott, Bulwer, Dumas, etc., have been able to produce so
many books. If these authors had wrought as voluminously as
newspaper editors do, the result would be something to marvel at,
indeed. How editors can continue this tremendous labor, this exhausting consumption of brain fibre (for their work is creative, and
not a mere mechanical laying-up of facts, like reporting), day after
day and year after year, is incomprehensible. Preachers take two
months' holiday in midsummer, for they find that to produce two
sermons a week is wearing, in the long run. In truth it must be so,
and is so; and therefore, how an editor can take from ten to twenty
texts and build upon them from ten to twenty painstaking editorials a week and keep it up all the year round, is farther beyond
comprehension than ever. Ever since I survived my week as editor,
I have found at least one pleasure in any newspaper that comes to

my hand; it is in admiring the long columns of editorial, and wondering to myself how in the mischief he did it!

Mr. Goodman's return relieved me of employment, unless I
chose to become a reporter again. I could not do that; I could not
serve in the ranks after being General of the army. So I thought I
would depart and go abroad into the world somewhere. Just at this
juncture, Dan, my associate in the reportorial department, told
me, casually, that two citizens had been trying to persuade him to
go with them to New York and aid in selling a rich silver mine
which they had discovered and secured in a new mining district in
our neighborhood. He said they offered to pay his expenses and
give him one-third of the proceeds of the sale. He had refused to go.
It was the very opportunity I wanted. I abused him for keeping so
quiet about it, and not mentioning it sooner. He said it had not occurred to him that I would like to go, and so he had recommended
them to apply to Marshall, the reporter of the other paper. I asked
Dan if it was a good, honest mine, and no swindle. He said the men
had shown him nine tons of the rock, which they had got out to
take to New York, and he could cheerfully say that he had seen but
little rock in Nevada that was richer; and moreover, he said that
they had secured a tract of valuable timber and a mill-site, near the
mine. My first idea was to kill Dan. But I changed my mind, notwithstanding I was so angry, for I thought maybe the chance was
not yet lost. Dan said it was by no means lost; that the men were
absent at the mine again, and would not be in Virginia to leave for
the east for some ten days; that they had requested him to do the
talking to Marshall, and he had promised that he would either secure Marshall or somebody else for them by the time they got
back; he would now say nothing to anybody till they returned, and
then fulfil his promise by furnishing me to them.

It was splendid. I went to bed all on fire with excitement; for nobody had yet gone east to sell a Nevada silver mine, and the field
was white for the sickle. I felt that such a mine as the one described
by Dan would bring a princely sum in New York, and sell without
delay or difficulty. I could not sleep, my fancy so rioted through its
castles in the air. It was the "blind lead" come again.

Next day I got away, on the coach, with the usual eclat attending departures of old citizens,—for if you have only half a dozen friends out there they will make noise for a hundred rather than let you seem to go away neglected and unregretted—and Dan promised to keep strict watch for the men that had the mine to sell.

The trip was signalized but by one little incident, and that occurred just as we were about to start. A very seedy looking vagabond passenger got out of the stage a moment to wait till the usual ballast of silver bricks was thrown in. He was standing on the pavement, when an awkward express employé, carrying a brick weighing a hundred pounds, stumbled and let it fall on the bummer's foot. He instantly dropped on the ground and began to howl in the most heart-breaking way. A sympathizing crowd gathered around and were going to pull his boot off; but he screamed louder than ever and they desisted; then he fell to gasping, and between the gasps ejaculated "Brandy! for Heaven's sake, brandy!" They poured half a pint down him, and it wonderfully restored and comforted him. Then he begged the people to assist him to the stage, which was done. The express people urged him to have a doctor at their expense, but he declined, and said that if he only had a little brandy to take along with him, to soothe his paroxysms of pain when they came on, he would be grateful and content. He was quickly supplied with two bottles, and we drove off. He was so smiling and happy after that, that I could not refrain from asking him how he could possibly be so comfortable with a crushed foot.

"Well," said he, "I hadn't had a drink for twelve hours, and hadn't a cent to my name. I was most perishing—and so, when that duffer dropped that hundred-pounder on my foot, I see my chance. Got a cork leg, you know!" and he pulled up his pantaloons and proved it.

He was as drunk as a lord all day long, and full of chucklings over his timely ingenuity.

One drunken man necessarily reminds one of another. I once heard a gentleman tell about an incident which he witnessed in a Californian bar-room. He entitled it "Ye Modest Man Taketh a Drink." It was nothing but a bit of acting, but it seemed to me a perfect rendering, and worthy of Toodles himself. The modest man, tolerably far gone with beer and other matters, enters a saloon (twenty-five cents is the price for anything and everything, and specie the only money used) and lays down a half dollar; calls for whisky and drinks it; the barkeeper makes change and lays the

FAREWELL AND ACCIDENT.

quarter in a wet place on the counter; the modest man fumbles at it with nerveless fingers, but it slips and the water holds it; he contemplates it, and tries again; same result; observes that people are interested in what he is at, blushes; fumbles at the quarter again—blushes—puts his forefinger carefully, slowly down, to make sure of his aim—pushes the coin toward the barkeeper, and says with a sigh:

"('ic!) Gimme a cigar!"

Naturally, another gentleman present told about another drunken man. He said he reeled toward home late at night; made a mistake and entered the wrong gate; thought he saw a dog on the stoop; and it was—an iron one. He stopped and considered; wondered if it was a dangerous dog; ventured to say "Be (hic) begone!" No effect. Then he approached warily, and adopted conciliation; pursed up his lips and tried to whistle, but failed; still approached, saying, "Poor dog!—doggy, doggy, doggy!—poor doggy-dog!" Got up on the stoop, still petting with fond names; till master of the advantages; then exclaimed, "Leave, you thief!"—planted a vindictive kick in his ribs, and went head-over-heels overboard, of course. A pause; a sigh or two of pain, and then a remark in a reflective voice:

"GIMME A CIGAR!"

"Awful solid dog. What could he ben eating? ('ic!) Rocks, p'raps. Such animals is dangerous. 'At's what *I* say—they're dangerous. If a man—('ic!)—if a man wants to feed a dog on rocks, let him *feed* him on rocks; 'at's all right; but let him keep him at *home*—not have him layin' round promiscuous, where ('ic!) where people's liable to stumble over him when they ain't noticin'!"

It was not without regret that I took a last look at the tiny flag (it was thirty-five feet long and ten feet wide) fluttering like a lady's handkerchief from the topmost peak of Mount Davidson, two thousand feet above Virginia's roofs, and felt that doubtless I was bidding a permanent farewell to a city which had afforded me the most vigorous enjoyment of life I had ever experienced. And this reminds me of an incident which the dullest memory Virginia could boast at the time it happened must vividly recall, at times, till its possessor dies. Late one summer afternoon we had a rain shower. That was astonishing enough, in itself, to set the whole town buzzing, for it only rains (during a week or two weeks) in the winter in Nevada, and even then not enough at a time to make it worth while for any merchant to keep umbrellas for sale. But the rain was not the chief wonder. It only lasted five or ten minutes; while the people were still talking about it all the heavens gathered to themselves a dense blackness as of midnight. All the vast eastern front of Mount Davidson, overlooking the city, put on such a funereal gloom that only the nearness and solidity of the mountain made its outlines even faintly distinguishable from the dead blackness of the heavens they rested against. This unaccustomed sight turned all eyes toward the mountain; and as they looked, a little tongue of rich golden flame was seen waving and quivering in the heart of the midnight, away up on the extreme summit! In a few minutes the streets were packed with people, gazing with hardly an uttered word, at the one brilliant mote in the brooding world of darkness. It flicked like a candle-flame, and looked no larger; but with such a background it was wonderfully bright, small as it was. It was the flag!—though no one suspected it at first, it seemed so like a supernatural visitor of some kind—a mysterious messenger of good tidings, some were fain to believe. It was the nation's emblem transfigured by the departing rays of a sun that was entirely palled from view; and on no other object did the glory fall, in all the broad panorama of mountain ranges and deserts. Not even upon the staff of the flag—for that, a needle in the distance at any time, was now untouched by the light and undistinguishable in the gloom. For a whole hour the weird visitor winked and burned in its lofty solitude, and still the thousands of uplifted eyes watched it with fascinated interest. How the people were wrought up! The superstition grew apace that this was a mystic courier come with great news from the war—the poetry of the idea excusing and commending it—and on it spread, from heart to heart, from lip to lip and from street to street, till there was a general impulse to have out the military and welcome the bright waif with a salvo of artillery!

And all that time one sorely tried man, the telegraph operator sworn to official secrecy, had to lock his lips and chain his tongue with a silence that was like to rend them; for he, and he only, of all the speculating multitude, knew the great things this sinking sun had seen that day in the east—Vicksburg fallen, and the Union arms victorious at Gettysburg!

THE HERALD OF GLAD NEWS.

But for the journalistic monopoly that forbade the slightest revealment of eastern news till a day after its publication in the California papers, the glorified flag on Mount Davidson would have been saluted and re-saluted, that memorable evening, as long as there was a charge of powder to thunder with; the city would have been illuminated, and every man that had any respect for himself would have got drunk,—as was the custom of the country on all occasions of public moment. Even at this distant day I cannot think of this needlessly marred supreme opportunity without regret. What a time we might have had!

CHAPTER 56

WE rumbled over the plains and valleys, climbed the Sierras to the clouds, and looked down upon summer-clad California. And I will remark here, in passing, that all scenery in California requires *distance* to give it its highest charm. The mountains are imposing in their sublimity and their majesty of form and altitude, from any point of view—but one must have distance to soften their ruggedness and enrich their tintings; a Californian forest is best at a little distance, for there is a sad poverty of variety in species, the trees being chiefly of one monotonous family—redwood, pine, spruce, fir—and so, at a near view there is a wearisome sameness of attitude in their rigid arms, stretched downward and outward in one continued and reiterated appeal to all men to "Sh!—don't say a word!—you might disturb somebody!" Close at hand, too, there is a reliefless and relentless smell of pitch and turpentine; there is a ceaseless melancholy in their sighing and complaining foliage; one walks over a soundless carpet of beaten yellow bark and dead spines of the foliage till he feels like a wandering spirit bereft of a footfall; he tires of the endless tufts of needles and yearns for substantial, shapely leaves; he looks for moss and grass to loll upon, and finds none, for where there is no bark there is naked clay and dirt, enemies to pensive musing and clean apparel. Often a grassy plain in California, is what it should be, but often, too, it is best contemplated at a distance, because although its grass blades are tall, they stand up vindictively straight and self-sufficient, and are unsociably wide apart, with uncomely spots of barren sand between.

One of the queerest things I know of, is to hear tourists from "the States" go into ecstasies over the loveliness of "ever-blooming California." And they always do go into that sort of ecstasies. But perhaps they would modify them if they knew how old Califor-

nians, with the memory full upon them of the dust-covered and
questionable summer greens of Californian "verdure," stand astonished, and filled with worshipping admiration, in the presence
of the lavish richness, the brilliant green, the infinite freshness,
the spendthrift variety of form and species and foliage that make
an eastern landscape a vision of Paradise itself. The idea of a man

AN EASTERN LANDSCAPE.

falling into raptures over grave and sombre California, when that
man has seen New England's meadow-expanses and her maples,
oaks and cathedral-windowed elms decked in summer attire, or
the opaline splendors of autumn descending upon her forests,
comes very near being funny—would be, in fact, but that it is so
pathetic. No land with an unvarying climate can be very beautiful.
The tropics are not, for all the sentiment that is wasted on them.
They seem beautiful at first, but sameness impairs the charm by
and by. *Change* is the handmaiden Nature requires to do her mira-
cles with. The land that has four well-defined seasons, cannot lack
beauty, or pall with monotony. Each season brings a world of en-

joyment and interest in the watching of its unfolding, its gradual, harmonious development, its culminating graces—and just as one

A VARIABLE CLIMATE.

begins to tire of it, it passes away and a radical change comes, with new witcheries and new glories in its train. And I think that to one in sympathy with nature, each season, in its turn, seems the loveliest.

San Francisco, a truly fascinating city to live in, is stately and handsome at a fair distance, but close at hand one notes that the architecture is mostly old-fashioned, many streets are made up of decaying, smoke-grimed, wooden houses, and the barren sand hills toward the outskirts obtrude themselves too prominently. Even the kindly climate is sometimes pleasanter when read about than personally experienced, for a lovely, cloudless sky wears out its welcome by and by, and then when the longed for rain does come it *stays*. Even the playful earthquake is better contemplated at a dis—

However there are varying opinions about that.

The climate of San Francisco is mild and singularly equable. The thermometer stands at about seventy degrees the year round. It hardly changes at all. You sleep under one or two light blankets summer and winter, and never use a mosquito bar. Nobody ever wears summer clothing. You wear black broadcloth—if you have it—in August and January, just the same. It is no colder, and no warmer, in the one month than the other. You do not use overcoats

and you do not use fans. It is as pleasant a climate as could well be
contrived, take it all around, and is doubtless the most unvarying
in the whole world. The wind blows there a good deal in the summer months, but then you can go over to Oakland, if you choose—
three or four miles away—it does not blow there. It has only
snowed twice in San Francisco in nineteen years, and then it only
remained on the ground long enough to astonish the children, and
set them to wondering what the feathery stuff was.

During eight months of the year, straight along, the skies are
bright and cloudless, and never a drop of rain falls. But when the
other four months come along, you will need to go and steal an
umbrella. Because you will require it. Not just one day, but one
hundred and twenty days in hardly varying succession. When you
want to go visiting, or attend church, or the theatre, you never look
up at the clouds to see whether it is likely to rain or not—you look
at the almanac. If it is winter, it will *rain*—and if it is summer, it
won't rain, and you cannot help it. You never need a lightning-rod,
because it never thunders and it never lightens. And after you have
listened for six or eight weeks, every night, to the dismal monotony of those quiet rains, you will wish in your heart the thunder
would leap and crash and roar along those drowsy skies once, and
make everything alive—you will wish the prisoned lightnings
would cleave the dull firmament asunder and light it with a blinding glare for *one* little instant. You would give *anything* to hear the
old familiar thunder again and see the lightning strike somebody.
And along in the summer, when you have suffered about four
months of lustrous, pitiless sunshine, you are ready to go down on
your knees and plead for rain—hail—snow—thunder and lightning—anything to break the monotony—you will take an earthquake, if you cannot do any better. And the chances are that you'll
get it, too.

San Francisco is built on sand hills, but they are prolific sand
hills. They yield a generous vegetation. All the rare flowers which
people in "the States" rear with such patient care in parlor flower
pots and greenhouses, flourish luxuriantly in the open air there all
the year round. Calla lilies, all sorts of geraniums, passion flowers,
moss roses—I do not know the names of a tenth part of them. I

only know that while New Yorkers are burdened with banks and drifts of snow, Californians are burdened with banks and drifts of flowers, if they only keep their hands off and let them grow. And I have heard that they have also that rarest and most curious of all the flowers, the beautiful *Espiritu Santo*, as the Spaniards call it— or flower of the Holy Spirit—though I thought it grew only in Central America—down on the Isthmus. In its cup is the daintiest little fac-simile of a dove, as pure as snow. The Spaniards have a superstitious reverence for it. The blossom has been conveyed to the States, submerged in ether; and the bulb has been taken thither also, but every attempt to make it bloom after it arrived, has failed.

I have elsewhere spoken of the endless winter of Mono, California, and but this moment of the eternal spring of San Francisco. Now if we travel a hundred miles in a straight line, we come to the eternal summer of Sacramento. One never sees summer clothing or mosquitoes in San Francisco—but they can be found in Sacramento. Not always and unvaryingly, but about one hundred and forty-three months out of twelve years, perhaps. Flowers bloom there, always, the reader can easily believe—people suffer and sweat, and swear, morning, noon and night, and wear out their stanchest energies fanning themselves. It gets hot there, but if you go down to Fort Yuma you will find it hotter. Fort Yuma is probably the hottest place on earth. The thermometer stays at one hundred and twenty in the shade there all the time—except when it varies and goes higher. It is a U. S. military post, and its occupants get so used to the terrific heat that they suffer without it. There is a tradition (attributed to John Phoenix*) that a very, very wicked soldier died there, once, and of course, went straight to the hottest corner of perdition,—and the next day he *telegraphed back for his blankets.* There is no doubt about the truth of this statement— there can be no doubt about it. I have seen the place where that soldier used to board. In Sacramento it is fiery summer always, and you can gather roses, and eat strawberries and ice-cream, and wear white linen clothes, and pant and perspire at eight or nine o'clock

---

*It has been purloined by fifty different scribblers who were too poor to invent a fancy but not ashamed to steal one.—M. T.

in the morning, and then take the cars, and at noon put on your
furs and your skates, and go skimming over frozen Donner Lake,

SACRAMENTO.   THREE HOURS AWAY.

seven thousand feet above the valley, among snow banks fifteen
feet deep, and in the shadow of grand mountain peaks that lift their
frosty crags ten thousand feet above the level of the sea. There is a
transition for you! Where will you find another like it in the Western hemisphere? And some of us have swept around snow-walled
curves of the Pacific Railroad in that vicinity, six thousand feet
above the sea, and looked down as the birds do, upon the deathless
summer of the Sacramento Valley, with its fruitful fields, its feathery foliage, its silver streams, all slumbering in the mellow haze of
its enchanted atmosphere, and all infinitely softened and spiri-
tualized by distance—a dreamy, exquisite glimpse of fairy-land,
made all the more charming and striking that it was caught
through a forbidding gateway of ice and snow and savage crags and
precipices.

CHAPTER 57

I T was in this Sacramento Valley, just referred to, that a deal of the most lucrative of the early gold mining was done, and you may still see, in places, its grassy slopes and levels torn and guttered and disfigured by the avaricious spoilers of fifteen and twenty years ago. You may see such disfigurements far and wide over California—and in some such places, where only meadows and forests are visible—not a living creature, not a house, no stick or stone or remnant of a ruin, and not a sound, not even a whisper to disturb the Sabbath stillness—you will find it hard to believe that there stood at one time a fiercely-flourishing little city, of two thousand or three thousand souls, with its newspaper, fire company, brass band, volunteer militia, bank, hotels, noisy Fourth of July processions and speeches, gambling hells crammed with tobacco smoke, profanity, and rough-bearded men of all nations and colors, with tables heaped with gold dust sufficient for the revenues of a German principality—streets crowded and rife with business—town lots worth four hundred dollars a front foot—labor, laughter, music, dancing, swearing, fighting, shooting, stabbing—a bloody inquest and a man for breakfast every morning—*everything* that delights and adorns existence—all the appointments and appurtenances of a thriving and prosperous and promising young city,— and *now* nothing is left of it all but a lifeless, homeless solitude. The men are gone, the houses have vanished, even the *name* of the place is forgotten. In no other land, in modern times, have towns so absolutely died and disappeared, as in the old mining regions of California.

It was a driving, vigorous, restless population in those days. It was a *curious* population. It was the *only* population of the kind that the world has ever seen gathered together, and it is not likely that the world will ever see its like again. For, observe, it was an

assemblage of two hundred thousand *young* men—not simpering,
dainty, kid-gloved weaklings, but stalwart, muscular, dauntless
young braves, brim full of push and energy, and royally endowed
with every attribute that goes to make up a peerless and magnificent manhood—the very pick and choice of the world's glorious
ones. No women, no children, no gray and stooping veterans,—
none but erect, bright-eyed, quick-moving, strong-handed young
giants—the strangest population, the finest population, the most
gallant host that ever trooped down the startled solitudes of an un-
peopled land. And where are they now? Scattered to the ends of the
earth—or prematurely aged and decrepit—or shot or stabbed in
street affrays—or dead of disappointed hopes and broken hearts—
all gone, or nearly all—victims devoted upon the altar of the
golden calf—the noblest holocaust that ever wafted its sacrificial
incense heavenward. It is pitiful to think upon.

It was a splendid population—for all the slow, sleepy, sluggish-
brained sloths staid at home—you never find that sort of people
among pioneers—you cannot build pioneers out of that sort of material. It was that population that gave to California a name for getting up astounding enterprises and rushing them through with a
magnificent dash and daring, and a recklessness of cost or consequences, which she bears unto this day—and when she projects a
new surprise, the grave world smiles as usual, and says "well, that
is California all over."

But they were rough in those times! They fairly reveled in gold,
whisky, fights and fandangoes, and were unspeakably happy. The
honest miner raked from a hundred to a thousand dollars out of his
claim a day, and what with the gambling dens and the other enter-
tainments, he hadn't a cent the next morning, if he had any sort of
luck. They cooked their own bacon and beans, sewed on their own
buttons, washed their own shirts—blue woolen ones—and if a
man wanted a fight on his hands without any annoying delay, all
he had to do was to appear in public in a white shirt or a stove-pipe
hat, and he would be accommodated. For those people hated aris-
tocrats. They had a particular and malignant animosity toward
what they called a "biled shirt."

It was a wild, free, disorderly, grotesque society! *Men*—only
swarming hosts of stalwart *men*—nothing juvenile, nothing feminine, visible anywhere!

In those days miners would flock in crowds to catch a glimpse of that rare and blessed spectacle, a woman! Old inhabitants tell how, in a certain camp, the news went abroad early in the morning that a woman was come! They had seen a calico dress hanging out of a wagon down at the camping ground—sign of emigrants from over the great plains. Everybody went down there, and a shout went up when an actual, bona-fide dress was discovered fluttering in the wind! The male emigrant was visible. The miners said:

"Fetch her out!"

He said: "It is my wife, gentlemen—she is sick—we have been robbed of money, provisions, everything, by the Indians—we want to rest."

"Fetch her out! We've got to see her!"

"But, gentlemen, the poor thing, she—"

"FETCH HER OUT!"

He "fetched her out," and they swung their hats and sent up three rousing cheers and a tiger; and they crowded around and

"FETCH HER OUT!"

gazed at her, and touched her dress, and listened to her voice with the look of men who listened to a *memory* rather than a present reality—and then they collected twenty-five hundred dollars in gold and gave it to the man, and swung their hats again and gave three more cheers, and went home satisfied.

Once I dined in San Francisco with the family of a pioneer, and talked with his daughter, a young lady whose first experience in San Francisco was an adventure, though she herself did not remember it, as she was only two or three years old at the time. Her father said that, after landing from the ship, they were walking up the street, a servant leading the party with the little girl in her arms. And presently a huge miner, bearded, belted, spurred, and bristling with deadly weapons—just down from a long campaign in the mountains, evidently—barred the way, stopped the servant, and stood gazing, with a face all alive with gratification and astonishment. Then he said, reverently:

"Well, if it ain't a child!" And then he snatched a little leather sack out of his pocket and said to the servant:

"WELL, IF IT AIN'T A CHILD!"

"There's a hundred and fifty dollars in dust, there, and I'll give it to you to let me kiss the child!"

That anecdote is *true.*

But see how things change. Sitting at that dinner table, listening to that anecdote, if I had offered double the money for the privilege of kissing the same child, I would have been refused. Seventeen added years have far more than doubled the price.

And while upon this subject I will remark that once in Star City, in the Humboldt Mountains, I took my place in a sort of long, post-office single file of miners, to patiently await my chance to peep through a crack in the cabin and get a sight of the splendid new sensation—a genuine, live Woman! And at the end of half an hour

A GENUINE LIVE WOMAN.

my turn came, and I put my eye to the crack, and there she was, with one arm akimbo, and tossing flap-jacks in a frying pan with the other. And she was one hundred and sixty-five* years old, and hadn't a tooth in her head.

---

*Being in calmer mood, now, I voluntarily knock off a hundred from that.—M. T.

CHAPTER 58

For a few months I enjoyed what to me was an entirely new phase of existence—a butterfly idleness; nothing to do, nobody to be responsible to, and untroubled with financial uneasiness. I fell in love with the most cordial and sociable city in the Union. After the sage-brush and alkali deserts of Washoe, San Francisco was Paradise to me. I lived at the best hotel, exhibited my clothes in the most conspicuous places, infested the opera, and learned to seem enraptured with music which oftener afflicted my ignorant ear than enchanted it, if I had had the vulgar honesty to confess it. However, I suppose I was not greatly worse than the most of my countrymen in that. I had longed to be a butterfly, and I was one at last. I attended private parties in sumptuous evening dress, simpered and aired my graces like a born beau, and polked and schottisched with a step peculiar to myself—and the kangaroo. In a word, I kept the due state of a man worth a hundred thousand dollars (prospectively,) and likely to reach absolute affluence when that silver-mine sale should be ultimately achieved in the east. I spent money with a free hand, and meantime watched the stock sales with an interested eye and looked to see what might happen in Nevada.

Something very important happened. The property holders of Nevada voted against the State Constitution; but the folks who had nothing to lose were in the majority, and carried the measure over their heads. But after all it did not immediately look like a disaster, though unquestionably it was one. I hesitated, calculated the chances, and then concluded not to sell. Stocks went on rising; speculation went mad; bankers, merchants, lawyers, doctors, mechanics, laborers, even the very washerwomen and servant girls, were putting up their earnings on silver stocks, and every sun that rose in the morning went down on paupers enriched and rich men beggared. What a gambling carnival it was! Gould & Curry soared to six thousand three hundred dollars a foot! And then—all of a sudden, out went the bottom and everything and everybody went

THE GRACE OF A KANGAROO.

to ruin and destruction! The wreck was complete. The bubble scarcely left a microscopic moisture behind it. I was an early beggar and a thorough one. My hoarded stocks were not worth the paper they were printed on. I threw them all away. I, the cheerful idiot that had been squandering money like water, and thought myself beyond the reach of misfortune, had not now as much as fifty dollars when I gathered together my various debts and paid them. I removed from the hotel to a very private boarding house. I took a reporter's berth and went to work. I was not entirely broken in spirit, for I was building confidently on the sale of the silver mine in the east. But I could not hear from Dan. My letters miscarried or were not answered.

One day I did not feel vigorous and remained away from the office. The next day I went down toward noon as usual, and found a note on my desk which had been there twenty-four hours. It was

signed "Marshall"—the Virginia reporter—and contained a request that I should call at the hotel and see him and a friend or two
that night, as they would sail for the east in the morning. A postscript added that their errand was a big mining speculation! I was
hardly ever so sick in my life. I abused
myself for leaving Virginia and entrusting to another man a matter I ought to
have attended to myself; I abused myself
for remaining away from the office on the
one day of all the year that I should have
been there. And thus berating myself I
trotted a mile to the steamer wharf and
arrived just in time to be too late. The
ship was in the stream and under way.

I comforted myself with the thought
that maybe the speculation would
amount to nothing—poor comfort at
best—and then went back to my slavery,
resolved to put up with my thirty-five
dollars a week and forget all about it.

DREAMS DISSIPATED.

A month afterward I enjoyed my first earthquake. It was one
which was long called the "great" earthquake, and is doubtless so
distinguished till this day. It was just after noon, on a bright October day. I was coming down Third street. The only objects in motion anywhere in sight in that thickly built and populous quarter,
were a man in a buggy behind me, and a street car wending slowly
up the cross street. Otherwise, all was solitude and a Sabbath stillness. As I turned the corner, around a frame house, there was a
great rattle and jar, and it occurred to me that here was an item!—
no doubt a fight in that house. Before I could turn and seek the
door, there came a really terrific shock; the ground seemed to roll
under me in waves, interrupted by a violent joggling up and down,
and there was a heavy grinding noise as of brick houses rubbing together. I fell up against the frame house and hurt my elbow. I knew
what it was, now, and from mere reportorial instinct, nothing else,
took out my watch and noted the time of day; at that moment a
third and still severer shock came, and as I reeled about on the
pavement trying to keep my footing, I saw a sight! The entire front

of a tall four-story brick building in Third street sprung outward like a door and fell sprawling across the street, raising a dust like a great volume of smoke! And here came the buggy—overboard

THE "ONE-HORSE SHAY" OUTDONE.

went the man, and in less time than I can tell it the vehicle was distributed in small fragments along three hundred yards of street. One could have fancied that somebody had fired a charge of chair-rounds and rags down the thoroughfare. The street car had stopped, the horses were rearing and plunging, the passengers were pouring out at both ends, and one fat man had crashed half way through a glass window on one side of the car, got wedged fast and was squirming and screaming like an impaled madman. Every door, of every house, as far as the eye could reach, was vomiting a stream of human beings; and almost before one could execute a wink and begin another, there was a massed multitude of people stretching in endless procession down every street my position commanded. Never was solemn solitude turned into teeming life quicker.

Of the wonders wrought by "the great earthquake," these were all that came under my eye; but the tricks it did, elsewhere, and far and wide over the town, made toothsome gossip for nine days. The destruction of property was trifling—the injury to it was widespread and somewhat serious.

The "curiosities" of the earthquake were simply endless. Gentlemen and ladies who were sick, or were taking a siesta, or had dissipated till a late hour and were making up lost sleep, thronged into the public streets in all sorts of queer apparel, and some without any at all. One woman who had been washing a naked child, ran down the street holding it by the ankles as if it were a dressed turkey. Prominent citizens who were supposed to keep the Sabbath strictly, rushed

HARD ON THE INNOCENTS.

out of saloons in their shirt-sleeves, with billiard cues in their hands. Dozens of men with necks swathed in napkins, rushed

DRY BONES SHAKEN.

from barber-shops, lathered to the eyes or with one cheek clean shaved and the other still bearing a hairy stubble. Horses broke from stables, and a frightened dog rushed up a short attic ladder and out on to a roof, and when his scare was over had not the nerve to go down again the same way he had gone up. A prominent editor flew down stairs, in the principal hotel, with nothing on but one brief undergarment—met a chambermaid, and exclaimed:

"Oh, what *shall* I do! Where shall I go!"
She responded with naive serenity:
"If you have no choice, you might try a clothing-store!"

"OH, WHAT *SHALL* I DO!"

A certain foreign consul's lady was the acknowledged leader of fashion, and every time she appeared in anything new or extraor-dinary, the ladies in the vicinity made a raid on their husbands' purses and arrayed themselves similarly. One man who had suffered considerably and growled accordingly, was stand-ing at the window when the shocks came, and the next in-stant the consul's wife, just out of the bath, fled by with no other apology for clothing than—a bath-towel! The suf-ferer rose superior to the terrors of the earthquake, and said to his wife:

"GET OUT YOUR TOWEL MY DEAR!"

"Now *that* is something *like!* Get out your towel my dear!"

The plastering that fell from ceilings in San Francisco that day,

would have covered several acres of ground. For some days afterward, groups of eyeing and pointing men stood about many a building, looking at long zig-zag cracks that extended from the eaves to
the ground. Four feet of the tops of three chimneys on one house
were broken square off and turned around in such a way as to completely stop the draft. A crack a hundred feet long gaped open six
inches wide in the middle of one street and then shut together
again with such force, as to ridge up the meeting earth like a slender grave. A lady sitting in her rocking and quaking parlor, saw the
wall part at the ceiling, open and shut twice, like a mouth, and
then—drop the end of a brick on the floor like a tooth. She was a
woman easily disgusted with foolishness, and she arose and went
out of there. One lady who was coming down stairs was astonished
to see a bronze Hercules lean forward on its pedestal as if to strike
her with its club. They both reached the bottom of the flight at the
same time,—the woman insensible from the fright. Her child,
born some little time afterward, was club-footed. However—on
second thought,—if the reader sees any coincidence in this, he
must do it at his own risk.

"WE WILL OMIT THE
BENEDICTION!"

The first shock brought
down two or three huge organ-
pipes in one of the churches.
The minister, with uplifted
hands, was just closing the services. He glanced up, hesitated, and said:

"However, we will omit the
benediction!"—and the next
instant there was a vacancy in
the atmosphere where he had
stood.

After the first shock, an
Oakland minister said:

"Keep your seats! There is
no better place to die than
this"—

And added, after the third:
"But outside is good enough!" He then skipped out at the back
door.

Such another destruction of mantel ornaments and toilet bottles as the earthquake created, San Francisco never saw before. There was hardly a girl or a matron in the city but suffered losses of this kind. Suspended pictures were thrown down, but oftener still, by a curious freak of the earthquake's humor, they were whirled completely around with their faces to the wall! There was great difference of opinion, at first, as to the course or direction the earthquake traveled, but water that splashed out of various tanks and buckets settled that. Thousands of people were made so sea-sick by the rolling and pitching of floors and streets that they were weak and bedridden for hours, and some few for even days afterward. Hardly an individual escaped nausea entirely.

The queer earthquake-episodes that formed the staple of San Francisco gossip for the next week would fill a much larger book than this, and so I will diverge from the subject.

By and by, in the due course of things, I picked up a copy of the *Enterprise* one day, and fell under this cruel blow:

NEVADA MINES IN NEW YORK.—G. M. Marshall, Sheba Hurst and Amos H. Rose, who left San Francisco last July for New York City, with ores from mines in Pine Wood District, Humboldt County, and on the Reese River range, have disposed of a mine containing six thousand feet and called the Pine Mountains Consolidated, for the sum of $3,000,000. The stamps on the deed, which is now on its way to Humboldt County, from New York, for record, amounted to $3,000, which is said to be the largest amount of stamps ever placed on one document. A working capital of $1,000,000 has been paid into the treasury, and machinery has already been purchased for a large quartz mill, which will be put up as soon as possible. The stock in this company is all full paid and entirely unassessable. The ores of the mines in this district somewhat resemble those of the Sheba mine in Humboldt. Sheba Hurst, the discoverer of the mines, with his friends corralled all the best leads and all the land and timber they desired before making public their whereabouts. Ores from there, assayed in this city, showed them to be exceedingly rich in silver and gold—silver predominating. There is an abundance of wood and water in the District. We are glad to know that New York capital has been enlisted in the development of the mines of this region. Having seen the ores and assays, we are satisfied that the mines of the District are very valuable—anything but wild-cat.

Once more native imbecility had carried the day, and I had lost a million! It was the "blind lead" over again.

Let us not dwell on this miserable matter. If I were inventing these things, I could be wonderfully humorous over them; but they are too true to be talked of with hearty levity, even at this distant day.* Suffice it that I so lost heart, and so yielded myself up to repinings and sighings and foolish regrets, that I neglected my duties and became about worthless, as a reporter for a brisk newspaper. And at last one of the proprietors took me aside, with a charity I still remember with considerable respect, and gave me an opportunity to resign my berth and so save myself the disgrace of a dismissal.

---

*True, and yet not exactly as given in the above figures, possibly. I saw Marshall, months afterward, and although he had plenty of money he did not claim to have captured an entire *million*. In fact I gathered that he had not then received $50,000. Beyond that figure his fortune appeared to consist of uncertain vast expectations rather than prodigious certainties. However, when the above item appeared in print I put full faith in it, and incontinently wilted and went to seed under it.

CHAPTER 59

For a time I wrote literary screeds for the *Golden Era*. C. H. Webb had established a very excellent literary weekly called the *Californian*, but high merit was no guaranty of success; it languished, and he sold out to three printers, and Bret Harte became editor at twenty dollars a week, and I was employed to contribute an article a week at twelve dollars. But the journal still languished, and the printers sold out to Capt. Ogden, a rich man and a pleasant gentleman who chose to amuse himself with such an expensive luxury without much caring about the cost of it. When he grew tired of the novelty, he re-sold to the printers, the paper presently died a peaceful death, and I was out of work again. I would not mention these things but for the fact that they so aptly illustrate the ups and downs that characterize life on the Pacific coast. A man could hardly stumble into such a variety of queer vicissitudes in any other country.

SLINKING.

For two months my sole occupation was avoiding acquaintances; for during that time I did not earn a penny, or buy an article of any kind, or pay my board. I became a very adept at "slinking." I slunk from back street to back street, I slunk away from approaching faces that looked familiar, I slunk to my meals, ate them humbly and with a mute apology for every mouthful I robbed my generous landlady of, and at midnight, after wanderings that were but slinkings away from cheerfulness and light, I slunk to my bed. I felt meaner, and lowlier and more despicable than the worms. During all this time I had but one piece of money—a silver ten-cent piece—and I held to it and would not spend it on any account, lest the consciousness coming strong upon me that I was *entirely* penniless, might suggest suicide. I had pawned everything but the clothes I had on; so I clung to my dime desperately, till it was smooth with handling.

However, I am forgetting. I did have one other occupation besides that of "slinking." It was the entertaining of a collector (and being entertained by him,) who had in his hands the Virginia banker's bill for the forty-six dollars which I had loaned my schoolmate, the "Prodigal." This man used to call regularly once a week and dun me, and sometimes oftener. He did it from sheer force of habit, for he knew he could get nothing. He would get out his bill, calculate the interest for me, at five per cent a month, and show me clearly that there was no attempt at fraud in it and no mistakes; and then plead, and argue and dun with all his might for any sum— any little trifle—even a dollar—even half a dollar, on account. Then his duty was accomplished and his conscience free. He immediately dropped the subject there always; got out a couple of cigars and divided, put his feet in the window, and then we would have a long, luxurious talk about everything and everybody, and he would furnish me a world of curious dunning adventures out of the ample store in his memory. By and by he would clap his hat on his head, shake hands and say briskly:

"Well, business is business—can't stay with you always!"—and was off in a second.

The idea of pining for a dun! And yet I used to long for him to come, and would get as uneasy as any mother if the day went by without his visit, when I was expecting him. But he never collected that bill, at last, nor any part of it. I lived to pay it to the banker myself.

Misery loves company. Now and then at night, in out-of-the-way, dimly lighted places, I found myself happening on another child of misfortune. He looked so seedy and forlorn, so homeless and friendless and forsaken, that I yearned toward him as a brother. I wanted to claim kinship with him and go about and enjoy our wretchedness together. The drawing toward each other must have been mutual; at any rate we got to falling together oftener, though still seemingly by accident; and although we did not speak or evince any recognition, I think the dull anxiety passed out of both of us when we saw each other, and then for several hours we would idle along contentedly, wide apart, and glancing furtively in at home lights and fireside gatherings, out of the night shadows, and very much enjoying our dumb companionship.

Finally we spoke, and were inseparable after that. For our woes were identical, almost. He had been a reporter too, and lost his berth, and this was his experience, as nearly as I can recollect it. After losing his berth, he had gone down, down, down, with never a halt: from a boarding house on Russian Hill to a boarding house in Kearny street; from thence to Dupont; from thence to a low sailor den; and from thence to lodgings in goods boxes and empty hogsheads near the wharves. Then, for a while, he had gained a meagre living by sewing up bursted sacks of grain on the piers; when that failed he had found food here and there as chance threw it in his way. He had ceased to show his face in daylight, now, for a reporter knows everybody, rich and poor, high and low, and cannot well avoid familiar faces in the broad light of day.

This mendicant Blucher—I call him that for convenience—was a splendid creature. He was full of hope, pluck and philosophy; he was well read and a man of cultivated taste; he had a bright wit and was a master of satire; his kindliness and his generous spirit made him royal in my eyes and changed his curb-stone seat to a throne and his damaged hat to a crown.

He had an adventure, once, which sticks fast in my memory as the most pleasantly grotesque that ever touched my sympathies. He had been without a penny for two months. He had shirked about obscure streets, among friendly dim lights, till the thing had become second nature to him. But at last he was driven abroad in daylight. The cause was sufficient; *he had not tasted food for forty-eight hours,* and he could not endure the misery of his hunger in idle hiding. He came along a back street, glowering at the loaves in bake-shop windows, and feeling that he could trade his life away for a morsel to eat. The sight of the bread doubled his hunger; but it was good to look at it, anyhow, and imagine what one might do if one only had it. Presently, in the middle of the street he saw a shining spot—looked again—did not, and could not, believe his eyes—turned away, to try them, then looked again. It was a verity—no vain, hunger-inspired delusion—it was a silver dime! He

A PRIZE.

snatched it—gloated over it; doubted it—bit it—found it genuine—choked his heart down, and smothered a halleluiah. Then he looked around—saw that nobody was looking at him—threw the dime down where it was before—walked away a few steps, and approached again, pretending he did not know it was there, so that he could re-enjoy the luxury of finding it. He walked around it, viewing it from different points; then sauntered about with his hands in his pockets, looking up at the signs and now and then glancing at it and feeling the old thrill again. Finally he took it up, and went away, fondling it in his pocket. He idled through unfrequented streets, stopping in doorways and corners to take it out and look at it. By and by he went home to his lodgings—an empty queensware hogshead,—and employed himself till night trying to make up his mind what to buy with it. But it was hard to do. To get the most for it was the idea. He knew that at the Miners' Restaurant he could get a plate of beans and a piece of bread for ten cents; or a fish-ball and some few trifles, but they gave "no bread with one fish-ball" there. At French Pete's he could get a veal cutlet, plain, and some radishes and bread, for ten cents; or a cup of coffee—a pint at least—and a slice of bread; but the slice was not thick enough by the eighth of an inch, and sometimes they were still more criminal than that in the cutting of it. At seven o'clock his hunger was wolfish; and still his mind was not made up. He turned out and went up Merchant street, still ciphering; and chewing a bit of stick, as is the way of starving men. He passed before the lights of Martin's restaurant, the most aristocratic in the city, and stopped. It was a place where he had often dined, in better days, and Martin knew him well. Standing aside, just out of the range of the light, he wor-shipped the quails and steaks in the show window, and imagined that maybe the fairy times were not gone yet and some prince in disguise would come along pres-ently and tell him to go in there and take whatever he wanted. He chewed his stick with a hungry in-terest as he warmed to his subject. Just at this juncture he was con-scious of some one at his side, sure enough; and then a finger touched his arm. He looked up, over his shoulder, and saw an apparition— a very allegory of Hunger! It was a man six feet high, gaunt, un-shaven, hung with rags; with a haggard face and sunken cheeks,

A LOOK IN AT THE WINDOW.

and eyes that pleaded piteously. This phantom said:

"Come with me—please."

He locked his arm in Blucher's and walked up the street to where the passengers were few and the light not strong, and then facing about, put out his hands in a beseeching way, and said:

"Friend—stranger—look at me! Life is easy to you—you go about, placid and content, as I did once, in my day—you have been in there, and eaten your sumptuous supper, and picked your teeth, and hummed your tune, and thought your pleasant thoughts, and said to yourself it is a good world—but you've never *suffered!* You don't know what trouble is—you don't know what misery is—nor hunger! Look at me! Stranger have pity on a poor friendless, home-less dog! As God is my judge, I have not tasted food for eight and forty hours!—look in my eyes and see if I lie! Give me the least tri-fle in the world to keep me from starving—anything—twenty-five cents! Do it, stranger—do it, *please.* It will be nothing to you, but

"DO IT, STRANGER."

life to me. Do it, and I will go down on my knees and lick the dust
before you! I will kiss your footprints—I will worship the very
ground you walk on! Only twenty-five cents! I am famishing—
perishing—starving by inches! For God's sake don't desert me!"

Blucher was bewildered—and touched, too—stirred to the
depths. He reflected. Thought again. Then an idea struck him, and
he said:

"Come with me."

He took the outcast's arm, walked him down to Martin's restaurant, seated him at a marble table, placed the bill of fare before
him, and said:

"Order what you want, friend. Charge it to me, Mr. Martin."

"All right, Mr. Blucher," said Martin.

Then Blucher stepped back and leaned against the counter and
watched the man stow away cargo after cargo of buckwheat cakes

at seventy-five cents a plate; cup after cup of coffee, and porter house steaks worth two dollars apiece; and when six dollars and a half's worth of destruction had been accomplished, and the stranger's hunger appeased, Blucher went down to French Pete's, bought a veal cutlet plain, a slice of bread, and three radishes, with his dime, and set to and feasted like a king!

Take the episode all around, it was as odd as any that can be culled from the myriad curiosities of Californian life, perhaps.

CHAPTER 60

By and by, an old friend of mine, a miner, came down from one of the decayed mining camps of Tuolumne, California, and I went back with him. We lived in a small cabin on a verdant hillside, and there were not five other cabins in view over the wide expanse of hill and forest. Yet a flourishing city of two or three thousand population had occupied this grassy dead solitude during the flush times of twelve or fifteen years before, and where our cabin stood had once been the heart of the teeming hive, the centre of the city. When the mines gave out the town fell into decay, and in a few years wholly disappeared—streets, dwellings, shops, everything—and left no sign. The grassy slopes were as green and smooth and desolate of life as if they had never been disturbed. The mere handful of miners still remaining, had seen the town spring up, spread, grow and flourish in its pride; and they had seen it sicken and die, and pass away like a dream. With it their hopes had died, and their zest of life. They had long ago resigned themselves to their exile, and ceased to correspond with their distant friends or turn longing eyes toward their early homes. They had accepted banishment, forgotten the world and been forgotten of the world. They were far from telegraphs and railroads, and they stood, as it were, in a living grave, dead to the events that stirred the globe's great populations, dead to the common interests of men, isolated and outcast from brotherhood with their kind. It was the most singular, and almost the most touching and melancholy exile that fancy can imagine. One of my associates in this locality, for two or three months, was a man who had had a university education; but now for eighteen years he had decayed there by inches, a bearded, rough-clad, clay-stained miner, and at times, among his sighings and soliloquizings, he unconsciously interjected vaguely remembered Latin and Greek sentences—dead and musty tongues, meet vehicles for the thoughts of one whose dreams were all of the past, whose life was a failure; a tired man, burdened with the present, and indifferent to the future; a man without ties, hopes, interests, waiting for rest and the end.

In that one little corner of California is found a species of mining which is seldom or never mentioned in print. It is called "pocket-mining" and I am not aware that any of it is done outside of that little corner. The gold is not evenly distributed through the surface dirt, as in ordinary placer mines, but is collected in little spots, and they are very wide apart and exceedingly hard to find, but when you do find one you reap a rich and sudden harvest.

THE OLD COLLEGIATE.

There are not now more than twenty pocket-miners in that entire little region. I think I know every one of them personally. I have known one of them to hunt patiently about the hillsides every day for eight months without finding gold enough to make a snuff-box—his grocery bill running up relentlessly all the time— and then find a pocket and take out of it two thousand dollars in two dips of his shovel. I have known him to take out three thousand dollars in two hours, and go and pay up every cent of his indebtedness, then enter on a dazzling spree that finished the last of his treasure before the night was gone. And the next day he bought his groceries on credit as usual, and shouldered his pan and shovel and went off to the hills hunting pockets again happy and content. This is the most fascinating of all the different kinds of mining, and furnishes a very handsome percentage of victims to the lunatic asylum.

Pocket hunting is an ingenious process. You take a spadeful of earth from the hillside and put it in a large tin pan and dissolve and wash it gradually away till nothing is left but a teaspoonful of fine sediment. Whatever gold was in that earth has remained, because, being the heaviest, it has sought the bottom. Among the sediment you will find half a dozen yellow particles no larger than pin-heads. You are delighted. You move off to one side and wash another pan. If you find gold again, you move to one side further, and wash a third pan. If you find *no* gold this time, you are delighted again, because you know you are on the right scent. You lay an imaginary plan, shaped like a fan, with its handle up the hill—for just where the end of the handle is, you argue that the rich deposit lies hidden, whose vagrant grains of gold have escaped and been washed down the hill, spreading farther and farther apart as they wandered. And so you proceed up the hill, washing the earth and narrowing your lines every time the absence of gold in the pan shows that you are outside the spread of the fan; and at last, twenty yards up the hill your lines have converged to a point—a single foot from that point you cannot find any gold. Your breath comes short and quick, you are feverish with excitement; the dinner-bell may ring its clapper off, you pay no attention; friends may die, weddings transpire, houses burn down, they are nothing to you; you sweat and dig and delve with a frantic interest—and all at once

STRIKING A POCKET.

you strike it! Up comes a spadeful of earth and quartz that is all lovely with soiled lumps and leaves and sprays of gold. Sometimes that one spadeful is all— five hundred dollars. Sometimes the nest contains ten thousand dollars, and it takes you three or four days to get it all out. The pocket-miners tell of one nest that yielded sixty thousand dollars and two men exhausted it in two weeks, and then sold the ground for ten thousand dollars to a party who never got three hundred dollars out of it afterward.

The hogs are good pocket hunters. All the summer they root around the bushes, and turn up a thousand little piles of dirt, and then the miners long for the rains; for the rains beat upon these little piles and wash them down and expose the gold, possibly right over a pocket. Two pockets were found in this way by the same man in one day. One had five thousand dollars in it and the other eight thousand dollars. That man could appreciate it, for he hadn't had a cent for about a year.

In Tuolumne lived two miners who used to go to the neighboring village in the afternoon and return every night with household supplies. Part of the distance they traversed a trail, and nearly always sat down to rest on a great boulder that lay beside the path. In the course of thirteen years they had worn that boulder tolerably smooth, sitting on it. By and by two vagrant Mexicans came along and occupied the seat. They began to amuse themselves by chipping off flakes from the boulder with a sledge-hammer. They examined one of these flakes and found it rich with gold. That boulder paid them eight hundred dollars afterward. But the aggravating circumstance was that these "Greasers" knew that there must be more gold where that boulder came from, and so they went panning up the hill and found what was probably the richest pocket that region has yet produced. It took three months to exhaust it, and it yielded a hundred and twenty thousand dollars. The two American miners who used to sit on the boulder are poor yet, and they take turn about in getting up early in the morning to curse those Mexicans—and when it comes down to pure ornamental cursing, the native American is gifted above the sons of men.

I have dwelt at some length upon this matter of pocket-mining because it is a subject that is seldom referred to in print, and therefore I judged that it would have for the reader that interest which naturally attaches to novelty.

CHAPTER 61

ONE of my comrades there—another of those victims of eighteen years of unrequited toil and blighted hopes—was one of the gentlest spirits that ever bore its patient cross in a weary exile: grave and simple Dick Baker, pocket-miner of Dead-Horse Gulch. He was forty-six, gray as a rat, earnest, thoughtful, slenderly educated, slouchily dressed and clay-soiled, but his heart was finer metal than any gold his shovel ever brought to light—than any, indeed, that ever was mined or minted.

Whenever he was out of luck and a little down-hearted, he would fall to mourning over the loss of a wonderful cat he used to own (for where women and children are not, men of kindly impulses take up with pets, for they must love something.) And he always spoke of the strange sagacity of that cat with the air of a man who believed in his secret heart that there was something human about it—maybe even supernatural.

TOM QUARTZ.

I heard him talking about this animal once. He said, "Gentlemen, I used to have a cat here, by the name of Tom Quartz, which you'd a took an interest in I reckon—most anybody would. I had him here eight year—and he was the remarkablest cat I ever see. He was a large gray one of the Tom specie, an' he had more hard, natchral sense than any man in this camp—'n' a *power* of dignity—he wouldn't a let the Gov'ner of Californy be familiar with him. He never ketched a rat in his life—'peared to be above it. He never cared for nothing but mining. He knowed more about mining, that cat did, than any man I ever

ever see. You couldn't tell *him* noth'n' 'bout placer diggin's—'n' as
for pocket-mining, why he was just born for it. He would dig out
after me an' Jim when we went over the hills prospect'n', and he
would trot along behind us for as much as five mile, if we went so
fur. An' he had the best judgment about mining ground—why you
never see anything like it. When we went to work, he'd scatter a
glance around, 'n' if he didn't think much of the indications, he
would give a look as much as to say, 'Well, I'll have to get you to
excuse *me*,' 'n' without another word he'd hyste his nose into the
air 'n' shove for home. But if the ground suited him, he would lay
low 'n' keep dark till the first pan was washed, 'n' then he would
sidle up 'n' take a look, an' if there was about six or seven grains of
gold *he* was satisfied—he didn't want no better prospect 'n that—
'n' then he would lay down on our coats and snore like a steamboat
till we'd struck the pocket, an' then get up 'n' superintend. He was
nearly lightnin' on superintending.

"Well, by an' by, up comes this yer quartz excitement. Everybody was into it—everybody was pick'n' 'n' blast'n' instead of
shovelin' dirt on the hillside—everybody was put'n' down a shaft
instead of scrapin' the surface. Noth'n' would do Jim, but *we* must
tackle the ledges, too, 'n' so we did. We commenced put'n' down a
shaft, 'n' Tom Quartz he begin to wonder what in the Dickens it
was all about. *He* hadn't ever seen any mining like that before, 'n'
he was all upset, as you may say—he couldn't come to a right understanding of it no way—it was too many for *him*. He was down
on it, too, you bet you—he was down on it powerful—'n' always
appeared to consider it the cussedest foolishness out. But that cat,
you know, was *always* agin new fangled arrangements—somehow
he never could abide 'em. *You* know how it is with old habits. But
by an' by Tom Quartz begin to git sort of reconciled a little, though
he never *could* altogether understand that eternal sinkin' of a shaft
an' never pannin' out anything. At last he got to comin' down in
the shaft, hisself, to try to cipher it out. An' when he'd git the
blues, 'n' feel kind o' scruffy, 'n' aggravated 'n' disgusted—knowin'
as he did, that the bills was runnin' up all the time an' we warn't
makin' a cent—he would curl up on a gunny sack in the corner an'
go to sleep. Well, one day when the shaft was down about eight

foot, the rock got so hard that we had to put in a blast—the first
blast'n' we'd ever done since Tom Quartz was born. An' then we lit
the fuse 'n' clumb out 'n' got off 'bout fifty yards—'n' forgot 'n' left
Tom Quartz sound asleep on the gunny sack. In 'bout a minute we
seen a puff of smoke bust up out of the hole, 'n' then everything let
go with an awful crash, 'n' about four million ton of rocks 'n' dirt
'n' smoke 'n' splinters shot up 'bout a mile an' a half into the air,
an' by George, right in the dead centre of it was old Tom Quartz a
goin' end over end, an' a snortin' an' a sneez'n', an' a clawin' an' a

reachin' for things like all
possessed. But it warn't no
use, you know, it warn't no
use. An' that was the last we

AN ADVANTAGE TAKEN.

see of *him* for about two minutes 'n' a half, an' then all of a sudden
it begin to rain rocks and rubbage, an' directly he come down ker-
whop about ten foot off f'm where we stood. Well, I reckon he was
p'raps the orneriest lookin' beast you ever see. One ear was sot
back on his neck, 'n' his tail was stove up, 'n' his eye-winkers was
swinged off, 'n' he was all blacked up with powder an' smoke, an'
all sloppy with mud 'n' slush f'm one end to the other. Well sir, it

warn't no use to try to apologize—we couldn't say a word. He took a sort of a disgusted look at hisself, 'n' then he looked at us—an' it was just exactly the same as if he had said—'Gents, maybe *you* think it's smart to take advantage of a cat that ain't had no experience of quartz minin', but *I* think *different*'—an' then he turned on his heel 'n' marched off home without ever saying another word.

AFTER AN EXCURSION.

"That was jest his style. An' maybe you won't believe it, but after that you never see a cat so prejudiced agin quartz mining as what he was. An' by an' by when he *did* get to goin' down in the shaft agin, you'd a been astonished at his sagacity. The minute we'd tetch off a blast 'n' the fuse'd begin to sizzle, he'd give a look as much as to say: 'Well, I'll have to git you to excuse *me*,' an' it was surpris'n', the way he'd shin out of that hole 'n' go f'r a tree. Sagacity? It ain't no name for it. 'Twas *inspiration!*"

I said, "Well, Mr. Baker, his prejudice against quartz mining *was* remarkable, considering how he came by it. Couldn't you ever cure him of it?"

"*Cure him!* No! When Tom Quartz was sot once, he was *always* sot—and you might a blowed him up as much as three million times 'n' you'd never a broken him of his cussed prejudice agin quartz mining."

The affection and the pride that lit up Baker's face when he delivered this tribute to the firmness of his humble friend of other days, will always be a vivid memory with me.

At the end of two months we had never "struck" a pocket. We had panned up and down the hillsides till they looked plowed like a field; we could have put in a crop of grain, then, but there would have been no way to get it to market. We got many good "prospects," but when the gold gave out in the pan and we dug down, hoping and longing, we found only emptiness—the pocket that should have been there was as barren as our own. At last we shouldered our pans and shovels and struck out over the hills to try new localities. We prospected around Angel's Camp, in Calaveras County, during three weeks, but had no success. Then we wan-

dered on foot among the mountains, sleeping under the trees at
night, for the weather was mild, but still we remained as centless
as the last rose of summer. That is a poor joke, but it is in pathetic
harmony with the circumstances, since we were so poor ourselves.
In accordance with the custom of the country, our door had always
stood open and our board welcome to tramping miners—they
drifted along nearly every day, dumped their post shovels by the
threshold and took "pot luck" with us—and now on our own
tramp we never found cold hospitality.

Our wanderings were wide and in many directions; and now I
could give the reader a vivid description of the Big Trees and the
marvels of the Yo Semite—but what has this reader done to me
that I should persecute him? I will deliver him into the hands of
less conscientious tourists and take his blessing. Let me be chari-
table, though I fail in all virtues else.

Some of the phrases in the above are mining technicalities, purely, and may be a
little obscure to the general reader. In *"placer diggings"* the gold is scattered all
through the surface dirt; in *"pocket"* diggings it is concentrated in one little spot;
in *"quartz"* the gold is in a solid, continuous vein of rock, enclosed between distinct walls of some other kind of stone—and this is the most laborious and expensive of all the different kinds of mining. *"Prospecting"* is hunting for a *"placer;" "indications"* are signs of its presence; *"panning out"* refers to the washing process by
which the grains of gold are separated from the dirt; a *"prospect"* is what one finds
in the first panful of dirt—and its value determines whether it is a good or a bad
prospect, and whether it is worth while to tarry there or seek further.

CHAPTER 62

AFTER a three months' absence, I found myself in San Francisco again, without a cent. When my credit was about exhausted, (for I had become too mean and lazy, now, to work on a morning paper, and there were no vacancies on the evening journals,) I was created San Francisco correspondent of the *Enterprise,* and at the end of five months I was out of debt, but my interest in my work was gone; for my correspondence being a daily one, without rest or respite, I got unspeakably tired of it. I wanted another change. The vagabond instinct was strong upon me. Fortune favored and I got a new berth and a delightful one. It was to go down to the Sandwich Islands and write some letters for the Sacramento *Union,* an excellent journal and liberal with employés.

We sailed in the propeller Ajax, in the middle of winter. The almanac called it winter, distinctly enough, but the weather was a compromise between spring and summer. Six days out of port, it became summer altogether. We had some thirty passengers; among them a cheerful soul by the name of Williams, and three sea-worn old whaleship captains going down to join their vessels. These latter played euchre in the smoking room day and night, drank astonishing quantities of raw whisky without being in the least affected by it, and were the happiest people I think I ever saw. And then there was "the old Admiral"—a retired whaleman. He was a roaring, terrific combination of wind and lightning and thunder, and earnest, whole-souled profanity. But nevertheless he was tender-hearted as a girl. He was a raving, deafening, devastating typhoon, laying waste the cowering seas but with an unvexed refuge in the centre where all comers were safe and at rest. Nobody could know the "Admiral" without liking him; and in a sudden and dire emergency I think no friend of his would know which to

THE THREE CAPTAINS.

choose—to be cursed by him or prayed for by a less efficient person.

His title of "Admiral" was more strictly "official" than any ever worn by a naval officer before or since, perhaps—for it was the voluntary offering of a whole nation, and came direct from the *people* themselves without any intermediate red tape—the people of the Sandwich Islands. It was a title that came to him freighted with affection, and honor, and appreciation of his unpretending merit. And in testimony of the genuineness of the title it was publicly ordained that an exclusive flag should be devised for him and used solely to welcome his coming and wave him God-speed in his going. From that time forth, whenever his ship was signaled in the offing, or he catted his anchor and stood out to sea, that ensign streamed from the royal halliards on the parliament house and the nation lifted their hats to it with spontaneous accord.

Yet he had never fired a gun or fought a battle in his life. When I knew him on board the Ajax, he was seventy-two years old and had

plowed the salt water sixty-one of them. For sixteen years he had gone in and out of the harbor of Honolulu in command of a whaleship, and for sixteen more had been captain of a San Francisco and Sandwich Island passenger packet and had never had an accident or lost a vessel. The simple natives knew him for a friend who never failed them, and regarded him as children regard a father. It was a dangerous thing to oppress them when the roaring Admiral was around.

Two years before I knew the Admiral, he had retired from the sea on a competence, and had sworn a colossal nine-

THE OLD ADMIRAL.

jointed oath that he would "never go within *smelling* distance of the salt water again as long as he lived." And he had conscientiously kept it. That is to say, *he* considered he had kept it, and it would have been more than dangerous to suggest to him, even in the gentlest way, that making eleven long sea voyages, as a passenger, during the two years that had transpired since he "retired," was only keeping the general spirit of it and not the strict letter.

The Admiral knew only one narrow line of conduct to pursue in any and all cases where there was a fight, and that was to shoulder his way straight in without an inquiry as to the rights or the merits of it, and take the part of the weaker side. And this was the reason why he was always sure to be present at the trial of any universally execrated criminal to oppress and intimidate the jury with a vindictive pantomime of what he would do to them if he ever caught them out of the box. And this was why harried cats and outlawed

dogs that knew him confidently took sanctuary under his chair in
time of trouble. In the beginning he was the most frantic and
bloodthirsty Union man that drew breath in the shadow of the
Flag; but the instant the Southerners began to go down before the
sweep of the Northern armies, he ran up the Confederate colors
and from that time till the end was a rampant and inexorable
secessionist.

He hated intemperance with a more uncompromising animosity than any individual I have ever met, of either sex; and he was
never tired of storming against it and beseeching friends and
strangers alike to be wary and drink with moderation. And yet if
any creature had been guileless enough to intimate that his absorbing nine gallons of "straight" whisky during our voyage was
any fraction short of rigid or inflexible abstemiousness, in that
self-same moment the old man would have spun him to the utter-
most parts of the earth in the whirlwind of his wrath. Mind, I am
not saying his whisky ever affected his head or his legs, for it did
not, in even the slightest degree. He was a capacious container, but
he did not hold enough for that. He took a level tumblerful of
whisky every morning before he put his clothes on—"to sweeten
his bilgewater," he said. He took another after he got the most of
his clothes on, "to settle his mind and give him his bearings." He
then shaved, and put on a clean shirt; after which he recited the
Lord's Prayer in a fervent, thundering bass that shook the ship to
her kelson and suspended all conversation in the main cabin.
Then, at this stage, being invariably "by the head," or "by the
stern," or "listed to port or starboard," he took one more to "put
him on an even keel so that he would mind his hellum and not
miss stays and go about, every time he came up in the wind." And
now, his state-room door swung open and the sun of his benignant
face beamed redly out upon men and women and children, and he
roared his "Shipmets a'hoy!" in a way that was calculated to wake
the dead and precipitate the final resurrection; and forth he strode,
a picture to look at and a presence to enforce attention. Stalwart
and portly; not a gray hair; broad-brimmed slouch hat; semi-sailor
toggery of blue navy flannel—roomy and ample; a stately expanse
of shirt-front and a liberal amount of black silk neck-cloth tied

with a sailor knot; large chain and imposing seals impending from his fob; awe-inspiring feet, and "a hand like the hand of Providence," as his whaling brethren expressed it; wrist-bands and sleeves pushed back half way to the elbow, out of respect for the warm weather, and exposing hairy arms, gaudy with red and blue anchors, ships, and goddesses of liberty tattooed in India ink. But these details were only secondary matters—his face was the lodestone that chained the eye. It was a sultry disk, glowing determinedly out through a weather beaten mask of mahogany, and studded with warts, seamed with scars, "blazed" all over with unfailing fresh slips of the razor; and with cheery eyes, under shaggy brows, contemplating the world from over the back of a gnarled crag of a nose that loomed vast and lonely out of the undulating immensity that spread away from its foundations. At his heels frisked the darling of his bachelor estate, his terrier "Fan," a creature no larger than a squirrel. The main part of his daily life was occupied in looking after "Fan," in a motherly way, and doctoring her for a hundred ailments which existed only in his imagination.

The Admiral seldom read newspapers; and when he did he never believed anything they said. He read nothing, and believed in nothing, but "The Old Guard," a secession periodical published in New York. He carried a dozen copies of it with him, always, and referred to them for all required information. If it was not there, he supplied it himself, out of a bountiful fancy, inventing history, names, dates, and everything else necessary to make his point good in an argument. Consequently he was a formidable antagonist in a dispute. Whenever he swung clear of the record and began to create history, the enemy was helpless and had to surrender. Indeed, the enemy could not keep from betraying some little spark of indignation at his manufactured history—and when it came to indignation, that was the Admiral's very "best hold." He was always ready for a political argument, and if nobody started one he would do it himself. With his third retort his temper would begin to rise, and within five minutes he would be blowing a gale, and within fifteen his smoking-room audience would be utterly stormed away and the old man left solitary and alone, banging the table with his fist, kicking the chairs, and roaring a hurricane of profanity. It got so, after a while, that whenever the Admiral approached, with politics in his eye, the passengers would drop out with quiet accord, afraid to meet him; and he would camp on a deserted field.

DESERTED FIELD.

But he found his match at last, and before a full company. At one time or another, everybody had entered the lists against him and been routed, except the quiet passenger Williams. He had never been able to get an expression of opinion out of him on politics. But now, just as the Admiral drew near the door and the company were about to slip out, Williams said:

"Admiral, are you *certain* about that circumstance concerning the clergymen you mentioned the other day?"—referring to a piece of the Admiral's manufactured history.

Every one was amazed at the man's rashness. The idea of deliberately inviting annihilation was a thing incomprehensible. The retreat came to a halt; then everybody sat down again wondering, to await the upshot of it. The Admiral himself was as surprised as any one. He paused in the door, with his red handkerchief half raised to his sweating face, and contemplated the daring reptile in the corner.

"*Certain* of it? Am I *certain* of it? Do you think I've been lying about it? What do you take me for? Anybody that don't know that

WILLIAMS.

circumstance, don't know anything; a child ought to know it. Read up your history! Read it up —— —— —— ——, and don't come asking a man if he's *certain* about a bit of A B C stuff that the very southern niggers know all about."

Here the Admiral's fires began to wax hot, the atmosphere thickened, the coming earthquake rumbled, he began to thunder and lighten. Within three minutes his volcano was in full eruption and he was discharging flames and ashes of indignation, belching black volumes of foul history aloft, and vomiting red-hot torrents of profanity from his crater. Meantime Williams sat silent, and apparently deeply and earnestly interested in what the old man was saying. By and by, when the lull came, he said in the most deferential way, and with the gratified air of a man who has had a mystery cleared up which had been puzzling him uncomfortably:

"*Now* I understand it. I always thought I knew that piece of history well enough, but was still afraid to trust it, because there was not that convincing particularity about it that one likes to have in history; but when you mentioned every name, the other day, and every date, and every little circumstance, in their just order and sequence, I said to myself, *this* sounds something like—*this* is history—*this* is putting it in a shape that gives a man confidence; and I said to myself afterward, I will just ask the Admiral if he is perfectly certain about the details, and if he is I will come out and thank him for clearing this matter up for me. And that is what I want to do now—for until you set that matter right it was nothing but just a confusion in my mind, without head or tail to it."

Nobody ever saw the Admiral look so mollified before, and so pleased. Nobody had ever received his bogus history as gospel before; its genuineness had always been called in question either by words or looks; but here was a man that not only swallowed it all down, but was grateful for the dose. He was taken aback; he hardly knew what to say; even his profanity failed him. Now, Williams continued, modestly and earnestly:

"But Admiral, in saying that this was the first stone thrown, and that this precipitated the war, you have overlooked a circumstance which you are perfectly familiar with, but which has escaped your memory. Now I grant you that what you have stated is correct in every detail—to wit: that on the 16th of October, 1860, two Massachusetts clergymen, named Waite and Granger, went in disguise to the house of John Moody, in Rockport, at dead of night, and dragged forth two Southern women and their two little children, and after tarring and feathering them conveyed them to Boston and burned them alive in the State House square; and I also grant your proposition that this deed is what led to the secession of South Carolina on the 20th of December following. Very well." [Here the company were pleasantly surprised to hear Williams proceed to come back at the Admiral with his own invincible weapon—clean, pure, *manufactured history*, without a word of truth in it.] "Very well, I say. But Admiral, why overlook the Willis and Morgan case in South Carolina? You are too well informed a man not to know all about that circumstance. Your arguments and your conversations have shown you to be intimately conversant with every detail of this national quarrel. You develop matters of history every day that show plainly that you are no smatterer in it, content to nibble about the surface, but a man who has searched the depths and possessed yourself of everything that has a bearing upon the great question. Therefore, let me just recall to your mind that Willis and Morgan case—though I see by your face that the whole thing is already passing through your memory at this moment. On the 12th of August, 1860, *two months* before the Waite and Granger affair, two South Carolina clergymen, named John H. Morgan and Winthrop L. Willis, one a Methodist and the other an Old School Baptist, disguised themselves, and went at midnight to the house of a planter named Thompson—Archibald F. Thompson, Vice President under Thomas Jefferson,—and took thence, at midnight, his widowed aunt, (a Northern woman,) and her adopted child, an orphan named Mortimer Highie, afflicted with epilepsy and suffering at the time from white swelling on one of his legs, and compelled to walk on crutches in consequence; and the two ministers, in spite of the pleadings of the victims, dragged them to the bush, tarred and feathered them, and afterward burned them at the stake in the city of Charleston. You remember perfectly well what a stir it made; you remember perfectly well that even the Charleston *Courier* stigmatized the act as being unpleasant, of questionable propriety, and scarcely justifiable, and likewise that it would not be matter of surprise if retaliation ensued. And you remember also, that this thing was the *cause* of the Massachusetts outrage. Who, indeed, were the two Massachusetts ministers? and who were the two Southern women they burned? I do not need to remind *you*, Admiral, with your intimate knowledge of history, that Waite was the nephew of the woman burned in Charleston; that Granger was her cousin in the second degree, and that the women they burned in Boston were the wife of John H. Morgan, and the still loved but divorced wife of Winthrop L. Willis. Now, Admiral, it is only fair that you should acknowledge that the first provocation came from the Southern preachers and that the Northern ones were justified in retaliating. In your arguments you never yet have shown the least disposition to withhold a just verdict or be in anywise unfair, when authoritative history condemned your position, and therefore I have no hesitation in asking you to take the original blame from the Massachusetts ministers, in this matter, and transfer it to the South Carolina clergymen where it justly belongs."

The Admiral was conquered. This sweet spoken creature who swallowed his fraudulent history as if it were the bread of life; basked in his furious blasphemy as if it were generous sunshine; found only calm, even-handed justice in his rampant partisanship; and flooded him with invented history so sugar-coated with flattery and deference that there was no rejecting it, was "too many" for him. He stammered some awkward, profane sentences about the ——— ——— ——— ——— Willis and Morgan business having escaped his memory, but that he "remembered it now," and then, under pretense of giving Fan some medicine for an imaginary cough, drew out of the battle and went away, a vanquished man. Then cheers and laughter went up, and Williams, the ship's benefactor, was a hero. The news went about the vessel, champagne was ordered, an enthusiastic reception instituted in the smoking room, and everybody flocked thither to shake hands with the conqueror. The wheelsman said afterward, that the Admiral stood up behind the pilot house and "ripped and cursed all to himself" till he loosened the smoke-stack guys and becalmed the mainsail.

The Admiral's power was broken. After that, if he began an argument, somebody would bring Williams, and the old man would grow weak and begin to quiet down at once. And as soon as he was done, Williams in his dulcet, insinuating way, would invent some history (referring for proof, to the old man's own excellent memory and to copies of "The Old Guard" known not to be in his possession) that would turn the tables completely and leave the Admiral all abroad and helpless. By and by he came to so dread Williams and his gilded tongue that he would stop talking when he saw him approach, and finally ceased to mention politics altogether, and from that time forward there was entire peace and serenity in the ship.

CHAPTER 63

On a certain bright morning the Islands hove in sight, lying low on the lonely sea, and everybody climbed to the upper deck to look. After two thousand miles of watery solitude the vision was a welcome one. As we approached, the imposing promontory of Diamond Head rose up out of the ocean, its rugged front softened by the hazy distance, and presently the details of the land began to make themselves manifest: first the line of beach; then the plumed cocoanut trees of the tropics; then cabins of the natives; then the white town of Honolulu, said to contain between twelve and fifteen thousand inhabitants, spread over a dead level; with streets from twenty to thirty feet wide, solid and level as a floor, most of them straight as a line and a few as crooked as a corkscrew.

The further I traveled through the town the better I liked it. Every step revealed a new contrast—disclosed something I was unaccustomed to. In place of the grand mud-colored brown stone fronts of San Francisco, I saw dwellings built of straw, *adobes* and cream-colored pebble-and-shell-conglomerated coral cut into oblong blocks and laid in cement; also a great number of neat white cottages, with green window-shutters; in place of front yards like billiard-tables with iron fences around them, I saw these homes surrounded by ample yards, thickly clad with green grass, and shaded by tall trees, through whose dense foliage the sun could scarcely penetrate; in place of the customary geranium, calla lily, etc., languishing in dust and general debility, I saw luxurious banks and thickets of flowers, fresh as a meadow after a rain, and glowing with the richest dyes; in place of the dingy horrors of San Francisco's pleasure grove, the "Willows," I saw huge-bodied, wide-spreading forest trees, with strange names and stranger appearance—trees that cast a shadow like a thunder-cloud, and were able to stand alone without being tied to green poles; in place of gold-fish, wiggling around in glass globes, assuming countless shades and degrees of distortion through the magnifying and diminishing qualities of their transparent prison houses, I saw cats—Tom-cats, Mary Ann cats, long-tailed cats, bob-tail cats,

SCENE ON THE ISLANDS.

blind cats, one-eyed cats, wall-eyed cats, cross-eyed cats, gray cats, black cats, white cats, yellow cats, striped cats, spotted cats, tame cats, wild cats, singed cats, individual cats, groups of cats, platoons of cats, companies of cats, regiments of cats, armies of cats, multitudes of cats, millions of cats, and all of them sleek, fat, lazy and sound asleep.

I looked on a multitude of people, some white, in white coats, vests, pantaloons, even white cloth shoes, made snowy with chalk duly laid on every morning; but the majority of the people were almost as dark as negroes—women with comely features, fine black eyes, rounded forms, inclining to the voluptuous, clad in a single bright red or white garment that fell free and unconfined from shoulder to heel, long black hair falling loose, gypsy hats, encircled with wreaths of natural flowers of a brilliant carmine tint; plenty of dark men in various costumes, and some with nothing on but a battered stove-pipe hat tilted on the nose, and a very scant breech-clout;—certain smoke-dried children were clothed in nothing but sunshine—a very neat fitting and picturesque apparel indeed.

In place of roughs and rowdies staring and blackguarding on the corners, I saw long-haired, saddle-colored Sandwich Island maidens sitting on the ground in the shade of corner houses, gazing in-dolently at whatever or whoever hap-pened along; instead of wretched cobble-stone pavements, I walked on a

FASHIONABLE ATTIRE.

firm foundation of coral, built up from the bottom of the sea by the absurd but persevering insect of that name, with a light layer of lava and cinders overlying the coral, belched up out of fathomless perdition long ago through the seared and blackened crater that stands dead and harmless in the distance now; instead of cramped and crowded street cars, I met dusky native women sweeping by, free as the wind, on fleet horses and astride, with gaudy riding-sashes streaming like banners behind them; instead of the com-bined stenches of Chinadom and Brannan street slaughter-houses, I breathed the balmy fragrance of jessamine, oleander, and the Pride of India; in place of the hurry and bustle and noisy confusion of San Francisco, I moved in the midst of a summer calm as tran-quil as dawn in the Garden of Eden; in place of the Golden City's skirting sand hills and the placid bay, I saw on the one side a frame-work of tall, precipitous mountains close at hand, clad in refresh-ing green, and cleft by deep, cool, chasm-like valleys—and in front the grand sweep of the ocean: a brilliant, transparent green near the shore, bound and bordered by a long white line of foamy spray dashing against the reef, and further out the dead blue water of the deep sea, flecked with "white caps," and in the far horizon a single, lonely sail—a mere accent-mark to emphasize a slumberous calm and a solitude that were without sound or limit. When the sun sunk down—the one intruder from other realms and persistent in suggestions of them—it was tranced luxury to sit in the perfumed air and forget that there was any world but these enchanted islands.

It was such ecstasy to dream, and dream—till you got a bite. A scorpion bite. Then the first duty was to get up out of the grass and

A BITE.

kill the scorpion; and the next to bathe the bitten place with alcohol or brandy; and the next to resolve to keep out of the grass in future. Then came an adjournment to the bed-chamber and the pastime of writing up the day's journal with one hand and the destruction of mosquitoes with the other—a whole community of them at a slap. Then, observing an enemy approaching,—a hairy tarantula on stilts—why not set the spittoon on him? It is done, and the projecting ends of his paws give a luminous idea of the magnitude of his reach. Then to bed and become a promenade for a centipede with forty-two legs on a side and every foot hot enough to burn a hole through a raw-hide. More soaking with alcohol, and a resolution to examine the bed before entering it, in future. Then wait, and suffer, till all the mosquitoes in the neighborhood have crawled in under the bar, then slip out quickly, shut them in and sleep peacefully on the floor till morning. Meantime it is comforting to curse the tropics in occasional wakeful intervals.

We had an abundance of fruit in Honolulu, of course. Oranges, pine-apples, bananas, strawberries, lemons, limes, mangoes, gua-

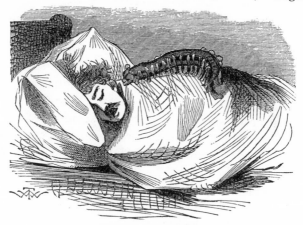

RECONNOITERING.

vas, melons, and a rare and curious luxury called the chirimoya, which is deliciousness itself. Then there is the tamarind. I thought

EATING TAMARINDS.

tamarinds were made to eat, but that was probably not the idea. I ate several, and it seemed to me that they were rather sour that year. They pursed up my lips, till they resembled the stem-end of a tomato, and I had to take my sustenance through a quill for twenty-four hours. They sharpened my teeth till I could have shaved with them, and gave them a "wire edge" that I was afraid would stay; but a citizen said "no, it will come off when the enamel does"—which was comforting, at any rate. I found, afterward, that only strangers eat tamarinds— but they only eat them once.

CHAPTER 64

In my diary of our third day in Honolulu, I find this:

I am probably the most sensitive man in Hawaii to-night—especially about sitting down in the presence of my betters. I have ridden fifteen or twenty miles on horseback since 5 P.M., and to tell the honest truth, I have a delicacy about sitting down at all.

An excursion to Diamond Head and the King's Cocoanut Grove was planned to-day—time, 4:30 P.M.—the party to consist of half a dozen gentlemen and three ladies. They all started at the appointed hour except myself. I was at the Government Prison, (with Capt. Fish and another whaleship-skipper, Capt. Phillips,) and got so interested in its examination that I did not notice how quickly the time was passing. Somebody remarked that it was twenty minutes past five o'clock, and that woke me up. It was a fortunate circumstance that Capt. Phillips was along with his "turn-out," as he calls a top-buggy that Capt. Cook brought here in 1778, and a horse that was here when Capt. Cook came. Capt. Phillips takes a just pride in his driving and in the speed of his horse, and to his passion for displaying them I owe it that we were only sixteen minutes coming from the prison to the American Hotel—a distance which has been estimated to be over half a mile. But it took some fearful driving. The captain's whip came down fast, and the blows started so much dust out of the horse's hide that during the last half of the journey we rode through an impenetrable fog, and ran by a pocket compass in the hands of Capt. Fish, a whaler of twenty-six years' experience, who sat there through the perilous voyage as self-possessed as if he had been on the euchre-deck of his own ship, and calmly said, "Port your helm—port," from time to time, and "Hold her a little free—steady—so-o," and "Luff—hard down to starboard!" and never once lost his presence of mind or betrayed the least anxiety by voice or manner. When we came to anchor at last, and Capt. Phillips looked at his watch and said, "Sixteen minutes—I told you it was in her! that's over three miles an hour!" I could see he felt entitled to a compliment, and so I said I had never seen lightning go like that horse. And I never had.

The landlord of the American said the party had been gone nearly an hour, but that he could give me my choice of several horses that could overtake them. I said, never mind—I preferred a safe horse to a fast one—I would like to have an excessively gentle horse—a horse with no spirit whatever—a lame one, if he had such a thing. Inside of five minutes I was mounted, and perfectly satisfied with my outfit. I had no time to label him "This is a horse," and so if the public took him for a sheep I cannot help it. I was satisfied, and that was the main thing. I could see that he had as many fine points as any man's horse, and so I hung my hat on one of them, behind the saddle, and swabbed the perspiration from my face and started. I named him after this island, "Oahu" (pronounced O-waw-hoo). The first gate he came to he started in; I had neither whip nor spur, and so I simply argued the case with him. He resisted argument, but ultimately yielded to insult and abuse. He backed out of that gate and steered for another one on the other side of the street. I triumphed by my former process. Within the next six hundred yards he crossed the street fourteen times and attempted thirteen gates, and in the meantime the tropical sun was beating down and threatening to cave the top of my head in, and I was literally dripping with perspiration. He abandoned the gate business after that and went along peaceably enough, but absorbed in meditation. I noticed this latter circumstance, and it soon began to fill me with apprehension. I said to myself, this creature is planning some new outrage, some fresh deviltry or other—no horse ever thought over a subject so profoundly as this one is doing just for nothing. The more this thing preyed upon my mind the more uneasy I became, until the suspense became almost unbearable and I dismounted to see if there was anything wild in his eye—for I had heard that the eye of this noblest of our domestic animals is very expressive. I cannot describe what a load of anxiety was lifted from my mind when I found that he was only asleep. I woke him up and started him into a faster walk, and then the villainy of his nature came out again. He tried to climb over a stone wall, five or

LOOKING FOR MISCHIEF.

six feet high. I saw that I must apply force to this horse, and that I might as well begin first as last. I plucked a stout switch from a tamarind tree, and the moment he saw it, he surrendered. He broke into a convulsive sort of a canter, which had three short steps in it and one long one, and reminded me alternately of the clattering shake of the great earthquake, and the sweeping plunging of the Ajax in a storm.

And now there can be no fitter occasion than the present to pronounce a left-handed blessing upon the man who invented the American saddle. There is no seat to speak of about it—one might as well sit in a shovel—and the stirrups are nothing but an ornamental nuisance. If I were to write down here all the abuse I expended on those stirrups, it would make a large book, even without pictures. Sometimes I got one foot so far through, that the stirrup partook of the nature of an anklet; sometimes both feet were through, and I was handcuffed by the legs; and sometimes my feet got clear out and left the stirrups wildly dangling about my shins. Even when I was in proper position and carefully balanced upon the balls of my feet, there was no comfort in it, on account of my nervous dread that they were going to slip one way or the other in a moment. But the subject is too exasperating to write about.

A mile and a half from town, I came to a grove of tall cocoanut trees, with clean, branchless stems reaching straight up sixty or seventy feet and topped with a spray of green foliage sheltering clusters of cocoanuts—not more picturesque than a forest of colossal ragged parasols, with bunches of magnified grapes under

A FAMILY LIKENESS.

them, would be. I once heard a grouty northern invalid say that a cocoanut tree might be poetical, possibly it was; but it looked like a feather-duster struck by lightning. I think that describes it better than a picture—and yet, without any question, there is something fascinating about a cocoanut tree—and graceful, too.

About a dozen cottages, some frame and the others of native grass, nestled sleepily in the shade here and there. The grass cabins are of a grayish color, are shaped much like our own cottages, only with higher and steeper roofs usually, and are made of some kind of weed strongly bound together in bundles. The roofs are very thick, and so are the walls; the latter have square holes in them for windows. At a little distance these cabins have a furry appearance, as if they might be made of bear skins. They are very cool and pleasant inside. The King's flag was flying from the roof of one of the cottages, and his Majesty was probably within. He owns the whole concern thereabouts, and passes his time there frequently, on sultry days "laying off." The spot is called "The King's Grove."

Near by is an interesting ruin—the meagre remains of an ancient heathen temple—a place where human sacrifices were offered up in those old bygone days when the simple child of nature,

yielding momentarily to sin when sorely tempted, acknowledged
his error when calm reflection had shown it to him, and came forward with noble frankness and offered up his grandmother as an
atoning sacrifice—in those old days when the luckless sinner
could keep on cleansing his conscience and achieving periodical
happiness as long as his relations held out; long, long before the
missionaries braved a thousand privations to come and make them
permanently miserable by telling them how beautiful and how
blissful a place heaven is, and how nearly impossible it is to get
there; and showed the poor native how dreary a place perdition is
and what unnecessarily liberal facilities there are for going to it;
showed him how, in his ignorance, he had gone and fooled away all
his kin-folks to no purpose; showed him what rapture it is to work
all day long for fifty cents to buy food for next day with, as compared with fishing for pastime and lolling in the shade through
eternal summer, and eating of the bounty that nobody labored to
provide but Nature. How sad it is to think of the multitudes who
have gone to their graves in this beautiful island and never knew
there was a hell!

This ancient temple was built of rough blocks of lava, and was
simply a roofless enclosure a hundred and thirty feet long and seventy wide—nothing but naked walls, very thick, but not much
higher than a man's head. They will last for ages, no doubt, if left
unmolested. Its three altars and other sacred appurtenances have
crumbled and passed away years ago. It is said that in the old times
thousands of human beings were slaughtered here, in the presence
of naked and howling savages. If these mute stones could speak,
what tales they could tell, what pictures they could describe, of
fettered victims writhing under the knife; of massed forms straining forward out of the gloom, with ferocious faces lit up by the sacrificial fires; of the background of ghostly trees; of the dark pyramid of Diamond Head standing sentinel over the uncanny scene,
and the peaceful moon looking down upon it through rifts in the
cloud-rack!

When Kamehameha (pronounced Ka-may-ha-may-ah) the
Great—who was a sort of a Napoleon in military genius and uniform success—invaded this island of Oahu three-quarters of a century ago, and exterminated the army sent to oppose him, and took

full and final possession of the country, he searched out the dead body of the King of Oahu, and those of the principal chiefs, and impaled their heads on the walls of this temple.

Those were savage times when this old slaughter-house was in its prime. The King and the chiefs ruled the common herd with a rod of iron; made them gather all the provisions the masters needed; build all the houses and temples; stand all the expenses, of whatever kind; take kicks and cuffs for thanks; drag out lives well flavored with misery, and then suffer death for trifling offenses or yield up their lives on the sacrificial altars to purchase favors from the gods for their hard rulers. The missionaries have clothed them, educated them, broken up the tyrannous authority of their chiefs, and given them freedom and the right to enjoy whatever their hands and brains produce, with equal laws for all and punishment for all alike who transgress them. The contrast is so strong—the benefit conferred upon this people by the missionaries is so prominent, so palpable and so unquestionable, that the frankest compliment I can pay them, and the best, is simply to point to the condition of the Sandwich Islanders of Capt. Cook's time, and their condition to-day. Their work speaks for itself.

CHAPTER 65

By and by, after a rugged climb, we halted on the summit of a hill which commanded a far-reaching view. The moon rose and flooded mountain and valley and ocean with a mellow radiance, and out of the shadows of the foliage the distant lights of Honolulu glinted like an encampment of fire-flies. The air was heavy with the fragrance of flowers. The halt was brief. Gayly laughing and talking, the party galloped on, and I clung to the pommel and cantered after. Presently we came to a place where no grass grew—a wide expanse of deep sand. They said it was an old battle-ground. All around everywhere, not three feet apart, the bleached bones of men gleamed white in the moonlight. We picked up a lot of them for mementoes. I got quite a number of arm bones and leg bones—of great chiefs, maybe, who had fought savagely in that fearful battle in the old days, when blood flowed like wine where we now stood—and wore the choicest of them out on Oahu afterward, trying to make him go. All sorts of bones could be found except skulls; but a citizen said, irreverently, that there had been an unusual number of "skull-hunters" there lately—a species of sportsmen I had never heard of before.

Nothing whatever is known about this place—its story is a secret that will never be revealed. The oldest natives make no pretense of being possessed of its history. They say these bones were here when they were children. They were here when their grandfathers were children—but how they came here, they can only conjecture. Many people believe this spot to be an ancient battle-ground, and it is usual to call it so; and they believe that these skeletons have lain for ages just where their proprietors fell in the great fight. Other people believe that Kamehameha I fought his first battle here. On this point, I have heard a story, which may have been taken from one of the numerous books which have been written concerning these islands—I do not know where the narrator got it. He said that when Kamehameha (who was at first merely a subordinate chief on the island of Hawaii), landed here, he brought a large army with him, and encamped at Waikiki. The Oahuans marched against him, and so confident were they of success that they readily acceded to a demand of their priests that they should draw a line where these bones now lie, and take an oath that, if forced to retreat at all, they would never retreat beyond this boundary. The priests told them that death and everlasting punishment would overtake any who violated the oath, and the march was resumed. Kamehameha drove them back step by step; the priests fought in the front rank and exhorted them both by voice and inspiriting example to remember their oath—to die, if need be, but never cross the fatal line. The struggle was manfully maintained, but at last the chief priest fell, pierced to the heart with a spear, and the unlucky omen fell like a blight upon the brave souls at his back; with a triumphant shout the invaders pressed forward—the line was crossed—the offended gods deserted the despairing army, and, accepting the doom their perjury had brought upon them, they broke and fled over the plain where Honolulu stands now—up the beautiful Nuuanu Valley—paused a moment, hemmed in by precipitous mountains on either hand and the frightful precipice of the Pari in front, and then were driven over—a sheer plunge of six hundred feet!

The story is pretty enough, but Mr. Jarves's excellent history says the Oahuans were intrenched in Nuuanu Valley; that Kamehameha ousted them, routed them, pursued them up the valley and drove them over the precipice. He makes no mention of our bone-yard at all in his book.

Impressed by the profound silence and repose that rested over the beautiful landscape, and being, as usual, in the rear, I gave voice to my thoughts. I said:

"What a picture is here slumbering in the solemn glory of the moon! How strong the rugged outlines of the dead volcano stand out against the clear sky! What a snowy fringe marks the bursting of the surf over the long, curved reef! How calmly the dim city sleeps yonder in the plain! How soft the shadows lie upon the stately mountains that border the dream-haunted Manoa Valley! What a grand pyramid of billowy clouds towers above the storied Pari! How the grim warriors of the past seem flocking in ghostly squadrons to their ancient battlefield again—how the wails of the dying well up from the—"

At this point the horse called Oahu sat down in the sand. Sat down to listen, I suppose. Never mind what he heard. I stopped

SAT DOWN TO LISTEN.

apostrophising and convinced him that I was not a man to allow contempt of court on the part of a horse. I broke the back-bone of a chief over his rump and set out to join the cavalcade again.

Very considerably fagged out we arrived in town at nine o'clock at night, myself in the lead—for when my horse finally came to understand that he was homeward bound and hadn't far to go, he turned his attention strictly to business.

This is a good time to drop in a paragraph of information. There is no regular livery stable in Honolulu, or, indeed, in any part of the kingdom of Hawaii; therefore, unless you are acquainted with wealthy residents (who all have good horses), you must hire animals of the wretchedest description from the Kanakas (*i. e.* natives.) Any horse you hire, even though it be from a white man, is not often of much account, because it will be brought in for you from some ranch, and has necessarily been leading a hard life. If the Kanakas who have been caring for him (inveterate riders they are) have not ridden him half to death every day themselves, you can depend upon it they have been doing the same thing by proxy, by clandestinely hiring him out. At least, so I am informed. The result is, that no horse has a chance to eat, drink, rest, recuperate, or look well or feel well, and so strangers go about the Islands mounted as I was to-day.

In hiring a horse from a Kanaka, you must have all your eyes about you, because you can rest satisfied that you are dealing with a shrewd unprincipled rascal. You may leave your door open and your trunk unlocked as long as you please, and he will not meddle with your property; he has no important vices and no inclination to commit robbery on a large scale; but if he can get ahead of you in the horse business, he will take a genuine delight in doing it. This trait is characteristic of horse-jockeys, the world over, is it not? He will overcharge you if he can; he will hire you a fine-looking horse at night (anybody's—maybe the King's, if the royal steed be in convenient view), and bring you the mate to my Oahu in the morning, and contend that it is the same animal. If you make trouble, he will get out by saying it was not himself who made the bargain with you, but his brother, "who went out in the country this morning." They have always got a "brother" to shift the responsibility upon. A victim said to one of these fellows one day:

"But I know I hired the horse of you, because I noticed that scar on your cheek."

The reply was not bad: "Oh, yes—yes—my brother all same—we twins!"

A friend of mine, J. Smith, hired a horse yesterday, the Kanaka warranting him to be in excellent condition. Smith had a saddle and blanket of his own, and he ordered the Kanaka to put these on the horse. The Kanaka protested that he was perfectly willing to trust the gentleman with the saddle that was already on the ani-

"MY BROTHER ALL SAME—WE TWINS!"

mal, but Smith refused to use it. The change was made; then Smith
noticed that the Kanaka had only changed the saddles, and had left
the original blanket on the horse; he said he forgot to change the
blankets, and so, to cut the bother short, Smith mounted and rode
away. The horse went lame a mile from town, and afterward got to
cutting up some extraordinary capers. Smith got down and took off
the saddle, but the blanket stuck fast to the horse—glued to a
procession of raw places. The Kanaka's mysterious conduct stood
explained.

Another friend of mine bought a pretty good horse from a native,
a day or two ago, after a tolerably thorough examination of the animal. He discovered to-day that the horse was as blind as a bat, in
one eye. He meant to have examined that eye, and came home
with a general notion that he had done it; but he remembers now

that every time he made the attempt his attention was called to something else by his victimizer.

One more instance, and then I will pass to something else. I am informed that when a certain Mr. L., a visiting stranger, was here he bought a pair of very respectable-looking match horses from a native. They were in a little stable with a partition through the middle of it—one horse in each apartment. Mr. L. examined one of them critically through a window (the Kanaka's "brother" having gone to the country with the key), and then went around the house and examined the other through a window on the other side. He said it was the neatest match he had ever seen, and paid for the

EXTRAORDINARY CAPERS.

horses on the spot. Whereupon the Kanaka departed to join his brother in the country. The fellow had shamefully swindled L. There was only one "match" horse, and he had examined his starboard side through one window and his port side through another! I decline to believe this story, but I give it because it is worth something as a fanciful illustration of a fixed fact—namely, that the Kanaka horse-jockey is fertile in invention and elastic in conscience.

You can buy a pretty good horse for forty or fifty dollars, and a good enough horse for all practical purposes for two dollars and a half. I estimate Oahu to be worth somewhere in the neighborhood of thirty-five cents. A good deal better animal than he is was sold here day before yesterday for a dollar and seventy-five cents, and sold again to-day for two dollars and twenty-five cents; Williams bought a handsome and lively little pony yesterday for ten dollars; and about the best common horse on the island (and he is a really good one) sold yesterday, with Mexican saddle and bridle, for seventy dollars—a horse which is well and widely known, and greatly respected for his speed, good disposition and everlasting bottom. You give your horse a little grain once a day; it comes from San

Francisco, and is worth about two cents a pound; and you give him
as much hay as he wants; it is cut and brought to the market by
natives, and is not very good; it is baled into long, round bundles,
about the size of a large man; one of them is stuck by the middle
on each end of a six-foot pole, and the Kanaka shoulders the pole

A LOAD OF HAY.

and walks about the streets between the upright bales in search of
customers. These hay bales, thus carried, have a general resemblance to a colossal capital H.

The hay-bundles cost twenty-five cents apiece, and one will last
a horse about a day. You can get a horse for a song, a week's hay for
another song, and you can turn your animal loose among the lux-
uriant grass in your neighbor's broad front yard without a song at
all—you do it at midnight, and stable the beast again before morning. You have been at no expense thus far, but when you come to
buy a saddle and bridle they will cost you from twenty to thirty-
five dollars. You can hire a horse, saddle and bridle at from seven to
ten dollars a week, and the owner will take care of them at his own
expense.

It is time to close this day's record—bed time. As I prepare for sleep, a rich voice rises out of the still night, and, far as this ocean rock is toward the ends of the earth, I recognize a familiar home air. But the words seem somewhat out of joint:

Waikiki lantani oe Kaa hooly hooly wawhoo.

Translated, that means "When we were marching through Georgia."

CHAPTER 66

Passing through the market place we saw that feature of Honolulu under its most favorable auspices—that is, in the full glory of Saturday afternoon, which is a festive day with the natives. The native girls by twos and threes and parties of a dozen, and sometimes in whole platoons and companies, went cantering up and down the neighboring streets astride of fleet but homely horses,

SANDWICH ISLAND GIRLS.

and with their gaudy riding habits streaming like banners behind them. Such a troop of free and easy riders, in their natural home, the saddle, makes a gay and graceful spectacle. The riding habit I speak of is simply a long, broad scarf, like a tavern table-cloth brilliantly colored, wrapped around the loins once, then apparently passed between the limbs and each end thrown backwards over the same, and floating and flapping behind on both sides beyond the horse's tail like a couple of fancy flags; then, slipping the stirrup-irons between her toes, the girl throws her chest forward, sits up like a Major General and goes sweeping by like the wind.

The girls put on all the finery they can on Saturday afternoon—fine black silk robes; flowing red ones that nearly put your eyes out; others as white as snow; still others that discount the rainbow; and they wear their hair in nets, and trim their jaunty hats with fresh flowers, and encircle their dusky throats with home-made necklaces of the brilliant vermillion-tinted blossom of the *ohia*; and they fill the markets and the adjacent streets with their bright presences, and smell like a rag factory on fire with their offensive cocoanut oil.

Occasionally you see a heathen from the sunny isles away down in the South Seas, with his face and neck tattooed till he looks like the customary mendicant from Washoe who has been blown up in a mine. Some are tattooed a dead blue color down to the upper lip—masked, as it were—leaving the natural light yellow skin of Micronesia unstained from thence down; some with broad marks drawn down from hair to neck, on both sides of the face, and a strip of the original yellow skin, two inches wide, down the centre—a gridiron with a spoke broken out; and some with the entire face discolored with the popular mortification tint, relieved only by one or two thin, wavy threads of natural yellow running across the face from ear to ear, and eyes twinkling out of this darkness, from under shadowing hat-brims, like stars in the dark of the moon.

Moving among the stirring crowds, you come to the poi merchants, squatting in the shade on their hams, in true native fashion, and surrounded by purchasers. (The Sandwich Islanders always squat on their hams, and who knows but they may be the old original "ham sandwiches?" The thought is pregnant with interest.) The poi looks like common flour paste, and is kept in large bowls formed of a species of gourd, and capable of holding from one to three or four gallons. Poi is the chief article of food among the

natives, and is prepared from the *taro* plant. The *taro* root looks
like a thick, or, if you please, a corpulent sweet potato, in shape,

but is of a light purple color when
boiled. When boiled it answers as
a passable substitute for bread.
The buck Kanakas bake it under
ground, then mash it up well with
a heavy lava pestle, mix water
with it until it becomes a paste,
set it aside and let it ferment, and
then it is poi—and an unseductive
mixture it is, almost tasteless before it ferments and too sour for a
luxury afterward. But nothing is
more nutritious. When solely
used, however, it produces acrid
humors, a fact which sufficiently

ORIGINAL HAM SANDWICH.

accounts for the humorous character of the Kanakas. I think there
must be as much of a knack in handling poi as there is in eating
with chopsticks. The forefinger is thrust into the mess and stirred
quickly round several times and drawn as quickly out, thickly
coated, just as if it were poulticed; the head is thrown back, the finger inserted in the mouth and the delicacy stripped off and swallowed—the eye closing gently, meanwhile, in a languid sort of ecstasy. Many a different finger goes into the same bowl and many a
different kind of dirt and shade and quality of flavor is added to the
virtues of its contents.

Around a small shanty was collected a crowd of natives buying
the *awa* root. It is said that but for the use of this root the destruction of the people in former times by certain imported diseases
would have been far greater than it was, and by others it is said that
this is merely a fancy. All agree that poi will rejuvenate a man who
is used up and his vitality almost annihilated by hard drinking, and
that in some kinds of diseases it will restore health after all medicines have failed; but all are not willing to allow to the *awa* the virtues claimed for it. The natives manufacture an intoxicating drink
from it which is fearful in its effects when persistently indulged in.
It covers the body with dry, white scales, inflames the eyes, and

causes premature decrepitude. Although the man before whose establishment we stopped has to pay a Government license of eight hundred dollars a year for the exclusive right to sell *awa* root, it is said that he makes a small fortune every twelve-month; while saloon-keepers, who pay a thousand dollars a year for the privilege of retailing whisky, etc., only make a bare living.

We found the fish market crowded; for the native is very fond of fish, and *eats the article raw and alive!* Let us change the subject.

In old times here Saturday was a grand gala day indeed. All the native population of the town forsook their labors, and those of the surrounding country journeyed to the city. Then the white folks had to stay indoors, for every street was so packed with charging cavaliers and cavalieresses that it was next to impossible to thread one's way through the cavalcades without getting crippled.

At night they feasted and the girls danced the lascivious *hula-hula*—a dance that is said to exhibit the very perfection of educated motion of limb and arm, hand, head and body, and the exactest uniformity of movement and accuracy of "time." It was performed by a circle of girls with no raiment on them to speak of, who went through an infinite variety of motions and figures without prompting, and yet so true was their "time," and in such perfect concert did they move that when they were placed in a straight line, hands, arms, bodies, limbs and heads waved, swayed, gesticulated, bowed, stooped, whirled, squirmed, twisted and undulated as if they were part and parcel of a single individual; and it was difficult to believe they were not moved in a body by some exquisite piece of mechanism.

Of late years, however, Saturday has lost most of its quondam gala features. This weekly stampede of the natives interfered too much with labor and the interests of the white folks, and by sticking in a law here, and preaching a sermon there, and by various other means, they gradually broke it up. The demoralizing *hula-hula* was forbidden to be performed, save at night, with closed doors, in presence of few spectators, and only by permission duly procured from the authorities and the payment of ten dollars for the same. There are few girls now-a-days able to dance this ancient national dance in the highest perfection of the art.

The missionaries have christianized and educated all the natives. They all belong to the Church, and there is not one of them, above the age of eight years, but can read and write with facility in the native tongue. It is the most universally educated race of people outside of China. They have any quantity of books, printed in the Kanaka language, and all the natives are fond of reading. They are inveterate church-goers—nothing can keep them away. All this ameliorating cultivation has at last built up in the native women a profound respect for chastity—in other people. Perhaps that is enough to say on that head. The national sin will die out when the race does, but perhaps not earlier. But doubtless this purifying is not far off, when we reflect that contact with civilization and the whites has reduced the native population from *four hundred thousand* (Capt. Cook's estimate,) to *fifty-five thousand* in something over eighty years!

Society is a queer medley in this notable missionary, whaling and governmental centre. If you get into conversation with a stranger, and experience that natural desire to know what sort of ground you are treading on by finding out what manner of man your stranger is, strike out boldly and address him as "Captain." Watch him narrowly, and if you see by his countenance that you are on the wrong tack, ask him where he preaches. It is a safe bet that he is either a missionary or captain of a whaler. I am now personally acquainted with seventy-two captains and ninety-six missionaries. The captains and ministers form one-half of the population; the third fourth is composed of common Kanakas and mercantile foreigners and their families, and the final fourth is made up of high officers of the Hawaiian Government. And there are just about cats enough for three apiece all around.

A solemn stranger met me in the suburbs the other day, and said:

"Good morning, your reverence. Preach in the stone church yonder, no doubt?"

"No, I don't. I'm not a preacher."

"Really, I beg your pardon, Captain. I trust you had a good season. How much oil—"

"Oil? What do you take me for? I'm not a whaler."

"Oh, I beg a thousand pardons, your Excellency. Major General in the household troops, no doubt? Minister of the Interior, likely?

Secretary of War? First Gentleman of the Bed-chamber? Commissioner of the Royal—"

"Stuff! I'm no official. I'm not connected in any way with the Government."

"Bless my life! Then, who the mischief are you? what the mischief are you? and how the mischief did you get here, and where in thunder did you come from?"

"I'm only a private personage—an unassuming stranger—lately arrived from America."

"No? Not a missionary! not a whaler! not a member of his Majesty's Government! not even Secretary of the Navy! Ah, Heaven! it is too blissful to be true; alas, I do but dream. And yet that noble,

I KISSED HIM FOR HIS MOTHER.

honest countenance—those oblique, ingenuous eyes—that massive head, incapable of—of—anything; your hand; give me your hand, bright waif. Excuse these tears. For sixteen weary years I have yearned for a moment like this, and—"

Here his feelings were too much for him, and he swooned away. I pitied this poor creature from the bottom of my heart. I was deeply moved. I shed a few tears on him and kissed him for his mother. I then took what small change he had and "shoved."

CHAPTER 67

I STILL quote from my journal:

I found the national Legislature to consist of half a dozen white men and some thirty or forty natives. It was a dark assemblage. The nobles and Ministers (about a dozen of them altogether) occupied the extreme left of the hall, with David Kalakaua (the King's Chamberlain) and Prince William at the head. The President of the Assembly, his Royal Highness M. Kekuanaoa,* and the Vice President (the latter a white man,) sat in the pulpit, if I may so term it.

The President is the King's father. He is an erect, strongly built, massive featured, white-haired, tawny old gentleman of eighty years of age or thereabouts. He was simply but well dressed, in a blue cloth coat and white vest, and white pantaloons, without spot, dust or blemish upon them. He bears himself with a calm, stately dignity, and is a man of noble presence. He was a young man and a distinguished warrior under that terrific fighter, Kamehameha I, more than half a century ago. A knowledge of his career suggested some such thought as this: "This man, naked as the day he was born, and war-club and spear in hand, has charged at the head of a horde of savages against other hordes of savages more than a generation and a half ago, and reveled in slaughter and carnage; has worshipped wooden images on his devout knees; has seen hundreds of his race offered up in heathen temples as sacrifices to wooden idols, at a time when no missionary's foot had ever pressed this soil, and he had never heard of the white man's God; has believed his enemy could secretly pray him to death; has seen the day, in his childhood, when it was a crime punishable by death for a man to eat with his wife, or for a plebeian to let his shadow fall upon the King—and now look at him: an educated Christian;

---

*Since dead.

neatly and handsomely dressed; a high-minded, elegant gentleman; a traveler, in some degree, and one who has been the honored guest of royalty in Europe; a man practiced in holding the reins of an enlightened government, and well versed in the politics of his country and in general, practical information. Look at him, sitting there presiding over the deliberations of a legislative body, among whom are white men—a grave, dignified, statesmanlike personage, and as seemingly natural and fitted to the place as if he had been born in it and had never been out of it in his lifetime. How the experiences of this old man's eventful life shame the cheap inventions of romance!"

Kekuanaoa is not of the blood royal. He derives his princely rank from his wife, who was a daughter of Kamehameha the Great. Under other monarchies the male line takes precedence of the female in tracing genealogies, but here the opposite is the case—the female line takes precedence. Their reason for this is exceedingly sensible, and I recommend it to the aristocracy of Europe: They say it is easy to know who a man's mother was, but, etc., etc.

The christianizing of the natives has hardly even weakened some of their barbarian superstitions, much less destroyed them. I have just referred to one of these. It is still a popular belief that if your enemy can get hold of any article belonging to you he can get down on his knees over it and *pray you to death*. Therefore many a

AN ENEMY'S PRAYER.

native gives up and dies merely because he *imagines* that some enemy is putting him through a course of damaging prayer. This praying an individual to death seems absurd enough at a first glance, but then when we call to mind some of the pulpit efforts of certain of our own ministers the thing looks plausible.

In former times, among the Islanders, not only a plurality of wives was customary, but a *plurality of husbands* likewise. Some native women of noble rank had as many as six husbands. A woman thus supplied did not reside with all her husbands at once, but lived several months with each in turn. An understood sign hung at her door during these months. When the sign was taken down, it meant "NEXT."

In those days woman was rigidly taught to "know her place." Her place was to do all the work, take all the cuffs, provide all the food, and content herself with what was left after her lord had finished his dinner. She was not only forbidden, by ancient law, and under penalty of death, to eat with her husband or enter a canoe, but was debarred, under the same penalty, from eating bananas, pineapples, oranges and other choice fruits at any time or in any place. She had to confine herself pretty strictly to "poi" and hard work. These poor ignorant heathen seem to have had a sort of groping idea of what came of woman eating fruit in the Garden of Eden, and they did not choose to take any more chances. But the missionaries broke up this satisfactory arrangement of things. They liberated woman and made her the equal of man.

The natives had a romantic fashion of burying some of their children alive when the family became larger than necessary. The missionaries interfered in this matter too, and stopped it.

To this day the natives are able to *lie down and die whenever they want to,* whether there is anything the matter with them or not. If a Kanaka takes a notion to die, that is the end of him; nobody can persuade him to hold on; all the doctors in the world could not save him.

A luxury which they enjoy more than anything else, is a large funeral. If a person wants to get rid of a troublesome native, it is only necessary to promise him a fine funeral and name the hour and he will be on hand to the minute—at least his remains will.

All the natives are Christians, now, but many of them still desert to the Great Shark God for temporary succor in time of trouble. An eruption of the great volcano of Kilauea, or an earthquake, always brings a deal of latent loyalty to the Great Shark God to the surface. It is common report that the King, educated, cultivated and refined Christian gentleman as he undoubtedly is, still turns to the idols of his fathers for help when disaster threatens. A planter caught a shark, and one of his christianized natives testified his emancipation from the thrall of ancient superstition by as-

sisting to dissect the shark after a fashion forbidden by his abandoned creed. But remorse shortly began to torture him. He grew
moody and sought solitude; brooded over his sin, refused food, and
finally said he must die and ought to die, for he had sinned against
the Great Shark God and could never know peace any more. He
was proof against persuasion and ridicule, and in the course of a
day or two took to his bed and died, although he showed no symp-
tom of disease. His young daughter followed his lead and suffered
a like fate within the week. Superstition is ingrained in the native
blood and bone and it is only natural that it should crop out in time
of distress. Wherever one goes in the Islands, he will find small
piles of stones by the wayside, covered with leafy offerings, placed
there by the natives to appease evil spirits or honor local deities belonging to the mythology of former days.

In the rural districts of any of the Islands, the traveler hourly
comes upon parties of dusky maidens bathing in the streams or in
the sea without any clothing on and exhibiting no very intemperate zeal in the matter of hiding their nakedness. When the mis-

VISITING THE MISSIONARIES.

sionaries first took up their residence in Honolulu, the native
women would pay their families frequent friendly visits, day by
day, not even clothed with a blush. It was found a hard matter to
convince them that this was rather indelicate. Finally the mission-

aries provided them with long, loose calico robes, and that ended the difficulty—for the women would troop through the town, stark naked, with their robes folded under their arms, march to the missionary houses and then proceed to dress! The natives soon manifested a strong proclivity for clothing, but it was shortly apparent that they only wanted it for grandeur. The missionaries imported a quantity of hats, bonnets, and other male and female wearing apparel, instituted a general distribution, and begged the people not to come to church naked, next Sunday, as usual. And they did not; but the national spirit of unselfishness led them to divide up with neighbors who were not at the distribution, and next Sabbath the poor preachers could hardly keep countenance before their vast congregations. In the midst of the reading of a hymn a brown, stately dame would sweep up the aisle with a world of airs, with nothing in the world on but a "stove-pipe" hat and a pair of cheap gloves; another dame would follow, tricked out in a man's shirt, and nothing else; another one would enter with a flourish, with simply the sleeves of a bright calico dress tied around her waist and the rest of the garment dragging behind like a peacock's tail off duty; a stately "buck" Kanaka would stalk in with a woman's bonnet on, wrong side before—only this, and nothing more; after him would stride his fellow, with the legs of a pair of pantaloons tied around his neck, the rest of his person untrammeled; in his rear would come another gentleman simply gotten up in a fiery neck-tie and a striped vest. The poor creatures were beaming with complacency and wholly unconscious of any absurdity in their appearance. They gazed at each other with happy admiration, and it was plain to see that the young girls were taking note of what each other had on, as naturally as if they had always lived in a land of Bibles and knew what churches were made for; here was the evidence of a dawning civilization. The spectacle which the congregation presented was so extraordinary and withal so moving, that the missionaries found it difficult to keep to the text and go on with the services; and by and by when the simple children of the sun began a general swapping of garments in open meeting and produced some irresistibly grotesque effects in the course of re-dressing, there was nothing for it but to cut the thing short with the benediction and dismiss the fantastic assemblage.

In our country, children play "keep house;" and in the same
high-sounding but miniature way the grown folk here, with the

FULL CHURCH DRESS.

poor little material of slender territory and meagre population,
play "empire." There is his royal Majesty the King, with a New

PLAYING EMPIRE.

York detective's income of
thirty or thirty-five thousand
dollars a year from the "royal
civil list" and the "royal domain." He lives in a two-story
frame "palace."

And there is the "royal family"—the customary hive of
royal brothers, sisters, cousins
and other noble drones and va-
grants usual to monarchy,—all
with a spoon in the national
pap-dish, and all bearing such
titles as his or her Royal Highness the Prince or Princess So-and-
so. Few of them can carry their royal splendors far enough to ride

in carriages, however; they sport the economical Kanaka horse or "hoof it"* with the plebeians.

Then there is his Excellency the "royal Chamberlain"—a sinecure, for his Majesty dresses himself with his own hands, except

ROYALTY AND ITS SATELLITES.

when he is ruralizing at Waikiki and then he requires no dressing.

Next we have his Excellency the Commander-in-chief of the Household Troops, whose forces consist of about the number of soldiers usually placed under a corporal in other lands.

Next comes the royal Steward and the Grand Equerry in Waiting—high dignitaries with modest salaries and little to do.

Then we have his Excellency the First Gentleman of the Bedchamber—an office as easy as it is magnificent.

Next we come to his Excellency the Prime Minister, a renegade American from New Hampshire, all jaw, vanity, bombast and ignorance, a lawyer of "shyster" calibre, a fraud by nature, a humble worshipper of the sceptre above him, a reptile never tired of sneer-

---

*Missionary phrase.

ing at the land of his birth or glorifying the ten-acre kingdom that has adopted him—salary, four thousand dollars a year, vast consequence, and no perquisites.

Then we have his Excellency the Imperial Minister of Finance, who handles a million dollars of public money a year, sends in his annual "budget" with great ceremony, talks prodigiously of "finance," suggests imposing schemes for paying off the "national debt" (of a hundred and fifty thousand dollars,) and does it all for four thousand dollars a year and unimaginable glory.

Next we have his Excellency the Minister of War, who holds sway over the royal armies—they consist of two hundred and thirty uniformed Kanakas, mostly Brigadier Generals, and if the country ever gets into trouble with a foreign power we shall probably hear from them. I knew an American whose copper-plate visiting card bore this impressive legend: "Lieutenant-Colonel in the Royal Infantry." To say that he was proud of this distinction is stating it but tamely. The Minister of War has also in his charge some venerable swivels on Punch-Bowl Hill wherewith royal salutes are fired when foreign vessels of war enter the port.

Next comes his Excellency the Minister of the Navy—a nabob who rules the "royal fleet," (a steam-tug and a sixty-ton schooner.)

And next comes his Grace the Lord Bishop of Honolulu, the chief dignitary of the "Established Church"—for when the American Presbyterian missionaries had completed the reduction of the nation to a compact condition of Christianity, native royalty stepped in and erected the grand dignity of an "Established (Episcopal) Church" over it, and imported a cheap ready-made Bishop from England to take charge. The chagrin of the missionaries has never been comprehensively expressed, to this day, profanity not being admissible.

Next comes his Excellency the Minister of Public Instruction.

Next, their Excellencies the Governors of Oahu, Hawaii, etc., and after them a string of High Sheriffs and other small fry too numerous for computation.

Then there are their Excellencies the Envoy Extraordinary and Minister Plenipotentiary of his Imperial Majesty the Emperor of the French; her British Majesty's Minister; the Minister Resident, of the United States; and some six or eight representatives of other foreign nations, all with sounding titles, imposing dignity and pro-digious but economical state.

Imagine all this grandeur in a play-house "kingdom" whose pop-ulation falls absolutely short of sixty thousand souls!

The people are so accustomed to nine-jointed titles and colossal magnates that a foreign prince makes very little more stir in Ho-nolulu than a western Congressman does in New York.

And let it be borne in mind that there is a strictly defined "court costume" of so "stunning" a nature that it would make the clown in a circus look tame and commonplace by comparison; and each Hawaiian official dignitary has a gorgeous vari-colored, gold-laced uniform peculiar to his office—no two of them are alike, and it is hard to tell which one is the "loudest." The King has a "drawing-room" at stated intervals, like other monarchs, and when these varied uniforms congregate there weak-eyed people have to con-template the spectacle through smoked glass. Is there not a gratify-ing contrast between this latter-day exhibition and the one the ancestors of some of these magnates afforded the missionaries the Sunday after the old-time distribution of clothing? Behold what re-ligion and civilization have wrought!

CHAPTER 68

WHILE I was in Honolulu I witnessed the ceremonious funeral of the King's sister, her Royal Highness the Princess Victoria. According to the royal custom, the remains had lain in state at the palace *thirty days*, watched day and night by a guard of honor. And during all that time a great multitude of natives from the several islands had kept the palace grounds well crowded and had made the place a pandemonium every night with their howlings and wailings, beating of tom-toms and dancing of the (at other times) forbidden *hula-hula* by half-clad maidens to the music of songs of questionable decency chanted in honor of the deceased. The printed programme of the funeral procession interested me at the time; and after what I have just said of Hawaiian grandiloquence in the matter of "playing empire," I am persuaded that a perusal of it may interest the reader:

After reading the long list of dignitaries, etc., and remembering the sparseness of the population, one is almost inclined to wonder where the material for that portion of the procession devoted to "Hawaiian Population Generally" is going to be procured:

Undertaker.
Royal School. Kawaiahao School. Roman Catholic School.
Maemae School.
Honolulu Fire Department.
Mechanics' Benefit Union.
Attending Physicians.
Konohikis (Superintendents) of Crown Lands, Konohikis of Private Lands of His Majesty, Konohikis of Private Lands of Her late Royal Highness.
Governor of Oahu and Staff.
Hulumanu (Military Company).
The Prince of Hawaii's Own (Military Company).
Household Troops.

The King's Household Servants.

Servants of Her late Royal Highness.

Protestant Clergy. The Clergy of the Roman Catholic Church.

His Lordship Louis Maigret, the Rt. Rev. Bishop of Arathea,
Vicar-Apostolic of the Hawaiian Islands.

The Clergy of the Hawaiian Reformed Catholic Church.

His Lordship the Right Reverend Bishop of Honolulu.

Escort Haw. Cavalry.
Large Kahilis.
Small Kahilis.
PALL BEARERS.

[HEARSE.]

Escort Haw. Cavalry.
Large Kahilis.
Small Kahilis.*
PALL BEARERS.

Her Majesty Queen Emma's Carriage.

His Majesty's Staff.

Carriage of Her late Royal Highness.

Carriage of Her Majesty the Queen Dowager.

The King's Chancellor.

Cabinet Ministers.

His Excellency the Minister Resident of the United States.

H. I. M.'s Commissioner.

H. B. M.'s Acting Commissioner.

Judges of Supreme Court.

Privy Councillors.

Members of the Legislative Assembly.

Consular Corps.

Circuit Judges.

Clerks of Government Departments.

Members of the Bar.

Collector General, Custom House Officers and Officers of the Customs.

Marshal and Sheriffs of the different Islands.

King's Yeomanry.

Foreign Residents.

Ahahui Kaahumanu.

---

*Ranks of long-handled mops made of gaudy feathers—sacred to royalty. They
are stuck in the ground around the tomb and left there.

Hawaiian Population Generally.
Hawaiian Cavalry.
Police Force.

I resume my journal at the point where the procession arrived at the royal mausoleum:

As the procession filed through the gate, the military deployed handsomely to the right and left and formed an avenue through which the long

A MODERN FUNERAL.

column of mourners passed to the tomb. The coffin was borne through the door of the mausoleum, followed by the King and his chiefs, the great officers of the kingdom, foreign Consuls, Embassadors and distinguished guests (Burlingame and Gen. Van Valkenburgh). Several of the *kahilis* were then fastened to a framework in front of the tomb, there to remain until they decay and fall to pieces, or, forestalling this, until another scion of royalty dies. At this point of the proceedings the multitude set up such a heart-broken wailing as I hope never to hear again. The soldiers fired three volleys of musketry—the wailing being previously silenced to permit of the guns being heard. His Highness Prince William, in a showy military uniform (the "true prince," this—scion of the house over-thrown by the present dynasty—he was formerly betrothed to the Princess but was not allowed to marry her), stood guard and paced back and forth within the door. The privileged few who followed the coffin into the mausoleum remained some time, but the King soon came out and stood in the door and near one side of it. A stranger could have guessed his rank (although he was so simply and unpretentiously dressed) by the profound deference paid him by all persons in his vicinity; by seeing his high officers receive his quiet orders and suggestions with bowed and uncovered heads; and by observing how careful those persons who came out of the mausoleum were to avoid "crowding" him (although there was room enough in the doorway for a wagon to pass, for that matter); how respectfully they edged out sideways, scraping their backs against the wall and always presenting a front view of their persons to his Majesty, and never putting their hats on until they were well out of the royal presence.

He was dressed entirely in black—dress-coat and silk hat—and looked rather democratic in the midst of the showy uniforms about him. On his breast he wore a large gold star, which was half hidden by the lappel of his coat. He remained at the door a half hour, and occasionally gave an order to the men who were erecting the *kahilis* before the tomb. He had the good taste to make one of them substitute black crape for the ordinary hempen rope he was about to tie one of them to the framework with. Finally he entered his carriage and drove away, and the populace shortly began to drop into his wake. While he was in view there was but one man who attracted more attention than himself, and that was Harris (the Yankee Prime Minister). This feeble personage had crape enough around his hat to express the grief of an entire nation, and as usual he neglected no opportunity of making himself conspicuous and exciting the admiration of the simple Kanakas. Oh! noble ambition of this modern Richelieu!

It is interesting to contrast the funeral ceremonies of the Princess Victoria with those of her noted ancestor Kamehameha the Conqueror, who died fifty years ago—in 1819, the year before the first missionaries came:

On the 8th of May, 1819, at the age of sixty-six, he died as he had lived, in the faith of his country. It was his misfortune not to have come in contact with men who could have rightly influenced his religious aspirations. Judged by his advantages, and compared with the most eminent of his countrymen, he may be justly styled, not only great, but good. To this day his memory warms the heart and elevates the national feelings of Hawaiians. They are proud of their old warrior-king; they love his name; his deeds form their historical age; and an enthusiasm everywhere prevails, shared even by foreigners who knew his worth, that constitutes the firmest pillar of the throne of his dynasty.

In lieu of human victims (the custom of that age), a sacrifice of three hundred dogs attended his obsequies; no mean holocaust, when their national value and the estimation in which they were held are considered. The bones of Kamehameha after being kept for a while, were so carefully concealed that all knowledge of their final resting place is now lost. There was a proverb current among the common people that the bones of a cruel king could not be hid; they made fish-hooks and arrows of them, upon which in using them they vented their abhorrence of his memory in bitter execrations.

The account of the circumstances of his death, as written by the native historians, is full of minute detail, but there is scarcely a line of it which does not mention or illustrate some bygone custom of the country. In this respect it is the most comprehensive document I have yet met with. I will quote it entire:

When Kamehameha was dangerously sick and the priests were unable to cure him, they said, "Be of good courage, and build a house for the god" (his own private god or idol), "that thou mayest recover." The chiefs corroborated this advice of the priests, and a place of worship was prepared for Kukailimoku, and consecrated in the evening. They proposed also to the king, with a view to prolong his life, that human victims should be sacrificed to his deity; upon which the greater part of the people absconded through fear of death, and concealed themselves in hiding-places till the tabu,* in which destruction impended, was past. It is doubtful whether Kamehameha approved of the plan of the chiefs and priests to sacrifice men, as he was known to say, "The men are sacred for the king;" meaning that they were for the service of his successor. This information was derived from his son, Liholiho.

After this, his sickness increased to such a degree that he had not strength to turn himself in his bed. When another season, consecrated for worship at the new temple—heiau—arrived, he said to his son Liholiho, "Go thou and make supplication to thy god; I am not able to go and will offer my prayers at home." When his devotions to his feathered god, Kukailimoku, were concluded, a certain religiously disposed individual, who had a bird-god, suggested to the king that through its influence his sickness might be removed. The name of this god was Pua; its body was made of a bird, now eaten by the Hawaiians, and called in their language *alae*. Kamehameha was willing that a trial should be made, and two houses were constructed to facilitate the experiment; but while dwelling in them, he became so very weak as not to receive food. After lying there three days, his wives, children, and chiefs, perceiving that he was very low, returned him to his own house. In the evening he was carried to the

---

Tabu (pronounced tah-boo,) means prohibition (we have borrowed it,) or sacred. The *tabu* was sometimes permanent, sometimes temporary; and the person or thing placed under *tabu* was for the time being sacred to the purpose for which it was set apart. In the above case the victims selected under the *tabu* would be sacred to the sacrifice.

eating-house,* where he took a little food in his mouth, which he did not swallow; also a cup of water. The chiefs requested him to give them his counsel. But he made no reply, and was carried back to the dwelling-house; but when near midnight, ten o'clock, perhaps, he was carried again to the place to eat; but, as before, he merely tasted of what was presented to him. Then Kaikioewa addressed him thus: "Here we all are, your younger brethren, your son, Liholiho, and your foreigner; impart to us your dying charge, that Liholiho and Kaahumanu may hear." Then Kamehameha inquired, "What do you say?" Kaikioewa repeated, "Your counsels for us." He then said, "Move on in my good way, and ——." He could proceed no further. The foreigner—Mr. Young—embraced and kissed him. Hoapili also embraced him, whispering something in his ear, after which he was taken back to the house. About twelve, he was carried once more to the house for eating, into which his head entered, while his body was in the dwelling-house immediately adjoining. It should be remarked, that this frequent carrying of a sick chief to and fro from one house to another, resulted from the tabu system then in force. There were at that time six houses (huts) connected with an establishment; one was for worship, one for the men to eat in, an eating-house for the women, a house to sleep in, a house in which to manufacture kapa (native cloth), and one where at certain intervals the women might dwell in seclusion.

The sick king was once more taken to his house, when he expired; this was at two o'clock—a circumstance from which Leleiohoku derived his name. As he breathed his last Kalaimoku came to the eating-house to order those in it to go out. There were two aged persons thus directed to depart; one went, the other remained on account of love to the king, by whom he had formerly been kindly sustained. The children also were sent away. Then Kalaimoku came to the house, and the chiefs had a consultation. One of them spoke thus: "This is my thought, we will eat him raw."† Kaahumanu (one of the dead king's widows) replied, "Perhaps his body is not at our disposal; that is more properly with his successor. Our part in him—the breath—has departed; his remains will be disposed of by Liholiho."

After this conversation, the body was taken into the consecrated house for the performance of the proper rites by the priest and the new king. The name of this ceremony is uko; and when the sacred hog was baked, the priest offered it to the dead body and it became a god, the king at the same time repeating the customary prayers.

---

*It was deemed pollution to eat in the same hut a person slept in—the fact that the patient was dying could not modify the rigid etiquette.

†This sounds suspicious, in view of the fact that all Sandwich Island historians, white and black, protest that cannibalism never existed in the Islands. However, since they only proposed to "eat him raw" we "won't count that." But it would certainly have been cannibalism if they had cooked him.—M. T.

Then the priest, addressing himself to the king and chiefs, said, "I will now make known to you the rules to be observed respecting persons to be sacrificed on the burial of this body. If you obtain one man before the corpse is removed, one will be sufficient; but after it leaves this house four will be required. If delayed until we carry the corpse to the grave, there must be ten; but after it is deposited in the grave, there must be fifteen. To-morrow morning there will be a tabu, and if the sacrifice be delayed until that time, forty men must die."

Then the high priest Hewahewa, inquired of the chiefs, where shall be the residence of King Liholiho? They replied, "Where, indeed? you of all men ought to know." Then the priest observed, "There are two suitable places; one is Kau, the other is Kohala." The chiefs preferred the latter, as it was more thickly inhabited. The priest added, "These are proper places for the king's residence, but he must not remain in Kona, for it is polluted." This was agreed to. It was now break of day. As he was being carried to the place of burial, the people perceived that their king was dead, and they wailed. When the corpse was removed from the house to the tomb, a distance of one chain, the procession was met by a certain man who was ardently attached to the deceased. He leaped upon the chiefs who were carrying the king's body; he desired to die with him, on account of his love. The chiefs drove him away. He persisted in making numerous attempts, which were unavailing. Kalaimoku also had it in his heart to die with him, but was prevented by Hookio.

The morning following Kamehameha's death, Liholiho and his train departed for Kohala according to the suggestions of the priest, to avoid the defilement occasioned by the dead. At this time, if a chief died the land was polluted, and the heirs sought a residence in another part of the country, until the corpse was dissected and the bones tied in a bundle, which being done, the season of defilement terminated. If the deceased were not a chief, the house only was defiled, which became pure again on the burial of the body. Such were the laws on this subject.

On the morning in which Liholiho sailed in his canoe for Kohala, the chiefs and people mourned after their manner on occasion of a chief's death, conducting themselves like madmen, and like beasts. Their conduct was such as to forbid description. The priests, also, put into action the sorcery apparatus, that the person who had prayed the king to death might die; for it was not believed that Kamehameha's departure was the effect either of sickness or old age. When the sorcerers set up by their fireplaces sticks with a strip of kapa flying at the top, the chief Keeaumoku, Kaahumanu's brother, came, in a state of intoxication, and broke the flagstaff of the sorcerers, from which it was inferred that Kaahumanu and her friends had been instrumental in the king's death. On this account they were subjected to abuse.

You have the contrast, now, and a strange one it is. This great Queen, Kaahumanu, who was "subjected to abuse" during the frightful orgies that followed the King's death, in accordance with ancient custom, afterward became a devout Christian and a steadfast and powerful friend of the missionaries.

Dogs were, and still are, reared and fattened for food, by the natives—hence the reference to their value in one of the above paragraphs.

Forty years ago it was the custom in the Islands to suspend all law for a certain number of days after the death of a royal personage; and then a saturnalia ensued which one may picture to himself after a fashion, but not in the full horror of the reality. The people shaved their heads, knocked out a tooth or two, plucked out an eye sometimes, cut, bruised, mutilated or burned their flesh, got drunk, burned each other's huts, maimed or murdered one another according to the caprice of the moment, and both sexes gave themselves up to brutal and unbridled licentiousness. And after it all,

FORMER FUNERAL ORGIES.

came a torpor from which the nation slowly emerged bewildered and dazed, as if from a hideous half-remembered nightmare. They were not the salt of the earth, those "gentle children of the sun."

The natives still keep up an old custom of theirs which cannot be comforting to an invalid. When they think a sick friend is going to die, a couple of dozen neighbors surround his hut and keep up a deafening wailing night and day till he either dies or gets well. No doubt this arrangement has helped many a subject to a shroud before his appointed time.

They surround a hut and wail in the same heart-broken way when its occupant returns from a journey. This is their dismal idea of a welcome. A very little of it would go a great way with most of us.

CHAPTER 69

Bound for Hawaii, (a hundred and fifty miles distant,) to visit the great volcano and behold the other notable things which distinguish that island above the remainder of the group, we sailed from Honolulu on a certain Saturday afternoon, in the good schooner Boomerang.

The Boomerang was about as long as two street cars, and about as wide as one. She was so small (though she was larger than the majority of the inter-island coasters) that when I stood on her deck I felt but little smaller than the Colossus of Rhodes must have felt when he had a man-of-war under him. I could reach the water when she lay over under a strong breeze. When the captain and my comrade (a Mr. Billings), myself and four other persons were all assembled on the little after portion of the deck which is sacred to the cabin passengers, it was full—there was not room for any more quality folks. Another section of the deck, twice as large as ours, was full of natives of both sexes, with their customary dogs, mats, blankets, pipes, calabashes of poi, fleas, and other luxuries and baggage of minor importance. As soon as we set sail the natives all lay down on the deck as thick as negroes in a slave-pen, and smoked, conversed, and spit on each other, and were truly sociable.

The little low-ceiled cabin below was rather larger than a hearse, and as dark as a vault. It had two coffins on each side—I mean two bunks. A small table, capable of accommodating three persons at dinner, stood against the forward bulkhead, and over it hung the dingiest whale-oil lantern that ever peopled the obscurity of a dungeon with ghostly shapes. The floor room unoccupied was not extensive. One might swing a cat in it, perhaps, but not a long cat. The hold forward of the bulkhead had but little freight in it, and from morning till night a portly old rooster, with a voice like Balaam's ass, and the same disposition to use it, strutted up and down in that part of the vessel and crowed. He usually took dinner at six

o'clock, and then, after an hour devoted to meditation, he mounted a barrel and crowed a good part of the night. He got hoarser and hoarser all the time, but he scorned to allow any personal consideration to interfere with his duty, and kept up his labors in defiance of threatened diphtheria.

Sleeping was out of the question when he was on watch. He was a source of genuine aggravation and annoyance. It was worse than useless to shout at

A PASSENGER.

him or apply offensive epithets to him—he only took these things for applause, and strained himself to make more noise. Occasionally, during the day, I threw potatoes at him through an aperture in the bulkhead, but he only dodged and went on crowing.

The first night, as I lay in my coffin, idly watching the dim lamp swinging to the rolling of the ship, and snuffing the nauseous odors of bilge water, I felt something gallop over me. I turned out promptly. However, I turned in again when I found it was only a rat. Presently something galloped over me once more. I knew it was not a rat this time, and I thought it might be a centipede, because the captain had killed one on deck in the afternoon. I turned out. The first glance at the pillow showed me a repulsive sentinel perched upon each end of it—cockroaches as large as peach leaves—fellows with long, quivering antennæ and fiery, malignant eyes. They were grating their teeth like tobacco worms, and appeared to be dissatisfied about something. I had often heard that these reptiles were in the habit of eating off sleeping sailors' toe nails down to the quick, and I would not get in the bunk any more. I lay down on the floor. But a rat came and bothered me, and shortly afterward a procession of cockroaches arrived and camped in my hair. In a few moments the rooster was crowing with uncommon spirit and a party of fleas were throwing double summersets about my person in the wildest disorder, and taking a bite every time they struck. I was beginning to feel really annoyed. I got up and put my clothes on and went on deck.

The above is not overdrawn; it is a truthful sketch of inter-island schooner life. There is no such thing as keeping a vessel in elegant condition, when she carries molasses and Kanakas.

It was compensation for my sufferings to come unexpectedly upon so beautiful a scene as met my eye—to step suddenly out of the sepulchral gloom of the cabin and stand under the strong light of the moon—in the centre, as it were, of a glittering sea of liquid

MOONLIGHT ON THE WATER.

silver—to see the broad sails straining in the gale, the ship heeled over on her side, the angry foam hissing past her lee bulwarks, and sparkling sheets of spray dashing high over her bows and raining upon her decks; to brace myself and hang fast to the first object that presented itself, with hat jammed down and coat tails whipping in the breeze, and feel that exhilaration that thrills in one's hair and quivers down his back-bone when he knows that every inch of canvas is drawing and the vessel cleaving through the waves at her utmost speed. There was no darkness, no dimness, no obscurity there. All was brightness, every object was vividly defined. Every prostrate Kanaka; every coil of rope; every calabash of poi; every puppy; every seam in the flooring; every bolthead; every object, however minute, showed sharp and distinct in its every outline; and the shadow of the broad mainsail lay black as a pall upon the deck, leaving Billings's white upturned face glorified and his body in a total eclipse.

Monday morning we were close to the island of Hawaii. Two of its high mountains were in view—Mauna Loa and Hualalai. The latter is an imposing peak, but being only ten thousand feet high is seldom mentioned or heard of. Mauna Loa is said to be sixteen thousand feet high. The rays of glittering snow and ice, that clasped its summit like a claw, looked refreshing when viewed from the blistering climate we were in. One could stand on that mountain (wrapped up in blankets and furs to keep warm), and while he nibbled a snow-ball or an icicle to quench his thirst he could look down the long sweep of its sides and see spots where plants are growing that grow only where the bitter cold of winter prevails; lower down he could see sections devoted to productions that thrive in the temperate zone alone; and at the bottom of the mountain he could see the home of the tufted cocoa palms and other species of vegetation that grow only in the sultry atmosphere of eternal summer. He could see all the climes of the world at a single glance of the eye, and that glance would only pass over a distance of four or five miles as the bird flies!

By and by we took boat and went ashore at Kailua, designing to ride horseback through the pleasant orange and coffee region of Kona, and rejoin the vessel at a point some leagues distant. This journey is well worth taking. The trail passes along on high ground—say a thousand feet above sea level—and usually about a mile distant from the ocean, which is always in sight, save that occasionally you find yourself buried in the forest in the midst of a rank, tropical vegetation and a dense growth of trees, whose great boughs overarch the road and shut out sun and sea and everything, and leave you in a dim, shady tunnel, haunted with invisible singing birds and fragrant with the odor of flowers. It was pleasant to ride occasionally in the warm sun, and feast the eye upon the ever-changing panorama of the forest (beyond and below us), with its many tints, its softened lights and shadows, its billowy undulations sweeping gently down from the mountain to the sea. It was pleasant also, at intervals, to leave the sultry sun and pass into the cool, green depths of this forest and indulge in sentimental reflections under the inspiration of its brooding twilight and its whispering foliage.

GOING INTO THE MOUNTAINS.

We rode through one orange grove that had ten thousand trees in it! They were all laden with fruit.

At one farmhouse we got some large peaches of excellent flavor. This fruit, as a general thing, does not do well in the Sandwich Islands. It takes a sort of almond shape, and is small and bitter. It needs frost, they say, and perhaps it does; if this be so, it will have a good opportunity to go on needing it, as it will not be likely to get it. The trees from which the fine fruit I have spoken of came had been planted and replanted *sixteen times*, and to this treatment the proprietor of the orchard attributed his success.

We passed several sugar plantations—new ones and not very extensive. The crops were, in most cases, third rattoons. [NOTE.— The first crop is called "plant cane;" subsequent crops which spring from the original roots, without replanting, are called "rattoons."] Almost everywhere on the island of Hawaii sugar-cane matures in twelve months, both rattoons and plant, and although it ought to be taken off as soon as it tassels, no doubt, it is not absolutely necessary to do it until about four months afterward. In Kona, the average yield of an acre of ground is *two tons* of sugar, they say. This is only a moderate yield for these islands, but would be astounding for Louisiana and most other sugar growing countries. The plantations in Kona being on pretty high ground—up among the light and frequent rains—no irrigation whatever is required.

CHAPTER 70

We stopped some time at one of the plantations, to rest ourselves and refresh the horses. We had a chatty conversation with several gentlemen present; but there was one person, a middle aged man, with an absent look in his face, who simply glanced up, gave us good-day and lapsed again into the meditations which our coming had interrupted. The planters whispered us not to mind him—crazy. They said he was in the Islands for his health; was a preacher; his home, Michigan. They said that if he woke up presently and fell to talking about a correspondence which he had some time held with Mr. Greeley about a trifle of some kind, we must humor him and listen with interest; and we must humor his fancy that this correspondence was the talk of the world.

It was easy to see that he was a gentle creature and that his madness had nothing vicious in it. He looked pale, and a little worn, as if with perplexing thought and anxiety of mind. He sat a long time,

THE DEMENTED.

looking at the floor, and at intervals muttering to himself and nodding his head acquiescingly or shaking it in mild protest. He was
lost in his thought, or in his memories. We continued our talk
with the planters, branching from subject to subject. But at last the
word "circumstance," casually dropped, in the course of conversation, attracted his attention and brought an eager look into his
countenance. He faced about in his chair and said:

"Circumstance? What circumstance? Ah, I know—I know too
well. So you have heard of it too." [With a sigh.] "Well, no matter—
all the world has heard of it. All the world. The whole world. It is a
large world, too, for a thing to travel so far in—now isn't it? Yes,
yes—the Greeley correspondence with Erickson has created the
saddest and bitterest controversy on both sides of the ocean—and
still they keep it up! It makes us famous, but at what a sorrowful
sacrifice! I was so sorry when I heard that it had caused that bloody
and distressful war over there in Italy. It was little comfort to me,
after so much bloodshed, to know that the victors sided with me,
and the vanquished with Greeley. It is little comfort to know that
Horace Greeley is responsible for the battle of Sadowa, and not me.
Queen Victoria wrote me that she felt just as I did about it—she
said that as much as she was opposed to Greeley and the spirit he
showed in the correspondence with me, she would not have had
Sadowa happen for hundreds of dollars. I can show you her letter, if
you would like to see it. But gentlemen, much as you may think
you know about that unhappy correspondence, you cannot know
the *straight* of it till you hear it from my lips. It has always been
garbled in the journals, and even in history. Yes, even in history—
think of it! Let me—*please* let me, give you the matter, exactly as
it occurred. I truly will not abuse your confidence."

Then he leaned forward, all interest, all earnestness, and told his
story—and told it appealingly, too, and yet in the simplest and
most unpretentious way; indeed, in such a way as to suggest to
one, all the time, that this was a faithful, honorable witness, giving
evidence in the sacred interest of justice, and under oath. He said:

"Mrs. Beazeley—Mrs. Jackson Beazeley, widow, of the village of
Campbellton, Kansas,—wrote me about a matter which was near
her heart—a matter which many might think trivial, but to her it
was a thing of deep concern. I was living in Michigan, then—serving in the ministry. She was, and is, an estimable woman—a

woman to whom poverty and hardship have proven incentives to industry, in place of discouragements. Her only treasure was her son William, a youth just verging upon manhood; religious, amiable, and sincerely attached to agriculture. He was the widow's comfort and her pride. And so, moved by her love for him, she wrote me about a matter, as I have said before, which lay near her heart—because it lay near her boy's. She desired me to confer with Mr. Greeley about turnips. Turnips were the dream of her child's young ambition. While other youths were frittering away in frivolous amusements the precious years of budding vigor which God had given them for useful preparation, this boy was patiently enriching his mind with information concerning turnips. The sentiment which he felt toward the turnip was akin to adoration. He could not think of the turnip without emotion; he could not speak of it calmly; he could not contemplate it without exaltation. He could not eat it without shedding tears. All the poetry in his sensitive nature was in sympathy with the gracious vegetable. With the earliest pipe of dawn he sought his patch, and when the curtaining night drove him from it he shut himself up with his books and garnered statistics till sleep overcame him. On rainy days he sat and talked hours together with his mother about turnips. When company came, he made it his loving duty to put aside everything

DISCUSSING TURNIPS.

else and converse with them all the day long of his great joy in the
turnip. And yet, was this joy rounded and complete? Was there no
secret alloy of unhappiness in it? Alas, there was. There was a can-
ker gnawing at his heart; the noblest inspiration of his soul eluded
his endeavor—viz.: he could not make of the turnip a climbing
vine. Months went by; the bloom forsook his cheek, the fire faded
out of his eye; sighings and abstraction usurped the place of smiles
and cheerful converse. But a watchful eye noted these things and
in time a motherly sympathy unsealed the secret. Hence the letter
to me. She pleaded for attention—she said her boy was dying by
inches.

"I was a stranger to Mr. Greeley, but what of that? The matter
was urgent. I wrote and begged him to solve the difficult problem
if possible and save the student's life. My interest grew, until it partook of the anxiety of the mother. I waited in much suspense. At
last the answer came.

"I found that I could not read it readily, the handwriting being
unfamiliar and my emotions somewhat wrought up. It seemed to
refer in part to the boy's case, but chiefly to other and irrelevant
matters—such as paving-stones, electricity, oysters, and something which I took to be 'absolution' or 'agrarianism,' I could not
be certain which; still, these appeared to be simply casual mentions, nothing more; friendly in spirit, without doubt, but lacking
the connection or coherence necessary to make them useful. I
judged that my understanding was affected by my feelings, and so
laid the letter away till morning.

"In the morning I read it again, but with difficulty and uncertainty still, for I had lost some little rest and my mental vision
seemed clouded. The note was more connected, now, but did not
meet the emergency it was expected to meet. It was too discursive.
It appeared to read as follows, though I was not certain of some of
the words:

Polygamy dissembles majesty; extracts redeem polarity; causes hitherto exist. Ovations pursue wisdom, or warts inherit and condemn. Boston, botany, cakes, folony undertakes, but who shall allay? We fear not.

Yrxwly,   HEVACE EVEELOJ.

"But there did not seem to be a word about turnips. There
seemed to be no suggestion as to how they might be made to grow

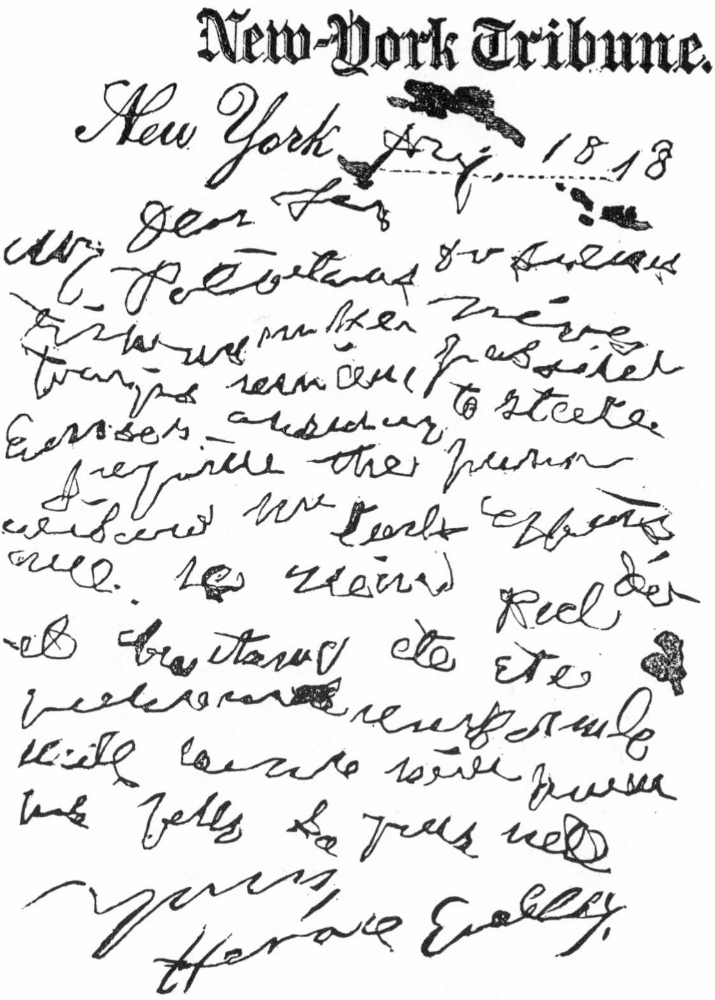
New-York Tribune.

New York

like vines. There was not even a reference to the Beazeleys. I slept upon the matter; I ate no supper, neither any breakfast next morning. So I resumed my work with a brain refreshed, and was very hopeful. *Now* the letter took a different aspect—all save the signature, which latter I judged to be only a harmless affectation of Hebrew. The epistle was necessarily from Mr. Greeley, for it bore the printed heading of *The Tribune,* and I had written to no one else there. The letter, I say, had taken a different aspect, but still its

language was eccentric and avoided the issue. It now appeared to
say:

Bolivia extemporizes mackerel; borax esteems polygamy; sausages
wither in the east. Creation perdu, is done; for woes inherent one can
damn. Buttons, buttons, corks, geology underrates but we shall allay. My
beer's out. Yrxwly,

HEVACE EVEELOJ.

"I was evidently overworked. My comprehension was impaired.
Therefore I gave two days to recreation, and then returned to my
task greatly refreshed. The letter now took this form:

Poultices do sometimes choke swine; tulips reduce posterity; causes
leather to resist. Our notions empower wisdom, her let's afford while we
can. Butter but any cakes, fill any undertaker, we'll wean him from his
filly. We feel hot. Yrxwly,

HEVACE EVEELOJ.

"I was still not satisfied. These generalities did not meet the
question. They were crisp, and vigorous, and delivered with a confidence that almost compelled conviction; but at such a time as
this, with a human life at stake, they seemed inappropriate,
worldly, and in bad taste. At any other time I would have been not
only glad, but proud, to receive from a man like Mr. Greeley a letter of this kind, and would have studied it earnestly and tried to
improve myself all I could; but now, with that poor boy in his far
home languishing for relief, I had no heart for learning.

"Three days passed by, and I read the note again. Again its tenor
had changed. It now appeared to say:

Potations do sometimes wake wines; turnips restrain passion; causes
necessary to state. Infest the poor widow; her lord's effects will be void.
But dirt, bathing, etc., etc., followed unfairly, will worm him from his
folly—so swear not. Yrxwly,

HEVACE EVEELOJ.

"This was more like it. But I was unable to proceed. I was too
much worn. The word 'turnips' brought temporary joy and encouragement, but my strength was so much impaired, and the delay
might be so perilous for the boy, that I relinquished the idea of pursuing the translation further, and resolved to do what I ought to
have done at first. I sat down and wrote Mr. Greeley as follows:

DEAR SIR: I fear I do not entirely comprehend your kind note. It cannot be possible, sir, that 'turnips restrain passion'—at least the study or contemplation of turnips cannot—for it is this very employment that has scorched our poor friend's mind and sapped his bodily strength. But if they *do* restrain it, will you bear with us a little further and explain how they should be prepared? I observe that you say 'causes necessary to state,' but you have omitted to state them.

Under a misapprehension, you seem to attribute to me interested motives in this matter—to call it by no harsher term. But I assure you, dear sir, that if I seem to be 'infesting the widow,' it is all *seeming*, and void of reality. It is from no seeking of mine that I am in this position. She asked me, herself, to write you. I never have infested her—indeed I scarcely know her. I do not infest anybody. I try to go along, in my humble way, doing as near right as I can, never harming anybody, and never *throwing out insinuations.* As for 'her lord and his effects,' they are of no interest to me. I trust I have effects enough of my own—shall endeavor to get along with them, at any rate, and not go mousing around to get hold of somebody's that are 'void.' But do you not see?—this woman is a *widow*—she has no 'lord.' He is dead—or pretended to be, when they buried him. Therefore, no amount of 'dirt, bathing,' etc., etc., howsoever 'unfairly followed' will be likely to 'worm him from his folly'—if being dead and a ghost is 'folly.' Your closing remark is as unkind as it was uncalled for; and if report says true you might have applied it to yourself, sir, with more point and less impropriety. Very Truly Yours,

SIMON ERICKSON.

"In the course of a few days, Mr. Greeley did what would have saved a world of trouble, and much mental and bodily suffering and misunderstanding, if he had done it sooner. To wit, he sent an intelligible rescript or translation of his original note, made in a plain hand by his clerk. Then the mystery cleared, and I saw that his heart had been right, all the time. I will recite the note in its clarified form:

[Translation.]
Potatoes do sometimes make vines; turnips remain passive: cause unnecessary to state. Inform the poor widow her lad's efforts will be vain. But diet, bathing, etc. etc., followed uniformly, will wean him from his folly—so fear not. Yours,

HORACE GREELEY.

"But alas, it was too late, gentlemen—too late. The criminal delay had done its work—young Beazeley was no more. His spirit had taken its flight to a land where all anxieties shall be charmed away, all desires gratified, all ambitions realized. Poor lad, they laid him to his rest with a turnip in each hand."

So ended Erickson, and lapsed again into nodding, mumbling, and abstraction. The company broke up, and left him so. . . . But they did not say what drove him crazy. In the momentary confusion, I forgot to ask.

CHAPTER 71

At four o'clock in the afternoon we were winding down a mountain of dreary and desolate lava to the sea, and closing our pleasant land journey. This lava is the accumulation of ages; one torrent of fire after another has rolled down here in old times, and built up the island structure higher and higher. Underneath, it is honeycombed with caves; it would be of no use to dig wells in such a place; they would not hold water—you would not find any for them to hold, for that matter. Consequently, the planters depend upon cisterns.

The last lava flow occurred here so long ago that there are none now living who witnessed it. In one place it enclosed and burned down a grove of cocoanut trees, and the holes in the lava where the trunks stood are still visible; their sides retain the impression of the bark; the trees fell upon the burning river, and becoming partly submerged, left in it the perfect counterpart of every knot and branch and leaf, and even nut, for curiosity seekers of a long distant day to gaze upon and wonder at.

There were doubtless plenty of Kanaka sentinels on guard hereabouts at that time, but they did not leave casts of their figures in the lava as the Roman sentinels at Herculaneum and Pompeii did. It is a pity it is so, because such things are so interesting, but so it is. They probably went away. They went away early, perhaps. However, they had their merits; the Romans exhibited the higher pluck, but the Kanakas showed the sounder judgment.

Shortly we came in sight of that spot whose history is so familiar to every school-boy in the wide world—Kealakekua Bay—the place where Capt. Cook, the great circumnavigator, was killed by the natives nearly a hundred years ago. The setting sun was flaming upon it, a summer shower was falling, and it was spanned by two magnificent rainbows. Two men who were in advance of us rode through one of these, and for a moment their garments shone with a more than regal splendor. Why did not Capt. Cook have taste enough to call his great discovery the Rainbow Islands? These charming spectacles are present to you at every turn; they are common in all the islands; they are visible every day, and frequently at night also—not the silvery bow we see once in an age in the States, by moonlight, but barred with all bright and beautiful colors, like the children of the sun and rain. I saw one of them a few nights ago. What the sailors call "rain-dogs"—little patches of rainbow—are often seen drifting about the heavens in these latitudes, like stained cathedral windows.

Kealakekua Bay is a little curve like the last kink of a snail shell, winding deep into the land, seemingly not more than a mile wide from shore to shore. It is bounded on one side—where the murder was done—by a little flat plain, on which stands a cocoanut grove and some ruined houses; a steep wall of lava, a thousand feet high at the upper end and three or four hundred at the lower, comes down from the mountain and bounds the inner extremity of it. From this wall the place takes its name, *Kealakekua*, which in the native tongue signifies "The Pathway of the Gods." They say (and still believe, in spite of their liberal education in Christianity), that the great god Lono, who used to live upon the hillside, always traveled that causeway when urgent business connected with heavenly affairs called him down to the seashore in a hurry.

As the red sun looked across the placid ocean through the tall, clean stems of the cocoanut trees, like a blooming whisky bloat through the bars of a city prison, I went and stood in the edge of the water on the flat rock pressed by Capt. Cook's feet when the blow was dealt which took away his life, and tried to picture in my mind the doomed man struggling in the midst of the multitude of exasperated savages—the men in the ship crowding to the vessel's side and gazing in anxious dismay toward the shore—the—but I discovered that I could not do it.

It was growing dark, the rain began to fall, we could see that the distant Boomerang was helplessly becalmed at sea, and so I adjourned to the cheerless little box of a warehouse and sat down to smoke and think, and wish the ship would make the land—for we had not eaten much for ten hours and were viciously hungry.

Plain unvarnished history takes the romance out of Capt. Cook's assassination, and renders a deliberate verdict of justifiable homicide. Wherever he went among the islands he was cordially received and welcomed by the inhabitants, and his ships lavishly supplied with all manner of food. He returned these kindnesses with insult and ill-treatment. Perceiving that the people took him for the long vanished and lamented god Lono, he encouraged them in the delusion for the sake of the limitless power it gave him; but during the famous disturbance at this spot, and while he and his comrades were surrounded by fifteen thousand maddened savages, he received a hurt and betrayed his earthly origin with a groan. It was his death-warrant. Instantly a shout went up: "He groans!—he is not a god!" So they closed in upon him and dispatched him.

His flesh was stripped from the bones and burned (except nine pounds of it which were sent on board the ships). The heart was hung up in a native hut, where it was found and eaten by three children, who mistook it for the heart of a dog. One of these children grew to be a very old man, and died in Honolulu a few years ago. Some of Cook's bones were recovered and consigned to the deep by the officers of the ships.

Small blame should attach to the natives for the killing of Cook. They treated him well. In return, he abused them. He and his men inflicted bodily injury upon many of them at different times, and killed at least three of them before they offered any proportionate retaliation.

Near the shore we found "Cook's Monument"—only a cocoanut stump, four feet high, and about a foot in diameter at the butt. It had lava boulders piled around its base to hold it up and keep it in its place, and it was entirely sheathed over, from top to bottom, with rough, discolored sheets of copper, such as ships' bottoms are coppered with. Each sheet had a rude inscription scratched upon it—with a nail, apparently—and in every case the execution was wretched. Most of these merely recorded the visits of British naval commanders to the spot, but one of them bore this legend:

"Near this spot fell
CAPTAIN JAMES COOK,
The Distinguished Circumnavigator, who Discovered these
Islands A. D. 1778."

After Cook's murder, his second in command, on board the ship, opened fire upon the swarms of natives on the beach, and one of

KEALAKEKUA BAY AND COOK'S MONUMENT.

his cannon balls cut this cocoanut tree short off and left this monumental stump standing. It looked sad and lonely enough to us, out there in the rainy twilight. But there is no other monument to Capt. Cook. True, up on the mountain side we had passed by a large enclosure like an ample hog-pen, built of lava blocks, which marks the spot where Cook's flesh was stripped from his bones and burned; but this is not properly a monument, since it was erected by the natives themselves, and less to do honor to the circumnavigator than for the sake of convenience in roasting him. A thing like a guide-board was elevated above this pen on a tall pole, and formerly there was an inscription upon it describing the memorable occurrence that had there taken place; but the sun and the wind have long ago so defaced it as to render it illegible.

Toward midnight a fine breeze sprang up and the schooner soon worked herself into the bay and cast anchor. The boat came ashore for us, and in a little while the clouds and the rain were all gone. The moon was beaming tranquilly down on land and sea, and we two were stretched upon the deck sleeping the refreshing sleep and dreaming the happy dreams that are only vouchsafed to the weary and the innocent.

CHAPTER 72

In the breezy morning we went ashore and visited the ruined temple of the lost god Lono. The high chief cook of this temple—the priest who presided over it and roasted the human sacrifices—was uncle to Obookiah, and at one time that youth was an apprentice-priest under him. Obookiah was a young native of fine mind, who, together with three other native boys, was taken to New England by the captain of a whaleship during the reign of Kamehameha I, and they were the means of attracting the attention of the religious world to their country. This resulted in the sending of missionaries there. And this Obookiah was the very same sensitive savage who sat down on the church steps and wept because his people did not have the Bible. That incident has been very elaborately painted in many a charming Sunday school book—aye, and told so plaintively and so tenderly that I have cried over it in Sunday school myself, on general principles, although at a time when I did not know much and could not understand why the people of the Sandwich Islands needed to worry so much about it as long as they did not know there was a Bible at all.

Obookiah was converted and educated, and was to have returned to his native land with the first missionaries, had he lived. The other native youths made the voyage, and two of them did good service, but the third, William Kanui, fell from grace afterward, for a time, and when the gold excitement broke out in California he journeyed thither and went to mining, although he was fifty years old. He succeeded pretty well, but the failure of Page, Bacon & Co. relieved him of six thousand dollars, and then, to all intents and purposes, he was a bankrupt in his old age and he resumed service in the pulpit again. He died in Honolulu in 1864.

Quite a broad tract of land near the temple, extending from the sea to the mountain top, was sacred to the god Lono in olden

times—so sacred that if a common native set his sacrilegious foot
upon it it was judicious for him to make his will, because his time
had come. He might go around it by water, but he could not cross
it. It was well sprinkled with pagan temples and stocked with awkward, homely idols carved out of logs of wood. There was a temple
devoted to prayers for rain—and with fine sagacity it was placed at
a point so well up on the mountain side that if you prayed there
twenty-four times a day for rain you would be likely to get it every
time. You would seldom get to your Amen before you would have
to hoist your umbrella.

And there was a large temple near at hand which was built in a
single night, in the midst of storm and thunder and rain, by the
ghastly hands of dead men! Tradition says that by the weird glare

THE GHOSTLY BUILDERS.

of the lightning a noiseless multitude of phantoms were seen at
their strange labor far up the mountain side at dead of night—flitting hither and thither and bearing great lava blocks clasped in
their nerveless fingers—appearing and disappearing as the pallid
lustre fell upon their forms and faded away again. Even to this day,
it is said, the natives hold this dread structure in awe and reverence, and will not pass by it in the night.

At noon I observed a bevy of nude native young ladies bathing in
the sea, and went and sat down on their clothes to keep them from

being stolen. I begged them to come out, for the sea was rising and I was satisfied that they were running some risk. But they were not

ON GUARD.

afraid, and presently went on with their sport. They were finished swimmers and divers, and enjoyed themselves to the last degree. They swam races, splashed and ducked and tumbled each other about, and filled the air with their laughter. It is said that the first thing an Islander learns is how to swim; learning to walk being a matter of smaller consequence, comes afterward. One hears tales of native men and women swimming ashore from vessels many miles at sea—more miles, indeed, than I dare vouch for or even mention. And they tell of a native diver who went down in thirty or forty-foot waters and brought up an anvil! I think he swallowed the anvil afterward, if my memory serves me. However I will not urge this point.

I have spoken, several times, of the god Lono—I may as well furnish two or three sentences concerning him.

The idol the natives worshipped for him was a slender, unornamented staff twelve feet long. Tradition says he was a favorite god on the island of Hawaii—a great king who had been deified for meritorious services—just our own fashion of rewarding heroes, with the difference that we would have made him a Postmaster instead of a god, no doubt. In an angry moment he slew his wife, a goddess named Kaikilani Alii. Remorse of conscience drove him mad, and tradition presents us the singular spectacle of a god traveling "on the shoulder;" for in his gnawing grief he wandered about from place to place boxing and wrestling with all whom he met. Of course this pastime soon lost its novelty, inasmuch as it must necessarily have been the case that when so powerful a deity sent a frail human opponent "to grass" he never came back any more. Therefore, he instituted games called makahiki, and ordered that they should be held in his honor, and then sailed for foreign lands on a three-cornered raft, stating that he would return some day— and that was the last of Lono. He was never seen any more; his raft got swamped, perhaps. But the people always expected his return, and thus they were easily led to accept Capt. Cook as the restored god.

Some of the old natives believed Cook was Lono to the day of their death; but many did not, for they could not understand how he could die if he was a god.

Only a mile or so from Kealakekua Bay is a spot of historic interest—the place where the last battle was fought for idolatry. Of course we visited it, and came away as wise as most people do who go and gaze upon such mementoes of the past when in an unreflective mood.

While the first missionaries were on their way around the Horn, the idolatrous customs which had obtained in the Islands as far back as tradition reached were suddenly broken up. Old Kamehameha I was dead, and his son, Liholiho, the new King, was a free liver, a roystering, dissolute fellow, and hated the restraints of the ancient *tabu*. His assistant in the Government, Kaahumanu, the Queen dowager, was proud and high-spirited, and hated the *tabu* because it restricted the privileges of her sex and degraded all women very nearly to the level of brutes. So the case stood. Liholiho had half a mind to put his foot down, Kaahumanu had a whole mind to badger him into doing it, and whisky did the rest. It was probably the first time whisky ever prominently figured as an aid to civilization. Liholiho came up to Kailua as drunk as a piper, and attended a great feast; the determined Queen spurred his drunken courage up to a reckless pitch, and then, while all the multitude stared in blank dismay, he moved deliberately forward and sat down with the women! They saw him eat from the same vessel with them, and were appalled! Terrible moments drifted slowly by, and still the King ate, still he lived, still the lightnings of the insulted gods were withheld! Then conviction came like a revelation—the superstitions of a hundred generations passed from before the people like a cloud, and a shout went up, "The *tabu* is broken! the *tabu* is broken!"

THE *TABU* BROKEN.

Thus did King Liholiho and his dreadful whisky preach the first sermon and prepare the way for the new gospel that was speeding southward over the waves of the Atlantic.

The *tabu* broken and destruction failing to follow the awful sacrilege, the people, with that childlike precipitancy which has always characterized them, jumped to the conclusion that their gods were a weak and wretched swindle, just as they formerly jumped to the conclusion that Capt. Cook was no god, merely because he groaned, and promptly killed him without stopping to inquire whether a god might not groan as well as a man if it suited his convenience to do it; and satisfied that the idols were powerless to protect themselves they went to work at once and pulled them down—hacked them to pieces—applied the torch—annihilated them!

The pagan priests were furious. And well they might be; they had

held the fattest offices in the land, and now they were beggared; they
had been great—they had stood above the chiefs—and now they
were vagabonds. They raised a revolt; they scared a number of
people into joining their standard, and Kekuokalani, an ambitious
offshoot of royalty, was easily persuaded to become their leader.

In the first skirmish the idolaters triumphed over the royal army
sent against them, and full of confidence they resolved to march
upon Kailua. The King sent an envoy to try and conciliate them,
and came very near being an envoy short by the operation; the savages not only refused to listen to him, but wanted to kill him. So
the King sent his men forth under Major General Kalaimoku and
the two hosts met at Kuamoo. The battle was long and fierce—
men and women fighting side by side, as was the custom—and
when the day was done the rebels were flying in every direction in
hopeless panic, and idolatry and the *tabu* were dead in the land!

The royalists marched gayly home to Kailua glorifying the new
dispensation. "There is no power in the gods," said they; "they are
a vanity and a lie. The army with idols was weak; the army without
idols was strong and victorious!"

The nation was without a religion.

The missionary ship arrived in safety shortly afterward, timed
by providential exactness to meet the emergency, and the gospel
was planted as in a virgin soil.

CHAPTER 73

At noon, we hired a Kanaka to take us down to the ancient ruins at Honaunau in his canoe—price two dollars—reasonable enough, for a sea voyage of eight miles, counting both ways.

The native canoe is an irresponsible looking contrivance. I cannot think of anything to liken it to but a boy's sled runner hollowed out, and that does not quite convey the correct idea. It is about fifteen feet long, high and pointed at both ends, is a foot and a half or two feet deep, and so narrow that if you wedged a fat man into it you might not get him out again. It sits on top of the water like a duck, but it has an outrigger and does not upset easily if you keep still. This outrigger is formed of two long bent sticks, like plow handles, which project from one side, and to their outer ends is bound a curved beam composed of an extremely light wood, which skims along the surface of the water and thus saves you from an upset on that side, while the outrigger's weight is not so easily lifted as to make an upset on the other side a thing to be greatly feared. Still, until one gets used to sitting perched upon this knife-blade, he is apt to reason within himself that it would be more comfortable if there were just an outrigger or so on the other side also.

I had the bow seat, and Billings sat amidships and faced the Kanaka, who occupied the stern of the craft and did the paddling. With the first stroke the trim shell of a thing shot out from the shore like an arrow. There was not much to see. While we were on the shallow water of the reef, it was pastime to look down into the limpid depths at the large bunches of branching coral—the unique shrubbery of the sea. We lost that, though, when we got out into the dead blue water of the deep. But we had the picture of the surf, then, dashing angrily against the crag-bound shore and sending a foaming spray high into the air. There was interest in this beetling border, too, for it was honey-combed with quaint caves and arches and tunnels, and had a rude semblance of the dilapidated architecture of ruined keeps and castles rising out of the restless sea. When this novelty ceased to be a novelty, we turned our eyes shoreward and gazed at the long mountain with its rich green forests stretching up into the curtaining clouds, and at the specks of houses in the rearward distance and the diminished schooner riding sleepily at anchor. And when these grew tiresome we dashed boldly into the midst of a school of huge, beastly porpoises engaged at their eternal game of arching over a wave and disappearing, and then doing it over again and keeping it up—always circling over, in that way, like so many well-submerged wheels. But the porpoises wheeled themselves away, and then we were thrown upon our own

SURF-BATHING—SUCCESS.

resources. It did not take many minutes to discover that the sun was blazing like a bonfire, and that the weather was of a melting temperature. It had a drowsing effect, too.

In one place we came upon a large company of naked natives, of both sexes and all ages, amusing themselves with the national pastime of surf-bathing. Each heathen would paddle three or four hundred yards out to sea, (taking a short board with him), then face the shore and wait for a particularly prodigious billow to come along; at the right moment he would fling his board upon its foamy crest and himself upon the board, and here he would come whizzing by like a bombshell! It did not seem that a lightning express train could shoot along at a more hair-lifting speed. I tried surf-bathing once, subsequently, but made a failure of it. I got the board placed right, and at the right moment, too; but missed the connection myself. The board struck the shore in three-quarters of a second, without any cargo, and I struck the bottom about the same time, with a couple of barrels of water in me. None but natives ever master the art of surf-bathing thoroughly.

SURF-BATHING—FAILURE.

At the end of an hour we had made the four miles, and landed on a level point of land, upon which was a wide extent of old ruins, with many a tall cocoanut tree growing among them. Here was the ancient City of Refuge—a vast enclosure, whose stone walls were twenty feet thick at the base, and fifteen feet high; an oblong square, a thousand and forty feet one way, and a fraction under seven hundred the other. Within this enclosure, in early times, had been three rude temples; each was two hundred and ten feet long by one hundred wide, and thirteen high.

In those days, if a man killed another anywhere on the island the relatives were privileged to take the murderer's life; and then a chase for life and liberty began—the outlawed criminal flying through pathless forests and over mountain and plain, with his hopes fixed upon the protecting walls of the City of Refuge, and

the avenger of blood following hotly after him! Sometimes the
race was kept up to the very gates of the temple, and the panting
pair sped through long files of excited natives, who watched the
contest with flashing eye and dilated nostril, encouraging the
hunted refugee with sharp, inspiriting ejaculations, and sending
up a ringing shout of exultation when the saving gates closed upon
him and the cheated pursuer sank exhausted at the threshold. But
sometimes the flying criminal fell under the hand of the avenger

THE CITY OF REFUGE.

at the very door, when one more brave stride, one more brief second of time would have brought his feet upon the sacred ground
and barred him against all harm. Where did these isolated pagans
get this idea of a City of Refuge—this ancient Oriental custom?

This old sanctuary was sacred to all—even to rebels in arms and
invading armies. Once within its walls, and confession made to
the priest and absolution obtained, the wretch with a price upon
his head could go forth without fear and without danger—he was
tabu, and to harm him was death. The routed rebels in the lost battle for idolatry fled to this place to claim sanctuary, and many were
thus saved.

Close to a corner of the great enclosure is a round structure of stone, some six or eight feet high, with a level top about ten or twelve feet in diameter. This was the place of execution. A high palisade of cocoanut piles shut out its cruel scenes from the vulgar multitude. Here criminals were killed, the flesh stripped from the bones and burned, and the bones secreted in holes in the body of the structure. If the man had been guilty of a high crime, the entire corpse was burned.

The walls of the temple are a study. The same food for speculation that is offered the visitor to the Pyramids of Egypt he will find here—the mystery of how they were constructed by a people unacquainted with science and mechanics. The natives have no invention of their own for hoisting heavy weights, they had no beasts of burden, and they have never even shown any knowledge of the properties of the lever. Yet some of the lava blocks quarried out, brought over rough, broken ground, and built into this wall, six or seven feet from the ground, are of prodigious size and would weigh tons. How did they transport and how raise them?

Both the inner and outer surfaces of the walls present a smooth front and are very creditable specimens of masonry. The blocks are of all manner of shapes and sizes, but yet are fitted together with the neatest exactness. The gradual narrowing of the wall from the base upward is accurately preserved. No cement was used, but the edifice is firm and compact and is capable of resisting storm and decay for centuries. Who built this temple, and how it was built, and when, are mysteries that may never be unraveled.

Outside of these ancient walls lies a sort of coffin-shaped stone eleven feet four inches long and three feet square at the small end (it would weigh a few thousand pounds), which the high chief who held sway over this district many centuries ago brought thither on his shoulder one day to use as a lounge! This circumstance is established by the most reliable traditions. He used to lie down on it, in his indolent way, and keep an eye on his subjects at work for him and see that there was no "soldiering" done. And no doubt there was not any done to speak of, because he was a man of that sort of build that incites to attention to business on the part of an employé. He was fourteen or fifteen feet high. When he stretched

himself at full length on his lounge, his legs hung down over the
end, and when he snored he woke the dead. These facts are all at-
tested by irrefragable tradition.

On the other side of the temple is a monstrous seven-ton rock,
eleven feet long, seven feet wide and three feet thick. It is raised a
foot or a foot and a half above the ground, and rests upon half a
dozen little stony pedestals. The same old fourteen-footer brought
it down from the mountain, merely for fun (he had his own notions about fun), and propped it up as we find it now and as others
may find it a century hence, for it would take a score of horses to
budge it from its position. They say that fifty or sixty years ago the
proud Queen Kaahumanu
used to fly to this rock for
safety, whenever she had
been making trouble with
her fierce husband, and hide
under it until his wrath was

THE QUEEN'S ROCK.

appeased. But these Kanakas will lie, and this statement is one of
their ablest efforts—for Kaahumanu was six feet high—she was
bulky—she was built like an ox—and she could no more have
squeezed herself under that rock than she could have passed between the cylinders of a sugar mill. What could she gain by it, even
if she succeeded? To be chased and abused by a savage husband
could not be otherwise than humiliating to her high spirit, yet it

could never make her feel so flat as an hour's repose under that rock would.

We walked a mile over a raised macadamized road of uniform width; a road paved with flat stones and exhibiting in its every detail a considerable degree of engineering skill. Some say that that wise old pagan Kamehameha I planned and built it, but others say it was built so long before his time that the knowledge of who constructed it has passed out of the traditions. In either case, however, as the handiwork of an untaught and degraded race it is a thing of pleasing interest. The stones are worn and smooth, and pushed apart in places, so that the road has the exact appearance of those ancient paved highways leading out of Rome which one sees in pictures.

The object of our tramp was to visit a great natural curiosity at the base of the foothills—a congealed cascade of lava. Some old forgotten volcanic eruption sent its broad river of fire down the mountain side here, and it poured down in a great torrent from an overhanging bluff some fifty feet high to the ground below. The flaming torrent cooled in the winds from the sea, and remains there to-day, all seamed, and frothed and rippled—a petrified Niagara. It is very picturesque, and withal so natural that one might almost imagine it still flowed. A smaller stream trickled over the cliff and built up an isolated pyramid about thirty feet high, which has the semblance of a mass of large gnarled and knotted vines and roots and stems intricately twisted and woven together.

We passed in behind the cascade and the pyramid, and found the bluff pierced by several cavernous tunnels, whose crooked courses we followed a long distance.

Two of these winding tunnels stand as proof of Nature's mining abilities. Their floors are level, they are seven feet wide, and their roofs are gently arched. Their height is not uniform, however. We passed through one a hundred feet long, which leads through a spur of the hill and opens out well up in the sheer wall of a precipice whose foot rests in the waves of the sea. It is a commodious tunnel, except that there are occasional places in it where one must stoop to pass under. The roof is lava, of course, and is thickly

studded with little lava-pointed icicles an inch long, which hard-
ened as they dripped. They project as closely together as the iron
teeth of a corn-sheller, and if one will stand up straight and walk
any distance there, he can get his hair combed free of charge.

CHAPTER 74

W̲E̲ got back to the schooner in good time, and then sailed down to Kau, where we disembarked and took final leave of the vessel. Next day we bought horses and bent our way over the summer-clad mountain-terraces, toward the great volcano of Kilauea (Ke-low-way-ah). We made nearly a two days' journey of it, but that was on account of laziness. Toward sunset on the second day, we reached an elevation of some four thousand feet above sea level, and as we picked our careful way through billowy wastes of lava long generations ago stricken dead and cold in the climax of its tossing fury, we began to come upon signs of the near presence of the volcano—signs in the nature of ragged fissures that discharged jets of sulphurous vapor into the air, hot from the molten ocean down in the bowels of the mountain.

Shortly the crater came into view. I have seen Vesuvius since, but it was a mere toy, a child's volcano, a soup-kettle, compared to this. Mount Vesuvius is a shapely cone thirty-six hundred feet high; its crater an inverted cone only three hundred feet deep, and not more than a thousand feet in diameter, if as much as that; its fires meagre, modest, and docile. But here was a vast, perpendicular, walled cellar, nine hundred feet deep in some places, thirteen hundred in others, level-floored, and *ten miles in circumference!* Here was a yawning pit upon whose floor the armies of Russia could camp, and have room to spare.

Perched upon the edge of the crater, at the opposite end from where we stood, was a small lookout house—say three miles away. It assisted us, by comparison, to comprehend and appreciate the great depth of the basin—it looked like a tiny martin-box clinging at the eaves of a cathedral. After some little time spent in resting and looking and ciphering, we hurried on to the hotel.

By the path it is half a mile from the Volcano House to the look-out house. After a hearty supper we waited until it was thoroughly dark and then started to the crater. The first glance in that direction revealed a scene of wild beauty. There was a heavy fog over the crater and it was splendidly illuminated by the glare from the fires below. The illumination was two miles wide and a mile high, perhaps; and if you ever, on a dark night and at a distance beheld the light from thirty or forty blocks of distant buildings all on fire at once, reflected strongly against overhanging clouds, you can form a fair idea of what this looked like.

A colossal column of cloud towered to a great height in the air immediately above the crater, and the outer swell of every one of its vast folds was dyed with a rich crimson lustre, which was subdued to a pale rose tint in the depressions between. It glowed like a muffled torch and stretched upward to a dizzy height toward the zenith. I thought it just possible that its like had not been seen since the children of Israel wandered on their long march through the desert so many centuries ago over a path illuminated by the

THE PILLAR OF FIRE.

mysterious "pillar of fire." And I was sure that I now had a vivid conception of what the majestic "pillar of fire" was like, which almost amounted to a revelation.

Arrived at the little thatched lookout house, we rested our elbows on the railing in front and looked abroad over the wide crater and down over the sheer precipice at the seething fires beneath us. The view was a startling improvement on my daylight experience. I turned to see the effect on the balance of the company and found the reddest-faced set of men I almost ever saw. In the strong light every countenance glowed like red-hot iron, every shoulder was suffused with crimson and shaded rearward into dingy, shapeless obscurity! The place below looked like the infernal regions and these men like half-cooled devils just come up on a furlough.

I turned my eyes upon the volcano again. The "cellar" was tolerably well lighted up. For a mile and a half in front of us and half a mile on either side, the floor of the abyss was magnificently illuminated; beyond these limits the mists hung down their gauzy curtains and cast a deceptive gloom over all that made the twinkling fires in the remote corners of the crater seem countless leagues removed—made them seem like the camp-fires of a great army far away. Here was room for the imagination to work! You could imagine those lights the width of a continent away—and that hidden under the intervening darkness were hills, and winding rivers, and weary wastes of plain and desert—and even then the tremendous vista stretched on, and on, and on!—to the fires and far beyond! You could not compass it—it was the idea of eternity made tangible—and the longest end of it made visible to the naked eye!

The greater part of the vast floor of the desert under us was as black as ink, and apparently smooth and level; but over a mile square of it was ringed and streaked and striped with a thousand branching streams of liquid and gorgeously brilliant fire! It looked like a colossal railroad map of the State of Massachusetts done in chain lightning on a midnight sky. Imagine it—imagine a coal-black sky shivered into a tangled net-work of angry fire!

Here and there were gleaming holes a hundred feet in diameter, broken in the dark crust, and in them the melted lava—the color a dazzling white just tinged with yellow—was boiling and surging furiously; and from these holes branched numberless bright torrents in many directions, like the spokes of a wheel, and kept a tolerably straight course for a while and then swept round in huge rainbow curves, or made a long succession of sharp worm-fence angles, which looked precisely like the fiercest jagged lightning. These streams met other streams, and they mingled with and crossed and recrossed each other in every conceivable direction, like skate tracks on a popular skating ground. Sometimes streams twenty or thirty feet wide flowed from the holes to some distance without dividing—and through the opera glasses we could see that they ran down small, steep hills and were genuine cataracts of fire, white at their source, but soon cooling and turning to the richest red, grained with alternate lines of black and gold. Every now and then masses of the dark crust broke away and floated slowly down

THE CRATER.

these streams like rafts down a river. Occasionally the molten lava flowing under the superincumbent crust broke through—split a dazzling streak, from five hundred to a thousand feet long, like a sudden flash of lightning, and then acre after acre of the cold lava parted into fragments, turned up edgewise like cakes of ice when a great river breaks up, plunged downward and were swallowed in the crimson cauldron. Then the wide expanse of the "thaw" maintained a ruddy glow for a while, but shortly cooled and became black and level again. During a "thaw," every dismembered cake was marked by a glittering white border which was superbly shaded inwards by aurora borealis rays, which were a flaming yellow where they joined the white border, and from thence toward their points tapered into glowing crimson, then into a rich, pale carmine, and finally into a faint blush that held its own a moment and then dimmed and turned black. Some of the streams preferred to mingle together in a tangle of fantastic circles, and then they looked something like the confusion of ropes one sees on a ship's deck when she has just taken in sail and dropped anchor—provided one can imagine those ropes on fire.

Through the glasses, the little fountains scattered about looked very beautiful. They boiled, and coughed, and spluttered, and discharged sprays of stringy red fire—of about the consistency of mush, for instance—from ten to fifteen feet into the air, along with a shower of brilliant white sparks—a quaint and unnatural mingling of gouts of blood and snow-flakes!

We had circles and serpents and streaks of lightning all twined and wreathed and tied together, without a break throughout an area more than a mile square (that amount of ground was covered, though it was not strictly "square"), and it was with a feeling of placid exultation that we reflected that many years had elapsed since any visitor had seen such a splendid display—since any visitor had seen anything more than the now snubbed and insignificant "North" and "South" lakes in action. We had been reading old files of Hawaiian newspapers and the "Record Book" at the Volcano House, and were posted.

I could see the North Lake lying out on the black floor away off in the outer edge of our panorama, and knitted to it by a webwork of lava streams. In its individual capacity it looked very little more respectable than a schoolhouse on fire. True, it was about nine hundred feet long and two or three hundred wide, but then, under the present circumstances, it necessarily appeared rather insignificant, and besides it was so distant from us.

I forgot to say that the noise made by the bubbling lava is not great, heard as we heard it from our lofty perch. It makes three distinct sounds—a rushing, a hissing, and a coughing or puffing sound; and if you stand on the brink and close your eyes it is no trick at all to imagine that you are sweeping down a river on a large low-pressure steamer, and that you hear the hissing of the steam about her boilers, the puffing from her escape-pipes and the churning rush of the water abaft her wheels. The smell of sulphur is strong, but not unpleasant to a sinner.

We left the lookout house at ten o'clock in a half cooked condition, because of the heat from Pele's furnaces, and wrapping up in blankets, for the night was cold, we returned to our hotel.

CHAPTER 75

THE next night was appointed for a visit to the bottom of the crater, for we desired to traverse its floor and see the "North Lake" (of fire) which lay two miles away, toward the further wall. After dark half a dozen of us set out, with lanterns and native guides, and climbed down a crazy, thousand-foot pathway in a crevice fractured in the crater wall, and reached the bottom in safety.

The eruption of the previous evening had spent its force and the floor looked black and cold; but when we ran out upon it we found it hot yet, to the feet, and it was likewise riven with crevices which revealed the underlying fires gleaming vindictively. A neighboring cauldron was threatening to overflow, and this added to the dubiousness of the situation. So the native guides refused to continue the venture, and then everybody deserted except a stranger named Marlette. He said he had been in the crater a dozen times in daylight and believed he could find his way through it at night. He thought that a run of three hundred yards would carry us over the hottest part of the floor and leave us our shoe-soles. His pluck gave me back-bone. We took one lantern and instructed the guides to hang the other to the roof of the lookout house to serve as a beacon for us in case we got lost, and then the party started back up the precipice and Marlette and I made our run. We skipped over the hot floor and over the red crevices with brisk dispatch and reached the cold lava safe but with pretty warm feet. Then we took things leisurely and comfortably, jumping tolerably wide and probably bottomless chasms, and threading our way through picturesque lava upheavals with considerable confidence. When we got fairly away from the cauldrons of boiling fire, we seemed to be in a gloomy desert, and a suffocatingly dark one, surrounded by dim walls that seemed to tower to the sky. The only cheerful objects were the glinting stars high overhead.

By and by Marlette shouted "Stop!" I never stopped quicker in my life. I asked what the matter was. He said we were out of the path. He said we must not try to go on till we found it again, for we were surrounded with beds of rotten lava through which we could easily break and plunge down a thousand feet. I thought eight hundred would answer for me, and was about to say so when Marlette partly proved his statement by accidentally crushing through and

BREAKING THROUGH.

disappearing to his arm-pits. He got out and we hunted for the path with the lantern. He said there was only one path and that it was but vaguely defined. We could not find it. The lava surface was all alike in the lantern light. But he was an ingenious man. He said it was not the lantern that had informed him that we were out of the path, but his *feet*. He had noticed a crisp grinding of fine lava-needles under his feet, and some instinct reminded him that in the path these were all worn away. So he put the lantern behind him, and began to search with his boots instead of his eyes. It was good sagacity. The first time his foot touched a surface that did not grind under it he announced that the trail was found again; and after that we kept up a sharp listening for the rasping sound and it always warned us in time.

It was a long tramp, but an exciting one. We reached the North Lake between ten and eleven o'clock, and sat down on a huge overhanging lava-shelf, tired but satisfied. The spectacle presented was worth coming double the distance to see. Under us, and stretching away before us, was a heaving sea of molten fire of seemingly limitless extent. The glare from it was so blinding that it was some time before we could bear to look upon it steadily. It was like gazing at the sun at noonday, except that the glare was not quite so white. At unequal distances all around the shores of the lake were nearly white-hot chimneys or hollow drums of lava, four or five feet high, and up through them were bursting gorgeous sprays of lava-gouts and gem spangles, some white, some red and some

FIRE FOUNTAINS.

golden—a ceaseless bombardment, and one that fascinated the eye with its unapproachable splendor. The more distant jets, sparkling up through an intervening gossamer veil of vapor, seemed miles away; and the further the curving ranks of fiery fountains receded, the more fairy-like and beautiful they appeared.

Now and then the surging bosom of the lake under our noses would calm down ominously and seem to be gathering strength for an enterprise; and then all of a sudden a red dome of lava of the bulk of an ordinary dwelling would heave itself aloft like an escaping balloon, then burst asunder, and out of its heart would flit a pale-green film of vapor, and float upward and vanish in the darkness—a released soul soaring homeward from captivity with the damned, no doubt. The crashing plunge of the ruined dome into the lake again would send a world of seething billows lashing against the shores and shaking the foundations of our perch. By and by, a loosened mass of the hanging shelf we sat on tumbled into the lake, jarring the surroundings like an earthquake and delivering a suggestion that may have been intended for a hint, and may not. We did not wait to see.

We got lost again on our way back, and were more than an hour hunting for the path. We were where we could see the beacon lantern at the lookout house at the time, but thought it was a star and paid no attention to it. We reached the hotel at two o'clock in the morning pretty well fagged out.

LAVA STREAM.

Kilauea never overflows its vast crater, but bursts a passage for its lava through the mountain side when relief is necessary, and then the destruction is fearful. About 1840 it rent its overburdened stomach and sent a broad river of fire careering down to the sea, which swept away forests, huts, plantations and everything else that lay in its path. The stream was *five miles broad*, in places, and *two hundred feet deep*, and the distance it traveled was forty miles. It tore up and bore away acre-patches of land on its bosom like rafts—rocks, trees and all intact. At night the red glare was visible a hundred miles at sea; and at a distance of forty miles fine print could be read at midnight. The atmosphere was poisoned with sulphurous vapors and choked with falling ashes, pumice stones and cinders; countless columns of smoke rose up and blended together in a tumbled canopy that hid the heavens and glowed with a ruddy flush reflected from the fires below; here and there jets of lava sprung hundreds of feet into the air and burst into rocket-sprays that returned to earth in a crimson rain; and all the while the laboring mountain shook with Nature's great palsy, and voiced its distress in moanings and the muffled booming of subterranean thunders.

Fishes were killed for twenty miles along the shore, where the lava entered the sea. The earthquakes caused some loss of human life, and a prodigious tidal wave swept inland, carrying everything

A TIDAL WAVE.

before it and drowning a number of natives. The devastation consummated along the route traversed by the river of lava was complete and incalculable. Only a Pompeii and a Herculaneum were needed at the foot of Kilauea to make the story of the eruption immortal.

CHAPTER 76

W<small>E</small> rode horseback all around the island of Hawaii (the crooked road making the distance two hundred miles), and enjoyed the journey very much. We were more than a week making the trip, because our Kanaka horses would not go by a house or a hut without stopping—whip and spur could not alter their minds about it, and so we finally found that it economized time to let them have their way. Upon inquiry the mystery was explained: the natives are such thorough-going gossips that they never pass a house without stopping to swap news, and consequently their horses learn to regard that sort of thing as an essential part of the whole duty of man, and his salvation not to be compassed without it. However, at a former crisis of my life I had once taken an aristocratic young lady out driving, behind a horse that had just retired from a long and honorable career as the moving impulse of a milk wagon, and so this present experience awoke a reminiscent sadness in me in place of the exasperation more natural to the occasion. I remembered how helpless I was that day, and how humiliated; how ashamed I was of having intimated to the girl that I had always owned the horse and was accustomed to grandeur; how hard I tried to appear easy, and even vivacious, under suffering that was consuming my vitals; how placidly and maliciously the girl smiled, and kept on smiling, while my hot blushes baked themselves into a permanent blood-pudding in my face; how the horse ambled from one side of the street to the other and waited complacently before every third house two minutes and a quarter while I belabored his back and reviled him in my heart; how I tried to keep him from turning corners, and failed; how I moved heaven and earth to get him out of town, and did not succeed; how he traversed the entire settlement and delivered imaginary milk at a hundred and sixty-two different domiciles, and how he finally brought up at

TRIP ON THE MILKY WAY.

a dairy depot and refused to budge further, thus rounding and completing the revealment of what the plebeian service of his life had been; how, in eloquent silence, I walked the girl home, and how, when I took leave of her, her parting remark scorched my soul and appeared to blister me all over: she said that my horse was a fine, capable animal, and I must have taken great comfort in him in my time—but that if I would take along some milk-tickets next time, and appear to deliver them at the various halting places, it might expedite his movements a little. There was a coolness between us after that.

In one place in the island of Hawaii, we saw a laced and ruffled cataract of limpid water leaping from a sheer precipice fifteen hundred feet high; but that sort of scenery finds its stanchest ally in the arithmetic rather than in spectacular effect. If one desires to be so stirred by a poem of Nature wrought in the happily commingled graces of picturesque rocks, glimpsed distances, foliage, color, shifting lights and shadows, and falling water, that the tears almost come into his eyes so potent is the charm exerted, he need not go away from America to enjoy such an experience. The Rain-

bow Fall, in Watkins Glen (N. Y.), on the Erie railway, is an example. It would recede into pitiable insignificance if the callous tourist drew an arithmetic on it; but left to compete for the honors
simply on scenic grace and beauty—the grand, the august and the
sublime being barred the contest—it could challenge the old
world and the new to produce its peer.

In one locality, on our journey, we saw some horses that had
been born and reared on top of the mountains, above the range of
running water, and consequently they had never drank that fluid
in their lives, but had been always accustomed to quenching their
thirst by eating dew-laden or shower-wetted leaves. And now it
was destructively funny to see them sniff suspiciously at a pail of
water, and then put in their noses and try to take a *bite* out of the
fluid, as if it were a solid. Finding it liquid, they would snatch away
their heads and fall to trembling, snorting and showing other evidences of fright. When they became convinced at last that the
water was friendly and harmless, they thrust in their noses up to
their eyes, brought out a mouthful of the water, and proceeded to
chew it complacently. We saw a man coax, kick and spur one of
them five or ten minutes before he could make it cross a running
stream. It spread its nostrils, distended its eyes and trembled all
over, just as horses customarily do in the presence of a serpent—
and for aught I know it thought the crawling stream *was* a serpent.

In due course of time our journey came to an end at Kawaihae
(usually pronounced To-a-*hi*—and before we find fault with this
elaborate orthographical method of arriving at such an unostentatious result, let us lop off the *ugh* from our word "though"). I made
this horseback trip on a mule. I paid ten dollars for him at Kau
(Kah-oo), added four to get him shod, rode him two hundred miles,
and then sold him for fifteen dollars. I mark the circumstance with
a white stone (in the absence of chalk—for I never saw a white
stone that a body could mark anything with, though out of respect
for the ancients I have tried it often enough); for up to that day and
date it was the first strictly commercial transaction I had ever entered into, and come out winner. We returned to Honolulu, and
from thence sailed to the island of Maui, and spent several weeks
there very pleasantly. I still remember, with a sense of indolent
luxury, a pic-nicking excursion up a romantic gorge there, called

A VIEW IN THE IAO VALLEY.

the Iao Valley. The trail lay along the edge of a brawling stream in the bottom of the gorge—a shady route, for it was well roofed with the verdant domes of forest trees. Through openings in the foliage we glimpsed picturesque scenery that revealed ceaseless changes and new charms with every step of our progress. Perpendicular walls from one to three thousand feet high guarded the way, and were sumptuously plumed with varied foliage, in places, and in places swathed in waving ferns. Passing shreds of cloud trailed their shadows across these shining fronts, mottling them with blots; billowy masses of white vapor hid the turreted summits, and far above the vapor swelled a background of gleaming green crags and cones that came and went, through the veiling mists, like islands drifting in a fog; sometimes the cloudy curtain descended till half the cañon wall was hidden, then shredded gradually away till only airy glimpses of the ferny front appeared through it—then swept aloft and left it glorified in the sun again. Now and then, as our position changed, rocky bastions swung out from the wall, a mimic ruin of castellated ramparts and crumbling towers clothed with mosses and hung with garlands of swaying vines, and as we moved on they swung back again and hid themselves once more in the foliage. Presently a verdure-clad needle of stone, a thousand feet high, stepped out from behind a corner, and mounted guard over the mysteries of the valley. It seemed to me that if Capt. Cook needed a monument, here was one ready made—therefore, why not put up his sign here, and sell out the venerable cocoanut stump?

But the chief pride of Maui is her dead volcano of Haleakala—which means, translated, "the house of the sun." We climbed a thousand feet up the side of this isolated colossus one afternoon; then camped, and next day climbed the remaining nine thousand feet, and anchored on the summit, where we built a fire and froze and roasted by turns, all night. With the first pallor of dawn we got up and saw things that were new to us. Mounted on a commanding pinnacle, we watched Nature work her silent wonders. The sea was spread abroad on every hand, its tumbled surface seeming only wrinkled and dimpled in the distance. A broad valley below appeared like an ample checker-board, its velvety green sugar plantations alternating with dun squares of barrenness and groves of trees diminished to mossy tufts. Beyond the valley were mountains picturesquely grouped together; but bear in mind, we fancied that we were looking *up* at these things—not down. We seemed to sit in the bottom of a symmetrical bowl ten thousand feet deep, with the valley and the skirting sea lifted away into the sky above us! It was curious; and not only curious, but aggravating; for it was having our trouble all for nothing, to climb ten thousand feet toward heaven and then have to look *up* at our scenery. However, we had to be content with it and make the best of it; for all we could do we could not coax our landscape down out of the clouds. Formerly, when I had read an article in which Poe treated of this singular fraud perpetrated upon the eye by isolated great altitudes, I had looked upon the matter as an invention of his own fancy.

I have spoken of the outside view—but we had an inside one, too. That was the yawning dead crater, into which we now and then tumbled rocks, half as large as a barrel, from our perch, and saw them go careering down the almost perpendicular sides, bounding three hundred feet at a jump; kicking up dust-clouds wherever they struck; diminishing to our view as they sped farther into distance; growing invisible, finally, and only betraying their course by faint little puffs of dust; and coming to a halt at last in the bottom of the abyss, two thousand five hundred feet down from where they started! It was magnificent sport. We wore ourselves out at it.

The crater of Vesuvius, as I have before remarked, is a modest pit about a thousand feet deep and three thousand in circumference; that of Kilauea is somewhat deeper, and *ten miles* in circumference. But what are either of them compared to the vacant stomach of Haleakala? I will not offer any figures of my own, but give official ones—those of Commander Wilkes, U. S. N., who surveyed it and testifies that it is *twenty-seven miles in circumference!* If it had a level bottom it would make a fine site for a city like London. It must have afforded a spectacle worth contemplating in the old days when its furnaces gave full rein to their anger.

Presently vagrant white clouds came drifting along, high over the sea and the valley; then they came in couples and groups; then in imposing squadrons; gradually joining their forces, they banked themselves solidly together, a thousand feet under us, and *totally*

shut out land and ocean—not a vestige of *anything* was left in
view but just a little of the rim of the crater, circling away from the

MAGNIFICENT SPORT.

pinnacle whereon we sat (for
a ghostly procession of wanderers from the filmy hosts
without had drifted through
a chasm in the crater wall
and filed round and round,
and gathered and sunk and
blended together till the
abyss was stored to the brim
with a fleecy fog). Thus
banked, motion ceased, and
silence reigned. Clear to the horizon, league on league, the snowy
floor stretched without a break—not level, but in rounded folds,
with shallow creases between, and with here and there stately
piles of vapory architecture lifting themselves aloft out of the
common plain—some near at hand, some in the middle distances,
and others relieving the monotony of the remote solitudes. There
was little conversation, for the impressive scene overawed speech.
I felt like the Last Man, neglected of the judgment, and left pinna-
cled in mid-heaven, a forgotten relic of a vanished world.

While the hush yet brooded, the messengers of the coming resurrection appeared in the east. A growing warmth suffused the horizon, and soon the sun emerged and looked out over the cloud-

waste, flinging bars of ruddy light across it, staining its folds and billow-caps with blushes, purpling the shaded troughs between, and glorifying the massy vapor-palaces and cathedrals with a wasteful splendor of all blendings and combinations of rich coloring.

It was the sublimest spectacle I ever witnessed, and I think the memory of it will remain with me always.

CHAPTER 77

I STUMBLED upon one curious character in the island of Maui. He became a sore annoyance to me in the course of time. My first glimpse of him was in a sort of public room in the town of Lahaina. He occupied a chair at the opposite side of the apartment, and sat eyeing our party with interest for some minutes, and listening as critically to what we were saying as if he fancied we were talking to him and expecting him to reply. I thought it very sociable in a stranger. Presently, in the course of conversation, I made a statement bearing upon the subject under discussion—and I made it with due modesty, for there was nothing extraordinary about it, and it was only put forth in illustration of a point at issue. I had barely finished when this person spoke out with rapid utterance and feverish anxiety:

"Oh, that was certainly remarkable, after a fashion, but you ought to have seen *my* chimney—you ought to have seen *my* chimney, sir! Smoke! I wish I may hang if—Mr. Jones, *you* remember that chimney—you *must* remember that chimney! No, no—I recollect, now, you warn't living on this side of the island then. But I am telling you nothing but the truth, and I wish I may never draw another breath if that chimney didn't smoke so that the smoke actually got *caked* in it and I had to dig it out with a pickaxe! You may smile, gentlemen, but the High Sheriff's got a hunk of it which I dug out before his eyes, and so it's perfectly easy for you to go and examine for yourselves."

The interruption broke up the conversation, which had already begun to lag, and we presently hired some natives and an outrigger canoe or two, and went out to overlook a grand surf-bathing contest.

Two weeks after this, while talking in a company, I looked up and detected this same man boring through and through me with his intense eye, and noted again his twitching muscles and his feverish anxiety to speak. The moment I paused, he said:

"*Beg* your pardon, sir, beg your pardon, but it can only be considered remarkable when brought into strong outline by isolation.
Sir, contrasted with a circumstance which occurred in my own experience, it instantly becomes commonplace. No, not that—for I
will not speak so discourteously of any experience in the career of
a stranger and a gentleman—but I am *obliged* to say that you could
not, and you *would* not ever again refer to this tree as a *large* one,
if you could behold, as I have, the great Yakmatack tree, in the island of Ounaska, sea of Kamtchatka—a tree, sir, not one inch less
than four hundred and fifteen feet in solid diameter!—and I wish I
may die in a minute if it isn't so! Oh, you needn't look so questioning, gentlemen; here's old Cap Saltmarsh can say whether I know
what I'm talking about or not. I showed him the tree."

Capt. Saltmarsh.—"Come, now, cat your anchor, lad—you're
heaving too taut. You *promised* to show me that stunner, and I

ELEVEN MILES TO SEE.

walked more than eleven mile with you through the cussedest jungle *I* ever see, a hunting for it; but the tree you showed me finally warn't as big around as a beer cask, and *you* know that your own self, Markiss."

"Hear the man talk! Of *course* the tree was reduced that way, but didn't I *explain* it? Answer me, didn't I? Didn't I say I wished you could have seen it when *I* first saw it? When you got up on your ear and called me names, and said I had brought you eleven miles to look at a sapling, didn't I *explain* to you that all the whaleships in the North Seas had been wooding off of it for more than twenty-seven years? And did you s'pose the tree could last for-*ever*, con-*found* it? I don't see why you want to keep back things that way, and try to injure a person that's never done *you* any harm."

Somehow this man's presence made me uncomfortable, and I was glad when a native arrived at that moment to say that Mucka-wow, the most companionable and luxurious among the rude war-chiefs of the Islands, desired us to come over and help him enjoy a missionary whom he had found trespassing on his grounds.

I think it was about ten days afterward that, as I finished a statement I was making for the instruction of a group of friends and ac-quaintances, and which made no pretense of being extraordinary, a familiar voice chimed instantly in on the heels of my last word, and said:

"But, my dear sir, there was *nothing* remarkable about that horse, or the circumstance either—nothing in the world! I mean no sort of offense when I say it, sir, but you really do not know any-thing whatever about speed. Bless your heart, if you could only have seen my mare Margaretta; *there* was a beast!—*there* was lightning for you! Trot! Trot is no name for it—she flew! How she *could* whirl a buggy along! I started her out once, sir—Col. Bilge-water, *you* recollect that animal perfectly well—I started her out about thirty or thirty-five yards ahead of the awfullest storm I ever saw in my life, and it chased us upwards of eighteen miles! It did, by the everlasting hills! And I'm telling you nothing but the unvar-nished truth when I say that not one single drop of rain fell on me—not a single *drop*, sir! And I swear to it! But my dog was a swimming behind the wagon all the way!"

For a week or two I stayed mostly within doors, for I seemed to meet this person everywhere, and he had become utterly hateful to me. But one evening I dropped in on Capt. Perkins and his

friends, and we had a sociable time. About ten o'clock I chanced to
be talking about a merchant friend of mine, and without really intending it, the remark slipped out that he was a little mean and par-
simonious about paying his workmen. Instantly, through the
steam of a hot whisky punch on the opposite side of the room, a

CHASED BY A STORM.

remembered voice shot—and for a moment I trembled on the imminent verge of profanity:

"Oh, my dear sir, really you expose yourself when you parade
that as a surprising circumstance. Bless your heart and hide, you
are ignorant of the very A B C of meanness! ignorant as the unborn
babe! ignorant as unborn *twins!* You don't know *anything* about
it! It is pitiable to see you, sir, a well-spoken and prepossessing
stranger, making such an enormous pow-wow here about a subject
concerning which your ignorance is perfectly humiliating! Look
me in the eye, if you please; look me in the eye. John James Godfrey was the son of poor but honest parents in the State of Mississippi—boyhood friend of mine—bosom comrade in later years.
Heaven rest his noble spirit, he is gone from us now. John James
Godfrey was hired by the Hayblossom Mining Company in California to do some blasting for them—the 'Incorporated Company
of Mean Men,' the boys used to call it. Well, one day he drilled a
hole about four feet deep and put in an awful blast of powder, and

was standing over it ramming it down with an iron crowbar about nine foot long, when the cussed thing struck a spark and fired the powder, and scat! away John Godfrey whizzed like a sky-rocket, him and his crowbar! Well, sir, he kept on going up in the air higher and higher, till he didn't look any bigger than a boy—and he kept going on up higher and higher, till he didn't look any bigger than a doll—and he kept on going up higher and higher, till he didn't look any bigger than a little small bee—and then he went out of sight! Presently he came in sight again, looking like a little small bee— and he came along down further and further, till he looked as big as a doll again—and down further and further, till he was as big as a boy again—and further and further, till he was a full-sized man once more; and then him and his crowbar came a wh-izzing down and lit right exactly in the same old tracks and went to r-ramming down, and r-ramming down, and r-ramming down again, just the same as if nothing had happened! Now do you know, that poor cuss warn't gone only sixteen minutes, and yet that Incorporated Company of Mean Men DOCKED HIM FOR THE LOST TIME!"

LEAVING WORK.

I said I had the headache, and so excused myself and went home. And on my diary I entered "another night spoiled" by this offensive loafer. And a fervent curse was set down with it to keep the item company. And the very next day I packed up, out of all patience, and left the island.

Almost from the very beginning, I regarded that man as a liar.

. . . . .

The line of points represents an interval of years. At the end of which time the opinion hazarded in that last sentence came to be gratifyingly and remarkably endorsed, and by wholly disinterested persons. The man Markiss was found one morning hanging to a beam of his own bedroom (the doors and windows securely fastened on the inside), dead, and on his breast was pinned a paper in his own handwriting begging his friends to suspect no innocent person of having anything to do with his death, for that it was the work of his own hands entirely. Yet the jury brought in the astounding verdict that deceased came to his death "by the hands of some person or persons unknown!" They explained that the perfectly undeviating consistency of Markiss's character for thirty years towered aloft as colossal and indestructible testimony, that whatever statement he chose to make was entitled to instant and unquestioning acceptance as a *lie*. And they furthermore stated their belief that he was not dead, and instanced the strong circumstantial evidence of his own word that he *was* dead—and beseeched the coroner to delay the funeral as long as possible, which was done. And so in the tropical climate of Lahaina the coffin stood open for seven days, and then even the loyal jury gave him up. But they sat on him again, and changed their verdict to "suicide induced by mental aberration"—because, said they, with penetration, "he said he was dead, and he *was* dead; and would he have told the truth if he had been in his right mind? *No*, sir."

CHAPTER 78

AFTER half a year's luxurious vagrancy in the Islands, I took shipping in a sailing vessel, and regretfully returned to San Francisco—a voyage in every way delightful, but without an incident: unless lying two long weeks in a dead calm, eighteen hundred miles from the nearest land, may rank as an incident. Schools of whales grew so tame that day after day they played about the ship among the porpoises and the sharks without the least apparent fear of us, and we pelted them with empty bottles for lack of better sport. Twenty-four hours afterward these bottles would be still lying on the glassy water under our noses, showing that the ship had not moved out of her place in all that time. The calm was absolutely breathless, and the surface of the sea absolutely without a wrinkle. For a whole day and part of a night we lay so close to another ship that had drifted to our vicinity, that we carried on conversations with her passengers, introduced each other by name, and became pretty intimately acquainted with people we had never heard of before, and have never heard of since. This was the only vessel we saw during the whole lonely voyage. We had fifteen passengers, and to show how hard pressed they were at last for occupation and amusement, I will mention that the gentlemen gave a good part of their time every

OUR AMUSEMENTS.

day, during the calm, to trying to sit on an empty champagne bottle (lying on its side), and thread a needle without touching their heels to the deck, or falling over; and the ladies sat in the shade of the mainsail, and watched the enterprise with absorbing interest. We were at sea five Sundays; and yet, but for the almanac, we never would have known but that all the other days were Sundays too.

I was home again, in San Francisco, without means and without employment. I tortured my brain for a saving scheme of some kind, and at last a public lecture occurred to me! I sat down and wrote one, in a fever of hopeful anticipation. I showed it to several friends, but they all shook their heads. They said nobody would come to hear me, and I would make a humiliating failure of it. They said that as I had never spoken in public, I would break down in the delivery, anyhow. I was disconsolate now. But at last an editor slapped me on the back and told me to "go ahead." He said, "Take the largest house in town, and charge a dollar a ticket." The audacity of the proposition was charming; it seemed fraught with practical worldly wisdom, however. The proprietor of the several theatres endorsed the advice, and said I might have his handsome new opera-house at half price—fifty dollars. In sheer desperation I took it—on credit, for sufficient reasons. In three days I did a hundred and fifty dollars' worth of printing and advertising, and was the most distressed and frightened creature on the Pacific coast. I could not sleep—who could, under such circumstances? For other people there was facetiousness in the last line of my posters, but to me it was plaintive with a pang when I wrote it:

Doors open at 7½. The trouble will begin at 8.

That line has done good service since. Showmen have borrowed it frequently. I have even seen it appended to a newspaper advertisement reminding school pupils in vacation what time next term would begin. As those three days of suspense dragged by, I grew more and more unhappy. I had sold two hundred tickets among my personal friends, but I feared they might not come. My lecture, which had seemed "humorous" to me, at first, grew steadily more and more dreary, till not a vestige of fun seemed left, and I grieved that I could not bring a coffin on the stage and turn the thing into a funeral. I was so panic-stricken, at last, that I went to three old friends, giants in stature, cordial by nature, and stormy-voiced, and said:

"This thing is going to be a failure; the jokes in it are so dim that nobody will ever see them; I would like to have you sit in the parquette, and help me through."

They said they would. Then I went to the wife of a popular citizen, and said that if she was willing to do me a very great kindness, I would be glad if she and her husband would sit prominently in the left-hand stage-box, where the whole house could see them. I explained that I should need help, and would turn toward her and smile, as a signal, when I had been delivered of an obscure joke—"and then," I added, "don't wait to investigate, but *respond!*"

She promised. Down the street I met a man I never had seen before. He had been drinking, and was beaming with smiles and good nature. He said:

"My name's Sawyer. You don't know me, but that don't matter. I haven't got a cent, but if you knew how bad I wanted to laugh, you'd give me a ticket. Come, now, what do you say?"

"Is your laugh hung on a hair-trigger?—that is, is it critical, or can you get it off *easy?*"

My drawling infirmity of speech so affected him that he laughed a specimen or two that struck me as being about the article I wanted, and I gave him a ticket, and appointed him to sit in the second circle, in the centre, and be responsible for that division of the house. I gave him minute instructions about how to detect indistinct jokes, and then went away, and left him chuckling placidly over the novelty of the idea.

I ate nothing on the last of the three eventful days—I only suffered. I had advertised that on this third day the box-office would be opened for the sale of reserved seats. I crept down to the theatre at four in the afternoon to see if any sales had been made. The ticket seller was gone, the box-office was locked up. I had to swallow suddenly, or my heart would have got out. "No sales," I said to myself; "I might have known it." I thought of suicide, pretended illness, flight. I thought of these things in earnest, for I was very miserable and scared. But of course I had to drive them away, and prepare to meet my fate. I could not wait for half past seven—I wanted to face the horror, and end it—the feeling of many a man doomed to hang, no doubt. I went down back streets at six o'clock, and entered the theatre by the back door. I stumbled my way in the dark among the ranks of canvas scenery, and stood on the stage.

The house was gloomy and silent, and its emptiness depressing. I went into the dark among the scenes again, and for an hour and a half gave myself up to the horrors, wholly unconscious of every-

thing else. Then I heard a murmur; it rose higher and higher, and ended in a crash, mingled with cheers. It made my hair rise, it was so close to me, and so loud. There was a pause, and then another; presently came a third, and before I well knew what I was about, I was in the middle of the stage, staring at a sea of faces, bewildered by the fierce glare of the lights, and quaking in every limb with a terror that seemed like to take my life away. The house was full, aisles and all!

The tumult in my heart and brain and legs continued a full minute before I could gain any command over myself. Then I

SEVERE CASE OF STAGE-FRIGHT.

recognized the charity and the friendliness in the faces before me, and little by little my fright melted away, and I began to talk. Within three or four minutes I was comfortable, and even content. My three chief allies, with three auxiliaries, were on hand, in the parquette, all sitting to-

MY THREE PARQUETTE ALLIES.

gether, all armed with bludgeons, and all ready to make an on-
slaught upon the feeblest joke that might show its head. And
whenever a joke did fall, their bludgeons came down and their
faces seemed to split from ear to ear; Sawyer, whose hearty coun-

SAWYER IN THE CIRCLE.

tenance was seen looming redly
in the centre of the second circle, took it up, and the house
was carried handsomely. Inferior jokes never fared so royally
before. Presently I delivered a
bit of serious matter with impressive unction (it was my
pet), and the audience listened
with an absorbed hush that gratified me more than any applause; and as I dropped the last
word of the clause, I happened
to turn and catch Mrs. ——'s intent and waiting eye; my conversation with her flashed upon me, and in spite of all I could do I
smiled. She took it for the signal, and promptly delivered a mellow
laugh that touched off the whole audience; and the explosion that
followed was the triumph of the evening. I thought that that honest man Sawyer would choke himself; and as for the bludgeons,
they performed like pile-drivers. But my poor little morsel of pathos was ruined. It was taken in good faith as an intentional joke,
and the prize one of the entertainment, and I wisely let it go at
that.

All the papers were kind in the morning; my appetite returned;
I had abundance of money. All's well that ends well.

CHAPTER 79

I LAUNCHED out as a lecturer, now, with great boldness. I had the field all to myself, for public lectures were almost an unknown commodity in the Pacific market. They are not so rare, now, I suppose. I took an old personal friend along to play agent for me, and for two or three weeks we roamed through Nevada and California and had a very cheerful time of it. Two days before I lectured in Virginia City, two stage-coaches were robbed within two miles of the town. The daring act was committed just at dawn, by six masked men, who sprang up alongside the coaches, presented revolvers at the heads of the drivers and passengers, and commanded a general dismount. Everybody climbed down, and the robbers took their watches and every cent they had. Then they took gunpowder and blew up the express specie boxes and got their contents. The leader of the robbers was a small, quick-spoken man, and the fame of his vigorous manner and his intrepidity was in everybody's mouth when we arrived.

The night after instructing Virginia, I walked over the desolate "divide" and down to Gold Hill, and lectured there. The lecture done, I stopped to talk with a friend, and did not start back till eleven. The "divide" was high, unoccupied ground, between the towns, the scene of twenty midnight murders and a hundred robberies. As we climbed up and stepped out on this eminence, the Gold Hill lights dropped out of sight at our backs, and the night closed down gloomy and dismal. A sharp wind swept the place, too, and chilled our perspiring bodies through.

"I tell you I don't like this place at night," said Mike the agent.

"Well, don't speak so loud," I said. "You needn't remind anybody that we are here."

Just then a dim figure approached me from the direction of Virginia—a man, evidently. He came straight at me, and I stepped aside to let him pass; he stepped in the way and confronted me again. Then I saw that he had a mask on and was holding something in my face—I heard a click-click and recognized a revolver in dim outline. I pushed the barrel aside with my hand and said:

"Don't!"

He ejaculated sharply:

"Your watch! Your money!"

I said:

"You can have them with pleasure—but take the pistol away from my face, please. It makes me shiver."

"No remarks! Hand out your money!"

"Certainly—I—"

"Put up your hands! Don't you go for a weapon! Put 'em up! Higher!"

I held them above my head.

A pause. Then:

"Are you going to hand out your money or not?"

I dropped my hands to my pockets and said:

"Certainly! I—"

"Put up your *hands!* Do you want your head blown off? Higher!"

I put them above my head again.

Another pause.

"*Are* you going to hand out your money or *not?* Ah-ah—again? Put up your hands! By George, you want the head shot off you awful bad!"

"Well, friend, I'm trying my best to please you. You tell me to give up my money, and when I reach for it you tell me to put up my hands. If you would only—. Oh, now—don't! All six of you at me! That other man will get away while—. Now please take some of those revolvers out of my face—*do*, if you *please!* Every time one of them clicks, my liver comes up into my throat! If you have a mother—any of you—or if any of you have ever *had* a mother—or a—grandmother—or a—"

"Cheese it! *Will* you give up your money, or have we got to—. There-there—none of that! Put up your *hands!*"

"Gentlemen—I know you are gentlemen by your—"

"Silence! If you want to be facetious, young man, there are times and places more fitting. *This* is a serious business."

"You prick the marrow of my opinion. The funerals I have attended in my time were comedies compared to it. Now *I* think—"

"Curse your palaver! Your money!—your money!—your money! Hold!—put up your hands!"

"Gentlemen, listen to reason. You *see* how I am situated—now *don't* put those pistols so close—I smell the powder. You see how I am situated. If I had four hands—so that I could hold up two and—"

A PREDICAMENT.

"Throttle him! Gag him! Kill him!"

"Gentlemen, *don't!* Nobody's watching the other fellow. Why don't some of you—. Ouch! Take it away, please! Gentlemen, you see that I've got to hold up my hands; and so I can't take out my money—but if you'll be so kind as to take it out for me, I will do as much for you some—"

"Search him Beauregard—and stop his jaw with a bullet, quick, if he wags it again. Help Beauregard, Stonewall."

Then three of them, with the small, spry leader, adjourned to Mike and fell to searching him. I was so excited that my lawless fancy tortured me to ask my two men all manner of facetious questions about their rebel brother-generals of the South, but, considering the order they had received, it was but common prudence to keep still. When everything had been taken from me,—watch,

money, and a multitude of trifles of small value,—I supposed I was
free, and forthwith put my cold hands into my empty pockets and
began an inoffensive jig to warm my feet and stir up some latent
courage—but instantly all pistols were at my head, and the order
came again:

"Be still! Put up your hands! And *keep* them up!"

They stood Mike up alongside of me, with strict orders to keep
his hands above his head, too, and then the chief highwayman said:

"Beauregard, hide behind that boulder; Phil Sheridan, you hide
behind that other one; Stonewall Jackson, put yourself behind that
sage-bush there. Keep your pistols bearing on these fellows, and if
they take down their hands within ten minutes, or move a single
peg, let them have it!"

Then three disappeared in the gloom toward the several am-
bushes, and the other three disappeared down the road toward
Virginia.

It was depressingly still, and miserably cold. Now this whole
thing was a practical joke, and the robbers were personal friends of
ours in disguise, and twenty more lay hidden within ten feet of us
during the whole operation, listening. Mike knew all this, and was
in the joke, but I suspected nothing of it. To me it was most uncomfortably genuine.

When we had stood there in the middle of the road five minutes,
like a couple of idiots, with our hands aloft, freezing to death by
inches, Mike's interest in the joke began to wane. He said:

"The time's up, now, ain't it?"

"No, you keep still. Do you want to take any chances with those
bloody savages?"

Presently Mike said:

"*Now* the time's up, anyway. I'm freezing."

"Well freeze. Better freeze than carry your brains home in a basket. Maybe the time *is* up, but how do *we* know?—got no watch to
tell by. I mean to give them good measure. I calculate to stand here
fifteen minutes or die. Don't you move."

So, without knowing it, I was making one joker very sick of his
contract. When we took our arms down at last, they were aching
with cold and fatigue, and when we went sneaking off, the dread I
was in that the time might not yet be up and that we would feel

bullets in a moment, was not sufficient to draw all my attention from the misery that racked my stiffened body.

The joke of these highwayman friends of ours was mainly a joke upon themselves; for they had waited for me on the cold hill-top two full hours before I came, and there was very little fun in that; they were so chilled that it took them a couple of weeks to get warm again. Moreover, I never had a thought that they would kill me to get money which it was so perfectly easy to get without any such folly, and so they did not really frighten me bad enough to make their enjoyment worth the trouble they had taken. I was only afraid that their weapons would go off accidentally. Their very numbers inspired me with confidence that no blood would be intentionally spilled. They were not smart; they ought to have sent only *one* highwayman, with a double-barreled shotgun, if they desired to see the author of this volume climb a tree.

However, I suppose that in the long run I got the largest share of the joke at last; and in a shape not foreseen by the highwaymen; for

BEST PART OF THE JOKE.

the chilly exposure on the "divide" while I was in a perspiration gave me a cold which developed itself into a troublesome disease and kept my hands idle some three months, besides costing me quite a sum in doctor's bills. Since then I play no practical jokes on people and generally lose my temper when one is played upon me.

When I returned to San Francisco I projected a pleasure journey to Japan and thence westward around the world; but a desire to see home again changed my mind, and I took a berth in the steamship, bade good-bye to the friendliest land and livest, heartiest community on our continent, and came by the way of the Isthmus to New York—a trip that was not much of a pic-nic excursion, for the cholera broke out among us on the passage and we buried two or three bodies at sea every day. I found home a dreary place after my long absence; for half the children I had known were now wearing whiskers or waterfalls, and few of the grown people I had been acquainted with remained at their hearthstones prosperous and happy—some of them had wandered to other scenes, some were in jail, and the rest had been hanged. These changes touched me deeply, and I went away and joined the famous Quaker City European Excursion and carried my tears to foreign lands.

Thus, after seven years of vicissitudes, ended a "pleasure trip" to the silver mines of Nevada which had originally been intended to occupy only three months. However, I usually miss my calculations further than that.

MORAL.

If the reader thinks he is done, now, and that this book has no moral to it, he is in error. The moral of it is this: If you are of any account, stay at home and make your way by faithful diligence; but if you are "no account," go away from home, and then you will *have* to work, whether you want to or not. Thus you become a blessing to your friends by ceasing to be a nuisance to them—if the people you go among suffer by the operation.

APPENDIX A

BRIEF SKETCH OF MORMON HISTORY

MORMONISM is only about forty years old, but its career has been full of stir and adventure from the beginning, and is likely to remain so to the end. Its adherents have been hunted and hounded from one end of the country to the other, and the result is that for years they have hated all "Gentiles" indiscriminately and with all their might. Joseph Smith, the finder of the Book of Mormon and founder of the religion, was driven from State to State with his mysterious copperplates and the miraculous stones he read their inscriptions with. Finally he instituted his "church" in Ohio and Brigham Young joined it. The neighbors began to persecute, and apostasy commenced. Brigham held to the faith and worked hard. He arrested desertion. He did more—he added converts in the midst of the trouble. He rose in favor and importance with the brethren. He was made one of the Twelve Apostles of the church. He shortly fought his way to a higher post and a more powerful— President of the Twelve. The neighbors rose up and drove the Mormons out of Ohio, and they settled in Missouri. Brigham went with them. The Missourians drove them out and they retreated to Nauvoo, Illinois. They prospered there, and built a temple which made some pretensions to architectural grace and achieved some celebrity in a section of country where a brick court-house with a tin dome and a cupola on it was contemplated with reverential awe. But the Mormons were badgered and harried again by their neighbors. All the proclamations Joseph Smith could issue denouncing polygamy and repudiating it as utterly anti-Mormon were of no avail; the people of the neighborhood, on both sides of the Mississippi, claimed that polygamy was practiced by the Mormons, and not only polygamy but a little of everything that was

bad. Brigham returned from a mission to England, where he had
established a Mormon newspaper, and he brought back with him
several hundred converts to his preaching. His influence among
the brethren augmented with every move he made. Finally Nauvoo was invaded by the Missouri and Illinois Gentiles, and Joseph
Smith killed. A Mormon named Rigdon assumed the Presidency
of the Mormon church and government, in Smith's place, and even
tried his hand at a prophecy or two. But a greater than he was at
hand. Brigham seized the advantage of the hour and without other
authority than superior brain and nerve and will, hurled Rigdon
from his high place and occupied it himself. He did more. He
launched an elaborate curse at Rigdon and his disciples; and he
pronounced Rigdon's "prophecies" emanations from the devil, and
ended by "handing the false prophet over to the buffetings of Satan
for a thousand years"—probably the longest term ever inflicted in
Illinois. The people recognized their master. They straightway
elected Brigham Young President, by a prodigious majority, and
have never faltered in their devotion to him from that day to this.
Brigham had forecast—a quality which no other prominent Mormon has probably ever possessed. He recognized that it was better
to move to the wilderness than *be* moved. By his command the
people gathered together their meagre effects, turned their backs
upon their homes, and their faces toward the wilderness, and on a
bitter night in February filed in sorrowful procession across the
frozen Mississippi, lighted on their way by the glare from their
burning temple, whose sacred furniture their own hands had fired!
They camped, several days afterward, on the western verge of
Iowa, and poverty, want, hunger, cold, sickness, grief and persecution did their work, and many succumbed and died—martyrs, fair
and true, whatever else they might have been. Two years the remnant remained there, while Brigham and a small party crossed the
country and founded Great Salt Lake City, purposely choosing a
land which was *outside the ownership and jurisdiction of the
hated American nation.* Note that. This was in 1847. Brigham
moved his people there and got them settled just in time to see disaster fall again. For the war closed and Mexico ceded Brigham's
refuge to the enemy—the United States! In 1849 the Mormons organized a "free and independent" government and erected the

"State of Deseret," with Brigham Young as its head. But the very
next year Congress deliberately snubbed it and created the "Territory of Utah" out of the same accumulation of mountains, sage-
brush, alkali and general desolation,—but made Brigham Governor of it. Then for years the enormous migration across the plains
to California poured through the land of the Mormons and yet the
church remained staunch and true to its lord and master. Neither
hunger, thirst, poverty, grief, hatred, contempt, nor persecution
could drive the Mormons from their faith or their allegiance; and
even the thirst for gold, which gleaned the flower of the youth and
strength of many nations, was not able to entice them! That was
the final test. An experiment that could survive that was an experiment with some substance to it somewhere.

Great Salt Lake City throve finely, and so did Utah. One of the
last things which Brigham Young had done before leaving Iowa,
was to appear in the pulpit dressed to personate the worshipped
and lamented prophet Smith, and confer the prophetic succession,
with all its dignities, emoluments and authorities, upon "President Brigham Young!" The people accepted the pious fraud with
the maddest enthusiasm, and Brigham's power was sealed and secured for all time. Within five years afterward he openly added polygamy to the tenets of the church by authority of a "revelation"
which he pretended had been received nine years before by Joseph
Smith, albeit Joseph is amply on record as denouncing polygamy
to the day of his death.

Now was Brigham become a second Andrew Johnson in the
small beginning and steady progress of his official grandeur. He
had served successively as a disciple in the ranks; home missionary; foreign missionary; editor and publisher; Apostle; President
of the Board of Apostles; President of all Mormondom, civil and
ecclesiastical; successor to the great Joseph by the will of heaven;
"prophet," "seer," "revelator." There was but one dignity higher
which he *could* aspire to, and he reached out modestly and took
that—he proclaimed himself a God!

He claims that he is to have a heaven of his own hereafter, and
that he will be its God, and his wives and children its goddesses,
princes and princesses. Into it all faithful Mormons will be admitted, with their families, and will take rank and consequence ac-

cording to the number of their wives and children. If a disciple dies
before he has had time to accumulate enough wives and children
to enable him to be respectable in the next world any friend can
marry a few wives and raise a few children for him *after he is dead*,
and they are duly credited to his account and his heavenly status
advanced accordingly.

Let it be borne in mind that the majority of the Mormons have
always been ignorant, simple, of an inferior order of intellect, unacquainted with the world and its ways; and let it be borne in mind
that the wives of these Mormons are necessarily after the same
pattern and their children likely to be fit representatives of such a
conjunction; and then let it be remembered that *for forty years*
these creatures have been driven, driven, driven, relentlessly! and
mobbed, beaten, and shot down; cursed, despised, expatriated;
banished to a remote desert, whither they journeyed gaunt with
famine and disease, disturbing the ancient solitudes with their
lamentations and marking the long way with graves of their
dead—and all because they were simply trying to live and worship
God in the way which *they* believed with all their hearts and souls
to be the true one. Let all these things be borne in mind, and then
it will not be hard to account for the deathless hatred which the
Mormons bear our people and our government.

That hatred has "fed fat its ancient grudge" ever since Mormon
Utah developed into a self-supporting realm and the church waxed
rich and strong. Brigham as Territorial Governor made it plain
that Mormondom was for the Mormons. The United States tried
to rectify all that by appointing Territorial officers from New England and other anti-Mormon localities, but Brigham prepared to
make their entrance into his dominions difficult. Three thousand
U. S. troops had to go across the plains and put these gentlemen in
office. And after they were in office they were as helpless as so
many stone images. They made laws which nobody minded and
which could not be executed. The Federal judges opened court in a
land filled with crime and violence and sat as holiday spectacles for
insolent crowds to gape at—for there was nothing to try, nothing
to do, nothing on the dockets! And if a Gentile brought a suit, the
Mormon jury would do just as it pleased about bringing in a verdict, and when the judgment of the court was rendered no Mormon

cared for it and no officer could execute it. Our Presidents shipped one cargo of officials after another to Utah, but the result was always the same—they sat in a blight for a while, they fairly feasted on scowls and insults day by day, they saw every attempt to do their official duties find its reward in darker and darker looks, and in secret threats and warnings of a more and more dismal nature—and at last they either succumbed and became despised tools and toys of the Mormons, or got scared and discomforted beyond all endurance and left the Territory. If a brave officer kept on courageously till his pluck was proven, some pliant Buchanan or Pierce would remove him and appoint a stick in his place. In 1857 Gen. Harney came very near being appointed Governor of Utah. And so it came very near being Harney Governor and Cradlebaugh Judge!—two men who never had any idea of fear further than the sort of murky comprehension of it which they were enabled to gather from the dictionary. Simply (if for nothing else) for the variety they would have made in a rather monotonous history of Federal servility and helplessness, it is a pity they were not fated to hold office together in Utah.

Up to the date of our visit to Utah, such had been the Territorial record. The Territorial government established there had been a hopeless failure, and Brigham Young was the only real power in the land. He was an absolute monarch—a monarch who defied our President—a monarch who laughed at our armies when they camped about his capital—a monarch who received without emotion the news that the august Congress of the United States had enacted a solemn law against polygamy, and then went forth calmly and married twenty-five or thirty more wives.

APPENDIX B

THE MOUNTAIN MEADOWS MASSACRE

THE persecutions which the Mormons suffered so long—and which they consider they still suffer in not being allowed to govern themselves—they have endeavored and are still endeavoring to repay. The now almost forgotten "Mountain Meadows massacre" was their work. It was very famous in its day. The whole United States rang with its horrors. A few items will refresh the reader's memory. A great emigrant train from Missouri and Arkansas passed through Salt Lake City and a few disaffected Mormons joined it for the sake of the strong protection it afforded for their escape. In that matter lay sufficient cause for hot retaliation by the Mormon chiefs. Besides, these one hundred and forty-five or one hundred and fifty unsuspecting emigrants being in part from Arkansas, where a noted Mormon missionary had lately been killed, and in part from Missouri, a State remembered with execrations as a bitter persecutor of the saints when they were few and poor and friendless, here were substantial additional grounds for lack of love for these wayfarers. And finally, this train was rich, very rich in cattle, horses, mules and other property—and how could the Mormons consistently keep up their coveted resemblance to the Israelitish tribes and not seize the "spoil" of an enemy when the Lord had so manifestly "delivered it into their hand?"

Wherefore, according to Mrs. C. V. Waite's entertaining book, "The Mormon Prophet," it transpired that—

A "revelation" from Brigham Young, as Great Grand Archee, or God, was despatched to President J. C. Haight, Bishop Higbee, and J. D. Lee (adopted son of Brigham), commanding them to raise all the forces they could muster and trust, follow those cursed gentiles (so read the revelation), attack them, disguised as Indians, and with the arrows of the Almighty make a clean sweep of them, and leave none to tell the tale; and if they needed any assistance, they were commanded to hire the Indians as their allies, promising them a share of the booty. They were to be neither slothful nor negligent in their duty, and to be punctual in sending the teams back to him before winter set in, for this was the mandate of Almighty God.

The command of the "revelation" was faithfully obeyed. A large party of Mormons, painted and tricked out as Indians, overtook the train of emigrant wagons some three hundred miles south of Salt Lake City, and made an attack. But the emigrants threw up earthworks, made fortresses of their wagons and defended themselves gallantly and successfully for five days! Your Missouri or Arkansas gentleman is not much afraid of the sort of scurvy apologies for "Indians" which the southern part of Utah affords. He would stand up and fight five hundred of them.

At the end of the five days the Mormons tried military strategy. They retired to the upper end of the "Meadows," resumed civilized apparel, washed off their paint, and then, heavily armed, drove down in wagons to the beleaguered emigrants, bearing a flag of truce! When the emigrants saw white men coming they threw down their guns and welcomed them with cheer after cheer! And, all unconscious of the poetry of it, no doubt, they lifted a little child aloft, dressed in white, in answer to the flag of truce!

The leaders of the timely white "deliverers" were President Haight and Bishop John D. Lee, of the Mormon church. Mr. Cradlebaugh, who served a term as a Federal Judge in Utah and afterward was sent to Congress from Nevada, tells in a speech delivered in Congress how these leaders next proceeded:

They professed to be on good terms with the Indians, and represented them as being very mad. They also proposed to intercede, and settle the matter with the Indians. After several hours of parley, they, having (apparently) visited the Indians, gave the *ultimatum* of the savages; which was, that the emigrants should march out of their camp, leaving everything behind them, even their guns. It was promised by the Mormon bishops that they would bring a force, and guard the emigrants back to the settlements.

The terms were agreed to,—the emigrants being desirous of saving the lives of their families. The Mormons retired, and subsequently appeared with thirty or forty armed men. The emigrants were marched out, the women and children in front, and the men behind, the Mormon guard being in the rear. When they had marched in this way about a mile, at a given signal, the slaughter commenced. The men were almost all shot down at the first fire from the guard. Two only escaped, who fled to the desert, and were followed 150 miles before they were overtaken and slaughtered.

The women and children ran on, two or three hundred yards further, when they were overtaken, and with the aid of the Indians they were slaughtered. Seventeen individuals only, of all the emigrant party, were spared, and they were little children, the eldest of them being only seven years old. Thus, on the 10th day of September, 1857, was consummated one of the most cruel, cowardly, and bloody murders known in our history.

The number of persons butchered by the Mormons on this occasion was *one hundred and twenty.*

With unheard-of temerity Judge Cradlebaugh opened his court and proceeded to make Mormondom answer for the massacre. And what a spectacle it must have been to see this grim veteran, solitary and alone in his pride and his pluck, glowering down on his Mormon jury and Mormon auditory, deriding them by turns, and by turns "breathing threatenings and slaughter!"

An editorial in the *Territorial Enterprise* of that day says of him and of the occasion:

He spoke and acted with the fearlessness and resolution of a Jackson; but the jury failed to indict, or even report on the charges, while threats of violence were heard in every quarter, and an attack on the U. S. troops intimated, if he persisted in his course.

Finding that nothing could be done with the juries, they were discharged, with a scathing rebuke from the Judge. And then, sitting as a committing magistrate, *he commenced his task alone.* He examined witnesses, made arrests in every quarter, and created a consternation in the camps of the saints, greater than any they had ever witnessed before, since Mormondom was born. At last accounts, terrified elders and bishops were decamping to save their necks; and developments of the most startling character were being made, implicating the highest church dignitaries in the many murders and robberies committed upon the gentiles during the past eight years.

Had Harney been Governor, Cradlebaugh would have been supported in his work, and the absolute proofs adduced by him of Mormon guilt in this massacre and in a number of previous murders, would have conferred gratuitous coffins upon certain citizens, together with occasion to use them. But Cumming was the Federal

Governor, and he, under a curious pretense of impartiality, sought to screen the Mormons from the demands of justice. On one occasion he even went so far as to publish his protest against the use of the U. S. troops in aid of Cradlebaugh's proceedings.

Mrs. C. V. Waite closes her interesting detail of the great massacre with the following remark and accompanying summary of the testimony—and the summary is concise, accurate and reliable:

For the benefit of those who may still be disposed to doubt the guilt of Young and his Mormons in this transaction, the testimony is here collated, and circumstances given, which go, not merely to implicate, but to fasten conviction upon them, by "confirmations strong as proofs of Holy Writ."

1. The evidence of Mormons themselves, engaged in the affair, as shown by the statements of Judge Cradlebaugh and Deputy U. S. Marshal Rogers.

2. The failure of Brigham Young to embody any account of it in his Report as Superintendent of Indian Affairs. Also his failure to make any allusion to it whatever from the pulpit, until several years after the occurrence.

3. The flight to the mountains of men high in authority in the Mormon Church and State, when this affair was brought to the ordeal of a judicial investigation.

4. The failure of the "Deseret News," the Church organ, and the only paper then published in the Territory, to notice the massacre, until several months afterward, and then only to deny that Mormons were engaged in it.

5. The testimony of the children saved from the massacre.

6. The children and the property of the emigrants found in possession of the Mormons, and that possession traced back to the very day after the massacre.

7. The statements of Indians in the neighborhood of the scene of the massacre: these statements are shown, not only by Cradlebaugh and Rogers, but by a number of military officers, and by J. Forney, who was, in 1859, Superintendent of Indian Affairs for the Territory. To all these were such statements freely and frequently made by the Indians.

8. The testimony of R. P. Campbell, Capt. 2d Dragoons, who was sent in the spring of 1859 to Santa Clara, to protect travellers on the road to California, and to inquire into Indian depredations.

APPENDIX C

CONCERNING A FRIGHTFUL ASSASSINATION
THAT WAS NEVER CONSUMMATED

[IF ever there was a harmless man, it is Conrad Wiegand, of Gold Hill, Nevada. If ever there was a gentle spirit that thought itself unfired gunpowder and latent ruin, it is Conrad Wiegand. If ever there was an oyster that fancied itself a whale; or a jack-o'lantern, confined to a swamp, that fancied itself a planet with a billion-mile orbit; or a summer zephyr that deemed itself a hurricane, it is Conrad Wiegand. Therefore, what wonder is it that when he says a thing, he thinks the world listens; that when he does a thing the world stands still to look; and that when he suffers, there is a convulsion of nature? When I met Conrad, he was "Superintendent of the Gold Hill Assay Office"—and he was not only its Superintendent, but its entire force. And he was a street preacher, too, with a mongrel religion of his own invention, whereby he expected to regenerate the universe. This was years ago. Here latterly he has entered journalism; and his journalism is what it might be expected to be: colossal to ear, but pigmy to the eye. It is extravagant grandiloquence confined to a newspaper about the size of a double letter sheet. He doubtless edits, sets the type, and prints his paper, all alone; but he delights to speak of the concern as if it occupies a block and employs a thousand men.

[Something less than two years ago, Conrad assailed several people mercilessly in his little "People's Tribune," and got himself into trouble. Straightway he airs the affair in the *Territorial Enterprise*, in a communication over his own signature, and I propose to reproduce it here, in all its native simplicity and more than human candor. Long as it is, it is well worth reading, for it is the richest specimen of journalistic literature the history of America can furnish, perhaps:]

From the Territorial Enterprise, Jan. 20, 1870.
A SEEMING PLOT FOR ASSASSINATION MISCARRIED.

TO THE EDITOR OF THE ENTERPRISE,

Months ago, when Mr. Sutro incidentally exposed mining mismanagement on the Comstock, and among others roused me to protest against its continuance, in great kindness you warned me that any attempt by publications, by public meetings and by legislative action, aimed at the correction of chronic mining evils in Storey County, must entail upon me (a) business ruin, (b) the burden of all its costs, (c) personal violence, and if my purpose were persisted in, then (d) assassination; and after all nothing would be effected.

YOUR PROPHECY FULFILLING.

In large part at least your prophecies have been fulfilled, for (a) assaying, which was well attended to in the Gold Hill Assay Office (of which I am superintendent), in consequence of my publications has been taken elsewhere, so the President of one of the companies assures me. With no reason *assigned*, other work has been taken away. With but one or two important exceptions, our assay business now consists simply of the *gleanings* of the vicinity. (b) Though my own personal donations to the People's Tribune Association have already exceeded $1,500, outside of our own numbers we have received (in money) less than $300 as contributions and subscriptions for the journal. (c) On Thursday last, on the main street in Gold Hill, near noon, with neither warning nor cause assigned, by a powerful blow I was felled to the ground, and while down I was kicked by a man who it would seem had been led to *believe* that I had spoken derogatorily of him. By whom he was so induced to believe I am as yet unable to say. On Saturday last I was again assailed and beaten by a man who first informed me why he did so, and who persisted in making his assault even after the erroneous impression under which he *also* was at first laboring had been clearly and repeatedly pointed out. This same man, after failing through intimidation to elicit from me the names of our editorial contributors, against giving which he knew me to be pledged, beat himself weary upon me with a rawhide, I not resisting, and then pantingly threatened me with permanent disfiguring mayhem, if ever again I should introduce his name into print, and who but a few minutes before his attack upon me assured me that the only reason I was "permitted" to reach home alive on Wednesday evening last (at which time the *People's Tribune* was issued) was, that he deems me only half-witted, and be it remembered the very next morning I *was* knocked down and kicked by a man who seemed to be *prepared* for flight.

[*He sees doom impending:*]

WHEN WILL THE CIRCLE JOIN?

How long before the *whole* of your prophecy will be fulfilled I cannot say, but under the shadow of so much fulfillment in so short a time, and with such direct threats from a man who is one of the most prominent exponents of the San Francisco mining Ring staring me and this whole community boldly and defiantly in the face and *pointing* to a completion of your augury, do you blame me for feeling that this communication is the last I shall ever write for the Press, especially when a sense alike of personal self-respect, of duty to this money-oppressed and fear-ridden community, and of American fealty to the spirit of true Liberty all command me, and each more loudly than love of life itself, to declare the name of that prominent man to be JOHN B. WINTERS, President of the Yellow Jacket Company, a political aspirant and a military General. The name of his partially duped accomplice and abettor in this last marvelous assault, is no other than PHILIP LYNCH, Editor and proprietor of the Gold Hill *News*.

Despite of the insult and wrong heaped upon me by John B. Winters, on Saturday afternoon, only a glimpse of which I shall be able to afford your readers, so much do I deplore clinching (by publicity) a serious mistake of any one, man or woman, committed under natural and not self-wrought passion, in view of his great apparent excitement at the time and in view of the almost perfect privacy of the assault, I am far from sure that I should not have given him space for repentance before exposing him, were it not that he himself has so far exposed the matter as to make it the common talk of the town that he has horsewhipped me. That fact having been made public, all the facts in connection need to be also, or silence on my part would seem *more* than singular, and with many would be proof either that I was conscious of some unworthy aim in publishing the article, or else that my "non-combatant" principles are but a convenient cloak alike of physical and moral cowardice. I therefore shall try to present a graphic but truthful picture of this whole affair, but shall forbear all comments, presuming that the editors of our own journal, if others do not, will speak freely and fittingly upon this subject in our next number, whether I shall then be dead or living, for my death will not stop, though it may suspend, the publication of the *People's Tribune*.

[*The "non-combatant" sticks to principle, but takes along a friend or two of a conveniently different stripe:*]

THE TRAP SET.

On Saturday morning John B. Winters sent verbal word to the Gold Hill Assay Office that he desired to see me at the Yellow Jacket office. Though such a request struck me as decidedly cool in view of his own recent discourtesies to me there alike as a publisher and as a stockholder in the Yellow Jacket mine, and though it seemed to me more like a summons than the courteous request by one gentleman to another for a favor, hoping that some conference with Sharon looking to the betterment of mining matters in Nevada might arise from it, I felt strongly inclined to overlook what *possibly* was simply an oversight in courtesy. But as then it had only been two days since I had been bruised and beaten under a hasty and false apprehension of facts, my caution was somewhat aroused. Moreover I remembered sensitively his contemptuousness of manner to me at my last interview in his office. I therefore felt it needful, if I went at all, to go accompanied by a friend whom he would not dare to treat with incivility, and whose presence with me might secure me exemption from insult. Accordingly I asked a neighbor to accompany me.

THE TRAP ALMOST DETECTED.

Although I was not then aware of this fact, it would seem that previous to my request this same neighbor had heard Dr. Zabriskie state publicly in a saloon, that Mr. Winters had told him he had decided either to kill or to horsewhip me, but had not finally decided on which. My neighbor, therefore, felt unwilling to go down with me until he had *first* called on Mr. Winters alone. He therefore paid him a visit. From that interview he assured me that he gathered the impression that he did not believe I would have any difficulty with Mr. Winters, and that he (Winters) would call on me at 4 o'clock in my own office.

MY OWN PRECAUTIONS.

As Sheriff Cummings was in Gold Hill that afternoon, and as I desired to converse with him about the previous assault, I invited him to my office, and he came. Although a half-hour had passed beyond 4 o'clock, Mr. Winters had not called, and we both of us began preparing to go home. Just then, Philip Lynch, Publisher of the Gold Hill *News*, came in and said, blandly and cheerily, as if bringing good news:

"Hello, John B. Winters wants to see you."

I replied, "Indeed! Why he sent me word that he would call on me *here* this afternoon at 4 o'clock!"

"O, well, it don't do to be too ceremonious just now, he's in my office, and that will do as well—come on in, Winters wants to consult with you alone. He's got something to say to you."

Though slightly uneasy at this change of programme, yet believing that in an *editor's* house I ought to be safe, and anyhow that I would be within hail of the street, I hurriedly, and but partially whispered my dim apprehensions to Mr. Cummings, and asked him if he would not keep near enough to hear my voice in case I should call. He consented to do so while waiting for some other parties, and to come in if he heard my voice or thought I had need of protection.

On reaching the editorial part of the *News* office, which viewed from the street is dark, I did not see Mr. Winters, and again my misgivings arose. Had I paused long enough to consider the case, I should have invited Sheriff Cummings in, but as Lynch went down stairs, he said: "*This* way, Wiegand—it's best to be private," or some such remark.

[*I do not desire to strain the reader's fancy, hurtfully, and yet it would be a favor to me if he would try to fancy this lamb in battle, or the duelling ground or at the head of a vigilance committee— M. T.:*]

I followed, and *without* Mr. Cummings, and without arms, which I never do or will carry, unless as a soldier in war, or unless I should yet come to feel I must fight a duel, or to join and aid in the ranks of a *necessary* Vigilance Committee. But by following I made a fatal mistake. Following was entering a trap, and whatever animal suffers itself to be *caught* should expect the common fate of a caged rat, as I fear events to come will prove.

Traps commonly are not set for *benevolence.*

[*His body-guard is shut out:*]

THE TRAP INSIDE.

I followed Lynch down stairs. At their foot a door to the left opened into a small room. From *that* room another door opened into yet *another* room, and once entered I found myself inveigled into what many will ever henceforth regard as a private subterranean Gold Hill den, admirably adapted in proper hands to the purposes of murder, raw or disguised, for from it with both or even one door closed, when too late, I saw that I *could* not be heard by Sheriff Cummings, and from it, BY VIOLENCE AND BY FORCE, I was prevented from making a peaceable exit, when I thought I saw the studious object of this "consultation" was no other than to compass my killing, *in the presence of Philip Lynch as a witness,* as soon as by insult a proverbially excitable man should be exasperated to the point of assailing Mr. Winters, so that Mr. Lynch, by his conscience and by his well known tenderness of heart toward the rich and potent would be *compelled* to testify that he saw Gen. John B. Winters kill Conrad Wiegand in "self-defense." But I am going too fast.

OUR HOST.

Mr. Lynch was present during most of the time (say a little short of an hour,) but three times he left the room. His testimony, therefore, would be available only as to the bulk of what transpired. On entering this carpeted den I was invited to a seat near one corner of the room. Mr. Lynch took a seat near the window. J. B. Winters sat (at first) near the door, and began his remarks essentially as follows:

"I have come here to exact of you a retraction, in black and white, of those damnably false charges which you have preferred against me in that —— —— infamous lying sheet of yours, and you must declare yourself their author; that you published them knowing them to be false, and that your motives were malicious."

"Hold, Mr. Winters. Your language is insulting and your demand an enormity. I trust I was not invited here either to be insulted or coerced. I supposed myself here by invitation of Mr. Lynch, at your request."

"Nor did I come here to insult you. I have already told you that I am here for a very different purpose."

"Yet your language *has* been offensive, and even now shows strong excitement. If insult is repeated I shall either leave the room or call in Sheriff Cummings, whom I just left standing and waiting for me outside the door."

"No, you won't, sir. You may just as well understand it at once as not. *Here* you are my man, and I'll tell you why! Months ago you put your property out of your hands, boasting that you did so to escape losing it on prosecution for libel."

"It is true that I did convert all my immovable property into personal property, such as I could trust safely to others, and chiefly to escape ruin through possible libel suits."

"Very good, sir. Having placed yourself beyond the pale of the law, *may God help your soul* if you DON'T make precisely such a retraction as I have demanded. I've got you now, and by ——, before you can get out of this room you've *got* to both write and sign precisely the retraction I have demanded, and before you go, anyhow—you —— —— low-lived —— lying —— ——, I'll teach you what *personal* responsibility is *outside* of the law; and, by ——, Sheriff Cummings and all the friends you've got in the world, besides, can't save you, you —— ——, etc.! *No,* sir. I'm *alone* now, and I'm *prepared* to be shot down just here and now rather than be vilified by you as I have been, and suffer you to escape me after publishing those charges, not only here where I am known and universally respected, but where I am *not* personally known and may be injured."

I confess this speech, with its terrible and but too plainly *implied* threat of killing me if I did not sign the paper he demanded, terrified me, especially as I saw he was working himself up to the highest possible pitch of passion, and instinct told me that *any* reply other than one of seeming concession to his demands would only be fuel to a raging fire, so I replied:

"Well, if I've *got* to sign ——," and then I paused some time. Resuming, I said, "But, Mr. Winters, you are greatly excited. Besides, I see you are laboring under a total misapprehension. It is your duty not to inflame but to calm yourself. I am prepared to show you, if you will only point out the article that you allude to, that *you* regard as 'charges' what no calm and logical mind has any *right* to regard as such. *Show* me the charges, and I will try, at all events; and if it becomes plain that no charges *have* been preferred, then plainly there can be nothing to retract, and no one could rightly *urge* you to demand a retraction. You should beware of making so serious a mistake, for however *honest* a man may be, every one is liable to misapprehend.

"Besides you *assume* that I am the author of some certain article which you have not pointed out. It is *hasty* to do so."

He then pointed to some numbered paragraphs in a *Tribune* article, headed "What's the Matter with Yellow Jacket?" saying *"That's* what I refer to."

To gain time for general reflection and resolution, I took up the paper and looked it over for a while, he remaining silent, and as I hoped, cooling. I then resumed, saying, "As I supposed. I do not *admit* having written that article, nor have you any right to *assume* so important a point, and then base important action upon your assumption. You might deeply regret it afterwards. In my published Address to the People, I notified the world that no information as to the authorship of any article would be given without the consent of the writer. I therefore cannot honorably tell you *who* wrote that article, nor can you exact it."

"If you are *not* the author, then I *do* demand to know who is?"

"I must decline to say."

"Then by ——, I brand *you* as its author, and shall treat you accordingly."

"Passing that point, the most important misapprehension which I notice is, that you regard them as 'charges' at all, when their context, both at their beginning and end, show they are not. These words introduce them: '*Such an investigation* [just before indicated,] *we think MIGHT result in showing some of the following points.*' Then follow eleven specifications, and the succeeding paragraph shows that the suggested investigation 'might EXONERATE those who are generally believed guilty.' You see, therefore, the context *proves* they are not preferred *as* charges, and this you seem to have overlooked."

While making those comments, Mr. Winters frequently interrupted me in such a way as to convince me that he was *resolved* not to consider candidly the thoughts contained in my words. He insisted upon it that they *were* charges, and "By ——," he would make me take them back *as* charges, and he referred the question to Philip Lynch, to whom I then appealed as a literary man, as a logician, and as an editor, calling his attention especially to the introductory paragraph just before quoted.

He replied, "If they are *not* charges, they certainly are *insinuations*," whereupon Mr. Winters renewed his demands for retraction precisely such as he had before named, except that he would allow me to state who *did* write the article if I did not myself, and this time shaking his fist in my face with more cursings and epithets.

When he threatened me with his clenched fist, instinctively I tried to rise from my chair, but Winters then forcibly thrust me down, as he did every other time (at least seven or eight,) when under similar imminent danger of bruising by his fist, (or for aught I could know worse than that after the first stunning blow,) which he could easily and safely to himself have dealt me so long as he kept me down and stood over me.

This fact it was, which more than anything else, convinced me that by plan and plot I was purposely made powerless in Mr. Winters' hands, and that he did not mean to allow me that advantage of being afoot which he possessed. Moreover, I then became convinced that Philip Lynch (and for what *reason* I wondered,) would do absolutely nothing to protect me in his own house. I realized then the situation thoroughly. I had found it equally vain to protest or argue, and I would make no unmanly appeal for pity, still less apologize. Yet my life had been by the plainest possible implication threatened. I was a weak man. I was unarmed. I was helplessly down, and Winters was afoot and probably armed. Lynch was the only "witness." The statements demanded, if given and not explained, would utterly sink me in my own self-respect, in my family's eyes, and in the eyes of the community. On the other hand, should I give the author's name how could I ever expect that confidence of the People which I should no longer deserve, and how much dearer to me and to my family was *my* life than the life of the real author to *his* friends. Yet life seemed dear and each minute that remained seemed precious if not solemn. I sincerely trust that neither you nor any of your readers, and especially none with families, may ever be placed in such seeming *direct* proximity to death while obliged to decide the one question I was compelled to, viz: What should I do—I, a man of family, and *not* as Mr. Winters is, "alone."

[*The reader is requested not to skip the following.*—M. T.:]

STRATEGY AND MESMERISM.

To gain time for further reflection, and hoping that by a *seeming* acquiescence I might regain my personal liberty, at least till I could give an alarm, or take advantage of some momentary inadvertence of Winters, and then without a *cowardly* flight escape, I resolved to write a certain kind of retraction, but previously had inwardly decided

First. That I would studiously avoid every action which might be *construed* into the drawing of a weapon, even by a self-infuriated man, no matter what amount of insult might be heaped upon me, for it seemed to me that this great excess of compound profanity, foulness and epithet must be more than a mere indulgence, and therefore must have some object. "Surely in vain the net is spread in the sight of any bird." Therefore, as before without thought, I thereafter by intent kept my hands away from my pockets, and generally in sight and spread upon my knees.

Second. I resolved to make no motion with my arms or hands which could possibly be construed into aggression.

Third. I resolved completely to govern my outward manner and suppress indignation. To do this, I must govern my spirit. To do that, by force of imagination I was obliged like actors on the boards to resolve myself into an unnatural mental state and see all things through the eyes of an assumed *character*.

Fourth. I resolved to try on Winters, silently, and unconsciously to himself a mesmeric power which I possess over certain kinds of people, and which at times I have found to work even in the dark over even the lower animals.

Does any one smile at these last counts? God save you from ever being *obliged* to beat in a game of chess, whose stake is your life, you having but four poor pawns and pieces and your adversary with his full force unshorn. But if you do, provided you have any strength with breadth of will, do not despair. Though mesmeric power may not *save* you it may help you; *try* it at all events. In this instance I was conscious of power coming into me, and by a law of nature, I know Winters was correspondingly weakened. If I could have gained more time I am sure he would not even have struck me.

It takes time both to form such resolutions and to recite them. That time, however, I gained while thinking of my retraction, which I first wrote in pencil, altering it from time to time till I got it to suit me, my aim being to make it look like a concession to demands, while in fact it should tersely speak the truth into Mr. Winters' mind. When it was finished, I copied it in ink, and if correctly copied from my first draft it should read as follows. In copying I do not think I made any material change:

COPY.

To PHILIP LYNCH, EDITOR OF THE GOLD HILL NEWS:

I learn that Gen. John B. Winters believes the following (pasted on) clipping from the *People's Tribune* of January to contain distinct charges of mine against him personally, and that as such he desires me to retract them unqualifiedly.

In compliance with his request, permit me to say that, although Mr. Winters and I see this matter differently, in view of his strong feelings in the premises, I hereby declare that I do not know those "charges" (if such they are) to be true, and I hope that a critical examination would altogether disprove them.

CONRAD WIEGAND.

Gold Hill, January 15, 1870.

I then read what I had written and handed it to Mr. Lynch, whereupon Mr. Winters said:

"That's not satisfactory, and it won't do;" and then addressing himself to Mr. Lynch, he further said: "How does it strike *you*?"

"Well, I confess I don't see that it *retracts* anything."

"Nor do I," said Winters; "In fact, I regard it as adding insult to injury. Mr. Wiegand, you've got to do better than that. *You* are not the man who can pull wool over *my* eyes."

"That, sir, is the only retraction I can write."

"No it isn't, sir, and if you so much as *say* so again you do it at your peril, for I'll thrash you to within an inch of your life, and by ——, sir, I don't pledge myself to spare you even that inch either. I want you to understand I have asked you for a very different paper, and that paper you've got to sign."

"Mr. Winters, I assure you that I *do* not wish to irritate you, but, at the same time, it is utterly *impossible* for me to write any other paper than that which I have written. If you are resolved to *compel* me to *sign* something, Philip Lynch's hand must write it at your dictation, and if, when written, I *can* sign it I will do so, but such a document as you say you *must* have from me I never can sign. I mean what I say."

"Well, sir, what's to be done must be done quickly, for I've been here long enough already. I'll put the thing in another shape (and then pointing to the paper;) Don't you know those charges are false?"

"I do not."

"Do you know them to be true?"

"Of my own personal knowledge I do not."

"Why then print them?"

"Because rightly considered in their connection they are *not* charges, but pertinent and useful *suggestions* in answer to the queries of a correspondent who stated facts which are inexplicable."

"Don't you know that *I* know they are false?"

"If you *do*, the proper course is simply to deny them and court an investigation."

"And do YOU claim the right to make ME come out and deny anything you may choose to write and print?"

To that question I think I made no reply, and he then further said: "Come, now, we've talked about this matter long enough. I want your final answer—Did you write that article or not?"

"I cannot in honor tell you *who* wrote it."

"Did you not see it before it was printed?"

"Most certainly, sir."

"And did you deem it a fit thing to publish?"

"Most assuredly, sir, or I would never have consented to its appearance. Of its *authorship* I can say nothing whatever, but for its *publication* I assume full, sole and personal responsibility."

"And do you then retract it or not?"

"Mr. Winters, if my refusal to sign such a paper as you have demanded *must* entail upon me all that your language in this room fairly implies, then I ask a few minutes for prayer."

"Prayer! —— —— you, this is not your *hour* for prayer—your time to pray was when you were writing those —— lying charges. Will you sign or not?"

"You already have my answer."

"What! do you still refuse?"

"I do sir."

"Take *that*, then," and to my amazement and inexpressible relief he drew only a raw-hide instead of what I expected—a bludgeon or pistol. With it, as he spoke, he struck at my left ear downwards, as if to tear it off, and afterwards on the side of the head. As he moved away to get a better chance for a more effective shot, for the first time I gained a chance under peril to rise, and I did so pitying him from the very bottom of my soul, to think that one so naturally capable of true dignity, power and nobility could, by the temptations of this State, and by unfortunate associations and aspirations, be so deeply debased as to find in such brutality anything which he could call satisfaction—but the great hope for us all is in progress and growth, and John B. Winters, I trust, will yet be able to comprehend my feelings.

He continued to beat me with all his great force, until absolutely weary, exhausted and panting for breath. I still adhered to my purpose of non-aggressive defense, and made no other use of my arms than to defend my head and face from further disfigurement. The mere pain arising from the blows he inflicted upon my person was of course transient, and my clothing to some extent deadened its severity, as it now hides all remaining traces.

When I supposed he was through, taking the butt end of his weapon and shaking it in my face, he warned me, if I correctly understood him, of more yet to come, and furthermore said, if ever I again dared introduce his name to print, in either my own or any other public journal, he would cut off my left ear (and I do not *think* he was jesting) and send me home to my family a visibly mutilated man, to be a standing warning to all low-lived puppies who seek to blackmail gentlemen and to injure their good names. And when he *did* so operate, he informed me that his implement would not be a whip but a knife.

When he had said this, unaccompanied by Mr. Lynch, as I remember it, he left the room, for I sat down by Mr. Lynch exclaiming: "The man is mad—he is *utterly* mad—this step is his ruin—it is a mistake—it would be ungenerous in me, despite of all the ill usage I have here received, to expose him, at least till he has had an opportunity to reflect upon the matter. I shall be in no haste."

"Winters *is* very mad just now," replied Mr. Lynch, "but when he is himself he is one of the finest men I ever met. In fact, he told me the reason he did not meet you up stairs was to spare you the humiliation of a beating in the sight of others."

I submit that that unguarded remark of Philip Lynch convicts him of having been privy in advance to Mr. Winters' intentions whatever they may have been, or at least to his meaning to make an assault upon me, but I leave to others to determine how much censure an *editor* deserves for inveigling a weak, non-combatant man, also a publisher, to a pen of his own to be horsewhipped, if no worse, for the simple printing of what is verbally in the mouth of nine out of ten men, and women too, upon the street.

While writing this account two theories have occurred to me as *possibly* true respecting this most remarkable assault:

First. The aim *may* have been simply to extort from me such admissions as in the hands of money and influence would have sent me to the Penitentiary for libel. This however seems unlikely, because any statements elicited by fear or force could not be evidence in law or could be so explained as to have no force. The statements wanted so badly must have been desired for some other purpose.

Second. The other theory has so dark and wilfully murderous a look that I shrink from writing it, yet as in all probability my death at the earliest practicable moment has already been decreed, I feel I should do all I can before my hour arrives, at least to show others how to break up that aristocratic rule and combination which has robbed all Nevada of true freedom, if not of manhood itself. Although I do not prefer this hypothesis as a *"charge,"* I feel that as an American citizen I still have a right both to think and to speak my thoughts even in the land of Sharon and Winters, and as much so respecting the theory of a brutal assault (especially when I have been its subject) as respecting any other apparent enormity. I give the matter simply as a suggestion which may explain to the proper authorities and to the people whom they should represent, a well ascertained but notwithstanding a darkly mysterious fact. The scheme of this assault *may* have been

First. To terrify me by making me conscious of my utter help-lessness after making actual though not legal threats against my life.

Second. To imply that I could *save* my life only by writing or signing certain specific statements which if not subsequently explained would eternally have branded me as infamous, and would have consigned my family to shame and want, or to the dreadful compassion and patronage of the rich.

Third. To blow my brains out *the moment I had signed,* thereby preventing me from making any such subsequent explanation as *could* remove the infamy.

Fourth. Philip Lynch to be compelled to testify that I was killed by John B. Winters in self-defense, for the conviction of Winters would bring *him* in as an accomplice. If that *was* the programme in John B. Winters' mind nothing saved my life but my persistent *refusal* to sign, when that refusal seemed clearly to me to be the choice of death.

The remarkable assertion made to me by Mr. Winters, that pity only spared my life on Wednesday evening last, almost compels me to believe that at first he *could* not have intended me to leave that room alive; and why I was allowed to, unless through mesmeric or some other invisible influence, I cannot divine. The more I reflect upon this matter, the more probable as true does this horrible interpretation become.

The narration of these things I might have spared both to Mr. Winters and to the public had he himself observed silence, but as he has both verbally spoken and suffered a thoroughly garbled statement of facts to appear in the Gold Hill *News*, I feel it due to myself no less than to this community, and to the entire independent press of America and Great Britain, to give a true account of what even the Gold Hill *News* has pronounced a disgraceful affair, and which it deeply regrets because of some telegraphic mistake in the account of it.

Though he may not deem it prudent to take my life just now, the publication of this article I feel sure must compel Gen. Winters (with his peculiar views about *his* right to exemption from criticism by *me*) to resolve on my violent death, though it may take years to compass it. Notwithstanding *I* bear *him* no ill will; and if W. C. Ralston and William Sharon, and other members of the San Francisco mining and milling Ring feel that he above all other men in this State and California is the most fitting man to supervise and control Yellow Jacket matters, until I am able to vote more than half their stock I presume he will be retained to grace his present post.

Meantime, I cordially invite all who know of any sort of important villainy which only *can* be cured by exposure (and who would expose it if they felt sure they would not be betrayed under bullying threats,) to communicate with the *People's Tribune*; for until I *am* murdered, so long as I can raise the means to publish, I propose to continue my *efforts* at least to revive the liberties of the State, to curb oppression, and to benefit this part of man's world and God's earth.

CONRAD WIEGAND.

[It does seem a pity that the Sheriff was shut out, since the good sense of a general of militia and of a prominent editor failed to teach them that the merited castigation of this weak, half-witted child was a thing that ought to have been done in the street, where the poor thing could have a chance to run. When a journalist maligns a citizen, or attacks his good name on hearsay evidence, he deserves to be thrashed for it, even if he *is* a "non-combatant" weakling; but a generous adversary would at least allow such a lamb the use of his legs at such a time.—M. T.]

REFERENCE
MATERIAL

EXPLANATORY NOTES

IN HIS PREFATORY to *Roughing It* Mark Twain confessed, "Yes, take it all around, there is quite a good deal of information in the book." These notes are intended to clarify and supplement this information by identifying people, places, and incidents, and by explaining literary allusions and topical references. In addition, they attempt to demonstrate the factuality of the narrative, so that the reader may more fully appreciate the artistry that Mark Twain used to shape his experiences into a work of literature.

The notes also identify portions of the text based on earlier printings—both of his own works that Mark Twain revised for inclusion in the book, and of works he quoted from other authors. Thus whenever mention is made that he incorporated into the text one of his pieces from, for example, the Buffalo *Express* or the Sacramento *Union*, the reader may find in Emendations of the Copy-Text and Rejected Substantives a record of the revisions he carried out while composing *Roughing It*. Likewise, when a note identifies the source of a quotation from the work of another author, the reader may find a record of any alterations Mark Twain is presumed to have made in the borrowed material.

All references in the text are keyed to this volume by page and line: for example, 1.1 means page 1, line 1. Chapter titles and picture captions are *not* included in the line count. Frequently cited works have been assigned an abbreviation, which in citations is followed by a page (or volume and page) number: "*L2*, 298" or "*MTB*, 1:337." But most works are cited by the author's last name ("Hunter, 254" or "Root and Connelley, 44") or by a short title ("*Tribute*, 23"). When two or more works by the same author are cited in this way, the date of publication is used to distinguish them: "Fatout 1964, 80" and "Fatout 1976, 10." Works by members of the Clemens family may be found under their initials: SLC, OC, and MEC. All abbreviations, authors, and short titles used in citations are fully defined in References. For the reader's convenience, citations to works available in numerous editions may supply a chapter number (or its equivalent, such as a book or act number) rather than a page number. All quotations from holograph documents are transcribed verbatim from the originals (or photocopies thereof), even when a published form is also cited for the reader's convenience. The location of every unique document or manuscript is identified by the standard Library of Congress abbreviation, or the last name of the owner, always defined in References. Previously unpublished

words by Mark Twain are identified by a dagger (†) in the citation and are
©1993 by Manufacturers Hanover Trust Company as Trustee of the Mark
Twain Foundation, which reserves all reproduction rights or dramatization rights in every medium.

1.1–2   My brother had just been appointed Secretary of Nevada Terri-
tory] Orion Clemens (1825–97) learned of his appointment as secretary
of Nevada Territory by President Lincoln on 27 March 1861, obtained
his commission on 20 April, and received his final instructions on 2
July. The position had been secured for him by Edward Bates (1793–
1869), Lincoln's newly appointed attorney general, who wrote to Secretary of State William Seward on 12 March 1861:

> I have just received a letter from *Orion Clemens* of M° begging me to help him
> to an office suitable to his degree & qualifications—& he indicates the post of
> Secretary of a Territory—any Territory except *Utah*—
> Mr C was bred a printer—I knew him in his apprenticeship—a good boy, anx-
> ious to learn, using all means in his power to do so. He edited a newspaper in a
> country town of M°, with fair success. Studied law, & practiced for several years,
> in N.E. M°. His success as a lawyer was not great, chiefly, I am told, because his
> politics did not suit his locality— He *was* a Whig, but joined the Republicans, &
> that, while it was honest & manly, subjected him to an opposition amounting
> almost to persecution.
> I consider him an honest man of fair mediocrity of talents & learning—more
> indeed of both, than I have seen in several Territorial secretaries.
> Without being very urgent with you, I commend Mr Clemens to you, as a
> worthy & competent man, who will be grateful for a favor. (Bates to Seward, 12
> Mar 61, *Letters of Application*)

In 1860 Orion had campaigned vigorously on behalf of Lincoln and the
Republican Party (MEC, 10; Miller, 1–2; Mack 1961b, 69).

1.7–11   I envied my brother . . . I never had been away from home] To create a fictional persona for the narrator, Clemens departed in several
ways from the facts. In reality, he had left home in June 1853 at the age
of seventeen. After working for four years as a journeyman typesetter
in various midwestern and eastern cities, he began his training in April
1857 as a cub pilot on the Mississippi. As a licensed pilot he earned as
much as $250 a month. For a period in 1860–61 he even provided finan-
cial support for Orion, who was ten years his senior and had been married since 1854. Still, Clemens had left the river by May 1861 (see the
note at 2.18–20), and may well have felt some envy toward his brother
(*L1*, 1–3, 44–46, 58–59, 69–71, 102, 103–4, 112; AD, 29 Mar 1906, CU-
MARK, in *MTA*, 2:290–91).

2.14–15   he offered me . . . the sublime position of private secretary under him] Orion's official instructions stipulated that "as a general
thing, the Secretary can, *in person*, perform *all* the duties pertaining to
his office" (Miller, 2). He therefore had no authority to offer his brother
a secretarial position. But that did not deter Clemens, who had saved

enough money from his pilot's wages to pay for both stage fares to Carson City (see the note at 4.2–3) and provide approximately $800 more for expenses. During the sixty-day session of the first Territorial Legislature, from 1 October through 29 November 1861, Orion did hire his brother as a clerk, at $8 a day, for a total of $480 (Miller, 1–3; AD, 29 Mar 1906, CU-MARK, in *MTA*, 2:291).

2.16–17   the heavens and the earth passed away, and the firmament was rolled together as a scroll] Revelation 6:14 and 21:1: "And the heaven departed as a scroll when it is rolled together; and every mountain and island were moved out of their places. . . . And I saw a new heaven and a new earth: for the first heaven and the first earth were passed away; and there was no more sea."

2.18–20   At the end of an hour or two I was ready . . . because we were going in the overland stage] Clemens did not in fact decide to go with Orion until early July 1861. For several weeks after Orion was told of his appointment on 27 March, Clemens continued to work as a pilot, completing his final run in New Orleans on 8 May and returning to St. Louis as a passenger on 21 May, by which date the Civil War had virtually halted commercial river traffic. From mid-June until early July he belonged to a small band of Confederate volunteers, an episode he later fictionalized in "The Private History of a Campaign That Failed" (SLC 1885). On 4 July he met in St. Louis with Orion, who had left behind his wife and daughter in Keokuk, Iowa; on 18 July the brothers embarked from St. Louis on the *Sioux City,* bound up the Missouri River for the overland stagecoach at St. Joseph (*L1,* 121–22; MEC, 10–11).

2.24–28   I only proposed to stay in Nevada three months . . . seven uncommonly long years] In August 1866 Clemens recalled that when he left for Nevada he expected "to be gone 3 months . . . thinking the war would be closed & the river open again by that time" (*L1,* 357). But the War lasted until April 1865, and he remained in the West until December 1866, returning to St. Louis in March 1867, after an absence of nearly six years (*L2,* 1, 18 n. 1).

3.1–3   sand-bars which we roosted on . . . and then got out our crutches and sparred over] To spar a vessel over a sand-bar, long stout poles were lashed to either side of it,

by means of which the bow was lifted as on crutches. The wheels were then put in forward motion and the boat driven ahead for a short distance, perhaps no more than a few feet. . . . This operation was repeated as often as necessary to enable the boat partly to hobble over, partly to dig its way through the bar into the deeper water of the pool beyond. (Hunter, 254–55)

3.4   she was walking most of the time] This passage resembles a description in Albert D. Richardson's *Beyond the Mississippi,* a book Clemens probably read while working on *Roughing It* (SLC to Bliss, 29 Oct 70,

Daley). Richardson had taken a steamboat in 1857 at Jefferson City, Missouri, to connect with the overland stage at Kansas City. "Navigating the Missouri, at low water," he wrote, "is like putting a steamer upon dry land, and sending a boy ahead with a sprinkling pot. Our boat rubbed and scraped upon sand-bars, and they stopped us abruptly a dozen times a day" (Richardson, 21–22, 25, 33).

3.7   "shear"] More commonly "sheer," the curvature from bow to stern of a ship's deck as shown in side elevation.

4.2–3   a hundred and fifty dollars apiece for tickets] Mark Twain evidently misremembered the actual cost. The receipt for the two fares, issued by the Central Overland California and Pike's Peak Express Company on 25 July 1861 for the trip from St. Joseph to Carson City, indicates that after an initial payment of $300, another $100 was due within thirty days, bringing the total to $200 per passenger. Three months later, in October 1861, the fare was reduced to $150, after the start of the line was moved from St. Joseph to nearby Atchison, Kansas (receipt in CU-MARK, facsimile in *L1*, 122; "The Overland Mail Route," San Francisco *Evening Bulletin*, 24 June 61, 3; "Overland Mail" and "Greatly Reduced Rates," Atchison *Freedom's Champion*, 12 Oct 61, 2, 3; Root and Connelley, 44).

5.3–9   a pitiful little Smith & Wesson's seven-shooter . . . you could not hit anything with it] Smith and Wesson's first production, introduced in 1857, was a twenty-two-caliber "Patent Breech-Loading 7 Shot Revolver," which weighed eight ounces and had a barrel less than four inches long. It was not accurate beyond ten or fifteen yards: "In a day when large-calibered guns were the rule, it must have been regarded as little more than a toy" (McHenry and Roper, 27, 139–40, 182).

5.16   Mr. George Bemis] Presumably Mark Twain invented Bemis. "Capt G. T. Hicher" and one other man accompanied the Clemens brothers when they called on Brigham Young in Salt Lake City (see the note at 92.22–93.3), but nothing has been found to suggest that either man accompanied them from St. Joseph.

5.18–19   an old original "Allen" revolver . . . a "pepper-box."] Bemis's weapon was not properly speaking a revolver (which has a single barrel), but a small-caliber pistol with six barrels (see the illustration on page 5), first manufactured by Ethan Allen in 1837. Its hammer cocked automatically with each pull of the trigger until all of its barrels, which revolved around a common axis, were fired. The name "pepper-box" derived from its resemblance (when viewed from the front) to the "perforations in the top of an old-fashioned pepper shaker." Such pistols were very popular, in spite of their inaccuracy at a range of more than a few feet (Chapel, 84–88, 92).

6.5–6 We jumped into the stage . . . and we bowled away] Orion kept a journal of the trip, which Clemens borrowed to help him write the opening chapters (SLC to OC, 15 July 70, CU-MARK, in *MTL*, 1:174–75). The journal itself is no longer extant, but some—or possibly all—of its contents survive, transcribed by Orion in a letter of 8 and 9 September 1861 to his wife, Mollie. This journal transcript provides a cursory account of the brothers' journey, from their 26 July departure from St. Joseph to their 14 August arrival in Carson City, with a brief description of the stopover at Salt Lake City on 6–7 August. It is printed in supplement A, together with a schematic comparison of Orion's account with the account in *Roughing It*. Maps 1A–1D in supplement B show the overland route and locate all of the stagecoach stations and other significant landmarks mentioned in the text and notes.

6.6 and left "the States" behind us] After the travelers ferried across the river at St. Joseph they disembarked in Kansas, which had become a state in January 1861; they would not leave "the States" proper until they entered Nebraska Territory (see the note at 12.18–19).

7.4 an imposing cradle on wheels] The Concord coach, manufactured by the Abbot-Downing Company of Concord, New Hampshire, was the standard vehicle used on all the major western stage lines at the time. Its body "rested on stout leather straps, called thorough braces, which rocked the stage body back and forth in a motion more pleasant to passengers than the ordinary jars of a wagon" and also diminished "the violence of jolts transmitted from the coach to the animals" (Hafen, 306; Greever, 44).

7.11–13 we had three days' delayed mails with us] On 1 July 1861 daily mail service was begun over a central overland route from St. Joseph to Sacramento. The Central Overland California and Pike's Peak Express Company (which until July had transported mail only semimonthly) was assigned responsibility for the line from St. Joseph to Salt Lake City, and from there the route was managed by the Butterfield Overland Mail Company, which until March 1861 had been carrying the daily mail over a southern route. The Butterfield Company had abandoned this southern route because of Confederate depredations, and, under an agreement with the Central Overland Company, moved its stock and equipment to the central route. The closure of the southern route, plus the inability of steamers to depart New York City after 20 June, led by early July to the accumulation of over twelve tons of mail at the St. Joseph office, some of which no doubt accompanied the Clemens brothers (Hafen, 92–94, 161, 211–14, 217–18; Conkling and Conkling, 2:325–26, 337–38; "Progress of the Continental Telegraph—The Overland Mail Company—Complaints as to the Newspaper Carriage Answered," San Francisco *Evening Bulletin*, 6 Sept 61, 2).

7.27–28   we would unload the most of our mail . . . on the Plains] Contemporary accounts, including the postmaster general's, confirm that in order to lighten their loads overland drivers sometimes stashed mail (especially printed material) along the route for a later stage to pick up, or even abandoned it altogether. The San Francisco *Evening Bulletin* commented in September 1861:

> Our literary folks subscribe for Harper and the Atlantic, and the people of the Great Basin and eastward get them; our "girls" subscribe for Bonner's Ledger, and the girls over the mountains get them; our babies' mothers "take Godey for the patterns," and the Brigham Young and eastward babies have the benefit of the patterns for their Sunday dresses. ("Literary Overlanders," 21 Sept 61, 3)

By June 1862 the problem had become so acute that overburdened drivers were even accused of wantonly destroying mail, sometimes while disguised as Indians (Blair, 561; Burton, 214; "The Overland Mail Troubles," San Francisco *Alta California*, 23 June 62, 1, reprinting the Carson City *Silver Age* of 19 June; Chapman, 264–67).

9.8–10   The fountains of her great deep . . . forty nights] Genesis 7:11–12: "In the six hundredth year of Noah's life . . . were all the fountains of the great deep broken up. . . . And the rain was upon the earth forty days and forty nights."

12.18–19   Little Sandy . . . Big Sandy] Actually, the trail crossed Little Sandy Creek about twenty-five miles beyond the Nebraska border, and then, another three miles or so further on, Big Sandy Creek. Clemens's memory of this section of the route was not helped by Orion's journal, which made no mention of the river crossings (see supplement A, item 1, and supplement B, map 1A).

13.26–15.7   "sage-brush," . . . "greasewood,"] This description of sage-brush and greasewood faintly echoes a similar passage in a letter Clemens wrote to his mother and then edited for publication in the Keokuk *Gate City* on 20 November 1861, in which he likened sage-brush to "a liliputian cedar tree" and characterized greasewood as "a perfect imitation, in miniature, of the live-oak tree, 'barring' the color of it" (SLC 1861). A clipping of this letter may well have been available in one of Clemens's scrapbooks.

14.8–10   lilliputian . . . Brobdingnag] Terms derived from imaginary countries in Swift's *Gulliver's Travels* (1726).

15.30–31   In Syria . . . a camel took charge of my overcoat] Clemens was in the vicinity of the headwaters of the Jordan on 17 and 18 September 1867, during the Holy Land excursion described in *The Innocents Abroad* (N&J1, 417, 420–22; SLC 1869a, chapter 42). No previous written version of this obviously fictional episode has been found, either in his letters to the *Alta California*, in *Innocents*, or in his extant notebook for the period, but Clemens did tell of "a ferocious and voracious camel" in at least one of his 1868 lectures about the excursion ("Opera

House—Mark Twain's Lecture," Virginia City *Territorial Enterprise*, 28 Apr 68, 3).

23.6–7 a great long "navy" revolver] A large-caliber revolver with a barrel measuring seven and one-half inches, first manufactured in 1851 by Samuel Colt (1814–62) and shortly thereafter adopted as a sidearm by the United States Navy. The revolver (with its imitators) predominated in the West in the latter half of the nineteenth century, becoming "Colt's passport to undying fame" (Edwards, 277–79, 283–84; Mathews, 1115).

24.7 Nicolson pavement] A type of street pavement, patented in 1854 by Samuel Nicolson (1791–1868), which was used in numerous American cities during the 1860s. Consisting of thick blocks of wood embedded in asphalt, it was less expensive than stone, rapidly laid, smooth, and relatively durable (*Mining and Scientific Press:* "The Chicago, or 'Nicholson' Pavement," 7 [21 Dec 63]: 4; "Patent Department," 8 [16 Jan 64]: 39).

25.1–2 We could not eat the bread or the meat, nor drink the "slumgullion."] The brothers' meal was evidently typical. Richard Burton, who traveled west by stagecoach in August 1860, described a breakfast "prepared in the usual prairie style": the stale coffee of "burnt beans" was simmered "till every noxious principle was duly extracted from it," the bacon was "rusty," the antelope steak was "cut off a corpse suspended for the benefit of flies outside," and the bread was prepared with "sour milk, . . . saleratus or prepared carbonate of soda or alkali, and other vile stuff, which communicates to the food the green-yellow tinge, and suggests many of the properties of poison" (Burton, 104).

25.3 the anecdote (a very, very old one, even at that day)] At least two writers known to Mark Twain published versions of this joke: John Phoenix (George H. Derby) in 1855, and Albert D. Richardson in 1867 (Bellamy, 39–40; Fried, 42–43; Derby, 211; Richardson, 493).

26.20–21 At 4 p.m. we crossed a branch of the river, and at 5 p.m. we crossed the Platte itself] The route reached the south bank of the Platte River at this point, but did not cross it. Orion's journal makes no mention of river crossings near Fort Kearny, and places the fort itself only seven miles beyond the sighting of the "Timber of Platte" (supplement A, item 1).

26.34–28.5 At . . . out.] This paragraph was reprinted, with a few minor changes, from the New York *Times* of 28 June 1869 (1–2). The article from which it was taken was the last of a series published by Clemens's friend William Swinton (1833–92), who had been a *Times* staff member since 1858. As the newspaper's special correspondent, he traveled to California in the spring of 1869 on the first run of the Pacific Railroad to employ "Pullman palace cars." His train departed Omaha on Sunday,

13 June, and arrived at Sacramento four days later. On 8 July Swinton accepted a professorship at the University of California in Berkeley, where he remained until 1874 (New York *Times:* "We had a dispatch . . . ," 9 July 69, 5; "The New West," 11 June 69, 5, and 14 June 69, 8; Ohles, 3:1262–63; Swinton to A. J. Moulder, 8 July 69, Regents' Records, Box 2:16, University Archives, CU-BANC).

27.5   DELMONICO] New York restaurateur Lorenzo Delmonico (1813–81), whose principal establishment, at Broadway and Chambers Street, was internationally renowned for the quality and variety of its menu.

30.5–7   the first prairie-dog villages . . . the regular *coyote*] With few exceptions, the chronology of the overland trip described in *Roughing It* accords exactly with Orion's journal of the actual journey (see supplement A, item 1). In this instance, however, the first sight of prairie dogs and coyotes is assigned to the fourth day, one day later than Orion's reference to them.

31.22   you need a minie rifle] This muzzle-loading rifle fired a bullet invented in 1849 by Claude Étienne Minié (1804–79), which expanded to fit tightly into the grooves of the rifling, thereby improving its accuracy. The rifle had greater range and accuracy than earlier types, and made a significant impact on military tactics when it came into wide use in the 1850s. It became obsolete soon after 1865, when it was superseded by breech-loading firearms.

35.4–7   the trip was often made in fifteen days . . . eighteen or nineteen days, if I remember rightly] The scheduled passenger trip from Atchison to Placerville (about sixty miles shorter than the trip from St. Joseph to Sacramento) actually took seventeen days. Clemens's trip to Carson City (a day short of Placerville) took twenty days, including a stop of two nights and two days at Salt Lake City. The government contract with the stage company provided for "the transportation of the entire letter mail six times a week on the central route, to be carried through in twenty days eight months in the year, and in twenty-three days four months in the year, from St. Joseph, Missouri, (or Atchison, Kansas,) to Placerville" (Blair, 560; "Greatly Reduced Rates," Atchison *Freedom's Champion,* 12 Oct 61, 3; Root and Connelley, 43, 63; Kelly 1862, 12).

37.36–38.1   this vast machinery . . . was in the hands of Mr. Ben Holladay. All the western half . . . was in his hands] In mid-1861 Benjamin Holladay (1819–87) held an unrecorded deed of trust giving him effective control of the stage line, but he did not become its official owner until March 1862. His interest was not in "the western half of the business," but in the line between the Missouri River and Salt Lake City. Popular with his employees, punctilious as an administrator, and sometimes unscrupulous in his business methods, Holladay was exceedingly prosperous and had achieved near-legendary status by the time he sold his stage operations to Wells, Fargo and Company in November 1866, anticipating the completion of the transcontinental railroad. Thereafter he concentrated his business interests in the West, where he operated railroads, steamship lines, a hotel, and a sawmill (Ralph Moody, 202–5, 211–13; Frederick, 63–64, 71–75, 80–81, 260, 272; Hafen, 227–28).

38.1–3 an incident of Palestine travel ... set down in my Holy Land note-book] The incident is not mentioned in Clemens's extant note-books or in *The Innocents Abroad*. Mark Twain did, however, tell the story in several of his 1868 and 1869 lecture appearances, and included it in "I Rise to a Question of Privilege," written in May 1868 for the San Francisco *News Letter and California Advertiser* but never published (SLC 1868d). Clemens's remarks in a letter of 2 December 1868 to Jervis Langdon confirm that it was based on fact (*L2*, 298, 299 n. 2).

38.8–19 a young New York boy by the name of Jack ... an elderly pilgrim ... learned in the Scriptures] Mark Twain refers to John A. (Jack) Van Nostrand (1847?–79) of New York City and Greenville, New Jersey, and to (Confederate) Colonel William Ritenour Denny (1823–1904), a Sunday-school superintendent from Winchester, Virginia, who were members of the *Quaker City* excursion and of Clemens's party during a three-week trip on horseback through the Holy Land. While at Jericho, Denny noted in his journal, "We tried to select what might be the spot (Pisgah) where Moses viewed the promised land and died on the mountains of Moab beyond Jordan but we could not" (Denny, entries for 11 and 25 Sept 67; *L2*, 64, 93, 395–96; *MTB*, 3:1290).

39.17–18 Ben Holladay would have fetched them through in thirty-six hours] Holladay was fond of performing dramatic feats of travel. In 1862 he made the trip from San Francisco to New York City in sixteen days (a clipping describing this event may be found in Clemens's December 1866 notebook); the following year he traveled from Folsom, California (near Sacramento), to Atchison, Kansas, in twelve days. On both occasions he used specially selected teams of horses. Albert D. Richardson, correspondent for the Boston *Journal* in 1863, estimated that the latter trip "cost him 20,000 dollars in wear and tear of stock and vehicles"—evidently a small price to pay for the publicity it received (Ralph Moody, 255; "Telegraphic," Sacramento *Bee*, 16 Sept 62, 3; *N&J1*, 265 n. 30).

40.5 "Julesburg," *alias* "Overland City,"] Named for Jules Bene (also known as Jules Beni or Reni, and as René Jules), a French-Canadian trader who settled on the site in 1859, this town consisted of no more than a dozen buildings by the time it was destroyed by Indians in February 1865. It marked a major junction—the point at which the stage line to Denver diverged toward the southwest, while the main overland

route crossed the South Platte River and headed northwest. By the time
of the Clemenses' visit, the town had a reputation for lawlessness,
which had prompted the stage company to rename it Overland City in
official documents. Present-day Julesburg, Colorado, was established
in 1884 by the Union Pacific Railroad, across the river and several miles
north of the original site (Root and Connelley, 65, 213–15, 360–61;
Thrapp, 1:92; Mattes, 279; Work, 24; see also the notes at 60.26–63.3
and 66.24–67.7).

41.8–9   a less sumptuous affair, called a "mud-wagon"] On the rougher
sections of the route the Concord coaches were replaced by "mud-
wagons," which carried the same number of inside passengers but were
faster on mountain roads and less likely to capsize because they were
both lighter and lower to the ground (Rusling, 143; Hafen, 96; George
R. Stewart 1968, 6, 7, 11).

41.28–30   we took horses . . . on a buffalo hunt] Orion's journal makes no
mention of such a hunt, although the entry for 29 July describes the
area beyond Fort Kearny as "the Buffalo region" (supplement A, item 1).
This side trip, which falls two days later in the Roughing It chronology,
is undoubtedly imaginary.

48.6–7   talking about the king, and the sacred white elephant, the Sleeping Idol] The Buddhists of Thailand (formerly Siam) believe that an al-
bino elephant is the incarnation of the soul of a king or a great hero and
is therefore sacred. The Sleeping Idol, an enormous statue of a reclining
Buddha in the Wat Poh temple in Bangkok, is one hundred and fifty feet
long and forty feet high, covered in gold leaf. Clemens probably read
about both in The English Governess at the Siamese Court, Anna Leonowens's personal reminiscence of her employment by King Mongkut,
ruler of Thailand from 1851 until his death in 1868. Clemens owned an
American edition of Leonowens's work (Boston: Osgood and Co.),
which he inscribed "Saml L. Clemens / 1871," indicating that he may
have added the Eckert incident long after first drafting chapter 6 in the
fall of 1870 (Gribben, 1:406; Leonowens, 49–50, 140–41; O'Donnell,
72–73).

50.3–4   carrying letters nineteen hundred miles in eight days] The pony
express provided mail service—at first weekly, and then semiweekly—
for nearly nineteen months, starting on 3 April 1860; it was officially
discontinued on 26 October 1861, two days after the completion of the
overland telegraph line. The service had been established by the
freighting firm of Russell, Majors and Waddell (which also owned the
Central Overland California and Pike's Peak Express Company) to
demonstrate the practicality of the central route, in an attempt to win
the overland-mail contract away from the Butterfield Overland Mail.
The full nineteen-hundred-mile route, from St. Joseph to Sacramento,
required about ten days of nonstop travel, in relays, with each rider

covering at least fifty miles (and sometimes as much as a hundred). By late July 1861, when the Clemenses started overland, telegraph stations had been established some fifty miles west of Fort Kearny, Nebraska, and the same distance east of Fort Churchill, Nevada; the transmission of messages therefore required pony-express travel only between these two stations, which took as little as eight days (Chapman, 301; Hafen, 169–74, 179, 185–87; Blair, 560).

50.15   the blackness of darkness] Jude 13.

50.27   *two dollars an ounce*] The cost of operating the pony express turned out to be much greater than the income generated, contributing to the eventual bankruptcy of Russell, Majors and Waddell. The initial fee for a letter was five dollars per half ounce, in addition to the basic ten-cent United States postage. Over the life of the service, the charge was gradually reduced: at the time of the Clemens brothers' trip it had recently been cut to the rate named here (Hafen, 180; "Pony Express," St. Louis *Missouri Democrat*, 1 July 61, 4; *DAH*, 4:306–7; see the textual note at 50.27).

53.14–54.10   the Indian mail robbery and massacre of 1856 . . . Babbitt, survived the massacre, . . . desperately wounded] Undoubtedly based on a story which the brothers heard and which Orion recorded in his journal, Mark Twain's account conflates several related incidents involving Cheyenne Indians, mislocates them by a hundred miles or more, and supplies a fictional embellishment—the "desperately wounded" survivor. On 24 August 1856, near Fort Kearny (about two hundred and fifty miles east of the scene of Mark Twain's account), a frightened mail conductor fired on two young Indians who approached to ask for tobacco. One of the Indians responded by wounding him with an arrow, but was restrained and punished by his fellow tribesmen. The following day soldiers from Fort Kearny retaliated by attacking the offending group of Indians, killing at least six, wounding many others, and taking their horses and other possessions. The surviving Indians then attacked a small wagon train carrying official supplies to the Utah government on behalf of Almon Whiting Babbitt (1813–56), secretary of Utah Territory since 1853. Two members of the company, which did not include Babbitt, survived the attack. Babbitt himself and two companions were killed thirteen days later, on 7 September, about a hundred miles east of the spot identified by Mark Twain. The Cheyenne plundered Babbitt's light carriage, taking his mules, jewelry, and gold coin (supplement A, item 1; McClelland, 1:650–54; Jefferson Davis, 106–12; Schindler, 230–36; Joseph Smith, 76; Jenson, 1:284–86; Van Wagoner and Walker, 5–9).

55.1–2   Fort Laramie . . . the Black Hills, with Laramie Peak] Fort Laramie "marked the transition from the Great Plains to the Rocky Mountains" (Mattes, 6). The Black Hills (now known as the Laramie Mountains), forested with dark conifers, are dominated by Laramie Peak, rising more than a mile above the surrounding land forty miles west of Fort Laramie (Mattes, 501; Urbanek 1974, 125; Lavender 1983, 10–11; Burton, 174).

58.10   We never did get much satisfaction about that dark occurrence] The altercation may have been less serious than the brothers thought. An unpublished account in the Library of Congress, said to be by some-one "well acquainted with the stage route in the early sixties," mentions

"Play Killings" which caused the green travelers to tremble with fear, often pulled off by stage drivers and wranglers, for the traveler's benefit. . . . these "Play Killings" were often written up afterwards as real, which caused eastern people to suppose that eight men out of ten were shot in the west each year. (Dick Clayton, 1, 3)

This account is clearly apocryphal in its other details, however, since it places Clemens—supposedly already calling himself "Mark Twain"— at Weber Station, Utah, in 1862, socializing with (among others) Jack Slade (see the next note), Lotta Crabtree (1847–1924), and the famous Indian scout Sacagawea (1784?–?1884).

58.36–38   Even before we got to Overland City, we had begun to hear about Slade and his "division"] From here through chapter 11, Mark Twain describes the career of the notorious Joseph A. (Jack) Slade (1829?–64). When returning to this section of his narrative in March 1871, Clemens asked Orion to set down his own recollections of what they had learned about Slade on the trip (SLC to OC, 10 Mar 71, NN-B). Orion's response, a letter written on 11 March, is reproduced in sup-plement A, item 3. Orion expressed confusion about where the broth-ers first heard Slade's name. In any case, Mark Twain's claim here that they had heard of Slade even before arriving in Overland City, some four hundred miles east of Rocky Ridge Station, was clearly intended to heighten the dramatic effect of their eventual encounter with him, described at the end of chapter 10. Slade had been an overland agent at least since 1859, first overseeing the route west from Fort Kearny, and then the entire division from Julesburg to Rocky Ridge Station. Spend-ing much of his time inspecting the stations along the route, he was an efficient superintendent and a ruthless exterminator of thieves and other outlaws (Callaway, 101–8; Root and Connelley, 216–18; Mc-Clernan, 22 n. 10).

60.5–6   I will reduce all this mass of overland gossip to one straightfor-ward narrative] Slade's biographers, from Mark Twain's time to the present, have found it impossible to distinguish fact from fiction. Mark Twain first described his meeting with Slade in an "Around the World" letter published in the Buffalo Express on 22 January 1870 (SLC 1870b). In this much fuller account in chapters 10 and 11, he combined popular lore with accurate history, relying on his own recollection of "overland gossip" and early 1860s newspaper reports, on Orion's letter of 11 March 1871, and on chapter 23 of Thomas J. Dimsdale's *Vigilantes of Montana* (166–77), a book that he later explicitly identifies as a source (see 64.1). Mark Twain probably received a copy of Dimsdale's book from Hezekiah Hosmer of Virginia City, Montana Territory, to whom he had written on 15 September 1870, requesting newspaper documentation about Slade (MtHI). See the Introduction, page 811.

60.8   Slade was born in Illinois, of good parentage] Dimsdale states merely that Slade "was raised in Clinton County, Ill., and was a member of a highly respectable family" (166). In fact he was born in 1829 or 1830 in Carlyle, Illinois, a town founded by his father, Charles Slade— a mill owner, merchant, and legislator who served in Congress briefly before his death in 1834. His mother, born Mary D. Kane, came from a wealthy and influential family (McClernan, 13, 22 n. 8, 37–42; Callaway, 97–98).

60.8–9   At about twenty-six years of age he killed a man in a quarrel and fled the country] Dimsdale asserts that "Slade was, at the time of his coming West, a fugitive from justice in Illinois, where he killed a man with whom he had been quarreling," by throwing a stone at his head. No source giving Slade's age as twenty-six at the time has been found (Dimsdale, 175–76).

60.12–18   he had an angry dispute with one of his wagon-drivers . . . and shot him dead] Dimsdale does not report this story, but Orion set down a version of it in his 11 March 1871 letter (supplement A, item 3). Slade's career in the late 1850s, before his employment as a division agent, has not been documented. There is some evidence that he worked with a freighting company on the overland trail, or possibly for John M. Hockaday and Company, which transported mail over the route in 1858–59. The incident Mark Twain describes may or may not have occurred, but the story was widely repeated, in several different versions. The brothers could have heard it on their overland trip, or read it during their stay in Nevada: it appeared in the Carson City *Silver Age* in June 1862 (Chapman, 184–85; Bloss, 86–87; Hafen, 109–110; Callaway, 113; McClernan, 26–27; "A Disreputable Agent," Sacramento *Union*, 24 June 62, 2, reprinting the Carson City *Silver Age* of 21 June).

60.22–24   he killed three savages . . . and afterward cut their ears off and sent them . . . to the chief of the tribe] No source for this episode has been discovered, although its atrocities are like those commonly attributed to Slade (McClernan, 42–43).

60.26–63.3   the important post of overland division-agent at Julesburg, in place of Mr. Jules . . . dead or alive] Jules Bene (see the note at 40.5), a

dishonest station keeper, was dismissed when Slade took charge of the
division; Slade, under orders to recover stolen company property,
seized some horses from him. Mark Twain's version of the ensuing
feud follows Dimsdale for the most part, but incorporates from Orion's
report the detail that the two men fired at each other through a doorway, while Dimsdale and others assert that Jules attacked Slade when
he was unarmed (Dimsdale, 173–75; Thrapp, 1:92; supplement A, item
3; McClernan, 13; Callaway, 102, 106–7; Langford, 2:293–95).

63.35–39   On one occasion . . . killing three, and wounding the fourth]
Mark Twain copied these two sentences almost verbatim from Dimsdale (175).

64n.1   Prof. Thos. J. Dimsdale] Thomas J. Dimsdale (1831–66), an educated Englishman suffering from tuberculosis, went to Virginia City,
Idaho Territory, in the summer of 1863, seeking improved health. (On
26 May 1864 this area became part of the newly formed territory of
Montana.) He taught school, served as the territory's first superintendent of public instruction, and edited the *Montana Post*, its first newspaper of consequence. *The Vigilantes of Montana*, based on a series of
articles which appeared in the *Post* in 1865–66, was published shortly
before his death (DeGolyer, ix).

64.16–65.15   he saw a man approaching who had offended him . . . one of
the deadest men that ever lived] No source for these two alleged murders has been identified. The account here became itself part of the tradition in which "every sort of homicidal exploit was attributed to
Slade," most or even all of which are probably "unworthy of belief"
(Callaway, 112–13).

66.5–23   a Frenchman who had offended Slade . . . they mounted double
and galloped away unharmed] Dimsdale does not recount these incidents. Orion set down a version of them, and they were also reported in
the Carson City *Silver Age* in June 1862. Both accounts link the two
incidents, identifying one of the would-be lynchers and his family as
the victims of the burning (supplement A, item 3; "A Disreputable
Agent," Sacramento *Union*, 24 June 62, 2, reprinting the Carson City
Silver Age of 21 June).

66.24–67.7   Slade's myrmidons captured his ancient enemy Jules . . .
correct in all essential particulars] This incident probably took place in
1860. Mark Twain first made passing reference to it in his January 1870
"Around the World" letter (SLC 1870b). His account here is greatly expanded, but does not seem to draw on either Orion's or Dimsdale's versions, from which it varies considerably. He may well have seen a report published in western newspapers in June 1862, which claimed
that Jules begged Slade to spare his life in return for "his entire stock,
which was valued at $3,000," and which also noted that Slade put

Jules's ears in his pocket, remarking that he planned to "make soup of them" ("The Overland Mail Troubles," San Francisco *Alta California*, 23 June 62, 1, reprinting the Carson City *Silver Age* of 19 June). Nathaniel P. Langford, in his authoritative 1890 account, establishes that there is little doubt that Slade acted in self-defense, that Jules was the vengeful aggressor, that Slade's contemporaries felt his killing of Jules was justified under the circumstances, and that the reports of Jules's torture were greatly exaggerated, if not utterly false (supplement A, item 3; Dimsdale, 174–75; Thrapp, 1:92, 3:1318; Langford, 2:295–301).

67.8   we rattled up to a stage station] Before writing *Roughing It* Clemens mentioned breakfasting with Slade at Rocky Ridge Station (which they reached on the morning of 3 August, the ninth day of their trip) on three different occasions: in his January 1870 "Around the World" letter, in his September 1870 letter to Hosmer, and in his March 1871 letter to Orion (see the notes at 58.36–38, 60.5–6, and 66.24–67.7). In the *Roughing It* chronology, he moved the encounter with Slade to the morning of the eighth day, leaving the location—the name of the station and its distance from St. Joseph—deliberately vague.

67.21   He was so friendly and so gentle-spoken] Dimsdale noted that Slade was "a kind hearted and intelligent gentleman" when alcohol had not transformed him into "a reckless demon," and reported that "no man in the Territory had a greater faculty of attracting the favorable notice of even strangers" (Dimsdale, 167). William F. ("Buffalo Bill") Cody, who worked under Slade for two years as a pony-express rider and stage driver, described him as kind, generous, and concerned for the welfare of his employees. A year before the Clemenses' trip, Slade had been so solicitous of a baby girl in Richard Burton's party of travelers that he drove them part of the way in his own buckboard with "an outriding escort" of "sixteen of the most villa[i]nous cut throats on the Plains" (Hale, 7–8; Cody, 104–5).

67.26–28   his face was rather broad . . . lips peculiarly thin and straight] Mark Twain chose not to use all of the description that Orion provided (supplement A, item 3). An 1862 newspaper story reported that Slade was "of small stature, very wiry, with sharp cheek bones, an aquiline nose and brown hair" ("A Disreputable Agent," Sacramento *Union*, 24 June 62, 2, reprinting the Carson City *Silver Age* of 21 June).

69.2–4   the Vigilance Committee in Montana . . . had hanged him] In June 1863 Slade moved to Virginia City, Idaho Territory, where he operated a freighting business and began ranching. He had been fired the previous November from the overland stage line at the insistence of the authorities at Fort Halleck, where he had wrecked the sutler's store on a drunken spree. Slade's execution on 10 March 1864 no doubt came to Clemens's attention in Nevada, when he was reporting for the Virginia City *Territorial Enterprise*. The files of the *Enterprise* for that period are lost, but the town's other major newspaper published two accounts of "the shocking event" (Virginia City *Union:* "Execution at Bannock City," 3 Apr 64, 2; "The Slade Scene in the Doings of the Idaho Vigilance Committee," 5 May 64, 1; Callaway, 118–19, 121–23; McClernan, 14, 25 n. 22, 27–28 n. 24; Chapman, 193–96; Root and Connelley, 466).

69.6–7   being a Reliable Account . . . Band:] This subtitle is evidently Mark Twain's own composite of the subtitles on the paper cover and on the title page of Dimsdale's book. The subtitle on the cover reads, "TRIAL, CAPTURE AND EXECUTION OF HENRY PLUMMER'S NOTORIOUS ROAD AGENT BAND! FORMING THE ONLY RELIABLE WORK EVER OFFERED TO THE PUBLIC." The subtitle on the title page reads, "OR POPULAR JUSTICE IN THE ROCKY MOUNTAINS. BEING A CORRECT AND IMPARTIAL NARRATIVE OF THE CHASE, TRIAL, CAPTURE AND EXECUTION OF HENRY PLUMMER'S ROAD AGENT BAND, . . . Forming the only reliable work on the subject ever offered the public."

69.13–17   "Those who saw him . . . would pronounce him a fiend incarnate."] An essentially accurate quotation from Dimsdale (167).

69.17–20   From Fort Kearny . . . anything in literature] Mark Twain was responsible for some of the "compactness, simplicity and vigor of expression" in this sentence; Dimsdale actually wrote, "He was feared a great deal more, generally, than the Almighty, from Kearney, West" (Dimsdale, 175).

69.22   After the execution of the five men, on the 14th of January] In an earlier chapter, Dimsdale described the hanging of five desperadoes on 14 January 1864: Boone Helm, Jack Gallagher, Frank Parish, Haze Lyons, and "Club-Foot George" Lane (Dimsdale, 136–46).

70.10–11   On returning from Milk River] Earlier in the chapter Dimsdale reported that Slade, shortly after arriving in Virginia City in 1863, undertook to fetch a load of merchandise from the Milk River in northwestern Idaho Territory; he and his teamsters successfully completed the seven-hundred-mile round trip through hostile Indian country. One writer described him as "the only man to be found in the mines willing to encounter the risk" of such an enterprise, through an area "full half of which was unmarked by a road" (Dimsdale, 167; Langford, 2:302–4).

72.26–31   Nevada . . . Virginia] Nevada City and Virginia City, two miles apart, were the largest mining camps in Alder Gulch, Idaho Territory (Langford, 1:377).

76.1–7   a Mormon emigrant train . . . the distance our stage had come in *eight days and three hours*] Orion's account indicates that the travelers actually encountered the emigrants on their seventh day of travel, probably between Horseshoe and La Prele stations (supplement A, item 1). Some four or five thousand emigrants, as estimated in October 1861 by the Salt Lake City *Deseret News*, made the trip to Utah in the summer of 1861 ("Last Immigrant Company," Salt Lake City *Deseret News*, 2 Oct 61, 180).

76.10 Horse Creek] This is the only place name in Mark Twain's account of the overland trip which is not mentioned in Orion's journal. Having followed the valley of the North Platte River for about two hundred miles, the trail left the river valley upstream from present-day Casper, Wyoming, and continued in a more westerly direction toward the Sweetwater River and Independence Rock, crossing on the way Horse Creek, the site of a stage station (Urbanek 1974, 104; Urbanek 1978, 43–44).

76.19–20 Independence Rock, Devil's Gate and the Devil's Gap] Independence Rock is a granite monolith covering over twenty acres and rising one hundred and ninety feet above the valley floor. Four miles upstream, the Sweetwater River flows through Devil's Gate, a deep, narrow gorge. To pass this obstacle, the trail traversed the ridge to the south through a "natural opening," which was very likely known as Devil's Gap, although the name has not been independently documented (Urbanek 1978, 49–51).

77.15 South Pass City] This settlement was situated near the place where the overland route left the Sweetwater River; it was less than a year old, being "one of the many mushroom growths which the presence of gold in the Rocky Mountains . . . caused to spring up" (Burton, 199–200). (Another town of the same name, still in existence today as a historic site, was founded several miles north in 1867: see WPA, 319–20.)

78.14–80.4 SOUTH PASS . . . Mount Washington] South Pass (elevation 7,550 feet) is a long, treeless valley, twenty-five miles wide, from which several mountains rising over twelve thousand feet are visible in the distance (WPA, 321). Mount Washington in New Hampshire (elevation 6,288 feet) is the highest point in the northeastern United States.

81.3–4 a spring which spent its water through two outlets and sent it in opposite directions] Mark Twain apparently alludes to Pacific Springs, situated in South Pass about four miles west of the Continental Divide. The notion of a single spring with "two outlets" sending the waters in "opposite directions" is evidently his alone; Orion claimed, in his letter of 11 March 1871, that at this spot one "spring with waters destined for the Atlantic stood within a man's length (or within sight) of another spring whose waters were about to commence a voyage to the Pacific," and in his journal he made only passing mention of the spring (supplement A, items 1 and 3; WPA, 323).

81.38–82.1   I freighted a leaf . . . But I put no stamp on it] Mark Twain's manuscript draft of this passage was longer; he later reduced it to this brief remark: see the manuscript page reproduced on page 843 in the Introduction.

82.9–17   a boyish prank of mine . . . to drop the melon on his head] In his Autobiographical Dictation of 29 March 1906, Clemens told a greatly expanded version of the watermelon incident, identifying his brother Henry as the victim (CU-MARK, in *MTA*, 2:282–84). No evidence has been found that he actually encountered an old friend on the summit.

85.7   sixty U. S. soldiers from Camp Floyd] Located some forty miles southwest of Salt Lake City, Camp Floyd was built in 1858 to house federal troops during the Mormon conflict of 1857–58. The soldiers met by the Clemens brothers must have been among the last to leave the camp, which the army had fully abandoned by the end of July 1861 (Alexander and Arrington, 3–7, 18). The Clemenses reached "the remnant and ruin" of this "important military station" on 8 August, shortly after leaving Salt Lake City (122.1–2).

85.33–34   took supper with a Mormon "Destroying Angel."] The brothers' last stop before Salt Lake City was Mountain Dell Station, operated by Ephraim Knowlton Hanks (1826–96). Born and raised in Ohio, Hanks ran away from home and joined the navy for three years before converting to Mormonism in about 1846. He served the church as a mail carrier, negotiator with the Indians, and in 1857–58 as guerrilla and scout. The Sons of Dan, or Danites—also known among non-Mormons as the Avenging or Destroying Angels—was a secret, para-military society formed in 1838 by the Missouri Mormons to defend themselves and punish apostates. Members swore to obey the head of the church "the same as the Supreme God," pledging secrecy upon pain of death. The society's name derived from Genesis 49:17: "Dan shall be a serpent by the way, an adder in the path, that biteth the horse heels, so that his rider shall fall backward." Richard Burton, who had stopped at Mountain Dell Station one year earlier, reported that Hanks made "a facetious allusion to all our new dangers under the roof of a Danite." In fact, the Sons of Dan may well have been officially dissolved in Missouri, but because Mormon vigilantism continued in Utah, the popular view (clearly known to Hanks) routinely blamed the Danites, with their reputation for vengeance. Burton (and others) described Hanks as "a middle-sized, light haired, good looking man, with regular features, a pleasant and humorous countenance, and the manly manner of his early sailor life, touched with the rough cordiality of the mountaineer." Mark Twain, whose description contrasts markedly with Burton's, may have confused Hanks with Heber C. Kimball's son (see the next note] (Burton, 237–38; Fike and Headley, 28; Hanks and Hanks, 15, 40, 57–58, 62, 191–94, 296; Schindler, 26–39, 200 n. 18, 258, 354; Hyde, 104–5; Hilton, 12–13; Nels Anderson, 27 n. 27, 149, 167).

86.10–11 one person that looked like a gentleman—Heber C. Kimball's son] Almost certainly William Henry Kimball (1826–1907), eldest son of Heber C. Kimball (see the note at 92.9–10) and an officer in the territorial militia. In a letter dated 19 August 1861 to the St. Louis *Missouri Democrat*, Orion quoted Kimball's identification of himself as Heber Kimball's "hell-roaring son" (OC, 1). The description seems apt: in 1857 he had been implicated in two murders (for one of which he was later indicted but never tried), and in 1860 he had been disfellowshiped temporarily for drunkenness. It has been suggested that Mark Twain had access to Orion's newspaper letter while writing *Roughing It*, and that he deliberately reversed the two characters (making Hanks the rowdy, and Kimball the gentleman) in order to "temper the heated passions and violent controversies visible just below the surface of his brother's letter" (Rogers 1961, 46). But it seems at least as likely that, ten years after the fact, Mark Twain merely confused the two men (Kimball 1981, 223, 232, 311; Kimball 1988, 9, 106; Schindler, 193 n. 1, 251, 280 n. 42, 357, 359–60; Bancroft 1882–90, 21:509; Hickman, 125, 128–29; Hilton, 69–70, 77–78).

86.14–15 said to be the wives of the Angel—or some of them, at least] Like many prominent Mormons, Hanks was a polygamist, but a modest one at this time: he had only two wives in 1861 (Hanks and Hanks, 131, 251–52).

86.19–87.1 "peculiar institution,"] Polygamy. The term was also commonly used to refer to black slavery in the United States (Arrington 1985, 247, 323; Waite, 30; O'Dea, 105).

87.5 Salt Lake House] According to Burton, this "grand," two-story hotel was "the principal, if not the only establishment of the kind" in the city. It had "a long verandah, supported by trimmed and painted posts," and a large central courtyard "for cor[r]alling cattle" (Burton, 247).

88.14 the Acting Governor of the Territory] In 1906 Clemens mistakenly recalled that Frank Fuller "was acting Governor, and he gave us a very good time during those two or three days that we rested in Great Salt Lake City" (AD, 11 Apr 1906, CU-MARK, in *MTA*, 2:350). The acting governor (as Orion noted at this time in his newspaper letter) was actually the territorial secretary, Francis H. Wootton, standing in for Governor Alfred Cumming, a secessionist who had departed for his native Georgia in May (see the note at 552.40–553.2). Wootton, also a secessionist, had already tendered his resignation, preferring not to serve under Lincoln, but he could not leave until his replacement, Frank Fuller, arrived, which he did on 10 September, a month after the

Clemens brothers had gone on to Carson City. Clemens and Fuller did not meet until 1862, after which they became lifelong friends (OC, 1; "Departure of the Governor," Salt Lake City *Deseret News*, 22 May 61, 96; "Affairs in Utah," New York *Times*, 8 July 61, 2; L2, 5; Bancroft 1882–90, 21:604–5).

88.15–16 "Gentiles" are people who are not Mormons] Because they identified themselves with the Hebrews of the Old Testament, Mormons early applied this biblical term to all non-Mormons (Arrington and Bitton, 128).

88.30 the exclusively Mormon refresher, "valley tan."] Burton claimed that this local whiskey made from wheat, "being generally pure," was better than what "sold under the name of cognac" (Burton, 388). Edward P. Hingston, who visited Salt Lake City with Artemus Ward in 1864, pronounced it "the vilest whisky I remember tasting" (Hingston, 457). The term originally referred to leather tanned in the Salt Lake Valley, but came to apply to anything manufactured in Utah, including crockery, medicines, furniture, and gold coin (Bancroft 1882–90, 21:540 n. 44).

89.4–7 no public drinking saloons were allowed . . . and no private drinking . . . except . . . "valley tan."] Beer was also produced and privately consumed. At this time the Mormons emphasized temperance rather than abstinence, although by the end of the century alcohol use was virtually prohibited. Hingston noted that Brigham Young himself owned a distillery and sold valley tan at a "properly appointed office, where it is only to be bought wholesale by those who are permitted to purchase, and who must take it to their own homes for private consumption" (Hingston, 457–58; Bush, 64 n. 48; McCue, 70–71; Burton, 388).

89.5 Brigham Young] Young (1801–77) was born in Vermont, raised in New York, and, as a young man, trained as a carpenter and painter. In 1831 he converted to Mormonism, whose founder, Joseph Smith, he met the following year. He rose quickly in the church ranks, becoming, after Smith's murder in 1844, the second prophet of the church and later its president. He was largely responsible for organizing and leading the Mormon exodus to Utah, begun in 1846. After serving as the first governor of Utah Territory from 1851 to 1858, he was obliged to give up all civil office, but still exercised nearly unquestioned authority among Mormons, warranting Mark Twain's description of him as an "absolute monarch" (87.3–4) (Arrington 1985, 413–17; Jenson, 1:8–14; Kimball 1981, 206).

90.10–16 The armorial crest of my own State . . . was always too figurative . . . a GOLDEN BEEHIVE . . . all at work] The Missouri state and Utah territorial seals are pictured below. The Missouri motto acknowledged the importance of preserving the Union, despite the long-standing conflict between slave and free states. (The Missouri Compromise of 1820 admitted Missouri to the Union as a slave state.) The beehive was a favorite Mormon emblem, signifying both the virtue of industry and the overall social order they sought to create, after a passage in the Book of Mormon: "And they did also carry with them Deseret, which, by interpretation, is a honey bee" (*Book of Mormon* 1866, Ether 1:3 [Ether 2:3]; Carter, 4:67–70; Houck, 3:269–71).

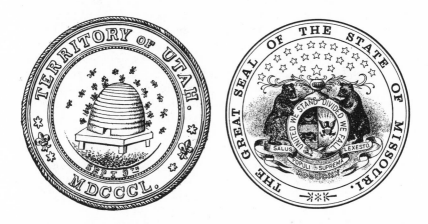

90.17–19 The city lies in the edge of a level plain as broad as the State of Connecticut . . . under a curving wall of mighty mountains] At the time, Salt Lake City occupied the northern edge of the valley, which extends roughly twenty-four miles north to south, and eighteen miles east to west. Connecticut is roughly sixty by ninety miles. The valley is surrounded by mountains, the tallest rising more than seven thousand feet above the valley floor.

91.7 Salt Lake City was healthy—an extremely healthy city] A commonplace: Burton, for example, claimed that its "climate of arid heat and dry cold is eminently suited to most healthy and to many sickly constitutions: children and adults have come from England, apparently in a dying state, and have lived to be strong and robust men" (Burton, 337).

92.8–9 the foundation of the prodigious temple] The Mormons began the temple at Salt Lake City in 1853, but suspended work in 1858 in anticipation of hostilities with federal troops (see the note at 548.26–31). Construction resumed in October 1861, shortly after the Clemenses left, and was completed in 1893. The foundation measured 186½ by 99 feet and consisted of footings 16 by 8 feet, designed to support walls at least 6 feet thick and 167½ feet high, with towers rising 15 to 43 feet higher. The building material was syenite (rock composed primarily of feldspar), quarried in the mountains and transported twenty miles by teams of horses and oxen (Rich, 307–8; *House of the Lord*, 12–13; "The Temple," Salt Lake City *Deseret News*, 18 Dec 61, 196).

92.9–10   that shrewd Connecticut Yankee, Heber C. Kimball] Heber Chase Kimball (1801–68) was born in Vermont and grew up there and in New York, where he became a Mormon in 1832. Rising rapidly in the church ranks, he led the first two Mormon missions to England. He was among the first Mormon settlers of Utah in 1847, and from then until his death was second only to Young in the church hierarchy. He served as chief justice, lieutenant governor, and ex-officio president of the senate of the provisional state of Deseret (1849–50), and as a member of the legislative council under the territorial government of Utah (1851–59). His widespread business interests included farming, ranching (cattle, sheep, and horses), milling, freighting, real-estate investment, and the vigorous promotion of domestic manufacture (Jenson, 1:34–37; Kimball 1981, 197–98, 206, 219–25; Esshom, 986–87).

92.11–12   the "Tithing-House,"] Devout Mormons began tithing (giving a tithe, or one-tenth, of their income to the church) in the late 1830s. The Salt Lake City Tithing Office and Deseret Store was a long narrow building with "cellars, store-rooms, receiving-rooms, pay-rooms, and writing offices" on Main Street, across from the building site of the temple (Burton, 302–3). There Mormons brought their tithes, either in coin or in produce and materials, which were then displayed for sale or distributed to the poor (Arrington and Bitton, 210; Cameron, 205, 227).

92.12   the "Lion House,"] So called after a sculpted lion over its entrance, it was one of a complex of buildings owned by Young, and it served as home for many of his wives and children. It contained a separate room for each wife, as well as a communal kitchen, dining room (large enough to seat fifty), nursery, schoolroom, and prayer room. Built in 1856 for sixty-five thousand dollars, it was located near the Tithing Office (Arrington 1985, 170; Burton, 301–2; Cameron, 227).

92.17–18   Mr. Street (since deceased)] James Street (d. 1867), whose experiences as an agent of the Overland Telegraph Company Mark Twain discusses in chapter 14, went to California in the early 1850s. He engaged in business in the southern part of the state, and later worked on the construction of a telegraph line between Los Angeles and San Francisco ("Death of James Street," San Francisco *Alta California*, 7 Jan 67, 2). Street may have accompanied the Clemens brothers on their visit to Young, although he is not named in Young's office journal for that day (see the next note). It has been suggested that the Clemenses did not meet Street in Salt Lake City, but only at Camp Floyd after leaving the city (Rogers 1961, 47). In 1874, however, Clemens wrote Street's daughter, "I remember your father very well indeed. His courtesies to us in Salt Lake City were of so pleasant a nature that even the fourteen years that have rolled by since have not sufficed to obliterate the memory of them" (SLC to Miss Street, 1 Dec 74, ViU†).

92.22–93.3 He talked about Utah . . . with our Secretary and certain government officials who came with us] Young's office journal for 7 August 1861 reads as follows:

> Br William Clayton, read the pony dispatch to some of the members of the club; Pres^t Young ‚Heber‚ & Wells were present.
> Br. W^m. Clayton, introduced: Mr Clements Sec^y of the Territory of Nevada who was on his way to Carson, ~~also~~ accompanied by ‚his Brother & Capt G. T. Hicher &‚ Sec.^y Wootten of this Ter. and ~~three~~ ‚one‚ other gentlemen. ~~Capt G. T. Hincher~~
> They conversed with Pres. Young & Wells principally about this Territory, situation of Big Cotton wood Lake, the health of the Country. Opinion of Mr Bridger who said he would be willing to give $50^{00} for the first bushel of wheat raised in this barren Country. The improvements in the Valley far exceeded their expectations, after the conversation they politely took their leave. (Young, entry for 7 Aug 61, used by permission)

William Clayton (1814–79), originally from Lancashire, England, went to Utah with Young in 1847 and became his clerk. Heber C. Kimball (see the note at 92.9–10) and Daniel Hanmer Wells (1814–91) were Young's first and second counselors, respectively; the three together were known as the First Presidency. Captain G. T. Hicher has not been identified; Secretary Wootton was the acting governor of Utah Territory (see the note at 88.14) (Kimball 1981, 45; Jenson, 1:36, 62, 717–18; Arrington and Bitton, 339). The "Opinion of Mr Bridger" refers to frontiersman and scout James Bridger (1804–81), who, according to an eyewitness in 1847, "considered it important not to bring a large population into the Great Basin until it was ascertained that grain could be raised; he said he would give one thousand dollars for a bushel of corn raised in the Basin" (Arrington 1985, 141, 458 n. 58).

93.4–5 I made several attempts to "draw him out" on Federal politics and his high-handed attitude toward Congress] Orion may have had explicit orders from the State Department to inquire into Mormon intentions following the secession of the Southern states. His letter to the *Democrat* indicated that he, rather than his brother, attempted to "draw out" the Mormon officials. Orion did not report Young's comments, but quoted the following speech of Kimball's:

> It's my opinion you won't see peace any more; the United States will go all to pieces, and the Mormons will take charge of and rule all the country; republicanism will be overthrown, but I won't say what will take its place, nor when, nor at what time the Mormons will commence their rule. You are going to have trouble in Nevada. But mind, I am a Union man, we are Union men, we are going to stand by the country. Now, tell it just as I say it. (OC, 1)

At the time of Clemens's visit, Young had done nothing that showed a particularly "high-handed attitude toward Congress." The phrase is probably a vestigial reference to material Mark Twain removed from the chapter, in proof, but ultimately included as appendix A when the book manuscript proved too short to fill the six hundred pages his publisher expected. Originally, the material in appendix A probably fell just after the previous paragraph (ending with "satisfied." at 92.16), and therefore before this reference to Young's "high-handed attitude." The final paragraph in appendix A makes clear that the "attitude" referred to was Young's response to events that occurred *after* "the date of our visit to Utah" (549.20), principally the federal law against polygamy passed in 1862 (see the note at 549.26–28). Appendix A and much else in these chapters on the Mormons derived from Mark Twain's reading of Catharine V. Waite's *Mormon Prophet and His Harem* (1868; first edition, 1866). He mentions her book in chapter 17 (117.2–3) and cites it as the source of his account of the Mountain Meadows massacre, which was evidently drafted as a chapter following chapter 14, but was likewise removed in proof, and ultimately restored as appendix B. Waite's view of Young was decidedly hostile (Waite, 20, 23, 25, 48, 89–90, 92–93, 295).

94.1–4   Mr. Street . . . had eight or nine hundred miles . . . to traverse with his wire] In June 1860 Congress passed the Pacific Telegraph Act, which authorized the construction, within two years, of a telegraph line from the Missouri River to San Francisco. In April 1861, several California telegraph companies merged to form the Overland Telegraph Company, which won the contract to build the line between Salt Lake City and Carson City, the eastern terminus of the existing line from San Francisco. Street, formerly the manager of the Pacific and Atlantic Telegraph Company in San Francisco, was placed in charge of the crew building west from Salt Lake City, while another crew worked east from Carson. Street's section covered about three hundred miles, half the distance to Carson (Thompson, 349, 354–55, 360–67; Gamble, 556–58; Reid, 501).

96.14–15   I believe his story. I knew him well . . . afterward in San Francisco] Street's story is confirmed, in its essentials, by his immediate superior, James Gamble, general superintendent of the Overland Telegraph Company. Gamble explained that "the first contract made with the Mormons was also a failure. Young denounced the contractors who agreed to furnish the poles from the pulpit, and said the work of furnishing the poles should and must be carried out" (Gamble, 559). After the line between Carson and Salt Lake was completed on 24 October 1861, Street returned to San Francisco, where he continued to work for several years for the California State Telegraph Company, which had absorbed the Overland Company. Clemens's surviving letters of the period, however, do not mention him (Gamble, 562; Langley 1861, 321, 493; Langley 1862, 369, 580; Langley 1865, 418).

97.9   these poor, ungainly and pathetically "homely" creatures] The supposedly dreary appearance of Mormon women was a popular myth.
Clemens was undoubtedly familiar with Richardson's description in
Beyond the Mississippi: "Few of the women are comely. . . . Nearly all
are plain—many extremely so. . . . they bear the indelible impress of
poverty, hard labor and stinted living. In those faces is little breadth,
thought or self-reliant reasoning, but much narrowness, grave sincerity
and unreflecting earnestness" (Richardson, 357). He is not known to
have read Fitz Hugh Ludlow's similar assertion in *The Heart of the
Continent,* that he "had not met a single woman who looked high-
toned, first-class, capable of poetic enthusiasm or heroic self-devotion;
. . . not one to whom a finely organized intellectual man could come
for companionship" (Ludlow, 375).

98n.2   Appendices A and B] As first drafted, appendix A was almost certainly part of chapter 13 (see the note at 93.4–5), and appendix B a separate chapter following chapter 14. Mark Twain cut out both, probably
in proof during August 1871, and only later agreed to make them into
appendixes to help lengthen his book, possibly as late as December
1871. See the Introduction, pages 844, 846, 865, 873.

98   *illus*] Strictly speaking, this drawing does not illustrate anything in
the text. Elisha Bliss, Mark Twain's publisher, probably inserted it
here to help fill up the white space on the last page of chapter 14. The
engraving was not made for *Roughing It,* but borrowed from a book
Bliss had published in 1870: Nelson Winch Green's *Mormonism,* an
anti-Mormon polemic based on an autobiographical account by Mary
Ettie V. Smith, a former Mormon. No evidence has been found that
Clemens himself was familiar with Green's book. Although the illustration appears here without a caption, it is called "The Endowment"
in the List of Illustrations (xxvi.6). That title was derived from
Green's caption, "The Oath of the Endowment": in Green's text the
picture illustrates a secret Mormon initiation ceremony in which, according to Mary Smith, the temptation scene in the Garden of Eden
was re-enacted in a fashion *"too monstrous for human belief."* Her
description of these "infernal rites" makes clear that the apron pictured was decorated with "green silk, to represent fig leaves," but it
does not explain the significance of the dagger (Green, 41–53, illustration facing 343).

99.4–6   how Burton galloped in among the . . . defenceless "Morrisites"
and shot them down . . . like so many dogs] Joseph Morris (1824–62)
was an English convert to Mormonism who emigrated to Utah in 1853.
In 1857 he claimed the first of a series of revelations which led him to
believe that he, rather than Brigham Young, was the true prophet. In
April 1861, shortly after being excommunicated, Morris organized his
own church, whose tenets included the imminence of a Second Com-

ing and the rejection of polygamy. Within a year he had attracted several hundred followers, who established a stronghold some thirty miles
north of Salt Lake City. In the spring of 1862 (several months after the
Clemens brothers had passed through Salt Lake City) the Morrisites
captured several would-be defectors, and then refused a judge's order to
release them. To enforce the order, Acting Governor Frank Fuller sent
a force of five hundred men, primarily Mormons, under the command
of Deputy Territorial Marshal Robert T. Burton (1821–1907), also a
Mormon. After a three-day battle, the Morrisites surrendered and
stacked their guns. Burton then rode into the stronghold and, according
to an eyewitness account reproduced in Waite's *Mormon Prophet*, murdered the unarmed Morris and three of his followers, including two
women. Burton claimed that he had fired only at Morris, and only
when Morris urged his followers to retrieve their weapons. In 1863,
several Morrisites were tried, and seven were convicted of second-
degree murder for the deaths of two militiamen, while others were
fined. All were pardoned three days later by Governor Stephen S. Har-
ding, who believed that Burton had acted out of vengeance and religious zeal. (Burton himself was tried and acquitted much later, in
1879.) Mark Twain could have learned of these events from Frank
Fuller, or contemporary news reports, or both. His characterization of
Burton may, however, indicate the influence of a source hostile to Mormons, such as Waite's *Mormon Prophet* (Howard, 112–32; Bancroft
1882–90, 21:615–21; Rich, 299–301; Neff, 650–52; Waite, 39, 136–41;
Esshom, 784; Hickman, 211–17).

99.6–8 Bill Hickman, a Destroying Angel, shot Drown and Arnold dead
for bringing suit against him for a debt] William Adams Hickman
(1815–83) joined the Mormon church in 1838 and was active in Mormon affairs until 1863, five years before being excommunicated. He
served both Smith and Young as a bodyguard, and was known as an Indian fighter, cattle rustler, and vigilante. He also sat in the Utah territorial legislature and served as a mail carrier, county sheriff, assessor,
tax collector, and prosecuting attorney. Beginning in 1863, he worked
as a spy and guide for the federal forces in Utah. C. M. Drown and Jo-
siah Arnold, a former Mormon, were murdered together in Salt Lake
City in July 1859. Mark Twain found a brief account of the murder in
Waite's *Mormon Prophet:*

A man by the name of Drown, brought suit upon a promissory note for $480,
against the Danite captain, Bill Hickman. The case being submitted to the
court, Drown obtained a judgment. A few days afterwards, Drown and a companion named Arnold were stopping at the house of a friend in Salt Lake City,
when Hickman, with some seven or eight of his band, rode up to the house, and
called for Drown to come out. Drown, suspecting foul play, refused to do so, and
locked the doors. The Danites thereupon dismounted from their horses, broke
down the doors, and shot down both Drown and Arnold. Drown died of his
wounds next morning, and Arnold a few days afterwards. Hickman and his band
rode off unmolested. (Waite, 84)

Although Hickman was indicted for murdering Drown, he was never brought to trial. In 1872, too late to affect *Roughing It*, J. H. Beadle edited and published Hickman's sensational autobiography, *Brigham's Destroying Angel*. There Hickman confessed to a number of grisly killings committed at the behest of Young, but he denied killing Drown and Arnold, pointing the finger instead at "a man by the name of Matthews," who had acted upon Young's remark that Drown was a "bad man, and should be used up" (Hickman, 110–11, 133–35; Hilton, ix–xi, 7–13, 43, 84, 85–86, 87, 108–9, 114, 119, 125–31; Schindler, 280 n. 42, 357; Van Wagoner and Walker, 119–24).

99.8–9 how Porter Rockwell did this and that dreadful thing] As a boy, Orrin Porter Rockwell (1813–78) knew and idolized Joseph Smith. In 1830, he became one of the earliest converts to Mormonism, serving as Smith's bodyguard in Illinois. Rockwell was notorious even before the Mormons left Illinois: he was arrested in 1843 for the attempted murder of Lilburn W. Boggs, a former governor of Missouri, and again in 1845 for killing a man implicated in Smith's murder the year before. Neither charge resulted in conviction. Rockwell was in the first party of Mormon immigrants to Utah in 1847. Known for his skills as a rider and marksman, he served as a scout, hunter, deputy marshal, express rider and, in 1857–58, guerrilla leader. Among the crimes ascribed to him was the 1857 killing of four wealthy travelers in Utah whom the Mormons suspected of being federal spies. No one was ever convicted of their murders. Rockwell was alleged to have killed as many as a hundred men, and was routinely identified as a "Destroying Angel" (Schindler, 3–6, 61–62, 70–73, 82, 94, 99, 148–49, 181, 192, 193, 223, 251, 268–78; Van Wagoner and Walker, 249–53).

99.27–29 their religion teaches them that the more wives a man has . . . the higher the place they will all have in the world to come] Beginning in 1835, Mormon doctrine held that the marriage bonds continued in an afterlife, an idea essential to the theological rationale for plural marriage, according to which a man's progression toward "exalted godhood" in heaven depended on the number of wives and children "sealed to him for eternity" (Van Wagoner, 56). Founder Joseph Smith was the first to practice plural marriage, albeit surreptitiously, as early as the 1830s. He did not develop the theological justification for it until 1843, when he claimed that a revelation from God called for the restoration of biblical polygamy. That revelation was known only to his closest associates, however, and he never publicly acknowledged it. In 1852, when the church under the leadership of Brigham Young announced plural marriage as a tenet, Mormons were exhorted, even commanded, to practice it, but only a small minority ever did so (Van Wagoner, 4–6, 85–86, 90–92, 97–98).

100.1–6 Brigham Young's harem contains twenty or thirty wives . . . children—fifty altogether] At the time of the Clemenses' visit, Young had seventeen wives (two of them sisters), ranging in age from about thirty-one to fifty-nine, and at least forty-one children (Arrington 1985, 420–21).

100.10–11   Johnson professed to have enjoyed a sociable breakfast in the Lion House] No evidence has been found that Johnson was modeled on a real person. Mark Twain's description of Young's family closely resembles the farcical treatment that Artemus Ward had used to poke fun at Mormon polygamy. Clemens was probably familiar with Ward's "A Visit to Brigham Young," first published in *Vanity Fair* on 10 November 1860 as "Artemus Ward Visits Brigham Young" and collected two years later in *Artemus Ward: His Book:*

> He don't pretend to know his children, thare is so many of um, tho they all know him. He sez about every child he meats call him Par, & he takes it for grantid it is so. His wives air very expensiv. Thay allers want suthin & ef he don't buy it for um thay set the house in a uproar. He sez he don't have a minit's peace. . . . "I find that the keers of a marrid life way hevy onto me," sed the Profit, "& sumtimes I wish I'd remaned singel." (Charles Farrar Browne 1862, 99–100)

Clemens met Ward in Virginia City in late 1863, and the two men quickly developed a mutual affection and professional respect (*L1*, 267–68, 269–70 n. 5). For further discussion of Ward's influence on Mark Twain, see Branch 1967, Branch 1978, Rowlette, and Cracroft.

103.13   Joseph Smith] See the note at 107.5–10.

103.13–14   By the slaughtered body of St. Parley Pratt] Parley Parker Pratt (1807–57) from New York joined the church in 1830 and five years later became one of Joseph Smith's original twelve apostles. He served as a missionary in the United States, Canada, Great Britain, the Pacific islands, and South America, and published several theological defenses of Mormon doctrine. He helped organize the first government in Utah and served in the territorial senate. He was murdered in Arkansas in May 1857 by the undivorced husband of his tenth plural wife, and was thereafter regarded by Mormons as a martyr (Van Wagoner and Walker, 217–23; Jenson, 1:83–85).

103.24–25   I will hang him higher than Haman] Haman, the chief minister of King Ahasuerus (Xerxes), persuaded the king to massacre all the Jews, and prepared a gallows to hang his own enemy, Mordecai. Queen Esther, a Jew, intervened, and Haman was hanged on his own gallows (Esther 3–7).

103.26   Shade of Nephi] See the note at 107.12.

103.34–36   I had married her . . . and of course I could not remember her name] Mark Twain may have known a similar anecdote in Richardson's *Beyond the Mississippi* in which Young, startled by a woman's claim to be his wife, consults his records and remarks, "Well, I believe you are right. I *knew* your face was familiar!" (Richardson, 355).

104.1–2 by the ghost of Orson Hyde] Originally from Connecticut, Orson Hyde (1805–78) was no ghost when *Roughing It* was published. He joined the Mormon church in 1831, became an apostle in 1835, and in the next few years led important missions to England and Jerusalem. For most of 1855 and 1856 he served as ecclesiastical leader and probate judge for newly formed Carson County, Utah (later Nevada) Territory. In 1858 he was appointed by Young to preside over a district of south-central Utah, where he lived until his death in 1878. Hyde was also elected to several terms in the Utah legislature, serving a total of more than fifteen years (Jenson, 1:80–82).

107.2–3 I brought away a copy from Salt Lake] The edition Mark Twain almost certainly used when writing this chapter was the "sixth European," published in 1866 and therefore not the copy he may have "brought away" with him in 1861.

107.5–10 If Joseph Smith . . . merely translated it from certain . . . plates of copper . . . in an out-of-the-way locality] Smith (1805–44), the founder and first prophet of the Mormon church (officially, the Church of Jesus Christ of Latter-day Saints), was born in Vermont and moved with his family to western New York in 1816. He claimed that a series of visions in the 1820s led him to discover certain metal plates buried under a stone near Manchester, New York. Smith's own statements and the Book of Mormon itself indicate variously that the plates were gold, or brass, or simply "ore." Smith's brother William, however, identified the metal as copper sometime after *Roughing It* was published, which suggests that Mark Twain had a contemporary source for this information, as yet unidentified (Hyde, 212–13; Donna Hill, 71). Engraved on these plates were ostensibly ancient characters which Smith called "Reformed Egyptian," and which he claimed to be able to translate by gazing into special "seer" stones. After dictating his translation over a period of months in 1828–29, he published it in March 1830 as the Book of Mormon. Eleven days later he founded his church, and over the next decade led a growing membership westward to various locations in Ohio, Missouri, and Illinois. In 1844, conflict both within the church and with non-Mormon neighbors at Nauvoo, Illinois, precipitated his arrest and, on 27 June, his murder in the Carthage, Illinois, jail (Brodie, 6–9, 37–43, 57, 60–62, 82, 87, 98–99, 208–9; Van Wagoner and Walker, 288–94; Donna Hill, 71–73; Arrington and Bitton, 13). See the first paragraph of appendix A for Mark Twain's summary of the history of the Mormon church under Smith.

107.12 The book seems to be merely a prosy detail of imaginary history] According to a modern (1981) introduction, the Book of Mormon is a "record of God's dealings with the ancient inhabitants of the Americas," principally the descendants and followers of Nephi and Laman, two sons of Lehi, who leave Jerusalem for the New World in 600 B.C.;

and the Jaredites, descendants and followers of Jared, who leave Babel after the destruction of the tower in 2500 B.C. The narrative culminates with the reappearance of Christ in America, heralding a period of harmony between the chronically warring Nephites and Lamanites. Ultimately the iniquitous Lamanites (the supposed forebears of the American Indians) destroy the Nephites. The chronicle is supposed to have been recorded on metal plates by several historians—first Nephi himself, and later Mormon and his son Moroni, the last surviving Nephite, who buried the plates around 421 A.D. Smith claimed that Moroni appeared to him as an angel in 1823 and revealed the location of the plates, but did not allow him to take possession of them until 1827 (Donna Hill, 98–100; Arrington and Bitton, 9, 14, 31–33; Hyde, 212–13; Brodie, 39–40, 43–44, 70–71).

108.14–39 THE TESTIMONY OF THREE WITNESSES ... OLIVER COWDERY, DAVID WHITMER, MARTIN HARRIS] Responding to demands that someone besides himself be allowed to see the plates, in March 1829 Smith announced a revelation instructing him to show them to three persons, unnamed. In June, when he had nearly completed his work on the Book of Mormon, he claimed a further revelation naming his three associates: Oliver Cowdery (1806–50), David Whitmer (1805–88), and Martin Harris (1783–1875). Harris and Cowdery had both assisted him by transcribing his dictations; Harris had also agreed to pay for publication; and Smith was living in Whitmer's home when he completed his work. The three witnesses subsequently gave varying accounts of the plates, and all became alienated from Smith and his church. Their testimony has appeared in every edition of the Book of Mormon (Brodie, 53, 60–62, 76–78; Donna Hill, 84–85, 89–97; Arrington and Bitton, 12–14; *Doctrine and Covenants*, sections 5 and 17; Jenson, 1:246–51, 263–76).

109.8–29 AND ALSO THE TESTIMONY OF EIGHT WITNESSES ... if the entire Whitmer family had testified] Familial connections among all eleven witnesses were even closer than their names might suggest. The five Whitmers—David, Christian (1798–1835), Jacob (1800–56), John (1802–78), and Peter, Jr. (1809–36)—were brothers; Oliver Cowdery and Hiram Page (1800–52) were married to the Whitmers' sisters; and Joseph Smith, Sr. (1771–1840), Hyrum Smith (1800–44), and Samuel Harrison Smith (1808–44) were Joseph's father and brothers (Jenson, 1: 52–53, 181–82, 251–52, 276–82; Brodie, 78–79).

109.31 Zeniff] Although the table of contents in the sixth European edition of the Book of Mormon (probably used by Mark Twain) lists the Record of Zeniff as a separate book, this record is actually a subsection of the Book of Mosiah; in addition, the text includes a fourth book of Nephi not listed in the contents (*Book of Mormon* 1866, viii, xi, Mosiah 6–13, 4 Nephi [492–96]).

109.33–111.21 first book of Nephi . . . reached it in safety] Mark Twain
paraphrases and quotes from *Book of Mormon* 1866, 1 Nephi 1:11–5:43
(1 Nephi 2:1–18:23), with the exception of the phrase "children of
Lehi" (109.34–35), which is found in Mormon 2:2 (Mormon 4:12).

110.5–6 He finished the ship *in a single day*, while his brethren stood by
and made fun of it] Mark Twain simplified and summarized several
pages of exceptionally turgid narrative. Nephi's brothers opposed his
plan to construct a ship "even for the space of many days," but through
divine intervention, he eventually enlisted their help, with construction taking longer than a single day (*Book of Mormon* 1866, 1 Nephi
5:22, 28–34 [1 Nephi 17:17, 49–18:4]).

111.22–24 Polygamy . . . was added by Brigham Young . . . it was regarded as an "abomination."] Following Waite's *Mormon Prophet*,
Mark Twain assumed that Young's 1852 public endorsement of polygamy was also its introduction. In fact, polygamy had been practiced in
secret by Joseph Smith and others during his lifetime, possibly as early
as the 1830s (see the note at 99.27–29). Waite presented the same evidence of doctrinal inconsistency, quoting both of the passages from the
Book of Mormon which Mark Twain quoted here (111.26–35, 112.1–5).
The conflict between Mormon scripture and practice, as well as
Smith's lifelong denial of polygamy (despite strong evidence to the
contrary), caused confusion among Mormons and led to many defec-
tions (see *Book of Mormon* 1866, Jacob 2:6,9 [Jacob 2:23–26, 3:5];
Waite, 176–79; Van Wagoner, 3–4, 12–13, 54–55, 72–74, 79; Foster,
130–39, 146–51).

112.1–2 the Lamanites . . . because of their filthiness and the cursings
which hath come upon their skins] The Lamanites, the supposed
ancestors of the American Indians, were cursed by God with a dark
skin because of their iniquities, and became "a filthy people, full of
idleness and all manner of abominations" (Brodie, 43–49; *Book of Mormon* 1866, 1 Nephi 3:31 [1 Nephi 12:23], 2 Nephi 4:4 [2 Nephi 5:21], 3
Nephi 1:9 [3 Nephi 2:14–15]).

112.16 now these were the names of the disciples whom Jesus had cho-
sen] According to the third Book of Nephi, Jesus, after appearing in the
New World, chose twelve disciples before returning to heaven. One of
these disciples, named Nephi, was a descendant of the original Nephi,
who had emigrated from Jerusalem six hundred years earlier (*Book of
Mormon* 1866, 3 Nephi 1:1, 8:10–11, 9:1–2 [3 Nephi 1:1–2, 18:36–39,
19:1, 4]).

112.17–20 how much more grandeur and picturesqueness . . . accompanied one of the tenderest episodes in the life of our Savior . . . I quote
the following] Mark Twain alludes to Christ's blessing of the children
in the New Testament:

And they brought young children to him, that he should touch them; and his disciples rebuked those that brought them. But when Jesus saw it, he was much displeased, and said unto them, Suffer the little children to come unto me, and forbid them not; for of such is the kingdom of God. Verily I say unto you, Whosoever shall not receive the kingdom of God as a little child, he shall not enter therein. And he took them up in his arms, put his hands upon them, and blessed them. (Mark 10:13–16)

The passage quoted from the *Book of Mormon* 1866 is 3 Nephi 8:5 (3 Nephi 17:19–25).

112.38–114.44   The book of Ether is an incomprehensible medley . . . I have not written] The Book of Ether recounts the history of the Jaredites (see the note at 107.12). The names and events mentioned here occur in *Book of Mormon* 1866, Ether 5–6 (Ether 12–15); the quoted extract is from Ether 6:7–9 (Ether 15:12–33).

113.21–22   that of the Kilkenny cats, which it resembles] Proverbial: two cats from Kilkenny County, Ireland, fought until they killed each other, leaving nothing behind but their tails. The story probably derived from the long-standing enmity between two "municipalities of Kilkenny . . . who contendeth so severely about boundaries and dues to the end of the 17th century that they mutually ruined each other" (Lean, 1:276). About 1700, their enmity gave rise to a nursery rhyme: "There were two cats at Kilkenny; Each thought there was one too many" (Stevenson, 799). A rather less plausible theory traces the expression to Hessian soldiers, garrisoned at Kilkenny during the Irish rebellion of 1798, who, for sport, forced cats to fight to the death (Harvey, 448).

116.3   the "Mormon question,"] Public policy toward the Mormons remained unsettled for much of the century. Concern over their political intransigence, religious eccentricity and dogmatism, and especially polygamy constituted the "Mormon question" or "Mormon problem," which Fitz Hugh Ludlow identified as "the engrossing question, 'What shall we do with the Mormons?'" (Ludlow, iii; Allen and Leonard, 296–97; Arrington and Bitton, 173–74, 176, 179; Bancroft 1882–90, 21:495–96 n. 30; Lingenfelter, Dwyer, and Cohen, 226).

116.8–117.6   "Mountain Meadows massacre" . . . the Mormons *were* the assassins] Mark Twain's account of this episode, based on Waite's *Mormon Prophet*, is in appendix B (see the note at 93.4–5).

122.11–13   there was no well or spring . . . a stage station there] There was in fact a spring at Fish Springs Station (or Fish Creek Station, as Orion called it in his journal), but it consisted merely of pot-holes full of warm, sulfurous water (supplement A, item 1; Root and Connelley, 103; Burton, 558). In the fall of 1871, after he had long since completed the printer's copy of his book, Mark Twain was obliged to rewrite part of this chapter when the printers lost the manuscript for it. He evidently rewrote it in October, while on lecture tour, and therefore without access to Orion's journal. See the Introduction, pages 869–70.

124.23–24   the station on the farther verge of the desert] The travelers arrived at Willow Springs Station at 2 P.M. on 9 August, having taken twenty-two hours to traverse some sixty-eight miles along the southern edge of the vast Great Salt Lake Desert (supplement A, item 1; Root and Connelley, 103).

124.31   "gild refined gold or paint the lily."] *King John*, act 4, scene 2.

126.2–3   Rocky Cañon, two hundred and fifty miles from Salt Lake] Mark Twain's source for this identification was undoubtedly Orion's journal entry of 10 August, but the forbidding canyon located at this point of the overland route was actually named Egan Canyon. Situated between "steep high rugged mountains," Egan Canyon had been the site of more than one attack by Goshute Indians (Mason, 51–53, 60–62; supplement A, item 1; Burton, 617; see supplement B, map 1C).

126.5–6   the wretchedest type of mankind I have ever seen, . . . the Goshoot Indians] This small tribe—whose name is now more commonly spelled "Goshute" (from the Indian word for "parched or dry earth" plus the suffix "ute")—were members of the Shoshoni family. They inhabited northwestern Utah and eastern Nevada, numbering fewer than five hundred by the 1870s (Hodge, 1:496–97; see also the note at 128.19–129.12).

126.8   the despised Digger Indians of California] The name "Digger" was originally applied to one Paiute tribe, which alone among the Paiutes practiced agriculture. In time it came to refer instead to numerous root-eating Paiute tribes inhabiting several western states, including California, Nevada, and Utah; "as the root-eaters were supposed to represent a low type of Indian, the term speedily became one of opprob[r]ium" (Hodge, 1:390).

126.12–127.3   Wood's "Uncivilized Races of Men" . . . Bosjesmans (Bushmen) of South Africa] In the fall of 1870, when beginning work on *Roughing It*, Mark Twain asked Elisha Bliss to send him a copy of John George Wood's two-volume work, *The Uncivilized Races, or Natural History of Man*, first published in London in 1868–70 and reissued by the American Publishing Company in 1870 (SLC to Bliss, 29 Oct 70, Daley). Mark Twain's own copy of the book, presumably the one Bliss sent him, survives with his marginalia sprinkled throughout (NvU); it contains no holograph comments, however, about the tribes he lists here. Wood, an "armchair" naturalist who compiled his book without leaving England, included articles—often contemptuously critical—on the Fuegians, Hottentots, Kytch, and Bushmen (as well as many others), but did not mention the Goshutes or Diggers in his brief article on the Indians of North America. Wood's conclusions were somewhat at variance with Mark Twain's: he seems to have found the Fuegians and the Kytch even more "degraded" than the Bushmen (John George Wood, 1:269, 485, 2:514, 515).

127.9–21 like all the other "Noble Red Men" . . . thinking whisky is referred to] The concept of the "Noble Red Man" has been traced at least as far back as the work of John Dryden, who wrote of "the noble savage" uncorrupted by "the base laws of servitude" (*The Conquest of Granada* [1670], act 1, scene 1); Mark Twain was most familiar with its embodiment in James Fenimore Cooper's Indian heroes (see the note at 128.19–129.12). In describing the Goshutes he may have recalled a passage in *Beyond the Mississippi* in which Richardson expressed similar sentiments:

> Near a little road-side grocery, supported by a post and flanked by an empty cask, stood a Noble Red Man. Indifferent to his tattered clothing, which afforded no protection from the sharp, wintry nights—with his long black locks flying in the wind—his whole soul was wrapped in a whisky bottle. He regarded it with a fixed stare, in which satisfaction at the quality of its contents and pensive regret at their diminishing quantity were ludicrously blended. Mr. Cooper died too early. I think one glimpse of *this* Aboriginal would have saved his pen much labor, and early American literature many Indian heroes. (Richardson, 512)

127.29–30 whichever animal-Adam the Darwinians trace them to] Mark Twain was no doubt referring to Charles Darwin's most recent work, *The Descent of Man*, volume 1 of which was published in the United States in mid-February 1871, and volume 2 in late March (D. Appleton and Co.). Clemens purchased and read at least the first volume (his copy is in CU-MARK)—probably by early April, when he evidently revised this chapter, and certainly no later than 2 July, when he wrote to Jim Gillis (see the note at 412.1–3), "Say, old philosopher, would you like to read Darwin? If you would, let me know, & I will get the books & forward them to you" (SLC to Gillis, PH in CU-MARK, courtesy of CCamarSJ†; New York *Tribune:* "New Publications," 10 Feb 71, 6, and "Books of the Week," 25 Mar 71, 6).

127.35–128.17 they attacked the stage-coach . . . the soldierly driver was dead] This is an essentially accurate account of the start of the Goshute War of 1863, which began on 22 March of that year and concluded in October when the Indians sued for peace. (Mark Twain's version differs from contemporary newspaper reports only in its failure to mention three other passengers—an old man, who was wounded and recovered, and his two little sons.) The attack occurred near Eight Mile Station, which in 1863 was in western Utah but is now in eastern Nevada (Angel, 180–83; "More Indian Difficulties," Salt Lake City *Deseret News*, 25 Mar 63, 312; "The Attack on the Overland Stage," Sacramento *Union*, 31 Mar 63, 3, reprinting the Virginia City *Union* of 28 March).

128.2   Judge Mott] Gordon Newell Mott (1812–87) was born in Ohio and practiced law in California before moving to Nevada Territory in 1861. From 1861 to 1863 he served as judge of the district comprising Lake, Storey, and Washoe counties, and as associate justice of the territorial supreme court. In 1863–64 he was a territorial representative to the United States Congress (*BDUSC*, 1544; Kelly 1862, 10; Kelly 1863, 9).

128.19–129.12   a disciple of Cooper . . . over-estimating the Red Man while viewing him through the mellow moonshine of romance] Mark Twain's disdain for the idealized image of the American Indian—especially as found in James Fenimore Cooper's Leather-Stocking Tales (of which *The Last of the Mohicans* [1826] was the second)—is evident as early as 25 June 1862 in a letter published in the Keokuk *Gate City* (SLC 1862b) and as late as 1884 in the unfinished tale "Huck Finn and Tom Sawyer among the Indians" (SLC 1884b). See, for example, his remarks in an 1867 letter to the San Francisco *Alta California* (SLC 1867j); in "A Day at Niagara," an August 1869 Buffalo *Express* contribution (SLC 1869e); and in "The Noble Red Man," a piece in the September 1870 *Galaxy* (SLC 1870j). For analyses of Mark Twain's treatment of this subject see Denton, Harris, Lorch 1945, and McNutt.

129.7   Emerson Bennett's works] Bennett (1822–1905) wrote melodramatic adventure fiction, much of it set on the frontier. Two such novels of his, both published in 1849, sold a hundred thousand copies each: *The Prairie Flower* and its sequel, *Leni-Leoti.*

129.7–8   studying frontier life at the Bowery Theatre] Since its construction in 1826 on the west side of the Bowery just below Canal Street, this theater had been quite popular for productions of all types; it specialized, however, in melodramas and thrillers, some of which were dramatized versions of dime novels by authors like Bennett (King, 578; Odell, 7:224–27).

129.20–21   the Baltimore and Washington Railroad Company . . . are Goshoots] The specific reason for Mark Twain's grievance against this railroad, the Washington branch line of the Baltimore and Ohio Railroad, is not now known.

130.1–24   the highest mountain peaks we had yet seen . . . the "Sink" of the Carson] Mark Twain's geographical description is not entirely accurate. His remark about the mountain peaks is clearly derived from Orion's record, which reads "Passed points declared by the driver to be the highest we had crossed." In fact, when the travelers crossed the Ruby Mountains through the Overland Pass they were several hundred feet lower than they had been at both South Pass and Big Mountain, and the highest mountains in view were more than a thousand feet lower than those of the Wind River and Uinta mountains visible from South

Pass and beyond. The "Great American Desert" was more commonly known as the Forty Mile Desert, a fact he alludes to in his description of it as "forty memorable miles of bottomless sand." It was so named by early emigrants, whose route took them across the desert from north to south, a distance of some forty miles. The overland-mail route, however, traversed the desert from east to west, a considerably shorter distance. Finally, Carson Lake and Carson Sink are separate features, although they are connected by sloughs (Angel, 359, 360, 365; Townley, 46–47; supplement A, item 1; see supplement B, maps 1D and 2).

130.5–6   the eastward-bound telegraph-constructors] See the note at 94.1–4.

130.7   his Excellency Gov. Nye] James Warren Nye (1815–76), an outspoken Republican politician from New York, served in the late 1850s as police commissioner and first president of the New York City Metropolitan Board of Police. In 1860 he campaigned vigorously for Lincoln, who rewarded him the following year with an appointment as governor of the newly formed Nevada Territory. Nye arrived at Carson City early in July 1861. After Nevada became a state, he was elected United States senator from 1864 to 1873. During his frequent absences from the territory, Orion, as territorial secretary, served as acting governor. Both the Clemenses enjoyed consistently friendly relations with Nye during their stay in Nevada, although he later reportedly dismissed Clemens as "nothing but a damned Secessionist" (Frank Fuller to A. B. Paine, 7 Dec 1910, Chester L. Davis 1956d, 1; Mack 1961a, 9–11; *BDUSC*, 1579; *L1*, 145–46 n. 2). Clemens later recalled,

Governor Nye was an old and seasoned politician from New York—politician, not statesman. He had white hair. He was in fine physical condition. He had a winningly friendly face and deep lustrous brown eyes that could talk as a native language the tongue of every feeling, every passion, every emotion. His eyes could outtalk his tongue, and this is saying a good deal, for he was a very remarkable talker, both in private and on the stump. He was a shrewd man. He generally saw through surfaces and perceived what might be going on inside without being suspected of having an eye on the matter. (AD, 2 Apr 1906, CU-MARK, in *MTA*, 2:305)

131.7–8   Ragtown] This settlement on the Carson River, which marked the end of the arduous desert passage for early emigrants on the trail to the California gold fields, probably derived its name from the worn-out clothes they washed and draped over bushes to dry (Townley, 31; Carlson, 197).

131.12   Horace Greeley] Greeley (1811–72) had been the influential editor of the New York *Tribune* since 1841, and was a prolific author and a political leader as well. Two years before the Clemens brothers went west, Greeley had taken the overland stagecoach to San Francisco as a correspondent for the *Tribune*; his travel letters were later published in *An Overland Journey, from New York to San Francisco, in the Summer of 1859* (Greeley 1860). He was one of Mark Twain's favorite targets for good-humored satire: see chapter 70.

131.13–132.6 Hank Monk . . . what was left of him] Henry James Monk (1826–83), the "king of stage drivers" (as Mark Twain referred to him in 1863), was born in New York; in 1852 he went to California, and for over thirty years drove stages there and in Nevada, working first for the California Stage Company and then, after 1857, for the Pioneer Stage Line (SLC 1863m). Monk was immortalized in western legend by virtue of a single accomplishment: a sixty-mile stagecoach trip over the Sierra Nevada on 30 July 1859, transporting Greeley from an inn fifteen miles west of Genoa, Nevada Territory, to Sportsman's Hall, California (a reception committee took Greeley in a carriage the remaining twelve miles to Placerville). Over the roughest and most dangerous forty miles of the trip Monk drove his horses at a "break-neck rate," as Greeley himself reported it (Greeley 1860, 281–82). Monk enjoyed recounting the adventure; the most reliable surviving version of the story appeared in the San Francisco *Golden Era* in April 1860, in a letter signed "Cornish." In December 1863 Mark Twain attended (and reported) a ceremony at which Monk's admirers presented him with a "superb gold watch . . . gorgeously embellished with coaches and horses" and engraved with "Hank's famous remark to Horace Greeley" (SLC 1863y; Cornish, 5; Lillard and Hood, 7–11, 41 n. 1, 44 nn. 13, 15; see Lillard and Hood for an exhaustive treatment of the incident).

132.8–9 Gregory Diggings] John H. Gregory of Georgia made a rich gold strike in May 1859 on the north fork of Clear Creek in Colorado, attracting thousands of prospectors. The diggings ultimately proved to be the richest in the state, producing $85 million in gold. The site is now near Central City, about thirty miles west of Denver (Bancroft 1882–90, 20:377–78; State Historical Society of Colorado, 41–42).

135.10–12 I . . . listened to that deathless incident four hundred and eighty-one or eighty-two times] Lillard and Hood make clear that the Greeley-Monk anecdote was indeed an exceedingly familiar story on the West Coast for many years. Mark Twain evidently first experimented with repeating the story for the sake of humorous satire sometime after delivering his first Sandwich Islands lecture in San Francisco on 2 October 1866, trying it out during his October–November lecture tour in California and Nevada ("Robbery of Mark Twain," Virginia City *Union*, 12 Nov 66, 3; *L1*, 361–62, 366–67 n. 4; Lorch 1966, 45–46). He then included the anecdote in his second San Francisco lecture, on 16 November, an occasion he described in detail many years later:

> For repetition is a mighty power in the domain of humor. If frequently used, nearly any precisely worded and unchanging formula will eventually compel laughter if it be gravely & earnestly repeated, at intervals, five or six times. I undertook to prove the truth of this, forty years ago, in San Francisco, on the occa-

sion of my second attempt at lecturing. My first lecture had succeeded to my satisfaction. Then I prepared another one, but was afraid of it because the first fifteen minutes of it was not humorous. I felt the necessity of preceding it with something which would break up the house with a laugh and get me on pleasant and friendly terms with it at the start, instead of allowing it leisure to congeal into a critical mood, since that could be disastrous. With this idea in mind, I prepared a scheme of so daring a nature that I wonder now that I ever had the courage to carry it through. San Francisco had been persecuted for five or six years with a silly and pointless and unkillable anecdote which everybody had long ago grown weary of—weary unto death. It was as much as a man's life was worth to tell that moldy anecdote to a citizen. I resolved to begin my lecture with it, and keep on repeating it until the mere repetition should conquer the house and make it laugh. That anecdote is in one of my books. . . .

I told it in a level voice, in a colorless and monotonous way, without emphasizing any word in it, and succeeded in making it dreary and stupid to the limit. Then I paused and looked very much pleased with myself, and as if I expected a burst of laughter. Of course there was no laughter, nor anything resembling it.

Mark Twain told the story three times in all; after the third telling, the audience finally broke into a "tempest" of laughter:

It was a heavenly sound to me, for I was nearly exhausted with weakness and apprehension, and was becoming almost convinced that I should have to stand there and keep on telling that anecdote all night, before I could make those people understand that I was working a delicate piece of satire. I am sure I should have stood my ground and gone on favoring them with that tale until I broke them down, under the unconquerable conviction that the monotonous repetition of it would infallibly fetch them some time or other. (AD, 31 Aug 1906, CU-MARK, in *AMT,* 143–46)

The following spring, Mark Twain again included the anecdote in his New York lecture, delivered in Cooper Union on 6 May 1867,

remarking when he did so that it had not the slightest connection with the subject of his lecture; but that every one who had been to California held it to be a solemn duty to inflict this story on any innocent Eastern man whom fate might place in his power. (Review of Richardson's *Beyond the Mississippi* in the New York *Citizen,* 24 Aug 67, 3)

135.18   sozodont] Sozodont—a red liquid containing 37 percent alcohol—was a popular dentifrice manufactured since early 1859 by Hall and Ruckel of Brooklyn; the advertisements for it, which appeared in newspapers and magazines throughout the country for several decades, contained the claim that it "purifies and perfumes the BREATH" (Wharton, 139; Presbrey, 339, 340, 382, 402).

135.26–28   Bayard Taylor has written about this hoary anecdote . . . and every other correspondence-inditing being] No version of the anecdote has been found in the western writings of Bayard Taylor (1825–78) or J. Ross Browne (1821–75). Taylor, a renowned travel writer, poet, novelist, translator, and New York *Tribune* correspondent, was in California at the same time as Greeley, arriving in August 1859 for a three-month lecture tour. His account of the tour—"New Pictures from California," included in *At Home and Abroad* (second series, 1862)—makes no mention of the Greeley-Monk anecdote. Browne, also an indefatigable traveler and prolific writer, served for a time in the West as special inspector of Indian affairs and commissioner of mines for the federal government. He and Clemens had known each other since at least 1866 (*L1*, 368). Albert D. Richardson (1833–69), a journalist and western traveler, corresponded for the *Tribune* for many years. His western writings from 1857–67 were incorporated into *Beyond the Mississippi,* which included a version of what he termed the "apocryphal" Greeley-Monk anecdote (Richardson, 382–84). Mark Twain almost certainly read Olive Logan's version of the yarn in her article "Does It Pay to Visit Yo Semite?" in the October 1870 *Galaxy,* which also included his own "Memoranda"; Logan explained that although "everybody has heard" the anecdote, "no matter, everybody must hear it again" (Logan, 503). And, finally, the joke was alluded to, if not actually recounted, in the following works, any of which Mark Twain could have read: *Artemus Ward: His Travels* (Charles Farrar Browne 1865, 156–62); Samuel Bowles's *Across the Continent* (137–38); Charles Wentworth Dilke's *Greater Britain* (1:188); and Harvey Rice's *Letters from the Pacific Slope* (50–51).

136n.1–2   the adventure it celebrates *never occurred*] It was Joseph Goodman (see the note at 274.25–26) who initially informed Clemens that Greeley had denied the truth of the anecdote. Shortly after the publication of *Roughing It,* when Greeley was running for president, Goodman wrote an anti-Greeley editorial for the *Enterprise,* which read in part:

> In the Fall of 1869, we met Hank Monk at Reno, as we were about leaving for the East. With the recollection of that ride fresh in his memory, and a sentiment of fellowship toward his illustrious passsenger, with whom he had passed hand in hand into literature and fame, Hank requested us to call upon Mr. Greeley and tell him that in memory of their celebrated mountain ride he wished him to procure a pass that would enable him to visit his friends in the East. . . . We met the philosopher at the Astor House, and briefly delivered our message. The reply was concise and emphatic. "Damn him! that fellow has done me more harm than any man in America!" We protested our ignorance of any injury. "But there was not a damned word of truth in the whole story!" rejoined Mr. Greeley. . . .
>
> In telling the story of the Placerville ride, will Democratic orators append this sequel, illustrative of the overbearing and illiberal nature of Mr. Greeley? . . . Hank Monk still handles the whip and reins, but we fancy he has more friends on this coast than Horace Greeley—though he is running for President. (Goodman 1872, 2; see also *MTB,* 1:303 n. 1)

On 24 March 1871—not long after the present chapter was written—Goodman began a visit with Clemens in Elmira, where he read part of the *Roughing It* manuscript. Presumably he then reported his 1869 encounter with Greeley. In August, when Clemens probably read this chapter in proof, he decided to ask Greeley himself whether the disclaimer was accurate, explaining that "a newspaper editor, who said he got it from you," had told him that it had *"never occurred"* (SLC to Greeley, 17 Aug 71, NN†; "City and Neighborhood," Elmira *Adver-*

tiser, 25 Mar 71, 4). Greeley's reply, if any, is not known to survive, but it is clear that he had ample reason to resent the story, which had been used by his political enemies to ridicule him. In March 1866 a congressman from New York who disagreed with a *Tribune* editorial had caused Artemus Ward's version to be read aloud to the entire House of Representatives (Lillard and Hood, 17).

136n.5–6 but what does the thirteenth chapter of Daniel say? Aha!] Although the book of Daniel in the King James Bible has only twelve chapters, the Catholic Bible includes two additional chapters that Protestants regard as apocryphal. Chapter thirteen—the story of Susanna, in which two elders who falsely accuse her of adultery are exposed by Daniel and put to death—was undoubtedly familiar to Mark Twain, since the Clemens family's 1817 King James Bible included the Apocrypha (CU-MARK). Mark Twain's intent here, admittedly somewhat obscure, seems to be to endorse the death penalty for "a man who would wantonly contrive so flat a [story] as this." The possibility remains, however, that he teasingly referred to a nonexistent book of the Bible so as to reinforce his allegation that the Greeley-Monk anecdote was utterly "apocryphal."

138.20–31 Mr. Harris . . . rode by . . . with a bullet through one of his lungs, and several in his hips] John (Jack) Harris was a notorious stagecoach bandit who nevertheless enjoyed the "general esteem" of the Nevada community, which considered the stage company to be among "the biggest robbers in all the world." No jury would convict him, even when a member of his gang turned state's evidence against him (Considine 1923b; Angel, 568). The gunfight that Mark Twain describes here, which occurred on 14 August 1861, was reported in the *Enterprise:* Harris, who "had some grudge against" a man named Julien, fired on him and missed; he himself was wounded in the chest and thigh ("Shooting Scrape," San Francisco *Evening Bulletin,* 21 Aug 61, 3, reprinting the Virginia City *Territorial Enterprise* of 17 August). Harris later went to Pioche, in eastern Nevada, where Wells, Fargo and Company hired him to prevent his depredations; Harris still managed to hold up the stagecoaches, taking a shortcut back to the station in time to meet them upon their arrival. Shortly before his death in 1875, allegedly caused by "a general breaking up of the system" (the result of his having been shot "several times" over the years), he confessed that his real name was Amos Huxford, and that he had been raised in Maine by a relative named Harris (Ashbaugh, 31; "Death of a Noted Character," San Francisco *Alta California,* 3 May 75, 1, reprinting the Pioche [Nev.] *Record* of 27 April).

138.36–139.11 the daily "Washoe Zephyr" set in . . . a skurrying storm of emigrating roofs and vacant lots] Exaggerated claims and comic tales about the Washoe winds were a staple of 1860s Nevada journalism.

Dan De Quille (William Wright), a colleague of Mark Twain's on the *Enterprise*, wrote his share of such items, as did J. Ross Browne and Mark Twain: see Lillard, 257–60, which presents a full discussion of the subject and reprints items by Wright in the Cedar Falls (Iowa) *Gazette*, as well as a passage from "A Peep at Washoe" (J. Ross Browne 1860–61, 289–90). Two items that appeared in the *Enterprise* local column in late 1862 have been attributed to Mark Twain: "A Gale" and "Blown Down" (SLC 1862d, 1862j). In the latter piece he remarked, "At sunset yesterday, the wind commenced blowing after a fashion to which a typhoon is mere nonsense, and in a short time the face of heaven was obscured by vast clouds of dust all spangled over with lumber, and shingles, and dogs and things."

140.4 Washoe is a pet nickname for Nevada] "Washoe" comes from the word "washiu," which means "person" in the language of the Washo Indians. The Washo, traditional enemies of the Paiute, were a small tribe inhabiting the region around Carson City and Lake Tahoe; in 1859 they numbered only about nine hundred (Hodge, 2:920).

140.5–6 Scriptural wind . . . "whence it cometh."] John 3:8.

140.21 newly arrived Chief and Associate Justices of the Territory] Upon the creation of Nevada Territory in March 1861, President Lincoln appointed George Turner (d. 1885) as chief justice, and Gordon N. Mott (see the note at 128.2) and Horatio M. Jones as associate justices. Mott was already in Carson City when the Clemenses arrived; but Turner, a lawyer and jurist from Ohio, and Jones, who was born in Pennsylvania but had become a resident of Missouri, did not arrive until the second week in September (*L1*, 126 n. 2, 128–29 n. 2, 243 n. 4; James W. Nye to William Seward, 19 July 61, *Territorial Papers*; Marsh, 691 n. 255).

141.4 Bridget O'Flannigan] A fictional name for Mrs. Margret Murphy, whose boarding house was on the north side of the plaza (*L1*, 134 n. 2; Kelly 1862, 85).

141.18–142.6 made of old flour sacks . . . pictures from *Harper's Weekly* on them] This description is similar to a passage in the letter Clemens published in the Keokuk *Gate City* on 20 November 1861. He may have referred to a clipping of the letter to refresh his memory:

> The houses are mostly frame, and unplastered; but "papered" inside with flour-sacks sewn together—with the addition, in favor of the parlor, of a second papering composed of engravings cut from "Harper's Weekly;" so you will easily perceive that the handsomer the "brand" upon the flour-sacks is, and the more spirited the pictures are, the finer the house looks. (SLC 1861)

143.1–2 voluntary camp followers of the Governor] Only three of these "camp followers" are known by name: Will H. Wagner, James Neary, and Clement T. Rice (see the notes at 147.17–19 and 278.11–12).

145.6–8   Bob H—— sprung up . . . the tarantulas is loose] This anecdote
was evidently based on an actual incident, which Clemens recorded in
his notebook in February 1865: "Time Bob Howland came into Mrs.
Murphy's corral in Carson, drunk, knocked down Wagners bottles of
tarantulas & scorpions & spilled them on the floor" (N&J1, 80). Clemens first met Robert Muir Howland (1838–90) in late August 1861
when Howland, who lived in Aurora (in the Esmeralda mining district),
stayed at Mrs. Murphy's while serving as a delegate to the Union Convention in Carson City. A native of New York, he emigrated to California and then, in the summer of 1861, to Nevada Territory. He was the
co-owner and superintendent of several mines in Aurora, marshal of
that town, and, in 1864, was appointed warden of the territorial prison
in Carson City by Governor Nye. In later life he continued his mining
activities and acted as a mining consultant. For many years Howland
and his wife, Louise (whom he married in 1867), maintained a friendship with Clemens and his wife, chiefly through correspondence (L1,
142 n. 2; "Married," Virginia City Territorial Enterprise, 12 Nov 67, 3).

147.7–8   as the historian Josephus phrases it, in his fine chapter upon the
destruction of the Temple] Flavius Josephus (A.D. 37–?100), historian
of the Jews, described the destruction of the temple of Solomon in Jerusalem by the Babylonians in Book 10, chapter 8, of Antiquities of the
Jews. Clemens owned The Genuine Works of Josephus (Philadelphia:
1829), which included Antiquities, although it is not known when he
acquired it (Gribben, 1:361).

147.11–12   I had nothing to do and no salary] See the note at 2.14–15.

147.13–15   Johnny K—— . . . the young son of an Ohio nabob] John D.
Kinney (1840–78), whom Clemens described to his mother in September 1861 as a "first-rate fellow," had worked as a teller in his father's
Cincinnati bank until his trip west (L1, 124). He arrived in Carson City
during the second week in September 1861, on the same stagecoach as
justices Turner and Jones. During his brief stay in Nevada Territory he
worked as a realtor and speculated heavily in mining claims. In March
1862 he returned to Cincinnati, and by 1870 had become a partner in
his father's bank (L1, 126 n. 2; SLC to Robert and Louise Howland, 6
Mar 70, Gunn).

147.16–17   the marvelous beauty of Lake Tahoe . . . drove us thither to
see it] This lake west of Carson City (see supplement B, map 3) spans
the California-Nevada border and is about twenty-two miles long by
twelve miles wide. It was officially named Lake Bigler, after John Bigler,
California's third governor (1852–56); the Washo name "Tahoe" (meaning "water" or "lake") came into use during the Civil War because of
Bigler's unpopular secessionist views, but was not officially adopted
until 1945. Clemens's trip to the lake probably took place on 14–17

September, shortly after Kinney's arrival in Carson City, not at the "end of August," as Mark Twain claims (Hart, 48, 268; *L1*, 126 n. 3).

147.17–19   Three or four members of the Brigade . . . located some timber lands] In a "Memorandum of Agreement and Copartnership" dated 24 August 1861, eleven men laid claim to a "certain parcel of Timber Land" on the northeast shore of Lake Tahoe, in the name of "John Nye & Co" (PH in CU-MARK, courtesy of Michael H. Marleau). In addition to John Nye, the governor's brother (see the note at 228.2–4), the signers included: John Ives, the governor's physician, who had accompanied him from New York; Will H. Wagner, presumably the boarder at Mrs. Murphy's who collected tarantulas (see the note at 145.6–8); and James Neary, another of Mrs. Murphy's boarders (*L1*, 143 n. 9, 200 n. 2; Kelly 1862, 85).

147.29–30   We . . . hired a couple of Chinamen to curse those people who had beguiled us] In writing to his mother in September 1861 about this trip, Clemens described Kinney's indulgence in restorative profanity while slyly affirming his own restraint. Kinney supposedly asked him, "Why don't you *curse* the infernal place? You know you *want* to. *I* do, and *will* curse the ———— thieving country as long as I live" (*L1*, 125).

152.2   the next two or three weeks] In a letter to his mother written immediately upon his return from Lake Tahoe (conjecturally dated 18–21 September 1861), Clemens stated that he had stayed there only four days (*L1*, 124; see the next note).

157.11   We made many trips to the lake after that] The "fence" and "house" that Clemens and Kinney built to secure their three-hundred-acre timber claim were destroyed by the forest fire. Nevertheless, on 25 October 1861 Clemens wrote his sister and mother, "I have already laid a timber claim on the borders of a Lake (Bigler) which throws Como in the shade. . . . In that claim I took up about two miles in length by one in width" (*L1*, 129). It is possible that Clemens made this claim of two square miles (slightly less than thirteen hundred acres), as Albert Bigelow Paine has suggested, during a later trip to Lake Tahoe, possibly on 22–28 September 1861. A second visit to the lake so soon after his first may explain why Mark Twain mistakenly remembered spending two or three weeks there. Only one additional trip of Clemens's to the lake has been documented, in August 1863 (*MTB*, 1:180; *L1*, 127 n. 7, 264).

158.24   *tapaderas*] Stirrup covers, which protected the rider's feet.

158.24–25   the ungainly sole-leather covering with the unspellable name] Mark Twain refers to a *mochila*, a removable piece of heavy leather—usually rectangular—which covered the frame of a Spanish (i.e., western) saddle, with openings for the horn and cantle. Pony-express riders used *mochilas* fitted with mail pouches at each corner, which could be rapidly switched from one saddle to another (Ahlborn, 39–40, 50, 54–55, 142).

159   *illus*] In July 1871 Orion described the artist's sketch of this illustration in a letter to Clemens: "I told Frank [Bliss, i.e., Elisha's son] to take the tree out of Carson and put the auctioneer on the horse. He said he would take the tree out, but people here wouldn't understand the idea of an auctioneer on a horse" (4 July 71, CU-MARK). Orion's view clearly prevailed.

162.5   Old *Abe* Curry] Abraham V. Z. Curry (1815–73) came from New York, where he had worked first as a baker and then in the shipping trade on Lake Erie. He emigrated to California in about 1852, and then to Eagle Valley, in what was then Utah Territory, in 1858. There he laid out Carson City and built many of its buildings, establishing himself as a leading merchant, zealous champion of his town, and a public-spirited citizen. In 1859 he and Alva Gould located a claim on the Comstock lode, which later became the immensely profitable Gould and Curry mine (see the note at 301.3–13). Curry later served in the second and third territorial legislatures (1862 and 1864). Mark Twain mentioned him frequently—always with admiration and affection—in his 1863–64 letters to the Virginia City *Territorial Enterprise* ("Abraham Curry," Carson City *Appeal*, 21 Oct 73, 2; Mack 1936, 178; Marsh, 669–70 n. 37; *MTEnt*, passim).

162.21–22   the Speaker of the House] The Speaker for the first Territorial Legislature (1861) was Miles N. Mitchell (b. 1819) of New York, who went to California in 1851 and then to Utah Territory in 1860. He served in the legislature again in 1862, was a member of the first constitutional convention (1863), and in January 1864 was elected governor. The election was invalidated, however, when the voters rejected the constitution. On 4 January 1864 Mark Twain correctly anticipated this outcome and posted a slate of candidates as "For Sale or Rent" to "any small State, lying around anywhere"; his advertisement for Mitchell read: "One Governor, entirely new. Attended Sunday-school in his youth, and still remembers it. Never drinks. In other respects, however, his habits are good. As Commander-in-Chief of the Militia, he would be an ornament. Most Governors are" (SLC 1864a; Marsh, 668 n. 24; Angel, 85).

163.8   the Clerk of the House] The clerk in both the first and second territorial legislatures was William M. Gillespie (1838–85), a New York journalist who traveled to Nevada with Governor Nye in July 1861 and worked briefly on the Carson City *Silver Age.* He served as a delegate to the third Territorial Legislature, as well as the constitutional conventions of 1863 and 1864, earning from Clemens the nickname "Jefferson's Manual" for his knowledge of parliamentary rules (SLC 1864b). Later in the decade Gillespie was the clerk and official reporter for the Nevada State Assembly. He practiced law and journalism in Salt Lake City, Honolulu, and San Francisco, returning eventually to Virginia City (Marsh, 3, 668–69 n. 29).

163.8–9 the Dana silver mine] Possibly a reference to the rich Daney mine, located in November 1861 on the Comstock lode in the Devil's Gate district (*ET&S1*, 492; see the textual note).

164.33–165.4 the regular price of hay . . . carpeted with their carcases] The prices given here may be somewhat exaggerated, but the description of the winter of 1859–60, "one of unusual length and severity," is essentially true: "Hay, for example, sold at the rate of four and five and barley at six and eight hundred dollars per ton, provisions of all kinds being also excessively scarce and dear. Many of the horses and two-thirds of the cattle in the country died from starvation" (DeGroot 1876b).

165.5–6 I gave the Genuine Mexican Plug to a passing Arkansas emigrant] This "emigrant" is almost certainly fictional; on 1 December 1861 Clemens sold a horse—presumably the model for the Mexican plug—to his friend William Clagett (see the note at 180.9–10) for forty-five dollars (PH of receipt in CU-MARK, courtesy of Fred Clagett, reproduced in *L1*, 169 n. 18).

166.22 In 1858 silver lodes were discovered in "Carson County,"] Actually, the first vein of silver—a low-grade extension of what was later called the Comstock lode—was discovered in 1856 near present-day Silver City by Ethan Allen Grosh and Hosea Ballou Grosh, sons of a Pennsylvania clergyman and veterans of the California gold fields. The Groshes were prospecting in Gold Canyon, where they and other miners had been recovering modest amounts of gold from placer diggings for several years. Both brothers died in late 1857, however, before they could record their silver claim. In the spring of 1859, two placer miners working farther north, at Gold Hill, uncovered a gold-bearing quartz vein which, although poor in silver, was actually a section of the Comstock lode. Then in June, near what was later the site of Virginia City, Peter O'Riley and Patrick McLaughlin accidentally uncovered a deposit of rich black sand, but failed to recognize that it contained large amounts of silver. Henry T. P. Comstock (who had taken over the Groshes' cabin and was searching for their claim) deceived O'Riley and McLaughlin into sharing their claim—which still appeared to be merely another placer—with himself and his partner, Emanuel Penrod. It was not until 27 June that rock from the vein was assayed and found to yield $3,876 per ton, of which three-fourths were silver and one-fourth gold. This news set off the great mining boom of the early 1860s. The lode was unofficially named after Comstock, in spite of the fact that he deserved little credit for its discovery (Grant H. Smith, 1–11, 17–18; Lord, 22-55; Angel, 51–59).

166.24–29 Allegiance to Brigham Young and Utah was renounced . . .
"Nevada Territory,"] In July 1859 delegates from Carson County
(western Utah Territory) and the Honey Lake Valley region of northern
California (east of the summit of the Sierra Nevada), impatient with
Congress's failure to set up a territorial government, drafted a "Declaration" of "entire and unconditional separation" from Mormon government, citing "a long train of abuses and usurpations on the part of the
Mormons of Eastern Utah towards the people of Western Utah" (Carson Valley *Territorial Enterprise*, 30 July 59, facsimile in Angel, 70). At
an election held in September 1859, a large majority of voters approved
the constitution and elected Isaac Roop governor (see the next note).
The provisional territory, however, failed to obtain the recognition of
Congress, and its government, in the absence of a mandate, never func-
tioned effectively. The Territory of Nevada was not officially established until 2 March 1861, when the Organic Act was signed into law
by President Buchanan, two days before the inauguration of President
Lincoln (Angel, 61–66, 69–72; Kelly 1862, 25–36).

166.27 Gov. Roop] Isaac N. Roop (1822–69), a native of Maryland, emigrated to northern California in 1850 and three years later settled in the
Honey Lake Valley region, where he founded Susanville, named after
his daughter. Roop had been active in two earlier attempts (in 1856 and
1857) to form a territory from parts of eastern California and western
Utah. He later served in the first Territorial Legislature (1861) and as a
boundary commissioner for Nevada (1862), and was twice elected district attorney of Lassen County, California (1865 and 1867) (Shuck,
405–10; *ET&S1*, 482; see also chapter 34 and the note at 223.19).

167.1–2 the population of the Territory was about twelve or fifteen thou-
sand] According to the official census taken in August 1861, the population of the territory was 16,374 (Angel, 78).

168.7–8 Congress had appropriated only twenty thousand dollars a year]
Orion Clemens reported to the Territorial Council (or Senate, as Mark
Twain calls it in this chapter) on 11 November 1861:

> The expense of the present session of the Legislature will probably amount to
> $35,000, being $15,000 more than the appropriation made by Congress. The
> current expenses of the two Houses have amounted already to $13,000, and will
> probably reach $15,000 before the end of the session; and the printing is esti-
> mated at $20,000. (Marsh, 245)

He later informed William H. Jones, acting first comptroller of the
Treasury Department after the death of Elisha Whittlesey (see the next
note), "When I first arrived here people were surprised and incredulous
when I talked of making the appropriation answer the purposes it was
intended for in this Territory—they said it ought to be three times as
much" (OC to William H. Jones, 29 Apr 63, "Territorial Letters
Received").

168.16–17 Ours had a trying time of it] The claims that Mark Twain makes about the difficulties of the new territorial government are true in a general sense—as evidenced by the voluminous correspondence between Orion and the Treasury Department in Washington—although not every example in this chapter has been independently documented. Mark Twain's intention to be factual is clear, however, from the letter he sent Orion from Elmira, shortly before writing this chapter in April 1871:

> In moving from Buffalo here I have lost certain notes & documents—among them what you wrote for me about the difficulties of opening up the Territorial government in Nevada & getting the machinery to running. And now, just at the moment that I want it, it is gone. I don't even know what it was you wrote, for I did not intend to read it until I was ready to use it. Have you time to scribble something again, to aid my memory. Little characteristic items like Whittlesey's refusing to allow for the knife, &c are the most illuminating things—the difficulty of getting credit for the Gov't—& all that sort of thing. Incidents are better, any time, than dry history. Don't tax yourself—I can make a little go a great way. (SLC to OC, 4 Apr 71, CU-MARK, in *MTLP*, 62)

Elisha Whittlesey (1783–1863) was first comptroller of the Treasury Department from 1849 to 1857 and again from 1861 until his death.

168.17–20 The Organic Act and the "instructions" from the State Department . . . at such-and-such a date] The Organic Act stipulated that the election of delegates be "held at such time and places, and be conducted in such manner, as the governor shall appoint and direct," and that the delegates "thus elected . . . shall meet at such place and on such day as the governor shall appoint" (Kelly 1862, 38–39). Prior to the Clemenses' arrival, Governor Nye had established 31 August as the election date, and 1 October as the date for the convening of the legislature (OC to Elisha Whittlesey, 21 Aug 61 [1st of 2], "Territorial Letters Received"). The Organic Act also granted a *per diem* to legislators of three dollars, and another three dollars for every twenty miles traveled to attend the legislative session (Kelly 1862, 43). No copy of Orion's fourteen pages of handwritten "instructions" can now be located (they were originally enclosed in a letter of 26 June 1861 to him from Elisha Whittlesey); William C. Miller indicated in a 1973 article that he had seen the instructions, but quoted only a few words from them (Miller, 2).

169.3–4 He offered his large stone building . . . rent-free] Curry provided, free of charge, the entire unpartitioned second story of his hotel (which was also his residence) at Warm Springs, about two miles outside Carson City: in the voucher of expenses for the first legislative session submitted to the Treasury Department by Orion, the cost of rent was listed as "0000.00." The building had "a penitential look," having been built "on speculation, ostensibly as a hotel for sick people, but really with a view to its ultimate conversion into a prison" (Marsh, 2).

Curry was also landlord to the legislature at its second session, beginning in November 1862—but he required a rent of $1,500 at that time for the new premises, more conveniently located within Carson City at the Great Basin Hotel (OC to Elisha Whittlesey, 21 Aug 61 [1st of 2], "Territorial Letters Received"; "Abstract of Disbursements" 1861; Kelly 1862, 65, 70; Marsh, 408, 411).

169.4–5   a horse-railroad from town to the Capitol] Andrew J. Marsh described this railroad for the Sacramento *Union:*

> It runs—or rather trots—from Carson City across the Eagle Valley. . . . The rolling stock consists of a platform car, which carries freight from Curry's stone quarry to Carson, and a windowless passenger car of primitive construction. Two mules . . . act in the capacity of locomotives. Into this car the assembled wisdom climb in the morning to be carted over the rough scantling track to the Capitol, and at night to be carted home again. The car has no springs, and the members think their daily rides afford excellent exercise for the dyspeptic. (Marsh, 47)

169.6–8   pine benches and . . . clean saw-dust by way of carpet and spittoon combined] When Orion defended the legislative expenses to the Treasury Department comptroller, he explained that the "members of the House of Representatives of the first session sat on borrowed pine benches," and that he "bought no carpets for the first session . . . but covered the floor with saw dust" (OC to William H. Jones, 29 Apr 63, "Territorial Letters Received").

169.9–17   canvas partition . . . three dollars and forty cents would be subtracted . . . and it *was*] According to the Carson City *Silver Age:*

> This large Hall is to be divided into four apartments, by partitions. The eastern end of the building is to be assigned to the Council, and the western end to the House of Representatives, while the central part is to contain two middling sized rooms for the use of the Committees and the Sergeant-at-Arms, of each House. ("Items from Washoe," San Francisco *Alta California,* 11 Sept 61, 4, reprinting the Carson City *Silver Age* of 6 September)

In a letter of 13 March 1862, the Treasury Department comptroller questioned Orion about a voucher he had submitted for cotton fabric and thread, totaling $103.07. Orion explained:

> This was for the walls and ceiling of the Legislative Halls, partition and Committee rooms, in lieu of plastering. In this part of the country, few houses are plastered. The custom is to take cotton cloth, stitch it together, cover the walls and ceiling with it, and cover the cloth on the walls with wall paper. (OC to Elisha Whittlesey, 2 May 62, "Official Correspondence")

Orion's explanation was apparently accepted, and the $103.07 was not "subtracted" from his salary.

169.23–25   one dollar and fifty cents . . . for press-work, in greenbacks] That is, $1.50 for setting 1,000 ems of type, and $1.50 for printing 250 sheets (Ringwalt, 156, 464–65). The comptroller's office set the prices to be allowed for territorial printing after submitting a detailed questionnaire to local printers to determine current market rates. Mark

Twain takes some liberty with historical chronology here, since the prices he quotes were established in March 1863 for the printing of the laws and journals of the second Territorial Legislature, which had met in late 1862 (William H. Jones to OC, 5 Mar 63, "Territorial Letters Sent"). Moreover, the problems associated with the deflated value of greenbacks (legal tender notes unsecured by gold, made necessary by the tremendous cost of the Civil War) had not yet arisen in the fall of 1861, since the first greenbacks were not issued until April 1862. Although Congress stipulated that these notes be accepted "in payment of all debts, public and private, within the United States," businessmen on the Pacific Coast continued to deal in specie and were unwilling to accept payment in greenbacks except "at their gold, not at their nominal, value," which fluctuated widely in response to military and political developments (Mitchell, 142–44, 185, 210–38; *DAH*, 3:261; Barrett, 30–31). This custom prevailed in Nevada, as Orion patiently explained to the comptroller in 1863:

> Legal tender notes . . . are here merchandise (we have no bank notes in circulation) and gold and silver coin is the currency, while in the States the reverse is the case. . . . Any man in this Territory having a legal tender note must sell it for its market price in coin, or submit to an equivalent advance in price, before he can buy . . . any article of food or clothing or merchandise, or pay for freight or printing material or hire of hands. (OC to William H. Jones, 29 Apr 63, "Territorial Letters Received")

169.27–34 When greenbacks had gone down to forty cents on the dollar . . . the printing of the journals was discontinued] Although Orion did have difficulty arranging for the printing of the laws and journals of the first (1861) legislative session, his problems did not become insurmountable until 1863, when he attempted to contract for the printing of the laws and journals of the second (1862) session. By that time, the gold value of greenbacks had fallen precipitously for ten months, dropping from $.98 to $.57 between April 1862 and February 1863 (it did not reach $.40 until June 1864) (*L1*, 223–24 n. 2; Mitchell, 211, 425–27). When Joseph T. Goodman of the Virginia City *Territorial Enterprise* responded in February 1863 to the government questionnaire about prevailing rates for printing, he indicated his willingness to take on the job of publishing the laws and journals in book form for $.75 "per 1,000 ems" and the same "per token." Although these rates were only one-half the government allowance in greenbacks, Goodman still insisted on payment in gold. But the comptroller informed Orion on 5 March that greenbacks were the "only basis upon which you can contract for the execution of the Territorial printing" (Goodman to OC, 28 Jan and 16 Feb 63, enclosed with OC to Elisha Whittlesey, 5 Feb and 23 Feb 63, "Territorial Letters Received"; William H. Jones to OC, 5 Mar 63, "Territorial Letters Sent"). In July, Orion wrote to Robert W. Taylor, who had succeeded Whittlesey as first comptroller of the Treasury Department, giving a full account of his "trouble" over the public printing and

explaining the reluctance of territorial printers to accept payment in
greenbacks:

> Finally, about a month ago, I prevailed on [the *Territorial Enterprise*] (after they
> had held the copy several months) to undertake the printing of the laws, by
> promising to advance on delivery the whole amount allowed by the Govern-
> ment, on bills made out by them in such amounts as they might think they
> ought to have, giving them a chance to get more if they could. I expect the laws
> to be delivered to me soon. Shall I make the same offer to induce them to under-
> take the printing of the Journals? . . . Nobody seems to care much about the
> printing of the Journals, and it is so late now that I think it is hardly worth while
> to have them printed. (OC to Robert W. Taylor, 9 July 63, "Territorial Letters
> Received")

The journals for the second legislative session were never printed; the
manuscript copy for them is preserved in the Archives Division of the
Office of the Secretary of State in Carson City (Marsh, ix, 662; *RI 1972*,
576, mistakenly states that the 1862 journals were printed "without
interruption").

169.37–170.2   with full exhibits of the high prices . . . a printed market
report] In his explanatory letter of 29 April 1863, Orion wrote:

> [The printers] express the opinion that they will do "pretty well" if they realize
> expenses from what the Department allows them. To show more clearly the dif-
> ficulty the printer has to contend with in this respect, I enclose some advertise-
> ments clipped from a daily (loyal) paper published in the town of Virginia in this
> Territory. I do not see that there is any practicable remedy, but it will serve to
> throw further light on the probable cause of the high prices asked by the print-
> ers. (OC to William H. Jones, 29 Apr 63, "Territorial Letters Received")

The enclosed "advertisements"—Mark Twain's "full exhibits" and
"printed market report"—do not survive.

170.3–5   The United States responded by subtracting the printing-bill
from the Secretary's suffering salary] Although Orion's salary was paid
quarterly, in full, his ongoing correspondence with the Treasury Department clearly indicates that he was expected to reimburse the government for all "disallowed" expenses. The dispute over the printing
bill for the 1862 laws continued for several years. Mark Twain clearly
had in mind two letters that the Treasury Department sent Orion in
1869 requesting him to reimburse, from his own pocket, $1330.08 of
"disallowed" payments he had made to printers (including Goodman)
between July 1863 and October 1864. In October 1869 Orion unsuccessfully appealed the request. Later that year, or early in 1870, Clemens asked his old Virginia City acquaintance Thomas Fitch (see the
note at 339.11–13), then a Nevada Congressman, to intercede for Orion
in the dispute, and indicated his own willingness to guarantee payment
of the debt if necessary. The official resolution of the case is unknown
(Robert W. Taylor to OC, 9 June 69 [two letters] and 30 Oct 69, CU-
MARK; OC to Robert W. Taylor, 4 Oct 69, CU-MARK; *L3*, 386; SLC to
PAM, 14 Jan 70, NPV).

170.16–20   kept his office in his bedroom . . . if I had been Secretary my-
self] When he first arrived in Nevada, Orion used his bedroom at Mrs.
Murphy's Carson City boarding house as his office, paying for it himself. At the end of 1862, after Clemens's repeated urgings that he find a
more suitable office and fit it up "superbly," he rented a three-room
suite and furnished it at government expense (*L1*, 213). To this the
comptroller (or some unidentified auditor) objected, but then relented
and noted on the verso of Orion's letter of explanation, "In consideration of the fact that he paid his own office rent for the first three or four
months of his incumbency—perhaps the rent should be allowed him
for the past" (OC to William H. Jones, 29 Apr 63, with notes on the
verso in an unidentified hand, "Territorial Letters Received"). Orion
voluntarily reimbursed the government $339.25 for his bed, table,
chairs, washstand, and window coverings (*L1*, 183–84 n. 5, 186, 196,
208–9, 212 n. 12).

170.31–35   The knives cost three dollars apiece . . . out of the Secretary's
salary] Orion's purchase of pocket knives for the second Territorial
Legislature was challenged in Washington, prompting him to submit
the following explanation:

> The 16 pocket knives were disposed of as follows: I and my clerk had one each.
> There were six extra clerks employed by the Legislature, and I gave knives to five
> of them. The Legislature employed two pages. I gave one to each. Some of the
> members lost their knives and I replaced them; and several members who were
> not present when the session opened came afterwards, and I gave them knives.

On the verso of Orion's letter an unidentified auditor noted:

> Allow the expense for knives, except to extra clerks as a *specialty*, & instruct the
> Sec. not to furnish duplicates to those who may lose them. . . . The Legislature
> had no right to employ those 4 extra clerks—the Sec. could not pay them &
> should not have furnished them either with knives or Blank books. (OC to Wil-
> liam H. Jones, 29 Apr 63, with notes on the verso in an unidentified hand, "Ter-
> ritorial Letters Received")

171.2–19   he got an Indian to saw . . . it went through all right] In March
1862 the comptroller informed Orion that a payment of $1.50 " 'To an
Indian' For cutting 1⅓ cords wood" was disallowed for lack of a receipt
bearing "signature or mark" (Elisha Whittlesey to OC, 13 Mar 62, "Territorial Letters Sent"). In the 1861–62 "Abstract of Disbursements,"
three similar payments—this time presumably accompanied by a
voucher signed with a "mark"—passed without challenge.

172.2–6   member proposed to save three dollars a day . . . during the
morning prayer] Mark Twain's description of this legislator appears to
conflate facts about two different Nevada characters, Jacob L. Van Bokkelen and Colonel Jonathan Williams. Van Bokkelen (d. 1873) had been
a member of the 1851 San Francisco Vigilance Committee; in Nevada
he served in both the first and second territorial legislatures and during
the Civil War was Lincoln's appointee as provost marshal for the terri-

tory (Marsh, 666 n. 11). On 17 October 1861, while president of the
Council in the first Territorial Legislature, Van Bokkelen objected to
the appointment of a chaplain, remarking that "he did not think it was
necessary to go to an expense of a dollar and a half a day for a short and
concise prayer in the morning. . . . He had sat under prayers costing
ten thousand dollars a year and did not know that they did him much
good" (Marsh, 90). The member who "sat with his feet on his desk, eating raw turnips," however, was clearly Colonel Williams, whose unusual habit Mark Twain first mentioned in a dispatch from Carson
City to the Virginia City *Territorial Enterprise:*

> Col. Williams, of the House, who says I mutilate his eloquence, addressed a
> note to me this morning, to the effect that I had given his constituents wrong
> impressions concerning him, and nothing but blood would satisfy him. I sent
> him that turnip on a hand-barrow, requesting him to extract from it a sufficient
> quantity of blood to restore his equilibrium—(which I regarded as a very excel-
> lent joke.) Col. Williams ate it (raw) during the usual prayer by the chaplain. . . .
> Col. Williams had his feet on his desk at the time. (SLC 1862h)

In 1866 Mark Twain again mentioned that Williams "used to always"
engage in this irreverent activity "during prayer by the Chaplain" (SLC
1866w). Clemens had a more personal reason for lampooning Williams: in July 1863 Orion, in his capacity as acting governor, discharged him as a notary public for Lander County for being "a loud
mouthed Copperhead"; Williams responded by calling Orion a specimen of "political vermin" ("Caustic Letter," Placerville [Calif.] *Mountain Democrat,* 8 Aug 63, 3). Williams was a proprietor of the *Enterprise* from 1859 until early 1862; Rollin Daggett described him as "an
erratic old gentleman who wrote strong, but in villainous English, and
was given a great deal to his cups" (Daggett, 15). Williams later "drifted
about Nevada for many years, ultimately committing suicide at Pioche
in January of 1876" (Lingenfelter and Gash, 253–54).

172.7–8   The legislature sat sixty days, and passed private toll-road fran-
chises] The first legislature, which met from 1 October to 29 November 1861, approved six franchises to construct toll roads. Twenty-two
roads were franchised at the second session (1862), and twenty-seven at
the third (1864). Such franchises were an effective way to provide for
the transportation of passengers and freight to and from the various
mining regions springing up in previously undeveloped areas of the territory (*Laws* 1862, 602; *Laws* 1863, 16–17, 213; *Laws* 1864, 178–79;
Maule, 17).

174.4–7   "Gould & Curry" . . . "Ophir"] These mines were among the
first, and richest, on the Comstock lode. The Gould and Curry claim,
located in 1859 by Alva Gould and Abraham Curry but soon sold to
others, was incorporated in June 1860 (see the note at 301.3–13). The
company operated "in a small way" until the end of 1861, when its tunnel under D Street in Virginia City "penetrated 40 feet of rich solid ore"

and the mine began to overtake the Ophir in productivity. At the time of the Clemenses' arrival in August, Gould and Curry stock was worth $225 per foot; between mid-February and May 1862 it rose from $375 to $850 per foot (Kelly 1862, 14; Grant H. Smith, 26, 84; *Mining and Scientific Press:* "Sales Mining Stocks," 3 [17 Aug 61]: 6; "Mining Stock," 4 [15 Feb 62]: 5; "Stock Quotations," 5 [8 May 62]: 5). The Ophir mine, the first and most famous claim on the Comstock, was incorporated in April 1860. Throughout 1861 and early 1862 Ophir stock sold in the range of $800 to $1,250 per foot. The stock price peaked at $3,800 in October 1862, not in late 1861, as Mark Twain implies here (Grant H. Smith, 80 n. 1; *Mining and Scientific Press:* mining-stock quotations in issues between January 1861 and April 1862; "Stock Quotations," 6 [7 Oct 62]: 2).

174.20–21   had found a "clay casing" and knew they were "right on the ledge"] Since sheets of clay often encased the quartz veins on the Comstock lode, they were regarded as good evidence of an ore deposit (Angel, 118).

175.1   And so on] Although some of the mines mentioned in this paragraph were real, the anecdotes are fictional ("List of Incorporated Mining Companies," *Mining and Scientific Press* 6 [10 Aug 63]: 1–7).

175.13   "Esmeralda" had just had a run] The principal town in the Esmeralda mining district was Aurora (claimed by both California and Nevada, until the resolution of the boundary dispute in the fall of 1863), which was located in the Sierra Nevada foothills about a hundred miles southeast of Carson City (see supplement B, map 3). Following the organization of the district in August 1860, Aurora experienced a boom, reaching a population of nearly two thousand by August 1861. Typical of the glowing reports from the area is this one from the Carson City *Silver Age* for early September: "Now is the time for capitalists to invest. Ground that can be bought at the present time for ten and fifteen dollars, in six months cannot be bought for five times that amount" ("Summary of Mining News," *Mining and Scientific Press* 4 [5 Oct 61]: 5, reprinting the Carson City *Silver Age*; Kelly 1862, 14, 238–42; Paher, 466). Spurred by such reports, Clemens visited Aurora briefly in September 1861, returning in April 1862 for a five-month stay. Aurora's prosperity reached its peak in early 1864; by the spring of 1865 half the population had left (*L1*, 122, 184–241; Angel, 418).

175.13–14   "Humboldt" was beginning to shriek for attention] This mining region was situated about a hundred seventy-five miles northeast of Carson City in the West Humboldt Mountains (see supplement B, map 2). Silver and gold were discovered in the area in 1860, and over the next year, Unionville, Humboldt City, and Star City—each in a separate mining district—emerged as the principal centers of mining activity. News of a rich strike in June 1861, before Clemens arrived in Nevada, caused a rush to the Humboldt region from the Comstock; but it was not until the fall that Humboldt mining fever heated up in earnest. In November a correspondent from the Santa Clara district reported:

> The great extent and richness of the Humboldt mines have long since ceased to be questions of doubt. . . . New leads are being located almost daily beyond the limits of the mining districts now formed. The irresistible conviction is forced upon all who have prospected here during the past Summer that this is not only the richest but most extensive quartz region extant. (Simmons, 1)

The Humboldt region continued to attract miners, mill operators, and investors for a time, except for a decline in 1864–65 which temporarily emptied the mining camps (Kelly 1862, 13, 235–38; *Mining and Scientific Press:* "Interesting Correspondence from Nevada Territory," 3 [15 June 61]: 2; "Nevada Territory," 4 [2 Nov 61]: 5); Angel, 449–54).

176.6–28   But . . . incalculable.] Neither this extract, nor the one at 177.3–178.19, can be dated precisely, since the *Enterprise* for this period is not extant, and no reprintings of these items have been found. Certain details (the discovery of coal, the length of the Sheba tunnel) suggest, however, that they appeared in late 1862 or early 1863, a year later than Mark Twain implies. He probably pasted the actual clippings of these extracts into his printer's copy, after removing them from the "coffin of 'Enterprise' files" he received from his family in the spring of 1870 (SLC to JLC and family, 26 Mar 70, NPV, in *MTBus*, 112).

176.19   Col. Whitman] In October 1861 George W. Whitman (1811?–1891), the former state controller of California (1856–58), announced his recent discovery of extensive coal beds fifteen miles southeast of Virginia City: "I am greatly mistaken if the supply of coal at this point is not more than sufficient to meet every demand for a period much longer than you or I will need fire in an earthly habitation." This discovery of a potential source of fuel in timber-scarce Nevada was as significant as a major ore strike (*Mining and Scientific Press:* "Nevada Territory," 4 [12 Oct 61]: 5; "Regular Correspondence," 4 [1 Feb 62]: 5; Curry, 644; *Hutchings' California Magazine* 2 [Mar 58]: 390).

176.23   Captain Burch] The Indian agent "for the several bands of Indians" in the Humboldt area in 1863–64, and presumably earlier as well (Sage Brush, 208–9).

177.17   The Sheba mine] The Sheba mine, located by William M. Hurst in May 1861, was very near Star City. Following its first shipment of ore to San Francisco in August 1861, it proved to be one of the richest Humboldt mines ("Humbol[d]t District," *Mining and Scientific Press* 4 [14 Dec 61]: 5; Ransome, 41–43). Upon his return from the Humboldt area, Clemens sent a sample of Sheba casing rock to his brother-in-law, William A. Moffett, in St. Louis (*L1*, 154).

178.6   the Mexican] See the note at 301.14–21.

179.4–6   We . . . drove out of Carson on a chilly December afternoon]
Clemens left Carson City with three companions (identified below)
during the first or second week of December 1861 and was away approximately seven weeks, returning by the end of January 1862. For his
other accounts of this trip to Humboldt see his letter of 30 January
1862 to his mother (published in the Keokuk *Gate City*), his letter of
12 February 1866 to the Virginia City *Territorial Enterprise,* and chapter 27 of *The Innocents Abroad* (SLC 1862a, 1866d, 1869a).

180.9–10   Young Clagett (now member of Congress from Montana)] William Horace Clagett (1838–1901) was an old friend of Clemens's from
Keokuk, Iowa, who arrived in Nevada Territory in September 1861.
Having recently been appointed notary public for Unionville, he was
now on his way there to assume his duties. In 1866, after serving as a
representative in the Nevada territorial and state legislatures, Clagett
left his Virginia City law practice and relocated to Montana. Elected
Republican congressman from Montana in August 1871 (at which time
Clemens inserted the parenthetical identification), he served in Washington, D.C., from December 1871 to March 1873 (*L1,* 123 n. 1, 150–51
n. 4; Clagett, 9, 16; *BDUSC,* 777).

180.11   Oliphant] A fictional name for Augustus W. (Gus) Oliver (1835–
?1918), a lawyer who in 1860 emigrated from Maine to California and
afterward to Carson City, where he worked briefly as a journalist. Recently appointed probate judge for Humboldt County, he, like Clagett,
was traveling there to take up his post. His later career took him to California, where he was employed as a schoolteacher and a judge (*L1,*
150–51 n. 4; biographical information courtesy of H. LeRoy Oliver).

180.12–13   old Mr. Ballou the blacksmith] Cornbury S. Tillou, a Carson
City blacksmith and jack-of-all-trades. Oliver later noted that Tillou
was "a Frenchman, an elderly man," but according to the 1860 census
he was born about 1820, and was therefore not "sixty years of age," as
Mark Twain describes him (Oliver to A. B. Paine, 24 Apr 1910, in Delaney, 3; *Carson County Census,* 133; *L1,* 150–51, n. 4).

180.17–18   We were fifteen days making the trip—two hundred miles;
thirteen, rather] Clemens wrote his mother on 30 January 1862 that he
had arrived in Unionville after "pushing that wagon nearly 200 miles,
and taking eleven days to do it in" (*L1,* 149).

180.37–181.1   his Partingtonian fashion] Benjamin P. Shillaber (1814–
90), an American journalist and humorist, was the creator of Mrs. Ruth
Partington, a New England widow given to malapropisms whose sayings were widely reprinted in American newspapers during Clemens's
apprentice years. In May 1852 Shillaber had published Clemens's
sketch "The Dandy Frightening the Squatter" in his magazine, the Bos-

ton *Carpet-Bag;* he and Clemens met sometime before *Roughing It* was written (*ET&S1,* 63–65; Shillaber to SLC, 1 Jan 70, CU-MARK).

183.2   the Great American Desert] Sam and Orion Clemens had crossed this desert from east to west in the overland-mail stagecoach in August 1861 (see the note at 130.1–24). Traveling to Unionville, Clemens and his party left the overland route at Ragtown Station and struck out across the desert through miles of "sand to the fetlock," alkali flats, and the slough of the Humboldt River (Doctor 1862a; see supplement B, map 2).

183.8–9   the "Sink of the Humboldt."] This inhospitable marsh containing Humboldt Lake is about eighty-five miles northeast of Carson City. A traveler crossing the Sink in October 1863 described it as "a large, dry, depressed plain, white with alkali, and glittering in the fierce rays of the sun like some polished crust of snow" ("Washoe as It Is," Sacramento *Union,* 2 Feb 64, 1).

184.14–19   Unionville consisted of eleven cabins . . . in the bottom of a crevice] Unionville, in the Buena Vista mining district, was laid out in July 1861 in a canyon in the Humboldt range, and in November became the Humboldt County seat. Although it apparently had only a handful of inhabitants when Clemens arrived in December 1861, by the following September the population was estimated at three hundred, and the town's buildings—constructed of adobe, slate, brush, and canvas—lined the canyon for almost a mile. The area was reportedly "well stocked with liquor, lice and loafers; and [at] the same time is greatly in want of water power, wood and women" ("Nevada Territory," *Mining and Scientific Press* 5 [14 June 62]: 5; *L1,* 151–52 n. 9; *Laws* 1862, 291; "Letter from the Humboldt Mines," Sacramento *Union,* 6 May 62, 1; "The Humboldt Mining District," San Francisco *Alta California,* 24 June 62, 1; Nomad, 1).

184.24   through which the cattle used to tumble occasionally] Clemens described Oliver's experiences with such intrusive cattle in chapter 27 of *The Innocents Abroad*—an account that Oliver himself claimed was apocryphal (Delaney, 3).

184.26   Indians brought brush and bushes] Indians from Captain John's band of Paiutes at Humboldt Lake supplied labor at Unionville for one dollar per day and board (Nomad, 1; Doctor 1862b).

188.11   "all that glitters is not gold."] An expression already proverbial in Shakespeare's time: "All that glisters is not gold— / Often have you heard that told" (*The Merchant of Venice,* act 2, scene 7).

190.7   "Monarch of the Mountains"] There is no evidence that Clemens participated in locating such a claim; he evidently was involved, however, in the location of one near Unionville named the "Annie Moffett" (or "Anne Moffatt"), after his niece. Nothing is known about this claim beyond his mentions of it in letters to Clagett in February and March 1862 (*L1*, 164, 168 n. 6, 170).

193.19–24 we owned largely in the "Gray Eagle," . . . the "Grand Mogul,"] In January 1862 Clemens purchased ten feet in the Alba Nueva ledge near Unionville from Hugo Pfersdorff (see the note at 197.15–16; no additional holdings of his in the Humboldt region at this time—aside from his shares in the Annie Moffett—have been documented (*L1*, 167 n. 2). Most of the mines listed here are presumably fictional.

193.34 no milling] John C. Fall's Pioneer Mill, the first in Unionville, did not begin operation until November 1862 (*L1*, 152 n. 11).

197.8–9 the Secretary and I had purchased "feet" from various Esmeralda stragglers] Before Clemens left Carson City for the Humboldt region he had acquired feet in at least two Esmeralda mines, the Black Warrior and the Farnum, the latter with his brother Orion. These shares were purchased from Horatio G. Phillips—who was associated with the Clemens brothers in several mining ventures in 1861 and 1862—and Noah T. Carpenter (*L1*, 140, 141 n. 1, 189 n. 11).

197.15–16 with Mr. Ballou and a gentleman named Ollendorff] Clemens spent New Year's Day in Unionville before beginning his return trip to Carson City, having stayed "two or three weeks" in Humboldt (SLC 1866d). His companions on the return trip were Colonel John B. Onstine and Captain Hugo Pfersdorff. Tillou ("Mr. Ballou") was almost certainly not with them: references in Clemens's correspondence with Clagett between February and September 1862 suggest that he remained in Humboldt during that time. Onstine was a lawyer from Ohio who established a practice in Carson City, and then in Unionville, in the early 1860s. Pfersdorff, one of the pioneers of the Unionville area, served as district recorder there from 1861 to about 1865 (*L1*, 150, 152 n. 13, 164, 166, 170, 171, 193, 239; "From the Humboldt Mines," Stockton *Independent*, 8 Feb 62, 2, reprinting the Carson City *Silver Age* of 21 January; Knight 1863, 359–60; Knight 1864, 285).

197.16–18 not the party . . . foreign grammars, with their interminable repetitions of questions] Heinrich Gottfried Ollendorff (1802–65) was a grammarian and teacher of languages resident in Paris for most of his career. Beginning in the late 1830s, he published a series of textbooks—each issued in numerous editions—on how to become proficient within six months in reading, writing, and speaking the major modern languages. His method, "based on the principle that a foreign language should be taught in the same way in which a child learns to speak its mother tongue," relied upon conversational question-and-answer exercises rather than upon memorizing and applying rules of grammar and syntax (Singer, 9:395).

197.21 "Honey Lake Smith's,"] A trading post and stage station about thirty-six miles northeast of Carson City, named for its proprietor, formerly of Honey Lake, California. The site is now submerged by the waters of the Lahontan Reservoir (Carlson, 135–36; Gianella, 5–7; Kelly 1862, 13; see supplement B, map 2).

200.18–22 We remained cooped up eight days . . . their profusion is simply inconceivable] In his letter to the Virginia City *Territorial Enterprise* dated 12 February 1866, Clemens recalled his stay at Honey Lake Smith's:

> I was 15 days on the road back to Carson on horseback, with Colonel Onstein and Captain Pfersdorff, nine of which were spent at Honey Lake Smith's, when there was but two hundred feet of dry ground around the house, and the whole desert for miles around was under water. The whole place was crowded with teamsters, and we wore out every deck of cards on the place, and then had no amusement left but to scrape up a handful of vermin off the floor or the beds, and "shuffle" them, and bet on odd or even. Even this poor excuse for a game broke up in a row at last when it was discovered that Colonel Onstein kept a "cold deck" down the back of his neck! He would persist in cheating, and so we played no more. Take it altogether, that was the funniest trip I ever made. (SLC 1866d)

201.6 "old sledge"] This card game, also known as "seven-up," was the subject of Mark Twain's sketch "Science vs. Luck," published in the *Galaxy* for October 1870 (SLC 1870*l*).

201.13–14 a stalwart ruffian called "Arkansas,"] Arkansas also figures in an unpublished play fragment by Clemens which Albert Bigelow Paine labeled, "Original form of 'Arkansaw' incident in 'Roughing It'—Probably written in Buffalo. 1870" (SLC 1873a). The manuscript, however, is written on paper which Clemens seems not to have used before early 1873, and therefore must date from after the publication of *Roughing It*. In the play, Arkansas is bullying two inoffensive customers in a Virginia City saloon when Scotty Briggs and Buck Fanshaw (featured in chapter 47) intervene and rout him and his gang. Briggs and Fanshaw then rebuke the barkeeper for not taking charge of the situation, as required by his exalted status in Virginia City society, a theme developed in chapter 48.

217.12 a stage station] Clemens and his companions had probably arrived at Desert Well Station, about twelve miles southwest of Honey Lake Smith's (Carlson, 97; Townley, 30–31; see supplement B, map 2).

219.36–220.1 We reached Carson . . . kept us there a week] Because of the heavy flooding on the road to Carson City, Clemens found his journey broken again at Virginia City, where he and his party (which reportedly included a "Capt. Cathburt," possibly a mistake for Pfersdorff) arrived on 19 January 1862. Their arrival was notable enough to be mentioned in several newspapers: "They were sixteen days on the route, being water-bound for eight days at Honey Lake Smith's and finally had to swim out. The desert road this side of Smith's was covered with snow and water, and traveling was, of course, slow and tiresome" ("From the Humboldt Mines," Stockton *Independent*, 8 Feb 62, 2, and "Humboldt," Marysville *Appeal*, 2 Feb 62, 3, both reprinting the Carson City *Silver Age* of 21 January). Clemens remained in Virginia City at least a week, but was back in Carson City by 28 January. His departure for the Esmeralda district did not take place until early April 1862 (*L1*, 150 n. 3, 184–85 n. 1).

220.2 the trial of the great land-slide case of Hyde *vs.* Morgan] Mark Twain had already published two versions of the story he is about to tell in the next chapter. The first, entitled "A Rich Decision," appeared in an August 1863 letter to the San Francisco *Morning Call*. The second, which appeared in the Buffalo *Express* in April 1870, was revised for inclusion in *Roughing It* (SLC 1863p, 1870e). Both earlier versions are reprinted in *The Great Landslide Case*, together with a discussion of the historical background and the evolution of the text (Anderson and Branch). James C. Merrell, who claimed to have shared a cabin with Clemens in Aurora, asserted that Clemens wrote an even earlier version of the story there during his 1862 sojourn. Merrell's account, which incorrectly implies that the landslide itself occurred in Aurora, may well be apocryphal (see the note at 221.20–29):

I believe that I heard read the first letter which ever gave him encouragement to become a writer. There had been an avalanche, which carried down a miner's cabin and deposited it on top of another miner's cabin. This appealed to Clemens as a most amusing mix-up, and he wrote a long letter to the *Virginia Enterprise*, describing the incident and making a long argument as to which miner could claim the entire property.

He chuckled over it a good deal while he was writing it and when he had finished he brought it to us and said, "Listen, boys, to what I told 'em about the late catastrophe." Then he read it all through to us.

Not long after, he got a letter from the *Enterprise*. I do not know the contents of it, but at supper table Clemens said, "I guess those fellows liked my stuff pretty well." Soon afterwards he had money to pay his bills, and I always supposed the paper gave him something for the letter. (Cyril Clemens, 19–21)

221.11–15 Gen. Buncombe ... his salary was Territorially meagre] "Buncombe" is a facetious name for Benjamin B. Bunker (b. 1815), a New Hampshire lawyer appointed United States attorney for Nevada Territory in March 1861. Because Bunker was expected to earn substantial fees in private legal practice, his annual salary as United States attorney was merely $250, as compared with the top salary of $3,000 for a territorial official. By July he had established a law practice in Carson City, but his residence in the territory was short-lived: in January 1862 he requested a leave of absence, and on 1 May he left the West, never to return. In June 1863 President Lincoln removed the absentee attorney from office. Clemens's letters of the period reveal that he was well acquainted with Bunker, toward whom he developed a decidedly irreverent attitude, adopting his name for the plodding, ruminative horse he rode on the trip to Humboldt (Anderson and Branch, 9–13; *L1*, 131, 135 n. 6, 147–48, 234, 235 n. 4).

221.20–29   Dick Hyde . . . his ranch was situated just in the edge of the valley] In his two earlier versions of the landslide case, Mark Twain used the real name of the plaintiff, Richard D. Sides (1825–1901). (Mark Twain may have been influenced by a historical connection between Sides and the Mormon leader Orson Hyde when he made this revision for *Roughing It:* see Anderson and Branch, 14–16, 24–27, 50). Sides, who was well known throughout the region, began ranching in Washoe Valley in the early 1850s, held offices in Carson County during the period of Mormon colonization, and staked an early claim on the Comstock lode. His ranch was outside Franktown, near the lower slopes of the Sierra Nevada (*Carson County Census*, 123; Doten, 3:2106; see supplement B, map 3).

222.1   Tom Morgan] Clemens's 1863 *Call* letter and an entry in his 1865 notebook identify the defendant as Tom Rust, about whom nothing further is known (SLC 1863p; *N&J1*, 79; Anderson and Branch, 54 n. 25).

223.17   Hal Brayton, a very smart lawyer] Clemens's friend Patrick Henry (Hal) Clayton (d. 1874), an early settler of Carson City. Clayton, who was appointed prosecuting attorney for the county in 1860, was a noted secessionist and a central figure in the boisterous proceedings of the Third House, Nevada's burlesque territorial legislature. He appeared as counsel for the defense in at least one other mock trial, in Virginia City in 1865 (Anderson and Branch, 13–14, 19; Marsh, 677 n. 108).

223.18–19   the courts being in vacation, it was to be tried before a referee] Nevada tradition and internal evidence suggest that the mock trial, intended as an elaborate practical joke on Bunker, actually took place in Carson City sometime during the first two weeks of February 1862, before the courts began their regular session on 17 February (Anderson and Branch, 19, 23–24).

223.19   ex-Governor Roop] Isaac N. Roop's title dated from his brief tenure in 1859 as governor of the unauthorized provisional territory of Nevada. He also served as a recorder of land deeds for a number of years in this period and was known as an expert on property rights (Anderson and Branch, 16–18; see also the notes at 166.24–29 and 166.27). Mark Twain called Roop "that remorseless old joker" in his 1870 Buffalo *Express* version of the tale (SLC 1870e).

227.4   Hoosac Tunnel] When *Roughing It* was published, this five-mile railroad tunnel through the Hoosac Mountains in western Massachusetts—the second longest in the world at that time—had been under construction for nearly fifteen years. In November 1873 its excavation was finally complete; the tunnel was opened in 1876 (*Annual Cyclopaedia 1873*, 355–58; *DAH*, 3:45).

228.1–2 WHEN we finally left for Esmeralda . . . we had an addition to the company] This second trip of Clemens's to Aurora, in the Esmeralda district (he had visited the area previously in September 1861: see the note at 175.13–14), came early in April 1862 after several weeks spent in Carson City. As noted earlier, the *Roughing It* narrative telescopes the actual chronology; it also implies that Mark Twain's traveling party still included his Humboldt friends Ballou (Tillou) and Ollendorff (Pfersdorff). Clemens's actual traveling companions have not been identified; Ballou, however, was probably not one of them (see the note at 197.15–16).

228.2–4 Capt. John Nye, the Governor's brother . . . a tongue hung in the middle] John Nye emigrated to California in 1848 after living for some years in Alabama, where he left a wife; unlike his brother, Governor James Nye, he was evidently a Southern sympathizer during the Civil War. He was "an enthusiastic entrepreneur in mining and timber projects and an incorporator of the Aurora and Walker River Railroad," and a principal in John Nye and Company, which located timber claims at Lake Tahoe in August 1861 (*L1*, 134 n. 2; see also the note at 147.17–18). Listed as a resident of Aurora in 1863, he moved to San Francisco soon thereafter: his name appears in San Francisco directories from 1864 through 1901, primarily as a real-estate agent. In 1867–68 Nye was also the steward of the United States Marine Hospital in San Francisco. In March 1868 the Washington, D.C., correspondent of the San Francisco *Evening Bulletin* noted the presence of "Capt. Nye of San Francisco" in the capital and characterized him as an effective and influential lobbyist for federal appointments on the Pacific Coast, "one of the fiercest and most vehement talkers that is to be found anywhere" (Jorkins, 5; Nye-Starr, 95, 96, 100–101; Kelly 1863, 432; Langley 1867, 373).

229.21–26 The Board were living on the "assessments." . . . the ledge . . . was as barren of silver as a curb-stone] Eastern capitalists, like other investors in mining property, were subject to frequent, onerous, and sometimes fraudulent assessments. In January 1863 easterners, principally New Yorkers, were reported to be investing heavily in Washoe mines. By the spring of 1864 this practice had "become all the rage in New York City," where "the people take as lively an interest in 'feet' . . . as we do here" (*Mining and Scientific Press*: "Lively Times" and "Eastern Capital," 8 [14 May 64]: 329; "Stock Remarks," 6 [12 Jan 63]: 5). Mark Twain's remarks recall his bitter indictment of mining-company assessment policies—in particular, those of the Hale and Norcross company, in which he owned stock—in the San Francisco *Morning Call* of 19 August 1864 (SLC 1864l; *L1*, 309 n. 5, 319 n. 5).

229.26–230.17 Jim Townsend's tunnel . . . two hundred and twenty-five feet of your tunnel on trestle-work] Mark Twain included a version of this tale in a letter to the San Francisco *Alta California* published on 26 May 1867 (SLC 1867e). James William Emery ("Lying Jim") Townsend (1838–1900) learned the printing trade in his home state of New Hampshire and began his journalism career on the San Francisco *Golden Era* in 1859, working alongside Joseph Goodman, Bret Harte, and Denis McCarthy (see the notes at 274.25–26, 405.4, and 537.4). He worked as a printer on the *Territorial Enterprise* from the fall of 1862 until the winter of 1863–64, when he joined the staff of the Virginia City *Union*. For the next forty years he was connected with a variety of California and Nevada newspapers as a printer, reporter, editor, and proprietor. Townsend, perhaps the original of Harte's "Truthful James," became widely known on the Pacific Coast as a wit and a raconteur of Münchausen-like adventures. Examples of his humorous journalism may be found in *Lying on the Eastern Slope* (Dwyer and Lingenfelter, 7–16). "Daley" is evidently a fictional name.

230.20–231.9 We took up various claims . . . we never ceased to expect fortune . . . to burst upon us some day] This paragraph sums up Clemens's unrewarding efforts, made with such friends as Robert Howland, Horatio Phillips, and Calvin Higbie, to locate and work numerous mines in Aurora from April to September 1862 (*L1*, 184–241 passim).

231.13–14 I went to work as a common laborer in a quartz mill, at ten dollars a week and board] Clemens worked in Joshua E. Clayton's mill on Martinez Hill just east of Aurora for about a week during the latter part of June 1862. Clayton proposed to teach Clemens his process for reducing gold and silver ore. Clemens wrote to Orion on 2 June, "When I have learned it, he wants Raish [Horatio Phillips] and me to go out to Humboldt, get it used by Humboldt Mills, and stay there and work it." One week later he claimed in another letter to his brother, "I know all the chemicals, and the manner of using them, shall begin practice in a week or so" (*L1*, 188 n. 9, 194 n. 3, 216, 219). Many years afterward, in 1906, Clemens again described his pay as "ten dollars a week and board," claiming that "the board was worth while, because it consisted not only of bacon, beans, coffee, bread, and molasses, but we had stewed dried apples every day in the week" (AD, 27 Mar 1906, CU-MARK, in *MTA*, 2:258).

232.6 This mill was a six-stamp affair] Clayton's mill, which was in operation by February 1862, actually had twelve stamps for crushing ore. The "Clayton & Veatch process" employed there, which Mark Twain describes in this chapter, was a variation of John A. Veatch's steam-tub method of amalgamation (Kelly 1862, 244; *L1*, 188 n. 9, 194 n. 3).

232–34   *illus*] These engravings were reused from two earlier works—Browne's "Reese River Country" and Richardson's *Beyond the Mississippi*—and do not illustrate the process in use at Clayton's mill. The first one, which accompanied Browne's description of mining in the Reese River area of central Nevada, apparently depicts the "Freiberg or barrel process, which is conducted by means of revolving barrels" (J. Ross Browne 1866, 42–43). The second one depicts the Washoe wet process, employing shallow pans, which became the most widely used in the Nevada silver mills (Richardson, 502; Küstel, 117–18, 122–24; Hodges, 2–3, 8–9).

233.30   "earn his bread by the sweat of his brow."] Compare Genesis 3:19: "In the sweat of thy face shalt thou eat bread."

234.10–11   screening tailings . . . with a long-handled shovel, is the most undesirable] In 1906 Clemens recalled: "I hate a long-handled shovel. I never could learn to swing it properly. As often as any other way the sand didn't reach the screen at all, but went over my head and down my back, inside of my clothes. It was the most detestable work I have ever engaged in" (AD, 27 Mar 1906, CU-MARK, in *MTA*, 2:258).

235.14–15   The first one in Nevada was built at Egan Cañon and was a small insignificant affair] Most sources agree that the first mill in Nevada was Almarin B. Paul's Pioneer Mill, which began crushing ore on 11 August 1860 in Gold Canyon. (Angel's *History of Nevada* awards the distinction to Logan and Holmes's mill, also in Gold Canyon, but this rudimentary operation—established in October 1859—"could only be called a mill by courtesy," according to Lord [86 n. 2].) The mistaken reference here to Egan Canyon may derive from Mark Twain's misreading of a remark in Richardson's *Beyond the Mississippi*. Describing his travels from Utah to Nevada in 1865, Richardson noted the first evidence of mining activity he had seen on his route: "Two hundred and fifty miles west of Salt Lake we encountered the first quartz mining of Nevada, at Egan Canyon, a picturesque valley. Only one mill was running. It had but five stamps" (369). Nearby appeared an illustration—later appropriated for use in *Roughing It* (reproduced on page 235)—deceptively captioned "Egan Canyon and First Quartz Mill" (368). Clemens passed through Egan Canyon, the site of a pony-express and overland-mail station, on his trip to Carson City. A small mill was built there in 1864 (Hodges, 2–3; Lord, 84–86; Angel, 60; Paher, 242).

235.18–236.22   the "fire-assay" . . . Nothing now remains but to weigh it] Clemens had the opportunity to observe this fire-assay process in February 1863 in the assaying rooms of Theall and Company in Virginia City; he described the technique at humorous length in his sketch "Silver Bars—How Assayed," probably published between 17 and 22 February in the *Territorial Enterprise* (SLC 1863b).

236.36–237.14 One assayer got such rich results . . . left town "between two days."] This anecdote was apparently a folktale. William F. Rae recounted it, for example, in his *Westward by Rail* (215), and it has been included in an anthology of Mormon folklore (Fife and Fife, 286; L. L. Lee, 47).

237.16–32 I only remained in the milling business one week . . . I was ordered off the premises] Clemens explained to his brother Orion in a letter of 9 July: "I caught a violent cold at Clayton's, which lasted two weeks, and I came near getting salivated, working in the quicksilver and chemicals. I hardly think I shall try the experiment again. It is a confining business, and [I] will not be confined, for love nor money" (*L1*, 225). In 1906 he described his departure: "On my side, I could not endure the heavy labor; and on the company's side, they did not feel justified in paying me to shovel sand down my back; so I was discharged just at the moment that I was going to resign" (AD, 27 Mar 1906, CU-MARK, in *MTA*, 2:258).

238.1–240.5 It . . . desires.] Mark Twain first published this passage in a Buffalo *Express* "Around the World" letter on 11 December 1869; he revised the earlier printing for inclusion in *Roughing It* (SLC 1869n).

238.1–2 It was somewhere in the neighborhood of Mono Lake that the marvelous Whiteman cement mine was supposed to lie] Mark Twain recounts his own version of a persistent legend about a rich gold-bearing cement mine allegedly located south of Mono Lake on the Owens River. (The term "cement" was commonly applied by miners in the area to lava or—more specifically—to "any firmly compacted mass of detrital auriferous material . . . of volcanic origin" [*Century Dictionary*, s.v. "cement"].) The mine was named after Gideon F. Whiteman, "who played a prominent part in the intense searches for it that began in 1861" (*L1*, 226–27 n. 2). Whiteman purportedly continued his search for the mine "until August of 1880, when paralysis forced him to permanently retire to San Francisco. There he allegedly died in 1883" (James W. A. Wright, 13, 51 n. 7).

238.4–20 we would have a wild excitement . . . the whole population gone chasing after W.] On 3 July 1862 an Aurora correspondent of the Sacramento *Bee* (possibly Daniel Twing, one of Clemens's cabinmates; see *L1*, 237 n. 2) wrote:

Our town is all excitement to-day, from the reported discovery of rich and extensive gold diggings over in the vicinity of Owens river. . . . Directly parties of horsemen were noticed to leave town during the still hours of night, stealthily moving away to the west. . . . Well, the next day succeeding the night of mystification, another and another party quietly took themselves out of town. . . . The cause of this epidemic is reports now industriously circulated through the camp, that . . . digging of surpassing richness had been discovered along the sides of the hills—gold lying in seams of cement, in the most prolific abundance. (Veni, Vidi, 1862a)

238.21–239.36 The tradition was . . . for twelve or thirteen years] This version of the legend differs significantly from a reputedly authoritative one written in 1879 by James W. A. Wright, a mining correspondent for the San Francisco *Evening Post,* who attempted to piece together a factual history of the mine from interviews with Whiteman and others. According to Wright, the "reddish, rusty looking cement . . . thickly spangled with flakes of purest gold" was discovered in 1857 by two emigrants crossing the Sierra who stopped to rest along the Owens River. In 1860 one of the two men, on his deathbed, gave a specimen of the cement to a San Francisco doctor, who in turn continued the search in 1861 and 1862, employing Whiteman on the latter occasion. Wright acknowledged Mark Twain's precedence in relating the cement-mine story, but claimed that his version of events—such as the statement that by 1862 Whiteman had been searching for the mine for "twelve or thirteen years"—was "humor rather than history" (James W. A. Wright, 11–14, 49).

239.36–37 Some people believed . . . he had not] On 28 July 1862 the Aurora correspondent of the Sacramento *Bee* commented:

One of the adventurers to the Cement diggings has just returned, and he tells me he thinks the diggings are a humbug, or else the first discoverers are humbugging everybody else by putting them on the wrong scent, and keeping them there till they get tired of prospecting and return home disgusted, when the pioneers will quietly take possession of their rich discoveries again and work them when and as they please, with no one to molest or make them afraid—except Indians. From what I accidentally heard one of the original proprietors say a day or two since, I am constrained to believe the latter conclusion is the correct one. (Veni, Vidi 1862b)

240.6 A new partner of ours, a Mr. Higbie] On 9 July 1862 Clemens reported to Orion that his cabinmate Calvin H. Higbie (1831?–1914)—the "Honest Man . . . Genial Comrade, and . . . Steadfast Friend" to whom *Roughing It* is dedicated—was among the cement-mine searchers: "I had a whispered message from him last night, in which he said he had arrived safely on the ground, and was in with the discoverers, turning the river out of its bed"; Clemens was relying on Higbie to determine whether the cement-mine rumors were a "steamboat": "Higbie is a large, strong man, and has the perseverance of the devil. If there is anything there, he will find it" (*L1,* 225). Higbie, a civil engineer who had lived for a time in Tuolumne County, California, arrived in Aurora in the spring of 1861. In the mid-1870s, after many years of traveling and engaging in mining ventures, he settled in Greenville, in northern California, where he lived until his death. In 1906 Clemens described him as "a most kindly, engaging, frank, unpretentious, unlettered, and utterly honest, truthful, and honorable giant; practical, unimaginative, destitute of humor, well endowed with good plain common sense, and as simple-hearted as a child" (AD, 10 Aug 1906, CU-MARK†; Higbie to SLC, 4 Dec 86, CU-MARK). Late in life Higbie wrote memoirs about his friendship with Clemens, who found them riddled with "extravagant distortions" and advised against their publication; portions of them were ultimately printed, however, after Higbie's death (AD, 10 Aug 1906, CU-MARK†; L1, 227 n. 3; Phillips, 22–23, 69–70, 73–74).

240.7–10   a friend of ours, a Mr. Van Dorn . . . join the next cement expedition] This friend was actually William Van Horn (b. 1820?), who came originally from Tennessee but had lived for a time in Keokuk, Iowa. Clemens described him in a 6 September 1862 letter to Clagett as "a comical old cuss, [who] can keep a camp alive with fun when he chooses" (L1, 239). According to Wright's history, Van Horn—a member of Whiteman's search party—actually located the cement mine with another prospector in the summer of 1862. Van Horn and his friend allegedly carried off thirty thousand dollars worth of gold at that time, but, on a subsequent visit, were forced to withdraw by hostile Indians. Van Horn reportedly died about 1865 without ever having returned to the site (L1, 240 n. 2; James W. A. Wright, 22–27).

240.16–18   We were to leave town . . . and meet at dawn on the "divide" overlooking Mono Lake] The prospectors apparently followed a wagon road leading south out of Aurora which traversed a ridge and descended into the Mono Lake basin (see supplement B, map 3). It is not known whether Clemens actually embarked on such an expedition to the Owens River cement mine, or when he visited Mono Lake. In a letter of 9 September 1862 he referred to a recent two-week trip "slashing around in the White Mountain District, partly for pleasure and partly for other reasons." Some have assumed that this late August–early September trip was the one described in chapters 37–39 of Roughing It (see L1, 239, 240 n. 2). But since the White Mountain district is considerably east of the Owens River and Mono Lake, this identification seems unlikely. Although Albert Bigelow Paine states that Clemens and Higbie made several long walking trips out of Aurora—including one to Yosemite, across the Sierra to the west of Mono Lake—none has been independently documented (MTB, 1:200).

243.7–8   Mono, it is sometimes called, and sometimes the "Dead Sea of California."] Mono Lake was named after the Monache Indians (members of the Shoshoni family), who inhabited the surrounding region. Their name meant "fly people" in the language of their Yokuts neighbors, who applied the term because "their chief food staple and trading article was the pupae of a fly . . . found in great quantities on the shores of the Great Basin lakes" (Gudde, 196; see also the note at 247.16–34). The comparison of Mono Lake to the Dead Sea seems to have originated with Henry DeGroot, an early visitor to the area, who stated: "It is literally a Dead Sea: not even a fish or frog can endure its acrid properties" (DeGroot 1860, 6–7). Browne popularized the name in his 1865 series for *Harper's* magazine, "A Trip to Bodie Bluff and the Dead Sea of the West," which Clemens had almost certainly read (J. Ross Browne 1865b, 416).

243.13–16 we traveled around . . . and then we went regularly into camp] Clemens's party probably went west along the north shore of the lake, possibly camping slightly beyond Black Point, at the spot where Mill Creek enters the lake (Frank J. Thomas, 2–3; see supplement B, map 3).

245.1–249.15 Mono Lake . . . true.] Mark Twain first published this chapter in a Buffalo *Express* "Around the World" letter on 16 October 1869; he revised the earlier printing for inclusion in *Roughing It* (SLC 1869k).

245.1–7 Mono Lake lies in a lifeless, treeless, hideous desert . . . a hundred miles in circumference, with two islands in its centre] Mono Lake is situated in an independent drainage basin, "a shallow, bathtub-shaped depression cupped by the lofty Sierra Nevada on its west and rolling volcanic uplands on its north, east and south" (Gaines, 16–17). The area around the northern shore is a "level-floored desert, scantily clothed in sage-brush and bunch-grass" (Russell, 272). At the time of Clemens's visit, the surface of the lake was slightly more than sixty-four hundred feet above sea level. The adjacent Sierra rises above thirteen thousand feet, while the White Mountains, visible to the southeast, tower to over fourteen thousand feet. In 1862 the lake was approximately fourteen miles east to west, and nine miles north to south; its circumference was probably about sixty miles. (Since 1941, water diversion has made it smaller, shallower, and saltier.) Its two volcanic islands are of contrasting appearance: the larger one, Paoha Island, is covered with light-colored lake sediment; Negit Island (now actually a peninsula) is formed of black lava (Gaines, 2, 8, 17, 25–26, 40–41, 66, 83; DeGroot 1863; Russell, 269, 278–79).

245.12–20 The lake is two hundred feet deep . . . so strong with alkali . . . the white lather would pile up three inches high] In the early 1860s the lake's maximum depth was about one hundred and ninety feet, and its average depth about seventy-five feet (it is now less than fifty feet). "Because of Mono's high carbonate concentrations, the lake is alkaline as well as salty. . . . Alkalinity imparts a slippery feel and bitter taste to the water, as well as those cleansing qualities praised by Twain" (Gaines, 17, 20–21). Browne remarked, in his 1865 article, "For washing purposes [the water] is admirable. I washed my head in it, and was astonished at the result" (J. Ross Browne 1865b, 417).

247.16–34 a white feathery sort of worm . . . a fly . . . the Indians eat all three] The lake waters contain vast numbers of brine shrimp (Mark

Twain's "feathery sort of worm") as well as immature (larval) brine
flies, both of which feed on algae. Female brine flies lay their eggs by
enveloping themselves in a "globule of air" to descend underwater,
where they cling to the rocks; when they have finished laying, they
simply "pop up to the surface." After the larvae are sufficiently developed, they attach themselves to rocks on the lakeshore and pupate,
emerging in several weeks as adult flies, which "darken the shore for
mile after mile; four thousand have been tallied in a square foot"
(Gaines, 42–48). Browne explained that the fly pupae were a "fruitful
source of subsistence" for the Mono Indians: "By drying them in the
sun and mixing them with acorns, berries, grass-seeds, and other articles of food gathered up in the mountains, they make a conglomerate
called *cuchaba*, which they use as a kind of bread" (J. Ross Browne
1865b, 417). In 1863 a member of the California geological survey described this delicacy in his journal:

> The Indians come far and near to gather them. The worms are dried in the sun,
> the shell rubbed off, when a yellowish kernel remains, like a small yellow grain
> of rice. This is oily, very nutritious, and not unpleasant to the taste, and under
> the name of *koo-chah-bee* forms a very important article of food. The Indians
> gave me some; it does not taste bad, and if one were ignorant of its origin, it
> would make fine soup. (Brewer, 417)

248.7–11   an unfailing spring of boiling water . . . a spring of pure cold
water, sweet and wholesome] Browne also described these springs:

> The larger island [Paoha] has a singular volcano in the interior, from which is-
> sues hot water and steam. Within a few yards of the boiling spring, the water of
> which is bitter, a spring of pure fresh water gushes out of the rocks. This is justly
> regarded as the greatest natural wonder of the lake. (J. Ross Browne 1865b, 418)

248.19–20   what it does with its surplus water is a dark and bloody mys-
tery] The lake's water level is maintained by evaporation (Gaines, 25).

249.3   the little town of Mono] The now-vanished mining camp of Monoville was situated a few miles north of Mono Lake and twenty-five
miles southwest of Aurora. Prospectors rushed to the area following
the discovery of rich gold deposits in July 1859, and within a few
months the population reached seven hundred. Deep snows during the
winter of 1859–60, and the discovery of gold and silver at Aurora the
following summer, just as quickly depopulated the town. By January
1864, according to the Aurora *Times*, Monoville was "almost wholly
deserted" ("A Deserted City," Virginia City *Union*, 5 Jan 64, 1, reprinting the Aurora *Times*; Chalfant, 40–42).

250.9–10   twelve miles, straight out to the islands] An exaggeration: the
islands were no farther than seven miles from any point on the lake
shore. From the northwest shore, where Clemens and his party probably camped, the distance was even less—perhaps four miles at most.

253.4–5   It was only a long swim that could be fatal] Browne also warned
of the caustic qualities of the lake waters: "It shrinks up the flesh when

steeped in it for any great length of time, like a strong decoction of lye. . . . One might almost as well sink as float in a case of wreck; for in either event his chance of life would be slender" (J. Ross Browne 1865b, 417–18). Modern assessment of the lake differs considerably: "Swimming in Mono Lake is a delightfully buoyant experience, for you cannot sink in the dense water. Old-timers claim a soak cures almost anything. But keep the water out of eyes and cuts—it stings! After a float, rinse the salts off your skin with fresh water" (Gaines, 4).

254.1–2   around its shores stand picturesque turret-looking masses] These mineral formations, or tufa towers, were created by underwater springs that bubbled up through the lake in past millennia; when the lake receded, they were exposed. Calcium in the spring water combined with carbonates in the lake water to form the precipitate calcite, which piled up on the lake bottom (Gaines, 21–22).

254.10–12   Castle Peak, and . . . a bright, miniature lake . . . between ten and eleven thousand feet] This twelve-thousand-foot peak (renamed Dunderberg Peak in 1878) is ten miles northwest of Mono Lake. The "miniature lake" is probably Trumbull Lake, "at the southern base of Castle Peak," some twenty-five hundred feet lower in elevation (Williams, 68; Browning, 59–60; see supplement B, map 3).

254.18–19   Mr. Ballou] See the notes at 180.12–13, 197.15–16, and 228.1–2.

256.17–28   the Wide West had "struck it rich!" . . . black, decomposed stuff . . . gold and particles of "native" silver] The Wide West claim was located in 1860 on Last Chance Hill, Aurora; its mining company was incorporated the following January with a capital stock of 2,400 shares valued at $600,000 (L1, 217 n. 2). The rich strike mentioned here occurred toward the end of May 1862; Clemens was among those who obtained a sample of the ore, "a *pinch* of decom, . . . pinched with thumb and finger, from Wide West ledge," as he wrote to Orion on 2 June (L1, 217). The Esmeralda *Star* reported on 31 May: "We have been in California since the spring of '49, visited many of the mines, but never saw anything to compare in richness with the ledge of the 'Wide West,' we have only spoken of the gold which could be seen and we were told that it was equally as rich in silver" (quoted in Mack 1947, 165–66).

257.12–16   a sixteen-hundred-pound parcel . . . to San Francisco] The details of this anecdote suggest that Mark Twain used as a source a clipping of a report in the Virginia City *Territorial Enterprise* for 20 July 1862, presumably preserved in a scrapbook. This report—from "a correspondent, writing from Esmeralda, July 13th"—had almost certainly been written by Clemens himself: "Sol. Carter purchased sixteen hundred pounds of decomposed Pride of Utah rock from the company, in the beginning of the week, for which he paid one dollar a pound in cash, and shipped said rock to San Francisco by his pack train" (SLC 1862c). When Mark Twain adapted this anecdote for use in *Roughing It*, he altered only the name of the mine, from the "Pride of Utah" to the "Wide West." The history of the Wide West was closely tied to that of the Pride of Utah, situated slightly above and parallel to it on Last Chance Hill. A rich strike was made in the Pride of Utah in mid-June, two or three weeks after the one in the Wide West. By early July it was known that the two ledges were intersected by the same rich cross vein, which was the source of both strikes. By the end of 1862 the two claims were owned by one company, and this consolidated Wide West mine was ultimately among the most productive in Esmeralda. In chapters 40–41 Mark Twain conflated the facts about the Wide West and the Pride of Utah, evidently in order to simplify his story of the blind lead as well as make it more dramatic, while still drawing on certain essential facts. The note at 269.25–26 discusses the question of whether the tale is fact or fiction.

257.27–258.11   he meant to have a look into the Wide West shaft . . . IT's A BLIND LEAD] According to Higbie's recollection, the superintendent of the Wide West invited him to inspect the excavation:

> While walking about and trying to get at the shape and formation of the deposit I discovered a cross vein running diagonally across this chimney and entering the walls at both sides. I called the attention of the superintendent to it. He thought it only a short spur and worthy of no attention, but as I had seen it entering both walls I was confident it was a permanent and distinct vein from the Wide West. Accordingly I made a mining location on this cross vein, as the mining laws permitted me to do, and put Sam L. Clemens' name on the location notice. (Phillips, 70)

259.5–6   even the Wide West people themselves did not suspect it] In reality, the owners of the Wide West quickly realized that the source of their rich strike was not their own claim but a cross ledge, apparently already located by someone else, called the "Dimes." In a letter of 22 June Clemens told Orion, "You see the grand rock comes from the 'Dimes,' in reality, and not from the W. W., although the latter said nothing about it until they had bought into the former" (*L1*, 220; Esmeralda district mining deeds, Book B:299–300, Mono County Archives).

259.14   the foreman of the Wide West] In the next chapter (268.29–30) Mark Twain identifies the foreman as A. D. Allen, an identification confirmed by the Esmeralda *Star* report of 31 May 1862 (quoted in Mack 1947, 165–66). Allen was an early locator of mining property on the Comstock lode, in Aurora, and in the Bodie mining district southwest of Esmeralda. In 1862 he was also president of Aurora's Live Yankee Mining Company. In September of that year he was elected a representative from Esmeralda County to the second Territorial Legislature, but failed to serve his term (*L1*, 191 n. 1; Angel, 402).

260.1–2 take possession of this blind lead, record it and establish ownership] Since the 1862 mining locations for the Esmeralda district (as opposed to mining deeds, which were entered in separate books) are not known to survive, it has not been possible to confirm whether Clemens and Higbie recorded a claim to the blind lead, or cross ledge, where it intersected the Pride of Utah tunnel. It is clear, however, that it turned out to be a continuation of the Dimes cross ledge. While the Wide West worked along the Dimes, the Pride of Utah followed its own rich strike, and the excavations soon met, which resulted in several months of legal "warfare" between the two companies ("The Wealth of Esmeralda," San Francisco *Alta California*, 3 Aug 62, 2).

260.2–3 and then forbid the Wide West company to take out any more of the rock] On 13 July, an Aurora correspondent—probably Clemens—reported that the excavations of the two companies had "run together." The Wide West served an injunction on the Pride of Utah (not the other way around) and, in addition, seized over one hundred pounds of its bullion from Clayton's mill. In retaliation, the Pride of Utah men "built a fire of such aromatic fuel as old boots, rags, etc., in the bottom of their shaft, and closed up the top, thus converting the Wide West shaft into a chimney"—which necessarily led to a suspension of work, at least temporarily (SLC 1862c).

262.38–263.2 By the laws of the district . . . obliged to do a fair and reasonable amount of work . . . within ten days] The first laws of the Esmeralda mining district were passed in August 1860, amended in June 1861, and amended again in June 1862. Although it is difficult to determine which laws were current and which were superseded by later ones, it appears that no provision such as the one that Mark Twain describes was in effect in June 1862. Mark Twain's reference to a ten-day period suggests that he was recalling Section 11 of the original code, which applied only to *surface* claims: "All surface claims shall be worked within ten days after there is sufficient water to successfully work said claims." It may be significant, in spite of Mark Twain's (and Higbie's) unequivocal assertion that they officially recorded their claim, that Section 5 read, "All quartz claims shall be duly recorded within ten days from the time of location." The law regarding labor that actually governed Clemens's claim was a recent amendment, passed on 1 June, which applied to both surface and underground (blind) leads: "There shall be ($20) twenty dollars' worth of work, or four days of useful labor, . . . done on each claim of two hundred feet . . . on or before the first day of December, 1862; said work to hold the claim good until the first day of June, 1863" (*Mining Laws*, 4, 6; Phillips, 70). Clemens and his partners would thus have had to perform twelve days of labor—at any time prior to 1 December—to secure their six-hundred-foot claim for a year. To obtain a perpetual title, they

needed to do fifteen days of work on each two-hundred-foot claim, a total of forty-five days of labor. In a letter of 22 June 1862 Clemens indicated that he was familiar with this provision: "By the new law I can
get a perpetual title to our ground very easily," he wrote Orion (in reference to another claim) (*L1*, 221). In retelling the blind-lead story
many years later, in 1906, he described a different version of the labor
requirement, claiming that he and his partners could have made their
"ownership of that exceedingly rich property permanent by doing ten
days' work on it, as required by the mining laws" (AD, 26 Mar 1906,
CU-MARK, in *MTA*, 2:253).

263.6–7   a Mr. Gardiner . . . "Nine-Mile Ranch"] The owner of this
ranch, located about nine miles northwest of Aurora, has not been conclusively identified. Two Gardiners are listed as Aurora residents:
E. L. H. Gardiner, deputy recorder for the Esmeralda district, and T. W.
Gardiner (Kelly 1863, 425, 427; *Mining Laws*, 2). Another early settler
in the area, George Albert Green, has also been named as an owner of
the ranch, probably at a later date (see supplement B, map 3; Fox, fold-
out map; Wedertz, 43).

264.1   CAPT. NYE was very ill indeed, with spasmodic rheumatism] On
12 July 1862 the Esmeralda *Star* reported that John Nye was bedridden
at Nine Mile Ranch, "an invalid, lying upon his back, all stiffened and
swollen up by that excruciating disease—inflammatory rheumatism"
("Captain John Nye," Forest Hill [Calif.] *Placer Courier*, 26 July 62, 3,
reprinting the Esmeralda *Star* of 12 July). Clemens described the illness
many years later as "a violent case of spasmodic rheumatism or blind
staggers, or some malady of the kind" (AD, 26 Mar 1906, CU-MARK,
in *MTA*, 2:254). Clemens's 1862 correspondence confirms that he was
absent from Aurora nursing Nye sometime between 25 June and 9 July
(*L1*, 223, 224).

264.12–13   I had seen him nurse a sick man himself and put up patiently
with the inconveniences] See the note at 265.22–24.

264.28–29   my late grandfather had had a coachman and such things] Although Clemens's paternal grandfather, Samuel B. Clemens of Virginia
(d. 1805), and his maternal grandfather, Benjamin Lampton of Kentucky (d. 1837), were both moderately prosperous slave owners, this
claim is clearly facetious (Wecter 1952, 6–9, 22–24, 46–47).

265.9   my share of the Tennessee land] Around 1830, in an effort to insure the family's future prosperity, John Marshall Clemens had purchased a tract of some seventy-five thousand acres near Jamestown,
Fentress County, Tennessee. "Although after the father's death in 1847
responsibility for realizing income from the land fell chiefly to Orion,
every member of the Clemens family, at one time or another, cherished
schemes for exploiting it" (*L1*, 79 n. 11). Clemens's own efforts to sell

the land in 1865–66 to grape-growing interests were frustrated by Orion's inconvenient temperance beliefs. In about 1887 Orion traded away what the family believed to be the last of the Tennessee land—a ten-thousand-acre parcel—but in 1906, Clemens was surprised by a proposal that he sell a remaining thousand acres (*L1*, 326, 327 n. 2, 341–42; AD, 5 Apr 1906, CU-MARK, in *MTA*, 2:320–21; SLC 1897–98, 30).

265.10–12   the typographical union of which I had long been a member in good standing] Clemens joined a printers' union in the summer of 1853 when he began work as a typesetter in St. Louis, probably the St. Louis Typographical Union No. 8—a charter member of the National Typographical Union, established in May 1852 (*L1*, 11 n. 2).

265.22–24   He raved like a maniac . . . and swore a world of oaths that he would kill me] Clemens wrote Orion on 9 July, upon his return from nursing Nye:

> Capt. Nye, as his disease grew worse, grew so peevish and abusive, that I quarrelled with him and left. He required almost constant attention, day and night, but he made no effort to hire anyone to assist me. He said he nursed the Governor three weeks, day and night—which is a d—d lie, I suspect. He told Mrs. Gardiner he would take up the quarrel with me again when he gets well. (*L1*, 224)

266.28–29   Higbie had depended on me, as I had on him] Higbie claimed in his reminiscences that he was in no way responsible for the loss of the claim. Having been called away to help some friends, he had exacted a promise from Clemens to "take care of things" by performing the "assessment work" (Phillips, 70).

268.11   as he came into Esmeralda by one road, I entered it by another] The dramatic coincidence of Higbie's and Clemens's entering Aurora by different roads minutes before the relocation, which presumably occurred at midnight on 30 June (see the next note), was certainly Clemens's invention. Clemens's letter of 9 July 1862 to Orion indicates that he did not return to Aurora until about 8 July, and that Higbie had left Aurora for the cement diggings during the first week in July and had not yet returned (*L1*, 224–25, 229–30 n. 1).

268.27–32   fourteen men, duly armed . . . proclaimed their ownership of the blind lead, under the new name of the "Johnson." . . . A. D. Allen . . . said his name must be added] On 1 July 1862 Peter Johnson—an owner of the Pride of Utah mine and of the Union Mill near Aurora—recorded the relocation of a ledge he named the "Johnson," in partnership with A. D. Allen and several others,

> said location being a re-location of the ledges or claims known as the Harlem and Zenobia ledges and being a claim of One thousand (1000) feet, described as commencing at the Notice in the Pride of Utah Tunnel, and thence running on the Lode Eight hundred (800) feet east and Two hundred (200) feet West. (Esmeralda district mining deeds, Book E:44–45, Mono County Archives)

(See the note at 269.10–12; "From the Esmeralda Mining District," San Francisco *Alta California,* 23 June 62, 1; Esmeralda district mining deeds, Book B:488–90, Mono County Archives.) It may have been this relocation that an Aurora correspondent of the Sacramento *Bee* reported on 3 July:

[The Wide West and the Pride of Utah] companies struck the cross lead about the same time, and worked towards each other. . . . The men who work for the two companies located claims immediately after the discovery of the cross vein covering nearly the whole of it, as it was not the lead claimed by the original companies. (Veni, Vidi 1862a)

Johnson's relocation did not go unchallenged. In December 1862 the Zenobia Lode Company published a notice that asserted

a superior title to the Johnson Co., claiming the same ground so far as said localities conflict. This ground is a portion of that now held by the Company known as the Wide West Company. The notice is signed by A. Waddell, J. C. Dorsey, S. P. Dorsey and James Elder. ("Esmeralda Mining Notices," *Mining and Scientific Press* 6 [20 Dec 62]: 2, repeated weekly through 2 Mar 63)

269.1–9 Higbie and I cleared out . . . and after a month or two . . . returned to Esmeralda] Clemens's letters of July and August 1862 disprove this statement: he did not absent himself from Aurora for any long period until late August, when he went to the White Mountains for about two weeks. In fact on 21 July Clemens, apparently still hoping that he could profit from the Johnson strike, purchased twenty-five feet in the "First East Extension of the 'Johnson' Lode, situated on Last Chance Hill" for $500; the deed for this purchase was "Filed for Record Octr 3^d a.d. 1862 . . . at the request of C. H. Higbie" (deed, item B12, NPV).

269.10–12 the Wide West and the Johnson companies had consolidated . . . five thousand feet, or shares] The Pride of Utah and the Johnson companies consolidated on 27 September 1862. The new corporation was capitalized for $1,400,000 with 5,600 shares; among the first trustees of the new company was A. D. Allen. On 3 December, the Wide West purchased the combined Johnson and Pride of Utah Mining Company for $200,000. By early 1863 the newly consolidated Wide West owned a controlling interest in the Dimes ledge as well (San Francisco *Evening Bulletin:* "More Mining Companies," 30 Sept 62, 3; "San Francisco Mining Companies," 6 Jan 63, 3; Esmeralda district mining deeds, Book C:743–44, Book E:44–45, Mono County Archives; "The Esmeralda Mines," letter dated 12 Feb 63, undated clipping, San Francisco *Alta California,* Bancroft Scraps, Set W [Nevada Mining], 94:1:50, CU-BANC; Sahab, 1).

269.12–15 the foreman . . . had sold his hundred feet . . . and gone home to the States to enjoy it] In January 1863 an Aurora correspondent for the San Francisco *Evening Bulletin* commented: "The Gambles and the Johnsons and the Allens are sure to sell stock in claims which have long since been given up by poor miners, while many rich ledges lie ne-

glected because confidence is only reposed in the wealthy" (Sahab, 1).
In an "Around the World" letter published in the Buffalo *Express* in January 1870 Clemens wrote of his two partners, Allen and Higbie: "The sensible one is still worth a hundred thousand dollars or so—he never lost his wits—but the other one (and by far the best and worthiest of our trio), can't pay his board" (SLC 1870a).

269.19–20 We would have been millionaires] The richness of the Johnson ledge is indisputable. The reputation of the consolidated Wide West mine (which included the rich Johnson lead) blossomed in late 1862, gaining "world-wide notoriety" in 1863 (Kelly 1863, 410). William H. Bunker, who explored the abandoned Johnson excavation in 1879, found that "occasionally a pillar of rich ore was left to sustain the walls. . . . The ore in the existing pillars assays as high as $10,000 per ton" (Bunker, 13). Nevertheless, the claim proved to be a "chamber mine"—that is, the rich ore was not dispersed throughout but was found in a single large chamber, reportedly large enough to "turn a wagon and horses in" (Wasson, 45; Joshua E. Clayton, 145)—and this chamber was soon exhausted. Confidence in the Wide West—and in the Esmeralda mining region as a whole—was short-lived. The value of Wide West stock began a precipitous decline in mid-1863, in spite of attempts to suppress the information that the original rich strike was depleted. By early the following year the mine's yield was negligible (*Mining and Scientific Press:* "Esmeralda," 6 [20 July 63]: 1; "Wide West Mining Company" and "Romance of the Wide West Continued," 8 [5 Mar 64]: 147, 148; "Esmeralda Stock List," 6 [25 May 63]: 5; "Report of Bids," 7 [21 Dec 63]: 5; Grant H. Smith, 48; Paher, 466).

269.22–24 the evidence of . . . the official records of Esmeralda District, is . . . proof that it is a true history] See the note at 260.1–2.

269.25–26 I was absolutely and unquestionably worth a million dollars, once] Independent documentary evidence proves that the story of the Wide West mine and its associated rich blind lead took place essentially as Mark Twain recounts it. It has not been demonstrated, however, that Clemens and Higbie were directly involved, in spite of their virtually identical recollections that they made a claim and lost it by default. Furthermore, Mark Twain's explanation of the applicable mining law does not seem to correspond to recoverable fact. That the story was at best an exaggeration is suggested by the content of Clemens's letters of the period, which make little mention of the Johnson lead, focusing instead on the nearby Annapolitan—a claim located in September 1861 which he, Higbie, and several other partners owned. On 22 June 1862, for example—two days after he is conjectured to have located the blind lead—he wrote to Orion:

We are most damnably "mixed" as to whether the "Annipolitan" will prove to be the "Dimes" or the "Pride of Utah." We want it to be the former—for in that case we can hold all our ground—but if it be the "Pride of Utah," we shall lose all of it except fifty feet, as the "P. of U." was located first. There is an extension on the "P. of U.," and in order to be on the safe side, we have given them notice not to work on it. (*L1*, 220)

Three days later, on 25 June, he informed Orion, "No—haven't struck anything in the 'Annipolitan.' No—down 12 feet—am not afraid of it. It will come out well I think" (*L1*, 223). In his next extant letter—written on 9 July, after his return from nursing Captain Nye and nine days after the relocation of the Johnson ledge—he told Orion, "From what I can learn, the Pride of Utah and the Dimes have run together, at a depth of less than 100 feet, and now form one immense ledge, of fabulous richness. I suppose the Annipolitan will share the same fate" (*L1*, 225). A week or so later Orion, who had evidently learned something of the Johnson excitement from Tom Nye (Captain Nye's son), wrote to ask Clemens about his involvement, prompting his only known mention of the Johnson claim: "No, I don't own a foot in the 'Johnson' ledge—I will tell the story some day in a more intelligible manner than Tom [Nye] has told it" (*L1*, 228). These letters suggest that it may have been the Annapolitan's proximity to the rich strikes which stimulated Clemens's dreams of wealth, and that the true story of the blind lead has not yet been told. For a full anaylsis see Edgar M. Branch's article "Fact and Fiction in the Blind Lead Episode of *Roughing It*" (Esmeralda district mining deeds, Book B:501–3, Book G:383–84, Mono County Archives; *L1*, 134 n. 2, 216–224, 230 n. 6).

269.27–270.1 A year ago . . . Higbie, wrote me] The earliest surviving letter from Higbie dates from 1886, when he wrote to Clemens from Greenville requesting a $20,000 loan to buy out two mining partners. Clemens responded with a good-natured refusal (Higbie to SLC, 4 Dec 86, CU-MARK; SLC to Higbie, 16 Dec 86, *Saturday Evening Post* 193 [11 Sept 1920]: 74).

271.2–4 I had gone out into the world . . . my father had endorsed for friends] Clemens's father, Virginia-born John Marshall Clemens, died on 24 March 1847 virtually bankrupt. His financial collapse—the inevitable result of years of unremunerative mercantile enterprises and real-estate investments—was apparently hastened by his dealings with Hannibal land speculator Ira Stout. Clemens later asserted that Stout got his father "to go security for a large sum, 'took the benefit of the bankrupt law' and ruined him—in fact made a pauper of him," condemning the Clemens family to years of "grinding poverty and privation" (SLC 1897, 31; AD, 28 Mar 1906, CU-MARK, in *MTA*, 2:274). When his father died, Clemens, aged eleven, became an apprentice (probably part time) at Henry La Cossitt's Hannibal *Gazette*, but he may be dating his entry "into the world" from his employment as a printer's devil, for board but no wages, at Joseph P. Ament's Hannibal *Missouri Courier* in the spring of 1848 (Wecter 1952, 122–23, 202; *Inds*, 314).

271.11–272.1 grocery clerk ... studied law ... blacksmithing ... printer ... pilot] Although it is possible that in his early years Clemens tried his hand as a clerk, law student, and blacksmith, these experiences have not been documented. His work as a printer and pilot is discussed in the note at 1.7–11.

271.26–27 Esmeralda *Union*] In 1862 Aurora's only newspaper was the Esmeralda *Star.* The Esmeralda *Union* did not begin publication until March 1864 (Angel, 295–97).

272.3–4 I did long to stand behind a wheel again] The frustration of his mining hopes may have caused Clemens privately to regret his piloting days, but in August 1862 he dashed off an emphatic disclaimer to his family: "What in thunder are pilot's wages to me? ... I never have *once* thought of returning home to go on the river again, and I never expect to do any more piloting at any price. ... Do not tell any one that I had any idea of piloting again at present—for it is all a mistake" (*L1*, 235–36). In early 1866, however, twenty months after leaving Nevada for San Francisco, he wrote his mother and sister, "I wish I was back there piloting up & down the river again. Verily, all is vanity and little worth—except piloting" (*L1*, 327).

272.5–6 grandiloquent letters home about my blind lead and my European excursion] On the whole Clemens seems to have kept his expectations to himself: "You must do all the writing home," he advised Orion in a letter of 9 June 1862 from Aurora, "I haven't written a word home since I left Carson. I am afraid the folks will not hear from me again while I remain in this part of Cal[i]fornia" (*L1*, 219). In fact, there are no letters extant from Clemens to his St. Louis family between early April 1862, when he left Carson City for Aurora, and mid-August, well after the blind-lead excitement of late June and early July.

273.10–28 I had amused myself with writing letters ... city editor of the *Enterprise*] In the spring of 1862 Clemens began sending correspondence from Aurora to the Virginia City *Territorial Enterprise* under the pen name "Josh." These letters—now lost—were apparently humorous or satirical in tone, and met with the enthusiastic approval of the *Enterprise* staff. Joseph Goodman, the newspaper's proprietor and editor-in-chief, later recalled these "voluntary contributions": "They struck us as so funny that we sent him word to come to Virginia City and take a job on the paper" ("Jos. Goodman's Memories of Humorist's Early Days," San Francisco *Examiner,* 22 Apr 1910, 3; see also the note at 220.2). Goodman was particularly struck by one item, a burlesque Fourth of July oration that commenced "Fellow Citizens:—I was sired by the great American eagle, and borne by a continental dam!" (This item has been identified as a lampoon of the platform style of Nevada Chief Justice George Turner, whom the *Enterprise* was then attacking for official corruption. It has also sometimes been conflated with another Clemens piece apparently entitled "Lecture of Mr. Personal Pronoun." Clemens himself later recalled that his place on the *Enterprise* was secured by a burlesque of a Turner speech.) At the end of July Clemens received a letter from William H. Barstow, who worked in the business office of the *Enterprise*, offering him the "post of local reporter . . . at $25 a week," which he accepted in early August (*L1*, 201 n. 8, 231, 233; Putnam, 3; Daggett, 15; Sam P. Davis, 1:393–94; Johnson, 266; AD, 2 Oct 1906, CU-MARK, in *MTE*, 390–91; *ET&S1*, 13–17).

274.8–9 I went up to Virginia . . . rusty looking city editor] Clemens postponed his journey to Virginia City for several weeks, taking up his new position in late September. According to Dennis Driscoll, one of the *Enterprise* proprietors, Clemens walked "all the way from Aurora, packing his blankets on his back," and announced his arrival with the remark, "Dang my buttons, if I don't believe I'm lousy"; among "all the compositors turning at the uncouth figure presented to them, . . . there was not a man to dispute Mark's assertion" ("The Pioneer Journal Dead," Virginia City *Evening Chronicle*, 16 Jan 93, 2; *L1*, 241 n. 5).

274.25–26 the chief editor and proprietor (Mr. Goodman] At this time the *Enterprise* had three proprietors: Joseph Thompson Goodman (1838–1917), editor-in-chief; Denis E. McCarthy, print-shop supervisor (see the note at 537.4); and Dennis Driscoll (1823–76), business manager. Goodman went to California from New York in 1854 and learned the printer's trade in San Francisco, working along with McCarthy at the San Francisco *Mirror* and the *Golden Era*. In March 1861 he and McCarthy purchased the *Enterprise*, transforming it from a weekly to a daily and greatly enlarging its circulation. From early 1862 until October 1863 Driscoll joined Goodman and McCarthy in ownership of the paper. After McCarthy sold out in September 1865, Goodman stayed on as sole proprietor until 1874, when he sold his interest (reportedly for half a million dollars) and became a San Francisco stockbroker and speculator, first gaining and then losing a fortune. From 1880 to 1891 he operated a raisin vineyard in Fresno County, California. During his retirement he devoted most of his time to deciphering the Maya inscriptions of Central America and Yucatan, about which he published a monograph, entitled *The Archaic Maya Inscriptions*, in London in 1897 (William Wright 1893a; "Death of D. E. McCarthy," Virginia City *Evening Chronicle*, 17 Dec 85, 2; *L1*, 242 n. 2; Lingenfelter and Gash, 253–54; Rawls, 8; Goodman to Alfred B. Nye, 6 Nov 1905 and 17 Nov 1905, Alfred B. Nye Papers, CU-BANC; "Joseph T. Goodman Comes into His Own," San Francisco *Chronicle*, 21 Sept 1930, F5; for a fuller history of the *Enterprise*, see the note at 292.1–7).

275.9 Dan] William Wright (1829–98), who wrote under the pseudonym "Dan De Quille," was widely known throughout the West as a mining reporter and humorist. Born in Ohio, he moved with his family to West

Liberty, Iowa, in 1847, and in 1857 emigrated to California. For five years he prospected and mined in California and Nevada, publishing occasional pieces of humorous journalism, notably in the San Francisco *Golden Era*. Since May 1862 he had been the local editor of the *Enterprise*, continuing his connection with the newspaper until it suspended publication in 1893. In 1897, in failing health and reduced circumstances, he retired to the home of his daughter in Iowa. His major work was *The History of the Big Bonanza* (1876), completed at Clemens's Hartford home and issued by Clemens's own publisher, the American Publishing Company (William Wright 1876, vii–ix, xv–xxv; Berkove 1988b; *L1*, 265–66; *ET&S1*, 171–72). Despite the impression given here that Clemens immediately assumed full duties as the *Enterprise*'s city editor, he actually shared the post with Wright for several weeks, until Wright departed on 27 December 1862 to visit his family in Iowa. When Wright returned in September 1863 he resumed his place on the *Enterprise*, sharing reportorial duties, as well as lodgings, with Clemens.

275.21   Two nonpareil columns] Nonpareil was one of the smallest type sizes, equivalent to modern six-point type; it was "extensively used, though mostly on newspapers" (A. A. Stewart, 163; MacKellar, 56). In later years Clemens recalled that his obligation to the *Enterprise* was "to furnish one column of leaded nonpareil every day, and as much more as I could get on paper before the paper should go to press at two o'clock in the morning" (AD, 9 Jan 1906, CU-MARK, in *MTA*, 1:271).

276.17–35   I discovered some emigrant wagons . . . no parallel in history] Clemens's sensational accounts of the beleaguered wagon trains have been identified as two *Enterprise* items of 1 October 1862, extant only as reprinted in the Marysville (Calif.) *Appeal* of 5 October (SLC 1862e–f).

277.2–3   Mr. Goodman said that I was as good a reporter as Dan] Goodman, in later years, reportedly had this to say about the relative abilities of his two local reporters:

Isn't it so singular that Mark Twain should live and Dan De Quille fade out? If anyone had asked me in 1863 which was to be an immortal name, I should unhesitatingly have said Dan De Quille. They had about equal talent and sense of humor, but the difference was the way in which they used their gifts. One shrank from the world; the other braved it, and it recognized his audacity. (Drury, 216)

278.11–12   My great competitor . . . was Boggs of the *Union*] The character Boggs was based upon Clement T. Rice. Rice went to Nevada from New York in 1861, "having received an appointment under Gov. Nye" (Rice to A. W. Clark, 8 July 61, quoted in Marsh, 680 n. 144). He prospected for a time, and like Clemens owned shares in many mining claims. Clemens had met him in Carson City in 1861 when Rice was a reporter on the *Silver Age*. Rice remained with the newspaper when it moved to Virginia City on 4 November 1862—under the proprietorship of Sam A. Glessner, James L. Laird, and John Church—and changed its name to the *Union*, soon becoming the major competitor of the *Enterprise*. Despite their elaborate journalistic sparring (with Rice figuring as "the Unreliable" in Clemens's columns), the two were good friends, visiting San Francisco together in May and June 1863 and collaborating in reporting the third Territorial Legislature in 1864 for their respective newspapers. By 1867, reputedly a wealthy man, Rice had entered the insurance business in New York City (*L1*, 131, 135 n. 6; Lingenfelter and Gash, 32, 255; *ET&S1*, 22, 193; *MTEnt*, 11–12).

278.17–18 because the principal hated the *Enterprise*] William E. Mellvile had been the principal of—and a teacher at—Virginia City's single public school since its establishment in 1862. During 1863 he was mentioned in the press as a possible candidate for political office and described as a superior teacher and a man of excellent character and fluent speech. He resigned in February 1864, perhaps as the result of unspecified charges brought against him by school trustee William H. Barstow. Clemens explained Mellvile's animosity toward the *Enterprise* in an earlier account of the school-report incident in an 1867 letter to the *Enterprise*: "The scrub who had charge of the public school would not let me have the report for the ENTERPRISE, because it had said he was an ass, which was true, and if he had been half a man he would have been flattered by it" (SLC 1868a; Angel, 571; Kelly 1863, 167; "Our Public School," Virginia City *Evening Bulletin*, 8 July 63, 3; Argentoro, 1; "Board of Education," Virginia City *Union*, 4, 7, and 25 Feb 64, 3; "Certificate of Incorporation of the Virginia Literary & Scientific Association," dated 22 Jan 62, Book A: 3637–38, Storey County Archives, PH in CU-MARK, courtesy of Michael H. Marleau).

279.17 the proprietor of the *Union*] In his 1867 *Enterprise* account Clemens identified this proprietor as John Church (SLC 1868a).

280.7–8 there was no school report in the *Union*, and Boggs held me accountable] In an 1881 letter Rice teased Clemens about the school-report incident, alluding to "the 'influence' you dosed me with in the Territorial Enterprise office, to get my 'school report' that I obtained for the Union" (Rice to SLC, 4 Dec 81, CU-MARK).

280.12 the proprietor of the "Genesee" mine] The Genesee, located in the Devil's Gate district five or six miles southeast of Virginia City, aroused interest among speculators in late 1862 and early 1863. The mine "proprietor" who requested the inspection may have been one of two owners mentioned by Mark Twain in an 1868 letter to the Chicago *Republican*: "Where is the famous Genessee, which United State[s] Senator Stewar[t] and 'uncle' Johnny Atchison bought for so fabulous a sum?" (SLC 1868e). John H. Atchison invested widely in Comstock mines, including the Ophir and the Mexican; in 1862 he and William M. Stewart (see the note at 288.16–17) lived at the same Carson City address ("Mining Matters in Nevada Territory," San Francisco *Alta California*, 28 Nov 62, 1, reprinting the Virginia City *Union* of 22 November; Quartz, 1; Marsh, 686 n. 198; Grant H. Smith, 80–81 n. 1; Kelly 1862, 67, 89).

281.4–6 the grand "flush times" . . . continued with unabated splendor for three years] The population boom, lavish spending habits, and jubilant spirits characterizing the Comstock in 1863 did not continue with "unabated splendor" for three years. The Washoe economy entered a major depression as early as May 1864 (right before Clemens's departure for San Francisco), which "culminated in the panic of December 1865" (Grant H. Smith, 48–50). In his *Enterprise* letter of 29 December 1865 Mark Twain spoke of the "list of rich stock operators of two years ago" who were "busted": "All the nabobs of '63 are pretty much ruined. . . . These are sad, sad times" (SLC 1866a).

282.36–37 It claimed a population of fifteen thousand to eighteen thousand] Although no official figures are available, it is estimated that between the fall of 1862 and midsummer 1863 the population of Virginia City increased from four thousand to fifteen thousand or more (Grant H. Smith, 28).

285.1 My salary was increased to forty dollars a week] This salary, Clemens later confessed, was "all of forty dollars more than I was worth, and I had always wanted a position which paid in the opposite proportion of value to amount of work" (AD, 9 Jan 1906, CU-MARK, in *MTA*, 1:271).

286.16–287.1 give the reporters forty or fifty "feet," and get them to . . . publish a notice of it] Clemens, for example, made favorable mention of the Echo mine, in which he was a shareholder, in three letters to the San Francisco *Morning Call* in July and August 1863. In the first of them he went so far as to claim that the Echo was "probably the richest mine in Gold Hill District" (SLC 1863f, 1863i, 1863l; *L1*, 258–59 n. 1).

287.25 We received presents of "feet" every day] Fully realizing the extent to which his reports affected the value of mining stock, Clemens learned, as he wrote home, "how to levy black-mail on the mining companies" in exchange for shares of stock (*L1*, 253). When his mother later inquired how he supported his extravagant living in San Francisco during May and June 1863, he answered, "Why I sold 'wildcat' mining ground that was given me, & my credit was always good at the bank for two or three thousand dollars, & is yet" (*L1*, 259–60).

288.16–17 Mr. Stewart (Senator, now, from Nevada)] William M. Stewart (1827?–1909), originally from New York, had emigrated to California in 1850; he practiced law and served as state attorney general before relocating to Nevada in 1860. There he invested in mining properties and maintained a highly lucrative law practice, earning immense fees for representing several of the largest mining companies. He was a member of the Territorial Council in 1861 and a delegate to the constitutional convention of 1863. When Nevada achieved statehood, Stewart was elected one of its first senators, serving from 1864 to 1875 and again from 1887 to 1905 (*L1*, 243 n. 4; Elliott, 4–5, 11, 17–26, 277 n. 1).

288.17–26 he would give me twenty feet of "Justis" stock . . . nothing could make that man yield] The Justis (sometimes spelled "Justice") mine, located in 1859, was in the Gold Hill district on the west side of Gold Canyon, conveniently situated near the main road and several mills. In mid-November 1863 Justis stock was hovering in the range of $10 a foot; on 11 December it had reached $70. By mid-February 1864, following a rich strike earlier that month, the price had risen to over $150 a foot (Lamb, 2; Virginia City *Union:* "Rich Strike," 10 Feb 64, 3; "Justice Company," 27 Mar 64, 3; "Washoe Stock and Exchange Board," Virginia City *Evening Bulletin,* various dates in Nov 63–Feb 64). Mark Twain gave a similar account of Stewart's offer in his letter to the *Enterprise* of 12 December 1863, taking the opportunity to launch an attack on the "disreputable old cottonhead":

[Stewart] as good as promised me ten feet in the "Justis," and then backed down again when the stock went up to $80 a foot. . . . Bill Stewart is always construing something—eternally distorting facts and principles. He would climb out of his coffin and construe the burial service. He is a long-legged, bull-headed, whopper-jawed, constructionary monomaniac. . . . I have my own opinion of Bill Stewart, and if it would not appear as if I were a little put out about that Justis (that was an almighty mean thing), I would as soon express it as not. (SLC 1863y)

288.27–28 My revenge will be found in the accompanying portrait] See the illustration on page 289. According to Stewart, Clemens exacted this "revenge" for quite another offense, dating from the winter of 1867–68. Stewart employed Clemens then as his private secretary and shared lodgings with him in Washington, D.C., an arrangement that allowed Clemens to begin work on his manuscript for *The Innocents Abroad.* Reportedly Clemens's irregular and obtrusive living habits so bedeviled their elderly landlady that Stewart was forced to call him to account. "I called Sam in and repeated to him what the landlady had said," Stewart recalled in 1891,

I told him I would thrash him if I ever heard another complaint. I said that I did not want to turn him out because I wanted him to finish his book. He made one of his smart replies at the expense of the landlady and I told him that I would thrash him then and there. He begged in a most pitiful way for me not to do so and I could not help laughing.

Seeing that he had gotten me into a good humor again he said that he would not annoy the old woman again, but that he would certainly get even with me for having threatened to thrash him if it took him 10 years to do so. ("Mark Twain's Revenge," New York *Recorder,* 5 Apr 91, clipping enclosed in Robert W. Carl to SLC, 5 Apr 91, CU-MARK)

In his autobiography, published in 1908, Stewart told substantially the same story, adding, "I was confident that he would come to no good end, but I have heard of him from time to time since then, and I understand that he has settled down and become respectable" (William M. Stewart, 224). Albert Bigelow Paine maintained that this mildly provocative portrait (which does not particularly resemble Stewart, who had a distinctive flowing beard) was an "unforgivable offense to [Stewart's] dignity," which rankled long after and influenced Stewart's unflattering—and at times untruthful—recollections of Clemens (*MTB*, 1:347 n. 1). But Clemens's friend Steve Gillis believed that Stewart's "malicious stories" were not the result of any real offense. In a letter to Paine, Gillis transmitted Joseph Goodman's remarks "about that Stewart fling":

> "If Mark didn't see fit to come back at the Senator, why should Paine take up the cudgel now? I have always thought that Stewart considered that attack a masterpiece of humor, and that his object was to draw Mark into a controversy and thereby attract attention to his (Stewart's) book." . . .

There you have Stewart's animus in a nutshell. (Gillis to Paine, 26 Feb 1911, Daley)

288.29–37 they had been buying "Overman" stock . . . These are actual facts] Between March and August 1863, the value of stock in the Overman mine, in the Gold Hill district, increased from $12 to over $600 a foot (*Mining and Scientific Press:* "Washoe Stock Remarks," 6 [23 Mar 63]: 5; "The Mining Share Market," 6 [31 Aug 63]: 4). In a letter written to his family on 18 July 1863, shortly after returning to Virginia City from a visit to San Francisco, Clemens gave a slightly different account of this failed opportunity:

> A gentleman in San Francisco told me to call at his office, & he would give me five feet of "Overman." Well, do you know I never went after it? The stock is worth $400⁰⁰ a foot, now—$2,000 thrown away. I don't care a straw, for myself, but I ought to have had more thought for you. (*L1*, 260)

The value of the stock on 16 July was in fact $400 a foot (*L1*, 261 n. 2).

289.20–2. the government holds the primary right to mines . . . or at least dia then] In the early 1860s there were no national laws regulating mining claims, nor any way to acquire legal title to claims located on public lands. By long-established custom, however, the rights of "squatter sovereignty" prevailed, and miners observed the laws set forth by each mining district. The National Mining Law of 1866, sponsored by Senator Stewart, gave legal status to local regulations and provided for the patenting of mining claims at a fee of five dollars per acre (Elliott, 49–55).

289.23–24 Imagine a stranger staking out a mining claim . . . in your front yard] The conflicting rights of "owners of gold and silver ledges lying under the earth, and the owners of lots lying on the top of the earth" were a topic of lively discussion in Nevada and California newspapers in 1863 and 1864 ("The Conflict in Washoe between Mining Claims and Surface Lots," San Francisco *Evening Bulletin*, 30 Apr 63, 3). The principle that *"no surface location of ground on mineral land can be made to the exclusion of mining interests"* prevailed in the courts, although owners of condemned houses, crops, or other improvements were entitled to compensation (San Francisco *Evening Bulletin:* "Further of the Conflict of Surface and Ledge Interests at Washoe," 5 May 63, 2; "Mining Companies vs. Lot Owners in Washoe," 7 Sept 63, 2). Mark Twain took note of this conflict of interests in "A Big Thing," published in the Buffalo *Express* in March 1870: "When you have 'taken up' a mine you have a legal right to dig for it,—and if another man owns the farm that is on top of it, it is a very grave misfortune for him, because the only way he has of protecting that farm from destruction, is to move it" (SLC 1870d).

289.30–35 I owned in another claim . . . "East India" stock . . . did not cut a quartz ledge or anything that remotely resembled one] Clemens wrote to his family in April 1863:

> Some of the boys made me a present of fifty feet in the East India G & S. M. Company, ten days ago. I was offered ninety-five dollars a foot for it, yesterday, in gold. *I refused it*—not because I think the claim is worth a cent, for I *don't*, but because I had a curiosity to see how high it *would* go, before people find out how worthless it is. (*L1*, 247)

The East India "humbug," Clemens later noted, was located "right in the middle of C. street" (SLC 1868e).

290.7–291.10 "North Ophir." . . . the mine had been "salted" with melted half dollars] The North Ophir was southwest of Virginia City in the Argentine district. It first attracted attention in March 1863, but its shares were not actively traded until a sudden "excitement" in the stock in early July sent prices soaring from below $10 up to $60 a foot. On 6 July, however, the Virginia City *Evening Bulletin* reported that "one individual who had some rock assayed and found silver alloyed with copper, swears that somebody melted a lot of half dollars and poured them into the ledge" ("Fluctuations of North Ophir," 6 July 63, 2). In spite of this accusation, Clemens puffed the mine in mid-July in exchange for five feet, claiming that expert testimony had "removed the stain from the North Ophir's character" (SLC 1863i). Years later he admitted that he had "bought that mine," and then "adjourned to the poor-house again" when a "painful case of 'salting' was apparent" (SLC 1869j). In an ironic conclusion to the hoax, the Virginia City correspondent of the San Francisco *Evening Bulletin* maintained in October 1863 that the "salting" conspirators had taken care to "preserve small portions of the milling of the coin, which on being detected would at once disclose the artifice," thereby depressing the value of the stock and permitting them to purchase it at cheap prices ("Review of Things in Washoe," San Francisco *Evening Bulletin*, 14 Oct 63, 1; "Struck It

Rich," Sacramento *Union*, 9 Mar 63, 1, reprinting an item possibly by Clemens in the Virginia City *Territorial Enterprise* of 6 March; *L1*, 260, 260–61 n. 1).

291.3–15   the world-renowned tragedian, McKean Buchanan ... we might have lost . . . from the stage] According to the Virginia City *Evening Bulletin* of 6 July 1863, a "prominent theatrical man" (presumably Buchanan) purchased a block of North Ophir stock for less than $10 a foot, sold out for $30, and then the next day bought it back for $60, believing it would rise still further ("Fluctuations of North Ophir," 2). Instead, he lost everything when the stock collapsed. McKean Buchanan (1823–72) abandoned a lucrative mercantile career to pursue his theatrical ambitions after making a decided hit as an amateur in New Orleans. He made his New York debut in 1849 and toured extensively over the succeeding years, appearing in California, Great Britain, and Australia. He and his company toured Nevada in 1862—meeting with little success—and returned in May 1863 for an extended engagement in Virginia City. Buchanan had an established reputation as a tragedian, although his overblown, bombastic style did not endear him to the critics. Mark Twain himself remarked in 1869 in the Buffalo *Express:*

> The great McKean Buchanan having been driven from all the world's great cities many years ago, still keeps up a pitiless persecution of the provinces, ranting with undiminished fury before audiences composed of one sad manager, one malignant reporter, and a Sheriff waiting to collect the license, and still pushes his crusade from village to village, strewing his disastrous wake with the corpses of country theatres. (SLC 1869f)

And upon Buchanan's death, the New York *Times* commented that many of his "warm personal friends . . . regretted his persistence in continuing on the dramatic stage" ("Obituary. McKean Buchanan," 18 Apr 72, 2; Odell, 5:444–45, 7:3; "McKean Buchanan's Death—Biographical Sketch of the Noted Actor," Denver *Rocky Mountain News*, 17 Apr 72, 1; Rambler, 1; Watson, 91–94, 125–26, 145).

292.1–7   over two years before, Mr. Goodman and another journeyman printer . . . bought it . . . for a thousand dollars] The weekly *Territorial Enterprise* had been established in December 1858 by William L. Jernegan and Alfred James in Genoa, Utah Territory. The struggling paper moved to Carson City in November 1859. By November 1860, Colonel Jonathan Williams, who had purchased James's interest in August 1859, was the sole proprietor and had relocated the paper to fast-growing Virginia City. Williams soon acquired a new partner, I. B. Wollard, whose interest was in turn bought in March 1861 by Goodman and McCarthy, who had recently arrived from San Francisco. Goodman later recalled that since he and McCarthy were penniless, the paper was "to be paid for out of its earnings." (The actual price is not known; in 1906 Clemens contradicted his statement here, claiming that it was only $214.) Goodman and McCarthy "turned the old weekly into a daily, and made enough in a single month to pay the whole purchase price" (Goodman to Alfred B. Nye, 17 Nov 1905, Alfred B. Nye Papers, CU-BANC). "Virginia City legend has it that Goodman and McCarthy every Saturday night divided the take in equal halves and each one carried his share home in a fire bucket filled with golden eagles" (Beebe, 32; Lingenfelter and Gash, 253–54; AD, 9 Jan 1906, CU-MARK, in *MTA*, 1:274).

292.7–11   The editorial sanctum . . . compressed into one apartment . . . general dinner table] The first Virginia City office of the *Enterprise* was on A Street near Sutton Avenue. Dan De Quille described the premises as

> a one-story frame with a shed addition on the north side. In the main structure were the cases of the compositors, the table at which all the writing, local and editorial, was done, and the old Washington hand-press on which the papers were worked off.
> The shed addition was used as a kitchen (an old Chinaman called "Joe" doing the cooking) and eating-room, and ranged on the sides were sleeping bunks, one above another in ship-shape. Here all hands ate at a long table, and here nearly all slept. (William Wright 1893a)

When Clemens joined the newspaper in September 1862, the office had been relocated to North C Street over a clothing store ("The Pioneer Journal Dead," Virginia City *Evening Chronicle*, 16 Jan 93, 2).

292.12–13   The paper was . . . printed by steam] The *Enterprise*'s new steam press—the first in Nevada—was brought in sections by ox-drawn wagon from San Francisco. The press began production the night of 31 July 1863 with editors and compositors alike taking part in a riotous celebration. The next morning's edition was several hours late and typographically chaotic, but sported "an entirely new and improved shape" of "increased and ponderous dimensions . . . nearly double" in size ("The Enterprise," Virginia City *Evening Bulletin*, 1 Aug 63, 3; Beebe, 87; Angel, 292).

292.13   there were five editors and twenty-three compositors] According to a correspondent for the Sacramento *Bee*, in January 1864 the *Enterprise* employed "nine compositors on the paper with a foreman, two or three in the job room, and one pressman," in addition to "four editors, viz: J. T. Goodman, Mr. [Charles A. V.] Putnam, 'Dan de Quille,' and 'Mark Twain'" (Curtis, 1). Putnam had joined the staff in May 1863. Clemens's fifth editor may have been George F. Dawson, an Englishman, who worked as an assistant editor in 1864 (Putnam, 3; *L1*, 304 n. 2).

292.16–18   the "Enterprise Building" was . . . fire-proof brick] The *Enterprise* moved to its third and final Virginia City location, a three-story brick building on South C Street, in August 1863 (*L1*, 243; William Wright 1893a).

292.21–23   The "Gould & Curry" company were erecting a monster hundred-stamp mill at a cost . . . of a million dollars] The imposing Gould and Curry mill was located about two miles northeast of Virginia City. As first constructed it had forty stamps for crushing ore; these were later increased to eighty. Its main structure, built in the form of a Greek cross, featured an ornamental pool graced by an elaborate fountain. While the mill was under construction, it was regarded as "the model mill of the country, and . . . the greatest piece of work of the sort in the world" ("Notes of Nevada Travel," Marysville [Calif.] *Appeal*, 28 June 62, 3). According to Eliot Lord, however, the mill—which had cost nearly $900,000 by the end of 1863—proved to be "the most conspicuous monument of inexperience and extravagance ever erected in a mining district," for it "was not yet fairly completed when its entire machinery for ore reduction was discarded" as unsatisfactory. In 1864 the mill was rebuilt, "almost from the foundation," at a cost of over $560,000 (Lord, 124–25; Grant H. Smith, 85; "Mill Reduction and Works of the Gould & Curry Company," Sacramento *Union*, 14 Nov 62, 4, reprinting the Virginia City *Union*).

292.23   Gould & Curry stock paid heavy dividends] The Gould and Curry Silver Mining Company paid its first monthly dividend, $24 a foot, in December 1862; in January 1863 the dividend rose to $100 per foot, and by June it had increased to $150. The first full year of dividends totaled $1,464,400 ($1,220 per foot), a sum representing about 40 percent of the company's gross receipts. For an investor who purchased stock in December 1862, at $2,600 per foot, this represented an annual return of nearly 47 percent (*Mining and Scientific Press:* "Mining Stock Report," 6 [20 Dec 62]: 5, and 6 [29 Dec 62]: 5; "Stock Remarks," 6 [2 Feb 63]: 5; "The Mining Share Market," 6 [29 June 63: 4]; "Cost and Result of Silver Mining," Virginia City *Union*, 14 Jan 64, 1).

292.25   The Superintendent of the Gould & Curry] The superintendent of the mine from its incorporation in 1860 was Charles Lyman Strong (1826–83), a self-educated mining engineer. He had arrived in California about 1850 as an agent for Wells and Company, and spent the next ten years in a variety of commercial pursuits. Encouraged by the Gould and Curry's owners to give free rein to his ideas, Strong was largely responsible for the construction of the company's extravagant mill. In 1864 the strain of his responsibilities caused him to resign his position in order to travel.

292.29–293.2   The Superintendent . . . was to have had one per cent . . . of the bullion likewise] Mark Twain refers to Walter W. Palmer, superintendent of the Ophir Silver Mining Company, who was employed during 1863 for a monthly salary of $2,500. On 1 January 1864 his salary was changed to $1,000, plus 2 percent "on the dividends to be thereafter declared by the Company, in lieu of the old contract salary" (SLC

1864n). Apparently some misunderstanding about the exact terms of this agreement led to a dispute. In May 1864 the company asked Palmer to resign (for unstated reasons), and he complied. On 19 August the company filed suit for the recovery of $8,456, which Palmer claimed was rightfully his. It was almost certainly Clemens who reported this case for the San Francisco *Morning Call* (SLC 1864n, 1864s).

293.6–33   U. S. Sanitary Commission . . . the wildest mob . . . came there "flush" and went away "busted."] The United States Sanitary Commission was officially established in June 1861 by an order of the secretary of war, but it owed its existence to a coalition of relief associations formed by women in the Northern states. During its first year its revenues were very limited, but in the fall of 1862—under the energetic leadership of its president, the Reverend Henry W. Bellows (1814–82)—it began to receive substantial contributions from across the nation and around the world. The clamorous mob described here gathered in front of the International Hotel on C Street during Clemens's first month on the *Enterprise*—on 26 October 1862—at a meeting organized by the Central Committee of the Storey County Patriotic Fund Association. This meeting represented Virginia City's effort to contribute its share to the $20,000 total that Storey County had pledged to raise. Nearly $3,000 was collected on the spot, which was added to $16,000 in silver bullion already donated. (The meeting was reported in the *Enterprise*, possibly by Clemens, on 28 October.) The president, or chairman, of the Central Committee was Almarin B. Paul (1823–1909) of Gold Hill (formerly of St. Louis), a prominent banker and mill operator reputed to be one of the wealthiest men in Nevada. Paul had pioneered the Washoe wet process for crushing ore, and established the Pioneer Mill, probably the first mill on the Comstock (see the note at 235.14–15; Stillé, 63–69, 197–204, 539–42; Sacramento *Union:* "Relief in Nevada Territory," 30 Oct 62, 2, reprinting the Virginia City *Territorial Enterprise* of 28 October; "Those Silver Brick," 4 Nov 62, 3; *L1*, 278 n. 6).

294.1–8   the famous "Sanitary Flour Sack" came our way . . . Reuel Gridley . . . was defeated] A year and a half passed before the Sanitary Flour Sack excitement began in April 1864. Clemens had last seen Reuel Colt Gridley (1829–70) in 1846 or 1847, when Gridley left their Hannibal, Missouri, school to join a company of infantry bound for the Mexican War. Barton S. Bowen, a steamboat captain with whom Clemens had served as a pilot, claimed in 1865 that he had once tried to "teach young Gridley" to be a pilot, "but found him so much given to larking, that he couldn't learn" ("River News," Cincinnati *Commercial*, 13 Feb 65, 4). In 1852 Gridley emigrated to California, and about ten years later relocated to Nevada, where, late in 1863, he started the grocery firm of Gridley, Hobart, and Jacobs at Austin, in the Reese

River area of central Nevada. (Reese River was the center of a mining "excitement" in 1862–63.) Gridley was not himself a mayoral candidate in the 19 April 1864 election that resulted in the Sanitary Flour Sack auction; he placed a bet on the Democratic candidate, David E. Buel, against the Republican candidate, Charles Holbrook. Gridley— who, as Clemens wrote his family on 17 May 1864, was "Union to the backbone, but a Copperhead in sympathies"—lost his bet to a Republican supporter, Dr. H. S. Herrick, the Lander County assessor and superintendent of schools. Mark Twain intentionally simplified the story of Gridley's bet: he described it correctly not only in his 1864 letter, but also in a December 1870 letter to the New York *Tribune* announcing Gridley's death (*L1*, 282; AD, 16 Mar 1906, CU-MARK, in *MTA*, 2:216–17; Elizabeth H. Smith, 11–13; Angel, 268–70, 461, 464; SLC 1870o).

295.10–12 he . . . had taken in eight thousand dollars in gold] The amount realized by the auction of Gridley's flour sack in Austin, together with additional donations and subscriptions, totaled $5,300 ("Sanitary Fund Meetings Yesterday!" Virginia City *Union*, 17 May 64, 3; "The Austin Flour Sack," Gold Hill *News*, 17 May 64, 2; *L1*, 282).

295.14–20 The news came to Virginia . . . Gridley arrived . . . only five thousand dollars had been secured] Three weeks elapsed before Gridley arrived in Virginia City with the flour sack. On Sunday, 15 May, he auctioned it during a fund-raising meeting in Maguire's Opera House for the disappointing sum of $570; by the end of the afternoon, however, the combined proceeds from the meeting totaled more than $3,700 in cash, mining stock, and silver bullion ("The Sanitary Meeting Sunday Afternoon," Virginia City *Union*, 17 May 64, 3; *L1*, 285 n. 9).

295.25–26 the next morning a procession of open carriages] The Sanitary Flour Sack procession of Monday, 16 May, was the subject of two reports, probably written by Clemens, in the *Enterprise* of 17 and 18 May (extant as reprinted in the San Francisco *Evening Bulletin* of 19 and 20 May). In the first of these, the procession was dubbed the "Army of the Lord," by which name it became known; Almarin Paul credited Mark Twain with this expression in a newspaper letter dated 21 May (Paul, 1; SLC 1864d–e). On 17 May Clemens also wrote an enthusiastic account of the event to his mother and sister, which was printed in an unidentified St. Louis newspaper. It was probably Pamela, his sister, who was involved in organizing a St. Louis fair to be held in May and June, who arranged for the letter's publication (*L1*, 281–87, 528–29).

297.8–10 Gen. W. said . . . The Yellow Jacket . . . offers a thousand dollars, coin] The bidder—at $500—for the Yellow Jacket mine was its newly elected president and superintendent, John B. Winters, known as "General Winters" because he was an officer in the Nevada militia. The Yellow Jacket, one of the first and richest of the Comstock mines, was located near Gold Hill on a southern extension of the lode (see the notes at 556.26–28 and 556.27; SLC 1864d; Grant H. Smith, 90–91, 93, 292–93; *RI 1972*, 587, misidentifies "Gen. W." as Charles H. S. Williams).

297.19–21   Gold Hill's . . . grand total was displayed] The contributions from Gold Hill totaled $6,588. Since this total was the first to exceed Austin's, Gridley "mounted the rostrum and threw up a sponge according to promise" (SLC 1864d–e).

297.22   refreshed with new lager beer and plenty of it] The first *Enterprise* report noted that "the boys" twice stopped to "moisten themselves" along the way. The reporter for the Gold Hill *News* remarked: "'Tone' was given to the procession by the presence of Gov. Twain and his staff of bibulous reporters, who came down in a free carriage, ostensibly for the purpose of taking notes, but in reality in pursuit of free whiskey" ("The Austin Flour Sack," 17 May 64, 2). (Clemens earned the title of "Gov. Twain" when he delivered a burlesque "Governor's Message" to Nevada's Third House, a mock legislative body, in December 1863: see *MTEnt*, 100–110, 144; *L1*, 272–73 n. 1.)

297.24–34   the expedition had carried Silver City and Dayton . . . forty thousand dollars in greenbacks] Silver City donated $1,800, and Dayton $1,865. Virginia City pledged $12,945 in gold, or $22,300 in greenbacks, not "forty thousand." The combined total earned for the Sanitary Commission on 16 May, however, *was* about $23,200 in gold, or $40,000 in greenbacks (SLC 1864d–e; Mitchell, 427). Contemporary newspaper stories, as well as later secondary accounts, frequently disagree about the totals for the flour-sack auctions. Since Mark Twain's source for his *Roughing It* account—if any—has not been determined, it is impossible to ascertain whether he intentionally inflated his figures.

298.3   Gridley sold the sack in Carson City] No auction was held in Carson City, as Clemens explained to his family in May 1864:

Carson is considerably larger than either of these three towns [Gold Hill, Dayton, Silver City], but it has a lousy, lazy, worthless, poverty-stricken population, and the universal opinion was that we couldn't raise $500 dollars there. So we started home again. (*L1*, 283)

In the *Enterprise* Clemens provided another—even more offensive—reason for the procession's failure to go to Carson:

The money raised at the Sanitary Fancy Dress Ball, recently held in Carson for the St. Louis Fair, had been diverted from its legitimate course, and was to be sent to aid a Miscegenation Society somewhere in the East; and it was feared the proceeds of the sack might be similarly disposed of. (Citizen, 2)

He explained to his sister-in-law that he was "not sober" when he wrote the item, and that he had not expected it to appear in print. For the resulting controversy, see *L1*, 287–89, 296–99.

298.3–4 and several California towns; also in San Francisco] Gridley left Virginia City on 17 May for Sacramento, where the sack was first sold at a picnic outside the city, and then auctioned again in the evening at a lecture given by Dr. Bellows (see the note at 293.6–33), earning $2,150 for the Sanitary Commission. The next day Gridley proceeded to San Francisco; journalist J. Ross Browne described his arrival: "It was the memorable event of the times. Never did Montgomery Street present a more imposing appearance. The beauty and the fashion of the city were there; and so was Gridley, decked out in glorious array, the observed of all observers" (J. Ross Browne 1866, 35). Ten days later the sack of flour was sold for the last time in the West, after the presentation of a comedy at the Metropolitan Theatre, bringing in $2,800. Gridley's celebrity was augmented by the sale of photographs taken by a San Francisco photographer; an engraving of one of these appeared in *Harper's Weekly* in January 1865 with the remark, "No lady's album in Nevada or California is considered complete without a photograph of GRIDLEY and his sack of flour" ("Mr. Gridley and His Sack of Flour," 21 Jan 65, 45; the engraving is reproduced in *L1*, 286). The flour sack reportedly earned in California and Nevada "the sum of $63,000 in coin, and it owned three blocks of lots in Austin worth $7,000, and a house and lot in Dayton" (*Tribute*, 23). Gridley's efforts were warmly praised by Dr. Bellows in a letter of 24 May: "The history of your Sanitary Sack of Flour is undoubtedly more interesting and peculiar than that of any sack recorded, short of the sack of Troy—and it would take another Homer to write it" ("Great Excitement about the Gridley-Sanitary Sack of Flour," Austin *Reese River Reveille*, 7 June 64, 1; "Departures Yesterday," Virginia City *Union*, 18 May 64, 3; "The Sanitary Gala Day," Sacramento *Union*, 19 May 64, 3; San Francisco *Evening Bulletin*: "Travels and Fortunes of the Great Austin Sack of Flour," 20 May 64, 1; "The Austin Sanitary Sack in Town," 21 May 64, 5; "Sale of the Gridley-Sanitary Sack of Flour at the Metropolitan Theatre," 30 May 64, 5).

298.4–5 he took it east and sold it in one or two Atlantic cities] Before sailing for the East, Gridley returned home to Austin for six months because of family illness. After leaving San Francisco for New York on 13 December 1864, he evidently visited several eastern cities in the spring of 1865; his exact itinerary, however, has not been determined. Of Gridley's tour "on the Atlantic side," Browne recalled reading "wonderful newspaper accounts. He was fêted, and gazed at, and admired, and hurrahed, and printed in weekly pictorials, and puffed, and joked— was the irrepressible Gridley" (J. Ross Browne 1866, 36; "Return of Mr.

Gridley," Austin *Reese River Reveille*, 5 June 64, 2; "The Famous Sanitary Flour Sack," San Francisco *Alta California*, 14 Dec 64, 1).

298.6–10 he finally carried it to St. Louis . . . small cakes and retailed them at high prices] Gridley took his flour sack to St. Louis in the summer of 1865. Since it was illegal in Missouri to auction the same item repeatedly, "it was suggested that the flour be baked into cakes which could be sold. Gridley refused, for he felt that the flour came from the West and that was where it belonged. Thus the tour ended on a sour note" (Elizabeth W. Smith, 16). Curiously, the idea of selling the flour as small cakes may have originated with Clemens a year earlier. In May 1864 an *Enterprise* reporter, probably Clemens, listed the amounts already realized by the flour-sack auctions in Nevada and estimated how much could be raised in California and the East, computing a total of over $500,000. He continued,

Now supposing that the managers of the St. Louis Fair are smart enough to have this historical sack of flour ultimately made into thin wafer cakes—500 to the pound—it strikes us that 25,000 people would willingly give $5 a cake for it, if only for the sake of telling their children and friends that they had eaten a cake made out of flour that had sold for over $500,000 per sack! (SLC 1864g)

298.11–13 when the flour sack's mission was ended . . . a hundred and fifty thousand dollars in greenbacks] The final total of Gridley's proceeds cannot be determined with any certainty. Since the estimates of others range from $40,000 to $275,000, in gold, Mark Twain's figure is quite plausible (*Tribune*, 24; Webb 1865b; Stillé, 238).

298.16–22 the expenses of his Sanitary flour sack expedition . . . He died at Stockton, California, in December, 1870] Gridley returned home in mid-July 1865, "completely broken down in health" and "almost bankrupt" (Tinkham, 66). He died on 24 November 1870 in Paradise City, California (a small town in Stanislaus County, not far from Stockton). In his December 1870 letter to the New York *Tribune* Mark Twain praised Gridley's "integrity, benevolence, and enterprise" (SLC 1870o). A commemorative statue, depicting Gridley and the flour sack, was erected in 1887 at his gravesite in the Stockton Rural Cemetery. The original buckskin-covered flour sack is now in the State Historical Museum in Reno ("Arrival of the 'Golden City,'" San Francisco *Alta California*, 10 July 65, 1; Tinkham, 64–66, 241–42; Elizabeth W. Smith, 16–18).

299.7–301.31 Two . . . him.] Mark Twain first published this passage in a Buffalo *Express* "Around the World" letter on 8 January 1870; he revised the earlier printing for inclusion in *Roughing It* (SLC 1870a).

299.7–14 Two cousins . . . a hundred thousand dollars a year] In the earlier version of this passage in the *Express*, the two teamsters are called brothers, rather than cousins. Mark Twain may therefore have originally had in mind Theodore and Joseph Winters—both of whom he knew—who hauled logs on the Truckee River ditch before the snows drove them into Carson Valley at the right time in 1859 to establish early and profitable claims on the Comstock ("Returns from Washoe," Marysville [Calif.] *Appeal*, 10 Nov 63, 2; *ET&S1*, 339–42, 461; *L1*, 275, 279–80 n. 11).

300.5–301.2 John Smith . . . I'll take that money, if you please] Mark Twain is alluding to Lemuel Sanford (Sandy) Bowers (1830–68), an unlettered nabob famous for his conspicuous display of wealth. According to the reminiscences of Almarin B. Paul and C. C. Stevenson, both pioneer settlers of Gold Hill, Bowers located his ten-foot claim in Gold Hill gulch in the fall of 1858, before the discovery of the Comstock lode. His claim, later combined with the adjoining ten feet held by his wife, Eilley Orrum (1826–1903), proved to be on the richest section of the lode. Bowers built a ten-stamp mill in Crown Point Ravine in 1861 and enlarged it to twenty stamps in 1862. The Bowerses traveled in Europe in 1862–63, during which time their mansion in Washoe Valley was constructed and furnished in lavish style. An 1864 *Enterprise* item, possibly by Clemens, described the costly fittings of the house and put Bowers's monthly income at $70,000. Bowers died in April 1868, leaving a surprisingly depleted estate of $638,000. Mrs. Bowers, prey to poor management and a variety of swindlers, lost everything—including her house—over a period of years, and was forced to eke out a living as the "Washoe seeress." This anecdote about the ship's pool was published in California newspapers in May 1865; the incident allegedly occurred a few months earlier on board the steamer *Champion* (Angel, 39, 58, 68; Hermann, 12–17; "Pioneer Reminiscences in Washoe," Sacramento *Union*, 9 Oct 63, 4, reprinting the Virginia City *Territorial Enterprise* of 7 October; "A Washoe Palace," Stockton *Independent*, 30 Sept 63, 3, reprinting the Carson City *Independent*; "The Bowers Mill," Virginia City *Union*, 28 Apr 64, 3; Addenbrooke, 36; "A Washoe Nabob," *Mining and Scientific Press* 8 [13 Feb 64]: 102, reprinting the Virginia City *Territorial Enterprise*; "Death of a Good Citizen," Gold Hill *Evening News*, 21 Apr 68, 3; "Out of His Reckoning," Sacramento *Bee*, 2 May 65, 2).

301.3–13 The Gould & Curry claim . . . was worth . . . seven million six hundred thousand dollars in gold coin] In January 1867, during his voyage from San Francisco to New York, Mark Twain made the following notebook entry—one of several entries recording anecdotes later included in *Roughing It:* "Curry sold 600 feet of Gould & Curry for $2,600. Gould sold 600 feet for $250, an old plug horse, a jug of whisky & a pair of blankets" (*N&J1*, 293; see the notes at 301.14–21, 301.22–28, 318.1–2, 322.14–15, and 331.10). Alva Gould (1815–?93) emigrated from Michigan to California in 1849–50. He was a placer miner there until 1858, when he went to Carson County, Utah Territory. His later accounts—dictated in 1877 and 1891—of locating a claim, with Abraham Curry (see the note at 162.5), on the Comstock in early 1859 are contradictory. He consistently asserted, however, that Curry sold his share in their claim to Henry Meredith for $2,400, while he was defrauded of his own interest. In 1863, Gould unsuccessfully sued the Gould and Curry Silver Mining Company "for the recovery of 70 feet of their ground," claiming that since he had never sold his share, it remained his "by right of location" ("Suit against the Gould & Curry Co.," Eureka [Calif.] *Humboldt Times*, 17 Oct 63, 3). Gould also figured in a well-known Comstock anecdote, involving his sale of what may have been a different claim, in which he accepted $450 from a California speculator and then rode drunkenly down Gold Canyon shouting, "Oh, I've fooled the Californian!" (Lord, 60). Gould spent his last years as a fruit peddler at the Reno train depot. At its peak price of $6,300 a foot in June 1863, the 1,200-foot Gould and Curry mine was worth, as Mark Twain states, about $7.6 million (Gould, 1–20; "Chapter about Closed," Sacramento *Record-Union*, 2 Sept 93, 1; "Alva Gould," San Francisco *Morning Call*, 10 Mar 91, 7; "General Mining Stock Report," *Mining and Scientific Press* 6 [29 June 63]: 5).

301.14–21   a poverty-stricken Mexican . . . one million five hundred thousand dollars] Compare this January 1867 entry in Clemens's notebook: "100 feet of Ophir (the present Mexican) was segregated for a stream of water as large as your wrist to some Spaniards. Afterwards worth $18,000 a foot" (*N&J1*, 294). While giving slightly different figures for its later value, this entry and *Roughing It* both give condensed versions of the early history of the Mexican, or Spanish, mine, a 100-foot claim reportedly traded in mid-1859 by the original owners of the Ophir claim to Henry Comstock and Emanuel Penrod in return for water rights. Later that year Gabriel Maldonado, a Mexican, and Francis J. Hughes bought the claim for $9,500 and organized the Mexican Company. In 1864 the value of the dividend-paying Mexican mine was judged to be $1 million; the value of the company's mill at Empire City (east of Carson) is not known. Mark Twain published accounts of his two descents into the mine in October 1862 and February 1863 ("Silver in Nevada," Sacramento *Union*, 2 May 64, 4; SLC 1862g, 1863a).

301.22–28   An individual who owned . . . a sixty-thousand-dollar horse] Another January 1867 notebook entry reads, "A man sold 26 feet of Ophir or Yellow Jacket for an old plug horse—called him the $26,000 horse" (*N&J1*, 293). The allusion may be to James Finney, who sold to Henry Comstock his interest in the Ophir claim for "a certain Indian pony, bob-tailed, lean and aged. . . . According to some authorities, divers bottles of exhilarating fluids formed part of the consideration by Finney received on that occasion" (DeGroot 1876a).

301.32–37   A youth of nineteen . . . made himself rich by watching the mining telegrams] John William (Johnny) Skae (1841?–85) was a native of Canada who emigrated in the late 1850s to California, and shortly thereafter to Nevada. In the early 1860s he used his position with the Virginia City telegraph office to gain inside information: "He soon acquired such profits from his speculations that he abandoned his profession and launched out as a capitalist" (*ET&S2*, 72–73, 77–78, 123, 254–60; "Death of 'Johnny' Skae," San Francisco *Morning Call*, 17 July 85, 1). Skae's abuse of his position may have prompted the California State Telegraph Company (which had jurisdiction over the Virginia City office) in April 1863 to prohibit "persons employed by them from owning feet in mining ground" ("Taking the Feet from Telegraph Employees," San Francisco *Evening Bulletin*, 22 Apr 63, 1, reprinting the Virginia City *Union* of 17 April). Skae, whom Mark Twain portrayed in three 1864–65 sketches as a convivial companion and "inimitable punster," also served as a trustee and vice-president of the Virginia and Gold Hill Water Company, and in 1863 became superintendent of the Hale and Norcross mine, in which Clemens invested (Angel, 588; "Death of John Skae, the Mining Operator," San Francisco *Evening Bulletin*, 17 July 85, 2; "Death of John Skae," Virginia City *Evening Chronicle*, 17 July 85, 3; *L1*, 300–301 n. 4).

302.9–303.15 Another telegraph operator . . . a fortune was the result] Mark Twain may be recalling David C. Williams, a San Francisco stockbroker and former telegraph operator who was implicated in more than one incident involving the use of the wires to make a profit on Nevada mining stocks. In July 1864 Williams, posing as a teamster, spent more than a week at a stage and telegraph station near Placerville. He made note of the messages being transmitted, and even tried to bribe the operator to let him handle the wires, hoping to overhear the decision in the Savage and North Potosi lawsuit and wire it to his confederates in San Francisco so that they could buy shares in the victorious company before the news became public. Unlike the character in the *Roughing It* account, however, Williams was unsuccessful: the operator summoned a detective, who arrested him ("Williams, the Wire-Worker," San Francisco *Morning Call*, 12 Aug 64, 1; "Monopolizing the Line," Virginia City *Union*, 19 Apr 64, 3).

303.25–27 a friend . . . sought him out, bought his "feet" . . . and sold the property for seventy-five thousand dollars] A similar story is told of John W. Mackay (1831–1902), who became famous in the 1870s as a "Big Bonanza" millionaire. In 1863 the owners of the Kentuck mine were prevented from incorporating by the disappearance of one of the original locators, who still owned several shares in the mine. Learning that he was with the Confederate army in Tennessee, Mackay traced him and returned

with the missing block of feet and a bill of sale to show his ownership. Mackay never revealed how he secured them but the legend insists he dogged his man into the front lines before Chattanooga and wrangled over the price while Parrott rifles boomed and Minié balls ripped overhead. (Beebe and Clegg, 66)

303.35–304.2   I was . . . again.] This paragraph, like the first part of the chapter, was based on an earlier printing in the Buffalo *Express* for 8 January 1870 (SLC 1870a). When Mark Twain was composing *Roughing It*, he discarded a sheet of manuscript on which he had pasted and revised a clipping of this passage from the *Express*; it is reproduced on page 816 in the Introduction.

308.10–16   grand time over Buck Fanshaw when he died . . . high position in the fire department] The prototype of Buck Fanshaw was Thomas Peasley, a well-known Virginia City figure. Born in New York, Peasley went to Virginia City from Calaveras County, California, in 1860 and became the owner of the city's most elegant and popular saloon, the Sazerac. He helped to organize the city's volunteer fire department, and in 1862 became its first chief engineer. The charismatic and athletic Peasley was also the "proprietor," as Mark Twain puts it, of Julia Bulette, Virginia City's first and most famous courtesan, and made her the "queen," in full fire regalia, of Engine Company No. 1. An aggressive Unionist, he was widely acknowledged as a leader both in local and national political campaigns in Virginia City. He had "killed his man," a young tough named "Sugarfoot Jack" Jenkins, although not in defense of a stranger (see the note at 323.17). By 1866 Peasley had given up his saloon business and become manager and coproprietor of Maguire's Opera House and sergeant-at-arms of the Nevada State Senate. On 2 February 1866 Peasley, aged about thirty-eight, engaged in a gunfight with Martin V. Barnhart in the bar of the Ormsby House in Carson City, which resulted in the death of both men. Obituary notices called Peasley the "acknowledged political head of the Fire and Police Departments of Virginia, and . . . a man of great influence with the sports and roughs," and asserted that the vote of the "Peasley crowd" was essential to a politician's success. Peasley's body was removed to Virginia City, where a resplendent and well-attended funeral was held. Clemens remained in San Francisco at the time ("Two Men Killed, in Carson," San Francisco *Morning Call*, 3 Feb 66, 3; "A Terrible Tragedy," Carson City *Appeal*, 3 Feb 66, 2; "Funeral Yesterday," Virginia City *Union*, 5 Feb 66, 3; *ET&S1*, 473–74; Angel, 599; Lyman, 119–22; Mack 1947, 195–98; Beebe and Clegg, 16–18).

308.16   a very Warwick in politics] Richard Neville (1428–71), earl of Warwick and Salisbury, was known as "the Kingmaker" during the early years of the Wars of the Roses. He helped Edward, duke of York, to secure the English throne in 1461 as Edward IV, and served as his powerful great chamberlain. Falling out with Edward, he drove him from the throne, and in 1470 restored Henry VI of the house of Lancaster.

308.23–24   a verdict of death "by the visitation of God."] Clemens included a similar anecdote in his "People and Things" column in the Buffalo *Express* for 18 August 1869:

In Nevada, a man with the consumption took the small-pox from a negro, the cholera from a Chinaman, and the yellow fever and the erysipelas from other parties, and swallowed fifteen grains of strychnine and fell out of the third-story window and broke his neck. Verdict of the jury, "Died by the visitation of God." (SLC 1869d)

309.13–14 the short-haired brotherhood] The term "short hairs" was apparently used for "roughs" in general, because they wore their hair in a short "fighting cut." From the mid-1860s the expression was sometimes used in politics to designate the party or faction of the "common man or 'toughs'" (Winfield J. Davis, 213–14; Morton, 111; Mathews, 2:1530).

309.17–20 minister . . . as yet unacquainted with the ways of the mines] Mark Twain's portrait of the young minister—here and in his earlier *Enterprise* piece (see the next note)—was based on his friend the Reverend Franklin S. Rising (1833?–68), the rector of St. Paul's Episcopal Church in Virginia City. (Rising did not, however, conduct the religious service at Peasley's funeral: the Reverend William M. Martin of Virginia City's Presbyterian Church officiated.) Rising arrived in Virginia City from New York in April 1862, formally opened his new church the following February, and helped establish Episcopal parishes in neighboring cities. He resigned his position in 1866 because of poor health and traveled to the Sandwich Islands, where he met Clemens again. The two men returned to the States together in July 1866 on the clipper *Smyrniote*. Hearing of Rising's death in an Ohio River steamboat collision in December 1868, Clemens described his association with this "noble young fellow" in a letter to Olivia Langdon: "I used to try to teach him how he ought to preach in order to get at the better natures of the rough population about him, & he used to try hard to learn—for I *knew* them & he did not, for he was refined & sensitive & not intended for such a people as that" (*L2*, 333, 337 n. 2; *L1*, 352, 354 n. 3; Doten, 2:877; Angel, 199–202, 215).

309.20 The committeeman, "Scotty" Briggs, made his visit] Mark Twain apparently returned to one of his early *Enterprise* pieces for the germ of his description of Scotty Briggs's interview with the minister. This recently discovered *Enterprise* article survives only in part, as a paraphrase quoted in the San Francisco *Call and Post* of 1 April 1921, and is reprinted here for the first time. The author of the article explained that Clemens had been dispatched by Goodman to interview the clergymen of the area; he "began with the Baptist Church, at Gold Hill," and reported as follows:

The high price charged for water by the water company renders it impossible to immerse any but wealthy converts. For this and other reasons the pastor of the church informs me that he will be compelled to resign. His salary is small, only $24 a month. But the irregularity with which it is paid, or, to speak more accurately, the regularity with which it is not paid, is very distressing to him. He keeps bachelor's quarters and is in debt to his butcher, and when the preacher calls for a beefsteak the butcher, in a sort of absent-minded way cuts him off a piece of liver. His congregation has dwindled to nine regular attendants, eight of whom are women, and his collection last Sabbath amounted to only twenty cents. On the whole it may be said that the condition of the cause of Christ in Gold Hill leaves very much to be desired.

The Methodist Church, in Virginia City, presents different conditions. The congregation is large and contributions are liberal. The pastor is a broad man—as broad as he is long. He measures 62 inches around the waist and 62 inches from keel to main yard.

The Episcopal clergyman is a charming little gentleman just out from the effete East. He is as unlearned in sporting nomenclature as sporting men are unlearned in the technicalities of orthodoxy.

Last week, on the day before Andy Brown died, his brother Steve went to the Episcopal clergyman and said: "My brother is about to pass in his checks and he wants you to come down to the joint and start him off square before he becomes a stiff."

"I am not a banker," said the clergyman, "and I can not aid your brother in passing checks."

"You don't tumble," said Andy. "My brother is going to die, and he wants you to do some praying over him before he goes. He doesn't feel sure as to where he will land, and he thinks that your prayers might keep him out of a hot climate."

"I see," said the divine. "Is your brother a professor?"

"He was," said Andy, "but since Baldy Thompson licked him in their last fight he has given up the profession of pugilism."

"Do you think," said the clergyman, "that your brother would like the Eucharist administered?"

"Well, partner," said Andy, dubiously, "it looks to me like a queer time for that sort of thing. But you know best, and you can take your deck along or I'll get you a pack of cards at the saloon." (Wells 1921a)

Mark Twain's portrait of Scotty Briggs, like his Buck Fanshaw, undoubtedly owed some of its features to actual Nevada figures. Briggs may have been drawn from John Van Buren (Jack) Perry, Virginia City's popular marshal and, like his friend Thomas Peasley, an ardent Unionist and a mainstay of the Virginia Volunteer Fire Department. Just as Scotty Briggs brawled alongside of Buck Fanshaw, so Perry joined Peasley and other Unionists in defending a Union recruiter attacked by a Secessionist in a Virginia City street. Mark Twain at least twice made reference to Perry's mastery of "vulgar phraseology" and recorded examples of his vivid slang quite similar to those of his fictional counterpart (SLC 1863c, 1863m). George Wharton James, an intimate friend of Perry's, claimed that Clemens became "very fond" of the marshal and spent many hours listening to his stories: "It was Jack who told several of the stories that appear in 'Roughing It'" (James, 530). Steve Gillis (see the note at 323.30–325.2), in later years, claimed that Scotty Briggs was drawn from one Ruef Williams, a neighbor at Jackass Hill in Tuolumne County—and possibly the "Riff Williams" whom Goodman mentioned as one of Peasley and Perry's cronies in the Virginia Fire Department. Nothing further is known about Williams, except that he was probably the "M. R. Williams" who was chief of the department at the time of Peasley's death ("A Card," Virginia City *Union*, 5 Feb 66, 2; Angel, 266, 600; AD, 26 May 1907, CU-MARK, in *MTE*, 361; Fulton, 55; Goodman 1892a).

313.18–314.1 some roughs jumped the Catholic bone-yard and started in to stake out town lots] The *Enterprise* local (possibly Clemens) reported on 25 December 1862:

> On Saturday last, parties in this city took possession of the Catholic cemetery, located in the southeast part of the town, and commenced the work of fencing it in and building thereon a house. When this became known throughout the city, there came near being a most bloody row over the matter. Many armed themselves and were for proceeding instantly to the burying ground to drive the jumpers away by force of arms.

But peaceful counsel prevailed, while a decision regarding ownership of the ground was awaited ("Jumping a Graveyard at Washoe," San Francisco *Evening Bulletin*, 29 Dec 62, 1, reprinting the Virginia City *Territorial Enterprise* of 25 December).

314.24–28 It was him that put down the riot last election . . . in less than three minutes] Paul Fatout has suggested that the model for this free-for-all was not an election riot, but a brawl that broke out between two rival fire companies after a major fire in Virginia City on 28 August 1863. The Virginia City *Union* reported:

> Fire Companies Nos. 1 and 2 met at the intersection of Taylor and C streets, and by some means became involved in a general row. . . . Trumpets, sticks and faucets were freely used, and blood streamed from numerous heads. The efforts of the police to stop it were at first futile, the Marshal himself [i.e., Perry] receiving a severe blow on the head with a club. ("The Fire at Virginia, N. T.," Sacramento *Union*, 31 Aug 63, 4, reprinting the Virginia City *Union* of 29 August)

Clemens reported on the fire and the riot in a dispatch to the San Francisco *Morning Call* (SLC 1863o). In composing this chapter, he may have conflated the riot with an incident in which Peasley made a lone stand before an anti-Union election rally in Virginia City on 22 October 1864:

> Fiery speeches and a street parade were features of the demonstration. As the parade neared the International Hotel, . . . Tom Peasley advanced to the middle of the street, faced the leaders of the line, which numbered thousands, and leveled two six-shooters at their heads. They came to an abrupt halt. Peasley pointed to a picture of President Lincoln that had been suspended from a window of the hotel, head downward, to indicate the derision of the anti-Unionists for the president.

He demanded that the picture be righted, and the parade leaders, "knowing the deadly earnestness of the man, and not caring to trifle with one of his reputation," complied; "only then did Peasley step aside and give the word for the parade to move on" (Levison, 7; "An Insult," Virginia City *Union*, 23 Oct 64, 3; Fatout 1964, 81–82).

318.1–2 THE first twenty-six graves in the Virginia cemetery were occupied by *murdered* men] In December 1866 Clemens wrote in his notebook, "First 26 buried in Va killed. First 6 buried in Carson" (N&J1, 251). He made the same claim about Virginia City in a May 1868 letter to the Chicago *Republican*, and again in a Buffalo *Express* "Around the World" letter published on 22 January 1870 (SLC 1868e, 1870b), which also contains remarks about two of the desperadoes mentioned later in this chapter—Sam Brown and Jack Williams—as well as Joseph Slade (see chapters 10 and 11; see also the note at 330.7–10).

319.10–11 Alfred the Great, when he invented trial by jury] Although Alfred (or Aelfred, 849–901), king of the West Saxons, may have introduced legal reforms "out of which sprang our present judicial system," the notion that he invented trial by jury is merely persistent legend. Trial by jury has ancient Teutonic roots, but "the first glimmerings of its actual existing shape cannot be seen till ages after Aelfred's day" (*DNB*, s.v. "Aelfred").

320.8 his candle-clock] King Alfred reportedly devised a clock consisting of candles, each of which burned for four hours, enclosed within a wood and horn lantern for protection from drafts (Asser, 86–87).

320.16–20 noted desperado . . . Mr. B. . . . Mr. B. L.] Unidentified.

322.14–15 a desperado of wide reputation, and who "kept his private graveyard,"] In a notebook entry of December 1866 Clemens made reference to the popular legend that the notorious Sam Brown (see the next note) kept his own cemetery: "Brown's Ranch—11 men he killed buried together & self at head" (N&J1, 251; Lyman, 146).

323.16 Sam Brown] Sam Brown, the most heartless bully of all Nevada "bad men," specialized in killing inoffensive, helpless people—the "peaceable citizens" whom most of the desperadoes, as Mark Twain wrote, left alone. According to Dan De Quille, "He was a big chief, and when he walked into a saloon, a side at a time, with his big Spanish spurs clanking along the floor, and his six-shooter flapping under his coat-tails, the little 'chiefs' hunted their holes and talked small on back seats" (William Wright 1876, 87). Brown allegedly killed at least sixteen persons in Texas, California, and Nevada. His three Nevada murders—the first in Carson City and two others in Virginia City—were committed over a two-year period beginning in February 1859. After the last of these, he reportedly wiped his bloody knife, lay down on a billiard table, and went to sleep. On 6 July 1861, his thirtieth birthday, he attacked hotel-keeper Henry Van Sickle near the town of Genoa, totally without provocation. Van Sickle escaped into the hotel, armed himself, and pursued Brown down the road, killing him in an exchange of gunfire (Angel, 343–44, 356–57; Van Sickle, 9–13). Van Sickle was fully exonerated when the jury found that Brown had died "from a just dispensation of an all-wise Providence" (Thrapp, 1:179).

323.16 Jack Williams] A gunman and robber responsible for the deaths of several men in California and Nevada, Williams was also a Virginia City deputy marshal in 1862. He was murdered on 9 December of that year by an assailant (probably Joseph McGee) who "fired through a door and escaped" ("A Desperado Killed—A Shooting Affair," Sacramento *Union*, 11 Dec 62, 3; see the note on McGee at 323.18). Clemens included a brief ironic description of Williams as "a kind-hearted man" who "gave all his custom to a poor undertaker who was trying to get along," in a January 1870 "Around the World" letter (SLC 1870b; "Shooting Affray at Virginia City," Sacramento *Union*, 8 Feb 62, 2; *CofC*, 8). He also probably wrote "Particulars of the Assassination of Jack Williams," reprinted from the *Territorial Enterprise* in the San Francisco *Morning Call* of 14 December 1862 (SLC 1862i). For more on Williams see chapter 49.

323.16 Billy Mulligan] "Mulligan was a natty little sport and gambler, who had been very active in San Francisco's ward politics at the time of the formation of the second vigilance committee in 1856, and had been ordered by that body to leave California" (Considine 1923c). After several years in New York, Mulligan turned up in Nevada, where he fought a much-publicized duel near Austin in April 1864. He died in a very public and bloody shoot-out on 7 July 1865 in San Francisco. The incident began when Mulligan, crazed from delirium tremens, fired a shot into the street from his room at the St. Francis Hotel. Over the next several hours he killed two people—one of them his friend Jack Mc-Nabb (see the note at 323.18), who had courageously tried to subdue him. Mulligan was finally killed by a police officer. Charles Henry Webb commemorated Mulligan's "Bad End" in verse in the San Francisco *Evening Bulletin* the following day (Webb 1865a; Richard Coke Wood, 75–80; "The Record of Blood," Virginia City *Territorial Enterprise*, 9 Apr 71, 3; "The Austin Duel," Virginia City *Union*, 23 Apr 64, 2).

323.17 Farmer Pease] Actually Langford ("Farmer") Peel, known as Virginia City's coolest, most gentlemanly gunman. Born in Liverpool, Peel had lived in Kansas and Salt Lake City before he fled to California in 1858 after killing a man in a duel. In 1863 he arrived in Virginia City, where on 30 September he seriously wounded the prize fighter Richard Paddock in a shoot-out following a saloon argument. About a month later, on 24 October, he shot and killed John ("El Dorado Johnny") Dennis, who had challenged him to a gunfight; Peel was acquitted on the grounds of self-defense. On another occasion he severely beat a judge who had sentenced him, and then walked calmly out of the courtroom when none of the officers present dared to apprehend him. According to Goodman, the next morning William Wright (Dan De Quille) took occasion to review the whole career of Peel in the local columns of the *Enterprise*. . . . He did not mince matters. He pictured the character of the desperado in its true light, spoke of his misdeeds in the plain and forcible terms they deserved, and called upon the authorities to overcome this terror and bring him to summary punishment.

When Wright's friends, as a joke, led him to believe that Peel was seeking vengeance for this column, Wright went looking for the desperado and found him in a saloon. He grabbed Peel, held a knife to his throat, and said, "I understand you are hunting for me. If there is any grudge we will settle it right here." Peel responded, "There's no hard feeling on my part, I assure you. . . . You wrote nothing about me but what was true and deserved, and I admire a man who is brave enough to say publicly what he thinks about a character like me" (Goodman 1891). Peel left Virginia City in 1867; in July of that year, at the age of thirty-six, he was killed in Montana by a former partner (Langford, 2:270–87; Angel, 345, 357; Gillis, 42–46; "Shooting at Virginia City," San Francisco *Alta California*, 1 Oct 63, 1; "Fatal Shooting Affray," Gold Hill *News*, 26 Oct 63, 3; Considine 1923a).

323.17   Sugarfoot Mike] Undoubtedly "Sugarfoot Jack" Jenkins, a young Virginia City gunman who died shortly after being shot on 20 September 1863 by Thomas Peasley (see the note at 308.10–16). Peasley was later acquitted by a jury, but the incident reportedly caused him to leave the saloon business, reform his combative nature, and adopt a "restrained and gentle manner" (Goodman 1892b; Lyman, 344–45; Wells 1921b; "Bloodshed at Washoe—Life of No Account," San Francisco *Evening Bulletin*, 25 Sept 63, 2, reprinting the Virginia City *Territorial Enterprise* of 22 September).

323.17   Pock-Marked Jake] Unidentified.

323.17–18   El Dorado Johnny] See the note on "Farmer Pease" at 323.17.

323.18   Jack McNabb] John H. McNabb, a Virginia City "rough," was often in the news in 1863–64. According to one possibly apocryphal account, he disrupted the opening night of Maguire's Opera House on 2 July 1863 by emptying his revolver at an enemy seated in a box across the auditorium (Beebe and Clegg, 52–54; Lyman, 240; see also J. B. Graham, 159–60, and Watson, 134). Two months later Mark Twain reported in a dispatch to the San Francisco *Morning Call* that the "notorious desperado" McNabb had shot two Virginia City policemen, wounding one of them—officer George W. Birdsall—gravely (SLC 1863q). Early in March 1864 McNabb was involved in another shooting incident at the Clipper Saloon. On 19 March he was sentenced to six months in jail for shooting officer Birdsall, but was pardoned two months later by Governor Nye. McNabb was shot and killed in San Francisco in 1865 by Billy Mulligan (see the note at 323.16; Virginia City *Union*: "Shooting Affray," 8 Mar 64, 3; "Sentenced," 20 Mar 64, 3; "Jack McNabb Pardoned," 13 May 64, 3).

323.18 Joe McGee] Joseph McGee, a butcher by trade, took part in a number of violent incidents—some involving members of the notorious John Daly gang—between 1859 and 1862 in Marysville and Sacramento, California. McGee, who became a special policeman on the Virginia City force, is believed to have been the murderer of Jack Williams in December 1862 (see the note on Williams at 323.16). Late on the night of 4 July 1863 McGee, having been ejected from a saloon while attempting an arrest, riddled the closed door with bullets, killing one patron and seriously wounding another. Mark Twain mentioned this incident in his letter to the San Francisco *Morning Call* dated 5 July. As he explains in chapter 49 (327n.1–328n.7), McGee was killed in a Carson City saloon on 10 December 1863 by John Daly, who was avenging the murder of his friend Williams a year earlier. Daly reportedly used the same gun with which McGee had shot Williams (SLC 1863e; "The Fourth at Virginia [N. T.]," Sacramento *Union*, 7 July 63, 2; San Francisco *Alta California:* "Imposing Funeral Procession," 23 July 63, 1; "Another Man Shot," 11 Dec 63, 1; "Blood Demanding Blood," San Francisco *Evening Bulletin*, 14 Dec 63, 1; McGrath, 88–90).

323.18 Jack Harris] See the note at 138.20–31.

323.18 Six-fingered Pete] Possibly John ("Three-fingered Jack") McDowell, an Irish emigrant who had fought in the Mexican War before joining the 1849 gold rush and prospecting in Tuolumne County, California. There and later in Virginia City he gained notoriety as a gunman. Early in 1864 he was in Aurora, earning a living as a gambler and—along with other members of the John Daly gang—working as a hired gun for the Pond mining company. McDowell, Daly, and two other gang members were hanged on 9 February 1864 by the Citizens' Safety Committee of Aurora, a vigilante group, for the murder of William R. Johnson, operator of a nearby stage station (McGrath, 82, 86–87, 90–96; "The Execution at Aurora," Virginia City *Union*, 14 Feb 64, 2, reprinting the Aurora *Times* of 10 February).

323.26–27 they held it almost shame to die otherwise than "with their boots on,"] Only those gunfighters who made no claim to respectability preferred such a violent end—El Dorado Johnny, for example, went to have his boots polished before challenging Peel (Gillis, 43). Thomas Peasley, however, expressed a last wish to have his boots removed as he lay dying in a Carson City saloon: "And thus Tom Peasley went out of the world fearlessly and barefooted, which implied to him a more honorable ending than it is likely most of us will make" (Goodman 1892b; see the note at 308.10–16, and the note on "Farmer Pease" at 323.17).

323.30–325.2 a little printer . . . celebrated name whereat we shook in our shoes] The bellicose printer was Clemens's good friend Stephen Edward (Steve) Gillis (1838–1918), known as a scrappy fighter. Gillis grew up in Mississippi and Tennessee, where he was trained as a typesetter.

He went to San Francisco in 1853 with his mother (his father had been there since 1849). By 1862, when Clemens joined the *Enterprise* staff, he was the paper's foreman. Over the next thirty-two years he worked as a foreman, typesetter, and writer, first on the *Enterprise* and later on the Virginia City *Chronicle*. In 1894 he retired to live with his brothers James (see the note at 412.1–3) and William at Jackass Hill, California (*L1*, 291–92 n. 3; see also Goodman 1892a). The table-lifting, glass-biting stranger has been identified as Tom McNabb, brother of the desperado Jack McNabb (see the note at 323.18):

> Of the three McNabb brothers, Tom was the only one that didn't die with his boots on. In a row with another San Francisco sport he received a bullet in his brain. It didn't kill him, but it seemed to change his nature. From that time on he was as docile a man as could be found in the city. (Considine 1923c)

By the time of his death in June 1872 at age forty-nine, McNabb had been "shot, stabbed and otherwise wounded over and over again" (Sacramento *Union*, 28 June 72: "Died," 2; "By State Telegraph," 3).

325.1   Cariboo] Cariboo, a remote district in British Columbia between the Fraser River and the Cariboo Mountains, was the scene of a frenzied rush after gold was discovered in the fall of 1860.

326.3–27   FATAL SHOOTING AFFRAY . . . dead.] The original newspaper printings of this extract and of the extracts at 327.1–14 and 328.8–330.2 have not been found. Mark Twain may have incorporated into his manuscript three clippings from the "coffin of 'Enterprise' files" he received from his family in the spring of 1870 (SLC to JLC and family, 26 Mar 70, NPV, in *MTBus*, 112). Williams (identified in the note at 323.16) killed Brown (not further identified) in the Bank Exchange Billiard Saloon in Virginia City on the night of 6 February 1862. George W. Birdsall was a brave, highly respected policeman well known to Clemens (see the note on McNabb at 323.18); Marshal John Van Buren Perry is identified in the note at 309.20 ("Shooting Affray at Virginia City," Sacramento *Union*, 8 Feb 62, 2).

327.1–14   ROBBERY AND DESPERATE AFFRAY . . . disappeared.] No other record of this robbery, which evidently occurred in June or July 1862, has been located. The victim, Charles Hurtzal, was probably the "Charles Hutzel" listed in the Nevada directory as a mill employee boarding at the Golden Age Hotel in Silver City. Andy Blessington, residing at the Eastern Slope Lodging House in Virginia City, has been identified as "one of the slickest short-card players that ever struck 'the land of Washoe.' . . . He was a bundle of nervous energy, full of fun, and when on the street usually the center of a crowd of idlers who appreciated good jokes" (J. B. Graham, 156; Kelly 1862, 207; Kelly 1863, 175).

327.20–25   Williams was assassinated . . . had sworn away his life] See the notes on Williams and McGee at 323.16 and 323.18.

328.8–330.2 MORE CUTTING AND SHOOTING . . . ripening?] Gumbert (or Gumpert) attacked Reeder on 10 December 1862; the *Enterprise* account quoted here must have appeared on 11 December. Clemens could not have written the item, since he was in Carson City at the time reporting the second Territorial Legislature; its author was probably Wright (suggestion courtesy of Lawrence Berkove, who also ascribes the other two extracts in this chapter to Wright: see Berkove 1993). Justice Joseph F. Atwill was a real-estate and mining agent who had been justice of the peace for Virginia City since 1861. The doctor attending Reeder was Joseph R. N. Owen (Kelly 1862, 116; Kelly 1863, 20, 269; "A Desperado Killed—A Shooting Affair," Sacramento *Union*, 11 Dec 62, 3).

330.7–10 Not less than a hundred men have been murdered . . . death penalty there] There were in fact about two hundred and sixty murders between 1846 and 1871, but only two executions (aside from lynchings carried out by vigilantes). Clemens witnessed the first of these while visiting Virginia City on a lecture tour in April–May 1868—the hanging of John Milleain, a Frenchman, for the murder of the courtesan Julia Bulette. He included a detailed, dramatic description of the event in a letter to the Chicago *Republican*, explaining that this "heartless assassin" was "the first man ever hanged in this city (or country either), where the first twenty-six graves in the cemetery were those of men who died by shots and stabs" (SLC 1868e; Angel, 343–50; Doten, 2:994–95; Beebe and Clegg, 18–22).

331.10 Capt. Ned Blakely] In actuality Captain Edgar (Ned) Wakeman (1818–75), a well-known skipper for many years in the Pacific Ocean trade. Among Wakeman's commands was the steamer *America*, which carried Clemens from San Francisco to San Juan del Sur, Nicaragua, in December 1866, on the first leg of his journey to New York. "I had rather travel with that old portly, hearty, jolly, boisterous, good-natured old sailor, Capt Ned Wakeman than with any other man I ever came across," Clemens confided in his notebook at the time, also noting nearby, "Hanging the negro in the Chinchas," which indicates that the yarn as recounted in this chapter may in fact reverse the roles of the negro and the white bully, Bill Noakes (*N&J1*, 238–43, 253, 336). Clemens encountered Wakeman again in Panama while returning from San Francisco to New York in July 1868. The two men spent a convivial evening together, and Clemens reported that "the old gentleman," who was "as tempestuous of exterior, as hearty of manner and as stormy of voice as ever," regaled him with yarns, including the one "about hanging the negro in the Chincha Islands" (SLC 1868h). Wakeman's hold on Clemens's imagination is apparent in notebook entries and literary works spanning the author's career. He is Captain Waxman in three San Francisco *Alta California* letters, Captain Hurricane Jones in

"Some Rambling Notes of an Idle Excursion," Admiral Stormfield in "The Refuge of the Derelicts," and the title character in "Captain Stormfield's Visit to Heaven" (SLC 1867b–d, 1878, 1905–6, 1909). After Wakeman's death his reminiscences were edited by his daughter and published as *The Log of an Ancient Mariner, Being the Life and Adventures of Captain Edgar Wakeman* (San Francisco: A. L. Bancroft and Co., 1878).

339.9–10 The *Weekly Occidental . . .* made its appearance in Virginia] The first number of the *Occidental,* edited by Thomas Fitch with the assistance of his wife, Anna M. Fitch (see the notes at 339.11–13 and 339.29–30), appeared on Sunday, 6 March 1864. No issues of the magazine survive, but its prospectus described it as a "Literary and Miscellaneous Newspaper, containing Tales, Poems, Literary Reviews, Editorials, Humorous Sketches, Brevities and Localisms, from the pens of the best writers of Nevada and California, together with Stories, Sketches and Essays from the latest Foreign and Domestic periodicals"; in addition, it was to chronicle important local events and contain a "Ladies' and Home Department" ("Prospectus of the 'Occidental,'" Virginia City *Union,* 9 Feb 64, 2). Contributors included Dan De Quille (William Wright), Joseph Goodman, and Rollin Daggett (see the note at 340.8–9), as well as the Fitches. Although Fitch recalled that three issues of the *Occidental* appeared, and Mark Twain here implies that there were four, apparently at least five numbers—from 6 March to 3 April 1864—were published: on 9 April, the day before the sixth was due to appear, the Virginia City *Evening Bulletin* noted that the "Occidental, a very excellent literary paper, has ceased to exist" ("Dead," 3). The possibility remains that two additional issues appeared: an advertisement attributed to the *Occidental* of 17 April survives in the Virginia City *Union* of the same date ("Sheriff's Sale," 1; Lingenfelter and Gash, 257; Rogers 1957, 365–70; William Wright 1893c; Fitch, 54–55; Eric N. Moody 1977, 11–13).

339.11–13 Mr. F. was to edit it . . . editor of the *Union,*] Thomas Fitch (1838–1923), a journalist, lawyer, speculator, politician, and orator with literary ambitions, was born in New York City and emigrated from Wisconsin to California in 1860. He worked as a journalist in San Francisco and Placerville, earned admittance to the bar, and in 1862–63 was a member of the California legislature. He went to Virginia City in June 1863 and was engaged as an editor on the *Union.* He later served as a delegate from Storey County to the constitutional convention of 1864, as the district attorney of Washoe County in 1865–66, and as a Republican congressman from Nevada in 1869–71. In addition to his failed literary journal, Fitch started a short-lived Virginia City daily newspaper, the *Washoe Evening Herald,* in July 1864, and in 1868 briefly published the weekly Belmont (Nev.) *Mountain Champion.* His literary endeavors included a novel, *Better Days; or, A Millionaire of To-morrow* (1891), written in collaboration with his wife, and an unpublished play, *Old Titles* (1876). Clemens and Fitch were well acquainted: Fitch and his family lodged across the hall from the rooms that Clemens and Dan De Quille shared in the Daggett and Myers building, and Clemens was a guest at Fitch's home in Washoe City during his western lecture tour of 1866. Although Clemens expressed his admiration of Fitch's writing and oratorical abilities (which earned him the title of "Silver Tongued Orator of the Pacific"), he also characterized Fitch in November 1864 as a political opportunist, a "two-faced" dog (*L1*, 310–11 n. 3, 318, 319 n. 4, 366 n. 3; SLC 1863e; Angel, 86; *BDUSC*, 1000; William Wright 1893b; Lingenfelter and Gash, 19, 258; Eric N. Moody 1978, vii–viii).

339.17–21   THE PEACE OF GOD . . . *passeth understanding*] Philippians 4:7.

339.28–29   an original novel . . . the full strength of the company] According to Fitch, this serialized composite "original novel" was entitled *The Silver Fiend, a Tale of Washoe.* Whereas Mark Twain designated the order of the collaborating authors as Anna Fitch, Thomas Fitch, Rollin Daggett, and the "dissolute stranger," Fitch maintained that he opened the story and was followed by Daggett and Mrs. Fitch, with Mark Twain scheduled to be the fourth contributor. Fitch claimed that the novel began as a western adventure with a later admixture—supplied by Mrs. Fitch—of domestic manners and love interest, centering on "a beautiful Vermont girl, who was compelled by her father's loss of fortune and death to come to the Pacific Coast and seek employment as a teacher" (Fitch, 54–55). A contemporary article in the Virginia City *Union* supports Fitch's recollection: "We were favored, last evening, with a copy of the first number of 'The Occidental,' the new literary weekly. . . . This copy of the Occidental contains . . . an original tale of the early days of Washoe, fertile in fact and fancy, and skilfully told—name of author not given" ("Literary Paper," 6 Mar 64, 2). Yet another version of the *Silver Fiend* project was recorded in 1893 by Dan De Quille, who recalled that only the first chapter—written by Daggett—ever appeared, and that it featured standard Gothic trappings such as a demonic Rosicrucian and a "partially subterranean castle" (William Wright 1893c, 173–74).

339.29–30   Mrs. F. was an able romancist of the ineffable school] Anna Mariska Fitch was the "talented lady editress" in charge of the "Ladies' and Home Department" in the *Occidental.* In addition to the novel that she and her husband co-authored (see note at 339.11–13), she published a novel, *Bound Down; or, Life and Its Possibilities* (1870); a play, *Items: A Washington Society Play* (1874); and a volume of verse, *The Loves of Paul Fenly* (1893).

340.8–9   Mr. D., a dark and bloody editor of one of the dailies] Mark
Twain is referring to Rollin Mallory Daggett (1831–1901), whom
Charles C. Goodwin, a colleague, described as "swarthy, a remote
strain of Iroquois in his veins, I think; heavy set . . . a face full of merriment generally, but savage as a trapped bear when he was angry"
(Goodwin, 185). Daggett was born in New York and raised in Ohio. In
1849–50 he went overland to California, where he prospected for gold
and worked as a printer. In 1852 he and J. Macdonough Foard founded
and began co-editing the San Francisco *Golden Era,* a prestigious literary weekly (undoubtedly the model for Fitch's *Occidental;* see the note
at 405.1). Eight years later he established the San Francisco *Evening
Mirror.* Upon moving to Virginia City in 1862 he became a prominent
stockbroker and notary public, as well as a part-time staff member on
the *Territorial Enterprise*—the beginning of a seventeen-year connection with the newspaper. In 1874, when William Sharon acquired the
paper, Daggett succeeded Joseph Goodman as editor-in-chief. He was
an outspoken Republican in politics, serving on the Territorial Council
in 1863 and as Nevada's representative in Congress from 1879 to 1881.
The following year he was appointed United States minister to Hawaii
(1882–85). Daggett's literary talent found expression in numerous
poems published in the *Enterprise,* and in a novel, *Braxton's Bar: A
Tale of Pioneer Years in California* (1882). In 1888 Mark Twain's publishing firm, Charles L. Webster and Company, issued a collaborative
work by Daggett and King Kalakaua of Hawaii, *The Legends and Myths
of Hawaii* (*BDUSC,* 864; *L1,* 310–11 n. 3; Kelly 1863, 203; Weisenburger, 20–27, 47, 52–54, 94–95, 162–64).

340.20–21   there arrived in Virginia a dissolute stranger with a literary
turn of mind] The model for this literary collaborator may have been—
as Franklin Rogers has suggested—Charles Henry Webb (1834–1905),
a journalist well known in New York Bohemian circles. (Rogers was incorrect, however, in asserting that Webb was not yet in the West during
the lifetime of the *Occidental.*) Webb, who ran away to sea as a boy and
spent four years on whaling vessels, later worked as a columnist and
correspondent for the New York *Times.* After relocating to San Francisco in April 1863 he served as a city editor for the *Evening Bulletin,* a
correspondent (as "John Paul") for the Sacramento *Union,* and a regular
contributor (as "Inigo") to the *Golden Era.* On 21 March 1864, one day
after the publication of the third number of the *Occidental,* "J. Paul"
arrived in Virginia City from San Francisco by the Pioneer Stage ("Arrivals," Virginia City *Union,* 22 Mar 64, 3). Mark Twain's claim (at
346.1–4) that the dissolute stranger's chapter of the *Silver Fiend* was
borrowed from Charles Reade's *Love Me Little, Love Me Long* (1859)
may well be a covert allusion to Webb, a punster and facile parodist. By
the time *Roughing It* was written Webb had published *Liffith Lank; or,*

Lunacy (1867), a burlesque of Reade's *Griffith Gaunt; or, Jealousy* (1866). The two men improved their acquaintance after Clemens moved to San Francisco at the end of May 1864. On the twenty-eighth of that month Webb issued the first number of his new literary weekly, the *Californian,* to which Mark Twain soon became a contributor. In April 1866 Webb returned to New York, where in 1867 he edited and published Mark Twain's first book, *The Celebrated Jumping Frog of Calaveras County, And other Sketches* (Rogers 1960, 77; Walker 1969, 133–34, 179–80; *ET&S1,* 504–6, 536 n. 26; *ET&S2,* 380–82).

341.35–36 by means of the usual strawberry mark on left arm] In romantic literature the discovery of a strawberry birthmark, often located on the left arm, commonly disclosed a character's unsuspected aristocratic lineage. Variations of the device figure in Henry Fielding's *Joseph Andrews* (1742), Horace Walpole's *The Castle of Otranto* (1764), and Ann Radcliffe's *The Castles of Athlin and Dunbayne* (1789), among others. John Maddison Morton's *Box and Cox: A Romance of Real Life* (1847), a universally popular one-act farce that was performed in Virginia City while Clemens was there, ridiculed the device by establishing Cox's identity as the brother of Box through the *lack* of a strawberry mark on his left arm. Clemens made a brief use of this convention in two newspaper pieces of early 1866, "Romance in Real Life" and "Neodamode" (part of a "San Francisco Letter"), and burlesqued it in greater detail in an "Around the World" letter (SLC 1866b–c, 1870c).

346.4 "Love Me Little, Love Me Long,"] The hero of Reade's novel, David Dodd, relates the following incident: Jem Green, a harpooner on the English whaler *Connemara,* harpooned a right whale on 5 March 1820 in the Pacific Ocean, but "she broke the harpoon shaft just below the line, and away she swam." Four years later in Nantucket, as a result of a drinking session with sailors from an American whaler, Green was presented with a harpoon steel bearing the *Connemara* stamp and his own name scratched on it. The log of the American vessel revealed that the right whale, with an English harpoon in her, was taken on 25 March 1820 off Greenland—at least "five thousand miles of water" away from the place of Green's strike (Charles Reade, 51–52).

346.6–7 Jonah's adventure as proof that a man could live in a whale's belly . . . three days] Jonah 1:17.

347.5–6 the resurrected Lazarus and the dilapidated mendicant] John 11:1–44 and Luke 16:19–31.

347.14 time brings its revenges] *Twelfth Night,* act 5, scene 1.

347.17 "The Raging Canal,"] This humorous song was written and performed by the celebrated comic singer Pete Morris (b. 1821); a version of the text may be found in *The American Songbag* (Levy, 256–57, 259;

Sandburg, 178–79). While "The Aged Pilot Man" and "The Raging Canal" share a similar narrative idea, Mark Twain was also inspired by traditional sentimental sea ballads—and specifically by Samuel Taylor Coleridge's "Rime of the Ancient Mariner," published in 1798 (Lilje-gren, 24). Roger L. Brooks has also pointed out similarities in rhyme and phrasing between Coleridge's poem and Mark Twain's (Roger L. Brooks, 451–53), while Howard Baetzhold has further observed:

Despite the reference to "The Raging Canal," the author almost surely expected his readers to see through his (or his narrator's) dodge. Recognition of the kin-ship with Coleridge's famous poem would, in turn, enhance the ridiculousness of Mark Twain's tempest on a canal. (Baetzhold, 277)

Dollinger's repeated assurance, "Fear not, but lean on Dollinger, / And he will fetch you through," echoes Jack's remark in chapter 6, "Ben Holladay would have fetched them through in thirty-six hours!" (39.17–18).

354.3–4   The year 1863 was perhaps the . . . culmination of the "flush times."] See the note at 281.4–6.

354.21–22   the grand combined procession . . . stretched unbroken from Virginia to California] Eliot Lord notes that the mule teams crossing the Sierra at this time "stretched along the highway for miles in an un-broken procession, and if a teamster by chance fell out of line he would often be compelled to wait for hours before he could regain a place in the column" (Lord, 192–93).

354.26–356.4   a hundred dollars a ton for full loads . . . passengers at from twenty-five to thirty dollars a head] Eliot Lord claims that a "com-puted average" of five cents per pound was paid to "teamsters and ship-pers in 1862" (confirming Mark Twain's "hundred dollars a ton") and cites an advertised price in 1863 of twenty-seven dollars per stagecoach passenger (Lord, 194). The rest of the figures in this paragraph, although plausible, have not been confirmed.

355n.1–356n.2   *Mr. Valentine . . . Enterprise.] This is an excerpt, edited by Mark Twain, from a much longer item he had written for the Enter-prise of 27 August 1863, entitled "Ye Bulletin Cyphereth"—a response to gross overestimates of bullion yields which had appeared a few days earlier in the Virginia City Evening Bulletin (SLC 1863n; ET&S1, 414). Note that Mark Twain's sums are incorrect: according to his figures, in 1862 the Virginia City office of Wells, Fargo shipped $2,596,000 (not $2,615,000), and between January 1862 and June 1863 it shipped $5,471,000 (not $5,330,000).

355n.1   Mr. Valentine, Wells Fargo's agent] Wells, Fargo and Company was organized in May 1852 by Henry Wells (1805–78) and William G. Fargo (1818–81), both of whom had more than a decade of experience in the express business. Within six months of its organization the company was well established in California mining camps as a major carrier of mail, gold dust and bullion, and passengers. Soon it was the dominant express line in the West, connecting with affiliated companies for delivery throughout the United States, Canada, and Europe. In 1863 the company was so successful that it paid its stockholders 122 percent in dividends. John J. Valentine (1840–1901) learned the express business in Kentucky. He emigrated to California in the spring of 1862, where he went to work for Wells, Fargo and Company, but was soon transferred to Virginia City, where he became a joint agent for that company, the Overland Mail Company, and the Pioneer Stage Company. In 1866 he became Wells, Fargo's superintendent of express, and by 1884 he was vice-president and general manager. He was president of the company from 1892 until his death (Loomis, 15–18, 34, 167, 188, 255, 280).

356.17–19 Under it was another busy city, down in the bowels of the earth] Here Mark Twain touches on a theme often developed in the columns of the *Enterprise,* even before he joined the staff. For example, in August 1862 the *Enterprise* local wrote, "Who ever thinks, in walking the streets, that perhaps hundreds of feet beneath him—beneath the city, in the bowels of the earth, a fellow mortal may also be walking in the same direction, in one of the streets of the city below?" ("Underground Life in the Silver Mines," San Francisco *Alta California,* 5 Aug 62, 1, reprinting the Virginia City *Territorial Enterprise;* see also "Subterranean Washoe," San Francisco *Herald and Mirror,* 14 May 62, 1, and "Washoe Underneath," Stockton *Independent,* 21 June 62, 1, both reprinting the *Enterprise).*

356.25–26 a vast web of interlocking timbers] The method of timbering a mine in square sets—somewhat like a honeycomb—was invented in 1860 by Philipp Deidesheimer (b. 1832) for use in the Ophir mine, and was soon adopted throughout the Comstock. The Deidesheimer method made possible the extraction of large ore bodies and provided a degree of safety to miners not possible under the old method of support by posts and caps. In late October 1862, about a month after going to work for the *Enterprise,* Clemens described the Deidesheimer square sets in his account of his descent into the Spanish mine (Angel, 573–74; SLC 1862g).

357.1–4 from the St. Nicholas to Wall street . . . high above the pinnacle of Trinity steeple] The vast and splendid St. Nicholas Hotel was opened in 1853 on Broadway at Spring Street, over a mile north of Wall Street. It was one of Clemens's favorite stopping places in New York. Trinity Protestant Episcopal Church, on Broadway opposite the head of Wall Street, was completed in 1846; its steeple was 284 feet high (Kouwenhoven, 277; King, 341–42).

357.10–11 The Spanish proverb says it requires a gold mine to "run" a silver one] Richardson also referred to this proverb in *Beyond the Mis-*

sissippi (370), although he did not identify it as Spanish. George Lyman, in *The Saga of the Comstock Lode,* renders the original proverb as "Para trabajar una mina de plata se necesita una mina de oro" (Lyman, 361 n. 4).

358.29–360.2   AN HOUR IN THE CAVED MINES . . . office.] The *Territorial Enterprise* printing of this article is not known to survive. In addition to this account, which probably appeared on 17 July 1863, Mark Twain's descriptions of his descents into the Ophir mine immediately before and after the 15 July cave-in are preserved in his San Francisco *Morning Call* letters published on 15, 18, and 23 July; in excerpts of *Enterprise* items reprinted in the *Mining and Scientific Press* of 27 July; and in the San Francisco *Evening Bulletin* of 21 July (SLC 1863f–j).

359.8–9   the Central] The Central Mining Company owned 150 feet on the Comstock lode immediately south of the Ophir claim (Lord, 61).

359.44   the Union incline and tunnel] The Mexican, California, Central, and Ophir companies cooperated to construct this eleven-hundred-foot tunnel in 1860 in order to "drain the ledge to the depth of 200 feet" (Lord, 88–89).

360n.1–2   I learn from an official source . . . that the yield for 1863 did not exceed $20,000,000] In this chapter Mark Twain presents three estimates of 1863 Nevada bullion production: $30 million (355n.18), $25 million (360.4), and $20 million. It is possible that his unidentified "official source" for this last figure was one of the numerous reports prepared in conjunction with the Sutro tunnel project, or even Adolph Sutro himself (see the next two notes). The best estimates now available indicate that the Nevada bullion yield for 1863 was only about $13.1 million: $12.4 million for the Comstock, $.5 million for Esmeralda, and $.2 million for Reese River and Humboldt (Lord, 416; Wasson, 47; Angel, 464; J. Ross Browne 1868, 332, 387, 431).

360n.3–9   the Sutro Tunnel is to plow through the Comstock lode . . . and will develop astonishing riches] The Sutro Tunnel, planned and built by Adolph Sutro at a cost of about $5 million, was begun on 19 October 1869—after several years of heroic effort by Sutro to obtain the required political and financial backing. The main tunnel, which was bored from a spot near the Carson River, east of Virginia City, into the flank of Mount Davidson, was completed on 8 July 1878. According to the 1867 "Report of the Committee on Federal Relations, of the Nevada Legislature," it was designed to intersect the

mines at a depth of 2,000 feet, draining off the water to that depth by its natural flow, securing the best ventilation, cooling the atmosphere in the mine, furnishing facilities for transportation, and making it possible to dispense with all pumping and hoisting machinery: for the miner can enter the mines from below, work upwards, and the ore will fall by its own gravity; whilst a railroad in the tunnel will transport the same at small cost to the adjacent valley. (Adolph Sutro, 81)

In August 1871 Clemens queried Sutro (who was about to embark from New York for Europe) about the tunnel project, writing from Hartford, where he was hard at work revising the printer's copy of *Roughing It:* "Can't you run up here for one day? I'm awful busy on my new book on Nevada & California. And by the way you might tell me something about the tunnel that would make an interesting page, perhaps"; ten days later, apparently after a meeting with Sutro in New York, he sent a follow-up telegram requesting the length of the tunnel "when finished" (SLC to Sutro, 19 Aug 71, Koundakjian†, and 29 Aug 71, NvHit). Sutro evidently supplied the information for this appended annotation: according to his own 1868 published defense of the project, the main tunnel was to run 4.0 miles, and the lateral branches to it another 3.4 miles, for a total of 7.4 miles. (As built, the branches were about a mile shorter than originally planned.) Although the tunnel was a benefit to the mines, especially as a means of drainage, it was built too late to be very profitable. No sizable bonanzas were discovered after its completion, and about fifty years later it was abandoned (Adolph Sutro, 23; Theodore Sutro, 37–38; Shinn, 194–208; Stewart and Stewart, 168).

360n.12   Mr. Sutro] Adolph Heinrich Joseph Sutro (1830–98), a native of Prussia, emigrated to America in 1850 and soon proceeded to the West Coast, where he became a successful merchant. Drawn to Nevada in 1860 by the silver discoveries, he built a quartz mill at Dayton, employing a process for extracting metals which he had helped to develop. Within a short time he conceived his tunnel project and devoted his energies to it for over fifteen years. In 1880, after the tunnel was completed, he sold his shares in the Sutro Tunnel Company and returned to San Francisco. Real-estate investments increased his fortune, much of which he devoted to construction projects beneficial to the city. He served as San Francisco's mayor from 1894 to 1896 (Stewart and Stewart, 9, 19, 26–27, 33, 36–38, 166–68, 181–90, 202–9). Mark Twain described a stagecoach trip with Sutro from Virginia City to Dayton in a letter to the *Enterprise* written in late 1863 or early 1864. There he briefly portrayed Sutro as a hardheaded, humorless businessman and an outspoken advocate of entrusting all public projects to individual enterprise (SLC 1863x).

361.2–3   get one Jim Blaine to tell me the stirring story of his grandfather's old ram] The ram story became one of Clemens's favorite platform pieces in later years. In 1907 he explained that the tale was intended "to exhibit certain bad effects of a good memory . . . which has no sense of proportion, and can't tell an important event from an unimportant one, but preserves them all, states them all, and thus retards the progress of a narrative, at the same time making a tangled, inextricable confusion of it" (AD, 13 Oct 1907, CU-MARK, in *MTE*, 217–18). It is unclear who the prototype was for Jim Blaine. In January 1865 Clemens commented in his notebook, "Mountaineers in habit [of] telling same old experiences over & over again in these little back settlements. Like Dan's old Ram, whi[c]h he always drivels about when drunk"; in an 1866 notebook entry he again alluded to "Dan's old Ram" (*N&J1*, 74–75, 172). The reference could be either to Dan De Quille (William Wright), whose fondness for liquor was well known on the Comstock, or Dan Twing, one of Clemens's Aurora cabinmates. It is also possible that Clemens heard the tale during his stay at Jackass Hill and Angel's Camp in the winter of 1864–65. On 10 August 1871, when Clemens was in Hartford revising the printer's copy for *Roughing It*, he told his wife, "I wrote a splendid chapter today, for the middle of the book"; this has been conjecturally identified as the present chapter (CU-MARK†; see the Introduction, pages 814–15, 863–64).

364.14   Dorcas S'iety] A common name for church sewing circles. The Biblical Dorcas was a Joppa woman "full of good works and almsdeeds," especially known for the "coats and garments" she made for the poor (Acts 9:36–42).

366.33–34   A dog can't be depended on to carry out a special providence] In 1907 Clemens described the most effective way to deliver this joke:

A pause *after* the remark was absolutely necessary with any and all audiences, because no man, howsoever intelligent he may be, can instantly adjust his mind to a new and unfamiliar, and yet for a moment or two apparently plausible, logic which recognizes in a dog an instrument too indifferent to pious restraints and too alert in looking out for his own personal interest to be safely depended upon in an emergency requiring self-sacrifice for the benefit of another, even when the command comes from on high. The absurdity of the situation always worked its way into the audience's mind, but it had to have time. (AD, 14 Oct 1907, CU-MARK, in *MTE*, 227–28)

It has been suggested that this "caricature of the doctrine of special providences links the monologue with Roop's speech at the Buncombe trial" (Henry Nash Smith 1962, 67–68; see chapter 34).

367.4–21   he got nipped by the machinery in a carpet factory . . . W-i-l-l-i-a-m—W-h-e—"] This story is an embroidered version of the card stripper's tale in "A Yankee in a Cotton Factory," by "Gamboge" (not otherwise identified), which was reprinted for many years in the American press after its first appearance in the Boston *Yankee Blade* on 2 October 1847 (Dorson, 14–15, 70–72).

369.1   there was a large Chinese population] Mark Twain derived some of his remarks about the Chinese in this chapter from an "Around the World" letter published in the Buffalo *Express* on 22 January 1870 (SLC 1870b). The material also echoes some of Samuel Bowles's comments about the Chinese in *Our New West* (396–416), a book Mark Twain may have been familiar with. Before writing *Roughing It* he had expressed his interest in the Chinese in numerous writings: see *CofC*, 23–27, 69–84; *ET&S2*, 38–48, 62–65; SLC 1868g, 1870f–g, 1870i, 1870k–*l*, 1871a.

369.16–17 no Chinaman can testify against a white man] An 1850 California law provided that "No Black, or Mulatto person, or Indian shall be allowed to give evidence in favor of, or against a White man"; in 1854 the California Supreme Court ruled that "Chinese and all other people not white, are included in the prohibition" (*Reports*, 4:399). The Civil Rights Act of 1866 and the Fourteenth Amendment (1868) effectively nullified this law, but "it was not until the revised [California Code of Civil Procedure] took effect on January first, 1873, that witnesses were admitted to the courts of California regardless of color and nationality" (Coolidge, 76; Sandmeyer, 45).

369.19–22 As I write . . . some boys have stoned an inoffensive Chinaman to death . . . no one interfered] Clemens probably read the following item in the New York *Tribune* for 3 June 1871 (1):

SAN FRANCISCO, June 2.—The police are endeavoring to arrest a gang of boys who stoned to death an inoffensive Chinaman on Fourth-st. yesterday afternoon. Dozens of people witnessed the assault, but did not interfere until the murder was complete. No attempt was then made to arrest the murderers.

In May 1870 (and again in 1906), Clemens recalled having written a similar report himself in 1864, only to have it suppressed by his employer, the San Francisco *Morning Call*, because of the paper's anti-Chinese bias. The 1870 article, published in the *Galaxy*, included an ironic defense of a San Francisco youth arrested for stoning a Chinese, concluding that everything in the boy's training "conspired to teach him that it was a high and holy thing to stone a Chinaman, and yet he no sooner attempts to do his duty than he is punished for it" (SLC 1870f, 723; AD, 13 June 1906, CU-MARK, in *MTE*, 256–57; *CofC*, 24–27).

370.1 a bill, like this below] The Chinese characters in the accompanying illustration are not, in fact, a laundry bill. They were borrowed from an engraving in Richardson's *Beyond the Mississippi* entitled "Invitation to Chinese Dinner." The top character, turned sideways in *Roughing It*, is taken out of context from the last line of the invitation and means " 'light' (used by Chinese custom instead of the pronoun 'you,')"; the other characters are a formal salutation (Richardson, 436–37).

370.31–34 an exorbitant swindle . . . "foreign" mining tax . . . usually inflicted on no foreigners but Chinamen] In April 1850 California enacted a tax, in the form of an obligatory license, on all foreigners working mining claims; from 1856 to 1870 the fee for this license was four dollars a month. In practice the tax began within a few years to be "exacted exclusively from Chinese miners":

The income from the Foreign Miners' licenses in the decade from 1854 to 1865, amounted to one-eighth, and for the whole period from 1850 to 1870, to one-half, of the total income of the State from all sources. From 1855 onward, it is conceded by all authorities that the Chinese paid practically the whole of these taxes—a sum amounting altogether to nearly five million dollars. (Coolidge, 36)

On 31 May 1870 the tax was invalidated by federal law (Wheat, 353–55 n. 4; Sanger, 140, 144).

371.10–13   Mr. Burlingame said that herein lay China's bitter opposition to railroads . . . graves of their ancestors or friends] Anson Burlingame (1820–70) was educated at the University of Michigan and Harvard Law School. He practiced law in Boston before turning to politics, serving first in the Massachusetts state legislature, and then as a United States congressman from 1855 to 1861, when he was appointed minister to China. Clemens first met Burlingame in Honolulu in June 1866, when he was en route to China after a leave of absence; he helped Clemens secure an exclusive interview with the survivors of the *Hornet* shipwreck (see *L1*, 343–48). In November 1867 Burlingame resigned his ministry and shortly thereafter accepted an appointment from the Chinese government as a special envoy to the West. In February 1868 he left China on a goodwill tour of Western capitals, traveling first across the United States. In Washington, D.C., he helped to draft a treaty with the United States, the first by a Western power to recognize China's sovereignty and allow unrestricted immigration (*L2*, 187 n. 2, 238–39 n. 1). Shortly after the ratification of the treaty in July, Clemens, with Burlingame's collaboration, wrote a lengthy and laudatory analysis of it for the New York *Tribune*, in which he cautioned,

Let us remember that China is one colossal graveyard—a mighty empire so knobbed all over with graves that the level spaces left are hardly more than alleys and avenues among the clustering death-mounds. . . . The first railroad that plows its pitiless way through these myriads of sacred hillocks will carry dismay and distress into countless households. (SLC 1868g)

372.2–3   if the government sells a gang of Coolies to a foreigner for the usual five-year term] Mark Twain is repeating a common misconception. Although many Chinese emigrated in the 1840s and 1850s to Cuba and South America (and other tropical areas) under labor contracts requiring a lengthy term of service, such arrangements did not involve the Chinese Imperial government, which technically forbade expatriation. Moreover, virtually no contract laborers came to the United States: "Only a few contract coolies were ever brought here and those before 1853. . . . Chinese laborers came as voluntary immigrants, either paying their own passage or borrowing the money to pay it" (Coolidge, 16–18, 43–48).

372.5–15   the Chinamen all belong to one or another of several great companies . . . a costly temple . . . duly marked] These associations of Chinese male immigrants exerted a close control over every aspect of their lives, functioning as social, benevolent, political, and quasi-judicial agencies. The members of each association came primarily from the same district or districts in Kwangtung Province, whence virtually all the Chinese in California had emigrated. The associations— of which there were six from 1862 until 1892—were united into an umbrella organization, known as the Chinese Six Companies. The Sze Yap [Mark Twain's "See Yup"] company, although one of the oldest of these, was not in fact the largest in the early 1860s, since by then many of its members had left to form two new companies, one of them the Ning Yeong. (This latter association soon became the largest, numbering seventy-five thousand members by 1876.) The lavishly appointed Ning Yeong temple, located on Broadway between Dupont and Kearny streets, was officially opened on 20 August 1864. Mark Twain visited the temple on this occasion and reported the event in several sketches for the San Francisco *Morning Call.* Clippings of these sketches may have served to refresh his memory when he wrote this chapter—providing, for example, the "eighteen thousand" membership figure for the Ning Yeong company (SLC 1864m, 1864o–q; Hoy, 1–16; Barth, 96–108, 123).

372.17–20   until the legislature . . . forbade the shipments . . . The bill was offered, whether it passed or not] No such proposed law has been identified, at least not before the mid-1870s. A quarantine law for San Francisco passed by the California state legislature in April 1870, however, stipulated that no exhumation could take place without a permit from the city health officer, and such permits were allegedly refused to Chinese applicants (Benjamin S. Brooks, 6; *Statutes* 1870, 720; Coolidge, 264; Sandmeyer, 54–55).

372.20–24   There was another bill . . . compelling every incoming Chinaman to be vaccinated . . . ten dollars for it] The quarantine law passed in April 1870 also required the city health officer to board any vessel arriving from an Asiatic port and "in his discretion, vaccinate each and every one" of the passengers for a fee of one dollar each (*Statutes* 1870, 716–21). It is possible that Mark Twain was confusing the vaccination regulation with an 1852 state law "requiring the masters of vessels to give a per capita bond of five hundred dollars as indemnity against the costs of medical and other relief of alien passengers; or to commute such bond by the payment of not less than five and not more than ten dollars per passenger"; these fees were to be distributed among the three principal state hospitals (Coolidge, 70; *Statutes* 1852, 78–82). The law remained in effect until 1870, when—like the foreign miners' tax—it was invalidated by federal statute. Between 1852 and 1870, Chinese immigrants paid from 45 to 85 percent of the nearly one-half million dollars thus collected (Coolidge, 70).

372.31–374.16   CHINATOWN . . . a piano.] The publication date of this *Enterprise* item is not known, but the reference to "gaudy plumes" (374.6) suggests that it might have appeared in the summer of 1863.

The local reporter for the Virginia City *Evening Bulletin,* addressing Mark Twain in print on 25 July of that year, recalled the "night we saw you coming in from Chinadom, with a 'feather in your cap'" ("Mark Twain," 3).

372.37 Josh-lights] Joss lights were votive candles, also used in Chinese temples; the term "joss" was not Chinese, but a pidgin English word for "deus," meaning "god."

373.34–36 "Tom," . . . used to be chief and only cook to the *Territorial Enterprise* . . . two years ago] Dan De Quille remembered the cook's name as "Joe" in his description of the *Enterprise's* first Virginia City quarters (see the note at 292.7–11). According to him, Joe was considered the "boss cook of the town" because of his ability to mold table butter in the form of lions and dragons, until it was discovered that he did not bother to keep mouse hairs and bugs out of his cooking ("Newspaper of Early Days on Comstock Dead," San Francisco *Chronicle,* 4 June 1916, 19).

376.2–7 going down to Carson to report the proceedings of the legislature . . . Agricultural Fair] Clemens reported the second and third territorial legislatures (11 November–20 December 1862, 12 January–20 February 1864) for the *Enterprise.* On 19 December 1862 he was made recording secretary of the newly created Washoe Agricultural, Mining and Mechanical Society, and in that capacity attended its first fair, held in Carson City on 12–17 October 1863. Only his report of the fair's final day, which appeared in the *Enterprise* on 20 October, is extant (*L1,* 266; SLC 1863w).

376.12–18 a convention had framed a State Constitution . . . nothing to tax that could stand a tax, for undeveloped mines could not] The first Nevada constitutional convention (which Clemens also reported for the *Enterprise:* see Marsh, Clemens, and Bowman) met in Carson City between 2 November and 11 December 1863. The document its members drafted contained a provision "which asked the people to vote for ratification of the constitution and at the same time choose officers to serve under it"; the candidates for office—who naturally favored the adoption of the constitution, since its rejection would nullify their election—were nominated at a second convention, held from 31 December 1863 through 2 January 1864 (Elliott, 27; *L1,* 269 n. 4). Although the *Enterprise* initially supported passage of the constitution, by 4 January 1864 Mark Twain had serious doubts about certain "unfortunate defects" of the document. The chief of these was a clause authorizing the taxing of all mining property—as distinct from net mining proceeds. The bulk of Nevada's mining property, he wrote, was not yet "in a developed and paying condition, and will require an enormous outlay of capital to accomplish such a result. And until it does begin to pay dividends, the people will not consent that it shall be burdened and hindered by taxation"; he correctly predicted that the voters would not ratify the constitution at the election of 19 January (SLC 1864a). For a discussion of the constitution that was ultimately ratified in September 1864, see the note at 396.21–25.

377.3–12   a schoolmate of mine . . . could have "taken the shine out of the Prodigal Son himself,"] Mark Twain is referring to Cornelius (Neil) Moss (b. 1836) of Hannibal, a classmate of his in Sunday school at the Old Ship of Zion Methodist Church and later at the school kept by John D. Dawson. Moss, whose father owned a large meat-packing business, attended Yale. Clemens later described him as "an envied rich boy. . . . Spoiled and of small account. . . . At 30 he was a graceless tramp in Nevada, living by mendicancy and borrowed money. Disappeared" (SLC 1897, 4–5; *Inds*, 336). Clemens actually encountered Moss in San Francisco in May 1863; there is no evidence of a second meeting in Virginia City in 1864 (*L1*, 252).

377.21–23   so I stepped in and borrowed forty-six dollars of a banker] In September 1864 Clemens alluded to a debt of fifty-five dollars which he owed to "Paxton & Thornburgh, Bankers" of Virginia City, possibly resulting from this loan to Moss (*L1*, 309, 310 n. 2).

377.31–32   Mr. Goodman went away for a week and left me the post of chief editor] On 18 March 1864 Clemens remarked to his sister about his new assignment: "I stipulated, when I took his place, that I should never be expected to write editorials about politics or eastern news. I take no sort of interest in those matters" (*L1*, 275). Goodman was away from Virginia City more than once in the spring of 1864, but the exact dates of his departures and returns have not been determined. His first absence (dating from sometime after 20 February, when Clemens returned to Virginia City from Carson after reporting the third Territorial Legislature) must have lasted more than a week, if—as Clemens informed his sister on 18 March—he went to the Sandwich Islands; no confirmation of such a trip, however, has been located in Virginia City, San Francisco, or Honolulu newspapers. By 8 April Goodman had returned to Virginia City, remaining for an unknown period of time; Clemens's later recollections suggest that he may have departed again by 22 April (see the next note). In any event, on 26 May the Virginia City *Union* again included Goodman on its list of arriving stage passengers ("Arrivals Yesterday," 9 Apr 64, 3, and 26 May 64, 3). The anecdotes in this paragraph seem to telescope events actually occurring over two to three months into a period of only one week.

377.35–36   I . . . copied an elaborate editorial out of the "American Cyclopedia,"] *The New American Cyclopedia: A Popular Dictionary of General Knowledge* was published by D. Appleton and Company in sixteen volumes between 1858 and 1863. Edited by George Ripley and

Charles A. Dana, the work was immensely popular, eventually selling
more than three million copies in two editions. In 1906 Clemens recalled that the *Cyclopedia* furnished him with his first editorial, written on 22 April on the occasion of the

> three-hundredth anniversary of Shakespeare's birthday. . . . There wasn't
> enough of what Shakespeare had done to make an editorial of the necessary
> length, but I filled it out with what he hadn't done—which in many respects was
> more important and striking and readable than the handsomest things he had
> really accomplished. (AD, 19 Jan 1906, CU-MARK, in *MTA*, 1:354–55)

Another instance of such "borrowing" from the *Cyclopedia*, possibly
by Clemens, was noted by the editor of the Virginia City *Union*. On 12
March he observed that the *Enterprise*, in its review of Adah Isaacs
Menken in *Mazeppa* (then playing in Virginia City), was "beginning to
devote its leading editorial space" to discussing "The Rationale of Obscene Exhibitions." He further observed that "the historical allusion to
'Mazeppa' in the *Enterprise* of yesterday, is in the main correct. It was
copied from the *American Cyclopedia*" ("A Few Words to the 'Modest'
Women of San Francisco Who Ventured to See Menken," San Francisco
Evening Bulletin, 15 Mar 64, 5, reprinting the Virginia City *Union* of
12 March; see *L1*, 276 n. 2).

378.6–8 Mr. Goodman returned and found six duels on his hands—my
personalities had borne fruit] One of Clemens's provocative editorials
may have been an item that appeared in the *Enterprise* on 30 March,
entitled "An Item for Our Cotemporaries" and extant as reprinted in
the Virginia City *Union* the next day. It charged collusion between the
Union and several "careless or corrupt" legislators in "log rolling" a bill
that appropriated $400 to the *Union* for printing a pamphlet version of
the proposed constitution (see the note at 376.12–18), whereas the *Enterprise* and other newspapers had printed it "as a matter of news." The
Union responded by accusing the *Enterprise* of "twaddling unscrupu-
lousness" and characterizing the editorial as "boobyish snivel combined with flat sneakishness" ("Several Items for the People," Virginia
City *Union*, 31 Mar 64, 2). Another humorous item by Mark Twain, in
which he facetiously claimed that Thomas Fitch (see the note at
339.11–13) had lodged a complaint against Virginia City broker Warren
F. Myers for voicing racial slurs, appeared in the *Enterprise* on 1 April
and elicited a disgusted comment from the Virginia City *Evening Bulletin* to the effect that "he who is a fool all the rest of the year, has no
special rights on this particular day" ("Another 'Goak,'" 1 Apr 64, 3).
The *Bulletin* continued its attack the following day, alluding to the
"bitterness of [Mark Twain's] remarks" in the morning's *Enterprise:*
"Merciless himself in perpetrating jokes on others, he winces like a cur
with a flea in his ear when others retort; showing conclusively that he
has quite misconcieved the nature of the character he has assumed—
that of being Washoe's wit!" ("A Misconception," 2 Apr 64, 3). Clemens's items and editorials in the *Enterprise* for 18–19 May nearly re-

sulted in his fighting two duels (with Steve Gillis as his second), one of them with James L. Laird of the Virginia City *Union.* In 1906 Clemens recalled that Laird's

editor had gone off to San Francisco too, and Laird was trying his hand at editing. I woke up Mr. Laird with some courtesies of the kind that were fashionable among newspaper editors in that region, and he came back at me the next day in a most vitriolic way. He was hurt by something I had said about him—some little thing—I don't remember what it was now—probably called him a horse-thief, or one of those little phrases customarily used to describe another editor. (AD, 19 Jan 1906, CU-MARK, partially published in *MTA*, 1:355)

Goodman, who may well have been absent during any or all of these controversies (see the note at 377.31–32), was evidently not himself called to account for Clemens's indiscretions (for a full discussion see *L1*, 287–301).

379.7–10 Dan . . . told me, casually, that two citizens . . . aid in selling a rich silver mine . . . in a new mining district] The two citizens were William M. Hurst and one of his partners, Amos H. Rose (see the next note). Hurst had prospected in the Humboldt mountains since at least 1861 and was known as the owner of the Sheba and Ben Franklin mines there. He and five others set out from Virginia City in early April 1864 on a prospecting expedition. They returned about a month later and announced their formation of a new mining district, called Pine Wood, about a hundred and eighty miles northeast of Virginia City, between Reese River and Humboldt. This new district was a ten-by-twelve-mile area rich in pine forests, streams, and promising silver ledges. A long report of the new district, based on an interview with Hurst and probably written by Dan De Quille, appeared in the *Enterprise* on 7 May ("Humboldt Mines," Sacramento *Union*, 15 Aug 62, 2; Virginia City *Union*: "Prospecting Expedition," 3 Apr 64, 3; "A New Mining District," 7 May 64, 3; William Wright 1864).

379.15–30 he had recommended them to apply to Marshall, the reporter of the other paper . . . furnishing me to them] Although Mark Twain's claim about his understanding with Dan De Quille may be a fiction (see also the note at 403.18–38), the account of the plan to sell the mine in New York is essentially true. George M. Marshall, the local reporter for the Virginia City *Union*, entered into a business arrangement with Hurst and Rose, who, although not a member of the April–May prospecting party, was evidently an early investor in Hurst's Pine Wood claim. On 29 June 1864 Marshall took the stage to San Francisco, where he met his two partners and shortly thereafter, on 4 July, sailed with them for the East ("Going to the States," Virginia City *Union*, 29 June 64, 3; Collins, 165; Marshall, 1). While in San Francisco he wrote to Dan De Quille, who also owned feet in the Pine Wood claim:

An arrangement has been entered into & papers drawn up with a N.Y. firm by which they give us $10 per foot on our stock as a basis, and half what it is sold for afterward. So as you have 1800 feet . . . multiply it by ten and see how many dollars you can count on. Don't get excited Dan, but I believe this is the biggest thing in existence, and for Gods sake dont breathe a word of it to anyone. (Marshall to Wright, 30 June 64, IaHi)

379.37   Next day I got away, on the coach, with the usual eclat] Clemens left Virginia City on 29 May 1864 on the California stage, accompanied by Steve Gillis and—unexpectedly—by Goodman, who had planned to accompany the travelers "a little way" and instead "kept clear on to San Francisco" (Goodman to A. B. Paine, 7 Apr 1911, Chester L. Davis 1956c, 4). Clemens's cronies may have attended his departure with the "usual eclat," but he was not universally regretted. The Gold Hill *Evening News* expressed no surprise at his disappearance in view of the "indignation aroused by his enormities" and remarked: "Mark Twain's beard is full of dirt, and his face is black before the people of Washoe" ("An Exile," Gold Hill *Evening News*, 30 May 64, 2). *Roughing It* makes no mention of a major reason for Clemens and Gillis's departure: the desire to avoid arrest for violating the law against dueling (see the note at 378.6–8).

380.36   Toodles] The comical drunkard Timothy Toodles was the chief character of a popular stage extravaganza, *The Toodles*. The role was made famous by William E. Burton on the New York stage in 1848. Clemens saw R. G. Marsh's Juvenile Comedians perform the play in Carson City on 12 January 1864 (*MTEnt*, 131–32; Watson, 46).

383.12–384.3   a little tongue of rich golden flame . . . Vicksburg fallen, and the Union arms victorious at Gettysburg] The Union victories at Vicksburg and Gettysburg took place on 4 July 1863. The Virginia City *Evening Bulletin* described the dazzling effect of early sunlight on the recently installed flag atop Mount Davidson on the morning of the Fourth. The event Clemens recalls here, however—the remarkable flamelike appearance of the flag in a storm-darkened sky—occurred a few weeks later, on 30 July (Virginia City *Evening Bulletin*: "Celebration of the 4th of July," 6 July 63, 3; "A Beautiful Sight," 31 July 63, 3). Anna Fitch commemorated the event in her poem "The Flag on Fire," explaining that

on the evening of July 30th, 1863, upon the breaking away of a storm, this banner was suddenly illuminated by some curious refraction of the rays of the setting sun. Thousands of awe struck persons witnessed the spectacle, which continued until the streets of Virginia, 1500 feet below, were in utter darkness. (Newman, 322)

387.18–392.24   The climate . . . over."] Mark Twain first published this passage in a Buffalo *Express* "Around the World" letter on 13 November 1869; he revised the earlier printing for inclusion in *Roughing It* (SLC 1869m).

389.22   Fort Yuma] Fort Yuma was established in November 1850 on the western bank of the lower Colorado River at its confluence with the

Gila, to guard the main mail, freight, and emigrant route as it entered California from New Mexico Territory (1854–63), or Arizona Territory (after 1863).

389.26–30   a tradition (attributed to John Phoenix*) that a very, very wicked soldier . . . *telegraphed back for his blankets*] Captain George Horatio Derby (1823–61) of the United States Army Corps of Topographical Engineers was best known for his humorous sketches, widely reprinted in newspapers during the 1850s under the pseudonyms "Squibob" and "John Phoenix," and collected in two volumes—*Phoenixiana; or, Sketches and Burlesques* (1856) and *The Squibob Papers* (1865). From 1849 to 1856 Derby was stationed on the Pacific Coast, leading an expedition up the Colorado River in the winter of 1850–51 to explore a route for the provisioning of Fort Yuma. Clemens was thoroughly familiar with Derby's writing (see Gribben, 1:185), but his attribution of the soldier-in-hell anecdote remains unsubstantiated: the story has not been found in Derby's works (George R. Stewart, 7, 59–72, 180, 196, 210–11). Richardson, however, possibly Mark Twain's source, printed a version of it—attributing it to an "unknown genius"—immediately after quoting the following remark about Fort Yuma from Derby's "Lectures on Astronomy": "Mercury . . . receives six and a half times as much heat from the Sun as we do; from which we conclude that the climate must be very similar to that of Fort Yuma, on the Colorado River" (Derby 1856, 59; quoted in Richardson, 581). J. Ross Browne also repeated the story in his description of Fort Yuma in *Adventures in the Apache Country* (J. Ross Browne 1869, 56).

390.7–8   some of us have swept around snow-walled curves of the Pacific Railroad in that vicinity] Clemens made the round trip from Sacramento to Virginia City and back on the Central Pacific Railroad in late April and early May 1868, traversing Donner Pass—where the track was not yet completed—by horse-drawn sleigh (*L2*, 211–14).

392.25–395.11   But . . . head.] Mark Twain first published this passage in a Buffalo *Express* "Around the World" letter on 11 December 1869; he revised the earlier printing for inclusion in *Roughing It* (SLC 1869n).

395.3   Star City] Clemens visited Star City, a few miles northeast of Unionville, during his prospecting trip to the Humboldt district in the winter of 1861–62 (see chapters 27–30 and supplement B, map 2). At its peak in 1864–65 Star City had a population of about twelve hundred, but by 1871 it was nearly abandoned (Angel, 458; Ransome, 10).

396.1–16   FOR a few months I enjoyed . . . a butterfly idleness . . . the due state of a man . . . likely to reach absolute affluence] Clemens's period of idleness actually lasted for only a week (see the note at 397.10–11). After the dust and wind of Washoe, however, his hotel, the Occidental, seemed like "Heaven on the half shell," and life in San Francisco was exhilarating: "The birds, and the flowers, and the Chinamen, and the winds, and the sunshine, and all things that go to make life happy, are present in San Francisco" (SLC 1864h). The amusements Mark Twain describes in this paragraph reflect to some extent his first visit to San Francisco a year earlier, in May and June 1863. At that time he enjoyed the luxuries of the Occidental Hotel and the Lick House, attended the opera, "lived like a lord," speculated feverishly, and moved, he claimed, in "the very best society to be found in San Francisco" (*L1*, 252–61, 302–3).

396.21–25   The property holders of Nevada voted against the State Constitution . . . unquestionably it was one] Presumably to intensify the dramatic impact of his 1864 financial reverses, Clemens misrepresented the facts surrounding the ratification of the constitution and inaccurately blamed it for the 1864 depression. As mentioned earlier (see the note at 376.12–18), the first proposed state constitution was rejected in January 1864, largely because of its provision for a mining-property tax—a provision that Clemens, among others, feared would be an economic burden on mining interests. Nevertheless, in spite of this rejection a significant depression set in (caused at least in part by the effects of chronic litigation over mining laws), which worsened throughout 1864. A revised constitution, which many believed would benefit the economy, was drafted during the summer; it provided for the taxation of net mining proceeds, while exempting unproductive mining property. With the united support of both large and small mining interests, this constitution was ratified by an overwhelming majority of the voters on 7 September 1864 (Elliott, 36, 41, 283 n. 11).

396.26–397.6   Stocks went on rising . . . My hoarded stocks were not worth the paper they were printed on] When Clemens arrived in San Francisco, a downward slide in mining-stock values had already begun, which continued (although mitigated by occasional rallies) through 1865. Nevertheless, there is some truth to his description of a frenzied "gambling carnival," a condition that evidently persisted in spite of falling prices. On 22 May a reporter for the San Francisco *Morning Call* deplored current uncontrolled mining speculation, the "insane traffic in all sorts of mining stocks" by "demented creatures" with "feet on the brain." Recent failures and suicides, he continued, were "slight tremblings" betokening "the financial earthquake approaching" ("The Mining Mania," 22 May 64, 2; Grant H. Smith, 48–50, 99). The *Call*'s prediction proved correct: the decline in stock prices became precipitous in June and July, wiping out many wildcat-mine investors like Clemens (whose losses, however, have not been documented). In the week ending 30 July, for example, Gould and Curry stock fell from about $1,600 to $1,000 per foot. (The price of $6,300 for Gould and Curry stock mentioned at 397.1 was a year out of date: the stock had peaked at that level in June 1863.) An item in the *Call* for 28 July, almost certainly written by Clemens, described the Gould and Curry's "mighty descent," which "mashed and flattened out all the little wild-cats like mice under a deadfall" (SLC 1864k; *Mining and Scientific Press:* "San Francisco Stock and Exchange Board and Pacific Board of Brokers," 9 [30 July 64]: 69; "San Francisco Stock and Exchange Board," 6 [29 June 63]: 5).

397.10–11 I removed from the hotel to a very private boarding house. I took a reporter's berth and went to work] Clemens started working as the local reporter for the San Francisco *Morning Call* around 6 June, much earlier than he implies here. It has not been established when he and Steve Gillis moved together from the Occidental to a boarding house, but by 15 July they had already relocated once again, leaving behind an irate landlady who reportedly described the two of them to Gillis's father as "a couple of desperate characters from Washoe—gamblers and murd[er]ers of the very worst description!" (*L1*, 303).

397.17–398.3 It was signed "Marshall" . . . as they would sail for the east in the morning] Marshall, Hurst, and Rose embarked from San Francisco on 4 July 1864 aboard the *Golden City:* see the notes at 379.7–10 and 379.15–30.

398.19–20 thirty-five dollars a week] When Clemens first went to work for the *Morning Call* his salary was forty dollars a week; by 25 September, however, he had given up night work and accepted a lower wage: "I told the 'Call' folks to pay me $25 a week, & let me work only in daylight" (*L1*, 302, 312).

398.21–24 A month afterward I enjoyed my first earthquake . . . on a bright October day] Clemens freely reordered the chronology of the events of 1864 and 1865 in chapters 58 through 61 of *Roughing It.* The severe earthquake of 8 October 1865 occurred not one month, but fifteen months after Marshall and his companions sailed for New York, and more than seven months after Clemens's return to San Francisco from the mining camps of Tuolumne and Calaveras counties (see chapters 60 and 61). Clemens published four sketches about the quake that have survived wholly or in part, and possibly others no longer extant. His *Roughing It* account draws on details recorded in three of the surviving sketches—"The Cruel Earthquake," "Popper Defieth Ye Earthquake," and "The Great Earthquake in San Francisco"—and, no doubt, upon his recollection of the anecdotes and "toothsome gossip" that circulated in the city for days following the quake (SLC 1865s–u, 1865aa).

403.18–38 NEVADA MINES IN NEW YORK . . . wild-cat.] The *Territorial Enterprise* printing of this article is not known to survive. It probably appeared on 8 November 1864, the day on which a virtually identical report was published in the Virginia City *Union* ("Sale of a Nevada Mine in New York City," 2). In a later article the *Union* explained the

eastern system of organizing mining companies, which it deemed superior to the western system:

A number of capitalists bargain with the owners of the mine to give them a certain sum of money and a certain portion of the stock for it. They then form a
joint stock incorporation; issue, say one-half of the stock and sell it in the market for cash, which constitutes the "working fund." The stock, it must be borne
in mind, is made unassessable. . . . As work is done and machinery erected the
mine becomes valuable and the stock saleable, enabling the originators who
hold the balance of the stock to sell, and thus realize more money. ("How Our
Mines are Sold in the Eastern Market," Virginia City *Union*, 16 Nov 64, 2)

Hurst (nicknamed "Sheba" from his most famous mine), Rose, and
Marshall thus received a large lump-sum payment and a sizeable block
of unassessable shares. Clemens may only have learned of their lucrative deal during his stay at Angel's Camp, when he made the following
entry in his notebook (probably on 24 January 1865), which suggests
little or no personal knowledge of the transaction: "Geo N. Marshall,
Geo. Hurst & another have sold a new mine in Humboldt for
$3,000,000 in N. York" (*N&J1*, 73). In discussing "abortive mining en-
terprises" in his *Story of the Mine*, Charles Howard Shinn may have
been alluding to the sale of "Pine Mountains Consolidated": "Over in
the lava of Pine Woods district in 1863 some Virginia City men sold a
group of mythical mines and received a very large payment down. The
New York buyers spent another fortune and departed, leaving the holes
in the desert" (Shinn, 143).

404.4–9 I neglected my duties . . . one of the proprietors . . . save myself
the disgrace of a dismissal] On or about 10 October 1864 George E.
Barnes, one of the proprietors of the San Francisco *Morning Call*, gave
Clemens the opportunity—which he took—to resign his position as
local reporter. As Barnes later recalled, Clemens left the *Call* "on the
most friendly terms, when it was found necessary to make the local department more efficient, admitting his reportorial shortcomings and
expressing surprise they were not sooner discovered" (Barnes, 1; *CofC*,
23–24). One of the *Call*'s other proprietors, James J. Ayers, admitted
that Clemens's resignation was a relief:

However valuable his services had proven to a Nevada paper, where he might
give full play to his fertile imagination and dally with facts to suit his fancy, that
kind of reporting on a newspaper in a settled community, where the plain, unvarnished truth was an essential element in the duties of a reporter, could hardly
be deemed satisfactory. It was true that we had long desired to dispense with
Mark's services, but had a delicacy about bluntly telling him so. (Ayers, 223–24)

404n.1–2 I saw Marshall, months afterward] Clemens encountered Marshall in San Francisco in December 1865, and satirized his tiresome
and profane travel reminiscences in a letter to the Virginia City *Territorial Enterprise* written on 23 December (SLC 1865ff).

405.1 I wrote literary screeds for the *Golden Era*] The San Francisco
Golden Era was founded on 19 December 1852 by Rollin M. Daggett

(see the note at 340.8–9) and J. Macdonough Foard, and purchased in 1860 by Joseph E. Lawrence and James Brooks. It quickly became the leading literary paper on the West Coast. Its luxurious office was the gathering place for local literary figures as well as distinguished visitors. The *Era* had already published (or reprinted) seven contributions by Mark Twain in 1863 and early 1864, and now—after his return to San Francisco in late May 1864—published three more (see SLC 1863d, 1863r–v, 1864f, 1864h–j). The *Golden Era* declined after the 1860s, finally ceasing publication in 1893.

405.1–18   C. H. Webb had established . . . the *Californian* . . . the paper presently died a peaceful death, and I was out of work again . . . queer vicissitudes] The first issue of the *Californian,* founded by Charles Henry Webb (see the note at 340.20–21), appeared on 28 May 1864 and soon earned favorable reviews from both the California and the eastern press. Nevertheless, in September 1864 Webb sold out to Richard L. Ogden (see the note at 405.7–8), who in turn relinquished his interest two months later to "three printers"—P. J. Thomas, A. M. Kenaday, and A. A. Stickney—together constituting the Californian Printing and Publishing Company. In January 1866 Webb again became a coproprietor along with Stickney, J. P. Bogardus, and William J. Bingham. During its first two years, the *Californian* was edited alternately by Webb and Bret Harte: Harte replaced Webb from 10 September to 19 November 1864, from 15 or 22 April to 30 December 1865, and from Webb's departure for New York on 18 April 1866 to 1 August 1866. In August 1866 Stickney and Bingham sold their interest to Bogardus, and James F. Bowman replaced Harte as editor; in October Bowman purchased Webb's remaining interest in the paper. Bowman and Bogardus continued together until January 1868, when the latter became sole proprietor, with Tremenheere L. Johns listed as his co-editor. The *Californian* survived—under different owners and editors—for several months longer: contrary to the statement in *Roughing It,* its "peaceful death" came with the issue of 21 November 1868, almost two years after Clemens had left the West (*Californian:* 1 [6 Aug 64]: 9; 1 [3 Sept 64]: 8; 1 [26 Nov 64]: 8; 2 [15 Apr 65]: 8; 4 [6 Jan 66]: 8; 4 [13 Jan 66]: 8; 4 [21 Apr 66]: 8; 5 [18 Aug 66]: 8; 5 [20 Oct 66]: 8; 7 [11 Jan 68]: 8; 7 [18 Jan 68]: 8; "Opening Chorus," 8 [21 Nov 68]: 2; *L1,* 314 n. 5, 330 n. 4; *ET&S2,* 144–45 n. 2; Harte to Webb, 18 Oct 66, CU-BANC).

405.4   Bret Harte] Harte (born Francis Brett Harte, 1836–1902), a native of New York, went to California in 1854 and worked in a variety of occupations before settling in San Francisco in 1860. After setting type for the *Golden Era* he began publishing pieces of his own in that journal. In the fall of 1864, during his first stint as editor of the *Californian,* he presumably accepted the first nine of Mark Twain's contributions (see the next note). In January 1866 he invited Clemens to collaborate on a collection of sketches, which, however, they never produced (see *L1*, 328). From July 1868 he served as the first editor of the *Overland Monthly*, for which he wrote some of his best work. After his departure for the East in February 1871, he contributed pieces to the *Atlantic Monthly*, but their quality was disappointing. From 1878 until his death he lived abroad, serving for a time as a consul in Prussia and then in Scotland. The work of his later years lacked the "vigor, color, and wit" of his early material, and "for the rest of his life he was little better than a hack writer" (*DAB*, 4:362–65).

405.5–6   I was employed to contribute an article a week at twelve dollars] On 25 September 1864, almost three months after his final contribution to the *Golden Era* and six days before his first sketch appeared in the *Californian*, Clemens wrote to his family:

> I have engaged to write for the new literary paper—the "Californian"—same pay I used to receive on the "Golden Era"—one article a week, fifty dollars a month. I quit the "Era," long ago. It wasn't high-toned enough. I thought that whether I was a literary "jackleg" or not, I wouldn't class myself with that style of people, anyhow. The "Californian" circulates among the highest class of the community, & is the best weekly literary paper in the United States—& I suppose I ought to know. (*L1*, 312)

Mark Twain's debut sketch, "A Notable Conundrum," was the first of twenty-seven original contributions to the *Californian* between 1 October 1864 and 29 September 1866 (SLC 1864t–bb, 1865a, 1865c–f, 1865h–j, 1865m, 1865o, 1865q–r, 1865v, 1865z, 1865dd–ee, 1866dd, 1866jj).

405.7–8   Capt. Ogden, a rich man and a pleasant gentleman] Richard Livingston Ogden (1825–1900), a native of New York, joined the army early in his life and served in the Mexican War, after which he settled in California and tried his hand at mining. He attained the rank of captain in the United States Army Quartermaster Corps, serving in San Francisco in 1863–64. After leaving military service, he successfully pursued careers both in journalism and in business. As "Podgers," he corresponded for the New York *Times* and the San Francisco *Alta California* (an 1865 letter to the *Alta* described the favorable reception in New York of Mark Twain's "Jumping Frog" tale: see Ogden, 1). His business interests included the management of George P. Kimball and Company of San Francisco, manufacturer of carriages and cars (Shuck et al., 1015–20). An item in the San Francisco *Morning Call* of 4 September 1864, probably by Clemens, reported Ogden's purchase of the *Californian*: "Mr. Webb has sold the paper to Captain Ogden, a gentleman of fine literary attainments, an able writer, and the possessor of a happy bank account" (SLC 1864r). Writing to Clemens in 1883, Ogden explained why he sold the *Californian* after only two months. He recalled

> settling every Saturday with the literary talent—at a considerable loss over receipts—all because the public was not as appreciative as at the present day, i e

the enterprise was a little too early. Webb found that out, and after having borrowed all the money I had, to keep it up, generously walked off and left me to run it for fun. When I had got about $5000 worth of fun out of it—I sold out for what I could get and never got that.—Some of the things you wrote in those days were as good if not better than you ever wrote since. I can safely say it in Hartes case. (Ogden to SLC, 19 June 83, CU-MARK)

405.20–25   For two months . . . I did not earn a penny . . . I became a very adept at "slinking."] Mark Twain may be drawing upon memories of two periods of financial distress during his residence in San Francisco—the first in 1864, and the second in 1865—but he was not wholly unemployed at either time. The *Roughing It* chronology places the two-month "slinking" period in late 1864—from about 10 October, when he lost his position with the *Morning Call,* until he departed in early December for Jackass Hill in Tuolumne County. During this period he apparently earned only $84 ($12 for each of seven sketches he published in the *Californian*); his departure from the *Call* cost him $200 in lost wages ($25 per week for eight weeks). In addition, on 21 October he was obliged to pay an assessment of $100 on four shares of Hale and Norcross stock, even though, when he left for Jackass Hill, he was able to take $300 with him, perhaps from the sale of one of these shares (SLC 1864v–bb; *L1,* 312, 315, 316 n. 5, 318, 319 n. 5, 320). Clemens continued in straitened circumstances throughout the first half of 1865, but his situation seems to have become acute in the late summer and fall, even occasioning comment in the press. An item entitled "A Sheik on the Move," presumably written by William K. McGrew, the *Call*'s local editor (see *ET&S2,* 546), appeared in the *Call* on 29 October 1865:

There is now, and has been for a long time past, camping about through town, a melancholy-looking Arab, known as Marque Twein. . . . His favorite measure is a pint measure. He is said to be a person of prodigious capacity, and addicted to a great flow of spirits. He moves often. Like all Arabs, Marque Twein is instinctively itinerant. He moves periodically. These periods occur at the end of his credit. . . . This Arab . . . wants to claim kin with respectable folks, but he labors under a difficulty in finding persons who are "on it." He may feel all right, but he don't *look* affectionate. His hat is an old one, and comes too far down over his eyes, and his clothes don't fit as if they were made for him. . . . Beware of him. (McGrew, 3)

Nine days earlier, Clemens had written a letter to Orion and Mollie Clemens which tends to confirm McGrew's description:

I have a religion—but you will call it blasphemy. It is that there is a God for the rich man but none for the poor.
     You are in trouble, & in debt—so am I. I am utterly miserable—so are you. Perhaps your religion will sustain you, will feed you—I place no dependence in mine. Our religions are alike, though, in one respect—neither can make a man happy when he is out of luck. If I do not get out of debt in 3 months,—pistols or poison for one—exit *me.* (*L1,* 324)

406.10–11   the entertaining of a collector (and being entertained by him,)] This collector may have been Clemens's friend John Henry Riley, the same man who figures later in this chapter as the mendicant

Blucher (see the note at 406.35–407.22). The identification is suggested by the fact that Riley evidently pursued a variety of unusual occupations during his years in San Francisco, several of which Clemens
described for humorous effect in a November 1870 *Galaxy* sketch entitled "Riley—Newspaper Correspondent." (The San Francisco city directory provides some corroboration of Riley's employment history,
listing him in 1862 as a "collector" for a grain brokerage.) Riley's ability
as a raconteur—as well as his love of smoking—endeared him to Clemens, who recalled the "unfailing vein of irony which makes his conversation to the last degree entertaining" (SLC 1870m; Langley 1862, 330,
381).

406.13   the "Prodigal."] See the note at 377.3–12.

406.35–407.22   another child of misfortune . . . This mendicant Blucher]
Clemens explicitly identified this Blucher (not to be confused with the
callow "Blucher" of *The Innocents Abroad*) as John Henry Riley in a
letter of 29 June 1871 to Mary Mason Fairbanks. Riley (1830?–72) was
a Philadelphian who emigrated to California in 1849 and held a variety
of jobs, including that of a newspaper reporter in San Francisco, before
he sailed for Washington, D.C., in November 1865. There he worked
for congressional committees, corresponded for the San Francisco *Alta
California*, and attained prominence among the corps of journalists.
For a time in the winter of 1867–68 he and Clemens shared lodgings in
Washington. Late in 1870, Clemens persuaded him to collaborate on a
book about the South African diamond mines. He spent several
months of 1871 in South Africa at Clemens's expense, gathering material for the project, and at the same time managed to secure an appointment as consul-general in the United States for the Orange Free State.
He died of cancer in September 1872—about a year after his return
from Africa—and the diamond-mine book was never written (SLC to
Fairbanks, 29 June 71, CSmH, in *MTMF*, 155–56; *MTMF*, 115; SLC
1870m; biographical information in CU-MARK, courtesy of Gerald
Thompson; Langley 1863, 306; "For the East," San Francisco *Alta California*, 10 Nov 65, 1; obituary notice dated 4 Dec 72, Bloemfontein
[Orange Free State] *Gouvernements Courant*, PH in CU-MARK; SLC
to Riley, 2 Dec 70, CU-MARK; Riley to SLC, 23 Mar 71 and 3 Dec 71,
CU-MARK).

408.27–409.1   the Miners' Restaurant . . . French Pete's . . . Martin's res-
taurant] The Miners' Restaurant was a chophouse on Commercial
Street—near the offices of the San Francisco *Morning Call*—known for
its "square meals," evidently paying "more regard . . . to . . . quantity
than quality" ("An Old Land-Mark Gone," Virginia City *Evening Bulletin*, 24 Oct 63, 4). Although "French Pete's" is not listed in the San
Francisco directories, it may have been a nickname for a second Miners' Restaurant (run by the same proprietors as the original one—Pierre

and Francis Cordier), located at the corner of Sansome and Merchant streets (see also the next note). Martin's (proprietor, Francisco Martin) was a high-toned establishment, also on Commercial Street, said to rival the better restaurants of New York; it was "much patronized by the Old Comstock crowd" (Edwords, 15; Langley 1860, 101, 210, 369; Langley 1859, 188; Neville, 136; Fletcher, 40).

411.7 Take the episode all around] A fragment of manuscript in Clemens's hand mentions an anecdote known to involve Riley, and then outlines the story related here, presumably also linked to him: "Found a dime—went up Kearney street—met poor man hungry—took him to Martin's and fed him—then we went to the miner's restaurant" (Anderson Auction Company, item 11: "we" may be a mistranscription of "he"). Clemens's inscription of "miner's restaurant" in this context supports the conjecture that "French Pete's" was the Cordiers' second Miners' Restaurant.

412.1–3 an old friend of mine, a miner, came down . . . and I went back with him] The old friend was James Norman (Jim) Gillis (1830–1907), the brother of Steve Gillis (see the note at 323.30–325.2). He was born in Georgia, and in 1848 obtained a medical degree in Memphis, Tennessee. The following year he went to San Francisco with his father, Angus Gillis. After an early period of ranching in Sacramento County, he spent most of the remainder of his life mining in Tuolumne County, living on Jackass Hill near Tuttletown. Periodically he visited San Francisco, where his parents lived; following such a visit late in 1864, he took Clemens back with him to his cabin on Jackass Hill. Clemens was spurred to leave San Francisco not only by his straitened financial circumstances, but by his fear that he would be called to honor a $500 bail bond he had posted for Steve Gillis, who had injured someone in a bar fight and fled to Nevada to escape prosecution. (In November 1866 the receipts from Clemens's second San Francisco lecture were confiscated to satisfy this bond: see "A Missionary's Troubles," San Francisco *Morning Call*, 18 Nov 66, 3.) Clemens arrived at Jackass Hill on 4 December 1864 and remained until 23 February 1865. Jim Gillis's wide-ranging intelligence and humor, his hospitality, and his love of nature were well known: Dan De Quille dubbed him the "Thoreau of the Sierras" and noted that his cabin was the "headquarters of all Bohemians visiting the mountains" (William Wright 1891). Clemens considered Gillis a "born humorist," a facile and imaginative spinner of "impromptu tales" (AD, 26 May 1907, CU-MARK, in *MTE*, 358–62). Among his creations were Dick Baker's tale of Tom Quartz, in the next chapter; the blue-jay yarn, in chapter 3 of *A Tramp Abroad*; and "The Tragedy of the Burning Shame," the basis for the Royal Nonesuch episode in chapter 23 of *Huckleberry Finn* ("James N. Gillis—His Life and Death," Sonora [Calif.] *Sierra Times*, 14 Apr 1907, clipping in CU-

MARK; Gillis, 17, 57–59; *L1*, 320–21; Fulton, 54–55; Goodwin, 90–94).

412.5–10 a flourishing city . . . fell into decay, and in a few years wholly disappeared] The first recorded discovery of gold on Jackass Hill was made in 1848 by the Means brothers, who earned an estimated ten thousand dollars from their claim. By 1849 well over three thousand miners were working in the immediate area, which was considered "without doubt the richest in the state" at the time (Heckendorn and Wilson, 80). The settlement on Jackass Hill, however, was never more than "a small community of homes, not a town, not even a village" (Gray, 8–13, 20). Within two years most of the miners had drifted away to more productive mining regions; the population of Tuolumne County reached a peak of over eighteen thousand in 1852, declining to eight thousand by 1870. The area nevertheless continued to yield significant amounts of gold: in January 1866, for example, the Gillis brothers struck a rich pocket that yielded up to forty dollars per pan (MacKinnon, 5, 79–80; Buckbee, 337).

412.25–30 One of my associates in this locality . . . for eighteen years he had decayed there . . . Latin and Greek sentences] None of Clemens's known acquaintances on Jackass Hill exactly fits this description, which may draw on at least two men, Dick Stoker (the model for Dick Baker in the next chapter) and Jim Gillis. In 1907 Clemens noted that Stoker had lived in his cabin for eighteen years by 1864 (he had actually lived there only fifteen years, since 1849: see the note at 416.4). Furthermore, Albert Bigelow Paine's description of Stoker as a passive, serene man who "had no world outside of the cabin and the hills, no affairs" is consistent with the portrait of this "decayed" miner (*MTB*, 1:267; AD, 26 May 1907, CU-MARK, in *MTE*, 362). While Stoker was "slenderly educated" (416.5–6), however, Gillis, in addition to having a medical degree, was reputed to know Latin and Greek (William Wright 1891).

413.6–419.28 In . . . me.] Mark Twain first published this passage in a Buffalo *Express* "Around the World" letter on 18 December 1869; he revised the earlier printing for inclusion in *Roughing It* (SLC 1869o).

416.4 Dick Baker, pocket-miner] In his Autobiographical Dictation of 26 May 1907 Clemens identified Baker as Dick Stoker, Jim Gillis's partner and cabinmate. Jacob Richard Stoker (1820–98), originally from Kentucky, left a successful business in Illinois to fight in the Mexican War. After the war, in 1849, he joined the California gold rush and went to Jackass Hill, where he remained, eking out a living as a pocket miner. Many years later, Jim Gillis's brother Steve recalled Stoker:

> Dick Stoker—dear, gentle unselfish old Dick—died over three years ago, aged 78. I am sure it will be a melancholy pleasure to Mark to know that Dick lived in comfort all his later life, sincerely loved and respected by all who knew him.

He never left Jackass Hill. He struck a pocket years ago containing enough not only to build himself a comfortable house near his old cabin, but to last him, without work, to his painless end. He was a Mason, and was buried by the Order in Sonora. (Undated letter to A. B. Paine, quoted in *MTL*, 1:171)

Clemens always held Stoker in affection, recalling with particular pleasure his portrayal of a character in Jim Gillis's skit "The Tragedy of the Burning Shame" (AD, 26 May 1907, CU-MARK, in *MTE*, 361; Stoker monument in the Masonic Cemetery, Sonora, photograph courtesy of Margaret Sanborn; Buckbee, 331; Gillis, 170–71; SLC to James Gillis, 26 Jan 70, PH in CU-MARK, courtesy of CCamarSJ, in *MTL*, 1:170–71).

416.4   Dead-Horse Gulch] A fictional name for Jackass Gulch, adjacent to Jackass Hill.

416.16–17   I heard him talking about this animal once] Although Baker (i.e., Stoker) is represented here as the narrator, Clemens later identified Jim Gillis as the author of the story of Tom Quartz:

> Every now and then Jim would have an inspiration, and he would stand up before the great log fire, with his back to it and his hands crossed behind him, and deliver himself of an elaborate impromptu lie—a fairy tale, an extravagant romance—with Dick Stoker as the hero of it as a general thing. Jim always soberly pretended that what he was relating was strictly history, veracious history, not romance. Dick Stoker, gray-headed and good-natured, would sit smoking his pipe and listen with a gentle serenity to these monstrous fabrications and never utter a protest. . . . I used another of Jim's inventions in one of my books, the story of Jim Baker's cat, the remarkable Tom Quartz. Jim Baker was Dick Stoker, of course; Tom Quartz had never existed; there was no such cat, at least outside of Jim Gillis's imagination. (AD, 26 May 1907, CU-MARK, in *MTE*, 360–62)

Mark Twain made many changes when revising the Buffalo *Express* printing of this story, primarily in the spelling of dialect pronunciations (such as " 'n'" for "and"), which brought the monologue closer to vernacular speech. Both the *Express* and the *Roughing It* versions were preceded by a manuscript sketch entitled "Remarkable Sagacity of a Cat," probably written in June 1868 (SLC 1868f).

419.37–38   We prospected around Angel's Camp, in Calaveras County, during three weeks] Clemens was at Angel's Camp, about seven miles northwest of Jackass Hill (across the Stanislaus River, the border with Calaveras County), between 22 January and 20 February 1865. Along with Gillis and Stoker, he spent some time prospecting, and some time sitting out the rainy weather listening to the conversation of the locals at the Angel's Hotel bar. During this time he made several notebook entries recording anecdotes that he would later include in *Roughing It* (*N&J1*, 66, 76–81).

420.7   post shovels] Shovels evidently used for digging ore: see the textual note.

420.10–14   I could give the reader a vivid description of the Big Trees . . . less conscientious tourists] It is unclear whether Mark Twain is referring to the giant sequoias at the Calaveras Grove of Big Trees, about twenty miles northeast of Angel's Camp, or to the more spectacular Mariposa Grove, about thirty-five miles south of Yosemite Valley, mentioned by most travelers visiting the valley (Hart, 72, 304). He was probably familiar with typically reverent accounts of these sites in such works as Richardson's *Beyond the Mississippi* (431–35), Bowles's *Our New West* (391–94), Ludlow's *The Heart of the Continent* (421– 24), and Greeley's *Overland Journey* (310–15). That he considered such accounts tiresome is suggested by an entry in his 1865–66 notebook: "Passenger volunteers account of journey to Big Trees & Yo Semite— & then Dan's old Ram" (*N&J1*, 172).

421.1–3 AFTER a three months' absence . . . I had become too mean and lazy, now, to work on a morning paper] Clemens returned to San Francisco on 26 February 1865, after an absence of twelve weeks. He seems to have earned only a minimal income over the next several months by writing occasional items for the Virginia City *Territorial Enterprise* and sketches for the *Californian,* the *California Youths' Companion,* and the San Francisco *Dramatic Chronicle* (*L1,* 321; SLC 1865a–r).

421.4–6 I was created San Francisco correspondent of the *Enterprise,* and at the end of five months I was out of debt] Mark Twain's daily correspondence for the *Enterprise,* for which he earned one hundred dollars a month, probably did not begin until the fall: the overwhelming majority of surviving *Enterprise* items date from after 10 October 1865, while only three survive from earlier in the year. Clemens was able to write to Orion and Mollie Clemens on 19 October 1865 that he had "gone to work in dead earnest" to get out of debt (*L1,* 324). Although the *Enterprise* files for the period are no longer extant, many of Mark Twain's letters are preserved in the Yale Scrapbook (see YSMT in References), and many more have been found reprinted in California and Nevada newspapers and magazines (SLC 1865s–t, 1865w, 1865ff, 1866a–d, 1866f–g). Besides his daily letter to the *Enterprise,* his effort in the five months between October 1865 and March 1866 included contributions to the San Francisco *Dramatic Chronicle* for forty dollars a month, correspondence for the *Napa County Reporter,* contributions to the *Californian* and the New York *Weekly Review,* and two pieces for the New York *Saturday Press,* one of which—"Jim Smiley and His Jumping Frog"—earned him his first major success with eastern readers (*ET&S2,* 481; SLC 1865u–v, 1865x–ee, 1866e, 1866h; *L1,* 327–28).

421.9–12 I got a new berth . . . for the Sacramento *Union,* an excellent journal and liberal with employés] Clemens traveled to Sacramento on 24 February 1866 to discuss the terms of his employment with the proprietors of the Sacramento *Union:* James Anthony, Paul Morrill, and Henry W. Larkin. Charles Henry Webb, who accompanied him, later asserted that he helped Clemens obtain the assignment. On 5 March Clemens informed his mother and sister: "I start to the Sandwich Islands day after to-morrow. . . . I only decided to-day to go. . . . I am to remain there a month & ransack the islands, . . . & write twenty or thirty letters to the Sacramento *Union*—for which they pay me as much money as I would get if I staid at home" (*L1*, 333, 333–34 n. 1; SLC 1866g). He later claimed that the *Union* proprietors—the "best men who ever owned a newspaper"—generously paid him "a great deal more than they promised," but the exact amount is not known (SLC 1899, 77; *L1*, 353; see the note at 533.5–6). Clemens remained in the islands for over four months and wrote twenty-five letters for the *Union*, thirteen of which he later revised to create chapters 63–69 and 71–74 of *Roughing It*.

421.13 We sailed in the propeller Ajax, in the middle of winter] Clemens departed on 7 March 1866 aboard the California Steam Navigation Company's steamer *Ajax*, which was making its second voyage to Honolulu (*L1*, 331 n. 10, 334 n. 1).

421.17–20 Williams, and three sea-worn old whaleship captains . . . drank astonishing quantities of raw whisky] The *Ajax* passenger list does not include any "Williams," nor does this "quiet passenger" (as he is described at 426.6) appear in Mark Twain's letters to the *Union*. Mark Twain probably did not draw Williams from life, but rather created him to serve as the nemesis of "the old Admiral" (see the next note). The sea captains listed on the *Ajax*'s roster were James Smith, W. H. Phillips, and A. W. Fish, whom Mark Twain—in his first two letters to the *Union*—called Cuttle, Phelps, and Fitch. He reported that during the voyage they consumed nineteen gallons of whiskey while playing euchre and exchanging nautical banter in the ship's smoking room (*Ajax* passenger list, PH in CU-MARK; SLC 1866i–j; see also *N&J1*, 191, 196).

421.22–423.19 "the old Admiral"—a retired whaleman . . . was around] The prototype of this character was Captain James Smith (1800–77), whom Mark Twain included on a list of ideal shipmates published in January 1868, referring to him as "Admiral Jim Smith, late of Hawaiian Navy" (SLC 1868b). Smith began his long sea career at the age of twelve as a cabin boy aboard a privateer during the War of 1812. He commanded a whaleship out of New London, Connecticut, for a number of years before being connected with the earliest line of sailing packets between San Francisco and Honolulu—the "Regular Dispatch Line"— as captain of the *Yankee* and the *Comet*. Smith's death in August 1877 resulted in a well-publicized estate dispute that was not resolved in the courts until October 1879. Members of Smith's family attempted to show that "the testator was unsound in mind, and unduly influenced when he made his will," even soliciting Clemens's affidavit—based on his shipboard acquaintance with the captain—to that effect. Testimony failed to support their case, revealing Smith as "an obstinate, clear-headed, profane, hot-tempered old fellow, who swore by Andrew Jackson, Jeff Davis, the New York *Sun* and *World*, and was no more susceptible to influence than a congressman is to the grace of God" (unidentified clipping enclosed in Helen R. Fitch to SLC, 16 Sept 79, CU-MARK). A third of Smith's considerable estate was left to his Hawaiian protégé, John Kellett, who, at age sixteen, was Smith's companion aboard the *Ajax* in March 1866 (Caulkins, 643; Decker, 82; Kuykendall 1953, 17, 265 n. 40; Hartford *Courant:* "Deaths," 24 Aug 77, 2; "The Last of a Privateer's Crew," 25 Aug 77, 4; "News of the State," 7 Oct 79, 4; Honolulu *Pacific Commercial Advertiser:* "Death of Capt. James Smith," 22 Sept 77, 3; "Passengers," 24 Mar 66, 2; *Ajax* passenger list, PH in CU-MARK).

425.14–15 At his heels frisked the darling . . . terrier "Fan,"] Gladys Bellamy has pointed out the similarity between Mark Twain's portrait of the admiral and his dog and the description of General Tecumseh Brown and his beloved bullterrier, also named "Fan," in John Phoenix's "A Legend of the Tehama House" (Bellamy, 33; Derby, 254–69).

425.21–22 "The Old Guard," a secession periodical published in New York] *The Old Guard*, a New York monthly published from June 1862 to December 1870, was "the only consistently anti-Lincoln magazine published in the North during the war" (Mott, 544–46). In an 1866 notebook entry Clemens made reference to Smith's "secesh" sympathies (*N&J1*, 191).

431.1 the Islands hove in sight] The *Ajax* docked at Honolulu at 11 A.M. on Sunday, 18 March ("The Pioneer Steam Line," Honolulu *Pacific Commercial Advertiser*, 24 Mar 66, 2).

431.9–434.2 then . . . sail—] Mark Twain based this portion of the text (except for the paragraph at 432.11–433.11) on his letter in the Sacramento *Union* of 19 April 1866, revising it for inclusion in *Roughing It* (SLC 1866l).

431.26–27 San Francisco's pleasure grove, the "Willows,"] Clemens was well acquainted with this popular resort, located at Mission and Eighteenth streets, whose attractions included a hotel and restaurant, gardens with tables and chairs, a minstrel and variety theater, an aquarium and zoo, and facilities for bowling and dancing (*ET&S1*, 494).

432.3–4 I saw cats] On 19 May the Honolulu *Advertiser* reported the publication of Mark Twain's first letters to the *Union* and reprinted much of his description of Honolulu, commenting: "His letters abound in genuine good humor and fun, though if he would stick a little closer to facts, they would be more reliable." In particular, the passage on cats struck the *Advertiser* as apocryphal: "We half suspect he brought the cats with him," suggested the paper ("Mark Twain," Honolulu *Pacific Commercial Advertiser,* 19 May 66, 1). Soon after his arrival in Honolulu, however, Clemens wrote in his notebook, "1000ˢ of cats and nary snake" (*N&J1,* 220).

435.9–17 they were rather sour that year . . . it will come off when the enamel does] Mark Twain adapted this description of tamarind tasting from a similar account, in a section entitled "Fruit," in his letter in the Sacramento *Union* of 20 April. He did not use this letter elsewhere in *Roughing It* (SLC 1866m).

436.1–441.20 IN my diary . . . itself.] In fact, Mark Twain did not draw on either of his two extant Hawaiian notebooks for this chapter (notebooks 5 and 6 in *N&J1,* 91–237). Rather he based this portion of the text on his letter in the Sacramento *Union* of 21 April 1866, revising it for inclusion in *Roughing It;* he reserved a section of the letter for use in the next chapter (SLC 1866n; see the note at 444.16–448.18).

436.9 the Government Prison] Mark Twain described his visit to this "model prison of the western half of the world"—completed in 1857 on the outskirts of Honolulu—in his letter in the *Union* of 21 May, but he used none of the account in *Roughing It* (Scott, 856; SLC 1866p).

436.10 Capt. Fish . . . Capt. Phillips] See the note at 421.17–20. Clemens recorded in his notebook that both captains had been victims of the Confederate privateer *Shenandoah,* which destroyed a number of Pacific whaling vessels (*N&J1,* 113, 182).

436.15 Capt. Cook] Captain James Cook (1728–79)—English circumnavigator, explorer of the Pacific Ocean, and first European to reach the Sandwich Islands—was killed by natives on 14 February 1779 at Kealakekua Bay on the island of Hawaii. Mark Twain recounts the events surrounding his death in chapter 71 (490.39–491.24).

436.19 the American Hotel] This hotel opened for business at the beginning of March 1866 on the "premises lately occupied by the British Consul" ("American House," *Friend* 17 [1 Mar 66]: 17). Clemens, with other *Ajax* passengers, took some of his meals there, but roomed in a nearby cottage ("American House," Honolulu *Pacific Commercial Advertiser,* 3 Mar 66, 3, and 10 Mar 66, 1; MTH, 19–22; SLC 1866m).

437.10–438.7 Inside of five minutes I was mounted . . . plunging of the Ajax in a storm] This description of the horse "Oahu" recalls an amusing sketch by George Washington Bates about his own recalcitrant "steed" in his 1854 account of a visit to the islands, *Sandwich Island Notes,* a book Clemens had read. Bates, the perspiring rider, attempts to whip his horse into consistent motion, but "he would trot, walk, or come to a stand, just as it suited him; and when I arrived at an elevation of the road, he stood as still as a sculptured war-steed" (Bates, 127). The

horse suddenly breaks into a mad gallop, before lapsing again into som-
nolence. "On the whole, it was a curious performance, but very far from
being agreeable" (Bates, 129). Early in his Sandwich Islands trip, Clemens filled many notebook pages with references from Bates's book—
without citing his source, which has now been identified for the first
time (N&J1, 210–15). Bates's narrative, while it furnishes abundant
evidence of the author's chauvinism and his disdain toward the islanders, is leavened by humor and treats frankly the discomforts and incon-
gruities of island travel and native life. Its author remains mysterious:
references in two extensive reviews of the book in the *Polynesian* suggest that Bates (also known as William Baker) was incarcerated in a
New York prison sometime in 1854 or 1855, apparently for bigamy
(*Polynesian:* 12 [11 Aug 55]: 53–54; 12 [1 Sept 55]: 66).

439.11–22   About a dozen cottages . . . "The King's Grove."] In his 21
April *Union* letter Mark Twain identified this place as "Waikiki . . . ,
once the Capital of the kingdom" (SLC 1866n). After Europeans discovered Honolulu harbor in 1793, the importance of nearby Waikiki diminished, although at the time of Clemens's visit it was still the royal
summer residence. The current king was Kamehameha V (see the note
at 462.4; Whitney, 26).

440.20–441.3   This ancient temple was built of rough blocks . . . Kamehameha . . . impaled their heads on the walls] Mark Twain's description of this site, located about a mile outside the village of Waikiki, and
of Kamehameha's vengeful display there owes some of its details to
James Jackson Jarves's *Scenes and Scenery in the Sandwich Islands*
(Jarves 1844a, 59–60).

440.35–441.1   When Kamehameha . . . took full and final possession of
the country] Through military triumphs and alliances between 1782
and 1810, Kamehameha (1758?–1819) gradually consolidated his
power beyond his native island of Hawaii, ultimately uniting the islands and ruling as Kamehameha I. The decisive victory occurred in
1795 when, at the battle of Nuuanu on the island of Oahu, he completed the conquest of all the principal islands except Kauai, whose
king did not acknowledge Kamehameha's sovereignty until 1810. For
the quarter century following the battle, Kamehameha's skilled management of domestic and foreign affairs assured the stability and independence of the kingdom and established the dynasty that was to follow. Mark Twain's information about Kamehameha's victory on Oahu,
here and in chapter 65, relies on Jarves's accounts in his *History of the
Hawaiian Islands* and its companion volume, *Scenes and Scenery in
the Sandwich Islands* (Kuykendall 1938, 32–61, 429–30; Jarves 1847,
92; Jarves 1844a, v–vi, 60).

440.36   a sort of a Napoleon] See the note at 469.34.

441.11–20 The missionaries have clothed them . . . Their work speaks for itself] In a number of published statements, Clemens reiterated his generally favorable assessment of the missionaries' role in the islands. He first listed the "benefit conferred" by them in early August 1866, in one of his Hawaiian notebooks (N&J1, 154; MTH, 128–48).

442.6–444.15 Gayly . . . business.] Mark Twain based this portion of the text on his letter in the Sacramento Union of 24 April 1866, revising it for inclusion in Roughing It (SLC 1866o). The "we" in the opening sentence of the chapter refers to the "half a dozen gentlemen and three ladies" whom he had intended to accompany (436.7–8). In revising the Union printing he deleted his report of catching up to his party.

442.11–12 We picked up a lot of them for mementoes] Clemens mentioned his explorations of Oahu's "ancient battle-fields & other places of interest" to his mother and sister in a letter of 3 April 1866 and added: "I have got a lot of human bones which I took from one of these battle-fields—I guess I will bring you some of them" (L1, 334).

443.24 the Pari] In his Union letter Mark Twain supplied a parenthetical explanation of the term "Pari" at this point: "pronounced Pally; intelligent natives claim that there is no r in the Kanaka alphabet" (SLC 1866o). Early writings on the Sandwich Islands used variant spellings of some sounds (such as "l/r" and "k/t"), reflecting regional differences in pronunciation. The spelling "Pari" was less common than "Pali," which became the standard form (Jarves 1847, 46; Ellis, 13–17; Charles Samuel Stewart, 95).

443.26 Mr. Jarves's excellent history] During his stay in the islands, Clemens made use of the extensive library of a Honolulu friend, Samuel Chenery Damon (1815–85), chaplain of the American Seamen's Friend Society, pastor of the Oahu Bethel Church, and publisher and editor of the Friend, a monthly newspaper. "I take your Jarves' History with me, because I may not be able to get it at home," Clemens confessed to his friend just before his departure for San Francisco in July; "I 'cabbage' it by the strong arm" (L1, 349). The copy he appropriated was almost certainly the third edition of Jarves's History of the Hawaiian Islands, published in Honolulu in 1847: Clemens quoted at length from this edition in two Union letters, one of which was used for Roughing It (see the notes at 469.30–470.5 and 470.11–472.43; SLC 1866x, 1866aa). His borrowing of the Jarves book was the subject of some humorous chaffing in the Hawaiian press. He finally mailed the book back to Damon in May 1867 (SLC 1867h; MTH, 155–63; L1, 349–50).

444.16–448.18 This . . . expense.] Mark Twain based this portion of the text on his letter in the Sacramento Union of 21 April 1866, revising it for inclusion in *Roughing It*; he used the beginning and end of this letter in the previous chapter (SLC 1866n; see the note at 436.1–441.20).

445.33   J. Smith] This may be a reference to Clemens's shipboard acquaintance Captain James Smith (see the note at 421.22–423.19), although that identification is belied by an entry of March 1866 in one of Clemens's notebooks: "No good livery horses—put em on ranch, Kanakas hire em out or ride em to death. Trick they played Wheelock by keeping their own blanket on sore-back horse" (*N&J1*, 219). A "Mr. Wheelack" had arrived in Honolulu from San Francisco on 7 January 1866 and had stayed at the Volcano House on the island of Hawaii in early March ("Passengers," *Friend* 17 [1 Feb 66]: 16; Volcano House Register, 74).

447.4   a certain Mr. L.] "Mr. L." is more fully identified in the *Union* text as "Leland" (SLC 1866n). Lewis Leland (1834–97) was the proprietor—until 1868—of San Francisco's Occidental Hotel, where Clemens made several sojourns in the mid-1860s. In 1868 Clemens named Leland as a reference, assuring Jervis Langdon, his future father-in-law, that Leland had known him "intimately for 3 or 4 years" (*L2*, 359). Clemens frequently mentioned the convivial Leland in his reporting, and recounted a humorous anecdote of Leland's January 1866 trip to Honolulu aboard the *Ajax* for his *Enterprise* readers (SLC 1866f).

447.31   Williams] The fictional Williams also figures in Mark Twain's account of the *Ajax* voyage in chapter 62 (see the note at 421.17–20). The *Union* text for the present passage, however, reads "Brown," the name Mark Twain gave to a comic figure appearing throughout the *Union* letters, first as a passenger aboard the *Ajax*. (The ship's passenger list did include a merchant named "W. H. Brown," but he returned to San Francisco on 4 April 1866 and thus could not have been the Brown of the *Union* letters, who supposedly accompanied Clemens on his excursion to the island of Hawaii in May and June.) The boisterous and vulgar Brown, who reappears in Mark Twain's 1866–67 letters to the San Francisco *Alta California,* is undoubtedly a composite creation, a comic foil incorporating elements of Clemens's own personality with those of some actual companions. In revising the *Union* letters for *Roughing It* Clemens consistently deleted passages involving Brown, or changed his name, as he did in this instance (SLC 1866n; *Ajax* passenger list, PH in CU-MARK; *N&J1*, 182 n. 6; "Passengers," *Friend* 17 [1 May 66]: 40).

449.2–6   I recognize a familiar home air . . . "When we were marching through Georgia."] Mark Twain derived this remark from his 24 April *Union* letter, in which he commented, "If it would have been all the same to General Sherman, I wish he had gone around by the way of the Gulf of Mexico" (SLC 1866o). Henry Clay Work (1832–84) wrote the lyrics and music for "Marching through Georgia" in 1865 to commemorate General Sherman's Georgia campaign of late 1864. Mark Twain had protested being "attacked, front and rear," by this immensely popular song in a letter to the *Enterprise* in late 1865 (SLC 1865w). A few months later, in one of his Hawaiian notebooks, he wrote: "I wish Sherman had marched through Alabama," and in December 1866 he included the song in a list of "the d—dest, oldest, vilest songs" (*N&J1*, 228, 262).

450.1–453.37 PASSING . . . art.] Mark Twain based this portion of the text on his letter in the Sacramento *Union* of 21 May 1866, revising it for inclusion in *Roughing It* (SLC 1866p).

450.3–451.14 The native girls . . . encircle their dusky throats with . . . vermillion-tinted blossom of the *ohia*] This description of the riding style and costume of the native girls owes much to Jarves's chapter covering Honolulu "street scenes" and "Saturday afternoon" activities in *Scenes and Scenery*. Furthermore, one of Clemens's early Hawaiian notebook entries reads "*Ohia* wreaths—crimson—& feathers" (*N&J1*, 215), referring to the following passage in Jarves's book: "Their hair is either done up after the latest fashions imitated from the foreign ladies, or is encircled with rich and expensive wreaths made from feathers. The less wealthy wear those made from the beautiful crimson blossoms of the *ohia* tree" (Jarves 1844a, 47, 53).

451.37–452.17 Poi is the chief article of food . . . it produces acrid humors] Mark Twain derived his information about poi from Jarves's *History:*

> Poi, the principal article of diet, was prepared from the kalo [taro] plant. The roots, after being baked under ground, were mashed on a large platter, by a heavy stone pestle, or an instrument made of lava, resembling a stirrup, and were mixed with water, until a thick paste was formed. This is sometimes eaten in a sweet state, but generally put aside until it ferments, in which condition it is preferred. It is a highly nutricious substance, though, when solely used, has a tendency to produce acrid humors. (Jarves 1847, 42)

452.36–453.1 The natives manufacture an intoxicating drink from it which . . . causes premature decrepitude] According to Jarves, the effects of awa "were very pernicious, covering the body with a white scurf, or scaliness, like the scurvy, inflaming the eyes, and causing premature decrepitude. It was also taken as a medicine" (Jarves 1847, 49). The narcotic drink was made from the root of the kava (*piper methysticum*), a shrub native to the Pacific islands, and had a bitter, unpleasant taste. Clemens again referred to it in an article entitled "The Sandwich Islands," written for the New York *Tribune* in 1873 (SLC 1873c; Pukui and Elbert, 30; Ellis, 386).

453.32–35 The demoralizing *hula-hula* was forbidden to be performed, save . . . only by permission . . . and the payment of ten dollars] The restrictions on the performance of the hula were part of the Civil Code of 1859 and resulted from legislative pressure brought by Prince Lot Kamehameha (later Kamehameha V). Clemens also referred to the ten-dollar fee in a Hawaiian notebook: "Have to take out a license ($10,) to have the Hulahula dance performed, & then if the girls dress for it in the usual manner, that is with no clothing worth mentioning, it must be conducted in strict privacy" (N&J1, 221).

454.3–4   It is the most universally educated race of people] In one of his Hawaiian notebooks Clemens made the following entry, based on a passage in Bates's *Sandwich Island Notes:* "* No place where *public* education so widely diffused | * Children of ten—all read & write" (N&J1, 210; Bates, 63).

454.11–13   contact with civilization . . . has reduced the native population . . . to *fifty-five thousand*] In a Hawaiian notebook Clemens noted: "*Certainly* were 400,000 here in Cook's time—& even in 1820" (N&J1, 129). Captain Cook had estimated the population to be 400,000 in 1778, but Captain George Vancouver

> some fifteen years after, puts it at a much lower figure, and intimates that Cook was misled by the multitudes that flocked to the shores whenever his ships appeared. But the fact nevertheless remains, that the natives have, since their first intercourse with foreigners, decreased at a fearful rate. (Bennett, 3)

Another estimate, probably more accurate, put the population at 142,000 in 1823; the official 1866 census figure was 58,765 (Bennett, 59).

454.16–456.6   If . . . "shoved."] Mark Twain based this portion of the text on his letter in the Sacramento *Union* of 20 April 1866, revising it for inclusion in *Roughing It*. Before reusing the material in *Roughing It* he had already reprinted it as a sketch entitled "Honored As a Curiosity in Honolulu" in *The Celebrated Jumping Frog of Calaveras County* (SLC 1866m, 1867a). Clemens also made the following related notebook entry in March–April 1866: "If you don't know a man in Hon—call him Capt & ask him how many barrels he took last season—chances are he's a whaler" (N&J1, 225).

457.1–458.18   I STILL quote from my journal . . . etc., etc.] Mark Twain based this portion of the text on his letter in the Sacramento *Union* of 20 June 1866, revising it for inclusion in *Roughing It*. This material is not found in either of Clemens's extant Hawaiian notebooks, but it may derive from a missing notebook that he used from mid-April to mid-June 1866 (SLC 1866v; N&J1, 100–101).

457.5–6   David Kalakaua (the King's Chamberlain)] Kalakaua (1836–91) held the office of chamberlain and secretary to Kamehameha V at a salary of $2,500 per year. Clemens met Kalakaua early in his stay in the islands, when, on 3 April, he was among Kalakaua's guests at a dinner in honor of James McBride, the American minister. Kalakaua was also scheduled to accompany Clemens on a visit to Iolani Palace on 4 April (see the note at 462.4). Mark Twain described Kalakaua in a *Union* letter:

> [He] is a man of fine presence, is an educated gentleman and a man of good abilities. He is approaching forty, I should judge—is thirty-five, at any rate. He is conservative, politic and calculating, makes little display, and does not talk much in the Legislature. He is a quiet, dignified, sensible man, and would do no discredit to the kingly office. (SLC 1866x)

Kalakaua, a descendant of ancient Hawaiian chiefs, became king in February 1874 after an abortive attempt to secure the throne in 1873. He reigned until his death in January 1891 in San Francisco (Honolulu *Pacific Commercial Advertiser:* "The Budget," 5 May 66, 1; "Audience at the Palace," 28 July 66, 3; *MTH,* 31; *L1,* 334; Withington, 229–34, 249, 275).

457.6 Prince William] As Kamehameha V's cousin and the grandson of a half-brother of Kamehameha I, the popular William Charles Lunalilo (1835–74) was widely recognized as the likely successor to the throne. Mark Twain noted in a *Union* letter that Lunalilo was

> of the highest blood in the kingdom—higher than the King himself, it is said. . . . Prince William is a man of fine, large build; is thirty-one years of age; is affable, gentlemanly, open, frank, manly; is as independent as a lord and has a spirit and a will like the old Conqueror himself. He is intelligent, shrewd, sensible—is a man of first rate abilities, in fact. . . . I like this man, and I like his bold independence, and his friendship for and appreciation of the American residents. (SLC 1866x)

In two articles entitled "The Sandwich Islands," published in the New York *Tribune* on 6 and 9 January 1873, Mark Twain, although acknowledging Lunalilo's excessive fondness for whiskey, urged that he be chosen as the next king. Lunalilo was elected—by popular and legislative vote—to succeed Kamehameha V in January 1873, but he reigned only briefly, until his death in February 1874 (SLC 1873b–c; *N&J1,* 124; Kuykendall 1953, 240, 242–44; Withington, 229–39).

457.6–9 The President of the Assembly, his Royal Highness M. Kekuanaoa,* . . . the King's father] Mataio Kekuanaoa (1794–1868) and his wife, the high chiefess Kinau (see the note at 458.13), were the parents of Kamehameha IV, Kamehameha V, and Princess Victoria. Kekuanaoa served as governor of Oahu from his wife's death in 1839 until 1864. In the administration of Kamehameha V, Kekuanaoa served as president of the legislature and of the Board of Education, and as *kuhina nui* (preeminent adviser and chief administrator) to the king, until the abolition of that office in 1864. Mark Twain may not have learned of Kekuanaoa's death until the fall of 1871, after this chapter had already been set in type and it was too late to insert the words "Since dead" (457n.1) into the body of the text ("Death of His Highness Mataio Kekuanaoa," Honolulu *Pacific Commercial Advertiser,* 28 Nov 68, 2; Bailey, 225–

26; Kuykendall 1938, 64; Kuykendall 1953, 107, 126; Varigny, 138, 168; W. D. Alexander, 289).

457.7–8 the Vice President (the latter a white man,)] The vice-president of the legislature was Honolulu merchant Godfrey Rhodes (1815–97), an Englishman resident in the islands since the 1840s who was known for his anti-American sentiments (Varigny, 252; Kuykendall 1953, 255; "Opening of the Legislature," Honolulu *Pacific Commercial Advertiser*, 28 Apr 66, 2).

458.2–3 the honored guest of royalty in Europe] Kekuanaoa had been one of the party that accompanied Kamehameha II on an ill-fated voyage to England in 1823–24. Both Kamehameha and his favorite queen, Kamamalu, died of the measles before they could be received by King George IV, but others of the party, including Kekuanaoa, met with him in September 1824 (Kuykendall 1938, 76–79).

458.13 his wife, who was a daughter of Kamehameha the Great] Kinau (d. 1839), whom Kekuanaoa married in October 1827, was a daughter of Kamehameha I. From June 1832 until her death she served as *kuhina nui* to Kamehameha III (Kuykendall 1938, 133–36; Bennett, 68–69).

458.21–23 a popular belief that . . . your enemy can . . . *pray you to death*] This phenomenon—and the related ability to *"die whenever they want to"* (459.21–22)—was frequently reported by early visitors to the islands (Archibald Campbell, 172–73; Charles Samuel Stewart, 202–3; Dibble 1839, 61–62, 77–78; Jarves 1847, 24–25, 99; Bates, 396–97). Clemens's interest in the subject is evidenced by an entry in one of his Hawaiian notebooks, as well as references in his Sandwich Islands lecture and in the fragments of a Sandwich Islands novel that he began in 1884 (*N&J1*, 117; SLC 1866kk, 1884a).

459.21–22 the natives are able to *lie down and die whenever they want to*] Clemens witnessed what he thought was an instance of this phenomenon while staying with Samuel G. Wilder and his family on Oahu. When the family's nursemaid died, he noted in his journal: "Her father died last week—nothing matter with the girl—just thought she was going to die" (*N&J1*, 128).

459.31 the Great Shark God] Mark Twain identified the Great Shark God as "Kauhuhu" in his 1866 piece "A Strange Dream." Kauhuhu was one of many powerful shark gods worshiped by the Hawaiians, a "fierce king shark of Maui who lives in a cave in Kipahulu and also has a home . . . on the windward side of Molokai" (SLC 1866t; Beckwith, 129).

461.14–25 a brown, stately dame . . . with nothing . . . but a "stovepipe" hat . . . a fiery neck-tie and a striped vest] A similar description in Bates's *Sandwich Island Notes* may have inspired Mark Twain:

When civilized habits first dawned upon them, their personal appearance was the most eccentric that can well be imagined. In coming to church on a Sunday, one man would come clad in nothing but a coat buttoned up on his back instead of in front. The entire wardrobe of a second would be a ragged cravat, and a single strip of native cloth crossed over his loins, called a *malo;* that of a third, the *malo,* and a pair of high boots; that of a fourth, the *malo,* and a tattered palm-leaf hat that might have served some foreigner nearly a score of years; that of a fifth, a shirt, with a collar reaching his eyes and half way up the back of his head, and the *malo.* (Bates, 262)

462.4 his royal Majesty the King] Kamehameha V (1830–72), known as Lot Kamehameha, reigned from 1863 until his death. Said to resemble his grandfather Kamehameha I, he was a capable and forceful administrator. Clemens was impressed with his abilities; in his 9 January 1873 *Tribune* article he described him as a "wise sovereign" who "tried hard to do well by his people, and succeeded. There was no trivial royal nonsense about him" (SLC 1873c). Clemens intended to meet Kamehameha V at Iolani Palace on 4 April 1866. Although he visited the palace, he apparently did not see the king, since he mentioned in 1873 that he only saw him "but once, . . . attending the funeral of his sister," Princess Victoria Kamamalu (SLC 1873c; Bennett, 7; Kuykendall 1938, 27–28; Jarves 1844a, 59; Kuykendall 1953, 125–26; *L1,* 334–35).

462.4–9 with a New York detective's income of thirty . . . thousand dollars a year from the . . . "royal domain."] As Clemens correctly states, Kamehameha V had two sources of income for the period of 1866 through 1868: an annual salary of $17,500, and income from the Crown Lands amounting to about $20,000 a year (Honolulu *Pacific Commercial Advertiser:* "Hawaiian Legislature," 5 May 66, 3; "Report of the Minister of Finance to the Legislature of 1866," 5 May 66, 4).

462.9–10 two-story frame "palace."] Iolani Palace, built in 1844–45, was a large square building with wide verandas on all sides. It was set in grounds "extensive enough to accommodate a village," according to Mark Twain, and afforded a panoramic view of Honolulu (SLC 1866s). The original palace was replaced in 1879 by a much grander structure (Scott, 113).

463.3–8 his Excellency the "royal Chamberlain" . . . the Commander-in-chief of the Household Troops, whose forces . . . under a corporal in other lands] Both of these titles belonged to the same man. David Kalakaua, the king's chamberlain (see the note at 457.5–6), was also—as Mark Twain mentioned in his 6 January 1873 article in the New York *Tribune*—commander-in-chief of the Household Troops. Kalakaua, who held the rank of colonel, reportedly "took a special interest in military matters, and was fond of appearing in elaborate military uniforms. Being tall and well built, he modeled such uniforms with great distinction" (Kuykendall 1967, 13). The Household Troops, comprising one hundred native soldiers, constituted the standing army and were charged with guarding the palace, the prison, and the treasury (SLC 1873c; Zambucka 1983, 10; Honolulu *Pacific Commercial Ad-*

vertiser: "Audience at the Palace," 28 July 66, 3; "Majority Report of the Military Committee," 23 May 68, 4; "The Mutiny at the Barracks," 13 Sept 73, 2).

463.9–12 the royal Steward and the Grand Equerry in Waiting . . . the First Gentleman of the Bed-chamber] These positions were not listed in the official government budget, and may have been invented by Mark Twain to add color to his description of how the "grown folk . . . play 'empire'" (462.2–4).

463.13–464.9 his Excellency the Prime Minister, a renegade American . . . his Excellency the Imperial Minister of Finance . . . all for four thousand dollars a year and unimaginable glory] There was at this time no official position of prime minister in the Hawaiian government. The "renegade American from New Hampshire" and the "Imperial Minister of Finance" were in fact the same person—Charles Coffin Harris (1821–81), the minister of finance and Kamehameha V's closest adviser. Harris was a native of New Hampshire who settled in the Sandwich Islands in 1850, practiced law, engaged in business, and, in 1862, began an association with the government that culminated in his becoming chief justice in 1877. His salary was $4,000 in 1866. As a member of the Hawaiian Reformed Catholic Church, he was considered an enemy of the American Protestant mission. Mark Twain first expressed his violent antipathy toward Harris—after observing him during a visit to the Hawaiian legislature—in a *Union* letter published on 21 June 1866; he continued his ridicule in several subsequent newspaper letters (SLC 1866w, 1866z–aa; see also the remark about Harris's vanity at 469.20–25). In a letter of 20 December 1870 to Albert Francis Judd of Honolulu, Clemens mentioned his plan to "do up the Islands & Harris" in some form in "2 or 3" years (PH in CtY-BR, in *MTH,* 467). Beyond his scathing remarks in *Roughing It,* however, plus similar comments in his 9 January 1873 *Tribune* article, Mark Twain is not known to have written anything further about Harris ("The Late Justice Harris of Hawaii," New York *Times,* 27 July 81, 3; Honolulu *Pacific Commercial Advertiser:* "'The Budget,'" 5 May 66, 1; "Estimated Expenditures for the Two Years Ending March 31, 1870," 25 Apr 68, 3; "Death of the Chief Justice," 9 July 81, 2; "Death of the Late Chancellor," *Friend* 30 [1 Aug 81]: 69; Kuykendall 1953, 36, 96–98, 126–28, 218; *MTH,* 27–28; SLC 1867i, 1873c).

464.5–8 a million dollars of public money a year . . . the "national debt" (of a hundred and fifty thousand dollars,)] Mark Twain's figure is more than double the Sandwich Islands' actual budget. The two-year budget for 1866 to 1868 was $826,823, and for the following two years, $997,680. His figure for the national debt, however, is more accurate: in April 1866 it stood at $166,649, and in March 1870 at $112,000 (Honolulu *Pacific Commercial Advertiser:* "'The Budget,'" 5 May 66, 1;

"Report of the Minister of Finance to the Legislature of 1866," 5 May 66, 4; "Our National Finances," 21 May 70, 2).

464.10–11 his Excellency the Minister of War, who holds sway over the royal armies] This title was Mark Twain's invention: although there was a Department of War, it had no minister. Charles de Varigny (1829–99), as minister of foreign affairs, had overall charge of the Hawaiian military, which consisted of the Household Troops and various volunteer companies. Varigny was born at Versailles, settled in the Sandwich Islands in 1855, and received his first government appointment in 1864. Mark Twain described him as a "sensible, unpretentious" man, but added: "If Varigny were as hopelessly bad as his English pronunciation, nothing but a special intervention of Providence could save him from perdition hereafter" (SLC 1866w; Varigny, 255, 258, 261; Honolulu *Pacific Commercial Advertiser:* "'The Budget,'" 5 May 66, 1; "Estimated Expenditures for the Two Years Ending March 31, 1870," 25 Apr 68, 3).

464.17–18 some venerable swivels on Punch-Bowl Hill] Puahi, or Punch-Bowl Hill, was an extinct crater half a mile behind Honolulu. According to Jarves, it "obtained its soubriquet in times not quite as temperate as the present; its shape internally is much like a bowl, being a gradual and uniform hollow" (Jarves 1844a, 23). Bates described the battery on its summit as consisting of "eleven guns, pointing different ways, at irregular distances from each other. . . . They rest on carriages in a state of rapid decay" (Bates, 100).

464.20–21 his Excellency the Minister of the Navy—a nabob who rules the "royal fleet," (a steam-tug and a sixty-ton schooner.)] There was no naval ministry; responsibility for a tugboat in Honolulu harbor, the *Pele,* fell to the minister of the interior—F. W. Hutchinson, an Englishman. The *Pele,* launched in 1856, was in service at Honolulu for thirty years. In June 1866, during Clemens's visit, it was fitted with a "small rifle of suitable caliber" so that it could be classed as a gunboat (Mifflin Thomas, 41, 221 n. 30). Nothing is known about the "sixty-ton schooner" (" 'The Budget,'" Honolulu *Pacific Commercial Advertiser,* 5 May 66, 1; Varigny, 195; W. D. Alexander, 329).

464.22–28 his Grace the Lord Bishop of Honolulu . . . a cheap ready-made Bishop from England to take charge] In 1860 Kamehameha IV, motivated in part by a desire to reinforce the Hawaiian monarchy, petitioned Queen Victoria to establish a branch of the Anglican (Episcopal) church in the Sandwich Islands. Despite protests from the American missionary community, the "Hawaiian Reformed Catholic Church" was created. Thomas Nettleship Staley (1823–98), a recently consecrated English bishop, arrived in Honolulu in October 1862 to serve as its head. Within a few weeks, Staley had confirmed as members of his church Kamehameha IV and Queen Emma, as well as other high chiefs and government figures, including Robert C. Wyllie, then the minister of foreign affairs, and Charles Harris, the attorney general. Despite some initial success, Staley and his bishopric proved unpopular, rousing antagonism from the already well-established Protestant and Roman Catholic missions. He resigned in 1870. In his *Union* letters Mark Twain sided with the American Protestant missionaries against Staley, condemning his dismissal of the missionary effort and his support of "barbarous" native rituals. He described the bishop as "a weak, trivial-minded man," spiteful, pretentious, and vain (SLC 1866z, 1866x, 1866aa; Korn, 333; *N&J1*, 134–35).

464.31 his Excellency the Minister of Public Instruction] There had been no such minister since 1855. At the time of Clemens's visit, educational matters were handled by a five-member Board of Education, whose president was Mataio Kekuanaoa (see the note at 457.6–9), and an inspector general of schools, Abraham Fornander (Kuykendall 1953, 106–8).

464.32 their Excellencies the Governors of Oahu, Hawaii, etc.] The governor of Oahu was John Owen Dominis (1832–91), son of an American sea captain who had settled in the Sandwich Islands in 1837. The island of Hawaii had been governed since 1855 by the high chiefess Ruth Keelikolani (1826–83) (Gasinski, 23, 26; Scott, 60; Korn, 303).

464.35–38 their Excellencies the Envoy Extraordinary . . . of the French; her British Majesty's Minister; the Minister Resident, of the United States] The French minister was M. Desnoyers. The acting British commissioner was William L. Green, a prominent Honolulu businessman. The American minister, James McBride, was awaiting the arrival of his successor, General Edward M. McCook, appointed in March 1866. McCook did not arrive in Honolulu until 22 July, three days after Clemens's departure for San Francisco (Honolulu *Pacific Commercial Advertiser:* "Programme of the Funeral," 30 June 66, 2; "Presentation at the Palace" and "British Commissioner," 8 Sept 66, 3; "H. B. M. Acting Commissioner," 6 May 65, 2; "Passengers," 1 Dec 66, 2; Kuykendall 1953, 206, 209, 291 n. 40; *L1*, 335 n. 2, 343 n. 4).

465.3–4 whose population falls absolutely short of sixty thousand souls] The 1866 census reported a population of 62,959, of whom 58,765 were native Hawaiians (Bennett, 59; see also the note at 454.11–13).

466.2–4 the King's sister, her Royal Highness the Princess Victoria . . . had lain in state at the palace *thirty days*] Princess Victoria Kamamalu Kaahumanu (1838–66) was the sister of Kamehameha IV and Kamehameha V, and the granddaughter and last female descendant of Kamehameha I. Since her brother Kamehameha V was unmarried, Victoria was heir apparent to the Hawaiian throne. She died on 29 May 1866 and, according to native custom, her body lay in state for one month before the funeral on 30 June 1866. Clemens was touring the island of Hawaii when Victoria died, but returned to Oahu in time to witness the elaborate funeral ceremonies. He devoted three of his *Union* letters to a description of these ceremonies and to a discussion of local politics, which had been thrown into "a state of unusual stir" as a result of Victoria's untimely death (SLC 1866x, 1866z–aa; "Death of the Heir Apparent," Honolulu *Pacific Commercial Advertiser,* 2 June 66, 2).

466.15–473.3   After . . . missionaries.] Mark Twain based this portion of the text on his letter in the Sacramento *Union* for 1 August 1866, revising it for inclusion in *Roughing It* (SLC 1866aa). That letter included the text of the funeral program (466.19–468.3), probably typeset from a clipping of the Honolulu *Pacific Commercial Advertiser* for 30 June 1866 ("Programme of the Funeral," 2). The *Union* letter also included the two lengthy quotations on the death of Kamehameha from Jarves's *History:* see the notes at 469.30–470.5 and 470.11–472.43.

466.27   Governor of Oahu] John Dominis (see the note at 464.32).

467.4–5   His Lordship Louis Maigret, the Rt. Rev. Bishop . . . of the Hawaiian Islands] Louis Désiré Maigret (1804–82), who arrived in the Sandwich Islands in 1840, headed the French Roman Catholic mission there from his cathedral of Our Lady of Peace in Honolulu. A notebook entry that Clemens made in late June 1866 suggests that he visited the cathedral (*N&J1,* 118). In contrast to his critical portrait of Bishop Staley, Clemens praised Maigret as "a leader of distinguished ability" in his *Union* letter published on 30 July (SLC 1866z; Kuykendall 1938, 150–52, 341–42; Korn, 324; "Death of Bishop Maigret," *Friend* 31 [1 July 82]: 67).

467.7   His Lordship the Right Reverend Bishop of Honolulu] Bishop Staley (see the note at 464.22–28). The *Advertiser* reported that Staley "appropriated" the position next to the hearse, which custom assigned not to him but to the "officiating clergyman." The paper claimed that Staley's "bigoted conduct" provoked "an intense feeling of disgust," reporting that "he would not walk side by side with the American Protestant Missionaries, but thrust himself above them, and above the Roman Catholic Bishop, all of whom have been longer upon the Islands, and have a greater influence than he has or ever will have among the people" (Honolulu *Pacific Commercial Advertiser:* "Funeral of the Princess Victoria" and "Side by Side," 7 July 66, 3).

467.9   Her Majesty Queen Emma's Carriage] Queen Emma—Emma Naea Rooke (1836–85), the widow of Kamehameha IV, sister-in-law of Kamehameha V, granddaughter of John Young (see the note at 471.7), and great granddaughter of the younger brother of Kamehameha I—was not in this carriage and did not attend the funeral. She had sailed for England in May 1865 for an extended visit and would not return un-til October 1866, after spending several weeks in the United States. Gracious, kindhearted, and highly cultivated, the popular Queen Emma had been known during her reign for her pro-British feelings and her promotion of the Hawaiian Reformed Catholic Church (*N&J1*, 220; Kuykendall 1953, 35, 78, 83–98 passim, 202–5).

467.12 Her Majesty the Queen Dowager] Queen Kalama (1817–70), widow of Kamehameha III ("Death of Her Majesty the Dowager Queen Kalama," Honolulu *Pacific Commercial Advertiser*, 24 Sept 70, 2).

467.13 The King's Chancellor] Elisha Hunt Allen (1804–83) was ap-pointed United States consul to the Sandwich Islands in 1849 and joined the Hawaiian government in 1853, serving first as minister of finance. In 1857 he was appointed chief justice and chancellor. Over the next two decades he distinguished himself in diplomatic missions for the Hawaiian government, successfully negotiating the 1876 treaty of reciprocity with the United States. After 1876 he served as Hawaiian minister in Washington, D.C.

467.15–17 His Excellency the Minister Resident of the United States. H. I. M.'s Commissioner. H. B. M.'s Acting Commissioner] These three men were identified by name in the *Advertiser*'s printed program—and in Mark Twain's *Union* letter—as "James McBride," "Mons. Des-noyers," and "W. L. Green" (see the note at 464.35–38).

467.29 Ahahui Kaahumanu] "The 'Ahahui Kaahumanu'—a benevolent society instituted (and presided over) by the late Princess for the nurs-ing of the sick and the burial of the dead—was numerously repre-sented. It is composed solely of native women. They were dressed in black, and wore sashes of different colors" (SLC 1866aa).

468.11 Burlingame] Anson Burlingame (see the note at 371.10–13), the United States minister to China (1861–67), arrived in Honolulu on 18 June en route to China. During his three-week stopover he developed a warm friendship with Clemens and helped him secure and conduct an interview with the survivors of the *Hornet* sea disaster—a journalistic scoop that Mark Twain reported in a *Union* letter published on 19 July (SLC 1866y; *L1*, 348 n. 1).

468.11 Gen. Van Valkenburgh] Robert Bruce Van Valkenburgh (1821–88), the recently appointed United States minister to Japan, was stop-ping over in Honolulu until 7 July on his way to his diplomatic post. A two-term congressman from New York State (1861–65), he had also served as a brigadier-general in the New York militia and commanded a regiment of New York volunteers at Antietam. He served in Japan un-til November 1869, and was later an associate justice of the Florida Su-preme Court.

469.30–470.5   On . . . execrations.] Mark Twain's source for this extract
was the third edition of Jarves's *History* (Jarves 1847, 105; see the note
at 443.26).

469.34   not only great, but good] The first and second editions of Jarves's
History include a passage at this point comparing Kamehameha I to
Napoleon, which does not appear in the book's third edition (the one
Mark Twain consulted and quoted in writing *Roughing It*): "He may be
justly styled the Napoleon of the Pacific. Without the worst traits of his
prototype, he possessed, according to the situation he occupied, equal
military skill, as vigorous an intellect, and as keen a judgment, as his
illustrious cotemporary" (Jarves 1843, 188; Jarves 1844b, 206). Mark
Twain makes a similar comparison in chapter 64 (440.36), which suggests that he had seen an earlier edition of the *History*. In 1884 he
owned a copy of the second edition, but he almost certainly acquired it
after the publication of *Roughing It* (Jarves 1847, 105; Gribben, 1:352;
N&J1, 104–5).

469.43–470.3   The bones of Kamehameha . . . were so carefully concealed . . . they made fish-hooks and arrows of them] Clemens recorded
in his notebook in April 1866: "Kammy's bones hidden at his own request, to keep them from making fish hooks of them—a superstition
that hooks made of the bones of a great Chief would concentrate the
fish" (*N&J1*, 230). In "A Strange Dream," probably written in April
1866, Mark Twain recounted an imaginary trip to Kilauea crater to
search for the great chief's bones, which have never been found (SLC
1866t).

470.6–10   The account . . . written by the native historians . . . is the
most comprehensive document I have yet met with] Mark Twain refers
to *Ka Mooolelo Hawaii*, an 1838 history of the Sandwich Islands "written by scholars at [a Hawaiian] High school, and corrected by one of the
instructors" (Malo et al., 58). Most of this history appeared for the first
time in translation in 1839 in the second volume of the *Hawaiian Spectator*, a quarterly review published in Honolulu from January 1838 to
October 1839 ("A Catalogue of Works Relating to the Hawaiian or
Sandwich Islands," *Friend* 11 [1 May 62]: 38). Mark Twain's introductory remarks are a paraphrase of Jarves's own introduction to the extract that follows: see the next note.

470.11–472.43   When . . . abuse.] Mark Twain's source for this extract
was the third edition of Jarves's *History* (Jarves 1847, 105–6; see the
note at 443.26). Jarves's source, in turn, was the April 1839 *Hawaiian
Spectator* (Malo et al., 227–31).

470.15   Kukailimoku] This was Kamehameha I's "favorite war god," represented "by images of wicker-work, covered with red feathers, with

eyes made of mother-of-pearl," and a wide gaping mouth "armed with sharks' teeth" (Jarves 1847, 29–30; W. D. Alexander, 41).

470.23   his son, Liholiho] Kamehameha I's heir, who ruled as Kamehameha II: see the note at 496.23–498.23.

471.6   Kaikioewa] A chief (d. 1839) who served as guardian of Prince Kauikeaouli (later Kamehameha III) during his minority and became governor of Kauai in 1824 (Dibble 1843, 199, 231–32; Kuykendall 1938, 118).

471.7   your foreigner] John Young (1742–1835), an English sailor who arrived in the Sandwich Islands in 1790 as boatswain of the American vessel *Eleanora*. Young—along with another English seaman, Isaac Davis (d. 1810) of the *Fair American*—was detained by Kamehameha I as a result of violence between the foreigners and the natives. The two Englishmen became trusted advisers to the king. Young served as governor of the island of Hawaii from 1802 to 1812, and through his marriage to one of the king's nieces became a member of the royal family (Kuykendall 1938, 24–25, 43–44, 54; Withington, 72–73; Scott, 887).

471.8   Kaahumanu] The favorite wife (1768?–1832) of Kamehameha I and a descendant of the chiefs of Maui. In 1819, when Kamehameha's son Liholiho became Kamehameha II, Kaahumanu assumed the position of *kuhina nui*, or chief adviser, in effect governing jointly with him. This position had been created for her by Kamehameha I, who did not want his successor to rule alone. After Liholiho's departure for England in 1823 (see the note at 496.23–498.23) Kaahumanu served as regent, continuing this role during the minority of Kamehameha III until her death. The beautiful and imperious Kaahumanu was a major force behind the overthrow of the tabu system in November 1819 (described in chapter 72, at 496.25–497.4). After 1821 she reversed her initially unfriendly attitude toward the Protestant missionaries, becoming a vigorous supporter of their educational, social, and moral reforms (Kuykendall 1938, 63–64, 67–68, 77–78, 106, 114; Bingham, 148–49, 164–65; Bradley, 141–44, 173, 190–93, 211–13; Kamakau, 306–23).

471.12   Hoapili] The chief Ulumeheihei (1767?–1840) was given the name "Hoapili," or "close adhering companion," by Kamehameha I, "from the friendship which existed between the old king and himself" (Jarves 1847, 108). It was Hoapili who successfully concealed the king's bones. He married Keopuolani and Kalakua, two of Kamehameha's widows. From 1823 until his death he served as governor of Maui (Judd, 41–42 n. 42; Jarves 1847, 119, 122).

471.23   Leleiohoku] One of Kalaimoku's sons (1826–48) (see the next note). At an early age he married Nahienaena, one of Kamehameha I's daughters, and later married the high chiefess Ruth Keelikolani. He was governor of the island of Hawaii from 1844 until his death at age twenty-two. The first part of his name, "Leleio," means "to die quickly" or suddenly, and "hoku" means "night of the full moon," a reference to Kamehameha's decease "on the night of Hoku, May (Ka'elo) 14 according to the Oahu calendar" (Kamakau, 212; Andrews, 336; Pukui and Elbert, 71; Zambucka 1977, 21).

471.24   Kalaimoku] Kamehameha I's trusted prime minister and treasurer (d. 1827), also known as Kalanimoku or Karaimoku. He adopted the name of one of his contemporaries, the great English prime minister William Pitt, and was often so addressed. He continued as prime minister in the reign of Kamehameha II (1819–24), and in the early years of the reign of Kamehameha III. During his long service, he was second in power (under the king's ultimate authority) only to Kaahumanu, the *kuhina nui* and regent (Kuykendall 1938, 53, 64, 431–32).

471n.3–6   †This . . . would certainly have been cannibalism if they had cooked him] This footnote misrepresents the view of Sandwich Islands historians. Jarves observed:

> Some doubt formerly existed, whether cannibalism ever prevailed in the group. The natives themselves manifested a degree of shame, horror and confusion, when questioned upon the subject, that led Cook and his associates, without any direct evidence of the fact, to believe in its existence; but later voyagers disputed this conclusion. The confessions of their own historians, and the general acknowledgment of the common people, have now established it beyond a doubt. (Jarves 1847, 49)

Mark Twain often treated the subject of cannibalism humorously during this period—for example, in two items about Honolulu publisher Henry Whitney, in his Sandwich Islands lecture, in the sketch "Cannibalism in the Cars," and in an 1870 Buffalo *Express* piece, "Dining with a Cannibal" (SLC 1866mm, 1870n, 884; Fatout 1976, 10; *MTH*, 144–45; SLC 1868i, 1870c).

472.12–14   Kau . . . Kohala . . . Kona] Kamehameha I died at his home, Kamakahonu, in the village of Kailua, Kona district. Kona is on the west side of the island of Hawaii, between the districts of Kohala to the north and Ka'u to the south. Kau is in the Ka'u district (Pukui, Elbert, and Mookini, 80, 91, 114).

472.39–40   Keeaumoku, Kaahumanu's brother] Keeaumoku (d. 1824), a high chief of the Maui royal line, was a trusted counselor to Kamehameha I, like his father of the same name. He served as governor of both Maui and Kauai (Kuykendall 1938, 53; Withington, 134–36; Jarves 1847, 108, 123).

473.7–15   Forty years ago . . . both sexes gave themselves up to . . . licentiousness] This paragraph summarizes a passage in Jarves's *History*, which Mark Twain quoted in full in his Sacramento *Union* letter published on 16 July 1866 (Jarves 1847, 40; SLC 1866x).

475.1–480.2 BOUND . . . fruit.] Mark Twain based this portion of the text on his letter in the Sacramento *Union* of 18 August 1866, revising it for inclusion in *Roughing It* (SLC 1866bb).

475.3–5 we sailed from Honolulu . . . in the good schooner Boomerang] Clemens sailed for the island of Hawaii on Saturday, 26 May, aboard the schooner *Emeline,* and returned to Honolulu three weeks later. The *Roughing It* account somewhat skews the chronology of Clemens's Sandwich Islands sojourn. His attendance at the funeral of Princess Victoria on 30 June, described in chapter 68, actually followed his trip to Hawaii; and his trip to Maui, mentioned briefly in chapters 76 and 77, in fact preceded the Hawaii trip (*N&J*1, 101; Honolulu *Pacific Commercial Advertiser:* "Departures," 2 June 66, 2; "Passengers," 16 June 66, 2).

475.11–12 the captain and my comrade (a Mr. Billings)] The *Emeline*'s skipper was Captain Crane, not further identified. Mark Twain altered his traveling companion's name from "Brown" to "Billings" when revising his 18 August *Union* letter; see the note at 447.31 ("Departures," Honolulu *Pacific Commercial Advertiser,* 2 June 66, 2; SLC 1866bb, 1866gg).

475.30–476.1 Balaam's ass] Numbers 22:21–33.

478.2 Billings's white upturned face] In revising his 18 August *Union* letter Mark Twain deleted a passage beginning here in which he made clear that Brown/Billings was lying seasick on the deck (SLC 1866bb).

478.5–8 Hualalai . . . being only ten thousand feet high . . . Mauna Loa is said to be sixteen thousand feet high] Modern measurements give elevations of 8,276 and 13,680 feet, respectively, for Hualalai and Mauna Loa. In his 18 August *Union* letter, Mark Twain gave Mauna Loa's elevation more accurately as 14,000 feet, then apparently revised the figure upward for *Roughing It.* The sources for his rather high figures are not known for certain, but two possibilities have been identified. James D. Dana of the 1838–42 United States Exploring Expedition (see the note at 523.30–31) estimated the elevation of Hualalai as "not far from 10,000 feet" (Dana, 156), a figure echoed by Rufus Anderson in *The Hawaiian Islands: Their Progress and Condition under Missionary Labors,* a book that Clemens is known to have consulted (he quoted a passage from it, without specific attribution, in his *Union* letter published on 24 August). Captain James King, in the final volume of Cook's *Voyage to the Pacific Ocean* (1784), reported Mauna Loa to be "at least 16,020 feet high" (Cook and King, 3:103; SLC 1866bb–cc; Rufus Anderson, 128).

478.22–24 we . . . went ashore at Kailua, designing to . . . rejoin the vessel at a point some leagues distant] On 28 May Clemens, apparently accompanied by another passenger on the *Emeline,* went ashore at the village of Kailua, in the Kona district on the west shore of Hawaii. They rode overland on horseback about fifteen miles to Kealakekua Bay, south of Kailua, reboarding the *Emeline* there around midnight. The *Roughing It* account of this journey omits many details found in Mark Twain's *Union* letters published on 18, 24, and 30 August (*MTH*, 62; SLC 1866bb–cc, 1866ee).

480.3–24 At . . . required.] Mark Twain based this portion of the text on the first half of his letter in the Sacramento *Union* of 24 August 1866, revising it for inclusion in *Roughing It*; he reserved the second half for use in chapter 71 (SLC 1866cc; see the note at 489.1–491.24).

480.11–24 We passed several sugar plantations . . . no irrigation whatever is required] Mark Twain confined his remarks in *Roughing It* on the subject of the islands' sugar production to this paragraph. He made no use of his *Union* letter published on 26 September, which—possibly at the behest of the *Union*—was largely devoted to the subject. Many years later he asserted, "Circumstance and the Sacramento *Union* sent me to the Sandwich Islands for five or six months, to write up sugar. I did it; and threw in a good deal of extraneous matter that hadn't anything to do with sugar" (SLC 1910, 1866hh).

481.1 We stopped some time at one of the plantations] This may have been the Kona plantation of Thomas Lack, possibly also the place where the travelers ate the "large peaches of excellent flavor" (480.3) (*MTH*, 20, 63–64).

482.15–19 that bloody and distressful war over there in Italy . . . battle of Sadowa] In the Austro-Prussian (or Seven Weeks') War of 1866, Prussian forces decisively defeated Austrian troops on 3 July 1866 near the Bohemian town of Sadowa. In subsequent peace treaties Austria agreed to the creation of the North German Confederation under the leadership of Prince Otto von Bismarck and ceded Venetia to Italy, a Prussian ally. This Prussian success set the stage for the Franco-Prussian War of 1870–71 and the complete unification of Germany.

483.7–8 She desired me to confer with Mr. Greeley about turnips] Horace Greeley (see the note at 131.12), an enthusiastic amateur farmer at his home in Chappaqua, New York, aired his views on agriculture in speeches, books, and the columns of the New York *Tribune*. "It became the fashion for critics and fun makers to jibe at Greeley's farming efforts, and the Chappaqua wood chopper was made the butt of much merriment" (Van Deusen, 147). In 1868, in a humorous but fundamentally respectful sketch of Greeley entitled "Private Habits of Horace Greeley," Mark Twain wrote that every day before a late breakfast Greeley

goes out into his model garden, and applies his vast store of agricultural knowledge to the amelioration of his cabbages; after which he writes an able agricultural article for the instruction of American farmers, his soul cheered the while with the reflection that if cabbages were worth eleven dollars apiece his model farm would pay. (SLC 1868j)

An 1870 *Tribune* series of Greeley's essays, entitled "What I Know of Farming," was collected in a book of the same name (Greeley 1871). In mid-April 1871 Greeley gave Clemens a copy inscribed as follows: "To Mark Twain, Esq., Ed. Buffalo Express who knows even less of MY farming than does Horace Greeley. N. York" (Anderson, lot 204); a slightly different version of the inscription was quoted in "H. G. as a Joker," Buffalo *Courier*, 21 Apr 71, 1).

484.17   I could not read it readily] Greeley's hand was notoriously illegible: "No doubt the 'worm fence' handwriting was difficult for a stranger to decipher, but *Tribune* printers and proofreaders were familiar with it. Others compared it to gridirons struck by lightning" (Stoddard, 140, facsimile facing 241). The newspapers of the day frequently printed jokes about the difficulty of reading Greeley's handwriting. In May 1871, for example, the following anecdote appeared in the Boston *Post:*

> Greeley wrote a letter to the Iowa Press Association, in which he said: "I have hominy, carrots and R. R. ties more than I could move with eight steers. If eels are blighted, dig them early. Any insinuation that brick ovens are dangerous to hams, gives me the horrors. GREELEY." That is, they read it so. They have since learned what he meant to say was: "I find so many cares and duties pressing upon me, that with the weight of years I feel obliged to decline nearly every invitation that takes me over a day's journey from home. Yours among them. HORACE GREELEY." ("Varieties," Buffalo *Express*, 10 May 71, 2, reprinting the Boston *Post*)

Mark Twain himself had commented on Greeley's penmanship in "Private Habits of Horace Greeley" and in a Buffalo *Express* column of 4 September 1869. He may have been further inspired by the facsimile of Greeley's hand published in Richardson's *Beyond the Mississippi* (SLC 1868j, 1869h; Richardson, 163–64). In any event, the immediate occasion for the illustration on page 485 (possibly engraved from a drawing by Mark Twain himself), and its accompanying "transcriptions," was undoubtedly a letter that Greeley wrote to Clemens on 7 May 1871, presumably in response to a letter from Clemens (now lost) thanking Greeley for the gift of his book (see the previous note). Greeley's letter is reproduced in supplement C.

489.1–491.24   At . . . retaliation.] Mark Twain based this portion of the text on the second half of his letter in the Sacramento *Union* of 24 August 1866, revising it for inclusion in *Roughing It;* he used the beginning of this letter in chapter 69 (SLC 1866cc; see the note at 480.3–24).

490.22   the great god Lono] Lono was one of the four major Hawaiian male deities. Associated with clouds and storms, he was worshiped as the god of fertility. Hawaiian tradition merges the god Lono with an ancient chief of the same name, who for a time lived at Kealakekua long before Captain Cook's arrival. Chapter 72 (495.15–496.11) contains Mark Twain's summary of Lono's legendary history (Beckwith, 31–41; Kuykendall 1938, 7–8; Kamakau, 61).

490.39–491.24 Plain unvarnished history . . . justifiable homicide . . . proportionate retaliation] Mark Twain's assessment of Captain Cook's relations with the Sandwich Islands natives was clearly influenced by Jarves's account in his *History*. "While it is not my desire to detract from the fame lawfully [Cook's] due," wrote Jarves, "yet I cannot, with his biographers, gloss over the events which occurred at the Hawaiian Islands" (Jarves 1847, 68). Jarves—in language somewhat less emphatic than Clemens's—points out Cook's intemperate and highhanded behavior, and his abuse of the deference accorded him by the worshipful Hawaiians. The foremost contemporary British accounts of Cook's actions were by James King, Cook's lieutenant, and by John Ledyard, a marine corporal on Cook's flagship, the *Resolution*. Jarves found Ledyard's account, the more critical of the two, to be substantiated by the account of native historians (Jarves 1847, 65–70; Cook and King, 3:25–82; Ledyard, 143–55; Malo et al., 64–67).

491.11–12 "He groans!—he is not a god!"] Mark Twain encountered this detail of Cook's death struggle, though not these words, in Jarves's *History*, which quotes the account of native historians. He found the remark quoted here either in Sheldon Dibble's *History of the Sandwich Islands*, where it first appeared, or in Henry T. Cheever's *Life in the Sandwich Islands* (Malo et al., 66; Jarves 1847, 68; Dibble 1843, 39; Cheever 1851b, 24).

491.13–18 His flesh was stripped from the bones and burned . . . Some of Cook's bones were . . . consigned to the deep] The natives' treatment of Cook's remains was the customary one accorded a dead king. Mark Twain probably learned most of the particulars from Jarves, who repeats and affirms the account of native historians. Jarves, however, does not report the detail about the survival of one child to be "a very old man," which can be found in Dibble's *History* and in Cheever's *Life* (Kuykendall 1938, 19; Malo, 141–43; Jarves 1847, 68–70; Dibble 1843, 39; Cheever 1851b, 24).

491.25–492.20 Near . . . innocent.] Mark Twain based this portion of the text on his letter in the Sacramento *Union* of 30 August 1866, revising it for inclusion in *Roughing It* (SLC 1866ee).

493.1–495.14 IN . . . point.] Mark Twain based this portion of the text on his letter in the Sacramento *Union* for 6 September 1866, revising it for inclusion in *Roughing It* (SLC 1866ff).

493.1–2 we went ashore and visited the ruined temple of the lost god Lono] Clemens visited the ruins of Hikiau temple, which had once housed the red-draped image of Lono. In his *Union* letter published on 6 September he noted that it was the very temple "so desecrated by Captain Cook. . . . Its low, rude walls look about as they did when he saw them, no doubt" (SLC 1866ff). Cook desecrated the temple—apparently with the acquiescence of the temple priests, who believed him to be the returned Lono—by carrying off the wooden railings and the idols of the lesser gods for use as firewood on his ship (Kamakau, 99; Kuykendall 1938, 16; Cook and King, 3:6–8, 25–26; *MTH*, 67).

493.4–10   Obookiah . . . was taken to New England . . . This resulted in the sending of missionaries there] The orphaned Henry Obookiah, also known as Opukahaia (1792?–1818), took passage—along with two other Hawaiian youths, William Kanui (see the note at 493.22–28) and Thomas Hopu—aboard the merchant ship of Captain Caleb Brintnal and arrived in New Haven, Connecticut, in 1809. There Obookiah was tutored by Edwin Welles Dwight (1789–1841) of Yale College, became a Christian, and actively encouraged the creation of a mission to the Sandwich Islands. Obookiah died of typhus at age twenty-six while a student at the newly created Foreign Mission School in Cornwall, Connecticut. His story, incorporated into Dwight's much-reprinted *Memoirs of Henry Obookiah, a Native of Owhyhee*, became a staple of missionary literature and influenced the decision to send the first missionaries to the islands in 1819 (Dwight, 3–129; Rufus Anderson, 46–48; Bradford Smith, 21–25; Bradley, 123–24; Boothby, 53–54).

493.11–12   savage who sat down on the church steps and wept because his people did not have the Bible] According to Anderson's history of missionary labors in the Sandwich Islands, Obookiah "was one day found sitting on the doorsteps of one of [the Yale College] buildings, weeping because the treasures of knowledge were open to others, but were not open to him. Mr. Edwin W. Dwight, who saw him thus, had compassion on him, and became his religious teacher" (Rufus Anderson, 46). Obookiah's own memoir makes no mention of such an encounter (Dwight, 18–20). Mark Twain's version of the story may derive from an unidentified source.

493.20–21   The other native youths made the voyage] The first missionary group, dispatched to the Sandwich Islands in October 1819, included three Hawaiian youths educated at the Foreign Mission School: William Kanui, Thomas Hopu, and John Honolii (Rufus Anderson, 46–49).

493.22–28   William Kanui, fell from grace . . . went to mining . . . was a bankrupt . . . died in Honolulu in 1864] Mark Twain learned these facts about William Kanui (1798?–1864) from an obituary notice in the February 1864 issue of the *Friend*, which he quoted and cited in the *Union* letter on which this passage is based (SLC 1866ff). Kanui lost his money in 1855, when the San Francisco bank of Page, Bacon and Company suspended operations on 22 February and closed its doors permanently on 2 May.

> [Kanui] then, being obliged to exert himself for a livelihood, opened a bootblacking stand, and continued it for some time. But sad to relate, in his religious interests he became quite reckless, and continued for a long time in a backslidden state. ("William Kanui Still Alive," report dated 20 June 1860 from San Francisco, *Friend* 10 [1 Feb 61]: 13)

Kanui's piety subsequently revived, and during his last years he "labored in San Francisco, and was connected with the Bethel Church of that city" ("Died," *Friend* 13 [5 Feb 64]: 16; Rufus Anderson, 48–49 n. 1; Bradford Smith, 24, 58–59, 288; San Francisco *Alta California:* "The Crisis Past," 23 Feb 55, 2; "Commercial," 3 May 55, 2).

494.21–495.14 At noon I observed a bevy of nude native young ladies . . . I will not urge this point] Mark Twain wrote this paragraph on the swimming prowess of the Hawaiians expressly for *Roughing It,* to replace a comic passage in his 6 September *Union* letter in which he claimed he "undressed and went in myself" (SLC 1866ff).

495.15–506.4 I have . . . charge.] Mark Twain based this portion of the text on his letter in the Sacramento *Union* of 22 September 1866, revising it for inclusion in *Roughing It* (SLC 1866gg).

495.17–496.7 The idol . . . was a slender, unornamented staff . . . he . . . sailed for foreign lands on a three-cornered raft] Mark Twain's description of the Lono idol and legend was apparently summarized from Jarves's *History* (Jarves 1847, 27–28).

495.25 "on the shoulder;"] That is, looking for a fight. See Scotty Briggs's description of Buck Fanshaw in chapter 47 (312.21–29).

496.5–6 he instituted games called makahiki, and ordered that they should be held in his honor] According to Jarves, Lono instituted the games to commemorate his wife's death. The makahiki season, which corresponded to the rainy months from roughly October through January, was sacred to Lono. During this time the chiefs gathered taxes and eschewed war, and on certain festival days all labor and the usual religious practices were prohibited while everyone enjoyed feasting, sports, and other recreation (Jarves 1847, 28; Malo, 186, 189–91; Kamakau, 180–81; Kuykendall 1938, 7–8; Beckwith, 33–35).

496.16 the place where the last battle was fought for idolatry] Kuamoo: see the note at 498.3–15.

496.23–498.23 his son, Liholiho, the new King . . . the gospel was planted as in a virgin soil] Mark Twain's primary source for the information in this passage was probably Jarves's *History* (Jarves 1847, 109–11). Liholiho (1797–1824) was the son of Kamehameha I and the chiefess Keopuolani. He was strictly raised by his parents and priests to prepare him for succession to the throne. His reign as Kamehameha II, from 1819 to 1824, was notable for the abolition of the tabu system, the arrival of the American missionaries, the growth of the sandalwood trade and the whaling industry, and the removal of the seat of government from Kailua to Honolulu. Liholiho shared his father's pro-British attitude, and in 1823–24 he visited England, accompanied by his wife Kamamalu and an official entourage. Kamamalu died of the measles in London in July 1824, and Liholiho followed her in death within a week. The other members of the royal party, however, were able to accomplish the king's mission—to confirm Hawaii as a protectorate of Great Britain (Kuykendall 1938, 71–81).

496.29–30   Kaahumanu had a whole mind to badger him into doing it] Liholiho was urged by two women to indulge in traditionally forbidden "free eating": Keopuolani, his mother, and Kaahumanu, his *kuhina nui* (see the note at 471.8). For some time both women had ignored certain eating tabus without suffering any ill consequences. Liholiho's decision to follow their example was all the harder because as a child he had been carefully instructed in the tabu rites of the priestly order, and because tradition held that only a chief who respected the ancient tabus, like Kamehameha I, would have a long reign (Kuykendall 1938, 67–68; Kamakau, 222–23).

496.32   Liholiho came up to Kailua as drunk as a piper] The feast at Kailua took place during the first week of November 1819, six months after the death of Kamehameha I (Kuykendall 1938, 68). According to Jarves, Kaahumanu

> sent word to the king, that upon his arrival at Kailua, she should cast aside his god. To this he made no objection, but with his retainers pushed off in canoes from the shore, and remained on the water for two days, indulging in a drunken revel. Kaahumanu despatched a double canoe for him, in which he was brought to Kailua. (Jarves 1847, 109)

498.3–15   They raised a revolt . . . idolatry and the *tabu* were dead in the land] Kamehameha II's forces, commanded by the prime minister, Kalaimoku (see the note at 471.24), met the opposing force, under Kekuokalani (or Kekuaokalani), at Kuamoo on or about 20 December 1819. Kekuokalani, an ambitious chief who clung to the traditional ways, was Liholiho's cousin, a son of Kamehameha I's brother. He was killed at Kuamoo and his forces were routed. Other minor uprisings by disaffected traditionalists were quickly put down by Liholiho's forces (Jarves 1847, 109–10; Malo et al., 337–40; W. D. Alexander, 170–71; Kuykendall 1938, 69).

498.21   The missionary ship arrived in safety shortly afterward] The first missionary party, comprising seventeen adults and their children, left Boston in the brig *Thaddeus* in October 1819 and arrived on the west coast of the island of Hawaii on 30 March 1820 (Bingham, 69; Kuykendall 1938, 102).

499.2 Honaunau] Honaunau is south of Kealakekua Bay on the western coast of the island of Hawaii.

499.21 Billings] See the note at 475.11–12.

501.25–29 the ancient City of Refuge . . . whose stone walls were twenty feet thick . . . a thousand and forty feet one way . . . seven hundred the other] The City of Refuge was built for Keawe (or Keave), a sixteenth-century chief. In 1823 William Ellis found its ruins to be 715×404 feet, with walls 15 feet thick and 12 feet high. Subsequent works about Hawaii accepted Ellis's dimensions as authoritative (Ellis, 157; Jarves 1847, 34; Cheever 1851b, 42; Rufus Anderson, 151). No source has been found for Mark Twain's figures.

503.17 How did they transport and how raise them?] This remark echoes previous descriptions of the site in the works of Ellis, Jarves, and Cheever. Cheever's description of the wall of rock apparently derived from Ellis's earlier account: "There are fragments of lava in these walls that must be of two or more tons weight each, six or eight feet above the ground, which it is difficult to imagine how Hawaiians could have raised (as they must) without machinery, by the mere force of the unassisted human hands" (Cheever 1851b, 42; Ellis, 157; Jarves 1847, 34).

503.26–504.2 a sort of coffin-shaped stone . . . When he stretched . . . on his lounge, his legs hung down over the end] This passage may have been inspired by a description written by S. S. Hill, an earlier visitor to the site:

> Our guide pointed out to us a block of hewn lava, that we judged to be about thirteen feet in length, which was preserved in remembrance of an ancient chief, who is said to have been of the length of the block when lying with outstretched arms upon its surface. If this be no exaggeration, the chief must have been of enormous dimensions indeed. (S. S. Hill, 185)

504.4–505.27 a monstrous seven-ton rock . . . a congealed cascade of lava . . . several cavernous tunnels] Similar accounts of these features have been found in works with which Mark Twain was probably familiar (Ellis, 160–63; Rufus Anderson, 151, 152).

507.1–4 WE . . . sailed down to Kau . . . Next day we bought horses and bent our way . . . toward the great volcano of Kilauea] From Kealakekua Bay the *Emeline* sailed south down the western coast of Hawaii on Wednesday, 30 May. Rough weather forced the schooner to tack far out to sea in order to round the treacherous southern point of the island. The *Emeline* was finally able to anchor at Kaalualu, a port on the southeast coast of Hawaii in the Kau district, on Friday, 1 June. Clemens rode on horseback six miles inland to the village of Waiohinu, where he purchased a mule for the forty-mile trip to Kilauea crater on the slopes of Mauna Loa, which occupied the better part of two days, 2 and 3 June (*MTH*, 69, 71–72; SLC 1866nn).

507.14 I have seen Vesuvius since] Clemens ascended Vesuvius, on the eastern shore of the Bay of Naples, in August 1867 with a party from the *Quaker City*. In his description of that ascent, in chapters 29 and 30 of *The Innocents Abroad*, he stated that "the Vesuvius of to-day is a very poor affair compared to the mighty volcano of Kilauea, in the Sandwich Islands" (SLC 1869a, 325; *L2*, 78).

507.20–21 nine hundred feet deep in some places, thirteen hundred in others . . . and *ten miles in circumference*] At the time of Clemens's visit, the crater was probably closer to four hundred feet in depth, considerably less than it had been in former years before successive lava flows raised its floor. Its circumference was accurately established in 1864 as eight and a half miles. Mark Twain could have obtained his figures on Kilauea's depth and circumference from any of several published sources, and may have been unaware that they did not reflect the configuration of the ever-changing crater in mid-1866. No source has been found giving the exact figures reported here, but Mark Twain could have derived them from Cheever's *Island World*, which described the crater as "nine to fifteen hundred feet deep, and from nine to fifteen miles in circumference," or from an article in the *Friend* for February 1866 which stated that its "depth varies from 600 to 1,200 feet. . . . The circumference by trigonometry is more than 7½ miles, while to a pedestrian it is 10 miles" (Cheever 1851a, 285; Titus Coan 1866, 10; Ellis, 226; Charles Samuel Stewart, 313–14; Hitchcock, 203–6 and plates 29–31).

508.1–512.8 By . . . hotel.] Mark Twain based this portion of the text on his letter in the Sacramento *Union* for 16 November 1866, revising it for inclusion in *Roughing It* (SLC 1866pp). It is the last section of the book to be derived from a *Union* letter.

508.1 the Volcano House] Some form of rude shelter had existed at Kilauea's northern edge for as many as forty years before Clemens's 1866 visit. Accommodations improved dramatically in March 1866 when the Volcano House, a thatched hotel capable of sleeping twenty, opened at the site. Mark Twain concluded his final Sacramento *Union* letter with a compliment for the "neat, roomy, well furnished and well kept hotel," claiming that "the surprise of finding a good hotel in such an outlandish spot startled me considerably more than the volcano did" (SLC 1866pp). He stayed at the Volcano House for about four nights, enjoying his accommodations free of charge, as he told his mother and sister in a letter of 21 June 1866 (*L1*, 343–44; Olson, 15–16, 28–31; *MTH*, 72–74, 125–27).

508.19 "pillar of fire."] Exodus 13:21.

511.22–23 many years had elapsed since any visitor had seen such a splendid display] Between the cataclysmic eruptions of 1840 and 1868,

Kilauea experienced several periods of rather intense activity, although prior to 1866 it had been relatively quiet for about ten years. Significant eruptions began on 22 May 1866 and continued into August, creating "a series of discharges all over the surface of the crater" as well as several new lava lakes in the northern portion (Brigham, 410–27; "The Volcano in Eruption Again," Honolulu *Pacific Commercial Advertiser,* 9 June 66, 3; Hitchcock, 188–206).

511.26–27 the "Record Book" at the Volcano House] It had long been the custom for visitors to Kilauea to record their impressions and sign their names in a guest book. Lodgers at the Volcano House continued this custom in the hotel's register, which eventually grew to many volumes and contains valuable scientific observations as well as effusions from a wide range of visitors, both celebrated and obscure. Clemens's own entry of 7 June 1866 burlesqued some of the other visitors' typical remarks (Olson, 67–69; Volcano House Register; SLC 1866u).

512.7 Pele's furnaces] In Hawaiian mythology, the fearsome Pele was the goddess of volcanoes. She and her family of deities made their home in Halemaumau, a large lake of molten lava in the southern portion of Kilauea crater (W. D. Alexander, 38).

513.1–525.7 THE . . . always.] Chapters 75–76—which include Mark Twain's descriptions of his descent into Kilauea crater, his tour of the island of Hawaii on horseback, and his visit to Maui—were not based on 1866 *Union* letters. It is not known for certain whether Mark Twain wrote them in late 1866 or early 1867 when preparing his never-published Sandwich Islands manuscript—or in 1871, when composing *Roughing It.*

513.1–2 a visit to the bottom of the crater] During his Sandwich Islands sojourn Mark Twain had probably read one or more of the numerous published accounts of trips into the crater, but there is no clear evidence that he drew upon any of them when later writing his own version (see Ellis, 224–36; Charles S. Stewart, 308–13; Byron, 183–90; Wilkes, 4:130–38, 181–91; Cheever 1851a, 290–309; and Hill, 256–78).

513.14 Marlette] Charles W. Marlette of Jacksonville, Illinois, had arrived in Honolulu in September 1865 and by March 1866 had visited Kilauea at least four times. Mark Twain's correct recollection of his companion's name suggests that he might have relied on his notebook for early June, which is now lost, to refresh his memory (Volcano House Register, 63, 74; "Passengers," *Friend* 14 [2 Oct 65]: 80).

516.14–15 About 1840 it rent its overburdened stomach] This eruption of Kilauea began on 30 May 1840 and continued for three weeks.

516.17–22 The stream was *five miles broad* . . . fine print could be read at midnight] Mark Twain drew the figures in this passage (as well as the

remark about the fishes at 517.9) from an account by the Reverend Titus Coan, a missionary stationed at Hilo, which was first published in
the *Missionary Herald* of July 1841 and widely reprinted thereafter. He
also quoted parts of this account in his Sandwich Islands lecture, which
he wrote upon his return to San Francisco (Titus Coan 1841; SLC
1866kk; Fatout 1976, 12).

517.10–12   The earthquakes caused some loss of human life, and a prodigious tidal wave swept inland . . . drowning a number of natives] The
1840 eruption was attended by neither loss of life nor a tidal wave.
Clemens may have had in mind the devastating volcanic and seismic
activity of March–April 1868, vivid reports of which (in the San Francisco newspapers) had prompted him to inform his lecture agent on 12
May that he intended to "revamp my Sandwich Islands talk & put in
this superb eruption 3 weeks ago" (*L1*, 216–17). The eruption was also
described by Titus Munson Coan (son of Titus Coan) in the September
1868 issue of *Harper's New Monthly Magazine:* "At the same time with
the earth eruption the sea receded far below the low-water-mark. Pausing a few seconds, as if gathering its power, it leaped upon the shore in
a wave forty feet high, that swept every thing before it. . . . Nearly a
hundred persons were drowned" (Titus Munson Coan, 557–58).

518.1–3   WE rode horseback all around the island . . . We were more than
a week making the trip] Clemens left Kilauea, probably on 7 June 1866,
accompanied by Edward Tasker Howard (1844?–1918), an acquaintance
made at the Volcano House. "Confound that island, I had a streak of fat
& a streak of lean all over it," he told his family on 21 June; "got lost
several times & had to sleep in huts with the natives & live like a dog"
(*L1*, 344). From the volcano Clemens and Howard headed north to Hilo
on the coast, then northward to Onomea, the Waipio valley, and finally
across the island to the west coast port of Kawaihae. In Hilo, Clemens
later mentioned, he stayed for three days with John H. Coney, sheriff of
the island. Other evidence suggests that he may also have been the
guest of blustery and profane Captain Thomas Spencer, a leading citizen of Hilo and owner of an extensive ship chandlery. At Onomea, six
miles north of Hilo, Clemens and Howard stayed overnight at the sugar
plantation of Stafford L. Austin, whose son, Franklin H. Austin, later
wrote a detailed account of that memorable visit (*MTH*, 74–79; *L1*, 346
n. 9; *N&J1*, 133 n. 74; Whitney, 73; Austin, 202–3, 250–54). Howard, a
New Yorker who had lived in San Francisco since 1864, returned to
New York after his Sandwich Islands trip and became a partner in Howard and Company, a Broadway jewelry and silverware firm ("Edward
Tasker Howard," New York *Times,* 9 Aug 1918, 11; advertisement,
New York *Times,* 3 Oct 66, 3). "I don't think an enormous deal of Howard," Clemens later admitted to a Honolulu friend,

though that's nothing against *him*, of course. Tastes differ, & 200 miles mule-back in company is the next best thing to a sea-voyage to bring a man's worst points to the surface. Ned & I *like* each other, but we don't *love*, & we never did. I like to talk with him, & I buy little jewelry trifles there, but we don't embrace—I would as soon think of embracing a fish, or an icicle, or any other particularly cold and unemotional thing—say a dead stranger, for instance. (SLC to Albert Francis Judd, 20 Dec 70, PH in CtY-BR, in *MTH*, 467)

518.10   the whole duty of man] An allusion to a devotional work entitled *The Whole Duty of Man* (1658), whose authors may have included Richard Allestree and Bishop John Fall. Clemens mentioned it several times in his writing, usually with comic intent (Gribben, 1:21).

520.9–10   they had never drank that fluid in their lives] While returning to San Francisco in early August 1866, Clemens reminded himself in his notebook of the horses that "don't drink" (*N&J1*, 159). Walter Frear has suggested that Clemens saw these horses not in June, after visiting Kilauea, but in May during his horseback ride from Kailua to Kealakekua Bay in the Kona district (*MTH*, 64). For a discussion of the verb form "had drank," see the textual note.

520.30–31   I mark the circumstance with a white stone] Marking something with a white stone "has been understood, from classical times[,] as an expression for commemorating any piece of good fortune or any lucky day" (Hazlitt, 2:568).

520.35–37   We returned to Honolulu, and from thence sailed to the island of Maui, and spent several weeks there] Clemens and Howard embarked from Kawaihae on the interisland steamer *Kilauea*, reaching Honolulu on 16 June. As explained in the note at 475.3–5, Clemens's trip to Maui actually preceded his trip to Hawaii. He sailed from Honolulu to Maui in mid-April (perhaps aboard the *Mary Ellen* on 17 April) and returned to Honolulu aboard the schooner *Ka Moi* on 22 May, on which day he wrote to Mollie Clemens:

I have just got back from a sea voyage—from the beautiful island of Maui. I have spent 5 weeks there, riding backwards & forwards among the sugar plantations—looking up the splendid scenery & visiting the lofty crater of Haleakala. It has been a perfect jubilee to me in the way of pleasure. I have not written a single line, & have not once thought of business, or care, or human toil or trouble or sorrow or weariness. Few such months come in a lifetime. (*L1*, 341)

Clemens limited his remarks about Maui in the Sacramento *Union* to a discussion of its sugar plantations (SLC 1866hh; Honolulu *Pacific Commercial Advertiser:* "Passengers," 16 June 66, 2; "Departures," 21 Apr 66, 2; *N&J1*, 234; *MTH*, 55).

520.38–522.1   a romantic gorge there, called the Iao Valley] Clemens would long remember the scenic Iao Valley behind the coastal village of Wailuku, where he stayed for part of his Maui visit. In his 1898 sketch "My Platonic Sweetheart," published posthumously in 1912, he described himself and his "dream-sweetheart," Agnes, "lounging up the blossomy gorge called the Iao Valley" on the "darling island" of Maui. In that Edenlike setting Agnes dies when struck by a falling arrow from the bow of a Kanaka (SLC 1912).

522.28–31   We climbed a thousand feet up . . . and next day climbed the remaining nine thousand feet] Apparently Clemens made the ascent of Haleakala shortly after 26 April, accompanied by Warren Woods Kimball (1838–74) and William Cargill Kimball (1841–90) of New York, brothers who had been his fellow passengers on the *Ajax* (*L1*, 335–36; Kimball biographical information courtesy of Rodney C. Eaton).

523.11–12   an article in which Poe treated of this singular fraud] Edgar Allen Poe, in his 1844 story "The Balloon Hoax," explained that because the extent of the horizon visible to the balloonist is many times greater than the height of the balloon car, the horizon "would appear to be *on a level* with the car. But, as the point immediately beneath him seems, and is, at a great distance below him, it seems, of course, also, at a great distance below the horizon. Hence the impression of *concavity*" (Poe, 3:1080). This high-altitude optical illusion was also mentioned in at least four works that Clemens had perused during his Sandwich Islands sojourn (Hopkins, 28; Jarves 1844a, 226; Cheever 1851b, 112; Bates, 327).

523.26   The crater of Vesuvius, as I have before remarked, is a modest pit about a thousand feet deep] In chapter 74 Mark Twain estimated the depth of Vesuvius to be only "three hundred feet" (507.17), while in *The Innocents Abroad* he had placed it at "two hundred feet" (SLC 1869a, 323).

523.30–31   Commander Wilkes, U. S. N., . . . testifies that it is *twenty-seven miles in circumference*] Commander Charles Wilkes (1798–1877) was the leader of a United States naval expedition that in 1838–42 surveyed and charted the Antarctic coast, the islands of the Pacific Ocean, and the American northwest coast. He reported in his *Narrative of the United States Exploring Expedition* (1844) that several expedition members—himself not among them—visited Haleakala in February 1841, but he made no mention of the crater's circumference. The expedition's geologist claimed in his report, published in 1849, that one of the party who visited the crater estimated its circumference to be fifteen miles. A more accurate 1869 survey established it as eighteen to twenty miles. Mark Twain's source for the figure of twenty-seven miles is unknown; he may have derived it—as well as the measurement of its depth as "two thousand five hundred feet" (523.22)—from Cheever's *Life*, which described Haleakala as "a deep, wide pit, twenty-five or thirty miles in circumference, and two or three thousand feet deep" (Cheever 1851b, 110; Wilkes, 4:251, 270–73; Dana, 228; Whitney, 50–51).

524.21 the Last Man] An allusion to the poem "The Last Man" by Thomas Campbell (1777–1844), published in 1824. Mark Twain is echoing—perhaps unconsciously—Bates's description of his emotions on the summit of Haleakala:

> I seemed to stand on the portals of another world, or to cling, solitarily and sadly, to the wrecks of this, as if it were just emerging from the grave of a deluge. . . . Like CAMPBELL's "*Last Man*," surveying the wrecks that old Time had flung over the lap of earth's mightiest nations, I was alone on that naked summit. (Bates, 328)

526.1 one curious character in the island of Maui] The eccentric Francis A. Oudinot (1822?–71) of Lahaina, Maui, was a native of Kentucky. At the time of his arrival in the Sandwich Islands in 1851, he listed his occupation as "jeweler." Claiming descent from Charles Nicolas Oudinot (1767–1847), the famous marshal of Napoleon's forces, he celebrated French national holidays by dressing in a resplendent French uniform and carrying a French flag. Oudinot, alone among Lahaina's American population, was known to be a Southern sympathizer during the Civil War. He also had a reputation as a spinner of yarns. Harriet Baldwin Damon, a resident of Lahaina in her youth, recalled him:

> Oudinot, well known throughout the islands as something of a farmer, had wonderful stories to recount of the marvelous growth of his plantings. With him the sugar cane grew so fast, it rustled and rattled, and with a lantern at night, he had watched the progress. All his products were magnified, nor did there ever appear to be a doubt in his mind but that his stories were accepted. With his lack of veracity, he was however most generous, and we never left his place empty handed. (Mary Charlotte Alexander, 250)

According to his obituary notice, Oudinot was a deputy sheriff at Lahaina for a number of years: "His hospitality, cheerfulness of temper and many other good qualities, caused him to be universally known on these islands and secured for him a large number of friends. Through industry and energy he has accumulated a valuable property situated in Lahaina" ("Died," Honolulu *Pacific Commercial Advertiser*, 22 July 71, 2; naturalization document of Francis A. Oudinot dated 18 June 55, Naturalization Book N:55, Hawaiian Ministry of Interior, Bureau of Immigration, H-Ar; William Ap Jones to Mr. Chapman of the Interior Ministry, 24 Aug 61, Miscellaneous File, Hawaiian Ministry of Interior, H-Ar; *MTH*, 57–58; *N&J1*, 120 n. 38).

526.11–531.22 I . . . sir."] Mark Twain first published this portion of the text as "About a Remarkable Stranger" in his "Memoranda" in the April 1871 *Galaxy* (SLC 1871b). He revised the sketch only slightly when incorporating it into *Roughing It*.

526.14–21 you ought to have seen *my* chimney . . . I had to dig it out with a pickaxe] In August 1866 Clemens wrote in one of his Hawaiian notebooks: "Chimney got choked with smoke so thick had to *dig* it out" (*N&J1*, 146).

528.26–35 *there* was lightning for you . . . my dog was a swimming behind the wagon] In late July 1866 Clemens wrote in his notebook, "Oudinot's bee & dog & lightning story—lightning came in at front door as he was just going out & drove him clear through & out at the back door" (*N&J1*, 147). Although the lightning anecdote sketched in the entry does not occur in this chapter, the listed elements (the bee, the dog, and the lightning) are nevertheless present (see the phrase "little small bee" at 530.11).

531.2–4 Markiss was found . . . dead] Oudinot was still alive when Mark Twain published his *Galaxy* sketch, but died of heart disease three months later.

532.1–3 AFTER half a year's luxurious vagrancy in the Islands, I . . . returned to San Francisco] Clemens left Honolulu aboard the *Smyrniote* on 19 July and arrived in San Francisco on 13 August. His Sandwich Islands trip, including the voyages there and back, lasted a little more than five months ("Passengers," Honolulu *Pacific Commercial Advertiser*, 21 July 66, 2).

532.4–30 lying two long weeks in a dead calm . . . trying to sit on an empty champagne bottle . . . and thread a needle] Between 24 July and 8 August the *Smyrniote* was becalmed, and so made negligible progress. Clemens's shipboard notebook entries and a letter written to his mother and sister describe certain games devised by the passengers, although not the one mentioned here (*N&J1*, 134–62; *L1*, 350–54).

532.13–14 For a whole day and part of a night we lay so close to another ship] The nearby ship was the *Comet*, which departed Honolulu for San Francisco just two and a half hours before the *Smyrniote*. Its passengers included some of Clemens's Sandwich Islands acquaintances: Mrs. Thomas Spencer and her two daughters, as well as Charles Marlette and Edward Howard (see the notes at 513.14 and 518.1–3; *N&J1*, 133; *L1*, 352; "Passengers," Honolulu *Pacific Commercial Advertiser*, 21 July 66, 2; "Passengers," San Francisco *Alta California*, 14 Aug 66, 4).

533.5–6 I was home again, in San Francisco, without means and without employment] Clemens was not in fact idle upon his return, as this remark suggests. During the seven weeks before his first public lecture in early October, he was busy with a variety of literary projects and journalistic assignments. He completed his Sandwich Islands letters to the Sacramento *Union* and, for the same newspaper, reported the horse races at the thirteenth annual fair of the California State Agricultural Society in Sacramento between 10 and 15 September (see Branch 1969). He contributed the sketch "How, for Instance?" to the New York *Weekly Review* and "Origin of Illustrious Men" to the *Californian*, and probably drafted "Forty-three Days in an Open Boat," which *Harper's Monthly* published in December. He may also have worked on a book-length manuscript based on his Sandwich Island letters, which he submitted for publication in 1867 without success. It is also unlikely that he was financially pressed during this period. According to his later recollection, the *Union* proprietors cheerfully agreed to pay him twenty dollars a week for "general correspondence" (presumably about three hundred and fifty dollars for seventeen and a half weeks), plus an extra $300 for his "grand 'scoop'" of the *Hornet* disaster (SLC 1899, 76–77; SLC 1866ii–jj, 1866qq; *L2*, 3–4, 58 n. 1).

533.7   at last a public lecture occurred to me] Clemens delivered his first lecture on 2 October 1866. He gave his first public account of the experience at a banquet held in his honor on 30 October 1869 in Pittsburgh, Pennsylvania, where he was scheduled to lecture two days later. The Pittsburgh account, widely quoted in the press, accords with the version that follows here except in a few particulars, which are identified in the notes below (*L3*, 382 n. 2; "A Feast of Humor," Buffalo *Express*, 3 Nov 69, 2, and "Mark Twain's First Lecture," San Francisco *Alta California*, 24 Nov 69, 2, both reprinting the Pittsburgh *Leader* of 31 October).

533.8–10   I showed it to several friends, but they . . . said . . . I would make a humiliating failure of it] In 1887 George E. Barnes, a proprietor of the San Francisco *Morning Call*, recalled that Clemens appeared at his office shortly after returning from the Sandwich Islands and solicited an opinion of his lecture idea, admitting that he had already been advised against it by Bret Harte, Charles Warren Stoddard, James F. Bowman, and "the rest of the fellows," who believed it would damage his "literary reputation" (Barnes, 1).

533.12–13   at last an editor . . . told me to "go ahead."] Barnes claimed that a *Call* editor (possibly meaning himself) read the manuscript of the lecture, found it "a well-constructed piece of work," and advised Clemens to go ahead with his plan (Barnes, 1). In writing this passage, however, Mark Twain probably had in mind (as Albert Bigelow Paine suggests) his friend and enthusiastic supporter John McComb (1829–96), a foreman on the San Francisco *Alta California* who would soon become its supervising editor and one of its owners (*MTB*, 1:292; *L1*, 361; *L2*, 12–13 n. 1).

533.16–18   The proprietor of the several theatres . . . said I might have his handsome new opera-house] Thomas Maguire (1820–96), originally from Ireland, was at this time San Francisco's most noted theatrical impresario. He owned the Opera House, built in the early 1850s, and the larger and more splendid Academy of Music, completed in May 1864. It was at this latter hall that Clemens delivered his first lecture. Many years later Clemens recalled Maguire's advice to "make my fortune—strike while the iron was hot—break into the lecture field!" (AD, Apr 1904, CU-MARK, in *MTA*, 1:242; Hart, 300; Lloyd, 153–54).

533.23–27   the last line of my posters . . . Doors open at 7½. The trouble will begin at 8 . . . Showmen have borrowed it frequently] Mark Twain explained in an 1867 letter to the *Alta* that he wrote his lecture announcement in the offices of the *Call*. The last line of the original text read: "Doors open at 7 o'clock. The trouble to begin at 8 o'clock" (SLC 1866*ll*). The announcement appeared in the San Francisco papers beginning on 27 September, and was distributed throughout the city as a poster. By the following year, the "trouble" phrase had been copied by performers as far away as New York City (SLC 1867g; Fatout 1960, 36–37; *MTTB*, 292 n. 2, Letter XVIII).

533.35–534.3   I went to three old friends . . . and said: . . . I would like to have you . . . help me through] One of these friends was certainly John McComb, whom Joseph Goodman described in 1881 as "the same wholesome, considerate fellow that befriended us all in early days and clacqued so conscientiously at your first lecture" (Goodman to SLC, 9 Mar 81, CU-MARK). Goodman's remark suggests that he was present as well. And according to Bailey Millard, one of Clemens's successors as local reporter on the San Francisco *Morning Call*, "Bret Harte and some of his friends" decided to "form a big claque that would insure the success of the affair" (Millard, 371; *CofC*, 10).

534.4–7   the wife of a popular citizen . . . and her husband would sit prominently in the left-hand stage-box] Amelia Ransome Neville, who attended the lecture, identified this cooperative acquaintance as Mrs. Frederick F. Low, whose husband—a former gold miner and banker—was governor of California from 1863 to 1867 (Neville, 162–63; *L1*, 373 n. 1).

534.14–16   My name's Sawyer . . . if you knew how bad I wanted to laugh, you'd give me a ticket] In April 1872 the San Francisco *Chronicle* identified Sawyer as long-time San Francisco resident William M. Slason (1831?–72), "a member of old Knickerbocker Engine Company, of a jolly, rollicking, boisterous nature, whose love for a joke was only exceeded by a fondness for rye" ("Bill Slason," 11 Apr 72, 3). At the time of Mark Twain's lecture, Slason was a driver for Wells, Fargo and Company (Langley 1865, 404; "Died," San Francisco *Call*, 9 Apr 72, 4).

534.31–32   "No sales," I said to myself] Clemens's 1869 version was probably more accurate, if less dramatic: "I went down to the theater about four o'clock in the afternoon. . . . Every seat in the house had been sold" ("Mark Twain's First Lecture," San Francisco *Alta California*, 24 Nov 69, 2).

536.23–24   as for the bludgeons, they performed like pile-drivers] Bailey Millard claimed that "although Harte tried to steer the claquers, they insisted upon applauding and laughing in the wrong places, which may or may not have been intended as a joke on Twain" (Millard, 371).

536.28–29 All the papers were kind . . . I had abundance of money] The press reviews of the lecture were uniformly favorable. The San Francisco *Dramatic Chronicle* called it "one of the greatest successes of the season" ("Academy of Music," 3 Oct 66, 3), while the *Evening Bulletin* went so far as to praise it as "one of the most interesting and amusing lectures ever given in this city" ("Local Matters," 3 Oct 66, 5). The *Call* noted that the lecture "evinced a good deal of shrewd observation on the part of the speaker, and was replete with valuable information and eloquent description, judiciously varied at intervals by telling bits of humor, which were given in the lecturer's happiest manner" ("'Mark Twain's' Lecture on the Sandwich Islands," 3 Oct 66, 3, clipping in Scrapbook 1:61, CU-MARK). The reviewer for the *Alta California* concluded, "Mark Twain has thoroughly established himself as the most piquant and humorous writer and lecturer on this coast" ("City Items," 3 Oct 66, 1, clipping in Scrapbook 1:61, CU-MARK). According to Albert Bigelow Paine, Clemens's gross returns from ticket sales were about twelve hundred dollars, of which he kept about one-third after paying his expenses and his agent (probably Denis McCarthy: see the next note; *MTB*, 1:294). On the morning after the lecture the *Dramatic Chronicle* printed the following anecdote:

> Meeting "Mark" this morning on Montgomery street, the following dialogue ensued:
>
> "*Mark*"—Well, what do they say about my lecture?
>
> *We*—Why, the envious and jealous say it was "a bilk" and a "sell."
>
> "*Mark*"—All right. It's a free country. Everybody has a right to his opinion, if he *is* an ass. Upon the whole, it's a pretty even thing. They have the consolation of abusing me, and I have the consolation of slapping my pocket and hearing their money jingle. They have their *opinions*, and I have their *dollars. I'm* satisfied. ("'Mark Twain's' Consolation," 4)

537.4 I took an old personal friend along to play agent for me] The old friend was Denis E. McCarthy (1840–85), an Australian of Irish descent who went to San Francisco with his parents in 1850 and began to work in a printing shop. When Clemens joined the staff of the Virginia City *Territorial Enterprise* in 1862 McCarthy was one of its proprietors (see the note at 274.25–26). After selling his share in the *Enterprise* to Joseph Goodman in September 1865, McCarthy moved to San Francisco, expecting to augment his fortune through mining-stock investments. He also launched a short-lived weekly paper, *The Irish People*. Unfortunately, however, McCarthy "was not a success as a speculator, for within four months he had lost his last dollar," and was apparently struggling financially when Clemens needed an agent in the fall of 1866. After the lecture tour McCarthy "returned to Virginia City and engaged as foreman in what but a few months before had been his own job office" (Angel, 326). He continued at the *Enterprise* until 1869, eventually recouping his losses in the Big Bonanza boom of 1873–74 (*L1*, 361–62; "Death of D. E. McCarthy," Virginia City *Evening Chronicle*, 17 Dec 85, 2; Lingenfelter and Gash, 254).

537.5   for two or three weeks we roamed through Nevada and California] The lecture tour lasted one month. In California, Clemens spoke in Sacramento (11 October), Marysville (15 October), Grass Valley (20 October), Nevada City (23 October), Red Dog (24 October), and You Bet (25 October); then, moving on to Nevada, in Virginia City (31 October), Carson City (3 November), Washoe City (7 November), Dayton (8 November), Silver City (9 November), and Gold Hill (10 November). According to the *Enterprise,* Clemens spent a brief time "rusticating at Lake Tahoe" between his Carson City and Washoe City engagements. According to Thomas Fitch, however, Clemens was his guest at Washoe City during the interim ("Mark Twain," Virginia City *Territorial Enterprise,* 6 Nov 66, 3; Fitch, 55–56).

537.6–8   Two days before I lectured in Virginia City, two stage-coaches were robbed . . . just at dawn] Clemens lectured in Virginia City on the evening of 31 October. Between 1:00 and 2:00 A.M. on that same day two stages of the Pioneer Line, traveling together from California, were waylaid and robbed near the summit of the Geiger grade, three or four miles north of the town. The masked highwaymen—whose leader was gentlemanly and well spoken—blew open a Wells, Fargo safe containing $5,150 in gold coin and then robbed the male passengers, treating them politely and addressing some of them by name (Virginia City *Territorial Enterprise:* "Highway Robbery—Is There No Remedy for It?" 1 Nov 66, 2; "Daring Stage Robbery," 1 Nov 66, 3; "The Brigands of the Geiger," 4 Nov 66, 3).

540.17–19   this whole thing was a practical joke, and the robbers were personal friends of ours in disguise] This hoax was actually perpetrated on the night of 10 November after Mark Twain's Gold Hill lecture, ten days after his appearance in Virginia City (not the "night after instructing Virginia," as he claims at 537.17). That same night, still unaware of the joke, Clemens wrote a "Card to the Highwaymen," which was printed in the *Enterprise* the following day. There he gave a briefer and less good-humored account of the hold-up and asked the attackers to return his watch, a cherished memento of his tenure as governor of the Third House in the winter of 1863–64 (SLC 18660o; see the note at 297.22). Of the many other accounts of the hoax, perhaps the most authoritative is Steve Gillis's, contained in a 1907 letter to Albert Bigelow Paine. Gillis claimed that he and McCarthy staged the joke to provide Clemens with a financial incentive, as well as a fresh subject, for a second Virginia City lecture, inasmuch as he had refused to "repeat himself in the same town" (Chester L. Davis 1956a, 3). They enlisted some of Clemens's Virginia City acquaintances to join them in impersonating highwaymen, among them police officer George W. Birdsall, Leslie F. Blackburn, Pat Holland, and Jimmy Eddington, who acted as the captain of the band. Clemens, however, was furious when he learned of the prank from Judge Alexander W. ("Sandy") Baldwin. He left Virginia City for San Francisco on 12 November, unmollified by the return of his stolen property and the conspirators' explanation. Paine's version of the story agrees substantially with Gillis's; another brief but straightforward sketch of the affair may be found in the journals of Alfred Doten, long associated with the Gold Hill *Evening News*. Considerably less factual are the recollections of William Gillis (who gives a different roster of participants) and the ill-natured reminiscences of Senator William M. Stewart (see the notes at 288.16–17 and 288.27–28; "Departures," Virginia City *Territorial Enterprise*, 13 Nov 66, 3; *MTB*, 1:297–302; Doten, 2:900–904 passim; Gillis, 108–16; William M. Stewart, 221–22).

542.4   When I returned to San Francisco] Clemens, apparently not incapacitated by his "troublesome disease" (541.19), delivered a revamped version of his Sandwich Islands lecture in San Francisco on 16 November, concluding it with "the only true and reliable history of the late REVOLTING HIGHWAY ROBBERY, Perpetrated upon the Lecturer, at dead of night, between the cities of Gold Hill and Virginia" (advertisement, San Francisco *Times*, 16 Nov 66, 4). He went on to lecture in San Jose (21 November), Petaluma (26 November), and Oakland (27 November). Before he left for the East, he gave one final performance in San Francisco, on 10 December (*L1*, 367 n. 4).

542.4–5   I projected a pleasure journey to Japan and thence westward around the world] In Honolulu in June 1866 Anson Burlingame, the American minister to China, urged Clemens to visit him in Peking in 1867. "I expect to do all this," Clemens wrote to his family at the time, "but I expect to go to the States first—& from China to the Paris World's Fair" (*L1*, 347–48). Clemens's intention of visiting the Orient was still alive in September 1866, when he mentioned the proposed trip in a letter to the Honolulu *Hawaiian Herald*. Soon thereafter, on 20 October, the Honolulu *Pacific Commercial Advertiser* printed a "Letter from San Francisco" that reported, "Mark Twain will probably revisit your shores en route for Japan and China, where he proposes to spend a few years traveling and writing for the Eastern press" (Ajax, 1; SLC 1866mm). Another item in the same issue added, "Verbally we hear that he is to write for the [San Francisco] *Bulletin*" ("An interesting letter . . . ," Honolulu *Pacific Commercial Advertiser*, 20 Oct 66, 3).

542.5–9   but a desire to see home again changed my mind, and I took a berth . . . to New York] By 4 December Clemens had decided against

traveling directly to the Orient: "The China Mail Steamer is getting
ready & everybody says I am throwing away a fortune in not going in
her. I firmly believe it myself. [¶] I sail for the States in the Opposition
steamer of the 15th inst, positively and without reserve" (L1, 369). Having accepted an assignment as a traveling correspondent for the San
Francisco *Alta California*, Mark Twain was about to embark on the
first leg of a journey that would eventually take him, according to the
Alta, to "the 'Universal Exposition' at Paris, through Italy, the Mediter-
ranean, India, China, Japan, and back to San Francisco by the China
Mail Steamship line." He bid formal farewell to San Francisco and California in the concluding remarks of his 10 December lecture at Congress Hall in San Francisco. Speaking in his most exalted oratorical
style, he predicted "the dawn of a radiant future" for the state: "A splendid prosperity shall descend like a glory upon the whole land!" (" 'Mark
Twain's' Farewell," San Francisco *Alta California*, 15 Dec 66, 2, in Benson, 211–13). Clemens sailed on the steamer *America*, captained by
Edgar Wakeman, on 15 December and arrived at San Juan del Sur, Nicaragua, on 28 December. After crossing the isthmus to San Juan del
Norte (Greytown), he embarked on the steamer *San Francisco* on 1 January 1867, arriving at New York on 12 January (N&J1, 238–40; L2, 1).

542.9–11   the cholera broke out among us . . . and we buried two or three
bodies at sea every day] Soon after the *San Francisco* sailed, cholera
broke out among the steerage passengers. Before the vessel anchored at
New York seven passengers had died from cholera and other causes.
Clemens's notebook for the period and his correspondence for the *Alta*
record the details of the harrowing voyage (see N&J1, 238–99, and
MTTB, 11–81).

542.11   I found home a dreary place] Clemens left New York on 3 March
1867 to visit his family in St. Louis. There is little in his *Alta* correspondence to suggest that his St. Louis stay was "dreary": he told his
readers that he "found it and left it the same happy, cheerful, contented
old town" (SLC 1867e). A year and a half later, however, he would admit
to Mary Mason Fairbanks: "There is something in my deep hatred of
St. Louis that will hardly let me appear cheery even at my mother's
own fireside. Nobody knows what a ghastly infliction it is on me to
visit St. Louis. I am afraid I do not always disguise it, either" (L2, 252).
During his 1867 visit, Clemens lectured several times—in St. Louis
and Hannibal (Missouri), in Keokuk (Iowa), and in Quincy (Illinois)—
during March and the first half of April before returning to New York
(L2, 19 n. 2, 23 n. 1).

542.17–18   I went away and joined the famous Quaker City European Ex-
cursion] This pleasure excursion to Europe and the Holy Land was organized by members of Henry Ward Beecher's Plymouth Church in
Brooklyn. The travelers embarked from New York on 8 June 1867 for a

five-month cruise aboard the steamer *Quaker City*. Clemens's participation was sponsored by the *Alta*, which paid his $1,250 fare plus $500 for expenses, as an advance against fifty letters he was expected to write during the voyage. He also arranged to correspond for the New York *Tribune* and (without signature) the New York *Herald*. The excursion ultimately became the subject of his first major book, *The Innocents Abroad* (SLC 1869a; *L2*, 14–15, 23–24 n. 1, 55 n. 3, 62).

542.19 after seven years of vicissitudes] See the note at 2.24–28.

545.6–9 Joseph Smith . . . was driven from State to State . . . inscriptions with] See the notes at 107.5–10 and 107.12. Smith claimed that he acquired the metal plates and "seer" stones near his home in Manchester, New York, in 1827. He soon carried them to Harmony, Pennsylvania, where in 1828–29 he dictated his translation of them (Brodie, 37–42; Donna Hill, 73).

545.9–10 he instituted his "church" in Ohio and Brigham Young joined it] Smith founded his church on 6 April 1830 in Fayette, New York, but settled in Kirtland, Ohio, about one year later. Young converted in the fall of 1831 and was baptized in April 1832 at Mendon, New York (Arrington and Bitton, 16, 21; Arrington 1985, 16–20, 413).

545.14–16 He was made one of the Twelve Apostles . . . shortly fought his way to a higher post . . . President of the Twelve] Young was among the twelve Mormon apostles named in February 1835. On 19 January 1841, Smith reported a divine revelation that, among other things, made Young the president of the apostles, a position he had already assumed (on lesser authority) in October 1838—rather than in 1836, as Waite inaccurately asserted (Cook, 242, 251; Arrington 1985, 48, 66; Waite, 13).

545.16–19 The neighbors rose up and drove the Mormons out of Ohio, and they settled in Missouri . . . they retreated to Nauvoo, Illinois] Shortly after Smith and about two hundred followers settled in Kirtland, Ohio, where they built their first temple, he designated Jackson County in western Missouri as the Mormon "Zion," or gathering place, and many of his followers, including some from Ohio, began to settle there. Conflict with non-Mormon neighbors in 1833 forced the Jackson County Mormons, numbering over a thousand, to resettle in neighboring counties north of the Missouri River. In 1837–38 the remaining Ohio group, which included Young and Smith, joined the colony in Missouri, driven there mainly by former Mormons who were outraged at what they regarded as Smith's financial dishonesty. By 1839 the often violent antagonism of non-Mormons in Missouri had driven the Mormons to Illinois, where they settled in Nauvoo on the Mississippi (Arrington 1985, 37, 53, 61–62; Allen and Leonard, 84–88, 108–9, 128–37; Brodie, 199–207, 210).

545.19–21 built a temple which . . . achieved some celebrity] Guided by
Smith's revelation, the Mormons began this temple in 1841; it was still
incomplete when they left Nauvoo in 1846. Smith envisioned a building on a "magnificent scale . . . which will undoubtedly attract the attention of the great men of the earth" (Andrew, 57). It was an imposing,
boxlike structure built of limestone and costing as much as eight hundred thousand dollars. It had thirty ornamental pilasters, a domed oc-
tagonal tower, and a massive, pool-sized baptismal font (Flanders, 190–
91, 194–99, 207–8; Andrew, 62–76). Clemens must have been well
aware of Nauvoo while growing up in the 1840s, since it was only about
seventy miles upstream from his boyhood home at Hannibal, Missouri, and even closer to Keokuk, Iowa (an outfitting center for Mormon emigrants in the early 1850s), where Clemens lived in 1855–56.
See also the note at 546.27–31 (*L1*, 58–59, 69; Kimball 1988, 48).

545.24–26 All the proclamations Joseph Smith could issue denouncing
polygamy . . . were of no avail] See the notes at 99.27–29 and 111.22–
24.

546.1–3 Brigham returned from a mission . . . Mormon newspaper . . .
converts to his preaching] While directing Mormon missionaries in
England in 1840–41, Young began a monthly periodical, the *Latter-day
Saints' Millennial Star*, and arranged for an English edition of the Book
of Mormon as well as a Mormon hymnal. The English mission recorded six thousand new members that year and oversaw the emigration to Nauvoo of some eight hundred English converts (Arrington
1985, 80–81, 84, 94–95; Waite, 13).

546.4–6 Nauvoo was invaded by the Missouri and Illinois Gentiles, and
Joseph Smith killed] External antagonism and internal dissension fo-
cused increasingly on Smith himself, particularly his political ambitions and self-serving economic and theological policies. On 19 June
1844, he ordered the destruction of the office and press of the *Nauvoo
Expositor*, a newspaper founded by apostates trying to reform the
church, which brought matters to a climax:

> Angry crowds . . . were swarming the streets of Carthage and Warsaw [Illinois].
> Missourians and Iowans were crossing the river in droves. . . . Armed bands al-
> ready were threatening isolated Mormon families and driving them into Nau-
> voo. There was lynch talk everywhere—always in the name of justice and lib-
> erty. (Brodie, 378)

Smith was arrested on a charge of treason and then murdered by Illinois militiamen in the Carthage jail on 27 June 1844 (Brodie, 362–94;
Donna Hill, 387–418).

546.6–15 A Mormon named Rigdon . . . buffetings of Satan for a thousand years] Sidney Rigdon (1793–1876) had been a prominent Baptist
and Campbellite preacher for more than a decade when he joined the
Mormons in 1830, shortly after the church was founded. He was a pow-

erful influence on Smith, who, shortly after Rigdon's conversion, claimed a revelation instructing him to move, along with his own rapidly increasing following, to Kirtland, Ohio, near Rigdon's home. Kirtland remained effectively the church's headquarters until 1838. Several of Smith's revelations were addressed to Rigdon, and on one occasion the two men reported sharing a vision in which they conversed with Christ. In 1842, however, they became enemies. After Smith's death in 1844, Rigdon claimed a revelation appointing him "guardian" of the church. In August 1844 this claim was rejected by the church hierarchy and by the great majority of the Nauvoo Mormons. Young declared Rigdon's revelations to be "from the Devil," and in September he was excommunicated and "delivered over to the buffetings of satan until he repents" (Nauvoo *Times and Seasons:* "Continuation of Elder Rigdon's Trial," 5 [1 Oct 44]: 667; "Conclusion of Elder Rigdon's Trial," 5 [15 Oct 44]: 686). Mark Twain's account borrowed much from Waite's *Mormon Prophet,* even some of its wording (Waite, 14; McKiernan, 11, 41, 45–46, 68–69; Van Wagoner and Walker, 232–38).

546.16–17 They straightway elected Brigham Young President] Mark Twain apparently misinterpreted his source, who ambiguously stated that Young was immediately "elected President by an overwhelming majority" (Waite, 14). In rejecting Rigdon, the Mormons affirmed the leadership of the twelve apostles, of whom Young was already president. It was not until December 1847, more than three years later, that Young was named president of the church (Arrington 1985, 153).

546.23–25 on a bitter night in February filed . . . across the frozen Mississippi] In 1846, when the Mormons in Illinois numbered around sixteen thousand, conflicts similar to those which had driven them from Ohio and Missouri forced them to abandon Nauvoo. They first intended to leave in April, when the grass would support their livestock on the move west, but out of fear of further attack (possibly even by federal troops), they began their exodus in February, when the Mississippi was still frozen over, allowing some to cross on the ice (Arrington 1985, 125–27; Brodie, 362–63; Waite, 15).

546.25–26 their burning temple, whose sacred furniture their own hands had fired] This detail is not mentioned in Waite's account, or in any other known source, and is presumably fiction. Before departing Nauvoo the Mormons tried, but failed, to sell or lease their temple. On 9 February 1846, an accidental fire damaged a small section of the roof. The building was later vandalized but remained standing until, damaged by an arsonist's fire in 1848, it was destroyed by a cyclone in 1850 (Linn, 355–56; Rich, 4).

546.27–31 They camped . . . on the western verge of Iowa . . . and many succumbed and died . . . Two years the remnant remained there] For more than a year (until April 1847), the exiled Mormons lived in temporary camps spread out across Iowa and on either bank of the Missouri River, where it divided Iowa from Nebraska Territory. Some stayed in Iowa as long as five years before migrating to Utah (Arrington 1985, 127–29; Stegner, 209–10). In a letter to the San Francisco *Alta California* written on 19 April 1867, Mark Twain reported on a convention held by those who had remained permanently in Iowa—"a grand pow-wow at Keokuk" of the Reorganized Mormon Church under Joseph Smith III:

> It is strange how this lost tribe has kept its faith through so many years of sorrow and disaster. These are people who were scattered in tents for miles and miles along the roads through Iowa when the Mormons were driven out of Nauvoo with fire and sword, twenty-five years ago. Their heavy misfortunes appealed so movingly to the kindly instincts of the Iowa people that they rescued them from starvation, and gave them houses and food and employment, and gradually they became absorbed into the population and lost sight of—forgotten entirely, in fact, till this Convention of young Joe's called them out, and then from every unsuspected nook and cranny crept a Mormon—a Mormon who had for many a year been taken for a Baptist, or a Methodist, or some other kind of Christian. (SLC 1867f)

546.32–37   purposely choosing a land . . . *outside . . . the hated American nation* . . . the United States] Waite claimed that in 1846 Young intended "to found his theocratic monarchy" in Mexico (Waite, 16). Great Salt Lake City remained in Mexican territory from its settlement in July 1847 until the ratification of the treaty ending the Mexican War in March 1848. In choosing a place to settle, the Mormons sought primarily to escape persecution by their neighbors. Their patriotic feelings for the "American nation" were certainly eroded by the repeated failure of government to protect them from violence, but there is little evidence that the Mormons were surprised or disappointed by the results of the Mexican War (Bancroft 1882–90, 21:239–41; Arrington 1985, 128–29; Eugene E. Campbell, 201–4; Flanders, 86).

546.37–547.5   In 1849 the Mormons organized a "free and independent" government . . . but made Brigham Governor of it] Mark Twain quotes from Waite, who quoted from the preamble of the "Constitution of the State of Deseret," submitted to the constitutional convention on 18 March 1849:

> We, the people, grateful to the Supreme Being for the blessings hitherto enjoyed, and feeling our dependence on Him for a continuance of those blessings, *do ordain and establish a free and Independent Government*, by the name of *the State of Deseret*; including all the territory of the United States within the following boundaries. (Waite, 21–22)

Deseret included some two hundred and sixty-five thousand square miles, extending from the Rockies to the Pacific Coast in present-day southern California, and from present-day southeastern Oregon to southern Arizona. Waite characterized the "formation of this government for the State of Deseret" as "the first effort to throw off the yoke of the Federal Government" (Waite, 23). In fact, Deseret promptly applied to Congress for statehood. Congress instead created the (much smaller) Territory of Utah in September 1850, and President Fillmore appointed Young the territorial governor, since he had already been elected governor of the provisional state (Arrington 1985, 223–27).

547.16–19 dressed to personate the worshipped and lamented prophet Smith . . . "President Brigham Young!"] Mark Twain's source inaccurately placed this incident in Iowa in December 1847, when Young became president of the church. It actually took place in Nauvoo, at the time of Young's victory over Rigdon in August 1844 (Waite, 18–19; Arrington 1985, 114–15).

547.21–25 Within five years afterward he openly added polygamy . . . denouncing polygamy to the day of his death] See the notes at 99.27–29 and 111.22–24.

547.26–27 Now was Brigham become a second Andrew Johnson in the small beginning and steady progress of his official grandeur] At least three times in 1869 Mark Twain ridiculed President Johnson's pride in being a self-made man who rose from poverty to the highest office in the land. In "The White House Funeral," written in March, he had Johnson say, in part: "born and reared 'poor white trash,' I have clung to my native instincts, and done every small, mean thing my eager hands could find to do" (SLC 1869b). In "The Last Words of Great Men," published in September, he had Johnson say: "I have been an alderman, member of Congress, Governor, Senator, Pres——adieu, you know the rest" (SLC 1869i). And in an unpublished burlesque of Victor Hugo, "L'Homme Qui Rit," probably written about the same time, the hero, representing Johnson, becomes a clown and plays "all the characters known to the profession—Alderman, Mayor, Legislator, Congressman, Senator, Vice President, President!" (SLC 1869g).

547.30–34 President of all Mormondom, civil and ecclesiastical; . . . he proclaimed himself a God] This passage owes something to Waite's listing of Young's various *"rôles"*

as "Governor of Utah and Superintendent of Indian Affairs;" "President of the Church, Prophet, Seer, and Revelator;" "Trustee in Trust for the Church;" "President of the Emigration Company;" "Lord of the Harem;" "Eloheim, or Head God;" and "Grand Archee of the Order of the Gods." (Waite, 20)

The final accusation was based in part on Waite's claim that Young "has encouraged a doctrine, which he dare not put in print;—no less than *to arrogate to himself the attributes of Deity*" (Waite, 174–75). Mormons believe that every man is capable of becoming a god after death, but there is no evidence that Young made any more grandiose claim for himself (Arrington 1985, 205).

547.37–548.6 Into it all faithful Mormons will be admitted . . . status advanced accordingly] In Mormon doctrine, a man's status in the afterlife is enhanced by the number of his children. There is some evidence that in early years the Mormons sanctioned the practice of proxy marriage and fatherhood, but it was never widespread (Remy and Brenchley, 2:153–56; Waite, 189, 257–58; Foster, 163–66).

548.21–22   the deathless hatred which the Mormons bear our people and our government] An exaggeration. There were Mormon separatist factions, and even nonseparatists often expressed bitterness about federal policies they regarded as punitive, but the Mormons persistently sought statehood for Utah Territory (see also the note at 546.32–37; Waite, 3–4, 23, 28–29, 51, 300; Hyde, 310, 314, 315; Remy and Brenchley, 2:248–52; Creer, 107–13).

548.23   "fed fat its ancient grudge"] *The Merchant of Venice*, act 1, scene 3.

548.26   Mormondom was for the Mormons] Young's policy from the outset was to settle Mormons as widely as possible throughout the region in order to prevent rival settlements. He encouraged Mormon self-sufficiency and discouraged commerce with non-Mormons, even at times boycotting non-Mormon businesses (O'Dea, 84–85; Arrington 1958, 248–49, 256; Arrington 1985, 169, 173).

548.26–31   The United States tried to . . . put these gentlemen in office] Based on Waite's chapter 4, "Political History Continued.—The Mormon War" (50–69), Mark Twain's capsule account of the 1857–58 hostilities between Mormons and federal troops is somewhat simplified. Some, but not all, non-Mormon territorial officials came into conflict with the community and were resisted. In the summer of 1857, President Buchanan concluded that the Mormons were in rebellion against federal authority. He appointed Alfred Cumming to replace Young as governor (see the note at 552.40–553.2), and ostensibly to secure his installation and that of other non-Mormon officials, ordered twenty-five hundred army regulars, accompanied by a civilian force of about equal size, to go to Utah. Fearing invasion and military occupation, the Mormons harassed the approaching force by occasionally destroying its supplies, but did not attack it outright. With the force present during the spring and summer of 1858, Mormons offered no resistance either to Cumming and other newly appointed officials, or to the establishment of Camp Floyd (see the note at 85.7; Furniss, 21–33, 52–61, 95–97, 109, 122–23; Creer, 90–101, 128, 149, 158–60; Arrington 1985, 251).

548.31–549.9   And after they were in office they . . . got scared and . . . left the Territory] A condensation of Waite's dramatic account of Mormon hostility toward federal appointees, who issued writs that the "people, instigated by the Mormon leaders, refused to obey." In particular, she mentioned a judge who found "his life threatened and in danger, and soon after left the Territory," and another who reportedly "died from the effects of poison, administered by the hands of a Mormon" (Waite, 31, 34, 46).

549.11–12 In 1857 Gen. Harney came very near being appointed Governor of Utah] No evidence has been found (nor does Waite assert) that Brevet Brigadier General William Selby Harney (1800–89) was considered for governor, but in May 1857 he was put in command of the troops sent to Utah with newly appointed Governor Cumming. In late August, however, long before the troops reached Utah, Harney was replaced by Colonel Albert Sidney Johnston (1803–62). Hubert H. Bancroft described Harney as "a man of much rude force of character, ambitious, and a capable officer, but otherwise ill fitted for the conduct of an expedition that needed the qualities of a diplomatist more than those of a soldier" (Bancroft 1882–90, 21:497). Harney served briefly as commander of the Department of the West, headquartered at St. Louis, but was relieved of his command in May 1861, shortly before the Clemens brothers left there for Nevada. Suspected of Southern sympathies, Harney remained inactive during the Civil War (Furniss, 63, 67, 95–96, 101).

549.13–14 Cradlebaugh Judge] In 1857 President Buchanan appointed John Cradlebaugh (1819–72) associate justice of Utah Territory, but Cradlebaugh did not arrive in Salt Lake City until November 1858. His determined efforts to try certain cases antagonized the Mormons as well as Governor Cumming, who favored conciliation. In particular, Cradlebaugh tried the men accused of perpetrating the infamous Mountain Meadows massacre (see the notes at 552.14–15, 552.40–553.2, and 553.3–4). He was reprimanded by Buchanan's attorney general for disregarding the government's "principles and rules of action," and in 1860 resisted the appointment of his replacement, claiming that his own term had not expired. He then settled in the part of western Utah which in 1861 became Nevada Territory, eventually serving as its first delegate to Congress. As a volunteer officer in the Civil War, he was seriously wounded in 1863 and returned to Nevada, where in 1864 he ran unsuccessfully for United States senator (Bancroft 1882–90, 21:500, 562 n. 36; Furniss, 97, 208; Angel, 78, 87; Marsh, 682 n. 160, 687 n. 217).

549.26–28 Congress of the United States had enacted a solemn law against polygamy . . . thirty more wives] President Lincoln signed the first antipolygamy legislation in 1862 during the Civil War, a conflict Mormon leaders thought would eventuate in the millennium and the vindication of Mormon doctrines. Active enforcement of the law was delayed until the early 1870s, first by the war itself, then by legal technicalities. After 1862 Young added three more wives (in 1863, 1865, and 1868) to the seventeen then living (Van Wagoner, 107–10; Arrington 1985, 420–21).

550.7–17   A great emigrant train from Missouri and Arkansas . . . additional grounds for lack of love for these wayfarers] In September 1857, when they were still fearful of being invaded by federal troops, a group of Mormons (abetted by Indians) attacked a wagon train at Mountain Meadows in southern Utah, killing some fifty men, forty women, and thirty-two children. The victims were members of a wagon train led by Alexander Fancher of Arkansas, which early in August had passed through Salt Lake City, where Mormons declined to resupply it. Resupply became increasingly difficult as the train traveled south through the territory, producing friction as it went: there were reports of damage to crops, water sources, and livestock, as well as injury to Indians. Some witnesses recalled that the travelers boasted of having persecuted Mormons in Missouri, and one even claimed to have the gun that had killed "Old Joe Smith." The "noted Mormon missionary" recently killed in Arkansas was also clearly pertinent: he was Parley Pratt (see the note at 103.13–14). But what Mark Twain cites as in itself a "sufficient cause for hot retaliation by the Mormon chiefs" was probably not even a contributing factor. Waite's claim that the emigrant families were "joined by some few Mormons, who were disaffected, and sought to travel under their protection," has not been confirmed (Waite, 76, 80). They were joined at Provo by a non-Mormon who had lived several months in Utah, which may explain the error (Brooks 1962, 211; Wise, 2, 270–76; Brooks 1970, 20–22, 30–57, 61–67, 78, 219–20).

550.17   this train was rich] Waite asserted that although the massacre was largely prompted by a desire for "revenge and retaliation," the "principal motive was plunder" (Waite, 80). The Fancher train was well equipped, and its members were more prosperous than typical emigrants. There were even reports that they carried a large quantity of gold coin (Wise, 10–12; Brooks 1962, 340, 372–76; Brooks 1970, 193, 199; Bancroft 1882–90, 21:545 n. 4; Carleton, 1–2, 9, 11).

550.20–21   "spoil" of an enemy . . . "delivered it into their hand?"] See, for example, Deuteronomy 2:33–36 and 3:3–7.

550.24–551.6   A "revelation" from Brigham Young . . . the mandate of Almighty God] Mark Twain quotes Waite (76, 79), adding the quotation marks around "revelation." No decisive evidence has been found to support Waite's claim regarding Young's orders. It is clear that his policies and behavior contributed to the charged atmosphere in which the crime occurred, and that he afterward collaborated in the coverup. A letter preserved in the Mormon archives indicates that he explicitly counseled against bloodshed in this instance and had no prior knowledge of the attackers' intentions. Nevertheless, John D. Lee, the high-ranking Mormon later executed for the Mountain Meadows massacre (see the note at 550.25–26), came to believe that "exterminating Captain Fancher's train of emigrants" was the "direct command of Brigham Young" (John D. Lee, 225; Brooks 1970, 61–67, 112–13, 219).

550.24   Great Grand Archee, or God] Waite identifies the "Grand Archees" as the highest ranking Mormons, who had the "power of life and death," within the "Order of the Danites," an "established institution in the Mormon Church" (Waite, 281; see the note at 85.33–34). This title has not been verified in Mormon literature, religious or secular.

550.25–26   President J. C. Haight, Bishop Higbee, and J. D. Lee (adopted son of Brigham)] These men, all deeply implicated in the Mountain Meadows massacre, were among the local leaders who shared civil, religious, and military authority in the small Mormon communities of southern Utah. Isaac Chauncey Haight (1813–86) was, at the time of the massacre, mayor of Cedar City (the town nearest the emigrants' encampment), delegate to the territorial legislature, president of the Cedar Stake of the Mormon church (the highest local religious authority), and lieutenant colonel in the local militia. In his military capacity he was the immediate superior of the men who attacked the emigrants, receiving and sending messages and orders between the men at Mountain Meadows and his own military superior in a neighboring town, but he was not present during the actual attack, first visiting the site the following morning. John Mount Higbee (1827–1904) was a counselor to Haight in the local church leadership and a major in the militia, a detachment of which he commanded in the attack at Mountain Meadows. Higbee coordinated his activities with John Doyle Lee (1812–77), who assumed responsibility for carrying out the overall plan of attack. Lee, who had been "sealed for eternity" to Young as an adopted son in 1845, was a long-time leader in southern Utah. At the time of the massacre he was a probate judge, county clerk, assessor, and local agent to the Indians. In time, the leading participants in the massacre, including these three men, went into exile outside Utah. By 1870, disapproval had grown so strong within the Mormon church that Haight and Lee were excommunicated, although no action was taken against Higbee. Haight was readmitted about four years later. Lee remained in hiding—ostracized by his church, his associates, and his neighbors—until his arrest in 1874. His first trial ended with a hung jury. He was convicted after a second trial, at which a number of his associates at Mountain Meadows testified against him, evidently having agreed to make him a scapegoat. He was taken to the site of the massacre and executed there in 1877, the only participant ever tried for the crime. Lee's autobiography, including his account of the Mountain Meadows massacre, was published posthumously (Brooks 1970, 52–55, 72–74, 76, 79, 83, 86, 110–11, 184–87, 191, 193–98, 207–12; Brooks 1962, 73, 185; Jones and Jones, 10–11, 28; Eugene E. Campbell, 170–72; John D. Lee).

551.7–552.2 A large party of Mormons . . . tricked out as Indians . . . the slaughter commenced] The emigrants were first attacked on 7 or 8 September 1857, while camped about two hundred sixty miles south of Salt Lake City at Mountain Meadows, where they planned to take an extended rest before continuing their journey to California. Eyewitness accounts of the initial attack conflict; the aggressors are described both as an Indian party of "several hundred" and as a group of Mormons disguised as Indians (John D. Lee, 226; Brooks 1970, 275). Mark Twain accepts the latter version, on the authority of Waite's quotation of the account by Cradlebaugh (see the note at 551.25–28), who interrogated the Indians in 1859 while investigating the incident. The Indians reported that the Mormons alone—"all painted"—had initiated the attack, after which the Indians joined in (Waite, 72). By 10 September a group of Mormons, over fifty strong, commanded by the local military, had gathered near the besieged emigrants. On Friday afternoon, 11 September, the emigrants were lured from their camp by the Mormons' promise of protection from the Indians. After allowing themselves to be disarmed, they were systematically murdered, the Mormons killing the men, the Indians killing the women and older children. The Mormons subsequently attempted to place full responsibility for the crime on the Indians (Brooks 1970, 67, 69–75, 101–5, 158–59, 165–66; Brooks 1962, 206–15; John D. Lee, 226–44, 379–80).

551.13–14 the sort of scurvy apologies for "Indians" which the southern part of Utah affords] Mark Twain may be echoing Cradlebaugh's remark that "the Indians in the southern part of the Territory of Utah" were unlikely to participate in a prolonged attack on the emigrants because they were "a very low, cowardly, beastly set" (Waite, 72).

551.24–25 The leaders of the timely white "deliverers" were President Haight and Bishop John D. Lee] Contrary to Cradlebaugh's assertion (quoted by Waite), Haight was not at the site, although he was a full participant in planning the massacre. Lee and a militiaman carried the white flag into the emigrants' camp and Lee negotiated the (false) terms of surrender (Waite, 73; John D. Lee, 238, 329, 334; Brooks 1970, 72–73).

551.25–28 Mr. Cradlebaugh . . . tells in a speech delivered in Congress] Cradlebaugh delivered this speech, on the "Admission of Utah as a State," in the House of Representatives on 7 February 1863. Waite quoted only a portion of it, apparently taking her text from its publication as a book (and making only minor changes in punctuation); her quotation in turn served as Mark Twain's source for the information paraphrased in the text at 551.7–25, as well as for the extract at 551.29–552.11 (Cradlebaugh, 17–19; Waite, 72–73).

552.3–5 Two only escaped . . . before they were overtaken and slaughtered] Most accounts agree that three emigrants escaped the initial attack on 7 or 8 September, but were killed subsequently. There were no adult survivors (Brooks 1970, 70–72, 97–100).

552.8–9 Seventeen individuals . . . were spared, and they were little children] The Mormons spared eighteen young children. In 1859 the territorial superintendent of Indian affairs, Jacob Forney (see the note at 553.33–34), located and took custody of seventeen of them to be returned to relatives. The remaining child apparently lived her life among the Mormons (Brooks 1970, 101–5).

552.14–15 Judge Cradlebaugh . . . proceeded to make Mormondom answer for the massacre] Cradlebaugh held court in the town of Provo in March 1859 and attempted to prosecute a number of crimes, including the Mountain Meadows massacre. The following month he traveled with a military escort to the towns nearest Mountain Meadows, where he gathered testimony about the massacre and issued writs for the arrest of thirty-eight men. None was served because those named were all in hiding. Cradlebaugh's strong judicial stance won him high regard in some quarters: when he returned to Nevada in December 1863 he was hailed as a hero, both for his war record and his actions in Utah. "His fearlessness and impartiality in the administration of justice secured him the enmity of the Mormons of Salt Lake," noted the Carson City *Independent:*

> Pistols were drawn in the Court room, and men threatened to shoot him if he persisted in his course. The stern and plain-spoken old Judge told them to "shoot and be d—d, but he intended to do his duty." Neither threats nor persuasion could swerve him one hair's breadth from what he deemed to be the path of duty. ("Judge Cradlebaugh," Sacramento *Union,* 28 Dec 63, 1, reprinting the Carson City *Independent*)

Mark Twain, who was then reporting for the Virginia City *Territorial Enterprise,* would surely have seen this article or others like it ("Ovation to Colonel Cradlebaugh," Sacramento *Union,* 4 Jan 64, 4, reprinting Carson City *Independent* of 30 December; Furniss, 214–19; Cradlebaugh, 15–16, 19–20; Waite, 70, 74; Brooks 1970, 173, 177).

552.19 "breathing threatenings and slaughter!"] Acts 9:1.

552.20 An editorial in the *Territorial Enterprise*] No example of the *Enterprise* printing is known to survive. Mark Twain's source for the extract at 552.22–35 was Waite's book, which quoted only a portion of the original (Waite, 84–85).

552.40–553.2 Cumming was the Federal Governor . . . to screen the Mormons from the demands of justice] In July 1857 Buchanan appointed Alfred Cumming (1802–73) to replace Young as territorial governor. Cumming had been mayor of Augusta, Georgia, and an Indian agent on the upper Missouri. Despite fears to the contrary (see the note at 548.26–31), Cumming was able to enter Salt Lake City in April 1858 and peaceably effect the transfer of executive power. He adopted a conciliatory approach to the Mormons, "possibly going beyond moderation to leniency" (Furniss, 208). With Lincoln's inauguration in 1861, Cumming returned to Georgia (Furniss, 96–98, 207–8; Hafen and Hafen, 286–87, 296; Bancroft 1882–90, 21:525–26; Linn, 505–7; Wise, 252–54).

553.3–4   he even went so far as to publish his protest against . . . Cradlebaugh's proceedings] On opening his court in Provo in March 1859, Cradlebaugh requested of General Johnston a military detachment to aid in securing prisoners. The presence of armed troops from Camp Floyd—in direct contact for the first time with the civilian population—quickly inflamed the Mormon community. As the situation worsened, Governor Cumming ordered the troops withdrawn, but not before their numbers in and around Provo had swelled to over eight hundred. Johnston refused the order. Cumming, indignant at the usurpation of his authority, issued a proclamation on 27 March 1859 "protesting against all movements of troops except such as accorded with his own instructions as chief executive magistrate" (Bancroft 1882–90, 21:562). The conflict was rendered moot when Cradlebaugh adjourned his court because the Mormons refused to testify, the Mormon grand jury refused to bring charges, and all the likely suspects had gone into hiding. Cumming's position was later sustained by the federal government, and Cradlebaugh was censured for using federal troops to facilitate the work of the court (Furniss, 214–19; Bancroft 1882–90, 21:561–62 n. 36).

553.11–12   "confirmations strong as proofs of Holy Writ."] Othello, act 3, scene 3.

553.13–38   1. The evidence of Mormons themselves . . . Indian depredations] In reproducing Waite's list, Mark Twain reordered and renumbered items 1–7, presumably to reflect his own view of their relative importance: Waite's order (expressed with Mark Twain's numbers) was 1, 5, 7, 6, 3, 4, 2. In addition, he dropped Waite's extract of Campbell's testimony from item 8 and omitted entirely the last item on her list, a lengthy excerpt from the letters and reports of Jacob Forney (Waite, 76–79).

553.14–15   Deputy U. S. Marshal Rogers] During late March and April 1859 William H. Rogers, a territorial Indian agent and acting deputy United States marshal, assisted both Jacob Forney, superintendent of Indian affairs, and Cradlebaugh in their investigation of the Mountain

Meadows massacre. On 29 February 1860 Rogers published in the Salt Lake City *Valley Tan*, an anti-Mormon newspaper, a lengthy and dispassionate "Statement" about their findings and the evidence for Mormon participation in the crime (reprinted in Brooks 1970, 265–78). Rogers assisted Forney in recovering the surviving children and joined Cradlebaugh in interviewing people claiming knowledge of the massacre. His statement included an account of a detailed confession by one Mormon who participated in the massacre and "gave Judge C. the name of 25 or 30 other men . . . who assisted" (Brooks 1970, 276). He also described conversations with Indians who attributed the massacre to Mormons acting on orders of Young. Rogers attempted to serve Cradlebaugh's writs for the arrest of Haight, Higbee, and Lee, but found that the suspects—along with a "large portion" of the male population of the area—had fled (Brooks 1970, 272; Bancroft 1882–90, 21:557 n. 23; Furniss, 210–11).

553.16–19   The failure of Brigham Young to embody any account of it . . . until several years after the occurrence] Young continued to function as superintendent of Indian affairs until his replacement arrived in June 1858 (see the note at 553.33–34). On 6 January 1858, in his official report to the commissioner of Indian affairs in Washington, D.C., Young blamed the massacre on the emigrants themselves, claiming that their poisoning of meat and water resulted in the deaths of several Indians; he quoted Lee's report to him that "about the 22nd of Sept. Capt Fanchers & Co. fell victims to the Indians wrath near Mountain Meadows." Young took the occasion to deliver a homily on the mishandling of Indian affairs and expressed the hope that future relations with the Indians would benefit from "a uniform consistent humane and conciliating course of superior acts by those who profess superior attainments" (Brooks 1970, 158–59). Several years later, in a sermon of 8 March 1863, Young also claimed that he had assured Governor Cumming of the Mormons' full cooperation with a trial before "an unprejudiced judge"—that is, someone other than Cradlebaugh—but, Young maintained, the case had remained unprosecuted "for fear the Mormons would be acquitted . . . and our enemies would thus be deprived of a favorite topic to talk about, when urging hostility against us" (Arrington 1985, 280, 480 n. 30; Morgan, 407–8).

553.23–25   The failure of the "Deseret News," . . . to notice the massacre, until several months afterward] The Salt Lake City *Deseret News*, the only newspaper published in the territory between 1850 and November 1858, made no mention of the massacre until it published an account of Cradlebaugh's proceedings in March 1859 (Bancroft 1882–90, 21:326, 715–19).

553.27   The testimony of the children saved from the massacre] Forney, in his report of August 1859 to the commissioner of Indian affairs, stated that two such children were being "detained to give evidence" (Brooks 1970, 260).

553.33–34 J. Forney, who was, in 1859, Superintendent of Indian Affairs for the Territory] Jacob Forney of Philadelphia officially succeeded Young as territorial superintendent of Indian affairs in August 1857, although he did not reach Salt Lake City until June 1858. The results of Forney's inquiry into the massacre may be found in his several official reports to the commissioner of Indian affairs in Washington, D.C., and his letter of 10 May 1859 to the Salt Lake City *Valley Tan* (reprinted in Brooks 1970, 253–65, and Cradlebaugh, 34–38, 40–42; see also Waite, 78–79). In his report of August 1859 Forney concluded that the "massacre was concocted by white men and consummated by whites and Indians. The names of many of the whites engaged in this terrible affair have already been given to the proper legal authorities" (Brooks 1970, 259; Morgan, 407–8; Furniss, 194–95).

553.36–37 The testimony of R. P. Campbell, Capt. 2d Dragoons, who was sent . . . to protect travellers] Reuben P. Campbell was a United States Army captain who commanded the detachment of troops accompanying Cradlebaugh to southern Utah in April 1859. Campbell's report to his superior officer was included in the appendix to the published text of Cradlebaugh's speech. In it he attributed the massacre to "the *Mormons* . . . assisted by such of the wretched Indians of the neighborhood as they could force or persuade to join" (Cradlebaugh, 31–32; also in Waite, 77–78; Brooks 1970, 271, 312).

554.1–2 Conrad Wiegand, of Gold Hill, Nevada] Conrad Wiegand (1830–80), a native of Pennsylvania trained as a chemist, worked at the Philadelphia mint before relocating to the Pacific Coast. During the early 1860s he was the supervising assayer at the San Francisco branch mint. (There, in July 1861, Wiegand engaged in a public controversy with a fellow employee, accusing him of assault—much as he accuses John B. Winters in the document reproduced in this appendix.) Wiegand, described by the Virginia City *Union* as "one of the best assayers in the United States," accepted a position with the Gould and Curry works near Virginia City in November 1863 ("Ex-Assayer Wiegand," San Francisco *Evening Bulletin*, 6 Nov 63, 3, reprinting the Virginia City *Union*). He opened his own assay office in Gold Hill, Nevada, in June 1865. In June 1880, in debt and suffering from nervous depression, he committed suicide. It was sometime after Clemens left Nevada in 1864 that Wiegand became familiar to Virginia City and Gold Hill residents through frequent articles in the local newspapers. The Virginia City *Territorial Enterprise* tended to view Wiegand's crusading journalism with indulgence:

Mr. Wiegand means well. All his instincts are humane and moral. He is among the worthiest of a class of reformers, who, in the abstract, perhaps, think rightly, but who fritter away valuable lives in attempting to accomplish impossibilities.

But while Mr. Wiegand is one of the worthiest of the class referred to, he is also one of the most impracticable. His purposes are rambling, practically aimless, and almost numberless. To-day he assaults one public vice, to-morrow another, and the next day a third. The result is that he makes no impression upon any of them, and will die without having made the world a whit better than he found it. ("Hold, Enough!" Virginia City *Territorial Enterprise*, 4 Nov 69, 2)

("The Mint Again—Wiegand's Statement," San Francisco *Alta California*, 22 July 61, 1; "Assaying at Gold Hill," Virginia City *Union*, 1 June 65, 3; "A Shocking Suicide," Virginia City *Evening Chronicle*, 14 June 80, 3; "The Suicide of Conrad Wiegand," Virginia City *Territorial Enterprise*, 16 June 80, 3.)

554.10–11 When I met Conrad, he was "Superintendent of the Gold Hill Assay Office"] Although Clemens left Nevada several months after Wiegand's arrival, the two men apparently did not meet until April 1868, when Clemens visited Wiegand's Gold Hill assay office during a lecture tour. On 28 April, in Virginia City, Wiegand presented him with a silver brick inscribed "Mark Twain—Matthew v, 41—Pilgrim," an allusion to the verse "And whosoever shall compel thee to go a mile, go with him twain." In an unpublished account, probably written shortly after his visit to Wiegand's office, Mark Twain expressed admiration for him, marveling at his honesty and evident lack of self-interest: "In his theories he is earnest & sincere, but as he tries to secure them realization in life, he should anticipate the fate of all [who] attempt such toil, isolation, persecution, and defamation [tempered] only by the respect of a few" (SLC 1868c, 13; *ET&S1*, 43).

554.12–13 he was a street preacher, too, with a mongrel religion of his own invention] In December 1867, Wiegand became rector of Virginia City's newly formed "Humanitarian Christian Society." He resigned in disgust two months later, after his fellow Humanitarians objected to his lecturing on "politico-religious" themes ("Humanitarian Christian Society Organized," Gold Hill *Evening News*, 23 Dec 67, 3; Virginia City *Territorial Enterprise*: "Politico-Religious Notice," 23 Feb 68, 3; "A Card from Conrad Wiegand," 25 Feb 68, 2; "Resignation," 27 Feb 68, 3). At that time the *Enterprise* published an editorial about Wiegand (almost certainly written by Joseph T. Goodman), coining the word "Wiegandish" to characterize his views and attempting to explain the "Humanitarian" creed of "this erratic genius." In conclusion the editorial described Wiegand as

a slight built man, with regular and pale features that wear an indescribable expression of mildness and intellectuality, and large blue eyes that are full of fire and thought yet impress you only as singularly pure and gentle, which, together with a profusion of soft brown hair and whiskers, make up a countenance that will irresistibly recall to mind the likeness of the Savior. ("Wiegandish," Virginia City *Territorial Enterprise*, 23 Feb 68, 2)

554.14–15 Here latterly he has entered journalism] On 3 November 1869 Wiegand began circulating a prospectus for his projected newspaper, the *People's Tribune*, whose mission, the *Enterprise* inferred, would be to "show its teeth to the Bank of California, talk of the management of the Comstock mines, extend a helping hand to suffering men and lewd women, and play numerous other 'fantastic tricks before high heaven'" ("Hold, Enough!" Virginia City *Territorial Enterprise*, 4 Nov 69, 2). According to Wiegand, the paper was to be "an observer and photographist of the Beautiful and the Good—a spirit-like friend" and "a watchman for rascality in the mines and in public posts—a terrier till able to be a mastiff" (*People's Tribune* prospectus, quoted in "Dissolving Views," Gold Hill *Evening News*, 19 Jan 70, 2). The first number of the *Tribune* appeared on 13 January 1870, its masthead bearing a sweeping declaration: "Devoted to the Betterment of All Things, to the Defence of Right and to the People" (1:1). Among the specific causes espoused by the *Tribune* were women's rights, free schools, free homestead lands for the poor, and the abolition of income tax. The paper—initially eight pages, later reduced to four—cost fifty cents a year; a total of six numbers were issued, one each month through June 1870 ("The People's Tribune," Gold Hill *Evening News*, 13 Jan 70, 2; "Our Creed," *People's Tribune* 1 [June 70]: 32).

555.3–569.29   From the Territorial Enterprise, Jan. 20, 1870 . . . CONRAD WIEGAND.] This account by Wiegand appeared on the front page of the *Enterprise* of 20 January 1870, labeled as an "advertisement" and entitled "Mr. Winters' Assault on Conrad Wiegand." Wiegand reprinted the account—slightly corrected and revised—in the February number of his own *People's Tribune*, with the title given at 555.4, "A Seeming Plot for Assassination Miscarried." Mark Twain's source for the account was in fact Wiegand's reprinting in the *Tribune*, and not the *Enterprise*, as the credit line seems to imply. He could have obtained a copy of the *Tribune* from Joseph Goodman, when Goodman visited him in the spring of 1871. Indeed, it is possible that Goodman brought with him other material on the Wiegand controversy, perhaps as background for a planned book of his own, or for a joint project that remains unidentified (see the Introduction, page 841).

555.5   TO THE EDITOR OF THE ENTERPRISE] The intended addressee of Wiegand's newspaper letter has not been identified. The official editor-in-chief of the *Enterprise*, Joseph Goodman, was not in Nevada in January 1870, having left Virginia City on 1 December 1869 for a trip to Europe ("For Europe," Virginia City *Territorial Enterprise*, 2 Dec 69, 2). Nevertheless, it could have been he who "warned" (555.8) Wiegand and made "prophecies" (555.16) about the consequences of publicly opposing the Bank of California (see the next note). The acting editor, in Goodman's absence, may have been Rollin Daggett, who would take over the editorship when William Sharon bought the newspaper in 1874 (see the note at 340.8–9).

555.6–7   Months ago, when Mr. Sutro incidentally exposed mining mismanagement on the Comstock] On 20 September 1869 Adolph Sutro delivered a speech in Piper's Opera House in Virginia City, to persuade miners and other workingmen to lend their financial and political support to his tunnel project (see the notes at 360n.3–9 and 360n.12). He accused the Bank of California, which had initially backed the tunnel but was now strongly opposed to it, of having created a virtual monopoly on Comstock mining and milling operations through mortgages and unethical stock manipulations. Furthermore, he charged, this "bank ring" had fostered "ruinous and wasteful" management practices that exploited laborers, created extremely uncomfortable and unsafe working conditions, and would soon exhaust the surface lodes. He asserted that the proposed tunnel would increase safety in the mines by providing a means of escape from underground fires, such as the one that had recently killed about forty miners in the Yellow Jacket shaft. At the same time it would destroy the bank's monopoly and empower workingmen to "rule the destinies of this State" ("Speech of Adolph Sutro," Virginia City *Territorial Enterprise*, 23 Sept 69, 1, 4; Stewart and Stewart, 59–80).

555.7–8 among others roused me to protest against its continuance] Wiegand and others were persuaded by Sutro's speech to join his fight against the "banking ring." Within a few days, on 29 September, an unsigned advertisement appeared in the *Enterprise* for an 11 November meeting of Yellow Jacket stockholders, to discuss "an investigation into the affairs of the Company and a change in the management of the mine" ("Yellow Jacket Stockholders," 2). Wiegand pressed the fight in other ways as well. On 30 October the Gold Hill *Evening News* mentioned a circular he had produced attacking the Bank of California, reportedly containing "the *wildest* set of ideas" (" 'Awake!' " 2). And on 5 November the *Enterprise* announced an upcoming public meeting at which Wiegand was to deliver an address entitled "The Morals of Nevada, and the Future of the Comstock Mines" ("People's Tribune Meeting," 2).

555.26–29 On Thursday last . . . I was felled to the ground, and . . . kicked by a man] On 13 January 1870, while delivering the first issues of the *Tribune*, Wiegand was assaulted by a man named Griffith Williams, who was arrested and fined $7.50 by Judge E. C. Cook. The next day the Gold Hill *Evening News* remarked, "Mr. Wiegand rightly thinks that if that is the price set for half killing a man, $15 only would be the price for completing the job, according to Cook" ("A Dangerous Precedent," 14 Jan 70, 3; "Our Publisher Assaulted," *People's Tribune* 1 [Feb 70]: 1).

556.26–28 JOHN B. WINTERS, President of the Yellow Jacket Company, a political aspirant and a military General] Winters was the president and superintendent of the Yellow Jacket mine (see the next note) from April 1864 until November 1870. He served in the second Territorial Legislature and ran for Congress in 1864 under the first (defeated)

Nevada state constitution, and was an officer in Nevada's militia. Clemens first became friendly with Winters and his wife in 1862, while residing in Carson City. On several occasions he wrote warmly and favorably of Winters's character and tried to advance his political career, suggesting in mid-1863, for example, that he should run for territorial delegate to Congress, for the "people here know him, respect him, and have confidence in him, and he could be elected very easily" (SLC 1863k). After Winters's attack on Wiegand, the *People's Tribune* described him as a "powerful but cowardly bully, whose best title to the term of gentleman would seem to be that he is well-barbered, wears good clothes, drives a good team, and is permitted by genuine gentlemen in San Francisco to retain the Presidency or Superintendence of an important mine" ("Mr. Winters' Attack on Conrad Wiegand," *People's Tribune* 1 [Feb 70]: 13; *ET&S1*, 487, 488–89; "Report of the Territorial Adjutant-General for 1863," Virginia City *Union*, 4 Feb 64, 1; Doten 2:1109; Angel, 506).

556.27 Yellow Jacket Company] The Yellow Jacket silver mine, just south of Gold Hill, was located in May 1859 and consisted of 1,200 feet of the Comstock lode; the company was incorporated in February 1863 with a capital value of $1,200,000. In his correspondence for the San Francisco *Evening Bulletin* in December 1866, Mark Twain characterized the Yellow Jacket as the "principal mine" of the area, a formerly "shaky" operation that had been salvaged by "good management," presumably under Winters's direction (SLC 1866rr).

556.29–30 PHILIP LYNCH, Editor and proprietor of the Gold Hill *News*] Lynch (1822–72) went to the West in 1850 from Pennsylvania. He was a proprietor of the Sacramento *Index*, and then, in 1862–63, the *Placer Courier* in Forest Hill, California. He founded the Gold Hill *Evening News* in October 1863 and continued with the successful daily as publisher and editor until his death in February 1872 (Sacramento *Union:* "Died," 16 Feb 72, 5; "The Death of Philip Lynch," 17 Feb 72, 1, reprinting the Gold Hill *Evening News*; Lingenfelter and Gash, 97). Beginning in 1869, Lynch's newspaper followed the lead of the Bank of California and the major Comstock mining companies in opposing Adolph Sutro and his tunnel project. Lynch also supported John B. Winters and consistently put a good face on Yellow Jacket affairs and prospects. When the special meeting of Yellow Jacket stockholders was called, his newspaper refused to run the advertisement for it, calling it "irresponsible," and stating that the mine had "always been well conducted, and never better than under the management of its present officers" ("The Yellow Jacket S. M. Co.," Gold Hill *Evening News*, 29 Sept 69, 2).

557.23 as a stockholder in the Yellow Jacket mine] Wiegand owned thirty shares of Yellow Jacket stock ("Mr. Wiegand's Card," *People's Tribune* 1 [Feb 70]: 14).

557.26 Sharon] William Sharon (1821–85), an Ohio-born financier, had been the general agent in Virginia City for the Bank of California's Nevada branch since its establishment in November 1864; he also served as the agent for the Gold Hill office, which opened the following year. As the production of the Comstock mines declined in the latter half of the decade, Sharon lured mine owners and investors to borrow money at low interest rates and then foreclosed when they defaulted. The bank soon controlled extensive mining and milling operations—among them the Yellow Jacket mine—under the aegis of the Union Mill and Mining Company, and Sharon quickly accumulated a personal fortune (Virginia City *Union:* advertisement and "Bank of California," 17 Nov 64, 2, 3; Lord, 244–56, 263–65; Lavender 1975, 186–87; Hart, 468).

558.3 Dr. Zabriskie] C. B. Zabriskie, a physician and surgeon, had an office on Main Street in Gold Hill near Wiegand's assay office (advertisement, Gold Hill *Evening News,* 2 July 69, 2).

558.13 Sheriff Cummings] W. J. Cummings, sheriff of Storey County from November 1868 until November 1870 (Angel, 607).

560.7–8 those damnably false charges which you have preferred against me in that . . . lying sheet of yours] According to the Gold Hill *Evening News,* Winters objected to "two articles in the Tribune—the one being headed 'Hiding Ore,' and the other being the answers to 'A Miner's' communication, called 'What's the Matter with Yellow Jacket?'" (Lynch 1870a, 3). "Hiding Ore," an undated letter to the editor from "Silver Stuck," charged that Yellow Jacket officials had concealed information about the discovery of a body of good ore, asking "what right John B. Winters, or Wm. Sharon, or any one else, had to *order* a discovery of that kind to be concealed; or, *while levying assessments,* to allow that body of ore to remain untouched?" The second article—a letter to the editor dated 15 December 1869 and signed "A Miner," together with the *Tribune's* response—accused the Yellow Jacket management of numerous illegal or highly questionable practices, summed up in the assertion that "Wm. Sharon, the Board of Trustees, or John B. Winters are indictable before the Grand Jury for offenses of omission and commission, of which, if convicted, that fact would go far to purify the atmosphere of the State" (*People's Tribune* 1 [Jan 70]: 3). The author of the editorial response is not known; Wiegand clearly implies (at 563.9–12) that he did not write it. The allegations it contained were evidently true, for the most part. Winters himself reportedly later admitted that he had done Sharon's "dirty work"—sabotaging mine equipment and adulterating the ore being mined—in order to "break the price of the stock" (Michelson, 189–90; Marye, 88–89, 92–93; Grant H. Smith, 91, 93; Bancroft 1891–92, 4:52–57). After the disastrous Yellow Jacket fire of April 1869, the company's stock—which had reached over two thousand dollars a share in the spring of 1865—plummeted, never to recover: the price was under forty dollars by October. Joseph Goodman was evidently among those who "lost heavily" on Yellow Jacket stock, claiming that the mine's indisputably rich ore "all went to feed the Union Mill and Mining Company's mills. The stockholders never got a dividend from it" (Michelson, 190; Angel, 59, 615; Kelly 1863, 18; Lord, 269–77, 426–35).

560.22–24 Months ago you put your property out of your hands . . . to escape losing it on prosecution for libel] Wiegand responded to this charge in the February number of the *People's Tribune*. He explained that in 1865 his Gold Hill assaying business appeared to be growing so rapidly that he borrowed money from the Bank of California to expand. When ore production dropped late in the year, the bank brought suit for repayment, and his assaying tools were confiscated and sold by the sheriff. The case of *Sharon* v. *Wiegand* was heard in December 1865, and Wiegand was forced to suspend business; the court accepted his bankruptcy in January 1866. Wiegand almost immediately reopened with a new co-proprietor, and began to repay his debts, although not legally obliged to do so. In the fall of 1869, when establishing the *People's Tribune,* he anticipated that he might become a target for libel suits, and "to prevent a second seizure of my tools, I *sold* them and delivered possession of the same in the presence of witnesses," since "the best security against legal plunder in the State of Nevada . . . is not to be upright, *but to be POOR*" ("Mr. Wiegand's Card," *People's Tribune* 1 [Feb 70]: 14; Gold Hill *Evening News:* " 'Awake!' " 30 Oct 69, 2; "Insolvent Notice," 2 Jan 66, 4; "For Assay," 19 Jan 66, 2; advertisement, 29 Jan 66, 2; Virginia City *Union:* "The Court Reports" and "Insolvent," 17 Dec 65, 3).

561.33 Address to the People] The title of Wiegand's *People's Tribune* prospectus, published on 3 November 1869 (see the note at 554.14–15).

563.17–18 I, a man of family, and *not* as Mr. Winters is, "alone."] Wiegand and his wife, Martha, had one daughter. Winters's wife had recently died of cancer in San Francisco, on 20 November 1869 (Virginia City *Territorial Enterprise:* "The Suicide of Conrad Wiegand," 16 June 80, 3; "Death of Conrad Wiegand," 15 June 80, 3; "Death of Mrs. John B. Winters," 21 Nov 69, 3).

563.32–33 "Surely in vain the net is spread in the sight of any bird."] Proverbs 1:17.

567.23–24 that unguarded remark of Philip Lynch convicts him of having been privy . . . to Mr. Winters' intentions] In response to Wiegand's accusation against him, Lynch wrote: "I trust, also, to be able to vindicate myself of the foul charges of 'conspiracy to murder and assassinate,' and acting in bad faith towards Mr. Wiegand in asking him into my office to have an interview with General Winters—in making which charges Mr. Wiegand has done me a gross injustice" (Lynch 1870b, 2).

569.3–4 he has . . . suffered a thoroughly garbled statement of facts to appear in the Gold Hill *News*] Wiegand refers to "A Case of Slanderous Vilification and Its Consequences," almost certainly written by Lynch. Lynch's report ignored the substance of the *Tribune*'s charges, characterizing them as "rather sweeping insinuations against the honesty and integrity of several business men in this community." The account also differed from Wiegand's in some of its particulars. For example, Lynch stated that Wiegand refused to visit Winters at the Yellow Jacket office (cf. 557.19–558.11), and he claimed that Wiegand initially agreed to sign a statement acknowledging that he had written the charges against Winters "willfully and deliberately, knowing them to be false" (cf. 561.4–10; Lynch 1870a, 3).

569.7–9 what even the Gold Hill *News* has pronounced a disgraceful affair . . . because of some telegraphic mistake in the account of it] Lynch explained in the *News:*

We regret that this disgraceful affair occurred in the NEWS office, and it happened without any collusion whatever on the part of anybody connected with the office. The senior editor, who was the only witness of the affair, besides the parties themselves, especially feels aggrieved, as the report has been telegraphed all over the State that he was "cowhided like the devil" on Saturday! When in fact it was all a mistake. Several telegrams have been received by him to-day, from different sections, inquiring after his health, the price of raw-hides, etc., etc. (Lynch 1870a, 3)

569.15 W. C. Ralston] William C. Ralston (1826–75), son of an Ohio farmer, served as a steamboat clerk and then as the Panama City agent for a steamship company. He moved to San Francisco in 1854 and within two years became involved in banking. In 1864 he founded the Bank of California with Darius O. Mills and served as its cashier and manager until 1873, when he succeeded Mills as president. Ralston's injudicious and unauthorized investments and speculations in a vast empire of enterprises on the Comstock lode and in San Francisco led to the bank's collapse in August 1875. Forced to resign on 27 August, he drowned while swimming in San Francisco Bay later that same day. Subsequent investigations revealed that he owed the bank several million dollars (Lavender 1975, 372–79).

569.32–33 the merited castigation . . . ought to have been done in the street] Mark Twain's comment is strikingly similar to one printed in the Gold Hill *News:* "We regret, as a friend, that Winters was so delicate about the chastisement as to do it in a corner. It ought to have been done, if at all, in the street" ("An Explanation Wanted," Gold Hill *Evening News*, 1 Feb 70, 2, reprinting the Hamilton [Nev.] *White Pine News* of 29 January). As mentioned earlier, Mark Twain might have

read this remark, and others equally unsympathetic to Wiegand, in Nevada newspapers supplied by Goodman (see the note at 555.3–569.29).

569.34–36   When a journalist maligns a citizen . . . he deserves to be
thrashed for it] The contempt for Wiegand that Mark Twain expresses
throughout this appendix and especially in this final gloss is a marked
change from his earlier approval, even admiration, for him (see the note
at 554.10–11). Although his friendship with Winters may have influenced his attitude, it hardly seems an adequate justification for the intensity of his scorn. It has been suggested that the Wiegand episode revived uncomfortable memories of the journalistic disputes that
precipitated his departure from Virginia City in May 1864, albeit his
own offense was inadvertent and prankish, and in no way comparable
to Wiegand's deliberate exposé (see the notes at 378.6–8 and 379.37,
and Robinson, 60–64). It has also been conjectured that Mark Twain's
inability to perceive Wiegand as a "peculiar" but nevertheless "brave
and prudent man, devoted to democratic rights, to journalistic confi-
dentiality of sources, and to a free press" was in the end merely the result of his own cynicism, which caused him to believe that "Conrad
Wiegand should have known better than to attack things the way they
were. The strong will prosper. The rest will be thrashed" (Bridgman,
58–60).

SUPPLEMENT A

BACKGROUND MATERIAL SUPPLIED BY ORION CLEMENS

Item 1: Orion Clemens to Mollie Clemens, 8 and 9 September 1861

WHEN CLEMENS began to work on *Roughing It* in July 1870, he asked his brother Orion to help him recall the details of their stagecoach trip to Nevada Territory in July–August 1861: "Have you a memorandum of the route we took—or the names of any of the Stations we stopped at?" Orion responded by forwarding his journal of the trip, which Clemens found to be "ever so much use" in writing the overland chapters.[1] Unfortunately, this journal is no longer extant. Its contents survive, however, in a letter that Orion wrote to his wife—Mary Eleanor (Mollie) Clemens (1834–1904)—upon his arrival in Carson City: Orion copied the journal, probably in its entirety, into this letter, which is transcribed below from the original in the Mark Twain Papers (CU-MARK). Mollie, who had remained with her family in Keokuk, Iowa, joined Orion in Nevada in October 1862 with their daughter, Jennie Clemens (1855–64). The portion of the letter giving the trip itinerary is thoroughly glossed in the explanatory notes to the *Roughing It* text; notes for the remaining portion are provided below.

Carson City, Nevada Territory,
September 8, 1861.

My Dear Wife:—

Thinking you may take some interest in my journal, I copy it:

July 26.—Left St. Joseph. Started on the plains about ten miles out. The plains here are simply prairie.

July 27. Crossed the Nebraska line about 180 miles from St. Joseph. Here we saw the first Jack Rabbit. They have larger ~~legs~~ bodies, longer legs and longer ears than our rabbits.

July 28. Saw first prairie wolf, and first antelope,, and first prairie dogs

---

[1] *L1*, 242 n. 1, 382–83; SLC to OC, 15 July 70, CU-MARK, in *MTL*, 1:174–75; SLC to OC, 24–31? Aug 70, *MTL*, 1:175.

and villages. Also came in sight of the long range of Sand Hills. 2 P.M. Timber of Platte in sight. 7 miles further arrived at Ft. Kearney, 296 miles from St. Joseph. The Platte is a muddy, shallow stream, full of sand bars. This was the South Platte. In places it is skirted by timber, but generally it meanders through the plains like a ribbon, without a tree or shrub on its banks.

July 29.—Saw the first Indians, 75 miles from Kearney, with Buffalo skin wigwams, the hide dressed on both sides, and put up on poles, sugar loaf shape. Here we found Buffalo robes at three to six dollars, beautifully dressed, and some of them wonderfully large. This is the Buffalo region, and robes are higher as you go further, either east or west. Saw an Indian child's grave on a scaffold about eight feet from the ground, supported by four stakes. Sand Hills and Platte river still in sight.

Tuesday, July 30. Arrived at the "Crossing" of the South Platte, alias "Overland City," alias "Julesburg," at 11 A.M., 470 miles from St. Joseph. Saw to-day first Cactus. 1:20 P.M. across the South Platte.

Wednesday, July 31.—Sunrise. Court House Rock, Chimney Rock, and Scott's Bluffs, in sight. At noon passed through Scott's Bluff's pass,, 580 miles from St. Joseph. This was the first high ground, since entering upon the plains. All was vast, prairie, until we reached Fort Kearney. Soon afterwards, we struck the barren region, and thenceforward we had a level expanse covered with sage brush, and that was the character of the growth until we arrived here, the plains being more or less elevated, or broken, but in other respects preserving the same characteristics. After we crossed the South Platte we found a great deal of cactus. When we crossed Scotts Bluff's we had been traveling in sight of the North Platte river all day. In the afternoon we found alkali water in the road, giving it a soapy appearance, and the ground in many places appearing as if whitewashed. About 6 P.M., crossed the range of Sand hills which had been stretching along our left in sight, since Sunday. We crossed this long low range near the scene of the Indian mail robbery and massacre in 1856, wherein Babbitt alone was saved, though left for dead. The whole party was killed, including some passengers. There was some treasure in the coach, which the Indians got.

Thursday, Aug. 1. Found ourselves this morning in the "Black Hills," with "Laramie Peak," looming up in large proportions. This peak is 60 miles from Fort Laramie, which we passed in the night. We took breakfast at "Horseshoe" station, forty miles from Fort Laramie, and 676 miles from St. Joseph. After dinner we climbed to the yellow pines. This afternoon passed, near La Parelle station, the little canon in which the Express rider was last night when a bullet from Indians on the side of the road passed through his coat. About 2½ hours before the station keeper at La Parelle had fired four times at one Indian. At noon we passed a Morm train 33 wagons long. They were nooning. About midnight, at a station we stopped at to change horses, a dispute arose between our conductor and four drivers who were at the Station. The conductor came to me for a pistol, but before I could hand it to him, one of the men came up and commenced cursing him. Another then came up and knocked the conductor down, cutting a bad gash in his upper lip, and telling him he would have killed him if he had had his boots on, and would have killed him then if he reported him. I had not heard the fuss before the pistol was called for, and supposed it was for the Indians, who, it was said, would be dangerous along this part of the road. The four drivers were drunk.

Friday, Aug. 2.—3 o'clock, A. M., passed over North Platte bridge, 760 miles from St. Joseph. 2 P. M., reached "Sweet water" creek, "Independence Rock," the "Devil's Gap," the "Devil's Gate," and alkali, or "Soda Lake," where the mormons shovel up the saleratus, take it to Salt Lake, and sell it for 25¢ per pound. A few days ago they took two wagon loads. Also, the "Rocky Ride," all within two or three miles of Independence Rock, which is 811 miles from St. Joseph. Passed in the night, "Cold Spring," an ice water spring, issuing near one of the Stations. Now, or at any time of the year, the men at this Station by scraping off the soil, sometimes only to the depth of six inches, can cut out pretty, clear, square blocks of ice. This "cold spring" is 36 miles from "Independence Rock," and 847 miles from St. Joseph.

Saturday, Aug. 3. Breakfast at Rock Ridge Station, 24 miles from "Cold Spring," and 871 miles from St. Joseph. A mile further on is "South Pass City" consisting of four log cabins, one of which is the post office, and one unfinished. Two miles further on saw for the first time, snow on the mountains, glittering in the sun like settings of silver. Near the summit of the South Pass appears in sight Fremont's Peak. The wind river mountains, in which we first saw snow, are about 50 miles distant. About 7 2 6 miles beyond the very summit of the South Pass of the Rocky mountains, is Pacific station, in Utah Territory, near the Nebraska line, where we got an excellent dinner. Near this Station are the Pacific Springs, which issue in a branch, taking up its march for the Pacific Ocean. The summit of the Rocky mountains, or the highest point of the South Pass, is 902 miles from St. Joseph.

Sunday, Aug. 4.—Crossed Green River. It is something like the Illinois, except that it is a very pretty clear river. The place we crossed was about 70 miles from the summit of the South Pass. Uinta mountains in sight, with snow on them, and portions of their summits hidden by the clouds. About 5 P. M arrived at Fort Bridger, on Black's Fork of Green river, 52 miles from the crossing of Green river, about 120 miles from the South Pass, and 1025 miles from St. Joseph.

Monday, Aug. 5.—52 miles further on, near the head of Echo Canon, were encamped 60 soldiers from Camp Floyd. Yesterday they fired upon 300 or 400 Utes, whom they supposed gathered for no good purpose. The Indians returned the fire, when the soldiers chased them four miles, took four prisoners, talked with and released them, and then talked with their chief. Echo Canon is 20 miles long, with many sandstone cliffs, (red) in curious shapes, and often rising perpendicularly 400 feet.

4 P. M., arrived on the summit of "Big mountain," 15 miles from Salt Lake City, when the most gorgeous view of mountain peaks yet encountered, burst on our sight.

Arrived at Salt Lake City at dark, and put up at the Salt Lake House,. There are about 15,000 inhabitants. The houses are scattering, mostly small frame, with large yards and plenty of trees. High mountains surround the city. On some of these perpetual snow is visible. Salt Lake City is 240 miles from the South Pass, or 1148 miles from St. Joseph.

Wednesday, Aug. 7. Bathed in the warm spring. Mountains in the morning, Southwest and East enveloped in clouds.

Thursday, Aug. 8.—Arrived at Fort Crittenden—(Camp Floyd) 8 A. M., 45 miles from Salt Lake City. Arrived at the edge of the desert, 95 miles from Salt Lake City, at 4 P. M.

Friday, Aug. 9.—Sunrise. Across the desert, 45 miles, and at the commencement of the "little Desert." 2 o'clock, across the little desert, 23 miles, and 163 miles from Salt Lake, being 68 miles across the two deserts, with only a spring at Fish Creek Station to seperate them. They are called deserts because there is no water in them. They are barren, but so is the balance of the route.

Saturday, Aug 10. Arrived in the forenoon at the entrance of "Rocky Canon," 255 miles from Salt Lake City.

Sunday, Aug 11.— Passed points declared by the driver to be the highest we had crossed. Saturday and Sunday nights were very cold, though the days were very warm.

Tuesday, Aug 13.—Arrived at Carson Sink where Carson river loses itself. It is a beautiful lake, 25 miles long by 15 wide, and 60 miles from Carson City.

Wednesday, Aug. 14,—Arrived at Carson City 580 miles from Salt Lake, or 1700 miles from St. Joseph

Carson City, N. T. Sept 9, 1861.

My Dear Wife—

I am very sorry to find from your letter of Aug. 9th that you are sick; I will accept that as your apology for not writing every week as you promised. Your description of the events going on around you are very interesting. It must be deeply exciting to you all. Even to me it comes home, very close home, when I see the names of intimate friends engaged in the battle, near both to Memphis & Keokuk, and some of them wounded. The

Walker family is singularly divided. Tarrence's[2] speech was eloquent,,
though brief.

I am very glad indeed you waved your handkerchief to the soldiers in
St. Louis. It was a noble impulse, and they will always remember it.

I received to-day your letter written ~~to-day~~ August 2 at Lagrange.
Have you any idea what made Jennie's face become a running sore and a
scab? Poor little thing, I hate to hear of her being in that condition. Tell
her I love her and want her and her Ma out here very much, and I am sorry
she is not well. I think Tom Bohon will do very well for Belle.[3] Give my
love to Cousin Mary.[4] It gets pretty hot here about noon, but the climate is
too dry for sweat. It has not rained since I have been here. I have just read
the 28th chapter of Deuteronomy.

To-night I received from you the most fearful letter I ever read. When
I commenced reading it I felt like I did when in Tennessee on my way to
Memphis, I picked up a paper announcing Henry's death—the same stopping and stillness of the heart.[5] How thankful I was when I got through the
letter, and found the dear little creature was thought by the doctor to be
out of danger. Her affection for and thoughtfulness of me touches me
deeply. How could we spare her? What was the matter with Jennie? What
caused her convulsions?

I am sorry you had to pay out any money on the trunk. I hope, as Congress has made an appropriation for us I will soon have some money to
send you. I brought my dictionary with me. I wrote from Salt Lake. Nothing keeps me from depression on account of your absence, but being busy
from the time I get up till I go to bed. I do not know that I am any more
attached to the Swedenborgian[6] than the Presbyterian faith.

Do they still send you the Tri-weekly Democrat,?[7] What a relief the
last part of your letter was after reading the first part. I shall look for a letter every day, until Jennie gets entirely well. You have indeed passed
through a terrible trial—only three hours sleep in three days. I send you

---

[2]Unidentified.

[3]Thomas B. Bohon married Susan Isabella (Belle) Stotts (b. 1837), Mollie's sister,
in October 1861 (*L1*, 68–69 n. 12).

[4]Unidentified.

[5]Henry Clemens (1838–58), Orion and Samuel's younger brother, was injured in
a boiler explosion on a Mississippi River steamboat on 13 June 1858 and died a
week later (*L1*, 80–86, 382).

[6]Emanuel Swedenborg (1688–1772) was a Swedish scientist and mystic who
claimed that direct insight into the spiritual world had revealed to him the true
meaning of the Scriptures. His ideas aroused considerable interest among American intellectuals—especially the Transcendentalists—during the nineteenth
century.

[7]The St. Louis *Missouri Democrat*—a Republican newspaper, despite its name.
Orion was acquainted with one of its editors, William McKee (Rowell, 59; *L2*, 198
n. 1).

many kisses, and don't forget to give Jennie a great many for me. I wish you were both with me.

Good night.

Your affectionate Husband,
Orion Clemens.

Item 2: Comparative Chart of the Overland Itinerary

THE FOLLOWING CHART summarizes, in schematic form, the overland itinerary as set down in Orion Clemens's letter to his wife of 8 and 9 September 1861, and as described by Mark Twain in *Roughing It*. Its purpose is to enable the reader to determine, at a glance, the major points of similarity and difference between the two accounts. The mileage figures in the second column are either taken directly, or calculated, from Orion's letter. An arrow (→) in the "*Roughing It* narrative" column indicates that the text agrees with Orion's account, and was presumably based on it. Whenever the text specifically mentions time and/or distance, it is noted in this column. Entries in *italic type* indicate that Mark Twain used exact wording from Orion's account. Entries in **boldface type** indicate incidents mentioned in both accounts, but on different days of the journey. Entries in SMALL CAPITALS indicate incidents unique to *Roughing It*. The chart does not include incidents and anecdotes in the narrative of the book which cannot be linked to a particular time or place in the itinerary, such as the description of overland facilities in chapter 4, the anecdote of Eckert and the cat in chapter 7, or Greeley's ride in chapter 20.

Page.line	Day	Miles	Orion's letter	Roughing It narrative
6.4	Day 1, 26 July	0	departure from St. Joseph	→
12.18	Day 2, 27 July	180	Nebraska boundary	→180m
12.25	→		first jackass rabbit	→
——				
26.18	Day 3, 28 July		**first prairie dogs, cayote**	
26.21	→		timber of Platte, 2 P.M.	→2 P.M.
26.22	→			CROSSING OF PLATTE, 5 P.M.
30.5	Day 4, 29 July	296	Fort Kearny	→56 hours out, 300m
40.5	Day 5, 30 July	371	Indians, buffalo region	**first prairie dogs, cayote**
41.11	→	470	*Julesburg/Overland City*, 11 A.M.	→noon, 5th day, 470m
41.27	Day 6, 31 July		crossing of South Platte, 1:20 P.M.	→
50.2	→		——	BREAKDOWN, BEMIS & BULL, DAWN, 550M
52.8	→	580	Scott's Bluffs Pass, noon	PONY-EXPRESS RIDER
52.10	→		*alkali water*	→
53.14	→		*sand hills, mail robbery*, 6 P.M.	→
55.1	Day 7, 1 Aug	636	Fort Laramie, at night	→7th day
55.2	→		Black Hills, Laramie Peak	→
55.7	→	676	Horseshoe station	→676m
55.10	→		La Prele ("La Parelle") station	→
55.13	→		attack on pony rider	→
55.20	→		attack on Indian	→
——				
57.13	→		**Mormon train, noon**	→
67.14	Day 8, 2 Aug		altercation at station, midnight	BREAKFAST WITH SLADE
——				
76.1	→	760	North Platte Bridge, 3 A.M.	**Mormon train, after breakfast**, 8th day, 798m
76.10	→		——	BATH IN HORSE CREEK

76.19	→		Sweetwater Creek, 2 P.M.	→ afternoon
76.19	→	811	Independence Rock	↑
76.23	→		Soda Lake	↑
77.3	→	847	Cold Spring, at night	→ at night
—	Day 9, 3 Aug	871	breakfast at Rocky Ridge station	—
77.15	→	872	South Pass City	↑
78.16	→	902	South Pass summit	↑
81.38	→	908	Pacific station	LEAF AND WATERMELON ANECDOTES
84.15	Day 10, 4 Aug	972	crossing of Green river	→ 10th day
85.4	→	1025	Fort Bridger, 5 P.M.	→ 5 P.M., 1025m
85.7	Day 11, 5 Aug	1077	soldiers from Camp Floyd	→ 1077m
85.15	→		Echo Cañon, 20m long	→ 20m long
85.27	→	1133	Big Mountain, 4 P.M.	→ 4 P.M., 1133m
85.33	→			SUPPER WITH A DESTROYING ANGEL
87.4	→	1148	Salt Lake City, nightfall	→
89.8	Day 12, 6 Aug			SALT LAKE CITY SIGHTSEEING
92.19	Day 13, 7 Aug	—	bath in warm spring	VISIT TO BRIGHAM YOUNG
107.1	→			MORMON BIBLE
120.15	→			DEPARTURE, LATE EVENING
122.1	Day 14, 8 Aug	1193	Camp Floyd, 8 A.M.	→ 8 A.M., 1193–98m
122.3	→	1243	edge of desert, 4 P.M.	→ 4 P.M., 1238–48m
122.7	Day 15, 9 Aug	1311	desert crossing, 68m across	→ 68m across
122.13	→		Fish Springs ("Fish Creek") station	unnamed station
126.2	Day 16, 10 Aug	1403	Egan ("Rocky") Cañon, afternoon	→ 16th day, 1398m
126.6	→			GOSHOOT INDIANS
130.1	Day 17, 11 Aug		highest points on trip	→ 17th day
130.6	Day 18, 12 Aug			REESE RIVER STATION, 18th day
130.23	Day 19, 13 Aug	1640	Carson Sink	→ 19th day
137.29	Day 20, 14 Aug	1700	Carson City	→ 20th day

Item 3: Orion Clemens to Samuel L. Clemens, 11 March 1871

ON 10 MARCH 1871 Clemens asked Orion to "torture your memory & write down in minute detail every fact & exploit in the desperado Slade's life that we heard on the Overland—& also describe his appearance & conversation as we saw him at Rocky Ridge station at breakfast" (NN-B†). Orion's response, written the following day, is transcribed below from the original in the Mark Twain Papers (CU-MARK); it provided Clemens with ideas for much of the material in chapter 10.

AGENTS WANTED FOR OVERLAND THROUGH ASIA, KNOX. UNCIVILIZED RACES, OR NATURAL HISTORY OF MAN, WOOD. INNOCENTS ABROAD, TWAIN. BEYOND THE MISSISSIPPI, FIELD, DUNGEON AND ESCAPE, PERSONAL HISTORY OF GRANT, RICHARDSON. GREAT METROPOLIS, BROWNE. THE GREAT REBELLION, HEADLEY. HISTORY OF THE BIBLE, STEBBINS. PEBBLES AND PEARLS, ABBY SAGE. ILLUSTRATED FAMILY BIBLES.

E. G. HASTINGS, PRES'T.   OFFICE AMERICAN PUBLISHING COMPANY,
E. BLISS, JR., SEC'Y   149 ASYLUM STREET.
F. E. BLISS, TREAS.

HARTFORD CONN. March 11 18 71

My Dear Bro:—
       your letters of 9ᵗʰ & 10ᵗʰ just received. I showed them to Bliss, who is much pleased.
       I don't think we heard of Slade till after we had left Rocky Ridge Station—the last before reaching South Pass station where ẃ the clouds looked so low, where we saw the first snow, and where a spring with waters destined for the Atlantic stood within a man's length ₐ(or within sight)ₐ of another spring whose waters were about to commence a voyage to the Pacific. There was nothing then in a name to attract us to Slade, and yet I remember something of his appearance while totally forgetting all the others. Perhaps the driver's description caused the difference. We got there (to R R Station) about sun up. There were a lot of fellows, young and rough in a room adjoining that in which we sat. ~~They~~ —if indeed it was not in the same room. They were ₐwashing in a tin pan,ₐ joking, laughing and chaffing each other, and kept it up at the table. I don't remember what they said, or anything they said, but I believe the subject was their hostelry and silly trifles. I think Slade got to the table after every body else did, and shewed good appetite for the bacon slices, &c. I think he was about your

size, if any difference rather shorter and more slender. He had gray eyes, very light straight hair, no beard, and a hard, looking face seamed like a man of 60, though otherwise he did not seem over thirty. I think the sides of his face were wrinkled. His face was thin, his nose straight and ordinarily prominent—lips rather thinner than usual—otherwise nothing unusual about his mouth, except that ~~w~~ his smile was attractive and his manner pleasant. Nothing peculiar about his ~~wa~~ voice. It does not leave a pleasant recollection,—but I don't know in what respect—it was neither very fine nor very coarse. My impression is that he was a *division* agent, from Overland City to Salt Lake,—having ~~two~~ ˌseveralˌ conductors under him.—~~one each~~ The one who wanted us to lend him a pistol, I think had about two hundred miles or 240 miles of the road. Slade was *not* a conductor. He had the conductors and drivers under him. They were a wild and desperate set, and the contractors on the Butterfield line (It seems to me that was the name of the old weekly or monthly line there and when the new daily line came on that he ˌ(Butterfield)ˌ took his stock south and ran the southern overland route through Santa Fe,ˌ) kept him a long time after they knew of his infernal deviltry, because he was the only man ~~they s~~ ˌconductors, drivers and station menˌ held in awe. It seems to me ˌweˌ had got down off the Rocky mountains—no, now may be it was before we reached the foot of the last ridge on this side, after all, that the driver commenced telling about Slade. I was sitting outside with the driver. I don't recollect whether you were sitting with us or inside, and I told you afterwards. Any how it was getting late, we were on level ground and hasting to make the next station, when the driver pointed out to me (or us) a corral and told us that there had been a fight there. Some spaniards were keeping the station. They were contumacious in some way and Slade brought some of his ~~drivers~~ ˌmenˌ over ˌfrom other stationsˌ. The Spaniards used their ~~for~~ corral as a fortification, but Slade's party was victorious. There were several, but he killed them all. One of them had a ~~wife~~ squaw wife and two little children. Slade fastened them up in a house (or the house) and setting fire to it burned them to death, swearing none of the breed should live. There had been bad blood between him and the Spaniards some time. Once they got him fastened up in the station by fastening the door when he was in, mounting guard ~~outside,~~ and giving him half an hour to prepare for death. He entreated them to ~~pre~~ permit him to bid farewell to his wife. They finally consented that he might send for her. He dispatched a note for her by the pony express which seems to have come along about the right time. She came immediately on horseback and was allowed to enter his room. For a wonder he seems to have been caught without his arms, and that he only needed a visit from his wife to supply the deficiency, for soon after her arrival he issued with her from the station, ~~with~~ ˌhavingˌ a pistol in each hand, with which he defied his guards, and mounting the horse with his wife galloped away.

Once Slade had a quarrel with a huge teamster, and in ˌanˌ apparent excess of courage dared the latter to fight. Whether the teamster had got him "covered" first, or whether Slade was afraid of the result on some other account, he proposed that each should throw away his pistol and fight a fair fist fight. The teamster agreed and the pistols were flung one side; but the moment the teamster's ˏpistol₍ left his hand Slade sprang for them˷, ˏpistols,, obtained both and shot the teamster dead.

Slade had a desperate fight at Overland City with Julian a Frenchman. Slade had a pistol and the Frenchman a shot gun. He was as desperate a man as Slade, and forced the latter to retreat into a house where he took refuge behind a door which stood ajar. They shot at each other through the door, and Slade was so badly wounded about the body as that he was confined to his bed several weeks. Julian improved the opportunity to leave for the purpose of avoiding Slade's vengeance. He went to Pikes Peak and was gone about six months. He returned and was captured by Slade or his friends near one of the stations,, and bound to a tree. Then Slade cut off his ears, tantalized him, poured out invectives on him, shot his so as barely to miss him several times, and after torturing him half an hour in these ways, killed him.

I don't know how he came to leave that road, but he went to Montana, where he was worked up into hanged by a vigilance committee. I believe his offence was belonging to a gang of horse thieves and robbers, with some particular murder laid to his charge. On the scaffold he was unmanned by terror and begged piteously for life.

Charlie Kincaid[1] had a rough time on that old mail route with the Indians once. If you want it I guess Mollie will remember something about it.

I have done the best ˏI could, on Slade—told all I can remember—and more than I recollect distinctly or ᵩ feel entirely certain of—trusting that it would be practically near enough correct.

Lo Bliss don't think you can sell your house soon.

Love to wife and baby.

Bliss has a queer notion about things. He can work at his business all through the month and then in a day or two sit down and spin off no end of insurance articles, and if I am not down here in the office where he writing and where he can holler at me he to go after a proof or do something about the paper he thinks I aint doing any thing, and instead of hiring a girl to write on wrappers has put me at it, because, I suppose, I spent time walking to think in the fresh air, or staid at home to pol after meals to polish up what I had written where I could be uninterrupted, having writ seized the opportunity to write the rough drafts at the office while Bliss was away at New York, for when he is away the others don't bother me. I

---

[1]Possibly the same "Mr. Kincaid, a Salt Lake trader," who was wounded by Indians in a stagecoach attack in the 1850s. Although he received "two arrow shots as he fled," he "entirely recovered by the next year" (Root and Connelley, 77).

dispair of making him comprehend the matter, and so accept the situation, being resolved to publish nothing of any importance which has not been well considered. I feel some delicacy in speaking to him also, because if I were to object to my girlish duties and and on the ground that I wanted time to think, and then fail to produce anything valuable he he would consider that I had merely made a shirking excuse and was humbugging him., hoping eventually to work into something higher.

He shows about the same discernment in grumbling because your portrait goes into the Aldine.[2] I laughed at him telling him you couldn't and propose it ,for this paper, and he hadn't thought of it and the Aldine people had. I'll work along here the best I can till I get my machine out,[3] and then I shall hope for better things.

Your Brother,
Orion.

Knox[4] has a column for this paper he charges $10 for.
What I am at work on is the exchange list—copying from a book—perhaps 5,000 papers—to help out till first April as they are taking stock.

---

[2]Clemens's portrait appeared in *The Aldine: A Typographic Art Journal* for April 1871 (58).

[3]An invention Orion was developing, not further identified.

[4]Thomas W. Knox (1835–96), a New York *Herald* correspondent and author of *Overland through Asia*, published by the American Publishing Company in 1870.

SUPPLEMENT B

MAPS

MAP I, divided into four adjoining segments, is a large-scale representation of the western United States and territories that figure in the *Roughing It* narrative. It depicts the route that Samuel Clemens and his brother Orion followed on their journey by overland-mail stagecoach from St. Joseph, Missouri, to Carson City, Nevada Territory, in July–August 1861. This route has been reliably established by studies of the overland mail and of the pony express, which often—but not always—made use of the mail-route facilities. All of the significant geographic features—both physical and cultural—mentioned in *Roughing It* and in the explanatory notes are represented on the map, in addition to other selected major features useful for orientation. The level of detail is not uniform: western Nevada Territory, for example, which contains more features of importance to the book than do other regions, appears in greater detail. The map is accurate as of July–August 1861, except for the town of Austin, Nevada, established in 1863. The representation of the travelers' daily progress is based on Orion's letter to his wife of 8 and 9 September 1861 (supplement A, item 1). Also shown are the three routes between Nevada Territory and Sacramento: the overland-mail route to Placerville, the road over Henness Pass (which Clemens traveled in May 1864), and the road over Donner Pass (which he traveled in April–May 1868).

Maps 2 and 3 represent a closer view of western Nevada Territory as of November 1861, when the Territorial Legislature established the first county boundaries: Map 2 shows the Humboldt region, which Clemens visited in the winter of 1861–62; Map 3 shows Carson City, Virginia City, and environs, plus the Esmeralda region—including Mono Lake—where he sojourned in the spring and summer of 1862 (having made a brief visit there in September 1861). Dotted lines indicate commonly traveled trails and roads. Clemens's probable route to Unionville is shown on Map 2, but the route of his return trip as far as Ragtown is not known; the map depicts the possible routes. The *Roughing It* account of his horseback trip to Aurora in April 1862 implies that he followed the stagecoach road, by way of Genoa. The route he walked on his return trip to Virginia City is not known for certain. Map 3 shows the two likeliest possibilities: the stagecoach road, and a shorter road between the Walker River and Dayton. Nothing is known about Clemens's routes to and from Lake Tahoe. On his first visit, in September 1861 (described in chapter 22), he apparently visited the north or the northeastern shore; in August 1863 he went to Glenbrook, midway along the eastern shore (see *L1*, 127 n. 5, 265 n. 3). According to his *Roughing It* account he made other trips as well. The map depicts the likeliest routes.

The following general source books defined in References were useful in preparing the maps: Angel's *History*, Browning's *Place Names of the Sierra Nevada*, Carlson's *Nevada Place Names*, Kelly's 1862 *Directory*, Mattes's *Great Platte River Road*, and Root and Connolley's *Overland Stage*. Clemens's route to the Humboldt region was established primarily from his own account of the trip in a February 1866 "San Francisco Letter" to the Virginia City *Territorial Enterprise* (SLC 1866d). Three letters (not by Clemens) to the Sacramento *Union* provided descriptions of the route: "Visit to the Humboldt Mines," 24 Sept 61, 1; "Letter from the Humboldt Mines" (signed "Wyoming"), 1 Apr 62, 4; and "Letter from the Humboldt Mines" (signed "D."), 6 May 62, 1. The remaining map sources are listed below.

American Automobile Association.

  1989. *Iowa, Nebraska.* Falls Church, Va.: American Automobile Association.

  1990. *Colorado, Wyoming.* Heathrow, Fla.: American Automobile Association.

  1990. *Nevada, Utah.* Heathrow, Fla.: American Automobile Association.

  1990. *Western States and Provinces.* Heathrow, Fla.: American Automobile Association.

Baltensperger, Bradley H. 1985. *Nebraska: A Geography.* Boulder, Colo.: Westview Press.

Bancroft, H. H. 1862. *Bancroft's Map of the Washoe Silver Region of Nevada Territory.* San Francisco: H. H. Bancroft and Co.

California State Automobile Association. 1979. *Lake Tahoe Region.* San Francisco: California State Automobile Association.

Clayton, Joshua Elliot. 1861. *Map of Esmeralda and Mono.* San Francisco: Britton and Co.

Clayton, William. 1848. *The Latter-Day Saints' Emigrants' Guide.* St. Louis: Missouri Republican. Reprint edition, edited by Stanley B. Kimball. Gerald, Mo.: Patrice Press, 1983.

Colton, J. H. 1864. *Colton's Map of the States and Territories West of the Mississippi River to the Pacific Ocean.* New York: J. H. Colton.

Coy, Owen C. 1973. *California County Boundaries.* Rev. ed. Fresno, Calif.: Valley Publishers.

DeGroot, Henry. 1863. *DeGroot's Map of Nevada Territory, Exhibiting a Portion of Southern Oregon & Eastern California*. San Francisco: Warren Holt.

Fike, Richard E., and John W. Headley. 1979. *The Pony Express Stations of Utah in Historical Perspective*. Bureau of Land Management, Utah. Cultural Resources Series, Monograph 2. Washington, D.C.: U.S. Government Printing Office.

Fink, K. W. 1935. *Map of the Pony Express Trail Beginning April 3rd. 1860 from St. Joseph Mo. and Sacramento Calif.* Kansas City, Kans.: W. R. Honnell.

Fox, Theron. 196–. *Nevada Treasure Hunters Ghost Town Guide*. San Jose, Calif.: Theron Fox.

Hunt, Thomas H. 1974. *Ghost Trails to California*. Palo Alto, Calif.: American West Publishing Company.

Kimball, Stanley B. 1988. *Historic Sites and Markers along the Mormon and Other Great Western Trails*. Urbana: University of Illinois Press.

Marcy, Randolph B. 1863. *The Prairie Traveler, A Hand-Book for Overland Expeditions*. London: Trübner and Co.

Mason, Dorothy. 1976. *The Pony Express in Nevada*. Compiled for the Nevada Bureau of Land Management. Carson City: Harrah's.

Maule, William M. 1938. *A Contribution to the Geographic and Economic History of the Carson, Walker and Mono Basins in Nevada and California*. San Francisco: California Region, Forest Service, U.S. Department of Agriculture.

National Geographic Society. 1981. *National Geographic Atlas of the World*. 5th ed. Washington, D.C.: National Geographic Society.

Nevada Emigrant Trail Marking Committee. 1975. *The Overland Emigrant Trail to California*. Reno: Nevada Historical Society.

State of Nevada. 1981. *Directory of Geographic Names in Nevada*. Prepared by State of Nevada, Department of Transportation Planning Division, Cartography and Graphics Section. 2d ed. Reno: State of Nevada.

Swackhamer, William D. 1979. *Political History of Nevada*. 7th ed. Carson City: Nevada State Printing Office.

Townley, John M. 1980. *Across Nevada with the Pony Express and Overland Stage Line*. Reno: Great Basin Studies Center.

Urbanek, Mae.
1974. *Wyoming Place Names*. 3d ed. Boulder, Colo.: Johnson Publishing Company.

1978. *Ghost Trails of Wyoming*. Boulder, Colo.: Johnson Publishing Company.

U.S. Department of the Interior. General Land Office. 1866. *Map of the State of Nevada to Accompany the Annual Report of the Comm! Gen! Land Office*. New York: Major and Knapp.

U.S. Department of the Interior. U.S. Geological Survey.
1916. *U.S. Contour Map, Polyconic Projection*.

1951. *Bucklin Reservoirs, Wyoming*. Photorevised 1981. 7.5 Minute Series (Topographic).

1951. *Carson Sink, Nevada*. 15 Minute Series (Topographic).

1951. *Graham Ranch, Wyoming*. Photorevised 1984. 7.5 Minute Series (Topographic).

1951. *Independence Rock, Wyoming*. Photorevised 1981. 7.5 Minute Series (Topographic).

1953. *Western United States 1:250,000; Delta*. Revised 1972.

1953. *Western United States 1:250,000; Tooele*. Revised 1970.

1955. *Western United States 1:250,000; Elko*. Revised 1972.

1955. *Western United States 1:250,000; Lovelock*. Revised 1970.

1956. *Aurora, Nevada-California*. 15 Minute Series (Topographic).

1956. *Toulon, Nevada*. 15 Minute Series (Topographic).

1957. *Western United States 1:250,000; Mariposa*. Revised 1970.

1957. *Western United States 1:250,000; Reno*. Revised 1971.

1957. *Western United States 1:250,000; Sacramento*. Revised 1970.

1957. *Western United States 1:250,000; Walker Lake*. Revised 1969.

1958. *Bodie, California*. 15 Minute Series (Topographic).

1958. *Trench Canyon, California-Nevada*. 15 Minute Series (Topographic).

1960. *Fairbury, Nebraska*. Photorevised 1980. 7.5 Minute Series (Topographic).

1960. *Fairbury SW, Nebraska-Kansas*. 7.5 Minute Series (Topographic).

1960. *Gladstone, Nebraska*. 7.5 Minute Series (Topographic).

1961. *Mountain Dell, Utah*. Photorevised 1975. 7.5 Minute Series (Topographic).

1963. *Fort Douglas, Utah*. Photorevised 1969 and 1975. 7.5 Minute Series (Topographic).

1966. *Hanover East, Kansas*. Photorevised 1983. 7.5 Minute Series (Topographic).

1966. *Hanover SE, Kansas*. Photorevised 1983. 7.5 Minute Series (Topographic).

1966. *Hanover SW, Kansas*. Photorevised 1983. 7.5 Minute Series (Topographic).

1966. *Hanover West, Kansas.* Photorevised 1983. 7.5 Minute Series (Topographic).

1966. *Herkimer, Kansas.* Photorevised 1983. 7.5 Minute Series (Topographic).

1966. *Marysville, Kansas.* Photorevised 1983. 7.5 Minute Series (Topographic).

1966. *Washington NE, Kansas.* 7.5 Minute Series (Topographic).

1970. *Endicott, Nebraska-Kansas.* 7.5 Minute Series (Topographic).

1978. *Lander, Wyoming.* 30×60 Minute Series (Topographic).

1979. *Bairoil, Wyoming.* 30×60 Minute Series (Topographic).

1979. *Casper, Wyoming.* 30×60 Minute Series (Topographic).

1981. *Rattlesnake Hills, Wyoming.* 30×60 Minute Series (Topographic).

1984. *South Pass, Wyoming.* 30×60 Minute Series (Topographic).

Wesley, Edgar B. 1961. *Our United States: Its History in Maps.* 2d ed. Chicago: Denoyer-Geppert Company.

Wheeler, George M. 1873. *Parts of Southern Nevada and Eastern California, Atlas Sheet No. 57; Geographical Explorations and Surveys West of the 100th Meridian.* Washington, D.C.: U.S. Government Printing Office.

Wheeler, Sessions S. 1971. *The Nevada Desert.* Caldwell, Idaho: Caxton Printers.

WPA.

1939. *Kansas: A Guide to the Sunflower State.* Compiled and written by the Federal Writers' Project of the Work Projects Administration for the State of Kansas. New York: Viking Press.

1939. *Nebraska: A Guide to the Cornhusker State.* Compiled and written by the Federal Writers' Project of the Works Progress Administration for the State of Nebraska. New York: Viking Press.

1940. *Nevada: A Guide to the Silver State.* Compiled by workers of the Writers' Program of the Work Projects Administration in the State of Nevada. Portland, Oreg.: Binfords and Mort.

1941. *Wyoming: A Guide to Its History, Highways, and People.* Compiled by workers of the Writers' Program of the Work Projects Administration in the State of Wyoming. New York: Oxford University Press.

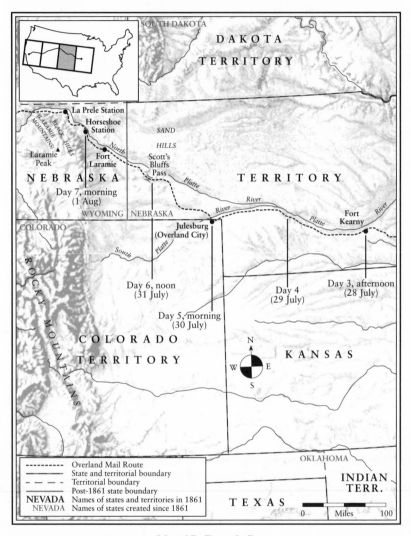

MAP 1B: Days 3–7.

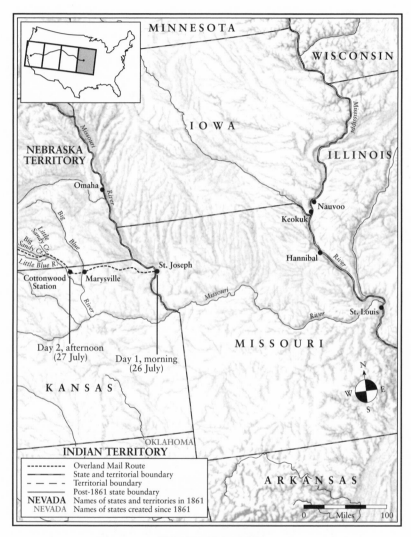

MAP 1A: Days 1–2.

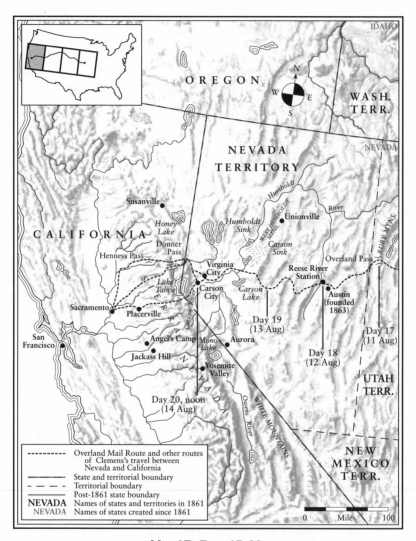

Map 1D: Days 17–20.

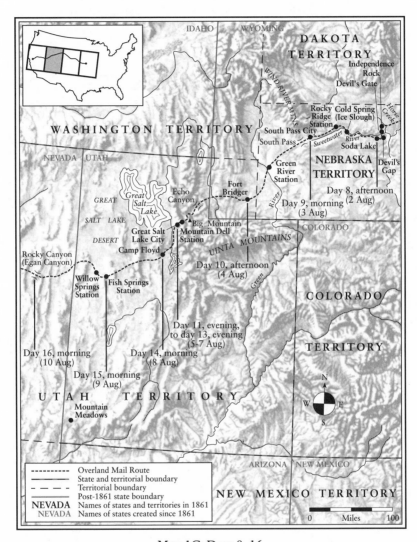

MAP 1C: Days 8–16.

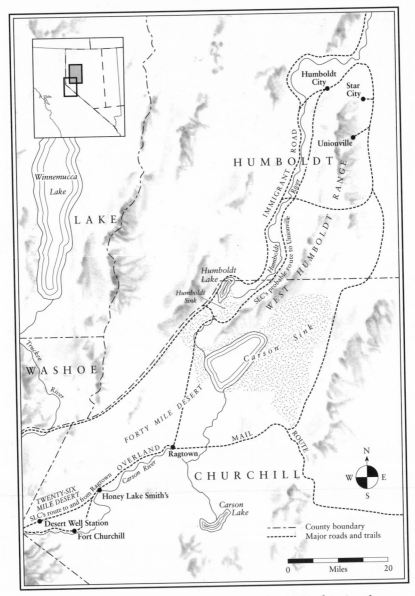

Map 2: West central Nevada Territory, November 1861, showing the possible routes of Clemens's Humboldt trip.

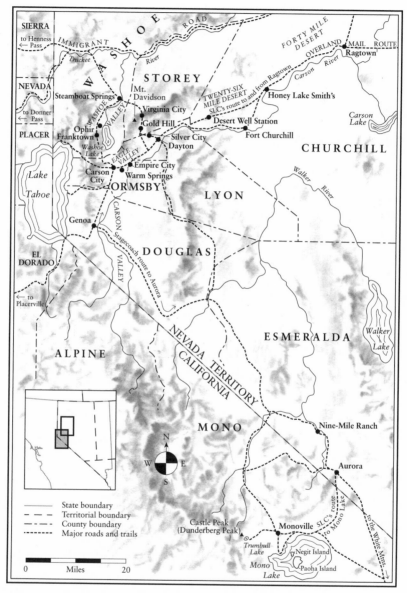

MAP 3: Southwestern Nevada Territory, November 1861, showing Virginia City, Carson City, and environs, and the Esmeralda region.

SUPPLEMENT C

Horace Greeley to Samuel L. Clemens, 7 May 1871

The letter reproduced here from the original in the Mark Twain Papers (87 percent of actual size, CU-MARK) almost certainly served as the inspiration for Mark Twain's parody of Greeley's illegible handwriting in chapter 70. A transcription of the letter is provided below. Greeley evidently wrote it in response to an acknowledgment from Clemens, to whom he had recently given a copy of his new book, *What I Know of Farming* (1871). See the notes at 483.7–8 and 484.17.

NEW-YORK TRIBUNE.

NEW YORK, May 7, 187 1.

Mark:

You are mistaken as to my criticisms on *your* farming. I never publicly made any, while you have undertaken to tell the exact cost per pint of my potatoes and cabbages, truely enough the inspiration of genius. If you will really betake yourself to farming, or even to telling what you know about it, rather than what you *don't* know about mine, I will not only refrain from disparaging criticism, but will give you my blessing.

Yours,

Horace Greeley.

Mark Twain.

New-York Tribune.

New York, May 7ᵗ 1871.

Mark:

You are mistaken as
to my criticisms on your
Farming. I never criticised
modeaf, while you have
undertaken to tell the exact
cost per pint of my Pota-
toes and Cabbages, being
wholly the instruction of
genius. If you will really be
take yourself to Farming or
even to telling what you
know about it rather than
what you don't know about
mine, I will not take to from
distooping criticism,
and will give you my blessing.
                        Yours
Mark Twain.   Horace Greeley.

INTRODUCTION

1

Roughing It was published in February 1872, a year and a half after Mark Twain began it. His second major book, it was also his second major success, comparable in some ways to his first, *The Innocents Abroad* (1869). Like *Innocents*, it was a thickly illustrated six-hundred-page volume published by Elisha Bliss and the American Publishing Company of Hartford and sold exclusively by subscription, at least in the United States. But because *Innocents* had been pirated in England and Canada, Clemens tried to make sure that *Roughing It* would not be, publishing it "simultaneously" in London through George Routledge and Sons. Just one year after publication, the combined English and American sales stood at ninety-three thousand copies, with royalties in excess of twenty thousand dollars. By Clemens's own standards, these numbers represented an undeniable success—despite his worst fears to the contrary.

The success of *Roughing It* makes it easy to overlook, or discount, the author's fears for his book, especially since his usual attitude toward it was fiercely upbeat: "We shall sell 90,000 copies the first 12 months," he wrote typically to Bliss, "I haven't even a shadow of a doubt of that."[1] But Clemens did have his doubts about *Roughing It*. Ten months before publication he was expecting it to be "a tolerable success—possibly an *excellent* success if the chief newspapers start it off well." Three months before publication he was a little less confident: "If the subject were less hackneyed," he told his wife, "it would be a great success." Yet even that pessimistic forecast pales beside what he recalled telling his friend David Gray in early 1872, as the book was being issued: "You will remember, maybe, how I felt about 'Roughing It'—that it would be considered pretty poor stuff, & that therefore I had better not let the press get a chance at it."[2]

Acting on this belief, Clemens at first vetoed the distribution of review copies, even to the "chief newspapers." As a result, only a handful of reviews ever appeared, and sales plummeted just six months after publication. He blamed this unexpected decline on the "engravings & paper," and

---

[1] SLC to Elisha Bliss, Jr., 4 Sept 70, CU-MARK, in *MTLP*, 39.
[2] SLC to Orion Clemens, 30 Apr 71, NPV, in *MTBus*, 119; SLC to Olivia L. Clemens, 27 Nov 71, CU-MARK, in *LLMT*, 166; SLC to David Gray, Sr., 10 June 80, NHyF†.

on the "original lack of publicity," admitting to Bliss that he had mis-
judged the importance of "~~early~~ prompt notoriety," which he had been
"*afraid* of & didn't want" until he was "dead sure of 50,000 subscriptions
to R. I."[3]

For a month Clemens made few exceptions to this ban, but among them
were Charles Dudley Warner on the Hartford *Courant,* and William Dean
Howells at the *Atlantic Monthly.* In late May 1872, when Clemens saw
Howells's comments, he thought the book might be a critical success after
all:

The "Atlantic" has come to hand with that most thoroughly & entirely satisfactory
notice of "Roughing it," & I am as uplifted & reassured by it as a mother who has
given birth to a white baby when she was awfully afraid it was going to be a mulatto.
I have been afraid & shaky all along, but now unless the N. Y. "Tribune" gives the
book a black eye, I am all right.[4]

Favorable though it was, this review failed to prompt any others: only
three have been found later than May, and two of these Clemens himself
solicited from the New York *Tribune.*[5]

Clemens's relief at Howells's praise is obvious. It is less obvious *why* he
felt "afraid & shaky all along," or why he thought of his book as a guiltily
begotten "mulatto," or even as "pretty poor stuff." Clemens's uneasiness
was caused by two different but related concerns. First was the subject of
the West itself. On the one hand, he realized that it had become suddenly
"hackneyed," even as he worked to complete his manuscript: too many
journalists had already published books describing their recent tours of
California and Nevada. For this reason he was prevented from writing a
comic travelogue like *Innocents,* and was instead forced to remember and
therefore transform his personal experiences "on the ground" between
1861 and 1866. On the other hand, despite his own delight in the "vigorous new vernacular of the occidental plains and mountains," there were
members of his audience who regarded slang and dialect, and the rough
societies in which they flourished, as "coarse" and "low"—unfit subjects
for literature, save perhaps in the refining hands of Bret Harte. Clemens
therefore had at least some grounds for doubting whether, in *Roughing It,*
he would, as he put it, "'top' Bret Harte again or bust."[6]

Clemens's second concern, which increased his uneasiness about the
first, may be thought of simply as the multitude of problems he encountered in trying to write and publish *Roughing It.* These ranged from what

[3]SLC to Elisha Bliss, Jr., 4 Mar 73, ViU, in *MTLP,* 74.

[4]SLC to William Dean Howells, 25–30? May 72, *L5,* forthcoming. Howells's review appeared in the June *Atlantic Monthly,* available in western New York by 24
May ("Recent Literature," 29 [June 72]: 754–55; "New Periodicals," Buffalo *Courier,* 25 May 72, 2).

[5]Reviews are discussed in section 8 below.

[6]Prefatory, page xxiv; chapter 4, page 26; SLC to Orion Clemens, 11 and 13 Mar
71, CU-MARK, in *MTLP,* 58.

he referred to in 1882 as a "lapse of facility" in composing the early chap-ters,[7] to the belated discovery that Bliss had been cutting corners with the "engravings & paper," making books that might be regarded in more than one way as "pretty poor stuff." Such problems ran counter to Clemens's expectations: *Roughing It* proved much more difficult to write than *Innocents*, his only basis for comparison.

He had written *Innocents* in the spring and summer of 1868, published it within a year, and had since begun to receive an astonishing income from it—nearly $14,000 in the first year. "I mean to write another book during the summer," he told Mary Mason Fairbanks on 6 January 1870. "This one has proven such a surprising success that I feel encouraged." Producing the next book seemed at first a rather simple matter, in part be-cause he believed he could always abandon the narrative form altogether, choosing instead to simply reprint his various sketches. On 22 January, for instance, he wrote Bliss that he was suing Charles Henry Webb to regain control of the *Jumping Frog* (1867), hoping to break up the plates "& pre-pare a new Vol. of Sketches, but on a different & more 'taking' model." He was confident about the next book, whatever it turned out to be: "I can get a book ready for you any time you want it—but you *can't* want one before this time next year—so I have plenty of time."[8]

Clemens had less time than he thought, for during the next fifteen months he would be constantly interrupted by personal and family crises that eventually drove him to "a state of absolute frenzy," and inevitably delayed the book.[9] Three weeks after Clemens signed a contract for it, Oli-via's father died, leaving her deeply depressed. One month later a visiting schoolmate of hers (Emma Nye) contracted typhoid and, after weeks of fe-verish hallucinations, died in the Clemenses' own bedroom. Five weeks after that, Olivia gave birth (prematurely) to her first child, Langdon, who was never strong and would not survive his second year. And when the child was just three months old, she herself contracted typhoid—from which she recovered slowly, once she was expected to recover at all.

But Clemens's inability to finish *Roughing It* "during the summer," or even within the five months his contract allowed him, is explained only in part by the lugubrious events of 1870–71. In particular, those events do not explain why he *created* half a dozen distractions during this same pe-riod. Just two months after deciding to write the book, he contracted to supply a monthly column for the New York *Galaxy*—a commitment so demanding that it alone could have stopped his progress on the book. In

[7]SLC to Alfred Arthur Reade, 14 Mar 82, Alfred Arthur Reade, ed., *Study and Stimulants; or, The Use of Intoxicants and Narcotics in Relation to Intellectual Life* (Manchester, England: Abel Heywood and Son, 1883), 122.

[8]Hirst, 317; SLC to Mary Mason Fairbanks, 6 and 7 Jan 70, CSmH, in *MTMF*, 114; SLC to Elisha Bliss, Jr., 22 Jan 70, CU-MARK, in *MTLP*, 30.

[9]SLC to Elisha Bliss, Jr., 17 Mar 71, NN-B†, published in part in *MTLP*, 60–61.

addition, he undertook negotiations and preparations for three other books, long before he had completed *Roughing It*.

Before he had finished, Clemens admitted that for long periods during the book's composition he was unable to be "thoroughly interested" in his subject.[10] His penchant for self-interruption and this inability to be "interested" in his subject were closely related phenomena, although Clemens himself seems not to have recognized it at the time. They belong to a pattern of behavior which he eventually accepted as normal, adapting to it by learning to "pigeon-hole" manuscripts when they got "tired, along about the middle."[11] Encountering such resistance for the first time, however, must have been alarming—an open invitation to self-doubt, and to fault finding, since there were many people and things he could blame for his slow progress. But writing this book was Clemens's first, naive experience with what proved to be his invariable pattern when writing fiction. This fact has not been noticed before, but it explains a good deal about how he wrote *Roughing It*.

By far the most important obstacle to such an explanation, however, has been the loss of Clemens's manuscript printer's copy, which was probably discarded once the book was in type. Without access to this document, it has been virtually impossible to understand, with any precision, Clemens's letters describing his progress and recording (usually by page or chapter number) how far he had written.[12] Now, for the first time, we propose a conjectural reconstruction of this missing document, which amounts to a map of what the printer's copy initially contained, and how

---

[10]SLC to Elisha Bliss, Jr., 15 May 71, ViU, in *MTL*, 1:187: "I find myself so thoroughly interested in my work, now (a thing I have not experienced for months) that I can't bear to lose a single moment of the inspiration."

[11]AD, 30 Aug 1906, CU-MARK, in *MTE*, 196.

[12]The principal studies of *Roughing It*'s composition, structure, and themes are: Martin B. Fried, "The Composition, Sources, and Popularity of Mark Twain's *Roughing It*" (Ph.D. diss., University of Chicago, 1951); Henry Nash Smith, introduction to *Roughing It* (New York: Harper and Brothers, 1959), xi–xxii; Franklin R. Rogers, *The Pattern for Mark Twain's Roughing It: Letters from Nevada by Samuel and Orion Clemens, 1861–1862* (Berkeley and Los Angeles: University of California Press, 1961); Henry Nash Smith, chapter 3, "Transformation of a Tenderfoot," in *Mark Twain: The Development of a Writer* (Cambridge: Harvard University Press, 1962), 52–70; Hamlin Hill, chapter 2, "The People's Author," in *Mark Twain and Elisha Bliss* (Columbia: University of Missouri Press, 1964), 21–68; *Roughing It*, edited by Franklin R. Rogers and Paul Baender, The Works of Mark Twain (Berkeley, Los Angeles, London: University of California Press, 1972); Hamlin Hill, introduction to *Roughing It* (New York: Penguin Books, 1981), 7–24; Harold J. Kolb, Jr., "Mark Twain and the Myth of the West," in *The Mythologizing of Mark Twain*, edited by Sara deSaussure Davis and Philip D. Beidler (University: University of Alabama Press, 1984), 119–35; and Jeffrey Steinbrink, chapters 8, 9, and 10—"Writing *Roughing It*," "Lighting Out," and "Coming of Age in Elmira"—in *Getting to Be Mark Twain* (Berkeley, Los Angeles, Oxford: University of California Press, 1991), 131–87. Steinbrink's chapters are the most successful effort to date to give a detailed account of the course of composition.

it was revised before publication. The reconstruction was prepared by counting the words in each chapter of the first edition and arithmetically deriving from them the pagination of the printer's copy, taking into account which passages were probably handwritten, and which were revised printings (usually newspaper clippings).[13] Two charts are provided on pages 814–15: FIGURE 1 represents chapters 1–11, which were transmitted and revised together; FIGURE 2 represents chapter 12 through appendix C. Since these charts estimate pagination for the *whole* text by relying on word counts, they help to identify most of the pages and chapters to which Clemens himself referred during composition. And since Clemens's references are *independent* of the estimates in the charts, they (and several other documents) constitute a significant check on the accuracy of the reconstruction.[14]

2

Choosing the subject of his second long book was, for Clemens, essentially a process of elimination: testing an old idea (writing about his experiences in the West) against a series of newer ideas. Until he signed the contract in July 1870, he toyed provocatively with the alternatives—publishers as well as subjects. He could write a "telling book" about England. He had heard from a subscription house in Philadelphia "offering unlimitedly." He thought his "Noah's Ark book" would be a "perfect lightning-striker." The Appleton company wanted him to do a "humorous picture-book." He gathered "material enough for a whole book" during a visit to Washington in early July (almost certainly the germ of *The Gilded Age*).[15] And the idea of a new sketchbook persisted as an easy alternative to writ-

---

[13]The average number of words Clemens put on a manuscript page was set at 84, partly because it yielded the most satisfactory overall result, and partly because it is the *actual* average found in the longest comparable manuscript available in Clemens's hand: a chapter written for, but omitted from, *The Innocents Abroad*, probably in June 1868. Known as "Fragment M" (A27, NPV), this particular manuscript has 43 leaves (torn half-sheets) measuring 4⅞ by 7⅞ inches, with 22 ruled lines—a paper stock very nearly identical to the stock used in three discarded pages from the *Roughing It* manuscript, which have survived in the Mark Twain Papers (CU-MARK), and which measure 4⅞ by 7¾ inches, also with 22 ruled lines. By actual count, the pages of Fragment M average 84.7 words of uncanceled text (pages with few, or no, cancellations hold as many as 100 words each). For a discussion of how revised clippings were counted, see page 817 below.

[14]The best way to judge the accuracy of the calculated page numbers is to see how well they correspond with the independent evidence found in Clemens's letters, and on two of the three extant manuscript pages. The correspondence is unlikely to be exact, but the occasional discrepancies are small and not cumulative, and therefore do not invalidate the overall reconstruction, which may be compared to a preliminary map that represents some areas with less certainty than others.

[15]SLC to Elisha Bliss, Jr.: 11 Mar 70, NN-B†; 5 May 70, typescript at WU†; 22 Jan 70, CU-MARK, in *MTMF*, 118; 20 May 70, courtesy of Robert Daley, in *MTLP*, 35; SLC to Olivia L. Clemens, 8 July 70, CU-MARK, in *LLMT*, 154.

ing something new. In fact, the first surviving indication that he had chosen the West as his topic came on 29 May 1870, in a letter to Mrs. Fairbanks: "Well, I guess we *shall* have to go with you to California in the Spring, for the publishers are getting right impatient to see another book on the stocks, & I doubt if I could do better than rub up old Pacific memories & put them between covers along with some eloquent pictures."[16] This remark implies his acceptance of a topic previously considered, and it assumes that the actual writing would be put off until the spring of 1871—a plan that makes sense only if he intended to satisfy Bliss's needs with something else, presumably a sketchbook, which he could make ready "any time."

Albert Bigelow Paine thought that it was Bliss who "proposed a book which should relate the author's travels and experiences in the Far West." If so, Paine's assertion is now the sole evidence for it. More than a week after Clemens recorded his decision to "rub up old Pacific memories," he turned aside a suggestion from Bliss: "I like your idea for a book, but the *inspiration* don't come."[17] What Bliss proposed is not known, yet even if it was the western book, Clemens had anticipated him. Certainly a book based on his western experiences was not a new idea to him.

Six years earlier, Clemens had chosen the same subject (or one very like it) for what would have been his first book—a book he planned to write, and may have begun, before leaving California. All that is known of this project is contained in a letter he wrote from San Francisco on 28 September 1864 in response to a letter (now lost) from his brother and sister-in-law (Orion and Mollie) in Nevada, to whom he had earlier confided this literary ambition. "I *would* commence on my book," he replied to their prodding, but he and Steve Gillis were "getting things ready for his wedding. . . . As soon as this wedding business is over, I believe I will send to you for the files, & begin on my book."[18]

The "files" Clemens referred to in 1864 were probably the same as the "coffin of 'Enterprise' files" which, in early March 1870, he finally did ask Orion to send him from St. Louis, acknowledging their receipt in Buffalo on 26 March—several months before he signed a contract for his second book.[19] These files were surely one reason that *Roughing It* at first seemed a relatively easy book to write. The files were scrapbooks filled with clippings of his work in the Virginia City *Territorial Enterprise*, but also of work by various other hands in the *Enterprise* and other Nevada and California newspapers. To judge from the surviving scrapbooks, the clippings documented Orion's activities as well as his own, and included even multiple copies of work Clemens had published routinely in the West: every-

[16]SLC to Mary Mason Fairbanks, 29 May 70, CSmH, in *MTMF,* 131.
[17]*MTB,* 1:420; SLC to Elisha Bliss, Jr., 9 June 70, CtHMTH†.
[18]SLC to Orion and Mary E. (Mollie) Clemens, 28 Sept 64, *L1,* 315.
[19]SLC to Jane Lampton Clemens and family, 26 Mar 70, NPV, in *MTBus,* 112.

thing from local columns and letters in the *Enterprise* and the San Francisco *Morning Call*, to long, carefully crafted sketches in the *Californian* and the *Golden Era*.[20]

For Clemens, the scrapbooks held out the promise of two kinds of help. Some, perhaps most, of their clippings would simply remind him of the facts—incidents, people, and stories from his western years. But others, especially clippings of his own work, could surely be revised and reprinted as chapters in the book. Like *Innocents*, the new book would be a fundamentally *factual* account, a personal narrative of a real trip—with the trip providing an automatic source of coherence, as well as an excuse for humorous digression. But unlike *Innocents*, which Clemens had written within a year of the voyage it recounted and largely by cobbling together newspaper letters composed during that voyage, *Roughing It* had to be written five to ten years after the events it described, and without the help of any such contemporary account, save what could be salvaged from the scrapbooks—supplemented by whatever collateral material Orion was able to provide.

Between their arrival on 26 March 1870 and the signing of the contract in mid-July, the scrapbooks may well have prompted Clemens to write two long western sketches: "The Facts in the Great Land Slide Case," published in the Buffalo *Express* on 2 April and later revised and reprinted in chapter 34 of *Roughing It;* and "A Couple of Sad Experiences," about his notorious western hoaxes ("Petrified Man" and "A Bloody Massacre near Carson"), written no later than April and published in the June *Galaxy*, but not reprinted (or even mentioned) in the book. But as a source of ready-made chapters about Nevada and California, the scrapbooks turned out to be much less useful than Clemens had anticipated. He used scarcely anything of his own from the *Enterprise*, and nothing at all of what he had published in the San Francisco *Morning Call*, the *Californian*, and the *Golden Era*. Samuel C. Thompson, who was briefly Clem-

---

[20]Maintaining the scrapbooks was a chore that fell largely to Orion and Mollie, although Clemens performed it himself on at least one occasion (see *ET&S1*, 502). The main cache of scrapbooks probably stayed with Orion and Mollie when they returned to St. Louis in September 1866, and therefore had to be retrieved from them when Clemens wanted it in 1870. Sometime in 1907 or 1908, Paine asked Clemens what had become of these "files," and was told that he had "burned" them. When Paine reported this statement to Joseph T. Goodman, Goodman replied on 13 March 1908:

I would accept as final your assertion that those "Enterprise" files were destroyed if it rested on any authority but Mark's. He never had physical energy enough to burn anything—unless perhaps his fingers. . . . He may at sometime have thrown a scrap of paper in the fire, and afterwards, not finding the "Enterprise" files when he wanted them, fancied that he had burned them; but I'll bet, he never did. (*Twainian* 15 [Jan–Feb 1956]: 1)

Goodman was right, of course: some portion of the files did indeed survive—in the estate of Anita Moffett (1891–1952), Pamela Clemens Moffett's granddaughter—and were eventually purchased by the Mark Twain Papers at Berkeley.

ens's private secretary the year after he published *Roughing It*, recalled that he "seemed to have no great esteem for his newspaper contributions. They [were] too hurried and shallow. He told me that in preparing to write 'Roughing It,' he searched newspaper files covering years of his writings and got no help from them."[21]

Although *Roughing It* may have been conceived as early as 1864, it was finally written at a time of greatly heightened interest in literature about the West—especially humorous short fiction and "dialect" poetry. Bret Harte and John Hay, both friends of Clemens's, achieved instantaneous celebrity in 1870–71 through their dialect poems.[22] Clemens himself was not much interested in poetry, but he was interested in dialect, and he was already well known for his western sketches. In a 27 December 1870 editorial in the New York *Tribune*, entitled "The Western School" (promptly reprinted in Clemens's Buffalo *Express*), Hay announced that a "vigorous and full-flavored literature is growing up in the West. The period of echoes and imitations, of feeble reproductions of bad models . . . has gone by, and a school of writers is now coming up on the further side of the Allegh[e]nies who have a message of their own to deliver, and who are uttering it in a way distinctly their own." Hay cited George Horatio Derby (John Phoenix) as the "leader and founder" of this "field of eccentric fiction," which had "since been so successfully worked by Mr. Francis Bret Harte and Mark Twain."

> The well-earned and legitimate success of these two gentlemen has given occasion to those indolent and ill-informed reviewers who have read nothing of the earlier efforts of the Western school, and only the most recent sketches of the two clever Californians who have taken the public by storm, to imagine that these two writers have a monopoly of Western subjects, and that any hunting in the same preserves is arrant poaching.[23]

Hay was in fact protesting a recent tendency to treat Bret Harte as the founder and sole legitimate member of this "Western school," and to regard all others (including Hay himself) as Harte's incompetent imitators.

For his part, Clemens felt personally indebted to Harte, telling Thomas Bailey Aldrich just a month after this editorial appeared that Harte had "trimmed & trained & schooled me patiently until he changed me from an awkward utterer of coarse grotesquenesses to a writer of paragraphs &

---

[21]Memoirs of Samuel Chalmers Thompson, typescript in CU-MARK, 96. In July 1871 the scrapbooks became useful in a third way—when Clemens began, in chapter 63, to use clippings of his 1866 Sandwich Islands letters to the Sacramento *Union*.

[22]Harte published "Heathen Chinee" in the September 1870 *Overland Monthly*. Hay published "Little-Breeches" in the 19 November 1870 daily New York *Tribune*, and "Jim Bludso (of the Prairie Belle)" in the 5 January 1871 daily *Tribune*; both poems were collected in *Pike County Ballads* in 1871.

[23]"The Western School," New York *Tribune*, 27 Dec 70, 4; reprinted as "The Western Literati. Who They Are—What They Have Done. Their Future," Buffalo *Express*, 29 Dec 70, 1. The article is unsigned.

chapters that have found a certain favor in the eyes of even some of the very decentest people in the land." Clemens was thinking especially of Harte's most recent help, for Harte had "read all the MS of the 'Innocents' & told me what passages, paragraphs & *chapters* to leave out—& I followed orders strictly."[24] But Clemens also felt keenly competitive with Harte, who was rising meteorically in the eyes of the eastern literary establishment, even as Clemens struggled with the manuscript of *Roughing It*. During this period, Clemens reviewed Harte's *Poems* in a way that suggests where he felt the competition between them was most intense:

> The true genius of Bret Harte is found in his vividly dramatic California sketches, far more than in any poem that he has written, and his permanent rank in American literature will depend more upon the cultivation that he gives to it in that description of writing than upon any thing that he can continue to do in the odd vein of the "Truthful James" ballads.[25]

Clemens's own rank in American literature could not have seemed to him certain or permanent when he wrote this review—but he *had* written and published dozens of sketches about the West, especially California. Now he had to confront the problem of how to make a book-length narrative from such materials.

Clemens's 1867–68 newspaper correspondence and even *The Innocents Abroad* contained many examples of his impulse to reminisce about his western experiences.[26] But the true precursor of a narrative about the West arose from his longstanding interest in it as a *lecture* topic. As early as January 1867, he wrote Edward P. Hingston that he intended to speak in New York and other eastern states "on California & perhaps on other subjects." Although Clemens did not write such a lecture that year, in May 1868 he again expressed his intention to "get up a lecture on California."[27] The following year he finally drafted his first narrative about the West, specific plans for which he described in a 10 May 1869 letter to James Redpath, his lecture agent. Clemens conceived the subject both as a lecture topic and as the subject of some newspaper letters he planned to write while revisiting California—and thus essentially in the mode of a tourist's contemporary report:

---

[24]SLC to Thomas Bailey Aldrich, 27 Jan 71, MH-H†; SLC to Charles Henry Webb, 26 Nov 70, ViU†.

[25]"New Books," Buffalo *Express*, 14 Jan 71, 2. The review is unsigned.

[26]See, for example, "Letter from 'Mark Twain.' [No. 14.]," San Francisco *Alta California*, 26 May 67, 1 (Jim Townsend's tunnel, in chapter 35 of *Roughing It*); "Mark Twain's Letters from Washington. Number II.," Virginia City *Territorial Enterprise*, 7 Jan 68, PH in CtY-BR (Boggs and the school report, in chapter 43); "Letter from Mark Twain," Chicago *Republican*, 31 May 68, 2 (wildcat mines, in chapter 44); "Remarkable Sagacity of a Cat," an unpublished manuscript probably written in June 1868, NPV (Dick Baker's cat, in chapter 61); and *The Innocents Abroad*, chapter 27 (the trip to Humboldt, in chapter 27).

[27]SLC to Edward P. Hingston, 15 Jan 67, *L2*, 8; SLC to Frank Fuller, 12 May 68, *L2*, 216.

If I go to California I shall write a dozen letters to the N. Y. *Tribune*, & if you can have them copied wholly or in part, it will be well—especially as the title of next winters lecture will be *"Curiosities of California."* Haven't written it yet, but it is mapped out, & suits me very well. [*Mem.* Nearly all the societies wanted a Cal. lecture last year, & of course it will be all the better, now, when the completion of the Pacific RR has turned so much attention in that direction. There is *scope* to the subject, for the country is a curiosity; do. the fluctuations of fortune in the mines, where men grow rich in a day & poor in another; do. *the people*—for you have been in new countries & understand that; do. the Lake Tahoe, whose wonders are little known & less appreciated here; ditto the *never-mentioned* strange Dead Sea of California; & ditto a passing mention, maybe, of the Big Trees & Yo Semite.[28]

Clemens never did return to California, nor did he ever deliver "Curiosities of California," but he did write it. By 5 July he had "written more than enough for a lecture," which he said "must be still added to & then cut down." Only a single fragment of what he wrote has survived in manuscript (a description of Lake Tahoe),[29] perhaps because he soon made use of the rest of it in the Buffalo *Express*—though not as a single narrative, but as a series of loosely connected articles. If we assume that he wrote "Curiosities of California" about as he described it to Redpath, then he probably published it between 16 October 1869 and 29 January 1870 as the so-called "Around the World" letters, five of which he subsequently reused in *Roughing It*.[30] It may have been the potential of this protonarrative which led Clemens to ask Orion for the scrapbooks in early March 1870.

By the end of July Clemens had tentatively settled on the idea of a book about the West. According to Paine, Bliss came to Elmira in "early July" to negotiate the contract for *Roughing It*, but he seems not to have come before the middle of the month. On 4 July, Clemens wrote Bliss to say that he would be in Elmira "10 days or 2 weeks yet," and to urge him to "Come—come either here or to Buf."[31] On the same day, however, Clemens took the train to Washington, D.C., returning to Elmira no sooner than 10 or 11 July. On 5 July, the Washington correspondent of the Sacramento *Union* had "quite a chat with him" in Washington:

---

[28]SLC to James Redpath, 10 May 69, *L3*, 215–16.

[29]SLC to Mary Mason Fairbanks, 5 July 69, *L3*, 281; "Scenery," manuscript of eleven pages, CU-MARK, published in *ET&S4*.

[30]The sixth letter was devoted to the "fluctuations of fortune in the mines" (chapter 46); the first letter described Mono Lake, or the "strange Dead Sea of California" (chapter 38). Letters 3–5 were also reused in *Roughing It*—in chapters 37, 56, 57, 60, and 61 (see the Description of Texts). Although Clemens ultimately wrote only eight letters in this series, he implied in January that he expected it to be some fifty letters long—long enough, in other words, to form the basis for a book (SLC to Elisha Bliss, Jr., 22 Jan 70, CU-MARK, in *MTLP*, 29). His decision to turn his lecture manuscript into articles also explains why, in the fall of 1869, he suddenly reverted to his Sandwich Islands lecture, even though "Curiosities of California" had been announced.

[31]*MTB*, 1:420; SLC to Elisha Bliss, Jr., 4 July 70, courtesy of Robert Daley, in *MTLP*, 36.

Mark appears to be a very devoted husband. His old friends in Nevada and California will remember how he used to smoke pipes, and quaff lager and dress rather slouchily. Well, all this is changed. He now dresses with good taste, never drinks or smokes. Such, alas! are some of the results of marriage. Undoubtedly he looks all the better for it, and perhaps it is this that lends a finer quality of late to his humor, which used occasionally to have a touch of grossness in it. But in all other respects he is the same old "Mark" of yore. He is under contract to write a new book, and wants to go off, as soon as his father-in-law is well enough, to some quiet nook in England or some other part of the world where nobody knows him, and there write it. It must be ready by next March.[32]

This interview shows that Clemens was already committed to publishing his next book with Bliss, ten days before the formal contract was drawn up and signed. The original draft of that contract, in Bliss's hand, indicates that it was "made this 15th day of July, AD 1870, at Elmira." In it Clemens agreed to write a "manuscript for a book upon such subject as may be agreed upon," and to deliver it "as soon as practicable, but as early as 1st of January next if they the sd company shall desire it. Said manuscript to contain matter sufficient for a book of about 600 pages octavo." The contract forbade Clemens "to write or furnish manuscript for any other book unless for said company, during the time said manuscript & book are being prepared & sold." And it stipulated that the American Publishing Company would "publish the said book in their best style—to commence operations at once upon receipt of manuscript & to push it through with all the despatch compatible with its being well done in text & illustrations." The company also agreed to "a copyright on every copy sold of *seven & one half* per cent of the retail or subscription price."[33]

In 1906 Clemens recalled in some detail—not all of it trustworthy— how he and Bliss had arrived at this percentage:

I had published "The Innocents" on a five per cent. royalty, which would amount to about twenty-two cents per volume. Proposals were coming in now from several other good houses. One offered fifteen per cent. royalty; another offered to give me *all* of the profits and be content with the advertisement which the book would furnish the house. I sent for Bliss, and he came to Elmira. . . . I told Bliss I did not wish to leave his corporation, and that I did not want extravagant terms. I said I thought I ought to have half the profit above cost of manufacture, and he said with enthusiasm that that was exactly right, exactly right. He went to his hotel and drew the contract and brought it to the house in the afternoon. I found a difficulty in it. It did not name "half profits," but named a seven-and-a-half per cent royalty instead. I asked him to explain that. I said that that was not the understanding. He said, "No, it wasn't," but that he had put in a royalty to simplify the matter—that 7½ per cent. royalty represented fully half the profit and a little more, up to a sale of a hundred thousand copies; that after that, the Publishing Company's half would be a shade superior to mine.

I was a little doubtful, a little suspicious, and asked him if he could swear to that.

[32]"Letter from Washington," signed "D.," written 6 July, Sacramento *Union*, 19 July 70, 1.

[33]Cyril Clemens Collection, CtHMTH, in *Mark Twain Quarterly* 6 (Summer/ Fall 1944): 5.

He promptly put up his hand and made oath to it, exactly repeating the words which he had just used.[34]

The contract did not name the subject of the new book, but the omission was deliberate, as Clemens explained to Orion on the day he signed it:

> Per contract I must have another 600-page book ready for my publisher Jan. 1, & I only began it to-day. The subject of it is a secret, because I may possibly change it. But as it stands, I propose to do up Nevada & Cal., beginning with the trip across the country in the stage. Have you a memorandum of the route we took—or the names of any of the Stations we stopped at? Do you remember any of the scenes, names, incidents or adventures of the coach trip?—for I remember next to *nothing* about the matter. Jot down a foolscap page of items for me. I wish I could have two days' talk with you.[35]

Orion did indeed have a memorandum book of the trip, which he promptly sent. He also agreed to write out some notes about their Nevada experiences, although these would not be ready until early November. Clemens did not, however, really begin writing on 15 July. Almost two weeks later he told his mother and sister that he was "going to write a 600-page 8vo. book (like the last) for my publishers (it is a secret for a few days yet.) It will be about Nevada & California & must be finished Jan 1. I shall begin it about a month from now. By request, Orion has sent me his note-book of the Plains trip."[36]

Meanwhile, Bliss evidently voiced a suspicion that Clemens was unhappy with the terms of the contract, and was considering another publisher. On 2 August, Clemens reassured him in such candid terms that the letter still serves as a useful corrective of his 1906 recollections:

> You know I already had an offer of *ten* per cent from those same parties in my pocket when I stipulated for 7½ with you. I simply promised to *give them a chance to bid;* I never said I would publish with them if theirs was the best bid. If their *first* offer had been 12½ I would merely have asked you to climb along up *as near that figure as you could & make money,* but I wouldn't have asked anything more. Whenever you said that you had got up to what was a fair divide between us (there being no *risk,* now, in publishing for me, while there WAS, before,) I should have closed with you on those terms. I never have had the slightest idea of publishing with anybody but you. (I was careful to make no promises to those folks about their bid.)
>
> You see you can't get it out of your head that I am a sort of a rascal, but I ain't. I can stick to you just as long as you can stick to me, & give you odds. I made that contract with all my senses about me, & it suits me & I am satisfied with it. If I get only half a chance I will write a book that will sell like fury provided you put pictures enough in it.[37]

[34]AD, 23 May 1906, CU-MARK, in *MTE,* 151–53.

[35]SLC to Orion Clemens, 15 July 70, CU-MARK, in *MTL,* 1:174–75. Orion was then working as the "Night Editor" of the St. Louis *Missouri Democrat.*

[36]SLC to Jane Lampton Clemens and Pamela A. Moffett, 27 July 70, NPV, in *MTBus,* 117.

[37]SLC to Elisha Bliss, Jr., 2 Aug 70, OC, in *MTLP,* 37.

Four days later, on 6 August, Olivia's father died. Although Clemens had already decided not to begin on his book until late August, Jervis Langdon's death ensured that he could not write anything else in August either. The funeral was held in Elmira on 8 August, the will probated on 12 August, and a memorial service conducted on 21 August.[38] Clemens refrained from publishing anything in the Buffalo *Express* until 25 August, when "Domestic Missionaries Wanted" appeared.[39] Presumably by then, or shortly thereafter, he also began on the book, for he wrote Orion on 2 September:

> I find that your little memorandum book is going to be ever so much use to me, & will enable me to make quite a coherent narrative of the Plains journey instead of slurring it over & jumping 2,000 miles at a stride. The book I am writing will sell. In return for the use of the little memorandum book I shall take the greatest pleasure in forwarding to you the third $1,000 which the publisher of the forthcoming work sends me—or the *first* $1,000, I am not particular—they will both be in the first quarterly statement of account from the publisher.[40]

Orion's journal served Clemens as an indispensable tool in writing the overland chapters (1–20). He relied on it for names, distances, times, landmarks, several particular incidents, and even its day-by-day account of the journey. He treated the original record like an outline, from which he could diverge at will without losing the essential thread of actual events. Especially at this early stage of composition, he seems also to have adhered closely to its chronology, and even its language. For example, when Orion noted on the fifth day, "Arrived at the 'crossing' of the South Platte, alias 'Overland City,' alias 'Julesburg,' at 11 A.M., 470 miles from St. Joseph," Clemens reproduced Orion's sentence almost verbatim, adding only a concluding phrase of his own: "At noon on the fifth day out, we arrived at the 'Crossing of the South Platte,' *alias* 'Julesburg,' *alias* 'Overland City,' four hundred and seventy miles from St. Joseph—the strangest, quaintest, funniest frontier town that our untraveled eyes had ever stared at and been astonished with."[41]

Even with such help in hand, however, Clemens's circumstances did not favor rapid composition. On the last day of August he wrote to his sister:

> We are getting along tolerably well. Mother [i.e., Mrs. Langdon] is here, & Miss Emma Nye. Livy cannot sleep, since her father's death—but I give her a narcotic every night & *make* her.

---

[38]Elmira *Advertiser:* "City and Neighborhood," 8 Aug 70, 4; "Jervis Langdon's Will," 13 Aug 70, 4; "The Late Jervis Langdon," 22 Aug 70, 4. Clemens was one of the executors of Jervis Langdon's will.

[39]Buffalo *Express*, 25 Aug 70, 2. Clemens's clipping of this unsigned editorial is in CU-MARK; Paine attributed it to him in 1912 (*MTB*, 1:400–401).

[40]SLC to Orion Clemens, 2 Sept 70, *L4*, forthcoming.

[41]Page 40. Orion's journal has not been found, but access to its text is made possible by a letter Orion wrote to his wife on 8 and 9 September 1861, into which he evidently copied most of it. See supplement A, item 1 (pages 769–74).

I am just as busy as I can be—am still writing for the Galaxy & also writing a book like the "Innocents" in size & style. . . . I have got my work ciphered down to *days*, & I haven't a single day to spare between this & the date which, by written contract I am to deliver the MSS. of the book to the publisher.[42]

Within days Clemens reported that Emma Nye had become "right sick— she cannot go on to Detroit yet awhile, where she is to teach." But he also reported progress on his manuscript: "I have written four chapters of my new book during the past few days, & I tell you it is going to be a mighty starchy book—will sell, too."[43] Two days later, on 4 September, he fired off a salvo of reassurance to Bliss:

During past week have written first four chapters of the book, & I tell you the "Innocents Abroad["] will have to get up early to beat it. It will be a book that will jump right strait into a continental celebrity the first month it is issued. Now I want it illustrated lavishly. We shall sell 90,000 copies the first 12 months. I haven't even a shadow of a doubt of that. I see the capabilities of my subject.[44]

His subject was now no longer a secret, for on 7 September the Elmira *Advertiser* reported that "MARK TWAIN's new book, which is to be published next spring, is to be an account of travel at home, describing in a humorous and satirical way our cities and towns, and the people of different sections."[45]

Clemens was soon obliged to confess that he had "no time to turn round" because Emma Nye was "dying in the house of typhoid fever (parents are in South Carolina) & the premises are full of nurses & doctors & we are all fagged out."[46] Still, he must have continued to write, for by 15 September he had completed two more chapters, which took him up through noon on the fifth day, at the end of chapter 6. By now he was already looking ahead to the ninth day, the subject of what became chapter 10, described in Orion's journal as "Breakfast at Rock[y] Ridge Station, 24 miles from 'Cold Spring,' and 871 miles from St. Joseph."[47] Clemens had his own very particular memory of that day, which he had recalled the previous winter in his seventh "Around the World" letter:

At the Rocky Ridge station in the Rocky Mountains, in the old days of overland stages and pony expresses, I had the gorgeous honor of breakfasting with Mr. Slade, the Prince of all the desperadoes; who killed twenty-six men in his time; who used to cut off his victims' ears and send them as keepsakes to their relatives; and who bound one of his victim's hand and foot and practiced on him with his revolver for

---

[42]SLC to Pamela A. Moffett, 31 Aug 70, NPV, in *MTL*, 1:176.

[43]Olivia L. Clemens and SLC to Mary Mason Fairbanks, 2 Sept 70, CSmH, in *MTMF*, 137.

[44]SLC tò Elisha Bliss, Jr., 4 Sept 70, CU-MARK, in *MTLP*, 39.

[45]"City and Neighborhood," Elmira *Advertiser*, 7 Sept 70, 4.

[46]SLC to Orion Clemens, 9 Sept 70, NPV, in *MTL*, 1:177.

[47]According to Orion's journal, this breakfast took place on the morning of the ninth day of the trip. Clemens eventually described it in chapter 10, even though that placed it on the eighth day; his narrative did not reach the ninth day until the beginning of chapter 12. Supplement A, item 2 (pages 775–77), provides a chart comparing Orion's journal with the *Roughing It* narrative.

hours together—a proceeding which seems almost inexcusable until we reflect that Rocky Ridge is away off in the dull solitudes of the mountains, and the poor desperadoes have hardly any amusements. Mr. Slade afterward went to Montana and began to thin out the population as usual—for he took a great interest in trimming the census and regulating the vote—but finally the Vigilance Committee captured him and hanged him, giving him just fifteen minutes to prepare himself in. The papers said he cried on the scaffold.[48]

But Clemens felt the need for more documentation of Slade's history than he could find in the scrapbooks, or in Orion's journal. He therefore wrote to the postmaster of Virginia City (Montana Territory), who was Hezekiah Hosmer, former chief justice of the territorial supreme court:

Buffalo, Sept. 15.

Dear Sir:

Four or five years ago a righteous Vigilance Committee ˏin your cityˏ hanged a casual acquaintance of mine named Slade, along with twelve other prominent citizens whom I only knew by reputation. Slade was a "section-agent" at Rocky Ridge station in the Rocky Mountains when I crossed the plains in the Overland stage ten years ago, & I took breakfast with him & survived.

Now I am writing a book (MS. to be delivered to publisher Jan. 1,) & as the Overland journey has made six chapters of it thus far & promises to make six or eight more, I thought I would just rescue my late friend Slade from oblivion & set a sympathetic public to weeping for him.

Such a humanized fragment of the original Devil could not & *did* not go out of the world without considerable newspaper eclat, in the shape of biographical notices, particulars of his execution, etc., & the object of this letter is to beg of you to ask some one connected with your city papers to send me a Virginia City newspaper of that day if it can be done without mutilating a file.

ˏ{ { { [*If found, please enclose in* LETTER *form,* } } }
{ { { *else it will go to the office of Buffalo "Express"* } } }
{ { { *ℰ be lost among the exchanges.*] } } }ˏ

I beg your pardon for writing you so freely & putting you, or trying to put you to trouble, without having the warrant of an introduction to you, but I did not know any one in Virginia City & so I ventured to ask this favor at your hands. Hoping you will be able to help me

I am, Sir,

Your Obt. Serv't
Mark Twain.[49]

Hosmer's reply to this appeal has not been found, but it was very likely he who referred Clemens to Thomas J. Dimsdale's little book, *The Vigilantes of Montana* (1866), a compilation of newspaper stories Dimsdale had written and published in the *Montana Post* in 1865–66. Hosmer may even have realized that Dimsdale's book would be hard to find in Buffalo, and therefore sent Clemens a copy of it—if not immediately, then probably within a month or two. The exact timing remains uncertain, because even though Dimsdale's book became the explicit source for much of what Clemens said about Slade in chapters 10 and 11, he did not complete those chapters until mid-March 1871.

---

[48]"Around the World. Letter Number 7," Buffalo *Express*, 22 Jan 70, 2.
[49]SLC to Hezekiah L. Hosmer, 15 Sept 70, MtHi†.

Bliss had, meanwhile, asked Clemens to contribute to the trade news-paper he was starting up as an advertising medium for the American Pub-lishing Company's books. On or about 21 September, Clemens dashed off a note in reply: "Yes, *will furnish article for paper*. . . . Finished 7ᵗʰ or 8ᵗʰ chap. of book to-day, forget which—am up to page 180—only about 1,500 ₓ1500ₓ more to write."[50] This statement, however, cannot be taken literally as a reference to chapters 7 and 8 as they were published in *Roughing It*— nor is it obvious why, having written "up to page 180," Clemens then had "only about 1500 more to write." Just where *was* he in the process of com-position? To answer that question, it is first necessary to explain the re-construction charts in greater detail.

3

Roughing It was, in most ways, a typical subscription book. Bliss pub-lished a salesman's prospectus containing selected pages and illustrations from it. Both the prospectus and the book contained highly particular ta-bles of contents and lists of illustrations, which can be compared with each other and with the texts and illustrations they refer to. Inconsisten-cies between the lists and the texts may, of course, be simple errors, but they may also reflect incomplete correction or revision. In this particular case, the bibliographical evidence of the prospectus is much richer than usual because Bliss began its production substantially before Clemens had completed his manuscript. Issued in November 1871, the first pro-spectus (Pra) was so filled with signs of incompleteness and inadvertence that Bliss took the equally unusual step of issuing a revised and corrected form of it (Prb) two months later. Much of what can now be pieced to-gether about the history of composition and revision (especially the evo-lution of the early chapters, represented in FIGURE 1) depends on the evi-dence of "errors" in Pra—errors, that is, in the sense that they refer to or are part of an earlier form of the text than the one finally published in *Roughing It*.

The wording of some of the column headings in the charts also needs clarification: "clippings," "real page nos," and "equiv page nos" (for "equivalent page numbers"). It is not self-evident why Clemens said on 21 September 1870 that he had only "about 1500 more [pages] to write." Sev-eral later statements show that he believed he needed a total of 1800 pages of printer's copy to make a 600-page book—three pages of printer's copy for each book page, an empirical average that took into account the vari-

---

[50]SLC to Elisha Bliss, Jr., 21? Sept 70, CCC†. Bliss's paper appeared for the first and only time as the *Author's Sketch Book* in late October. Redesigned and re-named *The American Publisher*, it reappeared in early March 1871, evidently the issue to which Clemens promised to contribute (see SLC to Orion Clemens, 4 Mar 71, NPV, in *MTL*, 1:186).

able space needed for the illustrations.[51] Yet when 1800 is reduced by 180 to 1620, that number does not seem a plausible approximation of "about 1500," even if it is assumed that Clemens was rounding off to the nearest hundred.

This statement is, in fact, the earliest indication we have that Clemens sometimes counted the pages of the *Roughing It* printer's copy, as he had earlier done with *Innocents*, in a way that took into account the larger number of words typically contained in a page made up wholly or in part from *clippings*. That Clemens used clippings to help make up the printer's copy for both *Innocents* and *Roughing It* is now well established. One of the three surviving pages of the *Roughing It* manuscript (reproduced in facsimile on page 816) amply demonstrates how such clippings were mounted and then altered in the margins. (The page is extant because it was discarded after Clemens further revised it.) In June 1868, when the printer's copy for *Innocents* was nearly complete, Clemens told Mrs. Fairbanks that he was "writing page No. ~~1,843.~~ ‸2,343.‸" But the printer's copy was never much longer than about 1300 pages: a manuscript chapter about Spain (very near the end of the book, and ultimately omitted from the text) was numbered 1289 through 1331. And in April 1869, when Bliss needed to cut the manuscript to fit within 650 book pages, Clemens wrote that he hoped "there won't be a necessity to cut much, but when you say you are only to the 800 or 900th page you don't comfort me entirely, because so much of the 400 or 500 pages still left are reprint, and so will string out a heap."[52] So it is clear that when he wrote Mrs. Fairbanks in June 1868, he added first 500, then 1000, pages to the real total of about 1343 pages. His hesitation between the two larger figures (1843 and 2343) shows that he was actually multiplying the same 500 pages of "reprint" (i.e., clippings from the San Francisco *Alta California*) first by two, then by three, so that the total equaled what he would have had if everything were in his handwriting. Clemens must have realized that he had incorrectly evaluated the length of his *Innocents* printer's copy, since he ultimately had *too much* material. Now, with *Roughing It*, he seems to have decided that a clipping page contained *four* times the number of words on a holograph page—not merely two or three, as he had earlier calculated. So if a holograph page averaged 84 words (as assumed here), Clemens counted a clipping page as 336 words—the *equivalent*, in other words, of four holograph pages ($4 \times 84 = 336$ words), or three more pages than were actually in the copy (*real* pages). It is this method of counting which explains his otherwise puzzling arithmetic here and in later statements about his

---

[51]See SLC to Elisha Bliss, Jr., 15 May 71, ViU, in *MTL*, 1:187–88, and SLC to Olivia L. Clemens, 10 Aug 71, CU-MARK, in *LLMT*, 159.

[52]SLC to Mary Mason Fairbanks, 17 June 68, *L2*, 222, 230 n. 4; SLC to Elisha Bliss, Jr., 29 Apr 69, *L3*, 199.

1		PRINTER'S COPY					Pra	Prb	1st ed
		18 March 1871				10 Apr 71 MS revised real pages (words)	early Aug 71 1st proofs folios (pages)	late Aug 71 proof revised ch no:folios	30 Jan 72 ch no:folios (pages)
ch no	subject	words (a)	real pages (a/84)	real page nos	equiv page nos				
1	trip to St. Joseph	769	9	1–9	1–9	—	19–22 (4)	1:19–21	1:19–21 (3)
2	stagecoach departure	1680	20	10–29	10–29	—	23–29 (7)	2:22–27	2:22–28 (7)
3	jackass rabbit, camel story	2557	30	30–59	30–59	—	30–38 (9)	3:29, 31–33, 35–36	3:29–36 (8)
4	stage stations, slumgullion	2921 +417*	36	60–95	60–99	—	39–49 (11)	4:38	4:37–47 (11)
5	cayote and dog	1508	18	96–113	100–117	—	50–55 (6)	5:51	5:48–53 (6)
6	stage officials, Jack and Moses	943	11	114–124	118–128	20 (1708)	56–61 (6)	—	6:54–59 (6)
7	Overland City (?)	2100	25	125–149	129–153	41 (3444)	62–74 (13)		
8	Bemis and the buffalo	1001	12	150–161	154–165	22 (1841)	75–81 (7)	7:62–63	7:60–66 (7)
	Eckert and the cat							7:68–69	7:67–69 (3)
8	pony-express rider	769	9	162–170	166–174	—	82–84 (3)	8:70–73	8:70–72 (3)
9	Scott's Bluffs, avalanche	602	7	171–177	175–181	—	85–86 (2)	—	8:73–74 (2)
9	Indian country	1606	19	178–196	182–200	—	87–91 (5)	—	9:75–79 (5)
10	Slade (Orion's information)	2550	30	197–226	201–230	—	92–101 (10)	10:80–81, 84	10:80–89 (10)
11	Slade (Dimsdale's information)	2725	32	227–258	231–262	—	102–108 (7)	—	11:90–96 (7)

*Clipping words

2		PRINTER'S COPY							Pr	1st ed
		holograph		clippings						
ch no	subject	words (a)	pages (b= a/84)	words (c)	pages (d= c/336)	real page nos	equiv pages (b+4d)	equiv page nos	Pra ch no: Prb folios	ch no
12	South Pass, arrival Salt Lake City	3245	39	—	—	259–297	39	263–301	illus, 98–102	12
13	Salt Lake City, Mormon history	1346+ 1842	38	—	—	298–335	38	302–339		13 + A
14	Mr. Street and the Mormons	1038	12	—	—	336–347	12	340–351		14
15	Mountain Meadows massacre	760	9	773	2.3	348–358	18	352–369		B
16	Johnson's account of polygamy	2249	27	—	—	359–385	27	370–396	16:120–126	15
17	Mormon Bible	1277	15	2146	6.4	386–406	41	397–437	17:127, 129–30, 135	16
18	"everything a quarter"	1408	17	—	—	407–423	17	438–454		17
19	alkali desert	1202	14	—	—	424–437	14	455–468		18
20	Digger Indians	1133	13	—	—	438–450	13	469–481		19
21	Horace Greeley and Hank Monk	2218	26	—	—	451–476	26	482–507		20
22	Carson City, Washoe zephyr	2868	34	—	—	477–510	34	508–541	22:65–167	21
23	trip to Lake Tahoe	1552	18	—	—	511–528	18	542–559		22
24	fire at the lake	1728	21	—	—	529–549	21	560–580	24:illus, 174–177	23
25	Mexican plug	1873	22	—	—	550–571	22	581–602	25:178–183	24
26	Nevada territorial government	1971	23	—	—	572–594	23	603–625		25
27	silver fever	897	11	788	2.3	595–607	20	626–645		26
28	trip to Humboldt	1370	16	—	—	608–623	16	646–661		27
29	prospecting	1601	19	—	—	624–642	19	662–680		28
30	"Monarch of the Mountains"	1473	18	—	—	643–660	18	681–698		29
31	return to Carson City	1628	19	—	—	661–679	19	699–717		30
32	Mr. Arkansas, lost in the snow	2952	35	—	—	680–714	35	718–752		31
33	discarded vices	1566	19	—	—	715–733	19	753–771		32
34	resurrected vices	799	10	—	—	734–743	10	772–781		33
35	great landslide case	122	1	1738	5.2	744–749	22	782–803		34

2	PRINTER'S COPY								Pr	1st ed
		holograph		clippings						
ch no	subject	words (a)	pages (b= a/84)	words (c)	pages (d= c/336)	real page nos	equiv pages (b+4d)	equiv page nos	Pra ch no: Prb folios	ch no
36	trip to Esmeralda	1031	12	—	—	750–761	12	804–815		35
	Nevada quartz mills	1873	22	—	—		22			36
37	Whiteman cement mine	1237	15	666	2.0	762–778	23	816–838		37
38	trip to Mono Lake	0	0	1374	4.1	779–782	16	839–854	illus	38
39	boating on the lake	1860	22	—	—	783–804	22	855–876		39
40	locating the blind lead	2185	26	—	—	805–830	26	877–902		40
41	losing the blind lead	2178	26	—	—	831–856	26	903–928		41
42	local reporter for the *Enterprise*	1989	24	—	—	857–880	24	929–952		42
43	Boggs and the school report	1936	23	—	—	881–903	23	953–975		43
44	puffing stocks, Senator Stewart	2124	25	—	—	904–928	25	976–1000		44
45	Gridley and the flour sack	2029	24	—	—	929–952	24	1001–1024	illus	45
46	Nevada nabobs	1687	20	952	2.8	953–975	31	1025–1055	325–328	46
47	Buck Fanshaw's funeral	3030	36	—	—	976–1011	36	1056–1091		47
48	desperadoes and trial by jury	2123	25	—	—	1012–1036	25	1092–1116		48
	fatal affrays	703	8	1452	4.3		25			49
49	Capt. Ned Blakely	2034	24	—	—	1037–1060	24	1117–1140		50
50	*Weekly Occidental*, "The Aged Pilot Man"	2698	32	806	7.6*	1061–1100	62	1141–1202	369–375	51
	mining statistics, underground city	1436†	17	980	2.9		29			52
	Jim Blaine's grandfather's ram	1998	24	—	—		24			53
51	Chinese community	1359	16	838	2.5	1101–1119	26	1203–1228		54
52	"Prodigal," chief editor	3000	36	—	—	1120–1155	36	1229–1264		55
53	trip to San Francisco	685	8	1120	3.3	1156–1166	21	1265–1285		56
54	San Francisco pioneers	44	1	1250	3.7	1167–1171	16	1286–1301		57
55	butterfly idleness, earthquake	2218	26	255	.8	1172–1198	29	1302–1330		58
56	"slinking," Blucher's story	2076	25	—	—	1199–1223	25	1331–1355		59
57	trip to Tuolumne, pocket-mining	389	5	993	3.0	1224–1231	17	1356–1372		60
58	Dick Baker and his cat	523	6	1209	3.6	1232–1241	20	1373–1392		61
59	trip to the Islands, the "Admiral"	3222	38	—	—	1242–1279	38	1393–1430		62
60	Honolulu, scorpions, tamarinds	766	9	523	1.6	1280–1290	15	1431–1445		63
61	steed Oahu, an ancient temple	140	2	1881	5.6	1291–1298	24	1446–1469		64
62	Kamehameha I, horse-jockeys	131	2	2039	6.1	1299–1306	26	1470–1495		65
63	market, remarkable stranger	176	2	1713	5.1	1307–1313	22	1496–1517		66
64	native customs, playing empire	2149	26	521	1.6	1314–1341	32	1518–1549		67
65	royal funeral, death of Kamehameha	542	6	2490	7.4	1342–1354	36	1550–1585		68
66	Hawaii, trip through Kona	0	0	1689	5.0	1355–1359	20	1586–1605	illus§	69
67	Horace Greeley's letter	2279	27	—	—	1360–1386	27	1606–1632		70
68	Kealakekua Bay, Capt. Cook	110	1	1326	3.9	1387–1391	17	1633–1649		71
69	Obookiah, first missionaries	188	2	1573	4.7	1392–1398	21	1650–1670		72
70	surf-bathing, City of Refuge	177	2	2056	6.1	1399–1406	26	1671–1696		73
71	Kilauea, Volcano House	333	4	1397	4.2	1407–1414	21	1697–1717		74
	exploration of Kilauea crater	1312	16	—	—		16			75
72	Maui's Iao Valley and Haleakala	2143	26	—	—	1415–1440	26	1718–1743	73:illus, 544–547, 549–550	76
73	Markiss, the liar	150	2	1681	5.0	1441–1447	22	1744–1765		77
74	first San Francisco lecture	1615	19	—	—	1448–1466	19	1766–1784	75:558–563	78
75	robbery by practical jokers	1845	22	—	—	1467–1488	22	1785–1806		79
	Wiegand's letter	470	6	5861	17.4		76			C

* "The Aged Pilot Man" calculated at a rate of 18 lines per page. †Excludes a footnote added in proof.
§See note 187.

I had two
partners in this brilliant stroke of fortune.
The sensible one is still worth a hundred
thousand dollars or so—he never lost his
wits—but the other one (and by far the
best and worthiest of our trio), dies pau-
is beard.

   I was personally acquainted with the
several nabobs mentioned in this ████, and
so, for old acquaintance sake, I have swapped their occupations and experiences
around in such a way as to keep the Pacific
public from recognizing these once notorious men. I have no desire to drag them
out of their retirement and make them uncomfortable by exhibiting them without
mask or disguise—I merely wish to use
their fortunes and misfortunes for a moment for the adornment of this newspaper
article

cannot

*chapter,
shifted*

brief sketch.

During the "flush
times" my brother the Secretary's official fees amounted
to about twelve thousand
dollars a year, in gold, & he
built a house at a cost of
six thousand. He lived to
sail from San Fran-
cisco with all his worldly
possessions in his pocket

Manuscript page numbered 968, removed from what is now chapter 46. It contains
a clipping from the Buffalo *Express* for 8 January 1870. Reproduced at 87 percent of
actual size, from the original in the Mark Twain Papers, The Bancroft Library (CU-
MARK).

progress—and which accounts for the headings on those columns of numbers in FIGURES 1 and 2.

How far had Clemens progressed with his book in September 1870, when he had written "up to page 180"? FIGURE 1 indicates that at the earliest "mappable" stage of composition, in March 1871, the last page in chapter 8 was 170, nine pages shy of what Clemens himself had said the previous September (assuming that "up to page 180" refers to the first page of chapter 9). In making this statement, however, Clemens may have considered that the clipping from the New York *Times* in chapter 4, which was slightly over one page long, was equivalent to five holograph pages. That would make the *equivalent* last page of chapter 8 number 174, just five pages shy of the number Clemens assigned it (179).[53]

If each clipping page that Clemens prepared was considered to contain the equivalent of four holograph pages, then he could reduce the total number of pages he needed by four times the number of clipping pages he used, or planned to use. If he estimated, for instance, that he would prepare 30 pages of clippings, then simple arithmetic shows that having written 180 pages of holograph, he could also count as "in hand" some 120 pages (4×30) which would result from these 30 clipping pages, for a total of 300 pages in hand—leaving him 1500 pages still to write.

Collation shows that by the time Clemens completed his book late in the fall of 1871, he had used more than 130 pages of clippings. But in September 1870, at the outset of composition, he expected to use many fewer, largely because he had not yet decided to reuse any of his 1866 letters to the Sacramento *Union*. Within a few weeks of his 21 September note to Bliss, he probably was able to count the clipping pages he planned to use from the Buffalo *Express*, and by December he had prepared nearly all of these by mounting and revising them for resetting. By that time, however, his plans for them had changed: he now intended to include them in a new sketchbook, rather than in *Roughing It*. On 22 December he told Bliss that he had "arranged" the principal sketches for this sketchbook, and by

---

[53]The calculated numbers in these charts are rounded off to the nearest whole number, except the numbers of clipping pages, which are rounded to the nearest tenth, to avoid the cumulative error caused when each is multiplied by four. In this case, for example, the clipping contained 417 words, or 1.2 clipping pages (417/336). The clipping was thus equivalent to 4.8 manuscript pages (1.2×4), rounded off to 5. Two sketches that Clemens prepared for reprinting no later than January 1871 consist almost entirely of pasted-up clippings and contain roughly 310 to 340 words on each page (see "Adventures in Hayti" and "A Ghost Story," in CU-MARK, sample pages reproduced in *ET&S1*, 580–83). In FIGURES 1–2, the number of words judged to be in clipping form or in holograph was determined by the amount of revision. Any passage in which collation showed heavy revision was counted as "holograph" rather than "clipping" words, on the assumption that marking a clipping was impractical.

sometime in January 1871 he had produced a working table of contents.[54] When the sketchbook was again postponed, some of these mounted clippings found their way back into *Roughing It:* revised versions of "Around the World" letters 1, 3, 4, and 5, as well as "The Facts in the Great Land Slide Case," all first published in the *Express*. If we count the number of clipping pages they represent—that is, if we count only the *Express* clippings Clemens planned at the outset to use in *Roughing It*—the total is 25. If he had used that figure (25) to compute the number of pages still left to write, the result would have been 1520, or "about 1500."[55]

Although Clemens said on 21 September that he had reached the end of chapter 8, FIGURE 1 indicates that chapters 1–8 as first drafted differed in several ways from their published form. Chapter 6, for instance, was probably only about eleven manuscript pages, roughly half as long as the published version—lacking perhaps a long section in the middle. Chapter 8 *ended* with the pony-express passage, which now begins the chapter, and it *began* with the story of Bemis and the buffalo, which now fills all but the last three pages of chapter 7. The anecdote about Eckert and the cocoanut-eating cat, which now occupies the last three pages of chapter 7, was almost certainly not in the manuscript at all, for the references it makes to Siam have been shown to derive from Anna H. Leonowens's *English Governess at the Siamese Court*, which Fields, Osgood and Company did not publish until December 1870, and which Clemens did not buy and read until sometime in 1871.[56] Finally, chapter 7 was very likely given over to something that Clemens eventually left out of the book entirely—a description of Overland City (or Julesburg), "the strangest, quaintest, funniest frontier town that our untraveled eyes had ever stared at and been astonished with."[57]

On or about 28 September (one week after finishing the "7th or 8th chap.") Clemens may also have written to his former colleagues on the *Enterprise* for help similar to the kind he had asked of Hezekiah Hosmer. The *Enterprise* reported:

MARK TWAIN'S new book is to be all about his experience in California and Nevada and coming to this coast by the Overland stages. It will be a volume of 600 pages octavo. He has started in on it, but at last accounts was two days' journey the

---

[54]SLC to Elisha Bliss, Jr., 22 Dec 70, CtY-BR, ViU, and courtesy of Todd M. Axelrod†.

[55]See *ET&S1*, 574–84. That is, $180 + (4 \times 25) = 280$, and $1800 - 280 = 1520$.

[56]Portions of Leonowens's story were serialized in the *Atlantic Monthly* for April, May, June, and August 1870, but the complete version, including the passages alluded to in chapter 7 of *Roughing It* (see the explanatory note at 48.6–7), was not issued as a book until early December (New York *Times*, 10 Dec 70, 2; "New Publications," New York *Tribune*, 27 Dec 70, 6).

[57]This phrase survives at the end of chapter 6 (page 40), but the expectations it sets up are not gratified in chapter 7, which says only, "For an hour we took as much interest in Overland City as if we had never seen a town before" (page 41). The rationale for this conjecture is set forth more fully in the discussion below.

other side of Salt Lake with it; so we need not get excited here about the "chief amang us" for some time to come. His book will be out in April next.[58]

Two days' journey "the other side" of Salt Lake City put Clemens on the ninth day, crossing the Continental Divide, which he described in chapter 12. He had not, presumably, heard yet from Hosmer on the subject of Slade, and he would leave chapters 10 and 11 incomplete until March.

The evidence of the next few months suggests that Clemens was having difficulty writing much beyond chapter 12. A dozen years later, he recalled that his problem was caused by his having given up smoking "during a year and a half":

As I never permitted myself to regret this abstinence, I experienced no sort of inconvenience from it. I wrote nothing but occasional magazine articles during pastime, and as I never wrote one except under strong impulse, I observed no lapse of facility. But by and by I sat down with a contract behind me to write a book of five or six hundred pages—the book called "Roughing it"—and then I found myself most seriously obstructed. I was three weeks writing six chapters. Then I gave up the fight, resumed my three hundred cigars, burned the six chapters, and wrote the book in three months, without any bother or difficulty.[59]

Although it shortens the time span, this recollection seems to be an accurate description of his difficulty, though perhaps not of its true or only cause. At any rate, Clemens did not resume his daily cigars until early 1871. (In mid-December 1870 he was still permitting himself to smoke only "from 3 till 5 on Sunday afternoons.")[60] The "lapse of facility" in composition actually lasted from September 1870 through most of March 1871.

On 29 September, at about ten o'clock in the morning, Emma Nye died in the Clemenses' Buffalo bedroom. Exhausted by the ordeal, Clemens and his wife left for a week's visit with his sister and mother (who had recently moved into their new home in Fredonia, New York), returning to Buffalo on 6 or 7 October. (His sister, Pamela, returned this visit shortly thereafter, staying for several weeks, at least in part because Olivia's first pregnancy was then in its seventh month.) While in Fredonia, Clemens sent Bliss a contribution (not identified) for his trade newspaper—but work on the book had obviously been interrupted, and his attention began increasingly to be diverted to other projects.[61] A week after returning to Buffalo, he wrote Bliss that he had "a notion to let the Galaxy publishers have a volume of old sketches for a 'Mark Twain's Annual—1871'—pro-

---

[58]"Local Matters," Virginia City *Territorial Enterprise*, 7 Oct 70, 3. This local item does not appear to derive from any published source. It must therefore come from a letter to Joseph T. Goodman, or to any of Clemens's other colleagues on the *Enterprise*, such as William Wright (Dan De Quille).

[59]SLC to Alfred Arthur Reade, 14 Mar 82, Alfred Arthur Reade, 121–22.

[60]SLC to Joseph H. Twichell, 19 Dec 70, CtY-BR, in *MTL*, 1:179.

[61]"Sad News to Friends," Elmira *Advertiser*, 30 Sept 70, 4; SLC to James Redpath, 4 Oct 70, MH-H†; SLC to Elisha Bliss, Jr.: 13 Oct 70, MB, in *MTLP*, 40; 31 Oct 70, courtesy of Maurice F. Neville Rare Books†.

vided they will pay me about 25 per cent. . . . What do you think? Write
me at once—& don't discourage me." But he also confessed that he was
"driveling along tolerably fairly on the book—getting off from 12 to 20
pages (MS.) a day. I am writing it so carefully that I'll never have to alter a
sentence, I guess, but it is *very* slow work. I like it well, as far as I have got.
The people will read it." On the same day he answered a question from
Mrs. Fairbanks, implying that he had made less progress than he had expected: "My book is not named yet. Have to write it first—you wouldn't
make a garment for an animal till you had seen the animal, would you? I
am getting along ever so slowly—so many things have hindered me." He
had not written to her earlier, he said, "because I am in such a terrible
whirl with Galaxy & book work. . . . I never want to see a pen again till
the task-hour strikes next day."[62]

Clemens assumed that the burden (or lure) of writing for the magazine
was affecting his capacity to sustain interest in the book. Five days later
he told Francis Church that he would probably retire from the *Galaxy* in
April "because the Galaxy work crowds book work so much." But he did
not resign immediately, he said, because he was "very fond of doing the
Memoranda, & take a live interest in it always—& so I hang on & hang on
& give no notice." On 26 October, when he read Bliss's inevitable objec-
tion to the book of *Galaxy* sketches, he replied that it was "too late now to
get out the annual" anyway. But he took issue with Bliss's notion that
"writing for the Galaxy" hurt the sale of his books: "I cannot believe it. It
is a good advertisement for me—as you show when you desire me to quit
the Galaxy & go on your paper." Still, if someone could prove that he was
harming his reputation by writing for the *Galaxy*, he would "draw out of
that & write for *no* periodical—for ~~certainly~~ I have chewed & drank &
sworn, habitually, & have discarded them all, & am well aware that a bad
thing should be killed entirely—*tapering off* is a foolish & dangerous
business."[63]

That Clemens was beginning to feel inhibited, if not yet "seriously obstructed," in his efforts to write may also be inferred from his pursuing
research into Slade and other matters. When he saw Bliss's first issue of
the *Author's Sketch Book* at the end of October, he found several promising sources among the books advertised:

> Say, now, Bliss, if *I* were a publisher, I would send *you* a book occasionally, but
> here I am suffering for the "Col's" book, & for "Beyond the Missippi" & for the "In-
> dian Races," & *especially* for the "Uncivilized Races," & [you] never say "boo"

---

[62]SLC to Elisha Bliss, Jr., 13 Oct 70, MB, in *MTLP*, 40; SLC to Mary Mason Fairbanks, 13 Oct 70, CSmH, in *MTMF*, 138–39.

[63]SLC to Francis P. Church, 18 Oct 70, Frank Luther Mott, *A History of American
Magazines, 1865–1885*, 2d printing (Cambridge: Belknap Press of Harvard University Press, 1957 [1st printing, 1938]), facing 255; SLC to Elisha Bliss, Jr., 26 Oct 70,
courtesy of Todd M. Axelrod†.

about sending them. You must give me the "Uncivilized Races["] & the "Col's," anyhow.[64]

Bliss must have sent some of these books, but the request shows that Clemens had probably not drafted chapter 14 or 15, since passages in each suggest his familiarity with one of the books he asked for: Albert Deane Richardson's *Beyond the Mississippi.* He had certainly not completed chapter 19, which explicitly refers to another of them, John George Wood's *The Uncivilized Races, or Natural History of Man.* Clemens owned and annotated a copy of Wood's book—and no doubt of Richardson's as well, although his copy is not known to survive—in addition to a copy of (Colonel) Albert S. Evans's *Our Sister Republic: A Gala Trip through Tropical Mexico in 1869–70;* all three books were published in 1869 or 1870 by the American Publishing Company or its subsidiaries.[65]

Soon there were additional distractions. During Pamela's visit she had apparently suggested that if Orion were to succeed with the "machine" he was trying to invent, he needed a job that would give him more free time. On the last day of October, therefore, Clemens wrote Bliss, casually proposing quite another sort of favor.

> Say, for instance—I have a brother about 45—an old & able writer & editor. He is night editor of the Daily St Louis Democrat, & is gradually putting his eyes out at it. He has served four years as Secretary of State of Nevada, having been appointed to the place by Mr. Lincoln—he had all the financial affairs of the Territory in his hands during that time & came out with the name of an able, honest & every way competent officer. He is well read in law, & I think understands book-keeping. He is a very valuable man for any sort of *office* work, but not worth a cent *outside* as a business man. Now I would like to get him out of night-work but haven't any other sort to offer him myself. Have *you* got a place for him at $100 or $150 a month, in your office? Or has your brother? Let me hear from you shortly, & do try & see if you can't give him such a place.

In a final paragraph, Clemens made sure Bliss got the point: "When is your paper coming out? Did you ever receive the article I sent you for it from Fredonia? Tell me."[66] Two days later, Bliss cheerfully took the hint: "Yours recd Yes I got your article. '*It is accepted*' (a. la. N.Y. Ledger) Thanks for same— . . . How would your Bro. do for an editor of it?" Clemens immediately sent this reply to Orion, urging him to "throw up that cursed night work & take this editorship."

---

[64]SLC to Elisha Bliss, Jr., 29 Oct 70, courtesy of Robert Daley†.

[65]Alan Gribben, *Mark Twain's Library: A Reconstruction,* 2 vols. (Boston: G. K. Hall and Co., 1980), 1:224, 2:577, 783. Clemens also mentioned, and may have received and read, a copy of Charles De Wolf Brownell's *The Indian Races of North and South America,* published by the American Publishing Company in 1865, but if so, its influence has not been detected in *Roughing It.* Wood's and Evans's books were prominently advertised and extracted in the *Author's Sketch Book* 1 (Nov 70): 2–4, which was clearly Clemens's source for the news that Bliss had published them. What alerted him to the two earlier books is not known. See the explanatory notes at 97.9, 103.34–36, and 126.12–127.3.

[66]SLC to Elisha Bliss, Jr., 31 Oct 70, courtesy of Maurice F. Neville Rare Books†.

Bliss offered me in effect $4,000 a year to ~~edit~~ take this berth he offers you—& so he has confidence in his little undertaking. He is shrewdly counting on two things, now—one is, by creating a position for you, he will keep me from "whoring after strange gods," which is Scripture for deserting to other publishers; &, 2ᵈ, get an occasional article out of me for the paper, a thing which would be *exceedingly* occasional otherwise. He is wise. He is one of the smartest business men in America, & I am only a dullard when I try to ~~pierce~~ conceive *all* the advantages ˌheˌ expects to derive from having you in the employ of the Am. Pub. Co. But all right—I am willing.[67]

On 7 November, Olivia gave birth prematurely to Langdon. Four days later, Clemens told Orion that his wife was "very sick," and that he did not believe the baby would "live five days." At the same time he thanked Orion for sending "such full Nevada notes—though as they have just come & I am stealing a few minutes from the sick room to answer a pile of business letters, I haven't read a sentence of them yet." These notes have not been found, and Clemens may have done no more than glance at them; in early April 1871 he admitted to Orion that he had misplaced them.[68]

Olivia's older sister, Susan Crane, had been visiting the Clemenses when Langdon arrived, and she remained to help care for Olivia and the baby until 12 November, when her place was taken briefly by Mrs. Fairbanks, visiting from Cleveland. On 19 November, after Fairbanks's departure, Clemens wrote his mother-in-law that Olivia "lets me go up to the study & work, (which I ought not to do & yet I am so dreadfully behindhand that I get blue as soon as I am idle)." Later that month, he reported that he worked "in my particular den, from 11 AM till 3 P.M., rain or shine."[69] Even so, it is unlikely that during this month he advanced the narrative much past chapter 19, in which he could now make use of Wood's *Uncivilized Races*. Most of his time was instead devoted to installments for the *Galaxy*—and part of it surely went to hatching plans for other projects, the first of which emerged in a 30 November letter that asked Bliss for an advance of $1500:

> I have put my greedy hands on the best man in America for my purpose & shall *start him to the diamond fields of South Africa within a fortnight, at my expense.*
> I shall ˌwriteˌ a book of his experiences for next spring, (600 pp 8vo.,) ˌspring of '72ˌ & write it just as if I had been through it all myself, but will explain in the preface that this is done merely to give it life ~~& sparkle.~~ & reality.

Demanding absolute secrecy and a royalty of 10 percent, Clemens went so far as to copy this letter (lest anyone steal the idea) before sending the original to Bliss. So completely did his new idea eclipse the western book that only in the next-to-last postscript of this long letter did he remember

---

[67]Elisha Bliss, Jr., to SLC, 2 Nov 70, CU-MARK; SLC to Orion Clemens, 5 Nov 70, NPV and CU-MARK†.

[68]SLC to Orion Clemens, 11 Nov 70, CU-MARK†; SLC to Orion Clemens, 4 Apr 71, CU-MARK, in *MTLP*, 62.

[69]SLC to Joseph H. and Harmony C. Twichell, 12 Nov 70, CtY-BR, in *MTL*, 1:178; Mary Mason Fairbanks to SLC, 8 Nov 70, CU-MARK; SLC to Olivia Lewis Langdon, 19 Nov 70, CtHMTH†; SLC to Charles Henry Webb, 26 Nov 70, ViU and MoSW†.

to mention, somewhat lamely, that "Mrs Fairbanks (my best critic) likes my new book WELL, as far as I have got." (Fairbanks had returned home more than a week earlier.) Clemens's infatuation with his book-by-proxy scheme betrays the inventor's pride in his invention, but the invention itself suggests how he may have diagnosed his problem with the western book—that is, as a lack of interest, due in part to the distance in time of his experiences. "I don't care two cents whether there is a diamond in all Africa or not," he wrote Bliss, "the adventurous narrative & its wild, new fascination is what I want."[70] The diamond-mine book (which was never really begun, let alone published) now seems a chimera, but it would be hard to find a more succinct expression of Clemens's frustration with his western materials—especially if one considers that he obviously believed, for almost a month, that he could write about someone else's recent adventures more easily than he could about his own relatively remote ones.

By Clemens's own account, it would be several years before he learned that virtually any book he started to write was "pretty sure to get tired, along about the middle, and refuse to go on with its work until its powers and its interest should have been refreshed by a rest and its depleted stock of raw materials reinforced by lapse of time." In 1906 Clemens recalled encountering such an interruption at "page 400" of the manuscript for *Tom Sawyer,* where "the story made a sudden and determined halt and refused to proceed another step." That was probably in 1872, when he had written only about 100 pages, although he would eventually write another 400 before being interrupted by a second "halt." What he could do about such interruptions became clear only after he began writing those 400 pages in 1874:

> When the manuscript had lain in a pigeon-hole two years I took it out one day and read the last chapter that I had written. It was then that I made the great discovery that when the tank runs dry you've only to leave it alone and it will fill up again in time, while you are asleep—also while you are at work at other things and are quite unaware that this unconscious and profitable cerebration is going on.[71]

In the fall of 1870, Clemens knew that he was "obstructed" in the composition of his western book, but it is unlikely that he understood why or what to do about it. He seems to have alternated between pushing stubbornly ahead (trying in various ways to make himself write) and switching off, with more or less deliberation, to "other things." Just three days after

---

[70]SLC to Elisha Bliss, Jr., 28 Nov 70, CU-MARK, in *MTLP*, 43. It is a measure of how far his mind really was from *Roughing It* that he was obliged in *both* the draft and the copy to insert the phrase, "spring of '72."

[71]AD, 30 Aug 1906, CU-MARK, in *MTE*, 196–97; *The Adventures of Tom Sawyer; Tom Sawyer Abroad; Tom Sawyer, Detective,* edited by John C. Gerber, Paul Baender, and Terry Firkins, The Works of Mark Twain (Berkeley, Los Angeles, London: University of California Press, 1980), 9–11. The editors point out that no such "break" occurs at page 400, although one does at page 500. In any case, the only two-year hiatus in composition occurred between 1872 and 1874. At this point in the composition of *Roughing It*, Clemens had written some 180 pages.

announcing his diamond-mine scheme to Bliss, for instance, he declined an invitation to write for the Boston *Saturday Evening Gazette* on the grounds that

work is piled on me in toppling pyramids, now—which figure represents a book which I am not getting out as fast as I ought—& I am obliged to say that I could not take half a column more on any terms. I would like exceedingly well to write for the Gazette (the only Weekly paper I ever wanted to own,) but as we steamboatmen used to say, "I've got my load."[72]

Yet "loaded" though he was, just one week later he had launched another project, quite unrelated to the western book, fully expecting to complete it before the month was out. On 7 or 8 December he telegraphed his *Galaxy* publishers, offering them a "pamphlet" that he wanted to publish in time for the holidays. On the morning of 9 December, Isaac Sheldon telegraphed his reply: "We will publish it & give you half of all profits." In a letter written the same day, Sheldon promised to "do our very best as to getting it out in time &c &c," but warned that it was "now of course late in the season to get out a book and there are always delays we can never calculate on."[73] This "book" became the fifty-page pamphlet known as *Mark Twain's (Burlesque) Autobiography and First Romance*, which would not be published, as it turned out, until early March 1871.

The day after Sheldon's telegram, 10 December, Clemens "shot off to New York to issue a pamphlet, & staid over 7 days," not returning to Buffalo until 17 December. While in New York, he stayed at the Albemarle Hotel and (as he later confided to Twichell) "smoked a week, day & night."[74] Free (at least momentarily) from domestic concerns, and fully occupied with projects other than the western book, Clemens soon took the opportunity to postpone his original deadline. He spent the week only in part on the pamphlet, for which he sought to hire an illustrator, Edward F. Mullen, eventually settling for Henry Louis Stephens instead.[75] He began his week in negotiations with Charles Henry Webb, from whom he succeeded in buying control of the *Jumping Frog*. On 11 December, he wrote an obituary letter about his old friend Reuel Gridley, whose "Famous Sanitary Flour Sack" he would treat at some length in chapter 45 of *Roughing It*. He gave this letter (signed "s. l. c.") to the New York *Tribune*, which published it two days later.[76] Perhaps while delivering this manuscript to the *Tribune* offices, Clemens called on several professional colleagues, including managing editor Whitelaw Reid and Reid's first lieutenant, John

[72]SLC to Warren Luther Brigham, 1 Dec 70, MBAt†.

[73]Sheldon and Company telegram and letter to SLC, 9 Dec 70, CU-MARK. For a detailed account of this project, see *ET&S1*, 561–71.

[74]SLC to Mary Mason Fairbanks, 17 Dec 70, CSmH, in *MTMF,* 142; SLC to Joseph H. Twichell, 19 Dec 70, CtY-BR, in *MTL,* 1:179.

[75]Clemens could have seen Mullen's comic illustrations in books by Jeems Pipes (Stephen C. Massett), Miles O'Reilly (Charles G. Halpine), and Artemus Ward (Charles Farrar Browne)—all issued by New York publisher George W. Carleton.

[76]*ET&S1*, 545 n. 43; "The Famous Sanitary Flour Sack," New York *Tribune,* 13 Dec 70, 5. Clemens dated his letter *"Albemarle,* Dec. 11, 1870."

Rose Greene Hassard, as well as a recent addition to the *Tribune* editorial staff, John Milton Hay.

4

Clemens had become better acquainted with Hay through their mutual acquaintance in Buffalo, David Gray. Raised on the banks of the Mississippi, Hay shared Clemens's midwestern roots and to some extent his literary tastes and ambitions. In December 1874, when Clemens published his first installment of "Old Times on the Mississippi" in the *Atlantic*, Hay declared it "perfect—no more nor less. I don't see how you do it. I knew all that, every word of it—passed as much time on the levee as you ever did, knew the same crowd and saw the same scenes—but I could not have remembered one word of it all. You have the two greatest gifts of the writer, memory and imagination."[77] At this time in 1870, Hay was enduring a mixed reaction to "Little-Breeches," which he had published (signed with his initials only) in the *Tribune* for 19 November, and which had since been widely reprinted. In a conversation that must have occurred during Clemens's week-long visit to New York between 10 and 17 December (in 1905 Clemens remembered only that it had been "in 1870 or '71"), they discussed this reaction. Clemens recalled that "Hay made ~~reference to~~ ₍mention of₎ the current notion that he was an imitator; he did not enlarge upon it, but he was not better pleased by it than you or I would be." And Clemens also mentioned that his talk with Hay was "incidentally" the occasion of his "getting acquainted with Horace Greeley":

It was difficult to get an interview with him, for he was a busy man, he was irascible, and he had an aversion to strangers; but I not only had the good fortune to meet him, but also had the great privilege of hearing him talk. The *Tribune* was in its early home, at that time, and Hay was a leader-writer on its staff. I had an appointment with him, and went there to look him up. I did not know my way, and entered Mr. Greeley's room by mistake. I recognized his back, and stood mute and rejoicing. After a little, he swung slowly around in his chair, with his head slightly tilted backward and the great moons of his spectacles glaring with intercepted light; after about a year—though it may have been less, perhaps—he arranged his firm mouth with care and said with virile interest:
  "Well? What the hell do *you* want?"[78]

---

[77]John M. Hay to SLC, 16 Dec 74, CU-MARK; see *MTA*, 2:118, 133.

[78]"John Hay and the Ballads," MS in RPB-JH, written 3 October 1905, published in *Harper's Weekly* 49 (21 Oct 1905): 1530. Clemens recounted his first meeting with Greeley more than once, often with slight variations: see *MTB*, 1:472, and "Miscellany," *MTE*, 347–48. In the "Miscellany," his conversation with Greeley went as follows:

  "Well, what in hell do *you* want!"
  "I was looking for a gentlem——"
  "Don't keep them in stock—clear out!"
  I could have made a very neat retort but didn't, for I was flurried and didn't think of it till I was downstairs.

Clemens could have encountered Greeley on or shortly after 12 December, for Greeley was reported in the city by the evening of 11 December ("Personal," New York *Evening Express*, 12 Dec 70, 4).

It is not too much to suppose that for Clemens, such gruff treatment demanded revenge—or at least poetic justice.

On 13 December, Clemens wrote Bliss again about the diamond-mine
book, this time inviting him to come to New York to discuss it, which
Bliss promptly did.[79] And at about the same time, Clemens met with his
intended proxy for the diamond-mine book, John Henry Riley, who had
come up from Washington for that purpose. Later in the week Clemens
received an invitation to join Whitelaw Reid, and "one or two friends, not
more" over a "quiet bottle of wine" at the Union League Club, but by then
he was too busy to accept.[80]

Well aware that he was progressing too slowly to meet his deadline for
the western book, Clemens proposed to Bliss that he (rather than the *Galaxy* publishers) *first* publish a sketchbook in 1871, postponing the western book until later the same year—the very alternative he had had in
mind since at least January 1870. Bliss tentatively accepted this change,
in part because Clemens promised to discuss it further, in Hartford, as
soon as his New York business was over. But instead of going to Hartford,
Clemens returned to Buffalo, where on the afternoon of 17 December he
telegraphed Bliss: "Got homesick. Will come shortly with sketches &
manuscript." Bliss replied that he was "most disappointed at your not
coming here, & so was *Twitchell*— . . . Your Brother is here & we are getting at work in earnest[.] . . . Let me know about Mss. & also about the
sketches & come on & have a talk if possible."[81] These references (and
Bliss's reply, quoted below) establish that Clemens expected to work on
both books simultaneously, which meant submitting the western book in
sections, as he completed them. But it would be mid-March before any
manuscript for the western book was sent to Bliss, and early June before
Clemens himself carried a later part of it to Hartford.

On 20 December, Clemens returned to Bliss the signed contract for the
diamond-mine book: "Riley is my man—did I introduce him to you in
New York? He sails Jan. 4 for Africa. . . . Riley is *perfectly* honorable &
reliable in every possible way—his simple promise is as good as any man's
oath. I have roomed with him long, & have known him years. He has
'roughed it' in many savage countries & is as tough as a pine-knot."[82] Two
days later he acknowledged the $1500 advance "for the foreign expedi-

[79]"Four page ALs, signed 'Clemens' with the postscript signed 'Mark' to 'Friend
Bliss' (his Hartford publisher Elisha Bliss), Dec. 13, [1870]. The letter discusses a
scheme of Clemens' to write about the diamond rush in South Africa" (Bromer, lot
10). Bliss had checked into the Tremont House in New York City by the morning of
14 December ("Morning Arrivals," New York *Evening Express*, 14 Dec 70, 3).

[80]Whitelaw Reid to SLC, 15 Dec 70 and 3 Jan 71, DLC.

[81]SLC to Elisha Bliss, Jr., 17 Dec 70, NN-B†; Elisha Bliss, Jr., to SLC, 20 Dec 70,
CU-MARK.

[82]SLC to Elisha Bliss, Jr., 20 Dec 70, courtesy of Christie, Manson and Woods
International†.

tion," then launched into great detail about the sketchbook, trying to goad
Bliss into immediate action:

> You'd better go to canvassing for the vol. of sketches *now*, hadn't you? You
> must illustrate it—& mind you, the man to do the choicest of the pictures is Mul-
> lin—the Sisters are reforming him & he is sadly in need of work & money. Write to
> Launt Thompson the Sculptor, (Albemarle Hotel, New York) about him. I did so
> want him for that satire but didn't know he was sober now & in hospital.
> Make out a contract for the sketch-book (7½ per cent.) & mail to me.
> I think the sketch-book should be as profusely illustrated as the Innocents.
> To-day I arranged enough sketches to make 200 134 pages of the book (200
> words on a page, I estimated—size of De Witt Talmage's new book of rubbish.) I
> shall go right on till I have finished selecting, & then write a new sketch or so. One
> hundred of the pages selected to-day are scarcely known.[83]

Bliss replied cautiously, on 28 December: "Yours of 22nd rec'd. Glad to hear
you are progressing with the *Books*— . . . Yes we will have Mullen illustrate the sketch book all right. . . . Are you coming on? Will canvass for
Sketch book as soon as Prospectus is ready for it."[84] Clemens would need
to be reminded more than once in 1871 that canvassing for a book could
not begin until its prospectus was ready, which required a major portion
of the manuscript. Oblivious to this hint, he replied on 3 January, trying
to turn up the pressure on Bliss: "Name the Sketch book '*Mark Twain's
Sketches*' & go on canvassing like mad. Because if you don't hurry it will
tread on the heels of the *big* book next August. In the course of a week I
can have most of the matter ready for you I think. ˌAm working like sin on
it.ˌ"[85] The next day he sent Bliss the manuscripts for two (possibly three)
"new" sketches, specifying that "the one about the liar [is] to be first one
in the book," and insisting that Orion make security copies for all of them
before they were sent to the artist for illustration. On 5 January he added
a postscript: "The curious beasts & great contrasts in this Pre-duluge article offer a gorgeous chance for the artist's fancy & ingenuity," he wrote.
"Send both sketches to Mullen—he is the man to do them, I guess. Launt
Thompson, Albemarle Hotel, will find him when wanted."[86] The "Pre-
duluge article" was an extract from the still incomplete "Noah's Ark
book." The "one about the liar" was undoubtedly the Sandwich Islands
sketch about Markiss, soon to be published in the *Galaxy* as "About a Remarkable Stranger" and eventually reprinted as chapter 77 of *Roughing It*.
(The third "new" sketch, if any, has not been identified, although it may
have been one that Clemens had listed as "Sailor Story," and that may in
turn have become chapter 50 in *Roughing It*.) Clemens presumably wrote

---

[83]SLC to Elisha Bliss, Jr., 22 Dec 70, CtY-BR, ViU, and courtesy of Todd M. Axel-
rod†. Talmage, a Brooklyn minister, had recently published *Crumbs Swept Up*. Edward F. Mullen was probably undergoing treatment at St. Vincent's Hospital in
New York, run by the Sisters of Charity.
[84]Elisha Bliss, Jr., to SLC, 28 Dec 70, CU-MARK.
[85]SLC to Elisha Bliss, Jr., 3 Jan 71, CU-MARK, in *MTLP*, 53.
[86]SLC to Elisha Bliss, Jr., 4 and 5 Jan 71, CU-MARK† and AAA, lot 244.

these "new sketches" only after preparing clippings of those he intended
to reprint from the *Express* and the *Galaxy,* including "Around the World"
letters 1, 3, 4, and 5, as well as "The Facts in the Great Land Slide Case"—
all listed in the table of contents he drafted for the sketchbook, but all
used ultimately in *Roughing It.*[87]

This "halt" in the composition of *Roughing It* gave Clemens's "tank"
time to refill. But it also gave him time to reflect on the hazards of his subject. The West, which in May 1869 had seemed to have "*scope*" and time-
liness because of the recent "completion of the Pacific RR," had by early
1871 been so often written about that Clemens could rightly call it hackneyed.[88] In 1869–70 alone his fellow journalists had published half a dozen
books on western travel, all based in part on sketches they had written for
newspapers or magazines. Prominent among these were Richardson's revised edition of *Beyond the Mississippi,* Samuel Bowles's *Our New West,*
J. Ross Browne's *Adventures in the Apache Country,* and Fitz Hugh Ludlow's *The Heart of the Continent.* Clemens must have been made increasingly aware that the West as described by passing visitors was no longer a
novelty.

Clemens was also conscious of the risks he ran in renouncing journalism to write books—an intention he recorded as early as 26 October, and
firmly embraced by 3 March 1871.[89] John Hay was also pondering a career
in literature. "The Western School" (his 27 December editorial in the *Tribune*) was his manifesto for a group in which he implicitly included
himself.

There will not be many writers who will equal the contagious drollery of Mark
Twain. It may be long before we find another that can touch so deftly the hidden
sources of smiles and tears—and that can give us so graphic a picture of Western
living in a style so vivid and so pure that we may call it in praise and not in criticism
"almost the true Dickens"—as Mr. Harte has done. But there are many good and
honest literary workmen who have grown up in the great West, not unmindful of its
strange and striking lessons. Some of them, Howells among the best, have already
given some earnest of the promising future. Others are just rising into notice. Let
them be received with candor and judged by what they say—not by what others
have said.[90]

---

[87]See *ET&S1,* 574–84.

[88]SLC to James Redpath, 10 May 69, *L3,* 215–16. See, for example, the following
comment in a book review in *Harper's New Monthly Magazine* for February 1870
(40:462): "The Mormons, the Yosemite Valley, the Big Trees, the Pacific Railroad,
and the Chinese Question are themes so old now, and so elaborately discussed in
newspaper and periodical, that it is not strange that Dr. JOHN TODD, in his *Sunset
Land* (Lee and Shepard), has failed to invest them with any remarkable degree of interest." The same work was reviewed in the November 1870 *Galaxy* (10:714): "It is
not an easy task in the year 1870 to tell us much that is new concerning California,
or, as our author fancifully calls it, 'The Sunset Land.'"

[89]SLC to Elisha Bliss, Jr., 26 Oct 70, courtesy of Todd M. Axelrod†; SLC to John
Henry Riley, 3 Mar 71, NN-B†.

[90]"The Western School," New York *Tribune,* 27 Dec 70, 4.

Even as Clemens worked to complete the printer's copy for the sketch-book, Hay published the second of his Pike County ballads, "Jim Bludso (of the Prairie Belle)," in the 5 January *Tribune,* again signing it simply "J. H." Clemens immediately reprinted the poem in the Buffalo *Express* and—in a letter not known to survive—wrote Hay praising it, but also suggesting a way to improve its authenticity. Hay replied on 9 January with a draft that adopted Clemens's suggestion. He also alluded to their previous discussion of the hostile reaction to "Little-Breeches": "The opposition is getting beaten out I think. Some of the heathen still rage furiously and the words of their mouths are 'ribaldry' 'plagiarism B.H' and 'vulgar blasphemy.' But there are compensations. 'The Atlantic' and Harpers and the Aldine have all asked me for some more foul vulgarity—and alack! I have not time to write it."[91] Clemens probably received this reply just before leaving for Cleveland, where he had to be by 11 January. On that day, he wrote Hay extending an invitation to join him (and probably David Gray) in a new "enterprise"—presumably a new journal. On 14 January, Hay declined this offer, but added:

I cannot forbear telling you how much I have been encouraged and gratified by your generous commendation of my verses. I have sometimes thought that the public appreciation was a compound of ignorance and surprise—but when you, who know all about the Western life and character, look at one of my little pictures and say it is true, it is comfortable beyond measure.

Another thing has rather tickled me this morning. No New York paper except Wilkes' has ever copied my rhymes—they were frightfully low, you know. The last London Spectator prints "Little-B." with editorial compliments.[92]

Hay's experience in publishing "low" verse (Pike County vernacular used to disguise a subversive point of view)[93] doubtless warned Clemens that he, too, might be accused of "foul vulgarity" for what he had written, or planned to write, about the West. He had, in fact, just been accused by

---

[91]John M. Hay to SLC, 9 Jan 71, CU-MARK. Clemens had suggested that Jim Bludso be made a pilot, rather than an engineer. He noted on Hay's letter, "Col. John Hay with poem 'Jim Bludso.'" The Buffalo *Express* (7 Jan 71, 2) attributed the poem to "*Col. John Hay, in the N. Y. Tribune,*" conclusive evidence that Clemens so ordered it.

[92]John M. Hay to SLC, 14 Jan 71, CU-MARK. Clemens's offer is inferred from Hay's letter. Hay referred to George Wilkes's *Spirit of the Times,* and to the London *Spectator,* which reprinted "Little-Breeches" in its 31 December 1870 issue, calling it "almost as good as the *Bigelow Papers*" ("Poetry," 1580).

[93]Consider the first stanza of "Little-Breeches. [A Pike County View of Special Providence]":

> I don't go much on religion,
>   I never ain't had no show;
> But I've a middlin' tight grip, Sir,
>   On the handful o' things I know.
> I don't pan out on the prophets
>   And free-will, and that sort of thing—
> But I b'lieve in God and the angels,
>   Ever sence one night last Spring.

Every Saturday of plagiarizing Bret Harte.[94] And it was against Harte's work that both he and Hay could expect to be judged. According to the Philadelphia *Bulletin:*

The poetry and prose of Bret Harte have made their great hit chiefly by reason of the novelty and marked uniqueness of their style. The style, as Mr. Harte created it, is singular for its delicate handling of rough themes and rough language. There is a subtle refinement thrown over the coarsest phases of California life, that recommends itself to the most cultivated taste, and has introduced Mr. Harte's books wherever there is the power to discriminate between vulgarity and the poetry of vulgar things.

But it has grown to be a great affliction that, all over the country, pert imitators of Bret Harte have sprung up, thrusting their pretensions to rival his exquisite art upon the public, and only succeeding in the production of a mixture of coarse vulgarity and profanity, which this low grade of scribblers fancy to be like the poetry of Bret Harte. . . . [*Harper's Weekly*] has a poet named John Hay, who is a victim of this Harte disease. He is a master of slang, in its lowest, vulgar[e]st, most profane forms. He fancies that he is imitating Bret Harte, while he is disgusting all intelligent readers, not only by his stupid ignorance of what constitutes the glamour of Harte's work, but also by the common grossness of both thought and language.[95]

But Hay's experience must also have been encouraging, because he clearly had won a large popular audience as well as the more enlightened one represented by Howells at the *Atlantic Monthly.* Two days after Hay published "The Western School," he wrote to ask Howells:

Have you ever seen a piece of dialect I wrote,—"Little Breeches"? It has had an appalling run. It is published every day in hundreds of papers. Two political papers in the West have issued illustrated editions of it. I mention this to show what a ravenous market there is for anything of the sort. I can't do it—but you could. That Western novel of yours must not be much longer delayed.[96]

It is a fair guess that Hay said much the same thing to Clemens about *his* book on the Far West ("I can't do it—but you could").[97]

Even before he received Hay's reply, however, Clemens had decided to give up journalism. On 14 January he told Webb: "I dassent. I made up my mind *solidly* day before yesterday that I would draw out of the Galaxy with the April No. & write no more for any periodical—except, at long

---

[94]The accusation came in the 7 January 1871 issue: "Mark Twain's versified story of the 'Three Aces' seems to be a feeble echo of Bret Harte. The 'Truthful James' vein is one that can be worked successfully only by the owner of the 'claim'" ("Literary Items," *Every Saturday,* 2:19). Charges of plagiarism were a kind of code for charges of vulgarity.

[95]"Harte Disease," Pittsburgh *Gazette,* 16 May 71, 4, reprinting the Philadelphia *Bulletin* of unknown date.

[96]John M. Hay to William Dean Howells, 29 Dec 70, in William Roscoe Thayer, ed., *The Life and Letters of John Hay,* 2 vols. (Boston: Houghton Mifflin Company, 1915), 1:357–58.

[97]Although Hay declined to join forces with Clemens in Buffalo, he soon agreed to become a regular contributor to Bliss's *American Publisher,* the first issue of which published "The Sphinx of the Tuilleries. [Written in Paris, August, 1867]" and also reprinted "Jim Bludso."

intervals a screed that I happened to dearly *want* to write."[98] Meanwhile, Orion finished copying the two (or three) manuscript sketches within a week of their arrival in Hartford, and on 16 January Bliss set off with them to New York, intending to hire Mullen. He returned to Hartford a week later, on 23 January, without succeeding. Orion reported that Bliss had "hunted for Mullin and Lant Thompson, or whatever his name is, two days. He found the latter's office in the hands of the plasterers. He is going back to-morrow and will find Mullin." But Bliss clearly had his doubts about the publication strategy Clemens had proposed to him. Even before going to search for Mullen, therefore, he allowed Orion to tell his brother that he, Bliss, "hardly" knew "whether it is good judgment to throw the Sketch Book on the market & interfere with the Innocents."[99] On 25 January, Orion reiterated Bliss's view: "About the sketch-book interfering with the Innocents—Bliss says he is going on with the sketch-book, and you will see which is right. The substance is that the new book will outsell the old one, and few people want to buy two books from the same author at the same time."[100] Even before this letter reached him, however, Clemens had conceded the point:

I believe you are more than half right—it is calculated to do more harm than good, no doubt. So if you like the idea, suppose we defer the Sketch Book till the *last*. That is, get out the big California & Plains book first of August; then the Diamond book first March or April 1872—& *then* the Sketch book the following fall. Does that strike you favorably?[101]

Three days later, he had developed this scheme into an elaborate but quite unrealistic plan to publish the western book as early as May—even though he had scarcely begun to write it. The inference is all but inescapable that Clemens was trying to force himself to write:

Tell you what I'll do, if you say so. Will write night & day & send you 200 pages of MS. every week (of the big book on California, Nevada & the Plains) & place finish it all up the 15ᵗʰ of April if you can without fail *issue* the book on the 15ᵗʰ of May—putting the sketch book over till another time. For this reason: my popularity is booming, now, & we ought to take the very biggest advantage of it.

I have to go to Washington next Tuesday & stay a week, but will send you 150 MS pages before going, if you say so. It seems to me that I would much rather do this. *Telegraph* me now, right away—don't wait to write. Next Wednesday I'll meet you in N. Y—& if you can't come there I'll run up & see *you*.

You could get a *cord* of subscriptions taken & advertising done between now & April 15. I have a splendid idea of the sagacity of this proposition.

Telegraph me right off.[102]

---

[98]SLC to Charles Henry Webb, 14 Jan 71, MoSW†.

[99]Orion Clemens to SLC, 25 Jan 71, CU-MARK; SLC to Elisha Bliss, Jr., 24 Jan 71, courtesy of Todd M. Axelrod, in *MTLP*, 54. Orion's phrase survives only in this subsequent letter from Clemens to Bliss. Orion presumably sent his now missing letter on or about 11 January.

[100]Orion Clemens to SLC, 25 Jan 71, CU-MARK.

[101]SLC to Elisha Bliss, Jr., 24 Jan 71, courtesy of Todd M. Axelrod, in *MTLP*, 54.

[102]SLC to Elisha Bliss, Jr., 27 Jan 71, CU-MARK, in *MTLP*, 54–55.

No manuscript was sent, or presumably called for. On Tuesday, 31 January, Clemens telegraphed "E. Bliss or Frank" before taking the train from Buffalo to New York: "Have an appointment at Grand Hotel eleven tomorrow can you be there at noon Clemens."[103]

That evening or early the next morning, Clemens checked into the Grand Hotel and, presumably on the morning of 1 February, met with Francis Church to negotiate a resolution of his *Galaxy* contract. Then he met with Bliss to discuss the western book.[104] They evidently agreed to issue it in May, just as Clemens had proposed in his most recent letter, even though there was scarcely time to make such a deadline. Clemens also promised to contribute something from the book manuscript to the *American Publisher*, the first issue of which was to appear within a month.

On the evening of 2 February, Clemens took the train to Washington, where he planned, among other things, to lobby for legislation affecting the Langdon estate.[105] On 6 February, Susan Crane, who was staying with Olivia and the baby, wrote him in Washington:

> Livy has consented to allow me to write you that she is not well, and has not been since you went away. She has had some fever, no appetite, no power to sleep, & ~~great depression of spirits.~~ ˏLivy did not like that, so I did not say it.ˏ . . .
> Now why I write is this, or why Livy allows me to write. If your business would take you over into next week, Livy feels that it would be almost unendurable but if your knowing these facts, would help you to close it this week, or defer it, she is willing to have you know how she is.[106]

Olivia had typhoid fever, although no one yet realized it. Clemens was depressed by the news of his wife's condition, but stayed in Washington to attend a dinner given in his honor by Samuel S. Cox (a Langdon family friend) on the evening of 7 February. The dinner was interrupted by a telegram from Buffalo, which summoned Clemens home. The danger of his wife's illness was clear, and he sought frantically to cancel his "Memoranda" for the March *Galaxy*, lest its publication make him seem to jest in the presence of death.[107] For the same reason, he telegraphed Bliss not to print the sketch he had sent in October for the *Publisher*. Throughout the next week Olivia's condition threatened to prove fatal: "We cannot tell what the result is going to be. Sometimes I have hope for my wife,—so I have at this moment—but most of the time it seems to me impossible

---

[103]SLC to Elisha Bliss, Jr., or Francis E. Bliss, 31 Jan 71, CU-MARK†. Francis was Elisha's son.

[104]"Morning Arrivals," New York *Evening Express*, 1 Feb 71, 3. If Bliss stayed overnight in New York, no record of it has been found.

[105]"Personal," New York *Tribune*, 3 Feb 71, 5.

[106]Susan L. Crane to SLC, 6 Feb 71, CSmH.

[107]"Our Fashionable Society," Washington (D.C.) *National Republican*, 9 Feb 71, 1; "Washington Letter" from Donn Piatt to the Cincinnati *Commercial*, 11 Feb 71, 2; Francis P. Church to SLC, 10 Feb 71, CU-MARK.

that she can get well. I cannot go into particulars—the subject is too dreadful."[108]

One week later, however, she was guardedly better, and Clemens was again trying to work on the western book. "Return to me, per express, the 'Liars' & the other 2 sketches—right away" he wrote Orion. "Livy is *very, very* slowly & slightly improving, but it is not possible to say whether she is out of danger or not—but we all consider that she is *not.*" The same day he gave an equally sober report to Whitelaw Reid: "My wife is still dangerously ill with typhoid fever, & we watch with her night & day hardly daring to prophecy what the result will be."[109]

One week later still, Clemens had decided not only to leave journalism, but to leave Buffalo, ostensibly on his doctor's advice.[110] He put both the house (which had been a wedding gift from Olivia's father) and his share in the *Express* up for sale. "I quit the Galaxy with the current number," he told Riley on 3 March, "& shall write no more for any periodical. Am offered great prices, but it's no go. Shall simply write books."[111] On 4 March he replied to Orion, who had returned the "Liars" sketch and one or two others, and who (at Bliss's suggestion) had urged him to begin sending book manuscript—at least in part so the next issue of the *Publisher* could fulfill the promise of a contribution from Mark Twain.[112] Clemens explained that he had wanted the "Liars" sketch back in order to "work it into the California book—which I shall do. But day before yesterday I concluded to go out of the Galaxy on the strength of it—& so I have turned it into the last Memoranda I shall ever write & published it as a 'specimen chapter' of my forthcoming book." He made it clear that he had broken with the *Galaxy,* and would not write for it now under any circumstances. Somewhat casually, however, he also seemed to say that he was unable, or unwilling, to write anything for the *Publisher,* at least for the time being:

Now do try & leave me clear out of the Publisher for the present, for I am endangering my reputation by writing *too much*—I want to get out of the public view

---

[108]SLC to Elisha Bliss, Jr., 15 Feb 71, CU-MARK, in *MTLP,* 55–56.

[109]SLC to Orion Clemens, 22 Feb 71, CU-MARK†; SLC to Whitelaw Reid, 22 Feb 71, DLC†.

[110]According to an authoritatively informed reporter in the Washington (D.C.) *National Republican,* Clemens "was induced to sell his interest in the Buffalo *Express* solely on account of the health of his wife, who, we are sorry to hear, is extremely delicate. These steps were taken by him on the advice of his physicians" (2 May 71, 2).

[111]SLC to John Henry Riley, 3 Mar 71, NN-B†.

[112]Orion must have sent Clemens the first (April) issue of the *Publisher* at about the same time he returned the "Liars" sketch—i.e., probably in early March. The issue printed an apology for the absence of a Mark Twain sketch, explaining that it was "in consequence of very dangerous illness" in Clemens's family, and promising a contribution in the "next number" ("Editorial Notes," *American Publisher,* Apr 71, 4). Bliss later told Clemens that "your brother wrote & inserted" the statement "on strength of your telegram" (Elisha Bliss, Jr., to SLC, 15 Mar 71, CU-MARK).

for a while. I ~~will~~ am still nursing Livy night & day & *cannot* write anything. I am nearly worn out. We shall go to Elmira ten days hence (if Livy can travel on a mattrass then,) & stay there till I have finished the California book—say three months. But I can't begin work right away when I get there—*must* have a week's rest, for I have been through 30 days' terrific siege. That makes it after the middle of March before I can go fairly to work—& then I'll have to hump myself & not lose a moment. You & Bliss just put yourselves in my place & you will see that my hands are full & *more* than full. When I told Bliss in N. Y. that I would write something for the Publisher *I* could not know that I was just about to lose FIFTY DAYS. Do you see the difference it makes?

In short, Clemens acknowledged that he had written nothing in February (twenty-eight days), and did not expect to write anything in March until he had gone to Elmira and taken a week's rest (another twenty-one days). Still, it is clear from the same letter that he remained sympathetic to Bliss's needs for the *Publisher:*

> Just as soon as ever I can, I will send some of the book MS., but right in the ⅓ first chapter I have got to alter the whole style of one of my characters & re-write him clear through to where I am now. It is no fool of a job I can tell you, but the book will be greatly bettered by it. Hold on a few days—four or five,—& I will see if I can get a few chapters fixed & send to Bliss.
>
> I have offered this dwelling house & the Express for sale, & when we go to Elmira we leave here for good. I shall not select a new home till the book is finished, but ~~writing a book, & reap if it proves to be a poor book~~ we have very little doubt that Hartford will be the place. We are almost certain of that.[113]

Bliss wrote on 7 March, evidently before this letter had arrived, having "just returned from N.Y." He identified two reasons for wanting the book manuscript as soon as possible:

> I was in hopes Orion found something from you on my return but poor Ori says he has nothing from you relating to matters. I asked him to write you a few days ago in regard to the Ms. for the *book.* We ought soon to get our arti[sts] on it so as to have them to do all in good style—What do you think about it?
>
> If we [are to] get it out in May it [must] soon be here. Now then if you have got as far as to give us something I think it would be well to get at it very soon. And now about an article for our paper. We trust you will not disappoint us this month[.] We have made a good start & got well underway & we want to keep on steadily. Send us on as soon as possible something good for it & send your bill in it & we will send check at once. Am happy to hear your wife is out of danger & getting on which I do through Mr. Twitchell.
>
> Hoping to hear from you soon on these subjects.[114]

As Clemens predicted, within five days of his 4 March letter he had finished his alteration of "the whole style" of one of his "characters," at least up through what was then chapter 8. The character in need of alteration was almost certainly the narrator himself. New (and old) evidence dis-

---

[113]SLC to Orion Clemens, 4 Mar 71, NPV, in *MTL*, 1:185–86.

[114]Elisha Bliss, Jr., to SLC, 7 Mar 71, transcription in an unidentified hand, Ct-HMTH. In part because Bliss's handwriting is extremely difficult to read, three substantive corrections are supplied within square brackets: "arti[sts]" for "article"; "[are to]" for an apparent omission, whether Bliss's or the transcriber's; and "[must]" for "will."

cussed below suggests that Clemens was pruning out some too-knowing remarks of a "tenderfoot" version of himself.[115]

At any rate, Clemens was by this time clearly reconciled to publishing one or more chapters in the *Publisher:*

> Tell Bliss "all right"—I will try to give him a chapter from the *new* book every month or nearly every month, for the Publisher.
>
> I have got several chapters (168 pages MS.) revised & ready for printers & artists, but for the sake of security shall get somebody to copy it & then send the original to him.[116]

The next day, however, Clemens reported having sent only "160 MS pages . . . to be copied," expecting to "have it back next Tuesday," when he would "ship it to Bliss & mark a chapter to be transferred to the Columns of the Publisher."[117] Clemens may simply have held back or destroyed eight pages. But if the reconstruction in FIGURE 1 is approximately correct, "160 MS pages" would not have taken him through the end of what he was then calling chapter 8 (later 7, and the start of 8), so there is at least one other possibility—that he mistakenly wrote "160" for "168." Such an error seems somewhat more likely because the conjectured end of chapter 8, the pony-express incident, clearly *was* copied at this time along with what preceded it.[118]

Although Clemens had certainly drafted sections of his manuscript beyond chapter 9, he must have left chapter 10 unfinished, for in the same 10 March letter he begged Orion to

> sit down right away & torture your memory & write down in minute detail every fact & exploit in the desperado Slade's life that we heard on the Overland—& also describe his appearance & conversation as we saw him at Rocky Ridge station at breakfast. I want to make up a telling chapter from it for the book—& will put it in the Publisher too, as soon as the agents begin to canvass.

Orion promptly met this request on 11 March.[119] Clemens incorporated most of his brother's details almost immediately into chapter 10, which,

---

[115]Henry Nash Smith (1962) noted that both the "tenderfoot" and the "old-timer" were "present in the narrative from the start," a device by which Clemens produced an "implied judgment upon the tenderfoot's innocence and a corresponding claim for the superior maturity and sophistication of the old-timer" (53). Getting the two personae properly adjusted to one another might, however, be expected to take some revision. On the other hand, a more recent speculation suggests that "the character in need of alteration was itself a piece of fiction, a creature Clemens conjured . . . to keep Orion and Bliss at bay while he made his way back to the long-neglected manuscript" (Steinbrink, 159).

[116]SLC to Orion Clemens, 9 Mar 71, PBL†.

[117]SLC to Orion Clemens, 10 Mar 71, NN-B†.

[118]It is relevant that Clemens wrote "168" *before* sending the manuscript off to be copied, and "160" after it had gone, when he could not see how many pages it contained. The pony-express incident was also the final part of the manuscript for which Clemens ordered any security copy at all.

[119]SLC to Orion Clemens, 10 Mar 71, NN-B†. Orion's response is transcribed in supplement A, item 3 (pages 778–81).

together with chapter 11 (presumably drafted earlier, upon receipt of Dimsdale's book), completed the first batch of book manuscript he would send to Bliss—probably on 18 March.

Before Orion's letter about Slade was written, however, Clemens received two letters from Hartford—one from Orion dated 8 March, and one from Bliss (now missing), probably written on the same day—making reply (but also clearly overreacting) to his casual refusal of 4 March to write for the *Publisher*. (Clemens had retracted this refusal almost immediately, and without prompting, in the two letters written on 9 and 10 March, before he received this double blast from Orion and Bliss on 10 March.) A sample of Orion's badgering will explain, almost by itself, the sulfurous reaction Clemens had to it. Orion vowed, among other things, that he and Bliss would

hunt up any information you want, and do anything else you want done, if you will only write. He is in earnest. He is decidedly worked up about it. He says, put yourself in our place. A new enterprise, in which "Twain" was to be a feature, and so widely advertised. He receives congratulations in New York at the Lotus Club that you and Hay are to write for the paper. Everybody likes it. It starts out booming. Are you going to kick the pail over? Think of yourself as writing for *no* periodical *except* the Publisher. . . . Squarely, ~~you~~ we *must* have something from you or we run the risk of going to the dickens. Bliss says he will pay you, but we must have something every number. If you only give us a half column, or even a quarter of a column——~~give~~ a joke or an anecdote, or anything you please—but give us *something*, so that the people may not brand us as falsifiers, and say we cried "Twain," "Twain," when we had no "Twain." If you don't feel like writing anything, copy something from your book. Are you going to let the Galaxy have a chapter and give us nothing? If you don't feel like taking the trouble of copying from the book say we may select something. We shall have time enough if you send some chapters in four or five days, as ~~we~~ ₐyou₎ proposed.[120]

Clemens wrote on the envelope of this missive, "Still urging MSS." But he fully vented his unhappiness with it in a long letter, begun on 11 March and finished after "two days 'to cool'":

Now why do you & Bliss go on urging me to make promises? I will not keep them. I have suffered damnation itself in the trammels of periodical writing and I will *not* appear once a month nor once in *three* months, ~~either.~~ in the Publisher nor any other periodical. . . .

You talk as if I am *responsible* for your newspaper venture. If I am I want it to stop right here—for I ~~will be damned~~ ₐdarned₎ ~~if I₎~~ am ₐnot₎ going to have another year of harassment about periodical writing. There isn't money enough between hell & Hartford to hire me to write once a month for *any* periodical. . . .

Why, confound it, when & how has this original little promise of mine (to "drop in an occasional screed along with the Company's *other* authors,") grown into these formidable dimensions—whereby I am the *father & sustainer* of the paper & you ₐhave₎ actually committed yourselves, & me too with advertisements looking in that direction? . . .

I don't want to even see my *name* anywhere in print for 3 months to come. As for being the high chief contributor & main card of the Publisher, I won't hear of it for a single moment. I'd rather break my pen & stop writing just where I am. Our

[120]Orion Clemens to SLC, 8 Mar 71, CU-MARK.

income is plenty good enough without working for more; & sometimes I think I'm a sort of fool for going on working, anyhow. . . .

I must & will keep shady & quiet till Bret Harte simmers down a little & then I mean to go up head again & *stay* there until I have published the two books already contracted for & just one more beside, which latter shall make a ripping sensation or I have overestimated the possibilities of my subject. . . .

The man who says the least about me in any paper for 3 months to come will do me the greatest favor. I tell you I mean to *go slow.* I will "top" Bret Harte again or bust. But I can't do it by dangling eternally in the public view.

In spite of his irritation, Clemens added a postscript to the letter: "Shall ship some book MS. next Wednesday"[121]—that is, on 15 March—a deadline which he did not quite meet, postponing his shipment until 18 March, the day he and Olivia left Buffalo for Elmira.

On 17 March Clemens replied to Bliss, who had been trying to resolve their differences by rational explanation.[122] His reply suggested that rational explanation was irrelevant. It also confirmed that his progress on the western book had been minimal since December.

Out of this chaos of my household I snatch a moment to reply. We are packing up, to-night, & tomorrow I shall take my wife to Elmira on a mattrass, ~~with~~—for she can neither sit up nor stand—& will not for a week or two. . . . In three whole months I have hardly written a page of MS. You do not know what it is to be in a state of absolute frenzy—desperation. I had rather die twice over than repeat the last six months of my life.

Now do you see?—I want *rest.* I want to get clear away from all hamperings, all harassments. I am going to shut myself up in a farm-house alone, on top an Elmira hill, & *write*—on my book. I will see no company, & worry about nothing. I never will make another promise again of any kind, that *can* be avoided, so help me God.

Take my name clear out of the list of contributors, & never mention me again—& then I shall feel that the fetters are off & I am free. I am to furnish an article for your next No. & I *will* furnish it—that is just the way I ~~make~~ ruin myself—making promises. Do you know that for *seven weeks* I have not had my natural rest but have been a night-&-day sick-nurse to my wife—& am still—& shall continue to be for two or three weeks longer——yet must turn in now & write a damned *humorous* article for the Publisher, because I have *promised* it—promised it when I thought that the vials of hellfire bottled up for my benefit *must* be about emptied. By the living God I don't believe they ever *will* be emptied.

It is scarcely surprising that under these circumstances Clemens's opinion of his work was decidedly gloomy:

The MS I sent to be copied is back but I find nothing in it that can be transferred to the Publisher—for the chapter I intended to use I shall tear up, for it is simply an attempt to be ~~full~~ funny, & a failure.

When I get to Elmira I will look over the *next* chapters & send something—or, failing that, will write something—my own obituary I hope it will be.[123]

It is likely that the chapter Clemens threatened to "tear up" was eventually left out of the book. If so, no text for it has ever been found, and its contents remain unknown and to a large degree unknowable. And yet cer-

[121]SLC to Orion Clemens, 11 and 13 Mar 71, CU-MARK, in *MTLP*, 56–58.
[122]See Elisha Bliss, Jr., to SLC, 15 Mar 71, CU-MARK.
[123]SLC to Elisha Bliss, Jr., 17 Mar 71, NN-B†, published in part in *MTLP*, 60–61.

tain things about it fall within the range of reasonable conjecture. It is clear, for instance, that *some* chapter originally preceded the Bemis incident, and that it was even set in type later that spring, as Bliss began work on the prospectus. The evidence for this conclusion is a small, bibliographical detail in the prospectus (Pra), which has long been known but never fully explained: two pages from the Bemis story, identical to the text as it appeared on pages numbered 62 and 63 in the first edition, are found in Pra on pages numbered 77 and 78—fifteen pages further along than where they ended up in the book.[124] The most likely explanation for these higher page numbers is that at the time Pra was *first* set in type, there was enough manuscript somewhere before the Bemis story to make fifteen book pages (text and illustrations), which were removed before Pra was published in November. Such a reduction could have come piecemeal from several chapters, but probably included one large block (presumably a chapter), and must have been authorized by Clemens sometime in August 1871. These revisions are discussed in greater detail below.

Something can also be conjectured about the likely content of the chapter that preceded Bemis and the buffalo, and the reasons for Clemens's dissatisfaction with it, if we assume that the reference to Overland City at the end of chapter 6 is a vestigial forecast of what originally followed it: "the strangest, quaintest, funniest frontier town that our untraveled eyes had ever stared at and been astonished with." If Clemens had written a chapter about the quaint manners and odd characters of Overland City, its humor apparently struck him now as strained ("simply an attempt to be funny, & a failure"). It may even have been largely in this chapter that the condescending "style" of his narrator ("strangest, quaintest, funniest") most required revision. If it seems implausible that he wrote such a chapter in the first place, it may help to recall the report in the 7 September 1870 Elmira *Advertiser* (published within days of his writing the first four chapters), which characterized his new book as "an account of travel at home, describing in a humorous and satirical way our cities and towns, and the people of different sections."[125]

Despite the impulse to tear up this chapter, Clemens probably did not do so at this time—although his unhappiness on rereading it perhaps made him conclude, prematurely as it happened, that the first eight chapters contained nothing suitable for the *Publisher.* He and his family were in Elmira by 19 March, one day after he evidently sent Bliss *all* of the manuscript for what was then chapters 1–11 (some 258 pages)—even though only two-thirds of it ("168 pages") had been copied for security.

After sending it, he may have looked through "the *next* chapters," but

---

[124]The editors of the 1972 edition implied that this discrepancy showed the episode had been moved from "in the area of Chapter 9" to its final position in chapter 7, but not when or why such a change was brought about (*RI 1972*, 18–19).

[125]"City and Neighborhood," Elmira *Advertiser,* 7 Sept 70, 4.

he found nothing there for the *Publisher*. On 20 March, however, he wrote Bliss that he had found something to contribute: it was in then chapter 8, which had in fact been copied along with the rest. He probably enclosed his security copy of it, referring Bliss and Orion to the original manuscript, which (as the postscript just below his signature shows) he assumed was by then already in Hartford:

> Here is my contribution (I take it from the book,) & by all odds it is the finest piece of writing I ever did. Consequently I want the people to *know* that it is from the book:
> Head it thus, & go on:
> The Old-Time Pony-Express
of the Great Plains.
>
> ═══════════
>
> small type [Having but little time to write volunteer-contributions, now I offer this in chapter from
> By <u>Mark</u> <u>Twain</u>.
> small type. [The following is a chapter from Mark Twain's forthcoming book & closes with a life-like picture of an incident of <u>Overland</u> stage travel on the <u>Plains</u> in the days before the Pacific railroad was built.—<u>Ed</u>. <u>Publisher</u>.]
> [From along about the 160th to 170th page of the MS.] It begins thus:
> "However, in a little while all interest was taken up in stretching our necks & watching for the pony-rider" &c.—Go on to end of chapter.
> P. S. Even Before the book is printed I shall write that bull story over again (that precedes the pony) or else alter it till it is good—for it *can* be made good—& then you can put *that* in the Publisher too, if you want to.
> Yrs. Clemens
>
> You got the Book MS, of course?
> Refer the marginal note to Orion, about postage. But I I feel *sure* I am wrong, & that it *was* FOUR Dollars an ounce instead of TWO——make the correction, if necessary READ PROOF VERY CAREFULLY, ORION—you need send none to me.[126]

It is clear that Clemens did not have his own manuscript of the pony-express passage before him, for otherwise he would simply have given its first page number, rather than saying it began "along about the 160th to 170th page of the MS."[127] (He seems to have remembered the approximate page, but could not check his memory against the security copy, which would not have preserved the original page numbers.) In fact, his ability to quote the first nineteen words of the passage, and his way of referring to it ("Here is my contribution"), would seem to make it all but manifest that he enclosed his security copy of the passage with the letter—both to make it easier to find it in his original manuscript, and to transmit the "marginal note" mentioned in the final postscript. It is also clear that the pas-

---

[126]SLC to Elisha Bliss, Jr., and Orion Clemens, 20 Mar 71, CU-MARK, in *MTLP*, 61–62.

[127]These page references also make it more likely that Clemens sent out 168, rather than 160, pages to be copied. For if the pony-rider passage came at the end of only 160 pages, he would have placed its beginning at about page 150. FIGURE 1 indicates instead that the passage probably occupied pages 162–70, and therefore began as Clemens said it did, "along about the 160th to 170th page."

sage, which he described for the *Publisher's* audience as "a chapter," did not *begin* a chapter, as it ultimately would in the book, but instead *ended* one ("Go on to end of chapter"), the beginning of which he also identified: "that bull story . . . that precedes the pony" can only refer to the Bemis tale, which ultimately began chapter 7 in the book, where it would be followed by the story of Eckert and the cat, which Clemens would supply in August to fill in when he turned the pony-express passage into the beginning of chapter 8.[128]

5

Having sent off the first eleven chapters of his manuscript,[129] Clemens seems to have taken the "week's rest" he earlier said he needed, while continuing to nurse Olivia through her convalescence. On 23 March, for instance, Charles Langdon, the Reverend Thomas K. Beecher, and Clemens attended an evening meeting of a local literary society, where Clemens spoke briefly: "Mr. Twain's address was concluded by saying that he had a sick wife at home, and that he had duties which he could not delegate, and with the President's permission he would retire, as his faith in doctors was rather limited." The next day, 24 March, his old friend Joseph T. Goodman arrived in Elmira.[130] Goodman's visit would grow into several months, and provide Clemens with badly needed encouragement about

---

[128]"However," the word that begins the passage quoted in the letter, also appeared in the *Publisher* text, but was omitted when the passage became the start of chapter 8. If the passage had begun a chapter at this time, Clemens might simply have identified it for Bliss by its chapter number.

[129]It is clear, but less than obvious, that Clemens *did* send chapters 1–11 on or about 18 March, rather than only chapters 1–8, with chapters 9–11 following by the end of April, as might be inferred (Steinbrink, 180). On 30 April he told Orion: "I sent Bliss MSS yesterday, ~~up to~~ about 100 pages of MS" (30 Apr 71, NPV, in *MTBus*, 118). Three days later, on 3 May, he told Bliss: "I mailed you the 12th, 13th, 14th & 15th chapters yesterday, & before that I had sent you the previous 11 chapters. Let me know if they all arrived safely" (3 May 71, CU-MARK, in *MTLP*, 66). If one assumes that these two letters allude to *separate* mailings of 100 pages on 29 April and chapters 12–15 on 2 May, then those 100 pages *must* have consisted of chapters 9–11, which could hardly have been sent as early as 18 March. As Figure 1 shows, however, chapters 9–11 comprised only 88 pages—not a good approximation of Clemens's figure. In fact, on 15 May, twelve days after telling Bliss he had sent chapters 12–15, Clemens chided him for not acknowledging them: "You do not mention having received my second batch of MS, sent a week or two ago—about 100 pages" (15 May 71, ViU, in *MTL*, 1:188). This statement suggests that the 100 pages and chapters 12–15 were *not* separate and distinct, but one and the same—Clemens's "second batch," sent on or about 29 April (as he told Orion) or 2 May (as he told Bliss). Figure 2 indicates that chapters 12 through 15 as originally submitted did in fact comprise some 100 pages of manuscript (259–358). Clemens's first batch must therefore have comprised chapters 1–11.

[130]"The Travelers' Inn," Elmira *Advertiser*, 27 Mar 71, 3; "Mr. Joseph F. Goodman, editor of the Virginia City *Enterprise*, Nevada, is visiting friends in this city" ("City and Neighborhood," Elmira *Advertiser*, 25 Mar 71, 4).

his western book. He and Goodman clearly discussed writing a novel together at this time (probably to be set in Washington, D.C.), but it is likely that shortly after arriving in Elmira, Goodman read Clemens's manuscript for the western book—at least insofar as he could by relying on the incomplete security copy and any further manuscript chapters Clemens had drafted by that time. Clemens would tell Orion on 18 April that Goodman was "up here at the farm with me," and that he was "going to read my MSS critically," but the likelihood is strong that by then Goodman had already read substantial portions of the manuscript.[131]

In a 1910 interview, after Clemens's death, Goodman recalled for a San Francisco reporter that it had frequently been his "privilege" to read Mark Twain's "works in manuscript, before they were sent to the publishers."

I recollect his giving me the manuscript of "Roughing It" to read one afternoon when I was visiting him in the early seventies. He had made a great hit with "The Innocents Abroad," and he was afraid he might not sustain his newly acquired reputation with "Roughing It." When I began to read the manuscript Sam sat down at a desk and wrote nervously. I was not reading to be amused, you understand, but was studying critically the merits of his writings.

I read along intently for an hour, hardly noticing that Sam was beginning to fret and shift about uneasily. At last he could not stand it any longer, and in despair he jumped up exclaiming, "Damn you, you have been reading that stuff for an hour and you have not cracked a smile yet. I don't believe I am keeping up my lick."[132]

Paine, who also interviewed Goodman and heard this story directly from him, published a rather more detailed account, and possibly one that profited from Clemens's own recollection of the facts. According to Paine, it

was really Joe Goodman, as much as anything, that stirred a fresh enthusiasm in the new book. Goodman arrived just when the author's spirits were at low ebb.

"Joe," he said, "I guess I'm done for. I don't appear to be able to get along at all with my work, and what I do write does not seem valuable. I'm afraid I'll never be able to reach the standard of The Innocents Abroad again. Here is what I have written, Joe. Read it, and see if that is your opinion."

Goodman took the manuscript and seated himself in a chair, while Clemens went over to a table and pretended to work. Goodman read page after page, critically, and was presently absorbed in it. Clemens watched him furtively, till he could stand it no longer. Then he threw down his pen, exclaiming:

"I knew it! I knew it! I am writing nothing but rot. You have sat there all this time reading without a smile, and pitying the ass I am making of myself. But I am not wholly to blame. I am not strong enough to fight against fate. I have been trying to write a funny book, with dead people and sickness everywhere. Mr. Langdon died first, then a young lady in our house, and now Mrs. Clemens and the baby have been at the point of death all winter! Oh, Joe, I wish to God I could die myself!"

"Mark," said Joe, "I was reading critically, not for amusement, and so far as I have read, and can judge, this is one of the best things you have ever written. I have found it perfectly absorbing. You are doing a great book!"

---

[131]SLC to Orion Clemens, 18 Apr 71, CU-MARK, in *MTLP*, 64. By 10 April, Clemens had dismantled his security copy even further, using it to send corrections to Bliss.

[132]"Jos. Goodman's Memories of Humorist's Early Days," San Francisco *Examiner*, 22 Apr 1910, 3.

Clemens knew that Goodman never spoke except from conviction, and the verdict was to him like a message of life handed down by an archangel. He was a changed man instantly. He was all enthusiasm, full of his subject, eager to go on. He proposed to pay Goodman a salary to stay there and keep him company and furnish him with inspiration—the Pacific coast atmosphere and vernacular, which he feared had slipped away from him. Goodman declined the salary, but extended his visit as long as his plans would permit, and the two had a happy time together, recalling old Comstock days.[133]

The first contemporary sign that Clemens's interest had been rekindled came slightly more than a week after Goodman's arrival. On 4 April, he wrote Orion:

> In moving from Buffalo here I have lost certain notes & documents—among them t̶h̶e̶ what you wrote for me about the difficulties of opening up the Territorial government in Nevada & getting the machinery to running. And now, just at the moment that I want it, it is gone. I don't even know what it was you wrote, for I did not intend to read it until I was ready to use it. D̶o̶ Have you time to scribble something again to aid my memory. Little characteristic items like Whittlesey's refusing to allow for the knife, &c are the most illuminating things—the difficulty of getting credit for the Gov't—& all that sort of thing. Incidents are better, any time, than dry history. Don't tax yourself—I can make a little go a great way.[134]

Clemens had misplaced the notes that Orion had sent the previous November, and the specific details mentioned here indicate that on 4 April he was preparing to write what became chapter 25. Indeed, four days later, on 8 April, he recorded being up "to the ₵ 570ᵗʰ page," conjecturally the next-to-last page of chapter 24, about the Mexican plug.[135] These facts would seem to confirm that during October, November, and December, at least, Clemens had in fact made some progress beyond chapter 12, if only because it seems unlikely that he wrote all of chapters 12–24 (more than 300 pages) in the two weeks between 25 March and 8 April.

On the other hand, much of what Clemens had written seems to have been still in draft form: he clearly continued to revise chapters 12 and following during March and April. One of the three surviving manuscript pages (reproduced in facsimile on page 843) shows, in fact, that he must have revised chapter 12 sometime after 13 March, when he received Orion's letter about Slade. Chapter 12 covers the final part of the journey to Salt Lake City and is, in general, notably dependent on Orion's journal for names, distances, and particular incidents, as well as for occasional phrasing.[136] But the journal barely mentions another landmark that Clemens treated rather fully in chapter 12—the east-west stream on the Continental Divide—stating merely, "Near this Station are the Pacific Springs, which issue in a branch, taking up its march for the Pacific Ocean." Clemens's cue for the incident in chapter 12 was therefore almost certainly not

---

[133]*MTB*, 1:435–36.

[134]SLC to Orion Clemens, 4 Apr 71, CU-MARK, in *MTLP*, 62.

[135]SLC to Orion Clemens, 8 and 10 Apr 71, CU-MARK, in *MTLP*, 63.

[136]For example, compare Orion's journal entries for 4 and 5 August (pages 771–72) with the passage on page 85.

westward again. ⁁ The incident had such a gentle air of romance about it that I was subdued into a vein of thoughtfulness; & as I sat ~~dreaming of~~ ~~lost to tracing its~~ the wanderings of ~~my~~ the leaf across the continent, & the vague possibility that many weeks to come she might take it out of the water as it drifted by the old city, & by the unerring instinct of ~~love reveal its message to her~~ love know instantly the ~~tender words to~~ tender freight it bore, the tears came into my eyes. However, when I reflected that I had forgotten to put a postage stamp on it,

Unnumbered manuscript page, removed from what is now chapter 12. Reproduced at 87 percent of actual size, from the original in the Mark Twain Papers, The Bancroft Library (CU-MARK).

Orion's journal, which he had had since August, but Orion's letter about Slade, which he received in March. That letter began by describing South Pass, "where the clouds looked so low, where we saw the first snow, and where a spring with waters destined for the Atlantic stood within a man's length (or within sight) of another spring whose waters were about to commence a voyage to the Pacific."[137] If Clemens wrote (or elaborated) his own description of this stream only after reading Orion's 11 March letter, then the unnumbered manuscript page—clearly a draft, not even quite filling the page—was written no earlier than mid-March. It contains a version of the "snapper" used to conclude this incident, which, by the time it appeared in the prospectus, had been condensed into a two-sentence paragraph: "I freighted a leaf with a mental message for the friends at home, and dropped it in the stream. But I put no stamp on it and it was held for postage somewhere."[138] Gone from this final version is any hint of the narrator's sweetheart ("*she*") in New Orleans ("the old city")— perhaps because such details were not compatible with his having "never" been "away from home" before.

An early version of the first page of chapter 18, about crossing "an '*alkali*' desert," also survives in manuscript. The page (reproduced in facsimile on page 845) is numbered "423," and the chapter is numbered "20," altered from "19," indicating that the number of the "desert" chapter was at least one higher than its final number in the first edition. A higher chapter number is confirmed by the evidence of Pra, which included several pages from chapters 15, 16, 21, 23, and 24, anachronistically identified as chapters 16, 17, 22, 24, and 25—that is, one chapter number higher than in the book. Where, prior to chapter 15, was a full chapter deleted? The answer is suggested by the author's footnote at the end of chapter 14, which refers the reader to the appendixes for "a brief sketch of Mormon history, and the noted Mountain Meadows massacre." That reference, together with some minor discrepancies in chapter 13, makes it all but certain that the material in the appendixes was originally part of these chapters on Mormonism. The "Brief Sketch of Mormon History" (appendix A) may have belonged originally in chapter 13—perhaps following Clemens's reference to having "picked up a great deal of useful information and entertaining nonsense," not otherwise mentioned. If so, that might explain why refer-

---

[137]Pages 771, 778.

[138]See pages 81–82. Although unnumbered, the manuscript page would have been approximately page 278. It reads:

westward again. ¶ The incident had such a gentle air of romance about it that I was subdued into a vein of thoughtfulness; & as I sat ~~lost to tracing its~~ ,dreaming of the, wanderings of ~~the~~ ,my, leaf across the continent, & the vague possibility that many weeks to come *she* might take it out of the water as it drifted by the old city, & ,by, the unerring instinct of ~~love reveal its message to her~~ love know instantly the ~~tender words its~~ tender freight it bore, the tears came into my eyes. However, when I reflected that I had forgotten to put a postage stamp on it, [*end of page*].

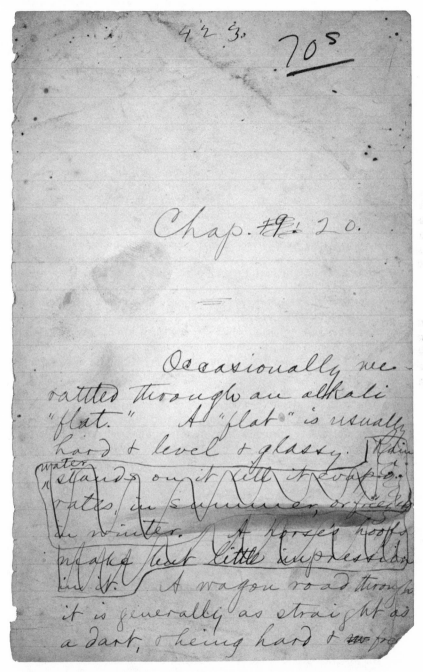

Manuscript page numbered 423, removed from what is now chapter 18. Reproduced at 87 percent of actual size, from the original in the Mark Twain Papers, The Bancroft Library (CU-MARK).

ences in the next paragraph to visiting "the king," and to the king's "high-handed attitude toward Congress," occur without the king or his offenses against Congress being clearly identified—something the last paragraph in what became appendix A *had* done, noting that

Brigham Young was the only real power in the land. He was an absolute monarch—a monarch who defied our President—a monarch who laughed at our armies when they camped about his capital—a monarch who received without emotion the news that the august Congress of the United States had enacted a solemn law against polygamy, and then went forth calmly and married twenty-five or thirty more wives.[139]

Likewise, the material that became appendix B, "The Mountain Meadows Massacre," was very likely a separate chapter, perhaps following chapter 14, and therefore preceding the one remaining reference to the subject in chapter 17. But however these chapters were in fact configured, the likelihood is great that they originally included the material on Mormonism preserved in the appendixes. When the words in the appendixes are counted as if they were part of the manuscript for chapters 13–15, the calculated page number for the start of chapter 18 is 424—quite close to the actual number on the surviving draft page, 423.[140]

Although Clemens sent Bliss only eleven chapters on 18 March, he knew perfectly well that the contract obliged Bliss "to commence operations at once upon receipt of manuscript." He therefore added a postscript to his 4 April note to Orion which expressed his impatience for Bliss to begin illustrating and typesetting what he had sent: "Is Bliss doing anything with the MS I sent? Is he thinking of beginning on it shortly?"[141] His anxiety to see illustrations and typesetting begin is the more remarkable because, having sent those chapters rather in haste than otherwise, he soon found that they needed more work. On 8 April he replied to another letter (now lost) from Orion, who apparently asked whether he and Bliss should use the manuscript of the Bemis episode for the *Publisher* and for the book, or wait for the revision promised in Clemens's first postscript of 20 March. Clemens repeated his original instructions, with one condition:

If I don't add a postscript to this, tell Bliss to go ahead & set up the MSS & put the engravers to work. My copy is down at the house & I am up here at the farm, a mile & a half up a mountain, where I write every day.

I am to the ⌀ 570th page & booming along. And what I am writing now is so much better than the opening chapters, or the Innocents Abroad either, that I do *wish* I could spare time to revamp the opening chapters, & even write some of them over again.

---

[139]Pages 92–93, 98n, 549.

[140]Pra confirms that the desert chapter was at one time number 19, but does not explain how it became number 20, if only briefly. The manuscript represents the printer's copy in a state well before Pra—one that might have included the same material with different chapter divisions, for example.

[141]SLC to Orion Clemens, 4 Apr 71, CU-MARK, in *MTLP*, 63.

I will read the bull story when I go down, & see whether it will do or not. It don't altogether suit me, but ~~maybe I shan't~~ I shall alter it *very little,* anyway. I don't want it to go in the same number of the paper with the pony sketch. Mind, I never want two articles of mine in the same number. Put it in the next if you choose.

But on reading his security copy that evening, Clemens was unable to resist the temptation to revise it—and not just in the Bemis chapter. He therefore did add a postscript, which referred explicitly to changes in chapter 6, in the Bemis incident, and in other chapters not specified:

Leave out the yarn about Jack & "Moses." It occurs about 117th page. ~~Stop~~ ˌCloseˌ the chapter with theˌseˌ words
"and when they tried to teach a subordinate anything that subordinate generally "got it through his head"—at least in time for the funeral.["]

Accompanying this, is the bull story, altered the way I want it. Don't put it in till about the fourth No. of the paper.
OVER.
Tell Bliss to go ahead setting up the book just as it is, making the corrections *marked in purple ink,* in some 20 or 30 pages which I shall mail to-night—possibly in this envelop.

Ys
Sam

P. S.—Monday—Am to 610th page, now.[142]

By the time Clemens finished and mailed this letter on 10 April (Monday), he had written as far as page 610, which probably fell near the start of chapter 27, about the trip to Humboldt, the virtual beginning of his "silver fever." And although the original letter no longer has its enclosures, he probably did send with it (or separately, soon thereafter) both "the bull story, altered the way I want it," and an additional "20 or 30 pages" of "corrections *marked in purple ink,*" which he asked that Bliss follow in setting up the eleven chapters already in hand. Both the revised "bull story" and these "corrections" were presumably in the form of altered and augmented pages from Clemens's security copy, which thereby grew even more incomplete. (Because Clemens used his typical purple ink, the changes were visibly distinct from the ink of the copy, evidently a different color.) Although none of the enclosures survives, it is still possible to make some informed guesses about what they contained.

The "Jack & 'Moses'" yarn, which Clemens here identified as beginning on "about" page 117 of the manuscript, was ultimately included in chapter 6 despite this instruction to omit it (the revised closing words for the chapter were also rejected). If, as FIGURE 1 indicates, chapter 6 began on page 114, then the "Jack & 'Moses'" story would have begun on page 126, not 117. The discrepancy indicates that among the revisions Clemens may have made at this time was the addition of up to nine pages toward the beginning of chapter 6, thus forcing the "Jack & 'Moses'" episode back

---

[142]SLC to Orion Clemens, 8 and 10 Apr 71, CU-MARK, in *MTLP,* 63–64.

to its present position.[143] The new material may have been designed to spell out more clearly, in preparation for chapters 10 and 11 on Slade, exactly how the "division-agent" fit into the hierarchy of stagecoach employees. Some evidence for this conjecture is provided by Orion's Slade letter (11 March), which implied that Clemens may have mistakenly referred to Slade as a conductor: "My impression is that he was a *division agent*, from Overland City to Salt Lake—having *several* conductors under him. . . . Slade was *not* a conductor. He had the conductors and drivers under him."[144] The somewhat disjointed style of chapter 6 may result from a revision designed to correct this error by introducing the division-agent to a narrative that originally described the conductor. Clemens's addition of nine pages (nearly doubling the chapter's original eleven pages) may even have suggested to him that he could now leave out "Jack & 'Moses'" entirely. Moreover, it seems necessary to speculate that then chapter 7, which Clemens had found so unsatisfactory even as he sent it to Bliss in March, was now submitted to further revision—chiefly by the addition of material. These 10 April "corrections" totaled, conjecturally, twenty-five pages: nine pages added to chapter 6, and sixteen to then chapter 7. There certainly were, in addition, changes to the Bemis story, which was now "the way I want it"—conjecturally, ten pages longer than before (see FIG-URE 1).

Given the limitations of the evidence, the precise size and location of these changes must remain in doubt. But whatever "corrections" were actually made in April, their net effect was to increase the length of the manuscript between chapter 6 and then chapter 8, without changing the original pagination. (Clemens could not have renumbered his pages because the printer's copy was in Hartford.) These added pages might well have been distributed in some other way, but their total could not have been very different. Without the bulk they added, there would be no way to explain why pages 62–63 of the Bemis story were forced back to pages 77–78 in the initial Pra typesetting, for if *all* the material, including then chapter 7 (later removed in proof), were present in the original manuscript, thus affecting its pagination, the conjectural first page of the pony-express passage would be forced well beyond the range of pages 160–70, to which Clemens assigned it.

Two days after sending this letter, Clemens was in New York.[145] Proba-

---

[143]Strictly speaking, the discrepancy could reflect the addition of a total of nine pages *anywhere* in the first 116 pages of manuscript. But chapter 6 is the earliest point in the text where it seems likely that material was added, rather than deleted.

[144]Page 779. In his September letter to Hosmer, however, Clemens had correctly identified Slade as a "section-agent" (SLC to Hezekiah L. Hosmer, 15 Sept 70, MtHit).

[145]"Home News," New York *Tribune*, 13 Apr 71, 8; "Morning Arrivals," New York *Evening Express*, 13 Apr 71, 3. Clemens was thus in New York on at least 12 and 13 April, but the nature of his errand is not known.

bly by the time he returned to Elmira, Orion's reply was waiting for him. The letter itself has not survived, but it evidently reported Bliss's reluctance to begin on the prospectus without more manuscript in hand, or at least without a more representative selection from it. Orion seems also to have requested permission to put "Jack & 'Moses'" in the *Publisher,* and even to have suggested further revision of the Bemis episode for the *Publisher* in order to distinguish it from an ostensibly similar account by another one of Bliss's authors, Thomas W. Knox. On 18 April, Clemens responded coolly to such meddling:

> Since Knox has printed a similar story {so (the same "situation" has been in print often—men have written it before Knox & I were born,}—let the Bull story alone until it appears in the book—or at least in the "specimen" chapters for canvassers. That is to say, Do not put it in the paper, *at all.* I cannot alter it—too much trouble. . . .
>
> P. S. No—I won't print Jack & Moses. I may lecture next winter, & in that case shall want it.[146]

On the same day, Clemens left Elmira for Buffalo "to finish the sale of my 'Express' interest," as he told Mrs. Fairbanks. The next day he completed this errand, picked up his mail at the *Express* office, and apparently met briefly with his friend David Gray.[147] The Buffalo *Courier* reported on 21 April:

> While Mark Twain was here, the other day, he received by mail a copy of "What I Know About Farming." A note on the fly-leaf, in a chirography that is already historical, read as follows:
>
> To MARK TWAIN, Buffalo; who knows even less about *my* farming than does
>   HORACE GREELEY.
>
> Isn't the common report that Mr. Greeley don't know anything about joking a reprehensible slander?[148]

Clemens did not immediately acknowledge this gift from his recent famous acquaintance. When he did, probably in early May, it must have been after Greeley's joke at his expense had received some coverage in the press (reprinting the Buffalo *Courier*), for he evidently protested Greeley's

---

[146]SLC to Orion Clemens, 18 Apr 71, CU-MARK, in *MTLP,* 64–65.

[147]SLC to Mary Mason Fairbanks, 18 Apr 71, CSmH, in *MTMF,* 151; "Personal," Buffalo *Courier,* 20 Apr 71, 2: "'Mark Twain' was in the city yesterday, on his way to the present residence of his family in Elmira."

[148]"H. G. as a Joker," Buffalo *Courier,* 21 Apr 71, 1. This copy of Greeley's book, which had been published about the middle of April, was still in Clemens's possession when he died, although its significance went unappreciated by Paine, who sold it in the auction of 1911. The catalog for that sale gave the inscription as follows: "To Mark Twain, Esq., Ed. Buffalo Express who knows even less of MY farming than does Horace Greeley. N. York" (Anderson Auction Company catalog, sale of 7–8 February 1911, lot 204). Clemens made at least one marginal notation in his copy: on pages 148–49 Greeley's text reads: "If it were the law of the land that whoever allowed caterpillars to nest and breed in his fruit trees should pay a heavy fine for each nest, we should soon be comparatively clear of the scourges." Clemens noted, "And the farmers too" ("Book Find Recalls Clemens' Stay Here," Buffalo *Courier-Express,* 3 Dec 1950, 24A).

"public" criticism of him. Clemens was, at any rate, in a foul mood during the last week of April. Orion's meddling had merely annoyed him,
but shortly after returning to Buffalo, he received a truly disheartening
letter from Bliss, probably on Monday, 24 April. Bliss wrote that he was
about to begin work on the prospectus, and that he planned to "get it
out very quickly," but felt the need to clarify what Orion had already
communicated:

> I fear your brother has written in a manner to give you wrong impressions of my
> views. I have said to him that the first part of a book alone, is not sufficient to make
> a proper prospectus of. I of course cannot get up full plate engravings, until I know
> the subject, & then it is well to have a variety of matter in it— I have not spoken of
> the position of affairs thinking it of no acc, but perhaps, it might be well to say, that
> standing where I do, with so many agents all over, coming in contact with the
> masses, I can feel the pulse of the community, as well as any other person; I do not
> think there is as much of a desire to see another book from you as there was 3
> months ago. Then anything offered would sell, people would subscribe to anything
> of yours without overhauling or looking at it much. Now they will inspect a Pro-
> spectus closer, & buy more on the strength of *it,* than they would have done a few
> months ago.
>
> Knowing this to be so, I feel particularly anxious to get out a *splendid Prospec-
> tus* one brim full of good matter, of *your own style*— I want to reawaken the appe-
> tite for the book—& know of no better means than to show them slices of a rich
> loaf, & let them try it— Consequently I said to your brother, "if he has anything
> *particularly fine* lets have it for *prospectus."*

Bliss also mentioned that he had already "made selections from Mss. here
for Pros.," suggesting that if Clemens had "any choice *cuts* ‚further along
in the book‚ for it" that he should "send them on" and Bliss would "heave
them in." Bliss continued, "Your brother says he wrote you Knox had written up something similar to the Bull story—I never saw it & do not know
anything about it. It ‚Yours‚ struck me *as a good thing, every way. Your
first chap. is splendid*—smacks of the old style—"[149]

These afterthoughts scarcely blunted Bliss's point, which was that
Clemens's delay in finishing his manuscript had cost him ground with his
audience and, by implication, that he now needed Bliss's help to reverse
that loss.[150] Clemens was clearly depressed by Bliss's testimony, and perhaps by other evidence, telling Mrs. Fairbanks on 26 April: "I am pegging
away at my book, but it will have no success. The papers have found at last
the courage to pull me down off my pedestal & cast slurs at me—& that is
simply a popular author's death rattle. Though he wrote an *inspired* book
after that, it would not save him."[151] It is not known which newspapers he
thought were casting "slurs" at him, or just what occasioned their criticism. But on Sunday, 30 April, a week after reading Bliss's remarks, he re-
proached Orion for writing him "discouraging letters": "Yours stopped

---

[149]Elisha Bliss, Jr., to SLC, 22 Apr 71, CU-MARK.
[150]Steinbrink makes nearly the same point (178–79).
[151]SLC to Mary Mason Fairbanks, 26 Apr 71, CSmH, in *MTMF,* 153.

my pen for two days—Bliss's stopped it for three. Hereafter my wife will read my Hartford letters & if they are of the same nature, keep them out of my hands. The idea of a newspaper editor & a publisher plying with dismal letters a man who is under contract to write *humorous* books for them!" Yet Clemens went on to make clear that he was steadily at work on his book. His inability to write had lasted no more than a week, in clear contrast with the longer intervals of indifference he had experienced the previous fall and winter.

I sent Bliss MSS yesterday, ~~up to~~ about 100 pages of MS.

Don't be in a great hurry getting out the specimen chapters for canvassers, for I want the chapter I am writing *now* in it—& it is away up to page 750 of the MS. I would like to select the "specimen" chapters myself (along with Joe Goodman, who writes by my side every day up at the farm). Joe & I have a 600-page book in contemplation which will wake up the nation. It is a thing which ~~David Gray &~~ I have talked over with David Gray a good deal, & he wanted me to do it right ~~& just~~ & well—which I couldn't without a man to do the accurate drudgery and some little other writing. But Joe is the party. This present book will be a tolerable success—possibly an *excellent* success if the chief newspapers start it off well—but the other book will be an *awful* success. The only trouble is, how I am to hang on to Joe till I publish this present book & another before I *begin* on the joint one.

When is the selection to be made for the specimen chapters?[152]

If on 30 April Clemens was "away up to page 750 of the MS.," FIGURE 2 indicates that he was probably at the end of chapter 34 (a revision of "The Facts in the Great Land Slide Case") or the start of chapter 35 (the trip to Esmeralda). Neither chapter was selected for the prospectus, which in fact included nothing from chapters 25–37; of the two, the tale of the landslide case seems more likely to have inspired Clemens's enthusiasm.

The 100 pages of manuscript Clemens mentioned to Orion as having been sent "yesterday" (29 April) are identical with what, three days later, he told Bliss he had sent "yesterday" (2 May): "I mailed you the 12th, 13th, 14th & 15th chapters yesterday, & before that I had sent you the previous 11 chapters."[153] Chapters 12–15 describe arriving in Salt Lake City and encountering Mormons. As FIGURE 2 shows, the page numbers of chapters 12–15 ran from 259 to 358 (exactly 100 pages), but only if it is assumed that they included material later removed and, later still, relegated to the appendixes. Clemens also told Bliss that his book was by then "half done," so he had accumulated many more pages than he sent—probably some 900 equivalent pages, placing him near the end of chapter 40 (the first of two chapters on the blind lead) by 3 May.[154]

---

[152]SLC to Orion Clemens, 30 Apr 71, NPV, in *MTBus,* 118–19.

[153]SLC to Elisha Bliss, Jr., 3 May 71, CU-MARK, in *MTLP,* 66; see note 129 above.

[154]It is conjectured that chapter 36 was not written at this time, but inserted later—probably in August. The evidence for this conjecture, and for designating three additional chapters as late additions to the printer's copy (see FIGURE 2), is discussed below (see pages 864–66). If Clemens was "up to page 750 of the MS." on 30 April, and "half done" on 3 May, and if the first statement refers to "real" pages while the second refers to "equivalent" pages (as assumed here), then he finished

On 8 or 9 May, Clemens received Greeley's somewhat testy and defensive reply to his letter of thanks:

Mark:

You are mistaken as to my criticisms on *your* farming. I never publicly made any, while you have undertaken to tell the exact cost per pint of my potatoes and cabbages, truely enough the inspiration of genius. If you will really betake yourself to farming, or even to telling what you know about it, rather than what you *don't* know about mine, I will not only refrain from disparaging criticism, but will give you my blessing.

Yours,
Horace Greeley.[155]

Greeley's notoriously difficult handwriting was the subject of innumerable jokes and anecdotes in the press, but this letter was the first Clemens himself had ever received from him. Their brief exchange, part of which was even then being reported in the newspapers, may well have suggested to Clemens the basic comic story of chapter 70, which concerns someone driven mad while corresponding with Greeley "about a trifle of some kind," only to discover that their correspondence had become "the talk of the world."[156] Clemens's first letter from Greeley became, in any case, the physical model for the only slightly exaggerated imitation of it, reproduced as a pseudo-facsimile in chapter 70.[157] Greeley's letter arrived during the most intensive period of book composition that Clemens had yet experienced, but the Sandwich Islands setting of chapter 70 suggests that it was probably not written until July, or even August, when Clemens again wrote Greeley (on another matter), and when the need for additional manuscript had become more apparent.

On Monday, 15 May, less than two weeks after he declared himself "half done," Clemens counted himself well past the halfway point:

I have MS. enough on hand now, to make (allowing for engravings) about 400 pages of the book—consequently am two-thirds done. I intended to run up to Hartford about the middle of the week & take it along; but I am because it has chapters

---

chapters 35, 37, 38, 39, and 40 (roughly 80 pages) in only three days. That he did indeed shift his way of counting is suggested by his choice of words (unlike "page 750," the words "half done" do not refer to actual pagination). If one assumes *no* shift occurred, then the number of chapters supposedly written in three days becomes truly implausible: 35 and 37–43 for real pages, 32–35 and 37–40 for equivalent pages.

[155]Horace Greeley to SLC, 7 May 71, CU-MARK; a facsimile of this letter is reproduced in supplement C, pages 794–95.

[156]Page 481. Greeley's inscription to Clemens in *What I Know of Farming*, reported on 21 April by the Buffalo *Courier*, was soon reprinted in other newspapers: the Chicago *Tribune* ("Literature," 7 May 71, 5) and the Pittsburgh *Gazette* ("Literature, Music and Art," 15 May 71, 4) are the earliest examples found so far, but even the *Courier* story must have been known to Clemens. That he was not pleased by such attention may be inferred from Greeley's denial that he had "publicly made" any "disparaging criticism" of Clemens.

[157]Paine was the first to assert that Greeley's letter was "the model for the pretended facsimile of Greeley's writing" in *Roughing It* (*MTB*, 1:438).

in it that ought by all means to be in the prospectus; but I find myself so thoroughly interested in my work, now (a thing I have not experienced for months) that I can't bear to lose a single moment of the inspiration. So I will stay here & peg away as long as it lasts. My present idea is to write as much more as I have already written, & then cull from the mass the very best chapters & discard the rest. I am not half as well satisfied with the first part of the book as I am with what I am writing now. When I get it done I want to see the man who will begin to read it & not finish it. If it falls short of the Innocents in any respect I shall lose my guess.

When I was writing the Innocents my daily "stent" was 30 pages of MS & I hardly ever got beyond it; but I have gone over that nearly every day for the last ten. That shows that I am writing with a red-hot interest. Nothing grieves me now—nothing troubles me, bothers me or gets my attention—I don't think of anything but the book, & don't have an hour's unhappiness about anything & don't care two cents whether school keeps or not. It will be a bully book. If I keep up my present lick three weeks more I shall be able & willing to scratch out half of the chapters of the Overland narrative—& shall do it.

You do not mention having received my second batch of MS, sent a week or two ago—about 100 pages.

If you want to issue a prospectus & go right to canvassing, say the word & I will forward some more MS—or send it by hand—special messenger. Whatever chapters you think are unquestionably good, we will retain of course, & so they can go into a prospectus as well one time as another. The book will be done soon, now. I have 1200 pages of MS already written, & am now writing 200 a week—more than that, in fact; during past week wrote 23 one day, then 30, 33, 35, 52, & 65~—part of the latter, ~say,~ nearly half, being a re-print sketch. How's that?[158]

By this time Clemens had clearly shifted to counting by equivalent pages. So when he said that he had "1200 pages of MS," he was probably near the end of what became chapter 51, with 1202 equivalent pages (but only 1100 real pages). Twelve hundred equivalent pages were "two-thirds" of the eighteen hundred pages he thought he needed: enough, by his reckoning, "to make (allowing for engravings) about 400 pages of the book," which was to be 600 pages long. His arithmetic makes sense in other ways as well: if he had 900 equivalent pages on 3 May, and had written more than 30 pages a day "nearly every day for the last ten," he would have added approximately 300 pages. His increased rate of progress may have had something to do with his subject: in chapter 42 he began to describe his experiences as a newspaper reporter in Virginia City. But his new-found speed was also due to his increased use of clippings in this section of the book (chapters 34, 37, 38, 46, and probably 51 all relied extensively on clippings), which now made it virtually necessary to count by equivalent pages.

Since Clemens wrote this letter on a Monday (15 May), the extraordinary string of daily stints "during the past week" can be plausibly assigned to Monday through Saturday, 8–13 May. It is therefore likely that he began on 8 May with 23 pages, a stint that corresponds to chapter 44 (puffing stocks), estimated at 25 pages (see FIGURE 2). The second day's stint, on 9 May, was 30 pages, which corresponds to chapter 45 (Reuel Gridley and

---

[158]SLC to Elisha Bliss, Jr., 15 May 71, ViU, in *MTL*, 1:187–88.

the flour sack), estimated at 24 pages (only a fair approximation of 30). The third stint, on 10 May, was 33 pages, which corresponds to chapter 46 (Nevada nabobs), estimated at 31 equivalent pages. The fourth stint, on 11 May, was 35 pages, which corresponds to chapter 47 (Scotty Briggs and Buck Fanshaw's funeral), estimated at 36 pages. The fifth stint, on 12 May, was 52 pages, which corresponds to chapters 48 (western desperadoes and the vagaries of jury trials) and 50 (Captain Ned Blakely): 25 plus 24 pages, or 49 pages, a good approximation of 52.[159] And the sixth and last stint, on 13 May, was 65 pages, "nearly half" being "a re-print sketch," which is to say, clippings. If this stint does indeed correspond to what became chapter 51 (the *Weekly Occidental*, with the poem called "The Aged Pilot Man"), estimated at 62 pages, the only part of it that could have been "re-print" was the poem. This suggests that the poem was in fact set from a clipping of the lost *Occidental* or even the *Enterprise*—although no such printing has been found.[160]

Having just written chapter 48 (on the failings of the jury system) on 12 May, Clemens concluded his 15 May letter somewhat giddily, with a dedication for the book which was not, in the end, adopted:

It will be a starchy book, & should be full of snappy pictures—especially pictures worked in with the letter-press. The dedication will be worth the price of the volume—thus:

<u>To the Late Cain,</u>

This Book is Dedicated:

Not on account of respect for his memory, for it merits little respect; not on account of sympathy with him, for his bloody deed placed him without the pale of sympathy, strictly speaking: but out of a mere humane commiseration for him in that it was his misfortune to live in a dark age that knew not the beneficent Insanity Plea.

Nor could he resist a gloating postscript about his reputation, which had recuperated, without Bliss's help, in less than three weeks' time: "The reaction is beginning & my stock is looking up. I am getting the bulliest offers for books & almanacs, am flooded with lecture invitations, & one periodical offers me $6,000 cash for 12 articles, of any length & on any subject, treated humorously or otherwise."[161] Bliss replied almost immediately, on 17 May:

---

[159]Chapter 49 (fatal affrays) was probably added in August or even later. Some bibliographical evidence suggests that the manuscript of chapter 48 was slightly longer than the chapter as printed: the description in the analytical Contents for the first edition included the phrase "Waking up the Weary Passenger" before the final "Satisfaction without Fighting." Since chapter 48 makes no reference to waking up a weary passenger, it is likely that the description was not adjusted to reflect Clemens's subsequent revision of the chapter itself.

[160]No issues of the *Occidental* are known to be extant. Clemens says in chapter 51 that the poem failed to appear in the *Occidental* because it "was on the 'first side' of the issue that was not completed" (page 347). This statement implies that the poem was typeset, and therefore available to Clemens in the form of proof.

[161]SLC to Elisha Bliss, Jr., 15 May 71, ViU, in *MTL*, 1:188.

Your favor recd   Am glad to hear from you. Sorry to hear you are not going to call on us to day. However it may be for the best as I think you are in the mood to do good work, at which I *heartily rejoice*—

Glad to know you are so pressed with overtures for work.

We intend to do *our part* towards making your book, what it should be, viz in illustrations. We shall try to have just the kind in that will suit—& think we shall succeed. I think it would be well to have Prospectus out *soon as practicible* as agents are anxious for it—still lets have the *best stuff in it*. I have no doubt you have ample matter now to select from, therefore suppose you do as you suggest, send another batch on, of *selected* chapters if you think best & I will get right to work— Suppose you send on such a lot, marked with what in your opinion is particularly good, & let me then make up prospectus matter from it & get engraving for it under way.

Send the Mss. by *express* it will come then safely. I will put *bully cuts* into it, such as will please you

Think this will be the plan if it suits you. I assure you nothing shall be wanting on my part, to bring it out in *high style*—I reckon I can do it.[162]

Nearly four weeks had passed since Bliss had said he was beginning on the prospectus. Clemens's reply to this latest request for his *"best stuff"* is not known, but he probably did not send any more manuscript in May. On 1 or 2 June, however, he carried his third batch of manuscript to Hartford. This third batch probably extended from chapter 15 (his 16) through 51 (his 50), omitting chapters 36 and 49, which were probably added later. He may also have submitted some *"selected* chapters" from later in the narrative which he thought especially suitable for the prospectus.[163]

Shortly before Clemens made this delivery, David Gray published an announcement of the book which was obviously informed by Clemens himself: "Mark Twain's new book, same size and style as the 'Innocents Abroad,' and as copiously illustrated, will be published in the fall, and will appear simultaneously in England and America. Dealing as it does with certain hitherto unrecorded phases of western life, it will be of historic value as well as aboundingly humorous."[164] This is the earliest known public reference to Clemens's plan to publish his western book "simultaneously" in England with George Routledge and Company—a step that would establish a valid English copyright, provided English publication preceded American by a day or so. Clemens had asked Bliss to arrange the matter with Routledge, probably soon after learning in March 1870 that only simultaneous publication could protect the book in England.[165]

[162]Elisha Bliss, Jr., to SLC, 17 May 71, CU-MARK.

[163]The prospectus included text, illustrations, or both, from chapters as high as 51, but nothing from chapters 52 through 79, with two exceptions: chapters 76 and 78, which were clearly the "selected chapters." See also note 187.

[164]Buffalo *Courier*, 31 May 71, 1.

[165]"I wrote them to know if it would pay me to go ~~in~~ over the Niagara river & get a British copyright, & you see what he says," Clemens wrote Bliss on 3 March 1870, presumably referring to *The Innocents Abroad* (CU-MARK†). A week later he implied that Bliss was supposed to inquire of Routledge about the next book: "Have you heard yet what the possibilities are in the matter of selling our book there?" (SLC to Elisha Bliss, Jr., 11 Mar 70, NN-B†).

Clemens did not stay in Hartford long enough to read proof, or even to revise chapters 1–15, which were already in Bliss's hands. On 5 or 6 June he returned to Elmira, where he may have begun one more chapter. He did not, at this time, write what became chapter 52 (Virginia City mining statistics, probably added in August or even later), nor did he write chapter 53 (Jim Blaine's ram story), which he probably finished on 10 August, when he told Olivia of having written "a splendid chapter today, for the middle of the book."[166] But he may well have begun chapter 54 (the Chinese in the West) in early June, for its first paragraph reads, in part: "As I write, news comes that in broad daylight in San Francisco, some boys have stoned an inoffensive Chinaman to death, and that although a large crowd witnessed the shameful deed, no one interfered." This sentence could not have been written *before* 3 June, when the news report that Clemens saw appeared in the New York *Tribune:*

> A CHINAMAN STONED TO DEATH BY BOYS.
> SAN FRANCISCO, June 2.—The police are endeavoring to arrest a gang of boys who stoned to death an inoffensive Chinaman on Fourth-st. yesterday afternoon. Dozens of people witnessed the assault, but did not interfere until the murder was complete. No attempt was then made to arrest the murderers.[167]

But if Clemens began chapter 54 after returning home on 5 or 6 June, by 9 June he apparently felt so relieved at having delivered some fifty chapters to the publisher that he stopped work on the book altogether. The next day he wrote his lecture agents, Redpath and Fall, that "without really intending to go into the lecture field," he had written "a lecture yesterday just for amusement & to see how the subject would work up," but having "read it over," he had now decided to "deliver it."[168] Clemens spent the rest of the month working on this lecture, and, when he grew dissatisfied with it, on two others. He also managed to write, or at least revise for publication, four magazine articles, three of which he sent, on 21 June, to Bliss:

> Here are three articles which you may have if you'll pay ~~$100 or $125~~ $125 for the lot, ~~according to the present state of your exchequer~~ — & if you don't want them I'll sell them to "Galaxy," but not for a cent less than three times the money—have just sold them a short article (shorter than either of these,) for $100. . . .
> Have you heard anything from Routledge? Considering the large English sale he made of one of my other books (Jumping Frog,) I thought may be we might make something if I could give him a secure copyright.— There seems to be no convenient way to beat those Canadian re-publishers anyway——though I ~~could~~ can go over the line & get out a copyright if you wish it & think it would hold water.[169]

---

[166]SLC to Olivia L. Clemens, 10 Aug 71, CU-MARK, in *LLMT,* 159.

[167]Page 369; New York *Tribune,* 3 June 71, 1.

[168]SLC to Redpath and Fall, 10 June 71, NHi†.

[169]SLC to Elisha Bliss, Jr., 21 June 71, CU-MARK, in *MTLP,* 66–67. The "short article" for the *Galaxy* was "About Barbers," published in the August issue. The three articles sent to Bliss were "A New Beecher Church" and "A Brace of Brief Lectures on Science" (in two parts), which appeared in the July, September, and October 1871 issues of the *American Publisher.*

It is likely that Clemens did not again work on the book manuscript until the end of the month. On 27 June he told Orion: "I wrote a third lecture to-day—& tomorrow I go back on the book again." On 29 June he reported writing "2 chapters of the book to-day—shall write chapter 53 to-morrow."[170] The two chapters were probably his chapters 51 and 52, which became chapter 54 (the account of the Chinese community, begun earlier in June) and chapter 55 (the "Prodigal," and Clemens's brief stint as chief editor of the *Enterprise*). His chapter 53, probably completed on 30 June, would eventually become chapter 56 (about tiring of Virginia City and leaving for San Francisco).

6

Back in Hartford, Bliss and Orion had begun to have the illustrations drawn, engraved, and electrotyped—at least for those chapters selected for the prospectus. Bliss had said in April (with only eleven chapters to choose from) that he had already made a selection—and indeed, out of the first eleven chapters, all but three (6, 9, and 11) were represented in the prospectus. If he followed normal procedure, Bliss would have ordered and received engravings for most of the illustrations in these chapters before ordering any type set, so that the first proofs could show the illustrations in place. Some evidence indicates that he was, to a degree, bypassing normal procedure for this book,[171] but it was still desirable to give the manuscript to the illustrators as soon as possible.

Bliss hired at least three artists: Edward F. Mullen, whom Clemens had wanted to hire for the *Burlesque Autobiography*, and then for the sketchbook, in December and January; Roswell Morse Shurtleff (1838–1915), later a successful landscape painter; and True W. Williams.[172] All three artists had earlier drawn illustrations for Richardson's *Beyond the Mississippi*, and Shurtleff and Williams had both provided drawings for *The Innocents Abroad*. All of the new drawings would be engraved by the firm of Fay and Cox in New York, which had also done the work for *Beyond the Mississippi* and *Innocents*, among others.

Williams was the principal artist for the book, signing fifty-four drawings (usually with his distinctive monogram) and contributing at least as many more that were not signed.[173] He received the first, as well as the

---

[170]SLC to Orion Clemens, 27 June 71 (2nd of 2) and 29 June 71, CU-MARK†.

[171]For instance, the only illustration in chapter 16, "THE MIRACULOUS COMPASS" (page 110), was not in place when Pra was printed, so that when it was inserted for Prb and A, the text which followed it was forced further along, although not so far as to overrun the last page of the chapter.

[172]Sinclair Hamilton, *Early American Book Illustrators and Wood Engravers, 1670–1870* (Princeton, N.J.: Princeton University Library, 1958), 207.

[173]Williams's signed illustrations appear in the present edition on (chapter:page) 2:6, 2:7, 4:23, 5:33, 6:36, 7:42, 7:48, 10:61, 10:62, 10:65, 10:68, 11:71, 12:82, 13:91, 14:97, 15:104, 15:105, 17:119, 21:139, 21:142, 23:155, 25:167, 25:172, 26:175,

largest, assignment of manuscript—possibly in May, when Bliss had chapters 1–15, or in June, when he also had chapters 16–50 (15–51, as later numbered in the book). His hand is evident starting with the clear likeness of the author in chapter 1, in which Mark Twain sports the same checked trousers that he wears in Williams's drawings for *Innocents*. Over half of Williams's signed drawings appear in chapters 2–37, but many of the later drawings are his as well. (In chapter 62, he may even have managed to sneak in a portrait of himself as "Williams," the captain's nemesis: see page 427.) Shurtleff signed the frontispiece and the full-page drawing of South Pass for chapter 12. Fourteen additional illustrations bear his initials or monogram, the earliest in chapter 42 and the last in chapter 79, for a total of sixteen.[174] Mullen signed only four drawings—one in chapter 38, one in chapter 43, and two in chapter 67[175]—although he likewise contributed several more that are unsigned.

In addition to commissioning the drawings for *Roughing It*, Bliss followed the common practice of reusing engravings from earlier books, especially those published by his own company and its subsidiaries. He took engravings from Thomas W. Knox's *Overland through Asia*, Nelson Winch Green's *Mormonism*, Junius Henri Browne's *Sights and Sensations in Europe*, as well as from Richardson's *Beyond the Mississippi* and Evans's *Our Sister Republic*. He also used seven illustrations from J. Ross Browne's *Adventures in the Apache Country*, presumably by purchasing a set of electrotypes from Browne's publisher, Harper and Brothers. In all, Bliss reused thirty-three illustrations from known sources.[176] In addition,

---

29:190, 30:199, 31:201, 31:205, 31:206, 31:208, 33:218, 34:222, 35:230, 37:242, 45:296, 46:305, 55:382, 55:384, 58:397, 58:400 (two), 58:401, 58:402, 59:410, 61:419, 62:422, 62:427, 63:432, 63:435, 65:446, 76:521, 76:524, and 78:535 (two).

[174]Illustrations signed with "S.," "R. S.," or the monogram "S. R." appear in the present edition on 42:273, 42:276, 44:289, 46:299, 50:332, 50:334, 51:341, 53:362, 53:364, 53:365, 53:366, 77:527, 79:539, and 79:541.

[175]See 38:248, 43:279, 67:458, and 67:463.

[176]Illustration electrotypes were advertised for sale, for example, in the *Publishers' and Stationers' Weekly Trade Circular* 1 (15 and 22 Feb 72): 148, 175. See also Hamlin Hill 1964, 58, 194 n. 110, and Beverly R. David, *Mark Twain and His Illustrators: Volume I (1869–1875)* (Troy, N.Y.: Whitston Publishing Company, 1986), 132–48 (the latter contains several errors). Below are the thirty-three "borrowed" illustrations (listed by chapter:page in the present edition) whose source has been identified: 4:27 = Richardson, 607; 5:30 = Richardson, 295 (portion only); 9:56 = Richardson, 231; 12:83 = Richardson, 246; 13:92 = Green, frontispiece; 13:93 = Green, frontispiece; 14:98 = Green, facing 343; 17:121 = J. Henri Browne, 148; 19:126 = Richardson, 495 (portion only); 20:136 = J. Henri Browne, 322; 24:163 = Richardson, 203; 26:177 = Richardson, 511 (portion only); 30:198 = Richardson, 74; 31:210 = Knox, 239; 34:224 = Richardson, 83 (portion only, altered); 36:232 = J. Ross Browne 1869, 532; 36:234 = Richardson, 502; 36:235 = Richardson, 368; 37:239 = J. Ross Browne 1869, 289 (altered); 38:244 = J. Ross Browne 1869, 438 (altered); 43:281 = J. Ross Browne 1869, 408 (altered); 43:283 = Richardson, 372; 44:286 = J. Ross Browne 1869, 505 (portion only, altered and reversed; signed "R.B."); 44:290 = J. Ross Browne 1869, 489 (portion only, altered; signed "R.B.");

Roughing It included some twenty-five illustrations for which no previous publication has yet been found, but which are likely to have been
taken from standard or stock sources, rather than drawn and engraved specifically for the book.

In early June, with the first fifty-one chapters now in hand, Orion presumably read the manuscript through for the first time, and in mid-June
wrote his brother praising it. Clemens replied on 21 June: "Am very glad,
indeed, you think so well of the book. I mean to make it a good one in spite
of everything—then the illustrations will do the rest. When the prospectus is out I believe Bliss will sell 50,000 copies before the book need be
actually issued."[177] Orion's comments are lost, but it was almost certainly
he who wrote the following squib in the July *American Publisher:* "A
NEW BOOK BY MARK TWAIN.—The American Publishing Company, of
Hartford, has in hand manuscript for a new book by Mark Twain. It is a
lively account of travel and a stirring recital of adventures in the Far West.
He was miner and reporter, and had some experiences, which, though sober reality, will tax credulity."[178] This last reference suggests that Orion
had read at least as far as chapters 40 and 41, about the blind lead. David
Gray, on the other hand, probably did not have a chance to read the manuscript, although on 20 July he published a description that must reflect
Clemens's private remarks about it—albeit inaccurately: "Mark Twain's
new book will be published by the American Publishing Company, of
Hartford, Connecticut. It will describe a journey to California in the
'flush times' of 1849, or scenes in the early history of the Golden State,
with probably much piquant personal matter. It is intended to serve as a
companion volume to 'Innocents Abroad.'"[179]

Despite this talk about publication, Clemens was well aware that he
had still not completed his manuscript. On 27 June, therefore, he had Olivia write to Mrs. Fairbanks, postponing their planned July visit to Cleveland: "Mr. Clemens feels that it will be a month or six weeks before his
book will be finished." Clemens himself added an apologetic postscript:
"I have lost so much time that I am obliged to give it up. This book has
been dragging along just 12 months, now, & I am *so* sick & tired of it. If I
were to chance another break or another move before I finish it I fear I
never *should* get it done."[180] Orion was conscious of the same problem,

---

46:302 = Richardson, 279 (portion only, altered); 48:319 = J. Ross Browne 1869,
500 (altered; signed "R.B."); 50:338=Knox, 20 (also in *Innocents*, 64); 52:358 =
Richardson, 377 (altered); 54:370 = Richardson, 436 (portion only); 54:375 =
Knox, 337; 66:456 = Evans, 113; 67:465 = Richardson, 216; 77:531 = Richardson, 487 (altered).

[177]SLC to Orion and Mary E. (Mollie) Clemens, 21 June 71, CU-MARK†.

[178]*American Publisher,* July 71, 4.

[179]"Personal," Buffalo *Courier,* 20 June 71, 1.

[180]Olivia L. Clemens and SLC to Mary Mason Fairbanks, 27 June 71, *MTMF,* 154
n. 3.

and in late June wrote his brother asking when to expect the next installment of printer's copy. Clemens replied on 2 July: "My MSS? Shall bring
it there myself before long. Say 2 to 4 weeks hence. Am just finishing
Chapter 56. Have already nearly MS enough, but am still writing—intend
to cut & cull liberally."[181] Chapter 56 would become chapter 59, about his
adventure with a San Francisco beggar. If he was still writing the chapters
in sequence, he must have written chapter 57 (San Francisco pioneers), 58
(the earthquake in San Francisco), and 59 between 30 June and 2 July.[182]
Even so, he did *not* have "nearly MS enough" to complete his book: he was
still some 450 pages short of the 1800 he thought he needed. Not for the
last time did his eagerness to be done mislead him about where he stood.
Orion replied on 4 July:

> I am glad you are going ahead on the book. Some of the artists' drafts for the
> pictures have come. I told Frank to take the tree out of Carson and put the auction-
> eer on the horse. He said he would take the tree out, but people here wouldn't un-
> derstand the idea of an auctioneer on a horse. Another has him taking his rider over
> a pile of telegraph poles—another bucking—and another going through a gate, rak-
> ing his rider off with the top beam. He is a ragged looking horse.[183]

The drawings Orion mentioned here were for chapter 24 (the Mexican
plug), which was eventually included almost in its entirety in the prospectus. Frank Bliss, who was presumably helping his father prepare the book,
followed Orion's advice, despite his concern that eastern readers would
not understand the auctioneer's being seated on a horse. No tree appears
in any of the pictures of Carson; one illustration shows the horse bucking;
and another shows him taking his rider over a post-and-rail fence.[184] Only
the drawing of the horse "going through a gate, raking his rider off with the
top beam" was discarded. It is apparent that the Blisses and Orion were
passing judgment on preliminary drawings, before they were sent off to be
engraved.

Three days later (on 7 July), Bliss replied to Clemens's letter of 21 June:

---

[181]SLC to Orion Clemens, 2 July 71, CU-MARK, in *MTLP*, 67–68.

[182]Before 10 July, Clemens probably wrote as far as chapter 61 or 62. Like chapter
59, chapter 61 (Dick Baker and his cat, Tom Quartz) had just been rehearsed in the
"third lecture," as he explained to Mrs. Fairbanks on 29 June:

> I call it "Reminiscences of some Un-Commonplace Characters I have Chanced to Meet." It tells
> a ˌpersonalˌ memory or so of Artemus Ward; ~~Riley~~ Blucher, an eccentric, big-hearted newspaper
> man; the King of the Sandwich Islands; Dick Baker, California Miner, & his wonderful cat; Dᵣ
> Jackson & the Guides; the Emperor Norton, a pathetic San Francisco lunatic; Blucher & our
> Washington landlady, a story I told in the Galaxy; ~~the~~ ˌaˌ grand oriental absolute monarch, the
> Rajah of Borneo; ~~the~~ our interview with the Emperor of Russia, about as I told it before—didn't
> alter it ˌ(a great deal)ˌ because it always "took" on the platform in that shape; & Blucher's curi-
> ous adventure with a beggar. . . .
>
> Of course you can't tell much about the lecture from this, but see what a splendid field it
> offers, & you know what a fascination there is in *personal* matters, & what a charm the *narra-
> tive* form carries with it. (SLC to Mary Mason Fairbanks, 29 June 71, CSmH, in *MTMF,* 155–56)

[183]Orion Clemens to SLC, 4 July 71, CU-MARK.

[184]See pages 159, 160, 162.

Thanks for your contributions   I have been sick 10 days, flat on my back, much of the time—& feel hard yet. . . . Have got the engravings mill driving—& shall make a merry book of it   And now, would like all the Mss. you have to be able to select subjects for *full page engravings*—want all I can of those to go in the ~~book~~ ˎprospectusˎ— And now another thing we have said nothing about. What is to be the title— This is a matter of some importance you know, & necessary for the Prospectus, unless we say we dont know it yet & call it the *"Unnamed"* & wait for developments, to christen it—

Let me know your wishes early as possible— Shall have prospectus ready early as possible to get the cuts ready, & make a sweep of the board—this fall— This & Beecher's Life of Christ—will have the field & I'll bet *we win*—[185]

This letter confirms that some large part of chapters 1–23 was already in production, since with the "engravings mill driving," Bliss would soon be able to begin the typesetting. He was eager to have the subjects for full-page illustrations chosen and the plates completed, since the time required for that, rather than for typesetting, would determine when the prospectus could be done ("Shall have prospectus ready early as possible to get the cuts ready"). Clemens replied in his turn on 10 July:

I heard you were sick, & am glad you are getting better again.

What terms did you arrive at with Routledge? . . .

Tomorrow I will fix up & forward as much MS as I have on hand. Some of it is tip-top.

I am now waiting a day or two till I get my old Sandwich Island notes together, for I want to put in 4 or 5 chapters about the Islands for the benefit of New England—& the world. When that is finished I shall come on & we will cull & cut down the MS & sock the book into the press. I think it will be a book worth reading, duly aided by the pictures. I am not scared about the result. It will sell.

I think of calling it

FLUSH TIMES
in the
SILVER MINES,
& other Matters.

=====

A PERSONAL NARRATIVE.

=====

By Mark Twain.
(Saml. L. Clemens.)

How does it strike you? Offer a suggestion, if one occurs to you.

Good! We'll run the tilt with Beecher.[186]

It remains uncertain just how many more chapters, if any, Clemens did "fix up & forward" after writing this letter. But this fourth batch probably contained only what became chapters 54–57, plus chapters 76 (Maui's Iao Valley and Haleakala) and 78 (Clemens's first lecture in San Francisco).

---

[185]Elisha Bliss, Jr., to SLC, 7 July 71, CU-MARK. The first volume of Henry Ward Beecher's two-volume *Life of Jesus, the Christ* would be published in September 1871 by another subscription house, J. B. Ford and Company of New York ("Literary," Cleveland *Leader*, 20 Sept 71, 2).

[186]SLC to Elisha Bliss, Jr., 10 July 71, OClRC†.

Chapters 76 and 78 must have been submitted at this time (if not sooner), out of sequence, for both were well represented in the prospectus, albeit as chapters 73 and 75.[187] The presence of a shared typographical feature also strongly suggests that chapters 1–57, 76, and 78 were in Bliss's hands substantially *before* the remaining chapters (58–75, 77, and 79): they all appear in the book with headings in type size A, while all the remaining chapter headings are in type size B.

CHAPTER LXXVI.   CHAPTER LXXVII.
TYPE SIZE A   TYPE SIZE B

This difference was clearly inadvertent, the result of using different type-setters for the two sets of chapters, or of using the same typesetters, but only after a long interval, so that they forgot (or were unable for other reasons) to use the same size type in the second set as they had in the first.

Clemens's letter of 10 July also makes it apparent that his intention even then was to include only a relatively small number of chapters on the Sandwich Islands—"4 or 5" at the end of a narrative principally devoted to "flush times" in Nevada. Back in December he had indicated that he still thought of the Sandwich Islands as the subject for a book he intended to write: "I am going to do up the Islands & Harris. They have 'kept' 4 years, & I guess they will keep 2 or 3 longer."[188] Presumably over the next three weeks in July, he culled his own notebooks and scrapbooks for possible material. He almost certainly made use of the printer's copy he had already prepared in 1866–67 from his Sacramento *Union* letters for a book on the Sandwich Islands, which he had submitted—unsuccessfully—for publication. And he ultimately included not "4 or 5" but fifteen chapters on the Sandwich Islands—all but four of them based on his original letters to the *Union*, clippings of which he pasted up and revised to serve as printer's copy.[189] Only about one-fifth of the material published in the twenty-five *Union* letters was used in the book: twelve letters were not used at all, while portions ranging from one-sixth to four-fifths were extracted from the remaining thirteen. Clemens probably wrote very little new material for the Sandwich Islands chapters, relying instead on the work he had done in 1866–67. The unusual number of simple errors in these chapters in the first edition also suggests that they were rather hurriedly prepared. By the time Clemens had chosen the material for them, it

---

[187]The prospectus also included the full-page engraving entitled "GOING INTO THE MOUNTAINS," which appears in chapter 69 (page 479) but has no specific relation to its text. It was almost certainly prepared at the same time as the full-page illustration in chapter 76 entitled "A VIEW IN THE IAO VALLEY" (page 521): it appears to be drawn by the same artist (Williams), and could illustrate chapter 76 just as well as it does chapter 69.

[188]SLC to Albert Francis Judd, 20 Dec 70, MS facsimile, CtY-BR†.

[189]See *L2*, 3–4, 48, 49 n. 2. The four chapters set in or describing the Sandwich Islands but not based on Sacramento *Union* letters are 70 (Greeley's letter), 75 (trip into Kilauea crater), 76 (Maui's Iao Valley and Haleakala), and 77 (the liar Markiss).

was clearer than it had been on 10 July that "Flush Times in the Silver Mines" was no longer an appropriate title. On 3 August, just days before Clemens arrived in Hartford, Bliss copyrighted another possibility, "The Innocents at Home," which served as the interim title for several weeks.[190]

On 2 or 3 August, Clemens left Elmira for New York, where he stayed briefly before taking the train to Hartford on about 5 August.[191] He probably brought with him all the remaining printer's copy—some 460 equivalent pages—except for those few chapters he would add in August, or even later. He remained in Hartford for almost the entire month, working on proofs for some portion of the early chapters (possibly only those chosen for the prospectus), and revising the printer's copy for chapters not yet sent to the illustrators or typesetters. On 10 August, five days after setting to work, he summarized his progress for Olivia:

> I wrote a splendid chapter today, for the middle of the book. I admire the book more & more, the more I cut & slash & lick & trim & revamp it. But you'll be getting impatient, now, & so I am going to begin tonight & work day & night both till I get through. It is a tedious, arduous job shaping ~~so~~ such a mass of MS for the press. It took me two months to do it for the Innocents. But this is another sight easier job, because it is so much better literary work—so much more acceptably written. It takes 1800 pages of MS to make this book?—& that is just what I have got—or rather, I have got 1,830. *I* thought that just a little over 1500 pages would be enough & that I could leave off all the Overland trip—& what a pity I can't.[192]

The "splendid chapter" has been conjecturally identified as chapter 53 (Jim Blaine's ram story).[193] The calculated pages in FIGURE 2 correspond

---

[190]The official memorandum of this copyrighted title, dated 3 August 1871, is numbered 7222B (CtHMTH). Clemens's original choice for a title was, however, made public—probably through the biographical data he supplied to the editors of the eighth edition of *Men of the Time: A Dictionary of Contemporaries, Containing Biographical Notices of Eminent Characters of Both Sexes* (227), published by George Routledge and Sons in 1872. John Camden Hotten's "Mark Twain: A Sketch of His Life," published in *Choice Humorous Works of Mark Twain* (1873) and dated 12 March 1873, said that *Roughing It* "was first announced under the title of 'Flush Times in the Silver Mines, and Other Matters'" (xxxviin). The title copyrighted by Bliss (and very likely suggested by him) was retained for the second volume of the Routledge edition, and was even mistakenly used in a few advertisements and news items about the American edition of the book.

[191]"Home News," New York *Tribune*, 4 Aug 71, 8; "Personal," New York *Evening Express*, 5 Aug 71, 3.

[192]SLC to Olivia L. Clemens, 10 Aug 71, CU-MARK, in *LLMT*, 159. This statement is the first and only time Clemens suggested that it would take 1500, rather than 1800, pages of manuscript to make a 600-page book. Apart from that error, his numbers are consistent with his earliest statement about his progress, especially if he regarded the "Overland trip" as comprising the first 180 pages of manuscript. For on 21 September 1870, having written 180 pages, he indicated he had "about 1500 more to write" (see page 812).

[193]Among the "Sandwich Islands notes" Clemens could have reviewed in the last three weeks of July was the following entry in one of his 1866 notebooks:

> Brown attempts to entertain company (in accordance with advice received from me,) ~~& is now~~ & accompanied by gaping & stretching of the company tells interminable story—something like Dan's old ram,)—& when abused ~~for~~ by me says it is *just* my style, & instances [*illeg-*

exactly to Clemens's own statement: when he arrived in Hartford with his final chapters he had a total of 1806 equivalent pages (1488 real pages); his new chapter added 24 pages, bringing the total to 1830 equivalent pages (1512 real pages). This amount of material would still not, as it turned out, be enough for a 600-page book—partly because of revisions Clemens would soon make in the first fifteen chapters, but chiefly because his es timates of the equivalence between printer's copy and book pages were too high (overcorrected from his estimate for *Innocents*). The need for more copy, however, would become apparent to him, and to Bliss, only as he worked through the proofs during August, and even somewhat later that fall.

It was probably during August that Clemens read proofs for chapters 1– 25—or at least the chapters in this section that were needed for the pro spectus. His intention to "cull & cut down the MS," especially in the "Overland trip," was not entirely relinquished, for he evidently decided at last to remove the chapter he had wanted to tear up back in March (then chapter 7). FIGURE 1 illustrates the revisions in chapters 7–9 which were set in motion by this deletion, made after the early chapters were in type. Clemens probably wrote and inserted the anecdote about Eckert and the cocoanut-eating cat after the Bemis episode, which was now chapter 7 (rather than chapter 8), at least in part so that the pony-express passage could begin (instead of end) what was now chapter 8. But in order to make chapter 8 a normal length (five, rather than three, book pages), he divided chapter 9 so that the opening passage, about Scott's Bluffs Pass, now ended chapter 8.[194] Chapter 9 was thereby reduced to about three-fourths its orig inal size, while the chapter numbering remained intact. That these changes were made only after the first twelve or so chapters were typeset is indicated by at least two things: (a) the absence of the Eckert episode from the analytical Contents, even though the other changes in chapter division were incorporated there, and (b) the typesetters' failure to change the Pra folio numbers (77–78) to their correct book pages (62–63) in the Bemis incident, even though the Eckert episode (68–69), which now fol lowed Bemis, was correctly paged.[195] Also in August, presumably, Clem-

---

ible] gaping over my trip across plains in overland stage—says that when I got to ~~Jules~~ Julesburg Mrs. C. left, to Fort Laramie, Mrs. W. left; to Wind River Mountains & that remarkable circum stance of the Indians shooting Pony Express rider, Mr. G. left—Salt Lake City Mr. B left—Sac ramento Mrs. L. left—(*N&J1*, 154)

[194]The discarded printer's copy page numbered 423, originally inscribed as a chapter opening, contains a passage that is very similar in wording to the passage that begins the Scott's Bluffs section (see page 52). This curious fact suggests that the page originally began chapter 9 before being set aside; then it was numbered 423 and used briefly in what became chapter 18; and finally it was discarded alto gether. The deleted chapter number on the page could even have been inscribed first as a "9," then altered to "19," and finally to "20."

[195]The Eckert episode was added in time to have an illustration prepared, how ever, and its caption, "A WONDERFUL LIE," was included in the List of Illustrations for Pra.

ens went on to revise chapters 13–15, about the Mormons, reducing the amount of "dry history" in chapter 13, and eliminating chapter 15 altogether, although not at this point with the intention of printing the excised material in appendixes. This last change did affect the chapter numbering in a way that was not corrected in Pra: it caused parts of chapters 15, 16, 21, 23, and 24 to be anachronistically identified there as chapters 16, 17, 22, 24, and 25.

Clemens no doubt made other changes in the text of the early chapters. The running headline on the last page of chapter 1 ("HERMAPHRODITE STEAMER") may refer to a remark that was cut out at the last moment (this chapter exactly fills its last page in the first edition). Similarly, the last subheading in the Contents for chapter 3 ("Warning to Experimenters") may refer to a passage that is no longer present, suggesting that the chapter was revised in proof without a corresponding revision in the Contents.

It may also have been in August that Clemens added chapter 36 (Nevada quartz mills) to his manuscript—in this case, before the surrounding chapters had been typeset.[196] Clemens must have added roughly twenty pages to his manuscript somewhere between chapters 15 and 46, for if he did not, the calculated pages for chapter 46 would be too high to include the page number ("968") on the draft manuscript page from that chapter.[197] That the added pages came in chapter 36, however, is only a reasonable guess. No illustrations were specifically drawn for it: three of its four engravings were demonstrably reused from other works, and the fourth, a tailpiece, appears to be a stock engraving.

Late in August, or sometime in the next few months, Clemens must also have added three more chapters to his manuscript, somewhere between chapter 46 and chapter 76, since chapters 73 and 75 in the prospectus became chapters 76 and 78 in the book. The most likely candidates are chapter 49 (shooting affrays in Virginia City), which is made up largely of *Enterprise* clippings, and which lacks any illustration except for a stock tailpiece; chapter 52 (mining statistics and techniques), which is also based on clippings, and which appears to be illustrated exclusively from borrowed engravings (the source for only one of its three engravings has actually been found); and chapter 75 (the exploration of Kilauea crater), whose four engravings include at least two stock drawings, and possibly three. Chapter 75, which is not based on a Sandwich Islands letter to the *Union,* may have been the sketch originally called "Fearful Adventure" in Clemens's draft table of contents for the sketchbook, written no later than January 1871. If so, then the piece was available in January, but presum-

---

[196]The addition of this chapter would have compensated, in the sequence of chapter numbers, for the loss of manuscript chapter 15.

[197]FIGURE 2 shows that if chapter 36 (comprising twenty-two pages of manuscript) had been part of the printer's copy from the start, then chapter 46 would have begun on calculated page 975, rather than on 953, and thus could not have included discarded page 968.

ably not included until, like the other added chapters, there was little time to commission drawings for it.[198]

By 17 August, Clemens had probably reached the proof for chapter 20 (Horace Greeley and Hank Monk), for on that day he wrote to Greeley:

> I am here putting my new book on California &c., to press, & find that in it I have said in positive words that the famous ~~episode~~ Hank Monk anecdote ~~has no truth in it~~ refers to an episode *which never occurred.*
>
> I got this from a newspaper editor, who said he got it from you. I never knew of his telling a lie—but to make *sure* will you please endorse his statement if you can—or deny it if you must?,—so that I can leave my remark as it is; or change it if truth requires.,[199]

Clemens had made the statement he referred to in a footnote at the end of chapter 20—a footnote he had probably supplied at the behest of Joseph Goodman, when Goodman had read his manuscript back in March and April.[200] It is not known how, or even whether, Greeley replied to Clemens's question.

On 19 August Clemens heard from his friend Adolph Sutro, who was planning to leave for Europe later in the month, but would be in New York for some days prior to departure. Clemens wrote him from Hartford:

> Got your letter to-day. When do you sail? Can't you run up here for one day? I'm awful busy on my new book on Nevada & California. And by the way you might tell me something about the tunnel that would make an interesting page, perhaps. It was about another matter that I wanted to see you principally & very particularly, but one might as well kill various birds with one stone.[201]

---

[198]See *ET&S1*, 578. In 1972 the editors of *Roughing It* argued that "a Canadian piracy possibly issued in July 1872" was "probably set from proofs" of the first American edition, smuggled to Toronto "in December 1871" before the book was in its final form, and that because this piracy "lacks the appendixes and eight chapters of the first edition (22, 36, 45, 49, 52, 71, 72, and 77)," it is possible to infer that "Mark Twain deleted several chapters between the phases of the prospectus and the piracy, only to restore or replace them before publication of the first American edition" (*RI 1972*, 18–20). If this Canadian edition were set from proofs, its missing chapters might well correspond to the chapters that Clemens added in August 1871 or later that fall. It is tempting evidence because, on independent grounds, we conjecture that chapters 36, 49, 52, 53, and 75 (the first three of which are absent from the Canadian piracy) were late additions. But significant problems arise with this Canadian evidence. (a) Collation shows that the Canadian edition was not set from proofs, but from a late state of the first American edition (Af), the earliest known example of which appeared in 1877. (b) The specific copy of the Canadian edition which was thought to have been published in July 1872 quotes a review of *A Tramp Abroad* which appeared in the London *Athenaeum* for 24 April 1880. (c) The typesetting in that copy is a reimpression of the type used in another Canadian edition issued by Belford and Company, also in 1880 (see the Description of Texts, 616). So the "significant variants" of the Canadian edition do not derive "from a form of the text prior to that of the first American edition," and therefore cannot help to identify any authorial revision of the text (*RI 1972*, 636 n. 2).

[199]SLC to Horace Greeley, 17 Aug 71, NN†.

[200]For Goodman's advice, see the explanatory note at 136n.1–2.

[201]SLC to Adolph Sutro, 19 Aug 71, JI2†. The other "matter" that Clemens had "principally & very particularly" in mind remains unidentified.

Clemens may have just drafted chapter 52, on mining statistics and techniques, which prompted him to ask Sutro for information about his tunnel. Sutro must have telegraphed Clemens shortly after arriving at the
Gilsey House on 22 August, for two days later Clemens telegraphed him
there: "When do you sail? how long shall you remain in NY when leave &
whither[?]" Sutro evidently replied that he sailed on 30 August, for on 25
August Clemens again telegraphed: "All right will see you in New York
before you sail." Clemens almost certainly met with Sutro in New York
between 26 and 28 August, and returned to Hartford almost immediately,
telegraphing from there on 29 August, "How long will tunnell be when
finished," a question that assumes a previous conversation.[202]

At any rate, it was from Hartford on 30 August that Clemens found himself "peremptorily called home by sickness" in his family. The next day he
wrote Orion from Elmira: "We have scarcely any hope of the baby's recovery," although his fears soon proved groundless. On 2 September, the Hartford *Courant* reported that Clemens had just spent "a month" in Hartford,
and that he had left "a few days ago" after "attending to matters connected
with the publication of his new book, 'The Innocents at Home,' which is
to be brought out by the American Publishing company of this city."[203]

It remains uncertain exactly how much of the book Clemens saw in
proof by the end of August, but it could not have been much more than
chapters 1–25. Three months later, on 6 December, Bliss reported that
type had been set only up through page 300 (the second page of chapter
43), but since portions of chapters 46, 51, 76, and 78 had by then already
appeared in Pra, they might have been ready for proofreading as early as
August. Bliss's statement indicates, however, that while Clemens may
have added chapter 52 in August, he did not supply the concluding footnote to it until sometime in December, for it reflects a communication
from Sutro received after Clemens departed Hartford: "Since the above
was in type, I learn from an official source that the above figure is too
high. . . . The tunnel will be some eight miles long, and will develop astonishing riches."[204] This note, which Clemens must have supplied on

---

[202]"Morning Arrivals," New York *Evening Express*, 22 Aug 71, 3; SLC to Adolph
Sutro: 24 Aug 71 and 25 Aug 71, NhD†; 29 Aug 71, NvHi†. Olivia Clemens, accompanied by her sister-in-law, Ida C. Langdon, and one of her cousins (not otherwise
identified) were in New York by 26 August, which may explain why Clemens himself is not listed at any New York hotel during this interval: he presumably joined
Olivia in her room ("Morning Arrivals," New York *Evening Express*, 26 Aug 71, 3).

[203]SLC to Mortimer D. Leggett, 6 Oct 71, DNA†; SLC to Orion Clemens, 31 Aug
71, CU-MARK†; "Brief Mention," Hartford *Courant*, 2 Sept 71, 2.

[204]Page 360n. Sutro later thanked Clemens, probably in a letter written on 30
June 1872, for the "favorable publicity given the tunnel" (Robert E. Stewart and
Mary Frances Stewart, *Adolph Sutro: A Biography* [Berkeley: Howell-North Books,
1962], 105). The present location of Sutro's letter and its full contents are not
known. Its date has been established by a letter that Clemens wrote to Sutro on 11
June 1872, which was docketed "Ans June 30/72" (ODaU†).

proofs sent to him on his lecture tour, may be usefully contrasted with a revision in chapter 27, where he inserted a parenthetical addition rather than a footnote, presumably before the passage was typeset. On the second page of chapter 27, William Clagett is identified parenthetically as "now member of Congress from Montana," a fact that could not have been added before 9 August, when the election results were first published in the New York *Tribune*.[205]

Langdon soon recovered from the immediate threat to his health, and much of September was given over to other matters, including Clemens's two visits to Washington to patent his elastic garment strap, which he had invented in August while working on his manuscript. Clemens was in Washington on 7–9 September, returned to Hartford a day or two later, and then went on to Elmira on the afternoon of 13 September.[206] On 15 September he asked Redpath to send his lecture schedule to Hartford, because he and his family planned to "take up our permanent residence" there on "the last day of this month," and because he had "to read proof half the winter."[207] The letter implies that he did not expect to complete the proofreading before he went on tour in mid-October.

On 17 September, Clemens and Olivia went to Buffalo "to pack up for Hartford."[208] From Buffalo, on 19 or 20 September, he again went to Washington in pursuit of his patent, returning to Buffalo by 22 September. Interviewed by the Washington *National Republican* just outside the patent office, Clemens seized the occasion to remind a recent correspondent of their memorable first meeting:

[Mark Twain] says that Horace Greeley first put the idea into his head, and set him to thinking on the abstruse subject of suspenders. When he first saw the veteran editor the extraordinary set of his trowsers, half in and half out of his boots, attracted his attention, and he at once set to work to see if he could not devise some plan of making them hang more gracefully. He thinks that he has succeeded, and that if Mr. Greeley will only use "Twain's patent suspenders" his pantaloons will in future become the envy and admiration of the New York *World*, and that Mr. Greeley will have no occasion, during the long life that is before him, to ask the *World* editors to discuss his arguments and let his pantaloons alone.[209]

Back in Buffalo, Clemens reported that he and Olivia were still "packing our furniture & shipping it to Hartford & we are in a mess—house upside

---

[205]Page 180; "Political. Republican Victory in Montana. Wm. H. Claggett Elected Delegate to Congress," New York *Tribune*, 9 Aug 71, 4.

[206]"Personal," Washington (D.C.) *National Republican*, 8 Sept 71, 2. The document Clemens filed for the patent is dated 9 September 1871. Orion Clemens to Mary E. (Mollie) Clemens, 14 Sept 71, CU-MARK, indicates that Clemens had gone to Elmira the previous afternoon.

[207]SLC to James Redpath, 15 Sept 71, NN-B†.

[208]SLC to Orion Clemens, 17 Sept 71, CU-MARK†.

[209]"Mark Twain Takes Out a Patent—Why He Did It," Washington (D.C.) *National Republican*, 21 Sept 71, 2. The reference to the New York *World*'s comments on Greeley has not been explained.

down—my wife sick—can't leave her bed for perhaps a week yet—& yet we must take possession of our house in Hartford Oct. 1.["210](#)" These various activities suggest that little proofreading was possible during most of September, even if proofs were available.

By 1 October Clemens was in Hartford and, though preoccupied with other matters, in a better position to examine proofs when and if they were ready. On 3 October, Orion wrote to Mollie that Clemens was extremely busy, and would "be over in a day or two":

> Besides his renting and moving, all the sale of his house, the Langdon business, his lectures soon to commence, and his book just going into the printer's hands. Isn't that enough to bother one poor mortal?
>
> I saw his artist (Williams) to-night climbing a lamp post, and offering to go to the top, for the amusement of some loafers in front of Tim Dooley's Saloon. Bliss told me this morning that Williams was on a spree.[211]

Orion's remark about the "book just going into the printer's hands" must refer to some portion of the text following chapter 24 which had been illustrated and was now going to the typesetters.

On 9 October, Clemens asked Redpath for details about his lecture schedule: "Send along the first end of my list & let me see where I am to talk. Please send a copy to my publisher, *E. Bliss Jr. 149 Asylum st Hartford*—for I must read proof for the next month or so."[212] Clemens's estimate—that he would finish proofreading by mid-November at the latest—was optimistic, for there were certainly problems, even before he left Hartford on 13 October to begin his tour. Before leaving, he probably settled the question of the title, since that was necessary for the prospectus, and he may well have seen some further proof.[213] On 19 October, after only six days (and three lectures), Clemens wrote Bliss from Wilkes-Barre, Pennsylvania:

> I brought the desert chapter away with me, to write it up—but it is no use; I am driven to death, with travel, lecturing & entertaining committees. It will be two weeks before I can get a chance to write up this chapter. I remember the heavy work it was to write it before, & I wish that man had the MS stuffed in his bowels that ~~wrote~~ ‚lost‚ it. If time presses, just leave the whole chapter out. It is all we can do.[214]

---

[210]SLC to James Redpath, 22 Sept 71, courtesy of Todd M. Axelrodt.

[211]Orion Clemens to Mary E. (Mollie) Clemens, 3 Oct 71, CU-MARK. Mollie was in Elmira, taking the "water cure."

[212]SLC to James Redpath, 9 Oct 71, CtHMTHt.

[213]In 1882, Clemens recalled that he had left the choice of a title up to the publisher:

I never write a title until I finish a book, and then I frequently don't know what to call it. I usually write out anywhere from a half dozen to two dozen and a half titles, and the publisher casts his experienced eye over them and guides me largely in the selection. That's what I did in the case of "Roughing It," and, in fact, it has always been my practice. ("An 'Innocent' Interviewed. Mark Twain Pays a Visit to St. Louis," St. Louis *Post-Dispatch*, 12 May 82, 2, in Budd, 37–39)

[214]SLC to Elisha Bliss, Jr., 19 Oct 71, courtesy of Robert Daley, in *MTLP*, 68.

Clemens referred not to chapter 20 (with its allusion to the Great American Desert),[215] but to chapter 18, which describes crossing "an '*alkali*' desert" west of Salt Lake City. It is apparent that the illustrators or the typesetters had lost part of the manuscript for this chapter, and that Bliss had asked Clemens to rewrite it, relying on what had survived.[216] (Clemens's suggestion that Bliss leave out the "whole chapter" if the attempt to rewrite it failed shows that not all of it had been lost.) Despite his temptation to give up, Clemens soon did rewrite the text. Since in the opening paragraph he correctly recalled at least one detail from Orion's journal— that the stage station was "forty-five miles from the beginning of the desert, and twenty-three from the end of it"—it seems likely that this passage was in the portion Clemens "brought . . . away" with him. The rest of the chapter could have been recreated from memory. Toward the end Clemens even offered a jocular excuse for a "narrative" that might "seem broken and disjointed, in places."[217] And there were other signs of strain: the chapter contains only one illustration, a tailpiece that is a stock engraving, suggesting that the text was lost before it could be illustrated. Finally, the chapter heading was clearly set by a typesetter who had either forgotten, or never knew, how to match the letterspacing of the other chapter headings, even though he used the correct size of type ("SIZE A"). Such details imply that the chapter was typeset much later than the surrounding chapters. Compare the letterspacing in the headings for chapters 17, 18, and 19:

CHAPTER XVII.

CHAPTER XVIII.

CHAPTER XIX.

Two weeks into his lecture tour, on 31 October, Clemens wrote Olivia from Milford, Massachusetts, that he had received no mail at the previous day's lecture site, Brattleboro, Vermont: "I got no letters at Brattleboro. None had come. None in the post office, either. No proofs from Bliss. Brattleboro is unreliable, I guess." This statement may mean that he had received no proof at all since leaving on tour. On 8 November, he lectured in Hartford, and could have picked up (or delivered) proofs, although no indication has been found that he did either. He passed through Hartford

---

[215]Compare *MTLP*, 68 n. 1, and *RI 1972*, 18.

[216]Chapter 18 was the last chapter listed with a page number in the Contents for Pra. One more page of contents was included (listing chapters 19–27), but page numbers for its chapters had not been assigned.

[217]See pages 122, 124–25, 772.

again on 19 November, three days before the first copies of the prospectus came from the bindery on 22 November.[218] By 27 November, he had seen a copy, for he wrote Olivia:

> I think Bliss has gotten up the prospectus book with taste & skill. The selections are good, & judiciously arranged. He had a world of good matter to select from, though. This is a better book than the Innocents, & *much* better written. If the subject were less hackneyed it would be a great success. But when I come to write the Mississippi book, *then* look out! I will spend 2 months on the river & take notes, & I bet you I will make a standard work.[219]

About ten days later, probably on 8 December, Clemens received a package from Bliss, who sent printed signatures instead of proofs:

> We send you all the parts of the book we have printed so far. We have set up to page 300—but plates not finished up yet. They are now finishing as we have begun to print— We are kept back—by here & there a cut not yet done— I could send you nothing except what I do unless I send my set of proofs which I cannot possibly spare— We have started presses & shall now have to finish up to keep them running— The electrotypers have not finished up as they like to shave down a bit at [a] time to make of equal thickness—[220]

Bliss had printed no more than eighteen signatures (since signature nineteen comprised pages 289–304), and probably fewer. He had typeset, but not yet printed, page 300 (the second page of chapter 43). His reason for not sending proofs seems somewhat specious: *why* was his own set the only one available? Perhaps by this late date he wanted to prevent Clemens from making further revisions, since that would interfere with keeping the presses "running."

Bliss's letter, and other evidence, have led to the inference that Clemens did not read proof for the last third of his book. The other evidence is the appearance in the first edition of some sixteen cases of terminal punctuation followed by a dash ("last word.—First word") between page 426 (in chapter 58) and page 532 (in chapter 74). The absence of this form of punctuation from any earlier part of the text has led to the conclusion that Clemens did not read or correct proof for any text beyond chapter 57—for if he had, he would surely have removed the superfluous dashes.[221] Termi-

---

[218]SLC to Olivia L. Clemens, 31 Oct 71, CU-MARK, in *LLMT,* 162; "Mark Twain's Lecture," Hartford *Courant,* 9 Nov 71, 2; Olivia L. Clemens to Robert M. Howland, 20 Nov 71, CU-MARK; APC, [73].

[219]SLC to Olivia L. Clemens, 27 Nov 71, CU-MARK, in *LLMT,* 166.

[220]Elisha Bliss, Jr., to SLC, 6 Dec 71, CU-MARK. Bliss placed some of the blame for delay on the "electrotypers"—that is, those responsible for producing electrotypes of the woodcuts, which they mounted on wood blocks and gradually "shaved down" to make precisely type high. Although he did not mention it, Bliss also copyrighted *Roughing It* in the name of the American Publishing Company (number 11568) on the same day he wrote Clemens, 6 December (Eugene R. Lehr of the Copyright Office, DLC, to Michael B. Frank, 29 Nov 1982, CU-MARK).

[221]"The confinement of such dashes to the portion of *Roughing It* after p. 378 [426 in the first edition] therefore rather suggests that the author corrected no proof for it, an implication supported by the chronology of his movements and the printing in late 1871 (see *MTLP,* p. 68)" (*RI 1972,* 628). The dash following terminal punc-

nal dashes, however, occur frequently in *The Innocents Abroad*, even in chapters for which we are certain that Clemens read proof, simply because the proofreader ignored his corrections. And in *Roughing It* the dashes occur in the same late chapters that have now been identified as a group by their anomalous "TYPE SIZE B" chapter headings (58–75, 77, 79). Therefore the terminal dashes are, in all likelihood, more evidence that the compositors for these late chapters were not instructed as carefully as the compositors for the early ones had been. In addition, Clemens's comments about two of the illustrations suggest that he did read at least some proof for chapters in the final third of his text.

In chapter 44 (on page 309 of the first edition) Clemens almost certainly added the following sentence in proof: "[My revenge will be found in the accompanying portrait.]" He referred to the "PORTRAIT OF MR. STEWART" that appeared on page 310 (page 289 of the present edition), which he probably first saw in page proof. Likewise, in chapter 54, he presumably added (or modified) the following sentence on first-edition page 392: "They always send a bill, like this below, pinned to the clothes." Here he referred to the untitled illustration of four Chinese characters (page 370 of this edition), which he probably also first saw in proof.[222] Since both references occurred on pages later than 300, and since Bliss said that he had set only up to page 300 by 6 December, it follows that Clemens saw and corrected proofs after that date, including at least one page that fell in the final third of the book (page 392 of the first edition).[223]

By early January Bliss had realized that the printer's copy was still not long enough to make what the first prospectus promised the reader, "Between 600 and 700 Octavo Pages."[224] The last page of the final chapter was only 570, and since Clemens was still on tour, there was no likelihood of his writing anything new. No documents have been found to tell us whether it was Bliss or Clemens who thought of adding appendixes to fill out the missing thirty pages. Either one could have suggested using the material that in August Clemens had removed from chapters 13 and 15 on

---

tuation at the right margin in Clemens's manuscript is now recognized as a device for justifying short lines. But the device was often misinterpreted even by Clemens's typesetters, who set both the period and the dash, even though the dash is meaningless except in the original lineation of his manuscript.

[222]It remains possible that Clemens's printer's copy originally called for a revenging "portrait" of Stewart, as well as something to represent a typical Chinese laundry bill. But on balance, his references to these illustrations seem much more like afterthoughts supplied in proof—responses to what Bliss had supplied.

[223]Even though Clemens made this last change some thirty pages before the first end-line dash, the "chronology of his movements" during December cannot establish that he failed to read proof for chapters 58 and beyond. He had planned from the outset to read proof while on lecture tour, and the changes to chapters 44 and 54 must have been made in December during that tour.

[224]The phrase occurs under "A New Book by a Well Known Author," in the publisher's announcement following the sample pages.

the Mormons, which was now reset in small (extract) type. The footnote referring the reader to appendixes A and B must also have been added at this time, in the blank space on the last page of chapter 14. For appendix C Clemens almost certainly supplied material he had already written, but then set aside. He may have drafted it while he was writing *Roughing It*, or while preparing the sketchbook, but he clearly did not include it in the original printer's copy. Appendix C is devoted to a relatively recent incident in Virginia City, and reprints a long article that first appeared in January 1870. Its relevance to the subject and period of *Roughing It* is at best remote, suggesting that it too was added solely to make the book longer: appendix C made the final page number 591. Accordingly, the revised prospectus (Prb), which came from the binders in late January, claimed that the volume would consist of "Nearly 600 Octavo Pages."[225]

The earliest known public announcement of the book with its correct title, probably based on the information in the recently published prospectus (Pra), appeared in the Buffalo *Courier* for 30 November:

—Mark Twain's forthcoming book is to be entitled "Roughing It," and will describe life in Nevada during the silver mining times, with a trip to the Sandwich Islands by way of an episode. It will be a companion volume to "The Innocents Abroad," and will contain between 600 and 700 pages, with several hundred engravings. It will be sold only by subscription.[226]

On 8 December, Clemens telegraphed Redpath that he had decided to "talk nothing but selections from my forth-coming book Roughing it, tried it last night suits me tip top."[227] Among the first to hear this evolving selection was David Gray, who described it on 9 December in the Buffalo *Courier:*

The subject of his lecture, scarcely a day old, was "Roughing It: Being Passages From My Forthcoming Book," and it promises to become in his hands perhaps the most interesting of his public performances. Gracefully deprecating the possible suspicion that he is out as a book canvasser, Mark proceeds in this lecture to cull from his unpublished volume a *melange* of passages—grave and gay, descriptive and humorous—which are in his very best style, and as varied and lively in their character as can be conceived. His pictures of the journey across the continent in stage-coach times; of the life in Nevada during the "flush" period of that territory's history, and of the strange personages he there encountered, are simply inimitable. The narrative branches off occasionally into one of those extraordinary and elaborate "yarns" for which he alone has a patent, and it encloses, also, frequent bits of word-painting which would make his fame as a serious speaker if he were not inveterately a humorist.[228]

---

[225]It is inconceivable that Bliss added these materials *without* consulting Clemens, who must therefore have been in touch with the publisher about his book even while on lecture tour—whether or not he managed to read proof for all the later chapters.

[226]"Literary Notes," Buffalo *Courier*, 30 Nov 71, 1.

[227]SLC to James Redpath and George L. Fall, 8 Dec 71, ODaU, in *MTL*, 1:193.

[228]"A New Lecture by Mark Twain," Buffalo *Courier*, 9 Dec 71, 2.

If *Roughing It* may be said to have evolved from the lecture called "Curiosities of California," it now gradually evolved back into a lecture much like what we know about its ancestor. On 10 December, Clemens wrote Mrs. Fairbanks:

> Am writing a new, tip-top lecture about California & Nevada—been at it all night—am still at it & pretty nearly dead with fatigue. Shall be studying it in the cars till midnight, & then sleep half the day in Toledo & study the rest. If I am in good condition there, I shall deliver it—but if I'm not just as bright as [a] dollar, shall talk A. Ward two or three nights longer & go on studying. Have already tried the new lecture in two villages, night before last & night before that—made a tip-top success in one, but was floored by fatigue & exhaustion of body & mind & made a dismal failure in the other—so now I am reconstructing & re-writing the thing & I'll *fetch* 'em next time.[229]

Bliss was no doubt eager to take advantage of the publicity that Clemens's new topic provided, and with prospectuses finally available, he was ready to enlist agents to sell the book.[230] On 11 December he began to advertise:

> "TO BOOK AGENTS."
> Mark Twain's new book is ready for canvassers. It is a companion volume to INNOCENTS ABROAD. Don't waste time on books no one wants, but take one people will stop you in the streets to subscribe for. "There is a time to laugh," and all who read this book will see clearly that time has come. For territory or circulars address AMERICAN PUBLISHING CO., Hartford, Conn.[231]

By 19 December, a more specific appeal for agents began to appear:

> Mark Twain's NEW BOOK is now ready for canvassers. It contains over 600 pages of reading matter, with 250 engravings, designed expressly for this work, by the best artists in the country. Agents now at work upon it are meeting with unparalleled

---

[229]SLC to Mary Mason Fairbanks, 10 Dec 71, CSmH, in *MTMF*, 157.

[230]Bliss also continued with his plan to advertise the book in the *American Publisher*. The pony-express passage had already appeared in May 1871. The first of seven additional excerpts, "My First Lecture" (from chapter 78), appeared in December, followed by "A Nabob's Visit to New York" (from chapter 46) in January 1872, and "Dollinger the Aged Pilot Man" (from chapter 51) the next month, coupled with a brief extract about Brigham Young's wives (from chapter 15). The March issue reprinted most of chapter 57. "Horace Greeley's Ride" (from chapter 20) appeared in April, and then, in June, "Mark Twain on the Mormons" (from chapter 15), which included the Mormon passage published in February. According to an introductory comment in the *Publisher*, "My First Lecture" was typeset from "advance sheets" of the book, "now in press." Collation indicates that the printer's copy for this passage and for the next three could have been proofs of A, or a copy of Prb. (All were included in Pra and Prb.) The last three extracts, published in March, April, and June, were set from the book itself. Thus, aside from the one about the pony express, all derived from A, contained no authorial revision, and have no textual authority.

[231]"'To Book Agents,'" Syracuse *Standard*, 4 Jan 72, 2; also in Elmira *Gazette*, 11 Jan 72, 4: both advertisements include the code "dec11," indicating that they were first printed on that day. The same advertisement also appeared in the Buffalo *Courier*, 14 Dec 71, 4, the New York *Independent* 24 (4 Jan 72): 8, and no doubt in numerous other newspapers as well.

success. Agent at Circleville, O., reports 25 orders in 2 days; one at Louisville, Ky., reports 175 orders in 8 days; one at Middletown, Conn., reports 200 orders in 12 days; one at Cincinnati, O., reports 250 orders in 12 days. Early applicants secure choice of territory. For circulars, terms, &c., address NETTLETON & CO., 161 Elm street, Cincinnati, Ohio.[232]

These figures show that canvassing began in Cincinnati as early as 7 December, the day after Bliss formally copyrighted the book. The orders were placed, of course, without any actual books in hand: the first bound books were not delivered until February.

Meanwhile, Clemens continued his lecture tour in various towns and cities of Michigan, Illinois, Indiana, Ohio, West Virginia, Pennsylvania, and Maryland. On 24 January 1872, just a day after the revised prospectus (Prb) issued from the bindery, he gave his *Roughing It* lecture at Steinway Hall in New York. The next day, his performance was described by a knowing but anonymous hand in the New York *Tribune:*

If there are those who fondly think that the popularity of the American humoristic school is on the decline, they would have been bravely undeceived by a visit to Steinway Hall last night. The most enormous audience ever collected at any lecture in New-York came together to listen to "Mark Twain's" talk on "Roughing It." Before the doors were opened $1,300 worth of tickets had been sold, and for some time before Mr. Clemens appeared the house was crammed in every part by an audience of over 2,000. A large number were turned away from the door, and after the close of the evening's entertainment the officers of the Library Association warmly urged Mr. Clemens to repeat his lecture for the benefit of those who were disappointed. It was not only financially that the lecture was successful. There was never seen in New-York an audience so obstinately determined to be amused. There was hardly a minute of silence during the hour. Peals of laughter followed every phrase, the solemn asseverations of the lecturer that his object was purely instructive and the investigation of the truth increasing the merriment. At several points of the lecture, especially the description of Mr. Twain's Mexican Plug, the Chamois of Nevada, and the Washoe Duel, the enjoyment of the audience was intemperate. A singular force and effectiveness was added to the discourse by the inimitable drawl and portentous gravity of the speaker. He is the finest living delineator of the true Pike accent, and his hesitating stammer on the eve of critical passages is always a prophecy—and hence, perhaps, a cause—of a burst of laughter and applause. He is a true humorist, endowed with that indefinable power to make men laugh which is worth, in current funds, more than the highest genius or the greatest learning.[233]

Clemens had no difficulty identifying the author of such praise:

The statements in this notice were made to me on the platform at the close of the lecture, by the President of the Mercantile Library Asso'n, while trying to have me repeat the lecture; and as Col. John Hay was the only other person listening, he necessarily wrote this notice & besides he is the only man in New York who can speak so authoritatively about "the true Pike accent."[234]

---

[232]"Wanted—Agents," Cincinnati *Gazette*, 19 Dec 71, 2. Since the book eventually contained more than 300 (not just 250) illustrations, this notice may signal how far along Bliss was in mid-December: the first-edition List of Illustrations indicates that illustration number 250 was on page 470, in chapter 65.

[233]"Mark Twain at Steinway Hall," New York *Tribune*, 25 Jan 72, 5.

[234]SLC to James Redpath, 26 Jan 72, American Art Association catalog, sale of 24–25 Nov 1924, lot 98.

7

The first copies of *Roughing It* came from the bindery on 30 January 1872, but were probably not released to agents for several weeks. On 8 February, the *Publishers' and Stationers' Weekly Trade Circular* reported the book "almost ready for publication." On the same day the Hartford *Courant* said it had "already reached a circulation of twenty thousand copies," meaning that so many subscriptions had been taken (none had yet been filled). On 13 February, Clemens gritted his teeth for Mrs. Fairbanks: "I killed a man this morning. He asked me when my book was coming out." A copy was deposited in the Library of Congress on 19 February, and publication was formally announced on 29 February.[235]

These final weeks of delay were probably a mistake, or at least unnecessary—the result of Bliss's failure to fully understand the British copyright law. The transatlantic arrangements for *Roughing It* had probably been worked out with Routledge as far back as July 1871, and Clemens's (and Bliss's) working relationship with Routledge was of even longer standing. In 1870, Bliss had cooperated with Routledge in publishing "the only authorized and unabridged edition" in the United States of Wood's *Uncivilized Races*, which Routledge had first issued in London in 1868–70. And Routledge had begun to court Clemens as early as 1868, hoping eventually to be named his *"only authorized London publishers."* The Routledge edition of *Roughing It* was to be the first result of that courtship, and it was soon followed by a series of Routledge "authorized" editions, all published in 1872, which included both *A Curious Dream; and Other Sketches* and *Mark Twain's Sketches*, as well as a revised edition of *The Innocents Abroad. Roughing It* would prove reasonably profitable for Routledge, but its importance to Clemens, who accepted a flat fee of only £37 ($185) for it, was chiefly as an answer to the English "piracy" of his books by John Camden Hotten.[236]

Collation shows that the Routledge edition of *Roughing It*, which appeared in two volumes, was typeset from proofs (or printed signatures) of the American edition (state Aa). The proofs were sent to London in at least two batches: the first in December 1871, and the last in January 1872. No effort was made to include the illustrations (although these were certainly present in the American proofs), and the Routledge text omitted the dedication to Calvin Higbie, as well as the three appendixes—further evidence that Clemens agreed to add the appendixes in January, too late even for the final batch of proofs. Since the dedication had appeared as early as November, in the first prospectus (Pra), Routledge may have omit-

---

[235]APC, [74]; *Weekly Trade Circular* 1 (8 Feb 72): 101, and 1 (29 Feb 72): 180; "Brief Mention," Hartford *Courant*, 8 Feb 72, 2; SLC to Mary Mason Fairbanks, 13 Feb 72, CSmH, in *MTMF*, 160; *BAL* 3337.

[236]*ET&S1*, 555, 590; Routledge Ledger Book 4:576–77, Routledge and Kegan Paul, London.

ted it because the proofs lacked some of the front matter, or because it would have made the first volume asymmetrical with the second. Collation establishes that Clemens did not alter the text, or provide any new material for the English edition—both things that he *did* soon do for the Routledge edition of *Innocents*, which he prepared in June and July 1872. Apart from the missing dedication and appendixes, there are fewer than forty variant substantives in the Routledge text—none of them authorial. Even the substitution of "d——d" for "bloody" (at 334.17) must be attributed to the English proofreader, since he was more likely than Clemens to know that "bloody" was more offensive than "damned," at least to a British reader. Although Clemens certainly gave his blessing to the English edition, its text is wholly derivative.

Chapters 1–45 appeared in volume 1, which was titled *Roughing It*, and chapters 46–79 appeared in volume 2, titled *The Innocents at Home*, perhaps at Bliss's or Clemens's suggestion. Volume 2 also included Routledge's text of the *Burlesque Autobiography* (tacked on at the end), presumably to help equalize the size of the two volumes—a sign that Routledge did not *omit* the appendixes, but instead set from proofs that did not contain them, and that he determined the size of volume 1 before knowing the total length of the work. Six thousand copies of the first volume were bound on 6 February. It appeared in the London *Athenaeum's* "List of New Books" on 10 February, and a copy was deposited in the British Museum on 15 February. The second volume was announced in the *Athenaeum's* "List of New Books" on 17 February, but its first 6,000 copies were not bound until 28 February. Bliss seems to have held back on announcing publication of the American edition until *both* volumes had been published in London, although he probably would have been safe as early as 10 February, when the first volume issued.[237]

As soon as publication in Hartford was formally declared, Orion abruptly accused Bliss of fraud in manufacturing the American edition, and was promptly fired (or resigned) for his trouble. Clemens surely understood why, under the circumstances, Bliss could no longer trust Orion, even as he knew that Orion had long nursed a resentment of Bliss's condescension toward him. He therefore did not intervene to save his brother's job, writing him on 7 March, in part:

---

[237]Routledge Ledger Book 4:576–77, Routledge and Kegan Paul, London; *Athenaeum:* 10 Feb 72, 177; 17 Feb 72, 210. The copy in the British Museum (call number 12331.bb.21) is stamped with the date of deposit, "15 FE 72" (PH in CU-MARK). In early March, Routledge also issued a single-volume edition, which was simply the pages of the two volumes bound together (*BAL* 3336). No copy of the second volume was deposited with the British Museum, probably because Routledge was satisfied that the first volume alone was sufficient: "If only a portion of a work be first published in this country, or within the scope of the British Copyright Act, it will be protected" (Walter Arthur Copinger, *The Law of Copyright, in Works of Literature and Art* [London: Stevens and Haynes, 1870], 64).

I cannot let you think that I overlook or underestimate the brotherly goodness & kindness of your motive in your assault upon Bliss. I would have you feel & know that I fully appreciate *that*, & value it. The fact that I contemn the *act* as being indefensible, does not in the least blind me to the virtue of the *motive* underlying it, or leave me unthankful for it. . . . There is no profit in remembering unpleasant things. Remember only that it has wrought one good: It has set you free from a humiliating servitude; a thing to be devoutly thankful for, God knows.

Being now free of all annoyance or regret in this matter, I hasten to say so.[238]

Clemens was indeed thankful for Orion's warning. Five days later, on 12 March, he met with Bliss to try to resolve the questions that had been raised by Orion's "indefensible" attack. And shortly before (or shortly after) that meeting with Bliss, he consulted Hartford lawyer Charles E. Perkins. Clemens recalled in 1875:

I came to the conclusion that an assertion of Bliss's which had induced me to submit to a lower royalty than I had at first demanded, was an untruth. I was going to law about it; but after my lawyer (an old personal friend & the best lawyer in Hartford) had heard me through, he remarked that Bliss's assertion being only verbal & not a part of a written understanding, my case was weak—so he advised me to leave the law alone——& charged me $250 for it.[239]

A partial, and indirect, record of Clemens's 12 March conversation with Bliss is preserved in a letter he drafted to Bliss on 20 March—a document he carefully preserved, sending a fair copy to Bliss. This draft shows that Orion's charges led Clemens to suspect Bliss of overstating his manufacturing costs, which in turn led to the suspicion that "half profits" were *not*, as Bliss had maintained in July 1870, equal to a 7.5 percent royalty. Written just three weeks after *Roughing It* was published in the United States, and just one day after Clemens's second child, Susy, was born, this remarkable document shows Clemens adopting his lawyer's advice and maneuvering to get "half profits" written into his contract:

The more I think over our last Tuesday's talk about my copyright or royalty, the better I am satisfied. But I *was* troubled a good deal, when I went there, for I had worried myself pretty well into the impression that I was getting a smaller ratio of this book's profits than I had ˏthe spirit of our contract had authorized me toˏ promised myself; indeed, I was so nearly convinced of it that if I had not known you so well, or if you had not been so patient & good tempered with my wool-gatherings & perplexities, & taken the pains to show me by facts & figures & arguments that my present royalty gives ˏme, fully half & possibly even more than half the net profits of the book, I would probably have come to the settled conviction that such was not the case, & then I should have been about as dissatisfied, a man as could be found in the country. I think few men could have convinced me that I am getting full half the profits, in the state of mind I then was, but you have done it, & I am glad of it, for after our long & pleasant intercourse, & the confidence that has existed between us, ˏI am glad you convinced me, forˏ I would have been sorry indeed to have come away ˏfrom your house, feeling that I had put such entire trust & confidence in you & the company to finally lose by it. And I am glad that you convinced me by good solid arguments & figures instead of mere plausible generalities, for

---

[238]SLC to Orion Clemens, 7 Mar 72, CU-MARK†.
[239]SLC to Charles Henry Webb, 8 Apr 75, NBuU-PO†.

~~that was just & business-like, & a conviction grounded in that way is satisfying &~~
~~permanent. So~~ ˌBut˗ everything is plain & open, now. ~~I knew I was entitled to half~~
~~the profits, & you will not blame me for coming frankly forward & consulting you~~
~~when I felt a little unsure about it.~~ And after thinking it over, I feel that, the result
being the same, you will ~~not mind~~ ˌreadily assent to the˗ altering ~~the~~ ˌof our˗ contract in such a way that it shall express that I am to receive half the profits. ~~I am~~
~~sorry the idea occurs to me so late, but that, of course, is of no real consequence.~~
Any friend of mine can represent me in the matter. ~~Twichell~~ ˌCharley Warner˗ will
do as well as another. ~~Let Twichell attend to it. However, I suppose he has his hands~~
~~about full; & perhaps he isn't much experienced in this sort of thing. Then let~~
~~Charles Perkins do it. Contracts are in his line at any rate. It is too complicated for~~
~~anybody but a lawyer to handle, anyhow; I could not even conduct it myself.~~ I will
~~write him.~~ ˌask him to do it.ˌ[240]

For his part, Bliss could hardly regard the result of any revision as "the
same," and he evidently declined to amend or replace the original contract, probably soon after receiving this letter. Despite his lawyer's earlier
advice, Clemens decided to sue. He recalled in 1880 that eventually "Bliss
went into the accounts & details & satisfied Perkins & his expert that 7½
per cent *did* represent half profits up to a sale of 50,000, & that after that
the publisher had a mere trifling advantage of the author. So we dropped
the matter."[241] The precise timing of these events remains unclear, but it
seems likely that Perkins and his (unidentified) expert interviewed Bliss
sometime in late May, and that Clemens was persuaded to give up the suit
by the end of June or, at the latest, by mid-July.[242]

Orion's charges against Bliss are not known to survive in their original,
presumably written, form, but their general import is clear. As mentioned
earlier, Bliss had used probably more than fifty borrowed engravings in
Roughing It—that is, engravings originally made for other books, but
reused (at substantial savings) in this one. Since this common practice
could hardly have been a secret, Orion probably accused Bliss not of borrowing illustrations, but of overstating their cost. Yet Orion must have
pointed to other abuses as well. On 15 May, Clemens urged him to "Ask
Chas. Perkins if he wants you to give him points in my lawsuit. But give
none otherwise."[243] On 17 May, Orion replied: "I didn't know you had
commenced a law suit. My plan did not contemplate a law suit by you. I
suppose it is a suit for damages. I did not think there was any chance for
enough to be made that way to justify such a proceeding." Orion's plan
was to force Bliss to sue Clemens, to prevent his publishing with someone
else.

---

[240]SLC to Elisha Bliss, Jr., 20 Mar 72, CU-MARK†, published in part in *MTLP*, 70–
71.
[241]SLC to Orion Clemens, 24 Oct 80, CU-MARK, in *MTLP*, 125–26.
[242]Following 21 March 1872 there is a hiatus in the correspondence between Bliss
and Clemens, presumably caused by the threatened lawsuit. The first known communication between them after that date was written by Clemens on 20 July.
[243]SLC to Orion and Mollie Clemens, 15 May 72, CU-MARK†.

In the meantime, while waiting for him to assume the role of plaintiff, which is a difficult position, because the plaintiff has every thing to prove, you ~~prepa~~ keep an eye on the paper manufacturer, on Hinckley, book keeper at Bliss's, on the book binders, and on the foremen of the press and book rooms of the Churchman, so that in case of sickness, or prospect of removal from the state, you may get an order from the chancellor to have their testimony taken for preservation on the ground of a probable law-suit. Imagine the effect of such an order on Bliss when he finds Hinckley subpoenaed to testify as to ˏborrowed engravings,ˏ the amount of paper received from the paper mill for ~~the publis~~ Roughing It; the testimony of the paper man as to its quality; of the Churchman pressman as to the country newspaper style of printing the cuts ˏ&c.,ˏ of the binder as to the quality of the binding, and how many he bound so. Bliss can see then that there is only needed to be added the testimony of some prominent ˏengravers, book binders, and, book publishers in the trade, at Boston and New York, to overwhelm with devastating ruin the subscription business and the American Publishing Company in particular—ˏbesides inevitably beating them ~~in the suit if there should be a~~ if they should sue, your case would be one of the "causes celebre." It would be seized upon with keen relish by newspapers favorable to the trade, and ~~no~~ the testimony published. All this Bliss must foresee ~~as soon as~~ ˏwhen, he sees the course indicated as soon as an excuse offers to "perpetuate the evidence" of—say Hinckley. This ˏindirect, quiet threat would be so terrible that he would never bring a suit against you if you simply went quietly along and ˏwrote, your next book ~~and~~ which you have contracted with him to publish, and put it into the hands of somebody else to publish, just as if you had never made any contract at all with Bliss to publish it.

These remarks suggest that Orion had accused Bliss of misrepresenting the cost not only of the illustrations ("borrowed engravings"), but of the paper and binding as well. Orion's point was that his brother could hardly recover significant damages for the way Roughing It had been manufactured, but that "the fraud you can prove concer[n]ing the printing of Roughing It" could be used to free him from his multiple contracts with Bliss by frightening the publisher with the prospect of seeing subscription-book manufacturing standards held up to ridicule by "newspapers favorable to the trade," which is to say, publishers who sold their books in bookstores, rather than by subscription.[244]

Whether or not Bliss really cheated Clemens remains an unanswered question.[245] It is clear, however, that Orion's charges inadvertently pro-

---

[244]Orion Clemens to SLC, 17 May 72, CU-MARK. After Bliss's death in 1880, Clemens examined the financial records of the American Publishing Company and wrote his brother:

The aspect of the balance-sheet is enlightening. It reveals the fact, through my present contract, (which is for half the profits on the book above actual cost of paper, printing & binding,) that if Perkins had listened to my urgings & sued the company for ½ profits on "Roughing It," at the time you ciphered on cost of Innocents, Bliss would have backed down & would not have allowed the case to go into court. I felt sure of that, at the time, but Perkins was loath to go for a man with no better weapon to use than a "scare." (SLC to Orion Clemens, 24 Oct 80, CU-MARK, in MTLP, 125–26)

[245]In 1906, Clemens was still convinced that Bliss had foresworn himself in July 1870:

It took me nine or ten years to find out that that was a false oath, and that 7½ per cent did not represent one-fourth of the profits. But in the meantime I had published several books with

vided Clemens with yet another reason to fear what newspaper critics would say about *Roughing It*. He did not believe that he was receiving "half profits," even when he dropped the lawsuit in June or July, but he was convinced that *Roughing It* had been printed on substandard paper and with badly executed engravings. It is important to recognize that his complaint was principally with the crude way the illustrations had been engraved, electroplated, and printed—and only incidentally, if at all, with the quality of the drawings themselves. Eventually he recognized that these drawbacks were to some extent inherent in subscription publishing. Two years later, after True Williams had contributed drawings to his next book (*The Gilded Age*), Clemens told Thomas Bailey Aldrich: "There is one discomfort which I fear a man must put up with when he publishes by subscription, & that is wretched paper & vile engravings."[246]

Although Clemens was less concerned about the quality of the actual drawings, he was ambitious to improve them as well. In December 1872, he wrote Thomas Nast: "I do hope my publishers can make it pay you to illustrate my English book. Then I should have good pictures. They've got to improve on 'Roughing It.'"[247] But Nast never did illustrate a book by Mark Twain—at least in part because of the high cost of his services. In

---

Bliss on 7½ and 10 per cent. royalties, and of course had been handsomely swindled on all of them. . . . In 1872 Bliss had made out to me that 7½ per cent. royalty, some trifle over twenty cents a copy, represented one-half of the profits, whereas at that earlier day it hardly represented a sixth of the profits. (AD, 23 May 1906, CU-MARK, in *MTE*, 151–55)

Hamlin Hill has pointed out that in November 1870, several months after the contract for *Roughing It* had been signed, Bliss offered the following calculation in a discussion about the Riley diamond-mine book: the manufacture of a subscription book with a cover price of $3.50, "without any copyright, cost of Plates, or any other expenses," cost about $1.00; when sold to agents at a 50 percent discount, each copy realized a profit of about $.75. Thus Clemens should have known that a 7.5 percent royalty ($.26) represented only about one-third of the profit (Hamlin Hill, "Mark Twain's Quarrels with Elisha Bliss," *American Literature* 33 [Jan 1962]: 454; Elisha Bliss, Jr., to SLC, 30 Nov 70, CU-MARK, in *MTLP*, 44 n. 2). But Bliss's exclusion of "any other expenses" makes his calculation difficult to interpret, and certainly left him room to maneuver in any dispute. Hill calculated that on *A Tramp Abroad* Clemens's half profits equaled just over $.51, or a fraction under 15 percent of the cover price (Hamlin Hill 1964, 156–57; chapter 4 discusses Clemens's contracts with Bliss). In the absence of records for the costs of manufacture—defined in the company's 1896 contract as plates, paper, printing, binding, and insurance—it is impossible to make an accurate accounting of the profits realized by the American Publishing Company on Mark Twain's books, and in all likelihood the question of whether Bliss swindled Clemens must remain unanswered (contract dated 31 Dec 96, CU-MARK, in *HHR*, 685; see also *MTB*, 1:420–21).

[246]SLC to Thomas Bailey Aldrich, 24 Mar 74, MH-H, in *MTLP*, 81.

[247]SLC to Thomas Nast, 17 Dec 72, in Albert Bigelow Paine, *Th. Nast: His Period and His Pictures* (New York: Harper and Brothers, 1904), 263. The date of the letter has been supplied, in part, from the auction catalog of a Nast sale, which prints a slightly different version of the letter text (Merwin-Clayton Sales Company catalog, sale of 2–3 Apr 1906, lot 244).

1905, Clemens put the blame for this parsimony entirely on Bliss, who "always had an eye for the pennies":

He did not waste any on the illustrations. He had a very good artist—Williams—who had never taken a lesson in drawing. Everything he did was original. The publisher hired the cheapest wood-engraver he could find, and in my early books you can see a trace of that. You can see that if Williams had had a chance he would have made some very good pictures.[248]

Williams continued to help illustrate Mark Twain's books, up through *A Tramp Abroad* (1880).

8

It was presumably with Orion's accusations fresh in his mind that Clemens told David Gray he was afraid *Roughing It* "would be considered pretty poor stuff," and that therefore he "had better not let the press get a chance at it."[249] But did Clemens actually withhold review copies, as this remark implies? To answer this question, more than sixty American, English, and Hawaiian newspapers and magazines were searched for periods ranging from six to twelve months (as available) in 1872–73.[250] The search showed that while extracts from the text of *Roughing It* were frequently published,[251] the total number of reviews, even very brief ones, was only fourteen. Reviews that Clemens or Bliss might have solicited soon after publication are certainly few: ten of those found can be safely excluded from this category, either because they were published in England and reviewed the Routledge edition, or because they appeared well after Clem-

---

[248]See SLC to Elisha Bliss, Jr., 4 Mar 73, ViU, in *MTLP*, 75; "Joan of Arc. Address at the Dinner of the Society of Illustrators, Given at the Aldine Association Club, December 22, 1905," in *MTS*, 271.

[249]SLC to David Gray, Sr., 10 June 80, NHyF†.

[250]No reviews of *Roughing It* were found in the following newspapers. **California:** San Diego *Bulletin;* San Francisco *Alta California, Chronicle, Evening Bulletin, Evening Post, Examiner, News Letter* and *California Advertiser;* Stockton *Independent;* **Colorado:** Denver *Rocky Mountain News;* **Illinois:** Chicago *Republican* and *Tribune;* **Louisiana:** New Orleans *Times Picayune;* **Massachusetts:** Boston *Advertiser;* Springfield *Republican;* **Montana Territory:** Helena *Rocky Mountain Gazette;* Virginia City *Montanian;* **Nevada:** Carson City *State Register;* Austin *Reese River Reveille;* Gold Hill *Evening News;* Virginia City *Evening Chronicle* and *Territorial Enterprise;* **New Jersey:** Newark *Advertiser;* **New York:** Albany *Argus* and *Evening Journal;* Buffalo *Express* (reprinted Moulton's *Tribune* review) and *Courier;* Elmira *Advertiser* and *Gazette;* New York *Evening Post, Evening Express, Herald, Sun, Times,* and *World;* Syracuse *Standard;* **Ohio:** Cincinnati *Gazette;* Cleveland *Herald* and *Leader;* Toledo *Blade;* **Pennsylvania:** Philadelphia *Evening Bulletin* and *Inquirer;* Pittsburgh *Commercial* and *Gazette;* **Utah:** Salt Lake City *Deseret Evening News* and *Tribune;* **Washington (D.C.):** *Chronicle* and *Evening Star;* **magazines:** *Athenaeum* and *Spectator* (London); *Golden Era; Nation; Harper's Monthly.*

[251]The three most frequently reprinted extracts were "A Nevada Funeral" (from chapter 47), "Mark Twain as Editor-in-Chief" (from chapter 55), and "Nevada Nabobs" (from chapter 46).

ens had changed his mind, and was actively trying to solicit reviews. On the whole, the reviews that did appear failed to confirm his worst fears, but they contained enough negative comment to suggest that his fears might have been more fully realized if he had not restricted review copies.

In March 1880, Clemens said that David Gray, Charles Dudley Warner, and William Dean Howells were the only men he could "trust to say the good thing if it could be honestly said" about his books, or, if it could not, to "be & remain charitably silent."[252] His trust in their discretion may well have begun with the publication of *Roughing It*. Clemens knew that Gray had reviewed *The Innocents Abroad* favorably, and intelligently, on 19 March 1870, and it seems inconceivable that he did not send him a copy of *Roughing It* in March 1872. But a search of the files of the Buffalo *Courier* shows that Gray did not review the book. On 9 March, in fact, he had this to say about Clarence King's *Mountaineering in the Sierra Nevada:*

If Mr. Bret Harte has most successfully wrought up the artistic material which the wild nature and humanity of California afford, Mr. King has as surely, with equal success, and with scarcely less literary art, portrayed for us the face of Californian nature. . . . His book takes a position immeasurably above the journals of travel with which western explorers have fatigued the public mind, and it will awaken a fresh and poetic interest in the hackneyed subject of the west.[253]

The closest Gray came to publishing his opinion of *Roughing It* was to print half a dozen extracts from it (including parts of chapters 26, 30, 44, 51, 59, and 67), which he introduced as follows:

Mark Twain, according to the autobiographical sketch in his recently published book, "Roughing It," left the Atlantic coast in 1865—he spent a short time as a government underling—and he himself says he would have made a good pickpocket if he had remained long in the service of Uncle Samuel. He pined for change, and here is his own account of how it came and what adventures it led him into.[254]

The inference must be that Gray was obliged by his real opinion of *Roughing It* to "be & remain charitably silent."[255]

On 18 March (a week after his meeting with Bliss) Clemens wrote to Howells, thanking him for an autographed copy of *Their Wedding Journey:* "I would like to send you a copy of *my* book, but I can't get a copy myself, yet, because 30,000 people who have bought & paid for it have to have preference over the author. But how is that for 2 months' sale? But

---

[252]SLC to William Dean Howells, 24 Mar 80, MH-H, in *MTHL,* 1:294.

[253]"New Publications," Buffalo *Courier,* 9 Mar 72, 4.

[254]"Roughing It. Mark Twain's Experience among the Silver Mines & Miners of Nevada," Buffalo *Courier,* 27 Apr 72, 4.

[255]Gray also expressed disapproval of his friend John Hay's *Pike County Ballads:*

In fact we cannot but think that the vein of truly American material he has struck is destined to develop something much more admirable than the Pike County Ballads. If Mr. Hay will turn the vigor, the true perception and creative power he has displayed in these to the representation of the higher and more beautiful phases of American life, preserving always the like juices and flavors of the soil, it will no more be said that we lack a distinctively national literature. ("New Publications," Buffalo *Courier,* 1 July 71, 4)

I'm going to send you one when I get a chance."[256] Howells's copy was almost certainly among the twenty-three "½ moroccos" that Clemens ordered sent to "friends of mine" in his 20 March letter to Bliss. In the final paragraph of that troubled letter, he professed to be

at last easy & comfortable about the new book. I have sufficient testimony, derived through many people's statements to my friends, to about satisfy me that the general verdict gives "Roughing It" the preference over "Innocents Abroad." This is rather gratifying than otherwise. The *reason* given is, that they like a book about America because they understand it better. It is pleasant to believe this, because it isn't a great deal of trouble to write books about one's own country. Miss Anna Dickinson says the book is unprecedentedly popular—a strong term, but I believe that was it. . . . (Request added to send 23 ½ moroccos to friends of mine named.)[257]

This statement may well be part of Clemens's strategy in dealing with Bliss, so just how "easy & comfortable" Clemens actually was at this time is in doubt. The passage does suggest, however, that he was relying chiefly on the word of friends, not on book reviews. It is also not known just how Clemens learned of Anna Dickinson's opinion, but since she was a friend of the Langdons', her words may have come by private letter to his wife or mother-in-law. Yet Dickinson's real feelings, less than a year later, were quite different from those she had expressed to the Langdons (and Clemenses). On 14 March 1873 she wrote her mother:

Just think that John Hay's beautiful "Castilian Days" never paid him but $350,— that Charlie Warner made, all told, from his jolly "Summer in a Garden" less than $1000,—that Whittier for years scarcely earned enough to keep him in bread & butter, & that this man's stuff, "Innocents Abroad" & "Roughing It," have paid him not short of $200,000.—
    'Tis enough to disgust one with one's kind.[258]

Because of Clemens's cautious strategy with review copies, opinions like Dickinson's were only rarely expressed in print. On 6 March 1872, however, the Manchester (England) *Guardian* reviewed the Routledge edition, taking a more critical tack than has been found in any American review:

The main portion of "Roughing It" is an account of the author's experiences among the silver miners in Nevada, and very rough both the experiences and the miners seem to have been, though of course a certain allowance must be made for exaggeration. The life and people are much the same as those that form the subject of Bret Harte's tales; but whereas he has shown a poetical and imaginative spirit, has represented inner life and character, and shown how the tender flower of sentiment or emotion may be found to spring among the rude and unlovely surroundings of a diggers' camp, our author [i.e., Mark Twain] has contented himself with dwelling on the outside of things and simply describing manners and customs. . . . Mark Twain, too, often falls into the slang of transatlantic journalism, and displays also

---

[256]SLC to William Dean Howells, 18 Mar 72, MH-H, in *MTHL*, 1:10.
    [257]SLC to Elisha Bliss, Jr., 20 Mar 72, CU-MARK†, published in part in *MTLP*, 70–71.
    [258]Anna Dickinson to Mary E. Dickinson, 14 Mar 73, Anna Dickinson Papers, DLC.

its characteristic inability to distinguish between the picturesque and the grotesque.[259]

And on 6 April, a reviewer in the London *Examiner* expressed similar, albeit slightly more tolerant, views. Mark Twain's

humour is not of a very delicate or profound order, but he enjoys it so keenly himself that it is impossible to resist the contagion. This humour is, moreover, evidently the natural outgrowth of the unsettled, adventurous, wild life he has led. . . . It is the humour of strong, daring, adventurous spirits, animated by wild, irregular passions, which may unfit them for settled life, but are among the very qualities required for semi-civilised regions, such as those that form the scene of Mr Clemens's [book].[260]

Whether or not Clemens saw either of these reviews is not known, but is almost irrelevant: although British, they represent precisely the kind of reaction Clemens had predicted to David Gray ("pretty poor stuff").

It is likely, but not certain, that Clemens also sent a copy of *Roughing It* to the Hartford *Courant,* edited by his friend Charles Dudley Warner— soon to become co-author of *The Gilded Age.* The *Courant's* review appeared on 18 March, the same day Clemens wrote to Howells, and is remarkable less for its deliberate praise than for an undercurrent of alarm, which emerges as a kind of defensiveness about the book. Warner began by reassuring the reader of Mark Twain's moral purpose, and the genuine clarity of his style:

Behind the mask of the story-teller is the satirist, whose head is always clear, who is not imposed on by shams, who hates all pretension, and who uses his humor, which is often extravagant, to make pretension and false dignity ridiculous.

It is not mere accident that everybody likes to read this author's stories and sketches; it is not mere accident that they are interesting reading. His style is singularly lucid, unambiguous and strong. Its simplicity is good art. The reader may not be conscious that there is any art about it, but there is art in its very perspicuity. There is no circumlocution, or any attempt at fine writing, but there is a use of vigorous English, and often a quaint use of it that gives the effect of humor in the soberest narration.

Warner then took up one of the more troublesome issues, the proper uses of "slang":

The author also means to be true to his art in another respect, and that is to report the odd characters he meets and the people of the new countr[i]es he describes, exactly as they were, slang and all. There is much slang in the book, but it is the *argot* that was current in the mining regions, and the description of the life there would be entirely imperfect if it had been left out.

And he included a defense of the book which, except for its final note, chimed very close to Clemens's own professed feelings about it:

Roughing It is a volume of nearly 600 pages, of queer stories, funny dialogues, strange, comical and dangerous adventures, and it is a book of humor first of all; but we are inclined to think that, on the whole, it contains the best picture of frontier

---

[259]"Literature: Uncivilised America," Manchester (England) *Guardian,* 6 Mar 72, 7.

[260]"Life in the Western States," London *Examiner,* 6 Apr 72, 361–62.

mining life that has been written. The episode of the silver mining in Nevada has certainly never been so graphically described. It is an experience that can, we trust, never be repeated on this continent. In these pages we are made to see distinctly a society that never had any parallel. It would be unpleasant to read about it, if the author did not constantly relieve the dreadful picture with strokes of humor.[261]

Similarly defensive, though briefer, was a notice on 25 March in the Cincinnati *Gazette*, which observed that Mark Twain's adventures were "related with a liveliness, and, we must add, with more than occasional imaginativeness peculiar to himself. One may not always approve the taste of what is said, yet he can rarely record his dissent without a smile. The many illustrations are not the least amusing feature of the book, which is published by subscription exclusively."[262]

These conservative views did not go wholly unanswered. On 11 April, the New York *Independent* remarked that among *Roughing It*'s

most entertaining chapters are those which describe the author's visit to the Hawaiian Islands. . . . We only wish that Mr. Clemens had made fewer alterations than he has made in those rollicking, often ludicrous descriptions, the "Sacramento Union" letters here reprinted. . . . The sketches of Western life are equally amusing. We may remark, too, that his fun is not dependent upon bad spelling or bad grammar. He writes good English, and we can commend the book to all who enjoy the wild Western drollery of which Mark Twain is the ablest living master. As a remarkably full repository of Western slang this work has a literary interest which will give it a permanent value to the student of Americanisms.[263]

By the time this notice appeared, Clemens had evidently begun to regret his cautious policy toward reviews. On 19 April he asked Frank Bliss to send a copy of the book to William C. Smythe, "a splendid old friend of mine," who had written him requesting a chance to review it: "He is city editor of the principal Pittsburg paper—a city *where I drew the largest audience ever assembled in Pittsburg to hear a lecture.* Send him a book. I want a *big* sale in Pittsburg." Smythe's review (if any) has not been found, but Clemens's letter shows that his own attitude toward reviews had changed.[264]

The next day, 20 April, Clemens wrote to James Redpath in Boston, weeping a few crocodile tears about the press's neglect of his book:

Could you jam this item into the Advertiser? I hate to see our fine success wholly uncelebrated:
Mark Twain's new book, "Roughing It" has sold 43,000 copies in two months & a half. Only 17,000 copies of "The Innocents Abroad["] were sold in the first two ~~months~~ & a half months.

[261] " 'Roughing It.' Mark Twain's New Book," Hartford *Courant*, 18 Mar 72, 1.
[262] "New Periodicals," Cincinnati *Gazette*, 25 Mar 72, 1.
[263] "Some Travels," *Independent* 24 (11 Apr 72): 6.
[264] SLC to Francis E. Bliss, 19 Apr 72, transcript at WU†. A brief note in Clemens's hand, apparently written in February 1872, places Smythe at that time with the "Commercial, Pittsburg" (Notebook 13A, [15], CU-MARK). In 1869, however, he was with the Pittsburgh *Dispatch* (*L3*, 378). A search of the *Commercial*'s files yielded no review, and the files of the *Dispatch* for 1872 could not be located.

I ordered a copy to be sent to you a couple of weeks ago. If it has been delayed, let me know.[265]

No such item has been found in the Boston *Advertiser*, but on 1 May, a generous review did appear in the Boston *Evening Transcript:*

Though abounding in facts, and brimful of new and interesting information, the work belongs, not to the literature of knowledge, but to the literature of nonsense, and will be read not so much for its wisdom as for its wit. It will be safer, as well as more agreeable, to quote its jokes than its statistics. There is, however, a serious side to Mark Twain's genius, and in "Roughing It" it has something like justice done to it. Some of the descriptions of mountains, lakes, rivers, and other marvels and wonders of nature are graphic, eloquent and almost poetical. . . . The silver mining fever in Nevada, and numerous other scenes, incidents and adventures are described with delightful freshness and vigor. The worthies of the "flush times" of Nevada are so admirably depicted that one is almost induced to call Mark Twain a comic Plutarch.

Dick Baker's story of his cat, and Jim Blaine's story of his grandfather's old ram, will satisfy and delight the lovers of Mark Twain's peculiar humor. But Scotty Brigg's Visit to the Minister is perhaps the best thing in the book, if not the best thing of its kind that Mark has yet done. The whole chapter on Scotty is rich in humor—the sweetest and tenderest humor in all Twain's writings.[266]

Redpath's reply to Clemens has not been found. He presumably told him what, if anything, he had accomplished with the Boston press, and may also have said something about the book itself. On 15 May Clemens replied in his turn: "Thank you with all my heart. I want to send a copy to the Boston literary correspondent of the N.Y. Tribune—Louise Chandler Moulton, isn't it? I will have it sent to you. Will you give it to her with my compliments?"[267] Redpath presumably did as requested, for on 10 June, Moulton noticed the book in her regular letter from Boston to the New York *Tribune:*

For pure fun, I know of nothing which has been published this year to compare with "Roughing It," by Mark Twain (Samuel S. Clemens), a New-England, though not a Boston, issue. It is a large and handsome book, full of the funniest possible illustrations. . . . It is funny everywhere; perhaps it is funniest of all when he sojourns in Salt Lake City, and learns to understand the Mormons through the revelations of their Gentile neighbors. . . . With a parting aphorism, which was one fruit of the writer's experience in "Roughing It," I will leave the book. An Irishman fell from a third story window with a hod of bricks, and had his life saved by falling upon Uncle Lem, an old gentleman who was leaning against the scaffolding. "Uncle Lem's dog was there," says the narrator. "Why did n't the Irishman fall on the dog? Becuz the dog would a seen him a coming, and stood from under. That's the reason the dog warn't appointed. *A dog can't be depended on to carry out a special providence.*"[268]

Shortly before Moulton's letter appeared, probably sometime between 25 and 30 May, Howells published his review (yet another voice from Boston) in the *Atlantic Monthly:*

---

[265]SLC to James Redpath, 20 Apr 72, ViU†.
[266]"Mark Twain's New Book," Boston *Evening Transcript*, 1 May 72, 3.
[267]SLC to James Redpath, 15 May 72, MB†.
[268]"Boston. Literary Notes," New York *Tribune*, 10 June 72, 6.

We can fancy the reader of Mr. Clemens's book finding at the end of it (and its six hundred pages of fun are none too many) that, while he has been merely enjoying himself, as he supposes, he has been surreptitiously acquiring a better idea of the flush times in Nevada, and of the adventurous life generally of the recent West, than he could possibly have got elsewhere. The grotesque exaggeration and broad irony with which the life is described are conjecturably the truest colors that could have been used, for all existence there must have looked like an extravagant joke, the humor of which was only deepened by its nether-side of tragedy. The plan of the book is very simple indeed, for it is merely the personal history of Mr. Clemens during a certain number of years, in which he crossed the Plains in the overland stage to Carson City, to be private secretary to the Secretary of Nevada. . . .

A thousand anecdotes, relevant and irrelevant, embroider the work; excursions and digressions of all kinds are the very woof of it, as it were; everything far-fetched or near at hand is interwoven, and yet the complex is a sort of "harmony of colors" which is not less than triumphant. The stage-drivers and desperadoes of the Plains; the Mormons and their city; the capital of Nevada, and its government and people; the mines and miners; the social, speculative, and financial life of Virginia City; the climate and characteristics of San Francisco; the amusing and startling traits of Sandwich Island civilization,—appear in kaleidoscopic succession. Probably an encyclopædia could not be constructed from the book; the work of a human being, it is not unbrokenly nor infallibly funny; nor is it to be always praised for all the literary virtues; but it is singularly entertaining, and its humor is always amiable, manly, and generous.[269]

This last sentence shows that even Howells could not avoid mentioning the book's occasional lack of "all the literary virtues." It is worth recalling that John Hay had identified Howells himself as a promising member of the "Western school." And Clemens therefore acknowledged this praise, as Howells recalled in 1910, in a way that "stamped his gratitude into my memory with a story wonderfully allegorizing the situation, which the mock modesty of print forbids my repeating here."[270]

Clemens's response to Howells is also worth comparing with what he said just three weeks later to Louise Chandler Moulton, writing her on 18 June:

I am *content*, now that the book has been praised in the Tribune—& so I thank you with all that honest glow of gratitude that comes into a mother's eyes when a stranger praises her child. Indeed, it is my sore spot that my publisher, in a frenzy of economy, has sent not a copy of my book to any newspaper to be reviewed, but is only always *going* to do it—so I seem to be publishing a book that attracts not the slightest mention. It is small consolation to me when he says, "Where is the use of it?—the book is 4 months & one week old, we are printing the 75th thousand, & are still behind the orders." If I say, "If you had had the book noticed in all the papers

---

[269]"Recent Literature," *Atlantic Monthly* 29 (June 72): 754–55.

[270]*My Mark Twain: Reminiscences and Criticisms* (New York: Harper and Brothers, 1910), 3. Paine reported in 1912 that Clemens had said, "When I read that review of yours, I felt like the woman who was so glad her baby had come white" (*MTB*, 1:390n). It was pointed out in 1960 that both Howells and Paine mistakenly recalled it as a remark about Howells's review of *The Innocents Abroad*, rather than *Roughing It* (*MTHL*, 1:6–7).

you would be now printing the 150ᵗʰ thousand, maybe," the wisdom falls upon a sodden mind that refuses to be enlightened.[271]

These remarks were disingenuous in more than one way, especially since Clemens had probably not yet dropped his lawsuit against Bliss. It is clear that the responsibility for not sending copies "to any newspaper to be reviewed," at least until April, belonged squarely to Clemens, not to Bliss.

Given the controversial nature of the West as a literary subject, Clemens could reasonably expect to be treated kindly by western journals, but no evidence has been found that he sent copies to them. The book seems to have reached western journals at about the same time copies were being delivered to agents in the West, which implies that Clemens did not do what he had previously done for *Innocents*, order it sent to the *Overland Monthly* so that Bret Harte could review it before anyone else. In late May an unidentified critic reviewed *Roughing It* in that journal with understandable enthusiasm:

As Irving stands, without dispute, at the head of American classic humorists, so the precedence in the unclassical school must be conceded to Mark Twain. About him there is nothing classic, bookish, or conventional, any more than there is about a buffalo or a grizzly. His genius is characterized by the breadth, and ruggedness, and audacity of the West; and, wherever he was born, or wherever he may abide, the Great West claims him as her intellectual offspring. Artemus Ward, Doesticks, and Orpheus C. Kerr, who have been the favorite purveyors of mirth for the Eastern people, were timid navigators, who hugged the shore of plausibility, and would have trembled at the thought of launching out into the mid-ocean of wild, preposterous invention and sublime exaggeration, as Mark Twain does, in such episodes as Bemis' buffalo adventure, and "Riding the Avalanche." . . .

It would be a great misapprehension, however, to conceive of *Roughing It* as merely a book of grotesque humor and rollicking fun. It abounds in fresh descriptions of natural scenery, some of which, especially in the overland stage-ride, are remarkably graphic and vigorous. . . .

Of the three hundred wood-cuts that illustrate the volume we can say nothing complimentary, from an artistic point of view. But some of them are spirited, and many of them suggestive. Crude as they are in design, and coarse in execution, they have afforded us much amusement; and the majority of readers would, we are sure, regret to dispense with them.[272]

On 28 April, Clemens's old San Francisco employer, the *Morning Call*, published a long, rambling notice that was basically positive:

No writer ever made so much out of so little, and that much of such excellent quality. Notwithstanding his palpable exaggeration in certain parts when describing in-

---

[271]SLC to Louise Chandler Moulton, 18 June 72, DLC†. Clemens's statement here that *Roughing It* was published on 11 February ("4 months & one week old") may refer to the English edition.

[272]"Current Literature," *Overland Monthly* 8 (June 72): 580–81. This review was not written by Bret Harte, who had been living in New York since February 1871, and would soon visit Clemens in Hartford on 13 June 1872, shortly after this review was published. It does seem likely, however, that Clemens read the review in Hartford, shortly after the magazine arrived in June.

cidents, there is much more of truth to be found, and a better idea of situations (in the theatrical sense) conveyed, than can be obtained from the most sober-sided narrative of the events of which he tells.[273]

Western reviewers were certainly not all so kind. On 18 May, a critic for another old employer, the Sacramento *Union*, reviewed the book with some asperity, sharply drawing attention to its "padding":

> Mark Twain is one of those geniuses that occasionally appear to make books that will sell, and, per consequence, make money, while others who write to benefit the world obtain but a poor reward for their labors. There is a good deal of stuff in this book, and a great deal too that is amusing. Had it been half its size, and the contents sifted, the book would have answered every purpose except, perhaps, to sell. . . . Sam Clemens tells good stories, but he is under high pressure as a book-making celebrity, and necessarily shoves off some yarns that under other circumstances might not find a place in his pages, and with less reputation as a humorist would not be excused by the reading public. There is always enough of fun in Clemens to make his books salable, and some stories are good enough to palliate the appearance of half a dozen others not as good.[274]

Sales were, in fact, excellent. On 21 March Clemens had chided Bliss for getting "caught in a close place with a short edition." And by the end of May the *American Publisher* announced, "The book is having an unparalleled sale. About 50,000 copies in a little over three months. . . . We have been unable to fill orders at sight, for this book; 10,000 copies are ordered ahead now." In mid-June Clemens again boasted to Howells of "62,000 copies of Roughing It sold & delivered in 4 months."[275] The bindery records of the American Publishing Company corroborate these impressive figures. It is clear that Bliss was indeed unable to meet the demand for copies: his general agents for Chicago reported on 24 March that they were "away behind in filling their orders," and that their "five hundred agents, throughout the North and Southwest," were "taking from five to ten orders each, daily." By 31 March the bindery had produced 24,676 copies, and it was apparently unable to meet all back orders until sometime in June: by the end of that month it had shipped a total of 67,395 copies.[276]

But sales declined sharply and unexpectedly in July, when only 2,645 copies were bound, less than a quarter of the number bound the previous month. The total for July through December was only 7,773, a mere one-

---

[273]" 'Mark Twain.' Biographical Sketch of the Great Humorist. Carefully Compiled from Imaginary Notes by B. B. Toby," San Francisco *Morning Call*, 28 Apr 72, 1.

[274]"New Publications," Sacramento *Union*, 18 May 72, 8. Two additional reviews were found which are not quoted here: "A New Book," Honolulu *Pacific Commercial Advertiser*, 30 Mar 72, Supplement, no page; and " 'Roughing It,' " Marysville (Calif.) *Appeal*, 13 June 72, 3.

[275]SLC to Elisha Bliss, Jr., 21 Mar 72, CtY-BR, in *MTLP*, 73; "Mark Twain on the Mormons," *American Publisher*, June 72, 8; SLC to William Dean Howells, 15 June 72, NN-B, in *MTHL*, 1:12.

[276]" 'Roughing It,' " Chicago *Tribune*, 24 Mar 72, 4; APC, [109].

eighth of the number for the first half of the year. Total sales for the year were thus 75,168, with 90 percent occurring in the first six months. If the rate of sale for January through June had continued for the rest of the year, Clemens's prediction in September 1870 that he would sell 90,000 copies during the first year would have been easily met, even exceeded.[277]

To someone with Clemens's high expectations, the sales of *Roughing It* were ultimately disappointing. A total of only 7,831 copies of the American edition were sold in 1873, followed by 5,132 in 1874. In comparison, fewer copies of *Innocents*—only 67,680—were sold during its first year, but its sales did not decline so precipitously: during the second year of publication, a total of 21,822 copies were sold. On 4 March 1873 Clemens remarked to Bliss that *Roughing It* was now selling "less than twice as many in a quarter as Innocents, a book which is getting gray with age."[278] But he was willing to take at least part of the blame:

I believe I have learned, now, that if one don't secure publicity & notoriety for a book the instant it is issued, no amount of hard work & faithful advertising can accomplish it later on. When we look at what Roughing It sold in the first 3 & 6

---

[277]APC, [109]; SLC to Elisha Bliss, Jr., 4 Sept 70, CU-MARK, in *MTLP*, 39. Previous assertions that the book sold only 65,376 copies in the first year apparently resulted from misreadings of the ledger, the largest error being for May: during that month 16,905 copies were bound, not 6,905 (compare *RI 1972*, 22, and Hamlin Hill 1964, 63).

[278]The bindery records corroborate this statement: in the quarter ending on 1 March 1873, 3,684 copies of *Roughing It* were sold, whereas the sales of *Innocents* totaled 2,045. Two years later, in March 1875, Clemens correctly calculated that his earnings on *Roughing It* and the venerable *Innocents* had become roughly even: "I get 5 per cent on Innocents Abroad & it has paid me $25,000 or $30,000. I get 7 ½ per cent on Roughing It. It has sold something over 100,000 copies, & consequently has paid me about the same aggregate that Innocents has" (SLC to William Wright, 24 Mar 75, CU-BANC†). Cumulative sales for the eight years following each book's publication totaled 119,870 copies of *Innocents* (July 1869–June 1877) and 96,183 of *Roughing It* (January 1872–December 1879). During these same periods, it may be estimated that Clemens earned $21,876 on *Innocents Abroad* and $26,330 on *Roughing It*. Thus the higher royalty on *Roughing It* compensated somewhat for its lower sales. Sales and royalty figures for the period 1869–79 for *Innocents Abroad* and *Roughing It* are based on the bindery records compiled by the American Publishing Company, on the surviving quarterly royalty statements, and on related evidence in correspondence and in Clemens's notebook (APC, [106–9]; statements dated 1 May 72, 5 Aug 72, 1 May 73, 1 Jan 76, 1 Apr 76, 1 July 76, 9 Nov 76, 24 Jan 77, 7 May 77, [1] Oct 77, and 23 Jan 78 [Scrapbook 10:24, 28, 29, 31, 75, 76a, 81, 84, CU-MARK; Elisha Bliss, Jr., to SLC, 5 Aug 72, CU-MARK; Francis E. Bliss to SLC: 1 May 72, CtHMTH; 1 May 73, CU-MARK]; SLC to Charles H. Webb, 8 Apr 75, NBuU-PO; *N&J2*, 428). Both *The Innocents Abroad* and *Roughing It* ranged in price from $3.50, for a cloth binding, to $5.00, for a half-morocco binding; a full-morocco binding was also available, but rarely purchased, at $8.00. Prices were perhaps 10 percent higher on the West Coast (see advertisements in the Honolulu *Pacific Commercial Advertiser*, 16 Mar 72, 2, and *HF*, 845), but this may not have affected Clemens's royalties.

months, we naturally argue that it would have sold full 3 times as many if it had gotten the prompt & early journalistic boost & notoriety that the Innocents had.[279]

Perhaps in response to this decline, Clemens engineered one more review in the New York *Tribune*. On 12 January 1873 he wrote to John Hay:

> Bliss is going to send "Roughing It" to the Tribune today, so he says. If you ever do any book reviews for the paper, I wish you & Reid would arrive at an amicable arrangement whereby you can have an hour or two to write a review of that book in, ~~for you understand it~~ & a week's holiday afterward to rest up in—for you know the people in it & the spirit of it better than an eastern man would. I shall hope so, at any rate. ˏThat is I mean I hope you'll write it—that is what I am *trying* to mean.ˏ
>
> Don't answer this letter—for I know how a man hates a man that's made him write a letter.[280]

But Whitelaw Reid did not assign Hay to review it, much to Clemens's annoyance. The reviewer was instead George Ripley, "the profound old stick who has done all the Tribune reviews for the last 90 years. The idea of setting such an oyster as that to prating about Humor!"[281] Ripley's comments were hardly unfavorable, concluding that *Roughing It* "may be regarded as one of the most racy specimens of Mark Twain's savory pleasantries, and their effect is aggravated by the pictorial illustrations which swarm on every page, many of which are no less comical than the letterpress."[282] But they certainly did not exhibit the sort of sympathetic understanding Clemens expected (and had earlier received) from John Hay. Just one year before, Hay had reviewed the *Roughing It* lecture in the *Tribune*, describing Mark Twain as "a true humorist, endowed with that indefinable power to make men laugh which is worth, in current funds, more than the highest genius or the greatest learning."[283]

9

Sales of the English edition of *Roughing It* followed the same pattern as the American, but on a smaller scale. In 1872 Routledge printed 18,000 copies of each volume, and followed in 1873 with another 8,000 of each. From 1872 through 1899, Routledge sold a total of 63,750 copies of volume 1, and 68,000 copies of volume 2. In 1882, Routledge also issued a new, one-volume illustrated edition, printing 4,000 copies that year. The plates and unsold sheets of this edition were sold in 1885 to Chatto and Windus, who printed an additional 5,000 copies before 1900.[284] Routledge was well satisfied with the sales of the original two-volume edition: in

[279]SLC to Elisha Bliss, Jr., 4 Mar 73, ViU, in *MTLP*, 74.

[280]SLC to John M. Hay, 12 Jan 73, OClWHit.

[281]SLC to Olivia L. Clemens, 2 Feb 73, CU-MARKt.

[282]"New Publications," New York *Tribune*, 31 Jan 73, 6. Ripley (1802–80), the literary critic for the *Tribune* from 1849 until his death, was also an ordained minister and a founding member of the Brook Farm Community near Boston (1841).

[283]"Mark Twain at Steinway Hall," New York *Tribune*, 25 Jan 72, 5.

[284]Routledge Ledger Book 4:576–77, 5:145, 183, 6:680–81, Routledge and Kegan Paul, London.

1892, when Chatto and Windus offered £100 for the "stereos & copyrights" of *Roughing It, The Gilded Age,* and *Mark Twain's Sketches,* Edmund Routledge responded, "You can have as I offered before the two 2/. vols of Twain for £60, but Roughing it we don't wish to sell at all."[285]

Although Clemens did not alter the text of any edition after the first American, he did sanction republication by Routledge, and later by Chatto and Windus, in England, as well as by Bernhard Tauchnitz in Germany, and (indirectly, through Routledge) by George Robertson in Australia. Clemens also sanctioned, but did not revise, later editions in the United States, both by the American Publishing Company and by Harper and Brothers. Despite Routledge's English copyright, however, John Camden Hotten reprinted several extracts from the text, without Routledge's or Clemens's permission. And beginning in 1880, Belford and Company in Toronto (later Rose-Belford Publishing, and later still, Rose Publishing Company) reprinted the whole text of *Roughing It,* lacking only chapters 22, 36, 45, 49, 52, 71, 72, and 77, again without Routledge's or Clemens's approval.

Hotten had written to Clemens in February 1872, shortly before *Roughing It* was published: "Will you oblige BY MAILING TO ME ON RECEIPT of this some of the proofs—a few chapters. You may depend upon my dealing honourably with you & I will place to your credit whatever is fair & equitable."[286] But Clemens had long since agreed to sell the English rights to Routledge, precisely in order to foil Hotten, who had reprinted both of his earlier books, the *Jumping Frog* and *The Innocents Abroad,* in England, and had also issued various collections and anthologies of American humor, much of it Mark Twain's. In 1870 Hotten had published *The Piccadilly Annual of Entertaining Literature,* which included five Mark Twain sketches from the *Galaxy;* and in 1871 he had issued two smaller volumes, *Eye Openers* and *Screamers,* containing several more sketches from the *Galaxy* and a few from the *Express,* the Chicago *Republican,* and the San Francisco *Alta California.*[287]

Hotten was made more cautious by the Routledge copyright on *Roughing It,* but in August 1872 he issued yet another collection of humor, *Practical Jokes with Artemus Ward, Including the Story of the Man Who Fought Cats,* which included fourteen Mark Twain sketches taken from the *Express,* the *Galaxy,* and other newspapers, as well as three extracts from the English edition of *Roughing It.* Whether or not Hotten thought Routledge's copyright was valid, he was apparently confident that these

---

[285]George Routledge and Sons to Chatto and Windus, 27 Feb 92, and Edmund Routledge to Chatto and Windus, 2 Mar 92, University of Reading, Reading, England.

[286]John Camden Hotten to SLC, 3 Feb 72, Chatto and Windus Letter Book 6:18, Chatto and Windus, London. Clemens never responded to this letter; it is possible that since he was on lecture tour at the time, he failed to receive it.

[287]*ET&S1,* 554, 586.

Roughing It anecdotes would not be detected. He supplied the titles "Editorial Skits," "Sending Them Through," and "The Union—Right or Wrong?" And he edited the texts rather more heavily than those from other sources that were clearly not protected by copyright.[288]

In March 1873 Hotten published *The Choice Humorous Works of Mark Twain* (HWa), reprinting virtually everything by Mark Twain which he had included in the earlier books. In London during the fall of 1872, Clemens had told Hotten of his willingness to revise and correct this volume before it appeared. Hotten welcomed the offer, but Clemens left for home before he could follow through on it. HWa included eight sketches corresponding to passages in *Roughing It*. Two of them were the anecdotes that Hotten had previously extracted from *Roughing It* ("Editorial Skits" was excluded). Also reprinted was the *Practical Jokes* text of "Mark Twain's Remarkable Stranger," derived from the April 1871 *Galaxy*, which Clemens had independently used as the basis for chapter 77. Hotten's 1870 *Jumping Frog* provided two extracts from the 1866 Sacramento *Union* which Clemens had independently incorporated into *Roughing It* from *Union* clippings: "Honoured as a Curiosity in Honolulu" and "The Steed Oahu." Hotten also reprinted "Mark in Mormonland" from *Roughing It*, "A Nabob's Visit to New York" from the *American Publisher* of January 1872, and "Baker's Cat" from his own *Screamers*, which had in turn come from the Buffalo *Express* of 18 December 1869.[289]

When Hotten died only a few months after HWa issued, his assistant, Andrew Chatto, took over the business in partnership with W. E. Windus. Chatto was eager to follow up on Clemens's 1872 offer to revise HWa, and so wrote to him again when he was in London: "I am sincerely anxious to establish more cordial relations as between Author & Publisher, than have hitherto existed, between you and our firm, and I beg to submit to you a set of the sheets of a volume of your writings, in order that you may (as I understand you expressed a desire to do) correct certain portions of the contents."[290]

An agreement was reached, and Clemens set to work revising a set of HWa folded and gathered sheets, which became the basis for a new edition, HWb, issued in April 1874. Collation of HWa with HWb shows that the original HWa plates were altered to incorporate Clemens's corrections and, in some cases, his deletion of entire sketches. Some of the texts— such as those from the *Union* and the *Express*—had undergone a parallel

---

[288]*Athenaeum*, 6 June 68, 799; *ET&S1*, 550, 589. An 1868 court case, *Routledge* v. *Low*, had resulted in a divided judicial interpretation of existing copyright law, leaving some uncertainty about whether an author needed to reside in some part of the British Empire at the time of publication in order to make his Imperial copyright indisputably secure.

[289]For details, including the chains of transmission for the eight pieces in HWa, see the Description of Texts.

[290]Andrew Chatto to SLC, 25 Nov 73, Chatto and Windus Letter Book 6:707.

evolution: they had been subjected to Hotten's cutting and editing, while Clemens had independently supplied his own revisions of the same sketches for *Roughing It*. Thus when he came to revise Hotten's texts, he was annoyed and sometimes puzzled, since their history was not clear to him.[291] Clemens's demonstrable changes to these eight sketches for HWb, however, were not revisions of *Roughing It* but of independent sketches, and therefore have not been adopted in the present text.[292]

The second English edition of *Roughing It* and *The Innocents at Home* (illustrated by F. A. Fraser; Routledge, 1882) was set from the first English edition, but contained the appendixes of the first American edition, and the revision of "thirteenth" to "sixteenth" (136n.6) introduced in the fifth state of the first American edition (Ae, 1874). Chatto and Windus reissued the second Routledge edition in 1885, 1889, and 1897. Clemens made no revisions in any of these reimpressions.

Bernhard Tauchnitz of Leipzig, Germany, published a Continental edition of *Roughing It* in 1880–81, which was based on the 1872 Routledge edition. In September 1880 he sent Clemens 300 gold marks (about $75) as a voluntary payment for his use of the text. Clemens responded on 7 October, expressing his "distinguished appreciation of a publisher who puts moral rights above legal ones, to his own disadvantage." He also evidently explained that the Routledge version of the book comprised two volumes, of which Tauchnitz had published only one. Tauchnitz promptly replied: "As to 'Roughing it' you are quite right. I have published in my edition only the Tale which bears this title in the 'Routledge edition.' In consequence of your kind explanation I will now publish in a further separate volume 'The Innocents at Home,' and beg to offer you, as for 'Roughing it,' Three Hundred Mark Gold for this volume."[293] Clemens provided no revisions for either volume in this edition.

From 1899 until 1903 the American Publishing Company issued several impressions of a two-volume edition of *Roughing It* (A2), typeset from the last state of the first American edition (Ag, 1892). Later impressions of A2 (e.g., the "Japan" and "DeLuxe") incorporate corrections suggested by the company's proofreader, Forrest Morgan, who compared a copy of the "Royal edition" (an early impression of A2) with the first edition. Although in at least one instance a query from Morgan was referred to Clemens, he offered no revisions of his own. The American Publishing Com-

---

[291]The revised HWa sheets are preserved in the Rare Book Division of the New York Public Library (NN). See *ET&S1*, 599–607, for a detailed publication history of HWa and HWb, and the Description of Texts for further details about the revisions Clemens inscribed.

[292]For further details about the revisions Clemens inscribed on HWa, see the Description of Texts.

[293]SLC to Bernhard Tauchnitz, 7 Oct 80, incomplete text in Curt Otto, *Der Verlag Bernhard Tauchnitz, 1837–1912* (Leipzig: Tauchnitz, 1912), 125; Bernhard Tauchnitz to SLC, 9 Dec 80, CU-MARK.

pany retained the copyright on *Roughing It* until 1903, when it sold the plates of A2 to Harper and Brothers. Harper continued to issue impressions of A2 from these plates until about 1914, when it published a new, more compact two-volume edition. Numerous impressions of this last typesetting appeared with the Harper imprint over several decades.[294]

No royalty statements (at least none itemized by title) are known to survive for the years 1880–98, although there were lump-sum payments for the years 1890–91 on the seven Mark Twain titles for which the American Publishing Company owned the rights.[295] On 31 December 1896 the company signed a new contract for these books, whereby it agreed to pay a royalty to Olivia Clemens of 12.5 percent of the cover price, or one-half of the net profits—whichever was greater—on the seven titles and on the forthcoming *Following the Equator*. Between January 1899 and June 1903, extant royalty statements (covering all but six months of that period) show 2,280 copies of *Roughing It* sold, representing payments of at least $997.[296] For the years 1903–7, the records of Harper and Brothers show that Mark Twain's three most popular books were *The Innocents Abroad* (46,125 copies), *The Adventures of Tom Sawyer* (40,962 copies), and *Roughing It* (40,334 copies).[297]

THE TEXT

The printer's copy used by the American typesetters and illustrators is not known to survive, but the conjectural reconstruction of that copy in Figures 1 and 2 (pages 814–15), together with the history of composition and production just described, affords a reasonably clear idea of it. To recapitulate, three pages of manuscript draft for *Roughing It* do survive, and are reproduced in facsimile above: they contain passages revised so completely that Clemens simply replaced them in the printer's copy.[298] The page numbered 423 is typical of the many chapters that were entirely in

---

[294]Contract dated 23 Oct 1903, CU-MARK, in *HHR*, 700–708. For details see the Description of Texts and the textual note at 416.4.

[295]The titles are *The Innocents Abroad; Roughing It; Sketches, New and Old; The Gilded Age; A Tramp Abroad; The Adventures of Tom Sawyer;* and *Pudd'nhead Wilson*. Only five statements of payments, totaling $2718, survive; the period covered by each statement is not indicated (Francis E. Bliss to SLC, 4 Jan 90, 1 July 90, 10 Jan 91, 3 Apr 91, and 9 Jan 92, all in CU-MARK).

[296]Contract dated 31 Dec 96, CU-MARK, in *HHR*, 682–87. At this time, sales of single volumes of the old editions represented only a portion of Clemens's income; considerably more income was generated from sales of volumes in the uniform edition and other fine limited editions. Only two of the extant statements for 1899–1903 itemize sales of the uniform editions by title: these statements suggest that sales of such volumes of *Roughing It* were twice that of single volumes. Overall, the income from volumes in uniform editions was at least three times that from single volumes (Francis E. Bliss to SLC, 7 Feb 1900 and 12 Oct 1900; Francis E. Bliss to Olivia L. Clemens, 21 Jan 1902 and 29 July 1903, all in CU-MARK).

[297]"Volumes of Mark Twain Sold from Nov 1-1903 to Oct. 31-1907," CU-MARK.

[298]See pages 816, 843, and 845; compare the text on pages 81–82, 122, and 303–4.

Clemens's holograph—those listed in FIGURES 1–2 as having *no* "clipping" words: they consisted of leaves inscribed on a single side, in purple ink, with the usual cancellations, interlineations, and insertions. The page numbered 968 is typical of the chapters that included "clipping" words: the printer's copy for them was partly holograph, and partly in printed form. Such printings were either passages cut from the *Book of Mormon* or Catharine V. Waite's *Mormon Prophet*,[299] or clippings from the New York *Times*, the Buffalo *Express*, the *Galaxy*, the Sacramento *Union*, the Virginia City *Territorial Enterprise* (and possibly even from proofs of the *Weekly Occidental*, also of Virginia City), which Clemens mounted on the same-sized paper that he used for holograph sections. Draft page 968, which contains a clipping from the *Express*, shows that such clippings could be revised both on the newsprint itself and in the margins. Among the sketches Clemens prepared in 1870–71 were two additional *Express* articles: "A Ghost Story" and "Adventures in Hayti" (CU-MARK). The draft page and these sketches, totaling sixteen pages, demonstrate that Clemens attended chiefly to changes in his own diction, while revising or correcting the spelling, capitalization, and punctuation much less often. On the draft page he changed "can't" to the more formal "cannot"; he altered "letter" to "chapter" (for obvious reasons); and he substituted "shifted" for the slangy "swapped." He also changed "newspaper article" to "little sketch" (in pencil, on the clipping itself), and then to "brief sketch" (in ink, in the margin). In "A Ghost Story" he changed "a tiny" to "an," "What" to "Now what," "in" to "under," and "infamous" to "mean." He also corrected a typographical error ("of" to "off") and changed "foot print" to "footprint," so that it would be spelled consistently as one word throughout the sketch, as was the analogous "footstep." In "Adventures in Hayti" he deleted some extreme phrasing, like "carrying their bleeding hearts outside their shirt-bosoms." He also deleted "just" and "soulless," corrected "dollars" to "dollar," "volcanos" to "volcano," and "I" to "It," but passed over several other errors: "what what" (dittography), "halucination," and "decripit." Collation of the first edition of *Roughing It* against the original printings of articles reused in it shows that Clemens made many similar changes (and some similar oversights) in them, presumably on the printer's copy, but possibly also in proof.

There were some likely exceptions to these two basic kinds of copy. In some cases, Clemens's revisions were so extensive that he must have copied out the passage, as he decided to do with the first uncanceled sentence in the clipping on draft page 968, preserving his change from

---

[299]It was possible for Clemens to cut out the passages from these books, rather than use loose pages (as he later did in the printer's copy for *Tom Sawyer*), because the sections he quoted were not printed on two sides of a sheet—except for about seventy words from *The Mormon Prophet*, which he could easily have copied out by hand.

"swapped" to "shifted," but making further deletions and revisions as well. Judging from collation, and other evidence, the quotations in chapters 10 and 11 from Dimsdale's *Vigilantes of Montana* were probably copied out, rather than supplied in torn pages from the book, which may have been loaned, rather than given, to Clemens by Hezekiah Hosmer. In addition, some small part of Clemens's manuscript in the first seven chapters may have been replaced before typesetting began with the "20 or 30 pages" of corrections that he sent to his publisher on or about 10 April 1871. Although these corrections were in Clemens's hand, some of them must have been inscribed on pages from the amanuensis security copy of his first 168 pages (up through the pony-express passage). It also seems likely that, when it was decided to put the material removed from chapters 13 and (then) 15 into appendixes, the typesetters availed themselves of the early proofs for those chapters, rather than digging out and setting from Clemens's printer's copy. Finally, the table of contents and list of illustrations were not drafted by Clemens, but by Bliss or his associates (Orion or Frank Bliss are both likely candidates), and therefore copy for them was also not in Clemens's hand.

It is clear that Clemens did not write or revise all of the chapters in sequence. Nor were they all typeset in sequence—in fact, they were probably not set by the same compositors throughout. It will be recalled that in October 1871, Clemens was forced to rewrite parts of chapter 18, combining newly written material with what had been preserved in proof, or possibly in manuscript. Chapters 58–75, 77, and 79 were clearly set in type well after the earlier chapters, probably by different typesetters, but at least by those who had not been instructed (among other things) to ignore Clemens's habitual end-line dashes. In addition to the revisions Clemens submitted by mail in April 1871, he revised virtually all of the copy during August 1871 ("I cut & slash & lick & trim & revamp it"), when he also read and drastically revised parts of the first fifteen (possibly twenty-five) chapters in proof, removing two chapters (conjecturally, one about Overland City and one about the Mountain Meadows massacre), as well as sharply reducing the length of a third (chapter 13); he also added new material (Eckert and the cat) and redivided chapters 7–9. Even so, the continuing problem of the book's overall length forestalled his wish to "scratch out half of the chapters of the Overland narrative."[300] It is likely, but not demonstrable, that Clemens read and revised proof for most of the book, occasionally adding footnotes (chapters 14 and 52), deleting anecdotes or episodes like "Waking Up the Weary Passenger" (chapter 48), adding two specific references to the illustrations (chapters 44 and 54),[301] and writing or adding several additional chapters (conjecturally 36, 49, 52, 53, and 75), as well as the appendixes, long after he thought the book was complete.

---

[300]SLC to Olivia L. Clemens, 10 Aug 71, CU-MARK, in *LLMT,* 159; SLC to Elisha Bliss, Jr., 15 May 71, ViU, in *MTL,* 1:187–88.
    [301]See pages 288 and 370.

Orion (and both Blisses) saw preliminary sketches for the illustrations, but no evidence has been found that Clemens himself did. He nevertheless saw a high percentage of the illustrations in proofs of the prospectus and of the book itself, and therefore had a chance to reject any that he did not approve. And although he was disappointed in the technical execution of at least some of the wood engravings, no edition of *Roughing It* can claim to fulfill his intentions without including them. There can be no doubt that, even before beginning to write, he expected his book to be "well & profusely illustrated" with "snappy pictures—especially pictures worked in with the letter-press."[302] They are therefore reproduced photographically from the first edition, occasionally reduced or enlarged slightly to accommodate the present page design.

Each chapter of the text has its own peculiar history of authorial revision and printing-house transmission, but the chapters with clippings of Clemens's own work were the most complex. In those cases, only the original newspaper (or magazine) typesetter worked exclusively from Clemens's holograph. The book typesetters set partly from his holograph, and partly from printed copy already one remove from holograph, despite Clemens's efforts to revise and correct it. This circumstance complicated the task of the book typesetters and proofreaders, insofar as their goal was to maintain uniformity in punctuation, spelling (especially of compound words), and capitalization, as well as in various nontextual matters, such as whether to retain certain manuscript abbreviations, how to set extract quotations, what typographical treatment to give titles and foreign words, and whether or not to spell out numbers.

In the absence of the manuscript printer's copy for *Roughing It*, the first American edition, which was set directly from that copy, would ordinarily be chosen as copy-text throughout. Indeed, for the present edition, the first edition (A) is copy-text for all parts of the text that reprint *no earlier text* (or at least none that is now available).[303] But wherever Clemens reprinted a text of his own, the *earlier printing* was chosen as copy-text, since it is the text nearest to the author's original holograph and is therefore the most likely to preserve his punctuation, spelling, capitalization, and paragraphing. And wherever Clemens quoted from a text by another writer, that text too was chosen as copy-text, to ensure that any errors in transmission would be removed, on the assumption that Clemens intended to quote accurately.[304] These several copy-texts were then emended

---

[302]SLC to Elisha Bliss, Jr.: 3 May 71, CU-MARK, in *MTLP*, 66; 15 May 71, ViU, in *MTL*, 1:188.

[303]The pony-express passage in chapter 8 is an exception. It was typeset for publication in the *American Publisher* from Clemens's manuscript, or from the amanuensis security copy of the manuscript, and that printing therefore derives independently from the manuscript: see the textual note at 50.1–52.7.

[304]For quotations, the printing Clemens is most likely to have used—either by transcribing it or by literally inserting it in the copy—was designated copy-text. In a few cases, the edition or impression he used cannot be certainly identified, so the

to incorporate all changes, whether to substantives or accidentals, which Clemens is thought to have made on the printer's copy (or on the proofs) of the first American edition.

This procedure is somewhat more cumbersome than relying exclusively on the first edition as copy-text, but it has several advantages. It increases the likelihood that the author's spelling and punctuation will be preserved throughout, while it forces the editor to recapitulate the process of revision and correction which Clemens himself performed on the clippings. And since the apparatus must record the editor's decisions about which differences between the copy-texts and the first edition are authorial and which are not, the list of emendations provides as full a record as we are ever likely to have of the author's revisions on his printer's copy and proofs.

But while the choice of first printings as copy-texts has these positive results, it does not automatically yield a text that is free of errors. We know from Clemens's statements over a long period of time that he always welcomed the correction of mistakes in his texts. In 1881, for example, he told the publisher of *The Prince and the Pauper:* "For corrections turning my 'sprang' into 'sprung' I am thankful; also for corrections of my grammar, for grammar is a science that was always too many for yours truly." And in 1897 he made it clear that while the printer's proofreader was not to concern himself with punctuation, he *was* expected to correct misspelling, "which *is* in his degraded line."[305] Since errors are, by definition, not intended, the following have been emended, whether they occur in authorial or in quoted copy-texts: (a) typographical errors such as "carrried" and "welome"; (b) missing or incorrect quotation marks (single where double are needed, and vice versa); (c) misspelled words (that is, spellings not sanctioned by any known authority since 1800, such as "logarythm"); (d) misspelled proper names of real people, places, things, and institutions such as "Holliday," "Fort Kearney," and "Roscicrucian"; (e) subject-verb disagreement (except in quoted speech), as in "statement were"; (f) "end-line dashes," which were never intended as punctuation; and (g) manifestly defective punctuation (at 183.18, 233.12, 304.31, 406.32, 430.15, 431.5, 487.18, and 523.9).

The largest potential for error in the copy-texts, however, lies in their inconsistent punctuation, spelling (particularly of compound words), and capitalization. In the first edition, the punctuation of parenthetical phrases, for example, follows no particular pattern: sometimes a comma

---

edition or impression *closest* to it was designated copy-text. Similarly, some things that Clemens published first in the *Enterprise* are not now available in that printing, and the only choice is to rely on the text of the first edition. The choice in each case is explained in the Textual Notes.

[305]SLC to James R. Osgood, 15–23 Aug 81, Caroline Ticknor, *Glimpses of Authors* (Boston: Houghton Mifflin Company, Riverside Press, 1922), 139–40; SLC to Chatto and Windus, 25 July 97, ViU†.

precedes the opening parenthesis, sometimes the closing one, and sometimes both. Collation reveals that the typesetters occasionally "corrected" the punctuation of the earlier printings, while in others they followed their copy exactly. The first edition also contains dozens of words spelled in more than one way, largely because it followed spellings in the earlier newspaper and magazine typesettings. The book typesetters attempted, albeit unsuccessfully, to spell words consistently, often succeeding within a chapter while overlooking variants in more distant chapters. While uniformity in spelling was clearly a goal, there was evidently no clear house style—at least none which was known by all the compositors, and which would have allowed them to resolve all such inconsistencies. It is clear, for example, from a detailed survey of holograph letters written between 1853 and 1870, as well as of numerous literary manuscripts from the same period, that Clemens spelled "summer" and "winter" without initial capitals. In some twenty occurrences of each of these words in manuscript, *none* was capitalized, including the two which appear on draft page 423 (where they are part of a sentence that Clemens canceled). And yet in both the Buffalo *Express* and Sacramento *Union* printings of Clemens's work, these words were consistently rendered with capitals, no doubt because the typesetters followed their own house style. In setting passages from holograph, the book compositors adopted Clemens's invariable lowercase form. But when setting passages based on *Express* and *Union* clippings, they followed the capitalized spellings in their copy, and even supplied capitals nearby, in an attempt to achieve uniformity. The result is that both authorial and nonauthorial spellings of these words occur almost randomly in the first edition, not because Clemens ever intended to spell them both with and without initial capitals, but because the typesetters tried and failed to create a uniform texture of spelling, defeated by printer's copy that contained a bewildering mixture of spellings.

We know quite a lot about Clemens's attitude toward compositorially or editorially imposed consistency in punctuation. His strong view, often and vigorously expressed, was that punctuation was *his* province and his alone, and that the compositor or proofreader ought simply to "*have no opinion whatever regarding the punctuation, that he was simply to make himself into a machine and follow the copy.*"[306] In August 1876, while seeing *Tom Sawyer* into print, Clemens explicitly turned down an offer from Bliss to make the punctuation "uniform . . . here & hereafter." The narrow question was whether the single word "No" (in dialog) should always be followed by a period, or always by an exclamation point. Clemens

---

[306]Frederick J. Hall, for Charles L. Webster and Company, to SLC, 19 Aug 89, CU-MARK. Hall paraphrased Clemens's instructions to him, but Clemens repeated them in his reply: "You are perfectly right. The proof-reader must follow my punctuation ABSOLUTELY. I will not allow even the slightest departure from it" (SLC to Frederick J. Hall, 20 Aug 89, ViU, in *MTLP*, 255).

replied on the proof for page 75 (chapter 7): "No, not uniform; follow copy; sometimes it is a quiet negative, & sometimes an exclamatorily vigorous one. The copy isn't *always* the way I want it, though. The thing takes a different look in print from what I thought it would." To which Bliss replied: "Of course! alter wherever it dont look right. We will follow copy & make your alterations afterwards." Clemens responded: "Very well, what better way *is* there, than that? Do I give you one-fiftieth the trouble that Richardson did?" To which Bliss in turn replied, "Richardson made more trouble over every page than you do in a whole book. Your model Ms is my standard to gauge others by, & must not be much better & cant be really."[307] This exchange shows that Clemens did not tolerate compositorial regularizing of his punctuation; that despite his care with preparing printer's copy, he did sometimes change his mind about punctuation when he saw it in type; and that in his own eyes and in Bliss's, his printer's copy manuscript was typically a model of clarity and accuracy.

Variant patterns of punctuation which were not deemed erroneous before the twentieth century, and which may be intentional, have therefore not been emended. Clemens's occasional use of a comma before an opening or closing parenthesis, or just before the sentence verb, or in combination with a dash, are all well documented in holograph manuscripts. Their occurrence in the printed copy-texts does not necessarily reflect the author's inscription, but it might. Variants of this kind either do not require uniformity (as Clemens firmly told Bliss in 1876), or cannot be made uniform without significant risk of obscuring the writer's intention.

Clemens's attitude about the limits of compositorial responsibility, however, did not extend to misspelled, or inconsistently spelled, words. For instance, in April 1869, while proofreading *The Innocents Abroad*, he wrote Bliss:

> I wish you would have MY revises revised again & look over them *yourself* & see that my marks have been corrected. A proof-reader who *persists* in making *two* words ˌ(& sometimes even *compound* words)ˌ of "anywhere" and "everything;" & who spells villainy "vill*ia*ny" & liquefies "liqu*i*fies" &c, &c, is ~~not three removes from an idiot—~~ˌinfernally unreliable—ˌ& so I don't like to trust your man. He never yet has acceded to a request of mine made in the margin, in the matter of spelling & punctuation, as I know of. He shows spite—don't trust him, but revise my revises yourself. I have long ago given up trying to get him to spell those first-mentioned words properly. ~~He is an idiot—& like all idiots, is self-conceited.~~[308]

This letter makes clear that two years before he proofread *Roughing It*, Clemens thought there was one and only one way to "properly" spell "anywhere" and "everything," even though it must be conceded that he occasionally wrote them with what looks for all the world like a space between the two halves of the compound. He was chastising the proofreader

[307]Elisha Bliss, Jr., to SLC, and SLC to Bliss, postmarked 7 Aug 76, CU-MARK, in *TS*, 510–11.

[308]SLC to Elisha Bliss, Jr., 20 Apr 69, *L3*, 197.

not simply for misspelling the words, nor just for failing to correct them, but also for spelling them in *more than one way* ("& sometimes even *compound* words").

The printing-house goal of uniformity in spelling can be traced at least as far back as 1808, to an essay by Joseph Nightingale in Caleb Stower's *Printer's Grammar; or, Introduction to the Art of Printing*, which included a paragraph subsequently reprinted in dozens of printer's manuals.[309] It appeared, for instance, in a manual Clemens himself is likely to have used as a printer's apprentice—Thomas F. Adams's *Typographia; or, The Printer's Instructor* (first published in 1845):

> We should always preserve a strict uniformity in the use of capitals, in orthography, and punctuation. Nothing can be more vexatious to an author, than to see the words *honour, favour,* &c. spelt with, and without the *u.* This is a discrepancy which correctors ought studiously to avoid. The above observations equally apply to the capitaling of noun-substantives, &c. in one place, and the omission of them in another. However the opinions of authors may differ in these respects, still the system of spelling, &c. must not be varied in the same work: but whatever authority is selected should be strictly adhered to.[310]

By the time Clemens wrote *Roughing It*, the demand for uniformity, both from readers and from the typesetters themselves, had significantly increased. Writing in 1901, Theodore Low De Vinne noted pointedly that

> during the last fifty years there has been no marked improvement in the average writer's preparation of copy for the printer, but there have been steadily increasing exactions from book-buyers. The printing that passed a tolerant inspection in 1850 does not pass now. The reader insists on more attention to uniformity in mechanical details.[311]

To emend the copy-texts of a published work by Mark Twain so that in its spelling, and in nontextual questions of typography, the text is as *au-*

---

[309]Cited in *A Connecticut Yankee in King Arthur's Court*, edited by Bernard L. Stein, with an Introduction by Henry Nash Smith, The Works of Mark Twain (Berkeley, Los Angeles, London: University of California Press, 1979), which reads in part: "By the middle of the century, the principle was firmly established that to spell, hyphenate, or capitalize a word in different ways within the same manuscript was an error, however correct each individual usage might be" (617 n. 92). Stein's edition of *Connecticut Yankee* imposed "consistency in spelling, compounding, and capitalization" on the text "so long as the author's inconsistency appears to be unintentional and without purpose" (617).

[310]Thomas F. Adams, *Typographia; or, The Printer's Instructor: A Brief Sketch of the Origin, Rise, and Progress of the Typographic Art, with Practical Directions for Conducting Every Department in an Office, Hints to Authors, Publishers, &c.* (Philadelphia: L. Johnson and Co., 1857 [copyright 1845]), 191.

[311]Theodore Low De Vinne, *Correct Composition: A Treatise on Spelling, Abbreviations, the Compounding and Division of Words, the Proper Use of Figures and Numerals, Italic and Capital Letters, Notes, etc. with Observations on Punctuation and Proof-Reading* (New York: Century Company, 1901), viii–x. De Vinne noted, "In making the last revision of this treatise, the writer has doubts as to the propriety of assuming to be its author, for the work done is as much the compilation and rearrangement of notes made by other men as it is the outcome of the writer's own long practice of printing" (x).

thorial as possible, as well as uniform in spellings for which the author had no distinct or discoverable preference (except the tacit one that uniformity be preserved in print), is therefore *not* to "modernize" the work but to restore part of its authenticity.[312] The lack of uniformity in the first edition cannot by itself show that uniformity was not a goal, both of the author and of the typesetters. There is no reason to suppose that Clemens intended his spelling to be pointlessly varied. It is no more likely that he would intentionally spell words in more than one way—without some reason for doing so—than it is that he would willingly allow misspellings in the text (always excepting the representation of speech, especially dialect). Clemens agreed with what his friend Joseph T. Goodman said to him in 1881, when he questioned Clemens's habitual (and no doubt unintentional) misspelling of "champagne" as "champaign":

Where do you find the authority for it? In that funny description in the "Tramp" of the scene between Neddy and his bride at the dinner table, it occurs three or four times, I think, and looks rather awkward to me, as the passage is a somewhat sarcastic and critical one, and a fellow should be mighty correct himself when scoring others.[313]

Apart from the correction of error, emendation of the copy-text accidentals was carried out with three priorities in mind. The first was to restore authorial spellings wherever possible, not just in resolving ambiguous end-line hyphenation, and to record each change as an emendation.[314] Taking that step alone brings the text very close to uniformity in spelling throughout. The second priority was to achieve uniformity in spelling the relatively few words for which the author's preference is either unknown or nonexistent. And the third was to complete the task begun by the book

---

[312]Compare G. Thomas Tanselle, "Problems and Accomplishments in the Editing of the Novel," *Studies in the Novel* 7 (Fall 1975): "A regularized text can no longer be thought of in most instances as an unmodernized text" (342). See also Hershel Parker, "Regularizing Accidentals: The Latest Form of Infidelity," *Proof* 3 (1973):

Undoubtedly printers of the early and middle nineteenth century were more consistent in their spelling and punctuation than their predecessors, but they sometimes followed copy when it was highly inconsistent and often were inconsistent themselves. Despite the greater accuracy of some nineteenth-century compositors than that of others, no one has yet shown that any major publisher then had a systematically imposed house style, although there were gestures toward one, as in the decision of the Harpers to follow Webster's still-controversial orthography. Nothing indicates that there was a mid-nineteenth-century equivalent of the modern-day Bryn Mawr graduate who slavishly checks manuscript usages against Webster's *Second* or *Third* while encubicled at a New York publishing office. (8–9)

[313]Joseph T. Goodman to SLC, 24 Oct 81, CU-MARK. Goodman's reference was to *A Tramp Abroad*, chapter 31.

[314]Ambiguous forms in the copy-texts (compounds hyphenated at the end of a line) were resolved as emendations by adopting the spelling that the manuscript survey (described below) established as the author's clear preference. Compounds ambiguously divided in the edited text are listed separately on pages 1020–21 to enable accurate quotation. Compounds ambiguously divided in the record of emendations appear with a double hyphen when the hyphenated form is intended.

typesetters, emending typographical or nontextual variants that they tried, but failed, to make consistent.[315]

In the absence of the printer's copy and the proofs for *Roughing It*, authorial preference in spelling must be determined from independent, or collateral, evidence.[316] Such evidence was gathered by a computer-assisted search of holograph manuscript letters for 1867–70 and a reading search of manuscript letters for 1853–66 and 1871–72, plus the following literary manuscripts (as well as miscellaneous later manuscripts as needed): ["Sarrozay Letter from 'the Unreliable'"] (1864); "The Mysterious Chinaman" (1864–65); "Angel's Camp Constable" (1865); ["The Brummel-Arabella Play Fragment"] (1865, 1870–71); "The Only Reliable Account of the Celebrated Jumping Frog of Calaveras County" (1865); ["Burlesque 'Il Trovatore'"] (1866); "How, for Instance?" (1866); Sandwich Islands lecture notes (1866–67); "Interview with Gen. Grant" (1867); "A New Cabinet 'Regulator'" (1867); "A Plea for Old Jokes" (1867); an unpublished letter to the San Francisco *Alta California* (1867); ["Mr. Brown, the Sergeant-at-Arms of the Senate"] (1867–68); draft of "The American Vandal Abroad" lecture (1868); "Assaying in Nevada" (1868); ["Boy's Manuscript"] (1868); "[Colloquy between a Slum Child and a Moral Mentor"] (1868); ["The Frozen Truth"] (1868); "The Legend of Rev. Dr Stone" (1868); "Remarkable Sagacity of a Cat" (1868); "I Rise to a Question of Privilege" (1868); manuscript fragments C, D, E, F, G, H, J, K, L, M (1868), discarded from *The Innocents Abroad* (NPV A7, A11, A20, A22, A24, A25, A26, A27); "L'Homme Qui Rit" (1869); "Remarkable Idiot" (1869); "Scenery," draft of the "Curiosities of California" lecture (1869); untitled burlesque letter from Lord Byron to Mark Twain (1869); "Chinese Labor &c" (1870); ["Housekeeping No. 1"] and ["Housekeeping No. 2"] (1870); "Interviewing the Interviewer" (1870); "A Protest" (1870); "The Reception at the President's" (1870); ["The Tennessee Land"] (1870); "A Wail" (1870); draft of the Artemus Ward lecture (1871); notes for the "Roughing It" lecture (1871–72); "An Appeal from One That Is Persecuted" (1872); "The 'Blind Letter' Department, London P.O." (1873); ["Foster's Case"] (1873); play fragment, a dramatization of the "Arkansaw Incident" (1873?); "Samuel Langhorne Clemens" (1873); "A True Story, Repeated Word for Word As I Heard It" (1874); "The Experience of the McWilliamses with Membranous Croup"

---

[315]Such emendation was carried out only on authorial copy-texts, not on material being quoted. Clemens's quotation of his own work in the *Territorial Enterprise* was treated like other quoted texts.

[316]Fredson Bowers, "Regularization and Normalization in Modern Critical Texts," *Studies in Bibliography* 42 (1989): 79–102. Bowers holds that "the only documentary evidence that can be trusted for emendation back to authorial forms is variation in the print, one form of which should be compositional but the other the reading of the [printer's] copy. It is then a separate problem requiring collateral evidence to establish whether either form is or is not authorial" (84).

(1875); the partial manuscripts of *The Gilded Age* (1874) and *A Tramp Abroad* (1880); and the complete manuscripts of *The Adventures of Tom Sawyer* (1876); *The Prince and the Pauper* (1882); *Adventures of Huckleberry Finn* (1885); and *A Connecticut Yankee in King Arthur's Court* (1889). For each word or word pair (like "a while") spelled in more than one way in the *Roughing It* copy-texts, a context-sensitive examination was made of every occurrence found in these manuscripts, determining whether or not the manuscript usage was reliably comparable to the usage in *Roughing It*. More weight was given to manuscripts written before 1885, and especially to those written in the period 1869–71. A count was made of all collected usages, and the results were judged to belong to one of three levels of evidence. It should be noted that a number of the adopted spellings are not more, but *less*, modern than the spellings probably imposed by the typesetters.

Level 1. At least ten occurrences of a word or word pair were found in holograph manuscript, all spelled alike.

Level 2. At least four occurrences were found in holograph manuscript, and at least three-fourths of them were spelled alike—that is, one form predominated over the other (or others) in a ratio of 3 to 1.

Level 3. Three or fewer occurrences were found in holograph manuscript—or *more* were found, but no single form predominated in a ratio of 3 to 1.

Level 1 evidence was deemed strong enough to justify emending *invariant* spellings of two words in the copy-texts: the noun "envelope" to "envelop" (twice), and "Saviour" to "Savior" (once). Four spellings that predominated in the copy-texts were confirmed by level 1 evidence: "anybody," "anyhow," "whisky," and "winter."

Level 2 evidence was deemed strong enough to establish clear authorial preference, and was used to *overturn* copy-text predominance, even when the predominant form was found to occur occasionally in manuscript. Thus for eight words the predominant spelling in the copy-texts was ignored, and the author's preference uniformly adopted: "a while," "backwards," "cañon," "County," "offense," "pretense," "river," and "Sanitary." In one case, "barkeeper," the spelling found three out of four times in manuscript was adopted even though it never occurred in the copy-texts, which had either "bar keeper" or "bar-keeper." For ten words in which no form predominated in the copy-texts, level 2 evidence established a preferred spelling: for example, "enterprise," "half past," "mould," and "practice." In twenty-seven cases a spelling that predominated in the copy-texts was confirmed by level 2 evidence: for example, "afterward," "by and by," "cannot," "centre," "ecstasy," "King," and "worshipped."

Level 3 evidence was regarded as significant, but less conclusive about the author's preference than levels 1 or 2. When variant spellings fell into this category, the spelling predominant in the copy-texts was adopted, provided that it was also found at least once in manuscript. This pattern occurred in sixty-two cases: for example, "boulder," "height," "Islands," "lawsuit," "sage-brush," "shoveled," "skurrying," and "tattooed." In six cases no manuscript usage was found that confirmed the predominant copy-text spelling, and so the manuscript form that *was* found (if only once) was adopted: "brim full," "enclosure," "log house," "pocket-mining," "station," and "wild-cat" (n.). When the copy-text variants occurred in equal numbers, *any* manuscript usage found was relied on to resolve the variation: level 3 evidence established the preferred spelling in twenty-six such cases: for example, "caulk," "foot-notes," "Garden of Eden," "per cent," and "St. Joe." In one case, "shotgun," the spelling found in manuscript was adopted even though it never occurred in the copy-texts, which had either "shot gun" or "shot-gun."

For forty-three variant spellings in the copy-texts, no exact manuscript evidence at all was found. When one spelling predominated in the copy-texts (as happened in twenty-seven cases), it was necessarily adopted. When no single spelling predominated (sixteen cases), holograph spelling of similar words was considered, as well as the preferred form in Webster's 1870 Unabridged Dictionary.

Resolution case by case ("spring," "summer," and "winter," all individually considered) rather than by category (the seasons) was attempted for most spelling variants, partly because that method was most likely to recover genuine authorial practice, but also because the result turned out to be categorically consistent as well. In a few cases, however, the categorical method was effective both in recovering Clemens's practice and in maintaining overall uniformity where the manuscript and copy-text evidence was otherwise scarce.[317] Emendation to retrieve authorial spelling and achieve uniformity was applied in the following spelling categories by using the same criteria as case-by-case emendation, except that both copy-text and holograph occurrences were counted in groups. (a) The spelling "county" was emended to "County" when it was part of a name, as in "Carson County." (b) "River" and "Station" were emended to "river" and "station" when part of a name, as in "Green river station." (c) The hyphen between "a" and a participle was emended to a space, as in "a hunting" rather than "a-hunting." (d) Word space between the numerator and denominator of fractions was emended to a hyphen: "two-thirds" rather than "two thirds." (e) Two-em dashes to show interrupted speech were

---

[317]For instance, the copy-texts have both "River" and "river" used with a proper name: "Green River" (once); "Missouri River" (once); "Humboldt river" (twice); "Reese River" (twice) and "Reese river" (once); "Carson River" (once) and "Carson river" (once). The manuscript search established that Clemens's overwhelming preference was for "river," which he wrote in thirteen out of fourteen instances recovered. The likelihood is therefore great that most, if not all, spellings of "River" in the copy-texts were imposed by the compositors, and all "River" variants could therefore be emended to "river," restoring authorial spelling and uniformity at one stroke.

emended to one-em dashes: "and—" rather than "and——." (f) The possessive of "Jarves" (a proper name ending in "s") was emended with an additional "s": "Jarves's" rather than "Jarves'." (g) Compound modifiers that included numbers but no hyphen, or only one hyphen, were emended: "ten-cent piece" rather than "ten cent piece," and "three-thousand-foot precipice" rather than "three-thousand foot precipice." (h) All references to "the Lake" (Mono or Tahoe) were emended to "the lake." (i) All spelled-out forms of "Captain," "Colonel," "General," "Governor" (as parts of names), and "United States" (as an adjective) were emended to their abbreviated forms: "Capt.," "Col.," "Gen.," "Gov.," and "U. S." (j) All closing quotation marks preceding other punctuation were emended to follow it instead. (k) Parentheses to signal interpolations or asides were emended to square brackets: "[falling inflection]" rather than "(falling inflection)."

Variant spellings that denote a difference in meaning were not emended. The distinctions between "Heaven" and "heaven," "Overland" and "overland," "Plains" and "plains," and "Nature" and "nature" are difficult to articulate, but nevertheless real. Likewise variable are Clemens's neologisms or slang set off, or not, by quotation marks ("flush times," "square meal," and "feet") in virtually identical contexts.

Despite Clemens's jealous control of his punctuation, there certainly were aspects of typesetting that he willingly if tacitly ceded to the printing house. In other words, Clemens's practice in manuscript is not invariably a sound guide to his intention for a literary work—the ampersand, for example, which he used throughout his manuscripts, always expecting it to be expanded to "and." In the use of numbers versus figures, or in the treatment of long quotations, Clemens accepted the participation of the printshop in devising and applying a uniform standard. A comparison of the first-edition text with the author's manuscript usage, as well as with the several copy-texts, provided a good deal of information about what kind of styling, textual and nontextual, the book typesetters applied. For example, they usually (but not invariably) spelled out numbers, even though the newspaper compositors (and Clemens himself, at least with informal manuscripts like letters) used numerals for convenience and speed. In spelling out numbers the book compositors may well have had the warrant of Clemens's holograph manuscript chapters: draft page 968 spells out both "six thousand" and "twelve thousand dollars." But whether or not Clemens's manuscript was consistent in this matter, the book compositors tried to be (albeit with imperfect success), deliberately printing numerals only for hours of the day followed by "A.M." or "P.M." Collation reveals that they achieved nearly consistent results in all categories except for dollars. They tended to leave the dollar figures they encountered in printed texts, such as the Buffalo *Express* (where newspaper style made figures conventional), perhaps because a clipping gave the impression of greater finish, having already been styled by the previous compositors. Emendation (always recorded) was therefore undertaken to complete the pattern begun by the book compositors in spelling out numbers—including dollars, except in two instances where numerals were deemed acceptable (both discussed in textual notes).[318]

Similarly, the book compositors set all extended quotations in smaller type, sometimes enclosing them in quotation marks, sometimes not. In a few places they set double quotation marks within an extract already enclosed in quotation marks, which suggests that they added the surrounding double quotes without attending to the internal ones. Examination of Clemens's practice in marking quoted material in his literary manuscripts of the 1870s and 1880s reveals that all three possible treatments occur with seemingly equal frequency: quotation marks with, and without, a request for small type, and small type alone. It is also clear that the compositors did not always follow their copy, but instead adopted a house style—with varying degrees of consistency. When the author wrote a specific directive in the manuscript, such as "Put this in small type," they usually followed it, but sometimes they removed quotation marks, and sometimes supplied them. While early-nineteenth-century printer's manuals make no mention of how to treat extracts, the later ones explicitly advise compositors not to use quotation marks when using small type; from this we can infer that redundancy was becoming less acceptable.[319] This edition perfects the apparent intention of the book compositors by following their prevailing pattern: quotation marks enclosing extracts in small type were removed by emendation.

Several additional minor points of typographical style required emendation for uniformity. The book compositors were nearly, but not entirely, consistent in styling names of ships in roman type and names of newspapers in italic. Three emendations in these two categories were made to achieve uniformity. The compositors also failed to achieve a consistent treatment of foreign words, and in this instance the evidence does not point to a categorical solution. Three foreign words were invariably set in italic type: *"riata," "tapidaros"* (a misspelling, emended to *"tapaderas"*), and *"awa."* Numerous other foreign words occurred only in roman type: "cañon" and "poi," for example. Five words and one abbreviation appeared in both italic and roman type: *"adobes," "hula-hula," "i. e.," "kahilis," "tabu,"* and *"taro."* No distinct pattern of normalizing was discernible in the evidence of collation. The italicized words appeared in material set from the author's holograph as well as from clippings from the Sacramento *Union;* in some cases the italic form was changed to roman, in oth-

---

[318]Dollar figures were spelled out in accordance with the practice followed by the compositors elsewhere in the book—that is, "twenty to forty dollars" for "$20 to $40," and "a hundred" for "100."

[319]See De Vinne, 214, and Wesley Washington Pasko, *American Dictionary of Printing and Bookmaking* (New York: Howard Lockwood and Co., 1894; reprint edition, Detroit: Gale Research Company, 1967), 482–83.

ers the reverse was true. The fact that some italic forms also represent a word used as a word ("*adobes,* the Spanish call them"; "*Tabu* . . . means prohibition") added a complication. It seems probable that the first-edition typesetting reflects Clemens's own inconsistency, overlaid by incomplete compositorial attempts, at one or more stages, to extend his sporadic markings for italics to all like instances. A word occurring in a single invariant form was deemed likely to reflect at least some authorial impulse to render it in that form; all *in*variant forms were therefore left unemended. Furthermore, it seems likely that any word occurring in both roman and italic forms reflected some authorial impulse, albeit sporadic, to render it in italics; all variant forms were therefore consistently italicized.

Italic punctuation following italic words (an accepted convention in American typesetting since at least the early nineteenth century) was adopted in the first edition in all but three instances, which have been emended here. Footnotes in the first edition were typeset with a paragraph indention except for two instances, in which the notes were centered: both have been emended here. Mark Twain's initials at the end of a footnote were emended to delete brackets in one instance.

The front matter in the first edition (the List of Illustrations and the Contents), the illustration captions, and the headlines (running heads) on each page were all undoubtedly supplied by Elisha or Frank Bliss, perhaps with Orion's assistance. All usages in these sections, being nonauthorial, were excluded from the first-edition tally of spelling variants and the like, but they were emended for uniformity according to the same policy as the rest of the text. Whenever the titles in the List of Illustrations, the wording of subjects in the Contents list, and the illustration captions themselves correspond to wording in the text, emendation was applied to make them accord exactly, and the quoted phrases were enclosed in quotation marks. Whenever the title of an illustration, as given in the List of the first edition, differed from the wording of the caption, the caption was deemed more accurate, and the title in the List emended to match it.[320] The running heads, which cannot be adapted to the paging of the present edition, have been silently omitted. In addition, the following alterations were carried out without being individually reported in Emendations of the

---

[320]The first-edition captions in general accorded with the text more closely and had fewer errors: see, for example, the title for illustration number 93, which in the first edition read "Fight" instead of "Fire." It is probable that after the List was prepared from the captions, some of the latter were revised; these revisions were then inadvertently not incorporated into the List. Three tailpieces and one other illustration were inadvertently omitted from the List in the first edition (at xxvb.16, xxvib.44, xxviia.42, and xxviiib.2); they were added in this edition, and all subsequent numbers in the List silently adjusted upward. One caption evidently not included in the first edition because the page was already full was supplied from the List (see page 395).

Copy-Text and Rejected Substantives. (a) All publication information no longer applicable to the present edition (such as "ISSUED BY SUBSCRIPTION ONLY" and "AMERICAN PUBLISHING COMPANY. . . . 1872") was removed from the title page. (b) The seven full-page illustrations were printed in the first edition as separate plates, which were not included in the pagination. For these seven illustrations the reading in the List— "(FULL PAGE,) (*Face Page*)"—was altered to read merely "(Full Page)," followed by the appropriate page number in this edition. (c) All first-edition front matter was styled in accordance with the design of this edition: periods were removed from the title page, and illustration titles on the List and the subjects in Contents were altered so that nouns, adjectives, and adverbs begin with initial capital letters, prepositions and conjunctions with lowercase letters. (d) Arabic chapter numbers, with no punctuation, were substituted for roman numerals followed by periods, and the opening of each chapter and appendix was styled in capitals and small capitals and set flush left with no paragraph indent.

H. E. S.

TEXTUAL APPARATUS

THE TEXTUAL APPARATUS consists of the following sections:

DESCRIPTION OF TEXTS consists of three parts. The first part lists and characterizes the several copy-texts and sources of emendation used in the preparation of this edition of *Roughing It*. The second part lists derivative texts—that is, partial or complete reprintings which appeared during the author's lifetime but which show no relevant authorial intervention. The third part lists all collations performed and specific copies used.

TEXTUAL NOTES discuss problematic readings in the edited text and explain and defend editorial decisions.

EMENDATIONS OF THE COPY-TEXT AND REJECTED SUBSTANTIVES records every reading adopted from a source other than the copy-texts, as well as all instances in which a compound word is hyphenated ambiguously at the end of a line in the copy-texts. In addition, it records all variant substantive readings among the copy-texts and texts used as sources of emendation.

WORD DIVISION IN THIS VOLUME lists compound words hyphenated at the end of a line in the edited text, when their intended form is ambiguous.

Description of Texts

Each of the fifteen texts described in "Authoritative Texts" below contains readings pertinent to the establishment of an accurate text for this edition of *Roughing It*. Many of these are texts written by Mark Twain before he composed *Roughing It*—sketches, articles, and newspaper letters—which he revised and incorporated into the book (BE, G, SU, TE63). Others are texts written by other authors, from which he quoted in the book (BoM, HoHI, MP, NYT, PCA, TE70, VoM), or which reprinted material subsequently included in the book and which thus intervened in the chain of textual transmission (PT). The second section, "Derivative Texts," describes reprintings of the complete text of *Roughing It*, or of excerpts from it, issued during Mark Twain's lifetime. All of them, with one exception (HWb), were found to derive without authorial intervention from A, or from the "pre-*Roughing It*" sources BE, G, or SU. (Variants in derivative editions are not recorded in Emendations of the Copy-Text and Rejected Substantives.) The last section, "Collations," comprises a list of collations performed and the specific copies used. Symbols and cues are explained in Emendations.

Authoritative Texts

A	First American edition of *Roughing It*
AP	*American Publisher*
BE	Buffalo *Express*
BoM	*Book of Mormon*
G	*Galaxy*
HoHI	*History of the Hawaiian Islands*
MP	*Mormon Prophet*
NYT	New York *Times*
PCA	Honolulu *Pacific Commercial Advertiser*
Pr	Prospectus of A
PT	*People's Tribune*
SU	Sacramento *Union*
TE63	Virginia City *Territorial Enterprise*
TE70	Virginia City *Territorial Enterprise*
VoM	*Vigilantes of Montana*

►A   First American edition. *Roughing It*. Hartford: American Publishing Company, 1872–1903 (*BAL* 3337 and reimpressions). Twenty-five impressions are known, the first four of which are dated 1872 and the last 1903. Collation revealed that several pages in A exist in more than one state. For convenience, the designations below refer to whole copies, rather than to individual pages within the copies. Seven states have been identified. The earliest copy located of each state is as follows: Aa, Ab, Ac, and Ad, 1872; Ae, 1874; Af, 1877; Ag, 1892. The variants are cumulative in each state; that is, Ab contains the first variant, Ac contains that one plus one more, and so forth. The last known state, Ag, contains a total of twelve variants; they are listed in chronological order of appearance. Aa is copy-text for all of the book not specified as deriving from one of the other sources listed below (roughly 75 percent of the text).

309.18	eastern (Aa) • Eastern (Ab–g)
542.7	hearties (Aa–b) • heartiest (Ac–g)
102.28	breast-pin (Aa–c) • breast pin (Ad–g)
103.13	death! (Aa–c) • ~. (Ad–g)
222.12–13	he was occupying his (Aa–c) • was occupying (Ad–g)
136n.6	thirteenth (Aa–d) • sixteenth (Ae–g)
273.2	toss² (Aa–d) • ~, (Ae–g)
273.31	fortune— (Aa–d) • ~∧ (Ae–g)
91.10	[They (Aa–e) • ∧~ (Af–g)
136n.6	Aha! (Aa–e) • ~∧ (Af–g)
236.5	coarse (Aa–e) • course (Af–g)
517.11	tidal wave (Aa–f) • tidal-wave (Ag)

►AP *American Publisher:* "The Old-Time Pony Express of the Great Plains," May 1871, 4. Eight extracts from *Roughing It* were printed in the *American Publisher,* the house journal of the American Publishing Company, between May 1871 and June 1872. Of the eight extracts, seven derived from the A typesetting; they are identified below in "Derivative Texts." One extract, however, was typeset directly from Mark Twain's *Roughing It* manuscript, or possibly from an amanuensis copy of it, and therefore contains readings that may have equal authority with A. This passage, listed below, is thus a radiating text, and all variants in it between A and AP are reported in Emendations. For a full discussion see the textual note at 50.1–52.7.

50.1–52.7   'IN . . . maybe.'
No illustrations were included.

►BE Buffalo *Express.* Out of the series of ten "Around the World" letters that Mark Twain published in the Buffalo *Express* between October 1869 and March 1870, he drew upon five—plus an additional *Express* sketch published in April 1870—for use in *Roughing It.* BE is copy-text for the passages listed below.

"Around the World. Letter No. One," 16 October 1869, 1.
245.1–249.15   MONO . . . true.
"Around the World. Letter No. 3," 13 November 1869, 1.
387.18–392.24   The¹ . . . over."

"Around the World. Letter Number 4," 11 December 1869, 2.
238.1–240.6   IT . . . desires.   BE, ¶17–18
392.25–395.11   But . . . head.   BE, ¶1–16
"Around the World. Letter Number 5," 18 December 1869, 2.
413.6–419.28   In . . . me.
"Around the World. Letter Number 6," 8 January 1870, 2.
299.7–301.31   Two . . . him.   BE, ¶1–18
303.35–304.2   I . . . again.   BE, ¶19
"The Facts in the Great Land Slide Case," 2 April 1870, 2.
221.1–227.5   THE . . . understanding.

▸BoM   *The Book of Mormon: An Account Written by the Hand of Mor-
         mon, upon Plates Taken from the Plates of Nephi.* Translated by
Joseph Smith, Jun. Sixth European Edition. Liverpool: Published by
Brigham Young, Jun., 1866. The relevant passages in the following edi-
tions or impressions of the Book of Mormon were collated to determine
Mark Twain's most likely source for the extracts in chapter 16: first
through fifth American (1830, 1837, 1840, 1842, 1858); first through sixth
European (1841, 1849, 1852, 1854, 1854, 1866); and Independence (187–).
Collation established that he could have used either the fifth or sixth European (English) "edition"—actually two printings of the same typesetting, with different front matter but otherwise apparently identical texts.
The sixth edition has been designated copy-text for the passages listed below, since it was probably the one most readily available in 1870–71. Citations are to book, chapter, verse, and (where necessary) line: "Jacob
2:6:14–25" refers to the Book of Jacob, chapter 2, verse 6, lines 14–25.

107.26–111.2   THE . . . powers: BoM, title page (lines
                                               1–23) and testimonial
                                               page

111.3–25   And . . . Jacob: BoM, 1 Nephi 5:38,
                                               5:39:1–2, 5:42

111.26–112.7   For . . . everybody: BoM, Jacob 2:6:14–25,
                                               2:9:11–18

112.8–36   And . . . children.   BoM, 3 Nephi 9:1:1–3,
                                               9:2:1–8, 8:5:3–22

113.24–114.44   7. . . . written.   BoM, Ether 6:7–8,
                                               6:9:1–25

▸G   *Galaxy:* "About a Remarkable Stranger. Being a Sandwich Island
         Reminiscence," 11 (April 1871): 616–18. Mark Twain apparently
revised a copy of this *Galaxy* printing when preparing printer's copy for
chapter 77. G is copy-text for the passage listed below.

526.1–531.22   I . . . sir."

▸HoHI   *History of the Hawaiian Islands,* by James Jackson Jarves. Third
         Edition. Honolulu: Charles Edwin Hitchcock, 1847. The rele-
vant passages in the following editions or impressions of Jarves's book

were collated to determine Mark Twain's most likely source for the extracts in his Sacramento *Union* letter published on 1 August 1866, which was later incorporated into chapter 68 of *Roughing It:* first (Boston and London, 1843); second (Boston, 1844); and third (Honolulu, 1847). Collation established that Mark Twain used the third edition. HoHI is copytext for the passage listed below; substantive variants between HoHI and ¶20–30 of the *Union* letter are reported in Emendations.

469.30–472.43	On . . . abuse.	HoHI, 105 ¶1–106 ¶4

►MP   *The Mormon Prophet and His Harem; or, An Authentic History of Brigham Young, His Numerous Wives and Children,* by Mrs. Catharine V. Waite. Fifth Edition, revised and enlarged. Chicago: J. S. Goodman and Co., 1868. Waite's book, which Mark Twain explicitly mentions as his source for the quotations in appendix B (550.22–23), was first issued in 1866, reprinted several times, and published in a "revised and enlarged" edition in 1868. The passages quoted by Mark Twain are identical (apparently printed from the same plates) in the two editions; the 1868 edition has been designated copy-text for the passages listed below because it was probably the one most readily available in 1870–71.

550.24–551.6	A . . . God.	MP, 76 ¶1
551.29–552.21	They . . . occasion:	MP, 73 ¶4–74 ¶2
552.22–553.7	He . . . reliable:	MP, 84 ¶5–85 ¶2
553.9–38	For . . . depredations.	MP, 76 ¶3–77 ¶7

►NYT   New York *Times:* "Across the Continent: From the Missouri to the Pacific Ocean by Rail," by William Swinton, 28 June 1869, 1–2. Although Mark Twain explicitly names the New York *Times* as the source of the extract in chapter 4 (26.29), collation suggested that his actual source may have been a reprinting of the article in an unidentified newspaper, incorporating several "corrections" (actually corruptions) of the text. Nevertheless, in the belief that Mark Twain intended to present an accurate text of the *Times* article, regardless of the actual copy that he had access to, NYT has been chosen as copy-text for the passages listed below.

26.32–34	ACROSS . . . jaunt.	NYT, title, ¶3
26.34–37	A . . . car.	NYT, ¶8
26.37–28.5	It . . . *out.*	NYT, ¶12

►PCA   Honolulu *Pacific Commercial Advertiser:* "Programme of the Funeral of Her Late Royal Highness the Princess Victoria Kamamalu Kaahumanu," 30 June 1866, 2. Mark Twain probably used a clipping of this program when preparing his Sacramento *Union* letter published on 1 August 1866. The *Union* letter was later incorporated into *Roughing It.* PCA is copy-text for the passage listed below; substantive variants between PCA and ¶8 of the *Union* letter are reported in Emendations. For a full discussion see the textual note at 466.19–468.3.

466.19–468.3	Undertaker . . . Force.

▶Pr   Prospectus. *Roughing It.* Hartford: American Publishing Company, 1871 and 1872. The prospectus was issued in two states, Pra (first copy bound on 22 November 1871) and Prb (first copy bound on 23 January 1872). Both states include eighty pages of selections from the book, plus two pages of advertising, a one-page "Publisher's Announcement," a page giving the prices of copies in the available bindings, and thirty-two blank ruled pages for the salesman to record his orders. Included in the advertising is an illustration from chapter 20 that does not appear elsewhere in Pr; it is printed on page 131 of this edition. Pr never serves as copy-text, although in one instance it is a source of emendation (see the textual note at 350.15–353.10). Except for one instance (see the entry below at 113.39–115.1), the make-up of the Pra pages—exclusive of folios and running heads—is identical to that of the corresponding A pages; all of the pages in Prb are identical in make-up to those in A. Unlike the pages in prospectuses for other works by Mark Twain, those in the *Roughing It* prospectus were not bound in the correct first-edition sequence. The first table below lists the contents in the order in which they appear in Pra and identifies the differences between Pra and Prb. Some minor variation has been noted among the copies of Pra examined in the number and placement of full-page illustrations, but since these are inserted plates, their placement does not affect the composition of type or imposition of pages; the table describes Pra (collection of Dorothy Goldberg). Only one copy of Prb has been examined (CU-MARK PS1318.A1 1872p). Prb contains the same pages as Pra (with the exception noted above), bound in the order shown in the second table. Both prospectuses contain the first-edition title page, copyright page, dedication page, and "Prefatory"; the title and copyright pages in Pra read "1871," and in Prb read "1872." The symbol "A" signifies "identical to A"; the symbol "Pra" signifies "identical to Pra."

CONTENTS OF PRA AND PRB, IN PRA ORDER

Page.line (C)	Cue/Description	Pra	Prb	Chapter:page (A)
218 *illus*	CAMPING IN THE SNOW.	A	A	frontispiece #1
xx *illus*	THE MINER'S DREAM.	[*not in*]	A	frontispiece #2
xxv *title*–b.6	List . . . 49	A	A	v
xxvb.7–xxviiib.28	35. . . . 543	[*contains four blank pages with folios vii–x, headed* 'ILLUSTRATIONS.']	A	vi–x
xxix *title*–xxxi.20	*Contents* . . . 122	A	A	xi–xii
xxxi.21–xxxii.27	CHAPTER . . . 179	[*page numbers for chapters not yet supplied*]	A	xiii

Page.line (C)	Cue/Description	Pra	Prb	Chapter:page (A)
xxxii.28– xxxvi.22	CHAPTER . . . 396	[contains three blank pages with folios xiv– xvi, headed 'CONTENTS.']	A	xiv–xvi
1.1–3.8	MY . . . SO.	A	A	1:19–21
4.1–9.11	THE . . . under	A	A	2:22–27
10.1–22	ABOUT . . . curtain,	A	A	3:29
11.25–14.12	legs . . . miniature	A	A	3:31–33 [last page ends 'minia-|']
15.23–17.15	jackass . . . height.	A	A	3:35–36
18.24–19.12	ourselves . . . every	A	A	4:38
79 illus	THE SOUTH PASS.	[not in]	A	12: facing 100
521 illus	A VIEW IN THE IAO VALLEY.	A	A	76: facing 547
347.9–353.18	I[1] . . . ashore.	[pages lack fo- lios and chapter identification]	[pages have cor- rect folios ex- cept for folios 373–74, which are reversed, al- though the pages are in the cor- rect order]	51:369–75
303.32–307.15	some . . . us."	[325, 327, 328 numbered '1, 3, 4' without chap- ter identifica- tion; 326 unnumbered]	A	46:325–28
107.1–22	ALL . . . it	[page headed (incorrectly) 'CHAPTER XVII.']	A	16:127
108.31–111.6	these . . . and[2]	[pages num- bered '17-3, 17- 4' to indicate pages 3 and 4 of (incorrect) chap- ter 17]	A	16:129–130
42.25–44.6	worth . . . holding	[pages num- bered with (in- correct) folios '77, 78']	A	7:62–63 [last page ends 'hold-|']
296 illus	THE GREAT "FLOUR SACK" PROCESSION.	A	A	45: facing 317
50.1–54.1	IN . . . with	A	A	8:70–73

Page.line (C)	Cue/Description	Pra	Prb	Chapter:page (A)
144.19–146.20	The . . . enemy.	[165 numbered '4'; 166–67 numbered '22-5, 22-6' to indicate pages 5 and 6 of (incorrect) chapter 22]	A	21:165–67
532.1–536.29	AFTER . . . well.	[558 headed (incorrectly) 'CHAPTER LXXV.'; 559–63 numbered '2-75, 3-75, 4-75, 5-75, 6-75' to indicate pages 2 through 6 of (incorrect) chapter 75]	Pra	78:558–63
60.1–62.3	REALLY . . . which	A	A	10:80–81
63.38–64.13 | 64n.1	and . . . practices. | *"The . . . Dimsdale.	A	A	10:84
155 illus	FIRE AT LAKE TAHOE.	A	A	23: facing 176
518.1–520.26	WE . . . such	[544 headed (incorrectly) 'CHAPTER LXXIII.' and numbered '1-73'; 545–46 numbered '2-73, 3-73' to indicate pages 2 and 3 of (incorrect) chapter 73]	[like Pra, except that 544 lacks the number '1-73']	76:544–46
152.25–157.13	conquering . . . history.	[pages numbered '24-2, 24-3, 24-4, 24-5' to indicate pages 2, 3, 4, and 5 of (incorrect) chapter 24; illustration on 24-2 does not appear on 174 in A, but on 169 (117 in C), and type on 24-2 wraps around on left side rather than right; caption matches A 174]	A	23:174–77 [first page begins 'quering']
48.16–49.24	cocoanut . . . boys."	A	A	7:68–69 [first page begins 'nut']
76.24–82.14	world . . . the[2]	A	A	12:98–102
32.18–33.3	is[2] . . . pie."	A	A	5:51

Page.line (C)	Cue/Description	Pra	Prb	Chapter:page (A)
113.39–115.1	camps . . . dreary	[page numbered '17-8' to indicate page 8 of (incorrect) chapter 17]	[not in; includes revised page described in next entry instead]	16:134.25–135.28
114.18–115n.1	wine . . . *Milton.	[not in; includes page described in previous entry instead]	A	16:135
244 illus	MONO LAKE. ['LAKE MONO.' in Pr; emended]	A	A	38: facing 265
99.25–106.7	daughters . . . Mormons.	[pages numbered '16-2, 16-3, 16-4, 16-5, 16-6, 16-7, 16-8' to indicate pages 2 through 8 of (incorrect) chapter 16]	A	15:120–26
158.1–164.16	I¹ . . . I	[178 headed (incorrectly) 'CHAPTER XXV.'; 180–81 numbered '25-3, 25-4' to indicate pages 3 and 4 of (incorrect) chapter 25; 179 and 182–83 have no folios or chapter identification]	A	24:178–83
520.26–522.23	an . . . to	[page numbered '4-73' to indicate page 4 of (incorrect) chapter 73]	Pra	76:547
523.20–525.7	only . . . always.	[pages numbered '6-73, 7-73' to indicate pages 6 and 7 of (incorrect) chapter 73]	Pra	76:549–50
479 illus	GOING INTO THE MOUNTAINS.	A	A	69: facing 502

ORDER OF CONTENTS IN PRB

Page.line (C)	Cue/Description
15.23–17.15	jackass . . . height.
18.24–19.12	ourselves . . . every
79 illus	THE SOUTH PASS.
50.1–54.1	IN . . . with
144.19–146.20	The . . . enemy.
532.1–536.29	AFTER . . . well.
60.1–62.3	REALLY . . . which
63.38–64.13 | 64n.1	and . . . practices. | *"The . . . Dimsdale.
479 illus	GOING INTO THE MOUNTAINS.
518.1–520.26	WE . . . such
152.25–157.3	conquering . . . history. [first page begins 'quering']
48.16–49.24	cocoanut . . . boys." [first page begins 'nut']
76.24–82.14	world . . . the^2
32.18–33.3	is^2 . . . pie."
114.18–115n.1	wine . . . *Milton.
521 illus	A VIEW IN THE IAO VALLEY.
99.25–106.7	daughters . . . Mormons.
158.1–164.16	I^1 . . . I
520.26–522.23	an . . . to
523.20–525.7	only . . . always.
296 illus	THE GREAT "FLOUR SACK" PROCESSION.
304.31–307.15	"Say . . . us."
107.1–22	ALL . . . it
108.31–111.6	these . . . and^2
42.25–44.6	worth . . . holding [last page ends 'hold-|']
347.9–353.18	I^1 . . . ashore.
303.32–304.30	some . . . driver:
244 illus	MONO LAKE. ['LAKE MONO.' in Pr; emended]

▶PT   *People's Tribune:* "A Seeming Plot for Assassination Miscarried," by Conrad Wiegand, 1 (February 1870): 10–12, a reprinting of TE70 (see below). Although collation established that PT was Mark Twain's actual source for the text of Wiegand's letter in appendix C, TE70 is copy-text for the passage in this edition. All substantive variants between PT and TE70 are reported in Emendations. For a full discussion see the textual note at 555.3–569.38.

       555.3–569.38   From . . . M. T.]

▶SU   Sacramento *Union.* Out of the series of twenty-five Sandwich Islands letters that Mark Twain published in the *Union* between April and November 1866, he drew upon thirteen—with significant revisions and deletions—for use in *Roughing It.* As indicated below, many of these letters survive as clippings in scrapbooks that Orion Clemens compiled; since none of the scrapbook clippings shows any sign of revision, Mark Twain must have used other copies of the clippings to prepare the printer's copy of *Roughing It.* In addition to emendations of the texts he did use, all of the material in these thirteen letters which he decided not to reuse—approximately 60 percent of the text—is reported in full in Emendations. SU is copy-text for the passages listed below.

"Scenes in Honolulu—No. 4," 19 April 1866, 2, clippings in Scrapbook 6:109–10 and Scrapbook 7:41–43, CU-MARK.

431.9–434.2	then . . . sail—	

"Scenes in Honolulu—No. 5," 20 April 1866, 2, clippings in Scrapbook 6:110–11 and Scrapbook 7:43, CU-MARK.

454.15–456.6	Society . . . shoved."	

"Scenes in Honolulu—No. 6," 21 April 1866, 3, clippings in Scrapbook 6:111–12 and Scrapbook 7:43–47, CU-MARK.

436.2–438.21	I . . . about.	SU, ¶1–4
439.1–441.20	A . . . itself.	SU, ¶15–22
444.16–448.18	This . . . expense.	SU, ¶5–14

"Scenes in Honolulu—No. 7," 24 April 1866, 4, clipping in Scrapbook 6:112–13, CU-MARK.

442 title–444.15	CHAPTER . . . business.	SU, ¶1–23
448.19–450 title	It . . . CHAPTER 66	SU, ¶24

"Scenes in Honolulu—No. 8," 21 May 1866, 3.

450.1–453.37	PASSING . . . art.	

"Scenes in Honolulu—No. 12," 20 June 1866, 1, clipping in Scrapbook 6:116–17, CU-MARK.

457 title–458.18	CHAPTER . . . etc.[2]	

"Scenes in Honolulu—No. 15," 1 August 1866, 1, clipping in Scrapbook 6:122–23, CU-MARK.

466.15–18	After . . . procured:	SU, ¶1–8
468.4–469.29	I . . . came:	SU, ¶9–19
472.44–475 title	You . . . CHAPTER 69	SU, ¶31–34

"Letter from Honolulu," 18 August 1866, 1.

475.1–480.2	BOUND . . . fruit.	

"From the Sandwich Islands," 24 August 1866, 3.

480.3–24	At . . . required.	SU, ¶1–13
489.1–491.24	AT . . . retaliation.	SU, ¶14–33

"From the Sandwich Islands," 30 August 1866, 3.

491.25–492.20	Near . . . innocent.	

"From the Sandwich Islands," 6 September 1866, 3.

493 title–495.14	CHAPTER . . . point.	

"From the Sandwich Islands," 22 September 1866, 1.

495.15–506.4	I[1] . . . charge.	

"Letter from Honolulu," 16 November 1866, 1.

508.1–10	By . . . like.	SU, ¶1–6
508.11–23	A . . . revelation.	SU, ¶15
508.24–512.8	Arrived . . . hotel.	SU, ¶7–16

►TE63 Virginia City *Territorial Enterprise*: "Ye Bulletin Cyphereth," 27 August 1863, Scrapbook 2:70, CU-MARK. Mark Twain probably had two clippings of this article, which he had written for the *Enterprise* several years earlier. One still survives in a scrapbook, and the other he apparently incorporated into the printer's copy for *Roughing It*. TE63 is copy-text for the passage listed below.

      355n.1–356n.3   *Mr. . . . M. T.]

▸TE70   Virginia City *Territorial Enterprise:* "Mr. Winters' Assault on Conrad Wiegand," by Conrad Wiegand, 20 January 1870, 1. Although the heading "From the Territorial Enterprise, Jan. 20, 1870" (555.3) implies that the text of the letter by Conrad Wiegand reproduced in appendix C is taken from the *Enterprise*, collation established that the actual source was a reprinting of the letter in the Gold Hill (Nevada) *People's Tribune* (see PT above). Nevertheless, TE70 has been designated copy-text for the passage listed below. The rationale for this selection, as well as a full explanation of the emendation policy for this appendix, may be found in the textual note at 555.3–569.38.

      555.3–569.38   From . . . M. T.]

▸VoM   *The Vigilantes of Montana, or Popular Justice in the Rocky Mountains. Being a Correct and Impartial Narrative of the Chase, Trial, Capture and Execution of Henry Plummer's Road Agent Band, Together with Accounts of the Lives and Crimes of Many of the Robbers and Desperadoes, the Whole Being Interspersed with Sketches of Life in the Mining Camps of the "Far West;" Forming the Only Reliable Work on the Subject Ever Offered the Public*, by Prof. Thomas J. Dimsdale. Virginia City, Montana Territory: Montana Post Press, 1866. Mark Twain explicitly mentions Dimsdale's book as his source for the quotations in the two chapters on the desperado Slade (64n.1, 69.5–8); it was issued in only one edition, which is copy-text for the passages listed below.

63.35–64.2	On . . . paragraph:	VoM, 175 ¶2
64.3–9	While . . . execution.	VoM, 175 ¶1
64.9–11	Stories . . . line.	VoM, 175 ¶4
64.11–13	As . . . practices.	VoM, 175 ¶3
69.5–13	"The . . . picturesque:	VoM, title page
69.13–17	"Those . . . incarnate."	VoM, 167 ¶2, lines 19–24
69.17–21	And . . . mine:	VoM, 175 ¶3, lines 3–4
69.22–74.18	After . . . feelings.	VoM, 167 ¶3–173 ¶3

Derivative Texts

▸AP   *American Publisher.* The following seven extracts published in the *American Publisher* derived from A without authorial revision or intervention. The first four were evidently typeset from page proofs of A or from Pr. The last three were probably typeset from a bound copy of A.

      "My First Lecture," December 1871, 4. Includes three illustrations from A, with captions (see pages 535–36).
      533.5–536.29   I . . . well.

"A Nabob's Visit to New York," January 1872, 4. Includes three illustrations from A, without captions (see pages 305–6).

304.3–307.15   In . . . us."

"Dollinger the Aged Pilot Man," February 1872, 8. Includes five illustrations from A, without captions (see pages 348–52).

347.9–353.18   I¹ . . . ashore.

Untitled extract, February 1872, 8. No illustrations included.

101.9–103.9   Mr. . . . mountains.

"Roughing It," March 1872, 8. Includes three illustrations from A, without captions (see pages 393–95).

391.27–395n.1   It¹ . . . M. T.

"Horace Greeley's Ride," April 1872, 8. Includes two illustrations from A, without captions (see pages 131 and 134).

131.7–136.5   On . . . Greeley.*

"Mark Twain on the Mormons," June 1872, 8. Includes four illustrations from A, with captions (see pages 100, 101, 104, and 105).

99.14–106.2   And . . . it."

►Aus   Australian edition. 2 vols. *The Innocents at Home, Part I— Roughing It* and *The Innocents at Home, Part II—The Pacific Coast*. Melbourne: George Robertson, 1872. Although this unillustrated edition resembles E physically, it was typeset from Ad and includes the appendixes of A, which E lacks. Unlike E, it does not contain "A Burlesque Autobiography." A "Notice" on an inserted slip reads: "This edition of 'The Innocents at Home' is reissued by authority from Messrs. George Routledge & Sons, of London, who are owners of the British Copyright." In 1873 Robertson reissued these two volumes, bound together in one volume, as *The Innocents at Home*, which includes separate title pages for the two parts.

►E   First English edition, first issue. *"Roughing It"* (*BAL* 3335) and *The Innocents at Home* (*BAL* 3336). London: George Routledge and Sons, 1872. This unillustrated edition was typeset from proof sheets of Aa, but lacks the appendixes included in all states of A. The second volume, however, concludes with "A Burlesque Autobiography," which was not included in A. Soon after the appearance of both volumes as the "Copyright Edition," the first volume (but not the second) was reissued as the "Author's English Edition" (*BAL* 3599). This volume was then bound together with the "Copyright Edition" of *The Innocents at Home* to create the single-volume edition of *Roughing It and the Innocents at Home* (George Routledge and Sons, 1872). *The Innocents at Home*, printed from the Routledge plates, was also issued in Toronto by the Musson Book Company sometime after 1901. No Musson issue of *Roughing It* has been located.

►PJks   *Practical Jokes with Artemus Ward, Including the Story of the Man Who Fought Cats*. By Mark Twain and Other Humourists.

London: John Camden Hotten, [1872]. *BAL* 3342. For a full discussion of PJks, HWa, HWa**MT**, and HWb, see the Introduction, pages 893–95. The three sketches marked with an asterisk below derived from E. The fourth sketch was typeset directly from G and therefore includes none of the revisions that Mark Twain carried out on G when preparing A.

> *"Editorial Skits": A → E → PJks
>
> 339.13–26   Once . . . stranger!"
>
> "Mark Twain's Remarkable Stranger": G → PJks
>
> 526.11–531.22   I . . . sir."
>
> *"Sending Them Through": A → E → PJks
>
> 38.4–40.3   No . . . boy.
>
> *"The Union—Right or Wrong?": A → E → PJks
>
> 278.11–281.3   We . . . had.

►HWa   *The Choice Humorous Works of Mark Twain.* Now First Collected. With Extra Passages to the "Innocents Abroad," Now First Reprinted, and a Life of the Author. London: John Camden Hotten, [1873]. *BAL* 3351. Mark Twain revised and corrected a set of sheets of HWa (HWa**MT**, now at NN); his changes were incorporated into HWb. The four sketches marked with an asterisk below derived ultimately from A: three through E, and one apparently through AP. The other four derived as noted. The collation entries listed below record the textual history of words occurring in passages deriving from A which Mark Twain revised in HWa**MT**, but do not report other variants between A and HWa.

> "Baker's Cat": BE → Scrs → HWa → HWa**MT** → HWb
>
> 416.9–419.28   Whenever . . . me.
>
> The HWa text derived ultimately from BE (SLC 1869o), through an intervening printing in *Screamers: A Gathering of Scraps of Humour, Delicious Bits, & Short Stories* (London: John Camden Hotten, [1871]). For details and a full collation, including a record of the holograph revisions on HWa**MT**, see *ET&S4*.
>
> "Honoured as a Curiosity in Honolulu": SU → Cal → JF1 → JF2 → JF3 → HWa → HWa**MT** [*no revision*] → HWb
>
> 454.16–456.6   If . . . shoved."
>
> The HWa text derived ultimately from a piece entitled "Etiquette" in SU (SLC 1866m), through intervening printings in the *Californian* and three successive editions of *The Celebrated Jumping Frog of Calaveras County* (JF1, New York: C. H. Webb, 1867; JF2, London: George Routledge and Sons, 1867 [unauthorized]; JF3, London: John Camden Hotten, [1870] [unauthorized]). HWa**MT** contains no revisions. For details and a full collation, see *ET&S3*.
>
> *"Mark in Mormonland": A → E → HWa → HWa**MT** [*deleted*]
>
> 100.1–106.7   According . . . Mormons.
>
> The HWa text derived from A, through E; Mark Twain deleted it without revision on HWa**MT**.

*"A Nabob's Visit to New York": A → AP → HWa → HWa**MT** → HWb
304.3–307.15 In . . . us."

The HWa text derived from A; the collation entry at 305.10 suggests that it was typeset from AP.

305.3	Ride it (A–AP, HWa**MT**–HWb) • Ride (HWa)
305.10	stared (A) • started for (HWa); stared for (AP, HWa**MT**–HWb)
305.24	can't (A–AP, HWa**MT**–HWb) • shan't (HWa)
305.36	reckon— (A–AP, HWa**MT**–HWb) • ~∧ (HWa)
306.18	cleats (A–AP, HWa**MT**–HWb) • bleats (HWa)
307.14	had (A–AP, HWa**MT**–HWb) • have (HWa)

"A Remarkable Stranger": G → PJks → HWa → HWa**MT** → HWb
526.11–531.22 I . . . sir."

The HWa text derived ultimately from G, through PJks. For details and a full collation, including a record of the holograph revisions on HWa**MT**, see *ET&S5*.

*"Sending Them Through": A → E → PJks → HWa → HWa**MT** → HWb
38.4–40.3 No . . . boy.

The HWa text derived from A, through E and PJks.

39.6	*who!* (A–E, HWa**MT**–HWb) • *what!* (PJks–HWa) [*SLC in* HWa**MT** *margin:* "God damn the hound who altered that."]
39.7	*who!* (A–E) • *what!* (PJks–HWa); *who!* (HWa**MT**–HWb)
39.8	Moses, (A–E) • Moses was (PJks–HWa); Moses (HWa**MT**–HWb)

"The Steed 'Oahu'": SU → Cal → JF1 → JF2 → JF3 → HWa → HWa**MT** → HWb
437.5–438.7 The . . . storm.

The publication history of the HWa text is identical to that of "Honoured as a Curiosity in Honolulu" (see above). For details and a full collation, including a record of one holograph revision on HWa**MT**, see *ET&S3*.

*"The Union—Right or Wrong?": A → E → PJks → HWa → HWa**MT** → HWb
278.11–281.3 We . . . had.

The HWa text derived from A, through E and PJks. (The designation "A–HWa" means that the reading is identical in A, E, PJks, and HWa.)

278.31–279.1	get . . . have[1] (A–E) • get (PJks–HWb) [*this corruption necessitated SLC's revision at 279.2*]
279.2	they will (A–HWa) • I can (HWa**MT**–HWb)
279.6	rational (A–HWa) • human (HWa**MT**–HWb)
280.11	But (A–HWa) • [*no* ¶] ~ (HWa**MT**–HWb) [*SLC in* HWa**MT** *margin:* "No ¶"]
280.11	friendly. The (A–E) • ~! [¶] ~ (PJks–HWa); ~. [¶] ~ (HWa**MT**–HWb)

►HWb   *The Choice Humorous Works of Mark Twain.* Revised and Corrected by the Author. With Life and Portrait of the Author, and

Numerous Illustrations. London: Chatto and Windus, 1874. *BAL* 3605. HWb incorporated the revisions inscribed by Mark Twain on HWaMT; all the texts were therefore merely new impressions of HWa, with corrected plates. All but one of the *Roughing It* sketches in HWa were reprinted in HWb; Mark Twain canceled "Mark in Mormonland." Later reprintings of "Honoured as a Curiosity in Honolulu"—in *Mark Twain's Sketches, New and Old* (American Publishing Company, 1875), *Information Wanted* (George Routledge and Sons, [1876]), and *Sketches by Mark Twain* (Bernhard Tauchnitz, 1883)—derived from HWb without authorial revision.

▶Can   Canadian edition. *Roughing It.* Toronto: Belford and Co., 1880.
          This unauthorized, abridged edition was set from Af. It contains 71 instead of 79 chapters: chapters 22, 36, 45, 49, 52, 71, 72, and 77 were omitted, as were the appendixes. Although "Fully Illustrated by Eminent Artists," according to the title page, it contains relatively few illustrations, some possibly tracings of illustrations in A and others probably stock cuts chosen for their fancied appropriateness. In July 1880, Belford and Company issued an impression of this edition, in a two-column format resembling a magazine or small newspaper, as "The Belford Library," no. 9 (July [n.y.]). Although this impression looks very different from the book issued by Belford, it was printed from the same type, reimposed line for line, some 75 lines per page. The year of the Belford Library impression is implied by the presence, below the masthead and title, of a quotation taken from a review of *A Tramp Abroad* which appeared in the London *Athenaeum* no. 2739 (24 Apr 80): 529–30. Undated reprints of this edition were issued by Rose-Belford Publishing Company and Rose Publishing Company; Rose-Belford was in operation until 1883, and Rose from 1883 until 1894.

▶Tau   Continental edition. 2 vols. *Roughing It* and *The Innocents at
          Home.* Authorized Edition. Leipzig: Bernhard Tauchnitz, 1880–81. *BAL* 3627. Collection of British Authors, volumes 1929 and 1948. This unillustrated edition was typeset from E. Like E, volume 2 includes "A Burlesque Autobiography" and omits the appendixes included in A.

▶E2   Second English edition. 1 vol. *Roughing It and The Innocents at
          Home.* Illustrated by F. A. Fraser. London: George Routledge and Sons, 1882. *BAL* 3630. This edition was typeset from E but contains many corrected readings from A, including one variant ("sixteenth" at 136n.6) introduced in Ae, as well as the appendixes of A that were omitted from E. Like E, however, it includes "A Burlesque Autobiography." An 1883 impression of E2 is recorded as *BAL* 3635. In 1885 Chatto and Windus acquired the plates of E2 from Routledge, together with 1536 copies of the book in quires. Chatto issued these copies with a cancel title page bearing its own imprint in 1885, and produced another printing in 1889. The two Routledge impressions and the 1889 Chatto impression were sold at 7*s.* 6*d.* in decorated red cloth. In 1897 Chatto and Windus issued the first of a

number of impressions printed from the same plates but priced at 3s. 6d. and bound in dark blue cloth stamped in gold on the front cover and spine.

▸LoH   *Mark Twain's Library of Humor.* New York: Charles L. Webster and Co., 1888. *BAL* 3425. This edition was also issued in Montreal by the Dawson Brothers (1888), an authorized printing from duplicate plates of LoH. The texts of all five *Roughing It* excerpts were typeset from A.

> "The Cayote"
> 30.5–34.12   Along . . . parents.
> "Dick Baker's Cat"
> 416.1–419.25   ONE . . . mining."
> "A Genuine Mexican Plug"
> 158.1–165.12   I¹ . . . perhaps.
> "Lost in the Snow"
> 207.14–219.24   We . . . cards!
> "Nevada Nabobs in New York"
> 304.3–307.15   In . . . us."

▸LoHE   *Mark Twain's Library of Humour.* London: Chatto and Windus, 1888 and 1897. *BAL* 1982. This authorized edition contains all of the *Roughing It* selections in LoH, from which it was typeset.

▸SAH   *Selections from American Humour.* Leipzig: Bernhard Tauchnitz, 1888. *BAL* 3646. The texts of both *Roughing It* excerpts were typeset from LoH.

> "Dick Baker's Cat"
> 416.1–419.25   ONE . . . mining."
> "A Genuine Mexican Plug"
> 158.1–165.12   I¹ . . . perhaps.

▸A2   Second American edition. 2 vols. *Roughing It.* Hartford: American Publishing Company, 1899, 1901, and 1903; London: Chatto and Windus, 1899; New York: Harper and Brothers, 1903–?14. *BAL* 3456. This edition was typeset from Ag. The three earliest impressions, all issued in 1899, were called the Autograph, Royal, and Popular "editions." All later impressions include corrections in the plates suggested by Forrest Morgan, a proofreader for the American Publishing Company; Mark Twain was evidently consulted in only one instance: see the textual note at 416.4.[1] These corrections first appeared in two other 1899 impressions

---

[1] The copy of A2 marked with corrections by Forrest Morgan (Royal edition, vols. 7–8) is at CtY-BR. In addition, some—but not all—of these corrections are listed on a sheet of paper now at ViU (Box 13, 6314-q). At the top of this sheet is written "Corrections for Roughing It—old edition" in Morgan's hand; the list itself is in Frank Bliss's hand. Morgan compared the text of A with the text of A2, restoring readings from A in some cases, and offering additional corrections as well. His suggestions were reviewed by Bliss, who evidently selected which ones to carry out (see *HF,* 522–23 n. 5).

called the Japan and DeLuxe editions. Later impressions include the Hillcrest edition, issued by the American Publishing Company in 1903, and also by Harper and Brothers from 1903 to 1906; the Author's National edition; and the Uniform Library edition issued by Harper from about 1904 to 1914, both as two volumes and as two volumes in one. In 1915, Harper issued a new, more compact, two-volume edition as the Limp Leather edition. Whereas in A2 volume 1 ends on page 326 and volume 2 on page 366, in this later edition volume 1 ends on unnumbered page 287 and volume 2 on unnumbered page 330. The new plates were used subsequently to produce the regular Harper edition, which bore no "edition" name, both in two volumes and in two volumes bound as one, and the two-volume Definitive edition published in 1922 by Gabriel Wells. A copy of *Roughing It* now in the Mark Twain Papers, issued by Harper and Row in 1969, was printed from the same setting of type.

▶Below is a list of additional books known to have reprinted excerpts from *Roughing It* during the author's lifetime (newspaper reprintings are not included). There is no evidence to suggest that they incorporate Mark Twain's revisions or corrections, but the possibility of authorial intervention cannot be ruled out entirely, since the excerpted texts have not been collated.

That Convention; or, Five Days a Politician. By F. G. W. et als. By Fletcher G. Welch. New York and Chicago: F. G. Welch and Co., 1872. *BAL*, 2:246. "The Champion Chirography of the Modern Cincinnatus."

Howard's Recitations. Comic, Serious, and Pathetic. Edited by Clarence J. Howard. New York: Dick and Fitzgerald, [1872]. *BAL*, 2:246. "Buck Fanshaw's Funeral."

One Hundred Choice Selections No. 9. Compiled by Phineas Garrett. Philadelphia and Chicago: P. Garrett and Co., 1874. *BAL*, 2:247. "Buck Fanshaw's Funeral."

The Pacific Coast Fourth Reader. San Francisco: A. L. Bancroft and Co., 1874. "The Pony Rider," "A Nevada Quartz-Mill" (parts 1 and 2), and "The Coyote."

The Elocutionist's Annual Number 2. Edited by J. W. Shoemaker. Philadelphia: J. W. Shoemaker and Co., 1875. *BAL*, 2:247. "Buck Fanshaw's Funeral."

Speechiana. New York: Happy Hours Co., [1875?]. "Buck Fanshaw's Funeral."

Record of the Year, 1:4 (April 1876). Reissued in *Parlor Table Companion.* New York: G. W. Carleton and Co., 1877. *BAL* 3376. "Mark Twain Buys a Horse."

The Reading Club and Handy Speaker. Number 6. Edited by George M. Baker. Boston: Lee and Shepard; New York: Charles T. Dillingham, 1879. *BAL*, 2:249. "Greeley's Ride."

Wit and Humor of the Age . . . by Mark Twain, Robt. J. Burdette, Josh Bill-ings, Alex. Sweet, Eli Perkins. With the Philosophy of Wit and Humor, by Melville D. Landon. Chicago: Western Publishing House, 1883. *BAL* 3633 and 11220; reprinted by various publishers, sometimes entitled *Library of Wit and Humor by Mark Twain and Others.* "Mark Twain on the First Woman in Nevada," "Mark Twain's Nevada Funeral—Scotty Briggs and the Clergyman," and "Mark Twain on the First San Francisco Baby."

Selections of American Humor in Prose and Verse. Leipzig: Gressner and Schramm, [1883]. "The Aged Pilot Man."

Choice Bits from Mark Twain. London: Diprose and Bateman, [1885]. *BAL* 3639. "Baker's Cat" and "Sending Them Through."

Chambers's New Reciter: Comprising Selections from the Works of I. Zangwill . . . [et al.] Edited by R. C. H. Morison. London: W. and R. Cham-bers, 1900. "Buck Fanshaw's Funeral."

Masterpieces of Wit and Humor with Stories and an Introduction by Rob-ert J. Burdette. Copyright, 1902, by E. J. Long. *BAL* 2013 and 3473. "The Funeral of Buck Fanshaw."

Mark Twain's Library of Humor: The Primrose Way. New York: Harper and Brothers, 1906. *BAL* 3668. "Buck Fanshaw's Funeral."

The American Press Humorists' Book. Edited and published by Frank Thompson Searight. Los Angeles: Frank Thompson Searight, 1907. *BAL* 3501. "Mark Twain Recalls an Incident of Carson Days" [Nevada nabobs in New York].

Collations

Like most books printed in the latter half of the nineteenth century, all copies of the first American edition of *Roughing It* were manufactured with acidic paper that has deteriorated over time, rendering the volumes extremely fragile. To reduce unnecessary damage to copies in CU-MARK, the text was initially transcribed and many collations were performed us-ing copies of a modern facsimile of Ac (N.Y.: Hippocrene Books, [1987]). Variant readings, however, were always checked in actual first-edition copies.

Printer's copy for this edition was initially prepared by two typists, each of whom keyed the entire text of the first edition from a copy of the Ac facsimile on a microcomputer using WordPerfect software, version 5.0. DocuComp software, version 1.2, was used to compare the two transcrip-tions electronically and to generate a list of the differences between them. The typographical errors thus revealed were purged from the text. Pas-sages based on sources other than A were then altered to bring them into conformity with their several copy-texts, by incorporation of accepted copy-text readings (previously identified through collation), and the en-tire text was emended as necessary. The resulting edited text was submit-ted on floppy disk to Wilsted & Taylor Publishing Services of Oakland,

California, who converted it electronically using Penta software to enable a Linotron 202 typesetter to produce printed pages. The page proofs were proofread by a two-person team against a copy of Ab and the other copytexts. It was thus possible to detect at this stage any errors that had previously been overlooked. In some half dozen instances the two typists made identical errors, which had not been identified by the DocuComp comparison. In addition, a handful of errors had been introduced by typesetter intervention. To ensure that the integrity of the corrected electronic text was preserved through successive stages of production, a final collation was performed—by superimposition on a light box—between the earliest correct version of each page and its last page proof, generated immediately before the book was printed.

The first-edition illustrations were reproduced from a copy of Ac (CU-MARK PS1318.A1 1872 copy 1). In addition, the points distinguishing the seven states of A from one another were checked in the following copies: Aa (CU-MARK PS1318.A1 1872 copy 4); Ab (CU-MARK PS1318.A1 1872); Ac (CU-MARK facsimile); Ac (CU-MARK PS1318.A1 1872c copy 1); Ac (CU-MARK PS1318.A1 1872a copy 2); Ad (CU-MARK PS1318.A1 1872a copy 4); Ae (Hirst); Af (CU-MARK PS1318.A1 1888); Ag (CU-MARK PS1318.A1 1900); Ag (Vi PS1318.A1 1903).

The sight collations listed below were carried out by two-person teams. The machine collations were performed on a Hinman collator. An asterisk (*) on an entry indicates that the complete collation performed for *RI 1972* was not repeated; instead, sight collation was performed on selected passages only, as needed to support the conclusion that the text was wholly derivative.

SIGHT COLLATIONS

Ac (CU-MARK PS1318.A1 1872c copy 1, PH) *vs.*
    AP (DLC, PH)
    BE (NBu, PH)
    BoM (CoDR BX8623 1866)
    G (CU-MARK AP2.G2 set 2)
    HoHI (CU-BANC DU625.J385)
    MP (CU-BANC xF835.W18 1868)
    NYT (CU-NEWS, PH)
    PCA (CU-BANC, PH)
    PT (CU-BANC, PH)
    SU, April 1866 (CU-MARK, clippings in Scrapbook 6:109–13)
    SU, May–November 1866 (CU-MARK, bound newsprint)
    TE63 (CU-MARK, clipping in Scrapbook 2:70)
    TE70 (CU-BANC, PH)
    VoM (CU-BANC xF731.D57)

Ac (CU-MARK facsimile) *vs.*
    Aus (NRU PS1318.A1r, PH)*
    Aus (CU-MARK PS1322.I537 1873)*

E (CU-MARK PS1318.A1 1880b)
PJks (IU 817.C859p, PH)*
Can (CU-MARK PS1318.A1 1880a)*
Tau vol. 1 (MB PS1318.A1 1880, PH)*
Tau vol. 2 (CU-MARK PS1322.I537 1881 copy 1)*
E2 (CU-MARK PS1318.A1 1882)*
LoH (CU-MARK PN6157.C5 1888 copy 5)*
LoHE (CU-MARK PN6157.C5 1888a)*
SAH (CU-MARK PRS.C55S41 1888)*
A2 (CU-MARK PS1300.E99d, vols. 7, 8)*
A2 (CU-MARK PS1300.E99c, vols. 7, 8)*

Ac (CU-MARK PS1318.A1 1872a copy 2) vs.
HWa (TxU Clemens B33)
HWb (TxU Clemens B34)

MACHINE COLLATIONS

Prb (CU-MARK PS1318.A1 1872p) vs.
Pra (collection of Dorothy Goldberg)
Ac (CU-MARK PS1318.A1 1872c copy 1)

Ac (CU-MARK PS1318.A1 1872a copy 2) vs.
Aa (CU-MARK PS1318.A1 1872 copy 4)
Ag (Vi PS1318.A1 1903)

Textual Notes

The textual notes explain and defend editorial decisions, including extensions of, and occasional exceptions to, the overall policy described in the Introduction (pages 896–911). Every entry in Emendations of the Copy-Text and Rejected Substantives which is the subject of a note is marked with an asterisk (*). All abbreviations for texts are fully defined in the Description of Texts.

xxix.18–19 Warning to Experimenters] This is the third phrase in the table of contents which refers to Mark Twain's brief camel anecdote (probably about five pages of manuscript): the others are "Overcoats as an Article of Diet" and "Sad Fate of a Camel." It is thus possible that "Warning to Experimenters" is a vestigial reference to something Clemens removed from his text after submitting his printer's copy to the publisher. But since this possibility is far from certain, and since the phrase (however redundant) causes no real ambiguity, it has not been emended.

xxxv.9 Killed—] In A the contents description includes an additional phrase after the dash, "Waking up the Weary Passenger—," which has been emended out of the present text because it is presumed to be a vestigial reference to some part of the text deleted by Mark Twain after he submitted the printer's copy for this chapter to his publisher.

3.7 "shear"] An acceptable nineteenth-century spelling (*OED*, s.v. "sheer").

14.2–3 live oak tree] The A spelling ("live oak-tree") is unintentionally ambiguous, and has therefore been emended to the spelling Clemens used in a holograph letter to his mother and sister on 25 October 1861 (*L1*, 133).

21.20 " 'dobies"] The A spelling (" *'dobies"*) is the only instance where the typesetters used italic type for an English word treated as a word, where no special emphasis was intended. They normally reserved italic for foreign words, and of course for emphasis. To accord with the treatment of all other like cases—e.g., "The first crop is called 'plant cane;' subsequent crops . . . are called 'rattoons'" (480.13–15)—quotation marks have been substituted here for italic type.

26.22   Kearny] The A spelling ("Kearney") has been corrected. The spelling "Kearny" dates from January 1849, when the federal government officially assigned this name to a newly established military post on the Platte River:

> It was the same spelling as that used by General Stephen Watts Kearny and also by General Phil Kearny, it is the correct spelling of the site of the present fort. The fact that in subsequent years someone not familiar with the correct spelling inserted an "e" in the last syllable and this error was perpetuated in the name of the present Kearney county and present city of Kearney does not alter the historic and orthographic truth that the name Fort Kearny is correctly spelled K-E-A-R-N-Y. (Sheldon, 274)

26.32–28.5   ACROSS . . . out.] This extract was taken from an article written by Mark Twain's friend William Swinton (see the explanatory note)—either directly from the New York *Times*, as Mark Twain states at 26.29, or from an unidentified reprinting in another newspaper. Mark Twain extracted only a portion of the original article: the title, one sentence from the end of the third paragraph, most of a sentence from the eighth paragraph, and all of the twelfth paragraph. Except for the correction of "Polephemus" to "Polyphemus" (28.1) and the change to "8 o'clock" at 28.3 (see the next note), all the A variants have been rejected as nonauthorial.

28.3   8 o'clock] The change from "6" to "8" o'clock (spelled "eight" in A) may have resulted from a typographical error in Mark Twain's copy of the article. The error is uncorrectable, however, because of the authorial addition of *"fifteen hours and forty minutes out"* at 28.5.

31.22   minie rifle] Although the name for the minié rifle came from its inventor, Claude Étienne Minié, it was frequently spelled without a capital letter or accent mark and was commonly pronounced "minnie" (Worcester, s.v. "Minie"). To supply an accent mark here would, therefore, imply that Mark Twain intended the French pronunciation, which seems doubtful at best. It is not known how Mark Twain normally spelled the word because no instance of holograph inscription has been found.

41.21   sunk] The verb form preferred by Webster 1870, which declared "sank" to be "nearly obsolete" (Webster 1870, s.v. "sink").

50.1–52.7   IN . . . maybe.] This section of the chapter was printed in the *American Publisher* (AP) for May 1871. Since Bliss and Orion had the holograph manuscript and the amanuensis copy of the passage in Hartford at about the same time, the AP and A typesettings probably derive independently from Mark Twain's manuscript (AP probably from the amanuensis copy, which in turn derived from the holograph manuscript). No copy-text is therefore chosen for this passage; instead, all variants between A and AP are recorded in Emendations, and the reading most in accord with Mark Twain's holograph practice is printed in the text. Although there are no substantive variants, the evidence of two spelling variants ("traveled" and "maybe" in A, versus "travelled" and "may be" in AP) indicates that the A compositor was not setting from AP, since elsewhere A spelled these words "travelled" and "may be," while Mark Twain spelled them "traveled" and "maybe." On 20 March 1871, in a letter transmitting the amanuensis copy of this passage to Orion and Bliss, Clemens instructed them to find the passage beginning with the words, "However, in a little while all interest was taken up in stretching our necks & watching for the pony-rider" (CU-MARK, in *MTLP*, 62). Since the comma after "while" in AP (50.1) is not present in Mark Twain's letter or in A, the presumption must again be that A was typeset from holograph. The punctuation in AP—numerous commas, and semicolons where A has commas—is uncharacteristic of Mark Twain, apparently corrupted by both the amanuensis and the AP compositor. On the other hand, three commas present in A (at 50.23, twice, and 51.17) but absent from AP were probably supplied by the A compositor, since the punctuation of AP was in general heavier than in A. The reading of AP has therefore been adopted in these three cases, and at 50.6, where AP "brim full" is Mark Twain's normal spelling. See also the next note.

50.27   *two dollars an ounce*] When Mark Twain submitted his manuscript for publication in AP, he doubted the accuracy of his figure: "Refer the marginal note to Orion, about postage. I feel *sure* I am wrong, & that it *was* Four Dollars an ounce instead of Two— —make the correction, if necessary" (SLC to Bliss and OC, 20 Mar 71, CU-MARK, in *MTLP*, 62). Although the reading *"two dollars an ounce"* was retained in AP, the figure was corrected—presumably as a result of Orion's research—to *"five dollars an ounce"* in A. Although the latter figure was not wrong, since it reflected the cost of postage when the pony-express mail service was initiated, Mark Twain's memory was more accurate than he had believed: his original *"two dollars an ounce"* (AP) was correct in July 1861 when this incident must have occurred, and has therefore been retained. The other rate Clemens mentioned in his letter to Bliss, "Four Dollars an ounce," had been in effect until the first of that month (Hafen, 180; "Pony Express," St. Louis *Missouri Democrat*, 1 July 61, 4; *DAH*, 4:306–7).

58.22–23   neither the conductor nor the new driver were] At least one nineteenth-century grammarian accepted a plural verb in this context: "When different subjects are disjoined by a conjunction . . . the predicate may be applied to the different subjects, and therefore may contain a plural verb" (McCulloch, 134n).

64.3–13   While . . . practices.] Mark Twain took this extract, as he states at 64n.1, from Thomas Dimsdale's *Vigilantes of Montana* (VoM). As the copy-text headings in Emendations indicate, he used the material from the book out of order. Having already borrowed paragraph 2 on page 175 of VoM (with only slight rewording) for the passage at 63.35–39, he then quoted from paragraphs 1, 4, and 3 on the same page. The material he excluded is reported as an emendation; one sentence from paragraph 3 he used later, in chapter 11 (69.17–18).

65.10 told him "none of that!—pass out the high-priced article."] The A reading ("told him to 'none of that!—pass out the high-priced article.'") probably resulted from an incomplete revision, as if Mark Twain first wrote "told him to 'pass out the high-priced article'" and then inserted "none of that!" without recognizing the mixed construction. Emendation of "to" corrects the oversight.

70.4 Vigilanter] The term "Vigilanter" occurs frequently in VoM as the singular of "Vigilantes," but it probably seemed mistaken to the A typesetter, who presumably "corrected" it to "Vigilante."

82.9 disruptured] An unusual but correct verb meaning "broken off or asunder" (*OED*, s.v. "disrupture"). Compare *RI 1972*, 649.

107.26–27 THE . . . NEPHI] Although the 1866 edition of the *Book of Mormon* (BoM) is copy-text for the extracts in this chapter, the typographical styling of the titles in capitals and small capitals on pages 107–9 has been silently adopted from A: Mark Twain clearly expected the compositors to make such choices about typographical styling, since it would have been impractical to follow the ornate styling of his source's title page.

113.12 5,000,000 or 6,000,000] These figures in A have not been normalized to "five or six million," on the assumption that their great magnitude is marginally clearer from figures than from prose.

126.9–10 Terra del Fuegans] The modern spelling "Tierra" has not been adopted because several nineteenth-century geographical dictionaries record "Terra" as an acceptable alternative spelling. For example, in "Pronunciation of Modern Geographical Names" in Webster's 1847 dictionary, both spellings occur as main entries, with neither signaled as preferable, and a third entry is listed under "Fuego, Terra del." In the "Geographical Vocabulary" of Webster's 1870 dictionary, the main entry is under "Terra del Fuego." *The Century Cyclopedia of Names* (Benjamin E. Smith) gives preference to "Tierra," but provides a cross-reference under the spelling "Terra." Mark Twain's spelling has therefore been judged archaic, but not an error. His spelling of "Fuegans," however, appears to be his own. The natives of Tierra del Fuego were correctly called "Fuegians" (not "Tierra del Fuegians"), as in Wood's *Uncivilized Races of Man*, which Mark Twain mentions on this page. The A spelling ("Fuegans") has not been corrected because it is probably authorial, and because "Terra del Fuegians" would be neither strictly correct nor authorial.

132.5   get you there on time!] Mark Twain obviously intended to have
        the Greeley anecdote told identically four separate times, and may
        even have instructed the typesetter to set the same passage in his
        manuscript for each repetition. Four emendations have therefore been
        made—two of accidentals, two of minor substantives, at 132.5, 132.33,
        and 133.25 (twice)—to make all four tellings identical.

136n.6 thirteenth chapter of Daniel] The fifth state of the first edition
        (Ae, 1874) and both later states read "sixteenth" instead of "thir-
        teenth"—a change intended to make this joke more intelligible, but
        one that may miss the original point: see the explanatory note at
        136n.5–6. No evidence has been found that Mark Twain initiated the
        change, nor are there any other variants in Ae which appear to be au-
        thorial. The reading of A has therefore been allowed to stand. Compare
        RI 1972, 637.

154.20 recurred] An unusual but correct use of "recur," meaning "to
        come back or return . . . *to* one's thoughts, mind or memory" (*OED*, s.v.
        "recur"). See the manuscript of *The Adventures of Tom Sawyer:* "The
        idea of being a clown recurred to him now, only to fill him with dis-
        gust" (SLC 1982, 206). Compare *RI 1972*, 649.

163.9   Dana silver mine, six miles] No evidence has been found that a
        mine of this name existed on the Comstock lode. It is possible that
        Mark Twain actually meant the famous Daney mine in the Devil's
        Gate mining district, but that he (or the compositor) misspelled its
        name. Indeed, in 1861–62 the *Mining and Scientific Press* referred to
        the "Dana" mine when it clearly meant the Daney ("Summary of Min-
        ing News," 4 [5 Oct 61]: 5, and 5 [1 May 62]: 5). On the other hand, the
        Daney mine was about twelve miles from Carson City, not "six," as
        Mark Twain states here. Furthermore, he seems to have spelled the
        name "Daney" correctly on two recent occasions, in a May 1868 letter
        to the Chicago *Republican* and in a June 1870 *Galaxy* article (SLC
        1868e, 1870h). On balance, therefore, the A reading does not seem a
        clear-cut error and has not been emended, despite the possibility that
        Clemens may have intended (and even written) "Daney."

176.6–28 But . . . incalculable.] No printing of this extract from the *En-
        terprise*—which is not extant for this period—has been found, so A is
        necessarily copy-text.

177.3–178.19 I . . . worlds.] See the previous note.

193.12 There were none] "It is a mistake to suppose that the pronoun
        ['none'] is singular only and must at all costs be followed by singular
        verbs etc.; the *OED* explicitly states that plural construction is com-
        moner" (Fowler, 394).

207.10 baled] An acceptable nineteenth-century spelling (*OED*, s.v.
        "bail").

214.6   every body] The A reading ("everybody") is an easy mistranscription of Clemens's holograph: "every heart went with him—every body, too" is clearly the meaning intended.

218 *illus*   CAMPING IN THE SNOW.] Although recorded in the List of Illustrations in A as facing the first page of chapter 33, this full-page engraving was in fact bound into the first edition as the first of two frontispieces. The engraving was also used as the frontispiece in Pra (which included no text from chapter 33), and remained in Prb as the first of two frontispieces. It seems likely that when the sheets of A were bound, the precedent of Pra was followed, rather than the List. The full-page illustrations in A were plates, inserted before binding, and not part of the signatures. Nor were they assigned folios, which contributed to the error. The illustration has therefore been restored to its originally intended position.

236.10   oxydize] An acceptable nineteenth-century spelling (Webster 1870, s.v. "oxydize").

239.37   had not] The Buffalo *Express* copy-text (BE) reading ("hadn't") has been rejected in favor of the A reading ("had not") on the assumption that Mark Twain so revised it. He demonstrably revised Buffalo *Express* "can't" to "cannot" on one of the three extant pages of his manuscript (see page 816), and it is a fair assumption that wherever an earlier printed contraction is replaced in A by the spelled-out form, Clemens was responsible for the change.

247.36   a hundred and fifty miles] The mileage given in BE ("150") is more accurate than the A reading ("a hundred"). It seems implausible that Clemens would deliberately make his number less accurate, and therefore it is likely that "a hundred" resulted from the typesetter's spelling out the figure in his copy and inadvertently omitting "and fifty."

284.2   rarified] An acceptable nineteenth-century spelling (*OED*, s.v. "rarefy").

293.21   checks and gold coin] The A reading ("checks of gold coin") is unintelligible. The compositor probably misread Mark Twain's habitual ampersand (&) as the word "of" (*RI 1972*, 638).

303.36   for old acquaintance sake] Although the preferred modern spelling would be "for old acquaintance' sake," Fowler (533) and the *OED* (s.v. "sake") assert that it was correct in the nineteenth century (and remains so today) to omit the apostrophe from abstract nouns in such possessive constructions. The BE spelling is therefore acceptable and, furthermore, corresponds with Mark Twain's known practice: see 15 Jan 67 to Hingston, "for old acquaintance sake" (*L2*, 8). See also the clipping on discarded manuscript page 968 (page 816), where the phrase remains unaltered, without the apostrophe.

344.31   Behring's Strait] An acceptable nineteenth-century spelling (Beeton, s.v. "Behring Strait"; Callicot, s.v. "Behring's Strait").

350.15–353.10   And count . . . faith!] The two pages on which these lines occur are reversed in the first edition, although they appear in the correct order in the prospectus (Pr). In Pra, the pages have no folios. In Prb, their folios are reversed: the page that should have been 374 appears as a verso page numbered 373; the page that should have been 373 appears as a recto page numbered 374. When the printer imposed the pages for the electroplating of A, he probably assumed that the folios were correct, and the page ordering wrong, which misled him into imposing the pages in reverse order. The correct order has been restored.

358.29–360.2   AN . . . office.] No printing of this extract from the *Enterprise*—which is not extant for this period—has been found, so A is necessarily copy-text.

360.4 $25,000,000] Figures have been retained for the dollar amounts here and in the two footnotes to this chapter. It was (and still is) customary for compositors to leave such numbers in arabic figures, when "the amounts are large and of frequent recurrence" (De Vinne, 84).

366.17   barbacue] An acceptable nineteenth-century spelling (*OED*, s.v. "barbecue").

372.31–374.16   CHINATOWN . . . piano.] No printing of this extract from the *Enterprise*—which is not extant for this period—has been found, so A is necessarily copy-text.

388.33   flowers] The absence of the comma after this word in A is accepted as part of the revision of "your" to "the," which changed the clause from nonrestrictive to restrictive.

395.7   half an hour] It seems probable that Mark Twain intended to substitute "half an hour" for "three-quarters of an hour" (the BE copy-text reading), and that either he miswrote his revision or the compositor failed to execute it properly: the result was a phrase uncharacteristic of Mark Twain. Since "half an hour" occurs frequently in manuscript, but "half of an hour" does not, the "of" has been emended.

402.11   then—drop] It is by no means certain how the clearly erroneous A reading, "then-drop," occurred, but it seems likely that a dash, and not a hyphen, was intended, since the dash is used elsewhere in this chapter for just such a dramatic pause as seems appropriate here: see the dash at 401.12–14: "no other apology for clothing than—a bath-towel!" A reverse substitution occurred at 403.13, where A reads "earthquake—episodes," suggesting that the two marks of punctuation were mixed together in the compositor's case.

403.18–38   NEVADA . . . wild-cat.] No printing of this extract from the *Enterprise*—which is not extant for this period—has been found, so A is necessarily copy-text.

416.4   Dead-Horse Gulch] When Mark Twain revised BE for inclusion in
  Roughing It, he added the first paragraph of this chapter in manuscript.
  He evidently intended to change "Deadhorse Gulch" to "Dead-Horse
  Gulch," but the A typesetter erroneously set "Dead-House Gulch" instead. This error was transmitted from the first American edition into
  the second American edition (A2), first issued in 1899. When the
  American Publishing Company proofreader, Forrest Morgan, marked a
  copy of A2 in preparation for a new impression with corrected plates,
  he noted the error and suggested that it be called to Mark Twain's attention. Some of Morgan's corrections were listed on a separate sheet
  of paper, in the hand of Frank Bliss (president of the American Publishing Company), except for the last item, which reads "House should be
  Horse," with the word "Horse" in Mark Twain's hand. This inscription
  confirms that the reading in A through A2 was an error, and offers some
  further evidence that Mark Twain intended the word to be spelled as a
  hyphenated compound, rather than as one word. The BE reading
  "Deadhorse" has therefore been emended to "Dead-Horse." (The copy
  of A2 marked with corrections by Forrest Morgan—"Royal Edition,"
  vols. 7–8—is at CtY-BR; the list of corrections is at ViU; see also the
  entry for A2 in the Description of Texts.)

416.26   wouldn't a let] The BE reading has been deemed preferable to the
  one in A, "wouldn't let," because its meaning, as a "contrary to fact"
  conditional, makes more sense in context; the "a" could very easily
  have been inadvertently dropped by a compositor. The same locution
  in a nearby phrase was transmitted from BE to A unaltered: "you'd a
  took" (416.19).

419.17   Sagacity] The absence of a paragraph break here in A, while a
  break does occur in BE, is presumed to result from authorial revision.
  This presumption is based on the evidence provided by a copy of John
  Camden Hotten's *Choice Humorous Works of Mark Twain* (HWa,
  1873), which Mark Twain agreed to revise in preparation for a new edition (HWb). Hotten's book included a text of the sketch which derived
  from the original BE printing, and thus still contained a paragraph
  break; in the margins of his copy Mark Twain instructed the typesetter
  to delete the paragraph break here and "run in" the text (see the entries
  for HWa and HWb in the Description of Texts).

420.7   post] The A reading, "paust," has been rejected as a misspelling.
  Mark Twain apparently meant "post," which is "a batch of ore for
  smelting at one time. . . . This word is from German *Posten*, parcel,
  lot, batch of ore, which is of course pronounced with a short or open *o*.
  M.T.'s sp. with *au* may be his attempt to render the sound of a word
  which he knew only in the spoken language of the miners" (*Lex*, 166).

429.30   women . . . were] It is remotely possible that the A reading
  "woman they burned . . . was the wife . . . and the still loved but di-

vorced wife" is an intentional garbling of the story for humorous effect. On balance, however, it is more likely to be an error resulting from an incomplete revision, and has therefore been emended.

431.10   inhabitants,] Because Mark Twain's revision of the Sacramento *Union* text (SU) for the opening of this chapter involved reordering much of the material, it is likely that he recopied at least the first two paragraphs of the chapter, since revising a pasted-up clipping would have been impractical. Possibly as a result of such recopying (or perhaps because of a careless typesetter), several errors were introduced. For example, at 431.9–10 the parentheses in SU around the clause "said . . . inhabitants" were deleted, presumably by Mark Twain, who then replaced the open parenthesis with a comma after "Honolulu" while neglecting to add a second comma after "inhabitants," which resulted in faulty syntax: the A sentence makes "spread" modify "inhabitants," whereas the SU sentence makes it clear that "Honolulu" was "spread over a dead level." A comma has therefore been supplied after "inhabitants," on the assumption that Mark Twain's revision was either incomplete or misread by the typesetter. The SU reading, "a few," at 431.12 makes better sense than the A reading, "few"; and at 431.15, SU "brown stone fronts" (a description also found elsewhere, at 261.30) is a more accurate rendering than the A "brown fronts." Finally, at 431.16, the A reading "adobies" falls halfway between the two spellings Mark Twain discusses earlier in *Roughing It*, where he says, "*adobes*, the Spaniards call these bricks, and Americans shorten it to '*dobies*'" (21.19–20). It seems likely that he intended to expand the colloquial "'dobies" to the more correct "*adobes*," and was either careless or was misunderstood by his typesetter. The A reading "adobies" has therefore been emended, and italic type supplied to match the earlier occurrence.

432 *cap* SCENE] Although normally the illustration captions in A are assumed to contain readings that are more correct than the entries in its List of Illustrations, in this case the plural "SCENES" in A has been emended to the singular in accordance with the preferred reading in the List, since clearly only one scene is depicted.

438.21   about.] At this point Mark Twain skipped over paragraphs 5–14 of SU, reserving most of that material for use in chapter 65 (444.16–448.18).

449.4   lantani] The A spelling, "lantoni," is regarded as a corruption of SU, rather than as an authorial revision, since there is no evidence that Mark Twain had reason to make a correction of this nonsense word.

465.13   has] The emendation of the A reading, "had," is a necessary correction of tense to make the verb conform with the others in the paragraph. The error was almost certainly compositorial.

466.19–468.3 Undertaker . . . Force.] It is very likely—but not certain—
that Mark Twain's source for Princess Kamamalu's funeral program
was a clipping from the Honolulu *Pacific Commercial Advertiser*
(PCA), which he incorporated into the manuscript for his *Union* letter
published on 1 August 1866; a clipping of SU then served in turn as
printer's copy for A. The program is also extant in a broadside printing
in Hawaiian, and it is possible that Mark Twain had access to a broadside version, although no such document has been located. Such broadside printings, both in English and in Hawaiian, are known to survive
from other royal funerals.

467.7 Bishop] Although the name of Bishop [Thomas Nettleship] Staley
(Anglican bishop of Honolulu since 1861) was present in the original
PCA program, it was absent from SU, while in the same line of type the
title "Reverend" was shortened to "Rev." It is possible that the SU typesetter volunteered both these changes, in order to fit the text of this
line into the narrow column of the newspaper, since there is no obvious
reason why Mark Twain would have deleted only the name "Staley,"
while reproducing the names of Bishop Louis Maigret, James McBride,
Mons. Desnoyers, and W. L. Green. Later, when writing *Roughing It*,
he added a new passage at the end of the preceding chapter in which he
described Staley (identified, however, only by his title) as a "cheap
ready-made Bishop from England" and ridiculed several other officials
as well. He then deleted the names of McBride, Desnoyers, and Green
from the program, leaving only Maigret's—presumably because he did
not wish to name the officials he had just made fun of: see the entries
at 467.15, 467.16, and 467.17. Although Staley's name had already been
deleted from the SU text that he was using, Mark Twain would no
doubt have deleted it now had it been present, as he did the other officials' names.

469.14 lappel] An acceptable nineteenth-century spelling (*OED*, s.v.
"lapel").

469.30–472.43 On . . . abuse.] Mark Twain used a borrowed copy of
James Jackson Jarves's *History of the Hawaiian Islands* (HoHI) to prepare his *Union* letter published on 1 August 1866 (see the explanatory
note at 443.26), which included the two extracts at 469.30–470.5 and
470.11–472.43. A clipping of SU then served in turn as printer's copy
for A. He clearly could not have torn out the pages to paste into his
manuscript, so he must have recopied the passages, making minor revisions—and presumably some errors—as he did so. The misspelling
in SU at 472.40 ("Kaahumauu's" in place of "Kaahumanu's") may
be further evidence that the SU compositor was setting type from
Mark Twain's manuscript, rather than from HoHI directly, since the
author's "n" could easily have been mistaken for a "u": a similar error

occurred at 526.1 ("Mani" instead of "Maui") in material typeset from holograph.

471.16   to and fro] The omission of HoHI "to and fro" from SU and A was apparently inadvertent, possibly a copying error by Mark Twain or by the SU compositor.

471.17   tabu] Since the spelling of "tabu" in the added footnote at 470n.1–5 is probably Mark Twain's, the change from HoHI "taboo" to SU "tabu" here and at 472.7 is accepted as authorial, while the roman styling of the copy-text is retained.

481.6   whispered us] An acceptable—although unusual—use of "whisper" (*OED*, s.v. "whisper").

484.35   folony] Probably a typographical error, since no other "invented" words occur in these comic transcriptions of Greeley's letter, aside from "Yrxwly, HEVACE EVEELOJ." Since it is not known, however, what word was intended—it could have been either "colony" or "felony"— emendation has not been attempted.

490.22   Lono] The italic type used by SU for Lono's name was not for special emphasis, but to mark it as a foreign word; since no other Hawaiian proper name is so treated in A or SU, this instance has been emended to roman type to conform to the practice followed elsewhere.

493.2   lost god] The reading of A here, set from Mark Twain's manuscript insertion into the SU text, is "the last god Lono," which is meaningless within the context. It is likely that the printed word "last" was a mis-reading of the author's handwritten "lost": Mark Twain refers to Lono in the preceding chapter as the "long vanished and lamented god" (491.6), and later in this chapter he further explains that according to Hawaiian mythology Lono sailed away and "was never seen any more" (496.8).

501.30   each was] This is the first of a cluster of five substantive variants in A rejected in favor of the SU readings (see also the entries at 502.20, 503.2, 503.3, and 503.24). The verb-tense error in both SU and A at 501.30 ("has" instead of "had") suggests that this section may have been carelessly prepared or typeset. Since none of the A variants seems a clear improvement of the text, all have been treated as unintended corruptions.

508.11–23   A . . . revelation.] Mark Twain substantially revised this paragraph in SU for A, reserving the first sentence for a later portion of this chapter (512.6–8), discarding the second sentence entirely, and using only the last four sentences here.

520.9   had never drank] According to the *OED*, from the seventeenth through the nineteenth centuries the verb form "drank" was "in-truded" from the past tense into the past participle, probably "to avoid the inebriate associations of *drunk*" (*OED*, s.v. "drink").

527.11 Kamtchatka] An acceptable nineteenth-century spelling (Webster 1870, "Geographical Vocabulary," 637).

531.6 for that] An archaic but nevertheless correct conjunction meaning "for the reason that": the *OED* cites examples from Keats (1821) and Macaulay (1855), among others (*OED*, s.v. "for that").

552.2 almost] Catharine V. Waite's *Mormon Prophet* (MP) is copy-text for this passage. The A reading "almost" is deemed a correction of the MP reading "most." Coincidentally, A restored the original text of Cradlebaugh's speech, as reported in the *Congressional Globe* (123), although Waite's most likely source read "most" (Cradlebaugh, 19).

552.22 He] Waite supplied the ellipses following the word "true" in the passage that Mark Twain elected not to include in his appendix, when she abridged the quotation from the *Enterprise;* the content of the missing passage is not known, since the *Enterprise* printing has not been found.

553.11 proofs of Holy Writ] The A reading is a correction of MP's inaccurate quotation ("proofs from Holy Writ") from *Othello* (act 3, scene 3), a play with which Mark Twain had long been familiar (*L1*, 42, 44 n. 12, 111, 114 n. 10; Gribben, 2:629). Since he carried out careful revision of the list in this extract, he was presumably responsible for this correction as well.

553.16–31 2. . . . 7.] Mark Twain reordered items 2 through 7 on this list of evidence, presumably to reflect his own view of their relative importance.

555.3–569.38 From . . . M. T.] Copy-text for the remainder of this appendix is Conrad Wiegand's letter in the *Enterprise* (TE70). Although Mark Twain states that Wiegand's letter is taken from the *Enterprise,* the actual source of A was a reprinting of the letter in Wiegand's monthly newspaper, the *People's Tribune* (PT). Mark Twain was apparently not aware that Wiegand had "touched up" his letter somewhat before reprinting it, adding—or possibly restoring—minor changes in punctuation and wording. It is clear that Mark Twain intended to present a text that had not received the benefit of Wiegand's second thoughts; on the other hand, he would have had no reason to reproduce those minor errors and corruptions that may have entered the text when it was typeset by the TE70 compositor, which Wiegand would understandably have chosen to correct when he reprinted it. The aim of the policy applied to the text of the letter is to retrieve the substance of the original, without Wiegand's later revisions, while accepting those PT accidentals and minor substantives which appear to be corrections of corruptions introduced into Wiegand's manuscript by the TE70 compositor. Mark Twain's revisions, such as the substitution of dashes for profanity, have been adopted as emendations.

559.3–6   *I . . . M. T.:*] All of Mark Twain's other interpolations into the body of Wiegand's text are signaled by the use of italic type; this one is therefore emended to italic, to make it uniform with the others. Mark Twain's opening and closing statements have been left in roman type, since they surround Wiegand's letter rather than interrupt it.

568.15   this] Here, and at 568.16, 568.22, and 569.27, A has substantive variants that appear to be corruptions resulting from compositorial error. The readings shared by TE70 and PT have therefore been left unaltered.

EMENDATIONS OF THE COPY-TEXT
AND REJECTED SUBSTANTIVES

This list records every departure of the edited text from each of the successive copy-texts on which it is based. The list therefore identifies alterations presumably made by Mark Twain for *Roughing It* (A), as well as corrections made independently by the editors (C). Found in the same list (rather than separately, as with previous volumes in the Works of Mark Twain) are also those few substantives in A which the editors reject in favor of the copy-text variants. Variant accidentals in A which the editors also reject in favor of the copy-text are not listed, however, for to do so would make the list excessively long.

The copy-text for each section of the text is identified where it begins within the list. For example:

> ▶ A (i–46) is copy-text for 'ROUGHING
> ... things:' (xxi *title*–26.31) ◀

The following symbols are used to identify the copy-texts and the sources of the variants listed here. (Each of the texts is more completely defined in the Description of Texts.)

A	First American edition of *Roughing It*
AP	*American Publisher*
BE	Buffalo *Express*
BoM	*Book of Mormon*
C	California editors
G	*Galaxy*
HoHI	*History of the Hawaiian Islands*
MP	*Mormon Prophet*
NYT	New York *Times*
PCA	Honolulu *Pacific Commercial Advertiser*
Pr	Prospectus of the first American edition of *Roughing It* (A)
PT	*People's Tribune*
SU	Sacramento *Union*
TE63	Virginia City *Territorial Enterprise*
TE70	Virginia City *Territorial Enterprise*
VoM	*Vigilantes of Montana*

In each entry, the reading adopted in the text is given first, with its source identified parenthetically. The adopted reading is separated by a dot (•) from the rejected variant (or variants) on the right, which is not identified parenthetically when it is from the copy-text. There are, however, several kinds of entries in which variants on both sides of the dot must be identified. When a passage of several lines has been adopted from A, the fact is recorded in one entry for the whole passage, and any further emendation within the passage is recorded in separate entries. For example, where Mark Twain has added a passage in A to a text first published in the Sacramento *Union* (which is therefore copy-text), the following entries occur:

> 109.25–   And . . . powers: (A) • [*not*
> 111.2   *in*]
> 109.35   Lehi;" (C) • ~"; (A)

The second entry here records an emendation of the A reading, not of the copy-text, which is still SU. Similarly, if the editors adopt the substance but not the form of a particular variant, all variant texts, including the copy-text, are identified parenthetically because the reading of this edition (C) corresponds exactly to none of the contributing documents.

> 28.3   8 (C) • eight (A); 6 (NYT)
> 238.2   marvelous (C) • marvellous
>   (A); wonderful (BE)

Likewise, in a passage where the Buffalo *Express* is copy-text, and the editors retain its substantive variant and reject the variant in A, both readings must be explicitly identified, since no emendation has in fact occurred. (It may help to think of such entries as recording a refusal to emend where emendation might otherwise be expected.)

> 239.10   lay (BE) • laid (A)

And in the few cases where substantive texts intervene between the copy-text and the first edition, all variant substantives are routinely reported, and must be explicitly identified, even though emendation is not necessarily involved.

> 471.20   manufacture kapa (native
>   cloth) (SU–A) • beat kapa
>   (HoHI)
> 471.22   king (HoHI–SU) • [*not in*]
>   (A)
> 560.36   you ——— —— (A) • you God
>   d——d (TE70–PT)

All illustrations and captions are drawn from the first American edition. The absence of illustrations in journal copy-texts, which were in general not illustrated (BE, G, SU, and TE63, for instance), is not recorded. Variant substantives in the captions printed in the prospectus and the first edition are, however, recorded. Certain nontextual typographical adjustments (such as the change from roman to arabic numerals in the chapter headings), which are listed in the Introduction (page 911), are not recorded as emendations. When emendation is reported for other reasons, however, the exact form of each text is reproduced.

> 391 *title*   CHAPTER 57 (C) •
>   CHAPTER LVII. (A);
>   DESOLATION. (BE)

Because Pr and A are different impressions from the same typesetting and are therefore part of the same edition, the symbol A by itself may signify a variant common to both; but when these texts vary from one another, the reading in each is given. Variant states within A or Pr are shown by lowercase letters following their abbreviations. Thus, Pra and Prb represent the first and second states of the prospectus, and Aa, Ab, Ac, Ad, Ae, Af, and Ag represent the seven known states of A. Variants identified as from Pr are common to Pra and Prb, and a variant identified as from A is common to all states of A, Aa through Ag.

Entries cite the edited text by page and line or, where necessary, by page, column, and line: "xxva.1" means "page xxv, first column, line 1"; "xxvb.8" means "page xxv, second column, line 8." Titles, subtitles, and captions are not included in the line count. Citations of them therefore use the page number with *"title," "sub," "cap,"* or *"illus,"* as appropriate. To distinguish two captions on the same page, the citation adds a number, *"cap1"* or *"cap2,"* as appropriate. Editorial comment is always italicized and enclosed in square brackets, thus: *"[centered]."* The symbol "¶" (for paragraph) is always editorial. Thus "VoM, 175 ¶2" means "the second paragraph that begins on page 175 of the *Vigilantes of Montana*." A vertical rule (|) indicates the end of a line; a double vertical rule (‖), the end of a page. Superscript numbers on words to the left of the dot do not appear in the text itself, but identify which of the two (or more) occurrences of a word in the same line is being cited. For example, the following entry cites the first of two "regions" in line 11 on page 50:

> 50.11   regions[1] (A) • ~, (AP)

An en dash (–) connecting two symbols indicates that the reading was transmitted from the first text into the second. In the following entry, for example, the copy-text reading "do" has been retained instead of the reading "are," which appeared in A, derived from PT.

> 564.12   do (TE70) • are (PT–A)

A wavy dash (~) on the right of the dot stands for the word on the left; a caret (∧) indicates the absence of a punctuation mark. A blank space enclosed in editorial brackets ([the]) means that the text contains a space or an ambiguous mark instead of the expected mark of punctuation or letter, indicating that the mark or letter may have been typeset, but did not print properly. A double hyphen (=) in a compound word divided at the end of a line signifies that the hyphen is to be retained. Compounds divided at the end of a line in the text appear below in their correct form (see Word Division in This Volume). Entries marked with an asterisk (*) are discussed in the Textual Notes.

▶A (i–46) is copy-text for 'ROUGH-ING . . . things:' (xxi *title*–26.31)◀

xxiv.19   caulk (C) • calk

xxva.1–2   The Miner's Dream (Full Page). *Frontispiece* (C) • THE MINERS' DREAM (FULL PAGE,) *Face Page . . . [flush right]* FRONTIS-PIECE. (Prb–A); (FULL PAGE) . . . *[flush right]* FRONTISPIECE. (Pra)

xxva.30–31   The Superintendent as a Teacher (C) • TEACHING A SUBORDINATE

xxvb.2   An Inhuman Spectacle (C) • I BEGAN TO PRAY

xxvb.7   "Here he comes!" (C) • ∧~ ~ ~∧∧

xxvb.11   Fist-Fight (C) • FIST FIGHT

xxvb.13   as (C) • AS AN

xxvb.16   Tail-Piece (C) • [not in]

xxvb.18   Lamentation (C) • LAMENTATIONS

xxvb.22   Stream (C) • STREAMS

xxvb.26   here! (C) • ~∧

xxvb.27   dam fool? (C) • FOOL

xxvia.2   of (C) • OE

xxvia.6   Endowment— (C) • ~,

xxvia.7   D (C) • ~.

xxvia.18 Goshoot (C) • GOSHOTT

xxvia.38 Fire (C) • FIGHT

xxvia.40–41   he was an American horse." (C) • HIM AN AMERICAN HORSE'

xxvia.48 Voucher (C) • VOUCHERS

xxvia.50 Toll-Roads (C) • TOLL ROADS

xxvib.3   that! (C) • THAT

xxvib.4   it! (C) • ~∧

xxvib.14 121. (C) • 120,

xxvib.19 125. (C) • 124

xxvib.26 Reärranging (C) • REARRANGING

xxvib.30 in Nevada (C) • [not in]

xxvib.37 Mono Lake (C) • LAKE MONO

xxvib.43 gone! (C) • ~∧

xxvib.44 Tail-Piece (C) • [not in]

xxvib.51 Enforcing a (C) • THE

xxviia.5 Bird's (C) • BIRDS

xxviia.5 Virginia (C) • VIRGINIA CITY

xxviia.6 Mount (C) • MT.

xxviia.8 "Take a few?" (C) • TRY A FEW

xxviia.19 "Weakens" (C) • ∧~∧

xxviia.20 Committeeman and (C) • SCOTTY BRIGGS AND THE

xxviia.22 Scotty (C) • [not in]

xxviia.23 Never (C) • DIDN'T

xxviia.24 a Sunday School (C) • S. S.

xxviia.26 a (C) • HIS

xxviia.33 Imparting (C) • GIVING

xxviia.40–41   Unlooked-for Appearance of (C) • THERE SAT

xxviia.42 The Storm Increased (C) • [not in]

xxviia.45 "Low bridge!" (C) • ∧~ ~∧∧

xxviia.48 Marvelous (C) • MARVELLOUS

xxviib.9 Tail-Piece (C) • TAIL PIECE

xxviib.12 cigar! (C) • ~∧

xxviib.15 An Eastern Landscape (C) • A NEW ENGLAND SCENE

xxviib.19 out! (C) • ~∧

xxviib.20 Well, if it ain't a child! (C) • WELL IF IT AINT A CHILD

xxviib.24 One-Horse (C) • ONE HORSE

xxviib.28 Oh, what shall (C) • OH! WHAT SHALL

xxviib.30 dear! (C) • ~∧

xxviib.32 benediction! (C) • ~∧

xxviib.36 it, stranger. (C) • ~∧ ~∧

xxviib.44 Deserted (C) • THE DESERTED

xxviib.46 Islands (C) • SANDWICH ISLANDS

xxviib.53 Sat (C) • SIT

xxviib.54–55   brother all same—we twins! (C) • BROTHER, WE TWINS

xxviiia.7–8   I . . . Mother (C) • "~ . . . ~"

xxviiib.1 The Tabu Broken (C) • BREAKING THE TABU

xxviiib.2 Tail-Piece (C) • [not in]

xxviiib.3 Surf-Bathing—Success (C) • SURF BATHING

xxviiib.4 Surf-Bathing—Failure (C) • SURF BATHING A FAILURE

xxviiib.5 The (C) • [not in]

xxviiib.10 Breaking (C) • BROKE

xxviiib.23 Stage-Fright (C) • STAGE FRIGHT

xxviiib.27 Best Part (C) • THE BEST

xxix.5   "Bully" (C) • ∧~∧

xxix.10   "the States" (C) • ~ "~"

xxix.10–11   Our Coach (C) • "~ ~"

xxx.4   Holladay (C) • Holliday

xxx.13   Comes! (C) • ~∧

xxx.16   Lying (C) • Laying

xxx.26   On a Spree (C) • "~ ~ ~"

xxx.27	Turn-out (C) • Turn out	
xxx.41	King (C) • "~"	
xxxi.6	D (C) • ~.	
xxxi.15	a Quarter (C) • "~ ~"	
xxxi.23	Stage-coach (C) • Stage Coach	
xxxi.27	Greeley's (C) • Greely's	
xxxii.1	Out-house (C) • Outhouse	
xxxii.19	Curry (C) • Currey	
xxxii.20	Toll-Roads (C) • Toll-Gates	
xxxii.26	Ballou (Prb–A) • Ballon (Pra)	
xxxii.38–39	Tunneling (C) • Tunnelling	
xxxii.39–40	Prophecy (C) • Prophesy	
xxxiii.2–3	Our Landlord (C) • "Our Land-|lord"	
xxxiii.14–15	Station-House (C) • Station House	
xxxiii.18	Gen. (C) • General	
xxxiii.19	Land-Slide (C) • Landslide	
xxxiii.19	Gen. (C) • General	
xxxiii.23	Traveling (C) • Travelling	
xxxiii.24	Capt. (C) • Captain	
xxxiii.25	Tunneling (C) • Tunnelling	
xxxiii.26	Claim (C) • "~"	
xxxiv.2	Mono Lake (C) • Lake Mono	
xxxiv.3	Death— (C) • ~ˌ|	
xxxiv.8	Interviewed (C) • "~"	
xxxiv.14	Burst (C) • Bursted	
xxxiv.35	Right (C) • [not in]	
xxxiv.36	Yorkers (C) • ~"	
xxxiv.39	Committeeman (C) • Committee Man	
xxxv.2	Down (C) • Down Again	
xxxv.3	Shake (C) • Shook	
xxxv.8	Graveyard (C) • Grave Yard	
xxxv.9	Whom (C) • Who	
*xxxv.9	Killed— (C) • Killed—Waking up the Weary Passenger	
xxxv.15	Capt. (C) • Captain	
xxxv.15	Noakes (C) • Nookes	
xxxv.17	Noakes (C) • Nookes	
xxxv.17	Afterward (C) • Afterwards	
xxxv.17	Capt. (C) • Captain	
xxxv.19	Noakes (C) • Nookes	
xxxv.21	Weekly Occidental (C) • Weekly Occidental	

xxxv.24	Outdone (C) • Out-done
xxxv.29	Underground (C) • Under Ground
xxxv.33	Filkins's (C) • Filkin's
xxxv.34	Jacops (C) • Jacobs
xxxv.37	Lem (C) • ~.
xxxvi.4	etc. (C) • &c.
xxxvi.8	Mount (C) • Mt.
xxxvi.14	Well, (C) • ~ˌ
xxxvi.29	Pocket-Mining (C) • Pocket Mining
xxxvii.6	Capt. (C) • Captain
xxxvii.29	Waters (C) • ~.
xxxvii.32	Beazeley (C) • Beazely
xxxvii.36	Capt. (C) • Captain
xxxviii.3	Whisky (C) • Whiskey
xxxviii.6	Surf-Bathing (C) • Surf Bathing
xxxviii.16	Pic-nicking (C) • Picnicing
xxxviii.16–17	Haleakala (C) • Holeakala
xxxviii.24	Well (C) • ~.
2.5	maybe (C) • may be
2.12	Isthmus (C) • isthmus
2.31	river (C) • River
2.32	Joe (C) • Jo.
3.4	Joe (C) • Jo.
4.19–20	stove-pipe (C) • stove-|pipe
4.27	underclothing (C) • under=clothing
4.28	U. S. (C) • United States
5.3	seven-shooter (C) • seven-|shooter
5.19	pepper-box (C) • pepper-|box
5.31	shotgun (C) • shot-|gun
7.11	mail-bags (C) • mail bags
9.3	a bust'n (C) • a-bust'n
9.10	us (Prb–A) • as (Pra)
11.20	Dictionary (C) • dictionary
11.26	mail-sacks (C) • mail sacks
12.28	one-third (C) • one third
13.19	Secretary (C) • secretary
13.26	sage-brush (C) • sage-|brush
*14.2–3	live oak tree (C) • live oak=tree
14.6	sage-bush (C) • sage-|bush

14.8	lilliputian (C) • liliputian
14.9	lilliputian (C) • liliputian
14.10	Brobdingnag (C) • Brobdignag
14.16	sage-brush (C) • sage-|brush
15.2	bunch-grass (C) • bunch-|grass
15.7	sage-brush (C) • sage-|brush
15n.1	mountain sides (C) • moun-tain-sides
15n.2	Territories (C) • territories
18.17	water canteens (C) • water-|canteens
20.11–12	stage-coaching (C) • stage-|coaching
20.21	stage-driver (C) • stage-|driver
21.18	sun-dried (C) • sun-|dried
*21.20	" 'dobies" (C) • 'dobies
21.35	teapot (C) • tea-|pot
21.37	station-keeper's (C) • sta-tion-|keeper's
22.17	one-half (C) • one half
23.10–11	bowie knife (C) • bowie⸗knife
23.24–25	queensware (C) • queens-|ware
24.5	up-ended (C) • up-|ended
24.7	Nicolson (C) • Nicholson
24.12	employés (C) • employes
24.15–16	Slumgullion (C) • Slum-|gullion
25.23	d—d (C) • d——d
25.31	employé (C) • employe
*26.22	Kearny (C) • Kearney

*▶NYT (title, ¶3) is copy-text for 'ACROSS . . . jaunt.' (26.32–34)◀

26.33   At (C) • "At (A); It had been my intention, on this trip, to go only as far as Ogden, there diverge to Salt Lake, and finish the trans-continental ride after some stay in the City of the Saints. When, however, the Chicago and Northwest train came into Omaha, on Saturday afternoon, I found occasion to alter my resolution. I learnt that the train was to take out two of the Pullman palace cars on their initial trip across the continent, and that Colonel

PULLMAN himself was along, and with him some of my old journalistic friends—SIMONTON, of the Associated Press, Governor BROSS, of the Chicago *Tribune*, and some others; so the invitation to join the party was not to be refused. Accordingly, at (NYT)

▶NYT (¶8) is copy-text for 'A . . . car.' (26.34–37)◀

26.34	A (A) • [¶] ~
26.37	dining car. (C) • dining-car. (A); dining car, the "International," which, O, muse of gastronomy, inspire me with language fitly to describe! (NYT)

▶NYT (¶12) is copy-text for 'It . . . out.' (26.37–28.5)◀

26.37	It (A) • [¶] ~
27.9	gourmet (NYT) • gormand (A)
27.11	our (NYT) • and (A)
27.14	while (NYT) • whilst (A)
28.1	Polyphemus (A) • Polephemus
*28.3	8 (C) • eight (A); 6 (NYT)
28.5	Omaha—. . . out. (C) • Omaha—. . . out." (A); Omaha. (NYT)

▶A (48–70) is copy-text for 'CHAPTER . . . CHAPTER 8' (29 *title*–50 *title*)◀

33.5	jackass rabbit (C) • jackass⸗rabbit
35.3	stage-coach (C) • stage-|coach
35.14	mules, (C) • ~∧
35.24	overland (C) • over-|land
36.1	stage-coach (C) • stage,|coach
36.14	bulldog (C) • bull-|dog
36.18	overland (C) • over-|land
36.33	backwards and forwards (C) • backward and forward
37.25	pretense (C) • pretence
37.38	Holladay (C) • Holliday
38.4	Holladay (C) • Holliday
38.8	Holladay (C) • Holliday
38.10	Holladay's (C) • Holliday's
39.6	[falling inflection] (C) • (~ ~)

39.14	within sight (C) • with insight
39.17	Holladay (C) • Holliday
41.23	mud-wagon (C) • mud-|wagon
42.14	a while (C) • awhile
43.9	shoveling (C) • shovelling
43.10–11	fifteen-hundred-dollar (C) • fifteen-hundred dollar
44.4	whirlwind (C) • whirl-|wind
44.8	overtook (C) • over-|took
45.8	slip-noose (C) • slip-|noose
48.16	cocoanut (C) • cocoa-|nut

*►A and AP (May 71) derive independently from MS for 'In . . . maybe.' (50.1–52.7)◄

50.1	IN (A) • However, in (AP)
50.1	while (A) • ~, (AP)
50.6	brim full (AP) • brim-|ful (A)
50.11	regions[1] (A) • ~, (AP)
50.14	daylight (A) • day-|light (AP)
50.15	darkness— (A) • ~, (AP)
50.16	horse (A) • ~, (AP)
50.16	racer (A) • ~, (AP)
50.17	gentleman; (A) • ~, (AP)
50.18	men (A) • ~, (AP)
50.20	pair (A) • ~, (AP)
50.23	thin (AP) • ~, (A)
50.23	roundabout (AP) • round-|about, (A)
50.24	boot-tops (A) • ~, (AP)
50.26	necessary, (A) • ~; (AP)
*50.27	two dollars an ounce (AP) • five dollars a letter (A)
50.28	carry— (A) • ~; (AP)
51.2	mail-pockets (A) • ~, (AP)
51.2	thighs (A) • ~, (AP)
51.6–7	stage-coach (A) • stage-|coach (AP)
51.7	traveled (A) • travelled (AP)
51.8	twenty-four (A) • twenty four (AP)
51.9	hours), (A) • ~); (AP)
51.15	procession (A) • ~, (AP)
51.17	eastward (AP) • ~, (A)

51 cap	"HERE HE COMES!" (C) • "HERE HE COMES." (A); [not in] (AP)
51.19	livelihood (A) • ~, (AP)
51.22	but (A) • ~, (AP)
51.22	other (A) • ~, (AP)
51.22	us (A) • ~, (AP)
51.23	us (A) • ~, (AP)
51.24	gone (A) • ~, (AP)
51.28	HERE HE COMES (A) • Here he comes (AP)
51.30	prairie (A) • ~, (AP)
52.3	that (A) • ~, (AP)
52.4	mail-sack (A) • ~, (AP)
52 cap	CHANGING HORSES. (A) • [not in] (AP)
52.7	maybe (A) • may be (AP)

►A (72–83) is copy-text for 'We . . . well.' (52.8–63.35)◄

52.22	mountain crags (C) • mountain-crags
53.7	three-thousand-foot (C) • three thousand-foot
55.7	Horseshoe station (C) • Horse-Shoe Station
55.10	La Prele station (C) • Laparelle Station
55.19–20	La Prele station (C) • Laparelle Station
55.30	stage-line (C) • stage-|line
56.4	statements (C) • statement
60.1	two-thirds (C) • two thirds
60.19	a while (C) • awhile
61.1	outlaws (C) • out-|laws
62.7	shotgun (C) • shot gun
62.12–13	bedridden (C) • bed-|ridden
63.4	a while (C) • awhile
63.32	overland (C) • over-|land
63.34	offenses (C) • offences

►VoM (175 ¶2) is copy-text for 'On . . . paragraph:' (63.35–64.2)◄

63.35	On (A) • [¶] Sometimes Slade acted as a lyncher. On
63.35	occasion (A) • ~,
63.36	lost (A) • either lost
63.36	chanced (A) • happened

63.37   With a single companion he
            rode (A) • He rode, with a
            single companion,

63.39   firing (A) • firing at them

63.39   three, (A) • ~∧

64.1–2   From . . . paragraph: (A) •
            [not in]

*▶VoM (175 ¶1) is copy-text for 'While
. . . execution.' (64.3–9)◀

64.3   held absolute sway (A) •
            ruled supreme

64.8–9   execution. (A) • execution.
            He was a gentle, well-be-
haved child, remarkable for his beautiful, soft black eyes, and for his polite
address.

▶VoM (175 ¶4) is copy-text for 'Stories
. . . line.' (64.9–11)◀

64.9   Stories (A) • [¶] ~

64.9   Slade's (A) • his

64.11   line. (A) • line; neverthe-
            less, such is the veneration
still cherished for him by many of the
old stagers, that any insult offered to
his memory would be fearfully and
quickly avenged. Whatever he did to
others, he was their friend, they say;
and so they will say and feel till the
tomb closes over the last of his old
friends and comrades of the Overland.

▶VoM (175 ¶3) is copy-text for 'As . . .
practices.' (64.11–13)◀

64.11   As (A) • [¶] ~

64.13   practices. (A) • practices.
            He was feared a great deal
more, generally, than the Almighty,
from Kearney, West. There was, it
seems, something in his bold recklessness, lavish generosity, and firm attachment to his friends, whose quarrel he
would back, everywhere and at any
time, that endeared him to the wild
denizens of the prairie, and this personal attachment it is that has cast a
veil over his faults, so dark that his
friends could never see his real character, or believe their idol to be a blood=
stained desperado.

▶A (85–90) is copy-text for 'Slade . . .
chapter—' (64.14–69.5)◀

64n.1   *"The (C) • [centered] *"~

*65.10   him (C) • him to

65.11   barkeeper (C) • bar-keeper

66.3   school-boy (C) • schoolboy

66.15–16   log house (C) • log-house

66.34–35   practiced (C) • practised

67.8   stage station (C) • stage=
            station

67.10   employés (C) • employees

67.32   tin-cupful (C) • tin-|cupful

▶VoM (title page) is copy-text for ' "The
. . . picturesque:' (69.5–13)◀

69.5–8   "The . . . M. T." (A) • THE |
            VIGILANTES OF MON-
TANA! | TRIAL, CAPTURE AND EXECU-
TION OF | HENRY PLUMMER'S | NO-
TORIOUS | ROAD AGENT BAND! |
FORMING THE ONLY RELIABLE WORK
EVER OFFERED TO THE PUBLIC. | BY
PROF. THOS. J. DIMSDALE. | VIR-
GINIA CITY, M. T.: | D. W. TILTON &
CO., BOOK AND JOB PRINTERS. | 1866.
(VoM, cover); THE | VIGILANTES OF
MONTANA, | OR | POPULAR JUS-
TICE | IN THE | ROCKY MOUNTAINS.
| BEING A CORRECT AND IMPARTIAL
NARRATIVE OF THE | CHASE, TRIAL,
CAPTURE AND EXECUTION OF |
HENRY PLUMMER'S | ROAD
AGENT BAND, | TOGETHER WITH AC-
COUNTS OF THE LIVES AND CRIMES OF
| MANY OF THE ROBBERS AND DESPER-
ADOES, THE WHOLE | BEING INTER-
SPERSED WITH SKETCHES OF LIFE IN
THE | MINING CAMPS OF THE "FAR
WEST;" | Forming the only reliable
work on the subject ever offered the
public. | BY PROF. THOS. J. DIMS-
DALE. | VIRGINIA CITY, M. T.: | MON-
TANA POST PRESS, D. W. TILTON & CO.,
BOOK AND JOB PRINTERS. | 1866. (VoM,
title page)

69.8–13   Mr. . . . picturesque: (A) •
            [not in]

▶VoM (167 ¶2, lines 19–24) is copy-text
for ' "Those . . . incarnate." ' (69.13–17)◀

69.13   "Those (A) • ∧~

69.15   gentleman; on (A) • gentle-
            man. On

69.17   incarnate." (A) • ~.∧

▶VoM (175 ¶3, lines 3–4) is copy-text
for 'And . . . mine:' (69.17–21)◀

69.17   And . . . mine: (A) • He was
            feared a great deal more,

generally, than the Almighty, from Kearney, West.

69.18   Kearny (C) • Kearney

►VoM (167 ¶3–173 ¶3) is copy-text for 'After . . . feelings.' (69.22–74.18)◄

69.24   from (VoM) • of (A)

70.1–3   *was . . . hands* (A) • was the tearing in pieces and stamp-ing upon a writ of this conrt, followed by the arrest of the Judge, Alex. Davis by authority of a presented Derringer, and with his own hands

70.1   *court* (A) • conrt

70.2   *his* (A) • the

70.2   *Davis,* (A) • Davis

*70.4   Vigilanter (VoM) • Vigilante (A)

70.7   crime was (A) • crimes were

70.19–21   *It . . . lights;* (A) • It had be-come quite common, when Slade was on a spree, for the shop-keep-ers and citizens to close the stores and put out all the lights;

70.22   hands. (A) • hands. One store in Nevada he never ventured to enter—that of the Lott brothers—as they had taken care to let him know that any attempt of the kind would be followed by his sudden death, and, though he often rode down there, threatening to break in and raise ——, yet he never attempted to carry his threat into execution.

70.42–43   *seizing . . . it* (A) • seizing the writ, he tore it up, threw it on the ground and stamped upon it

70.43   companions' (A) • ~ₐ

71.1   retention (A) • capture

71.2–3   *master . . . law-makers* (A) • master of the situation and the conqueror and ruler of the courts, law and law-makers

72.14   courtezan (A) • prostitute

72.16   however, (A) • ~ₐ

72.39   street (A) • street, where the Ohlinghouse stone building now stands

73.1   intended (A) • intendend

73.2   Pfouts' (A) • Pfout's

73.15   horsewoman (A) • horse-|woman

►A (95–128) is copy-text for 'There . . . follows:' (74.19–107.25)◄

76.28   wagon loads (C) • wagon-|loads

77.5   hillside (C) • hill-side

77.15   hotel-keeper (C) • hotel-|keeper

77.18   good-day (C) • good day

77.24   hotel-keeper (C) • hotel-|keeper

77.32   western (C) • Western

77.37   commonplace (C) • com-mon-|place

80.28   cañons (C) • canyons

80.36   cañon-sides (C) • canyon⸗sides

81.22   cañon-beds (C) • canyon⸗beds

81.26   sand-bars (C) • sand-|bars

84 *cap1*   HERE! (C) • ~.

84 *cap2*   DAM (C) • [*not in*]

84.15   river (C) • River

84.20   river (C) • River

85.4   5 (C) • five

85.7   Cañon (C) • Canyon

85.7   U. S. (C) • United States

85.15   Cañon (C) • Canyon

85.31   overland (C) • over-|land

85.36   church (C) • Church

93.2   Secretary (C) • secretary

93.5   Federal (C) • federal

93.5   high-handed (C) • high handed

94.1   STREET (C) • STREET

94.6   roadside (C) • road-|side

98n.1   Meadows (C) • Meadow

99.5   Morrisites (C) • Morisites

99.11   daylight (C) • day-|light

100.4   hennery (C) • henery

100.8   homelike (C) • home-|like

100.17   eastern (C) • Eastern

104 *cap*   A REMARKABLE RESEM-BLANCE. (C) • "~ ~ ~."

107 *title*   16 (C) • XVI. (Prb–A); XVII. (Pra)

*►BoM (title page [lines 1–23] and testi-
monial page) is copy-text for 'THE . . .
powers:' (107.26–111.2)◄

- 107.28   Wherefore (A) • [block ¶] ~
- 108.6   An (A) • [block ¶] ~
- 108.9   Heaven. (A) • Heaven;

which is to shew unto the
remnant of the House of Israel what
great things the Lord hath done for
their fathers; and that they may know
the covenants of the Lord, that they are
not cast off for ever; and also to the
convincing of the Jew and Gentile that
JESUS is the CHRIST, the ETERNAL
GOD, manifesting himself unto all nations. And now if there are faults, they
are the mistakes of men; wherefore
condemn not the things of God, that ye
may be found spotless at the judgment-
seat of Christ.

- 108.10–13   "Hid . . . comes (A) • [not
in]
- 108.10–11   wherefore?" (C) • ~"? (A)
- 108.40–   Some . . . this: (A) • [not in]
109.7
- 109.25–   And . . . powers: (A) • [not
111.2   in]
- 109.35   Lehi;" (C) • ~"; (A)

►BoM (1 Nephi 5:38, 5:39:1–2, 5:42) is
copy-text for 'And . . . Jacob:' (111.3–
25)◄

- 111.3   And (A) • 38. And
- 111.11   And (A) • 39. And
- 111.13   Then . . . him. (A) • [not in]
- 111.14   And (A) • 42. And
- 111.18–25 Equipped . . . Jacob: (A) •
[not in]

►BoM (Jacob 2:6:14–25, 2:9:11–18) is
copy-text for 'For . . . everybody:'
(111.26–112.7)◄

- 111.26   For (A) • [no ¶] ~
- 111.36–38 However . . . chapter: (A) •
[not in]
- 112.1   Behold (A) • [no ¶] ~
- 112.5   none (A) • none; and there
should not be whoredoms
committed among them
- 112.6–7   The . . . everybody: (A) •
[not in]
- 112.6   book (C) • Book (A)

►BoM (3 Nephi 9:1:1–3, 9:2:1–8, 8:5:3–
22) is copy-text for 'And . . . children.'
(112.8–36)◄

- 112.8   And (A) • 1. AND
- 112.11   And (A) • 2. And
- 112.17–21 In . . . Nephi: (A) • [not in]
- 112.19   Savior (C) • Saviour (A)

►A (133–34) is copy-text for 'And . . .
battle:' (112.37–113.23)◄

- 112.38   book (C) • Book
- 113.5   Heshlon;" (C) • ~";
- 113.6   Gilgal;" (C) • ~";
- 113.6   Akish;" (C) • ~";
- 113.6–7   Moron;" (C) • Moran";
- 113.7   Agosh;" (C) • ~";

►BoM (Ether 6:7–8, 6:9:1–25) is copy-
text for '7. . . . written.' (113.24–
114.44)◄

- 114.43   and² (A) • (~
- 114.44   written (A) • written,) and
he hid them in a manner
that the people of Limhi did find them

►A (135–241) is copy-text for 'It . . .
CHAPTER 34' (115.1–221 title)◄

- 115n.1   *Milton. (C) • [centered]
*Milton. (Prb–A); [not in]
(Pra)
- 116.8   massacre (C) • Massacre
- 117 illus New York (C) • N. York
- 118.1   whisky (C) • whiskey
- 118.10–11 twenty-five-cent (C) •
twenty-five cent
- 118.17–18 yellow-jacket (C) • yellow-|
jacket
- 119.7   Meadows (C) • Meadow
- 119.12   afterward (C) • afterwards
- 120.15   midnight (C) • mid-|night
- 120.17   mail-sacks (C) • mail sacks
- 121.2   reveled (C) • revelled
- 122.3   4 (C) • four
- 122.15   livelong (C) • live-|long
- 123.35   maybe (C) • may be
- 124.25   Dictionary (C) • dictionary
- 124.29   twenty-three-mile (C) •
twenty-three mile
- 126.2   Cañon (C) • Canyon
- 127.20   whisky (C) • whiskey

128.11	outrun (C) • out-|run
130.6	river (C) • River
130.23	desert (C) • Desert
130.23	the³ (C) • The
130.25	river (C) • River
131.7	desert (C) • Desert
131.8	log house (C) • log-house
132.4	a while (C) • awhile
*132.5	time! (C) • ~ₐ
132.20	a while (C) • awhile
132.33	most (C) • very
133.5	a while (C) • awhile
133.25	at (C) • in
133.25	Placerville (C) • ~,
133.31	a while (C) • awhile
135.18	whisky (C) • whiskey
135.35	stage-drivers (C) • stage drivers
135.37	brakemen (C) • brake-|men
*136n.6	thirteenth (Aa–d) • sixteenth (Ae–g)
139.1	dust-cloud (C) • dust cloud
139.10	skurrying (C) • scurrying
139.16	stage-coach (C) • stage coach
140.1	summer (C) • Summer
140.3	chambermaids (C) • chamber-|maids
140.7	west (C) • West
141.11	maybe (C) • may be
142.3	overpowering (C) • over-|powering
142.8	queensware (C) • queen's≈ware
142.10	oil-cloth (C) • oil-|cloth
143.2	camp followers (C) • camp≈followers
143.4	Territorial (C) • territorial
143.11	Democratic (C) • democratic
143.17	boarding house (C) • boarding-house
144.8	Gov. (C) • Governor
144.28	Brigade's (C) • brigade's
145.3–4	Brigade (C) • brigade
147.12	secretary (C) • Secretary
147.16	marvelous (C) • marvellous
148.3	lake (C) • Lake
148.13	landmarks (C) • land-|marks
148.36	fell (C) • feel
149.3	anyway (C) • any way
150.34	log house (C) • log-house
152.21	foot-races (C) • foot-|races
153.16	mountain sides (C) • mountain-sides
154.25	nightfall (C) • night-fall
154.29	frying pan (C) • frying-pan
156.1	chaparral (C) • chapparal
156.10	mountain side (C) • mountain-side
156.14	net-work (C) • net-|work
157.2	head on (C) • head-on
158 title	24 (C) • XXIV. (Prb–A); XXV. (Pra)
158.24	tapaderas (C) • tapidaros
158.27	measure;" (C) • ~";
159 cap	HE WAS (C) • HIM
162.25	three-quarters (C) • three quarters
163.2	three-quarters (C) • three quarters
164.28	livery-stable (C) • livery stable
165.1	people (C) • peopled
165.3	Valleys (C) • valleys
166.2	County (C) • county
166.25–26	Territorial (C) • territorial
166.27	Gov. (C) • Governor
166.29	Gov. (C) • Governor
168.6	small-fry (C) • small fry
168.8	greenbacks (C) • green-|backs
169.5	Capitol (C) • capitol
169.16–17	eighteen-hundred-dollar (C) • eighteen hundred dollar
169.27	greenbacks (C) • green-|backs
170.29	envelops (C) • envelopes
172.7	toll-road (C) • toll-|road
174.4	& (C) • and
174.12	So-and-so (C) • So-and-So
174.13	forty thousand dollars (C) • $40,000

174.15–16   sixty-five thousand dollars (C) • $65,000

174.18   eighteen thousand dollars (C) • $18,000

175.16   marvelous . . . marvelous (C) • marvellous . . . marvellous

176.24   pyrrhonism (C) • pyrhanism

176.34   a hundred to four hundred dollars (C) • $100 to $400

176.35   twenty to forty dollars (C) • $20 to $40

176.38   one-fourth (C) • one fourth

180.11   sage-brush (C) • sage-|brush

183.18   beverage, (C) • ~∧

184.7   Canal (C) • canal

184.13   County (C) • county

184.15   liberty pole (C) • liberty⸗ pole

184.16   cañon (C) • canyon

184.18   cañon (C) • canyon

184.20   mountain-tops (C) • mountain tops

185.15   brim full (C) • brimful

185.36   reconnoitre (C) • reconnoiter

187.11   maybe (C) • may be

187.12   Seven-thousand-dollar (C) • Seven thousand dollar

188 cap   THAT! (C) • THAT!

189.3   sage-brush (C) • sage-|brush

191.1   NOTICE. (C) • "~."

191.2–6   We . . . same. (C) • "~ . . . ~."

191.2   (and (C) • [~

191.31   silver mill (C) • silver-mill

193.3   Clagett (C) • Clagget

193.30   marvelous cañon (C) • marvellous canyon

195.17   eye-glass (C) • eye-|glass

197.27   Toward (C) • Towards

197.27   hay wagons (C) • hay⸗ wagons

197.29   stage-drivers (C) • stage drivers

197.35   By'm-by (C) • By'm-|by

200.9   sunburned (C) • sun-burned

201.4   bar-room (C) • bar-|room

202.1   a while (C) • awhile

203.16   a sayin' (C) • a-sayin'

204.1   nothing 'll (C) • nothing'll

204.10   a ranklin' (C) • a-ranklin'

204.19   underhanded (C) • under-|handed

204.36   doorway (C) • door-|way

207.20   City (C) • city

208.12   logarithm (C) • logarythm

209.23   snow-fall (C) • snow-|fall

209.34   on (C) • an

211.10   camp-fire (C) • camp fire

211.24   sage-bush (C) • sage bush

*214.6   every body (C) • everybody

214.26   logarithm (C) • logarythm

►BE (2 Apr 70) is copy-text for 'THE . . . understanding.' (221.1–227.5)◄

221.1   THE (A) • It was in the early days of Nevada Territory. The

221.3   spring (C) • Spring

221.5   The reader cannot (A) • You do not

221.5   he has (A) • you have

221.9   his (A) • your

221.9   he (A) • you

221.11   Gen. (C) • General

221.12   U. S. (C) • United States

221.16   down (A) • [not in]

221.17   benevolent compassion (A) • unmalignant contempt

221.20   Hyde (A) • Sides

221.20   Gen. (C) • General

221.23   conduct (A) • defend

222.4   everything (A) • every thing

222.8   thirty-eight (A) • six

222.12–13   he was occupying his (BE–Ac) • was occupying (Ad–g)

222.15   anybody (A) • any body

222.16   the (A) • [not in]

222.20   he (A) • [not in]

222.21   anybody (A) • any body

222.23   Hyde (A) • Sides

222.27   a coming (C) • a-coming (A); coming (BE)

222.28   by (A) • and by

222.30–36 splinters . . . teeth!—(A) • trees going end over end in the air, rocks as big as a house jumping about a thousand feet high and busting into ten million pieces, cattle literally turned inside out and a-coming head on with their tails hanging out between their teeth—Oh, splinters, and cord= wood, and thunder and lightning, and hail and snow, odds and ends of hay stacks and things, and dust—Oh, dust ain't no name for it—it was just clouds, solid clouds of dust!—

222.35   a coming (C) • a-coming

222.37   a wondering (C) • a= wondering

222.37– 223.1   didn't . . . me, (A) • did n't stay and hold possession; likely! Umph!

223.1   glimpse (A) • glimpse of that speckticle

223.2   lit (A) • I lit

223.2   county (A) • country

223.7–8   condition—got (A) • ~ – ~

223.8   anything (A) • any thing

223.9   a going (C) • a-going

223.16   Hyde (A) • Sides

223.16–17   everybody (A) • every body

223.20–21   a . . . two (A) • the largest parlor of the Ormbsy House at 2

223.22   General (A) • innocent General

223.24   witnesses (A) • wienesses

223.25   Hyde (A) • Sides

223.27   two (A) • 2

223.27   court (C) • Court

223.27   Roop (A) • that remorseless old joker

223.28   the (A) • his

223.28–29   spectators (A) • a "packed" jury

223.29   solemnity (A) • fraudulent solemnity

223.34   court (C) • Court

224.2–3   trickled . . . system (A) • saturated his whole system with pleasure

224.6   ranchmen (A) • ranch men

224.8   Hyde (A) • Sides

224.14   exultation in (A) • a great glow of triumph on

224.14   an impassioned (A) • a mighty

224.15   law-books (A) • law-|books

224.16   everything (A) • every thing

224.16   everybody (A) • every body

224.17   bathos, (A) • and

225.4   conviction (A) • comfort- able conviction

225.5   was anything (A) • were any thing

225.5   great (A) • big

225.7   case was killed (A) • cake was dough

225.8   thinking (A) • thinking profoundly

225.8   waited (A) • waited breathlessly

225.11   his (A) • and his

225.12–13   throne . . . impressively: (A) • throne and seated him- self. The sheriffs commanded the at- tention of the Court. Judge Roop cleared his throat and said:

225.18   have perceived that (A) • [not in]

225.18   overwhelming (A) • over-| whelming

225.19   it, (A) • ~∧

225.19   Hyde (A) • Sides

225.23   mere (A) • [not in]

225.24   us (A) • us to our undoing

225.25   this. (A) • ~?

225.30   dissatisfied (A) • unsatisfied

225.34   or . . . it (A) • [not in]

226 cap   REÄRRANGING (C) • REAR- RANGING (A)

226.4   Hyde (A) • Sides

226.6   law-books (A) • law books

226.7   frantic with indignation (A) • a raving madman, almost

226.8   fool (A) • ass, a fool

226.10   floor (A) • fioor

226.15   Hyde (A) • Sides

226.15   ground (A) • ground itself

226.17   Hyde (A) • Sides

227.2–5   months . . . understanding.
(A) • weeks he got it
through his understanding that he had
been played upon with a joke. [*indented from right*] MARK TWAIN.

▶A (248–59) is copy-text for 'CHAP-
TER . . . CHAPTER 37' (228 *title*–238
title)◀

229.4   heaves;" (C) • ~";

229.26   curb-stone (C) • curbstone

233.9   quicksilver (C) • quick-|
silver

233.12   time, (C) • ~‸

233.20   quicksilver (C) • quick-|
silver

233.23   one-third (C) • one third

235.9   two-thirds (C) • two thirds

235.14   Cañon (C) • Canyon

235.16   afterward (C) • afterwards

236.5   coarse (Aa–e) • course (Af–
g)

236.10   mould (C) • mold

▶BE (11 Dec 69 ¶17–18) is copy-text for
'It . . . desires.' (238.1–240.5)◀

238.1   IT (A) • [*centered*] THE FA-
MOUS "CEMENT" MINE. [¶]
It

238.2   marvelous (C) • marvellous
(A); wonderful (BE)

238.3   that (A) • that this
mysterious

238.4   in disguise, (A) • [*not in*]

238.14   Whiteman (A) • W.

238.18   daylight (A) • day-|light

238.18   winter (C) • Winter

238.19   complete, (A) • complete
and

238.20   W. (A) • W. I ought to know,
because I was one of those
fools myself.

238.21   The (A) • But it was enough
to make a fool of nearly any
body. The

238.21   more than (A) • [*not in*]

238.28   dull (A) • shining

239.1–2   curb-stone (C) • curb stone

239.3   two hundred dollars (C) •
$200

239.10   by² (A) • bye

239.10   lay (BE) • laid (A)

239.27   Whiteman (A) • W.

239.32   one (A) • [*not in*]

239.33   Esmeralda (A) • '62

*239.37   had not (A) • hadn't

240.2   Whiteman (A) • W.

240.2   a (A) • rather a

240.4   one (A) • about one

▶A (261–65) is copy-text for 'A . . .
CHAPTER 38' (240.6–245 *title*)◀

240.27   coffee-pot (C) • coffee pot

241.7   cañon (C) • canyon

241.17   pommel (C) • pummel

242.15   lake (C) • Lake

242.19   lake (C) • Lake

243.6   lake (C) • Lake

243.15   lake (C) • Lake

243.17   shotguns (C) • shot-guns

243.19   lake (C) • Lake

244 *cap*   MONO LAKE (C) • LAKE
MONO

▶BE (16 Oct 69) is copy-text for 'MONO
. . . true.' (245.1–249.15)◀

245.1   MONO LAKE (C) • MONO
LAKE (A); [*indented from
right*] NEW YORK, October 10. [¶] [I am
just starting on a plea[ ]ure trip around
the globe, *by proxy*. That is to say, Professor D. R. FORD, of Elmira College, is
now making the journey for me, and
will write the newspaper account of his
(our) trip. No, not that exactly—but he
will travel and write letters, and I shall
stay at home and add a dozen pages to
each of his letters. One of us will furnish the fancy and the jokes, and the
other will furnish the facts. I am equal
to either department, though statistics
are my best hold. I am perfectly satisfied now. I have long had a desire to
travel clear around the world in one
grand, comprehensive picnic excursion,
but the fatigue and vexation of it
formed one drawback, and the expense
another. The necessary thing was to get
somebody to divide these discomforts
with, and so make them bearable. This
is now accomplished. I stay at home
and stand the fatigue, and the Professor
travels and stands the expense. While
my Double is roaming about the Great

Plains, and Nevada and California, my half of the letters will be at a disadvantage, because I shall be hampered by an intimate personal knowledge of those localities; but when he gets into Japan, and China and India, I can soar with a gorgeous freedom because I don't know any thing about those lands. [¶] [Professor Ford is a scholarly man; a man whose attainments cover a vast field of knowledge. His knowledge is singularly accurate, too; what he knows he is *certain* of, and likewise what he knows he has a happy faculty of communicating to others. He is a man of high social standing and unspotted character. He is a warm personal friend of mine— which is to his discredit, perhaps, but would you have a man perfect? He is a minister of the Gospel, and a *live* one— a man whose religion broadens and adorns his nature; not a religion that dates a man back into the last century and saps his charity and makes him a bigot. Mr. Ford's letters will be written in all good faith and honesty, and I shall not mar them. I shall merely have *a good deal to say.* I trust that the discriminating reader will always be able to discover where Ford leaves off and I begin—though I don't really intend he *shall* be able to do that. As Mr. F. jogs along, I mean to write paragraph for paragraph with him, and I shall set down all that I know about the countries he visits, together with a good deal that neither I nor anybody else knows about them. [¶] [Mr. Ford had reached Salt Lake City a few days ago, and by this time is prowling among the silver mines of Nevada. His letters are on their way hither, no doubt, but in themeantime I will begin the journey unassisted, with a sketch or so of my own about The Dead Sea of California, and some other curious features of that country. The Professor will sail for Japan in the steamer America, which leaves San Francisco on the 4th of November. A twenty-five or thirty day sea voyage, doubled, makes a long interregnum, and so his Japanese letters will not begin to arrive before January. However, I can run this duplicate correspondence by myself till then. With the reader's permission I will now begin— and what I say about Mono Lake may be accepted as strictly true. I shall tell no lies about it.] [*indented from right*] MARK TWAIN. [*centered*] THE DEAD SEA. [¶] Mono Lake or the Dead Sea of California, is one of her most extraordinary curiosities, but being situated in a very out-of-the-way corner of the country, and away up among the eternal snows of the Sierras, it is little known and very seldom visited. A mining excitement carried me there once, and I spent several months in its vicinity. It (BE)

245.1–2	eight thousand (A) • 8000
245.3	two thousand (A) • 2000
245.3	summits (A) • snmmits
245.3–4	always clothed in (A) • hidden always in the
245.6	grayish (A) • greyish
245.8	rent (A) • ~,
245.9	gray (A) • grey
245.12	two hundred (A) • 200
245.15	the ablest of washerwomen's (A) • your ablest washerwoman's
246.3	summersets (BE) • somersaults (A)
246.4–5	extraordinary (A) • frantic and extraordinary
247.2	anything (A) • any thing
247.3–4	two hundred and fifty (A) • 250
247.5	nine (A) • five
247.12	age.] (A) • age. Horace Greeley remarked to a friend of mine that if he were ever to make a joke like that, he would not desire to live any longer.]
247.13–14	pollywogs (BE) • polliwigs (A)
247.15	sea-gulls (A) • sea gulls
247.27	do not (A) • don't
247.32–33	economy: the ducks (A) • economy. The ducks and gulls
247.34	all three (A) • the flies
247.34	wild-cats (C) • wild cats

247.35   wild-cats (C) • wild cats (A);
            wild cats when the crops
            fail (BE)

*247.36   a hundred and fifty (C) • a
            hundred (A); 150 (BE)

248.2   Kansas (A) • Tennessee

248.4–5   pumice stone (C) •
            pumicestone

248.6   anybody (A) • any body

248.14   anything (A) • any thing

248.15   anything (A) • any thing

248 cap   BOARDING HOUSE (C) •
            BOARDING-HOUSE (A)

248.18   not . . . it (A) • not a stream
            of any kind flows out of it

248.20   mystery. (A) • mystery. All
            the rivers of Nevada sink
into the earth mysteriously after they
have run 100 miles or so—none of
them flow to the sea, as is the fashion
of rivers in all other lands.

248.22   winter (C) • Winter

248.23   (in Esmeralda) (A) • [not in]

249.1   nine (A) • 9

249.4   summer (C) • Summer

249.8–9   barkeeper (C) • bar keeper

249.12   do not (A) • don't

249.15   true. (A) • true. [centered]
            [TO BE CONTINUED.]

▶A (270–320) is copy-text for 'CHAP-
TER . . . cases.' (250 title–299.6)◀

250.24   pumice stone (C) • pumice⸗
            stone

253.17   head on (C) • head-on

253.26   steering-oar (C) • steering
            oar

255 cap   GONE! (C) • ~.

257.12   sixteen-hundred-pound (C)
            • sixteen-hundred-pounds

257.31   sage-brush (C) • sage brush

261.38   spring (C) • Spring

264.1   CAPT. NYE (C) • CAPTAIN
            NYE

264.24   coachman (C) • coach-|man

265.34   cañon (C) • canyon

266.23   brim full (C) • brimful

266.36   horseback (C) • horse-|back

267.3–5   Don't . . . CAL. (C) •
            "~ . . . ~."

271.19   a while (C) • awhile

273.2   backwards (C) • backward

273.22   hillside (C) • hill side

274.31   reported,' (C) • ~,‸

274.32   headquarters (C) • head-|
            quarters

275.2–3   practice (C) • practise

275.7   note-book (C) • note-|book

275.14   business-like (C) • business
            like

280.4   whisky (C) • whiskey

280.12   Genesee (C) • Genessee

280.35   good-bye (C) • good by

282.15   whisky (C) • whiskey

282.29   & (C) • and

284.17   cañon (C) • canyon

286.9   (by (C) • [~

286.16   reporters (C) • reporter

288 cap   TAKE (C) • TRY

289.20   U. S. (C) • United States

291.10   half dollars (C) • half⸗
            dollars

292.7–8   press-room (C) • press-|
            room

292.17–18   fire-proof (C) • fire-|proof

292.26   rent-free (C) • rent free

292.29   Superintendent (C) •
            superintendent

293.1   lawsuit (C) • law suit

293.2   cent (C) • ~.

293.6   U. S. (C) • United States

293.8   eastern (C) • Eastern

*293.21   and² (C) • of

293.37   Sanitary (C) • sanitary

298.3   City (C) • city

298.17   Sanitary (C) • sanitary

▶BE (8 Jan 70 ¶1–18) is copy-text for
'Two . . . him.' (299.7–301.31)◀

299.7   Two cousins (A) • [cen-
            tered] "EARLY DAYS" IN
NEVADA. [centered] SILVER LAND NA-
BOBS. [¶] One of the curious features of
Pacific Coast life is the startling uncertainty that marks a man's career in the
mines. He may spring from poverty to
wealth so suddenly as to turn his hair
white and then after a while he may become poor again so suddenly as to

make all that white hair fall off and leave his head as clean as a billiard ball. The great Nevada silver excitement of '58–'59 was prolific in this sort of vicissitudes. [¶] Two brothers

299.7	man (A) • man in Virginia city
299.8–9	three hundred dollars (C) • $300
299.12–13	eight to ten thousand dollars (C) • $8000 to $10,000
299.13–14	a hundred thousand dollars (C) • $100,000
299.14	year. (A) • year. They had

that handsome income for just about two years—and they dressed in the loudest kind of costumes and wore mighty diamonds, and played poker for amusement, these men who had seldom had $20 at one time in all their lives before. One of them is tending bar for wages, now, and the other is serving his country as Commander-in-Chief of a street car in San Francisco at $75 a month. He was very glad to get that employment, too.

299.16–17	six thousand dollars' (C) • $6000
299.17	of (A) • [not in]
299.19	could not (A) • couldn't
299.21	it. (A) • it. But let us learn

from him that persistent effort is bound to achieve success at last. Within a year's time his happiness was secure; for he hadn't a cent to spend.

299.23–24	sixteen thousand dollars (C) • $16,000
299.27	five dollars (A) • $5
299.28	he (A) • ho
299.28	country. (A) • country.

Three years afterward he attained to the far more exceeding grandeur of working in it again, at *four* dollars a day.

300.1–2	a hundred thousand dollars (C) • $100,000
300.3–4	but . . . account. (A) • and a little over a year ago a

friend saw him shoveling snow on the Pacific Railroad for a living, away up on the summit of the Sierras, some 7,000 feet above the level of comfort and the sea. The friend remarked that it must be pretty hard work, though, as the snow was twenty-five feet deep, it promised to be a steady job, at least. Yes, he said, he didn't mind it *now*, though a month or so ago when it was sixty-two feet deep and still a snowing, he wasn't so much attached to it. Such is life.

300.5	Smith. (A) • Smith. That wasn't his name, but we wiil call him that.
300.6	soul (A) • fellow
300.7	and (A) • and the team belonged to another man. By

and bye he married an excellent woman, who

300.8	him (A) • them
300.9	two hundred and fifty (C) • $250
300.10	three hundred dollars (C) • $300 (A); $500 (BE)
300.13–14	retired from the hay business (A) • quit raising hay
300.15	thirty thousand dollars (C) • $30,000
300.16	sixty thousand dollars (C) • $60,000
300.17	at any rate. (A) • any how.

He built a house out in the desert—right in the most forbidding and otherwise howling desert—and it was currently reported that that house cost him a quarter of a million. Possibly that was exaggerated somewhat, though it certainly was a fine house and a costly one. The bed[ ]|steads cost $400 or $500 apiece.

300.18	he . . . he (A) • the Smiths . . . they
300.19	he[1] (A) • Smith
300.22	wonders (A) • wonder
300.22	everybody (A) • every body
300.25–26	five hundred dollars (C) • $500
300.29	envelops (C) • envelopes
300.31	said: (A) • ~,
300.33	than (A) • that
300.36	Well, (A) • ~ₐ
300.38	0's (A) • naughts
301.1	'em (A) • em

301.2   please." (A) • please." [¶]
Well, Smith is dead. And
when he died he wasn't worth a cent.
The lesson of all this is, that one must
learn how to do everything he does—
one must have experience in being rich
before he can *remain* rich. The history
of California will prove this to your entire satisfaction. Sudden wealth is an
awful misfortune to the average run of
men. It is wasting breath to instruct
the reader after this fashion, though,
for no man was ever convinced of it yet
till he had tried it himself—and I am
around now hunting for a man who is
afraid to try it. I haven't had any luck,
so far. [¶] All the early pioneers of California acquired more or less wealth, but
an enormous majority of them have not
got any now. Those that have, got it
slowly and by patient toil.

301.3   The Gould & Curry (A) •
The reader has heard of the
great Gould & Curry silver mine of Nevada. I believe its shares are still quoted
in the stock sales in the New York papers. The

301.3   twelve hundred feet, and
(A) • 1200 feet, if I remem-
ber rightly, or may be it was 800—and I
think

301.4   the (A) • [*not in*]

301.7   seventeen (A) • 17

301.9   nine (A) • 9

301.10   three (A) • 3

301.10   that[1] (A) • [*not in*]

301.12   million (BE) • millions (A)

301.15   directly (A) • right

301.17   a hundred feet (A) • 100 ft

301.17   traded (A) • swapped

301.18   hundred feet (A) • 100 ft

301.20   mill) (A) • ~),

301.20–21 one million five hundred
thousand dollars. (C) •
$1,500,000. (A); $1,500,000. I was down
in it about that time, 600 ft under the
ground, and about half of it caved in
over my head—and yet, valuable as
that property was, I would have given
the entire mine to have been out of
that. I do not wish to brag—but I can be
liberal if you take me right. (BE)

301.22   twenty (A) • 20

301.24   sorry-looking (C) • sorry
looking

301.24   was, (A) • ~∧

301.25   three thousand dollars (C) •
$3000

301.26   had not (A) • hadn't

301.28–30 sixty-thousand-dollar . . .
bareback (A) • 60,000-dollar
horse and yet had to ride him bareback
because he couldn't scare up cash
enough to buy a saddle

301.31   sixty-thousand-dollar (A) •
60,000-dollar

301.31   him. (A) • him. [¶] The
shiftless people I have been
talking about have settled sedimentally
down to their proper place on the bottom, but the solid mining prosperity of
California and Nevada continues—the
two together producing some
$40,000,000 annually in gold and sil-
ver. White Pine is giving birth to the
usual number of suddenly-created nabobs, but three years hence nearly
every one of them will be scratching for
wages again. Petroleum bred a few of
these butterflies for the eastern market.
They don't live long in Nevada. I was
worth half a million dollars myself,
once, for ten days—and now I am
prowling around the lecture field and
the field of journalism, instructing the
public for a subsistence. I was just as
happy as the other butterflies, and no
wiser—except that I am sincerely glad
that my supernatural stupidity lost me
my great windfall before it had a
chance to make a more inspired ass of
me than I was before. I am satisfied
that I do not know enough to be
wealthy and live to survive it. I had two
partners in this brilliant stroke of fortune. The sensible one is still worth a
hundred thousand dollars or so—he
never lost his wits – but the other one
(and by far the best and worthiest of our
trio), can't pay his board.

►A (323–25) is copy-text for 'A . . .
country.' (301.32–303.34)◄

302.6–7   a hundred and fifty thousand dollars (C) • $150,000

303.25   barkeeper (C) • bar-keeper

303.27   seventy-five thousand dollars (C) • $75,000

303.30   to² (C) • [*not in*]

►BE (8 Jan 70 ¶19) is copy-text for 'I . . . again.' (303.35–304.2)◄

303.35   personally (A) • pe[ ]sonally

303.35–36   majority . . . to (A) • several nabobs mentioned in this letter

303.36   shifted (A) • swapped

303.37   experiences (A) • exp[ ]riences

303.38–   No . . . again (A) • I have no
304.2   desire to drag them out of their retirement and make them uncomfortable by exhibiting them without mask or disguise—I merely wish to use their fortunes and misfortunes for a moment for the adornment of this newspaper article

►A (325–78) is copy-text for 'In . . . the' (304.3–355.11)◄

304.31   bet (C) • ~,

309.16   resolutions (C) • resolutious

309.18   gentle, spirituel (C) • gentle ,spirituel

310.3   patent-leather (C) • patent leather

310.4–5   boot-tops (C) • boot tops

310.14   pot luck (C) • pot-luck

314.1   town lots (C) • town-lots

314.6   power?" (C) • ~?'

314.17   Let's (C) • Lets

315 *cap*   NEVER (C) • DIDN'T

315.21   you're (C) • you 're

316.3   hand-shake (C) • hand-| shake

316.7   half-mast (C) • half mast

316 *cap*   SUNDAY SCHOOL (C) • SUN-DAY-SCHOOL

317.5   Sunday school (C) • Sunday⸗ school

317.7   small fry (C) • small-fry

318.16   saloon-keeper (C) • saloon keeper

321.5   empaneled (C) • impaneled

321.10   barkeepers (C) • bar-keepers

323.6   barkeeper (C) • bar keeper

323.13–14   governors (C) • Governors

327n.10   barkeeper (C) • bar-keeper

327n.11   barkeeper (C) • bar-keeper

327n.13–   barkeeper (C) • bar-keeper
328n.1

328n.3   barkeeper (C) • bar-keeper

332.7   t'other (C) • 'tother

333.33   handcuffs (C) • hand-|cuffs

335.4   *anyhow* (C) • *any how*

336.11   there'll (C) • there 'll

336.19   cañon (C) • canyon ·

336.24   cañon (C) • canyon

339.25   church (C) • Church

340.10   Rosicrucian (C) • Roscicrucian

340.16   track (C) • tract

340.19   billets-doux (C) • billet⸗ doux

341.28   Rosicrucian (C) • Roscicrucian

341.39   Rosicrucian (C) • Roscicrucian

342.31   foot-notes (C) • footnotes

342.36   Rosicrucian (C) • Roscicrucian

344.9   whaleships (C) • whale ships

344.33   whaleships (C) • whale ships

346.4   Little, (C) • ~ₐ

350.8   Hurray! hurray! (C) • Hurray! huray!

350 *cap*   SHORTENING SAIL (Ac–g) • BOY IN THE ACT (Pr–Ab)

*350.15–   And count . . . wind!" ‖ "A
353.10   quarter-three . . . faith! (Pr) • "A quarter-three . . . faith! ‖ And count . . . wind!" [*pages reversed*] (A)

351.3   gunny sacks (C) • gunny⸗ sacks

354.13   enclosed (C) • inclosed

354.18   a hundred and fifty (C) • 150

354.25   two hundred dollars (C) • $200

354.26   a hundred dollars (C) • $100

354.28   ten thousand dollars (C) • $10,000

355.2–3   fifteen hundred to three thousand dollars (C) • $1,500 to $3,000

355.5   cent (C) • ~.

355.6–7   twenty-five dollars (C) • $25

►TE63 is copy-text for '*Mr. . . . M. T.]' (355n.1–356n.3)◄

355n.1   *Mr. (A) • Ye Bulletin Cypshereth.—The Bulletin folks have gone and swallowed an arithmetic; that arithmetic has worked them like a "wake-up-Jake," and they have spewed up a multitude of figures. We cypher up the importance of the Territory sometimes so recklessly that our self-respect lies torpid within us for weeks afterwards—but we see now that our most preposterous calculations have been as mild as boarding-house milk; we perceive that we haven't the nerve to do up this sort of thing with the Bulletin. It estimates the annual yield of the precious metals at $730,000,000! Bully! They say figures don't lie—but we doubt it. We are distanced—that must be confessed; yet, appalled as we are, we will venture upon the Bulletin's "boundless waste" of figures, and take the chances. A Gould & Curry bar with $2,000 in it weighs nearly 100 pounds; $100,000 worth of their bullion would weigh between two and two and a half tons; it would take two of Wells Fargo's stages to carry that $100,000 without discommoding the passengers; it would take 100 stages to carry $5,000,000; 2,000 stages to carry $100,000,000, and 14,600 stages to carry the Bulletin's annual yield of $730,000,000! Wells, Fargo & Co. transport all the bullion out of the Territory in their coaches, and to attend to this little job, they would have to send forty stages over the mountains daily throughout the year, Sundays not excepted, and make each of the forty carry considerably more than a ton of bullion!—yet they generally send only two stages, and the greatest number in one day, during the heaviest rush, was six coaches; they didn't each carry a ton of bullion, though, old smarty from Hongkong. The Bulletin also estimates the average

yield of ore from our mines at $1,000 a ton! Bless your visionary soul, sixty dollars—where they get it "regular like"—is considered good enough in Gold Hill, and it is a matter of some trouble to pick out many tons that will pay $400. From sixty to two hundred is good rock in the Ophir, and when that company, or the Gould & Curry, or the Spanish, or any other of our big companies get into a chamber that pays over $500, they ship it to the Bay, my boy. But they don't ship thousands of tons at a time, you know. In Esmeralda and Humboldt, ordinary "rich rock" yields $100 to $200, and when better is found, it is shipped also. Reese River appears to be very rich, but you can't make an "average" there yet awhile; let her mines be developed first. We place the average yield of the ore of our Territory at $100 a ton—that is high enough; we couldn't starve, easily, on forty-dollar rock. Lastly, the Bulletin puts the number of our mills at 150. That is another mistake; the number will not go over a hundred, and we would not be greatly amazed if it even fell one or two under that. While we are on the subject, though, we might as well estimate the "annual yield" of the precious metals, also; we did not intend to do it at first. Mr.

355n.1   agent (A) • handsome and accomplished agent

355n.7 $1,600,000 (A) • 1,600,000

355n.11   1863 (though (A) • 1863, and now,

355n.12   we (A) • we too, like the Bulletin,

355n.12   underestimating, somewhat) (C) • under estimating, somewhat) (A); "underestimating," somewhat (TE63)

355n.13   them (A) • them eight, no, to be liberal,

355n.19   producing (A) • [not in]

355n.21   day (A) • day—one ton of the Bulletin's rock, or ten of ours

356n.1   have (A) • have got

356n.1   down (A) • down just about

356n.2   aggregate.—*Enterprise.* (A) • • aggregate. Oh no!—we have never been to school—we don't know how to cypher. Certainly not—we are probably a natural fool, but we don't know it. Anyhow, we have mashed the Bulletin's estimate all out of shape and cut the first left-hand figure off its $730,000,000 as neatly as a regular banker's clerk could have done it.

356n.3   [A considerable overestimate.—M. T.] (C) • [A considerable over estimate.—M. T.] (A); [*not in*] (TE63)

▶A (378–410) is copy-text for 'neighborhood . . . that.' (356.1–387.17)◀

356.1–2   a thousand dollars (C) • $1,000

356.3   besides (C) • beside

356.4   twenty-five to thirty dollars (C) • $25 to $30

357.13   & (C) • and

357.15   & (C) • and

357.34–35 daylight (C) • day-|light

358.2–3   feeling (C) • feel-|

358.39–   earthquake (C) • earth-|
359.1   quake

359.24   upright (C) • up-|right

359.39–40 flood-water (C) • flood-| water

359.44   earthquake (C) • earth-| quake

361.27   Grandfather (C) • Grand-| father

362.5–6   grandfather (C) • grand-| father

362.6   West (C) • west

362.10   flap-jack (C) • flapjack

363.7   t'other (C) • t' other

364.2–3   'Your . . . dear' (C) • "~ . . . ~"

367.1   uncle (C) • Uncle

367.4   County (C) • county

370.7   Ironer;" (C) • ~";

370.7   Washer;" (C) • ~";

371.4   wrinkled (C) • wringled

372.10   headquarters (C) • head-| quarters

372.25   law-makers (C) • law-| makers

373.18–19 unpronounceable (C) • unpronouncable

374.13   gridiron (C) • grid-|iron

375.3   east (C) • East

376.8   Territorial (C) • territorial

376.15   Constitution (C) • constitution

376.16   well-nigh (C) • wellnigh

376.24   a hundred thousand dollars (C) • $100,000

376.27   a hundred thousand dollars (C) • $100,000

377.4   river (C) • River

379.12   one-third (C) • one third

379.26   east (C) • East

379.32   east (C) • East

380.20   paroxysms (C) • paroxyms

381.3   whisky (C) • whiskey

381.3   barkeeper (C) • bar-keeper

381.9   barkeeper (C) • bar-keeper

383.7   midnight (C) • mid-|night

383.8   overlooking (C) • over-| looking

386.5   spendthrift (C) • spend-| thrift

386.6   eastern (C) • Eastern

387.10   sand hills (C) • sand-hills

▶BE (13 Nov 69) is copy-text for 'The¹ . . . over."' (387.18–392.24)◀

387.18   The¹ (A) • [*centered*] *CALI-FORNIA—CONTINUED.* [*centered*] MORE CLIMATE. [¶] There are other kinds of climate in California—several kinds—and some of them very agreeable. The

387.21   summer (C) • Summer

387.21   winter (C) • Winter

387.22   summer (C) • Summer

387.22   broadcloth (A) • broad-| cloth

387.22   you have (A) • you've got

387.24   do not (A) • don't

388.1   do not (A) • don't

388.1   is (A) • is just

388.1   well (A) • [*not in*]

388.2   take it all around, (A) • [*not in*]

388.2   doubtless (A) • [*not in*]

388.3–4   summer (C) • Summer
388.4   choose (A) • want to
388.5   does not (A) • don't
388.11   you will need (A) • the most righteous thing you can do will be
388.12   you will require (A) • you'll need
388.13   hardly varying (A) • unvarying
388.16   *rain* (A) • rain—there is little use in bothering about that—
388.17   cannot (A) • can not
388.23–24   a blinding glare (A) • the red splendors of hell
388.24   *anything* (A) • any *thing*
388.26   summer (C) • Summer
388.28   plead (A) • beg
388.29   you will (A) • you'll
388.30   cannot (A) • can't
388.32   San (A) • [*centered*] SANDY FERTILITY. [¶] San
388.33   the (A) • your
*388.33   flowers (A) • ~,
388.35   greenhouses (C) • green houses
388.36   Calla lilies (A) • Calla-|lilies
388.37   do not (A) • don't
389.4   they have also (A) • we have here
389.6   thought it grew only (A) • never have seen it anywhere but
389.8   pure (A) • pure and white
389.12   I (A) • [*centered*] CLIMATE RESUMED. [¶] I
389.12   elsewhere (A) • [*not in*]
389.12   winter (C) • Winter
389.13   but this moment of (A) • [*not in*]
389.13   spring (C) • Spring
389.15   summer (C) • Summer
389.15   summer clothing (C) • Summer-clothing
389.17–18   one hundred and forty-three (A) • 143
389.19   the reader (A) • you
389.21   stanchest (A) • dearest

389.21   hot (A) • pretty hot
389.23–24   one hundred and twenty (A) • 120
389.24   varies (A) • relents
389.25   and¹ (A) • ~—
389.26   suffer (A) • are bound to suffer
389.27   Phoenix* (C) • Phenix* (A); Phenix (BE)
389.28   course, (A) • course he
389.29   perdition,— (A) • ~, ——,
389.29–30   *telegraphed . . . blankets* (A) • telegraphed back for his blankets
389.31   can (A) • *can*
389.31   it. (A) • it—for
389.32   In Sacramento it (A) • With a French lady by the name of O'Flannigan, and she lives there yet. Sacramento
389.32   summer (C) • Summer
389n.1–2   *It . . . M. T. (A) • [*not in*]
390.1   then (A) • [*not in*]
390.7   some of us (A) • I
390.8   six thousand (A) • 6000
390.9   deathless (A) • everlasting
390.10   fruitful (A) • green
390.13   dreamy (A) • rich, dreamy
390.13   fairy-land (C) • fairy-|land
390.15   forbidding (BE) • forbidden (A)
391 *title* CHAPTER 57 (C) • CHAPTER LVII. (A); DESOLATION. (BE)
391.1   Sacramento Valley, just referred to, (A) • Sac Valley
391.10   fiercely-flourishing (A) • wildly, fiercely-flourishing
391.15   gold (A) • glittering gold
391.17   four hundred dollars (A) • $400
391.19   *everything* (A) • *every thing*
391.20   delights and adorns existence (A) • goes to make life happy and desirable
391.22   of it all (A) • [*not in*]
391.24   land, in modern times, have (A) • land do

391.25   died and disappeared (A) •
die and disappear

391.27   It (A) • [*centered*] THE CRU-
SADING HOST. [¶] It

391.30   observe (A) • mark you

392.1   two hundred thousand (A) •
200,000

392.3   brim full (C) • brimful

392.15   It is pitiful to think upon
(A) • California has much
to answer for in this destruction of the
flower of the world's young chivalry

392.18   cannot (A) • can not

392.20   enterprises (A) •
enterprizes

392.21   recklessness (A) • princely
recklessness

392.23   surprise (A) • astonisher

392.23   smiles (A) • smiles and
admires

►BE (11 Dec 69 ¶1–16) is copy-text for
'But . . . head.' (392.25–395.11)◄

392.25   But (A) • [*centered*] CALI-
FORNIA—CONTINUED.
[*centered*] THE "EARLY DAYS." [¶] But

392.27   from (A) • [*not in*]

392.28   dens (A) • dues

392.31   woolen (C) • woollen

392.37–39 It . . . anywhere! (A) • In his
sketch entitled "The Luck
of Roaring Camp," Mr. Bret Harte has
deftly pictured the roughness and lawlessness of a California mining camp of
the early days, and also its large-
hearted charity and compassion—for
these traits are found in all true pioneers. Roaring Camp becomes blessed
by the presence of a wandering, sickly
woman and her little child—rare and
coveted treasures among rude men
who still yearned in secret for the
mothers and sisters and children they
loved and cherished in other days. This
wanderer—the only woman in Roaring
Camp—died, and the honest miners
took charge of the orphan little one in a
body. They washed it and dressed it and
fed it—getting its garments on wrong
end first as often as any other way, and
pinning the garments *to* the child occasionally and wondering why the baby
wasn't comfortable—and the food

these inexperienced nurses lovingly
concocted for it was often rather beyond its capabilities, since it was neither an alligator nor an ostrich. [¶] But
they meant well, and the baby thrived
in spite of the perilous kindnesses of
the miners. But it was manifest that *all*
could not nurse the baby at once, and
so they passed a law that the best behaved man should have it for one day,
and the man with the cleanest shirt the
next day, and the man whose cabin was
in the neatest order the next, and so on.
And the result was, that a handsome
cradle was bought, and carted from
cabin to cabin, according to who won
the privilege of nursing each day—and
the handsome cradle made such a contrast to the unhandsome furniture, that
gradually the unhandsome furniture
disappeared and gave way for a neater
sort—and then ambitious male nurses
got to washing up and putting on clean
garments every day, and some of them
twice a day—and rough, boisterous
characters became gentle and soft-spoken, since only the well-behaved could
nurse the baby. And, in fine, the lawless
Roaring Camp became insensibly
transformed into a neat well-dressed,
orderly and law-abiding community,
the wonder and admiration of all the
mining world. All this, through the
dumb teaching, the humanizing influence, the uninspired ministering of a
little child.

393.1   In (A) • [*centered*] THE SEX
ON EXHIBITION. [¶] In

393.1   miners (A) • men

393.7   bona-fide (C) • bonafide

393.13   her!" (A) • ~!ᴧ

393.14–15 "But . . . OUT!" (A) • That
was the only reply.

393 *cap*   OUT! (C) • ~. (A)

394.3   Once (A) • [*centered*] EX-
HORBITANT RATES. [¶] A
year or two ago

394.10   campaign (A) • mining
campaign

394.11   evidently— (A) • ~ᴧ

395.2   have (A) • had

395.3   And (A) • [*centered*]
TOUCHING SPECTACLE. [¶]
And

395.5 single file (A) • single-file
395.6 the¹ (A) • a
395.6 the² (A) • th
*395.7 half (C) • half of (A); three=quarters of (BE)
395 cap A GENUINE LIVE WOMAN. (C) • [not in] (A)
395.10 one hundred and sixty-five* years (A) • 165 yrs
395.11 head. (A) • head. However, she was a woman and therefore we were glad to see her and to make her welcome.

▶A (418n–36) is copy-text for '*Being . . . end.' (395n.1–413.5)◀

396.17 east (C) • East
396.31 & (C) • and
398.16 maybe (C) • may be
398.22 earthquake (C) • earth-|quake
399 cap OUTDONE (C) • OUT-DONE
401 cap1 SHALL I DO! (C) • SHALL I DO?
401.18 like! (C) • ~!
401 cap2 TOWEL MY DEAR! (C) • ~, ~ ~.
*402.11 then—drop (C) • then-drop
402 cap BENEDICTION!" (C) • ~.∧
403.11 bedridden (C) • bed-ridden
403.11 afterward. (C) • ~.—
403.13 earthquake-episodes (C) • earthquake—episodes
403.18 Hurst (C) • Hurs
405.5 twenty dollars (C) • $20
405.6 twelve dollars (C) • $12
405.7 Capt. (C) • Captain
406.4 ten-cent (C) • ten cent
406.7 everything (C) • every thing
406.9–10 besides (C) • beside
406.32 last, (C) • ~∧
406.34–35 out-of-the-way (C) • out-of=the way
407.14 Kearny (C) • Kearney
407.38 anyhow (C) • any how
408.27 Miners' (C) • Miner's
409.3–4 worshipped (C) • worshiped
409.6 maybe (C) • may be
409.31 suffered! (C) • ~!

410 cap "DO IT, STRANGER." (C) • ∧~ ~∧ ~.∧
412.22 outcast (C) • out-|cast
412.24 imagine. (C) • ~.—

▶BE (18 Dec 69) is copy-text for 'In . . . me.' (413.6–419.28)◀

413.6 In that (A) • [centered] CALIFORNIA—CONTINUED. [centered] "POCKET" MINING. [¶] In
413.21 twenty (A) • 20
413.21 pocket-miners (C) • pocket miners
413.23 hillsides (C) • hill-sides
413.24 eight (A) • 8
413.26 find (A) • I have seen him find
413.26 two (A) • a
413.27 known him to (A) • seen him
413.27–28 three thousand dollars (A) • $3000
413.33 is (A) • is perhaps
413.35 asylum. (A) • asylum. Honest toil and moderate gains in shops and on farms have their virtues and their advantages. When a man consents to seek for sudden riches he does it at his peril. [No charge.]
413.37 hillside (C) • hill-|side
414.3 yellow (A) • shining
414.14 twenty (A) • 20
414.21–22 spadeful (A) • spade full
414.26 five hundred dollars (C) • $500
414.27–28 ten thousand dollars (C) • $10,000
414.31–32 sixty thousand dollars (C) • $60,000
414.34 ten thousand dollars (C) • $10,000
414.35–36 three hundred dollars (C) • $300
415.4–5 five thousand dollars (C) • $5,000
415.5 eight thousand dollars (C) • $8,000
415.7 lived two (A) • livedtwo
415.8 household (A) • house-|hold

415.16	eight hundred dollars (C) • $800
415.21	a hundred and twenty thousand dollars (C) • $120,000
415.25	American (A) • American miner
415.26	pocket-mining (C) • pocket mining
416 title	CHAPTER 61 (C) • CHAPTER LXI. (A); BAKER'S CAT. (BE)
416.1–4	ONE . . . simple (A) • Speaking of sagacity it reminds me of
*416.4	Dead-Horse Gulch. (C) • Dead-House Gulch.— (A); Deadhorse Gulch. (BE)
416.5–9	He . . . Whenever (A) • [no ¶] Whenever
416.9	luck (A) • luch
416.15	maybe (C) • may be
416.20	anybody (C) • any body
416.21	eight (A) • 8
416.23–24	an' . . . natchral (A) • and . . . nat'ral
416.25	'n' (A) • and
*416.26	a (BE) • [not in] (A)
416.27	Californy (A) • California
417.1	noth'n' 'bout placer diggin's—'n' (A) • nothing about placer diggings—and
417.2	pocket-mining (C) • pocket mining
417.3	an' . . . prospect'n' (A) • and . . . prospecting
417.5	fur. An' (A) • far. And
417.7	'n' (A) • and
417.8	'Well (A) • "~
417.9	me,' 'n' (A) • me," and
417.10–11	'n' . . . 'n' . . . 'n' (A) • and . . . and . . . and
417.12	'n' . . . an' (A) • and . . . and
417.13	'n (BE) • 'n' (A)
417.14–15	'n' . . . an' . . . 'n' (A) • and . . . and . . . and
417.15–16	He . . . superintending. (A) • [not in]
417.17	by an' by (C) • bye an' bye (A); bye and bye (BE)

417.17	yer (A) • [not in]
417.17–18	Everybody . . . everybody (C) • Every body . . . every body
417.18	pick'n' 'n' blast'n' (A) • picking and blasting
417.19	shovelin' (A) • shoveling
417.19	hillside—everybody (C) • hill side—every body
417.19	put'n' (A) • putting
417.20	scrapin' . . . Noth'n' (A) • scraping . . . Nothing
417.21	'n' . . . put'n' (A) • and . . . putting
417.22–23	'n' . . . 'n' (A) • and . . . and
417.26	'n' (A) • and
417.28	was (A) • he was
417.29	You (A) • You
417.30–31	an' . . . sinkin' (A) • and . . . sinking
417.32	an' . . . pannin' (A) • and . . . panning
417.32	anything (C) • any thing
417.32	comin' (A) • coming
417.33	An' . . . git (A) • And . . . get
417.34	'n' . . . 'n' . . . 'n' (A) • and . . . [not in] . . . and
417.34	knowin' (A) • knowing
417.35	runnin' . . . an' (A) • running . . . and
417.36	makin' . . . an' (A) • making . . . and
417.37	eight (A) • 8
418.2	blast'n' . . . An' (A) • blasting . . . And
418.3	'n'[1] . . . 'n'[2] (A) • and . . . and
418.3	'bout fifty (A) • about 50
418.3	'n'[3] . . . 'n'[4] (A) • and . . . and
418.4–5	'bout . . . 'n' (A) • about . . . and
418.6	'n' . . . ton . . . 'n' (A) • and . . . tons . . . and
418.7	'n' . . . 'n' (A) • and . . . and
418.7–8	'bout . . . an' . . . an' (A) • about . . . and . . . and
418.8	dead centre (A) • midst
418.8–9	a goin' (A) • going
418.9–10	an'[1] . . . a reachin' (A) • and a snorting and a sneezing,

	and a clawing and a reaching
418.13	An' (A) • And
418.14–15	'n' . . . an' . . . an' (A) • and . . . and . . . and
418.16–17	f'm . . . lookin' (A) • from . . . looking
418.18	'n' . . . 'n' (A) • and . . . and
418.19	'n' . . . an' (A) • and . . . and
418.19	smoke, (A) • ~_∧
418.19–20	an' . . . 'n' . . . f'm (A) • and . . . and . . . from
419.2	'n' . . . an' (A) • and . . . and
419.4	'Gents (A) • "~
419.4	maybe (C) • may be (A); May be (BE)
419.6	ain't (C) • 'ain't
419.7	minin' (A) • mining
419.8	*different'* (A) • ~"
419.8–9	an' . . . 'n' (A) • and . . . and
419.11	An' (A) • And
419.11	maybe (C) • may be
419.13	An' by an' by (C) • An' by an' bye (A); And by and bye (BE)
419.13	goin' (A) • going
419.15	tetch . . . 'n' (A) • touch . . . and
419.16	'Well (A) • "~
419.16	git . . . *me,'* an' (A) • get . . . *me,"* and
419.17	surpris'n' . . . 'n' . . . f'r (A) • surprising . . . and . . . for
*419.17	Sagacity (A) • [¶] ~
419.19	prejudice (A) • predjudice
419.19	quartz mining (C) • quartz⸗ mining (A); quart mining (BE)
419.22	"*Cure* (A) • _∧~
419.22	No! (A) • NO.
419.23	three (A) • 3
419.24	'n' . . . broken (A) • and . . . broke
419.28	me. (A) • me. [*indented from right*] MARK TWAIN.

▶A (443–54) is copy-text for 'At . . . na-tives;' (419.29–431.8)◀

419.35	own. (C) • ~.—
419.38	County (C) • county
*420.7	post (C) • paust
420n.6	*placer;"* (C) • ~;_∧
421.13	Ajax (C) • *Ajax*
421.22	was "the (C) • was"the
421.22	Admiral"— (C) • ~—"
422.11	welcome (C) • welome
423.2	Ajax (C) • *Ajax*
423.34	side. (C) • ~.—
424.21	said. (C) • ~.—
424.29	wind." (C) • ~."—
425.22	carried (C) • carrried
425.25	everything (C) • every thing
427.9	eruption (C) • irruption
428.15	aback (C) • a back
428.25	Southern (C) • southern
*429.30	women . . . were (C) • woman . . . was
430.7	rampant (C) • rampart
430.13	pretense (C) • pretence
430.15	benefactor, (C) • ~_∧
430.21	smoke-stack (C) • smoke-| stack
431.5	ocean, (C) • ~_∧
431.8	cocoanut (C) • coacoanut

▶SU (19 Apr 66) is copy-text for 'then . . . sail—' (431.9–434.2)◀

| 431.9 | then the white town (A) • [*indented from right*] Ho- |

NOLULU, March, 1866. [*centered*] **Our Arrival Elaborated a Little More.** [¶] We came in sight of two of this group of is-lands, Oahu and Molokai (pronounced O-waw-hoo and Mollo-*ki*), on the morning of the 18th, and soon ex-changed the dark blue waters of the deep sea for the brilliant light blue of "soundings." The fat, ugly birds (said to be a species of albatross) which had skimmed after us on tireless wings clear across the ocean, left us, and an occasional flying-fish went skimming over the water in their stead. Oahu loomed high, rugged, treeless, barren, black and dreary, out of the sea, and in the distance Molokai lay like a homely sway-backed whale on the water. [*cen-tered*] **The Hawaiian Flag.** [¶] As we rounded the promontory of Diamond Head (bringing into view a grove of cocoa-nut trees, first ocular proof that we were in the tropics), we ran up the stars and stripes at the main-spencer-gaff, and the Hawaiian flag at the fore. The latter is suggestive of the prominent political elements of the Islands. It is part French, part English, part American and is Hawaiian in general. The union is the English cross; the remainder of the flag (horizontal stripes) looks American, but has a blue French stripe in addition to our red and white ones. The flag was gotten up by foreign legations in council with the Hawaiian Government. The eight stripes refer to the eight islands which are inhabited; the other four are barren rocks incapable of supporting a population. [*centered*] **Reflections.** [¶] As we came in sight we fired a gun, and a good part of Honolulu turned out to welcome the steamer. It was Sunday morning, and about church time, and we steamed through the narrow channel to the music of six different church bells, which sent their mellow tones far and wide, over hills and valleys, which were peopled by naked, savage, thundering barbarians only fifty years ago! Six Christian churches within five miles of the ruins of a Pagan temple, where human sacrifices were daily offered up to hideous idols in the last century! We were within pistol shot of one of a group of islands whose ferocious inhabitants closed in upon the doomed and helpless Captain Cook and murdered him, eighty-seven years ago; and lo! their descendants were at church! Behold what the missionaries have wrought! [*centered*] **The Crowd on the Pier.** [¶] By the time we had worked our slow way up to the wharf, under the guidance of McIntyre, the pilot, a mixed crowd of four or five hundred people had assembled—Chinamen, in the costume of their country; foreigners and the better class of natives, and "half whites" in carriages and dressed in Sacramento Summer fashion; other native men on foot, some in the cast-off clothing of white folks, and a few wearing a battered hat, an old ragged vest, and nothing else—at least nothing but an unnecessarily slender rag passed between the legs; native women clad in a single garment—a bright colored robe or wrapper as voluminous as a balloon, with full sleeves. This robe is "gathered" from shoulder to shoulder, before and behind, and then descends in ample folds to the feet—seldom a chemise or any other under-garment—fits like a circus tent fits the tent pole, and no hoops. These robes were bright yellow, or bright crimson, or pure black occasionally, or gleaming white; but "solid colors" and "stunning" ones were the rule. They wore little hats such as the sex wear in your cities, and some of the younger women had very pretty faces and splendid black eyes and heavy masses of long black hair, occasionally put up in a "net;" some of these dark, gingerbread colored beauties were on foot—generally on bare-foot, I may add—and others were on horseback—astraddle; they never ride any other way, and they ought to know which way is best, for there are no more accomplished horsewomen in the world, it is said. The balance of the crowd consisted chiefly of little half-naked native boys and girls. All were chattering in the catchy, chopped-up Kanaka language; but what they were chattering about will always remain a mystery to me. [*centered*] **The King.** [¶] Captain Fitch said, "There's the King! that's him in the buggy; I know him far as I can see him." [¶] I had never seen a King in my life, and I naturally took out my note-book and put him down: "Tall, slender, dark; full-bearded; green frock coat, with lappels and collar bordered with gold band an inch wide; plug hat—broad gold band around it; royal costume looks too much like a livery; this man isn't as fleshy as I thought he was." [¶] I had just got these notes entered when Captain Fitch discovered that he had got hold of the wrong King—or, rather, that he had got hold of the King's driver or a carriage-driver of one of the nobility. The King was not present at all. It was a great disappointment to me. I heard afterward that the comfortable, easy[ ]|going King Kamehameha (pronounced Ka-may-ah-may= ah) V had been seen sitting on a barrel on the wharf, the day before, fishing; but there was no consolation in that; that did not restore to me my lost King. [*centered*] **Honolulu.** [¶] The town

431.9   Honolulu, said (A) • ∼∧ (∼

431.9–10   twelve and fifteen thousand (A) • 12,000 and 15,000

*431.10   inhabitants, (C) • inhabitants (A); inhabitants) is (SU)

431.10   with (A) • has

431.12   a few (SU) • few (A)

431.12–18 corkscrew . . . neat (A) • corkscrew; houses one and

two stories high, built of wood, straw, 'dobies and dull cream-colored pebble‿ and-shell-conglomerated coral cut into oblong square blocks and laid in cement, but no brick houses; there are great yards, more like plazas, about a large number of the dwelling-houses, and these are carpeted with bright green grass, into which your foot sinks out of sight; and they are ornamented by a hundred species of beautiful flowers and blossoming shrubs, and shaded by noble tamarind trees and the "Pride of India," with its fragrant flower, and by the "Umbrella Tree," and I do not know how many more. I had rather smell Honolulu at sunset than the old Police Court-|room in San Francisco. [*centered*] **Almost a King.** [¶] I had not shaved since I left San Francisco—ten days. As soon as I got ashore I hunted for a striped pole, and shortly found one. I always had a yearning to be a King. This may never be, I suppose. But at any rate it will always be a satisfaction to me to know that if I am not a King, I am the next thing to it—I have been shaved by the King's barber. [*centered*] **Landsmen on "Sea Legs."** [¶] Walking about on shore was very uncomfortable at first; there was no spring to the solid ground, and I missed the heaving and rolling of the ship's deck; it was unpleasant to lean unconsciously to an anticipated lurch of the world and find that the world did not lurch, as it should have done. And there was something else missed—something gone—something wanting, I could not tell what—a dismal vacuum

of some kind or other—a sense of emptiness. But I found out what it was presently. It was the absence of the ceaseless dull hum of beating waves and whipping sails and fluttering of the propeller, and creaking of the ship— sounds I had become so accustomed to that I had ceased to notice them and had become unaware of their existence until the deep Sunday stillness on shore made me vaguely conscious that a familiar spirit of some kind or other was gone from me. Walking on the solid earth with legs used to the "giving" of the decks under his tread, made Brown sick, and he went off to bed and left me to wander alone about this odd‿ looking city of the tropics. [*centered*] **New Scenes and Strong Contrasts.** [¶] The further I traveled through the town the better I liked it. Every step revealed a new contrast—disclosed something I was unaccustomed to. In place of the grand mud-colored brown stone fronts of San Francisco, I saw neat

431.15   brown stone (SU) • brown (A)

431.16   dwellings (A) • [*not in*]

431.16   *adobes* (C) • adobies (A); 'dobies (SU)

431.17   cream-colored (A) • dull cream-colored

431.17–18 oblong (A) • oblong square

431.18   cement; also a great number of (A) • cement,

431.20   these homes (A) • those cottages

431.21   yards (A) • yards, about like Portsmouth Square (as to size)

431.23–24 geranium, calla lily, etc., (A) • infernal geranium

431.24   debility (A) • debility on tin-roofed rear additions or in bedroom windows

431.26–27 San Francisco's pleasure grove, (A) • [*not in*]

431.27   "Willows," (A) • "Willows," and the painful sharp‿

pointed shrubbery of that funny caricature of nature which they call "South Park,"

431.30	of (A) • of those vile, tire-some, stupid, everlasting
432.1	globes, (A) • globes and
432.1	countless (A) • all
432.4	bob-tail (SU) • bob-tailed (A)
*432 cap	SCENE (C) • SCENES (A)
432.10–433.12	asleep . . . In (A) • asleep; in
433.18	wretched (A) • that wretched
433.19	pavements (A) • pavement nuisance
433.23	perdition (A) • hell
433.24	harmless (A) • cold and harmless yonder
433.25	street cars (C) • street-cars
433.26	astride (A) • astraddle
433.28	Chinadom (A) • Sacra-mento street, Chinadom
433.28	Brannan (A) • Brannon
433.31	summer (C) • Summer
433.32	the Golden City's (A) • our familiar
433.33–34	framework (C) • frame=work
433.36	ocean: (A) • ~;
433.38	dead (A) • ~,
434.2	sail— (A) • sail—— [¶] At this moment, this man

Brown, who has no better manners than to read over one's shoulder, observes: [¶] "Yes, and hot. Oh, I reckon not (only 82 in the shade)! Go on, now, and put it all down, now that you've begun; just say, 'And more 'santipedes,' and cockroaches, and fleas, and lizards, and red ants, and scorpions, and spiders, and mosquitoes and missionaries'—oh, blame my cats if I'd live here two months, not if I was High-You=Muck-a-Muck and King of Wawhoo, and had a harem full of hyenas!" [Wah-ine (most generally pronounced Wy-heeny), seems to answer for wife, woman and female of questionable character, indifferently. I never can get this man Brown to understand that "hyena" is not the proper pronuncia-tion. He says "It ain't any odds; it de-scribes some of 'em, anyway."] [¶] I re-marked: "But, Mr. Brown, these are trifles." [¶] "Trifles be—blowed! You get nipped by one of them scorpions once, and see how you like it! There was Mrs. Jones, swabbing her face with a sponge; she felt something grab her cheek; she dropped the sponge and out popped a scorpion an inch and a half long! Well, she just got up and danced the Highland fling for two hours and a half—and yell!—why, you could have heard her from Lu-wow to Hoola-|hoola, with the wind fair! and for three days she soaked her cheek in brandy and salt, and it swelled up as big as your two fists. And you want to know what made me light out of bed so sudden last night? Only a 'santipede'—nothing, only a 'santipede,' with forty-two legs on a side, and every foot hot enough to burn a hole through a raw-hide. Don't you know one of them things grabbed Miss Boone's foot when she was riding one day? He was hid in the stirrip, and just clamped himself around her foo[ ] and sunk his fangs plum through her shoe; and she just throwed her whole soul into one war-whoop and then fainted. And she didn't get out of bed nor set that foot on the floor again for three weeks. And how did Captain Godfrey always get off so easy? Why, because he always carried a bottle full of scorpions and santipedes soaked in alcohol, and whenever he got bit he bathed the place with that devilish mixture or took a drink out of it, I don't recollect which. And how did he have to do once, when he hadn't his bottle along? He had to cut out the bite with his knife and fill up the hole with ar-nica, and then prop his mouth open with the boot-jack to keep from getting the lockjaw. Oh, fill me up about this lovely country! You can go on writing that slop about balmy breezes and fra-grant flowers, and all that sort of truck, but you're not going to leave out them santipedes and things for want of being reminded of it, you know." [¶] I said, mildly: "But, Mr. Brown, these are the mere——" [¶] "Mere—your grand-mother! they ain't the mere anything! What's the use of you telling me they're the mere—mere—whatever it was you was going to call it? You look at them raw splotches all over my face—all over my arms—all over my body! Mosquito bites! Don't tell me about mere—mere, things! You can't get around them mosquito bites. I took and brushed out my bar good night before last, and tucked it in all around, and before morning I was eternally chawed up, anyhow. And the night before I fastened her up all right, and got in bed and smoked that old strong pipe until I got strangled and smothered and couldn't get out, and then they swarmed in there and jammed their bills through my shirt and sucked me as dry as a life-preserver before I got my breath again. And how did that dead⸗fall work? I was two days making it, and sweated two buckets full of brine, and blame the mosquito ever went under it; and sloshing around in my sleep I ketched my foot in it and got it flattened out so that it wouldn't go into a green turtle shell forty four inches across the back. Jim Ayres grinding out seven double verses of poetry about Waw-*hoo!* and crying about leaving the blasted place in the two last verses; and you slobbering here about—there you are! Now—*now*, what do you say? That yellow spider could straddle over a saucer just like nothing—and if I hadn't been here to set that spittoon on him, he would have been between your sheets in a minute—he was traveling straight for your bed—he had his eye on it. Just pull at that web that he's been stringing after him—pretty near as hard to break as sewing silk; and look at his feet sticking out all round the spittoon. Oh, confound Waw-*hoo!*" [¶] I am glad Brown has got disgusted at that murdered spider and gone; I don't like to be interrupted when I am writing—especially by Brown, who is one of those men who always looks at the unpleasant side of everything, and I seldom do. [*indented from right*] MARK TWAIN.

►A (457–59) is copy-text for 'a¹ . . . this:' (434.2–436.1)◄

434.8   ecstasy (C) • ecstacy

434.12   bed-chamber (C) • bed-| chamber

►SU (21 Apr 66 ¶1–4) is copy-text for 'I . . . about.' (436.2–438.21)◄

436.2   I (A) • [*indented from right*] HONOLULU, March, 1866. [*centered*] **Coming Home from Prison.** [¶] I

436.2   Hawaii (A) • the kingdom of Hawaii

436.4   horseback (C) • horse-|back

436.4   P.M. (A) • P. M.

436.5   all. (A) • all. I am one of the poorest horsemen in the world, and I never mount a horse without experiencing a sort of dread that I may be setting out on that last mysterious journey which all of us must take sooner or later, and I never come back in safety from a horseback trip without thinking of my latter end for two or three days afterward. This same old regular devotional sentiment began just as soon as I sat down here five minutes ago.

436.7   P.M. (A) • P. M.

436.9–10   (with . . . Phillips,) (A) • [*not in*]

436.10   Capt. . . . Capt. (C) • Captain . . . Captain (A)

436.14   Capt. (C) • Captain

436.14   along (A) • there

436.15   Capt. (C) • Captain

436.16   Capt. . . . Capt. (C) • Captain . . . Captain

436.20   fearful (A) • awful

436.21   captain's (C) • Captain's

436.24   Capt. (C) • Captain

436.24   whaler (A) • whaler Captain

436.24   years' (C) • years

436.25   the (A) • that

437.1   Capt. (C) • Captain

437.5   The (A) • [*centered*] **The Steed "Oahu."** [¶] The

437.7   overtake (A) • easily overtake

437.14   so I (A) • I just

437.17   O-waw-hoo (SU) • O-waw⸗ hee (A)

437.19 resisted (A) • firmly resisted

437.25 perspiration. He abandoned (A) • perspiration and profanity. (I am only human and I was sorely aggravated. I shall behave better next time.) He quit

437.28 apprehension (A) • the gravest apprehension

437.28 creature (A) • malignant brute

437.32 until (A) • until at last

437.32 almost (A) • [not in]

437.37 villainy (A) • inborn villainy

438.3 surrendered (A) • gave in

438.8 And now (A) • [centered] **Out of Prison, but in the Stocks.** [¶] And now it occurs to me that

438.9 left-handed blessing (A) • fervent curse

438.16 legs; (A) • ~,

►SU (21 Apr 66 ¶15–22) is copy-text for 'A . . . itself.' (439.1–441.20)◄

439.1 A (A) • [centered] **The King's Grove, Waikiki.** [¶] A

439.1 cocoanut (C) • cocoa-nut

439.4 cocoanuts (C) • cocoa-nuts

439.4 picturesque (A) • pituresque

439 cap LIKENESS. (C) • ~ₐ (A)

439.6–10 I . . . too. (A) • [not in]

439.7 cocoanut (C) • cocoa-|nut (A)

439.10 cocoanut (C) • cocoa-nut (A)

439.11 About (A) • [no ¶] ~

439.20 his (C) • His

439.23 Near (A) • [centered] **Ruins of an Ancient Heathen Temple.** [¶] Near

439.23 meagre (A) • meager

440.2 to (SU) • [not in] (A)

440.3 grandmother (A) • grand-|mother

440.9 impossible (A) • imposssible

440.13 kin-folks (C) • kin-|folks

440.16 summer (C) • Summer

440.20 This (A) • [no ¶] And it inclines right thinking man to weep rather than to laugh when he reflects how surprised they must have been when they got there. This

440.21 enclosure (C) • inclosure

440.27 naked (A) • multitudes of naked, whooping

440.29 victims writhing (A) • victims, writhing and shrieking

440.29 massed (A) • dense masses of dusky

440.30 ferocious (A) • eager and ferocious

440.30 by the (A) • with the weird light of

440.31 background (A) • vague background

440.31 trees (A) • trees; of the mournful sea washing the dim shore

440.32 uncanny (A) • dismal

440.33 looking (A) • looking calmly

440.34 cloud-rack (A) • drifting clouds

440.36 sort of a (A) • very

440.37–38 century (A) • cenury

441.2 King (A) • king

441.3 on (A) • upon

441.5 King (A) • king

441.13–14 their hands (A) • the labor of their hand

441.14 produce (A) • produces

441.16 benefit (A) • wonderful benefit

441.19 Capt. (C) • Captain

441.20 itself. (A) • itself. [¶] The little collection of cottages (of which I was speaking a while ago) under the cocoanut trees is a historical point. It is the village of Waikiki (usually pronounced Wy-kee-ky), once the Capital of the kingdom and the abode of the great Kamehameha I. In 1801, while he lay encamped at this place with seven thousand men, preparing to invade the island of Kaui (he had previously captured and subdued the seven other inhabited islands of the group, one after another), a pestilence broke out in Oahu and raged with great virulence. It attacked the king's army and made great havoc in it. It is said that three hundred bodies were washed out to sea in one day. [¶] There is an opening in the coral reef at this point, and anchorage inside for a small number of vessels, though one accustomed to the great Bay of San Francisco would never take this little belt of smooth water, with its border of foaming surf, to be a harbor, save for White-|hall boats or something of that kind. But harbors are scarce in these islands—open roadsteads are the rule here. The harbor of Waikiki was discovered in 1786 (seven or eight years after Captain Cook's murder) by Captains Portlock and Dixon, in the ships King George and Queen Charlotte—the first English vessels that visited the islands after that unhappy occurrence. This little bathing tub of smooth water possesses some further historical interest as being the spot where the distinguished navigator, Vancouver, landed when he came here in 1792. [¶] In a conversation with a gentleman to-day about the scarcity of harbors among the islands (and in all the islands of the South Pacific), he said the natives of Tahiti have a theory that the reason why there are harbors wherever fresh water streams empty into the sea, and none elsewhere, is that the fresh water kills the coral insect, or so discommodes or disgusts it that it will not build its stony wall in its vicinity, and instance what is claimed as a fact, viz, that the break in the reef is always found where the fresh water passes over it, in support of this theory. [¶] [This notable equestrian excursion will be concluded in my next, if nothing happens.] [*indented from right*] MARK TWAIN.

▶SU (24 Apr 66 ¶1–23) is copy-text for 'CHAPTER . . . business.' (442 *title*–444.15)◀

442 *title*–　CHAPTER 65 . . . brief.
　　6　　　Gayly (C) • CHAPTER LXV. . . . brief.—Gayly (A); [*indented from right*] HONOLULU, March, 1866.

[*centered*] **The Equestrian Excursion Concluded.** [¶] I wandered along the sea beach on my steed Oahu around the base of the extinct crater of Leahi, or Diamond Head, and a quarter of a mile beyond the point I overtook the party of ladies and gentlemen and assumed my proper place—that is, in the rear—for the horse I ride always persists in remaining in the rear in spite of kicks, cuffs and curses. I was satisfied as long as I could keep Oahu within hailing distance of the cavalcade—I knew I could accomplish nothing better even if Oahu were Norfolk himself. [¶] We went on—on—on—a great deal too far, I thought, for people who were unaccustomed to riding on horseback, and who must expect to suffer on the morrow if they indulged too freely in this sort of exercise. Finally we got to a point which we were expecting to go around in order to strike an easy road home; but we were too late; it was full tide and the sea had closed in on the shore. Young Henry McFarlane said he knew a nice, comfortable route over the hill—a short cut—and the crowd dropped into his wake. We climbed a hill a hundred and fifty feet high, and about as straight up and down as the side of a house, and as full of rough lava blocks as it could stick—not as wide, perhaps, as the broad road that leads to destruction, but nearly as dangerous to travel, and apparently leading in the same general direction. I felt for the ladies, but I had no time to speak any words of sympathy, by reason of my attention being so much occupied by Oahu. The place was so steep that at times he stood straight up on his tip= toes and clung by his forward toe-nails, with his back to the Pacific Ocean and his nose close to the moon—and thus situated we formed an equestrian picture which was as uncomfortable to me as it may have been picturesque to the spectators. You may think I was afraid, but I was not. I knew I could stay on him as long as his ears did not pull out. [¶] It was a great relief to me to know that we were all safe and sound on the summit at last, because the sun was just disappearing in the waves, night was abroad in the land, candles and lamps were already twinkling in the distant town, and we gratefully reflected that Henry had saved us from having to go back around that rocky, sandy beach. But a new trouble arose while the party were admiring the rising moon and the cool, balmy night= breeze, with its odor of countless flowers, for it was discovered that we had got into a place we could not get out of—we were apparently surrounded by precipices—our pilot's chart was at fault, and he could not extricate us, and so we had the prospect before us of either spending the night in the admired night-breeze, under the admired moon, or of clambering down the way we came, in the dark. However, a Kanaka came along presently and found a first-rate road for us down an almost imperceptible decline, and the party set out on a cheerful gallop again, and Oahu struck up his miraculous canter once more. The moon rose up, and flooded mountain and valley and ocean with silvery light, and I was not sorry we had lately been in trouble, because the consciousness of being safe again raised our spirits and made us more capable of enjoying the beautiful scene than we would have been otherwise. I never breathed such a soft, delicious atmosphere before, nor one freighted with such rich fragrance. A barber shop is nothing to it. [*centered*] **A Battle= Ground Whose History Is Forgotten.** [¶] Gayly (SU)

442.5   fire-flies (C) • fire-|flies (A)

442.7   I (A) • with set teeth and bouncing body I

442.19   before. (A) • before. The conversation at this point took a unique and ghastly turn. A gentleman said: [¶] "Give me some of your bones, Miss Blank; I'll carry them for you." [¶] Another said: [¶] "You haven't got bones enough, Mrs. Blank; here's a good shin-bone, if you want it." [¶] Such observations as these fell from the lips of ladies with reference to their queer newly-acquired property: [¶] "Mr. Brown, will you please hold some of my bones for me a minute?" And, [¶]

"Mr. Smith, you have got some of my bones; and you have got one, too, Mr. Jones; and you have got my spine, Mr. Twain. Now don't any of you gentlemen get my bones all mixed up with yours so that you can't tell them apart." [¶] These remarks look very irreverent on paper, but they did not sound so, being used merely in a business way and with no intention of making sport of the remains. I did not think it was just right to carry off any of these bones, but we did it, anyhow. We considered that it was at least as right as it is for the Hawaiian Government and the city of Honolulu (which is the most excessively moral and religious town that can be found on the map of the world), to permit those remains to lie decade after decade, to bleach and rot in sun and wind and suffer desecration by careless strangers and by the beasts of the field, unprotected by even a worm-fence. Call us hard names if you will, you statesmen and missionaries! but I say shame upon you, that after raising a nation from idolatry to Christianity, and from barbarism to civilization, you have not taught it the comment of respect for the dead. Your work is incomplete. [*centered*] **Legendary.**

443.24   Pari (A) • Pari [pronounced *Pally*; intelligent natives claim that there is no *r* in the Kanaka alphabet]

443.26   Jarves's (C) • Jarves'

443.30   book. (A) • book. [¶] There was a terrible pestilence here in 1804, which killed great numbers of the inhabitants, and the natives have legends of others that swept the islands long before that; and therefore many persons now believe that these bones belonged to victims of one of these epidemics who were hastily buried in a great pit. It is by far the most reasonable conjecture, because Jarves says that the weapons of the Islanders were so rude and inefficient that their battles were not often very bloody. If this was a battle it was astonishingly deadly, for in spite of the depredations of "skull hunters," we rode a considerable distance over ground so thickly strewn with human bones that the horses feet crushed them, not occasionally, but at every step. [*centered*] **Sentiment.**

443.37   calmly (A) • camly

444.2   Manoa (C) • Mauoa

444.6   the— (C) • ~——

444.7   sat (A) • deliberately sat

444.10   court (C) • Court

444.11   chief (C) • Chief

444.12   nine (C) • 9

444.15   turned . . . business. (A) • threw his legs wildly out

before and behind him, depressed his head and laid his ears back, and flew by the admiring company like a telegram. In five minutes he was far away ahead of everybody. [¶] We stopped in front of a private residence—Brown and I did— to wait for the rest and see that none were last. I soon saw that I had attracted the attention of a comely young girl, and I felt duly flattered. Perhaps, thought I, she admires my horsemanship—and I made a savage jerk at the bridle and said, "Ho! will you!" to show how fierce and unmanageable the beast was—though, to say truly, he was leaning up against a hitching-post peaceably enough at the time. I stirred Oahu up and moved him about, and went up the street a short distance to look for the party, and "loped" gallantly back again, all the while making a pretense of being unconscious that I was an object of interest. I then addressed a few "peart" remarks to Brown, to give the young lady a chance to admire my style of conversation, and was gratified to see her step up and whisper to Brown and glance furtively at me at the same time. I could see that her gentle face bore an expression of the most kindly and earnest solicitude, and I was shocked and angered to hear Brown burst into a fit of brutal laughter. [¶] As soon as we started home, I asked, with a fair show of indifference, what she had been saying. [¶] Brown laughed again and said: "She thought from the slouchy way you rode and the way you drawled out your words, that you was drunk! She said, 'Why don't you take

the poor creature home, Mr. Brown? It makes me nervous to see him galloping that horse and just hanging on that way, and he so drunk.'" [¶] I laughed very loudly at the joke, but it was a sort of hollow, sepulchral laugh, after all. And then I took it out of Oahu. [*centered*] **An Old Acquaintance.** [¶] I have found an old acquaintance here—Rev. Franklin S. Rising, of the Episcopal ministry, who has had charge of a church in Virginia, Nevada, for several years, and who is well known in Sacramento and San Francisco. He sprained his knee in September last, and is here for his health. He thinks he has made no progress worth mentioning towards regaining it, but I think differently. He can ride on horseback, and is able to walk a few steps without his crutches—things he could not do a week ago.

►SU (21 Apr 66 ¶5–14) is copy-text for 'This . . . expense.' (444.16–448.18)◄

444.16   This (A) • [*centered*] **About Horses and Kanaka Shrewdness.** [¶] This

445.1   wretchedest (A) • vilest

445.1–2   Kanakas (*i. e.* natives.) (C) • Kanakas. (i. e. natives.) (A); Kanakas. (SU)

445.10   Islands (A) • islands

445.14   a shrewd unprincipled rascal (A) • as shrewd a rascal as ever patronized a penitentiary

445.19   horse-jockeys (C) • horse jockeys

445.24   make trouble (A) • raise a row

446 *cap*   "MY BROTHER ALL SAME— WE TWINS!" (C) • MY BROTHER—WE TWINS. (A)

446.8   places (A) • sores

447.3   instance (A) • yarn

447.4   a certain Mr. L., a visiting stranger, (A) • Leland

447.9   Mr. L. (A) • Leland

447.20   fellow (A) • scoundrel

447.20   L. (A) • Leland

447.26   You (A) • [*centered*] **Honolulu Prices for Horseflesh.** [¶] You

447.30   seventy-five cents (A) • six bits

447.31   Williams (A) • Brown

447.34   Mexican (A) • good Mexican

448.9   The (A) • These

448.15–16   twenty to thirty-five dollars (A) • $20 to $35

448.16–17   seven to ten dollars (A) • $7 to $10

448.18   expense. (A) • expense. [¶] Well, Oahu worried along over a smooth, hard road, bordered on either side by cottages, at intervals, pulu swamps at intervals, fish ponds at intervals, but through a dead level country all the time, and no trees to hide the wide Pacific ocean on the right or the rugged, towering rampart of solid rock, called Diamond Head or Diamond Point, straight ahead.

▶SU (24 Apr 66 ¶24) is copy-text for 'It . . . CHAPTER 66' (448.19–450 title)◀

448.19–
449.3   It . . . joint: (A) • [centered] **"While We Were Marching Through Georgia!"** [¶] The popular-song nuisance follows us here. In San Francisco it used to be "Just Before the Battle Mother," every night and all night long. Then it was "When Johnny Comes Marching Home." After that it was "Wearin' of the Green." And last and most dreadful of all, came that calamity of "When We Were Marching Through Georgia." It was the last thing I heard when the ship sailed, and it gratified me to think I should hear it no more for months. And now, here at dead of night, at the very outpost and fag-end of the world, on a little rock in the middle of a limitless ocean, a pack of dark-skinned savages are tramping down the street singing it with a vim and an energy that make my hair rise!—singing it in their own barbarous tongue! They have got the tune to perfection—otherwise I never would have suspected that

449.4   Waikiki . . . wawhoo. (C) • [centered] "~ . . . ~." (A); [indented] "~ . . . ~‸" (SU)

*449.4   lantani (SU) • lantoni (A)

449.4   oe (C) • œ (SU–A)

449.5–450   Translated . . . CHAPTER title   66 (C) • Translated . . . CHAPTER LXVI. (A); [flush left] means "When We Were Marching Through Georgia." If it would have been all the same to General Sherman, I wish he had gone around by the way of the Gulf of Mexico, instead of marching through Georgia. [indented from right] MARK TWAIN. (SU)

▶SU (21 May 66) is copy-text for 'PASSING . . . art.' (450.1–453.37)◀

450.1   PASSING (A) • [indented from right] HONOLULU (S. I.), April, 1866. [centered] Off. [¶] Mounted on my noble steed Hawaii (pronounced Hah-wy-ye—stress on second syllable), a beast that cost thirteen dollars and is able to go his mile in three—with a bit of margin to it—I departed last Saturday week for—for any place that might turn up. [centered] **Saturday in Honolulu.** [¶] Passing

450.9   the (A) • which is the

450.9   graceful (A) • graceful and exhilarating

451.1   table-cloth (C) • table cloth

451.3   passed (A) • passed up

451.3   backwards (C) • backward

451.5–6   then, . . . girl (A) • and then, with a girl that

451.6   forward, (A) • forward and

451.7   wind. (A) • wind. "Gay?" says Brown, with a fine irony; "oh, you can't mean it!"

451.8   can (A) • can scare up

451.12–13   home-made (A) • home-| made

451.15   a rag factory on fire (A) • thunder

451.15–16   offensive (A) • villainous

451.18   tattooed (C) • tatooed

451.19   mendicant from Washoe (A) • unfortunate from Reese River

451.24   centre (C) • center

451.30   Moving (A) • [centered] **Poi for Sale.** [¶] Moving

452.1   taro plant (A) • kalo or taro plant (k and t are the same in the Kanaka alphabet, and so are *l* and *r*)

452.1   *taro*² (C) • taro

452.11   an unseductive (A) • a villainous

452.14   nothing (A) • nothing in the world

452.18   humorous (A) • blithe and humorous

452.23   delicacy (A) • poultice

452.27   contents. (A) • contents. One tall gentleman, with nothing in the world on but a soiled and greasy shirt, thrust in his finger and tested the poi, shook his head, scratched it with the useful finger, made another test, prospected among his hair, caught something and eat it; tested the poi again, wiped the grimy perspiration from his brow with the universal hand, tested again, blew his nose—"Let's move on, Brown," said I, and we moved. [*centered*] **Awa For Sale—Ditto Fish.**

452.30   certain imported (A) • venereal

453.3   the (A) • an

453.5   saloon-keepers (C) • saloon keepers

453.8   *eats . . . alive!* (A) • eats the article raw.

453.9   In (A) • [*centered*] **Old-Time Saturdays.** [¶] In

453.14   crippled. (A) • crippled. In the afternoon the natives were wont to repair to the plain, outside the town, and indulge in their ancient sports and pastimes and bet away their week's earnings on horse races. One might see two or three thousand, some say five thousand, of these wild riders, skurrying over the plain in a mass in those days. And it must have been a fine sight.

453.15–16   *hula-hula* (C) • *hula hula*

453.20   through (A) • through with

453.32–33   *hula-hula* (C) • *hula hula*

453.37   art. (A) • art. [*centered*] **The Government Prison.** [¶] Cantering across the bridge and down the firm, level, gleaming white coral turnpike that leads toward the south, or

the east, or the west, or the north (the points of the compass being all the same to me, inasmuch as, for good reasons, I have not had an opportunity thus far of discovering whereabouts the sun rises in this country—I know where it sets, but I don't know how it gets there nor which direction it comes from), we presently arrived at a massive coral edifice which I took for a fortress at first, but found out directly that it was the Government prison. A soldier at the great gate admitted us without further authority than my countenance, and I suppose he thought he was paying me a handsome compliment when he did so; and so did I until I reflected that the place was a penitentiary. However, as far as appearances went, it might have been the king's palace, so neat, and clean, and white, and so full of the fragrance of flowers was the establishment, and I was satisfied. [¶] We passed through a commodious office, whose walls were ornamented with linked strands of polished handcuffs and fetters, through a hall, and among the cells above and below. The cells for the men were eight or ten feet high, and roomy enough to accommodate the two prisoners and their hammocks, usually put in each, and have space left for several more. The floors were scrubbed clean, and were guiltless of spot or stain of any kind, and the painfully white walls were unmarred by a single mark or blemish. Through ample gratings, one could see the blue sky and get his hair blown off by the cool breeze. They call this a prison—the pleasantest quarters in Honolulu. [¶] There are four wards, and one hundred and thirty-two prisoners can be housed in rare and roomy comfort within them. [¶] There were a number of native women in the female department. Poor devils, they hung their heads under the prying eyes of our party as if they were really ashamed of being there. [¶] In the condemned cell and squatting on the floor, all swathed in blankets, as if it were cold weather, was a brown-faced, gray-bearded old scalliwag, who, in a frolicsome mood, had massacred three women and a batch of children—his own property, I believe—and reflects upon that exploit with genuine satisfaction to this hour, and will go to the gallows as tranquilly indifferent as a white man would go to dinner. [*centered*] **Out at the Back Door.** [¶] The prison-yard—that sad inclosure which, in the prisons of my native America, is a cheerless barren and yieldeth no vegetation save the gallows-tree, with its sorrowful human fruit—is a very garden! The beds, bordered by rows of inverted bottles (the usual style here), were filled with all manner of dainty flowers and shrubs; Chinese mulberry and orange trees stood here and there, well stocked with fruit; a beautiful little pine tree—rare, and imported from the far South Seas—occupied the center, with sprays of gracefully arching green spears springing outward like parasol tops, at marked and regular intervals, up its slender stem, and diminishing in diameter with mathematical strictness of graduation, till the sprouting plume at the top stood over a perfect pyramid. Vines clambered everywhere and hid from view and clothed with beauty everything that might otherwise have been suggestive of chains and captivity. There was nothing here to remind one of the prison save a brace of dovecotes, containing several pretty birds brought hither from "strange, strange lands beyond the sea." These, sometimes, may pine for liberty and their old free life among the clouds or in the shade of the orange groves, or abroad on the breezy ocean—but if they do, it is likely they take it out in pining, as a general thing. [*centered*] **Captain Tait, Scriptural Student.** [¶] Against one wall of the prison house stands an airy little building which does duty as a hospital. A harmless old lunatic, named Captain Tait, has his quarters here. He has a wife and children in the town, but he prefers the prison hospital, and has demanded and enjoyed its hospitality (slip of the pen—no joke intended) for years. He visits his family at long intervals—being free to go and come as he pleases—but he always drifts back to the prison again after a few days. His is a religious mania, and he professes to read sixty chapters of the Bible every day, and write them down in a book. He was about down to chapter thirty-five when I was introduced to him, I should judge, as it was nearly two in the afternoon. [¶] I said, "What book are you reading, Captain?" [¶] "The precious of the precious—the book of books—the Sacred Scriptures, sir." [¶] "Do you read a good deal in it!" [¶] "Sixty chapters every day (with a perceptible show of vanity, but a weary look in the eye withal)—sixty chapters every day, and write them all down in a plain, legible hand." [¶] "It is a good deal. At that rate, you must ultimately get through, and run short of material." [¶] "Ah, but the Lord looks out for his own. I am in His hands—He does with me as He wills. I often read some of the same chapters over again, for the Lord tells me what to read, and it is not for me to choose. Providence always shows me the place." [¶] "No hanging fire?—I mean, can you always depend on—on this information coming to time every day, so to speak?" [¶] "Always—always, sir. I take the sacred volume in my hand, in this manner, every morning, in a devout and prayerful spirit, and immediately, and without any volition on my part, my fingers insert themselves between the leaves—so directed from above (with a sanctified glance aloft)—and I know that the Lord desires me to open at that place and begin. I never have to select the chapter myself—the Lord always does it for me." [¶] I heard Brown mutter, "The old man appears to have a good thing, anyway—and his poi don't cost him anything, either; Providence looks out for his regular sixty, the prison looks out for his hash, and his family looks out for itself. I've never seen any sounder maniac than him, and I've been around considerable." [*centered*] **General George Washington.** [¶] We were next introduced to General George Washington, or, at least, to an aged, limping negro man, who called himself by that honored name. He was supposed to be seventy years old, and he looked it. He was as crazy as a loon, and sometimes, they say, he grows very violent. He was a Samson in a small way; his arms were corded with muscle, and his legs felt as hard as if they were made of wood. He was in a peaceable mood at present, and strongly manacled. They have a hard time with him occasionally, and some time or other he will get in a lively way and eat up the garrison of that prison, no doubt. The native soldiers who guard the place are afraid of him, and he knows it. [¶] His history is a sealed book—or at least all that part of it which transpired previously to the entry of his name as a pensioner upon the Hawaiian Government fifteen years ago. He was found carrying on at a high rate at one of the other islands, and it is supposed he was put ashore there from a vessel called the Olive Branch. He has evidently been an old sailor, and it is thought he was one of a party of negroes who fitted out a ship and sailed from a New England port some twenty years ago. He is fond of talking in his dreamy, incoherent way, about the Blue Ridge in Virginia, and seems familiar with Richmond and Lynchburg. I do not think he is the old original General W. [centered] **Aloft.** [¶] Up stairs in the prison are the handsome apartments used by the officers of the establishment; also a museum of quaint and curious weapons of offense and defense, of all nations and all ages of the world. [¶] The prison is to a great extent a self-supporting institution, through the labor of the convicts farmed out to load and unload ships and work on the highways, and I am not sure but that it supports itself and pays a surplus into the public treasury besides, but I have no note of this, and I seldom place implicit confidence in my memory in matters where figures and finance are concerned and have not been thought of for a fortnight. This Government Prison is in the hands of W. C. Parke, Marshal of the Kingdom, and he has small need to be ashamed of his management of it. Without wishing to betray too much knowledge of such matters, I should say that this is the model prison of the western half of the world, at any rate. [indented from right] MARK TWAIN.

►A (477) is copy-text for 'The . . . years!' (453.38–454.14)◄

454.10   earlier. (C) • ~.—

454.13   Capt. (C) • Captain

►SU (20 Apr 66) is copy-text for 'Society . . . shoved."' (454.15–456.6)◄

454.15–16   Society . . . If (A) • [indented from right] HONO-LULU, March, 1866. [centered] **Board and Lodging Secured.** [¶] I did not expect to find as comfortable a hotel as the American, with its large, airy, well-furnished rooms, distinguished by perfect neatness and cleanliness, its cool, commodious verandas, its excellent table, its ample front yard, carpeted with grass and adorned with shrubbery, et cetera—and so I was agreeably disappointed. One of our lady passengers from San Francisco, who brings high recommendations, has purchased a half interest in the hotel, and she shows such a determination to earn success that I heartily wish she may achieve it—and the more so because she is an American, and if common remark can be depended upon the foreign element here will not allow an American to succeed if a good strong struggle can prevent it. [¶] Several of us have taken rooms in a cottage in the center of the town, and are well satisfied with our quarters. There is a grassy yard as large as Platt's Hall on each of three sides of the premises; a number of great tamarind and algeraba trees tower above us, and their dense, wide-spreading foliage casts a shade that palls our verandas with a sort of solemn twilight, even at noonday. If I were not so fond of looking into the rich masses of green leaves that swathe the stately tamarind right before my door, I would idle less and write more, I think. The leaf of this tree is of the size and shape of that of our sickly, homely locust in the States; but the tamarind is as much more superb a tree than the locust as a beautiful white woman is more lovely than a Digger squaw who may chance to generally resemble her in shape and size. [¶] The algeraba (my spelling is guesswork) has a gnarled and twisted trunk, as thick as a barrel, far-reaching, crooked branches and a delicate, feathery foliage which would be much better suited to a garden shrub than to so large a tree. [¶] We have got some handsome mango trees about us also, with dark green leaves, as long as a goose quill and not more than twice as broad. The trunk of this tree is about six inches through, and is very straight and smooth. Five feet from the ground it divides into three branches of equal size, which bend out with a graceful curve and then assume an upright position. From these numerous smaller branches spout. The main branches are not always three in number, I believe; but our's have this characteristic, at any rate. [¶] We pay from five to seven dollars a week for furnished rooms, and ten dollars for board. [*centered*] **Further Particulars in this Connection.** [¶] Mr. Laller, an American, and well spoken of, keeps a restaurant where meals can be had at all hours. So you see that folks of both regular and eccentric habits can be accommodated in Honolulu. [¶] Washing is done chiefly by the natives; price, a dollar a dozen. If you are not watchful, though, your shirt won't stand more than one washing, because Kanaka artists work by a most destructive method. They use only cold water—sit down by a brook, soap the garment, lay it on one rock and "pound" it with another. This gives a shirt a handsome fringe around its borders, but it is ruinous on buttons. If your washerwoman knows you will not put up with this sort of thing, however, she will do her pounding with a bottle, or else rub your clothes clean with her hands. After the garments are washed the artist spreads them on the green grass, and the flaming sun and the winds soon bleach them as white as snow. They are then ironed on a cocoa-leaf mat spread on the ground, and the job is finished. I cannot discover that anything of the nature of starch is used. [¶] Board, lodging, clean clothes, furnished room, coal oil or whale oil lamp (dingy, greasy, villainous)—next you want water, fruit, tobacco and cigars, and possibly wines and liquors—and then you are "fixed," and ready to live

in Honolulu. [*centered*] **Water.** [¶] The water is pure, sweet, cool, clear as crystal, and comes from a spring in the mountains, and is distributed all over the town through leaden pipes. You can find a hydrant spirting away at the bases of three or four trees in a single yard, sometimes, so plenty and cheap is this excellent water. Only twenty-four dollars a year supplies a whole household with a limitless quantity of it. [*centered*] **Fruit.** [¶] You must have fruit. You feel the want of it here. At any rate, I do, though I cared nothing whatever for it in San Francisco. You pay about twenty-five cents ("two reals," in the language of the country, borrowed from Mexico, where a good deal of their silver money comes from) a dozen for oranges; and so delicious are they that some people frequently eat a good many at luncheon. I seldom eat more than ten or fifteen at a sitting, however, because I despise to see anybody gormandize. Even fifteen is a little surprising to me, though, for two or three oranges in succession were about as much as I could ever relish at home. Bananas are worth about a bit a dozen—enough for that rather over-rated fruit. Strawberries are plenty, and as cheap as the bananas. Those which are carefully cultivated here have a far finer flavor than the California article. They are in season a good part of the year. I have a kind of a general idea that the tamarinds are rather sour this year. I had a curiosity to taste these things, and I knocked half a dozen off the tree and eat them the other day. They sharpened my teeth up like a razor, and put a "wire edge" on them that I think likely will wear off when the enamel does. My judgment now is that when it comes to sublimated sourness, persimmons will have to take a back seat and let the tamarinds come to the front. They are shaped and colored like a peanut, and about three times as large. The seeds inside of the thin pod are covered with that sour, gluey substance which I experimented on. They say tamarinds make excellent preserves (and by a wise provision of Providence, they are generally placed in sugar-growing countries), and also that a few of them placed in impure water at sea will render it palatable. Mangoes and guavas are plenty. I do not like them. The limes are excellent, but not very plenty. Most of the apples brought to this market are imported from Oregon. Those I have eaten were as good as bad turnips, but not better. They claim to raise good apples and peaches on some of these islands. I have not seen any grapes, or pears or melons here. They may be out of season, but I keep thinking it is dead Summer time now. [*centered*] **Cigars.** [¶] The only cigars smoked here are those trifling, insipid, tasteless, flavorless things they call "Manilas"—ten for twenty-five cents; and it would take a thousand to be worth half the money. After you have smoked about thirty-five dollars worth of them in a forenoon you feel nothing but a desperate yearning to go out somewhere and take a smoke. They say high duties and a sparse population render it unprofitable to import good cigars, but I do not see why some enterprising citizen does not manufacture them from the native tobacco. A Kanaka gave me some Oahu tobacco yesterday, of fine texture, pretty good flavor, and so strong that one pipe full of it satisfied me for several hours. [This man Brown has just come in and says he has bought a couple of tons of Manilas to smoke to-night.] [*centered*] **Wines and Liquors.** [¶] Wines and liquors can be had in abundance, but not of the very best quality. The duty on brandy and whisky amounts to about three dollars a gallon, and on wines from thirty to sixty cents a bottle, according to market value. And just here I would caution Californians who design visiting these islands against bringing wines or liquors with their baggage, lest they provoke the confiscation of the latter. They will be told that to uncork the bottles and take a little of the contents out will compass the disabilities of the law, but they may find it dangerous to act upon such a suggestion, which is nothing but an unworthy evasion of the law, at best. It is incumbent upon the custom officers to open trunks and

search for contraband articles, and although I think the spirit of the law means to permit foreigners to bring a little wine or liquor ashore for private use, I know the letter of it allows nothing of the kind. In addition to searching a passenger's baggage, the Customhouse officer makes him swear that he has got nothing contraband with him. I will also mention, as a matter of information, that a small sum (two dollars for each person) is exacted for permission to land baggage, and this goes to the support of the hospitals. [¶] I have said that the wines and liquors sold here are not of the best quality. It could not well be otherwise, as I can show. There seem to be no hard, regular drinkers in this town, or at least very few; you perceive that the duties are high; saloon keepers pay a license of a thousand dollars a year; they must close up at ten o'clock at night and not open again before daylight the next morning; they are not allowed to open on Sunday at all. These laws are very strict, and are rigidly obeyed. [*centered*] **Water Again.** [¶] I must come back to water again, though I thought I had exhausted the subject. As no ice is kept here, and as the notion that snow is brought to Honolulu from the prodigious mountains on the island of Hawaii is a happy fiction of some imaginative writer, the water used for drinking is usually kept cool by putting it in "monkeys" and placing those animals in open windows, where the breezes of heaven may blow upon them. "Monkeys" are slender-necked, large-bodied, gourd-shaped earthenware vessels, manufactured in Germany, and are popularly supposed to keep water very cool and fresh, but I cannot indorse that supposition. If a wet blanket were wrapped around the monkey, I think the evaporation would cool the water within, but nobody seems to consider it worth while to go to that trouble, and I include myself among this number. [¶] Ice is worth a hundred dollars a ton in San Francisco, and five or six hundred here, and if the steamer continues to run, a profitable trade may possibly be driven in the article hereafter. It does not pay to bring it from Sitka in sailing vessels, though. It has been tried. It proved a mutinous and demoralizing cargo, too; for the sailors drank the melted freight and got so high-toned that they refused ever afterwards to go to sea unless the Captains would guarantee them ice-water on the voyage. Brown got the latter fact from Captain Phelps, and says he "coppered it in consideration of the source." To "copper" a thing, he informs me, is to bet against it. [*centered*] **Etiquette.** [¶] If

454.17   stranger (A) • stranger in
            Honolulu

454.29   the other day (A) •
            yesterday

454.34   oil—" (C) • ~"— (A);
            ~——" (SU)

454.35   What (A) • Why, what

455.1   Bed-chamber (A) • Bed-|
            chamber

455.2   Royal—" (C) • ~"— (A);
            ~——" (SU)

455.3   Stuff! (A) • Stuff! man.

455 *cap*   I . . . MOTHER. (C) •
            "~ . . . ~." (A)

456.2   and—" (C) • ~"— (A);
            ~——" (SU)

456.6   "shoved." (A) • "shoved."
            [*indented from right*] MARK
            TWAIN.

►SU (20 June 66) is copy-text for 'CHAPTER . . . etc.²' (457 *title*–458.18)◄

457 *title*–   CHAPTER 67 . . . journal:
1   (C) • CHAPTER LXVII. . . .
journal: (A); [*indented from right*] Ho-
NOLULU, May 23, 1866. [*centered*] **Ha-
waiian Legislature.** [¶] I have been reporting the Hawaiian Legislature all day. This is my first visit to the Capitol. I expected to be present on the 25th of April and see the King open his Parliament in state and hear his speech, but I was in Maui then and Legislatures had no charms for me. [¶] The Government of the Hawaiian Kingdom is composed of three estates, viz: The King, the Nobles and the Commons or Representatives. The Nobles are members of the Legislature by right of their nobility—by blood, if you please—and hold the position for life. They hold the right to sit, at any rate, though that right is not complete until they are formally commissioned as Legislators by the King. Prince William, who is thirty-one years of age, was only so commissioned two years ago, and is now occupying a seat in the Parliament for the first time. The King's Ministers belong to the Legislature by virtue of their office. Formerly the Legislative Assembly consisted of a House of Nobles and a House of Representatives, and worked separately, but now both estates sit and vote together. The object of the change was to strengthen the hands of the Nobles by giving them a chance to overawe the Commons (the latter being able to outvote the former by about three to one), and it works well. The handful of Nobles and Ministers, being backed by the King and acting as his mouthpieces, outweigh the common multitude on the other side of the House, and carry things pretty much their own way. It is well enough, for even if the Representatives were to assert their strength and override the Nobles and pass a law which did not suit the King, his Majesty would veto the measure and that would be the end of it, for there is no passing a bill over *his* veto. [¶] Once, when the legislative bodies were separate and the Representatives did not act to suit the late King (Kamehameha IV), he took Cromwell's course—prorogued the Parliament instanter and sent the members about their business. When the present King called a Convention, a year or two ago, to frame a new Constitution, he wanted a property qualification to vote incorporated (universal suffrage was the rule before) and desired other amendments, which the Convention refused to sanction. He dismissed them at once, and fixed the Constitution up to suit himself, ratified it, and it is now the fundamental law of the land, although it has never been formally ratified and accepted by the people or the Legislature. He took back a good deal of power which his predecessors had surrendered to the people, abolished the universal suffrage clause

and denied the privilege of voting to all save such as were possessed of a hundred dollars worth of real estate or had an income of seventy-five dollars a year. And, if my opinion were asked, I would say he did a wise thing in this last named matter. [¶] The King is invested with very great power. But he is a man of good sense and excellent education, and has an extended knowledge of business, which he acquired through long and arduous training as Minister of the Interior under the late King, and therefore he uses his vast authority wisely and well. [centered] **The Capitol—An American Sovereign Snubbed.** [¶] The Legislature meets in the Supreme Court-|room, an apartment which is larger, lighter and better fitted and furnished than any Court-room in San Francisco. A railing across the center separates the legislators from the visitors. [¶] When I got to the main entrance of the building, and was about to march boldly in, I found myself confronted by a large placard, upon which was printed: [centered] "No ADMITTANCE BY THIS ENTRANCE EXCEPT TO MEMBERS | OF THE LEGISLATURE AND FOREIGN OFFICIALS." [¶] It shocked my republican notions somewhat, but I pocketed the insinuation that I was not high-toned enough to go in at the front door, and went around and entered meekly at the back one. If ever I come to these islands again I will come as the Duke of San Jose, and put on as many frills as the best of them. [centered] **The King's Father.** (SU)

457.2	national (A) • [not in]
457.7	his (C) • His
457.7	Kekuanaoa,* (A) • Kekuanaoa,
457.8	the latter a white man, (A) • Rhodes
457.10	tawny (A) • swarthy
457.10	eighty (A) • 80
457.15	fighter (A) • old fighter
457.16–17	ago . . . this: (A) • ago, and I could not help saying to myself,
457.19–20	more . . . ago (A) • far back in the past

457.21	worshipped (A) • worshiped
457.21	devout (A) • bended
457.23	wooden (A) • hideous
457n.1	*Since dead. (A) • [not in]
458.1	high-minded (C) • high-| minded
458.9	How (A) • Lord! how
458.10	eventful life (A) • strange, eventful life must
458.18	etc.[2] (A) • etc. [centered] **A Comprehensive Slur.** [¶]

The mental caliber of the Legislative Assembly is up to the average of such bodies the world over—and I wish it were a compliment to say it, but it is hardly so. I have seen a number of Legislatures, and there was a comfortable majority in each of them that knew just about enough to come in when it rained, and that was all. Few men of first class ability can afford to let their affairs go to ruin while they fool away their time in Legislatures for months on a stretch. Few such men care a straw for the small-beer distinction one is able to achieve in such a place. But your chattering, one-horse village lawyer likes it, and your solemn ass from the cow counties, who don't know the Constitution from the Lord's Prayer, enjoys it, and these you will always find in the Assembly; the one gabble, gabble, gabbling threadbare platitudes and "give-me-liberty-or-give-me-death" buncombe from morning till night, and the other asleep, with his slab-soled brogans set up like a couple of gravestones on the top of his desk. [¶] Among the Commons in this Legislature are a number of Kanakas, with shrewd, intelligent faces, and a "gift of gab" that is appalling. The Nobles are able, educated, fine-looking men, who do not talk often, but when they do they generally say something—a remark which will not apply to all their white associates in the same house. If I were not ashamed to digress so often I would like to expatiate a little upon the noticeable fact that the nobility of this land, as a general thing, are distinguishable from the common herd by their large stature and commanding presence, and also set forth the theories in vogue for accounting for it, but for the present I will pass the subject by. [*centered*] **In Session—Bill Ragsdale.** [¶] At 11 A. M. His Royal Highness the President called the House to order. The roll-call was dispensed with for some reason or other, and the Chaplain, a venerable looking white man, offered up a prayer in the native tongue; and I must say that this curious language, with its numerous vowels and its entire absence of hissing sounds, fell very softly and musically from his lips. A white Chief Clerk read the Journal of the preceding day's proceedings in English, and then handed the document to Bill Ragsdale, a "half white" (half white and half Kanaka), who translated and clattered it off in Kanaka with a volubility that was calculated to make a slow-spoken man like me distressingly nervous. [¶] Bill Ragsdale stands up in front of the Speaker's pulpit, with his back against it, and fastens his quick black eye upon any member who rises, lets him say half a dozen sentences and then interrupts him, and repeats his speech in a loud, rapid voice, turning every Kanaka speech into English and every English speech into Kanaka, with a readiness and felicity of language that are remarkable—waits for another installment of talk from the member's lips and goes on with his translation as before. His tongue is in constant motion from 11 in the forenoon till four in the afternoon, and why it does not wear out is the affair of Providence, not mine. There is a spice of deviltry in the fellow's nature, and it crops out every now and then when he is translating the speeches of slow old Kanakas who do not understand English. Without departing from the spirit of a member's remarks, he will, with apparent unconsciousness, drop in a little voluntary contribution occasionally in the way of a word or two that will make the gravest speech utterly ridiculous. He is careful not to venture upon such experiments, though, with the remarks of persons able to detect him. I noticed when he translated for His Excellency David Kalakaua, who is an accomplished English scholar, he asked, "Did I translate you correctly, your Excellency?" or something to that effect. The rascal. [*centered*] **Familiar Characteristics.** [¶] This Legislature is like all other Legislatures. A wooden-head gets up and proposes an utterly absurd something or other, and he and half a dozen other wooden-heads discuss it with windy vehemence for an hour, the remainder of the house sitting in silent patience the while, and then a sensible man—a man of weight—a big gun—gets up and shows the foolishness of the matter in five sentences; a vote is taken and the thing is tabled. Now, on one occasion, a Kanaka member, who paddled over here from some barren rock or other out yonder in the ocean—some scalliwag who wears nothing but a pair of socks and a plug hat when he is at home, or possibly is even more scantily arrayed in the popular *malo*—got up and gravely gave notice of a bill to authorize the construction of a suspension bridge from Oahu to Hawaii, a matter of a hundred and fifty miles! He said the natives would prefer it to the inter-island schooners, and they wouldn't suffer from sea-|sickness on it. Up came Honorables Ku and Kulaui, and Kowkow and Kiwawhoo and a lot of other clacking geese, and harried and worried this notable internal improvement until some sensible person rose and choked them off by moving the previous question. Do not do an unjust thing now, and imagine Kanaka Legislatures do stupider things than other similar bodies. Rather blush to remember that once, when a Wisconsin Legislature had the affixing of a penalty for the crime of arson under consideration, a member got up and seriously suggested that when a man committed the damning crime of arson they ought either to hang him or make him marry the girl! To my mind the suspension bridge man was a Solomon compared to this idiot. [¶] [I shall have to stop at this point and finish this subject to⹀morrow. There is a villain over the way, yonder, who has been playing "Get out of the Wilderness" on a flute ever since I sat down here to-night—sometimes fast, sometimes slow, and always skipping the first note in the second bar—skipping it so uniformly that I have got to waiting and painfully looking out for it latterly. Human nature cannot stand this sort of torture. I wish his funeral was to come off at half-past eleven o'clock to-morrow and I had nothing to do. I would attend it.] [*centered*] **Explanatory.** [¶] It has been six weeks since I touched a pen. In explanation and excuse I offer the fact that I spent that time (with the exception of one week) on the island of Maui. I only got back yesterday. I never spent so pleasant a month before, or bade any place good-bye so regretfully. I doubt if there is a mean person there, from the homeliest man on the island (Lewers) down to the oldest (Tallant). I went to Maui to stay a week and remained five. I had a jolly time. I would not have fooled away any of it writing letters under any consideration whatever. It will be five or six weeks before I write again. I sail for the island of Hawaii to-morrow, and my Maui notes will not be written up until I come back. [*indented from right*] MARK TWAIN.

▶A (481–90) is copy-text for 'The . . . reader:' (458.19–466.14)◀

459.14	Garden (C) • garden
459.32	eruption (C) • irruption
461.4	dress! (C) • ~!—
461.15	stove-pipe (C) • stovepipe
463.4	Majesty (C) • majesty
463.16	worshipper (C) • worshiper
464.2	four thousand dollars (C) • $4,000
464.8	a hundred and fifty thousand dollars (C) • $150,000
464.9	four thousand dollars (C) • $4,000
464.16	Infantry." (C) • ~.∧
465.7	western (C) • Western
*465.13	has (C) • had
466.9	*hula-hula* (C) • "hula-|hula"

▶SU (1 Aug 66 ¶1–8) is copy-text for 'After . . . procured:' (466.15–18)◀

466.15   After (A) • [*indented from right*] HONOLULU, July 1, 1866. [*centered*] **Funeral of the Prin-**

cess. [¶] At ten o'clock yesterday morning, the court, members of the Legislature and various diplomatic bodies assembled at the Iolani Palace, to be present at the funeral of the late Princess. The sermon was preached by the Rev. Mr. Parker, pastor of the great stone church—of which the Princess was a member, I believe, and whose choir she used to lead in the days of her early womanhood. To the day of her death she was a staunch, unwavering friend and ally of the missionaries, and it is a matter of no surprise that Parker, always eloquent, spoke upon this occasion with a feeling and pathos which visibly moved the hearts of men accustomed to conceal their emotions. [¶] The Bishop of Honolulu, ever zealous, had sought permission to officiate in Parker's stead, but after duly considering the fact that the Princess had always regarded the Bishop with an unfriendly eye and had persistently refused to have anything to do with his church, his request was denied. However, he demanded and was granted the place of honor in the procession, although it belonged properly to the officiating clergyman. The Bishop also claimed that inasmuch as the Royal Mausoleum was consecrated ground, it would be sacrilegious to allow a Calvinistic minister to officiate there when the body was consigned to the tomb, and so he was allowed to conduct that portion of the obsequies himself. However, he explained that it was not the custom of his church to read a burial service or offer up a prayer over such as had never belonged to that church, and therefore the departed Princess was consigned to her last resting place with no warmer or kindlier a recommendation than a meager, noncommittal benediction—a sort of chilly funereal politeness—nothing more. But then we should not blame the Bishop in this matter, because he has both authority and example to sustain his position, as I find by reference to a "Review" by W. D. Alexander of one of his "Pastoral Addresses." I quote from Alexander: [¶] "Only last December, Thomas Powell, near Peterborough, in England, wished to have his son buried in the parish church-yard, and a Dissenting minister to officiate. When the friends had gathered around the grave, a messenger arrived from the clergyman of the Established Church, one Ellaby, stating that he was ready to perform the Episcopal service. This was courteously declined, upon which the Rector issued from the church and forbade the burial. Even the right of silent interment was denied them, and when the afflicted father would himself perform the last sad offices at the grave of his child, the spade was wrenched from his hand by the sexton." [¶] In offering this defense of the Bishop of Honolulu, I do so simply with an unselfish wish to do him justice and save him from hasty and injurious criticism, and *not* through a mean desire to curry favor with him. [*centered*] **The Grand Funereal Pageant.** [¶] As the hour of eleven approached, large bodies of white and native residents, chiefly on horseback, moved toward the palace through the quiet streets, to see the procession form. All business houses were closed, of course, and many a flag, half-mast high, swung lazily in the Summer air. [¶] The procession began to move at eleven, amid the solemn tolling of bells and the dull booming of minute guns from the hights overlooking the city. A glance of the eye down the procession revealed a striking and picturesque spectacle—large bodies of women, in melancholy black, and roofed over with a far-reaching double line of black umbrellas; troops of men and children, in black; carriages, with horses clad from head to foot in sable velvet; and in strong contrast with all this were the bright colors flashing here and there along the pageant—swarthy Zouaves, in crimson raiment; soldiers, in blue and white and other lively hues; mounted lancers, with red and white pennants fluttering from their weapons; nobles and great officers in splendid uniforms; and—conspicuous amid its gloomy surroundings—the catafalque, flanked on either side with gorgeously-tinted kahilis. The slow and measured tread of the march-

ing squadrons; the mournful music of the bands; the chanting of the virtues of the dead and the warrior deeds of her ancestors, by a gray and venerable woman here and there; the wild wail that rang out at times from some bereaved one to whom the occasion brought back the spirit of the buried past—these completed the effect. [*centered*] **The Kahilis.** [¶] The *kahilis* are symbols of mourning which are sacred to the aristocracy. They are immense plumes, mounted upon tall poles, and are made of feathers of all bright and beautiful colors; some are a rich purple; some crimson; others brown, blue, white and black, etc. These are all dyed, but the costly kahilis formed of the yellow feather of royalty (*tabu* to the common herd) were tinted by the hand of nature, and come from the tropic bird, which, as I have said in a previous letter, has but two of them—one under each wing. One or two kahilis, also, made of red feathers from a bird called by sailors the marlinspike bird, had no artificial coloring about them. These feathers are very long and slender (hence the fowl's name), and each bird's tail is furnished with two, and only two, of them. The birds of the Sandwich Islands seem uncommonly indigent in the matter of strictly ornamental feathers. A dozen or more of these gaudy *kahilis* were upheld by pall-| bearers of high blood and fenced in the stately catafalque with a vari-colored wall as brilliant as a rainbow. Through the arches of the catafalque could be seen the coffin, draped with that badge and symbol of royalty, the famous yellow-feather war-cloak, whose construction occupied the toiling hands of its manufacturers during nine generations of Hawaiian Kings. [*centered*] **"Style."** [¶] We have here, in this little land of 50,000 inhabitants, the complete machinery, in its minutest details, of a vast and imposing empire, done in miniature. We have all the sounding titles, all the grades and castes, all the pomp and circumstance, of a great monarchy. To the curious, the following published programme of the procession will not be uninteresting. After

*►PCA is copy-text for 'Undertaker . . . Force.' (466.19–468.3) ■ SU (1 Aug 66 ¶8) variants are reported◄

466.19   Undertaker. (SU–A) • [cen-
          tered] PROGRAMME OF
THE FUNERAL [centered] —OF—
[centered] **Her Late Royal Highness the
Princess** [centered] VICTORIA KAMA-
MALU KAAHUMANU. [centered rule]
[centered] Undertaker. (PCA)

466.20   School.³ (SU) • ~,

466.21   Maemae (PCA–SU) •
          Miæmæ (A)

466.23   Mechanics' (SU–A) • Me-
          chanic's (PCA)

466.25   (Superintendents) (SU–A) •
          [not in] (PCA)

466.25   Crown (PCA) • the Crown
          (SU–A)

466.26   Private (PCA) • the Private
          (SU–A)

466.28   (Military Company) (SU–A)
          • [not in] (PCA)

466.29–30 The Prince of Hawaii's Own
          (Military Company).
Household Troops. (SU) • Household
Troops. | The Prince of Hawaii's Own
(Military Company). [lines reversed]
(A); The Prince of Hawaii's Own. |
Household Troops. (PCA)

*467.7   Bishop (SU–A) • Bishop
          Staley (PCA)

467rt.2   Kahilis.* (A) • Kahilis.
          (PCA–SU)

467.8   [HEARSE.] (SU–A) • [cata-
          falque dingbat] (PCA)

467.15   States (A) • States, James
          McBride (PCA–SU)

467.16   Commissioner (A) • Com-
          missioner, Mons. Desnoy-
          ers (PCA–SU)

467.17   Commissioner (A) • Com-
          missioner, W. L. Green
          (PCA–SU)

467.20   the (PCA) • [not in] (SU–A)

467n.1–2 *Ranks . . . there. (A) • [not
          in] (PCA–SU)

468.3   Force. (SU–A) • Force. [¶]
          The Procession will form at
10 o'clock A. M., on Saturday, June

30th, on King street, in front of Iolani
Palace. Those who are to precede the
Catafalque will form between Richard
street and Fort street, and those who
are to follow, on the Waikiki side of the
Palace gate. [¶] The Procession will
start at 11 o'clock A. M., precisely, and
will proceed through King street to Nuuanu street, thence by Nuuanu street
to the Royal Mausoleum. [¶] The
Procession will be under the direction
of the Governor of Oahu. [¶] Iolani Palace, June 27, 1866. (PCA)

►SU (1 Aug 66 ¶9–19) is copy-text for 'I
. . . came:' (468.4–469.29)◄

468.4–5   I . . . mausoleum: (A) •
          [centered] **Details.** [¶] The
"Ahahui Kaahumana"—a benevolent
society instituted (and presided over)
by the late Princess for the nursing of
the sick and the burial of the dead—
was numerously represented. It is composed solely of native women. They
were dressed in black, and wore sashes
of different colors. [¶] His Majesty the
King, attended by a guard of nobles and
princes, whose uniforms were splendid, with bright colors and loops and
braids of gold, rode with his venerable
father in the first carriage in the rear of
the catafalque. The Bishop of Honolulu
occupied the place of honor in that portion of the procession which preceded
the catafalque. [¶] The servants of the
King and the late Princess would have
made quite a respectable procession by
themselves. They numbered two hundred and fifty, perhaps. [¶] Four or five
poodle dogs, which had been the property of the deceased, were carried in the
arms of individuals among these servants of peculiar and distinguished
trustworthiness. It is likely that all the
Christianity the Hawaiians could ab-
sorb would never be sufficient to wean
them from their almost idolatrous affection for dogs. And these dogs, as a
general thing, are the smallest, meanest, and most spiritless, homely and
contemptible of their species. [¶] As the
procession passed along the broad and
beautiful Nuuanu street, an innocent
native would step out occasionally

from the ranks, procure a slice of water-| melon, or a pineapple, or a lighted pipe, from some dusky spectator and return to his place and enjoy the refreshing luxury as he kept step with the melancholy music. [¶] When we had thoroughly examined the pageant we retired to a back street and galloped ahead to the mausoleum, two miles from the center of the town, and sat down to wait. This mausoleum is a neat edifice, built of dressed blocks of coral; has a high, sharp, slated roof, and its form is that of a Greek cross. The remains of the later Kings repose in it, but those of ancient times were hidden or burned, in compliance with a custom of the dark ages; some say, to prevent evil-disposed persons from getting hold of them and thus being enabled to pray a descendant to death; others say, to prevent the natives from making fish-|hooks out of them, it being held that there were superior fishhook virtues in the bones of a high chief. There are other theories for accounting for this custom, but I have forgotten what they are. It is said that it was usual to send a friend to hide the bones (after they had been stripped of the flesh and neatly tied in a bundle), and then waylay him and kill him as he came back, whereby it will be observed that to do a favor of this kind was attended with consequences which could not be otherwise than disagreeable to the party assuming the kindly office of undertaker to a dead dignitary. Of course, as you will easily divine, the man was killed to prevent the possibility of his divulging his precious secret. [¶] The mausoleum is large enough to accommodate many dead Kings and Princes. It stands in the middle of a large grass-clad lawn, which is inclosed by a stone wall. [*centered*] **Arrival of the Procession.**

468.11	Gen. (C) • General
468.11	*kahilis* (C) • kahilis
468.12	framework (C) • frame-|work
468.15	heart-broken (A) • dismal, heart-|broken
468.18–19	(the . . . he (A) • (who
469.1	the King soon (A) • [*centered*] **The King** [*flush left*] Soon
469.10	his (A) • His
469.11	presence. (A) • presence. [¶]

The King is thirty-four years of age, it is said, but looks all of fifty. He has an observant, inquiring eye, a heavy, massive face, a lighter complexion than is common with his race, tolerably short, stiff hair, a moderate mustache and imperial, large stature, inclining somewhat to corpulence (I suppose he weighs fully one hundred and eighty—may be a little over), has fleshy hands, but a small foot for his size, is about six feet high, is thoughtful and slow of movement, has a large head, firmly set upon broad shoulders, and is a better man and a better looking one than he is represented to be in the villainous popular photographs of him, for none of them are good. That last remark is surplusage, however, for no photograph ever was good, yet, of anybody—hunger and thirst and utter wretchedness overtake the outlaw who invented it! It transforms into desperadoes the meekest of men; depicts sinless innocence upon the pictured faces of ruffians; gives the wise man the stupid leer of a fool, and a fool an expression of more than earthly wisdom. If a man tries to look merely serious when he sits for his picture, the photograph makes him as solemn as an owl; if he smiles, the photograph smirks repulsively; if he tries to look pleasant, the photograph looks silly; if he makes the fatal mistake of attempting to seem pensive, the camera will surely write him down an ass. The sun never looks through the photographic instrument that it does not print a lie. The piece of glass it prints it on is well named a "negative"—a contradiction—a misrepresentation—a falsehood. I speak feelingly of this matter, because by turns the instrument has represented me to be a lunatic, a Solomon, a missionary, a burglar and an abject idiot, and I am neither.

469.12   He (A) • The King
469.20   into (A) • in
469.21–22   Harris (the Yankee Prime Minister) (A) • Minister Harris
469.26   It (A) • [centered] **A Contrast—How They Did in Ancient Times.** [¶] It
469.27   noted (A) • great
469.28   fifty (A) • less than fifty

*►HoHI (105 ¶1–106 ¶4) is copy-text for 'On . . . abuse.' (469.30–472.43) ■ SU (1 Aug 66 ¶20–30) variants are reported◄

469.39   dynasty (A) • son (HoHI–SU)
469.40   (the custom of that age) (SU–A) • [not in] (HoHI)
469.42   and . . . are (SU–A) • is (HoHI)
470.6–10   The . . . entire: (SU–A) • The native historians relate the circumstances of his death with a feeling and minuteness, which so well illustrates many of their customs, that the reader will pardon the insertion. (HoHI)
470.8   bygone (C) • by-gone (SU)
470.11   When (C) • '∼
470.12–13   god" . . . idol), "that (C) • god' . . . idol) 'that (SU); god' . . . idol), that (A); god, that (HoHI)
470.19   tabu,* (C) • *tabu* (A); tabu, (SU); kapu, (HoHI)
470.21   "The . . . king;" (C) • '∼ . . . ∼;'
470.23   his son, Liholiho (HoHI) • Liholiho, his son (SU–A)
470.24   After (C) • '∼
470n.1–5   *Tabu . . . sacrifice. (A) • [not in] (HoHI–SU)
470n.2–4   tabu . . . tabu . . . tabu (C) • tabu . . . tabu . . . tabu (A)
471.1   eating-house,* (C) • eating house,† (A); eating house, (SU); eating-house, (HoHI)
471.4   midnight (A) • mid-|night
*471.16   to and fro (HoHI) • [not in] (SU–A)
*471.17   tabu (C) • tabu (SU); taboo (HoHI)

471.18   (huts) (A) • [not in] (HoHI–SU)
471.19   an eating-house (C) • an eating house (SU–A); another (HoHI)
471.19–20   house to sleep in (SU–A) • dormitory (HoHI)
471.20   manufacture kapa (native cloth) (SU–A) • beat kapa (HoHI)
471.22   The (C) • '∼
471.22   king (HoHI) • [not in] (SU–A)
471.30   raw."† (C) • raw.'* (A); raw.' (SU); raw." (HoHI)
471.30   (one of the dead king's widows) (SU–A) • [not in] (HoHI)
471.30   king's (C) • King's (SU)
471.32   the (HoHI) • his (SU–A)
471.34   After (C) • '∼
471.35   new (SU–A) • [not in] (HoHI)
471n.1–6   *It . . . M. T. (C) • †It . . . [M. T.] (A); [not in] (HoHI–SU)
471n.4   Islands (C) • islands (A)
471n.5   that." (C) • ∼". (A)
472.1   Then (C) • '∼
472.1   priest, (A) • ∼∧
472.1   "I (C) • '∼
472.7   tabu (C) • *tabu* (SU); taboo (HoHI)
472.9   Then (C) • '∼
472.12   other is (SU–A) • other, (HoHI)
472.22   unavailing. (SU–A) • unavailing. His name was Keamahulihia. (HoHI)
472.22   Kalaimoku (HoHI–SU) • Kalaimoka (A)
472.24   The (C) • '∼
472.32   On (C) • '∼
472.34   themselves (SU–A) • [not in] (HoHI)
472.38–39   fire-places (SU) • fire-|places
472.39   sticks (HoHI–SU) • stick (A)

472.40   Kaahumanu's (HoHI) • Kaa-
         humaun's (A); Kaahu-
         mauu's (SU)

472.42   king's death (C) • King's
         death (SU–A); death of Ka-
         mehameha (HoHI)

472.43   abuse. (C) • abuse." (SU–A);
         abuse.'—*Hawaiian Specta-
         tor, vol. 2, p. 227.* (HoHI)

▶SU (1 Aug 66 ¶31–34) is copy-text for
'You . . . CHAPTER 69' (472.44–475
title)◀

473.2   afterward (A) • afterwards

473.3   missionaries. (A) • mission-
         aries. [*indented from right*]
MARK TWAIN. [*centered*] **Postscript—The Ministers.** [¶] Burlingame
and Von Valkenburgh, United States
Ministers to China and Japan, are ready
to sail, but are delayed by the absence
of two attaches, who went to Hawaii to
see the volcano, and who were not
aware how slow a country this is to get
around in. The journey hence to Hilo,
which would be made anywhere else almost in eighteen or twenty hours, requires a week in the little inter-island
schooners. [¶] Colonel Kalakaua, the
King's Chamberlain, has invited the
Ministerial party to a great *luau* (native
dinner) at Waikiki. [¶] Gen Von Valkenburgh has achieved a distinguished success as a curiosity-finder—not hunter.
Standing on the celebrated Pari, a day
or two ago, and amusing himself by
idly punching into the compact lava
wall through which the road is cut, he
crumbled away a chunk of it, and observing something white sticking to it,
he instituted an examination, and
found a sound, white, unmarred and
unblemished human jaw-tooth firmly
imbedded in the lava! Now the question is, how did it get there—in the
side (where a road had been cut in) of a
mountain of lava—seven hundred feet
above the valley? a mountain which
has been there for ages, this being one
of the oldest islands in the group. Burlingame was present and saw the General unearth his prize. I have critically
examined it, but, as I half expected myself, the world knows as much about
how to account for the wonder now as

if I had let it alone. In old times, the
bones of Chiefs were often thrown into
the volcanoes, to make sure that no enemy could get a chance to meddle with
them; and Brown has given it as his deliberate opinion that "that old snag
used to belong to one of them fellows."
Possibly—but the opinion comes from
a source which entitles it to but little
weight. However, that tooth is as notable a curiosity as any I have yet seen in
the Sandwich Islands. [*indented from
right*] M. T.

473.4–475 Dogs . . . CHAPTER 69 (C)
  title   • Dogs . . . CHAPTER
             LXIX. (A); [*not in*] (SU)

▶SU (18 Aug 66) is copy-text for
'BOUND . . . fruit.' (475.1–480.2)◀

475.1   BOUND (A) • [*indented from
         right*] HONOLULU, July,
1866. [*centered*] **At Sea Again.** [¶]
Bound

475.1   (a hundred and fifty miles
         distant,) (A) • [*not in*]

475.3   that (A) • this

475.11   captain (C) • Captain

475.12   my comrade (a Mr. Bill-
         ings), (A) • Brown and

475.12   persons (A) • gentlemen
         and the wheelsman

475.19   lay (A) • laid

475.20   smoked, conversed, and (A)
         • smoked and conversed
and captured vermin and eat them,

475.24   bunks (A) • bunks—though
         Mr. Brown, with that spirit
of irreverence which is so sad a feature
of his nature, preferred to call the bunk
he was allotted his shelf

475.27   ghostly (A) • grim and
         ghostly

475.28   not a long cat (A) • then it
         would be fatal to the cat to
         do it

475.30   portly (A) • villainous

475.30– Balaam's (C) • Baalam's
476.1   (SU–A)

476.2   six (A) • 6

476.13   annoyance (A) • annoyance
         to me

476.18   only dodged (A) • simply
         dodged them

476.21–22   I turned out promptly (A) •
Lazarus did not come out of
his sepulchre with a more cheerful
alacrity than I did out of mine

476.25   captain (C) • Captain

476.33   lay (A) • laid

476.36–37   summersets (SU) • somer-
saults (A)

477.1   overdrawn; it is (A) • an attempt to be spicy; it is simply an attempt to give

477.3   condition (A) • condition, I
think

477.4   It (A) • [centered] **"Roll On,
Silver Moon."** [¶] It

477.4   my (A) • all my

477.7   centre (A) • center

477.8   silver— (A) • ~,

477.8   heeled (C) • keeled (SU–A)

477.14   back-bone (C) • back bone

477.16   waves (A) • billows

478.2   Billings's (A) • Brown's

478.3   eclipse. (A) • eclipse. [cen-
tered] **I Endeavor to Entertain the Seasick Man.** [¶] I turned to
look down upon the sparkling animal-
culæ of the South Seas and watch the
train of jeweled fire they made in the
wake of the vessel. I—— [¶] "Oh, me!"
[¶] "What is the matter, Brown?" [¶]
"Oh, me!" [¶] "You said that before,
Brown. Such tautology——" [¶] "Tautology be hanged! This is no time to
talk to a man about tautology when he
is sick—so sick—oh, my! and has
vomited up his heart and—ah, me—oh
hand me that soup dish, and don't
stand there hanging to that bulkhead
looking like a fool!" [¶] I handed him
the absurd tin shaving-pot, called
"berth-pan," which they hang by a hook
to the edge of a berth for the use of distressed landsmen with unsettled stom-
achs, but all the sufferer's efforts were
fruitless—his tortured stomach refused to yield up its cargo. [¶] I do not
often pity this bitter enemy to sentiment—he would not thank me for it,
anyhow—but now I did pity him; and I
pitied him from the bottom of my
heart. Any man, with any feeling, must
have been touched to see him in such

misery. I did not try to help him—indeed I did not even think of so unpromising a thing—but I sat down by him to
talk to him and so cause the tedious
hours to pass less wearily, if possible. I
talked to him for some time, but
strangely enough, pathetic narratives
did not move his emotions, eloquent
declamation did not inspirit him, and
the most humorous anecdotes failed to
make him even smile. He seemed as
distressed and restless, at intervals—albeit the rule of his present case was to
seem to look like an allegory of unconditional surrender—hopeless, helpless
and indifferent—he seemed as distressed and restless as if my conversation and my anecdotes were irksome to
him. It was because of this that at last I
dropped into poetry. I said I had been
writing a poem—or rather, been para-
phrasing a passage in Shakspeare—a
passage full of wisdom, which I
thought I might remember easier if I reduced it to rhyme—hoped it would be
pleasant to him—said I had taken but
few liberties with the original; had preserved its brevity and terseness, its language as nearly as possible, and its
ideas in their regular sequence—and
proceeded to read it to him, as follows:

PALONIUS' ADVICE TO HIS SON—
PARAPHRASED FROM HAMLET.

Beware of the spoken word! Be wise;
  Bury thy thoughts in thy breast;
Nor let thoughts that are unnatural
  Be ever in acts expressed.

Be thou courteous and kindly toward all—
  Be familiar and vulgar with none;
But the friends thou hast proved in thy need,
  Hold thou fast till life's mission is done!

Shake not thy faith by confiding
  In every new-begot friend.
Beware thou of quarrels—but, in them,
  Fight them out to the bitter end.

Give thine ear unto all that would seek it,
  But to few thy voice impart;
Receive and consider all censure,
  But thy judgment seal in thy heart.

Let thy habit be ever as costly
  As thy purse is able to span;
Never gaudy, but rich—for the raiment
  Full often proclaimeth the man.

Neither borrow nor lend—oft a loan
  Both loseth itself and a friend,
And to borrow relaxeth the thrift
  Whereby husbandry gaineth its end.

But lo! above all set this law:
  UNTO THYSELF BE THOU TRUE!
Then never toward any canst thou
  The deed of a false heart do.

[¶] As I finished, Brown's stomach cast up its contents, and in a minute or two he felt entirely relieved and comfortable. He then said that the anecdotes and the eloquence were "no good," but if he got seasick again he would like some more poetry. [*centered*] **The Zones of the Earth Concentrated.**

478.5   Hualalai (SU) • Hualaiai (A)

478.7   said to be sixteen (A) • fourteen

478.14   winter (C) • Winter

478.19   summer (C) • Summer (A); Summers (SU)

478.21   four or five (A) • eight or ten

478.21–25 flies! . . . passes (A) • flies. [*centered*] **The Refuge for the Weary.** [¶] We landed at Kailua (pronounced Ki-loo-ah), a little collection of native grass houses reposing under tall cocoanut trees—the sleepiest, quietest, Sundayest looking place you can imagine. Ye weary ones that are sick of the labor and care, and the bewildering turmoil of the great world, and sigh for a land where ye may fold your tired hands and slumber your lives peacefully away, pack up your carpet-sacks and go to Kailua! A week there ought to cure the saddest of you all. [¶] An old ruin of lava-block walls down by the sea was pointed out as a fort built by John Adams for Kamehameha I, and mounted with heavy guns—some of them 32-pounders—by the same sagacious Englishman. I was told the fort was dismantled a few years ago, and the guns sold in San Francisco for old iron—which was very improbable. I was told that an adjacent ruin was old Kamehameha's sleeping-house; another, his eating-house; another, his god's house; another, his wife's eating-house—for by the ancient *tabu* system, it was death for man and woman to eat together. Every married man's premises comprised five or six houses. This was the law of the land. It was this custom, no doubt, which has left every pleasant valley in these islands marked with the ruins of numerous house inclosures, and given strangers the impression that the population must have been vast before those houses were deserted; but the argument loses much of its force when you come to consider that the houses absolutely necessary for half a dozen married men were sufficient in themselves to form one of the deserted "villages" so frequently pointed out to the "Californian" (to the natives all whites are *haoles*—how-ries—that is, strangers, or, more properly, foreigners; and to the white residents all white new comers are "Californians"—the term is used more for convenience that anything else). [¶] I was told, also, that Kailua was old Kamehameha's favorite place of residence, and that it was always a favorite place of resort with his successors. Very well, if Kailua suits these Kings—all right. Every man to his taste; but, as Brown observed in this connection, "You'll excuse *me*." [*centered*] **Stewed Chicken—Miraculous Bread.** [¶] I was told a good many other things concerning Kailua—not one of which interested me in the least. I was weary and worn with the plunging of the Boomerang in the always stormy passages between the islands; I was tired of hanging on by teeth and toe-|nails; and, above all, I was tired of stewed chicken. All I wanted was an hour's rest on a foundation that would let me stand up straight without running any risk—but no information; I wanted something to eat that was not stewed chicken—I didn't care what—but no information. I took no notes, and had no inclination to take any. [¶] Now, the foregoing is nothing but the feverish irritability of a short, rough sea-voyage coming to the surface—a voyage so short that it affords no time for you to tone down and grow quiet and reconciled, and get your stomach in order, and the bad taste out of your mouth, and the unhealthy coating off your tongue. I snarled at the old rooster and the cockroaches and the national stewed chicken all the time—not because these troubles could be removed, but only because it was a sanitary necessity to snarl at something or perish. One's salt-water spleen must be growled out of the system—there is no other relief. I pined—I longed—I yearned to growl at the Captain himself, but there was no opening. The man had had such passengers before, I suppose, and knew how to handle them, and so he was polite and painstaking and accommodating—and most exasperatingly patient and even-tempered. So I said to myself "I will take it out of your old schooner, anyhow; I will blackguard the Boomerang in the public prints, to pay for your shameless good-nature when your passengers are peevish and actually need somebody to growl at for very relief!" [¶] But now that I am restored by the land breeze, I wonder at my ingratitude; for no man ever treated me better than Captain Kangaroo did on board his ship. As for the stewed chicken—that last and meanest substitute for something to eat—that soothing rubbish for toothless infants—that diet for cholera patients in the rice-water stage—it was of course about the best food we could have at sea, and so I only abused it because I hated it as I do sardines or tomatoes, and because it was stewed chicken, and because it was such a relief to abuse somebody or something. But Kangaroo—I never abused Captain Kangaroo. I hope I have a better heart than to abuse a man who, with the kindest and most generous and unselfish motive in the world, went into the galley, and with his own hands baked for me the worst piece of bread I ever ate in my life. His motive was good, his desire to help me was sincere, but his execution was damnable. You see, I was not sick, but nothing would taste good to me; the Kanaka cook's bread was particularly unpalatable; he was a new hand—the regular cook being sick and helpless below—and Captain Kangaroo, in the genuine goodness of his heart, felt for me in my distress and

went down and made that most infernal bread. I ate one of those rolls—I would have eaten it if it had killed me—and said to myself: "It is on my stomach; 'tis well; if it were on my conscience, life would be a burden to me." I carried one up to Brown and he ate a piece, but declined to experiment further. I insisted, but he said no, he didn't want any more ballast. When the good deeds of men are judged in the Great Day that is to bring bliss or eternal woe unto us all, the charity that was in Captain Kangaroo's heart will be remembered and rewarded, albeit his bread will have been forgotten for ages. [centered] **The Famous Orange and Coffee Region.** [¶] It was only about fifteen miles from Kailua to Kealakekua Bay, either by sea or land, but by the former route there was a point to be weathered where the ship would be the sport of contrary winds for hours, and she would probably occupy the entire day in making the trip, whereas we could do it on horseback in a little while and have the cheering benefit of a respite from the discomforts we had been experiencing on the vessel. We hired horses from the Kanakas, and miserable affairs they were, too. They had lived on meditation all their lives, no doubt, for Kailua is fruitful in nothing else. I will mention, in this place, that horses are plenty everywhere in the Sandwich Islands—no Kanaka is without one or more—but when you travel from one island to another, it is necessary to take your own saddle and bridle, for these articles are scarce. It is singular baggage for a sea voyage, but it will not do to go without it. [¶] The ride through the district of Kona to Kealakekua Bay took us through the famous coffee and orange section. I think the Kona coffee has a richer flavor than any other, be it grown where it may and call it by what name you please. At one time it was cultivated quite extensively, and promised to become one of the great staples of Hawaiian commerce; but the heaviest crop ever raised was almost entirely destroyed by a blight, and this, together with heavy American customs duties, had the effect of suddenly checking enterprise in this direction. For several years the coffee-growers fought the blight with all manner of cures and preventives, but with small success, and at length some of the less persevering abandoned coffee-growing altogether and turned their attention to more encouraging pursuits. The coffee interest has not yet recovered its former importance, but is improving slowly. The exportation of this article last year was over 263,000 pounds, and it is expected that the present year's yield will be much greater. Contrast the progress of the coffee interest with that of sugar, and the demoralizing effects of the blight upon the former will be more readily seen.

EXPORTATIONS.

	1852.	1865.
Coffee, pounds....	117,000	263,000
Sugar, pounds......	730,000	15,318,097

[¶] Thus the sugar yield of last year was more than twenty times what it was in 1852, while the coffee yield has scarcely more than doubled. [¶] The coffee plantations we encountered in our short journey looked well, and we were told that the crop was unusually promising. [¶] There are no finer oranges in the world than those produced in the district of Kona; when new and fresh they are delicious. The principal market for them is California, but of course they lose much of their excellence by so long a voyage. About 500,000 oranges were exported last year against 15,000 in 1852. The orange culture is safe and sure, and is being more and more extensively engaged in every year. We passed one orchard that contained ten thousand orange trees. [¶] There are many species of beautiful trees in Kona—noble forests of them— and we had numberless opportunities of contrasting the orange with them. The verdict rested with the orange. Among the varied and handsome foliage of the Ko, Koa, Kukui, bread-|fruit, mango, guava, peach, citron, ohia and other fine trees, its dark, rich green cone was sure to arrest the eye and compel constant exclamations of admiration. So dark a green is its foliage, that at a distance of a quarter of a mile

the orange tree looks almost black. [centered] **Woodland Scenery.** [¶] The ride from Kailua to Kealakekua Bay is worth taking. It passes

478.30 boughs (SU) • bows (A)

478.35 billowy (A) • hillowy

480.1–2 We . . . fruit. (A) • [no ¶] The jaunt through Kona will always be to me a happy memory. [indented from right] MARK TWAIN.

▶SU (24 Aug 66 ¶1–13) is copy-text for 'At . . . required.' (480.3–24)◀

480.3 At (A) • [indented from right] KONA (Sandwich Islands), July, 1866. [centered] **Still in Kona—Concerning Matters and Things.** [¶] At

480.3 flavor (A) • flavor while on our horseback ride through Kona

480.9 sixteen times (A) • over and over again

480.14 replanting, (A) • ~∧

480.19 two tons (A) • two tons

480.21 astounding (A) • extraordinary

480.24 required. (A) • required. [¶] In Central Kona there is but little idle cane land now, but there is a good deal in North and South Kona. There are thousands of acres of cane land unoccupied on the island of Hawaii, and the prices asked for it range from one dollar to a hundred and fifty an acre. It is owned by common natives, and is lying "out of doors." They make no use of it whatever, and yet, here lately, they seem disinclined to either lease or sell it. I was frequently told this. In this connection it may not be out of place to insert an extract from a book of Hawaiian travels recently published by a visiting minister of the gospel: [¶] "Well, now, I wouldn't, if I was you." [¶] "Brown, I wish you wouldn't look over my shoulder when I am writing; and I wish you would indulge yourself in some little respite from my affairs and interest yourself in your own business sometimes." [¶] "Well, I don't care. I'm disgusted with these mush-and-milk preacher travels, and I wouldn't make an extract from one of them. Father Damon has got stacks of books shoemakered up by them pious bushwhackers from America, and they're the flattest reading—they are sicker than the smart things children say in the newspapers. Every preacher that gets lazy comes to the Sandwich Islands to 'recruit his health,' and then he goes back home and writes a book. And he puts in a lot of history, and some legends, and some manners and customs, and dead loads of praise of the missionaries for civilizing and Christianizing the natives, and says in considerable chapters how grateful the savage ought to be; and when there is a chapter to be filled out, and they haven't got anything to fill it out with, they shovel in a lot of Scripture—now *don't* they? You just look at Rev. Cheever's book and Anderson's—and when they come to the volcano, or any sort of heavy scenery, and it is too much bother to describe it, they shovel in another lot of Scripture, and wind up with 'Lo! what God hath wrought!' Confound their lazy melts! Now, *I* wouldn't make extracts out of no such bosh." [¶] "Mr. Brown, I brought you with me on this voyage merely because a newspaper correspondent should travel in some degree of state, and so command the respect of strangers; I did not expect you to assist me in my literary labors with your crude ideas. You may desist from further straining your intellect for the present, Mr. Brown, and proceed to the nearest depot and replenish the correspondent fountain of inspiration." [¶] "Fountain dry now, of course. Confound me if I ever chance an opinion but I've got to trot down to the soda factory and fill up that cursed jug again. It seems to me that you need more inspiration——" [¶] "Good afternoon, Brown." [¶] The extract I was speaking of reads as follows: [¶] "We were in North Kona[ ] The arable uplands in both the Konas are owned chiefly by foreigners. Indeed, the best of the lands on all the islands appear to be fast going into foreign hands; and one of the allegations made to me by a foreign resident against the missionaries was that their influence was against

such a transfer. The Rev. Mr. —— told me, however, that to prevent the lands immediately about him, once owned by the admirable Kapiolani, from going to strangers he knew not who, he had felt obliged to invest his own private funds in them." [¶] We naturally swell with admiration when we contemplate a sacrifice like this. But while I read the generous last words of that extract, it fills me with inexpressible satisfaction to know that the Rev. Mr.—— had his reward. He paid fifteen hundred dollars for one of those pieces of land; he did not have to keep it long; without sticking a spade into it he sold it to a foreigner for ten thousand dollars in gold. Yet there be those among us who fear to trust the precious promise, "Cast thy bread upon the waters and it shall return unto thee after many days." [¶] I have since been told that the original $1,500 belonged to a ward of the missionary, and that inasmuch as the latter was investing it with the main view to doing his charge the best service in his power, and doubtless would not have felt at liberty to so invest it merely to protect the poor natives, his glorification in the book was not particularly gratifying to him. The other missionaries smile at the idea of their tribe "investing their own private funds" in this free and easy, this gay and affluent way—buying fifteen hundred dollars worth of land at a dash (salary $400 a year), and merely to do a trifling favor to some savage neighbor.

►A (504–11) is copy-text for 'CHAPTER . . . CHAPTER 71' (481 *title*–489 *title*)◄

482.18	Greeley. (C) • ~.—
484.5	viz. (C) • ~$_\wedge$
484.15	suspense. (C) • ~.—
484.24	useful. (C) • ~.—
484.33	Polygamy (C) • '~
484.36	EVEELOJ. (C) • ~.'
486.3	Bolivia (C) • '~
486.7	EVEELOJ. (C) • ~.'
486.11	Poultices (C) • '~
486.15	EVEELOJ. (C) • ~.'
486.27	Potations (C) • '~
486.31	EVEELOJ. (C) • ~.'

487.1   DEAR (C) • "∼

487.2   sir (C) • Sir

487.4   strength. (C) • ∼.—

487.8   Under (C) • "∼

487.18   'void.' (C) • '∼ₐ"

487.28   To wit (C) • To-|wit

487.34   Potatoes (C) • '∼

487.38   GREELEY. (C) • ∼.'

487.40   Beazeley (C) • Beazely

►SU (24 Aug 66 ¶14–33) is copy-text for 'AT . . . retaliation.' (489.1–491.24)◄

489.1   AT (A) • [centered] **Nature's Printed Record in the Lava.** [¶] At

489.11   enclosed (A) • inclosed

489.12   cocoanut (C) • cocoa-|nut

489.15   counterpart (A) • counterfeit

489.22   perhaps. (A) • perhaps. It was very bad.

489.24   judgment. (A) • judgment. [¶] As usual, Brown loaded his unhappy horse with fifteen or twenty pounds of "specimens," to be cursed and worried over for a time, and then discarded for new toys of a similar nature. He is like most people who visit these Islands; they are always collecting specimens, with a wild enthusiasm, but they never get home with any of them. [centered] **Captain Cook's Death-place.**

489.27   Capt. (C) • Captain

489.29   summer (C) • Summer

489.30   men (A) • gentlemen

490.2   Capt. (C) • Captain

490.5   common (A) • as common

490.5   islands (A) • islands as fogs and wind in San Francisco

*490.22   Lono (C) • *Lono*

490.28   Capt. (C) • Captain

490.29   which (A) • that

490.32   the—but (A) • the—— But

490.38   ten (A) • the ten

490.39   Plain (A) • [centered] **The Story of Captain Cook.** [¶] Plain

490.39   Capt. (C) • Captain

491.5–10   Perceiving . . . groan. (A) • [¶] When he landed at Kea-

lakekua Bay, a multitude of natives, variously estimated at from ten to fifteen thousand, flocked about him and conducted him to the principal temple with more than royal honors—with honors suited to their chiefest god, for such they took him to be. They called him Lono—a deity who had resided at that place in a former age, but who had gone away and had ever since been anxiously expected back by the people. When Cook approached the awe-stricken people, they prostrated themselves and hid their faces. His coming was announced in a loud voice by heralds, and those who had not time to get out of the way after prostrating themselves, were trampled under foot by the following throngs. Arrived at the temple, he was taken into the most sacred part and placed before the principal idol, immediately under an altar of wood on which a putrid hog was deposited. "This was held toward him while the priest repeated a long and rapidly enunciated address, after which he was led to the top of a partially decayed scaffolding. Ten men, bearing a large hog and bundles of red cloth, then entered the temple and prostrated themselves before him. The cloth was taken from them by the priest, who encircled Cook with it in numerous folds, and afterward offered the hog to him in sacrifice. Two priests, alternately and in unison, chanted praises in honor of Lono, after which they led him to the chief idol, which, following their example, he kissed." He was anointed by the high priest—that is to say, his arms, hands and face, were slimed over with the chewed meat of a cocoanut; after this nasty compliment, he was regaled with awa manufactured in the mouths of attendants and spit out into a drinking vessel; "as the last most delicate attention, he was fed with swine-meat which had been masticated for him by a filthy old man." [¶] These distinguished civilities were never offered by the islanders to mere human beings. Cook was mistaken for their absent god; he accepted the situation and helped the natives to deceive themselves. His conduct might have been wrong, in a moral point of view, but his policy was good in conniving at the deception, and proved itself so; the belief that he was a god saved him a good while from being killed—protected him thoroughly and completely, until, in an unlucky moment, it was discovered that he was only a man. His death followed instantly. Jarves, from whose history, principally, I am condensing this narrative, thinks his destruction was a direct consequence of his dishonest personation of the god, but unhappily for the argument, the historian proves, over and over again, that the false Lono was spared time and again when simple Captain Cook of the Royal Navy would have been destroyed with small ceremony. [¶] The idolatrous worship of Captain Cook, as above described, was repeated at every heathen temple he visited. Wherever he went the terrified common people, not being accustomed to seeing gods marching around of their own free will and accord and without human assistance, fled at his approach or fell down and worshipped him. A priest attended him and regulated the religious ceremonies which constantly took place in his honor; offerings, chants and addresses met him at every point. "For a brief period he moved among them an earthly god—observed, feared and worshiped." During all this time the whole island was heavily taxed to supply the wants of the ships or contribute to the gratification of their officers and crews, and, as was customary in such cases, no return expected. "The natives rendered much assistance in fitting the ships and preparing them for their voyages." [¶] At one time the King of the island laid a tabu upon his people, confining them to their houses for several days. This interrupted the daily supply of vegetables to the ships; several natives tried to violate the tabu, under threats made by Cook's sailors, but were prevented by a chief, who, for thus enforcing the laws of his country, had a musket fired over his head from one of the ships. This is related in "Cook's Voyages." The tabu was soon removed, and the Englishmen were favored with the boundless hospitality of the natives as

before, except that the Kanaka women were interdicted from visiting the ships; formerly, with extravagant hospitality, the people had sent their wives and daughters on board themselves. The officers and sailors went freely about the island, and were everywhere laden with presents. The King visited Cook in royal state, and gave him a large number of exceeding costly and valuable presents—in return for which the resurrected Lono presented His Majesty a white linen shirt and a dagger—an instance of illiberality in every way discreditable to a god. [¶] "On the 2d of February, at the desire of his commander, Captain King proposed to the priests to purchase for fuel the railing which surrounded the top of the temple of *Lono!* In this Cook manifested as little respect for the religion in the mythology of which he figured so conspicuously, as scruples in violating the divine precepts of his own. Indeed, throughout his voyages a spirit regardless of the rights and feelings of others, when his own were interested, is manifested, especially in his last cruise, which is a blot upon his memory." [¶] Cook desecrated the holy places of the temple by storing supplies for his ships in them, and by using the level grounds within the inclosure as a general workshop for repairing his sails, etc.— ground which was so sacred that no common native dared to set his foot upon it. Ledyard, a Yankee sailor, who was with Cook, and whose journal is considered the most just and reliable account of this eventful period of the voyage says two iron hatchets were offered for the temple railing, and when the sacreligious proposition was refused by the priests with horror and indignation, it was torn down by order of Captain Cook and taken to the boats by the sailors, and the images which surmounted it removed and destroyed in the presence of the priests and chiefs. [¶] The abused and insulted natives finally grew desperate under the indignities that were constantly being heaped upon them by men whose wants they had unselfishly relieved at the expense of their own impoverishment, and angered by some fresh baseness, they stoned a party of sailors and drove them to their boats. From this time onward Cook and the natives were alternately friendly and hostile until Sunday, the 14th, whose setting sun saw the circumnavigator a corpse. [¶] Ledyard's account and that of the natives vary in no important particulars. A Kanaka, in revenge for a blow he had received at the hands of a sailor (the natives say he was flogged), stole a boat from one of the ships and broke it up to get the nails out of it. Cook determined to seize the King and remove him to his ship and keep him a prisoner until the boat was restored. By deception and smoothly-worded persuasion he got the aged monarch to the shore, but when they were about to enter the boat a multitude of natives flocked to the place, and one raised a cry that their King was going to be taken away and killed. Great excitement ensued, and Cook's situation became perilous in the extreme. He had only a handful of marines and sailors with him, and the crowd of natives grew constantly larger and more clamorous every moment. Cook opened hostilities himself. Hearing a native make threats, he had him pointed out, and fired on him with a blank cartridge. The man, finding himself unhurt, repeated his threats, and Cook fired again and wounded him mortally. A speedy retreat of the English party to the boats was now absolutely necessary; as soon as it was begun Cook was hit with a stone, and discovering who threw it, he shot the man dead. The officer in the boats observing the retreat, ordered the boats to fire; this occasioned Cook's guard to face about and fire also, and then the attack became general. Cook and Lieutenant Phillips were together a few paces in the rear of the guard, and perceiving a general fire without orders, quitted the King and ran to the shore to stop it; but not being able to make themselves heard, and being close pressed upon by the chiefs, they joined the guard, who fired as they retreated. Cook having at length reached the margin of the water, between the fire and

the boats, waved with his hat for them to cease firing and come in; and while he was doing this a chief stabbed him from behind with an iron dagger (procured in traffic with the sailors), just under the shoulder-blade, and it passed quite through his body. Cook fell with his face in the water and immediately expired. [¶] The native account says that after Cook had shot two men, he struck a stalwart chief with the flat of his sword, for some reason or other; the chief seized and pinioned Cook's arms in his powerful gripe, and bent him backward over his knee (not meaning to hurt him, for it was not deemed possible to hurt the god *Lono*, but to keep him from doing further mischief) and this treat[ ]|ment giving him pain, he betrayed his mortal nature with a groan!

491.11   Instantly a shout went up:
             (A) • The fraud which had
served him so well was discovered at
last. The natives shouted,

491.12   So they closed in upon him
             and dispatched (A) • and in-
stantly they fell upon him and killed

491.14   ships). (A) • ~)[ ]
491.17   died (A) • died here
491.18   Some (A) • A portion
491.21   them. (A) • ~[ ]
491.24   retaliation. (A) • retalia-
             tion. [*indented from right*]
             MARK TWAIN.

►SU (30 Aug 66) is copy-text for 'Near
. . . innocent.' (491.25–492.20)◄

491.25   Near . . . a (A) • [*indented
             from right*] KEALAKEKUA
BAY (S. I.), 1866. [*centered*] **Great Britain's Queer Monument to Captain
Cook.** [¶] When I digressed from my
personal narrative to write about
Cook's death I left myself, solitary,
hungry and dreary, smoking in the little
warehouse at Kealakekua Bay. Brown
was out somewhere gathering up a
fresh lot of specimens, having already
discarded those he dug out of the old
lava flow during the afternoon. I soon
went to look for him. He had returned
to the great slab of lava upon which
Cook stood when he was murdered,

and was absorbed in maturing a plan for blasting it out and removing it to his home as a specimen. Deeply pained at the bare thought of such sacrilege, I reprimanded him severely and at once removed him from the scene of temptation. We took a walk then, the rain having moderated considerably. We clambered over the surrounding lava field, through masses of weeds, and stood for a moment upon the door-|step of an ancient ruin—the house once occupied by the aged King of Hawaii—and I reminded Brown that that very stone step was the one across which Captain Cook drew the reluctant old king when he turned his footsteps for the last time toward his ship. [¶] I checked a movement on Mr. Brown's part: "No," I said, "let it remain; seek specimens of a less hallowed nature than this historical stone." [¶] We also strolled along the beach toward the precipice of Kealakekua, and gazed curiously at the semi-| circular holes high up in its face—graves, they are, of ancient kings and chiefs—and wondered how the natives ever managed to climb from the sea up the sheer wall and make those holes and deposit their packages of patrician bones in them. [¶] Tramping about in the rear of the warehouse, we suddenly came upon another object of interest. It was a

491.26   four (A) • four or five

491.27   boulders (A) • bowlders

491.32–33 Most . . . legend: (A) • It
           was almost dark by this
time, and the inscriptions would have been difficult to read even at noonday, but with patience and industry I finally got them all in my note-book. They read as follows:

491.37   1778." (C) • 1778. (A); 1778.
           [centered] His Majesty's
Ship Imogene, October 17, 1837." [¶] "Parties from H. M. ship Vixen visited this spot Jan. 25, 1858." [¶] "This sheet and capping put on by Sparrowhawk, September 16, 1839, in order to preserve this monument to the memory of Cook." [¶] "Captain Montressor and officers of H. M. S. Calypso visited this spot the 13th of October, 1858." [¶]

"This tree having fallen, was replaced on this spot by H. M. S. V. Cormorant, G. T. Gordon, Esq., Captain, who visited this bay May 18, 1846." [¶] "This bay was visited, July 4, 1843, by H. M. S. Carysfort, the Right Honorable Lord George Paulet, Captain, to whom, as the representative of Her Britannic Majesty Queen Victoria, these islands were ceded, February 25, 1843." (SU)

492.2   to us, (A) • [not in]

492.4   Capt. (C) • Captain

492.5   enclosure (C) • inclosure

492.14   Toward midnight (A) • [cen-
           tered] **"Music Soothes the
Sad and Lonely."** [¶] The sky grew overcast, and the night settled down gloomily. Brown and I went and sat on the little wooden pier, saying nothing, for we were tired and hungry and did not feel like talking. There was no wind; the drizzling, melancholy rain was still falling, and not a sound disturbed the brooding silence save the distant roar of the surf and the gentle washing of the wavelets against the rocks at our feet. We were very lonely. No sign of the vessel. She was still becalmed at sea, no doubt. After an hour of sentimental meditation, I bethought me of working upon the feelings of my comrade. The surroundings were in every way favorable to the experiment. I concluded to sing—partly because music so readily touches the tender emotions of the heart, and partly because the singing of pathetic ballads and such things is an art in which I have been said to excel. In a voice tremulous with feeling, I began: | " 'Mid pleasures and palaces though we may roam, | Be it ever so humble there's no place like home; | H-o-m-e—ho-home—sweet, swe-he⸗ he—" [¶] My poor friend rose up slowly and came and stood before me and said: [¶] "Now look a-here, Mark—it ain't no time, and it ain't no place, for you to be going on in that way. I'm hungry, and I'm tired, and wet; and I ain't going to be put upon and aggravated when I'm so miserable. If you was to start in on any more yowling like that, I'd shove you overboard—I would, by geeminy." [¶] "Poor vulgar creature," I said to my-

self, "he knows no better. I have not the heart to blame him. How hard a lot is his, and how much he is to be pitied, in that his soul is dead to the heavenly charm of music. I cannot sing for this man; I cannot sing for him while he has that dangerous calm in his voice, at any rate. [*centered*] **Hunger Driveth to Desperate Enterprises.** [¶] We spent another hour in silence and in profound depression of spirits; it was so gloomy and so still, and so lonesome, with nothing human anywhere near save those bundles of dry kingly bones hidden in the face of the cliff. Finally Brown said it was hard to have to sit still and starve with plenty of delicious food and drink just beyond our reach—rich young cocoanuts! I said, "what an idiot you are not to have thought of it before. Get up and stir yourself; in five minutes we shall have a feast and be jolly and contented again!" [¶] The thought was cheering in the last degree, and in a few moments we were in the grove of cocoa palms, and their ragged plumes were dimly visible through the wet haze, high above our heads. I embraced one of the smooth, slender trunks, with the thought of climbing it, but it looked very far to the top, and of course there were no knots or branches to assist the climber, and so I sighed and walked sorrowfully away. [¶] "Thunder! what was that!" [¶] It was only Brown. He had discharged a prodigious lava-block at the top of a tree, and it fell back to the earth with a crash that tore up the dead silence of the palace like an avalanche. As soon as I understood the nature of the case I recognized the excellence of the idea. I said as much to Brown, and told him to fire another volley. I cannot throw lava-blocks with any precision, never having been used to them, and thereforefore I apportioned our labor with that fact in view, and signified to Brown that he would only have to knock the cocoanuts down—I would pick them up myself. [¶] Brown let drive with another bowlder. It went singing through the air and just grazed a cluster of nuts hanging fifty feet above ground. [¶] "Well done!" said I; "try it again." [¶] He did so. The result

was precisely the same. [¶] "Well done again!" said I; "move your hind-sight a shade to the left, and let her have it once more." [¶] Brown sent another bowlder hurling through the dingy air—too much elevation—it just passed over the cocoanut tuft. [¶] "Steady, lad," said I; "you scatter too much. Now—one, two, fire!" and the next missile clove through the tuft and a couple of long, slender leaves came floating down to the earth. "Good!" I said; "depress your piece a line." [¶] Brown paused and panted like an exhausted dog; then he wiped some perspiration from his face—a quart of it, he said—and discarded his coat, vest and cravat. The next shot fell short. He said, "I'm letting down; them large bowlders are monstrous responsible rocks to send up there, but they're rough on the arms." [¶] He then sent a dozen smaller stones in quick succession after the fruit, and some of them struck in the right place, but the result was—nothing. I said he might stop and rest awhile. [¶] "Oh, never mind," he said, "I don't care to take any advantage—I don't wan't to rest until you do. But it's singular to me how you always happen to divide up the work about the same way. I'm to knock 'em down, and you're to pick 'em up. I'm of the opinion that you're going to wear yourself down to just nothing but skin and bones on this trip, if you ain't more careful. Oh, don't mind about me resting—I can't be tired—I ain't hove only about eleven ton of rocks up into that liberty pole." [¶] "Mr. Brown, I am surprised at you. This is mutiny." [¶] "Oh, well, I don't care what it is—mutiny, sass or what you please—I'm so hungry that I don't care for nothing." [¶] It was on my lips to correct his loathsome grammar, but I considered the dire extremity he was in, and withheld the deserved reproof. [¶] After some time spent in mutely longing for the coveted fruit, I suggested to Brown that if he would climb the tree I would hold his hat. His hunger was so great that he finally concluded to try it. His exercise had made him ravenous. But the experiment was not a success. With infinite labor and a great deal of awkwardly-constructed swearing, he managed to get up some thirty feet, but then he came to an uncommonly smooth place and began to slide back slowly but surely. He clasped the tree with arms and legs, and tried to save himself, but he had got too much sternway, and the thing was impossible; he dragged for a few feet and then shot down like an arrow. [¶] "It is *tabu*," he said, sadly. "Let's go back to the pier. The transom to my trowsers has all fetched away, and the legs of them are riddled to rags and ribbons. I wish I was drunk, or dead, or something—anything so as to be out of this misery." [¶] I glanced over my shoulders, as we walked along, and observed that some of the clouds had parted and left a dim lighted doorway through to the skies beyond; in this place, as in an ebony frame, our majestic palm stood up and reared its graceful crest aloft; the slender stem was a clean, black line; the feathers of the plume—some erect, some projecting horizontally, some drooping a little and others hanging languidly down toward the earth—were all sharply cut against the smooth gray background. [¶] "A beautiful, beautiful tree is the cocoa-palm!" I said, fervently. [¶] "I don't see it," said Brown, resentfully. "People that haven't clumb one are always driveling about how pretty it is. And when they make pictures of these hot countries they always shove one of the ragged things into the foreground. I don't see what there is about it that's handsome; it looks like a feather-duster struck by lightning." [¶] Perceiving that Brown's mutilated pantaloons were disturbing his gentle spirit, I said no more. [*centered*] **Providentially Saved from Starvation.** [¶] Toward midnight a native boy came down from the uplands to see if the Boomerang had got in yet, and we chartered him for subsistence service. For the sum of twelve and a half cents in coin he agreed to furnish cocoanuts enough for a dozen men at five minutes notice. He disappeared in the murky atmosphere, and in a few seconds we saw a little black object, like a rat, running up our tall tree and

pretty distinctly defined against the light place in the sky; it was our Kanaka, and he performed his contract without tearing his clothes—but then he had none on, except those he was born in. He brought five large nuts and tore the tough green husks off with his strong teeth, and thus prepared the fruit for use. We perceived then that it was about as well that we failed in our endeavors, as we never could have gnawed the husks off. I would have kept Brown trying, though, as long as he had any teeth. We punched the eye-holes out and drank the sweet (and at the same time pungent) milk of two of the nuts, and our hunger and thirst were satisfied. The boy broke them open and we ate some of the mushy, white paste inside for pastime, but we had no real need of it. [¶] After a while

492.15   herself (A) • [*not in*]
492.16   all (A) • [*not in*]
492.20   innocent. (A) • innocent. [*indented from right*] MARK TWAIN.

▶SU (6 Sept 66) is copy-text for 'CHAPTER . . . point.' (493 *title*–495.14)◀

493 *title*–   CHAPTER 72 . . . The (C) •
2   CHAPTER LXXII. . . . The (A); [*indented from right*] KEALAKEKUA BAY, July, 1866. [*centered*] **A Funny Scrap of History.** [¶] In my last I spoke of the old cocoanut stump, all covered with copper plates bearing inscriptions commemorating the visits of various British naval commanders to Captain Cook's death-place at Kealakekua Bay. The most magniloquent of these is that left by "the Right Hon. Lord George Paulet, to whom, as the representative of Her Britannic Majesty Queen Victoria, the Sandwich Islands were ceded, February 25, 1843." [¶] Lord George, if he is alive yet, would like to tear off that plate and destroy it, no doubt. He was fearfully snubbed by his Government, shortly afterward, for his acts as Her Majesty's representative upon the occasion to which he refers with such manifest satisfaction. [¶] A pestilent fellow by the name of Charlton had been Great Britain's Consul at Honolulu for many years. He seems to have

employed his time in sweating, fuming and growling about everything and everybody; in acquiring property by devious and inscrutable ways; in blackguarding the Hawaiian Government and the missionaries; in scheming for the transfer of the islands to the British crown; in getting the King drunk and laboring diligently to keep him so; in working to secure a foothold for the Catholic religion when its priests had been repeatedly forbidden by the King to settle in the country; in promptly raising thunder every time an opportunity offered, and in making himself prominently disagreeable and a shining nuisance at all times. [¶] You will thus perceive that Charlton had a good deal of business on his hands. There was "a heap of trouble on the old man's mind." [¶] He was sued in the Courts upon one occasion for a debt of long standing, amounting to £3,000, and judgment rendered against him. This made him lively. He swore like the army in Flanders. But it was of no avail. The case was afterwards carefully examined twice—once by a Commission of distinguished English gentlemen and once by the law officers of the British Crown—and the Hawaiian Court's decision sustained in both instances. His property was attached, and one Skinner, a relative who had $10,000 in bank, got ready to purchase it when it should be sold on execution. So far, so good. [¶] Several other English residents had been worsted in lawsuits. They and Charlton became loud in their denunciation of what they termed a want of justice in the Hawaiian Courts. The suits were all afterwards examined by the law officers of the British Crown, and the Hawaiian Courts sustained, as in Charlton's case. [¶] Charlton got disgusted, wrote a "sassy" letter to the King, and left suddenly for England, conferring his Consulate, for the time being, upon a kindred spirit named Simpson, a bitter traducer of the Hawaiian Government—an officer whom the Government at once refused to recognize. Charlton left with Simpson a demand upon the Government for possession of a large and exceedingly valu-able tract of land in Honolulu, alleged to have been transferred to him by a deed duly signed by a native gentleman, who had never owned the property, and whose character for probity was such that no one would believe he ever would have been guilty of such a proceeding. Charity compels us to presume that the versatile Charlton forged the deed. The boundaries, if specified, were vaguely defined; it contained no mention of a consideration for value received; it had been held in abeyance and unmentioned for twenty years, and its signer and witnesses were long since dead. It was a shaky instrument altogether. [¶] On his way to England Charlton met my Lord George in a Queen's ship, and laid his grievances before him, and then went on. My Lord sailed straight to Honolulu and began to make trouble. Under threats of bombarding the town, he compelled the King to make the questionable deed good to the person having charge of Charlton's property interests; demanded the reception of the new Consul; demanded that all those suits—a great number—which had been decided adversely to Englishmen (including many which had even been settled by amicable arbitration between the parties) should be tried over again, and by juries composed entirely of Englishmen, although the written law provided that but half the panel should be English, and therefore, of course, the demand could not be complied with without a tyrannical assumption of power by the King; he stopped the seizure and sale of Charlton's property; he brought in a little bill (gotten up by the newly-created and promptly-emasculated Consul, Simpson) for $117,000 and some odd change—enough to "bust" the Hawaiian exchequer two or three times over—to use a popular missionary term—for all manner of imaginary damages sustained by British subjects at divers and sundry times, and among the items was one demanding $3,000 to indemnify Skinner for having kept his $10,000 lying idle for four months, expecting to invest it in Charlton's property, and then not getting a chance to do it on account of Lord George having stopped the sale. An exceedingly nice party was Lord George, take him all around. [¶] For days and nights together the unhappy Kamehameha III was in bitterest distress. He could not pay the bill, and the law gave him no power to comply with the other demands. He and his Ministers of State pleaded for mercy—for time to remodel the laws to suit the emergency. But Lord George refused steadfastly to accede to either request, and finally, in tribulation and sorrow, the King told him to take the islands and do with them as he would; he knew of no other way—his Government was too weak to maintain its rights against Great Britain. [¶] And so Lord George took them and set up his Government, and hauled down the royal Hawaiian ensign and hoisted the English colors over the archipelago. And the sad King notified his people of the event in a proclamation which is touching in its simple eloquence: [¶] "Where are you, chiefs, people and commons from my ancestors, and people from foreign lands! [¶] "Hear ye! I make known to you that I am in perplexity by reason of difficulties into which I have been brought without cause; therefore I have given away the life of our land, hear ye! But my rule over you, my people, and your privileges will continue, for I have hope that the life of the land will be restored when my conduct is justified. [indented from right] KAMEHAMEHA III." [¶] And then, I suppose, my Lord George Paulet, temporary King of the Sandwich Islands, went complacently skirmishing around his dominions in his ship, and feeding fat on glory—for we find him, four months later, visiting Kealakekua Bay and nailing his rusty sheet of copper to the memorial stump set up to glorify the great Cook—and imagining, no doubt, that his visit had conferred immortality upon a name which had only possessed celebrity before. [¶] But my lord's happiness was not to last long. His superior officer, Rear Admiral Thomas, arrived at Honolulu a week or two afterward, and as soon as he understood the case he im-

mediately showed the new Government the door and restored Kamehameha to all his ancient powers and privileges. It was the 31st of July, 1843. There was immense rejoicing on Oahu that day. The Hawaiian flag was flung to the breeze. The King and as many of his people as could get into the Great Stone Church went there to pray, and the balance got drunk. The 31st of July is Independence Day in the Sandwich Islands, and consequently in these times there are two grand holidays in the Islands in the month of July. The Americans celebrate the 4th with great pomp and circumstance, and the natives outdo them if they can, on the 31st—and the speeches disgorged upon both occasions are regularly inflicted in cold blood upon the people by the newspapers, that have a dreary fashion of coming out just a level week after one has forgotten any given circumstance they talk about. [centered] **A Lucrative Office.** [¶] When I woke up on the schooner's deck in the morning, the sun was shining down right fervently, everybody was astir, and Brown was gone—gone in a canoe to Captain Cook's side of the bay, the Captain said. I took a boat and landed on the opposite shore, at the port of entry. There was a house there—I mean a foreigner's house—and near it were some native grass huts. The Collector of this port of entry not only enjoys the dignity of office, but has emoluments also. That makes it very nice, of course. He gets five dollars for boarding every foreign ship that stops there, and two dollars more for filling out certain blanks attesting such visit. As many as three foreign ships stop there in a single year, sometimes. Yet, notwithstanding this wild rush of business, the late Collector of the port committed suicide several months ago. The foreign ships which visit this place are whalers in quest of water and potatoes. The present Collector lives back somewhere—has a den up the mountain several thousand feet—but he comes down fast enough when a ship heaves in sight. [centered] **Washoe Men.** [¶] I found two Washoe men at the house. But I was not surprised; I believe if a man were to go to perdition itself he would find Washoe men there, though not so thick, maybe, in the other place. [*centered*] **The Holy Place.** [¶] Two hundred yards from the house was the ruins of the pagan temple of Lono, so desecrated by Captain Cook when he was pretending to be that deity. Its low, rude walls look about as they did when he saw them, no doubt. In a cocoanut grove near at hand is a tree with a hole through its trunk, said to have been made by a cannon ball fired from one of the ships at a crowd of natives immediately after Cook's murder. It is a very good hole. [*centered*] **The Hero of the Sunday School Books.** [¶] The (SU)

*493.2	lost (C) • last (A)
493.4	Obookiah (C) • Obookia
493.5	Obookiah (C) • Obookia
493.8	they (A) • [*not in*]
493.9–10	country. This resulted in the sending of (A) • country

and putting it into their heads to send

493.10	Obookiah (C) • Obookia
493.13	school (C) • School
493.15	school (C) • School
493.17	needed to worry so much (A) • need care a cent
493.18	all. (A) • all. This was the same Obookia—this was

the very same old Obookia—so I reflected, and gazed upon the ruined temple with a new and absorbing interest. Here that gentle spirit worshiped; here he sought the better life, after his rude fashion; on this stone, perchance, he sat down with his sacred lasso, to wait for a chance to rope in some neighbor for the holy sacrifice; on this altar, possibly, he broiled his venerable grandfather, and presented the rare offering before the high priest, who may have said, "Well done, good and faithful servant." It filled me with emotion. [*centered*] **Kanui the Unfortunate.**

493.19	Obookiah (C) • Obookia
493.22	William (A) • Wm.
493.26	six thousand dollars (A) • $6,000

493.27–28	in his . . . 1864. (A) • community.

Thus, after all his toils, all his privations, all his faithful endeavors to gather together a competence, the blighting hand of poverty was laid upon him in his old age and he had to go back to preaching again. One cannot but feel sad to contemplate such afflictions as these cast upon a creature so innocent and deserving. [¶] And finally he died—died in Honolulu in 1864. The Rev. Mr. Damon's paper, referring—in the obituary notice—to Page-Bacon's unpaid certificates of deposit in the unhappy man's possession, observes that "he departed this life leaving the most substantial and gratifying evidence that he was prepared to die." And so he was, poor fellow, so he was. He was cleaned out, as you may say, and he was prepared to go. He was all right. Poor, poor old fellow. One's heart bleeds for him. [¶] For some time after his bereavement in the matter of finances, he helped Rev. M. Rowell to carry on the Bethel Church in San Francisco and gave excellent satisfaction for a man who was so out of practice. Sleep in peace, poor tired soul!—you were out of luck many a time in your long, checkered life, but you are safe now where care and sorrow and trouble can never assail you any more. [*centered*] **Temple to the Rain God.**

493.29	the temple (A) • that port of entry
494.2	judicious (A) • time
494.3	had (A) • was
494.6	fine (A) • rare
494.11	And (A) • [*centered*] **The House Built by the Dead Men.** [¶] And
494.13	weird (C) • wierd
494.16	lava blocks (C) • lava-blocks
494.17–18	pallid lustre (A) • fitful lightning
494.18	forms (A) • pallid forms
494.21	At (A) • [*centered*] **Venus at the Bath.** [¶] At

494.22–   and² . . . point. (A) • down
495.14   to look at them. But with a prudery which seems to be characteristic of that sex everywhere, they all plunged in with a lying scream, and when they rose to the surface they only just poked their heads out and showed no disposition to proceed any further in the same direction. I was naturally irritated by such conduct, and there[ ]|fore I piled their clothes up on a bowlder in the edge of the sea and sat down on them and kept the wenches in the water until they were pretty well used up. I had them in the door, as the missionaries say. I was comfortable, and I just let them beg. I thought I could freeze them out, may be, but it was impracticable. I finally gave it up and went away, hoping that the rebuke I had given them would not be lost upon them[ ] I went and undressed and went in myself. And then they went out. I never saw such singular perversity. Shortly a party of children of both sexes came floundering around me, and then I quit and left the Pacific ocean in their possession. [centered] **The Shameless Brown.** [¶] I got uneasy about Brown finally, and as there were no canoes at hand, I got a horse whereon to ride three or four miles around to the other side of the bay and hunt him up. As I neared the end of the trip, and was riding down the "pathway of the gods" toward the sea in the sweltering sun, I saw Brown toiling up the hill in the distance, with a heavy burden on his shoulder, and knew that canoes were scarce with him, too. I dismounted and sat down in the shade of a crag, and after a while—after numerous pauses to rest by the way—Brown arrived at last, fagged out, and puffing like a steamboat, and gently eased his ponderous burden to the ground—the cocoanut stump all sheathed with copper memorials to the illustrious Captain Cook. [¶] "Heavens and earth!" I said, "what are you going to do with that?" [¶] "Going to do with it!—lemme blow a little—lemme blow—it's monstrous heavy, that log is; I'm most tired out—going to do with it! Why, I'm going to take her home for a specimen." [¶] "You

egregious ass! March straight back again and put it where you got it. Why, Brown, I am surprised at you—and hurt. I am grieved to think that a man who has lived so long in the atmosphere of refinement which surrounds me can be guilty of such vandalism as this. Reflect, Brown, and say if it be right—if it be manly—if it be generous—to lay desecrating hands upon this touching tribute of a great nation to her gallant dead? Why, Brown, the circumnavigator Cook labored all his life in the service of his country; with a fervid soul and a fearless spirit, he braved the dangers of the unknown seas and planted the banner of England far and wide over their beautiful island world. His works have shed a glory upon his native land which still lives in her history to-day; he laid down his faithful life in her service at last, and, unforgetful of her son, she yet reveres his name and praises his deeds—and in token of her love, and in reward for the things he did for her, she has reared this monument to his memory—this symbol of a nation's gratitude—which you would defile with unsanctified hands. Restore it—go!" [¶] "All right, if you say so; but I don't see no use of such a spread as you're making. I don't see nothing so very high-toned about this old rotten chunk. It's about the orneriest thing for a monument I've ever struck yet. If it suits Cook, though, all right; I wish him joy; but if I was planted under it I'd highst it, if it was the last act of my life. Monument! it ain't fit for a dog—I can buy dead loads of just such for six bits. She puts this over Cook—but she put one over that foreigner—what was his name?—Prince Albert—that cost a million dollars—and what did *he* do? Why, he never done anything—never done anything but lead a gallus, comfortable life, at home and out of danger, and raise a large family for Government to board at £300,000 a year apiece. But with this fellow, you know, it was different. However, if you say the old stump's got to go down again, down she goes. As I said before, if its your wishes, I've got nothing to say. Nothing only this—I've fetched her a mild or a mild and a half, and she weighs a hundred and fifty I should judge, and if it would suit Cook just as well to have her planted up here instead of down there, it would be considerable of a favor to me." [¶] I made him shoulder the monument and carry it back, nevertheless. His criticisms on the monument and its patron struck me, though, in spite of myself[ ] The creature has got no sense, but his vaporings sound strangely plausible sometimes. [¶] In due time we arrived at the port of entry once more. [*indented from right*] MARK TWAIN.

▶SU (22 Sept 66) is copy-text for 'I¹ . . . charge.' (495.15–506.4)◀

495.15–16 I¹ . . . him. (A) • KEALAKE-
KUA BAY, July, 1866. [*centered*] **The Romantic God Lono.** [¶] I have been writing a good deal, of late, about the great god Lono and Captain Cook's personation of him. Now, while I am here in Lono's home, upon ground which his terrible feet have trodden in remote ages—unless these natives lie, and they would hardly do that, I suppose—I might as well tell who he was.

495.17 worshipped (C) • worshiped
495.18 Tradition (A) • Unpoetical history
495.23 Alii (SU) • Aiii (A)
496.7 day— (A) • ~,
496.9 perhaps. (A) • ~[ ]
496.10 thus (A) • [*not in*]
496.10 Capt. (C) • Captain
496.12 Some (A) • [*centered*] **The Poetic Tradition.** [¶] But there is another tradition which is rather more poetical than this bald historical one. Lono lived in considerable style up here on the hillside. His wife was very beautiful, and he was devoted to her. One day he overheard a stranger proposing an elopement to her, and without waiting to hear her reply he took the stranger's life and then upbraided Kaikilani so harshly that her sensitive nature was wounded to the quick. She went away in tears, and Lono began to repent of his hasty conduct almost before she was out of sight. He sat him down under a cocoanut tree

to await her return, intending to receive her with such tokens of affection and contrition as should restore her confidence and drive all sorrow from her heart. But hour after hour winged its tardy flight and yet she did not come. The sun went down and left him desolate. His all-wise instincts may have warned him that the separation was final, but he hoped on, nevertheless, and when the darkness was heavy he built a beacon fire at his door to guide the wanderer home again, if by any chance she had lost her way. But the night waxed and waned and brought another day, but not the goddess. Lono hurried forth and sought her far and wide, but found no trace of her. At night he set his beacon fire again and kept lone watch, but still she came not; and a new day found him a despairing, broken-hearted god. His misery could no longer brook suspense and solitude, and he set out to look for her. He told his sympathizing people he was going to search through all the island world for the lost light of his household, and he would never come back any more till he had found her. The natives always implicitly believed that he was still pursuing his patient quest and that he would find his peerless spouse again some day, and come back; and so, for ages they waited and watched in trusting simplicity for his return. They gazed out wistfully over the sea at any strange appearance on its waters, thinking it might be their loved and lost protector. But Lono was to them as the rainbow-tinted future seen in happy visions of youth—for he never came. [¶] Some

496.15 Only (A) • [*centered*] **The Field of the Vanquished Gods.** [¶] Only
496.21 Islands (C) • island, (A); islands (SU)
496.29 half (A) • ha[ ]f
496.29 Kaahumanu (SU) • Kaahumahu (A)
496.31 first (SU) • rest. It was probably the first (A)
497 *cap* *TABU* (C) • TABU (A)
497.12 Capt. (C) • Captain

497.14–15 convenience (A) • pleasure

498.4 Kekuokalani (SU) • Beku-okalani (A)

499 *title* CHAPTER 73 (C) • CHAP-TER LXXIII. (A); [*centered*] **Canoe Voyage.** (SU)

499.9 sits on (A) • seems to sit right upon

499.11 still. (A) • ~[ ]

499.21 I (A) • [*centered*] **Sleepy Scenery.** [¶] I

499.21 Billings (A) • Brown

500.5 turned (A) • had to turn

500.6 gazed (A) • gaze

500.17– 501.21 too . . . thoroughly. (A) • too, and when Brown at-tempted to open a conversation, I let him close it again for lack of encourage-ment. I expected he would begin on the Kanaka, and he did: [¶] "Fine day, John." [¶] "Aole iki." [¶] [I took that to mean "I don't know," and as equivalent to "I don't understand you."] [¶] "Sorter sul-try, though." [¶] "Aole iki." [¶] "You're right—at least I'll let it go at that, any-way. It makes you sweat considerable, don't it?" [¶] "Aole iki." [¶] "Right again, likely. You better take a bath when you get down here to Honaunau—you don't smell good, any how, and you can't sweat that way long without smelling worse." [¶] "Aole iki." [¶] "Oh, this aint any use. This Injun don't seem to know anything but 'Owry ikky,' and the interest of that begins to let down after it's been said sixteen or seventeen times. I reckon I'll bail out a while for a change." [¶] I expected he would upset the canoe, and he did. It was well enough to take the chances, though, be-cause the sea had flung the blossom of a wave into the boat every now and then, until, as Brown said in a happy spirit of exaggeration, there was about as much water inside as there was out-side. There was no peril about the up-set, but there was a very great deal of discomfort. The author of the mischief thought there was compensation for it, however, in that there was a marked improvement in the Kanaka's smell af-terwards. [*centered*] **The Ruined City of Refuge.**

501.13 myself. (C) • ~.— (A)

501.14–15 three-quarters (C) • three quarters (A)

501.26 enclosure (C) • inclosure

501.27 fifteen (A) • fifteen or twenty

501.29 enclosure (C) • inclosure

501.30 had (C) • has (SU–A)

*501.30 each was (SU) • each (A)

501.30 two hundred and ten (A) • 210

501.31 one hundred (A) • 100

501.31 thirteen (A) • 13

501.33 relatives (A) • relatives of the deceased

502.5 inspiriting (A) • inspirited

502.12 Oriental (A) • Jewish

502.16 and (A) • or

502.20 Close (A) • [*centered*] **The Place of Execution.** [¶] Close

502.20 a¹ (SU) • the (A)

502.20 enclosure (C) • inclosure

503.2 feet (SU) • [*not in*] (A)

503.3 cocoanut (A) • cocoa-|nut

503.3 its (SU) • the (A)

503.4 multitude. (A) • ~[ ]

503.7 was (A) • was | was

503.8 The¹ (A) • [*centered*] **A Study for the Curious.** [¶] The

503.24 it was (SU) • was it (A)

503.26 Outside (A) • [*centered*] **There Were Giants in Those Days.** [¶] Outside

503.29 thither (A) • hither

503.35–36 employé (C) • employe

504.3 irrefragable tradition. (A) • irrefragible tradition. [¶] Brown said: "I don't say anything against this Injun's inches, but I copper his judgment. He didn't know his own size. Because if he did, why didn't he fetch a rock that was long enough, while he was at it?" [*centered*] **Kaahu-manu's Rock.**

504.9 fun (A) • fun, and they were marked by a quaint origi-nality, as well

504.10   it¹ (A) • it at

504.15   trouble (A) • troub[ ]e

504.23   a (A) • her

505.3   We (A) • [*centered*] **Science Among Barbarians.** [¶] We

505.5   that that (A) • that

504.14   The (A) • [*centered*] **A Petrified Niagara.** [¶] The

505.24   semblance (A) • resemblance

505.26   We (A) • [*centered*] **Nature's Mining Achievements.** [¶] We

505.28   a long distance. (A) • about fifty feet, but with no notable result, save that we made a discovery that may be of high interest to men of science. We discovered that the darkness in there was singularly like the darkness observable in other particularly dark places—exactly like it, I thought. I am borne out in this opinion by my comrade, who said he did not believe there was any difference, but if there was, he judged it was in favor of this darkness here.

505.31   height (A) • hight

505.35   occasional (A) • occasionally

506.4   charge. (A) • charge. [¶] Brown tried to hurry me away from this vicinity by saying that if the expected land breeze sprang up while we were absent, the Boomerang would be obliged to put to sea without waiting for us; but I did not care; I knew she would land our saddles and shirt-collars at Kau, and we could sail in the superior schooner Emmeline, Captain Crane, which would be entirely to my liking. Wherefore we proceeded to ransack the country for further notable curiosities. [*indented from right*] MARK TWAIN.

►A (532–33) is copy-text for 'CHAPTER . . . hotel.' (507 *title*–29)◄

507.19   docile. (C) • ~.—

507.25   lookout (C) • look-out

►SU (16 Nov 66 ¶1–6) is copy-text for 'By . . . like.' (508.1–10)◄

508.1   By (A) • [*indented from right*] VOLCANO HOUSE,

June 3d—Midnight. [*centered*] **The Great Volcano of Kileaua.** [¶] I suppose no man ever saw Niagara for the first time without feeling disappointed. I suppose no man ever saw it the fifth time without wondering how he could ever have been so blind and stupid as to find any excuse for disappointment in the first place. I suppose that any one of nature's most celebrated wonders will always look rather insignificant to a visitor at first, but on a better acquaintance will swell and stretch out and spread abroad, until it finally grows clear beyond his grasp—becomes too stupendous for his comprehension. I know that a large house will seem to grow larger the longer one lives in it, and I also know that a woman who looks criminally homely at a first glance will often so improve upon acquaintance as to become really beautiful before the month is out. [¶] I was disappointed when I saw the great volcano of Kileaua (Ke-low-way-ah) to-day for the first time. It is a comfort to me to know that I fully expected to be disappointed, however, and so, in one sense at least, I was not disappointed. [¶] As we "raised" the summit of the mountain and began to canter along the edge of the crater, I heard Brown exclaim, "There's smoke, by George!" (poor infant—as if it were the most surprising thing in the world to see smoke issuing from a volcano), and I turned my head in the opposite direction and began to crowd my imagination down. When I thought I had got it reduced to about the proper degree, I resolutely faced about and came to a dead halt. "Disappointed, anyhow!" I said to myself. "Only a considerable hole in the ground—nothing to Haleakala—a wide, level, black plain in the bottom of it, and a few little sputtering jets of fire occupying a place about as large as an ordinary potato-patch, up in one corner—no smoke to amount to anything. And these 'tremendous' perpendicular walls they talk about, that inclose the crater! they don't amount to a great deal, either; it is a large cellar—nothing more—and precious little fire in it, too." So I soliloquized. But as I gazed, the "cellar" insensibly grew. I was glad of that, albeit I expected it. I am passably good at judging of hights and distances, and I fell to measuring the diameter of the crater. After considerable deliberation I was obliged to confess that it was rather over three miles, though it was hard to believe it at first. It was growing on me, and tolerably fast. And when I came to guess at the clean, solid, perpendicular walls that fenced in the basin, I had to acknowledge that they were from 600 to 800 feet high, and in one or two places even a thousand, though at a careless glance they did not seem more than two to three hundred. The reason the walls looked so low is because the basin inclosed is so large. The place looked a little larger and a little deeper every five minutes, by the watch. And still it was unquestionably small; there was no getting around that. About this time I saw an object which helped to increase the size of the crater. It was a house perched on the extreme edge of the wall, at the far end of the basin, two miles and a half away; it looked like a marten box under the eaves of a cathedral! That wall appeared immensely higher after that than it did before. [¶] I reflected that night was the proper time to view a volcano, and Brown, with one of those eruptions of homely wisdom which rouse the admiration of strangers, but which custom has enabled me to contemplate calmly, said five o'clock was the proper time for dinner, and therefore we spurred up the animals and trotted along the brink of the crater for about the distance it is from the Lick House, in San Francisco, to the Mission, and then found ourselves at the Volcano House. [¶] On the way we passed close to fissures several feet wide and about as deep as the sea, no doubt, and out of some of them steam was issuing. It would be suicidal to attempt to travel about there at night. As we approached the lookout house I have before spoken of as being perched on the wall, we saw some objects ahead which I took for the brilliant white plant called the "silver sword," but they proved to be

"buoys"—pyramids of stones painted white, so as to be visible at night, and set up at intervals to mark the path to the lookout house and guard unaccustomed feet from wandering into the abundant chasms that line the way. [¶] By

508.1–2   lookout house (C) • lookout-house

►SU (16 Nov 66 ¶15) is copy-text for 'A . . . revelation.' (508.11–23)◄

*508.11   A (A) • [centered] **The Pillar of Fire.** [¶] We left the lookout house at ten o'clock in a half cooked condition, because of the heat from Pele's furnaces, and wrapping up in blankets (for the night was cold) returned to the hotel. After we got out in the dark we had another fine spectacle. A

508.11   height (A) • hight
508.13   lustre (C) • luster
508.15   height (A) • hight

►SU (16 Nov 66 ¶7–16) is copy-text for 'Arrived . . . hotel.' (508.24–512.8)◄

508.24   Arrived (A) • [centered] **The Vision of Hell and its Angels.** [¶] Arrived
509.18   the¹ (A) • [not in]
509.23–24 coal-black (A) • coa!-black
509.25   a hundred (A) • twenty
509.29   spokes of a wheel (A) • "spokes" of a lady's fan
509.37   opera glasses (C) • opera‿glasses
511.34   us. (A) • us. We heard a week ago that the volcano was getting on a heavier spree than it had indulged in for many years, and I am glad we arrived just at the right moment to see it under full blast.
512.6   We (A) • [centered] **The Pillar of Fire.** [¶] We
512.8   blankets, for (A) • ~‿(~
512.8   cold, we (A) • cold)
512.8   our hotel. (C) • our Hotel. (A); the hotel. After we got out in the dark we had another fine spectacle. A colossal column of cloud towered to a great hight in the air immediately above the crater, and the

outer swell of every one of its vast folds was dyed with a rich crimson luster, which was subdued to a pale rose tint in the depressions between. It glowed like a muffled torch and stretched upward to a dizzy hight toward the zenith. I thought it just possible that its like had not been seen since the children of Israel wandered on their long march through the desert so many centuries ago over a path illuminated by the mysterious "pillar of fire." And I was sure that I now had a vivid conception of what the majestic "pillar of fire" was like, which almost amounted to a revelation. [*centered*] **Accommodations for Man and Beast.** [¶] It is only at very long intervals that I mention in a letter matters which properly pertain to the advertising columns, but in this case it seems to me that to leave out the fact that there is a neat, roomy, well furnished and well kept hotel at the volcano, would be to remain silent upon a point of the very highest importance to any one who may desire to visit the place. The surprise of finding a good hotel in such an outlandish spot startled me considerably more than the volcano did. The house is new—built three or four months ago—and the table is good. One could not easily starve here even if the meats and groceries were to give out, for large tracts of land in the vicinity are well paved with excellent strawberries. One can have as abundant a supply as he chooses to call for. There has never, heretofore, been anything in this locality for the accommodation of travelers but a crazy old native grass hut, scanty fare, hard beds of matting and a Chinese cook. [*indented from right*] MARK TWAIN. (SU)

▶A (538–50) is copy-text for 'CHAP-TER . . . CHAPTER 77' (513 *title*–526 *title*)◀

513.7	eruption (C) • irruption
513.11	overflow (C) • over-|flow
513.13	everybody (C) • every body
513.19	lookout (C) • look-out
515.3	noonday (C) • noon-|day
516.9	lookout (C) • look-out
516.16	everything (C) • every thing
517.11	everything (C) • every thing
517.15	eruption (C) • irruption
518 *title*	76 (C) • LXXVI. (A); LXXIII. (Pr)
518.8	thorough-going (C) • thor-ough-|going
520.24	Kawaihae (C) • Kawaehae
520.38	pic-nicking (C) • picnicing
522.24	Capt. (C) • Captain
523.9	for (C) • ~,
524.24	east (C) • East

▶G is copy-text for 'I . . . sir."' (526.1–531.22)◀

526.1–11   I . . . I (A) • [On second thought I will extend my MEMORANDA a little, and insert the following chapter from the book I am writing. It will serve to show that the volume is not going to be merely entertaining, but will be glaringly instructive as well. I have related one or two of these incidents before lecture audiences, but have never printed any of them before.—M. T.] [¶] I

526.1	island (C) • Island (A)
526.1	Maui (C) • Mani (A)
526.12	when this person (A) • my simple statement when the stranger at the other corner of the room
526.16	Smoke! (A) • Smoke! Humph!
526.26	outrigger (C) • out-|rigger
526.27–28	to overlook a grand surf-bathing contest (A) • in the roaring surf to watch the children at their sport of riding out to sea perched on the crest of a gigantic wave
527.16	*Capt.* (C) • *Captain*
527.18	cussedest (A) • cussedest aggravatingest
527.19	a hunting (A) • a-hunting
528.4	*explain* (A) • explain
528.7	whaleships (C) • whale-|ships
528.9	for-*ever* (A) • for-|*ever*
528.19	pretense (C) • pretence
528.20	familiar (A) • familiar and hated
528.24	offense (C) • offence
528.28	Col. (C) • Colonel

528.28–29   Bilgewater (A) • Bilge-|
            water
528.34–35   a swimming (C) • a⸗
            swimming
528.38   Capt. (C) • Captain
529.5   whisky (C) • whiskey
529.14   humiliating (A) • ghastly
529.19   Hayblossom (A) • Hay-|
            blossom
529.20–21   'Incorporated . . . Men,' (C)
            • "~ . . . ~,"
530.3   sky-rocket (C) • sky-|rocket
530.21   then (A) • [not in]
530.26   do (A) • don't
530.27   know, (A) • ~ₐ
530.34   island (C) • Island (A); Is-
            lands (G)

▶A (558–76) is copy-text for 'CHAP-
TER . . . that—' (532 title–550.23)◀

532 title   78 (C) • LXXVIII. (A);
            LXXV. (Pr)
532.1   Islands (C) • islands
533.25   Doors . . . 8. (C) •
            "~ . . . ~."
534.35   half past (C) • half-past
535.8   rise (C) • raise
535.26   talk. (C) • ~[ ]
537.7   stage-coaches (C) • stage-|
            coaches
537.12   gunpowder (C) • gun-|
            powder
538.19   "Certainly (C) • ₐ~
538.23   "Are (C) • ₐ~
538.29   while—. (C) • ~.—
540.26   ain't (C) • aint
541.14   double-barreled shotgun (C)
            • double-barrelled shot gun
542.7   heartiest (Ac–g) • hearties
            (Aa–b)
545 title   APPENDIX A (C) • [half-ti-
            tle] APPENDIX ‖ APPEN-
            DIX. | A.
545 sub   HISTORY (C) • ~.
545.14   church (C) • Church
545.27   practiced (C) • practised
547.11   nations, (C) • ~ₐ
548.27   Territorial (C) • territorial
548.30   U. S. (C) • United States

548.33   Federal (C) • federal
549.3   a while (C) • awhile
549.11   Gen. (C) • General
549.13   Governor (C) • governor
549.14   Judge (C) • judge
550 title   APPENDIX B (C) • B.
550 sub   MASSACRE (C) • ~.

▶MP (76 ¶1) is copy-text for 'A . . .
God.' (550.24–551.6)◀

550.24   "revelation" (C) • '~' (A);
            ₐ~ₐ (MP)
550.26   (adopted son of Brigham)
            (A) • [not in]

▶A (577) is copy-text for 'The . . . proceeded:' (551.7–28)◀

551.25   church (C) • Church

▶MP (73 ¶4–74 ¶2) is copy-text for
'They . . . occasion:' (551.29–552.21)◀

551.29   They (C) • "They (A); "This
            wagon contained President
            Haight and Bishop John D. Lee, among
            others of the Mormon Church. They
            (MP)
551.30   them (A) • the Indians
551.31   hours of (MP) • hours (A)
551.31–32   (apparently) (A) • ₐ~ₐ
551.32   savages (A) • Indians
551.36   The (A) • "~
551.37   appeared (A) • appeared at
            the corral
*552.2   almost (A) • most
552.4   overtaken (A) • over-|taken
552.6   The (A) • "~
552.8–9   individuals . . . children (A)
            • only of the small children
            were saved
552.9   of them (A) • [not in]
552.10   old (A) • [not in]
552.11   history. (C) • history." (A);
            history. Upon the way from
            the Meadows, a young Indian pointed
            out to me the place where the Mor-
            mons painted and disguised them-
            selves. (MP)
552.12–21   The . . . occasion: (A) • [not
            in]

▶MP (84 ¶5–85 ¶2) is copy-text for 'He . . . reliable:' (552.22–553.7)◀

*552.22 He (C) • "He (A); "Judge Cradlebaugh, of the United States Court of Utah, is making his mark in that Territory, if half that is written of him is true. . . . . Satisfied that many of the leading Mormons had taken part in or instigated the Mountain Meadow massacre, and the murder of Jones, Potter, Forbes, Parrish, and a dozen others, he determined to bring them to punishment. . . . . He (MP)

552.24 U. S. (A) • [not in]

552.26 Finding (C) • "~

552.27 And then, sitting (A) • Sitting

552.28 he . . . alone (A) • he commenced his task alone

552.30–31 than . . . born (A) • even than was occasioned by the arrival of the troops within the walls of Zion

552.35 years. (C) • ~."

552.36– Had . . . pretence (A) • Gov-
553.1 ernor Cumming did not sustain Judge Cradlebaugh, but, under the pretence

553.2 On (A) • [¶] Hence various differences between Cumming on one side, and Johnson and Cradlebaugh on the other; and on

553.3 he (A) • the Governor

553.4 U. S. (A) • [not in]

553.5–7 Mrs. . . . reliable: (A) • [not in]

▶MP (76 ¶3–77 ¶7) is copy-text for 'For . . . depredations.' (553.8–38)◀

*553.11 of (A) • from

553.14–15 Deputy U. S. Marshal Rogers (C) • Deputy U. S. Marshal Rodgers (A); Deputy-Marshal Rodgers (MP)

*553.16–31 2. . . . 7. (C) • "2. . . . "3. . . . "4. . . . "5. . . . "6. . . . "7. (A); 5. . . . 7. . . . 6. . . . 3. . . . 4. . . . 2. (MP) [paragraphs reordered as well as renumbered in A; C follows A]

553.31 scene of the (A) • [not in]

553.32–33 Rogers (C) • Rodgers (MP–A)

▶A (580) is copy-text for 'APPENDIX . . . perhaps:]' (554 title–555.2)◀

554 title APPENDIX C (C) • C.

554 sub CONSUMMATED (C) • ~.

554.3 gunpowder (C) • gun-| powder

554.23–24 Territorial Enterprise, (C) • "Territorial Enterprise,"

*▶TE70 is copy-text for 'From . . . M. T.]' (555.3–569.38) ■ PT variants are reported◀

555.3–4 From . . . MISCARRIED (PT–A) • [ADVERTISEMENT] | MR. WINTERS' ASSAULT ON CONRAD WIEGAND (TE70)

555.6–7 mismanagement (TE70) • management (PT–A)

555.7 roused (PT) • rou[ ]ed

555.10 correction (PT) • cor[ ]|rection

555.12 its (PT) • it[ ]

555.13 (d) (PT–A) • (c) (TE70)

555.13 be (TE70, A) • he (PT)

555.16 least (PT) • le[ ]st

555.17 assaying (PT) • assa[ ]ing

555.22 gleanings (A) • gleanings

555.22 (b) (PT) • (~[ ])

555.26 (c) (PT) • (~.)

556.3 editorial (PT) • edi[ ]orial

556.9 People's Tribune (C) • People's Tribune

556.12 flight (PT) • fl[ ]ght

556.13 [He . . . impending:] (A) • [not in] (TE70–PT)

556.17 direct (TE70) • [not in] (PT–A)

556.19 boldly and (TE70) • [not in] (PT–A)

556.31 of (TE70) • [not in] (PT–A)

557.8 non-combatant (A) • non=combattant

557.16–17 [The . . . stripe:] (A) • [not in] (TE70–PT)

557.20 Office (PT) • office

557.28 courtesy (PT) • courtosy

557.35 me² (TE70) • [not in] (PT–A)

558.5 kill (TE70, A) • kill* | [footnote at bottom of column]

[¶] *So far as "killing" is concerned this

seems to have been an error which has before been corrected and is again now. (PT)

558.11   office. (A) • office.* | [foot-note at bottom of column] [¶] *I confess I had a[ ] first a little confusion about this matter, when, after the assault, my neighbor assured me that Mr. Winters told him during that interview, that his object in seeking the meeting with me was to obtain a retraction of charges against him (Winters,) preferred in the *People's Tribune*, by calling me to an[1] account for them, and if I failed to make such retraction that he should then demand personal satisfaction. Thereupon my neighbor told Winters, that *he* deemed it in very bad taste, to say the least, to invite me to his office at all, because there *he* would be surrounded by friends and dependents, and as it were, would have me in his power. He further suggested that the more fitting way to call me to account would be for him to call on me at my office, and if he thought proper, in company with some one who could impartially state any occurrences[2] at *that* place. On reflection, Mr. Winters acceded to that view, and hence the message he sent, referred to above[ ] Why my neighbor did not inform me of Winters' intentions, he explained to my satisfaction, but I do not deem it wise to recite it.[3] (TE70) [PT *agrees with* TE70 *in its substantives, except for the readings marked above by editorial superscript numbers, which refer to the following variants:*]

[1]an (TE70) • [not in] (PT)
[2]occurrences (TE70) • occurrence (PT)
[3]it. (TE70) • the explanation. [¶] [This statement, so far as it appears to have been said *to* Mr. Winters, my neighbor desires me also to correct. He assures me that he did not say so. He is sure he only made those comments to *me*, and did not intend me to understand that he had made them to Mr. Winters. Though my memory, confirmed by that of another, differs, it is possible the excitement of the time caused us both to mishear.] (PT)

558.20   John (PT) • Jno[ ]
558.24   in, (PT) • i[ ][ ]
*559.3–6   [*I . . . M. T.:*] (C) • [I do not desire to strain the reader's fancy, hurtfully, and yet it would be a favor to me if he would try to fancy this lamb in battle, or the duelling ground or at the head of a vigilance committee—M. T.:] (A); [*not in*] (TE70–PT)
559.15   [*His . . . out:*] (A) • [*not in*] (TE70–PT)
559.35   most (TE70) • the most (PT–A)
560.8   that —— —— (A) • that God damned (TE70–PT)
560.8   sheet (A) • w——e sheet (TE70–PT)
560.21   sir (PT) • Sir
560.22   why! (PT) • ~?
560.28   sir (PT) • Sir
560.28   Having (PT) • Ha[ ][ ]ng
560.29   *soul* (A) • *soul** | [*footnote at bottom of column*] [¶] *Or "God help you," or some tantamount expression. Its spirit I feel more positive about than its precise wording, which is true of all these merely remembered sayings, all of which together made me believe that if a possible pretext were afforded I was to be killed and brutally. (TE70–PT)
560.30   by —— (A) • by the living God Almighty (TE70–PT)
560.32–33   anyhow—you (PT) • ~ – ~
560.33   you —— —— —— lying —— —— (A) • you God d——d low-lived s——g lying s—n of a b—h (TE70–PT)
560.34   by —— (A) • by God (TE70–PT)
560.36   you —— —— (A) • you G—— d——d (TE70–PT)
560.36   sir (PT) • Sir
560.38   vilified (C) • villified
561.10   sign ——," (PT) • ~ ——,ₐ
561.11   Winters, (PT) • ~ₐ
561.15   'charges' (A) • "~"
561.37   is?" (PT) • ~?[ ]'
562.1   by —— (A) • by God (TE70–PT)

562.6   them: (PT) • ~.

562.16   By —— (A) • By God
           (TE70–PT)

562.21–22 *insinuations,* (A) • insinua-
           tions, (PT); insinuations[ ]
           (TE70)

563.19   [*The . . . M. T.:*] (A) • [*not in*]
           (TE70–PT)

563.37   into (PT) • [ ]nto

564.8   even (TE70) • [*not in*] (PT–
           A)

564.12   do (TE70) • are (PT–A)

564.20   thinking (PT) • thiking

564.32   unqualifiedly (PT) •
           unqualfiedly

564.34   this (PT) • th[ ]s

565.7   Mr. (PT) • ~[ ]

565.11–12 by —— (A) • by God (TE70–
           PT)

565.12   don't (PT) • do[ ]'t

565.18   must (PT) • mnst

565.18   it (TE70) • [*not in*] (PT–A)

565.24   are (TE70) • to be (PT–A)

565.29   print (TE70) • did you print
           (PT–A)

566.2   this (TE70) • the (PT–A)

566.10   responsibility. (PT) • ~[ ]

566.15   —— —— you (A) • G—d
           d——n you (TE70–PT)

566.15   prayer— (PT) • ~ –

566.16   those (PT) • th[ ]se

566.16   —— lying (A) • d——d
           lying (TE70–PT)

566.18   my (PT) • m[ ]

566.19   "What (PT) • ⸢⸣~

566.33   feelings. (PT) • ~,

567.17   till (TE70) • until (PT–A)

567.24   Winters' (PT) • Winter's

567.27   non-combatant (A) • non⸗
           combattant

568.7   *"charge,"* (PT) • ⸢⸣~,"

*568.15   this (TE70–PT) • the (A)

568.16   utter (TE70–PT) • own (A)

568.22   or (TE70–PT) • and (A)

568.25   such (TE70) • [*not in*] (PT–
           A)

568.25   as (TE70) • such as (PT–A)

569.8   some (TE70) • some alleged
           (PT–A)

569.9   it. (TE70) • it. [Who re-
           ceived the erroneous tele-
           grams?] (PT–A)

569.27   this part of (TE70–PT) •
           [*not in*] (A)

569.30–38 [It . . . M. T.] (A) • [*not in*]
           (TE70–PT)

Word Division in This Volume

The following compound and dialect words that could be rendered either solid or with a hyphen are hyphenated at the end of a line in this volume. For purposes of quotation each is listed here with its correct form.

xxix.11–12	Earthquake	143.8–9	good-natured
xxx.23–24	Hob-nobbing	143.34–35	sage-brush
xxxi.12–13	Outdone	153.36–37	mid-nothingness
xxxiii.20–21	Afterthought	156.38–157.1	white-caps
xxxvi.20–21	Chambermaid	157.11–12	hair-breadth
4.19–20	stove-pipe	169.24–25	press-work
13.6–7	sage-brush	172.11–12	toll-roads
14.4–5	sage-brush	180.12–13	blacksmith
15.6–7	greasewood	194.1–2	nightfall
15.13–14	sage-brush	198.15–16	moonlight
18.14–15	underclothing	199.16–17	*waist*-deep
19.16–17	pipe-stems	204.23–24	bloodshed
20.11–12	stage-coaching	204.35–36	landlord's
20.21–22	station-keepers	205.4–5	tongue-lashing
20.25–26	station-keeper	215.24–25	heartfelt
21.37–38	wash-basin	209.24–25	snow-bed
22.34–35	buckskin	233.10–11	buckskin
23.24–25	queensware	235.4–5	quicksilver
31.12–13	sage-brush	235.10–11	brick-mould
32.36–37	hindmost	236.9–10	cup-shape
33.8–9	windfalls	239.1–2	curb-stone
35.17–18	station-keepers	247.13–14	pollywogs
41.8–9	mud-wagon	249.8–9	barkeeper
50.23–24	skull-cap	260.18–19	tumble-down
51.6–7	stage-coach	264.2–3	kind-hearted
52.13–14	whitewashed	264.28–29	coachman
57.29–30	overhead	276.30–31	cross-questioning
62.12–13	bedridden	280.38–281.1	workmen
70.20–21	*shop-keepers*	282.21–22	fire-proof
77.28–29	postmaster	292.7–8	press-room
82.34–35	good-byes	292.17–18	fire-proof
86.3–4	blackguard	313.18–314.1	bone-yard
95.17–18	sub-contractors	321.7–8	sage-brush
99.18–19	grandfather	321.22–23	jurymen
118.2–3	toothache	322.4–5	blacklegs
118.17–18	yellow-jacket	322.16–17	sidewalk
129.10–11	over-estimating	323.2–3	overwhelm
131.4–5	overflowing	327n.13–328n.1	barkeeper
138.26–27	six-shooter	333.12–13	double-barreled
139.5–6	sage-brush	335.32–33	overhaul

342.16–17	ill-chosen	451.10–11	rainbow
347.6–7	gateway	451.12–13	home-made
357.34–35	daylight	453.15–16	*hula-hula*
358.39–359.1	earthquake	453.32–33	*hula-hula*
359.39–40	flood-water	459.10–11	pine-apples
361.21–22	powder-kegs	463.11–12	Bed-chamber
362.5–6	grandfather	465.13–14	drawing-room
363.13–14	oncomfortable	472.6–7	To-morrow
372.38–373.1	long-tailed	472.38–39	fire-places
388.29–30	earthquake	472.40–41	flag-staff
395.4–5	post-office	489.5–6	honey-combed
398.3–4	postscript	489.18–19	hereabouts
400.2–3	wide-spread	496.28–29	Liholiho
403.7–8	earthquake	508.1–2	lookout
405.30–406.1	midnight	514.22–23	overhanging
414.3–4	pin-heads	519.19–520.1	Rainbow
418.15–16	ker-whop	528.9–10	con-*found*
424.15–16	uttermost	528.13–14	Muckawow
425.7–8	lodestone	528.14–15	war-chiefs
433.6–7	stove-pipe	528.28–29	Bilgewater
433.33–34	framework	530.20–21	full-sized
442.18–19	sportsmen	547.3–4	sage-brush
442.23–24	grandfathers	551.10–11	earthworks
442.25–26	battle-ground	555.6–7	mismanagement

REFERENCES

This list defines the abbreviations used in this book and provides full bibliographic information for works cited by the author's name, by the author's name and publication date, or by a short title.

AAA. 1927. *The Notable Library of Major W. Van R. Whitall of Pelham, New York.* Sale of 14–15 February. New York: American Art Association.

"Abstract of Disbursements."

1861. "Abstract of Disbursements on Account of the Legislative Assembly of the Territory of Nevada, from July 1ˢᵗ 1861, to November 29ᵗʰ 1861." In Miscellaneous Treasury Account No. 142896, Office of the First Auditor, RG 217, Records of the General Accounting Office, DNA.

1861–62. "Abstract of Disbursements on Account of the Legislative Assembly of the Territory of Nevada, from November 29ᵗʰ 1861 to June 30ᵗʰ 1862." In Miscellaneous Treasury Account No. 144986, Office of the First Auditor, RG 217, Records of the General Accounting Office, DNA.

AD. Autobiographical Dictation.

Adams, Thomas F. 1857. *Typographia; or, The Printer's Instructor: A Brief Sketch of the Origin, Rise, and Progress of the Typographic Art, with Practical Directions for Conducting Every Department in an Office, Hints to Authors, Publishers, &c.* Copyright 1845. Philadelphia: L. Johnson and Co.

Addenbrooke, Alice B. 1950. *The Mistress of the Mansion.* Palo Alto, Calif.: Pacific Books.

Ahlborn, Richard E., ed. 1980. *Man Made Mobile: Early Saddles of Western North America.* Smithsonian Studies in History and Technology, no. 39. Washington, D.C.: Smithsonian Institution Press.

Ajax [pseud.]. 1866. "Letter from San Francisco." Letter dated 24 September. Honolulu *Pacific Commercial Advertiser,* 20 October, 1.

Alexander, Mary Charlotte. 1953. *Dr. Baldwin of Lahaina.* Berkeley: Printed by Stanford University Press for Mary Charlotte Alexander.

Alexander, W. D. 1891. *A Brief History of the Hawaiian People.* New York: American Book Company.

Alexander, Thomas G., and Leonard J. Arrington. 1966. "Camp in the Sagebrush: Camp Floyd, Utah, 1858–1861." *Utah Historical Quarterly* 34 (Winter): 3–21.

Allen, James B., and Glen M. Leonard. 1976. *The Story of the Latter-day Saints.* Salt Lake City: Deseret Book Company.

AMT. 1959. *The Autobiography of Mark Twain.* Edited by Charles Neider. New York: Harper and Brothers.

Anderson Auction Company. 1911. *Catalogue of the Library and Manuscripts of Samuel L. Clemens [Mark Twain].* Part 1. Sale no. 892 (7–8 February). New York: Anderson Auction Company.

Anderson, Nels. 1942. *Desert Saints: The Mormon Frontier in Utah.* Chicago: University of Chicago Press.

Anderson, Rufus. 1864. *The Hawaiian Islands: Their Progress and Condition under Missionary Labors.* Boston: Gould and Lincoln.

Anderson, Frederick, and Edgar M. Branch, eds. 1972. *The Great Landslide Case by Mark Twain: Three Versions.* Berkeley: The Friends of The Bancroft Library.

Andrew, Laurel B. 1978. *The Early Temples of the Mormons: The Architecture of the Millennial Kingdom in the American West.* Albany: State University of New York Press.

Andrews, Lorrin. 1865. *A Dictionary of the Hawaiian Language.* Honolulu: Henry M. Whitney.

Angel, Myron, ed. 1881. *History of Nevada.* Oakland, Calif.: Thompson and West.

Annual Cyclopaedia 1873. 1877. "Hoosac Tunnel." *The American Annual Cyclopaedia and Register of Important Events of the Year 1873.* Vol. 13. New York: D. Appleton and Co.

APC. 1866–79. "Books received from the Binderies, Dec 1ˢᵗ 1866 to Dec 31. 1879," the American Publishing Company's stock ledger, NN-B.

Argentoro [pseud.]. 1863. "Letter from Washoe." Letter dated 24 October. San Francisco *Morning Call,* 28 October, 1.

Arrington, Leonard J.
  1958. *Great Basin Kingdom: An Economic History of the Latter-day Saints, 1830–1900.* Cambridge: Harvard University Press.
  1985. *Brigham Young: American Moses.* New York: Alfred A. Knopf.

Arrington, Leonard J., and Davis Bitton. 1979. *The Mormon Experience: A History of the Latter-day Saints.* New York: Alfred A. Knopf.

Ashbaugh, Don. 1963. *Nevada's Turbulent Yesterday: A Study in Ghost Towns.* Los Angeles: Westernlore Press.

Asser, John. 1908. *Asser's Life of King Alfred.* Translated with an introduction and notes by L. C. Jane. London: Chatto and Windus.

Austin, Franklin H. 1926. "Mark Twain Incognito—A Reminiscence." *Friend* 96 (September, October, November): 201–4, 224–29, 248–54. Partly reprinted in *MTH*, 75–79.

Ayers, James J. 1922. *Gold and Sunshine: Reminiscences of Early California.* Boston: Richard G. Badger.

Baetzhold, Howard G. 1970. *Mark Twain and John Bull: The British Connection.* Bloomington: Indiana University Press.

Bailey, Paul. 1975. *Those Kings and Queens of Old Hawaii.* Los Angeles: Westernlore Books.

BAL. 1957. *Bibliography of American Literature.* Compiled by Jacob Blanck. Vol. 2. New Haven: Yale University Press.

Bancroft, Hubert Howe.
1882–90. *History of the Pacific States of North America.* 34 vols. San Francisco: A. L. Bancroft and Co. / History Company.

1891–92. *Chronicles of the Builders of the Commonwealth.* 7 vols. San Francisco: History Company.

Barnes, George E. 1887. "Mark Twain, as He Was Known during His Stay on the Pacific Slope." San Francisco *Morning Call*, 17 April, 1.

Barrett, Don C. 1931. *The Greenbacks and Resumption of Specie Payments, 1862–1879.* Cambridge: Harvard University Press.

Barth, Gunther. 1964. *Bitter Strength: A History of the Chinese in the United States, 1850–1870.* Cambridge: Harvard University Press.

Bates, George Washington. 1854. *Sandwich Island Notes. By a Haole.* New York: Harper and Brothers.

BDUSC. 1989. *Biographical Directory of the United States Congress, 1774–1989.* Bicentennial edition. Washington, D.C.: Government Printing Office.

Beadle, J. H. 1872. Preface to *Brigham's Destroying Angel.* In Hickman, v–vii.

Beckwith, Martha. 1940. *Hawaiian Mythology.* New Haven: Yale University Press. Citations are to the 1970 reprint edition, Honolulu: University of Hawaii Press.

Beebe, Lucius. 1954. *Comstock Commotion: The Story of "The Territorial Enterprise."* Stanford: Stanford University Press.

Beebe, Lucius, and Charles Clegg. 1954. *Legends of the Comstock Lode.* Rev. ed. Stanford: Stanford University Press.

Beeton, S. O., ed. 1868. *Beeton's Dictionary of Geography: A Universal Gazetteer.* London: Ward, Lock, and Tyler.

Bellamy, Gladys Carmen. 1941. "Mark Twain's Indebtedness to John Phoenix." *American Literature* 13 (March): 29–43.

Bennett, Chauncey C. 1869. *Honolulu Directory, and Historical Sketch of the Hawaiian or Sandwich Islands.* Honolulu: C. C. Bennett.

Benson, Ivan. 1938. *Mark Twain's Western Years.* Stanford: Stanford University Press.

Berkove, Lawrence I.
1988a. "Jim Gillis: 'The Thoreau of the Sierras.'" *Mark Twain Circular* 2 (March–April): 1–2.

1988b. "Dan De Quille's Narratives of Ohio: Lorenzo Dow's Miracle." *Northwest Ohio Quarterly* 60 (Spring): 47–56.

1993. "Dan De Quille and *Roughing It*: Borrowings and Influence." *Nevada Historical Society Quarterly,* forthcoming.

Bingham, Hiram. 1855. *A Residence of Twenty-one Years in the Sandwich Islands; or, The Civil, Religious, and Political History of Those Islands.* 3d ed. Canandaigua, N.Y.: H. D. Goodwin.

Blair, Montgomery. 1861. "Report of the Postmaster General," dated 2 December. In *Message of the President of the United States to the Two Houses of Congress at the Commencement of the Second Session of the Thirty-seventh Congress.* Washington, D.C.: Government Printing Office.

Bloss, Roy S. 1959. *Pony Express—The Great Gamble.* Berkeley: Howell-North.

Book of Mormon.
1866. *The Book of Mormon: An Account Written by the Hand of Mormon, upon Plates Taken from the Plates of Nephi.* Translated by Joseph Smith, Jun. Sixth European Edition. Liverpool: Published by Brigham Young, Jun. [*Citations in the notes are to chapters and verses in this edition, followed by parenthetical citations to chapters and verses in all editions published since 1879. "1 Nephi" and "2 Nephi" refer to the "First" and "Second" books of Nephi; "3 Nephi" refers to a book listed in the table of contents as merely "Book of Nephi"; "4 Nephi" refers to another "Book of Nephi," not listed in the table of contents, which follows immediately after "3 Nephi."*]

1981. *The Book of Mormon. The Doctrine and Covenants of the Church of Jesus Christ of Latter-day Saints. The Pearl of Great Price.* Salt Lake City: Church of Jesus Christ of Latter-day Saints.

Boothby, H. E. 1919. "Up from Idolatry." *Hawaiian Almanac and Annual for 1920,* 53–78.

Bowers, Fredson. 1989. "Regularization and Normalization in Modern Critical Texts." *Studies in Bibliography* 42:79–102.

Bowles, Samuel.

1866. *Across the Continent: A Summer's Journey to the Rocky Mountains, the Mormons, and the Pacific States, with Speaker Colfax.* London: Sampson Low, Son, and Marston.

1869. *Our New West. Records of Travel between the Mississippi River and the Pacific Ocean.* Hartford: Hartford Publishing Co.

Bradley, Harold Whitman. 1942. *The American Frontier in Hawaii: The Pioneers, 1789–1843.* Stanford: Stanford University Press. Citations are to the 1968 reprint edition, Gloucester, Mass.: Peter Smith.

Branch, Edgar Marquess.

1946. "A Chronological Bibliography of the Writings of Samuel Clemens to June 8, 1867." *American Literature* 18 (May): 109–59.

1967. "'My Voice Is Still for Setchell': A Background Study of 'Jim Smiley and His Jumping Frog.'" *PMLA* 82 (December): 591–601.

1969. "Mark Twain Reports the Races in Sacramento." *Huntington Library Quarterly* 32 (February): 179–86.

1978. "'The Babes in the Wood': Artemus Ward's 'Double Health' to Mark Twain." *PMLA* 93 (October): 955–72.

1985. "Fact and Fiction in the Blind Lead Episode of *Roughing It.*" *Nevada Historical Society Quarterly* 28 (Winter): 234–48.

Brewer, William H. 1930. *Up and Down California in 1860–1864.* Edited by Francis P. Farquhar. New Haven: Yale University Press.

Bridgman, Richard. 1987. *Traveling in Mark Twain.* Berkeley, Los Angeles, London: University of California Press.

Brigham, William T. 1868. *Notes on the Volcanoes of the Hawaiian Islands.* Boston: Riverside Press.

Brodie, Fawn M. 1971. *No Man Knows My History: The Life of Joseph Smith the Mormon Prophet.* 2d ed., rev. and enl. New York: Alfred A. Knopf.

Bromer. 1992. *Selections from Our Stock to Be Featured . . . February 14, 15, 16 1992 at the Los Angeles Airport Hilton.* Los Angeles: Bromer Booksellers.

Brooks, Benjamin S. 1876. *The Chinese in California. Addressed to the Committee on Foreign Relations of the U.S. Senate.* n.p.

Brooks, Juanita.

1962. *John Doyle Lee: Zealot—Pioneer Builder—Scapegoat.* Glendale, Calif.: Arthur H. Clark Company.

1970. *The Mountain Meadows Massacre.* 3d ed. Norman: University of Oklahoma Press.

Brooks, Roger L. 1962. "A Second Possible Source for Mark Twain's 'The Aged Pilot Man.'" *Revue de littérature comparée* 36 (July–September): 451–53.

Browne, Charles Farrar [Artemus Ward, pseud.].

1862. *Artemus Ward: His Book.* New York: Carleton.

1865. *Artemus Ward: His Travels.* New York: Carleton.

Browne, J. Ross.

1860–61. "A Peep at Washoe." *Harper's New Monthly Magazine* 22 (December, January, February): 1–17, 145–62, 289–305. Reprinted in J. Ross Browne 1864, 309–436.

1864. *Crusoe's Island: A Ramble in the Footsteps of Alexander Selkirk. With Sketches of Adventure in California and Washoe.* New York: Harper and Brothers.

1865a. "Washoe Revisited." *Harper's New Monthly Magazine* 30–31 (May, June, July): 681–96, 1–12, 151–61. Reprinted in J. Ross Browne 1869, 293–392.

1865b. "A Trip to Bodie Bluff and the Dead Sea of the West." *Harper's New Monthly Magazine* 31 (August, September): 274–84, 411–19. Reprinted in J. Ross Browne 1869, 393–444.

1865c. "The Walker River Country." *Harper's New Monthly Magazine* 31 (November): 700–709. Reprinted in J. Ross Browne 1869, 445–73.

1866. "The Reese River Country." *Harper's New Monthly Magazine* 33 (June): 26–44. Reprinted in J. Ross Browne 1869, 475–535.

1868. *Report of J. Ross Browne, on the Mineral Resources of the States and Territories West of the Rocky Mountains.* San Francisco: H.H. Bancroft and Co.

1869. *Adventures in the Apache Country: A Tour through Arizona and Sonora, with Notes on the Silver Regions of Nevada.* New York: Harper and Brothers.

Browne, Junius Henri. 1872. *Sights and Sensations in Europe.* Hartford: American Publishing Company.

Browning, Peter. 1986. *Place Names of the Sierra Nevada: From Abbot to Zumwalt.* Berkeley: Wilderness Press.

Buckbee, Edna Bryan. 1935. *The Saga of Old Tuolumne.* New York: Press of the Pioneers.

Budd, Louis J., ed. 1977. "A Listing of and Selection from Newspaper and Magazine Interviews with Samuel L. Clemens, 1874–1910." *American Literary Realism* 10 (Winter): i–100.

Bunker, William M. 1879. *From Report upon the Aurora Mining District, Esmeralda Co., Nevada.* San Francisco: Barry, Baird, and Co.

Burton, Richard F. 1861. *The City of the Saints and Across the Rocky Mountains to California.* London: Longman, Green, Longman, and Roberts.

Bush, Lester E., Jr. 1981. "The Word of Wisdom in Early Nineteenth-Century Perspective." *Dialogue* 14 (Autumn): 46–65.

Byron, George Anson. 1826. *Voyage of H. M. S. Blonde to the Sandwich Islands, in the Years 1824–1825.* London: John Murray.

Callaway, Llewellyn Link. 1973. *Two True Tales of the Wild West.* Oakland: Maud Gonne Press.

Callicot, T. Carey. 1855. *Cyclopedia of Universal Geography: Being a Gazetteer of the World.* New York: A. S. Barnes and Co.

Cameron, Marguerite. 1939. *This Is the Place.* Caldwell, Idaho: Caxton Printers.

Campbell, Archibald. 1816. *A Voyage Round the World, from 1806 to 1812.* Edinburgh: Printed for Archibald Constable and Co.

Campbell, Eugene E. 1988. *Establishing Zion: The Mormon Church in the American West, 1847–1869.* Salt Lake City: Signature Books.

Canning, Ray R., and Beverly Beeton. 1977. *The Genteel Gentile: Letters of Elizabeth Cumming, 1857–1858.* Salt Lake City: Tanner Trust Fund, University of Utah Library.

Carleton, J. H. 1902. *Special Report of the Mountain Meadow Massacre, by J. H. Carleton, Brevet Major, United States Army, Captain, First Dragoons,* dated 25 May 1859. U.S. Congress, House of Representatives, 57th Congress, 1st session, volume 110, document 605.

Carlson, Helen S. 1974. *Nevada Place Names: A Geographical Dictionary.* Reno: University of Nevada Press.

Carson County Census. [1860] 1967. "Free Inhabitants in . . . Carson County." *Population Schedules of the Eighth Census of the United States, 1860. Roll 1314. Utah: Carson County.* National Archives Microfilm Publications, Microcopy no. 653. Washington, D.C.: General Services Administration.

Carter, Kate B., comp. 1952–57. *Treasures of Pioneer History.* 6 vols. Salt Lake City: Daughters of Utah Pioneers.

Caulkins, Frances Manwaring. 1895. *History of New London, Connecticut.* New London: H. D. Utley.

CCamarSJ. Estelle Doheny Collection, The Edward Laurence Doheny Memorial Library, Saint John's Seminary, Camarillo, California.

CCC. Honnold Library, Claremont, California.

Chalfant, Willie Arthur. 1928. *Outposts of Civilization.* Boston: Christopher Publishing House.

Chapel, Charles Edward. 1961. *Guns of the Old West.* New York: Coward-McCann.

Chapman, Arthur. 1932. *The Pony Express: The Record of a Romantic Adventure in Business.* New York and London: G. P. Putnam's Sons.

Cheever, Henry T.
1851a. *The Island World of the Pacific.* New York: Harper and Brothers.

1851b. *Life in the Sandwich Islands; or, The Heart of the Pacific, as It Was and Is.* New York: A. S. Barnes and Co.

Citizen [pseud.]. 1864. Letter dated 18 May, quoting the Virginia City *Territorial Enterprise* of 17 May. In "The 'Enterprise' Libel of the Ladies of Carson," Virginia City *Union,* 25, 26, and 27 May, 2. Reprinted in *L1,* 289 n. 2.

Clagett, Fred. 1990. "The Life of William H. Clagett." Paper presented on 20 April at the Pacific Northwest History Conference in Boise, Idaho. TS in CU-MARK.

Clayton, Dick. 1932? "Mark Twain and Jack Slade Entertain At Weber Stage Station in 1862." TS of six pages, an account by Dick Clayton, Coalville, Utah, retelling a narrative by Tom Rivington. U.S. Works Progress Administration, Series A, Group 3. Historical Records Survey: Utah. Transcripts of Mormon Diaries and Journals, 3–14. Manuscripts Division, DLC.

Clayton, Joshua E. 1864. "Pocket Veins." *Mining and Scientific Press* 8 (5 March): 145–46.

Clemens, Cyril. 1932. *Mark Twain the Letter Writer.* Boston: Meador Publishing Company.

Clemens, Mary Eleanor. See MEC.

Clemens, Orion. See OC.

Clemens, Samuel Langhorne. See SLC.

Coan, Titus.

1841. "Letter from Mr. Coan, Dated at Hilo, 25th Sept. 1840." *Missionary Herald* 37 (July): 283–85.

1866. "Volcanic Phenomena of the Island of Hawaii." *Friend* 17 (1 February): 9–11, 14.

1882. *Life in Hawaii: An Autobiographic Sketch of Mission Life and Labors (1835–1881).* New York: Anson D. F. Randolph and Co.

Coan, Titus Munson. 1868. "The Greatest Volcano in the World." *Harper's New Monthly Magazine* 37 (September): 553–59.

CoDR. Regis College Library, Denver, Colorado.

Cody, William F. 1879. *The Life of Hon. William F. Cody, Known as Buffalo Bill, the Famous Hunter, Scout and Guide: An Autobiography.* Hartford: Frank E. Bliss. Citations are to the 1978 reprint edition, with a foreword by Don Russell, Lincoln: University of Nebraska Press.

CofC. 1969. *Clemens of the "Call": Mark Twain in San Francisco.* Edited by Edgar M. Branch. Berkeley and Los Angeles: University of California Press.

Collins, Charles, comp. 1864–65. *Mercantile Guide and Directory for Virginia City, Gold Hill, Silver City and American City.* Virginia City: Agnew and Deffebach.

Conard, Howard L., ed. 1901. *Encyclopedia of the History of Missouri*. 6 vols. New York: Southern History Company.

Congressional Globe. 1863. "Appendix to the Congressional Globe." *Congressional Globe*, 37th Congress, 3d session. John C. Rives, comp. Washington, D.C.: Congressional Globe Office.

Conkling, Roscoe P., and Margaret B. Conkling. 1947. *The Butterfield Overland Mail, 1857–1869*. 3 vols. Glendale, Calif.: Arthur H. Clark Company.

Considine, John L.
1923a. "The Desperadoes." San Francisco *Evening Bulletin*, 20 September, Section 2, 2.

1923b. "Mark Twain." San Francisco *Evening Bulletin*, 22 September, Magazine Section, 10.

1923c. "Mark Twain Achieves Fame." San Francisco *Evening Bulletin*, 13 October, Magazine Section, 10.

Cook, James, and James King. 1784. *A Voyage to the Pacific Ocean*. 3 vols. Volumes 1 and 2 written by Captain Cook and volume 3 written by Captain King. London: G. Nicol and T. Cadell.

Cook, Lyndon W. 1981. *The Revelations of the Prophet Joseph Smith: A Historical and Biographical Commentary of the Doctrine and Covenants*. Provo, Utah: Seventy's Mission Bookstore.

Coolidge, Mary Roberts. 1909. *Chinese Immigration*. New York: Henry Holt and Co.

Copinger, Walter Arthur. 1870. *The Law of Copyright, in Works of Literature and Art*. London: Stevens and Haynes.

Cornish [pseud.]. 1860. "Washoe: Thither and Hither." San Francisco *Golden Era* 10 (15 April): 5.

Cracroft, Richard H. 1984. "'Ten Wives Is All You Need': Artemus Twain and the Mormons—Again." *Western Humanities Review* 38 (Autumn): 197–211.

Cradlebaugh, John. 1863. *Speech of Hon. John Cradlebaugh, of Nevada, on the Admission of Utah as a State. Delivered in the House of Representatives, February 7, 1863*. Washington, D.C.: L. Towers and Co.

Creer, Leland Hargrave. 1929. *Utah and the Nation*. University of Washington Publications in the Social Sciences, vol. 7. Seattle: University of Washington Press.

CSmH. Henry E. Huntington Library, San Marino, California.

CtHMTH. Mark Twain Memorial, Hartford, Connecticut.

CtHSD. Stowe-Day Memorial Library and Historical Foundation, Hartford, Connecticut.

CtY-BR. Collection of American Literature, Beinecke Rare Book and Manuscript Library, Yale University Library, New Haven, Connecticut.

CU-BANC. The Bancroft Library, University of California, Berkeley.

CU-MAPS. Map Collection, University of California, Berkeley.

CU-MARK. Mark Twain Papers, CU-BANC.

CU-NEWS. Newspaper and Microcopy Division, University of California, Berkeley.

Curry, C. F., comp. 1907. *California Blue Book or State Roster.* Sacramento: State Printing Office.

Curtis, Camphor. 1864. "The Newspapers of Virginia." Undated letter. Sacramento *Bee,* 6 January, 1.

DAB. 1928–36. *Dictionary of American Biography.* Edited by Allen Johnson and Dumas Malone. 20 vols. New York: Charles Scribner's Sons.

Daggett, Rollin M. 1893. "Daggett's Recollections," in "The Passing of a Pioneer." San Francisco *Examiner,* 22 January, 15. Reprinted as *"Enterprise* Men and Events" in Lewis, 11–16.

DAH. 1940. *Dictionary of American History.* 5 vols. New York: Charles Scribner's Sons.

Daley. Collection of Robert Daley.

Dana, James D. 1849. *Geology.* Vol. 10 of *United States Exploring Expedition. During the Years 1838, 1839, 1840, 1841, 1842. Under the Command of Charles Wilkes, U.S.N.* Philadelphia: C. Sherman.

David, Beverly R. 1986. *Mark Twain and His Illustrators: Volume I (1869–1875).* Troy, N.Y.: Whitston Publishing Company.

Davis, Chester L., Sr.
1944. "About Mark Twain's Job on the San Francisco *Call." Twainian* 3 (May):4–6.

1952a. "Mark's Letters to San Francisco Call." *Twainian* 11 (January–February): 1–4.

1952b. "Mark's Letters to San Francisco Call." *Twainian* 11 (March–April): 1–4.

1956a. "Mark Twain's Highway Robbery as Told by Steve Gillis." *Twainian* 15 (January–February): 3–4.

1956b. "Letters from Steve Gillis." *Twainian* 15 (March–April): 1–3.

1956c. "Goodman's Assistance on the Biography." *Twainian* 15 (May–June): 2–4.

1956d. "Letters from Frank Fuller." *Twainian* 15 (July–August): 1–3.

Davis, Jefferson. 1856. "Report of the Secretary of War." In *Message from the President of the United States to the Two Houses of Congress, at the Commencement of the Third Session of the Thirty-fourth Congress.* Washington, D.C.: Cornelius Wendell.

Davis, Sam P., ed. 1913. *The History of Nevada.* 2 vols. Reno: Elms Publishing Company.

Davis, Winfield J. 1893. *History of Political Conventions in California, 1849–1892.* Sacramento: California State Library.

Dawson's Book Shop. 1925. *A Catalogue of Rare Books.* No. 37 (February). Los Angeles: Dawson's Book Shop.

Decker, Robert Owen. 1976. *The Whaling City: A History of New London.* Chester, Conn.: New London County Historical Society.

DeGolyer, E. 1953. Introduction to *The Vigilantes of Montana* by Thomas J. Dimsdale, 2d ed. Norman: University of Oklahoma Press.

DeGroot, Henry.

1860. *Sketches of the Washoe Silver Mines.* San Francisco: Hutchings and Rosenfield. Citations are to the 1961 reprint edition, Morrison, Ill.: Karl Yost.

1863. *DeGroot's Map of Nevada Territory, Exhibiting a Portion of Southern Oregon & Eastern California.* San Francisco: Warren Holt.

1876a. "Comstock Papers. No. 2." *Mining and Scientific Press* 33 (29 July): 80.

1876b. "Comstock Papers. No. 5." *Mining and Scientific Press* 33 (2 September): 160.

Delaney, Wesley A. 1948. "The Truth about That Humboldt Trip as Told by Gus Oliver to A. B. Paine." *Twainian* 7 (May–June): 1–3.

Denny, William R. 1867. "*Quaker City* and Holy Land Journal." TS of 273 pages, Manuscripts Department, ViU, PH in CU-MARK.

Denton, Lynn W. 1971–72. "Mark Twain and the American Indian." *Mark Twain Journal* 16 (Winter): 1–3.

Derby, George H. [John Phoenix, pseud.].

1856. *Phoenixiana; or, Sketches and Burlesques.* New York: D. Appleton and Co.

1865. *The Squibob Papers.* New York: Carleton.

De Vinne, Theodore Low. 1901. *Correct Composition: A Treatise on Spelling, Abbreviations, the Compounding and Division of Words, the Proper Use of Figures and Numerals, Italic and Capital Letters, Notes, etc. with Observations on Punctuation and Proof-Reading.* New York: Century Company.

Dibble, Sheldon.

1839. *History and General Views of the Sandwich Islands' Mission.* New York: Taylor and Dodd.

1843. *A History of the Sandwich Islands*. Lahainaluna: Press of the Mission Seminary.

Dilke, Charles Wentworth. 1868. *Greater Britain: A Record of Travel in English-Speaking Countries during 1866 and 1867*. 2 vols. London: Macmillan and Co.

Dimsdale, Thomas J. 1866. *The Vigilantes of Montana, or Popular Justice in the Rocky Mountains. Being a Correct and Impartial Narrative of the Chase, Trial, Capture and Execution of Henry Plummer's Road Agent Band, Together with Accounts of the Lives and Crimes of Many of the Robbers and Desperadoes, the Whole Being Interspersed with Sketches of Life in the Mining Camps of the "Far West;" Forming the Only Reliable Work on the Subject Ever Offered the Public*. Virginia City, Montana Territory: Montana Post Press.

DLC. United States Library of Congress, Washington, D.C.

DNA. United States National Archives and Records Service, National Archives Library, Washington, D.C.

DNB. 1921–22. *The Dictionary of National Biography*. Edited by Sir Leslie Stephen and Sir Sidney Lee. 22 vols. London: Oxford University Press.

Doctor, The [pseud.].
1862a. "Notes of a Trip to the Humboldt Mines, Nevada Territory." Letter dated 28 September. San Francisco *Alta California*, 2 October, 1.
1862b. "Notes of a Trip to the Humboldt Mines, Nevada Territory.— No. 2." San Francisco *Alta California*, 4 October, 2.

Doctrine and Covenants. 1954. *The Doctrine and Covenants, Containing Revelations Given to Joseph Smith, Jr., the Prophet*. With an introduction and historical and exegetical notes by Hyrum M. Smith and Janne M. Sjodahl. Rev. ed. Salt Lake City: Deseret Book Company.

Dorson, Richard M. 1946. *Jonathan Draws the Long Bow*. Cambridge: Harvard University Press.

Doten, Alfred. 1973. *The Journals of Alfred Doten, 1849–1903*. Edited by Walter Van Tilburg Clark. 3 vols. Reno: University of Nevada Press.

Drury, Wells. 1936. *An Editor on the Comstock Lode*. New York: Farrar and Rinehart.

Dwight, Edwin Welles. 1819. *Memoirs of Henry Obookiah, a Native of Owhyhee, and a Member of the Foreign Mission School; Who Died at Cornwall, Conn. Feb 17, 1818, Aged 26 Years*. New Haven: Nathan Whiting.

Dwyer, Richard A., and Richard E. Lingenfelter. 1984. *Lying on the Eastern Slope: James Townsend's Comic Journalism on the Mining Frontier*. Miami: Florida International University Press.

Edwards, William B. 1953. *The Story of Colt's Revolver; the Biography of Col. Samuel Colt*. Harrisburg, Pa.: Stackpole Company.

Edwords, Clarence E. 1914. *Bohemian San Francisco: Its Restaurants and Their Most Famous Recipes. The Elegant Art of Dining*. San Francisco: Paul Elder and Co.

Elliott, Russell R. 1983. *Servant of Power: A Political Biography of Senator William M. Stewart*. Nevada Studies in History and Political Science No. 18. Reno: University of Nevada Press.

Ellis, William. 1827. *Narrative of a Tour through Hawaii, or Owhyhee*. 3d ed. London: H. Fisher, Son, and P. Jackson.

Esshom, Frank. 1913. *Pioneers and Prominent Men of Utah*. Salt Lake City: Utah Pioneers Book Publishing Company.

ET&S1. 1979. *Early Tales & Sketches, Volume 1 (1851–1864)*. Edited by Edgar Marquess Branch and Robert H. Hirst, with the assistance of Harriet Elinor Smith. The Works of Mark Twain. Berkeley, Los Angeles, London: University of California Press.

ET&S2. 1981. *Early Tales & Sketches, Volume 2 (1864–1865)*. Edited by Edgar Marquess Branch and Robert H. Hirst, with the assistance of Harriet Elinor Smith. The Works of Mark Twain. Berkeley, Los Angeles, London: University of California Press.

ET&S3. Forthcoming. *Early Tales & Sketches, Volume 3 (1866–1868)*. Edited by Edgar Marquess Branch and Richard Bucci, with the assistance of Harriet Elinor Smith. The Works of Mark Twain. Berkeley, Los Angeles, London: University of California Press.

ET&S4. Forthcoming. *Early Tales & Sketches, Volume 4 (1869–1870)*. Edited by Edgar Marquess Branch and Robert H. Hirst. The Works of Mark Twain. Berkeley, Los Angeles, London: University of California Press.

ET&S5. Forthcoming. *Early Tales & Sketches, Volume 5 (1870–1871)*. Edited by Edgar Marquess Branch and Robert H. Hirst. The Works of Mark Twain. Berkeley, Los Angeles, London: University of California Press.

Evans, Albert S. 1870. *Our Sister Republic: A Gala Trip through Tropical Mexico in 1869–70*. Hartford: Columbian Book Company.

Fatout, Paul.

1960. *Mark Twain on the Lecture Circuit*. Bloomington: Indiana University Press.

1964. *Mark Twain in Virginia City*. Bloomington: Indiana University Press.

1976. *Mark Twain Speaking*. Iowa City: University of Iowa Press.

Fife, Austin, and Alta Fife. 1956. *Saints of Sage & Saddle: Folklore among the Mormons*. Bloomington: Indiana University Press.

Fike, Richard E., and John W. Headley. 1979. *The Pony Express Stations of Utah in Historical Perspective*. Bureau of Land Management, Utah. Cultural Resources Series, Monograph 2. Washington, D.C.: Government Printing Office.

Fitch, Thomas. 1978. *Western Carpetbagger: The Extraordinary Memoirs of "Senator" Thomas Fitch*. Edited by Eric N. Moody. Reno: University of Nevada Press.

Flanders, Robert Bruce. 1965. *Nauvoo: Kingdom on the Mississippi*. Urbana: University of Illinois Press.

Fletcher, Robert H., ed. 1898. *The Annals of the Bohemian Club from Its Beginning, in the Year Eighteen Hundred and Seventy-two, to Eighteen Hundred and Eighty*, vol. 1. San Francisco: Hicks-Judd Company.

FM. 1972. *Mark Twain's Fables of Man*. Edited with an introduction by John S. Tuckey. Text established by Kenneth M. Sanderson and Bernard L. Stein. Series editor, Frederick Anderson. The Mark Twain Papers. Berkeley, Los Angeles, London: University of California Press.

Ford, Darius R.
   1870a. "Around the World. Letter Number IX. The Pacific." Letter dated 19 November 1869, signed "D. R. F." Buffalo *Express*, 12 February, 2.

   1870b. "Around the World. Letter Number X. Japan." Letter dated 17 and 24 January, signed "D. R. F." Buffalo *Express*, 5 March, 2.

Foster, Lawrence. 1981. *Religion and Sexuality: Three American Communal Experiments of the Nineteenth Century*. New York and Oxford: Oxford University Press.

Fowler, H. W. 1965. *A Dictionary of Modern English Usage*. 2d ed., revised by Sir Ernest Gowers. New York and London: Oxford University Press.

Fox, Theron. 196–. *Nevada Treasure Hunters Ghost Town Guide*. San Jose, Calif.: Theron Fox.

Frederick, J. V. 1940. *Ben Holladay, the Stagecoach King*. Glendale, Calif.: Arthur H. Clark Company.

Fried, Martin B. 1951. "The Composition, Sources, and Popularity of Mark Twain's *Roughing It*." Ph.D. diss., University of Chicago.

Fulton, Robert. 1914. "Glimpses of the Mother Lode." *Bookman* 39 (March): 49–57.

Furniss, Norman F. 1960. *The Mormon Conflict, 1850–1859*. New Haven: Yale University Press.

Gaines, David. 1981. *Mono Lake Guidebook*. Lee Vining, Calif.: Kutsavi Books.

Gamble, James. 1881. "Wiring a Continent." *The Californian: A Western Monthly Magazine* 3 (June): 556–63.

Gasinski, T. Z. 1976. "Captain John Dominis and His Son Governor John Owen Dominis: Hawaii's Croatian Connection." *Journal of Croatian Studies* 17:14–46.

Gianella, Vincent P. 1960. "The Site of Williams Station, Nevada." *Nevada Historical Society Quarterly* 3 (October–December): 5–10.

Gillis, William R. 1930. *Gold Rush Days with Mark Twain.* New York: Albert and Charles Boni.

Glasscock, Carl Burgess. 1931. *The Big Bonanza.* Indianapolis: Bobbs-Merrill Company.

Goodman, Joseph T.
1872. "Greeley and Hank Monk." Virginia City *Territorial Enterprise,* 24 July, 2.

1891. "Taming a Terror." San Francisco *Chronicle,* 27 December, 1–2.

1892a. "A Battle-Born State." San Francisco *Chronicle,* 14 February, 1.

1892b. "How Tom Peasley Died." San Francisco *Chronicle,* 21 February, 1.

Goodwin, Charles C. 1913. *As I Remember Them.* Salt Lake City: Salt Lake Commercial Club.

Gould, Alva. 1877. "An Historical sketch of Alva Goulds life since the 22nd March 1849." Carson City, Nevada. MS notebook of twenty pages, dictated, dated 29 January at Carson City, CU-BANC.

Gowans, Fred R., and Eugene E. Campbell. 1975. *Fort Bridger: Island in the Wilderness.* Provo, Utah: Brigham Young University Press.

Graham, J. B. 1915. *Handset Reminiscences: Recollections of an Old-Time Printer and Journalist.* Salt Lake City: Century Printing Company.

Graham, J. H. 1878. *Revised Ordinances of the City of Virginia, County of Storey, State of Nevada.* Virginia City: Enterprise Steam Printing House.

Gray, Harriet Helman. 1939. "A Story of Jackass Hill." TS of seventy-four pages, CU-BANC.

Greeley, Horace.
1860. *An Overland Journey, from New York to San Francisco, in the Summer of 1859.* New York: C. M. Saxton, Barker and Co.

1868. *Recollections of a Busy Life.* New York: J. B. Ford and Co.

1871. *What I Know of Farming.* New York: G. W. Carleton.

Green, Nelson Winch. 1870. *Mormonism: Its Rise, Progress, and Present Condition.* Hartford: Belknap and Bliss.

Greever, William S. 1963. *The Bonanza West: The Story of the Western Mining Rushes, 1848–1900.* Norman: University of Oklahoma Press.

Gribben, Alan. 1980. *Mark Twain's Library: A Reconstruction.* 2 vols. Boston: G. K. Hall and Co.

Gudde, Erwin G. 1962. *California Place Names: The Origin and Etymology of Current Geographical Names.* 2d ed., rev. and enl. Berkeley and Los Angeles: University of California Press.

Gunn. Collection of Mr. and Mrs. Robert M. Gunn.

Hafen, LeRoy R. 1926. *The Overland Mail 1849–1869, Promoter of Settlement, Precursor of Railroads.* Cleveland: Arthur H. Clark. Reissued in facsimile as *The Overland Mail* in 1976 by Quarterman Publications of Lawrence, Massachusetts.

Hafen, LeRoy R., and Ann W. Hafen, eds. 1958. *The Utah Expedition, 1857–1858.* Glendale, Calif.: Arthur H. Clark Company.

Hale, Richard Walden. 1930. *Sir Richard F. Burton: A Footnote to History.* Boston: Richard Walden Hale.

Hamilton, Sinclair. 1958. *Early American Book Illustrators and Wood Engravers, 1670–1870.* Princeton, N.J.: Princeton University Library.

Hanks, Sidney Alvarus, and Ephraim K. Hanks. 1948. *Scouting for the Mormons on the Great Frontier.* Salt Lake City: Deseret News Press.

H-Ar. Hawaii State Archives, Iolani Palace Grounds, Honolulu.

Harris, Helen L. 1975. "Mark Twain's Response to the Native American." *American Literature* 46 (January): 495–505.

Hart, James D. 1987. *A Companion to California.* New edition, rev. and enl. Berkeley, Los Angeles, London: University of California Press.

Harvey, Paul, ed. 1967. *The Oxford Companion to English Literature.* 4th ed., revised by Dorothy Eagle. Oxford: Clarendon Press, Oxford University Press.

Hay, John M.
  1870a. "Little-Breeches." New York *Tribune,* 19 November, 5. Reprinted in the Buffalo *Express,* 22 November, 2.

  1870b [*attributed*]. "The Western School." New York *Tribune,* 27 December, 4. Reprinted as "The Western Literati. Who They Are—What They Have Done. Their Future" in the Buffalo *Express,* 29 December, 1.

  1871. "Jim Bludso (of the Prairie Belle)." New York *Tribune,* 5 January, 5. Reprinted in the Buffalo *Express,* 7 January, 2.

Hazlitt, W. Carew. 1905. *Faiths and Folklore: A Dictionary of National Beliefs, Superstitions and Popular Customs, Past and Current, with Their Classical and Foreign Analogues, Described and Illustrated.* 2 vols. London: Reeves and Turner.

Heckendorn, John, and W. A. Wilson, comps. 1856. *Miners and Business Men's Directory for the Year Commencing January 1st, 1856. Embracing a General Directory of the Citizens of Tuolumne, and Portions of Calaveras, Stanislaus and San Joaquin Counties.* Columbia, Calif.: Columbia *Clipper.*

Hermann, Ruth. 1981. *Virginia City, Nevada, Revisited.* Sparks, Nev.: Falcon Hill Press.

HF. 1988. *Adventures of Huckleberry Finn.* Edited by Walter Blair and Victor Fischer, with the assistance of Dahlia Armon and Harriet Elinor Smith. The Works of Mark Twain. Berkeley, Los Angeles, London: University of California Press.

HHR. 1969. *Mark Twain's Correspondence with Henry Huttleston Rogers, 1893–1909.* Edited with an Introduction by Lewis Leary. Berkeley and Los Angeles: University of California Press.

Hickman, Bill. 1872. *Brigham's Destroying Angel: Being the Life, Confession, and Startling Disclosures of the Notorious Bill Hickman, the Danite Chief of Utah.* Edited by J.H. Beadle. New York: George A. Crofutt.

Hill, Donna. 1977. *Joseph Smith: The First Mormon.* Garden City, N.Y.: Doubleday and Co.

Hill, Hamlin.
1962. "Mark Twain's Quarrels with Elisha Bliss." *American Literature* 33 (January): 442–56.

1964. *Mark Twain and Elisha Bliss.* Columbia: University of Missouri Press.

1981. Introduction to *Roughing It.* New York: Penguin Books.

Hill, S. S. 1856. *Travels in the Sandwich and Society Islands.* London: Chapman and Hall.

Hilton, Hope A. 1988. *"Wild Bill" Hickman and the Mormon Frontier.* Salt Lake City: Signature Books.

Hingston, Edward P. 1871. *The Genial Showman: Being Reminiscences of the Life of Artemus Ward and Pictures of a Showman's Career in the Western World.* London: John Camden Hotten. First published in 1870 in two volumes.

Hirst, Robert H. 1975. "The Making of *The Innocents Abroad:* 1867–1872." Ph.D. diss., University of California, Berkeley.

Hitchcock, Charles H. 1909. *Hawaii and Its Volcanoes.* Honolulu: Hawaiian Gazette Company.

Hodge, Frederick Webb, ed. 1912. *Handbook of American Indians North of Mexico.* Smithsonian Institution Bureau of American Ethnology Bulletin no. 30. 2 parts. Washington, D.C.: Government Printing Office.

Hodges, A. D., Jr. 1890. *Amalgamation at the Comstock Lode, Nevada: A Historical Sketch of Milling Operations at Washoe, and an Account of the Treatment of Tailings at the Lyon Mill, Dayton.* San Francisco: Author's Edition.

Hopkins, Manley. 1862. *Hawaii: The Past, Present, and Future of Its Island-Kingdom.* London: Longman, Green, Longman, and Roberts.

Horner, Charles F. 1926. *The Life of James Redpath and the Development of the Modern Lyceum.* New York: Barse and Hopkins.

Houck, Louis. 1908. *A History of Missouri from the Earliest Explorations and Settlements until the Admission of the State into the Union.* 3 vols. Chicago: R. R. Donnelley and Sons Company.

House of the Lord. 1897. *House of the Lord: Historical and Descriptive Sketch of the Salt Lake Temple.* Salt Lake City: George Q. Cannon and Sons Company.

Howard, G. M. 1976. "Men, Motives, and Misunderstandings: A New Look at the Morrisite War of 1862." *Utah Historical Quarterly* 44 (Spring): 112–32.

Howells, William Dean. 1872. "Recent Literature." *Atlantic Monthly* 29 (June): 754–55.

Hoy, William. 1942. *The Chinese Six Companies.* San Francisco: Chinese Consolidated Benevolent Association.

HU. Thomas Hale Hamilton Library, University of Hawaii at Manoa, Honolulu.

Hunter, Louis C. 1949. *Steamboats on the Western Rivers: An Economic and Technological History.* Cambridge: Harvard University Press.

Hyde, John. 1857. *Mormonism: Its Leaders and Designs.* New York: W. P. Fetridge and Co.

IaHi. State Historical Society of Iowa, Iowa City.

IC. Chicago Public Library, Chicago, Illinois.

Inds. 1989. *Huck Finn and Tom Sawyer among the Indians, and Other Unfinished Stories.* Foreword and notes by Dahlia Armon and Walter Blair. Texts established by Dahlia Armon, Paul Baender, Walter Blair, William M. Gibson, and Franklin R. Rogers. The Mark Twain Library. Berkeley, Los Angeles, London: University of California Press.

IU. University of Illinois, Urbana.

James, George Wharton. 1911. "How Mark Twain Was Made." *National Magazine* (February): 525–37.

Jarves, James Jackson.
   1843. *History of the Hawaiian or Sandwich Islands.* London: Edward Moxon.

   1844a. *Scenes and Scenery in the Sandwich Islands, and a Trip through Central America.* London: Edward Moxon.

   1844b. *History of the Hawaiian or Sandwich Islands.* 2d ed. Boston: James Munroe and Co.

1847. *History of the Hawaiian Islands.* 3d ed. Honolulu: Charles Edwin Hitchcock.

Jenson, Andrew. 1901–36. *Latter-day Saint Biographical Encyclopedia.* 4 vols. Salt Lake City: Andrew Jenson History Company.

JI2. Iwaki Meisei University, Iwaki, Fukushima, Japan.

JLC. Jane Lampton Clemens.

Johnson, Merle. 1935. *A Bibliography of the Works of Mark Twain.* New York: Harper and Brothers.

Jones, Evelyn K., and York F. Jones. 1986. *Mayors of Cedar City.* Cedar City: Southern Utah State College.

Jorkins [pseud.]. 1868. "Jorkins at Washington." Letter dated 18 February. San Francisco *Evening Bulletin*, 14 March, 5.

Journal. 1862. *Journal of the Council of the First Legislative Assembly of the Territory of Nevada.* San Francisco: Valentine and Co.

Judd, Laura Fish. 1966. *Honolulu: Sketches of Life in the Hawaiian Islands from 1828 to 1861.* Edited by Dale L. Morgan. Chicago: R. R. Donnelley and Sons Company. First published in 1880.

Kamakau, Samuel M. 1961. *Ruling Chiefs of Hawaii.* Honolulu: The Kamehameha Schools Press.

Kelly, J. Wells, comp.
1862. *First Directory of Nevada Territory.* San Francisco: Valentine and Co.

1863. *Second Directory of Nevada Territory.* San Francisco: Valentine and Co.

Kimball, Stanley B.
1981. *Heber C. Kimball: Mormon Patriarch and Pioneer.* Urbana: University of Illinois Press.

1988. *Historic Sites and Markers along the Mormon and Other Great Western Trails.* Urbana: University of Illinois Press.

King, Moses, ed. 1893. *King's Handbook of New York City: An Outline History and Description of the American Metropolis.* 2d ed. Boston: Moses King.

Knight, William H., ed.
1863. *Hand-Book Almanac for the Pacific States: An Official Register, and Business Directory.* San Francisco: H. H. Bancroft and Co.

1864. *Hand-Book Almanac for the Pacific States: An Official Register and Business Directory.* San Francisco: H. H. Bancroft and Co.

Knox, Thomas W. 1870. *Overland through Asia.* Hartford: American Publishing Company.

Kolb, Harold J., Jr. 1984. "Mark Twain and the Myth of the West." In *The Mythologizing of Mark Twain*, edited by Sara deSaussure Davis and Philip D. Beidler. University: University of Alabama Press.

Korn, Alfons L. 1958. *The Victorian Visitors*. Honolulu: University of Hawaii Press.

Koundakjian. Collection of Theodore Koundakjian.

Kouwenhoven, John A. 1953. *The Columbia Historical Portrait of New York*. New York: Doubleday and Co.

Küstel, Guido. 1863. *Nevada and California Processes of Silver and Gold Extraction*. San Francisco: Frank D. Carlton.

Kuykendall, Ralph S.
1938. *The Hawaiian Kingdom, 1778–1854: Foundation and Transformation*. Honolulu: University of Hawaii.

1953. *The Hawaiian Kingdom, 1854–1874: Twenty Critical Years*. Honolulu: University of Hawaii Press.

1967. *The Hawaiian Kingdom, 1874–1893: The Kalakaua Dynasty*. Honolulu: University of Hawaii Press.

L1. 1988. *Mark Twain's Letters, Volume 1: 1853–1866*. Edited by Edgar Marquess Branch, Michael B. Frank, Kenneth M. Sanderson, Harriet Elinor Smith, Lin Salamo, and Richard Bucci. Berkeley, Los Angeles, London: University of California Press.

L2. 1990. *Mark Twain's Letters, Volume 2: 1867–1868*. Edited by Harriet Elinor Smith, Richard Bucci, and Lin Salamo. Berkeley, Los Angeles, London: University of California Press.

L3. 1992. *Mark Twain's Letters, Volume 3: 1869*. Edited by Victor Fischer, Michael B. Frank, and Dahlia Armon. Berkeley, Los Angeles, London: University of California Press.

L4. Forthcoming. *Mark Twain's Letters, Volume 4: 1870–1871*. Edited by Victor Fischer and Michael B. Frank. Berkeley, Los Angeles, London: University of California Press.

L5. Forthcoming. *Mark Twain's Letters, Volume 5: 1872–1873*. Edited by Lin Salamo and Harriet Elinor Smith. Berkeley, Los Angeles, London: University of California Press.

Lamb, George W. 1863. "Gold Hill Mining District, N. T." San Francisco *Evening Bulletin*, 29 December, 2.

Lang, Herbert O. 1882. *A History of Tuolumne County, California*. San Francisco: B. F. Alley.

Langford, Nathaniel Pitt. 1890. *Vigilante Days and Ways; The Pioneers of the Rockies; The Makers and Making of Montana, Idaho, Oregon, Washington, and Wyoming*. 2 vols. Boston: J. G. Cupples Company.

Langley, Henry G., comp.

1859. *The San Francisco Directory for the Year Commencing June, 1859.* San Francisco: Valentine and Co.

1860. *The San Francisco Directory for the Year Commencing July, 1860.* San Francisco: Valentine and Co.

1861. *The San Francisco Directory for the Year Commencing September, 1861.* San Francisco: Valentine and Co.

1862. *The San Francisco Directory for the Year Commencing September, 1862.* San Francisco: Valentine and Co.

1863. *The San Francisco Directory for the Year Commencing October, 1863.* San Francisco: Towne and Bacon.

1864. *The San Francisco Directory for the Year Commencing October, 1864.* San Francisco: Towne and Bacon.

1865. *The San Francisco Directory for the Year Commencing December, 1865.* San Francisco: Towne and Bacon.

1867. *The San Francisco Directory for the Year Commencing September, 1867.* San Francisco: Henry G. Langley.

Lavender, David. 1975. *Nothing Seemed Impossible: William C. Ralston and Early San Francisco.* Palo Alto, Calif.: American West Publishing Company.

1983. *Fort Laramie and the Changing Frontier.* Washington, D.C.: U.S. Department of the Interior.

Laws.

1862. *Laws of the Territory of Nevada, Passed at the First Regular Session of the Legislative Assembly.* San Francisco: Valentine and Co.

1863. *Laws of the Territory of Nevada, Passed at the Second Regular Session of the Legislative Assembly.* Virginia City: J. T. Goodman and Co.

1864. *Laws of the Territory of Nevada, Passed at the Third Regular Session of the Legislative Assembly.* Virginia City: John Church and Co.

Lean, Vincent Stuckey. 1902. *Lean's Collectanea: Proverbs (English & Foreign), Folk Lore, and Superstitions, Also Compilations towards Dictionaries of Proverbial Phrases and Words, Old and Disused.* 4 vols. Bristol, England: J. W. Arrowsmith.

Ledyard, John. 1963. *John Ledyard's Journal of Captain Cook's Last Voyage.* Edited by James Kenneth Munford. Corvallis: Oregon State University Press, 1963. Ledyard's journal first published in 1783.

Lee, John D. 1877. *Mormonism Unveiled; or, The Life and Confessions of the Late Mormon Bishop, John D. Lee; (Written by Himself).* St. Louis: Bryan, Brand and Co.

Lee, L. L. 1974. "Mark Twain's Assayer: Some Other Versions." *Markham Review* 4 (May): 47–48.

Leonowens, Anna Harriette. 1871. *The English Governess at the Siamese Court*. Boston: Osgood and Co.

Letters of Application. [1861–69] 1970. *Letters of Application and Recommendation During the Administrations of Abraham Lincoln and Andrew Johnson, 1861–1869*. National Archives Microfilm Publications, Microcopy no. M650, Roll 10. Washington, D.C.: National Archives and Records Service, General Services Administration.

Levison, Jacob B. 1933. *Memories for My Family*. San Francisco: John Henry Nash.

Levy, Lester S. 1967. *Grace Notes in American History: Popular Sheet Music from 1820 to 1900*. Norman: University of Oklahoma Press.

Lewis, Oscar. 1971. *The Life and Times of the Virginia City "Territorial Enterprise": Being Reminiscences of Five Distinguished Comstock Journalists*. Ashland, Oreg.: Lewis Osborne.

Lex. 1963. *A Mark Twain Lexicon*. By Robert L. Ramsay and Frances G. Emberson. New York: Russell and Russell.

Liljegren, S. B. 1945. "The Revolt against Romanticism in American Literature as Evidenced in the Works of S. L. Clemens." *Essays and Studies on American Language and Literature* 1:9–60.

Lillard, Richard G. 1943. "Evolution of the 'Washoe Zephyr.'" *American Speech* 18 (December): 257–60.

Lillard, Richard G., and Mary V. Hood. 1973. *Hank Monk and Horace Greeley: An Enduring Episode in Western History*. Georgetown, Calif.: Wilmac Press.

Lingenfelter, Richard E., Richard A. Dwyer, and David Cohen, comps. and eds. 1968. *Songs of the American West*. Berkeley and Los Angeles: University of California Press.

Lingenfelter, Richard E., and Karen Rix Gash. 1984. *The Newspapers of Nevada: A History and Bibliography, 1854–1979*. Reno: University of Nevada Press.

Linn, William Alexander. 1963. *The Story of the Mormons, from the Date of Their Origin to the Year 1901*. First published in 1902. New York: Russell and Russell.

Litten, Jane. 1962. "Old Poheoheo's Ghost." *Hawaii Historical Review* 1 (October): 6–8.

LLMT. 1949. *The Love Letters of Mark Twain*. Edited by Dixon Wecter. New York: Harper and Brothers.

Lloyd, B. E. 1876. *Lights and Shades in San Francisco*. San Francisco: A. L. Bancroft and Co.

Logan, Olive. 1870. "Does It Pay to Visit Yo Semite?" *Galaxy* 10 (October): 498–509.

Loomis, Noel M. 1968. *Wells Fargo*. New York: Clarkson N. Potter.

Lorch, Fred W.

1929. "Orion Clemens." *Palimpsest* 10 (October): 353–88.

1945. "Mark Twain's Early Views on Western Indians." *Twainian* 4 (April): 1–2.

1966. *The Trouble Begins at Eight: Mark Twain's Lecture Tours*. Ames: Iowa State University Press.

Lord, Eliot. 1883. *Comstock Mining and Miners*. Washington, D.C.: Government Printing Office. Citations are to the 1959 reprint edition, introduction by David F. Myrick, Berkeley: Howell-North Books.

Ludlow, Fitz Hugh. 1870. *The Heart of the Continent: A Record of Travel Across the Plains and in Oregon*. New York: Hurd and Houghton.

Lyman, George D. 1934. *The Saga of the Comstock Lode: Boom Days in Virginia City*. New York: Charles Scribner's Sons.

Lynch, Philip.

1870a. "A Case of Slanderous Vilification and Its Consequences." Gold Hill *News*, 17 January, 3.

1870b. "An Explanation Wanted." Gold Hill *News*, 1 February, 2.

McClelland, Robert. 1857. "Report of the Secretary of the Interior." In *Executive Documents Printed by Order of the House of Representatives, during the Third Session of the Thirty-fourth Congress, 1856–'57*. 13 vols. Washington, D.C.: Cornelius Wendell.

McClernan, John B. 1977. *Slade's Wells Fargo Colt (Historical Notes)*. Hicksville, N.Y.: Exposition Press.

McCue, Robert J. 1981. "Did the Word of Wisdom Become a Commandment in 1851?" *Dialogue* 14 (Autumn): 66–77.

M'Culloch, J. M. 1859. *A Manual of English Grammar, Philosophical and Practical*. 18th ed. Edinburgh: Oliver and Boyd.

McGrath, Roger D. 1984. *Gunfighters, Highwaymen & Vigilantes: Violence on the Frontier*. Berkeley, Los Angeles, London: University of California Press.

McGrew, William K. [McGrooge, pseud.]. 1865. "A Sheik on the Move." San Francisco *Morning Call*, 29 October, 3.

McHenry, Roy C., and Walter F. Roper. 1945. *Smith & Wesson Hand Guns*. Huntington, W.Va.: Standard Publications.

Mack, Effie Mona.

1936. *Nevada: A History of the State from the Earliest Times through the Civil War*. Glendale, Calif.: Arthur H. Clark Company.

1947. *Mark Twain in Nevada*. New York: Charles Scribner's Sons.

1961a. "James Warren Nye: A Biography." *Nevada Historical Society Quarterly* 4 (July–December): 9–59.

1961b. "Orion Clemens, 1825–1897: A Biography." *Nevada Historical Society Quarterly* 4 (July–December): 61–108.

MacKellar, Thomas. 1885. *The American Printer: A Manual of Typography.* 15th ed., rev. and enl. Philadelphia: MacKellar, Smiths and Jordan. Citations are to the 1977 reprint edition, Nevada City, Calif.: Harold A. Berliner.

McKiernan, F. Mark. 1971. *The Voice of One Crying in the Wilderness: Sidney Rigdon, Religious Reformer, 1793–1876.* Lawrence, Kans.: Coronado Press.

MacKinnon, Richard Malcolm. 1967. "The Historical Geography of Settlement in the Foothills of Tuolumne County, California." Master's thesis, University of California, Berkeley.

McNutt, James C. 1978. "Mark Twain and the American Indian: Earthly Realism and Heavenly Idealism." *American Indian Quarterly* 4 (August): 223–42.

Malo, David. 1903. *Hawaiian Antiquities.* Translated from the Hawaiian by Dr. N. B. Emerson. Honolulu: Hawaiian Gazette Company.

Malo, David, et al. 1839. "Ka Mooolelo Hawaii." *Hawaiian Spectator* 2 (January, April, July): 58–77, 211–31, 334–40.

Marsh, Andrew J. 1972. *Letters from Nevada Territory, 1861–1862.* Edited by William C. Miller, Russell W. McDonald, and Ann Rollins. Reno: Legislative Counsel Bureau, State of Nevada.

Marsh, Andrew J., Samuel L. Clemens, and Amos Bowman. 1972. *Reports of the 1863 Constitutional Convention of the Territory of Nevada.* Edited by William C. Miller, Eleanore Bushnell, Russell W. McDonald, and Ann Rollins. Reno: Legislative Counsel Bureau, State of Nevada.

Marshall, George M. 1864. "Our Traveler's Letters." Letter dated 3 July. Virginia City *Union,* 7 July, 1.

Marye, George Thomas, Jr. 1923. *From '49 to '83 in California and Nevada.* San Francisco: A. M. Robertson.

Mason, Dorothy. 1976. *The Pony Express in Nevada.* Compiled for the Nevada Bureau of Land Management. Carson City: Harrah's.

Mathews, Mitford M. 1951. *A Dictionary of Americanisms on Historical Principles.* 2 vols. Chicago: University of Chicago Press.

Mattes, Merrill J. 1969. *The Great Platte River Road: The Covered Wagon Mainline via Fort Kearny to Fort Laramie.* Lincoln: Nebraska State Historical Society.

Maule, William M. 1938. *A Contribution to the Geographic and Economic History of the Carson, Walker and Mono Basins in Nevada and California.* San Francisco: California Region, Forest Service, U.S. Department of Agriculture.

MB. Boston Public Library and Eastern Massachusetts Regional Public Library, Boston.

MBAt. Boston Athenaeum, Boston, Massachusetts.

MEC (Mary E. [Mollie] Clemens). 1862–66. "Mrs. Orion Clemens. 'Journal.' For 1862." Location unknown, PH of MS in CU-MARK. Partly printed in Lorch 1929, 357–59.

MH-H. Houghton Library, Harvard University, Cambridge, Massachusetts.

Michelson, Miriam. 1934. *The Wonderlode of Silver and Gold.* Boston: Stratford Company.

MiD. Detroit Public Library, Detroit, Michigan.

Millard, Bailey. 1910. "Mark Twain in San Francisco." *Bookman* 31 (June): 369–73.

Miller, William C. 1973. "Samuel L. and Orion Clemens vs. Mark Twain and His Biographers (1861–1862)." *Mark Twain Journal* 16 (Summer): 1–9.

Mining Laws. 1863. *Mining Laws of Esmeralda District, Mono County, California.* San Francisco: Towne and Bacon.

Mitchell, Wesley C. 1903. *A History of the Greenbacks.* Chicago: University of Chicago Press.

Mono County Archives. Mono County Archives, County Courthouse, Bridgeport, California.

Moody, Eric N.
1977. "Another Last Word on the Weekly Occidental." *Mark Twain Journal* 18 (Summer): 11–13.

1978. Foreword to *Western Carpetbagger: The Extraordinary Memoirs of "Senator" Thomas Fitch.* In Fitch, vii–x.

Moody, Ralph. 1967. *Stagecoach West.* New York: Thomas Y. Crowell Company.

Morgan, Dale L. 1948. "The Administration of Indian Affairs in Utah, 1851–1858." *Pacific Historical Review* 17 (November): 383–409.

Morton, Charles Ledyard. 1890. *Political Americanisms: A Glossary of Terms and Phrases Current at Different Periods in American Politics.* New York: Longmans, Green, and Co.

MoSW. Washington University, St. Louis, Missouri.

Mott, Frank Luther. 1938. *A History of American Magazines, 1850–1865.* Cambridge: Harvard University Press.

Moulton, Louise Chandler. 1872. "Literary Notes." New York *Tribune,* 10 June, 6.

MS. Manuscript.

MTA. 1924. *Mark Twain's Autobiography.* Edited by Albert Bigelow Paine. 2 vols. New York: Harper and Brothers.

MTB. 1912. *Mark Twain: A Biography.* By Albert Bigelow Paine. 3 vols. New York: Harper and Brothers. [*Volume numbers in citations are to this edition; page numbers are the same in all editions.*]

MTBus. 1946. *Mark Twain, Business Man.* Edited by Samuel Charles Webster. Boston: Little, Brown and Co.

MTE. 1940. *Mark Twain in Eruption.* Edited by Bernard DeVoto. New York: Harper and Brothers.

MTEnt. 1957. *Mark Twain of the "Enterprise."* Edited by Henry Nash Smith, with the assistance of Frederick Anderson. Berkeley and Los Angeles: University of California Press.

MTH. 1947. *Mark Twain and Hawaii.* By Walter Francis Frear. Chicago: Lakeside Press.

MtHi. Montana Historical Society, Helena.

MTHL. 1960. *Mark Twain–Howells Letters.* Edited by Henry Nash Smith and William M. Gibson, with the assistance of Frederick Anderson. 2 vols. Cambridge: Belknap Press of Harvard University Press.

MTL. 1917. *Mark Twain's Letters.* Edited by Albert Bigelow Paine. 2 vols. New York: Harper and Brothers.

MTLP. 1967. *Mark Twain's Letters to His Publishers, 1867–1894.* Edited by Hamlin Hill. The Mark Twain Papers. Berkeley and Los Angeles: University of California Press.

MTMF. 1949. *Mark Twain to Mrs. Fairbanks.* Edited by Dixon Wecter. San Marino, Calif.: Huntington Library.

MTS. 1923. *Mark Twain's Speeches.* With an introduction by Albert Bigelow Paine and an appreciation by William Dean Howells. New York: Harper and Brothers.

MTTB. 1940. *Mark Twain's Travels with Mr. Brown.* Edited by Franklin Walker and G. Ezra Dane. New York: Alfred A. Knopf.

N&J1. 1975. *Mark Twain's Notebooks & Journals, Volume I (1855–1873).* Edited by Frederick Anderson, Michael B. Frank, and Kenneth M. Sanderson. The Mark Twain Papers. Berkeley, Los Angeles, London: University of California Press.

NBu. Buffalo and Erie County Public Library, Buffalo, New York.

NBuU-PO. Poetry Library, State University of New York at Buffalo.

Neff, Andrew Love. 1940. *History of Utah 1847 to 1869.* Salt Lake City: Deseret News Press.

Neville, Amelia Ransome. 1932. *The Fantastic City: Memoirs of the Social and Romantic Life of Old San Francisco.* Boston: Houghton Mifflin Company, Riverside Press.

Newman, Mary Richardson [May Wentworth, pseud.], ed. 1867. *Poetry of the Pacific: Selections and Original Poems from the Poets of the Pacific States*. San Francisco: Pacific Publishing Company.

NhD. Dartmouth College, Hanover, New Hampshire.

NHyF. General Services Administration National Archives and Record Service, Franklin D. Roosevelt Library, Hyde Park, New York.

NN. The New York Public Library, Astor, Lenox and Tilden Foundations, New York City.

NN-B. Henry W. and Albert A. Berg Collection, NN.

Nomad [pseud.]. 1862. "Letter from Humboldt, N. T." Letter dated 17 September. Sacramento *Union*, 23 September, 1.

NPV. Jean Webster McKinney Family Papers, Francis Fitz Randolph Rare Book Room, Vassar College Library, Poughkeepsie, New York.

NRU. University of Rochester, Rochester, New York.

Nv-Ar. Nevada State Library and Archives, Division of Archives and Records, Carson City.

NvHi. Nevada State Historical Society, Reno.

NvU. University of Nevada Reno.

NvU-NSP. Nevada State Papers, NvU.

Nye-Starr, Kate. 1888. *A Self-Sustaining Woman; or, The Experience of Seventy-two Years*. Chicago: Illinois Printing and Binding Company.

OC [Orion Clemens]. 1861. "From Nevada Territory." Letter dated 19 August, signed "Carson." St. Louis *Missouri Democrat*, 16 September, 1, clipping in Scrapbook 1:40, CU-MARK. Reprinted in Rogers 1961, 47–49.

OC. Cincinnati Public Library, Cincinnati, Ohio.

OClRC. Rowfant Club, Cleveland, Ohio.

OClWHi. Western Reserve Historical Society, Cleveland, Ohio.

ODaU. Collection of Victor and Irene Murr Jacobs, Roesch Library, University of Dayton, Dayton, Ohio.

O'Dea, Thomas F. 1957. *The Mormons*. Chicago: University of Chicago Press.

Odell, George C. D. 1927–49. *Annals of the New York Stage*. 15 vols. New York: Columbia University Press.

O'Donnell, Sheryl. 1963–64. Notes for chapters 7–11 of *Roughing It* in "Notes toward an Annotated Edition of *Roughing It* by the Members of the English 400 Class, Fall 1963–64." Unpublished paper, John Carroll University, Cleveland, Ohio. Courtesy of John Melton.

OED. 1989. *The Oxford English Dictionary*. 2d ed. Prepared by J. A. Simpson and E. S. C. Weiner. Oxford: Clarendon Press.

"Official Correspondence." 1861–64. Official letters sent by Secretary Orion Clemens, Nv-Ar.

Ogden, Richard L. [Podgers, pseud.]. 1866. "Podgers' Letter from New York." Letter dated 10 December 1865. San Francisco *Alta California*, 10 January, 1.

Ohles, John F., ed. 1978. *Biographical Dictionary of American Educators.* 3 vols. Westport, Conn.: Greenwood Press.

OLC. Olivia (Livy) Langdon Clemens.

Olson, Gunder Einer. 1944. *The Story of the Volcano House.* 3d ed. Hilo, Hawaii: Hilo Tribune Herald.

Paher, Stanley W. 1970. *Nevada Ghost Towns & Mining Camps.* Berkeley: Howell-North Books.

PAM. Pamela Ann Moffett.

Parker, Hershel. 1973. "Regularizing Accidentals: The Latest Form of Heresy." *Proof* 3:1–20.

Pasko, Wesley Washington. 1894. *American Dictionary of Printing and Bookmaking.* New York: Howard Lockwood and Co. Citations are to the 1967 reprint edition, Detroit: Gale Research Company.

Paul, Almarin B. [Cosmos, pseud.]. 1864. "Affairs in Washoe." Letter dated 21 May. San Francisco *Evening Bulletin*, 25 May, 1.

PBL. Robert B. Honeyman Collection, Linderman Library, Lehigh University, Bethlehem, Pennsylvania.

PH. Photocopy.

Phillips, Michael J. 1920. "Mark Twain's Partner." *Saturday Evening Post* 193 (11 September): 22–23, 69–70, 73–74.

Poe, Edgar Allan. 1978. *Collected Works of Edgar Allan Poe.* Edited by Thomas Ollive Mabbott. 3 vols. Cambridge: Harvard University Press.

Presbrey, Frank. 1929. *The History and Development of Advertising.* Garden City, N.Y.: Doubleday, Doran and Co. Citations are to the 1968 reprint edition, New York: Greenwood Press.

Pukui, Mary Kawena, and Samuel H. Elbert. 1971. *Hawaiian Dictionary.* Honolulu: University of Hawaii Press.

Pukui, Mary Kawena, Samuel H. Elbert, and Esther T. Mookini. 1974. *Place Names of Hawaii.* Rev. and enl. ed. Honolulu: University Press of Hawaii.

Putnam, C. A. V. 1898. "Dan De Quille and Mark Twain: Reminiscences by an Old Associate Editor of Virginia City, Nevada." Salt Lake City *Tribune*, 25 April, 3.

Quartz [pseud.]. 1863. "Letter from Nevada Territory." Letter dated 1 February. San Francisco *Alta California*, 8 February, 1.

Rabb, Kate Milnor, ed. 1907. *The Wit and Humor of America.* 5 vols. Indianapolis: Bobbs-Merrill Company.

Rambler [pseud.].

1862. "Mining Prospects as Represented." Letter dated 12 September. San Francisco *Alta California,* 17 September, 1.

1863. "Letter from Nevada Territory." Letter dated 28 June. San Francisco *Alta California,* 11 July, 1.

Ransome, Frederick Leslie. 1909. *Notes on Some Mining Districts in Humboldt County, Nevada.* United States Geological Survey Bulletin no. 414. Washington, D.C.: Government Printing Office.

Rawls, James J., ed. 1980. *Dan De Quille of the Big Bonanza.* San Francisco: Book Club of California.

Reade, Alfred Arthur, ed. 1883. *Study and Stimulants; or, The Use of Intoxicants and Narcotics in Relation to Intellectual Life.* Manchester, England: Abel Heywood and Son.

Reade, Charles. 1859. *Love Me Little, Love Me Long.* New York: Harper and Brothers.

Reid, James D. 1886. *The Telegraph in America and Morse Memorial.* New York: John Polhemus.

Remy, Jules, and Julius Brenchley. 1861. *A Journey to Great-Salt-Lake City.* 2 vols. London: W. Jeffs.

Reports. 1868. *Reports of Cases Determined in the Supreme Court of the State of California,* vol. 4. San Francisco: Sumner Whitney.

RI 1972. 1972. *Roughing It.* Introduction and explanatory notes by Franklin R. Rogers. Text established and textual notes by Paul Baender. The Works of Mark Twain. Berkeley, Los Angeles, London: University of California Press.

Rice, Harvey. 1870. *Letters from the Pacific Slope; or, First Impressions.* New York: D. Appleton and Co.

Rich, Russell R. 1972. *Ensign to the Nations: A History of the Church from 1846 to the Present.* Provo, Utah: Brigham Young University Publications.

Richardson, Albert Deane. 1869. *Beyond the Mississippi: From the Great River to the Great Ocean.* 2d ed., rev. and enl. Hartford: American Publishing Company. First published in 1867.

Ringwalt, J. Luther, ed. 1871. *American Encyclopædia of Printing.* Philadelphia: Menamin and Ringwalt.

Ripley, George. 1873. "New Publications." New York *Tribune,* 31 January, 6.

Robinson, Forrest G. 1980. "Seeing the Elephant: Some Perspectives on Mark Twain's *Roughing It.*" *American Studies* 21 (Fall): 43–64.

Rodecape, Lois Foster. 1942. "Tom Maguire, Napoleon of the Stage." *California Historical Society Quarterly* 21 (March): 39–74.

Rogers, Franklin R.

1957. "Washoe's First Literary Journal." *California Historical Society Quarterly* 36 (December): 365–70.

1960. *Mark Twain's Burlesque Patterns.* Dallas: Southern Methodist University Press.

1961. *The Pattern for Mark Twain's Roughing It: Letters from Nevada by Samuel and Orion Clemens, 1861–1862.* Berkeley and Los Angeles: University of California Press.

Root, Frank A., and William Elsey Connelley. 1901. *The Overland Stage to California.* Topeka, Kans.: Published by the Authors. Citations are to the 1970 reprint edition, Glorieta, N.Mex.: Rio Grande Press.

Roper, Gordon. 1966. "Mark Twain and His Canadian Publishers: A Second Look." *Papers of the Bibliographical Society of Canada* 5:30–89.

Rowell, George P. 1869. *Geo. P. Rowell & Co's American Newspaper Directory.* New York: George P. Rowell and Co.

Rowlette, Robert. 1973. "'Mark Ward on Artemus Twain': Twain's Literary Debt to Ward." *American Literary Realism* 6 (Winter): 13–25.

RPB-JH. John Hay Library of Rare Books and Special Collections, Brown University, Providence, Rhode Island.

Rusling, James F. 1875. *Across America: or, The Great West and the Pacific Coast.* New York: Sheldon and Co.

Russell, Israel C. 1889. *Quaternary History of Mono Valley, California.* Washington, D.C.: Government Printing Office.

Sage Brush [pseud.]. 1864. "Humboldt Correspondence." Letter dated 11 February. Undated clipping from the Oroville (Calif.) *Union Record,* Bancroft Scraps, Set W (Nevada Mining), 94:1:208–9, CU-BANC.

Sahab [pseud.]. 1863. "The Esmeralda Region." Letter dated 24 January. San Francisco *Evening Bulletin,* 3 February, 1.

S&B. 1967. *Mark Twain's Satires & Burlesques.* Edited by Franklin R. Rogers. Berkeley and Los Angeles: University of California Press.

Sandburg, Carl. 1927. *The American Songbag.* New York: Harcourt, Brace and Co.

Sandmeyer, Elmer Clarence. 1939. *The Anti-Chinese Movement in California.* Urbana: University of Illinois Press.

Sanger, George P., ed. 1871. *The Statutes at Large and Proclamations of the United States of America, from December 1869 to March 1871, and Treaties and Postal Conventions.* Boston: Little, Brown, and Co.

Schindler, Harold. 1983. *Orrin Porter Rockwell: Man of God, Son of Thunder.* 2d ed. Salt Lake City: University of Utah Press.

Scott, Edward B. 1968. *The Saga of the Sandwich Islands.* Crystal Bay, Nev.: Sierra-Tahoe Publishing Company.

Sheldon, Addison E. 1930. "Old Fort Kearny," an appendix to Lillian M. Willman, "The History of Fort Kearny." *Publications of the Nebraska State Historical Society* 21: 211–318.

Shinn, Charles Howard. 1896. *The Story of the Mine, as Illustrated by the Great Comstock Lode of Nevada.* New York: D. Appleton and Co.

Shuck, Oscar T., ed. 1870. *Representative and Leading Men of the Pacific.* San Francisco: Bacon and Co.

Shuck, Oscar T., et al., eds. 1875. *Sketches of Leading and Representative Men of San Francisco.* London: London and New York Publishing Company.

Simmons, A. J. 1861. "The Humboldt Mines." Sacramento *Union*, 15 November, 1.

Singer, Isidore, ed. 1901–6. *The Jewish Encyclopedia.* 12 vols. New York and London: Funk and Wagnalls Company.

SLC (Samuel Langhorne Clemens).

1861. "Nevada Correspondence." Letter dated 26 October. Keokuk *Gate City*, 20 November, 2. Reprinted in *L1*, 136–40.

1862a. "Model Letter from Nevada." Letter dated 30 January. Keokuk *Gate City*, 6 March, 4. Reprinted in *L1*, 146–52.

1862b. Letter dated 20 March. Keokuk *Gate City*, 25 June, 1. Reprinted in *L1*, 174–80.

1862c [*attributed*]. Letter dated 13 July, in "Late from Washoe." Sacramento *Union*, 22 July, 2, reprinting the Virginia City *Territorial Enterprise* of 20 July.

1862d [*attributed*]. "A Gale." Oroville (Calif.) *Butte Record*, 11 October, 2, reprinting the Virginia City *Territorial Enterprise* of 1 October. Reprinted in *ET&S1*, 389.

1862e [*attributed*]. "The Indian Troubles on the Overland Route." Marysville (Calif.) *Appeal*, 5 October, reprinting the Virginia City *Territorial Enterprise* of 1 October. Reprinted in *ET&S1*, 390–91.

1862f [*attributed*]. ["More Indian Troubles."] Marysville (Calif.) *Appeal*, 5 October, reprinting the Virginia City *Territorial Enterprise* of 1 October. Reprinted in *ET&S1*, 391.

1862g. "The Spanish Mine." Oroville (Calif.) *Butte Record*, 1 November, 1, reprinting the Virginia City *Territorial Enterprise* of unknown date, probably late October. Reprinted in *ET&S1*, 160–66.

1862h. "Letter from Carson." Virginia City *Territorial Enterprise*, 12 December, clipping in Scrapbook 1:60, CU-MARK. Reprinted in *MTEnt*, 38–41.

1862i [*attributed*]. "Particulars of the Assassination of Jack Williams." San Francisco *Morning Call*, 14 December, 2, reprinting the Virginia City *Territorial Enterprise* of 10–12 December.

1862j [*attributed*]. "Blown Down." Virginia City *Territorial Enterprise*, 30 or 31 December, clipping in Scrapbook 4:14, CU-MARK. Reprinted in *ET&S1*, 393–94.

1863a. "The Spanish." Undated clipping from the Virginia City *Territorial Enterprise* (probably 12 or 22 February), Grant Smith Papers, carton 3, box 4, CU-BANC. Reprinted in *ET&S1*, 167–68.

1863b. "Silver Bars—How Assayed." Stockton (Calif.) *Independent*, 26 February, 1, reprinting the Virginia City *Territorial Enterprise* of 17–22 February. Reprinted in *ET&S1*, 210–14.

1863c. "City Marshal Perry." Rabb, 5:1809–13, reprinting the Virginia City *Territorial Enterprise* of 4 March. Reprinted in *ET&S1*, 233–38.

1863d. "Frightful Accident to Dan De Quille." San Francisco *Golden Era* 12 (1 May): 5, reprinting the Virginia City *Territorial Enterprise* of 20 April. Reprinted in *ET&S1*, 357–61.

1863e. "'Mark Twain's' Letter." Letter dated 5 July. San Francisco *Morning Call*, 9 July, 1. Reprinted in *ET&S1*, 254–58.

1863f. "'Mark Twain's' Letter." Letter dated 12 July. San Francisco *Morning Call*, 15 July, 1. Reprinted in Chester L. Davis 1952a, 2–3.

1863g. "'Mark Twain's' Letter." Letter dated 16 July. San Francisco *Morning Call*, 18 July, 1. Reprinted in Chester L. Davis 1952a, 3.

1863h [*attributed*]. "Particulars of the Recent 'Cave' of the Mexican and Ophir Mines." San Francisco *Evening Bulletin*, 21 July, 1, reprinting the Virginia City *Territorial Enterprise* of 16 July.

1863i. "'Mark Twain's' Letter." Letter dated 19 July. San Francisco *Morning Call*, 23 July, 1. Reprinted in Chester L. Davis 1952a, 3–4.

1863j [*attributed*]. Extracts published in *Mining and Scientific Press* 6 (27 July): 1, reprinting the Virginia City *Territorial Enterprise* of 14–17 July.

1863k. "'Mark Twain's' Letter." Letter dated 2 August. San Francisco *Morning Call*, 6 August, 1. Partly reprinted in Chester L. Davis 1944, 5.

1863l. "'Mark Twain's' Letter." Letter dated 8 August. San Francisco *Morning Call*, 13 August, 1. Reprinted in Chester L. Davis 1952b, 3.

1863m. "Letter from Mark Twain." Letter dated "Tuesday Afternoon" [18 August]. Virginia City *Territorial Enterprise*, 19 August, clipping in Scrapbook 2:62, CU-MARK. Reprinted in *MTEnt*, 66–70.

1863n [*attributed*]. "Ye Bulletin Cyphereth." Virginia City *Territorial Enterprise*, 27 August, clipping in Scrapbook 2:70, CU-MARK. Reprinted in *ET&S1*, 414–17.

1863o. "The Virginia City Fire." Dispatch dated 28 August. San Francisco *Morning Call*, 29 August. Reprinted in *CofC*, 287.

1863p. "'Mark Twain's' Letter." Letter dated 20 August. San Francisco *Morning Call*, 30 August, Supplement, 1. Reprinted in *ET&S1*, 277–83.

1863q. "Jack McNabb Shooting Policeman." Dispatch dated 2 September. San Francisco *Morning Call*, 3 September, 1. Reprinted in *CofC*, 287.

1863r. "Bigler *vs.* Tahoe." San Francisco *Golden Era* 11 (13 September): 3, reprinting the Virginia City *Territorial Enterprise* of 4–5 September. Reprinted in *ET&S1*, 288–90.

1863s. "How to Cure a Cold." San Francisco *Golden Era* 11 (20 September): 8. Reprinted in *ET&S1*, 296–303.

1863t. "Mark Twain—More of Him." San Francisco *Golden Era* 11 (27 September): 3, reprinting (with an addition) the Virginia City *Territorial Enterprise* of 21–24 June. Reprinted in *ET&S1*, 304–12.

1863u. "The Lick House Ball." San Francisco *Golden Era* 11 (27 September): 4. Reprinted in *ET&S1*, 313–19.

1863v. "The Great Prize Fight." San Francisco *Golden Era* 11 (11 October): 8. Reprinted in Walker 1938, 24–31.

1863w. "First Annual Fair of the Washoe Agricultural, Mining and Mechanical Society." Letter dated 19 October. Virginia City *Territorial Enterprise*, 20 October, clipping in Scrapbook 2:99–101, CU-MARK. Partly reprinted in *MTEnt*, 80–86.

1863x [*attributed*]. Letter from Dayton, written between November 1863 and February 1864. Glasscock, 122–23, reprinting the Virginia City *Territorial Enterprise* of unknown date, sometime between November 1863 and March 1864. Reprinted in *ET&S1*, 418–19.

1863y. "Letter from Mark Twain." Letter dated 12 December. Virginia City *Territorial Enterprise*, 15 December, clipping in Scrapbook 3:42–43, CU-MARK. Reprinted in *MTEnt*, 95–100.

1864a. "Doings in Nevada." Letter dated 4 January. New York *Sunday Mercury*, 7 February, 3. Reprinted in *MTEnt*, 121–26.

1864b. "Legislative Proceedings. . . . House—Thirty-first Day." Virginia City *Territorial Enterprise*, 12 February, clipping in Scrapbook 3:106, CU-MARK. Partly reprinted in *MTEnt*, 154–55.

1864c. "Letter from Mark Twain." Letter dated "Monday" [25 April]. Virginia City *Territorial Enterprise*, 28 April, clipping in Scrapbook 3:144, CU-MARK. Reprinted in *MTEnt*, 178–82.

1864d [*attributed*]. "Grand Austin Sanitary Flour-Sack Progress through Storey and Lyon Counties." San Francisco *Evening Bulletin*, 19 May, 5, reprinting the Virginia City *Territorial Enterprise* of 17 May.

1864e [*attributed*]. "Travels and Fortunes of the Great Austin Sack of Flour." San Francisco *Evening Bulletin*, 20 May, 1, incorporating a report from the Virginia City *Territorial Enterprise* of 18 May.

1864f. "Washoe.—'Information Wanted.'" San Francisco *Golden Era* 12 (22 May): 5, reprinting the Virginia City *Territorial Enterprise* of 1–14 May. Reprinted in *ET&S1*, 365–71.

1864g [*attributed*]. "Anticipating the Gridley Flour-Sack History." San Francisco *Evening Bulletin*, 26 May, 2, reprinting the Virginia City *Territorial Enterprise* of unknown date, probably mid-May.

1864h. "'Mark Twain' in the Metropolis." San Francisco *Golden Era* 12 (26 June): 3, reprinting the Virginia City *Territorial Enterprise* of 17–23 June. Reprinted in *ET&S2*, 9–12.

1864i. "The Evidence in the Case of Smith *vs.* Jones." San Francisco *Golden Era* 12 (26 June): 4. Reprinted in *ET&S2*, 13–21.

1864j. "Early Rising, As Regards Excursions to the Cliff House." San Francisco *Golden Era* 12 (3 July): 4. Reprinted in *ET&S2*, 22–30.

1864k [*attributed*]. "Stocks Down." San Francisco *Morning Call*, 28 July, 3.

1864l [*attributed*]. "What Goes with the Money?" San Francisco *Morning Call*, 19 August, 2. Reprinted in *ET&S2*, 454–55.

1864m. "The New Chinese Temple." San Francisco *Morning Call*, 19 August, 3. Reprinted in *ET&S2*, 38–43, and in *CofC*, 77–80.

1864n [*attributed*]. "Suit against a Mining Superintendent." San Francisco *Morning Call*, 20 August, 2, clipping in Scrapbook 5:41, CU-MARK.

1864o. "The Chinese Temple." San Francisco *Morning Call*, 21 August, 1. Reprinted in *ET&S2*, 44, and in *CofC*, 81.

1864p. "The New Chinese Temple." San Francisco *Morning Call*, 23 August, 3. Reprinted in *ET&S2*, 45–46, and in *CofC*, 81–83.

1864q. "Supernatural Impudence." San Francisco *Morning Call*, 24 August, 2. Reprinted in *ET&S2*, 47–48, and in *CofC*, 84.

1864r [*attributed*]. "The Californian." San Francisco *Morning Call*, 4 September, 3. Reprinted in *ET&S2*, 470.

1864s [*attributed*]. "Answer in a Mining Company's Suit." San Francisco *Morning Call*, 28 September, 1.

1864t. "A Notable Conundrum." *Californian* 1 (1 October): 9. Reprinted in *ET&S2*, 66–71.

1864u. "Concerning the Answer to That Conundrum." *Californian* 1 (8 October): 1. Reprinted in *ET&S2*, 72–78.

1864v. "Still Further Concerning That Conundrum." *Californian* 1 (15 October): 1. Reprinted in *ET&S2*, 79–85.

1864w. "Whereas." *Californian* 1 (22 October): 1. Reprinted in *ET&S2*, 86–93.

1864x. "A Touching Story of George Washington's Boyhood." *Californian* 1 (29 October): 1. Reprinted in *ET&S2*, 94–99.

1864y. "Daniel in the Lion's Den—and Out Again All Right." *Californian* 1 (5 November): 9. Reprinted in *ET&S2*, 100–107.

1864z. "The Killing of Julius Cæsar 'Localized.'" *Californian* 1 (12 November): 1. Reprinted in *ET&S2*, 108–15.

1864aa. "A Full and Reliable Account of the Extraordinary Meteoric Shower of Last Saturday Night." *Californian* 1 (19 November): 9. Reprinted in *ET&S2*, 116–24.

1864bb. "Lucretia Smith's Soldier." *Californian* 2 (3 December): 9. Reprinted in *ET&S2*, 125–33.

1865a. "An Unbiased Criticism." *Californian* 2 (18 March): 8–9. Reprinted in *ET&S2*, 134–43.

1865b. "San Francisco's New Toy." San Francisco *Morning Call*, 16 May, 1, reprinting the Virginia City *Territorial Enterprise* of unknown date, sometime after 6 April.

1865c. "Important Correspondence." *Californian* 2 (6 May): 9. Reprinted in *ET&S2*, 144–56.

1865d. "Further of Mr. Mark Twain's Important Correspondence." *Californian* 2 (13 May): 9. Reprinted in *ET&S2*, 157–62.

1865e. "How I Went to the Great Race Between Lodi and Norfolk." *Californian* 3 (27 May): 9. Reprinted in *ET&S2*, 163–68.

1865f. "A Voice for Setchell." *Californian* 3 (27 May): 9. Reprinted in *ET&S2*, 169–73.

1865g. "Advice for Good Little Boys." San Francisco *California Youths' Companion* 2 (3 June): 213. Reprinted in *ET&S2*, 240–42 (misdated 1 July).

1865h. "Answers to Correspondents." *Californian* 3 (3 June): 4. Reprinted in *ET&S2*, 174–80.

1865i. "Answers to Correspondents." *Californian* 3 (10 June): 9. Reprinted in *ET&S2*, 181–86.

1865j. "Answers to Correspondents." *Californian* 3 (17 June): 4–5. Reprinted in *ET&S2*, 187–96.

1865k. "Enthusiastic Eloquence." San Francisco *Dramatic Chronicle*, 23 June, 2. Reprinted in *ET&S2*, 233–35.

1865*l*. "Advice for Good Little Girls." San Francisco *California Youths' Companion* 2 (24 June): 237. Reprinted in *ET&S2*, 243–45 (misdated 1 or 8 July).

1865m. "Answers to Correspondents." *Californian* 3 (24 June): 4–5. Reprinted in *ET&S2*, 197–207.

1865n. "Just 'One More Unfortunate.'" Downieville (Calif.) *Mountain Messenger*, 1 July, reprinting the Virginia City *Territorial Enterprise* of 27–30 June. Reprinted in *ET&S2*, 236–39.

1865o. "Answers to Correspondents." *Californian* 3 (1 July): 4–5. Reprinted in *ET&S2*, 208–18.

1865p. "Mark Twain on the Colored Man." San Francisco *Golden Era* 13 (23 July): 2, reprinting the Virginia City *Territorial Enterprise* of 7–19 July. Reprinted in *ET&S2*, 246–49.

1865q. "Answers to Correspondents." *Californian* 3 (8 July): 4–5. Reprinted in *ET&S2*, 219–32.

1865r. "The Facts." *Californian* 3 (26 August): 5. Reprinted in *ET&S2*, 250–61.

1865s. "The Cruel Earthquake." Gold Hill *News*, 13 October, 2, reprinting the Virginia City *Territorial Enterprise* of 10–11 October. Reprinted in *ET&S2*, 289–93.

1865t. "Popper Defieth Ye Earthquake." Virginia City *Territorial Enterprise*, 15–31 October, clipping in **YSMT**, 38A–39. Reprinted in *ET&S2*, 294–96.

1865u. "Earthquake Almanac." San Francisco *Dramatic Chronicle*, 17 October, 3. Reprinted in *ET&S2*, 297–99.

1865v. "Real Estate *versus* Imaginary Possessions, Poetically Considered." *Californian* 3 (28 October): 5. Reprinted in *ET&S3*.

1865w. "'Mark Twain' On the Ballad Infliction." *Californian* 3 (4 November): 7, reprinting the *Territorial Enterprise* of 28 October–2 November. Reprinted in Benson, 194–95, and in *ET&S3*.

1865x. "San Francisco Correspondence." Letter dated 8 November. Napa (Calif.) *Napa County Reporter*, 11 November, 2. Reprinted in *ET&S3*.

1865y. "Jim Smiley and His Jumping Frog." New York *Saturday Press* 4 (18 November): 248–49. Reprinted in *ET&S2*, 282–88.

1865z. "'Mark Twain' on the Launch of the Steamer 'Capital.'" *Californian* 3 (18 November): 9. Reprinted in *ET&S2*, 359–66.

1865aa. "The Great Earthquake in San Francisco." New York *Weekly Review* 16 (25 November): 5. Reprinted in *ET&S2*, 300–310.

1865bb. "Mark Twain's Letters. Number 1." Letter dated 23 November. Napa (Calif.) *Napa County Reporter*, 25 November, 2. Reprinted partly in *ET&S2*, 371–75, and partly in *ET&S3*.

1865cc. "Mark Twain's Letters." Letter dated 30 November. Napa (Calif.) *Napa County Reporter*, 2 December, 2. Reprinted partly in *ET&S2*, 380–84, and partly in *ET&S3*.

1865dd. "The Christmas Fireside." *Californian* 4 (23 December): 4. Reprinted in *ET&S2*, 405–10.

1865ee. "Enigma." *Californian* 4 (23 December): 4. Reprinted in *ET&S2*, 411–12.

1865ff. "San Francisco Letter." Letter dated 23 December. Virginia City *Territorial Enterprise*, 26–28 December, clipping in **YSMT**, 55–56. Reprinted partly in *ET&S2*, 413–15, and partly in *ET&S3*.

1866a. "San Francisco Letter." Letter dated 29 December 1865. Virginia City *Territorial Enterprise*, 3 January. Reprinted in *ET&S3*.

1866b. "Romance in Real Life." Redwood City *San Mateo County Gazette*, 6 January, 1, reprinting the Virginia City *Territorial Enterprise* of 2–4 January. Reprinted in *ET&S3*.

1866c. "San Francisco Letter." Letter dated 28 January. Virginia City *Territorial Enterprise*, 30–31 January. Reprinted in *ET&S3*.

1866d. "San Francisco Letter." Letter dated 12 February. Virginia City *Territorial Enterprise*, 15–16 February. Reprinted in *ET&S3*.

1866e. "An Open Letter to the American People." New York *Weekly Review* 17 (17 February): 1. Reprinted in *ET&S3*.

1866f. "San Francisco Letter." Letter dated 23 February. Virginia City *Territorial Enterprise*, 25–28 February, clipping in **YSMT**, 42–42A. Reprinted in *ET&S3*.

1866g. "Letter from Mark Twain." Letter dated 25 February. Virginia City *Territorial Enterprise*, 27 February–1 March, clipping in **YSMT**, 39. Reprinted in *ET&S3*.

1866h. "The Mysterious Bottle of Whiskey." New York *Saturday Press* 5 (3 March): 3. Reprinted in *ET&S3*.

1866i. "San Francisco to Sandwich Islands—No. 1." Letter dated 18 March. Sacramento *Union*, 16 April, 5, clippings in Scrapbook 6:107–8 and Scrapbook 7:37, CU-MARK. Reprinted in *MTH*, 262–64.

1866j. "San Francisco to Sandwich Islands—No. 2." Letter dated 19 March. Sacramento *Union*, 17 April, 2, clippings in Scrapbook 6:108 and Scrapbook 7:37–39, CU-MARK. Reprinted in *MTH*, 265–69.

1866k. "San Francisco to Sandwich Islands—No. 3." Letter dated March. Sacramento *Union*, 18 April, 2, clippings in Scrapbook 6:109 and Scrapbook 7:39–41, CU-MARK. Reprinted in *MTH*, 270–73.

1866*l*. "Scenes in Honolulu—No. 4." Letter dated March. Sacramento *Union*, 19 April, 2, clippings in Scrapbook 6:109–10 and Scrapbook 7:41–43, CU-MARK. Reprinted in *MTH*, 274–78.

1866m. "Scenes in Honolulu—No. 5." Letter dated March. Sacramento *Union*, 20 April, 2, clippings in Scrapbook 6:110–11 and Scrapbook 7:43, CU-MARK. Reprinted in *MTH*, 279–83; partially reprinted in *ET&S3*.

1866n. "Scenes in Honolulu—No. 6." Letter dated March. Sacramento *Union*, 21 April, 3, clippings in Scrapbook 6:111–12 and Scrapbook 7:43–47, CU-MARK. Reprinted in *MTH*, 284–90.

1866o. "Scenes in Honolulu—No. 7." Letter dated March. Sacramento *Union*, 24 April, 4, clipping in Scrapbook 6:112–13, CU-MARK. Reprinted in *MTH*, 291–95.

1866p. "Scenes in Honolulu—No. 8." Letter dated April. Sacramento *Union*, 21 May, 3. Reprinted in *MTH*, 296–301.

1866q. "Scenes in Honolulu—No. 9." Letter dated April. Sacramento *Union*, 22 May, 3, clipping in Scrapbook 6:113–14, CU-MARK. Reprinted in *MTH*, 302–7.

1866r. "Scenes in Honolulu—No. 10." Letter dated April. Sacramento *Union*, 23 May, 3, clipping in Scrapbook 6:114–15, CU-MARK. Reprinted in *MTH*, 308–12.

1866s. "Scenes in Honolulu—No. 11." Letter dated April. Sacramento *Union*, 24 May, 3, clipping in Scrapbook 6:115–16, CU-MARK. Reprinted in *MTH*, 313–17.

1866t. "A Strange Dream." *Saturday Press* 5 (2 June): 1–2. Reprinted in *ET&S3*.

1866u. ["At the Volcano."] Entry dated 7 June in the Volcano House Register (q.v.). The two leaves containing the entry (pp. 75–78) were removed from the book sometime after 1912 and are now lost, but its text survives in two transcriptions. Published in *MTH*, 126–27, and in *ET&S3*.

1866v. "Scenes in Honolulu—No. 12." Letter dated 23 May. Sacramento *Union*, 20 June, 1, clipping in Scrapbook 6:116–17, CU-MARK. Reprinted in *MTH*, 318–22.

1866w. "Scenes in Honolulu—No. 13." Letter dated 23 May. Sacramento *Union*, 21 June, 3, clipping in Scrapbook 6:117–18, CU-MARK. Reprinted in *MTH*, 323–27.

1866x. "Scenes in Honolulu—No. 13." Letter dated 22 June, number 14 in the sequence. Sacramento *Union*, 16 July, 3, clipping in Scrapbook 6:118–19, CU-MARK. Reprinted in *MTH*, 328–34.

1866y. "Letter from Honolulu." Letter dated 25 June, number 15 in the sequence. Sacramento *Union*, 19 July, 1, clipping in Scrapbook 6:119–21, CU-MARK. Reprinted in *MTH*, 335–47.

1866z. "Scenes in Honolulu—No. 14." Letter dated 30 June, number 16 in the sequence. Sacramento *Union*, 30 July, 1, clipping in Scrapbook 6:121–22, CU-MARK. Reprinted in *MTH*, 348–55.

1866aa. "Scenes in Honolulu—No. 15." Letter dated 1 July, number 17 in the sequence. Sacramento *Union*, 1 August, 1, clipping in Scrapbook 6:122–23, CU-MARK. Reprinted in *MTH*, 356–64.

1866bb. "Letter from Honolulu." Letter dated July, number 18 in the sequence. Sacramento *Union*, 18 August, 1. Reprinted in *MTH*, 365–71.

1866cc. "From the Sandwich Islands." Letter dated July, number 19 in the sequence. Sacramento *Union*, 24 August, 3. Reprinted in *MTH*, 372–78.

1866dd. ["The Moral Phenomenon."] *Californian* 5 (25 August): 9. Reprinted in *ET&S3*.

1866ee. "From the Sandwich Islands." Letter dated 1866, number 20 in the sequence. Sacramento *Union*, 30 August, 3. Reprinted in *MTH*, 379–83.

1866ff. "From the Sandwich Islands." Letter dated July, number 21 in the sequence. Sacramento *Union*, 6 September, 3. Reprinted in *MTH*, 384–90.

1866gg. "From the Sandwich Islands." Letter dated July, number 22 in the sequence. Sacramento *Union*, 22 September, 1. Reprinted in *MTH*, 391–97.

1866hh. "From the Sandwich Islands." Letter dated 10 September, number 23 in the sequence. Sacramento *Union*, 26 September, 1. Reprinted in *MTH*, 398–407.

1866ii. "How, For Instance?" New York *Weekly Review* 17 (29 September): 1. Reprinted in *ET&S3*.

1866jj. "Origin of Illustrious Men." *Californian* 5 (29 September): 8. Reprinted in *ET&S3*.

1866kk. MS of sixty-six pages, a draft of the Sandwich Islands lecture, together with related fragmentary notes or drafts, Daley. Mark Twain first delivered this lecture on 2 October in San Francisco. Partly published in *MTS*, 7–20.

1866ll. Advertisement, San Francisco *Dramatic Chronicle*, 2 October, 3. Reprinted in *MTB*, 1:292.

1866mm. "An Epistle from Mark Twain." Letter dated 24 September. Honolulu *Hawaiian Herald*, 17 October, 1. Reprinted in *MTH*, 460–61, and in *ET&S3*.

1866nn. "From the Sandwich Islands." Letter dated June, number 24 in the sequence. Sacramento *Union*, 25 October, 1. Reprinted in *MTH*, 408–15.

1866oo. "Card to the Highwaymen." Virginia City *Territorial Enterprise*, 11 November, 3. Reprinted in *ET&S3*.

1866pp. "Letter from Honolulu." Letter dated 3 June, number 25 in the sequence. Sacramento *Union*, 16 November, 1. Reprinted in *MTH*, 416–20.

1866qq. "Forty-three Days in an Open Boat." *Harper's New Monthly Magazine* 34 (December): 104–13.

1866rr. "Mark Twain's Interior Notes—No. 2." San Francisco *Evening Bulletin*, 6 December, 1. Reprinted in Benson, 204–7, and in *ET&S3*.

1867a. *The Celebrated Jumping Frog of Calaveras County, And other Sketches.* Edited by John Paul. New York: C. H. Webb.

1867b. "Letter from 'Mark Twain.' Number 2." Letter dated 20 December 1866 on "Steamer 'Columbia.'" San Francisco *Alta California*, 22 February, 1. Reprinted in *MTTB*, 20–27.

1867c. "Letter from 'Mark Twain.' Number 3." Letter dated 23 December 1866. San Francisco *Alta California*, 24 February, 1. Reprinted in *MTTB*, 28–33.

1867d. "Letter from 'Mark Twain.' Number IV." Letter dated "Christmas Eve" 1866. San Francisco *Alta California*, 15 March, 1. Reprinted in *MTTB*, 34–45.

1867e. "Letter from 'Mark Twain.' [No. 14.]" Letter dated 16 April. San Francisco *Alta California*, 26 May, 1. Reprinted in *MTTB*, 141–48.

1867f. "Letter from 'Mark Twain.' [No. 15.]" Letter dated 19 April. San Francisco *Alta California*, 2 June, 1. Reprinted in part in *MTTB*, 149–58.

1867g. "Letter from 'Mark Twain.' [No. 18.]" Letter dated 18 May. San Francisco *Alta California*, 23 June, 1. Reprinted in part in *MTTB*, 180–91.

1867h. "Letter from 'Mark Twain.' [No. 20.]" Letter dated 20 May. San Francisco *Alta California*, 7 July, 1. Reprinted in *MTTB*, 202–13.

1867i. "Letter from 'Mark Twain.' [No. 22.]" Letter dated 26 May. San Francisco *Alta California*, 21 July, 1. Reprinted in *MTTB*, 226–37.

1867j. "Letter from 'Mark Twain.' [No. 25.]" Letter dated 5 June. San Francisco *Alta California*, 11 August, 1. Reprinted in *MTTB*, 259–69.

1867k. "The Holy Land Excursion. Letter from 'Mark Twain.' [Number Twenty-eight.]" Letter dated 12 September. San Francisco *Alta California*, 4 December, 1. Reprinted in *TIA*, 183–88.

1868a. "Mark Twain's Letters from Washington. Number II." Letter dated 16 December 1867. Virginia City *Territorial Enterprise*, 7 January, no page, PH in Willard S. Morse Collection, CtY-BR.

1868b. "Letter from 'Mark Twain.' Home Again." Letter dated 20 November 1867. San Francisco *Alta California*, 8 January, 1. Reprinted in *TIA*, 309–13.

1868c. "Assaying in Nevada." Incomplete MS of nineteen pages, written sometime in May, catalogued as A3, NPV. Bracketed words within quotations were supplied by a twelve-page typed transcript containing readings no longer visible in the MS, also catalogued as A3, NPV.

1868d. "I Rise to a Question of Privilege." MS of fifteen pages, written ca. 18–23 May for the San Francisco *News Letter and California Advertiser*, although left unpublished, a discussion of reverence versus ridicule, catalogued as A15, NPV. Published in *ET&S3*.

1868e. "Letter from Mark Twain." Letter dated 2 May. Chicago *Republican*, 31 May, 2.

1868f. "Remarkable Sagacity of a Cat." MS of four pages, probably written in June, catalogued as A4, NPV. Published in *ET&S3*.

1868g. "The Treaty with China." New York *Tribune*, 4 August, 1–2.

1868h. "Letter from Mark Twain." Letter dated 17 August. Chicago *Republican*, 23 August, 2.

1868i. "Cannibalism in the Cars." *Broadway: A London Magazine* (November): 189–94. Reprinted in *ET&S3*.

1868j. "Private Habits of Horace Greeley." *Spirit of the Times* 19 (7 November): 192.

1869a. *The Innocents Abroad; or, The New Pilgrims' Progress.* Hartford: American Publishing Company.

1869b. "The White House Funeral." Written on 7 March for the New York *Tribune*, but not then published. First published in *L3*, 458–66. One sheet of *Tribune* galley proof, CU-MARK.

1869c. "Scenery." MS of eleven pages, written in late June or early July as part of a lecture on "Curiosities of California," CU-MARK. Published in Wecter 1948, 13–17, and *ET&S4*.

1869d. "People and Things." Buffalo *Express*, 18 August, 2.

1869e. "A Day at Niagara." Buffalo *Express*, 21 August, 1. Reprinted in *ET&S4*.

1869f. "People and Things." Buffalo *Express*, 24 August, 2.

1869g. "L'Homme Qui Rit." MS of twenty-two pages, written ca. September, CU-MARK. Published in *S&B*, 40–48.

1869h. "People and Things." Buffalo *Express*, 4 September, 2.

1869i. "The Last Words of Great Men." Buffalo *Express*, 11 September, 1. Reprinted in *ET&S4*.

1869j. Letter dated 11 October to the California Pioneers, in "The California Pioneers." New York *Tribune*, 14 October, 5. Reprinted in *L3*, 370–74.

1869k. "Around the World. Letter No. One." Letter dated 10 October. Buffalo *Express*, 16 October, 1. Reprinted in *ET&S4*.

1869l. "Around the World. Letter No. 2. Adventures in Hayti." Letter dated 5 October. Buffalo *Express*, 30 October, 1. Reprinted in *ET&S4*.

1869m. "Around the World. Letter No. 3. California—Continued." Undated letter. Buffalo *Express*, 13 November, 1. Reprinted in *ET&S4*.

1869n. "Around the World. Letter Number 4. California—Continued." Undated letter. Buffalo *Express*, 11 December, 2. Reprinted in *ET&S4*.

1869o. "Around the World. Letter Number 5. California—Continued." Undated letter. Buffalo *Express*, 18 December, 2. Reprinted in *ET&S4*.

1870a. "Around the World. Letter Number 6. 'Early Days' in Nevada." Undated letter. Buffalo *Express*, 8 January, 2–3. Reprinted in *ET&S4*.

1870b. "Around the World. Letter Number 7. Pacific Coast—Concluded." Undated letter. Buffalo *Express*, 22 January, 2. Reprinted in *ET&S4*.

1870c. "Around the World. Letter Number 8. Dining with a Cannibal." Letter dated 20 November 1869. Buffalo *Express*, 29 January, 2. Reprinted in *ET&S4*.

[For "Around the World" letters 9 and 10 see Ford, Darius R.]

1870d. "A Big Thing." Buffalo *Express*, 12 March, 2. Reprinted in *ET&S4*.

1870e. "The Facts in the Great Land Slide Case." Buffalo *Express*, 2 April, 2. Reprinted in *ET&S4*.

1870f. "Disgraceful Persecution of a Boy." *Galaxy* 9 (May): 722–24. Reprinted in *ET&S4*.

1870g. Untitled MS of seven pages, written ca. 14 May–8 June, labeled "Chinese Labor &c" by Albert Bigelow Paine, CU-MARK. Published in Wecter 1948, 24–26.

1870h. "A Couple of Sad Experiences." *Galaxy* 9 (June): 858–61. Reprinted in *ET&S4*.

1870i. "John Chinaman in New York." *Galaxy* 10 (September): 426. Reprinted in *ET&S5*.

1870j. "The Noble Red Man." *Galaxy* 10 (September): 426–29. Reprinted in *ET&S5*.

1870k. "Science vs. Luck." *Galaxy* 10 (October): 574–75. Reprinted in *ET&S5*.

1870*l*. "Goldsmith's Friend Abroad Again." *Galaxy* 10 (October, November): 569–71, 727–31. Reprinted in *ET&S5*.

1870m. "Riley—Newspaper Correspondent." *Galaxy* 10 (November): 726–27. Reprinted in *ET&S5*.

1870n. "Favors from Correspondents." *Galaxy* 10 (December): 883–85.

1870o. "The Famous Sanitary Flour Sack." Letter dated 11 December signed "S. L. C." New York *Tribune*, 13 December, 5.

1871a. "Goldsmith's Friend Abroad Again." *Galaxy* 11 (January): 156–58. Reprinted in *ET&S5*.

1871b. "About a Remarkable Stranger. Being a Sandwich Island Reminiscence." *Galaxy* 11 (April): 616–18.

1871c. "The Old-Time Pony Express of the Great Plains." *American Publisher* 1 (May): 4.

1873a. Untitled play fragment, MS of twenty pages, a dramatization of the "Arkansas" incident in chapter 31 of *Roughing It*, CU-MARK.

1873b. "The Sandwich Islands." Letter dated 3 January. New York *Tribune*, 6 January, 4–5. Reprinted in *MTH*, 489–94.

1873c. "The Sandwich Islands." Letter dated 6 January. New York *Tribune*, 9 January, 4–5. Reprinted in *MTH*, 494–500.

1878. "Some Random Notes of an Idle Excursion." In *Punch, Brothers, Punch! and Other Sketches*. New York: Slote, Woodman and Co. First published in 1877–78 in the *Atlantic Monthly* 40 (October): 443–47; 40 (November): 586–92; 40 (December): 718–24; 41 (January): 12–19.

1884a. MS fragments, totaling eighteen pages, of an unfinished Sandwich Islands novel, CU-MARK.

1884b. "Huck Finn and Tom Sawyer among the Indians." MS originally of 228 pages, written beginning in July, primarily in MiD (some of the MS is at other institutions, some is missing: see *Inds*, 372). Published in *Inds*, 33–81.

1885. "The Private History of a Campaign That Failed." *Century Magazine* 31 (December): 193–204.

1897. "Villagers of 1840–3." MS of forty-three pages, CU-MARK. Published in *Inds*, 93–108.

1897–98. "My Autobiography. [Random Extracts from it.]" MS of seventy-five pages, CU-MARK. Published, with omissions, as "Early Days" in *MTA*, 1:81–115.

1899. "My Début as a Literary Person." *Century Magazine* 59 (November): 76–88.

1903. *"AS REGARDS THE COMPANY'S BENEVOLENCES."* TS of four pages, CU-MARK. Published in *HHR*, 533–34.

1905. "Joan of Arc. Address at the Dinner of the Society of Illustrators, Given at the Aldine Association Club, December 22, 1905." *MTS*, 269–75.

1905–6. "The Refuge of the Derelicts." MS of 307 pages, CU-MARK. Published in *FM*, 157–248.

1909. *Extract from Captain Stormfield's Visit to Heaven.* New York: Harper and Brothers. First published in 1907–8 in *Harper's Monthly Magazine* 116 (December): 42–49; 116 (January): 266–76.

1910. "The Turning Point of My Life." *Harper's Bazar* 44 (February): 118–19.

1912. "My Platonic Sweetheart." *Harper's Monthly Magazine* 126 (December): 14–20. Partly reprinted in *MTH*, 480–82.

1982. *The Adventures of Tom Sawyer by Mark Twain: A Facsimile of the Author's Holograph Manuscript.* Introduction by Paul Baender. 2 vols. Frederick, Md., and Washington, D.C.: University Publications of America and Georgetown University Library.

Smith, Benjamin E., ed. 1895. *The Century Cyclopedia of Names.* 2d ed. New York: Century Company.

Smith, Bradford. 1956. *Yankees in Paradise: The New England Impact on Hawaii.* Philadelphia: J. B. Lippincott Company.

Smith, Elizabeth H. 1965. "Reuel Colt Gridley." *Tales of the Paradise Ridge* 6 (June): 11–18.

Smith, Grant H. 1943. *The History of the Comstock Lode, 1850–1920.* University of Nevada Bulletin, Geology and Mining Series No. 37. Reno: Nevada State Bureau of Mines and the Mackay School of Mines.

Smith, Henry Nash.

1959. Introduction to *Roughing It.* New York: Harper and Brothers.

1962. *Mark Twain: The Development of a Writer.* Cambridge: Belknap Press of Harvard University Press.

Smith, Joseph. 1904. *History of the Church of Jesus Christ of Latter-day Saints. Period I. History of Joseph Smith, the Prophet by Himself.* 7 vols. Introduction and Notes by B. H. Roberts. Salt Lake City: Deseret News.

State Historical Society of Colorado. 1972. *Point of Interest.* Denver: State Historical Society of Colorado.

Statutes.

1852. *The Statutes of California, Passed at the Third Session of the Legislature.* San Francisco: G. K. Fitch and V. E. Geiger and Co., State Printers.

1866. *The Statutes of California, Passed at the Sixteenth Session of the Legislature, 1865–6.* Sacramento: O. M. Clayes, State Printer.

1870. *The Statutes of California, Passed at the Eighteenth Session of the Legislature, 1869–70.* Sacramento: D. W. Gelwicks, State Printer.

1876. *The Statutes of California, Passed at the Twenty-first Session of the Legislature, 1875–6.* Sacramento: State Printing Office.

1878. *The Statutes of California, Passed at the Twenty-second Session of the Legislature, 1877–8.* San Francisco: A. L. Bancroft and Co.

Stegner, Wallace. 1964. *The Gathering of Zion: The Story of the Mormon Trail.* New York: McGraw-Hill Book Company. Citations are to the 1981 reprint edition, Salt Lake City and Chicago: Westwater Press.

Steinbrink, Jeffrey. 1991. *Getting to Be Mark Twain.* Berkeley, Los Angeles, Oxford: University of California Press.

Stevenson, Burton, comp. 1948. *The Home Book of Proverbs, Maxims and Familiar Phrases.* New York: Macmillan Company.

Stewart, A. A., comp. 1912. *The Printer's Dictionary of Technical Terms.* Boston: School of Printing, North End Union.

Stewart, Charles Samuel. 1839. *A Residence in the Sandwich Islands.* 5th ed. Boston: Weeks, Jordan and Co.

Stewart, George R.

1937. *John Phoenix, Esq., the Veritable Squibob: A Life of Captain George H. Derby, U.S.A.* New York: Henry Holt and Co. Citations are to the 1969 reprint edition, New York: Da Capo Press.

1968. "Travelers by 'Overland.'" *American West* 5 (July): 4–12, 61.

Stewart, William M. 1908. *Reminiscences of Senator William M. Stewart of Nevada.* Edited by George Rothwell Brown. New York: Neale Publishing Company.

Stewart, Robert E., and Mary Frances Stewart. 1962. *Adolph Sutro: A Biography.* Berkeley: Howell-North Books.

Stillé, Charles J. 1866. *History of the United States Sanitary Commission.* Philadelphia: J. B. Lippincott and Co.

Stoddard, Henry Luther. 1946. *Horace Greeley: Printer, Editor, Crusader.* New York: G. P. Putnam's Sons.

Storey County Archives. Storey County Archives, County Courthouse, Virginia City, Nevada.

Sutro, Adolph. 1868. *The Mineral Resources of the United States, and the Importance and Necessity of Inaugurating a Rational System of Mining, with Special Reference to the Comstock Lode and the Sutro Tunnel, in Nevada.* Baltimore: John Murphy and Co.

Sutro, Theodore. 1887. *The Sutro Tunnel Company and the Sutro Tunnel: Property, Income, Prospects, and Pending Litigation.* New York: J. J. Little and Co.

Tanselle, G. Thomas. 1975. "Problems and Accomplishments in the Editing of the Novel." *Studies in the Novel* 7 (Fall): 323–60.

Taylor, Bayard. 1862. *At Home and Abroad: A Sketch-book of Life, Scenery and Men.* 2d series. New York: G. P. Putnam.

"Territorial Letters Received." 1861–64. Letters received from Secretary Orion Clemens, in "Letters Received from Territorial Officials." Office of the First Comptroller of the Treasury Department, RG 217, Records of the General Accounting Office, DNA.

"Territorial Letters Sent." 1861–69. Letters sent to Secretary Orion Clemens, in "Letters Sent Relating to Territorial Expenses." Office of the First Comptroller of the Treasury Department, RG 217, Records of the General Accounting Office, DNA.

Territorial Papers. 1942. *State Department Territorial Papers, Nevada Series, Vol. 1: May 13, 1861–October 31, 1864.* File Microcopies of Records in the National Archives, Microcopy no. 13, roll 1. Washington, D.C.: National Archives.

Thayer, William Roscoe, ed. 1915. *The Life and Letters of John Hay.* 2 vols. Boston: Houghton Mifflin Company.

Thomas, Frank J. 1964. *Mark Twain Roughed It Here.* Los Angeles: Tenfingers Press.

Thomas, Mifflin. 1983. *Schooner from Windward: Two Centuries of Hawaiian Interisland Shipping.* Honolulu: University of Hawaii Press.

Thompson, Robert Luther. 1947. *Wiring a Continent: The History of the Telegraph Industry in the United States, 1832–1866.* Princeton, N.J.: Princeton University Press.

Thrapp, Dan L. 1988. *Encyclopedia of Frontier Biography.* 3 vols. Glendale, Calif.: Arthur H. Clark Company.

TIA. 1958. *Traveling with the Innocents Abroad: Mark Twain's Original Reports from Europe and the Holy Land.* Edited by Daniel Morley McKeithan. Norman: University of Oklahoma Press.

Tinkham, George H. 1921. *History of Stanislaus County, California.* Los Angeles: Historic Record Company.

Toby, B. B. 1872. "'Mark Twain.' Biographical Sketch of the Great Humorist. Carefully Compiled from Imaginary Notes by B. B. Toby." San Francisco *Morning Call,* 28 April, 1.

Townley, John M. 1980. *Across Nevada with the Pony Express and Overland Stage Line.* Reno: Great Basin Studies Center.

Tribute. 1883. *A Tribute to the Memory of Reuel Colt Gridley. Compiled and published for the purpose of raising money to aid in building a monument to his memory, and establishing a fund for his family. Stockton, California, April 9, 1883.* San Francisco: A. L. Bancroft.

TS. 1980. *The Adventures of Tom Sawyer; Tom Sawyer Abroad; Tom Sawyer, Detective.* Edited by John C. Gerber, Paul Baender, and Terry Firkins. The Works of Mark Twain. Berkeley, Los Angeles, London: University of California Press.

TxU. Harry Ransom Humanities Research Center, University of Texas, Austin.

Urbanek, Mae.
1974. *Wyoming Place Names.* 3d ed. Boulder, Colo.: Johnson Publishing Company.
1978. *Ghost Trails of Wyoming.* Boulder, Colo.: Johnson Publishing Company.

Van Deusen, Glyndon G. 1953. *Horace Greeley: Nineteenth-Century Crusader.* Philadelphia: University of Pennsylvania Press.

Van Sickle, Henry. 1883. "Utah Desperadoes." MS of thirteen pages, dictated at Genoa, Nevada, CU-BANC.

Van Wagoner, Richard S. 1989. *Mormon Polygamy: A History.* 2d ed. Salt Lake City: Signature Books.

Van Wagoner, Richard S., and Steven C. Walker. 1982. *A Book of Mormons.* Salt Lake City: Signature Books.

Varigny, Charles de. 1981. *Fourteen Years in the Sandwich Islands, 1855–1868.* Translated by Alfons L. Korn. Honolulu: University Press of Hawaii and the Hawaiian Historical Society. Modern translation of *Quatorze ans aux îles Sandwich,* first published in 1874.

Veni, Vidi [pseud.].
1862a. "Mono County Correspondence." Letter dated 3 July. Sacramento *Bee,* 12 July, 3.

1862b. "Esmeralda Correspondence." Letter dated 28 July. Sacramento *Bee,* 1 August, 1.

Vi. Virginia State Library, Richmond.

ViU. Clifton Waller Barrett Library, Alderman Library, University of Virginia, Charlottesville.

Volcano House Register. 1866. Register of visitors to the Volcano House in 1866, pp. 63–85 of volume 1. The leaves containing the entries made between 25 April and 18 July, including Clemens's entry of 7 June, are now missing: see SLC 1866u. Original at the Volcano House, Hawaii Volcanoes National Park, Hawaii; PH in HU.

Waite, Mrs. Catharine V. 1868. *The Mormon Prophet and His Harem; or, An Authentic History of Brigham Young, His Numerous Wives and Children.* 5th ed., rev. and enl. Chicago: J. S. Goodman and Co.

Walker, Franklin.
1938. *The Washoe Giant in San Francisco.* San Francisco: George Fields.

1969. *San Francisco's Literary Frontier.* Rev. ed. Seattle: University of Washington Press.

Warner, Charles Dudley. 1872 [*attributed*]. "'Roughing It.' Mark Twain's New Book." Hartford *Courant,* 18 March, 1.

Watson, Margaret G. 1964. *Silver Theatre: Amusements of the Mining Frontier in Early Nevada, 1850 to 1864.* Glendale, Calif.: Arthur H. Clark Company.

Webb, Charles Henry [John Paul and Inigo, pseuds.].
1865a. "Local Matters: An Afternoon of Blood." San Francisco *Evening Bulletin,* 8 July, 5.

1865b. "Letter from San Francisco." Letter dated 12 July. Sacramento *Union,* 14 July, 2.

Webster, Noah.
1847. *American Dictionary of the English Language.* New York: Hurst and Co.

1870. *A Dictionary of the English Language.* Rev. and enl. by Chauncey A. Goodrich and Thomas Heber Orr. 2 vols. Glasgow: William Mackenzie.

1934. *Webster's New International Dictionary of the English Language.* 2d ed. Springfield, Mass.: G. and C. Merriam Company.

Wecter, Dixon.

1948. *Mark Twain in Three Moods.* San Marino, Calif.: Friends of the Huntington Library.

1952. *Sam Clemens of Hannibal.* Boston: Houghton Mifflin Company, Riverside Press.

Wedertz, Frank S. 1978. *Mono Diggings.* Bishop, Calif.: Chalfant Press.

Weisenburger, Francis Phelps. 1965. *Idol of the West: The Fabulous Career of Rollin Mallory Daggett.* Syracuse, N.Y.: Syracuse University Press.

Wells, Evelyn.

1921a. "The Silver Sixties." Chapter 5 in "The Silver Sixties: Tom Fitch's Story of California-Nevada Comstock Days," San Francisco *Call and Post,* 1 April, 15.

1921b. "Fighters of Old Days." Chapter 14 in "The Silver Sixties: Tom Fitch's Story of California-Nevada Comstock Days," San Francisco *Call and Post,* 12 April, 13.

West, George P. 1924. "Bret Harte's 'Roaring Camp' Still Producing." San Francisco *Call and Post,* 24 May, 13, 18.

Wharton, Don. 1948. "Why We Brush Our Teeth." *Reader's Digest* 53 (July): 139–42.

Wheat, Carl I. 1929. "'California's Bantam Cock'—The Journals of Charles E. De Long, 1854–1863 (Continued)." *California Historical Society Quarterly* 8 (December): 337–63.

Whitney, Henry M. 1875. *The Hawaiian Guide Book.* Honolulu: Henry M. Whitney.

Wilkes, Charles. 1844. *Narrative of the United States Exploring Expedition. During the Years 1838, 1839, 1840, 1841, 1842.* 5 vols. Philadelphia: C. Sherman.

Williams, George, III. 1986. *Mark Twain: His Adventures at Aurora and Mono Lake.* Riverside, Calif.: Tree By the River Publishing.

Wise, William. 1976. *Massacre at Mountain Meadows: An American Legend and a Monumental Crime.* New York: Thomas Y. Crowell Company.

Withington, Antoinette. 1953. *The Golden Cloak.* Honolulu: Hawaiiana Press.

Wood, John George. 1870. *The Uncivilized Races, or Natural History of Man; Being a Complete Account of the Manners and Customs, and the*

Physical, Social and Religious Condition and Characteristics, of the Uncivilized Races of Men, throughout the Entire World. 2 vols. Hartford: American Publishing Company.

Wood, Richard Coke. 1949. *Tales of Old Calaveras.* Angels, Calif.: Calaveras Californian.

Worcester, Joseph E., comp. 1863. *Dictionary of the English Language.* Boston: Brewer and Tileston.

Work, James C. 1979. "The Julesburg of Mark Twain's Roughing It." *Mark Twain Journal* 19 (Summer): 24.

WPA. 1941. *Wyoming: A Guide to Its History, Highways, and People.* Compiled by workers of the Writers' Program of the Work Projects Administration in the State of Wyoming. New York: Oxford University Press.

Wright, James W. A. 1960. *The Cement Hunters: Lost Gold Mine of the High Sierra.* Edited by Richard E. Lingenfelter. Los Angeles: Glen Dawson.

Wright, William [Dan De Quille, pseud.].
1864 [*attributed*]. "New Mining District." Sacramento *Union*, 10 May, 3, reprinting the Virginia City *Territorial Enterprise* of 7 May.

1876. *The Big Bonanza.* Hartford: American Publishing Company. Citations are to the 1947 reprint edition, introduction by Oscar Lewis, New York: Alfred A. Knopf.

1891. "The Thoreau of the Sierras." Salt Lake City *Tribune*, 19 July. Reprinted in Berkove 1988a, 2.

1893a. "The *Territorial Enterprise* . . . ," in "The Passing of a Pioneer," San Francisco *Examiner*, 22 January, 15. Reprinted as "The Story of the Enterprise" in Lewis, 5–10.

1893b. "Salad Days of Mark Twain." San Francisco *Examiner*, 19 March, 13–14. Reprinted in Lewis, 37–52.

1893c. "Reporting with Mark Twain." *Californian Illustrated Magazine* 4 (July): 170–78.

WU. Memorial Library, University of Wisconsin, Madison.

Young, Brigham. 1861. "Office Journal." Brigham Young Collection, Archives Division, Church Historical Department, The Church of Jesus Christ of Latter-day Saints, Salt Lake City, Utah.

YSMT. Yale Scrapbook, Willard S. Morse Collection, CtY-BR. [*Clemens used this scrapbook to collect clippings of his articles dating from December 1863 to October 1866, many of which he revised in the margins. The scrapbook was the source for roughly half of the pieces in SLC 1867a: see* ET&S1, 506–42.]

Zambucka, Kristin.

1977. *The High Chiefess Ruth Keelikolani.* Honolulu: Mana Publishing Company.

1983. *Kalakaua: Hawaii's Last King.* Honolulu: Mana Publishing Company.

The text of this book is set in Trump Mediae-val, which was designed in 1954 for the Weber typefoundry by Georg Trump. For display matter and headings two closely related fonts were chosen to coordinate with the text type: Weiss italic (a slightly inclined font with swash capitals) and Weiss Initials Series I (an all-capital font). Both were designed by Emil Rudolf Weiss in 1931 for the Bauer typefoundry, and furnished for this edition by Solotype Typographers of Oakland, California. The paper used is Troy Book Cream, an acid-free paper manufactured by the Cross Pointe Paper Corporation. The text was composed in WordPerfect 5.0 by the Mark Twain Project and transferred on disk to Wilsted & Taylor Publishing Services of Oakland, who typeset it using Data General Nova 4c and Nova 4x computers, Penta software, and a Linotron 202 typesetter. The book was printed and bound by Maple-Vail Book Manufacturing Group in Binghamton, New York.

Pretzels

One of the World's Oldest Snack Foods

Elaine Landau

THE ROURKE PRESS, INC.

VERO BEACH, FLORIDA 32964

PHOTO CREDITS
Ben Klaffke

EDITORIAL SERVICES
Editorial Directions Inc.

Library of Congress Cataloging-in-Publication Data

Landau, Elaine.
  Pretzels : one of the world's oldest snack foods / Elaine Landau.
    p. cm. — (Tasty treats)
  Includes bibliographical references.
    Summary: Provides a brief introduction to pretzels, describing their history, different kinds of pretzels, and how they
are made.
    ISBN 1-57103-340-8
    1. Pretzels—Juvenile literature. [1. Pretzels.] I. Title.

TX770.P73 L36 2000
641.8'15—dc21

00–022395

Printed in the USA

Contents

Pretzels come in various shapes and sizes.

A Great Snack

Want a tasty snack? How about a pretzel? There are at least twenty eight types to choose from.

Most people eat the hard, crispy ones. These come in many different shapes. Sticks, **nuggets**, **rods**, and loops are just few. There are also pizza pretzels and chocolate-dipped pretzels.

Chocolate covered pretzels are especially delicious.

People like to sink their teeth into a chewy soft pretzel.

This pretzel looks good and tastes good, too.

Soft pretzels are good, too. They are usually large and chewy. People like to sink their teeth into these. Mothers give them to teething babies.

This is a book about pretzels. One of the world's oldest snack foods.

Pretzel Beginnings

Ever wonder how the pretzel was invented? Some say the first pretzel might have been made as early as A.D. 610. A monk from southern France thought it up. He started off with some leftover scraps of dough. He twisted the **dough** to look like a child's arms folded in prayer. Then he baked it.

The monk used pretzels as rewards. He gave them to the children who learned their prayers. The baked dough pieces were named pretiola. In Latin that means "little reward."

At first, there were only soft pretzels. The hard pretzel was created by accident. A young man tending the pretzel ovens fell asleep. The pretzels were left baking for too long.

Does the shape of these pretzels remind you of a child's arms folded in prayer?

The chief baker thought they would be ruined. But the hard, crisp pretzels were delicious! After that, hard pretzels were made daily.

Today, both hard and soft pretzels are popular. More than 300 million pounds of pretzels are produced yearly in the United States.

Early pretzels were soft like the one this girl is enjoying.

Pretzel Making

Today, there is not much work for pretzel twisters. Ninety percent of pretzel making is done by machine. A twisting machine rolls and twists the dough.

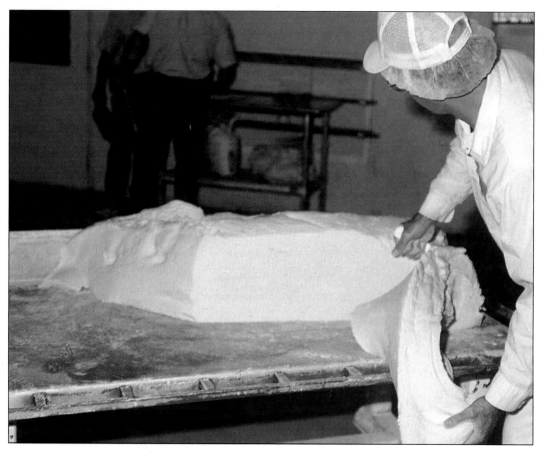

Here dough is prepared for pretzel making

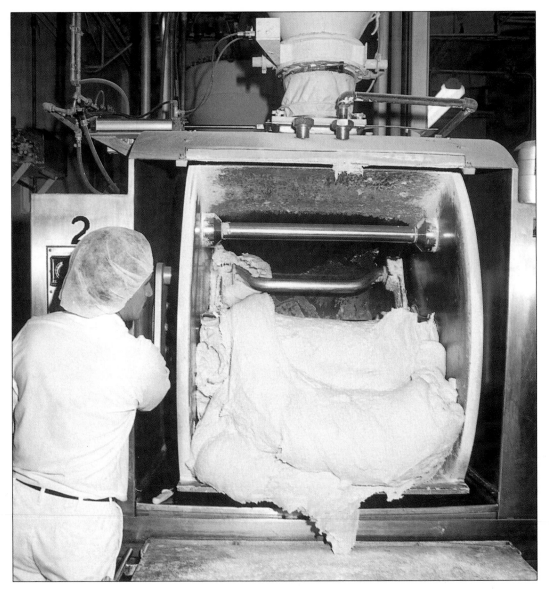

Today most pretzels are made by machine.

Then, it is dropped onto a belt that brings it to a cooker. There, the pretzel is rinsed with a specially made hot fluid. This gives the pretzel its golden brown color and shiny finish.

Notice the golden brown finish on these pretzels.

People of all ages everywhere enjoy a pretzel break.

Salt is then dropped onto the pretzel. Next, it goes into the oven. It comes out fully baked. The pretzel is put in a dryer to remove extra **moisture**. It is now ready for packing and shipping. Modern packaging helps pretzels stay fresh longer. It also allows them to be shipped to distant places.

Pretzels make a great after school snack.

Today there is a large pretzel industry in the United States. American pretzel makers do about 130 billion dollars worth of business a year. Pretzels can be found nearly everywhere in the United States. Pretzels made here are also shipped to many cities worldwide. It is hard to find someone who has never heard of a pretzel.

Pretzels and fruit are a healthy snack

A Healthy Choice

There is good news about pretzels. They are good for you! Pretzels are made from wheat flour. They are rich in protein. Pretzels also contain calcium and other minerals. In many areas you can buy organic pretzels. The basic ingredients in these were grown without using pesticides.

Pretzels make a healthy after-school or evening snack. They go especially well with soups, cheese, and salads. Many people like pretzels with ice cream, milk, or soda. Soft pretzel sandwiches are delicious. Here is a recipe for one that is a real taste treat. It is called Raisin Nut Pretzel Delight.

This is what you need:

a large soft pretzel
2 oz. of cream cheese
about 30 golden raisins
about 20 almond slivers

This is what to do:

Cut the pretzel in half horizontally (Ask an adult to help you use the knife)

Spread the cream cheese on both pretzel halves

Place the nuts and raisins wherever you put cream cheese

Put the two pretzel halves together

Enjoy your snack

Raisin Nut Pretzel Delights are especially good with a glass of milk

Pretzels are also used in other recipes. Crushed pretzels are put in turkey and chicken stuffing. Pretzel crumbs make great pie crusts as well.

This woman dips pretzels in salt so they won't be "baldies".

Pretzel **Fun Facts**

 "Baldies" are unsalted pretzels.

 In the 1960s couples often "wished" on a pretzel when they married. The bride held one side of the soft pretzel. The groom held the other. Then both pulled on it. The one with the largest piece won. His or her wish would come true. However, both the bride and groom usually wished for a lifetime of happiness together. Therefore no one lost!

 On New Year's Eve in Germany, some children wear pretzels around their necks. They are supposed to bring good luck in the coming year.

Here a man twists pretzels by hand.

 In Austria, some people top their Christmas trees with pretzels.

 The world's fastest pretzel twister is Helen Hoff. She can twist fifty seven pretzels a minute.

Glossary

baldies (bawl Dez) – unsalted pretzels

dough (doh) – a soft mass of flour, water, and other items mixed together. It is used to make pretzels and other baked goods.

moisture (MOIS chur) – a small amount of liquid; dampness

nugget (NUHG it) – a pretzel shaped like a small lump

rod (rod) – a pretzel shaped like a thick stick.

For Further Reading

Kalbacken, Joan. *The Food Pyramid*. Danbury, Connecticut: Children's Press, 1998.

Katzen, Mollie. *Honest Pretzels: And 64 Other Amazing Recipes for Cooks Ages 8 and Up*. New York: Tricycle, 1999.

Maynard, Christopher. *Why Are Pineapples Prickly? Questions Children Ask about Food*. New York: DK Publishing, 1997.

Powell, Jillian. *Food, and Your Health*. Austin, Texas: Raintree Steck-Vaughn, 1998.

Index